H. G. Wells, Ayn Rand, Mark Twain...

Time Voyage - Boxed Set

OK Publishing 2024

H. G. Wells, Ayn Rand, Mark Twain…
Timeless Tales of Time Travel - Ultimate Collection

Published by
MUSAICUM
Books

- Advanced Digital Solutions & High-Quality book Formatting -

musaicumbooks@okpublishing.info

2024 OK Publishing

ISBN 978-80-272-7931-9

Authors

H. G. Wells
Ayn Rand
Mark Twain
H. Beam Piper
Philip K. Dick
Fritz Leiber
Andre Norton
Lester Del Rey
August Derleth
Frederik Pohl

Contents

H. G. Wells

The Time Machine

Chapter I

The Time Traveller (for so it will be convenient to speak of him) was expounding a recondite matter to us. His grey eyes shone and twinkled, and his usually pale face was flushed and animated. The fire burned brightly, and the soft radiance of the incandescent lights in the lilies of silver caught the bubbles that flashed and passed in our glasses. Our chairs, being his patents, embraced and caressed us rather than submitted to be sat upon, and there was that luxurious after-dinner atmosphere when thought roams gracefully free of the trammels of precision. And he put it to us in this way — marking the points with a lean forefinger — as we sat and lazily admired his earnestness over this new paradox (as we thought it) and his fecundity.

'You must follow me carefully. I shall have to controvert one or two ideas that are almost universally accepted. The geometry, for instance, they taught you at school is founded on a misconception.'

'Is not that rather a large thing to expect us to begin upon?' said Filby, an argumentative person with red hair.

'I do not mean to ask you to accept anything without reasonable ground for it. You will soon admit as much as I need from you. You know of course that a mathematical line, a line of thickness nil, has no real existence. They taught you that? Neither has a mathematical plane. These things are mere abstractions.'

'That is all right,' said the Psychologist.

'Nor, having only length, breadth, and thickness, can a cube have a real existence.'

'There I object,' said Filby. 'Of course a solid body may exist. All real things — '

'So most people think. But wait a moment. Can an *instantaneous* cube exist?'

'Don't follow you,' said Filby.

'Can a cube that does not last for any time at all, have a real existence?'

Filby became pensive. 'Clearly,' the Time Traveller proceeded, 'any real body must have extension in *four* directions: it must have Length, Breadth, Thickness, and — Duration. But through a natural infirmity of the flesh, which I will explain to you in a moment, we incline to overlook this fact. There are really four dimensions, three which we call the three planes of Space, and a fourth, Time. There is, however, a tendency to draw an unreal distinction between the former three dimensions and the latter, because it happens that our consciousness moves intermittently in one direction along the latter from the beginning to the end of our lives.'

'That,' said a very young man, making spasmodic efforts to relight his cigar over the lamp; 'that... very clear indeed.'

'Now, it is very remarkable that this is so extensively overlooked,' continued the Time Traveller, with a slight accession of cheerfulness. 'Really this is what is meant by the Fourth Dimension, though some people who talk about the Fourth Dimension do not know they mean it. It is only another way of looking at Time. *There is no difference between Time and any of the three dimensions of Space except that our consciousness moves along it* . But some foolish people have got hold of the wrong side of that idea. You have all heard what they have to say about this Fourth Dimension?'

'I have not,' said the Provincial Mayor.

'It is simply this. That Space, as our mathematicians have it, is spoken of as having three dimensions, which one may call Length, Breadth, and Thickness, and is always definable by reference to three planes, each at right angles to the others. But some philosophical people have been asking why *three* dimensions particularly — why not another direction at right angles to the other three? — and have even tried to construct a Four-Dimension geometry. Professor Simon Newcomb was expounding this to the New York Mathematical Society only a month or so ago. You know how on a flat surface, which has only two dimensions, we can represent a figure of a three-dimensional solid, and similarly they think that by models of three dimensions they could represent one of four — if they could master the perspective of the thing. See?'

'I think so,' murmured the Provincial Mayor; and, knitting his brows, he lapsed into an introspective state, his lips moving as one who repeats mystic words. 'Yes, I think I see it now,' he said after some time, brightening in a quite transitory manner.

'Well, I do not mind telling you I have been at work upon this geometry of Four Dimensions for some time. Some of my results are curious. For instance, here is a portrait of a man at eight years old, another at fifteen, another at seventeen, another at twenty-three, and so on. All these are evidently sections, as it were, Three-Dimensional representations of his Four-Dimensioned being, which is a fixed and unalterable thing.

'Scientific people,' proceeded the Time Traveller, after the pause required for the proper assimilation of this, 'know very well that Time is only a kind of Space. Here is a popular scientific diagram, a weather record. This line I trace with my finger shows the movement of the barometer. Yesterday it was so high, yesterday night it fell, then this morning it rose again, and so gently upward to here. Surely the mercury did not trace this line in any of the dimensions of Space generally recognized? But certainly it traced such a line, and that line, therefore, we must conclude was along the Time-Dimension.'

'But,' said the Medical Man, staring hard at a coal in the fire, 'if Time is really only a fourth dimension of Space, why is it, and why has it always been, regarded as something different? And why cannot we move in Time as we move about in the other dimensions of Space?'

The Time Traveller smiled. 'Are you sure we can move freely in Space? Right and left we can go, backward and forward freely enough, and men always have done so. I admit we move freely in two dimensions. But how about up and down? Gravitation limits us there.'

'Not exactly,' said the Medical Man. 'There are balloons.'

'But before the balloons, save for spasmodic jumping and the inequalities of the surface, man had no freedom of vertical movement.'

'Still they could move a little up and down,' said the Medical Man.

'Easier, far easier down than up.'

'And you cannot move at all in Time, you cannot get away from the present moment.'

'My dear sir, that is just where you are wrong. That is just where the whole world has gone wrong. We are always getting away from the present moment. Our mental existences, which are immaterial and have no dimensions, are passing along the Time-Dimension with a uniform velocity from the cradle to the grave. Just as we should travel *down* if we began our existence fifty miles above the earth's surface.'

'But the great difficulty is this,' interrupted the Psychologist. 'You *can* move about in all directions of Space, but you cannot move about in Time.'

'That is the germ of my great discovery. But you are wrong to say that we cannot move about in Time. For instance, if I am recalling an incident very vividly I go back to the instant of its occurrence: I become absentminded, as you say. I jump back for a moment. Of course we have no means of staying back for any length of Time, any more than a savage or an animal has of staying six feet above the ground. But a civilized man is better off than the savage in this respect. He can go up against gravitation in a balloon, and why should he not hope that ultimately he may be able to stop or accelerate his drift along the Time-Dimension, or even turn about and travel the other way?'

'Oh, *this* ,' began Filby, 'is all — '

'Why not?' said the Time Traveller.

'It's against reason,' said Filby.

'What reason?' said the Time Traveller.

'You can show black is white by argument,' said Filby, 'but you will never convince me.'

'Possibly not,' said the Time Traveller. 'But now you begin to see the object of my investigations into the geometry of Four Dimensions. Long ago I had a vague inkling of a machine — '

'To travel through Time!' exclaimed the Very Young Man.

'That shall travel indifferently in any direction of Space and Time, as the driver determines.'

Filby contented himself with laughter.

'But I have experimental verification,' said the Time Traveller.

'It would be remarkably convenient for the historian,' the Psychologist suggested. 'One might travel back and verify the accepted account of the Battle of Hastings, for instance!'

'Don't you think you would attract attention?' said the Medical Man. 'Our ancestors had no great tolerance for anachronisms.'

'One might get one's Greek from the very lips of Homer and Plato,' the Very Young Man thought.

'In which case they would certainly plough you for the Little-go. The German scholars have improved Greek so much.'

'Then there is the future,' said the Very Young Man. 'Just think! One might invest all one's money, leave it to accumulate at interest, and hurry on ahead!'

'To discover a society,' said I, 'erected on a strictly communistic basis.'

'Of all the wild extravagant theories!' began the Psychologist.

'Yes, so it seemed to me, and so I never talked of it until — '

'Experimental verification!' cried I. 'You are going to verify *that* ?'

'The experiment!' cried Filby, who was getting brain-weary.

'Let's see your experiment anyhow,' said the Psychologist, 'though it's all humbug, you know.'

The Time Traveller smiled round at us. Then, still smiling faintly, and with his hands deep in his trousers pockets, he walked slowly out of the room, and we heard his slippers shuffling down the long passage to his laboratory.

The Psychologist looked at us. 'I wonder what he's got?'

'Some sleight-of-hand trick or other,' said the Medical Man, and Filby tried to tell us about a conjurer he had seen at Burslem; but before he had finished his preface the Time Traveller came back, and Filby's anecdote collapsed.

The thing the Time Traveller held in his hand was a glittering metallic framework, scarcely larger than a small clock, and very delicately made. There was ivory in it, and some transparent crystalline substance. And now I must be explicit, for this that follows — unless his explanation is to be accepted — is an absolutely unaccountable thing. He took one of the small octagonal tables that were scattered about the room, and set it in front of the fire, with two legs on the hearthrug. On this table he placed the mechanism. Then he drew up a chair, and sat down. The only other object on the table was a small shaded lamp, the bright light of which fell upon the model. There were also perhaps a dozen candles about, two in brass candlesticks upon the mantel and several in sconces, so that the room was brilliantly illuminated. I sat in a low armchair nearest the fire, and I drew this forward so as to be almost between the Time Traveller and the fireplace. Filby sat behind him, looking over his shoulder. The Medical Man and the Provincial Mayor watched him in profile from the right, the Psychologist from the left. The Very Young Man stood behind the Psychologist. We were all on the alert. It appears incredible to me that any kind of trick, however subtly conceived and however adroitly done, could have been played upon us under these conditions.

The Time Traveller looked at us, and then at the mechanism. 'Well?' said the Psychologist.

'This little affair,' said the Time Traveller, resting his elbows upon the table and pressing his hands together above the apparatus, 'is only a model. It is my plan for a machine to travel through time. You will notice that it looks singularly askew, and that there is an odd twinkling appearance about this bar, as though it was in some way unreal.' He pointed to the part with his finger. 'Also, here is one little white lever, and here is another.'

The Medical Man got up out of his chair and peered into the thing. 'It's beautifully made,' he said.

'It took two years to make,' retorted the Time Traveller. Then, when we had all imitated the action of the Medical Man, he said: 'Now I want you clearly to understand that this lever, being pressed over, sends the machine gliding into the future, and this other reverses the motion. This saddle represents the seat of a time traveller. Presently I am going to press the lever, and off the machine will go. It will vanish, pass into future Time, and disappear. Have a good look at the thing. Look at the table too, and satisfy yourselves there is no trickery. I don't want to waste this model, and then be told I'm a quack.'

There was a minute's pause perhaps. The Psychologist seemed about to speak to me, but changed his mind. Then the Time Traveller put forth his finger towards the lever. 'No,' he said suddenly. 'Lend me your hand.' And turning to the Psychologist, he took that individual's hand in his own and told him to put out his forefinger. So that it was the Psychologist himself who sent forth the model Time Machine on its interminable voyage. We all saw the lever turn. I am absolutely certain there was no trickery. There was a breath of wind, and the lamp flame jumped. One of the candles on the mantel was blown out, and the little machine suddenly swung round, became indistinct, was seen as a ghost for a second perhaps, as an eddy of faintly glittering brass and ivory; and it was gone — vanished! Save for the lamp the table was bare.

Everyone was silent for a minute. Then Filby said he was damned.

The Psychologist recovered from his stupor, and suddenly looked under the table. At that the Time Traveller laughed cheerfully. 'Well?' he said, with a reminiscence of the Psychologist. Then, getting up, he went to the tobacco jar on the mantel, and with his back to us began to fill his pipe.

We stared at each other. 'Look here,' said the Medical Man, 'are you in earnest about this? Do you seriously believe that that machine has travelled into time?'

'Certainly,' said the Time Traveller, stooping to light a spill at the fire. Then he turned, lighting his pipe, to look at the Psychologist's face. (The Psychologist, to show that he was not unhinged, helped himself to a cigar and tried to light it uncut.) 'What is more, I have a big machine nearly finished in there' — he indicated the laboratory — 'and when that is put together I mean to have a journey on my own account.'

'You mean to say that that machine has travelled into the future?' said Filby.

'Into the future or the past — I don't, for certain, know which.'

After an interval the Psychologist had an inspiration. 'It must have gone into the past if it has gone anywhere,' he said.

'Why?' said the Time Traveller.

'Because I presume that it has not moved in space, and if it travelled into the future it would still be here all this time, since it must have travelled through this time.'

'But,' I said, 'If it travelled into the past it would have been visible when we came first into this room; and last Thursday when we were here; and the Thursday before that; and so forth!'

'Serious objections,' remarked the Provincial Mayor, with an air of impartiality, turning towards the Time Traveller.

'Not a bit,' said the Time Traveller, and, to the Psychologist: 'You think. You can explain that. It's presentation below the threshold, you know, diluted presentation.'

'Of course,' said the Psychologist, and reassured us. 'That's a simple point of psychology. I should have thought of it. It's plain enough, and helps the paradox delightfully. We cannot see it, nor can we appreciate this machine, any more than we can the spoke of a wheel spinning, or a bullet flying through the air. If it is travelling through time fifty times or a hundred times faster than we are, if it gets through a minute while we get through a second, the impression it creates will of course be only one-fiftieth or one-hundredth of what it would make if it were not travelling in time. That's plain enough.' He passed his hand through the space in which the machine had been. 'You see?' he said, laughing.

We sat and stared at the vacant table for a minute or so. Then the Time Traveller asked us what we thought of it all.

'It sounds plausible enough tonight,' said the Medical Man; 'but wait until tomorrow. Wait for the common sense of the morning.'

'Would you like to see the Time Machine itself?' asked the Time Traveller. And therewith, taking the lamp in his hand, he led the way down the long, draughty corridor to his laboratory. I remember vividly the flickering light, his queer, broad head in silhouette, the dance of the shadows, how we all followed him, puzzled but incredulous, and how there in the laboratory we beheld a larger edition of the little mechanism which we had seen vanish from before our eyes. Parts were of nickel, parts of ivory, parts had certainly been filed or sawn out of rock crystal. The thing was generally complete, but the twisted crystalline bars lay unfinished upon the bench beside some sheets of drawings, and I took one up for a better look at it. Quartz it seemed to be.

'Look here,' said the Medical Man, 'are you perfectly serious? Or is this a trick — like that ghost you showed us last Christmas?'

'Upon that machine,' said the Time Traveller, holding the lamp aloft, 'I intend to explore time. Is that plain? I was never more serious in my life.'

None of us quite knew how to take it.

I caught Filby's eye over the shoulder of the Medical Man, and he winked at me solemnly.

Chapter II

I think that at that time none of us quite believed in the Time Machine. The fact is, the Time Traveller was one of those men who are too clever to be believed: you never felt that you saw all round him; you always suspected some subtle reserve, some ingenuity in ambush, behind his lucid frankness. Had Filby shown the model and explained the matter in the Time Traveller's words, we should have shown *him* far less scepticism. For we should have perceived his motives; a pork butcher could understand Filby. But the Time Traveller had more than a touch of whim among his elements, and we distrusted him. Things that would have made the frame of a less clever man seemed tricks in his hands. It is a mistake to do things too easily. The serious people who took him seriously never felt quite sure of his deportment; they were somehow aware that trusting their reputations for judgment with him was like furnishing a nursery with eggshell china. So I don't think any of us said very much about time travelling in the interval between that Thursday and the next, though its odd potentialities ran, no doubt, in most of our minds: its plausibility, that is, its practical incredibleness, the curious possibilities of anachronism and of utter confusion it suggested. For my own part, I was particularly preoccupied with the trick of the model. That I remember discussing with the Medical Man, whom I met on Friday at the Linnaean. He said he had seen a similar thing at Tubingen, and laid considerable stress on the blowing out of the candle. But how the trick was done he could not explain.

The next Thursday I went again to Richmond — I suppose I was one of the Time Traveller's most constant guests — and, arriving late, found four or five men already assembled in his drawingroom. The Medical Man was standing before the fire with a sheet of paper in one hand and his watch in the other. I looked round for the Time Traveller, and — 'It's halfpast seven now,' said the Medical Man. 'I suppose we'd better have dinner?'

'Where's — —?' said I, naming our host.

'You've just come? It's rather odd. He's unavoidably detained. He asks me in this note to lead off with dinner at seven if he's not back. Says he'll explain when he comes.'

'It seems a pity to let the dinner spoil,' said the Editor of a well-known daily paper; and thereupon the Doctor rang the bell.

The Psychologist was the only person besides the Doctor and myself who had attended the previous dinner. The other men were Blank, the Editor aforementioned, a certain journalist, and another — a quiet, shy man with a beard — whom I didn't know, and who, as far as my observation went, never opened his mouth all the evening. There was some speculation at the dinner-table about the Time Traveller's absence, and I suggested time travelling, in a half-jocular spirit. The Editor wanted that explained to him, and the Psychologist volunteered a wooden account of the 'ingenious paradox and trick' we had witnessed that day week. He was in the midst of his exposition when the door from the corridor opened slowly and without noise. I was facing the door, and saw it first. 'Hallo!' I said. 'At last!' And the door opened wider, and the

Time Traveller stood before us. I gave a cry of surprise. 'Good heavens! man, what's the matter?' cried the Medical Man, who saw him next. And the whole tableful turned towards the door.

He was in an amazing plight. His coat was dusty and dirty, and smeared with green down the sleeves; his hair disordered, and as it seemed to me greyer — either with dust and dirt or because its colour had actually faded. His face was ghastly pale; his chin had a brown cut on it — a cut half healed; his expression was haggard and drawn, as by intense suffering. For a moment he hesitated in the doorway, as if he had been dazzled by the light. Then he came into the room. He walked with just such a limp as I have seen in footsore tramps. We stared at him in silence, expecting him to speak.

He said not a word, but came painfully to the table, and made a motion towards the wine. The Editor filled a glass of champagne, and pushed it towards him. He drained it, and it seemed to do him good: for he looked round the table, and the ghost of his old smile flickered across his face. 'What on earth have you been up to, man?' said the Doctor. The Time Traveller did not seem to hear. 'Don't let me disturb you,' he said, with a certain faltering articulation. 'I'm all right.' He stopped, held out his glass for more, and took it off at a draught. 'That's good,' he said. His eyes grew brighter, and a faint colour came into his cheeks. His glance flickered over our faces with a certain dull approval, and then went round the warm and comfortable room. Then he spoke again, still as it were feeling his way among his words. 'I'm going to wash and dress, and then I'll come down and explain things... Save me some of that mutton. I'm starving for a bit of meat.'

He looked across at the Editor, who was a rare visitor, and hoped he was all right. The Editor began a question. 'Tell you presently,' said the Time Traveller. 'I'm — funny! Be all right in a minute.'

He put down his glass, and walked towards the staircase door. Again I remarked his lameness and the soft padding sound of his footfall, and standing up in my place, I saw his feet as he went out. He had nothing on them but a pair of tattered, bloodstained socks. Then the door closed upon him. I had half a mind to follow, till I remembered how he detested any fuss about himself. For a minute, perhaps, my mind was wool-gathering. Then, 'Remarkable Behaviour of an Eminent Scientist,' I heard the Editor say, thinking (after his wont) in headlines. And this brought my attention back to the bright dinner-table.

'What's the game?' said the Journalist. 'Has he been doing the Amateur Cadger? I don't follow.' I met the eye of the Psychologist, and read my own interpretation in his face. I thought of the Time Traveller limping painfully upstairs. I don't think any one else had noticed his lameness.

The first to recover completely from this surprise was the Medical Man, who rang the bell — the Time Traveller hated to have servants waiting at dinner — for a hot plate. At that the Editor turned to his knife and fork with a grunt, and the Silent Man followed suit. The dinner was resumed. Conversation was exclamatory for a little while, with gaps of wonderment; and then the Editor got fervent in his curiosity. 'Does our friend eke out his modest income with a crossing? or has he his Nebuchadnezzar phases?' he inquired. 'I feel assured it's this business of the Time Machine,' I said, and took up the Psychologist's account of our previous meeting. The new guests were frankly incredulous. The Editor raised objections. 'What *was* this time travelling? A man couldn't cover himself with dust by rolling in a paradox, could he?' And then, as the idea came home to him, he resorted to caricature. Hadn't they any clothes-brushes in the Future? The Journalist too, would not believe at any price, and joined the Editor in the easy work of heaping ridicule on the whole thing. They were both the new kind of journalist — very joyous, irreverent young men. 'Our Special Correspondent in the Day after Tomorrow reports,' the Journalist was saying — or rather shouting — when the Time Traveller came back. He was dressed in ordinary evening clothes, and nothing save his haggard look remained of the change that had startled me.

'I say,' said the Editor hilariously, 'these chaps here say you have been travelling into the middle of next week! Tell us all about little Rosebery, will you? What will you take for the lot?'

The Time Traveller came to the place reserved for him without a word. He smiled quietly, in his old way. 'Where's my mutton?' he said. 'What a treat it is to stick a fork into meat again!'

'Story!' cried the Editor.

'Story be damned!' said the Time Traveller. 'I want something to eat. I won't say a word until I get some peptone into my arteries. Thanks. And the salt.'

'One word,' said I. 'Have you been time travelling?'

'Yes,' said the Time Traveller, with his mouth full, nodding his head.

'I'd give a shilling a line for a verbatim note,' said the Editor. The Time Traveller pushed his glass towards the Silent Man and rang it with his fingernail; at which the Silent Man, who had been staring at his face, started convulsively, and poured him wine. The rest of the dinner was uncomfortable. For my own part, sudden questions kept on rising to my lips, and I dare say it was the same with the others. The Journalist tried to relieve the tension by telling anecdotes of Hettie Potter. The Time Traveller devoted his attention to his dinner, and displayed the appetite of a tramp. The Medical Man smoked a cigarette, and watched the Time Traveller through his eyelashes. The Silent Man seemed even more clumsy than usual, and drank champagne with regularity and determination out of sheer nervousness. At last the Time Traveller pushed his plate away, and looked round us. 'I suppose I must apologize,' he said. 'I was simply starving. I've had a most amazing time.' He reached out his hand for a cigar, and cut the end. 'But come into the smoking-room. It's too long a story to tell over greasy plates.' And ringing the bell in passing, he led the way into the adjoining room.

'You have told Blank, and Dash, and Chose about the machine?' he said to me, leaning back in his easy-chair and naming the three new guests.

'But the thing's a mere paradox,' said the Editor.

'I can't argue tonight. I don't mind telling you the story, but I can't argue. I will,' he went on, 'tell you the story of what has happened to me, if you like, but you must refrain from interruptions. I want to tell it. Badly. Most of it will sound like lying. So be it! It's true — every word of it, all the same. I was in my laboratory at four o'clock, and since then... I've lived eight days... such days as no human being ever lived before! I'm nearly worn out, but I shan't sleep till I've told this thing over to you. Then I shall go to bed. But no interruptions! Is it agreed?'

'Agreed,' said the Editor, and the rest of us echoed 'Agreed.' And with that the Time Traveller began his story as I have set it forth. He sat back in his chair at first, and spoke like a weary man. Afterwards he got more animated. In writing it down I feel with only too much keenness the inadequacy of pen and ink — and, above all, my own inadequacy — to express its quality. You read, I will suppose, attentively enough; but you cannot see the speaker's white, sincere face in the bright circle of the little lamp, nor hear the intonation of his voice. You cannot know how his expression followed the turns of his story! Most of us hearers were in shadow, for the candles in the smoking-room had not been lighted, and only the face of the Journalist and the legs of the Silent Man from the knees downward were illuminated. At first we glanced now and again at each other. After a time we ceased to do that, and looked only at the Time Traveller's face.

Chapter III

'I told some of you last Thursday of the principles of the Time Machine, and showed you the actual thing itself, incomplete in the workshop. There it is now, a little travel-worn, truly; and one of the ivory bars is cracked, and a brass rail bent; but the rest of it's sound enough. I expected to finish it on Friday, but on Friday, when the putting together was nearly done, I found that one of the nickel bars was exactly one inch too short, and this I had to get remade; so that the thing was not complete until this morning. It was at ten o'clock to-day that the first of all Time Machines began its career. I gave it a last tap, tried all the screws again, put one more drop of oil on the quartz rod, and sat myself in the saddle. I suppose a suicide who holds a pistol to his skull feels much the same wonder at what will come next as I felt then. I took the starting lever in one hand and the stopping one in the other, pressed the first, and almost immediately the second. I seemed to reel; I felt a nightmare sensation of falling; and, looking round, I saw the laboratory exactly as before. Had anything happened? For a moment I suspected that my intellect had tricked me. Then I noted the clock. A moment before, as it seemed, it had stood at a minute or so past ten; now it was nearly halfpast three!

'I drew a breath, set my teeth, gripped the starting lever with both hands, and went off with a thud. The laboratory got hazy and went dark. Mrs. Watchett came in and walked, apparently without seeing me, towards the garden door. I suppose it took her a minute or so to traverse the place, but to me she seemed to shoot across the room like a rocket. I pressed the lever over to its extreme position. The night came like the turning out of a lamp, and in another moment came tomorrow. The laboratory grew faint and hazy, then fainter and ever fainter. Tomorrow night came black, then day again, night again, day again, faster and faster still. An eddying murmur filled my ears, and a strange, dumb confusedness descended on my mind.

'I am afraid I cannot convey the peculiar sensations of time travelling. They are excessively unpleasant. There is a feeling exactly like that one has upon a switchback — of a helpless headlong motion! I felt the same horrible anticipation, too, of an imminent smash. As I put on pace, night followed day like the flapping of a black wing. The dim suggestion of the laboratory seemed presently to fall away from me, and I saw the sun hopping swiftly across the sky, leaping it every minute, and every minute marking a day. I supposed the laboratory had been destroyed and I had come into the open air. I had a dim impression of scaffolding, but I was already going too fast to be conscious of any moving things. The slowest snail that ever crawled dashed by too fast for me. The twinkling succession of darkness and light was excessively painful to the eye. Then, in the intermittent darknesses, I saw the moon spinning swiftly through her quarters from new to full, and had a faint glimpse of the circling stars. Presently, as I went on, still gaining velocity, the palpitation of night and day merged into one continuous greyness; the sky took on a wonderful deepness of blue, a splendid luminous color like that of early twilight; the jerking sun became a streak of fire, a brilliant arch, in space; the moon a fainter fluctuating band; and I could see nothing of the stars, save now and then a brighter circle flickering in the blue.

'The landscape was misty and vague. I was still on the hillside upon which this house now stands, and the shoulder rose above me grey and dim. I saw trees growing and changing like puffs of vapour, now brown, now green; they grew, spread, shivered, and passed away. I saw huge buildings rise up faint and fair, and pass like dreams. The whole surface of the earth seemed changed — melting and flowing under my eyes. The little hands upon the dials that registered my speed raced round faster and faster. Presently I noted that the sun belt swayed up and down, from solstice to solstice, in a minute or less, and that consequently my pace was over a year a minute; and minute by minute the white snow flashed across the world, and vanished, and was followed by the bright, brief green of spring.

'The unpleasant sensations of the start were less poignant now. They merged at last into a kind of hysterical exhilaration. I remarked indeed a clumsy swaying of the machine, for which I was unable to account. But my mind was too confused to attend to it, so with a kind of madness growing upon me, I flung myself into futurity. At first I scarce thought of stopping, scarce thought of anything but these new sensations. But presently a fresh series of impressions grew up in my mind — a certain curiosity and therewith a certain dread — until at last they took complete possession of me. What strange developments of humanity, what wonderful advances upon our rudimentary civilization, I thought, might not appear when I came to look nearly into the dim elusive world that raced and fluctuated before my eyes! I saw great and splendid architecture rising about me, more massive than any buildings of our own time, and yet, as it seemed, built of glimmer and mist. I saw a richer green flow up the hillside, and remain there, without any wintry intermission. Even through the veil of my confusion the earth seemed very fair. And so my mind came round to the business of stopping.

'The peculiar risk lay in the possibility of my finding some substance in the space which I, or the machine, occupied. So long as I travelled at a high velocity through time, this scarcely mattered; I was, so to speak, attenuated — was slipping like a vapour through the interstices of intervening substances! But to come to a stop involved the jamming of myself, molecule by molecule, into whatever lay in my way; meant bringing my atoms into such intimate contact with those of the obstacle that a profound chemical reaction — possibly a far-reaching explosion — would result, and blow myself and my apparatus out of all possible dimensions — into the Unknown. This possibility had occurred to me again and again while I was making the machine; but then I had cheerfully accepted it as an unavoidable risk — one of the risks a man has got to take! Now the risk was inevitable, I no longer saw it in the same cheerful light. The fact is that, insensibly, the absolute strangeness of everything, the sickly jarring and swaying of the machine, above all, the feeling of prolonged falling, had absolutely upset my nerve. I told myself that I could never stop, and with a gust of petulance I resolved to stop forthwith. Like an impatient fool, I lugged over the lever, and incontinently the thing went reeling over, and I was flung headlong through the air.

'There was the sound of a clap of thunder in my ears. I may have been stunned for a moment. A pitiless hail was hissing round me, and I was sitting on soft turf in front of the overset machine. Everything still seemed grey, but presently I remarked that the confusion in my ears was gone. I looked round me. I was on what seemed to be a little lawn in a garden, surrounded by rhododendron bushes, and I noticed that their mauve and purple blossoms were dropping in a shower under the beating of the hailstones. The rebounding, dancing hail hung in a cloud over the machine, and drove along the ground like smoke. In a moment I was wet to the skin. "Fine hospitality," said I, "to a man who has travelled innumerable years to see you."

'Presently I thought what a fool I was to get wet. I stood up and looked round me. A colossal figure, carved apparently in some white stone, loomed indistinctly beyond the rhododendrons through the hazy downpour. But all else of the world was invisible.

'My sensations would be hard to describe. As the columns of hail grew thinner, I saw the white figure more distinctly. It was very large, for a silver birch-tree touched its shoulder. It was of white marble, in shape something like a winged sphinx, but the wings, instead of being carried vertically at the sides, were spread so that it seemed to hover. The pedestal, it appeared to me, was of bronze, and was thick with verdigris. It chanced that the face was towards me; the sightless eyes seemed to watch me; there was the faint shadow of a smile on the lips. It was greatly weatherworn, and that imparted an unpleasant suggestion of disease. I stood looking at it for a little space — half a minute, perhaps, or half an hour. It seemed to advance and to recede as the hail drove before it denser or thinner. At last I tore my eyes from it for a moment and saw that the hail curtain had worn threadbare, and that the sky was lightening with the promise of the sun.

'I looked up again at the crouching white shape, and the full temerity of my voyage came suddenly upon me. What might appear when that hazy curtain was altogether withdrawn? What might not have happened to men? What if cruelty had grown into a common passion? What if in this interval the race had lost its manliness and had developed into something in-human, unsympathetic, and overwhelmingly powerful? I might seem some old-world savage animal, only the more dreadful and disgusting for our common likeness — a foul creature to be incontinently slain.

'Already I saw other vast shapes — huge buildings with intricate parapets and tall columns, with a wooded hillside dimly creeping in upon me through the lessening storm. I was seized with a panic fear. I turned frantically to the Time Machine, and strove hard to readjust it. As I did so the shafts of the sun smote through the thunderstorm. The grey downpour was swept aside and vanished like the trailing garments of a ghost. Above me, in the intense blue of the summer sky, some faint brown shreds of cloud whirled into nothingness. The great buildings about me stood out clear and distinct, shining with the wet of the thunderstorm, and picked out in white by the unmelted hailstones piled along their courses. I felt naked in a strange world. I felt as perhaps a bird may feel in the clear air, knowing the hawk wings above and will swoop. My fear grew to frenzy. I took a breathing space, set my teeth, and again grappled fiercely, wrist and knee, with the machine. It gave under my desperate onset and turned over. It struck my chin violently. One hand on the saddle, the other on the lever, I stood panting heavily in attitude to mount again.

'But with this recovery of a prompt retreat my courage recovered. I looked more curiously and less fearfully at this world of the remote future. In a circular opening, high up in the wall of the nearer house, I saw a group of figures clad in rich soft robes. They had seen me, and their faces were directed towards me.

'Then I heard voices approaching me. Coming through the bushes by the White Sphinx were the heads and shoulders of men running. One of these emerged in a pathway leading straight to the little lawn upon which I stood with my machine. He was a slight creature — perhaps four feet high — clad in a purple tunic, girdled at the waist with a leather belt. Sandals or buskins — I could not clearly distinguish which — were on his feet; his legs were bare to the knees, and his head was bare. Noticing that, I noticed for the first time how warm the air was.

'He struck me as being a very beautiful and graceful creature, but indescribably frail. His flushed face reminded me of the more beautiful kind of consumptive — that hectic beauty of which we used to hear so much. At the sight of him I suddenly regained confidence. I took my hands from the machine.

Chapter IV

'In another moment we were standing face to face, I and this fragile thing out of futurity. He came straight up to me and laughed into my eyes. The absence from his bearing of any sign of fear struck me at once. Then he turned to the two others who were following him and spoke to them in a strange and very sweet and liquid tongue.

'There were others coming, and presently a little group of perhaps eight or ten of these exquisite creatures were about me. One of them addressed me. It came into my head, oddly enough, that my voice was too harsh and deep for them. So I shook my head, and, pointing to my ears, shook it again. He came a step forward, hesitated, and then touched my hand. Then I felt other soft little tentacles upon my back and shoulders. They wanted to make sure I was real. There was nothing in this at all alarming. Indeed, there was something in these pretty little people that inspired confidence — a graceful gentleness, a certain childlike ease. And besides, they looked so frail that I could fancy myself flinging the whole dozen of them about like ninepins. But I made a sudden motion to warn them when I saw their little pink hands feeling at the Time Machine. Happily then, when it was not too late, I thought of a danger I had hitherto forgotten, and reaching over the bars of the machine I unscrewed the little levers that would set it in motion, and put these in my pocket. Then I turned again to see what I could do in the way of communication.

'And then, looking more nearly into their features, I saw some further peculiarities in their Dresden-china type of prettiness. Their hair, which was uniformly curly, came to a sharp end at the neck and cheek; there was not the faintest suggestion of it on the face, and their ears were singularly minute. The mouths were small, with bright red, rather thin lips, and the little chins ran to a point. The eyes were large and mild; and — this may seem egotism on my part — I fancied even that there was a certain lack of the interest I might have expected in them.

'As they made no effort to communicate with me, but simply stood round me smiling and speaking in soft cooing notes to each other, I began the conversation. I pointed to the Time Machine and to myself. Then hesitating for a moment how to express time, I pointed to the sun. At once a quaintly pretty little figure in chequered purple and white followed my gesture, and then astonished me by imitating the sound of thunder.

'For a moment I was staggered, though the import of his gesture was plain enough. The question had come into my mind abruptly: were these creatures fools? You may hardly understand how it took me. You see I had always anticipated that the people of the year Eight Hundred and Two Thousand odd would be incredibly in front of us in knowledge, art, everything. Then one of them suddenly asked me a question that showed him to be on the intellectual level of one of our five-year-old children — asked me, in fact, if I had come from the sun in a thunderstorm! It let loose the judgment I had suspended upon their clothes, their frail light limbs, and fragile features. A flow of disappointment rushed across my mind. For a moment I felt that I had built the Time Machine in vain.

'I nodded, pointed to the sun, and gave them such a vivid rendering of a thunderclap as startled them. They all withdrew a pace or so and bowed. Then came one laughing towards me, carrying a chain of beautiful flowers altogether new to me, and put it about my neck. The idea was received with melodious applause; and presently they were all running to and fro for flowers, and laughingly flinging them upon me until I was almost smothered with blossom. You who have never seen the like can scarcely imagine what delicate and wonderful flowers countless years of culture had created. Then someone suggested that their plaything should be exhibited in the nearest building, and so I was led past the sphinx of white marble, which had seemed to watch me all the while with a smile at my astonishment, towards a vast grey edifice of fretted stone. As I went with them the memory of my confident anticipations of a profoundly grave and intellectual posterity came, with irresistible merriment, to my mind.

'The building had a huge entry, and was altogether of colossal dimensions. I was naturally most occupied with the growing crowd of little people, and with the big open portals that yawned before me shadowy and mysterious. My general impression of the world I saw over their heads was a tangled waste of beautiful bushes and flowers, a long neglected and yet weedless garden. I saw a number of tall spikes of strange white flowers, measuring a foot perhaps across the spread of the waxen petals. They grew scattered, as if wild, among the variegated shrubs, but, as I say, I did not examine them closely at this time. The Time Machine was left deserted on the turf among the rhododendrons.

'The arch of the doorway was richly carved, but naturally I did not observe the carving very narrowly, though I fancied I saw suggestions of old Phoenician decorations as I passed through, and it struck me that they were very badly broken and weatherworn. Several more brightly clad people met me in the doorway, and so we entered, I, dressed in dingy nineteenth-century garments, looking grotesque enough, garlanded with flowers, and surrounded by an eddying mass of bright, soft-colored robes and shining white limbs, in a melodious whirl of laughter and laughing speech.

'The big doorway opened into a proportionately great hall hung with brown. The roof was in shadow, and the windows, partially glazed with coloured glass and partially unglazed, admitted a tempered light. The floor was made up of huge blocks of some very hard white metal, not plates nor slabs — blocks, and it was so much worn, as I judged by the going to and fro of past generations, as to be deeply channelled along the more frequented ways. Transverse to the length were innumerable tables made of slabs of polished stone, raised perhaps a foot from the floor, and upon these were heaps of fruits. Some I recognized as a kind of hypertrophied raspberry and orange, but for the most part they were strange.

'Between the tables was scattered a great number of cushions. Upon these my conductors seated themselves, signing for me to do likewise. With a pretty absence of ceremony they began to eat the fruit with their hands, flinging peel and stalks, and so forth, into the round openings in the sides of the tables. I was not loath to follow their example, for I felt thirsty and hungry. As I did so I surveyed the hall at my leisure.

'And perhaps the thing that struck me most was its dilapidated look. The stained-glass windows, which displayed only a geometrical pattern, were broken in many places, and the curtains that hung across the lower end were thick with dust. And it caught my eye that the corner of the marble table near me was fractured. Nevertheless, the general effect was extremely rich and picturesque. There were, perhaps, a couple of hundred people dining in the hall, and most of them, seated as near to me as they could come, were watching me with interest, their little eyes shining over the fruit they were eating. All were clad in the same soft and yet strong, silky material.

'Fruit, by the by, was all their diet. These people of the remote future were strict vegetarians, and while I was with them, in spite of some carnal cravings, I had to be frugivorous also. Indeed, I found afterwards that horses, cattle, sheep, dogs, had followed the Ichthyosaurus into extinction. But the fruits were very delightful; one, in particular, that seemed to be in season all the time I was there — a floury thing in a three-sided husk — was especially good, and I made it my staple. At first I was puzzled by all these strange fruits, and by the strange flowers I saw, but later I began to perceive their import.

'However, I am telling you of my fruit dinner in the distant future now. So soon as my appetite was a little checked, I determined to make a resolute attempt to learn the speech of these new men of mine. Clearly that was the next thing to do. The fruits seemed a convenient thing to begin upon, and holding one of these up I began a series of interrogative sounds and gestures. I had some considerable difficulty in conveying my meaning. At first my efforts met with a stare of surprise or inextinguishable laughter, but presently a fair-haired little creature seemed to grasp my intention and repeated a name. They had to chatter and explain the business at great length to each other, and my first attempts to make the exquisite little sounds of their language caused an immense amount of amusement. However, I felt like a schoolmaster amidst children, and persisted, and presently I had a score of noun substantives at least at my command; and then I got to demonstrative pronouns, and even the verb "to eat." But it was slow work, and the little people soon tired and wanted to get away from my interrogations, so I determined, rather of necessity, to let them give their lessons in little doses when they felt inclined. And very little doses I found they were before long, for I never met people more indolent or more easily fatigued.

'A queer thing I soon discovered about my little hosts, and that was their lack of interest. They would come to me with eager cries of astonishment, like children, but like children they would soon stop examining me and wander away after some other toy. The dinner and my conversational beginnings ended, I noted for the first time that almost all those who had surrounded me at first were gone. It is odd, too, how speedily I came to disregard these little people. I went out through the portal into the sunlit world again as soon as my hunger was satisfied. I was continually meeting more of these men of the future, who would follow me a little distance, chatter and laugh about me, and, having smiled and gesticulated in a friendly way, leave me again to my own devices.

'The calm of evening was upon the world as I emerged from the great hall, and the scene was lit by the warm glow of the setting sun. At first things were very confusing. Everything was so entirely different from the world I had known — even the flowers. The big building I had left was situated on the slope of a broad river valley, but the Thames had shifted perhaps a mile from its present position. I resolved to mount to the summit of a crest, perhaps a mile and a half away, from which I could get a wider view of this our planet in the year Eight Hundred and Two Thousand Seven Hundred and One A.D. For that, I should explain, was the date the little dials of my machine recorded.

'As I walked I was watching for every impression that could possibly help to explain the condition of ruinous splendour in which I found the world — for ruinous it was. A little way up the hill, for instance, was a great heap of granite, bound together by masses of aluminium, a vast labyrinth of precipitous walls and crumpled heaps, amidst which were thick heaps of very beautiful pagoda-like plants — nettles possibly — but wonderfully tinted with brown about the leaves, and incapable of stinging. It was evidently the derelict remains of some vast structure, to what end built I could not determine. It was here that I was destined, at a later date, to have a very strange experience — the first intimation of a still stranger discovery — but of that I will speak in its proper place.

'Looking round with a sudden thought, from a terrace on which I rested for a while, I realized that there were no small houses to be seen. Apparently the single house, and possibly even the household, had vanished. Here and there among the greenery were palace-like buildings, but the house and the cottage, which form such characteristic features of our own English landscape, had disappeared.

'"Communism," said I to myself.

'And on the heels of that came another thought. I looked at the half-dozen little figures that were following me. Then, in a flash, I perceived that all had the same form of costume, the same soft hairless visage, and the same girlish rotundity of limb. It may seem strange, perhaps, that I had not noticed this before. But everything was so strange. Now, I saw the fact plainly enough. In costume, and in all the differences of texture and bearing that now mark off the sexes from each other, these people of the future were alike. And the children seemed to my eyes to be but the miniatures of their parents. I judged, then, that the children of that time were extremely precocious, physically at least, and I found afterwards abundant verification of my opinion.

'Seeing the ease and security in which these people were living, I felt that this close resemblance of the sexes was after all what one would expect; for the strength of a man and the softness of a woman, the institution of the family, and the differentiation of occupations are mere militant necessities of an age of physical force; where population is balanced and abundant, much childbearing becomes an evil rather than a blessing to the State; where violence comes but rarely and offspring are secure, there is less necessity — indeed there is no necessity — for an efficient family, and the specialization of the sexes with reference to their children's needs disappears. We see some beginnings of this even in our own time, and in this future age it was complete. This, I must remind you, was my speculation at the time. Later, I was to appreciate how far it fell short of the reality.

'While I was musing upon these things, my attention was attracted by a pretty little structure, like a well under a cupola. I thought in a transitory way of the oddness of wells still existing, and then resumed the thread of my speculations. There were no large buildings towards the top of the hill, and as my walking powers were evidently miraculous, I was presently left alone for the first time. With a strange sense of freedom and adventure I pushed on up to the crest.

'There I found a seat of some yellow metal that I did not recognize, corroded in places with a kind of pinkish rust and half smothered in soft moss, the arm-rests cast and filed into the resemblance of griffins' heads. I sat down on it, and I surveyed the broad view of our old world under the sunset of that long day. It was as sweet and fair a view as I have ever seen. The sun had already gone below the horizon and the west was flaming gold, touched with some horizontal bars of purple and crimson. Below was the valley of the Thames, in which the river lay like a band of burnished steel. I have already spoken of the great palaces dotted about among the variegated greenery, some in ruins and some still occupied. Here and there rose a white or silvery figure in the waste garden of the earth, here and there came the sharp vertical line of some cupola or obelisk. There were no hedges, no signs of proprietary rights, no evidences of agriculture; the whole earth had become a garden.

'So watching, I began to put my interpretation upon the things I had seen, and as it shaped itself to me that evening, my interpretation was something in this way. (Afterwards I found I had got only a half-truth — or only a glimpse of one facet of the truth.)

'It seemed to me that I had happened upon humanity upon the wane. The ruddy sunset set me thinking of the sunset of mankind. For the first time I began to realize an odd consequence of the social effort in which we are at present engaged. And yet, come to think, it is a logical consequence enough. Strength is the outcome of need; security sets a premium on feebleness. The work of ameliorating the conditions of life — the true civilizing process that makes life more and more secure — had gone steadily on to a climax. One triumph of a united humanity over Nature had followed another. Things that are now mere dreams had become projects deliberately put in hand and carried forward. And the harvest was what I saw!

'After all, the sanitation and the agriculture of to-day are still in the rudimentary stage. The science of our time has attacked but a little department of the field of human disease, but even so, it spreads its operations very steadily and persistently. Our agriculture and horticulture destroy a weed just here and there and cultivate perhaps a score or so of wholesome plants, leaving the greater number to fight out a balance as they can. We improve our favourite plants and animals — and how few they are — gradually by selective breeding; now a new and better peach, now a seedless grape, now a sweeter and larger flower, now a more convenient breed of cattle. We improve them gradually, because our ideals are vague and tentative, and our knowledge is very limited; because Nature, too, is shy and slow in our clumsy hands. Some day all this will be better organized, and still better. That is the drift of the current in spite of the eddies. The whole world will be intelligent, educated, and cooperating; things will move faster and faster towards the subjugation of Nature. In the end, wisely and carefully we shall readjust the balance of animal and vegetable life to suit our human needs.

'This adjustment, I say, must have been done, and done well; done indeed for all Time, in the space of Time across which my machine had leaped. The air was free from gnats, the earth from weeds or fungi; everywhere were fruits and sweet and delightful flowers; brilliant butterflies flew hither and thither. The ideal of preventive medicine was attained. Diseases had been stamped out. I saw no evidence of any contagious diseases during all my stay. And I shall have to tell you later that even the processes of putrefaction and decay had been profoundly affected by these changes.

'Social triumphs, too, had been effected. I saw mankind housed in splendid shelters, gloriously clothed, and as yet I had found them engaged in no toil. There were no signs of struggle, neither social nor economical struggle. The shop, the advertisement, traffic, all that commerce which constitutes the body of our world, was gone. It was natural on that golden evening that I should jump at the idea of a social paradise. The difficulty of increasing population had been met, I guessed, and population had ceased to increase.

'But with this change in condition comes inevitably adaptations to the change. What, unless biological science is a mass of errors, is the cause of human intelligence and vigour? Hardship and freedom: conditions under which the active, strong, and subtle survive and the weaker go to the wall; conditions that put a premium upon the loyal alliance of capable men, upon self-restraint, patience, and decision. And the institution of the family, and the emotions that arise therein, the fierce jealousy, the tenderness for offspring, parental self-devotion, all found their justification and support in the imminent dangers of the young. *Now* , where are these imminent dangers? There is a sentiment arising, and it will grow, against connubial jealousy, against fierce maternity, against passion of all sorts; unnecessary things now, and things that make us uncomfortable, savage survivals, discords in a refined and pleasant life.

'I thought of the physical slightness of the people, their lack of intelligence, and those big abundant ruins, and it strengthened my belief in a perfect conquest of Nature. For after the battle comes Quiet. Humanity had been strong, energetic, and intelligent, and had used all its abundant vitality to alter the conditions under which it lived. And now came the reaction of the altered conditions.

'Under the new conditions of perfect comfort and security, that restless energy, that with us is strength, would become weakness. Even in our own time certain tendencies and desires, once necessary to survival, are a constant source of failure. Physical courage and the love of battle, for instance, are no great help — may even be hindrances — to a civilized man. And in a state of physical balance and security, power, intellectual as well as physical, would be out of place. For countless years I judged there had been no danger of war or solitary violence, no danger from wild beasts, no wasting disease to require strength of constitution, no need of toil. For such a life, what we should call the weak are as well equipped as the strong, are indeed no longer weak. Better equipped indeed they are, for the strong would be fretted by an energy for which there was no outlet. No doubt the exquisite beauty of the buildings I saw was the outcome of the last surgings of the now purposeless energy of mankind before it settled down into perfect harmony with the conditions under which it lived — the flourish of that triumph which began the last great peace. This has ever been the fate of energy in security; it takes to art and to eroticism, and then come languor and decay.

'Even this artistic impetus would at last die away — had almost died in the Time I saw. To adorn themselves with flowers, to dance, to sing in the sunlight: so much was left of the artistic spirit, and no more. Even that would fade in the end into a contented inactivity. We are kept keen on the grindstone of pain and necessity, and, it seemed to me, that here was that hateful grindstone broken at last!

'As I stood there in the gathering dark I thought that in this simple explanation I had mastered the problem of the world — mastered the whole secret of these delicious people. Possibly the checks they had devised for the increase of population had succeeded too well, and their numbers had rather diminished than kept stationary. That would account for the abandoned ruins. Very simple was my explanation, and plausible enough — as most wrong theories are!

Chapter V

'As I stood there musing over this too perfect triumph of man, the full moon, yellow and gibbous, came up out of an overflow of silver light in the northeast. The bright little figures ceased to move about below, a noiseless owl flitted by, and I shivered with the chill of the night. I determined to descend and find where I could sleep.

'I looked for the building I knew. Then my eye travelled along to the figure of the White Sphinx upon the pedestal of bronze, growing distinct as the light of the rising moon grew brighter. I could see the silver birch against it. There was the tangle of rhododendron bushes, black in the pale light, and there was the little lawn. I looked at the lawn again. A queer doubt chilled my complacency. "No," said I stoutly to myself, "that was not the lawn."

'But it *was* the lawn. For the white leprous face of the sphinx was towards it. Can you imagine what I felt as this conviction came home to me? But you cannot. The Time Machine was gone!

'At once, like a lash across the face, came the possibility of losing my own age, of being left helpless in this strange new world. The bare thought of it was an actual physical sensation. I could feel it grip me at the throat and stop my breathing. In another moment I was in a passion of fear and running with great leaping strides down the slope. Once I fell headlong and cut my face; I lost no time in stanching the blood, but jumped up and ran on, with a warm trickle down my cheek and chin. All the time I ran I was saying to myself: "They have moved it a little, pushed it under the bushes out of the way." Nevertheless, I ran with all my might. All the time, with the certainty that sometimes comes with excessive dread, I knew that such assurance was folly, knew instinctively that the machine was removed out of my reach. My breath came with pain. I suppose I covered the whole distance from the hill crest to the little lawn, two miles perhaps, in ten minutes. And I am not a young man. I cursed aloud, as I ran, at my confident folly in leaving the machine, wasting good breath thereby. I cried aloud, and none answered. Not a creature seemed to be stirring in that moonlit world.

'When I reached the lawn my worst fears were realized. Not a trace of the thing was to be seen. I felt faint and cold when I faced the empty space among the black tangle of bushes. I ran round it furiously, as if the thing might be hidden in a corner, and then stopped abruptly, with my hands clutching my hair. Above me towered the sphinx, upon the bronze pedestal, white, shining, leprous, in the light of the rising moon. It seemed to smile in mockery of my dismay.

'I might have consoled myself by imagining the little people had put the mechanism in some shelter for me, had I not felt assured of their physical and intellectual inadequacy. That is what dismayed me: the sense of some hitherto unsuspected power, through whose intervention my invention had vanished. Yet, for one thing I felt assured: unless some other age had produced its exact duplicate, the machine could not have moved in time. The attachment of the levers —

I will show you the method later — prevented any one from tampering with it in that way when they were removed. It had moved, and was hid, only in space. But then, where could it be?

'I think I must have had a kind of frenzy. I remember running violently in and out among the moonlit bushes all round the sphinx, and startling some white animal that, in the dim light, I took for a small deer. I remember, too, late that night, beating the bushes with my clenched fist until my knuckles were gashed and bleeding from the broken twigs. Then, sobbing and raving in my anguish of mind, I went down to the great building of stone. The big hall was dark, silent, and deserted. I slipped on the uneven floor, and fell over one of the malachite tables, almost breaking my shin. I lit a match and went on past the dusty curtains, of which I have told you.

'There I found a second great hall covered with cushions, upon which, perhaps, a score or so of the little people were sleeping. I have no doubt they found my second appearance strange enough, coming suddenly out of the quiet darkness with inarticulate noises and the splutter and flare of a match. For they had forgotten about matches. "Where is my Time Machine?" I began, bawling like an angry child, laying hands upon them and shaking them up together. It must have been very queer to them. Some laughed, most of them looked sorely frightened. When I saw them standing round me, it came into my head that I was doing as foolish a thing as it was possible for me to do under the circumstances, in trying to revive the sensation of fear. For, reasoning from their daylight behaviour, I thought that fear must be forgotten.

'Abruptly, I dashed down the match, and, knocking one of the people over in my course, went blundering across the big dining-hall again, out under the moonlight. I heard cries of terror and their little feet running and stumbling this way and that. I do not remember all I did as the moon crept up the sky. I suppose it was the unexpected nature of my loss that maddened me. I felt hopelessly cut off from my own kind — a strange animal in an unknown world. I must have raved to and fro, screaming and crying upon God and Fate. I have a memory of horrible fatigue, as the long night of despair wore away; of looking in this impossible place and that; of groping among moonlit ruins and touching strange creatures in the black shadows; at last, of lying on the ground near the sphinx and weeping with absolute wretchedness. I had nothing left but misery. Then I slept, and when I woke again it was full day, and a couple of sparrows were hopping round me on the turf within reach of my arm.

'I sat up in the freshness of the morning, trying to remember how I had got there, and why I had such a profound sense of desertion and despair. Then things came clear in my mind. With the plain, reasonable daylight, I could look my circumstances fairly in the face. I saw the wild folly of my frenzy overnight, and I could reason with myself. "Suppose the worst?" I said. "Suppose the machine altogether lost — perhaps destroyed? It behoves me to be calm and patient, to learn the way of the people, to get a clear idea of the method of my loss, and the means of getting materials and tools; so that in the end, perhaps, I may make another." That would be my only hope, perhaps, but better than despair. And, after all, it was a beautiful and curious world.

'But probably, the machine had only been taken away. Still, I must be calm and patient, find its hiding-place, and recover it by force or cunning. And with that I scrambled to my feet and looked about me, wondering where I could bathe. I felt weary, stiff, and travel-soiled. The freshness of the morning made me desire an equal freshness. I had exhausted my emotion. Indeed, as I went about my business, I found myself wondering at my intense excitement overnight. I made a careful examination of the ground about the little lawn. I wasted some time in futile questionings, conveyed, as well as I was able, to such of the little people as came by. They all failed to understand my gestures; some were simply stolid, some thought it was a jest and laughed at me. I had the hardest task in the world to keep my hands off their pretty laughing faces. It was a foolish impulse, but the devil begotten of fear and blind anger was ill curbed and still eager to take advantage of my perplexity. The turf gave better counsel. I found a groove ripped in it, about midway between the pedestal of the sphinx and the marks of my feet where, on arrival, I had struggled with the overturned machine. There were other signs of removal about, with queer narrow footprints like those I could imagine made by a sloth.

This directed my closer attention to the pedestal. It was, as I think I have said, of bronze. It was not a mere block, but highly decorated with deep framed panels on either side. I went and rapped at these. The pedestal was hollow. Examining the panels with care I found them discontinuous with the frames. There were no handles or keyholes, but possibly the panels, if they were doors, as I supposed, opened from within. One thing was clear enough to my mind. It took no very great mental effort to infer that my Time Machine was inside that pedestal. But how it got there was a different problem.

'I saw the heads of two orange-clad people coming through the bushes and under some blossom-covered apple-trees towards me. I turned smiling to them and beckoned them to me. They came, and then, pointing to the bronze pedestal, I tried to intimate my wish to open it. But at my first gesture towards this they behaved very oddly. I don't know how to convey their expression to you. Suppose you were to use a grossly improper gesture to a delicate-minded woman — it is how she would look. They went off as if they had received the last possible insult. I tried a sweet-looking little chap in white next, with exactly the same result. Somehow, his manner made me feel ashamed of myself. But, as you know, I wanted the Time Machine, and I tried him once more. As he turned off, like the others, my temper got the better of me. In three strides I was after him, had him by the loose part of his robe round the neck, and began dragging him towards the sphinx. Then I saw the horror and repugnance of his face, and all of a sudden I let him go.

'But I was not beaten yet. I banged with my fist at the bronze panels. I thought I heard something stir inside — to be explicit, I thought I heard a sound like a chuckle — but I must have been mistaken. Then I got a big pebble from the river, and came and hammered till I had flattened a coil in the decorations, and the verdigris came off in powdery flakes. The delicate little people must have heard me hammering in gusty outbreaks a mile away on either hand, but nothing came of it. I saw a crowd of them upon the slopes, looking furtively at me. At last, hot and tired, I sat down to watch the place. But I was too restless to watch long; I am too Occidental for a long vigil. I could work at a problem for years, but to wait inactive for twenty-four hours — that is another matter.

'I got up after a time, and began walking aimlessly through the bushes towards the hill again. "Patience," said I to myself. "If you want your machine again you must leave that sphinx alone. If they mean to take your machine away, it's little good your wrecking their bronze panels, and if they don't, you will get it back as soon as you can ask for it. To sit among all those unknown things before a puzzle like that is hopeless. That way lies monomania. Face this world. Learn its ways, watch it, be careful of too hasty guesses at its meaning. In the end you will find clues to it all." Then suddenly the humour of the situation came into my mind: the thought of the years I had spent in study and toil to get into the future age, and now my passion of anxiety to get out of it. I had made myself the most complicated and the most hopeless trap that ever a man devised. Although it was at my own expense, I could not help myself. I laughed aloud.

'Going through the big palace, it seemed to me that the little people avoided me. It may have been my fancy, or it may have had something to do with my hammering at the gates of bronze. Yet I felt tolerably sure of the avoidance. I was careful, however, to show no concern and to abstain from any pursuit of them, and in the course of a day or two things got back to the old footing. I made what progress I could in the language, and in addition I pushed my explorations here and there. Either I missed some subtle point or their language was excessively simple — almost exclusively composed of concrete substantives and verbs. There seemed to be few, if any, abstract terms, or little use of figurative language. Their sentences were usually simple and of two words, and I failed to convey or understand any but the simplest propositions. I determined to put the thought of my Time Machine and the mystery of the bronze doors under the sphinx as much as possible in a corner of memory, until my growing knowledge would lead me back to them in a natural way. Yet a certain feeling, you may understand, tethered me in a circle of a few miles round the point of my arrival.

'So far as I could see, all the world displayed the same exuberant richness as the Thames valley. From every hill I climbed I saw the same abundance of splendid buildings, endlessly varied in material and style, the same clustering thickets of evergreens, the same blossom-laden trees and tree-ferns. Here and there water shone like silver, and beyond, the land rose into blue undulating hills, and so faded into the serenity of the sky. A peculiar feature, which presently attracted my attention, was the presence of certain circular wells, several, as it seemed to me, of a very great depth. One lay by the path up the hill, which I had followed during my first walk. Like the others, it was rimmed with bronze, curiously wrought, and protected by a little cupola from the rain. Sitting by the side of these wells, and peering down into the shafted darkness, I could see no gleam of water, nor could I start any reflection with a lighted match. But in all of them I heard a certain sound: a thud — thud — thud, like the beating of some big engine; and I discovered, from the flaring of my matches, that a steady current of air set down the shafts. Further, I threw a scrap of paper into the throat of one, and, instead of fluttering slowly down, it was at once sucked swiftly out of sight.

'After a time, too, I came to connect these wells with tall towers standing here and there upon the slopes; for above them there was often just such a flicker in the air as one sees on a hot day above a sun-scorched beach. Putting things together, I reached a strong suggestion of an extensive system of subterranean ventilation, whose true import it was difficult to imagine. I was at first inclined to associate it with the sanitary apparatus of these people. It was an obvious conclusion, but it was absolutely wrong.

'And here I must admit that I learned very little of drains and bells and modes of conveyance, and the like conveniences, during my time in this real future. In some of these visions of Utopias and coming times which I have read, there is a vast amount of detail about building, and social arrangements, and so forth. But while such details are easy enough to obtain when the whole world is contained in one's imagination, they are altogether inaccessible to a real traveller amid such realities as I found here. Conceive the tale of London which a negro, fresh from Central Africa, would take back to his tribe! What would he know of railway companies, of social movements, of telephone and telegraph wires, of the Parcels Delivery Company, and postal orders and the like? Yet we, at least, should be willing enough to explain these things to him! And even of what he knew, how much could he make his untravelled friend either apprehend or believe? Then, think how narrow the gap between a negro and a white man of our own times, and how wide the interval between myself and these of the Golden Age! I was sensible of much which was unseen, and which contributed to my comfort; but save for a general impression of automatic organization, I fear I can convey very little of the difference to your mind.

'In the matter of sepulture, for instance, I could see no signs of crematoria nor anything suggestive of tombs. But it occurred to me that, possibly, there might be cemeteries (or crematoria) somewhere beyond the range of my explorings. This, again, was a question I deliberately put to myself, and my curiosity was at first entirely defeated upon the point. The thing puzzled me, and I was led to make a further remark, which puzzled me still more: that aged and infirm among this people there were none.

'I must confess that my satisfaction with my first theories of an automatic civilization and a decadent humanity did not long endure. Yet I could think of no other. Let me put my difficulties. The several big palaces I had explored were mere living places, great dining-halls and sleeping apartments. I could find no machinery, no appliances of any kind. Yet these people were clothed in pleasant fabrics that must at times need renewal, and their sandals, though undecorated, were fairly complex specimens of metalwork. Somehow such things must be made. And the little people displayed no vestige of a creative tendency. There were no shops, no workshops, no sign of importations among them. They spent all their time in playing gently, in bathing in the river, in making love in a half-playful fashion, in eating fruit and sleeping. I could not see how things were kept going.

'Then, again, about the Time Machine: something, I knew not what, had taken it into the hollow pedestal of the White Sphinx. Why? For the life of me I could not imagine. Those waterless wells, too, those flickering pillars. I felt I lacked a clue. I felt — how shall I put it? Suppose you found an inscription, with sentences here and there in excellent plain English, and interpolated therewith, others made up of words, of letters even, absolutely unknown to you? Well, on the third day of my visit, that was how the world of Eight Hundred and Two Thousand Seven Hundred and One presented itself to me!

'That day, too, I made a friend — of a sort. It happened that, as I was watching some of the little people bathing in a shallow, one of them was seized with cramp and began drifting downstream. The main current ran rather swiftly, but not too strongly for even a moderate swimmer. It will give you an idea, therefore, of the strange deficiency in these creatures, when I tell you that none made the slightest attempt to rescue the weakly crying little thing which was drowning before their eyes. When I realized this, I hurriedly slipped off my clothes, and, wading in at a point lower down, I caught the poor mite and drew her safe to land. A little rubbing of the limbs soon brought her round, and I had the satisfaction of seeing she was all right before I left her. I had got to such a low estimate of her kind that I did not expect any gratitude from her. In that, however, I was wrong.

'This happened in the morning. In the afternoon I met my little woman, as I believe it was, as I was returning towards my centre from an exploration, and she received me with cries of delight and presented me with a big garland of flowers — evidently made for me and me alone. The thing took my imagination. Very possibly I had been feeling desolate. At any rate I did my best to display my appreciation of the gift. We were soon seated together in a little stone arbour, engaged in conversation, chiefly of smiles. The creature's friendliness affected me exactly as a child's might have done. We passed each other flowers, and she kissed my hands. I did the same to hers. Then I tried talk, and found that her name was Weena, which, though I don't know what it meant, somehow seemed appropriate enough. That was the beginning of a queer friendship which lasted a week, and ended — as I will tell you!

'She was exactly like a child. She wanted to be with me always. She tried to follow me everywhere, and on my next journey out and about it went to my heart to tire her down, and leave her at last, exhausted and calling after me rather plaintively. But the problems of the world had to be mastered. I had not, I said to myself, come into the future to carry on a miniature flirtation. Yet her distress when I left her was very great, her expostulations at the parting were sometimes frantic, and I think, altogether, I had as much trouble as comfort from her devotion. Nevertheless she was, somehow, a very great comfort. I thought it was mere childish affection that made her cling to me. Until it was too late, I did not clearly know what I had inflicted upon her when I left her. Nor until it was too late did I clearly understand what she was to me. For, by merely seeming fond of me, and showing in her weak, futile way that she cared for me, the little doll of a creature presently gave my return to the neighbourhood of the White Sphinx almost the feeling of coming home; and I would watch for her tiny figure of white and gold so soon as I came over the hill.

'It was from her, too, that I learned that fear had not yet left the world. She was fearless enough in the daylight, and she had the oddest confidence in me; for once, in a foolish moment, I made threatening grimaces at her, and she simply laughed at them. But she dreaded the dark, dreaded shadows, dreaded black things. Darkness to her was the one thing dreadful. It was a singularly passionate emotion, and it set me thinking and observing. I discovered then, among other things, that these little people gathered into the great houses after dark, and slept in droves. To enter upon them without a light was to put them into a tumult of apprehension. I never found one out of doors, or one sleeping alone within doors, after dark. Yet I was still such a blockhead that I missed the lesson of that fear, and in spite of Weena's distress I insisted upon sleeping away from these slumbering multitudes.

'It troubled her greatly, but in the end her odd affection for me triumphed, and for five of the nights of our acquaintance, including the last night of all, she slept with her head pillowed on my arm. But my story slips away from me as I speak of her. It must have been the night before her rescue that I was awakened about dawn. I had been restless, dreaming most disagreeably that I was drowned, and that sea anemones were feeling over my face with their soft palps. I woke with a start, and with an odd fancy that some greyish animal had just rushed out of the chamber. I tried to get to sleep again, but I felt restless and uncomfortable. It was that dim grey hour when things are just creeping out of darkness, when everything is colourless and clear cut, and yet unreal. I got up, and went down into the great hall, and so out upon the flagstones in front of the palace. I thought I would make a virtue of necessity, and see the sunrise.

'The moon was setting, and the dying moonlight and the first pallor of dawn were mingled in a ghastly half-light. The bushes were inky black, the ground a sombre grey, the sky colourless and cheerless. And up the hill I thought I could see ghosts. There several times, as I scanned the slope, I saw white figures. Twice I fancied I saw a solitary white, ape-like creature running rather quickly up the hill, and once near the ruins I saw a leash of them carrying some dark body. They moved hastily. I did not see what became of them. It seemed that they vanished among the bushes. The dawn was still indistinct, you must understand. I was feeling that chill, uncertain, early-morning feeling you may have known. I doubted my eyes.

'As the eastern sky grew brighter, and the light of the day came on and its vivid colouring returned upon the world once more, I scanned the view keenly. But I saw no vestige of my white figures. They were mere creatures of the half light. "They must have been ghosts," I said; "I wonder whence they dated." For a queer notion of Grant Allen's came into my head, and amused me. If each generation die and leave ghosts, he argued, the world at last will get overcrowded with them. On that theory they would have grown innumerable some Eight Hundred Thousand Years hence, and it was no great wonder to see four at once. But the jest was unsatisfying, and I was thinking of these figures all the morning, until Weena's rescue drove them out of my head. I associated them in some indefinite way with the white animal I had startled in my first passionate search for the Time Machine. But Weena was a pleasant substitute. Yet all the same, they were soon destined to take far deadlier possession of my mind.

'I think I have said how much hotter than our own was the weather of this Golden Age. I cannot account for it. It may be that the sun was hotter, or the earth nearer the sun. It is usual to assume that the sun will go on cooling steadily in the future. But people, unfamiliar with such speculations as those of the younger Darwin, forget that the planets must ultimately fall back one by one into the parent body. As these catastrophes occur, the sun will blaze with renewed energy; and it may be that some inner planet had suffered this fate. Whatever the reason, the fact remains that the sun was very much hotter than we know it.

'Well, one very hot morning — my fourth, I think — as I was seeking shelter from the heat and glare in a colossal ruin near the great house where I slept and fed, there happened this strange thing: Clambering among these heaps of masonry, I found a narrow gallery, whose end and side windows were blocked by fallen masses of stone. By contrast with the brilliancy outside, it seemed at first impenetrably dark to me. I entered it groping, for the change from light to blackness made spots of colour swim before me. Suddenly I halted spellbound. A pair of eyes, luminous by reflection against the daylight without, was watching me out of the darkness.

'The old instinctive dread of wild beasts came upon me. I clenched my hands and steadfastly looked into the glaring eyeballs. I was afraid to turn. Then the thought of the absolute security in which humanity appeared to be living came to my mind. And then I remembered that strange terror of the dark. Overcoming my fear to some extent, I advanced a step and spoke. I will admit that my voice was harsh and ill-controlled. I put out my hand and touched something soft. At once the eyes darted sideways, and something white ran past me. I turned with my heart in my mouth, and saw a queer little ape-like figure, its head held down in a peculiar manner, running across the sunlit space behind me. It blundered against a block of granite, staggered aside, and in a moment was hidden in a black shadow beneath another pile of ruined masonry.

'My impression of it is, of course, imperfect; but I know it was a dull white, and had strange large greyish-red eyes; also that there was flaxen hair on its head and down its back. But, as I say, it went too fast for me to see distinctly. I cannot even say whether it ran on all-fours, or only with its forearms held very low. After an instant's pause I followed it into the second heap of ruins. I could not find it at first; but, after a time in the profound obscurity, I came upon one of those round well-like openings of which I have told you, half closed by a fallen pillar. A sudden thought came to me. Could this Thing have vanished down the shaft? I lit a match, and, looking down, I saw a small, white, moving creature, with large bright eyes which regarded me steadfastly as it retreated. It made me shudder. It was so like a human spider! It was clambering down the wall, and now I saw for the first time a number of metal foot and hand rests forming a kind of ladder down the shaft. Then the light burned my fingers and fell out of my hand, going out as it dropped, and when I had lit another the little monster had disappeared.

'I do not know how long I sat peering down that well. It was not for some time that I could succeed in persuading myself that the thing I had seen was human. But, gradually, the truth dawned on me: that Man had not remained one species, but had differentiated into two distinct animals: that my graceful children of the Upper-world were not the sole descendants of our generation, but that this bleached, obscene, nocturnal Thing, which had flashed before me, was also heir to all the ages.

'I thought of the flickering pillars and of my theory of an underground ventilation. I began to suspect their true import. And what, I wondered, was this Lemur doing in my scheme of a perfectly balanced organization? How was it related to the indolent serenity of the beautiful Upper-worlders? And what was hidden down there, at the foot of that shaft? I sat upon the edge of the well telling myself that, at any rate, there was nothing to fear, and that there I must descend for the solution of my difficulties. And withal I was absolutely afraid to go! As I hesitated, two of the beautiful Upper-world people came running in their amorous sport across the daylight in the shadow. The male pursued the female, flinging flowers at her as he ran.

'They seemed distressed to find me, my arm against the overturned pillar, peering down the well. Apparently it was considered bad form to remark these apertures; for when I pointed to this one, and tried to frame a question about it in their tongue, they were still more visibly distressed and turned away. But they were interested by my matches, and I struck some to amuse them. I tried them again about the well, and again I failed. So presently I left them, meaning to go back to Weena, and see what I could get from her. But my mind was already in revolution; my guesses and impressions were slipping and sliding to a new adjustment. I had now a clue to the import of these wells, to the ventilating towers, to the mystery of the ghosts; to say nothing of a hint at the meaning of the bronze gates and the fate of the Time Machine! And very vaguely there came a suggestion towards the solution of the economic problem that had puzzled me.

'Here was the new view. Plainly, this second species of Man was subterranean. There were three circumstances in particular which made me think that its rare emergence above ground was the outcome of a long-continued underground habit. In the first place, there was the bleached look common in most animals that live largely in the dark — the white fish of the Kentucky caves, for instance. Then, those large eyes, with that capacity for reflecting light, are common features of nocturnal things — witness the owl and the cat. And last of all, that evident confusion in the sunshine, that hasty yet fumbling awkward flight towards dark shadow, and that peculiar carriage of the head while in the light — all reinforced the theory of an extreme sensitiveness of the retina.

'Beneath my feet, then, the earth must be tunnelled enormously, and these tunnellings were the habitat of the new race. The presence of ventilating shafts and wells along the hill slopes — everywhere, in fact, except along the river valley — showed how universal were its ramifications. What so natural, then, as to assume that it was in this artificial Underworld that such work as was necessary to the comfort of the daylight race was done? The notion was so plausible that I at once accepted it, and went on to assume the *how* of this splitting of the human species. I dare say you will anticipate the shape of my theory; though, for myself, I very soon felt that it fell far short of the truth.

'At first, proceeding from the problems of our own age, it seemed clear as daylight to me that the gradual widening of the present merely temporary and social difference between the

Capitalist and the Labourer, was the key to the whole position. No doubt it will seem grotesque enough to you — and wildly incredible! — and yet even now there are existing circumstances to point that way. There is a tendency to utilize underground space for the less ornamental purposes of civilization; there is the Metropolitan Railway in London, for instance, there are new electric railways, there are subways, there are underground workrooms and restaurants, and they increase and multiply. Evidently, I thought, this tendency had increased till Industry had gradually lost its birthright in the sky. I mean that it had gone deeper and deeper into larger and ever larger underground factories, spending a still-increasing amount of its time therein, till, in the end —! Even now, does not an Eastend worker live in such artificial conditions as practically to be cut off from the natural surface of the earth?

'Again, the exclusive tendency of richer people — due, no doubt, to the increasing refinement of their education, and the widening gulf between them and the rude violence of the poor — is already leading to the closing, in their interest, of considerable portions of the surface of the land. About London, for instance, perhaps half the prettier country is shut in against intrusion. And this same widening gulf — which is due to the length and expense of the higher educational process and the increased facilities for and temptations towards refined habits on the part of the rich — will make that exchange between class and class, that promotion by intermarriage which at present retards the splitting of our species along lines of social stratification, less and less frequent. So, in the end, above ground you must have the Haves, pursuing pleasure and comfort and beauty, and below ground the Have-nots, the Workers getting continually adapted to the conditions of their labour. Once they were there, they would no doubt have to pay rent, and not a little of it, for the ventilation of their caverns; and if they refused, they would starve or be suffocated for arrears. Such of them as were so constituted as to be miserable and rebellious would die; and, in the end, the balance being permanent, the survivors would become as well adapted to the conditions of underground life, and as happy in their way, as the Upper-world people were to theirs. As it seemed to me, the refined beauty and the etiolated pallor followed naturally enough.

'The great triumph of Humanity I had dreamed of took a different shape in my mind. It had been no such triumph of moral education and general cooperation as I had imagined. Instead, I saw a real aristocracy, armed with a perfected science and working to a logical conclusion the industrial system of to-day. Its triumph had not been simply a triumph over Nature, but a triumph over Nature and the fellow-man. This, I must warn you, was my theory at the time. I had no convenient cicerone in the pattern of the Utopian books. My explanation may be absolutely wrong. I still think it is the most plausible one. But even on this supposition the balanced civilization that was at last attained must have long since passed its zenith, and was now far fallen into decay. The too-perfect security of the Upper-worlders had led them to a slow movement of degeneration, to a general dwindling in size, strength, and intelligence. That I could see clearly enough already. What had happened to the Under-grounders I did not yet suspect; but from what I had seen of the Morlocks — that, by the by, was the name by which these creatures were called — I could imagine that the modification of the human type was even far more profound than among the "Eloi," the beautiful race that I already knew.

'Then came troublesome doubts. Why had the Morlocks taken my Time Machine? For I felt sure it was they who had taken it. Why, too, if the Eloi were masters, could they not restore the machine to me? And why were they so terribly afraid of the dark? I proceeded, as I have said, to question Weena about this Underworld, but here again I was disappointed. At first she would not understand my questions, and presently she refused to answer them. She shivered as though the topic was unendurable. And when I pressed her, perhaps a little harshly, she burst into tears. They were the only tears, except my own, I ever saw in that Golden Age. When I saw them I ceased abruptly to trouble about the Morlocks, and was only concerned in banishing these signs of the human inheritance from Weena's eyes. And very soon she was smiling and clapping her hands, while I solemnly burned a match.

Chapter VI

'It may seem odd to you, but it was two days before I could follow up the newfound clue in what was manifestly the proper way. I felt a peculiar shrinking from those pallid bodies. They were just the half-bleached colour of the worms and things one sees preserved in spirit in a zoological museum. And they were filthily cold to the touch. Probably my shrinking was largely due to the sympathetic influence of the Eloi, whose disgust of the Morlocks I now began to appreciate.

'The next night I did not sleep well. Probably my health was a little disordered. I was oppressed with perplexity and doubt. Once or twice I had a feeling of intense fear for which I could perceive no definite reason. I remember creeping noiselessly into the great hall where the little people were sleeping in the moonlight — that night Weena was among them — and feeling reassured by their presence. It occurred to me even then, that in the course of a few days the moon must pass through its last quarter, and the nights grow dark, when the appearances of these unpleasant creatures from below, these whitened Lemurs, this new vermin that had replaced the old, might be more abundant. And on both these days I had the restless feeling of one who shirks an inevitable duty. I felt assured that the Time Machine was only to be recovered by boldly penetrating these underground mysteries. Yet I could not face the mystery. If only I had had a companion it would have been different. But I was so horribly alone, and even to clamber down into the darkness of the well appalled me. I don't know if you will understand my feeling, but I never felt quite safe at my back.

'It was this restlessness, this insecurity, perhaps, that drove me further and further afield in my exploring expeditions. Going to the southwestward towards the rising country that is now called Combe Wood, I observed far off, in the direction of nineteenth-century Banstead, a vast green structure, different in character from any I had hitherto seen. It was larger than the largest of the palaces or ruins I knew, and the facade had an Oriental look: the face of it having the lustre, as well as the pale-green tint, a kind of bluish-green, of a certain type of Chinese porcelain. This difference in aspect suggested a difference in use, and I was minded to push on and explore. But the day was growing late, and I had come upon the sight of the place after a long and tiring circuit; so I resolved to hold over the adventure for the following day, and I returned to the welcome and the caresses of little Weena. But next morning I perceived clearly enough that my curiosity regarding the Palace of Green Porcelain was a piece of self-deception, to enable me to shirk, by another day, an experience I dreaded. I resolved I would make the descent without further waste of time, and started out in the early morning towards a well near the ruins of granite and aluminium.

'Little Weena ran with me. She danced beside me to the well, but when she saw me lean over the mouth and look downward, she seemed strangely disconcerted. "Goodbye, little Weena," I said, kissing her; and then putting her down, I began to feel over the parapet for the climbing hooks. Rather hastily, I may as well confess, for I feared my courage might leak away! At first she watched me in amazement. Then she gave a most piteous cry, and running to me, she began to pull at me with her little hands. I think her opposition nerved me rather to proceed. I shook her off, perhaps a little roughly, and in another moment I was in the throat of the well. I saw her agonized face over the parapet, and smiled to reassure her. Then I had to look down at the unstable hooks to which I clung.

'I had to clamber down a shaft of perhaps two hundred yards. The descent was effected by means of metallic bars projecting from the sides of the well, and these being adapted to the needs of a creature much smaller and lighter than myself, I was speedily cramped and fatigued by the descent. And not simply fatigued! One of the bars bent suddenly under my weight, and almost swung me off into the blackness beneath. For a moment I hung by one hand, and after that experience I did not dare to rest again. Though my arms and back were presently acutely painful, I went on clambering down the sheer descent with as quick a motion as possible. Glancing upward, I saw the aperture, a small blue disk, in which a star was visible, while little Weena's head showed as a round black projection. The thudding sound of a machine below grew louder and more oppressive. Everything save that little disk above was profoundly dark, and when I looked up again Weena had disappeared.

'I was in an agony of discomfort. I had some thought of trying to go up the shaft again, and leave the Underworld alone. But even while I turned this over in my mind I continued to descend. At last, with intense relief, I saw dimly coming up, a foot to the right of me, a slender loophole in the wall. Swinging myself in, I found it was the aperture of a narrow horizontal tunnel in which I could lie down and rest. It was not too soon. My arms ached, my back was cramped, and I was trembling with the prolonged terror of a fall. Besides this, the unbroken darkness had had a distressing effect upon my eyes. The air was full of the throb and hum of machinery pumping air down the shaft.

'I do not know how long I lay. I was roused by a soft hand touching my face. Starting up in the darkness I snatched at my matches and, hastily striking one, I saw three stooping white creatures similar to the one I had seen above ground in the ruin, hastily retreating before the light. Living, as they did, in what appeared to me impenetrable darkness, their eyes were abnormally large and sensitive, just as are the pupils of the abysmal fishes, and they reflected the light in the same way. I have no doubt they could see me in that rayless obscurity, and they did not seem to have any fear of me apart from the light. But, so soon as I struck a match in order to see them, they fled incontinently, vanishing into dark gutters and tunnels, from which their eyes glared at me in the strangest fashion.

'I tried to call to them, but the language they had was apparently different from that of the Over-world people; so that I was needs left to my own unaided efforts, and the thought of flight before exploration was even then in my mind. But I said to myself, "You are in for it now," and, feeling my way along the tunnel, I found the noise of machinery grow louder. Presently the walls fell away from me, and I came to a large open space, and striking another match, saw that I had entered a vast arched cavern, which stretched into utter darkness beyond the range of my light. The view I had of it was as much as one could see in the burning of a match.

'Necessarily my memory is vague. Great shapes like big machines rose out of the dimness, and cast grotesque black shadows, in which dim spectral Morlocks sheltered from the glare. The place, by the by, was very stuffy and oppressive, and the faint halitus of freshly shed blood was in the air. Some way down the central vista was a little table of white metal, laid with what seemed a meal. The Morlocks at any rate were carnivorous! Even at the time, I remember wondering what large animal could have survived to furnish the red joint I saw. It was all very indistinct: the heavy smell, the big unmeaning shapes, the obscene figures lurking in the shadows, and only waiting for the darkness to come at me again! Then the match burned down, and stung my fingers, and fell, a wriggling red spot in the blackness.

'I have thought since how particularly ill-equipped I was for such an experience. When I had started with the Time Machine, I had started with the absurd assumption that the men of the Future would certainly be infinitely ahead of ourselves in all their appliances. I had come without arms, without medicine, without anything to smoke — at times I missed tobacco frightfully — even without enough matches. If only I had thought of a Kodak! I could have flashed that glimpse of the Underworld in a second, and examined it at leisure. But, as it was, I stood there with only the weapons and the powers that Nature had endowed me with — hands, feet, and teeth; these, and four safety-matches that still remained to me.

'I was afraid to push my way in among all this machinery in the dark, and it was only with my last glimpse of light I discovered that my store of matches had run low. It had never occurred to me until that moment that there was any need to economize them, and I had wasted almost half the box in astonishing the Upper-worlders, to whom fire was a novelty. Now, as I say, I had four left, and while I stood in the dark, a hand touched mine, lank fingers came feeling over my face, and I was sensible of a peculiar unpleasant odour. I fancied I heard the breathing of a crowd of those dreadful little beings about me. I felt the box of matches in my hand being gently disengaged, and other hands behind me plucking at my clothing. The sense of these unseen creatures examining me was indescribably unpleasant. The sudden realization of my ignorance of their ways of thinking and doing came home to me very vividly in the darkness. I shouted at them as loudly as I could. They started away, and then I could feel them approaching me again. They clutched at me more boldly, whispering odd sounds to each other. I shivered violently, and shouted again — rather discordantly. This time they were not so seriously alarmed, and they made a queer laughing noise as they came back at me. I will confess I was horribly frightened. I determined to strike another match and escape under the protection of its glare. I did so, and eking out the flicker with a scrap of paper from my pocket, I made good my retreat to the narrow tunnel. But I had scarce entered this when my light was blown out and in the blackness I could hear the Morlocks rustling like wind among leaves, and pattering like the rain, as they hurried after me.

'In a moment I was clutched by several hands, and there was no mistaking that they were trying to haul me back. I struck another light, and waved it in their dazzled faces. You can scarce imagine how nauseatingly inhuman they looked — those pale, chinless faces and great, lidless, pinkish-grey eyes! — as they stared in their blindness and bewilderment. But I did not stay to look, I promise you: I retreated again, and when my second match had ended, I struck my third. It had almost burned through when I reached the opening into the shaft. I lay down on the edge, for the throb of the great pump below made me giddy. Then I felt sideways for the projecting hooks, and, as I did so, my feet were grasped from behind, and I was violently tugged backward. I lit my last match... and it incontinently went out. But I had my hand on the climbing bars now, and, kicking violently, I disengaged myself from the clutches of the Morlocks and was speedily clambering up the shaft, while they stayed peering and blinking up at me: all but one little wretch who followed me for some way, and wellnigh secured my boot as a trophy.

'That climb seemed interminable to me. With the last twenty or thirty feet of it a deadly nausea came upon me. I had the greatest difficulty in keeping my hold. The last few yards were a frightful struggle against this faintness. Several times my head swam, and I felt all the sensations of falling. At last, however, I got over the well-mouth somehow, and staggered out of the ruin into the blinding sunlight. I fell upon my face. Even the soil smelt sweet and clean. Then I remember Weena kissing my hands and ears, and the voices of others among the Eloi. Then, for a time, I was insensible.

Chapter VII

'Now, indeed, I seemed in a worse case than before. Hitherto, except during my night's anguish at the loss of the Time Machine, I had felt a sustaining hope of ultimate escape, but that hope was staggered by these new discoveries. Hitherto I had merely thought myself impeded by the childish simplicity of the little people, and by some unknown forces which I had only to understand to overcome; but there was an altogether new element in the sickening quality of the Morlocks — a something inhuman and malign. Before, I had felt as a man might feel who had fallen into a pit: my concern was with the pit and how to get out of it. Now I felt like a beast in a trap, whose enemy would come upon him soon.

'The enemy I dreaded may surprise you. It was the darkness of the new moon. Weena had put this into my head by some at first incomprehensible remarks about the Dark Nights. It was not now such a very difficult problem to guess what the coming Dark Nights might mean. The moon was on the wane: each night there was a longer interval of darkness. And I now understood to some slight degree at least the reason of the fear of the little Upper-world people for the dark. I wondered vaguely what foul villainy it might be that the Morlocks did under the new moon. I felt pretty sure now that my second hypothesis was all wrong. The Upper-world people might once have been the favoured aristocracy, and the Morlocks their mechanical servants: but that had long since passed away. The two species that had resulted from the evolution of man were sliding down towards, or had already arrived at, an altogether new relationship. The Eloi, like the Carolingian kings, had decayed to a mere beautiful futility. They still possessed the earth on sufferance: since the Morlocks, subterranean for innumerable generations, had come at last to find the daylit surface intolerable. And the Morlocks made their garments, I inferred, and maintained them in their habitual needs, perhaps through the survival of an old habit of service. They did it as a standing horse paws with his foot, or as a man enjoys killing animals in sport: because ancient and departed necessities had impressed it on the organism. But, clearly, the old order was already in part reversed. The Nemesis of the delicate ones was creeping on apace. Ages ago, thousands of generations ago, man had thrust his brother man out of the ease and the sunshine. And now that brother was coming back changed! Already the Eloi had begun to learn one old lesson anew. They were becoming reacquainted with Fear. And suddenly there came into my head the memory of the meat I had seen in the Underworld. It seemed odd how it floated into my mind: not stirred up as it were by the current of my meditations, but coming in almost like a question from outside. I tried to recall the form of it. I had a vague sense of something familiar, but I could not tell what it was at the time.

'Still, however helpless the little people in the presence of their mysterious Fear, I was differently constituted. I came out of this age of ours, this ripe prime of the human race, when Fear does not paralyse and mystery has lost its terrors. I at least would defend myself. Without further delay I determined to make myself arms and a fastness where I might sleep. With that refuge as a base, I could face this strange world with some of that confidence I had lost in realizing to what creatures night by night I lay exposed. I felt I could never sleep again until my bed was secure from them. I shuddered with horror to think how they must already have examined me.

'I wandered during the afternoon along the valley of the Thames, but found nothing that commended itself to my mind as inaccessible. All the buildings and trees seemed easily practicable to such dexterous climbers as the Morlocks, to judge by their wells, must be. Then the tall pinnacles of the Palace of Green Porcelain and the polished gleam of its walls came back to my memory; and in the evening, taking Weena like a child upon my shoulder, I went up the hills towards the southwest. The distance, I had reckoned, was seven or eight miles, but it must have been nearer eighteen. I had first seen the place on a moist afternoon when distances are deceptively diminished. In addition, the heel of one of my shoes was loose, and a nail was working through the sole — they were comfortable old shoes I wore about indoors — so that I was lame. And it was already long past sunset when I came in sight of the palace, silhouetted black against the pale yellow of the sky.

'Weena had been hugely delighted when I began to carry her, but after a while she desired me to let her down, and ran along by the side of me, occasionally darting off on either hand to pick flowers to stick in my pockets. My pockets had always puzzled Weena, but at the last she had concluded that they were an eccentric kind of vase for floral decoration. At least she utilized them for that purpose. And that reminds me! In changing my jacket I found...'

The Time Traveller paused, put his hand into his pocket, and silently placed two withered flowers, not unlike very large white mallows, upon the little table. Then he resumed his narrative.

'As the hush of evening crept over the world and we proceeded over the hill crest towards Wimbledon, Weena grew tired and wanted to return to the house of grey stone. But I pointed out the distant pinnacles of the Palace of Green Porcelain to her, and contrived to make her understand that we were seeking a refuge there from her Fear. You know that great pause that comes upon things before the dusk? Even the breeze stops in the trees. To me there is always an air of expectation about that evening stillness. The sky was clear, remote, and empty save for a few horizontal bars far down in the sunset. Well, that night the expectation took the colour of my fears. In that darkling calm my senses seemed preternaturally sharpened. I fancied I could even feel the hollowness of the ground beneath my feet: could, indeed, almost see through it the Morlocks on their anthill going hither and thither and waiting for the dark.

In my excitement I fancied that they would receive my invasion of their burrows as a declaration of war. And why had they taken my Time Machine?

'So we went on in the quiet, and the twilight deepened into night. The clear blue of the distance faded, and one star after another came out. The ground grew dim and the trees black. Weena's fears and her fatigue grew upon her. I took her in my arms and talked to her and caressed her. Then, as the darkness grew deeper, she put her arms round my neck, and, closing her eyes, tightly pressed her face against my shoulder. So we went down a long slope into a valley, and there in the dimness I almost walked into a little river. This I waded, and went up the opposite side of the valley, past a number of sleeping houses, and by a statue — a Faun, or some such figure, *minus* the head. Here too were acacias. So far I had seen nothing of the Morlocks, but it was yet early in the night, and the darker hours before the old moon rose were still to come.

'From the brow of the next hill I saw a thick wood spreading wide and black before me. I hesitated at this. I could see no end to it, either to the right or the left. Feeling tired — my feet, in particular, were very sore — I carefully lowered Weena from my shoulder as I halted, and sat down upon the turf. I could no longer see the Palace of Green Porcelain, and I was in doubt of my direction. I looked into the thickness of the wood and thought of what it might hide. Under that dense tangle of branches one would be out of sight of the stars. Even were there no other lurking danger — a danger I did not care to let my imagination loose upon — there would still be all the roots to stumble over and the tree-boles to strike against.

'I was very tired, too, after the excitements of the day; so I decided that I would not face it, but would pass the night upon the open hill.

'Weena, I was glad to find, was fast asleep. I carefully wrapped her in my jacket, and sat down beside her to wait for the moonrise. The hillside was quiet and deserted, but from the black of the wood there came now and then a stir of living things. Above me shone the stars, for the night was very clear. I felt a certain sense of friendly comfort in their twinkling. All the old constellations had gone from the sky, however: that slow movement which is imperceptible in a hundred human lifetimes, had long since rearranged them in unfamiliar groupings. But the Milky Way, it seemed to me, was still the same tattered streamer of stardust as of yore. Southward (as I judged it) was a very bright red star that was new to me; it was even more splendid than our own green Sirius. And amid all these scintillating points of light one bright planet shone kindly and steadily like the face of an old friend.

'Looking at these stars suddenly dwarfed my own troubles and all the gravities of terrestrial life. I thought of their unfathomable distance, and the slow inevitable drift of their movements out of the unknown past into the unknown future. I thought of the great precessional cycle that the pole of the earth describes. Only forty times had that silent revolution occurred during all the years that I had traversed. And during these few revolutions all the activity, all the traditions, the complex organizations, the nations, languages, literatures, aspirations, even the mere memory of Man as I knew him, had been swept out of existence. Instead were these frail creatures who had forgotten their high ancestry, and the white Things of which I went in terror. Then I thought of the Great Fear that was between the two species, and for the first time, with a sudden shiver, came the clear knowledge of what the meat I had seen might be. Yet it was too horrible! I looked at little Weena sleeping beside me, her face white and starlike under the stars, and forthwith dismissed the thought.

'Through that long night I held my mind off the Morlocks as well as I could, and whiled away the time by trying to fancy I could find signs of the old constellations in the new confusion. The sky kept very clear, except for a hazy cloud or so. No doubt I dozed at times. Then, as my vigil wore on, came a faintness in the eastward sky, like the reflection of some colourless fire, and the old moon rose, thin and peaked and white. And close behind, and overtaking it, and overflowing it, the dawn came, pale at first, and then growing pink and warm. No Morlocks had approached us. Indeed, I had seen none upon the hill that night. And in the confidence of renewed day it almost seemed to me that my fear had been unreasonable. I stood up and found my foot with the loose heel swollen at the ankle and painful under the heel; so I sat down again, took off my shoes, and flung them away.

'I awakened Weena, and we went down into the wood, now green and pleasant instead of black and forbidding. We found some fruit wherewith to break our fast. We soon met others of the dainty ones, laughing and dancing in the sunlight as though there was no such thing in nature as the night. And then I thought once more of the meat that I had seen. I felt assured now of what it was, and from the bottom of my heart I pitied this last feeble rill from the great flood of humanity. Clearly, at some time in the Long-Ago of human decay the Morlocks' food had run short. Possibly they had lived on rats and suchlike vermin. Even now man is far less discriminating and exclusive in his food than he was — far less than any monkey. His prejudice against human flesh is no deep-seated instinct. And so these inhuman sons of men — —! I tried to look at the thing in a scientific spirit. After all, they were less human and more remote than our cannibal ancestors of three or four thousand years ago. And the intelligence that would have made this state of things a torment had gone. Why should I trouble myself? These Eloi were mere fatted cattle, which the ant-like Morlocks preserved and preyed upon — probably saw to the breeding of. And there was Weena dancing at my side!

'Then I tried to preserve myself from the horror that was coming upon me, by regarding it as a rigorous punishment of human selfishness. Man had been content to live in ease and delight upon the labours of his fellow-man, had taken Necessity as his watchword and excuse, and in the fullness of time Necessity had come home to him. I even tried a Carlyle-like scorn of this wretched aristocracy in decay. But this attitude of mind was impossible. However great their intellectual degradation, the Eloi had kept too much of the human form not to claim my sympathy, and to make me perforce a sharer in their degradation and their Fear.

'I had at that time very vague ideas as to the course I should pursue. My first was to secure some safe place of refuge, and to make myself such arms of metal or stone as I could contrive. That necessity was immediate. In the next place, I hoped to procure some means of fire, so that I should have the weapon of a torch at hand, for nothing, I knew, would be more efficient against these Morlocks. Then I wanted to arrange some contrivance to break open the doors of bronze under the White Sphinx. I had in mind a battering ram. I had a persuasion that if I could enter those doors and carry a blaze of light before me I should discover the Time Machine and escape. I could not imagine the Morlocks were strong enough to move it far away. Weena I had resolved to bring with me to our own time. And turning such schemes over in my mind I pursued our way towards the building which my fancy had chosen as our dwelling.

Chapter VIII

'I found the Palace of Green Porcelain, when we approached it about noon, deserted and falling into ruin. Only ragged vestiges of glass remained in its windows, and great sheets of the green facing had fallen away from the corroded metallic framework. It lay very high upon a turfy down, and looking northeastward before I entered it, I was surprised to see a large estuary, or even creek, where I judged Wandsworth and Battersea must once have been. I thought then — though I never followed up the thought — of what might have happened, or might be happening, to the living things in the sea.

'The material of the Palace proved on examination to be indeed porcelain, and along the face of it I saw an inscription in some unknown character. I thought, rather foolishly, that Weena might help me to interpret this, but I only learned that the bare idea of writing had never entered her head. She always seemed to me, I fancy, more human than she was, perhaps because her affection was so human.

'Within the big valves of the door — which were open and broken — we found, instead of the customary hall, a long gallery lit by many side windows. At the first glance I was reminded of a museum. The tiled floor was thick with dust, and a remarkable array of miscellaneous objects was shrouded in the same grey covering. Then I perceived, standing strange and gaunt in the centre of the hall, what was clearly the lower part of a huge skeleton. I recognized by the oblique feet that it was some extinct creature after the fashion of the Megatherium. The skull and the upper bones lay beside it in the thick dust, and in one place, where rainwater had dropped through a leak in the roof, the thing itself had been worn away. Further in the gallery was the huge skeleton barrel of a Brontosaurus. My museum hypothesis was confirmed. Going towards the side I found what appeared to be sloping shelves, and clearing away the thick dust, I found the old familiar glass cases of our own time. But they must have been airtight to judge from the fair preservation of some of their contents.

'Clearly we stood among the ruins of some latter-day South Kensington! Here, apparently, was the Palaeontological Section, and a very splendid array of fossils it must have been, though the inevitable process of decay that had been staved off for a time, and had, through the extinction of bacteria and fungi, lost ninety-nine hundredths of its force, was nevertheless, with extreme sureness if with extreme slowness at work again upon all its treasures. Here and there I found traces of the little people in the shape of rare fossils broken to pieces or threaded in strings upon reeds. And the cases had in some instances been bodily removed — by the Morlocks as I judged. The place was very silent. The thick dust deadened our footsteps. Weena, who had been rolling a sea urchin down the sloping glass of a case, presently came, as I stared about me, and very quietly took my hand and stood beside me.

'And at first I was so much surprised by this ancient monument of an intellectual age, that I gave no thought to the possibilities it presented. Even my preoccupation about the Time Machine receded a little from my mind.

'To judge from the size of the place, this Palace of Green Porcelain had a great deal more in it than a Gallery of Palaeontology; possibly historical galleries; it might be, even a library! To me, at least in my present circumstances, these would be vastly more interesting than this spectacle of oldtime geology in decay. Exploring, I found another short gallery running transversely to the first. This appeared to be devoted to minerals, and the sight of a block of sulphur set my mind running on gunpowder. But I could find no saltpeter; indeed, no nitrates of any kind. Doubtless they had deliquesced ages ago. Yet the sulphur hung in my mind, and set up a train of thinking. As for the rest of the contents of that gallery, though on the whole they were the best preserved of all I saw, I had little interest. I am no specialist in mineralogy, and I went on down a very ruinous aisle running parallel to the first hall I had entered. Apparently this section had been devoted to natural history, but everything had long since passed out of recognition. A few shrivelled and blackened vestiges of what had once been stuffed animals, desiccated mummies in jars that had once held spirit, a brown dust of departed plants: that was all! I was sorry for that, because I should have been glad to trace the patent readjustments by which the conquest of animated nature had been attained. Then we came to a gallery of simply colossal proportions, but singularly ill-lit, the floor of it running downward at a slight angle from the end at which I entered. At intervals white globes hung from the ceiling — many of them cracked and smashed — which suggested that originally the place had been artificially lit. Here I was more in my element, for rising on either side of me were the huge bulks of big machines, all greatly corroded and many broken down, but some still fairly complete. You know I have a certain weakness for mechanism, and I was inclined to linger among these; the more so as for the most part they had the interest of puzzles, and I could make only the vaguest guesses at what they were for. I fancied that if I could solve their puzzles I should find myself in possession of powers that might be of use against the Morlocks.

'Suddenly Weena came very close to my side. So suddenly that she startled me. Had it not been for her I do not think I should have noticed that the floor of the gallery sloped at all. The end I had come in at was quite above ground, and was lit by rare slit-like windows. As you went down the length, the ground came up against these windows, until at last there was a pit like the "area" of a London house before each, and only a narrow line of daylight at the top. I went slowly along, puzzling about the machines, and had been too intent upon them to notice the gradual diminution of the light, until Weena's increasing apprehensions drew my attention. Then I saw that the gallery ran down at last into a thick darkness. I hesitated, and then, as I looked round me, I saw that the dust was less abundant and its surface less even. Further away towards the dimness, it appeared to be broken by a number of small narrow footprints. My sense of the immediate presence of the Morlocks revived at that. I felt that I was wasting my time in the academic examination of machinery. I called to mind that it was already far advanced in the afternoon, and that I had still no weapon, no refuge, and no means of making a fire. And then down in the remote blackness of the gallery I heard a peculiar pattering, and the same odd noises I had heard down the well.

'I took Weena's hand. Then, struck with a sudden idea, I left her and turned to a machine from which projected a lever not unlike those in a signal-box. Clambering upon the stand, and grasping this lever in my hands, I put all my weight upon it sideways. Suddenly Weena, deserted in the central aisle, began to whimper. I had judged the strength of the lever pretty correctly, for it snapped after a minute's strain, and I rejoined her with a mace in my hand more than sufficient, I judged, for any Morlock skull I might encounter. And I longed very much to kill a Morlock or so. Very inhuman, you may think, to want to go killing one's own descendants! But it was impossible, somehow, to feel any humanity in the things. Only my disinclination to leave Weena, and a persuasion that if I began to slake my thirst for murder my Time Machine might suffer, restrained me from going straight down the gallery and killing the brutes I heard.

'Well, mace in one hand and Weena in the other, I went out of that gallery and into another and still larger one, which at the first glance reminded me of a military chapel hung with tattered flags. The brown and charred rags that hung from the sides of it, I presently recognized as the decaying vestiges of books. They had long since dropped to pieces, and every semblance of print had left them. But here and there were warped boards and cracked metallic clasps that told the tale well enough. Had I been a literary man I might, perhaps, have moralized upon the futility of all ambition. But as it was, the thing that struck me with keenest force was the enormous waste of labour to which this sombre wilderness of rotting paper testified. At the time I will confess that I thought chiefly of the *Philosophical Transactions* and my own seventeen papers upon physical optics.

'Then, going up a broad staircase, we came to what may once have been a gallery of technical chemistry. And here I had not a little hope of useful discoveries. Except at one end where the roof had collapsed, this gallery was well preserved. I went eagerly to every unbroken case. And at last, in one of the really airtight cases, I found a box of matches. Very eagerly I tried them. They were perfectly good. They were not even damp. I turned to Weena. "Dance," I cried to her in her own tongue. For now I had a weapon indeed against the horrible creatures we feared. And so, in that derelict museum, upon the thick soft carpeting of dust, to Weena's huge delight, I solemnly performed a kind of composite dance, whistling *The Land of the Leal* as cheerfully as I could. In part it was a modest *cancan* , in part a step dance, in part a skirt-dance (so far as my tail-coat permitted), and in part original. For I am naturally inventive, as you know.

'Now, I still think that for this box of matches to have escaped the wear of time for immemorial years was a most strange, as for me it was a most fortunate thing. Yet, oddly enough, I found a far unlikelier substance, and that was camphor. I found it in a sealed jar, that by chance, I suppose, had been really hermetically sealed. I fancied at first that it was paraffin wax, and smashed the glass accordingly. But the odour of camphor was unmistakable. In the universal decay this volatile substance had chanced to survive, perhaps through many thousands of centuries. It reminded me of a sepia painting I had once seen done from the ink of a fossil Belemnite that must have perished and become fossilized millions of years ago. I was about to throw it away, but I remembered that it was inflammable and burned with a good bright flame — was, in fact, an excellent candle — and I put it in my pocket. I found no explosives, however, nor any means of breaking down the bronze doors. As yet my iron crowbar was the most helpful thing I had chanced upon. Nevertheless I left that gallery greatly elated.

'I cannot tell you all the story of that long afternoon. It would require a great effort of memory to recall my explorations in at all the proper order. I remember a long gallery of rusting stands of arms, and how I hesitated between my crowbar and a hatchet or a sword. I could not carry both, however, and my bar of iron promised best against the bronze gates. There were numbers of guns, pistols, and rifles. The most were masses of rust, but many were of some new metal, and still fairly sound. But any cartridges or powder there may once have been had rotted into dust. One corner I saw was charred and shattered; perhaps, I thought, by an explosion among the specimens. In another place was a vast array of idols — Polynesian, Mexican, Grecian, Phoenician, every country on earth I should think. And here, yielding to an irresistible impulse, I wrote my name upon the nose of a steatite monster from South America that particularly took my fancy.

'As the evening drew on, my interest waned. I went through gallery after gallery, dusty, silent, often ruinous, the exhibits sometimes mere heaps of rust and lignite, sometimes fresher. In one place I suddenly found myself near the model of a tin-mine, and then by the merest accident I discovered, in an airtight case, two dynamite cartridges! I shouted "Eureka!" and smashed the case with joy. Then came a doubt. I hesitated. Then, selecting a little side gallery, I made my essay. I never felt such a disappointment as I did in waiting five, ten, fifteen minutes for an explosion that never came. Of course the things were dummies, as I might have guessed from their presence. I really believe that had they not been so, I should have rushed off incontinently and blown Sphinx, bronze doors, and (as it proved) my chances of finding the Time Machine, all together into nonexistence.

'It was after that, I think, that we came to a little open court within the palace. It was turfed, and had three fruit-trees. So we rested and refreshed ourselves. Towards sunset I began to consider our position. Night was creeping upon us, and my inaccessible hiding-place had still to be found. But that troubled me very little now. I had in my possession a thing that was, perhaps, the best of all defences against the Morlocks — I had matches! I had the camphor in my pocket, too, if a blaze were needed. It seemed to me that the best thing we could do would be to pass the night in the open, protected by a fire. In the morning there was the getting of the Time Machine. Towards that, as yet, I had only my iron mace. But now, with my growing knowledge, I felt very differently towards those bronze doors. Up to this, I had refrained from forcing them, largely because of the mystery on the other side. They had never impressed me as being very strong, and I hoped to find my bar of iron not altogether inadequate for the work.

Chapter IX

'We emerged from the palace while the sun was still in part above the horizon. I was determined to reach the White Sphinx early the next morning, and ere the dusk I purposed pushing through the woods that had stopped me on the previous journey. My plan was to go as far as possible that night, and then, building a fire, to sleep in the protection of its glare. Accordingly, as we went along I gathered any sticks or dried grass I saw, and presently had my arms full of such litter. Thus loaded, our progress was slower than I had anticipated, and besides Weena was tired. And I began to suffer from sleepiness too; so that it was full night before we reached the wood. Upon the shrubby hill of its edge Weena would have stopped, fearing the darkness before us; but a singular sense of impending calamity, that should indeed have served me as a warning, drove me onward. I had been without sleep for a night and two days, and I was feverish and irritable. I felt sleep coming upon me, and the Morlocks with it.

'While we hesitated, among the black bushes behind us, and dim against their blackness, I saw three crouching figures. There was scrub and long grass all about us, and I did not feel safe from their insidious approach. The forest, I calculated, was rather less than a mile across. If we could get through it to the bare hillside, there, as it seemed to me, was an altogether safer resting-place; I thought that with my matches and my camphor I could contrive to keep my path illuminated through the woods. Yet it was evident that if I was to flourish matches with my hands I should have to abandon my firewood; so, rather reluctantly, I put it down. And then it came into my head that I would amaze our friends behind by lighting it. I was to discover the atrocious folly of this proceeding, but it came to my mind as an ingenious move for covering our retreat.

'I don't know if you have ever thought what a rare thing flame must be in the absence of man and in a temperate climate. The sun's heat is rarely strong enough to burn, even when it is focused by dewdrops, as is sometimes the case in more tropical districts. Lightning may blast and blacken, but it rarely gives rise to widespread fire. Decaying vegetation may occasionally smoulder with the heat of its fermentation, but this rarely results in flame. In this decadence, too, the art of fire-making had been forgotten on the earth. The red tongues that went licking up my heap of wood were an altogether new and strange thing to Weena.

'She wanted to run to it and play with it. I believe she would have cast herself into it had I not restrained her. But I caught her up, and in spite of her struggles, plunged boldly before me into the wood. For a little way the glare of my fire lit the path. Looking back presently, I could see, through the crowded stems, that from my heap of sticks the blaze had spread to some bushes adjacent, and a curved line of fire was creeping up the grass of the hill. I laughed at that, and turned again to the dark trees before me. It was very black, and Weena clung to me convulsively, but there was still, as my eyes grew accustomed to the darkness, sufficient light for me to avoid the stems. Overhead it was simply black, except where a gap of remote blue sky shone down upon us here and there. I struck none of my matches because I had no hand free. Upon my left arm I carried my little one, in my right hand I had my iron bar.

'For some way I heard nothing but the crackling twigs under my feet, the faint rustle of the breeze above, and my own breathing and the throb of the bloodvessels in my ears. Then I seemed to know of a pattering about me. I pushed on grimly. The pattering grew more distinct, and then I caught the same queer sound and voices I had heard in the Underworld. There were evidently several of the Morlocks, and they were closing in upon me. Indeed, in another minute I felt a tug at my coat, then something at my arm. And Weena shivered violently, and became quite still.

'It was time for a match. But to get one I must put her down. I did so, and, as I fumbled with my pocket, a struggle began in the darkness about my knees, perfectly silent on her part and with the same peculiar cooing sounds from the Morlocks. Soft little hands, too, were creeping over my coat and back, touching even my neck. Then the match scratched and fizzed. I held it flaring, and saw the white backs of the Morlocks in flight amid the trees. I hastily took a lump of camphor from my pocket, and prepared to light it as soon as the match should wane. Then I looked at Weena. She was lying clutching my feet and quite motionless, with her face to the ground. With a sudden fright I stooped to her. She seemed scarcely to breathe. I lit the block of camphor and flung it to the ground, and as it split and flared up and drove back the Morlocks and the shadows, I knelt down and lifted her. The wood behind seemed full of the stir and murmur of a great company!

'She seemed to have fainted. I put her carefully upon my shoulder and rose to push on, and then there came a horrible realization. In manoeuvring with my matches and Weena, I had turned myself about several times, and now I had not the faintest idea in what direction lay my path. For all I knew, I might be facing back towards the Palace of Green Porcelain. I found myself in a cold sweat. I had to think rapidly what to do. I determined to build a fire and encamp where we were. I put Weena, still motionless, down upon a turfy bole, and very hastily, as my first lump of camphor waned, I began collecting sticks and leaves. Here and there out of the darkness round me the Morlocks' eyes shone like carbuncles.

'The camphor flickered and went out. I lit a match, and as I did so, two white forms that had been approaching Weena dashed hastily away. One was so blinded by the light that he came straight for me, and I felt his bones grind under the blow of my fist. He gave a whoop of dismay, staggered a little way, and fell down. I lit another piece of camphor, and went on gathering my bonfire. Presently I noticed how dry was some of the foliage above me, for since my arrival on the Time Machine, a matter of a week, no rain had fallen. So, instead of casting about among the trees for fallen twigs, I began leaping up and dragging down branches. Very soon I had a choking smoky fire of green wood and dry sticks, and could economize my camphor. Then I turned to where Weena lay beside my iron mace. I tried what I could to revive her, but she lay like one dead. I could not even satisfy myself whether or not she breathed.

'Now, the smoke of the fire beat over towards me, and it must have made me heavy of a sudden. Moreover, the vapour of camphor was in the air. My fire would not need replenishing for an hour or so. I felt very weary after my exertion, and sat down. The wood, too, was full of a slumbrous murmur that I did not understand. I seemed just to nod and open my eyes. But all was dark, and the Morlocks had their hands upon me. Flinging off their clinging fingers I hastily felt in my pocket for the matchbox, and — it had gone! Then they gripped and closed with me again. In a moment I knew what had happened. I had slept, and my fire had gone out, and the bitterness of death came over my soul. The forest seemed full of the smell of burning wood. I was caught by the neck, by the hair, by the arms, and pulled down. It was indescribably horrible in the darkness to feel all these soft creatures heaped upon me. I felt as if I was in a monstrous spider's web. I was overpowered, and went down. I felt little teeth nipping at my neck. I rolled over, and as I did so my hand came against my iron lever. It gave me strength. I struggled up, shaking the human rats from me, and, holding the bar short, I thrust where I judged their faces might be. I could feel the succulent giving of flesh and bone under my blows, and for a moment I was free.

'The strange exultation that so often seems to accompany hard fighting came upon me. I knew that both I and Weena were lost, but I determined to make the Morlocks pay for their meat. I stood with my back to a tree, swinging the iron bar before me. The whole wood was full of the stir and cries of them. A minute passed. Their voices seemed to rise to a higher pitch of excitement, and their movements grew faster. Yet none came within reach. I stood glaring at the blackness. Then suddenly came hope. What if the Morlocks were afraid? And close on the heels of that came a strange thing. The darkness seemed to grow luminous. Very dimly I began to see the Morlocks about me — three battered at my feet — and then I recognized, with incredulous surprise, that the others were running, in an incessant stream, as it seemed, from behind me, and away through the wood in front. And their backs seemed no longer white, but reddish. As I stood agape, I saw a little red spark go drifting across a gap of starlight between the branches, and vanish. And at that I understood the smell of burning wood, the slumbrous murmur that was growing now into a gusty roar, the red glow, and the Morlocks' flight.

'Stepping out from behind my tree and looking back, I saw, through the black pillars of the nearer trees, the flames of the burning forest. It was my first fire coming after me. With that I looked for Weena, but she was gone. The hissing and crackling behind me, the explosive thud as each fresh tree burst into flame, left little time for reflection. My iron bar still gripped, I followed in the Morlocks' path. It was a close race. Once the flames crept forward so swiftly on my right as I ran that I was outflanked and had to strike off to the left. But at last I emerged upon a small open space, and as I did so, a Morlock came blundering towards me, and past me, and went on straight into the fire!

'And now I was to see the most weird and horrible thing, I think, of all that I beheld in that future age. This whole space was as bright as day with the reflection of the fire. In the centre was a hillock or tumulus, surmounted by a scorched hawthorn. Beyond this was another arm of the burning forest, with yellow tongues already writhing from it, completely encircling the space with a fence of fire. Upon the hillside were some thirty or forty Morlocks, dazzled by the light and heat, and blundering hither and thither against each other in their bewilderment. At first I did not realize their blindness, and struck furiously at them with my bar, in a frenzy of fear, as they approached me, killing one and crippling several more. But when I had watched the gestures of one of them groping under the hawthorn against the red sky, and heard their moans, I was assured of their absolute helplessness and misery in the glare, and I struck no more of them.

'Yet every now and then one would come straight towards me, setting loose a quivering horror that made me quick to elude him. At one time the flames died down somewhat, and I feared the foul creatures would presently be able to see me. I was thinking of beginning the fight by killing some of them before this should happen; but the fire burst out again brightly, and I stayed my hand. I walked about the hill among them and avoided them, looking for some trace of Weena. But Weena was gone.

'At last I sat down on the summit of the hillock, and watched this strange incredible company of blind things groping to and fro, and making uncanny noises to each other, as the glare of the fire beat on them. The coiling uprush of smoke streamed across the sky, and through the rare tatters of that red canopy, remote as though they belonged to another universe, shone the little stars. Two or three Morlocks came blundering into me, and I drove them off with blows of my fists, trembling as I did so.

'For the most part of that night I was persuaded it was a nightmare. I bit myself and screamed in a passionate desire to awake. I beat the ground with my hands, and got up and sat down again, and wandered here and there, and again sat down. Then I would fall to rubbing my eyes and calling upon God to let me awake. Thrice I saw Morlocks put their heads down in a kind of agony and rush into the flames. But, at last, above the subsiding red of the fire, above the streaming masses of black smoke and the whitening and blackening tree stumps, and the diminishing numbers of these dim creatures, came the white light of the day.

'I searched again for traces of Weena, but there were none. It was plain that they had left her poor little body in the forest. I cannot describe how it relieved me to think that it had escaped the awful fate to which it seemed destined. As I thought of that, I was almost moved to begin a massacre of the helpless abominations about me, but I contained myself. The hillock, as I have said, was a kind of island in the forest. From its summit I could now make out through a haze of smoke the Palace of Green Porcelain, and from that I could get my bearings for the White Sphinx. And so, leaving the remnant of these damned souls still going hither and thither and moaning, as the day grew clearer, I tied some grass about my feet and limped on across smoking ashes and among black stems, that still pulsated internally with fire, towards the hiding-place of the Time Machine. I walked slowly, for I was almost exhausted, as well as lame, and I felt the intensest wretchedness for the horrible death of little Weena. It seemed an overwhelming calamity. Now, in this old familiar room, it is more like the sorrow of a dream than an actual loss. But that morning it left me absolutely lonely again — terribly alone. I began to think of this house of mine, of this fireside, of some of you, and with such thoughts came a longing that was pain.

'But as I walked over the smoking ashes under the bright morning sky, I made a discovery. In my trouser pocket were still some loose matches. The box must have leaked before it was lost.

Chapter X

'About eight or nine in the morning I came to the same seat of yellow metal from which I had viewed the world upon the evening of my arrival. I thought of my hasty conclusions upon that evening and could not refrain from laughing bitterly at my confidence. Here was the same beautiful scene, the same abundant foliage, the same splendid palaces and magnificent ruins, the same silver river running between its fertile banks. The gay robes of the beautiful people moved hither and thither among the trees. Some were bathing in exactly the place where I had saved Weena, and that suddenly gave me a keen stab of pain. And like blots upon the landscape rose the cupolas above the ways to the Underworld. I understood now what all the beauty of the Over-world people covered. Very pleasant was their day, as pleasant as the day of the cattle in the field. Like the cattle, they knew of no enemies and provided against no needs. And their end was the same.

'I grieved to think how brief the dream of the human intellect had been. It had committed suicide. It had set itself steadfastly towards comfort and ease, a balanced society with security and permanency as its watchword, it had attained its hopes — to come to this at last. Once, life and property must have reached almost absolute safety. The rich had been assured of his wealth and comfort, the toiler assured of his life and work. No doubt in that perfect world there had been no unemployed problem, no social question left unsolved. And a great quiet had followed.

'It is a law of nature we overlook, that intellectual versatility is the compensation for change, danger, and trouble. An animal perfectly in harmony with its environment is a perfect mechanism. Nature never appeals to intelligence until habit and instinct are useless. There is no intelligence where there is no change and no need of change. Only those animals partake of intelligence that have to meet a huge variety of needs and dangers.

'So, as I see it, the Upper-world man had drifted towards his feeble prettiness, and the Underworld to mere mechanical industry. But that perfect state had lacked one thing even for mechanical perfection — absolute permanency. Apparently as time went on, the feeding of the Underworld, however it was effected, had become disjointed. Mother Necessity, who had been staved off for a few thousand years, came back again, and she began below. The Underworld being in contact with machinery, which, however perfect, still needs some little thought outside habit, had probably retained perforce rather more initiative, if less of every other human character, than the Upper. And when other meat failed them, they turned to what old habit had hitherto forbidden. So I say I saw it in my last view of the world of Eight Hundred and Two Thousand Seven Hundred and One. It may be as wrong an explanation as mortal wit could invent. It is how the thing shaped itself to me, and as that I give it to you.

'After the fatigues, excitements, and terrors of the past days, and in spite of my grief, this seat and the tranquil view and the warm sunlight were very pleasant. I was very tired and sleepy, and soon my theorizing passed into dozing. Catching myself at that, I took my own hint, and spreading myself out upon the turf I had a long and refreshing sleep.

'I awoke a little before sunsetting. I now felt safe against being caught napping by the Morlocks, and, stretching myself, I came on down the hill towards the White Sphinx. I had my crowbar in one hand, and the other hand played with the matches in my pocket.

'And now came a most unexpected thing. As I approached the pedestal of the sphinx I found the bronze valves were open. They had slid down into grooves.

'At that I stopped short before them, hesitating to enter.

'Within was a small apartment, and on a raised place in the corner of this was the Time Machine. I had the small levers in my pocket. So here, after all my elaborate preparations for the siege of the White Sphinx, was a meek surrender. I threw my iron bar away, almost sorry not to use it.

'A sudden thought came into my head as I stooped towards the portal. For once, at least, I grasped the mental operations of the Morlocks. Suppressing a strong inclination to laugh, I stepped through the bronze frame and up to the Time Machine. I was surprised to find it had been carefully oiled and cleaned. I have suspected since that the Morlocks had even partially taken it to pieces while trying in their dim way to grasp its purpose.

'Now as I stood and examined it, finding a pleasure in the mere touch of the contrivance, the thing I had expected happened. The bronze panels suddenly slid up and struck the frame with a clang. I was in the dark — trapped. So the Morlocks thought. At that I chuckled gleefully.

'I could already hear their murmuring laughter as they came towards me. Very calmly I tried to strike the match. I had only to fix on the levers and depart then like a ghost. But I had overlooked one little thing. The matches were of that abominable kind that light only on the box.

'You may imagine how all my calm vanished. The little brutes were close upon me. One touched me. I made a sweeping blow in the dark at them with the levers, and began to scramble into the saddle of the machine. Then came one hand upon me and then another. Then I had simply to fight against their persistent fingers for my levers, and at the same time feel for the studs over which these fitted. One, indeed, they almost got away from me. As it slipped from my hand, I had to butt in the dark with my head — I could hear the Morlock's skull ring — to recover it. It was a nearer thing than the fight in the forest, I think, this last scramble.

'But at last the lever was fitted and pulled over. The clinging hands slipped from me. The darkness presently fell from my eyes. I found myself in the same grey light and tumult I have already described.

Chapter XI

'I have already told you of the sickness and confusion that comes with time travelling. And this time I was not seated properly in the saddle, but sideways and in an unstable fashion. For an indefinite time I clung to the machine as it swayed and vibrated, quite unheeding how I went, and when I brought myself to look at the dials again I was amazed to find where I had arrived. One dial records days, and another thousands of days, another millions of days, and another thousands of millions. Now, instead of reversing the levers, I had pulled them over so as to go forward with them, and when I came to look at these indicators I found that the thousands hand was sweeping round as fast as the seconds hand of a watch — into futurity.

'As I drove on, a peculiar change crept over the appearance of things. The palpitating greyness grew darker; then — though I was still travelling with prodigious velocity — the blinking succession of day and night, which was usually indicative of a slower pace, returned, and grew more and more marked. This puzzled me very much at first. The alternations of night and day grew slower and slower, and so did the passage of the sun across the sky, until they seemed to stretch through centuries. At last a steady twilight brooded over the earth, a twilight only broken now and then when a comet glared across the darkling sky. The band of light that had indicated the sun had long since disappeared; for the sun had ceased to set — it simply rose and fell in the west, and grew ever broader and more red. All trace of the moon had vanished. The circling of the stars, growing slower and slower, had given place to creeping points of light. At last, some time before I stopped, the sun, red and very large, halted motionless upon the horizon, a vast dome glowing with a dull heat, and now and then suffering a momentary extinction. At one time it had for a little while glowed more brilliantly again, but it speedily reverted to its sullen red heat. I perceived by this slowing down of its rising and setting that the work of the tidal drag was done. The earth had come to rest with one face to the sun, even as in our own time the moon faces the earth. Very cautiously, for I remembered my former headlong fall, I began to reverse my motion. Slower and slower went the circling hands until the thousands one seemed motionless and the daily one was no longer a mere mist upon its scale. Still slower, until the dim outlines of a desolate beach grew visible.

'I stopped very gently and sat upon the Time Machine, looking round. The sky was no longer blue. Northeastward it was inky black, and out of the blackness shone brightly and steadily the pale white stars. Overhead it was a deep Indian red and starless, and south-eastward it grew brighter to a glowing scarlet where, cut by the horizon, lay the huge hull of the sun, red and motionless. The rocks about me were of a harsh reddish colour, and all the trace of life that I could see at first was the intensely green vegetation that covered every projecting point on their southeastern face. It was the same rich green that one sees on forest moss or on the lichen in caves: plants which like these grow in a perpetual twilight.

'The machine was standing on a sloping beach. The sea stretched away to the southwest, to rise into a sharp bright horizon against the wan sky. There were no breakers and no waves, for not a breath of wind was stirring. Only a slight oily swell rose and fell like a gentle breathing, and showed that the eternal sea was still moving and living. And along the margin where the water sometimes broke was a thick incrustation of salt — pink under the lurid sky. There was a sense of oppression in my head, and I noticed that I was breathing very fast. The sensation reminded me of my only experience of mountaineering, and from that I judged the air to be more rarefied than it is now.

'Far away up the desolate slope I heard a harsh scream, and saw a thing like a huge white butterfly go slanting and fluttering up into the sky and, circling, disappear over some low hillocks beyond. The sound of its voice was so dismal that I shivered and seated myself more firmly upon the machine. Looking round me again, I saw that, quite near, what I had taken to be a reddish mass of rock was moving slowly towards me. Then I saw the thing was really a monstrous crab-like creature. Can you imagine a crab as large as yonder table, with its many legs moving slowly and uncertainly, its big claws swaying, its long antennae, like carters' whips, waving and feeling, and its stalked eyes gleaming at you on either side of its metallic front? Its back was corrugated and ornamented with ungainly bosses, and a greenish incrustation blotched it here and there. I could see the many palps of its complicated mouth flickering and feeling as it moved.

'As I stared at this sinister apparition crawling towards me, I felt a tickling on my cheek as though a fly had lighted there. I tried to brush it away with my hand, but in a moment it returned, and almost immediately came another by my ear. I struck at this, and caught something threadlike. It was drawn swiftly out of my hand. With a frightful qualm, I turned, and I saw that I had grasped the antenna of another monster crab that stood just behind me. Its evil eyes were wriggling on their stalks, its mouth was all alive with appetite, and its vast ungainly claws, smeared with an algal slime, were descending upon me. In a moment my hand was on the lever, and I had placed a month between myself and these monsters. But I was still on the same beach, and I saw them distinctly now as soon as I stopped. Dozens of them seemed to be crawling here and there, in the sombre light, among the foliated sheets of intense green.

'I cannot convey the sense of abominable desolation that hung over the world. The red eastern sky, the northward blackness, the salt Dead Sea, the stony beach crawling with these foul, slow-stirring monsters, the uniform poisonous-looking green of the lichenous plants, the thin air that hurts one's lungs: all contributed to an appalling effect. I moved on a hundred years, and there was the same red sun — a little larger, a little duller — the same dying sea, the same chill air, and the same crowd of earthy crustacea creeping in and out among the green weed and the red rocks. And in the westward sky, I saw a curved pale line like a vast new moon.

'So I travelled, stopping ever and again, in great strides of a thousand years or more, drawn on by the mystery of the earth's fate, watching with a strange fascination the sun grow larger and duller in the westward sky, and the life of the old earth ebb away. At last, more than thirty million years hence, the huge red-hot dome of the sun had come to obscure nearly a tenth part of the darkling heavens. Then I stopped once more, for the crawling multitude of crabs had disappeared, and the red beach, save for its livid green liverworts and lichens, seemed lifeless. And now it was flecked with white. A bitter cold assailed me. Rare white flakes ever and again came eddying down. To the northeastward, the glare of snow lay under the starlight of the sable sky and I could see an undulating crest of hillocks pinkish white. There were fringes of ice along the sea margin, with drifting masses further out; but the main expanse of that salt ocean, all bloody under the eternal sunset, was still unfrozen.

'I looked about me to see if any traces of animal life remained. A certain indefinable apprehension still kept me in the saddle of the machine. But I saw nothing moving, in earth or sky or sea. The green slime on the rocks alone testified that life was not extinct. A shallow sandbank had appeared in the sea and the water had receded from the beach. I fancied I saw some black object flopping about upon this bank, but it became motionless as I looked at it, and I judged that my eye had been deceived, and that the black object was merely a rock. The stars in the sky were intensely bright and seemed to me to twinkle very little.

'Suddenly I noticed that the circular westward outline of the sun had changed; that a concavity, a bay, had appeared in the curve. I saw this grow larger. For a minute perhaps I stared aghast at this blackness that was creeping over the day, and then I realized that an eclipse was beginning. Either the moon or the planet Mercury was passing across the sun's disk. Naturally, at first I took it to be the moon, but there is much to incline me to believe that what I really saw was the transit of an inner planet passing very near to the earth.

'The darkness grew apace; a cold wind began to blow in freshening gusts from the east, and the showering white flakes in the air increased in number. From the edge of the sea came a ripple and whisper. Beyond these lifeless sounds the world was silent. Silent? It would be hard to convey the stillness of it. All the sounds of man, the bleating of sheep, the cries of birds, the hum of insects, the stir that makes the background of our lives — all that was over. As the darkness thickened, the eddying flakes grew more abundant, dancing before my eyes; and the cold of the air more intense. At last, one by one, swiftly, one after the other, the white peaks of the distant hills vanished into blackness. The breeze rose to a moaning wind. I saw the black central shadow of the eclipse sweeping towards me. In another moment the pale stars alone were visible. All else was rayless obscurity. The sky was absolutely black.

'A horror of this great darkness came on me. The cold, that smote to my marrow, and the pain I felt in breathing, overcame me. I shivered, and a deadly nausea seized me. Then like a red-hot bow in the sky appeared the edge of the sun. I got off the machine to recover myself. I felt giddy and incapable of facing the return journey. As I stood sick and confused I saw again the moving thing upon the shoal — there was no mistake now that it was a moving thing — against the red water of the sea. It was a round thing, the size of a football perhaps, or, it may be, bigger, and tentacles trailed down from it; it seemed black against the weltering blood-red water, and it was hopping fitfully about. Then I felt I was fainting. But a terrible dread of lying helpless in that remote and awful twilight sustained me while I clambered upon the saddle.

Chapter XII

'So I came back. For a long time I must have been insensible upon the machine. The blinking succession of the days and nights was resumed, the sun got golden again, the sky blue. I breathed with greater freedom. The fluctuating contours of the land ebbed and flowed. The hands spun backward upon the dials. At last I saw again the dim shadows of houses, the evidences of decadent humanity. These, too, changed and passed, and others came. Presently, when the million dial was at zero, I slackened speed. I began to recognize our own petty and familiar architecture, the thousands hand ran back to the starting-point, the night and day flapped slower and slower. Then the old walls of the laboratory came round me. Very gently, now, I slowed the mechanism down.

'I saw one little thing that seemed odd to me. I think I have told you that when I set out, before my velocity became very high, Mrs. Watchett had walked across the room, travelling, as it seemed to me, like a rocket. As I returned, I passed again across that minute when she traversed the laboratory. But now her every motion appeared to be the exact inversion of her previous ones. The door at the lower end opened, and she glided quietly up the laboratory, back foremost, and disappeared behind the door by which she had previously entered. Just before that I seemed to see Hillyer for a moment; but he passed like a flash.

'Then I stopped the machine, and saw about me again the old familiar laboratory, my tools, my appliances just as I had left them. I got off the thing very shakily, and sat down upon my bench. For several minutes I trembled violently. Then I became calmer. Around me was my old workshop again, exactly as it had been. I might have slept there, and the whole thing have been a dream.

'And yet, not exactly! The thing had started from the southeast corner of the laboratory. It had come to rest again in the northwest, against the wall where you saw it. That gives you the exact distance from my little lawn to the pedestal of the White Sphinx, into which the Morlocks had carried my machine.

'For a time my brain went stagnant. Presently I got up and came through the passage here, limping, because my heel was still painful, and feeling sorely begrimed. I saw the *Pall Mall*

Gazette on the table by the door. I found the date was indeed to-day, and looking at the time-piece, saw the hour was almost eight o'clock. I heard your voices and the clatter of plates. I hesitated — I felt so sick and weak. Then I sniffed good wholesome meat, and opened the door on you. You know the rest. I washed, and dined, and now I am telling you the story.

'I know,' he said, after a pause, 'that all this will be absolutely incredible to you. To me the one incredible thing is that I am here tonight in this old familiar room looking into your friendly faces and telling you these strange adventures.'

He looked at the Medical Man. 'No. I cannot expect you to believe it. Take it as a lie — or a prophecy. Say I dreamed it in the workshop. Consider I have been speculating upon the destinies of our race until I have hatched this fiction. Treat my assertion of its truth as a mere stroke of art to enhance its interest. And taking it as a story, what do you think of it?'

He took up his pipe, and began, in his old accustomed manner, to tap with it nervously upon the bars of the grate. There was a momentary stillness. Then chairs began to creak and shoes to scrape upon the carpet. I took my eyes off the Time Traveller's face, and looked round at his audience. They were in the dark, and little spots of colour swam before them. The Medical Man seemed absorbed in the contemplation of our host. The Editor was looking hard at the end of his cigar — the sixth. The Journalist fumbled for his watch. The others, as far as I remember, were motionless.

The Editor stood up with a sigh. 'What a pity it is you're not a writer of stories!' he said, putting his hand on the Time Traveller's shoulder.

'You don't believe it?'

'Well — —'

'I thought not.'

The Time Traveller turned to us. 'Where are the matches?' he said. He lit one and spoke over his pipe, puffing. 'To tell you the truth...I hardly believe it myself.... And yet...'

His eye fell with a mute inquiry upon the withered white flowers upon the little table. Then he turned over the hand holding his pipe, and I saw he was looking at some half-healed scars on his knuckles.

The Medical Man rose, came to the lamp, and examined the flowers. 'The gynaeceum's odd,' he said. The Psychologist leant forward to see, holding out his hand for a specimen.

'I'm hanged if it isn't a quarter to one,' said the Journalist. 'How shall we get home?'

'Plenty of cabs at the station,' said the Psychologist.

'It's a curious thing,' said the Medical Man; 'but I certainly don't know the natural order of these flowers. May I have them?'

The Time Traveller hesitated. Then suddenly: 'Certainly not.'

'Where did you really get them?' said the Medical Man.

The Time Traveller put his hand to his head. He spoke like one who was trying to keep hold of an idea that eluded him. 'They were put into my pocket by Weena, when I travelled into Time.' He stared round the room. 'I'm damned if it isn't all going. This room and you and the atmosphere of every day is too much for my memory. Did I ever make a Time Machine, or a model of a Time Machine? Or is it all only a dream? They say life is a dream, a precious poor dream at times — but I can't stand another that won't fit. It's madness. And where did the dream come from?...I must look at that machine. If there is one!'

He caught up the lamp swiftly, and carried it, flaring red, through the door into the corridor. We followed him. There in the flickering light of the lamp was the machine sure enough, squat, ugly, and askew; a thing of brass, ebony, ivory, and translucent glimmering quartz. Solid to the touch — for I put out my hand and felt the rail of it — and with brown spots and smears upon the ivory, and bits of grass and moss upon the lower parts, and one rail bent awry.

The Time Traveller put the lamp down on the bench, and ran his hand along the damaged rail. 'It's all right now,' he said. 'The story I told you was true. I'm sorry to have brought you out here in the cold.' He took up the lamp, and, in an absolute silence, we returned to the smoking-room.

He came into the hall with us and helped the Editor on with his coat. The Medical Man looked into his face and, with a certain hesitation, told him he was suffering from overwork, at which he laughed hugely. I remember him standing in the open doorway, bawling good night.

I shared a cab with the Editor. He thought the tale a 'gaudy lie.' For my own part I was unable to come to a conclusion. The story was so fantastic and incredible, the telling so credible and sober. I lay awake most of the night thinking about it. I determined to go next day and see the Time Traveller again. I was told he was in the laboratory, and being on easy terms in the house, I went up to him. The laboratory, however, was empty. I stared for a minute at the Time Machine and put out my hand and touched the lever. At that the squat substantial-looking mass swayed like a bough shaken by the wind. Its instability startled me extremely, and I had a queer reminiscence of the childish days when I used to be forbidden to meddle. I came back through the corridor. The Time Traveller met me in the smoking-room. He was coming from the house. He had a small camera under one arm and a knapsack under the other. He laughed when he saw me, and gave me an elbow to shake. 'I'm frightfully busy,' said he, 'with that thing in there.'

'But is it not some hoax?' I said. 'Do you really travel through time?'

'Really and truly I do.' And he looked frankly into my eyes. He hesitated. His eye wandered about the room. 'I only want half an hour,' he said. 'I know why you came, and it's awfully good of you. There's some magazines here. If you'll stop to lunch I'll prove you this time travelling up to the hilt, specimen and all. If you'll forgive my leaving you now?'

I consented, hardly comprehending then the full import of his words, and he nodded and went on down the corridor. I heard the door of the laboratory slam, seated myself in a chair, and took up a daily paper. What was he going to do before lunch-time? Then suddenly I was reminded by an advertisement that I had promised to meet Richardson, the publisher, at two. I looked at my watch, and saw that I could barely save that engagement. I got up and went down the passage to tell the Time Traveller.

As I took hold of the handle of the door I heard an exclamation, oddly truncated at the end, and a click and a thud. A gust of air whirled round me as I opened the door, and from within came the sound of broken glass falling on the floor. The Time Traveller was not there. I seemed to see a ghostly, indistinct figure sitting in a whirling mass of black and brass for a moment — a figure so transparent that the bench behind with its sheets of drawings was absolutely distinct; but this phantasm vanished as I rubbed my eyes. The Time Machine had gone. Save for a subsiding stir of dust, the further end of the laboratory was empty. A pane of the skylight had, apparently, just been blown in.

I felt an unreasonable amazement. I knew that something strange had happened, and for the moment could not distinguish what the strange thing might be. As I stood staring, the door into the garden opened, and the manservant appeared.

We looked at each other. Then ideas began to come. 'Has Mr. — — gone out that way?' said I.

'No, sir. No one has come out this way. I was expecting to find him here.'

At that I understood. At the risk of disappointing Richardson I stayed on, waiting for the Time Traveller; waiting for the second, perhaps still stranger story, and the specimens and photographs he would bring with him. But I am beginning now to fear that I must wait a lifetime. The Time Traveller vanished three years ago. And, as everybody knows now, he has never returned.

Epilogue

One cannot choose but wonder. Will he ever return? It may be that he swept back into the past, and fell among the blood-drinking, hairy savages of the Age of Unpolished Stone; into the abysses of the Cretaceous Sea; or among the grotesque saurians, the huge reptilian brutes of the Jurassic times. He may even now — if I may use the phrase — be wandering on some plesiosaurus-haunted Oolitic coral reef, or beside the lonely saline lakes of the Triassic Age. Or did he go forward, into one of the nearer ages, in which men are still men, but with the riddles of our own time answered and its wearisome problems solved? Into the manhood of the race: for I, for my own part, cannot think that these latter days of weak experiment, fragmentary theory, and mutual discord are indeed man's culminating time! I say, for my own part. He, I know — for the question had been discussed among us long before the Time Machine was made — thought but cheerlessly of the Advancement of Mankind, and saw in the growing pile of civilization only a foolish heaping that must inevitably fall back upon and destroy its makers in the end. If that is so, it remains for us to live as though it were not so. But to me the future is still black and blank — is a vast ignorance, lit at a few casual places by the memory of his story. And I have by me, for my comfort, two strange white flowers — shrivelled now, and brown and flat and brittle — to witness that even when mind and strength had gone, gratitude and a mutual tenderness still lived on in the heart of man.

Ayn Rand

Anthem

Part One

It is a sin to write this. It is a sin to think words no others think and to put them down upon a paper no others are to see. It is base and evil. It is as if we were speaking alone to no ears but our own. And we know well that there is no transgression blacker than to do or think alone. We have broken the laws. The laws say that men may not write unless the Council of Vocations bid them so. May we be forgiven!

But this is not the only sin upon us. We have committed a greater crime, and for this crime there is no name. What punishment awaits us if it be discovered we know not, for no such crime has come in the memory of men and there are no laws to provide for it.

It is dark here. The flame of the candle stands still in the air. Nothing moves in this tunnel save our hand on the paper. We are alone here under the earth. It is a fearful word, alone. The laws say that none among men may be alone, ever and at any time, for this is the great transgression and the root of all evil. But we have broken many laws. And now there is nothing here save our one body, and it is strange to see only two legs stretched on the ground, and on the wall before us the shadow of our one head.

The walls are cracked and water runs upon them in thin threads without sound, black and glistening as blood. We stole the candle from the larder of the Home of the Street Sweepers. We shall be sentenced to ten years in the Palace of Corrective Detention if it be discovered. But this matters not. It matters only that the light is precious and we should not waste it to write when we need it for that work which is our crime. Nothing matters save the work, our secret, our evil, our precious work. Still, we must also write, for-may the Council have mercy upon us! —we wish to speak for once to no ears but our own.

Our name is Equality 7-2521, as it is written on the iron bracelet which all men wear on their left wrists with their names upon it. We are twenty-one years old. We are six feet tall, and this is a burden, for there are not many men who are six feet tall. Ever have the Teachers and the Leaders pointed to us and frowned and said:

"There is evil in your bones, Equality 7-2521, for your body has grown beyond the bodies of your brothers." But we cannot change our bones nor our body.

We were born with a curse. It has always driven us to thoughts which are forbidden. It has always given us wishes which men may not wish. We know that we are evil, but there is no will in us and no power to resist it. This is our wonder and our secret fear, that we know and do not resist.

We strive to be like all our brother men, for all men must be alike. Over the portals of the Palace of the World Council, there are words cut in the marble, which we repeat to ourselves whenever we are tempted:

"WE ARE ONE IN ALL AND ALL IN ONE.
THERE ARE NO MEN BUT ONLY THE GREAT WE,
ONE, INDIVISIBLE AND FOREVER."

We repeat this to ourselves, but it helps us not.

These words were cut long ago. There is green mould in the grooves of the letters and yellow streaks on the marble, which come from more years than men could count. And these words are the truth, for they are written on the Palace of the World Council, and the World Council is the body of all truth. Thus has it been ever since the Great Rebirth, and farther back than that no memory can reach.

But we must never speak of the times before the Great Rebirth, else we are sentenced to three years in the Palace of Corrective Detention. It is only the Old Ones who whisper about it in the evenings, in the Home of the Useless. They whisper many strange things, of the towers which rose to the sky, in those Unmentionable Times, and of the wagons which moved without horses, and of the lights which burned without flame. But those times were evil. And those times passed away, when men saw the Great Truth which is this: that all men are one and that there is no will save the will of all men together.

All men are good and wise. It is only we, Equality 7-2521, we alone who were born with a curse. For we are not like our brothers. And as we look back upon our life, we see that it has ever been thus and that it has brought us step by step to our last, supreme transgression, our crime of crimes hidden here under the ground.

We remember the Home of the Infants where we lived till we were five years old, together with all the children of the City who had been born in the same year. The sleeping halls there were white and clean and bare of all things save one hundred beds. We were just like all our brothers then, save for the one transgression: we fought with our brothers. There are few offenses blacker than to fight with our brothers, at any age and for any cause whatsoever. The Council of the Home told us so, and of all the children of that year, we were locked in the cellar most often.

When we were five years old, we were sent to the Home of the Students, where there are ten wards, for our ten years of learning. Men must learn till they reach their fifteenth year. Then they go to work. In the Home of the Students we arose when the big bell rang in the tower and we went to our beds when it rang again. Before we removed our garments, we stood in the great sleeping hall, and we raised our right arms, and we said all together with the three Teachers at the head:

"We are nothing. Mankind is all. By the grace of our brothers are we allowed our lives. We exist through, by and for our brothers who are the State. Amen."

Then we slept. The sleeping halls were white and clean and bare of all things save one hundred beds.

We, Equality 7-2521, were not happy in those years in the Home of the Students. It was not that the learning was too hard for us. It was that the learning was too easy. This is a great sin, to be born with a head which is too quick. It is not good to be different from our brothers, but it is evil to be superior to them. The Teachers told us so, and they frowned when they looked upon us.

So we fought against this curse. We tried to forget our lessons, but we always remembered. We tried not to understand what the Teachers taught, but we always understood it before the Teachers had spoken. We looked upon Union 5-3992, who were a pale boy with only half a brain, and we tried to say and do as they did, that we might be like them, like Union 5-3992, but somehow the Teachers knew that we were not. And we were lashed more often than all the other children.

The Teachers were just, for they had been appointed by the Councils, and the Councils are the voice of all justice, for they are the voice of all men. And if sometimes, in the secret darkness of our heart, we regret that which befell us on our fifteenth birthday, we know that it was through our own guilt. We had broken a law, for we had not paid heed to the words of our Teachers. The Teachers had said to us all:

"Dare not choose in your minds the work you would like to do when you leave the Home of the Students. You shall do that which the Council of Vocations shall prescribe for you. For the Council of Vocations knows in its great wisdom where you are needed by your brother men, better than you can know it in your unworthy little minds. And if you are not needed by your brother man, there is no reason for you to burden the earth with your bodies."

We knew this well, in the years of our childhood, but our curse broke our will. We were guilty and we confess it here: we were guilty of the great Transgression of Preference. We preferred some work and some lessons to the others. We did not listen well to the history of all the Councils elected since the Great Rebirth. But we loved the Science of Things. We wished to know. We wished to know about all the things which make the earth around us. We asked so many questions that the Teachers forbade it.

We think that there are mysteries in the sky and under the water and in the plants which grow. But the Council of Scholars has said that there are no mysteries, and the Council of Scholars knows all things. And we learned much from our Teachers. We learned that the earth is flat and that the sun revolves around it, which causes the day and the night. We learned the names of all the winds which blow over the seas and push the sails of our great ships. We learned how to bleed men to cure them of all ailments.

We loved the Science of Things. And in the darkness, in the secret hour, when we awoke in the night and there were no brothers around us, but only their shapes in the beds and their snores, we closed our eyes, and we held our lips shut, and we stopped our breath, that no shudder might let our brothers see or hear or guess, and we thought that we wished to be sent to the Home of the Scholars when our time would come.

All the great modern inventions come from the Home of the Scholars, such as the newest one, which was found only a hundred years ago, of how to make candles from wax and string; also, how to make glass, which is put in our windows to protect us from the rain. To find these things, the Scholars must study the earth and learn from the rivers, from the sands, from the winds and the rocks. And if we went to the Home of the Scholars, we could learn from these also. We could ask questions of these, for they do not forbid questions.

And questions give us no rest. We know not why our curse makes us seek we know not what, ever and ever. But we cannot resist it. It whispers to us that there are great things on this earth of ours, and that we can know them if we try, and that we must know them. We ask, why must we know, but it has no answer to give us. We must know that we may know.

So we wished to be sent to the Home of the Scholars. We wished it so much that our hands trembled under the blankets in the night, and we bit our arm to stop that other pain which we could not endure. It was evil and we dared not face our brothers in the morning. For men may wish nothing for themselves. And we were punished when the Council of Vocations came to give us our life Mandates which tell those who reach their fifteenth year what their work is to be for the rest of their days.

The Council of Vocations came on the first day of spring, and they sat in the great hall. And we who were fifteen and all the Teachers came into the great hall. And the Council of Vocations sat on a high dais, and they had but two words to speak to each of the Students. They called the Students' names, and when the Students stepped before them, one after another, the Council said: "Carpenter" or "Doctor" or "Cook" or "Leader." Then each Student raised their right arm and said: "The will of our brothers be done."

Now if the Council has said "Carpenter" or "Cook," the Students so assigned go to work and they do not study any further. But if the Council has said "Leader," then those Students go into the Home of the Leaders, which is the greatest house in the City, for it has three stories. And there they study for many years, so that they may become candidates and be elected to the City Council and the State Council and the World Council-by a free and general vote of all men. But we wished not to be a Leader, even though it is a great honor. We wished to be a Scholar.

So we awaited our turn in the great hall and then we heard the Council of Vocations call our name: "Equality 7-2521." We walked to the dais, and our legs did not tremble, and we looked up at the Council. There were five members of the Council, three of the male gender and two of the female. Their hair was white and their faces were cracked as the clay of a dry river bed. They were old. They seemed older than the marble of the Temple of the World Council. They sat before us and they did not move. And we saw no breath to stir the folds of their white togas. But we knew that they were alive, for a finger of the hand of the oldest rose, pointed to us, and fell down again. This was the only thing which moved, for the lips of the oldest did not move as they said: "Street Sweeper."

We felt the cords of our neck grow tight as our head rose higher to look upon the faces of the Council, and we were happy. We knew we had been guilty, but now we had a way to atone for it. We would accept our Life Mandate, and we would work for our brothers, gladly and willingly, and we would erase our sin against them, which they did not know, but we knew. So we were happy, and proud of ourselves and of our victory over ourselves. We raised our right arm and we spoke, and our voice was the clearest, the steadiest voice in the hall that day, and we said:

"The will of our brothers be done."

And we looked straight into the eyes of the Council, but their eyes were as cold blue glass buttons.

So we went into the Home of the Street Sweepers. It is a grey house on a narrow street. There is a sundial in its courtyard, by which the Council of the Home can tell the hours of the day and when to ring the bell. When the bell rings, we all arise from our beds. The sky is green and cold in our windows to the east. The shadow on the sundial marks off a half-hour while we dress and eat our breakfast in the dining hall, where there are five long tables with twenty clay plates and twenty clay cups on each table. Then we go to work in the streets of the City, with our brooms and our rakes. In five hours, when the sun is high, we return to the Home and we eat our midday meal, for which one-half hour is allowed. Then we go to work again. In five hours, the shadows are blue on the pavements, and the sky is blue with a deep brightness which is not bright. We come back to have our dinner, which lasts one hour. Then the bell rings and we walk in a straight column to one of the City Halls, for the Social Meeting. Other columns of men arrive from the Homes of the different Trades. The candles are lit, and the Councils of the different Homes stand in a pulpit, and they speak to us of our duties and of our brother men. Then visiting Leaders mount the pulpit and they read to us the speeches which were made in the City Council that day, for the City Council represents all men and all men must know. Then we sing hymns, the Hymn of Brotherhood, and the Hymn of Equality, and the Hymn of the Collective Spirit. The sky is a soggy purple when we return to the Home. Then the bell rings and we walk in a straight column to the City Theatre for three hours of Social Recreation. There a play is shown upon the stage, with two great choruses from the Home of the Actors, which speak and answer all together, in two great voices. The plays are about toil and how good it is. Then we walk back to the Home in a straight column. The sky is like a black sieve pierced by silver drops that tremble, ready to burst through. The moths beat against the street lanterns. We go to our beds and we sleep, till the bell rings again. The sleeping halls are white and clean and bare of all things save one hundred beds.

Thus have we lived each day of four years, until two springs ago when our crime happened. Thus must all men live until they are forty. At forty, they are worn out. At forty, they are sent to the Home of the Useless, where the Old Ones live. The Old Ones do not work, for the State takes care of them. They sit in the sun in summer and they sit by the fire in winter. They do not speak often, for they are weary. The Old Ones know that they are soon to die. When a miracle happens and some live to be forty-five, they are the Ancient Ones, and the children stare at them when passing by the Home of the Useless. Such is to be our life, as that of all our brothers and of the brothers who came before us.

Such would have been our life, had we not committed our crime which changed all things for us. And it was our curse which drove us to our crime. We had been a good Street Sweeper and like all our brother Street Sweepers, save for our cursed wish to know. We looked too long at the stars at night, and at the trees and the earth. And when we cleaned the yard of the Home of the Scholars, we gathered the glass vials, the pieces of metal, the dried bones which they had discarded. We wished to keep these things and to study them, but we had no place to hide them. So we carried them to the City Cesspool. And then we made the discovery.

It was on a day of the spring before last. We Street Sweepers work in brigades of three, and we were with Union 5-3992, they of the half-brain, and with International 4-8818. Now Union 5-3992 are a sickly lad and sometimes they are stricken with convulsions, when their mouth froths and their eyes turn white. But International 4-8818 are different. They are a tall, strong youth and their eyes are like fireflies, for there is laughter in their eyes. We cannot look upon International 4-8818 and not smile in answer. For this they were not liked in the Home of the Students, as it is not proper to smile without reason. And also they were not liked because they took pieces of coal and they drew pictures upon the walls, and they were pictures which made men laugh. But it is only our brothers in the Home of the Artists who are permitted to draw pictures, so International 4-8818 were sent to the Home of the Street Sweepers, like ourselves.

International 4-8818 and we are friends. This is an evil thing to say, for it is a transgression, the great Transgression of Preference, to love any among men better than the others, since we must love all men and all men are our friends. So International 4-8818 and we have never spoken of it. But we know. We know, when we look into each other's eyes. And when we look thus without words, we both know other things also, strange things for which there are no words, and these things frighten us.

So on that day of the spring before last, Union 5-3992 were stricken with convulsions on the edge of the City, near the City Theatre. We left them to lie in the shade of the Theatre tent and we went with International 4-8818 to finish our work. We came together to the great ravine behind the Theatre. It is empty save for trees and weeds. Beyond the ravine there is a plain, and beyond the plain there lies the Uncharted Forest, about which men must not think.

We were gathering the papers and the rags which the wind had blown from the Theatre, when we saw an iron bar among the weeds. It was old and rusted by many rains. We pulled with all our strength, but we could not move it. So we called International 4-8818, and together we scraped the earth around the bar. Of a sudden the earth fell in before us, and we saw an old iron grill over a black hole.

International 4-8818 stepped back. But we pulled at the grill and it gave way. And then we saw iron rings as steps leading down a shaft into a darkness without bottom.

"We shall go down," we said to International 4-8818.

"It is forbidden," they answered.

We said: "The Council does not know of this hole, so it cannot be forbidden."

And they answered: "Since the Council does not know of this hole, there can be no law permitting to enter it. And everything which is not permitted by law is forbidden."

But we said: "We shall go, none the less."

They were frightened, but they stood by and watched us go.

We hung on the iron rings with our hands and our feet. We could see nothing below us. And above us the hole open upon the sky grew smaller and smaller, till it came to be the size of a button. But still we went down. Then our foot touched the ground. We rubbed our eyes, for we could not see. Then our eyes became used to the darkness, but we could not believe what we saw.

No men known to us could have built this place, nor the men known to our brothers who lived before us, and yet it was built by men. It was a great tunnel. Its walls were hard and smooth to the touch; it felt like stone, but it was not stone. On the ground there were long thin tracks of iron, but it was not iron; it felt smooth and cold as glass. We knelt, and we crawled forward, our hand groping along the iron line to see where it would lead. But there was an unbroken night ahead. Only the iron tracks glowed through it, straight and white, calling us to follow. But we could not follow, for we were losing the puddle of light behind us. So we turned and we crawled back, our hand on the iron line. And our heart beat in our fingertips, without reason. And then we knew.

We knew suddenly that this place was left from the Unmentionable Times. So it was true, and those Times had been, and all the wonders of those Times. Hundreds upon hundreds of years ago men knew secrets which we have lost. And we thought: "This is a foul place. They are damned who touch the things of the Unmentionable Times." But our hand which followed the track, as we crawled, clung to the iron as if it would not leave it, as if the skin of our hand were thirsty and begging of the metal some secret fluid beating in its coldness.

We returned to the earth. International 4-8818 looked upon us and stepped back.

"Equality 7-2521," they said, "your face is white."

But we could not speak and we stood looking upon them.

They backed away, as if they dared not touch us. Then they smiled, but it was not a gay smile; it was lost and pleading. But still we could not speak. Then they said:

"We shall report our find to the City Council and both of us will be rewarded."

And then we spoke. Our voice was hard and there was no mercy in our voice. We said:

"We shall not report our find to the City Council. We shall not report it to any men."

They raised their hands to their ears, for never had they heard such words as these.

"International 4-8818," we asked, "will you report us to the Council and see us lashed to death before your eyes?"

They stood straight all of a sudden and they answered: "Rather would we die."

"Then," we said, "keep silent. This place is ours. This place belongs to us, Equality 7-2521, and to no other men on earth. And if ever we surrender it, we shall surrender our life with it also."

Then we saw that the eyes of International 4-8818 were full to the lids with tears they dared not drop. They whispered, and their voice trembled, so that their words lost all shape:

"The will of the Council is above all things, for it is the will of our brothers, which is holy. But if you wish it so, we shall obey you. Rather shall we be evil with you than good with all our brothers. May the Council have mercy upon both our hearts!"

Then we walked away together and back to the Home of the Street Sweepers. And we walked in silence.

Thus did it come to pass that each night, when the stars are high and the Street Sweepers sit in the City Theatre, we, Equality 7-2521, steal out and run through the darkness to our place. It is easy to leave the Theatre; when the candles are blown out and the Actors come onto the stage, no eyes can see us as we crawl under our seat and under the cloth of the tent. Later, it is easy to steal through the shadows and fall in line next to International 4-8818, as the column leaves the Theatre. It is dark in the streets and there are no men about, for no men may walk through the City when they have no mission to walk there. Each night, we run to the ravine, and we remove the stones which we have piled upon the iron grill to hide it from the men. Each night, for three hours, we are under the earth, alone.

We have stolen candles from the Home of the Street Sweepers, we have stolen flints and knives and paper, and we have brought them to this place. We have stolen glass vials and powders and acids from the Home of the Scholars. Now we sit in the tunnel for three hours each night and we study. We melt strange metals, and we mix acids, and we cut open the bodies of the animals which we find in the City Cesspool. We have built an oven of the bricks we gathered in the streets. We burn the wood we find in the ravine. The fire flickers in the oven and blue shadows dance upon the walls, and there is no sound of men to disturb us.

We have stolen manuscripts. This is a great offense. Manuscripts are precious, for our brothers in the Home of the Clerks spend one year to copy one single script in their clear handwriting. Manuscripts are rare and they are kept in the Home of the Scholars. So we sit under the earth and we read the stolen scripts. Two years have passed since we found this place. And in these two years we have learned more than we had learned in the ten years of the Home of the Students.

We have learned things which are not in the scripts. We have solved secrets of which the Scholars have no knowledge. We have come to see how great is the unexplored, and many lifetimes will not bring us to the end of our quest. But we wish no end to our quest. We wish nothing, save to be alone and to learn, and to feel as if with each day our sight were growing sharper than the hawk's and clearer than rock crystal.

Strange are the ways of evil. We are false in the faces of our brothers. We are defying the will of our Councils. We alone, of the thousands who walk this earth, we alone in this hour are doing a work which has no purpose save that we wish to do it. The evil of our crime is not for the human mind to probe. The nature of our punishment, if it be discovered, is not for the human heart to ponder. Never, not in the memory of the Ancient Ones' Ancients, never have men done that which we are doing.

And yet there is no shame in us and no regret. We say to ourselves that we are a wretch and a traitor. But we feel no burden upon our spirit and no fear in our heart. And it seems to us that our spirit is clear as a lake troubled by no eyes save those of the sun. And in our heart-strange are the ways of evil! —in our heart there is the first peace we have known in twenty years.

Part Two

Liberty 5-3000... Liberty five-three thousand ... Liberty 5-3000....

We wish to write this name. We wish to speak it, but we dare not speak it above a whisper. For men are forbidden to take notice of women, and women are forbidden to take notice of men. But we think of one among women, they whose name is Liberty 5-3000, and we think of no others. The women who have been assigned to work the soil live in the Homes of the Peasants beyond the City. Where the City ends there is a great road winding off to the north, and we Street Sweepers must keep this road clean to the first milepost. There is a hedge along the road, and beyond the hedge lie the fields. The fields are black and ploughed, and they lie like a great fan before us, with their furrows gathered in some hand beyond the sky, spreading forth from that hand, opening wide apart as they come toward us, like black pleats that sparkle with thin, green spangles. Women work in the fields, and their white tunics in the wind are like the wings of sea-gulls beating over the black soil.

And there it was that we saw Liberty 5-3000 walking along the furrows. Their body was straight and thin as a blade of iron. Their eyes were dark and hard and glowing, with no fear in them, no kindness and no guilt. Their hair was golden as the sun; their hair flew in the wind, shining and wild, as if it defied men to restrain it. They threw seeds from their hand as if they deigned to fling a scornful gift, and the earth was a beggar under their feet.

We stood still; for the first time did we know fear, and then pain. And we stood still that we might not spill this pain more precious than pleasure.

Then we heard a voice from the others call their name: "Liberty 5-3000," and they turned and walked back. Thus we learned their name, and we stood watching them go, till their white tunic was lost in the blue mist.

And the following day, as we came to the northern road, we kept our eyes upon Liberty 5-3000 in the field. And each day thereafter we knew the illness of waiting for our hour on the northern road. And there we looked at Liberty 5-3000 each day. We know not whether they looked at us also, but we think they did. Then one day they came close to the hedge, and suddenly they turned to us. They turned in a whirl and the movement of their body stopped, as if slashed off, as suddenly as it had started. They stood still as a stone, and they looked straight upon us, straight into our eyes. There was no smile on their face, and no welcome. But their face was taut, and their eyes were dark. Then they turned as swiftly, and they walked away from us.

But the following day, when we came to the road, they smiled. They smiled to us and for us. And we smiled in answer. Their head fell back, and their arms fell, as if their arms and their thin white neck were stricken suddenly with a great lassitude. They were not looking upon us, but upon the sky. Then they glanced at us over their shoulder, as we felt as if a hand had touched our body, slipping softly from our lips to our feet.

Every morning thereafter, we greeted each other with our eyes. We dared not speak. It is a transgression to speak to men of other Trades, save in groups at the Social Meetings. But once, standing at the hedge, we raised our hand to our forehead and then moved it slowly, palm down, toward Liberty 5-3000. Had the others seen it, they could have guessed nothing, for it looked only as if we were shading our eyes from the sun. But Liberty 5-3000 saw it and understood. They raised their hand to their forehead and moved it as we had. Thus, each day, we greet Liberty 5-3000, and they answer, and no men can suspect.

We do not wonder at this new sin of ours. It is our second Transgression of Preference, for we do not think of all our brothers, as we must, but only of one, and their name is Liberty 5-3000. We do not know why we think of them. We do not know why, when we think of them, we feel all of a sudden that the earth is good and that it is not a burden to live. We do not think of them as Liberty 5-3000 any longer. We have given them a name in our thoughts. We call them the Golden One. But it is a sin to give men names which distinguish them from other men. Yet we call them the Golden One, for they are not like the others. The Golden One are not like the others.

And we take no heed of the law which says that men may not think of women, save at the Time of Mating. This is the time each spring when all the men older than twenty and all the women older than eighteen are sent for one night to the City Palace of Mating. And each of the men have one of the women assigned to them by the Council of Eugenics. Children are born each winter, but women never see their children and children never know their parents. Twice have we been sent to the Palace of Mating, but it is an ugly and shameful matter, of which we do not like to think.

We had broken so many laws, and today we have broken one more. Today, we spoke to the Golden One.

The other women were far off in the field, when we stopped at the hedge by the side of the road. The Golden One were kneeling alone at the moat which runs through the field. And the drops of water falling from their hands, as they raised the water to their lips, were like sparks of fire in the sun. Then the Golden One saw us, and they did not move, kneeling there, looking at us, and circles of light played upon their white tunic, from the sun on the water of the moat, and one sparkling drop fell from a finger of their hand held as frozen in the air.

Then the Golden One rose and walked to the hedge, as if they had heard a command in our eyes. The two other Street Sweepers of our brigade were a hundred paces away down the road. And we thought that International 4-8818 would not betray us, and Union 5-3992 would not understand. So we looked straight upon the Golden One, and we saw the shadows of their lashes on their white cheeks and the sparks of sun on their lips. And we said:

"You are beautiful, Liberty 5-3000."

Their face did not move and they did not avert their eyes. Only their eyes grew wider, and there was triumph in their eyes, and it was not triumph over us, but over things we could not guess.

Then they asked:

"What is your name?"

"Equality 7-2521," we answered.

"You are not one of our brothers, Equality 7-2521, for we do not wish you to be."

We cannot say what they meant, for there are no words for their meaning, but we know it without words and we knew it then.

"No," we answered, "nor are you one of our sisters."

"If you see us among scores of women, will you look upon us?"

"We shall look upon you, Liberty 5-3000, if we see you among all the women of the earth."

Then they asked:

"Are Street Sweepers sent to different parts of the City or do they always work in the same places?"

"They always work in the same places," we answered, "and no one will take this road away from us."

"Your eyes," they said, "are not like the eyes of any among men."

And suddenly, without cause for the thought which came to us, we felt cold, cold to our stomach.

"How old are you?" we asked.

They understood our thought, for they lowered their eyes for the first time.

"Seventeen," they whispered.

And we sighed, as if a burden had been taken from us, for we had been thinking without reason of the Palace of Mating. And we thought that we would not let the Golden One be sent to the Palace. How to prevent it, how to bar the will of the Councils, we knew not, but we knew suddenly that we would. Only we do not know why such thought came to us, for these ugly matters bear no relation to us and the Golden One. What relation can they bear?

Still, without reason, as we stood there by the hedge, we felt our lips drawn tight with hatred, a sudden hatred for all our brother men. And the Golden One saw it and smiled slowly, and there was in their smile the first sadness we had seen in them. We think that in the wisdom of women the Golden One had understood more than we can understand.

Then three of the sisters in the field appeared, coming toward the road, so the Golden One walked away from us. They took the bag of seeds, and they threw the seeds into the furrows of earth as they walked away. But the seeds flew wildly, for the hand of the Golden One was trembling.

Yet as we walked back to the Home of the Street Sweepers, we felt that we wanted to sing, without reason. So we were reprimanded tonight, in the dining hall, for without knowing it we had begun to sing aloud some tune we had never heard. But it is not proper to sing without reason, save at the Social Meetings.

"We are singing because we are happy," we answered the one of the Home Council who reprimanded us.

"Indeed you are happy," they answered. "How else can men be when they live for their brothers?"

And now, sitting here in our tunnel, we wonder about these words. It is forbidden, not to be happy. For, as it has been explained to us, men are free and the earth belongs to them; and all things on earth belong to all men; and the will of all men together is good for all; and so all men must be happy.

Yet as we stand at night in the great hall, removing our garments for sleep, we look upon our brothers and we wonder. The heads of our brothers are bowed. The eyes of our brothers are dull, and never do they look one another in the eyes. The shoulders of our brothers are hunched, and their muscles are drawn, as if their bodies were shrinking and wished to shrink out of sight. And a word steals into our mind, as we look upon our brothers, and that word is fear.

There is fear hanging in the air of the sleeping halls, and in the air of the streets. Fear walks through the City, fear without name, without shape. All men feel it and none dare to speak.

We feel it also, when we are in the Home of the Street Sweepers. But here, in our tunnel, we feel it no longer. The air is pure under the ground. There is no odor of men. And these three hours give us strength for our hours above the ground.

Our body is betraying us, for the Council of the Home looks with suspicion upon us. It is not good to feel too much joy nor to be glad that our body lives. For we matter not and it must not matter to us whether we live or die, which is to be as our brothers will it. But we, Equality 7-2521, are glad to be living. If this is a vice, then we wish no virtue.

Yet our brothers are not like us. All is not well with our brothers. There are Fraternity 2-5503, a quiet boy with wise, kind eyes, who cry suddenly, without reason, in the midst of day or night, and their body shakes with sobs they cannot explain. There are Solidarity 9-6347, who are a bright youth, without fear in the day; but they scream in their sleep, and they scream: "Help us! Help us! Help us!" into the night, in a voice which chills our bones, but the Doctors cannot cure Solidarity 9-6347.

And as we all undress at night, in the dim light of the candles, our brothers are silent, for they dare not speak the thoughts of their minds. For all must agree with all, and they cannot know if their thoughts are the thoughts of all, and so they fear to speak. And they are glad when the candles are blown for the night. But we, Equality 7-2521, look through the window upon the sky, and there is peace in the sky, and cleanliness, and dignity. And beyond the City there lies the plain, and beyond the plain, black upon the black sky, there lies the Uncharted Forest.

We do not wish to look upon the Uncharted Forest. We do not wish to think of it. But ever do our eyes return to that black patch upon the sky. Men never enter the Uncharted Forest, for there is no power to explore it and no path to lead among its ancient trees which stand as guards of fearful secrets. It is whispered that once or twice in a hundred years, one among the men of the City escape alone and run to the Uncharted Forest, without call or reason. These men do not return. They perish from hunger and from the claws of the wild beasts which roam the Forest. But our Councils say that this is only a legend. We have heard that there are many Uncharted Forests over the land, among the Cities. And it is whispered that they have grown over the ruins of many cities of the Unmentionable Times. The trees have swallowed the ruins, and the bones under the ruins, and all the things which perished. And as we look upon the Uncharted Forest far in the night, we think of the secrets of the Unmentionable Times. And we wonder how it came to pass that these secrets were lost to the world. We have heard the legends of the great fighting, in which many men fought on one side and only a few on the other. These few were the Evil Ones and they were conquered. Then great fires raged over the land. And in these fires the Evil Ones and all the things made by the Evil Ones were burned. And the fire which is called the Dawn of the Great Rebirth, was the Script Fire where all the scripts of the Evil Ones were burned, and with them all the words of the Evil Ones. Great mountains of flame stood in the squares of the Cities for three months. Then came the Great Rebirth.

The words of the Evil Ones... The words of the Unmentionable Times... What are the words which we have lost?

May the Council have mercy upon us! We had no wish to write such a question, and we knew not what we were doing till we had written it. We shall not ask this question and we shall not think it. We shall not call death upon our head.

And yet... And yet... There is some word, one single word which is not in the language of men, but which had been. And this is the Unspeakable Word, which no men may speak nor hear. But sometimes, and it is rare, sometimes, somewhere, one among men find that word. They find it upon scraps of old manuscripts or cut into the fragments of ancient stones. But when they speak it they are put to death. There is no crime punished by death in this world, save this one crime of speaking the Unspeakable Word.

We have seen one of such men burned alive in the square of the City. And it was a sight which has stayed with us through the years, and it haunts us, and follows us, and it gives us no rest. We were a child then, ten years old. And we stood in the great square with all the children and all the men of the City, sent to behold the burning. They brought the Transgressor out into the square and they led them to the pyre. They had torn out the tongue of the Transgressor, so that they could speak no longer. The Transgressor were young and tall. They had hair of gold and eyes blue as morning. They walked to the pyre, and their step did not falter. And of all the faces on that square, of all the faces which shrieked and screamed and spat curses upon them, theirs was the calmest and the happiest face.

As the chains were wound over their body at the stake, and a flame set to the pyre, the Transgressor looked upon the City. There was a thin thread of blood running from the corner of their mouth, but their lips were smiling. And a monstrous thought came to us then, which has never left us. We had heard of Saints. There are the Saints of Labor, and the Saints of the Councils, and the Saints of the Great Rebirth. But we had never seen a Saint nor what the likeness of a Saint should be. And we thought then, standing in the square, that the likeness of a Saint was the face we saw before us in the flames, the face of the Transgressor of the Unspeakable Word.

As the flames rose, a thing happened which no eyes saw but ours, else we would not be living today. Perhaps it had only seemed to us. But it seemed to us that the eyes of the Transgressor had chosen us from the crowd and were looking straight upon us. There was no pain in their eyes and no knowledge of the agony of their body. There was only joy in them, and pride, a pride holier than is fit for human pride to be. And it seemed as if these eyes were trying to tell us something through the flames, to send into our eyes some word without sound. And it seemed as if these eyes were begging us to gather that word and not to let it go from us and from the earth. But the flames rose and we could not guess the word....

What-even if we have to burn for it like the Saint of the Pyre-what is the Unspeakable Word?

Part Three

We, Equality 7-2521, have discovered a new power of nature. And we have discovered it alone, and we alone are to know it.

It is said. Now let us be lashed for it, if we must. The Council of Scholars has said that we all know the things which exist and therefore the things which are not known by all do not exist. But we think that the Council of Scholars is blind. The secrets of this earth are not for all men to see, but only for those who will seek them. We know, for we have found a secret unknown to all our brothers.

We know not what this power is nor whence it comes. But we know its nature, we have watched it and worked with it. We saw it first two years ago. One night, we were cutting open the body of a dead frog when we saw its leg jerking. It was dead, yet it moved. Some power unknown to men was making it move. We could not understand it. Then, after many tests, we found the answer. The frog had been hanging on a wire of copper; and it had been the metal of our knife which had sent the strange power to the copper through the brine of the frog's body. We put a piece of copper and a piece of zinc into a jar of brine, we touched a wire to them, and there, under our fingers, was a miracle which had never occurred before, a new miracle and a new power.

This discovery haunted us. We followed it in preference to all our studies. We worked with it, we tested it in more ways than we can describe, and each step was as another miracle unveiling before us. We came to know that we had found the greatest power on earth. For it defies all the laws known to men. It makes the needle move and turn on the compass which we stole from the Home of the Scholars; but we had been taught, when still a child, that the loadstone points to the north and that this is a law which nothing can change; yet our new power defies all laws. We found that it causes lightning, and never have men known what causes lightning. In thunderstorms, we raised a tall rod of iron by the side of our hole, and we watched it from below. We have seen the lightning strike it again and again. And now we know that metal draws the power of the sky, and that metal can be made to give it forth.

We have built strange things with this discovery of ours. We used for it the copper wires which we found here under the ground. We have walked the length of our tunnel, with a candle lighting the way. We could go no farther than half a mile, for earth and rock had fallen at both ends. But we gathered all the things we found and we brought them to our work place. We found strange boxes with bars of metal inside, with many cords and strands and coils of metal. We found wires that led to strange little globes of glass on the walls; they contained threads of metal thinner than a spider's web.

These things help us in our work. We do not understand them, but we think that the men of the Unmentionable Times had known our power of the sky, and these things had some relation to it. We do not know, but we shall learn. We cannot stop now, even though it frightens us that we are alone in our knowledge.

No single one can possess greater wisdom than the many Scholars who are elected by all men for their wisdom. Yet we can. We do. We have fought against saying it, but now it is said. We do not care. We forget all men, all laws and all things save our metals and our wires. So much is still to be learned! So long a road lies before us, and what care we if we must travel it alone!

Part Four

Many days passed before we could speak to the Golden One again. But then came the day when the sky turned white, as if the sun had burst and spread its flame in the air, and the fields lay still without breath, and the dust of the road was white in the glow. So the women of the field were weary, and they tarried over their work, and they were far from the road when we came. But the

Golden One stood alone at the hedge, waiting. We stopped and we saw that their eyes, so hard and scornful to the world, were looking at us as if they would obey any word we might speak.

And we said:

"We have given you a name in our thoughts, Liberty 5-3000."

"What is our name?" they asked.

"The Golden One."

"Nor do we call you Equality 7-2521 when we think of you."

"What name have you given us?" They looked straight into our eyes and they held their head high and they answered:

"The Unconquered."

For a long time we could not speak. Then we said:

"Such thoughts as these are forbidden, Golden One."

"But you think such thoughts as these and you wish us to think them."

We looked into their eyes and we could not lie.

"Yes," we whispered, and they smiled, and then we said: "Our dearest one, do not obey us."

They stepped back, and their eyes were wide and still.

"Speak these words again," they whispered.

"Which words?" we asked. But they did not answer, and we knew it.

"Our dearest one," we whispered.

Never have men said this to women.

The head of the Golden One bowed slowly, and they stood still before us, their arms at their sides, the palms of their hands turned to us, as if their body were delivered in submission to our eyes. And we could not speak.

Then they raised their head, and they spoke simply and gently, as if they wished us to forget some anxiety of their own.

"The day is hot," they said, "and you have worked for many hours and you must be weary."

"No," we answered.

"It is cooler in the fields," they said, "and there is water to drink. Are you thirsty?"

"Yes," we answered, "but we cannot cross the hedge."

"We shall bring the water to you," they said.

Then they knelt by the moat, they gathered water in their two hands, they rose and they held the water out to our lips.

We do not know if we drank that water. We only knew suddenly that their hands were empty, but we were still holding our lips to their hands, and that they knew it, but did not move.

We raised our head and stepped back. For we did not understand what had made us do this, and we were afraid to understand it.

And the Golden One stepped back, and stood looking upon their hands in wonder. Then the Golden One moved away, even though no others were coming, and they moved, stepping back, as if they could not turn from us, their arms bent before them, as if they could not lower their hands.

Part Five

We made it. We created it. We brought it forth from the night of the ages. We alone. Our hands. Our mind. Ours alone and only.

We know not what we are saying. Our head is reeling. We look upon the light which we have made. We shall be forgiven for anything we say tonight....

Tonight, after more days and trials than we can count, we finished building a strange thing, from the remains of the Unmentionable Times, a box of glass, devised to give forth the power of the sky of greater strength than we had ever achieved before. And when we put our wires to this box, when we closed the current-the wire glowed! It came to life, it turned red, and a circle of light lay on the stone before us.

We stood, and we held our head in our hands. We could not conceive of that which we had created. We had touched no flint, made no fire. Yet here was light, light that came from nowhere, light from the heart of metal.

We blew out the candle. Darkness swallowed us. There was nothing left around us, nothing save night and a thin thread of flame in it, as a crack in the wall of a prison. We stretched our hands to the wire, and we saw our fingers in the red glow. We could not see our body nor feel it, and in that moment nothing existed save our two hands over a wire glowing in a black abyss.

Then we thought of the meaning of that which lay before us. We can light our tunnel, and the City, and all the Cities of the world with nothing save metal and wires. We can give our brothers a new light, cleaner and brighter than any they have ever known. The power of the sky can be made to do men's bidding. There are no limits to its secrets and its might, and it can be made to grant us anything if we but choose to ask.

Then we knew what we must do. Our discovery is too great for us to waste our time in sweeping the streets. We must not keep our secret to ourselves, nor buried under the ground. We must bring it into the sight of all men. We need all our time, we need the work rooms of the Home of the Scholars, we want the help of our brother Scholars and their wisdom joined to ours. There is so much work ahead for all of us, for all the Scholars of the world.

In a month, the World Council of Scholars is to meet in our City. It is a great Council, to which the wisest of all lands are elected, and it meets once a year in the different Cities of the earth. We shall go to this Council and we shall lay before them, as our gift, this glass box with the power of the sky. We shall confess everything to them. They will see, understand and forgive. For our gift is greater than our transgression. They will explain it to the Council of Vocations, and we shall be assigned to the Home of the Scholars. This has never been done before, but neither has a gift such as ours ever been offered to men.

We must wait. We must guard our tunnel as we had never guarded it before. For should any men save the Scholars learn of our secret, they would not understand it, nor would they believe us. They would see nothing, save our crime of working alone, and they would destroy us and our light. We care not about our body, but our light is...

Yes, we do care. For the first time do we care about our body. For this wire is as a part of our body, as a vein torn from us, glowing with our blood. Are we proud of this thread of metal, or of our hands which made it, or is there a line to divide these two?

We stretch out our arms. For the first time do we know how strong our arms are. And a strange thought comes to us: we wonder, for the first time in our life, what we look like. Men never see their own faces and never ask their brothers about it, for it is evil to have concern for their own faces or bodies. But tonight, for a reason we cannot fathom, we wish it were possible to us to know the likeness of our own person.

Part Six

We have not written for thirty days. For thirty days we have not been here, in our tunnel. We had been caught. It happened on that night when we wrote last. We forgot, that night, to watch the sand in the glass which tells us when three hours have passed and it is time to return to the City Theatre. When we remembered it, the sand had run out.

We hastened to the Theatre. But the big tent stood grey and silent against the sky. The streets of the City lay before us, dark and empty. If we went back to hide in our tunnel, we would be found and our light found with us. So we walked to the Home of the Street Sweepers.

When the Council of the Home questioned us, we looked upon the faces of the Council, but there was no curiosity in those faces, and no anger, and no mercy. So when the oldest of them asked us: "Where have you been?" we thought of our glass box and of our light, and we forgot all else. And we answered:

"We will not tell you."

The oldest did not question us further. They turned to the two youngest, and said, and their voice was bored:

"Take our brother Equality 7-2521 to the Palace of Corrective Detention. Lash them until they tell."

So we were taken to the Stone Room under the Palace of Corrective Detention. This room has no windows and it is empty save for an iron post. Two men stood by the post, naked but for leather aprons and leather hoods over their faces. Those who had brought us departed, leaving us to the two Judges who stood in a corner of the room. The Judges were small, thin men, grey and bent. They gave the signal to the two strong hooded ones.

They tore the clothes from our body, they threw us down upon our knees and they tied our hands to the iron post. The first blow of the lash felt as if our spine had been cut in two. The second blow stopped the first, and for a second we felt nothing, then the pain struck us in our throat and fire ran in our lungs without air. But we did not cry out.

The lash whistled like a singing wind. We tried to count the blows, but we lost count. We knew that the blows were falling upon our back. Only we felt nothing upon our back any longer. A flaming grill kept dancing before our eyes, and we thought of nothing save that grill, a grill, a grill of red squares, and then we knew that we were looking at the squares of the iron grill in the door, and there were also the squares of stone on the walls, and the squares which the lash was cutting upon our back, crossing and re-crossing itself in our flesh.

Then we saw a fist before us. It knocked our chin up, and we saw the red froth of our mouth on the withered fingers, and the Judge asked:

"Where have you been?"

But we jerked our head away, hid our face upon our tied hands, and bit our lips.

The lash whistled again. We wondered who was sprinkling burning coal dust upon the floor, for we saw drops of red twinkling on the stones around us.

Then we knew nothing, save two voices snarling steadily, one after the other, even though we knew they were speaking many minutes apart:

"Where have you been where have you been where have you been where have you been?..."

And our lips moved, but the sound trickled back into our throat, and the sound was only:

"The light... The light... The light...."

Then we knew nothing.

We opened our eyes, lying on our stomach on the brick floor of a cell. We looked upon two hands lying far before us on the bricks, and we moved them, and we knew that they were our hands. But we could not move our body. Then we smiled, for we thought of the light and that we had not betrayed it.

We lay in our cell for many days. The door opened twice each day, once for the men who brought us bread and water, and once for the Judges. Many Judges came to our cell, first the humblest and then the most honored Judges of the City. They stood before us in their white togas, and they asked:

"Are you ready to speak?"

But we shook our head, lying before them on the floor. And they departed.

We counted each day and each night as it passed. Then, tonight, we knew that we must escape. For tomorrow the World Council of Scholars is to meet in our City.

It was easy to escape from the Palace of Corrective Detention. The locks are old on the doors and there are no guards about. There is no reason to have guards, for men have never defied the Councils so far as to escape from whatever place they were ordered to be. Our body is healthy and strength returns to it speedily. We lunged against the door and it gave way. We stole through the dark passages, and through the dark streets, and down into our tunnel.

We lit the candle and we saw that our place had not been found and nothing had been touched. And our glass box stood before us on the cold oven, as we had left it. What matter they now, the scars upon our back!

Tomorrow, in the full light of day, we shall take our box, and leave our tunnel open, and walk through the streets to the Home of the Scholars. We shall put before them the greatest gift ever offered to men. We shall tell them the truth. We shall hand to them, as our confession, these pages we have written. We shall join our hands to theirs, and we shall work together, with the power of the sky, for the glory of mankind. Our blessing upon you, our brothers! Tomorrow, you will take us back into your fold and we shall be an outcast no longer. Tomorrow we shall be one of you again. Tomorrow...

Part Seven

It is dark here in the forest. The leaves rustle over our head, black against the last gold of the sky. The moss is soft and warm. We shall sleep on this moss for many nights, till the beasts of the forest come to tear our body. We have no bed now, save the moss, and no future, save the beasts.

We are old now, yet we were young this morning, when we carried our glass box through the streets of the City to the Home of the Scholars. No men stopped us, for there were none about from the Palace of Corrective Detention, and the others knew nothing. No men stopped us at the gate. We walked through empty passages and into the great hall where the World Council of Scholars sat in solemn meeting.

We saw nothing as we entered, save the sky in the great windows, blue and glowing. Then we saw the Scholars who sat around a long table; they were as shapeless clouds huddled at the rise of the great sky. There were men whose famous names we knew, and others from distant lands whose names we had not heard. We saw a great painting on the wall over their heads, of the twenty illustrious men who had invented the candle.

All the heads of the Council turned to us as we entered. These great and wise of the earth did not know what to think of us, and they looked upon us with wonder and curiosity, as if we were a miracle. It is true that our tunic was torn and stained with brown stains which had been blood. We raised our right arm and we said:

"Our greeting to you, our honored brothers of the World Council of Scholars!"

Then Collective 0-0009, the oldest and wisest of the Council, spoke and asked:

"Who are you, our brother? For you do not look like a Scholar."

"Our name is Equality 7-2521," we answered, "and we are a Street Sweeper of this City."

Then it was as if a great wind had stricken the hall, for all the Scholars spoke at once, and they were angry and frightened.

"A Street Sweeper! A Street Sweeper walking in upon the World Council of Scholars! It is not to be believed! It is against all the rules and all the laws!"

But we knew how to stop them.

"Our brothers!" we said. "We matter not, nor our transgression. It is only our brother men who matter. Give no thought to us, for we are nothing, but listen to our words, for we bring you a gift such as had never been brought to men. Listen to us, for we hold the future of mankind in our hands."

Then they listened.

We placed our glass box upon the table before them. We spoke of it, and of our long quest, and of our tunnel, and of our escape from the Palace of Corrective Detention. Not a hand moved in that hall, as we spoke, nor an eye. Then we put the wires to the box, and they all bent forward and sat still, watching. And we stood still, our eyes upon the wire. And slowly, slowly as a flush of blood, a red flame trembled in the wire. Then the wire glowed.

But terror struck the men of the Council. They leapt to their feet, they ran from the table, and they stood pressed against the wall, huddled together, seeking the warmth of one another's bodies to give them courage.

We looked upon them and we laughed and said:

"Fear nothing, our brothers. There is a great power in these wires, but this power is tamed. It is yours. We give it to you."

Still they would not move.

"We give you the power of the sky!" we cried. "We give you the key to the earth! Take it, and let us be one of you, the humblest among you. Let us all work together, and harness this power, and make it ease the toil of men. Let us throw away our candles and our torches. Let us flood our cities with light. Let us bring a new light to men!"

But they looked upon us, and suddenly we were afraid. For their eyes were still, and small, and evil.

"Our brothers!" we cried. "Have you nothing to say to us?"

Then Collective 0-0009 moved forward. They moved to the table and the others followed.

"Yes," spoke Collective 0-0009, "we have much to say to you."

The sound of their voices brought silence to the hall and to beat of our heart.

"Yes," said Collective 0-0009, "we have much to say to a wretch who have broken all the laws and who boast of their infamy!

"How dared you think that your mind held greater wisdom than the minds of your brothers? And if the Councils had decreed that you should be a Street Sweeper, how dared you think that you could be of greater use to men than in sweeping the streets?"

"How dared you, gutter cleaner," spoke Fraternity 9-3452, "to hold yourself as one alone and with the thoughts of the one and not of the many?"

"You shall be burned at the stake," said Democracy 4-6998.

"No, they shall be lashed," said Unanimity 7-3304, "till there is nothing left under the lashes."

"No," said Collective 0-0009, "we cannot decide upon this, our brothers. No such crime has ever been committed, and it is not for us to judge. Nor for any small Council. We shall deliver this creature to the World Council itself and let their will be done."

We looked upon them and we pleaded:

"Our brothers! You are right. Let the will of the Council be done upon our body. We do not care. But the light? What will you do with the light?"

Collective 0-0009 looked upon us, and they smiled.

"So you think that you have found a new power," said Collective 0-0009. "Do all your brothers think that?"

"No," we answered.

"What is not thought by all men cannot be true," said Collective 0-0009.

"You have worked on this alone?" asked International 1-5537.

"Many men in the Homes of the Scholars have had strange new ideas in the past," said Solidarity 8-1164, "but when the majority of their brother Scholars voted against them, they abandoned their ideas, as all men must."

"This box is useless," said Alliance 6-7349.

"Should it be what they claim of it," said Harmony 9-2642, "then it would bring ruin to the Department of Candles. The Candle is a great boon to mankind, as approved by all men. Therefore it cannot be destroyed by the whim of one."

"This would wreck the Plans of the World Council," said Unanimity 2-9913, "and without the Plans of the World Council the sun cannot rise. It took fifty years to secure the approval of all the Councils for the Candle, and to decide upon the number needed, and to re-fit the Plans so as to make candles instead of torches. This touched upon thousands and thousands of men working in scores of States. We cannot alter the Plans again so soon."

"And if this should lighten the toil of men," said Similarity 5-0306, "then it is a great evil, for men have no cause to exist save in toiling for other men."

Then Collective 0-0009 rose and pointed at our box.

"This thing," they said, "must be destroyed."

And all the others cried as one:

"It must be destroyed!"

Then we leapt to the table.

We seized our box, we shoved them aside, and we ran to the window. We turned and we looked at them for the last time, and a rage, such as it is not fit for humans to know, choked our voice in our throat.

"You fools!" we cried. "You fools! You thrice-damned fools!"

We swung our fist through the windowpane, and we leapt out in a ringing rain of glass.

We fell, but we never let the box fall from our hands. Then we ran. We ran blindly, and men and houses streaked past us in a torrent without shape. And the road seemed not to be flat before us, but as if it were leaping up to meet us, and we waited for the earth to rise and strike us in the face. But we ran. We knew not where we were going. We knew only that we must run, run to the end of the world, to the end of our days.

Then we knew suddenly that we were lying on a soft earth and that we had stopped. Trees taller than we had ever seen before stood over us in great silence. Then we knew. We were in the Uncharted Forest. We had not thought of coming here, but our legs had carried our wisdom, and our legs had brought us to the Uncharted Forest against our will.

Our glass box lay beside us. We crawled to it, we fell upon it, our face in our arms, and we lay still.

We lay thus for a long time. Then we rose, we took our box and walked on into the forest.

It mattered not where we went. We knew that men would not follow us, for they never enter the Uncharted Forest. We had nothing to fear from them. The forest disposes of its own victims. This gave us no fear either. Only we wished to be away, away from the City and from the air that touches upon the air of the City. So we walked on, our box in our arms, our heart empty.

We are doomed. Whatever days are left to us, we shall spend them alone. And we have heard of the corruption to be found in solitude. We have torn ourselves from the truth which is our brother men, and there is no road back for us, and no redemption.

We know these things, but we do not care. We care for nothing on earth. We are tired.

Only the glass box in our arms is like a living heart that gives us strength. We have lied to ourselves. We have not built this box for the good of our brothers. We built it for its own sake. It is above all our brothers to us, and its truth above their truth. Why wonder about this? We have not many days to live. We are walking to the fangs awaiting us somewhere among the great, silent trees. There is not a thing behind us to regret.

Then a blow of pain struck us, our first and our only. We thought of the Golden One. We thought of the Golden One whom we shall never see again. Then the pain passed. It is best. We are one of the Damned. It is best if the Golden One forget our name and the body which bore that name.

Part Eight

It has been a day of wonder, this, our first day in the forest.

We awoke when a ray of sunlight fell across our face. We wanted to leap to our feet, as we have had to leap every morning of our life, but we remembered suddenly that no bell had rung and that there was no bell to ring anywhere. We lay on our back, we threw our arms out, and we looked up at the sky. The leaves had edges of silver that trembled and rippled like a river of green and fire flowing high above us.

We did not wish to move. We thought suddenly that we could lie thus as long as we wished, and we laughed aloud at the thought. We could also rise, or run, or leap, or fall down again. We were thinking that these were thoughts without sense, but before we knew it our body had risen in one leap. Our arms stretched out of their own will, and our body whirled and whirled, till it raised a wind to rustle through the leaves of the bushes. Then our hands seized a branch and swung us high into a tree, with no aim save the wonder of learning the strength of our body. The branch snapped under us and we fell upon the moss that was soft as a cushion. Then our body, losing all sense, rolled over and over on the moss, dry leaves in our tunic, in our hair, in our face. And we heard suddenly that we were laughing, laughing aloud, laughing as if there were no power left in us save laughter.

Then we took our glass box, and we went on into the forest. We went on, cutting through the branches, and it was as if we were swimming through a sea of leaves, with the bushes as waves rising and falling and rising around us, and flinging their green sprays high to the treetops. The trees parted before us, calling us forward. The forest seemed to welcome us. We went on, without thought, without care, with nothing to feel save the song of our body.

We stopped when we felt hunger. We saw birds in the tree branches, and flying from under our footsteps. We picked a stone and we sent it as an arrow at a bird. It fell before us. We made a fire, we cooked the bird, and we ate it, and no meal had ever tasted better to us. And we thought suddenly that there was a great satisfaction to be found in the food which we need and obtain by our own hand. And we wished to be hungry again and soon, that we might know again this strange new pride in eating.

Then we walked on. And we came to a stream which lay as a streak of glass among the trees. It lay so still that we saw no water but only a cut in the earth, in which the trees grew down, upturned, and the sky lay at the bottom. We knelt by the stream and we bent down to drink. And then we stopped. For, upon the blue of the sky below us, we saw our own face for the first time.

We sat still and we held our breath. For our face and our body were beautiful. Our face was not like the faces of our brothers, for we felt not pity when looking upon it. Our body was not like the bodies of our brothers, for our limbs were straight and thin and hard and strong. And we thought that we could trust this being who looked upon us from the stream, and that we had nothing to fear with this being.

We walked on till the sun had set. When the shadows gathered among the trees, we stopped in a hollow between the roots, where we shall sleep tonight. And suddenly, for the first time this day, we remembered that we are the Damned. We remembered it, and we laughed.

We are writing this on the paper we had hidden in our tunic together with the written pages we had brought for the World Council of Scholars, but never given to them. We have much to speak of to ourselves, and we hope we shall find the words for it in the days to come. Now, we cannot speak, for we cannot understand.

Part Nine

We have not written for many days. We did not wish to speak. For we needed no words to remember that which has happened to us.

It was on our second day in the forest that we heard steps behind us. We hid in the bushes, and we waited. The steps came closer. And then we saw the fold of a white tunic among the trees, and a gleam of gold.

We leapt forward, we ran to them, and we stood looking upon the Golden One.

They saw us, and their hands closed into fists, and the fists pulled their arms down, as if they wished their arms to hold them, while their body swayed. And they could not speak.

We dared not come too close to them. We asked, and our voice trembled:

"How did you come to be here, Golden One?"

But they whispered only:

"We have found you...."

"How did you come to be in the forest?" we asked.

They raised their head, and there was a great pride in their voice; they answered:

"We have followed you."

Then we could not speak, and they said:

"We heard that you had gone to the Uncharted Forest, for the whole City is speaking of it. So on the night of the day when we heard it, we ran away from the Home of the Peasants. We found the marks of your feet across the plain where no men walk. So we followed them, and we went into the forest, and we followed the path where the branches were broken by your body."

Their white tunic was torn, and the branches had cut the skin of their arms, but they spoke as if they had never taken notice of it, nor of weariness, nor of fear.

"We have followed you," they said, "and we shall follow you wherever you go. If danger threatens you, we shall face it also. If it be death, we shall die with you. You are damned, and we wish to share your damnation."

They looked upon us, and their voice was low, but there was bitterness and triumph in their voice.

"Your eyes are as a flame, but our brothers have neither hope nor fire. Your mouth is cut of granite, but our brothers are soft and humble. Your head is high, but our brothers cringe. You walk, but our brothers crawl. We wish to be damned with you, rather than blessed with all our brothers. Do as you please with us, but do not send us away from you."

Then they knelt, and bowed their golden head before us.

We had never thought of that which we did. We bent to raise the Golden One to their feet, but when we touched them, it was as if madness had stricken us. We seized their body and we pressed our lips to theirs. The Golden One breathed once, and their breath was a moan, and then their arms closed around us.

We stood together for a long time. And we were frightened that we had lived for twenty-one years and had never known what joy is possible to men.

Then we said:

"Our dearest one. Fear nothing of the forest. There is no danger in solitude. We have no need of our brothers. Let us forget their good and our evil, let us forget all things save that we are together and that there is joy as a bond between us. Give us your hand. Look ahead. It is our own world, Golden One, a strange, unknown world, but our own."

Then we walked on into the forest, their hand in ours.

And that night we knew that to hold the body of women in our arms is neither ugly nor shameful, but the one ecstasy granted to the race of men.

We have walked for many days. The forest has no end, and we seek no end. But each day added to the chain of days between us and the City is like an added blessing.

We have made a bow and many arrows. We can kill more birds than we need for our food; we find water and fruit in the forest. At night, we choose a clearing, and we build a ring of fires around it. We sleep in the midst of that ring, and the beasts dare not attack us. We can see their eyes, green and yellow as coals, watching us from the tree branches beyond. The fires smoulder as a crown of jewels around us, and smoke stands still in the air, in columns made blue by the moonlight. We sleep together in the midst of the ring, the arms of the Golden One around us, their head upon our breast.

Some day, we shall stop and build a house, when we shall have gone far enough. But we do not have to hasten. The days before us are without end, like the forest.

We cannot understand this new life which we have found, yet it seems so clear and so simple. When questions come to puzzle us, we walk faster, then turn and forget all things as we watch the Golden One following. The shadows of leaves fall upon their arms, as they spread the branches apart, but their shoulders are in the sun. The skin of their arms is like a blue mist, but their shoulders are white and glowing, as if the light fell not from above, but rose from under their skin. We watch the leaf which has fallen upon their shoulder, and it lies at the curve of their neck, and a drop of dew glistens upon it like a jewel. They approach us, and they stop, laughing, knowing what we think, and they wait obediently, without questions, till it pleases us to turn and go on.

We go on and we bless the earth under our feet. But questions come to us again, as we walk in silence. If that which we have found is the corruption of solitude, then what can men wish for save corruption? If this is the great evil of being alone, then what is good and what is evil?

Everything which comes from the many is good. Everything which comes from one is evil. This have we been taught with our first breath. We have broken the law, but we have never doubted it. Yet now, as we walk through the forest, we are learning to doubt.

There is no life for men, save in useful toil for the good of all their brothers. But we lived not, when we toiled for our brothers, we were only weary. There is no joy for men, save the joy shared with all their brothers. But the only things which taught us joy were the power we created in our wires, and the Golden One. And both these joys belong to us alone, they come from us alone, they bear no relation to all our brothers, and they do not concern our brothers in any way. Thus do we wonder.

There is some error, one frightful error, in the thinking of men. What is that error? We do not know, but the knowledge struggles within us, struggles to be born. Today, the Golden One stopped suddenly and said:

"We love you."

But they frowned and shook their head and looked at us helplessly.

"No," they whispered, "that is not what we wished to say."

They were silent, then they spoke slowly, and their words were halting, like the words of a child learning to speak for the first time:

"We are one... alone... and only... and we love you who are one... alone... and only."

We looked into each other's eyes and we knew that the breath of a miracle had touched us, and fled, and left us groping vainly.

And we felt torn, torn for some word we could not find.

Part Ten

We are sitting at a table and we are writing this upon paper made thousands of years ago. The light is dim, and we cannot see the Golden One, only one lock of gold on the pillow of an ancient bed. This is our home.

We came upon it today, at sunrise. For many days we had been crossing a chain of mountains. The forest rose among cliffs, and whenever we walked out upon a barren stretch of rock we saw great peaks before us in the west, and to the north of us, and to the south, as far as our eyes could see. The peaks were red and brown, with the green streaks of forests as veins upon them, with blue mists as veils over their heads. We had never heard of these mountains, nor seen them marked on any map. The Uncharted Forest has protected them from the Cities and from the men of the Cities.

We climbed paths where the wild goat dared not follow. Stones rolled from under our feet, and we heard them striking the rocks below, farther and farther down, and the mountains rang with each stroke, and long after the strokes had died. But we went on, for we knew that no men would ever follow our track nor reach us here.

Then today, at sunrise, we saw a white flame among the trees, high on a sheer peak before us. We thought that it was a fire and stopped. But the flame was unmoving, yet blinding as liquid metal. So we climbed toward it through the rocks. And there, before us, on a broad summit, with the mountains rising behind it, stood a house such as we had never seen, and the white fire came from the sun on the glass of its windows.

The house had two stories and a strange roof flat as a floor. There was more window than wall upon its walls, and the windows went on straight around the corners, though how this kept the house standing we could not guess. The walls were hard and smooth, of that stone unlike stone which we had seen in our tunnel.

We both knew it without words: this house was left from the Unmentionable Times. The trees had protected it from time and weather, and from men who have less pity than time and weather. We turned to the Golden One and we asked:

"Are you afraid?"

But they shook their head. So we walked to the door, and we threw it open, and we stepped together into the house of the Unmentionable Times.

We shall need the days and the years ahead, to look, to learn, and to understand the things of this house. Today, we could only look and try to believe the sight of our eyes. We pulled the heavy curtains from the windows and we saw that the rooms were small, and we thought that not more than twelve men could have lived here. We thought it strange that men had been permitted to build a house for only twelve.

Never had we seen rooms so full of light. The sunrays danced upon colors, colors, more colors than we thought possible, we who had seen no houses save the white ones, the brown ones and the grey. There were great pieces of glass on the walls, but it was not glass, for when we looked upon it we saw our own bodies and all the things behind us, as on the face of a lake. There were strange things which we had never seen and the use of which we do not know. And there were globes of glass everywhere, in each room, the globes with the metal cobwebs inside, such as we had seen in our tunnel.

We found the sleeping hall and we stood in awe upon its threshold. For it was a small room and there were only two beds in it. We found no other beds in the house, and then we knew that only two had lived here, and this passes understanding. What kind of world did they have, the men of the Unmentionable Times?

We found garments, and the Golden One gasped at the sight of them. For they were not white tunics, nor white togas; they were of all colors, no two of them alike. Some crumbled to dust as we touched them. But others were of heavier cloth, and they felt soft and new in our fingers.

We found a room with walls made of shelves, which held rows of manuscripts, from the floor to the ceiling. Never had we seen such a number of them, nor of such strange shape. They were not soft and rolled, they had hard shells of cloth and leather; and the letters on their pages were so small and so even that we wondered at the men who had such handwriting. We glanced through the pages, and we saw that they were written in our language, but we found many words which we could not understand. Tomorrow, we shall begin to read these scripts.

When we had seen all the rooms of the house, we looked at the Golden One and we both knew the thought in our minds.

"We shall never leave this house," we said, "nor let it be taken from us. This is our home and the end of our journey. This is your house, Golden One, and ours, and it belongs to no other men whatever as far as the earth may stretch. We shall not share it with others, as we share not our joy with them, nor our love, nor our hunger. So be it to the end of our days."

"Your will be done," they said.

Then we went out to gather wood for the great hearth of our home. We brought water from the stream which runs among the trees under our windows. We killed a mountain goat, and we brought its flesh to be cooked in a strange copper pot we found in a place of wonders, which must have been the cooking room of the house.

We did this work alone, for no words of ours could take the Golden One away from the big glass which is not glass. They stood before it and they looked and looked upon their own body.

When the sun sank beyond the mountains, the Golden One fell asleep on the floor, amidst jewels, and bottles of crystal, and flowers of silk. We lifted the Golden One in our arms and we carried them to a bed, their head falling softly upon our shoulder. Then we lit a candle, and we brought paper from the room of the manuscripts, and we sat by the window, for we knew that we could not sleep tonight.

And now we look upon the earth and sky. This spread of naked rock and peaks and moonlight is like a world ready to be born, a world that waits. It seems to us it asks a sign from us, a spark, a first commandment. We cannot know what word we are to give, nor what great deed this earth expects to witness. We know it waits. It seems to say it has great gifts to lay before us, but it wishes a greater gift for us. We are to speak. We are to give its goal, its highest meaning to all this glowing space of rock and sky.

We look ahead, we beg our heart for guidance in answering this call no voice has spoken, yet we have heard. We look upon our hands. We see the dust of centuries, the dust which hid the great secrets and perhaps great evils. And yet it stirs no fear within our heart, but only silent reverence and pity.

May knowledge come to us! What is the secret our heart has understood and yet will not reveal to us, although it seems to beat as if it were endeavoring to tell it?

Part Eleven

I am. I think. I will.

My hands... My spirit... My sky... My forest... This earth of mine.... What must I say besides? These are the words. This is the answer.

I stand here on the summit of the mountain. I lift my head and I spread my arms. This, my body and spirit, this is the end of the quest. I wished to know the meaning of things. I am the meaning. I wished to find a warrant for being. I need no warrant for being, and no word of sanction upon my being. I am the warrant and the sanction.

It is my eyes which see, and the sight of my eyes grants beauty to the earth. It is my ears which hear, and the hearing of my ears gives its song to the world. It is my mind which thinks, and the judgement of my mind is the only searchlight that can find the truth. It is my will which chooses, and the choice of my will is the only edict I must respect.

Many words have been granted me, and some are wise, and some are false, but only three are holy: "I will it!"

Whatever road I take, the guiding star is within me; the guiding star and the loadstone which point the way. They point in but one direction. They point to me.

I know not if this earth on which I stand is the core of the universe or if it is but a speck of dust lost in eternity. I know not and I care not. For I know what happiness is possible to me on earth. And my happiness needs no higher aim to vindicate it. My happiness is not the means to any end. It is the end. It is its own goal. It is its own purpose.

Neither am I the means to any end others may wish to accomplish. I am not a tool for their use. I am not a servant of their needs. I am not a bandage for their wounds. I am not a sacrifice on their altars.

I am a man. This miracle of me is mine to own and keep, and mine to guard, and mine to use, and mine to kneel before!

I do not surrender my treasures, nor do I share them. The fortune of my spirit is not to be blown into coins of brass and flung to the winds as alms for the poor of the spirit. I guard my treasures: my thought, my will, my freedom. And the greatest of these is freedom.

I owe nothing to my brothers, nor do I gather debts from them. I ask none to live for me, nor do I live for any others. I covet no man's soul, nor is my soul theirs to covet.

I am neither foe nor friend to my brothers, but such as each of them shall deserve of me. And to earn my love, my brothers must do more than to have been born. I do not grant my love without reason, nor to any chance passer-by who may wish to claim it. I honor men with my love. But honor is a thing to be earned.

I shall choose friends among men, but neither slaves nor masters. And I shall choose only such as please me, and them I shall love and respect, but neither command nor obey. And we shall join our hands when we wish, or walk alone when we so desire. For in the temple of his spirit, each man is alone. Let each man keep his temple untouched and undefiled. Then let him join hands with others if he wishes, but only beyond his holy threshold.

For the word "We" must never be spoken, save by one's choice and as a second thought. This word must never be placed first within man's soul, else it becomes a monster, the root of all the evils on earth, the root of man's torture by men, and of an unspeakable lie.

The word "We" is as lime poured over men, which sets and hardens to stone, and crushes all beneath it, and that which is white and that which is black are lost equally in the grey of it. It is the word by which the depraved steal the virtue of the good, by which the weak steal the might of the strong, by which the fools steal the wisdom of the sages.

What is my joy if all hands, even the unclean, can reach into it? What is my wisdom, if even the fools can dictate to me? What is my freedom, if all creatures, even the botched and the impotent, are my masters? What is my life, if I am but to bow, to agree and to obey?

But I am done with this creed of corruption.

I am done with the monster of "We," the word of serfdom, of plunder, of misery, falsehood and shame.

And now I see the face of god, and I raise this god over the earth, this god whom men have sought since men came into being, this god who will grant them joy and peace and pride.

This god, this one word:

Part Twelve

It was when I read the first of the books I found in my house that I saw the word "I." And when I understood this word, the book fell from my hands, and I wept, I who had never known tears. I wept in deliverance and in pity for all mankind.

I understood the blessed thing which I had called my curse. I understood why the best in me had been my sins and my transgressions; and why I had never felt guilt in my sins. I understood that centuries of chains and lashes will not kill the spirit of man nor the sense of truth within him.

I read many books for many days. Then I called the Golden One, and I told her what I had read and what I had learned. She looked at me and the first words she spoke were:

"I love you."

Then I said:

"My dearest one, it is not proper for men to be without names. There was a time when each man had a name of his own to distinguish him from all other men. So let us choose our names. I have read of a man who lived many thousands of years ago, and of all the names in these books, his is the one I wish to bear. He took the light of the gods and he brought it to men, and he taught men to be gods. And he suffered for his deed as all bearers of light must suffer. His name was Prometheus."

"It shall be your name," said the Golden One.

"And I have read of a goddess," I said, "who was the mother of the earth and of all the gods. Her name was Gaea. Let this be your name, my Golden One, for you are to be the mother of a new kind of gods."

"It shall be my name," said the Golden One.

Now I look ahead. My future is clear before me. The Saint of the pyre had seen the future when he chose me as his heir, as the heir of all the saints and all the martyrs who came before him and who died for the same cause, for the same word, no matter what name they gave to their cause and their truth.

I shall live here, in my own house. I shall take my food from the earth by the toil of my own hands. I shall learn many secrets from my books. Through the years ahead, I shall rebuild the achievements of the past, and open the way to carry them further, the achievements which are open to me, but closed forever to my brothers, for their minds are shackled to the weakest and dullest ones among them.

I have learned that my power of the sky was known to men long ago; they called it Electricity. It was the power that moved their greatest inventions. It lit this house with light which came from those globes of glass on the walls. I have found the engine which produced this light. I shall learn how to repair it and how to make it work again. I shall learn how to use the wires which carry this power. Then I shall build a barrier of wires around my home, and across the paths which lead to my home; a barrier light as a cobweb, more impassable than a wall of granite; a barrier my brothers will never be able to cross. For they have nothing to fight me with, save the brute force of their numbers. I have my mind.

Then here, on this mountaintop, with the world below me and nothing above me but the sun, I shall live my own truth. Gaea is pregnant with my child. Our son will be raised as a man. He will be taught to say "I" and to bear the pride of it. He will be taught to walk straight and on his own feet. He will be taught reverence for his own spirit.

When I shall have read all the books and learned my new way, when my home will be ready and my earth tilled, I shall steal one day, for the last time, into the cursed City of my birth. I shall call to me my friend who has no name save International 4-8818, and all those like him, Fraternity 2-5503, who cries without reason, and Solidarity 9-6347 who calls for help in the night, and a few others. I shall call to me all the men and the women whose spirit has not been killed within them and who suffer under the yoke of their brothers. They will follow me and I shall lead them to my fortress. And here, in this uncharted wilderness, I and they, my chosen friends, my fellow-builders, shall write the first chapter in the new history of man.

These are the things before me. And as I stand here at the door of glory, I look behind me for the last time. I look upon the history of men, which I have learned from the books, and I wonder. It was a long story, and the spirit which moved it was the spirit of man's freedom. But what is freedom? Freedom from what? There is nothing to take a man's freedom away from him, save other men. To be free, a man must be free of his brothers. That is freedom. That and nothing else.

At first, man was enslaved by the gods. But he broke their chains. Then he was enslaved by the kings. But he broke their chains. He was enslaved by his birth, by his kin, by his race. But he broke their chains. He declared to all his brothers that a man has rights which neither god nor king nor other men can take away from him, no matter what their number, for his is the right of man, and there is no right on earth above this right. And he stood on the threshold of the freedom for which the blood of the centuries behind him had been spilled.

But then he gave up all he had won, and fell lower than his savage beginning.

What brought it to pass? What disaster took their reason away from men? What whip lashed them to their knees in shame and submission? The worship of the word "We."

When men accepted that worship, the structure of centuries collapsed about them, the structure whose every beam had come from the thought of some one man, each in his day down the ages, from the depth of some one spirit, such spirit as existed but for its own sake. Those men who survived those eager to obey, eager to live for one another, since they had nothing else to vindicate them-those men could neither carry on, nor preserve what they had received. Thus did all thought, all science, all wisdom perish on earth. Thus did men-men with nothing to offer save their great number-lost the steel towers, the flying ships, the power wires, all the things they had not created and could never keep. Perhaps, later, some men had been born with the mind and the courage to recover these things which were lost; perhaps these men came before the Councils of Scholars. They were answered as I have been answered-and for the same reasons.

But I still wonder how it was possible, in those graceless years of transition, long ago, that men did not see whither they were going, and went on, in blindness and cowardice, to their fate. I wonder, for it is hard for me to conceive how men who knew the word "I" could give it up and not know what they lost. But such has been the story, for I have lived in the City of the damned, and I know what horror men permitted to be brought upon them.

Perhaps, in those days, there were a few among men, a few of clear sight and clean soul, who refused to surrender that word. What agony must have been theirs before that which they saw coming and could not stop! Perhaps they cried out in protest and in warning. But men paid no heed to their warning. And they, these few, fought a hopeless battle, and they perished with their banners smeared by their own blood. And they chose to perish, for they knew. To them, I send my salute across the centuries, and my pity.

Theirs is the banner in my hand. And I wish I had the power to tell them that the despair of their hearts was not to be final, and their night was not without hope. For the battle they lost can never be lost. For that which they died to save can never perish. Through all the darkness, through all the shame of which men are capable, the spirit of man will remain alive on this earth. It may sleep, but it will awaken. It may wear chains, but it will break through. And man will go on. Man, not men.

Here on this mountain, I and my sons and my chosen friends shall build our new land and our fort. And it will become as the heart of the earth, lost and hidden at first, but beating, beating louder each day. And word of it will reach every corner of the earth. And the roads of the world will become as veins which will carry the best of the world's blood to my threshold. And all my brothers, and the Councils of my brothers, will hear of it, but they will be impotent against me. And the day will come when I shall break all the chains of the earth, and raze the cities of the enslaved, and my home will become the capital of a world where each man will be free to exist for his own sake.

For the coming of that day shall I fight, I and my sons and my chosen friends. For the freedom of Man. For his rights. For his life. For his honor.

And here, over the portals of my fort, I shall cut in the stone the word which is to be my beacon and my banner. The word which will not die, should we all perish in battle. The word which can never die on this earth, for it is the heart of it and the meaning and the glory.

The sacred word:

EGO

Mark Twain

A Connecticut Yankee in King Arthur's Court

A Word of Explanation

It was in Warwick Castle that I came across the curious stranger whom I am going to talk about. He attracted me by three things: his candid simplicity, his marvelous familiarity with ancient armor, and the restfulness of his company — for he did all the talking. We fell together, as modest people will, in the tail of the herd that was being shown through, and he at once began to say things which interested me. As he talked along, softly, pleasantly, flowingly, he seemed to drift away imperceptibly out of this world and time, and into some remote era and old forgotten country; and so he gradually wove such a spell about me that I seemed to move among the specters and shadows and dust and mold of a gray antiquity, holding speech with a relic of it! Exactly as I would speak of my nearest personal friends or enemies, or my most familiar neighbors, he spoke of Sir Bedivere, Sir Bors de Ganis, Sir Launcelot of the Lake, Sir Galahad, and all the other great names of the Table Round — and how old, old, unspeakably old and faded and dry and musty and ancient he came to look as he went on! Presently he turned to me and said, just as one might speak of the weather, or any other common matter —

"You know about transmigration of souls; do you know about transposition of epochs — and bodies?"

I said I had not heard of it. He was so little interested — just as when people speak of the weather — that he did not notice whether I made him any answer or not. There was half a moment of silence, immediately interrupted by the droning voice of the salaried cicerone:

"Ancient hauberk, date of the sixth century, time of King Arthur and the Round Table; said to have belonged to the knight Sir Sagramor le Desirous; observe the round hole through the chain-mail in the left breast; can't be accounted for; supposed to have been done with a bullet since invention of firearms — perhaps maliciously by Cromwell's soldiers."

My acquaintance smiled — not a modern smile, but one that must have gone out of general use many, many centuries ago — and muttered apparently to himself:

"Wit ye well, *I saw it done* ." Then, after a pause, added: "I did it myself."

By the time I had recovered from the electric surprise of this remark, he was gone.

All that evening I sat by my fire at the Warwick Arms, steeped in a dream of the olden time, while the rain beat upon the windows, and the wind roared about the eaves and corners. From time to time I dipped into old Sir Thomas Malory's enchanting book, and fed at its rich feast of prodigies and adventures, breathed in the fragrance of its obsolete names, and dreamed again. Midnight being come at length, I read another tale, for a nightcap — this which here follows, to wit:

HOW SIR LAUNCELOT SLEW TWO GIANTS, AND MADE A CASTLE FREE

Anon withal came there upon him two great giants,
well armed, all save the heads, with two horrible
clubs in their hands. Sir Launcelot put his shield
afore him, and put the stroke away of the one
giant, and with his sword he clave his head asunder.
When his fellow saw that, he ran away as he were

wood [*demented], for fear of the horrible strokes,
and Sir Launcelot after him with all his might,
and smote him on the shoulder, and clave him to
the middle. Then Sir Launcelot went into the hall,
and there came afore him three score ladies and
damsels, and all kneeled unto him, and thanked
God and him of their deliverance. For, sir, said
they, the most part of us have been here this
seven year their prisoners, and we have worked all
manner of silk works for our meat, and we are all
great gentlewomen born, and blessed be the time,
knight, that ever thou wert born; for thou hast
done the most worship that ever did knight in the
world, that will we bear record, and we all pray
you to tell us your name, that we may tell our
friends who delivered us out of prison. Fair
damsels, he said, my name is Sir Launcelot du
Lake. And so he departed from them and betaught
them unto God. And then he mounted upon his
horse, and rode into many strange and wild
countries, and through many waters and valleys,
and evil was he lodged. And at the last by
fortune him happened against a night to come to
a fair courtilage, and therein he found an old
gentlewoman that lodged him with a goodwill,
and there he had good cheer for him and his horse.
And when time was, his host brought him into a
fair garret over the gate to his bed. There
Sir Launcelot unarmed him, and set his harness
by him, and went to bed, and anon he fell on
sleep. So, soon after there came one on
horseback, and knocked at the gate in great
haste. And when Sir Launcelot heard this he rose
up, and looked out at the window, and saw by the
moonlight three knights come riding after that
one man, and all three lashed on him at once
with swords, and that one knight turned on them
knightly again and defended him. Truly, said
Sir Launcelot, yonder one knight shall I help,
for it were shame for me to see three knights
on one, and if he be slain I am partner of his
death. And therewith he took his harness and
went out at a window by a sheet down to the four
knights, and then Sir Launcelot said on high,
Turn you knights unto me, and leave your
fighting with that knight. And then they all
three left Sir Kay, and turned unto Sir Launcelot,
and there began great battle, for they alight
all three, and strake many strokes at Sir
Launcelot, and assailed him on every side. Then
Sir Kay dressed him for to have holpen Sir
Launcelot. Nay, sir, said he, I will none of

your help, therefore as ye will have my help
let me alone with them. Sir Kay for the pleasure
of the knight suffered him for to do his will,
and so stood aside. And then anon within six
strokes Sir Launcelot had stricken them to the earth.

And then they all three cried, Sir Knight, we
yield us unto you as man of might matchless. As
to that, said Sir Launcelot, I will not take
your yielding unto me, but so that ye yield
you unto Sir Kay the seneschal, on that covenant
I will save your lives and else not. Fair knight,
said they, that were we loath to do; for as for
Sir Kay we chased him hither, and had overcome
him had ye not been; therefore, to yield us unto
him it were no reason. Well, as to that, said
Sir Launcelot, advise you well, for ye may
choose whether ye will die or live, for an ye be
yielden, it shall be unto Sir Kay. Fair knight,
then they said, in saving our lives we will do
as thou commandest us. Then shall ye, said Sir
Launcelot, on Whitsunday next coming go unto the
court of King Arthur, and there shall ye yield
you unto Queen Guenever, and put you all three
in her grace and mercy, and say that Sir Kay
sent you thither to be her prisoners. On the morn
Sir Launcelot arose early, and left Sir Kay
sleeping; and Sir Launcelot took Sir Kay's armor
and his shield and armed him, and so he went to
the stable and took his horse, and took his leave
of his host, and so he departed. Then soon after
arose Sir Kay and missed Sir Launcelot; and
then he espied that he had his armor and his
horse. Now by my faith I know well that he will
grieve some of the court of King Arthur; for on
him knights will be bold, and deem that it is I,
and that will beguile them; and because of his
armor and shield I am sure I shall ride in peace.
And then soon after departed Sir Kay, and
thanked his host.

As I laid the book down there was a knock at the door, and my stranger came in. I gave him a
pipe and a chair, and made him welcome. I also comforted him with a hot Scotch whisky; gave
him another one; then still another — hoping always for his story. After a fourth persuader,
he drifted into it himself, in a quite simple and natural way:

THE STRANGER'S HISTORY

I am an American. I was born and reared in Hartford, in the State of Connecticut — anyway, just over the river, in the country. So I am a Yankee of the Yankees — and practical; yes, and nearly barren of sentiment, I suppose — or poetry, in other words. My father was a blacksmith, my uncle was a horse doctor, and I was both, along at first. Then I went over to the great arms factory and learned my real trade; learned all there was to it; learned to make everything: guns, revolvers, cannon, boilers, engines, all sorts of labor-saving machinery. Why, I could make anything a body wanted — anything in the world, it didn't make any difference what; and if there wasn't any quick new-fangled way to make a thing, I could invent one — and do it as easy as rolling off a log. I became head superintendent; had a couple of thousand men under me.

Well, a man like that is a man that is full of fight — that goes without saying. With a couple of thousand rough men under one, one has plenty of that sort of amusement. I had, anyway. At last I met my match, and I got my dose. It was during a misunderstanding conducted with crowbars with a fellow we used to call Hercules. He laid me out with a crusher alongside the head that made everything crack, and seemed to spring every joint in my skull and made it overlap its neighbor. Then the world went out in darkness, and I didn't feel anything more, and didn't know anything at all — at least for a while.

When I came to again, I was sitting under an oak tree, on the grass, with a whole beautiful and broad country landscape all to myself — nearly. Not entirely; for there was a fellow on a horse, looking down at me — a fellow fresh out of a picture-book. He was in old-time iron armor from head to heel, with a helmet on his head the shape of a nail-keg with slits in it; and he had a shield, and a sword, and a prodigious spear; and his horse had armor on, too, and a steel horn projecting from his forehead, and gorgeous red and green silk trappings that hung down all around him like a bedquilt, nearly to the ground.

"Fair sir, will ye just?" said this fellow.

"Will I which?"

"Will ye try a passage of arms for land or lady or for —"

"What are you giving me?" I said. "Get along back to your circus, or I'll report you."

Now what does this man do but fall back a couple of hundred yards and then come rushing at me as hard as he could tear, with his nail-keg bent down nearly to his horse's neck and his long spear pointed straight ahead. I saw he meant business, so I was up the tree when he arrived.

He allowed that I was his property, the captive of his spear. There was argument on his side — and the bulk of the advantage — so I judged it best to humor him. We fixed up an agreement whereby I was to go with him and he was not to hurt me. I came down, and we started away, I walking by the side of his horse. We marched comfortably along, through glades and over brooks which I could not remember to have seen before — which puzzled me and made me wonder — and yet we did not come to any circus or sign of a circus. So I gave up the idea of a circus, and concluded he was from an asylum. But we never came to an asylum — so I was up a stump, as you may say. I asked him how far we were from Hartford. He said he had never heard of the place; which I took to be a lie, but allowed it to go at that. At the end of an hour we saw a faraway town sleeping in a valley by a winding river; and beyond it on a hill, a vast gray fortress, with towers and turrets, the first I had ever seen out of a picture.

"Bridgeport?" said I, pointing.

"Camelot," said he.

My stranger had been showing signs of sleepiness. He caught himself nodding, now, and smiled one of those pathetic, obsolete smiles of his, and said:

"I find I can't go on; but come with me, I've got it all written out, and you can read it if you like."

In his chamber, he said: "First, I kept a journal; then by and by, after years, I took the journal and turned it into a book. How long ago that was!"

He handed me his manuscript, and pointed out the place where I should begin:

"Begin here — I've already told you what goes before." He was steeped in drowsiness by this time. As I went out at his door I heard him murmur sleepily: "Give you good den, fair sir."

I sat down by my fire and examined my treasure. The first part of it — the great bulk of it — was parchment, and yellow with age. I scanned a leaf particularly and saw that it was a palimpsest. Under the old dim writing of the Yankee historian appeared traces of a penmanship which was older and dimmer still — Latin words and sentences: fragments from old monkish legends, evidently. I turned to the place indicated by my stranger and began to read — as follows.

Chapter I. Camelot

"Camelot — Camelot," said I to myself. "I don't seem to remember hearing of it before. Name of the asylum, likely."

It was a soft, reposeful summer landscape, as lovely as a dream, and as lonesome as Sunday. The air was full of the smell of flowers, and the buzzing of insects, and the twittering of birds, and there were no people, no wagons, there was no stir of life, nothing going on. The road was mainly a winding path with hoof-prints in it, and now and then a faint trace of wheels on either side in the grass — wheels that apparently had a tire as broad as one's hand.

Presently a fair slip of a girl, about ten years old, with a cataract of golden hair streaming down over her shoulders, came along. Around her head she wore a hoop of flame-red poppies. It was as sweet an outfit as ever I saw, what there was of it. She walked indolently along, with a mind at rest, its peace reflected in her innocent face. The circus man paid no attention to her; didn't even seem to see her. And she — she was no more startled at his fantastic make-up than if she was used to his like every day of her life. She was going by as indifferently as she might have gone by a couple of cows; but when she happened to notice me, *then* there was a change! Up went her hands, and she was turned to stone; her mouth dropped open, her eyes stared wide and timorously, she was the picture of astonished curiosity touched with fear. And there she stood gazing, in a sort of stupefied fascination, till we turned a corner of the wood and were lost to her view. That she should be startled at me instead of at the other man, was too many for me; I couldn't make head or tail of it. And that she should seem to consider me a spectacle, and totally overlook her own merits in that respect, was another puzzling thing, and a display of magnanimity, too, that was surprising in one so young. There was food for thought here. I moved along as one in a dream.

As we approached the town, signs of life began to appear. At intervals we passed a wretched cabin, with a thatched roof, and about it small fields and garden patches in an indifferent state of cultivation. There were people, too; brawny men, with long, coarse, uncombed hair that hung down over their faces and made them look like animals. They and the women, as a rule, wore a coarse tow-linen robe that came well below the knee, and a rude sort of sandal, and many wore an iron collar. The small boys and girls were always naked; but nobody seemed to know it. All of these people stared at me, talked about me, ran into the huts and fetched out their families to gape at me; but nobody ever noticed that other fellow, except to make him humble salutation and get no response for their pains.

In the town were some substantial windowless houses of stone scattered among a wilderness of thatched cabins; the streets were mere crooked alleys, and unpaved; troops of dogs and nude children played in the sun and made life and noise; hogs roamed and rooted contentedly about, and one of them lay in a reeking wallow in the middle of the main thoroughfare and suckled her family. Presently there was a distant blare of military music; it came nearer, still nearer, and soon a noble cavalcade wound into view, glorious with plumed helmets and flashing mail and flaunting banners and rich doublets and horse-cloths and gilded spearheads; and through the muck and swine, and naked brats, and joyous dogs, and shabby huts, it took its gallant way, and in its wake we followed.

Followed through one winding alley and then another, — and climbing, always climbing — till at last we gained the breezy height where the huge castle stood. There was an exchange of bugle blasts; then a parley from the walls, where men-at-arms, in hauberk and morion, marched back and forth with halberd at shoulder under flapping banners with the rude figure of a dragon displayed upon them; and then the great gates were flung open, the drawbridge was lowered, and the head of the cavalcade swept forward under the frowning arches; and we, following, soon found ourselves in a great paved court, with towers and turrets stretching up into the blue air on all the four sides; and all about us the dismount was going on, and much greeting and ceremony, and running to and fro, and a gay display of moving and intermingling colors, and an altogether pleasant stir and noise and confusion.

Chapter II. King Arthur's Court

The moment I got a chance I slipped aside privately and touched an ancient common looking man on the shoulder and said, in an insinuating, confidential way:

"Friend, do me a kindness. Do you belong to the asylum, or are you just on a visit or something like that?"

He looked me over stupidly, and said:

"Marry, fair sir, me seemeth — "

"That will do," I said; "I reckon you are a patient."

I moved away, cogitating, and at the same time keeping an eye out for any chance passenger in his right mind that might come along and give me some light. I judged I had found one, presently; so I drew him aside and said in his ear:

"If I could see the head keeper a minute — only just a minute — "

"Prithee do not let me."

"Let you *what* ?"

"*Hinder* me, then, if the word please thee better. Then he went on to say he was an under-cook and could not stop to gossip, though he would like it another time; for it would comfort his very liver to know where I got my clothes. As he started away he pointed and said yonder was one who was idle enough for my purpose, and was seeking me besides, no doubt. This was an airy slim boy in shrimp-colored tights that made him look like a forked carrot, the rest of his gear was blue silk and dainty laces and ruffles; and he had long yellow curls, and wore a plumed pink satin cap tilted complacently over his ear. By his look, he was good-natured; by his gait, he was satisfied with himself. He was pretty enough to frame. He arrived, looked me over with a smiling and impudent curiosity; said he had come for me, and informed me that he was a page.

"Go 'long," I said; "you ain't more than a paragraph."

It was pretty severe, but I was nettled. However, it never phazed him; he didn't appear to know he was hurt. He began to talk and laugh, in happy, thoughtless, boyish fashion, as we walked along, and made himself old friends with me at once; asked me all sorts of questions about myself and about my clothes, but never waited for an answer — always chattered straight ahead, as if he didn't know he had asked a question and wasn't expecting any reply, until at last he happened to mention that he was born in the beginning of the year 513.

It made the cold chills creep over me! I stopped and said, a little faintly:

"Maybe I didn't hear you just right. Say it again — and say it slow. What year was it?"

"513."

"513! You don't look it! Come, my boy, I am a stranger and friendless; be honest and honorable with me. Are you in your right mind?"

He said he was.

"Are these other people in their right minds?"

He said they were.

"And this isn't an asylum? I mean, it isn't a place where they cure crazy people?"

He said it wasn't.

"Well, then," I said, "either I am a lunatic, or something just as awful has happened. Now tell me, honest and true, where am I?"

"IN KING ARTHUR'S COURT."

I waited a minute, to let that idea shudder its way home, and then said:

"And according to your notions, what year is it now?"

"528 — nineteenth of June."

I felt a mournful sinking at the heart, and muttered: "I shall never see my friends again — never, never again. They will not be born for more than thirteen hundred years yet."

I seemed to believe the boy, I didn't know why. *Something* in me seemed to believe him — my consciousness, as you may say; but my reason didn't. My reason straightway began to clamor; that was natural. I didn't know how to go about satisfying it, because I knew that the testimony of men wouldn't serve — my reason would say they were lunatics, and throw out their evidence. But all of a sudden I stumbled on the very thing, just by luck. I knew that the only total eclipse of the sun in the first half of the sixth century occurred on the 21st of June, A.D. 528, O.S., and began at 3 minutes after 12 noon. I also knew that no total eclipse of the sun was due in what to *me* was the present year — i.e., 1879. So, if I could keep my anxiety and curiosity from eating the heart out of me for forty-eight hours, I should then find out for certain whether this boy was telling me the truth or not.

Wherefore, being a practical Connecticut man, I now shoved this whole problem clear out of my mind till its appointed day and hour should come, in order that I might turn all my attention to the circumstances of the present moment, and be alert and ready to make the most out of them that could be made. One thing at a time, is my motto — and just play that thing for all it is worth, even if it's only two pair and a jack. I made up my mind to two things: if it was still the nineteenth century and I was among lunatics and couldn't get away, I would presently boss that asylum or know the reason why; and if, on the other hand, it was really the sixth century, all right, I didn't want any softer thing: I would boss the whole country inside of three months; for I judged I would have the start of the best-educated man in the kingdom by a matter of thirteen hundred years and upward. I'm not a man to waste time after my mind's made up and there's work on hand; so I said to the page:

"Now, Clarence, my boy — if that might happen to be your name — I'll get you to post me up a little if you don't mind. What is the name of that apparition that brought me here?"

"My master and thine? That is the good knight and great lord Sir Kay the Seneschal, foster brother to our liege the king."

"Very good; go on, tell me everything."

He made a long story of it; but the part that had immediate interest for me was this: He said I was Sir Kay's prisoner, and that in the due course of custom I would be flung into a dungeon and left there on scant commons until my friends ransomed me — unless I chanced to rot, first. I saw that the last chance had the best show, but I didn't waste any bother about that; time was too precious. The page said, further, that dinner was about ended in the great hall by this time, and that as soon as the sociability and the heavy drinking should begin, Sir Kay would have me in and exhibit me before King Arthur and his illustrious knights seated at the Table Round, and would brag about his exploit in capturing me, and would probably exaggerate the facts a little, but it wouldn't be good form for me to correct him, and not over safe, either; and when I was done being exhibited, then ho for the dungeon; but he, Clarence, would find a way to come and see me every now and then, and cheer me up, and help me get word to my friends.

Get word to my friends! I thanked him; I couldn't do less; and about this time a lackey came to say I was wanted; so Clarence led me in and took me off to one side and sat down by me.

Well, it was a curious kind of spectacle, and interesting. It was an immense place, and rather naked — yes, and full of loud contrasts. It was very, very lofty; so lofty that the banners depending from the arched beams and girders away up there floated in a sort of twilight; there was a stone-railed gallery at each end, high up, with musicians in the one, and women, clothed in stunning colors, in the other. The floor was of big stone flags laid in black and white squares, rather battered by age and use, and needing repair. As to ornament, there wasn't any, strictly speaking; though on the walls hung some huge tapestries which were probably taxed as works of art; battle-pieces, they were, with horses shaped like those which children cut out of paper or create in gingerbread; with men on them in scale armor whose scales are represented by round holes — so that the man's coat looks as if it had been done with a biscuit-punch. There was a fireplace big enough to camp in; and its projecting sides and hood, of carved and pillared stonework, had the look of a cathedral door. Along the walls stood men-at-arms, in breastplate and morion, with halberds for their only weapon — rigid as statues; and that is what they looked like.

In the middle of this groined and vaulted public square was an oaken table which they called the Table Round. It was as large as a circus ring; and around it sat a great company of men dressed in such various and splendid colors that it hurt one's eyes to look at them. They wore their plumed hats, right along, except that whenever one addressed himself directly to the king, he lifted his hat a trifle just as he was beginning his remark.

Mainly they were drinking — from entire ox horns; but a few were still munching bread or gnawing beef bones. There was about an average of two dogs to one man; and these sat in expectant attitudes till a spent bone was flung to them, and then they went for it by brigades and divisions, with a rush, and there ensued a fight which filled the prospect with a tumultuous chaos of plunging heads and bodies and flashing tails, and the storm of howlings and barkings deafened all speech for the time; but that was no matter, for the dog-fight was always a bigger interest anyway; the men rose, sometimes, to observe it the better and bet on it, and the ladies and the musicians stretched themselves out over their balusters with the same object; and all broke into delighted ejaculations from time to time. In the end, the winning dog stretched himself out comfortably with his bone between his paws, and proceeded to growl over it, and gnaw it, and grease the floor with it, just as fifty others were already doing; and the rest of the court resumed their previous industries and entertainments.

As a rule, the speech and behavior of these people were gracious and courtly; and I noticed that they were good and serious listeners when anybody was telling anything — I mean in a dog-fightless interval. And plainly, too, they were a childlike and innocent lot; telling lies of the stateliest pattern with a most gentle and winning naivety, and ready and willing to listen to anybody else's lie, and believe it, too. It was hard to associate them with anything cruel or dreadful; and yet they dealt in tales of blood and suffering with a guileless relish that made me almost forget to shudder.

I was not the only prisoner present. There were twenty or more. Poor devils, many of them were maimed, hacked, carved, in a frightful way; and their hair, their faces, their clothing, were caked with black and stiffened drenchings of blood. They were suffering sharp physical pain, of course; and weariness, and hunger and thirst, no doubt; and at least none had given them the comfort of a wash, or even the poor charity of a lotion for their wounds; yet you never heard them utter a moan or a groan, or saw them show any sign of restlessness, or any disposition to complain. The thought was forced upon me: "The rascals — *they* have served other people so in their day; it being their own turn, now, they were not expecting any better treatment than this; so their philosophical bearing is not an outcome of mental training, intellectual fortitude, reasoning; it is mere animal training; they are white Indians."

Chapter III. Knights of the Table Round

Mainly the Round Table talk was monologues — narrative accounts of the adventures in which these prisoners were captured and their friends and backers killed and stripped of their steeds and armor. As a general thing — as far as I could make out — these murderous adventures were not forays undertaken to avenge injuries, nor to settle old disputes or sudden fallings out; no, as a rule they were simply duels between strangers — duels between people who had never even been introduced to each other, and between whom existed no cause of offense whatever. Many a time I had seen a couple of boys, strangers, meet by chance, and say simultaneously, "I can lick you," and go at it on the spot; but I had always imagined until now that that sort of thing belonged to children only, and was a sign and mark of childhood; but here were these big boobies sticking to it and taking pride in it clear up into full age and beyond. Yet there was something very engaging about these great simple-hearted creatures, something attractive and lovable. There did not seem to be brains enough in the entire nursery, so to speak, to bait a fishhook with; but you didn't seem to mind that, after a little, because you soon saw that brains were not needed in a society like that, and indeed would have marred it, hindered it, spoiled its symmetry — perhaps rendered its existence impossible.

There was a fine manliness observable in almost every face; and in some a certain loftiness and sweetness that rebuked your belittling criticisms and stilled them. A most noble benignity and purity reposed in the countenance of him they called Sir Galahad, and likewise in the king's also; and there was majesty and greatness in the giant frame and high bearing of Sir Launcelot of the Lake.

There was presently an incident which centered the general interest upon this Sir Launcelot. At a sign from a sort of master of ceremonies, six or eight of the prisoners rose and came forward in a body and knelt on the floor and lifted up their hands toward the ladies' gallery and begged the grace of a word with the queen. The most conspicuously situated lady in that massed flower-bed of feminine show and finery inclined her head by way of assent, and then the spokesman of the prisoners delivered himself and his fellows into her hands for free pardon, ransom, captivity, or death, as she in her good pleasure might elect; and this, as he said, he was doing by command of Sir Kay the Seneschal, whose prisoners they were, he having vanquished them by his single might and prowess in sturdy conflict in the field.

Surprise and astonishment flashed from face to face all over the house; the queen's gratified smile faded out at the name of Sir Kay, and she looked disappointed; and the page whispered in my ear with an accent and manner expressive of extravagant derision —

"Sir *Kay* , forsooth! Oh, call me pet names, dearest, call me a marine! In twice a thousand years shall the unholy invention of man labor at odds to beget the fellow to this majestic lie!"

Every eye was fastened with severe inquiry upon Sir Kay. But he was equal to the occasion. He got up and played his hand like a major — and took every trick. He said he would state the case exactly according to the facts; he would tell the simple straightforward tale, without comment of his own; "and then," said he, "if ye find glory and honor due, ye will give it unto him who is the mightiest man of his hands that ever bare shield or strake with sword in the ranks of Christian battle — even him that sitteth there!" and he pointed to Sir Launcelot. Ah, he fetched them; it was a rattling good stroke. Then he went on and told how Sir Launcelot, seeking adventures, some brief time gone by, killed seven giants at one sweep of his sword, and set a hundred and forty-two captive maidens free; and then went further, still seeking adventures, and found him (Sir Kay) fighting a desperate fight against nine foreign knights, and straightway took the battle solely into his own hands, and conquered the nine; and that night Sir

Launcelot rose quietly, and dressed him in Sir Kay's armor and took Sir Kay's horse and gat him away into distant lands, and vanquished sixteen knights in one pitched battle and thirty-four in another; and all these and the former nine he made to swear that about Whitsuntide they would ride to Arthur's court and yield them to Queen Guenever's hands as captives of Sir Kay the Seneschal, spoil of his knightly prowess; and now here were these half dozen, and the rest would be along as soon as they might be healed of their desperate wounds.

Well, it was touching to see the queen blush and smile, and look embarrassed and happy, and fling furtive glances at Sir Launcelot that would have got him shot in Arkansas, to a dead certainty.

Everybody praised the valor and magnanimity of Sir Launcelot; and as for me, I was perfectly amazed, that one man, all by himself, should have been able to beat down and capture such battalions of practiced fighters. I said as much to Clarence; but this mocking featherhead only said:

"An Sir Kay had had time to get another skin of sour wine into him, ye had seen the accompt doubled."

I looked at the boy in sorrow; and as I looked I saw the cloud of a deep despondency settle upon his countenance. I followed the direction of his eye, and saw that a very old and white-bearded man, clothed in a flowing black gown, had risen and was standing at the table upon unsteady legs, and feebly swaying his ancient head and surveying the company with his watery and wandering eye. The same suffering look that was in the page's face was observable in all the faces around — the look of dumb creatures who know that they must endure and make no moan.

"Marry, we shall have it again," sighed the boy; "that same old weary tale that he hath told a thousand times in the same words, and that he *will* tell till he dieth, every time he hath gotten his barrel full and feeleth his exaggeration-mill a-working. Would God I had died or I saw this day!"

"Who is it?"

"Merlin, the mighty liar and magician, perdition singe him for the weariness he worketh with his one tale! But that men fear him for that he hath the storms and the lightnings and all the devils that be in hell at his beck and call, they would have dug his entrails out these many years ago to get at that tale and squelch it. He telleth it always in the third person, making believe he is too modest to glorify himself — maledictions light upon him, misfortune be his dole! Good friend, prithee call me for evensong."

The boy nestled himself upon my shoulder and pretended to go to sleep. The old man began his tale; and presently the lad was asleep in reality; so also were the dogs, and the court, the lackeys, and the files of men-at-arms. The droning voice droned on; a soft snoring arose on all sides and supported it like a deep and subdued accompaniment of wind instruments. Some heads were bowed upon folded arms, some lay back with open mouths that issued unconscious music; the flies buzzed and bit, unmolested, the rats swarmed softly out from a hundred holes, and pattered about, and made themselves at home everywhere; and one of them sat up like a squirrel on the king's head and held a bit of cheese in its hands and nibbled it, and dribbled the crumbs in the king's face with naive and impudent irreverence. It was a tranquil scene, and restful to the weary eye and the jaded spirit.

This was the old man's tale. He said:

"Right so the king and Merlin departed, and went until an hermit that was a good man and a great leech. So the hermit searched all his wounds and gave him good salves; so the king was there three days, and then were his wounds well amended that he might ride and go, and so departed. And as they rode, Arthur said, I have no sword. No force,[1] said Merlin, hereby is a sword that shall be yours and I may. So they rode till they came to a lake, the which was a fair water and broad, and in the midst of the lake Arthur was ware of an arm clothed in white samite, that held a fair sword in that hand. Lo, said Merlin, yonder is that sword that I spake of. With that they saw a damsel going upon the lake. What damsel is that? said Arthur. That is the Lady of the lake, said Merlin; and within that lake is a rock, and therein is as fair a place as any on earth, and richly beseen, and this damsel will come to you anon, and then speak ye fair to her that she will give you that sword. Anon withal came the damsel unto Arthur and saluted him, and he her again. Damsel, said Arthur, what sword is that, that yonder the arm holdeth above the water? I would it were mine, for I have no sword. Sir Arthur King, said the damsel, that sword is mine, and if ye will give me a gift when I ask it you, ye shall have it. By my faith, said Arthur, I will give you what gift ye will ask. Well, said the damsel, go ye into yonder barge and row yourself to the sword, and take it and the scabbard with you, and I will ask my gift when I see my time. So Sir Arthur and Merlin alight, and tied their horses to two trees, and so they went into the ship, and when they came to the sword that the hand held, Sir Arthur took it up by the handles, and took it with him.

And the arm and the hand went under the water; and so they came unto the land and rode forth. And then Sir Arthur saw a rich pavilion. What signifieth yonder pavilion? It is the knight's pavilion, said Merlin, that ye fought with last, Sir Pellinore, but he is out, he is not there; he hath ado with a knight of yours, that hight Egglame, and they have fought together, but at the last Egglame fled, and else he had been dead, and he hath chased him even to Carlion, and we shall meet with him anon in the highway. That is well said, said Arthur, now have I a sword, now will I wage battle with him, and be avenged on him. Sir, ye shall not so, said Merlin, for the knight is weary of fighting and chasing, so that ye shall have no worship to have ado with him; also, he will not lightly be matched of one knight living; and therefore it is my counsel, let him pass, for he shall do you good service in short time, and his sons, after his days. Also ye shall see that day in short space ye shall be right glad to give him your sister to wed. When I see him, I will do as ye advise me, said Arthur. Then Sir Arthur looked on the sword, and liked it passing well. Whether liketh you better, said Merlin, the sword or the scabbard? Me liketh better the sword, said Arthur. Ye are more unwise, said Merlin, for the scabbard is worth ten of the sword, for while ye have the scabbard upon you ye shall never lose no blood, be ye never so sore wounded; therefore, keep well the scabbard always with you. So they rode into Carlion, and by the way they met with Sir Pellinore; but Merlin had done such a craft that Pellinore saw not Arthur, and he passed by without any words. I marvel, said Arthur, that the knight would not speak. Sir, said Merlin, he saw you not; for and he had seen you ye had not lightly departed. So they came unto Carlion, whereof his knights were passing glad. And when they heard of his adventures they marveled that he would jeopard his person so alone. But all men of worship said it was merry to be under such a chieftain that would put his person in adventure as other poor knights did."

* * * * *

Chapter IV. Sir Dinadan the Humorist

It seemed to me that this quaint lie was most simply and beautifully told; but then I had heard it only once, and that makes a difference; it was pleasant to the others when it was fresh, no doubt.

Sir Dinadan the Humorist was the first to awake, and he soon roused the rest with a practical joke of a sufficiently poor quality. He tied some metal mugs to a dog's tail and turned him loose, and he tore around and around the place in a frenzy of fright, with all the other dogs bellowing after him and battering and crashing against everything that came in their way and making altogether a chaos of confusion and a most deafening din and turmoil; at which every man and woman of the multitude laughed till the tears flowed, and some fell out of their chairs and wallowed on the floor in ecstasy. It was just like so many children. Sir Dinadan was so proud of his exploit that he could not keep from telling over and over again, to weariness, how the immortal idea happened to occur to him; and as is the way with humorists of his breed, he was still laughing at it after everybody else had got through.

He was so set up that he concluded to make a speech — of course a humorous speech. I think I never heard so many old played-out jokes strung together in my life. He was worse than the minstrels, worse than the clown in the circus. It seemed peculiarly sad to sit here, thirteen hundred years before I was born, and listen again to poor, flat, worm-eaten jokes that had given me the dry gripes when I was a boy thirteen hundred years afterwards. It about convinced me that there isn't any such thing as a new joke possible. Everybody laughed at these antiquities — but then they always do; I had noticed that, centuries later. However, of course the scoffer didn't laugh — I mean the boy. No, he scoffed; there wasn't anything he wouldn't scoff at. He said the most of Sir Dinadan's jokes were rotten and the rest were petrified. I said "petrified" was good; as I believed, myself, that the only right way to classify the majestic ages of some of those jokes was by geologic periods. But that neat idea hit the boy in a blank place, for geology hadn't been invented yet. However, I made a note of the remark, and calculated to educate the commonwealth up to it if I pulled through. It is no use to throw a good thing away merely because the market isn't ripe yet.

Now Sir Kay arose and began to fire up on his history-mill with me for fuel. It was time for me to feel serious, and I did. Sir Kay told how he had encountered me in a far land of barbarians, who all wore the same ridiculous garb that I did — a garb that was a work of enchantment, and intended to make the wearer secure from hurt by human hands. However he had nullified the force of the enchantment by prayer, and had killed my thirteen knights in a three hours' battle, and taken me prisoner, sparing my life in order that so strange a curiosity as I was might be exhibited to the wonder and admiration of the king and the court. He spoke of me all the time, in the blandest way, as "this prodigious giant," and "this horrible sky-towering monster," and "this tusked and taloned man-devouring ogre", and everybody took in all this bosh in the naivest way, and never smiled or seemed to notice that there was any discrepancy between these watered statistics and me. He said that in trying to escape from him I sprang into the top of a tree two hundred cubits high at a single bound, but he dislodged me with a stone the size of a cow, which "all-to brast" the most of my bones, and then swore me to appear at Arthur's court for sentence. He ended by condemning me to die at noon on the 21st; and was so little concerned about it that he stopped to yawn before he named the date.

I was in a dismal state by this time; indeed, I was hardly enough in my right mind to keep the run of a dispute that sprung up as to how I had better be killed, the possibility of the killing being doubted by some, because of the enchantment in my clothes. And yet it was nothing but an ordinary suit of fifteen-dollar slopshops. Still, I was sane enough to notice this detail, to wit: many of the terms used in the most matter-of-fact way by this great assemblage of the first ladies and gentlemen in the land would have made a Comanche blush.

Indelicacy is too mild a term to convey the idea. However, I had read "Tom Jones," and "Roderick Random," and other books of that kind, and knew that the highest and first ladies and gentlemen in England had remained little or no cleaner in their talk, and in the morals and conduct which such talk implies, clear up to a hundred years ago; in fact clear into our own nineteenth century — in which century, broadly speaking, the earliest samples of the real lady and real gentleman discoverable in English history — or in European history, for that matter — may be said to have made their appearance. Suppose Sir Walter, instead of putting the conversations into the mouths of his characters, had allowed the characters to speak for themselves? We should have had talk from Rebecca and Ivanhoe and the soft lady Rowena which would embarrass a tramp in our day. However, to the unconsciously indelicate all things are delicate. King Arthur's people were not aware that they were indecent and I had presence of mind enough not to mention it.

They were so troubled about my enchanted clothes that they were mightily relieved, at last, when old Merlin swept the difficulty away for them with a commonsense hint. He asked them why they were so dull — why didn't it occur to them to strip me. In half a minute I was as naked as a pair of tongs! And dear, dear, to think of it: I was the only embarrassed person there. Everybody discussed me; and did it as unconcernedly as if I had been a cabbage. Queen Guenever was as naively interested as the rest, and said she had never seen anybody with legs just like mine before. It was the only compliment I got — if it was a compliment.

Finally I was carried off in one direction, and my perilous clothes in another. I was shoved into a dark and narrow cell in a dungeon, with some scant remnants for dinner, some moldy straw for a bed, and no end of rats for company.

Chapter V. An Inspiration

I was so tired that even my fears were not able to keep me awake long.

When I next came to myself, I seemed to have been asleep a very long time. My first thought was, "Well, what an astonishing dream I've had! I reckon I've waked only just in time to keep from being hanged or drowned or burned or something.... I'll nap again till the whistle blows, and then I'll go down to the arms factory and have it out with Hercules."

But just then I heard the harsh music of rusty chains and bolts, a light flashed in my eyes, and that butterfly, Clarence, stood before me! I gasped with surprise; my breath almost got away from me.

"What!" I said, "you here yet? Go along with the rest of the dream! scatter!"

But he only laughed, in his lighthearted way, and fell to making fun of my sorry plight.

"All right," I said resignedly, "let the dream go on; I'm in no hurry."

"Prithee what dream?"

"What dream? Why, the dream that I am in Arthur's court — a person who never existed; and that I am talking to you, who are nothing but a work of the imagination."

"Oh, la, indeed! and is it a dream that you're to be burned tomorrow? Ho-ho — answer me that!"

The shock that went through me was distressing. I now began to reason that my situation was in the last degree serious, dream or no dream; for I knew by past experience of the lifelike intensity of dreams, that to be burned to death, even in a dream, would be very far from being a jest, and was a thing to be avoided, by any means, fair or foul, that I could contrive. So I said beseechingly:

"Ah, Clarence, good boy, only friend I've got, — for you *are* my friend, aren't you? — don't fail me; help me to devise some way of escaping from this place!"

"Now do but hear thyself! Escape? Why, man, the corridors are in guard and keep of men-at-arms."

"No doubt, no doubt. But how many, Clarence? Not many, I hope?"

"Full a score. One may not hope to escape." After a pause — hesitatingly: "and there be other reasons — and weightier."

"Other ones? What are they?"

"Well, they say — oh, but I daren't, indeed daren't!"

"Why, poor lad, what is the matter? Why do you blench? Why do you tremble so?"

"Oh, in sooth, there is need! I do want to tell you, but — "

"Come, come, be brave, be a man — speak out, there's a good lad!"

He hesitated, pulled one way by desire, the other way by fear; then he stole to the door and peeped out, listening; and finally crept close to me and put his mouth to my ear and told me his fearful news in a whisper, and with all the cowering apprehension of one who was venturing upon awful ground and speaking of things whose very mention might be freighted with death.

"Merlin, in his malice, has woven a spell about this dungeon, and there bides not the man in these kingdoms that would be desperate enough to essay to cross its lines with you! Now God pity me, I have told it! Ah, be kind to me, be merciful to a poor boy who means thee well; for an thou betray me I am lost!"

I laughed the only really refreshing laugh I had had for some time; and shouted:

"Merlin has wrought a spell! *Merlin* , forsooth! That cheap old humbug, that maundering old ass? Bosh, pure bosh, the silliest bosh in the world! Why, it does seem to me that of all the childish, idiotic, chuckleheaded, chicken-livered superstitions that ev — oh, damn Merlin!"

But Clarence had slumped to his knees before I had half finished, and he was like to go out of his mind with fright.

"Oh, beware! These are awful words! Any moment these walls may crumble upon us if you say such things. Oh call them back before it is too late!"

Now this strange exhibition gave me a good idea and set me to thinking. If everybody about here was so honestly and sincerely afraid of Merlin's pretended magic as Clarence was, certainly a superior man like me ought to be shrewd enough to contrive some way to take advantage of such a state of things. I went on thinking, and worked out a plan. Then I said:

"Get up. Pull yourself together; look me in the eye. Do you know why I laughed?"

"No — but for our blessed Lady's sake, do it no more."

"Well, I'll tell you why I laughed. Because I'm a magician myself."

"Thou!" The boy recoiled a step, and caught his breath, for the thing hit him rather sudden; but the aspect which he took on was very, very respectful. I took quick note of that; it indicated that a humbug didn't need to have a reputation in this asylum; people stood ready to take him at his word, without that. I resumed.

"I've known Merlin seven hundred years, and he — "

"Seven hun — "

"Don't interrupt me. He has died and come alive again thirteen times, and traveled under a new name every time: Smith, Jones, Robinson, Jackson, Peters, Haskins, Merlin — a new alias every time he turns up. I knew him in Egypt three hundred years ago; I knew him in India five hundred years ago — he is always blethering around in my way, everywhere I go; he makes me tired. He don't amount to shucks, as a magician; knows some of the old common tricks, but has never got beyond the rudiments, and never will. He is well enough for the provinces — one-night stands and that sort of thing, you know — but dear me, *he* oughtn't to set up for an expert — anyway not where there's a real artist. Now look here, Clarence, I am going to stand your friend, right along, and in return you must be mine. I want you to do me a favor. I want you to get word to the king that I am a magician myself — and the Supreme Grand High-yu-Muck-amuck and head of the tribe, at that; and I want him to be made to understand that I am just quietly arranging a little calamity here that will make the fur fly in these realms if Sir Kay's project is carried out and any harm comes to me. Will you get that to the king for me?"

The poor boy was in such a state that he could hardly answer me. It was pitiful to see a creature so terrified, so unnerved, so demoralized. But he promised everything; and on my side he made me promise over and over again that I would remain his friend, and never turn against him or cast any enchantments upon him. Then he worked his way out, staying himself with his hand along the wall, like a sick person.

Presently this thought occurred to me: how heedless I have been! When the boy gets calm, he will wonder why a great magician like me should have begged a boy like him to help me get out of this place; he will put this and that together, and will see that I am a humbug.

I worried over that heedless blunder for an hour, and called myself a great many hard names, meantime. But finally it occurred to me all of a sudden that these animals didn't reason; that *they* never put this and that together; that all their talk showed that they didn't know a discrepancy when they saw it. I was at rest, then.

But as soon as one is at rest, in this world, off he goes on something else to worry about. It occurred to me that I had made another blunder: I had sent the boy off to alarm his betters with a threat — I intending to invent a calamity at my leisure; now the people who are the readiest and eagerest and willingest to swallow miracles are the very ones who are hungriest to see you perform them; suppose I should be called on for a sample? Suppose I should be asked to name my calamity? Yes, I had made a blunder; I ought to have invented my calamity first. "What shall I do? what can I say, to gain a little time?" I was in trouble again; in the deepest kind of trouble...

"There's a footstep! — they're coming. If I had only just a moment to think.... Good, I've got it. I'm all right."

You see, it was the eclipse. It came into my mind in the nick of time, how Columbus, or Cortez, or one of those people, played an eclipse as a saving trump once, on some savages, and I saw my chance. I could play it myself, now, and it wouldn't be any plagiarism, either, because I should get it in nearly a thousand years ahead of those parties.

Clarence came in, subdued, distressed, and said:

"I hasted the message to our liege the king, and straightway he had me to his presence. He was frighted even to the marrow, and was minded to give order for your instant enlargement, and that you be clothed in fine raiment and lodged as befitted one so great; but then came Merlin and spoiled all; for he persuaded the king that you are mad, and know not whereof you speak; and said your threat is but foolishness and idle vaporing. They disputed long, but in the end, Merlin, scoffing, said, 'Wherefore hath he not *named* his brave calamity? Verily it is because he cannot.' This thrust did in a most sudden sort close the king's mouth, and he could offer naught to turn the argument; and so, reluctant, and full loth to do you the discourtesy, he yet prayeth you to consider his perplexed case, as noting how the matter stands, and name the calamity — if so be you have determined the nature of it and the time of its coming. Oh, prithee delay not; to delay at such a time were to double and treble the perils that already compass thee about. Oh, be thou wise — name the calamity!"

I allowed silence to accumulate while I got my impressiveness together, and then said:

"How long have I been shut up in this hole?"

"Ye were shut up when yesterday was well spent. It is 9 of the morning now."

"No! Then I have slept well, sure enough. Nine in the morning now! And yet it is the very complexion of midnight, to a shade. This is the 20th, then?"

"The 20th — yes."

"And I am to be burned alive tomorrow." The boy shuddered.

"At what hour?"

"At high noon."

"Now then, I will tell you what to say." I paused, and stood over that cowering lad a whole minute in awful silence; then, in a voice deep, measured, charged with doom, I began, and rose by dramatically graded stages to my colossal climax, which I delivered in as sublime and noble a way as ever I did such a thing in my life: "Go back and tell the king that at that hour I will smother the whole world in the dead blackness of midnight; I will blot out the sun, and he shall never shine again; the fruits of the earth shall rot for lack of light and warmth, and the peoples of the earth shall famish and die, to the last man!"

I had to carry the boy out myself, he sunk into such a collapse. I handed him over to the soldiers, and went back.

Chapter VI. The Eclipse

In the stillness and the darkness, realization soon began to supplement knowledge. The mere knowledge of a fact is pale; but when you come to *realize* your fact, it takes on color. It is all the difference between hearing of a man being stabbed to the heart, and seeing it done. In the stillness and the darkness, the knowledge that I was in deadly danger took to itself deeper and deeper meaning all the time; a something which was realization crept inch by inch through my veins and turned me cold.

But it is a blessed provision of nature that at times like these, as soon as a man's mercury has got down to a certain point there comes a revulsion, and he rallies. Hope springs up, and cheerfulness along with it, and then he is in good shape to do something for himself, if anything can be done. When my rally came, it came with a bound. I said to myself that my eclipse would be sure to save me, and make me the greatest man in the kingdom besides; and straightway my mercury went up to the top of the tube, and my solicitudes all vanished. I was as happy a man as there was in the world. I was even impatient for tomorrow to come, I so wanted to gather in that great triumph and be the center of all the nation's wonder and reverence. Besides, in a business way it would be the making of me; I knew that.

Meantime there was one thing which had got pushed into the background of my mind. That was the half-conviction that when the nature of my proposed calamity should be reported to those superstitious people, it would have such an effect that they would want to compromise. So, by and by when I heard footsteps coming, that thought was recalled to me, and I said to myself, "As sure as anything, it's the compromise. Well, if it is good, all right, I will accept; but if it isn't, I mean to stand my ground and play my hand for all it is worth."

The door opened, and some men-at-arms appeared. The leader said:

"The stake is ready. Come!"

The stake! The strength went out of me, and I almost fell down. It is hard to get one's breath at such a time, such lumps come into one's throat, and such gaspings; but as soon as I could speak, I said:

"But this is a mistake — the execution is tomorrow."

"Order changed; been set forward a day. Haste thee!"

I was lost. There was no help for me. I was dazed, stupefied; I had no command over myself, I only wandered purposely about, like one out of his mind; so the soldiers took hold of me, and pulled me along with them, out of the cell and along the maze of underground corridors, and finally into the fierce glare of daylight and the upper world. As we stepped into the vast enclosed court of the castle I got a shock; for the first thing I saw was the stake, standing in the center, and near it the piled fagots and a monk. On all four sides of the court the seated multitudes rose rank above rank, forming sloping terraces that were rich with color. The king and the queen sat in their thrones, the most conspicuous figures there, of course.

To note all this, occupied but a second. The next second Clarence had slipped from some place of concealment and was pouring news into my ear, his eyes beaming with triumph and gladness. He said:

"Tis through *me* the change was wrought! And main hard have I worked to do it, too. But when I revealed to them the calamity in store, and saw how mighty was the terror it did engender, then saw I also that this was the time to strike! Wherefore I diligently pretended, unto this and that and the other one, that your power against the sun could not reach its full until the morrow; and so if any would save the sun and the world, you must be slain to-day, while your enchantments are but in the weaving and lack potency. Odsbodikins, it was but a dull lie, a most indifferent invention, but you should have seen them seize it and swallow it, in the frenzy of their fright, as it were salvation sent from heaven; and all the while was I laughing in my sleeve the one moment, to see them so cheaply deceived, and glorifying God the next, that He was content to let the meanest of His creatures be His instrument to the saving of thy life. Ah how happy has the matter sped! You will not need to do the sun a *real* hurt — ah, forget not that, on your soul forget it not! Only make a little darkness — only the littlest little darkness, mind, and cease with that. It will be sufficient. They will see that I spoke falsely, — being ignorant, as they will fancy — and with the falling of the first shadow of that darkness you shall see them go mad with fear; and they will set you free and make you great! Go to thy triumph, now! But remember — ah, good friend, I implore thee remember my supplication, and do the blessed sun no hurt. For *my* sake, thy true friend."

I choked out some words through my grief and misery; as much as to say I would spare the sun; for which the lad's eyes paid me back with such deep and loving gratitude that I had not the heart to tell him his goodhearted foolishness had ruined me and sent me to my death.

As the soldiers assisted me across the court the stillness was so profound that if I had been blindfold I should have supposed I was in a solitude instead of walled in by four thousand people. There was not a movement perceptible in those masses of humanity; they were as rigid as stone images, and as pale; and dread sat upon every countenance. This hush continued while I was being chained to the stake; it still continued while the fagots were carefully and tediously piled about my ankles, my knees, my thighs, my body. Then there was a pause, and a deeper hush, if possible, and a man knelt down at my feet with a blazing torch; the multitude strained forward, gazing, and parting slightly from their seats without knowing it; the monk raised his hands above my head, and his eyes toward the blue sky, and began some words in Latin; in this attitude he droned on and on, a little while, and then stopped. I waited two or three moments; then looked up; he was standing there petrified. With a common impulse the multitude rose slowly up and stared into the sky. I followed their eyes, as sure as guns, there was my eclipse beginning! The life went boiling through my veins; I was a new man! The rim of black spread slowly into the sun's disk, my heart beat higher and higher, and still the assemblage and the priest stared into the sky, motionless. I knew that this gaze would be turned upon me, next. When it was, I was ready. I was in one of the most grand attitudes I ever struck, with my arm stretched up pointing to the sun. It was a noble effect. You could *see* the shudder sweep the mass like a wave. Two shouts rang out, one close upon the heels of the other:

"Apply the torch!"

"I forbid it!"

The one was from Merlin, the other from the king. Merlin started from his place — to apply the torch himself, I judged. I said:

"Stay where you are. If any man moves — even the king — before I give him leave, I will blast him with thunder, I will consume him with lightnings!"

The multitude sank meekly into their seats, and I was just expecting they would. Merlin hesitated a moment or two, and I was on pins and needles during that little while. Then he sat down, and I took a good breath; for I knew I was master of the situation now. The king said:

"Be merciful, fair sir, and essay no further in this perilous matter, lest disaster follow. It was reported to us that your powers could not attain unto their full strength until the morrow; but — "

"Your Majesty thinks the report may have been a lie? It *was* a lie."

That made an immense effect; up went appealing hands everywhere, and the king was assailed with a storm of supplications that I might be bought off at any price, and the calamity stayed. The king was eager to comply. He said:

"Name any terms, reverend sir, even to the halving of my kingdom; but banish this calamity, spare the sun!"

My fortune was made. I would have taken him up in a minute, but I couldn't stop an eclipse; the thing was out of the question. So I asked time to consider. The king said:

"How long — ah, how long, good sir? Be merciful; look, it groweth darker, moment by moment. Prithee how long?"

"Not long. Half an hour — maybe an hour."

There were a thousand pathetic protests, but I couldn't shorten up any, for I couldn't remember how long a total eclipse lasts. I was in a puzzled condition, anyway, and wanted to think. Something was wrong about that eclipse, and the fact was very unsettling. If this wasn't the one I was after, how was I to tell whether this was the sixth century, or nothing but a dream? Dear me, if I could only prove it was the latter! Here was a glad new hope. If the boy was right about the date, and this was surely the 20th, it *wasn't* the sixth century. I reached for the monk's sleeve, in considerable excitement, and asked him what day of the month it was.

Hang him, he said it was the *twenty-first* ! It made me turn cold to hear him. I begged him not to make any mistake about it; but he was sure; he knew it was the 21st. So, that featherheaded boy had botched things again! The time of the day was right for the eclipse; I had seen that for myself, in the beginning, by the dial that was near by. Yes, I was in King Arthur's court, and I might as well make the most out of it I could.

The darkness was steadily growing, the people becoming more and more distressed. I now said:

"I have reflected, Sir King. For a lesson, I will let this darkness proceed, and spread night in the world; but whether I blot out the sun for good, or restore it, shall rest with you. These are the terms, to wit: You shall remain king over all your dominions, and receive all the glories and honors that belong to the kingship; but you shall appoint me your perpetual minister and executive, and give me for my services one per cent of such actual increase of revenue over and above its present amount as I may succeed in creating for the state. If I can't live on that, I sha'n't ask anybody to give me a lift. Is it satisfactory?"

There was a prodigious roar of applause, and out of the midst of it the king's voice rose, saying:

"Away with his bonds, and set him free! and do him homage, high and low, rich and poor, for he is become the king's right hand, is clothed with power and authority, and his seat is upon the highest step of the throne! Now sweep away this creeping night, and bring the light and cheer again, that all the world may bless thee."

But I said:

"That a common man should be shamed before the world, is nothing; but it were dishonor to the *king* if any that saw his minister naked should not also see him delivered from his shame. If I might ask that my clothes be brought again — "

"They are not meet," the king broke in. "Fetch raiment of another sort; clothe him like a prince!"

My idea worked. I wanted to keep things as they were till the eclipse was total, otherwise they would be trying again to get me to dismiss the darkness, and of course I couldn't do it. Sending for the clothes gained some delay, but not enough. So I had to make another excuse. I said it would be but natural if the king should change his mind and repent to some extent of what he had done under excitement; therefore I would let the darkness grow a while, and if at the end of a reasonable time the king had kept his mind the same, the darkness should be dismissed. Neither the king nor anybody else was satisfied with that arrangement, but I had to stick to my point.

It grew darker and darker and blacker and blacker, while I struggled with those awkward sixth-century clothes. It got to be pitch dark, at last, and the multitude groaned with horror to feel the cold uncanny night breezes fan through the place and see the stars come out and twinkle in the sky. At last the eclipse was total, and I was very glad of it, but everybody else was in misery; which was quite natural. I said:

"The king, by his silence, still stands to the terms." Then I lifted up my hands — stood just so a moment — then I said, with the most awful solemnity: "Let the enchantment dissolve and pass harmless away!"

There was no response, for a moment, in that deep darkness and that graveyard hush. But when the silver rim of the sun pushed itself out, a moment or two later, the assemblage broke loose with a vast shout and came pouring down like a deluge to smother me with blessings and gratitude; and Clarence was not the last of the wash, to be sure.

Chapter VII. Merlin's Tower

Inasmuch as I was now the second personage in the Kingdom, as far as political power and authority were concerned, much was made of me. My raiment was of silks and velvets and cloth of gold, and by consequence was very showy, also uncomfortable. But habit would soon reconcile me to my clothes; I was aware of that. I was given the choicest suite of apartments in the castle, after the king's. They were aglow with loud-colored silken hangings, but the stone floors had nothing but rushes on them for a carpet, and they were misfit rushes at that, being not all of one breed. As for conveniences, properly speaking, there weren't any. I mean *little* conveniences; it is the little conveniences that make the real comfort of life. The big oaken chairs, graced with rude carvings, were well enough, but that was the stopping place. There was no soap, no matches, no looking-glass — except a metal one, about as powerful as a pail of water. And not a chromo. I had been used to chromos for years, and I saw now that without my suspecting it a passion for art had got worked into the fabric of my being, and was become a part of me.

It made me homesick to look around over this proud and gaudy but heartless barrenness and remember that in our house in East Hartford, all unpretending as it was, you couldn't go into a room but you would find an insurance-chromo, or at least a three-color God-Bless-Our-Home over the door; and in the parlor we had nine. But here, even in my grand room of state, there wasn't anything in the nature of a picture except a thing the size of a bedquilt, which was either woven or knitted (it had darned places in it), and nothing in it was the right color or the right shape; and as for proportions, even Raphael himself couldn't have botched them more formidably, after all his practice on those nightmares they call his "celebrated Hampton Court cartoons." Raphael was a bird. We had several of his chromos; one was his "Miraculous Draught of Fishes," where he puts in a miracle of his own — puts three men into a canoe which wouldn't have held a dog without upsetting. I always admired to study R.'s art, it was so fresh and unconventional.

There wasn't even a bell or a speaking-tube in the castle. I had a great many servants, and those that were on duty lolled in the anteroom; and when I wanted one of them I had to go and call for him. There was no gas, there were no candles; a bronze dish half full of boardinghouse butter with a blazing rag floating in it was the thing that produced what was regarded as light. A lot of these hung along the walls and modified the dark, just toned it down enough to make it dismal. If you went out at night, your servants carried torches. There were no books, pens, paper or ink, and no glass in the openings they believed to be windows. It is a little thing — glass is — until it is absent, then it becomes a big thing. But perhaps the worst of all was, that there wasn't any sugar, coffee, tea, or tobacco. I saw that I was just another Robinson Crusoe cast away on an uninhabited island, with no society but some more or less tame animals, and if I wanted to make life bearable I must do as he did — invent, contrive, create, reorganize things; set brain and hand to work, and keep them busy. Well, that was in my line.

One thing troubled me along at first — the immense interest which people took in me. Apparently the whole nation wanted a look at me. It soon transpired that the eclipse had scared the British world almost to death; that while it lasted the whole country, from one end to the other, was in a pitiable state of panic, and the churches, hermitages, and monkeries overflowed with praying and weeping poor creatures who thought the end of the world was come. Then had followed the news that the producer of this awful event was a stranger, a mighty magician at Arthur's court; that he could have blown out the sun like a candle, and was just going to do it when his mercy was purchased, and he then dissolved his enchantments, and was now recognized and honored as the man who had by his unaided might saved the globe from destruction and its peoples from extinction. Now if you consider that everybody believed that, and not only believed it, but never even dreamed of doubting it, you will easily understand that there was not a person in all Britain that would not have walked fifty miles to get a sight of me. Of course I was all the talk — all other subjects were dropped; even the king became suddenly a person of minor interest and notoriety. Within twenty-four hours the delegations began to arrive, and from that time onward for a fortnight they kept coming. The village was crowded, and all the countryside. I had to go out a dozen times a day and show myself to these reverent and awe-stricken multitudes.

It came to be a great burden, as to time and trouble, but of course it was at the same time compensatingly agreeable to be so celebrated and such a center of homage. It turned Brer Merlin green with envy and spite, which was a great satisfaction to me. But there was one thing I couldn't understand — nobody had asked for an autograph. I spoke to Clarence about it. By George! I had to explain to him what it was. Then he said nobody in the country could read or write but a few dozen priests. Land! think of that.

There was another thing that troubled me a little. Those multitudes presently began to agitate for another miracle. That was natural. To be able to carry back to their far homes the boast that they had seen the man who could command the sun, riding in the heavens, and be obeyed, would make them great in the eyes of their neighbors, and envied by them all; but to be able to also say they had seen him work a miracle themselves — why, people would come a distance to see *them* . The pressure got to be pretty strong. There was going to be an eclipse of the moon, and I knew the date and hour, but it was too far away. Two years. I would have given a good deal for license to hurry it up and use it now when there was a big market for it. It seemed a great pity to have it wasted so, and come lagging along at a time when a body wouldn't have any use for it, as like as not. If it had been booked for only a month away, I could have sold it short; but, as matters stood, I couldn't seem to cipher out any way to make it do me any good, so I gave up trying. Next, Clarence found that old Merlin was making himself busy on the sly among those people. He was spreading a report that I was a humbug, and that the reason I didn't accommodate the people with a miracle was because I couldn't. I saw that I must do something. I presently thought out a plan.

By my authority as executive I threw Merlin into prison — the same cell I had occupied myself. Then I gave public notice by herald and trumpet that I should be busy with affairs of state for a fortnight, but about the end of that time I would take a moment's leisure and blow up Merlin's stone tower by fires from heaven; in the meantime, whoso listened to evil reports about me, let him beware. Furthermore, I would perform but this one miracle at this time, and no more; if it failed to satisfy and any murmured, I would turn the murmurers into horses, and make them useful. Quiet ensued.

I took Clarence into my confidence, to a certain degree, and we went to work privately. I told him that this was a sort of miracle that required a trifle of preparation, and that it would be sudden death to ever talk about these preparations to anybody. That made his mouth safe enough. Clandestinely we made a few bushels of first-rate blasting powder, and I superintended my armorers while they constructed a lightning-rod and some wires. This old stone tower was very massive — and rather ruinous, too, for it was Roman, and four hundred years old. Yes, and handsome, after a rude fashion, and clothed with ivy from base to summit, as with a shirt of scale mail. It stood on a lonely eminence, in good view from the castle, and about half a mile away.

Working by night, we stowed the powder in the tower — dug stones out, on the inside, and buried the powder in the walls themselves, which were fifteen feet thick at the base. We put in a peck at a time, in a dozen places. We could have blown up the Tower of London with these charges. When the thirteenth night was come we put up our lightning-rod, bedded it in one of the batches of powder, and ran wires from it to the other batches. Everybody had shunned that locality from the day of my proclamation, but on the morning of the fourteenth I thought best to warn the people, through the heralds, to keep clear away — a quarter of a mile away. Then added, by command, that at some time during the twenty-four hours I would consummate the miracle, but would first give a brief notice; by flags on the castle towers if in the daytime, by torch-baskets in the same places if at night.

Thunder-showers had been tolerably frequent of late, and I was not much afraid of a failure; still, I shouldn't have cared for a delay of a day or two; I should have explained that I was busy with affairs of state yet, and the people must wait.

Of course, we had a blazing sunny day — almost the first one without a cloud for three weeks; things always happen so. I kept secluded, and watched the weather. Clarence dropped in from time to time and said the public excitement was growing and growing all the time, and the whole country filling up with human masses as far as one could see from the battlements. At last the wind sprang up and a cloud appeared — in the right quarter, too, and just at nightfall. For a little while I watched that distant cloud spread and blacken, then I judged it was time for me to appear. I ordered the torch-baskets to be lit, and Merlin liberated and sent to me. A quarter of an hour later I ascended the parapet and there found the king and the court assembled and gazing off in the darkness toward Merlin's Tower. Already the darkness was so heavy that one could not see far; these people and the old turrets, being partly in deep shadow and partly in the red glow from the great torch-baskets overhead, made a good deal of a picture.

Merlin arrived in a gloomy mood. I said:

"You wanted to burn me alive when I had not done you any harm, and latterly you have been trying to injure my professional reputation. Therefore I am going to call down fire and blow up your tower, but it is only fair to give you a chance; now if you think you can break my enchantments and ward off the fires, step to the bat, it's your innings."

"I can, fair sir, and I will. Doubt it not."

He drew an imaginary circle on the stones of the roof, and burnt a pinch of powder in it, which sent up a small cloud of aromatic smoke, whereat everybody fell back and began to cross themselves and get uncomfortable. Then he began to mutter and make passes in the air with his hands. He worked himself up slowly and gradually into a sort of frenzy, and got to thrashing around with his arms like the sails of a windmill. By this time the storm had about reached us; the gusts of wind were flaring the torches and making the shadows swash about, the first heavy drops of rain were falling, the world abroad was black as pitch, the lightning began to wink fitfully. Of course, my rod would be loading itself now. In fact, things were imminent. So I said:

"You have had time enough. I have given you every advantage, and not interfered. It is plain your magic is weak. It is only fair that I begin now."

I made about three passes in the air, and then there was an awful crash and that old tower leaped into the sky in chunks, along with a vast volcanic fountain of fire that turned night to noonday, and showed a thousand acres of human beings groveling on the ground in a general collapse of consternation. Well, it rained mortar and masonry the rest of the week. This was the report; but probably the facts would have modified it.

It was an effective miracle. The great bothersome temporary population vanished. There were a good many thousand tracks in the mud the next morning, but they were all outward bound. If I had advertised another miracle I couldn't have raised an audience with a sheriff.

Merlin's stock was flat. The king wanted to stop his wages; he even wanted to banish him, but I interfered. I said he would be useful to work the weather, and attend to small matters like that, and I would give him a lift now and then when his poor little parlor-magic soured on him. There wasn't a rag of his tower left, but I had the government rebuild it for him, and advised him to take boarders; but he was too high-toned for that. And as for being grateful, he never even said thank you. He was a rather hard lot, take him how you might; but then you couldn't fairly expect a man to be sweet that had been set back so.

Chapter VIII. The Boss

To be vested with enormous authority is a fine thing; but to have the onlooking world consent to it is a finer. The tower episode solidified my power, and made it impregnable. If any were perchance disposed to be jealous and critical before that, they experienced a change of heart, now. There was not any one in the kingdom who would have considered it good judgment to meddle with my matters.

I was fast getting adjusted to my situation and circumstances. For a time, I used to wake up, mornings, and smile at my "dream," and listen for the Colt's factory whistle; but that sort of thing played itself out, gradually, and at last I was fully able to realize that I was actually living in the sixth century, and in Arthur's court, not a lunatic asylum. After that, I was just as much at home in that century as I could have been in any other; and as for preference, I wouldn't have traded it for the twentieth. Look at the opportunities here for a man of knowledge, brains, pluck, and enterprise to sail in and grow up with the country. The grandest field that ever was; and all my own; not a competitor; not a man who wasn't a baby to me in acquirements and capacities; whereas, what would I amount to in the twentieth century? I should be foreman of a factory, that is about all; and could drag a seine down street any day and catch a hundred better men than myself.

What a jump I had made! I couldn't keep from thinking about it, and contemplating it, just as one does who has struck oil. There was nothing back of me that could approach it, unless it might be Joseph's case; and Joseph's only approached it, it didn't equal it, quite. For it stands to reason that as Joseph's splendid financial ingenuities advantaged nobody but the king, the general public must have regarded him with a good deal of disfavor, whereas I had done my entire public a kindness in sparing the sun, and was popular by reason of it.

I was no shadow of a king; I was the substance; the king himself was the shadow. My power was colossal; and it was not a mere name, as such things have generally been, it was the genuine article. I stood here, at the very spring and source of the second great period of the world's history; and could see the trickling stream of that history gather and deepen and broaden, and roll its mighty tides down the far centuries; and I could note the upspringing of adventurers like myself in the shelter of its long array of thrones: De Montforts, Gavestons, Mortimers, Villierses; the war-making, campaign-directing wantons of France, and Charles the Second's scepter-wielding drabs; but nowhere in the procession was my full-sized fellow visible. I was a Unique; and glad to know that that fact could not be dislodged or challenged for thirteen centuries and a half, for sure. Yes, in power I was equal to the king. At the same time there was another power that was a trifle stronger than both of us put together. That was the Church. I do not wish to disguise that fact. I couldn't, if I wanted to. But never mind about that, now; it will show up, in its proper place, later on. It didn't cause me any trouble in the beginning — at least any of consequence.

Well, it was a curious country, and full of interest. And the people! They were the quaintest and simplest and trustingest race; why, they were nothing but rabbits. It was pitiful for a person born in a wholesome free atmosphere to listen to their humble and hearty outpourings of loyalty toward their king and Church and nobility; as if they had any more occasion to love and honor king and Church and noble than a slave has to love and honor the lash, or a dog has to love and honor the stranger that kicks him! Why, dear me, *any* kind of royalty, howsoever modified, *any* kind of aristocracy, howsoever pruned, is rightly an insult; but if you are born and brought up under that sort of arrangement you probably never find it out for yourself, and don't believe it when somebody else tells you. It is enough to make a body ashamed of his race to think of the sort of froth that has always occupied its thrones without shadow of right or reason, and the seventh-rate people that have always figured as its aristocracies — a company of monarchs and nobles who, as a rule, would have achieved only poverty and obscurity if left, like their betters, to their own exertions.

The most of King Arthur's British nation were slaves, pure and simple, and bore that name, and wore the iron collar on their necks; and the rest were slaves in fact, but without the name; they imagined themselves men and freemen, and called themselves so. The truth was, the nation as a body was in the world for one object, and one only: to grovel before king and Church and noble; to slave for them, sweat blood for them, starve that they might be fed, work that they might play, drink misery to the dregs that they might be happy, go naked that they might wear silks and jewels, pay taxes that they might be spared from paying them, be familiar all their lives with the degrading language and postures of adulation that they might walk in pride and think themselves the gods of this world. And for all this, the thanks they got were cuffs and contempt; and so poor-spirited were they that they took even this sort of attention as an honor.

Inherited ideas are a curious thing, and interesting to observe and examine. I had mine, the king and his people had theirs. In both cases they flowed in ruts worn deep by time and habit, and the man who should have proposed to divert them by reason and argument would have had a long contract on his hands. For instance, those people had inherited the idea that all men without title and a long pedigree, whether they had great natural gifts and acquirements or hadn't, were creatures of no more consideration than so many animals, bugs, insects; whereas I had inherited the idea that human daws who can consent to masquerade in the peacock-shams of inherited dignities and unearned titles, are of no good but to be laughed at. The way I was looked upon was odd, but it was natural. You know how the keeper and the public regard the elephant in the menagerie: well, that is the idea. They are full of admiration of his vast bulk and his prodigious strength; they speak with pride of the fact that he can do a hundred marvels which are far and away beyond their own powers; and they speak with the same pride of the fact that in his wrath he is able to drive a thousand men before him. But does that make him one of *them* ? No; the raggedest tramp in the pit would smile at the idea. He couldn't comprehend it; couldn't take it in; couldn't in any remote way conceive of it. Well, to the king, the nobles, and all the nation, down to the very slaves and tramps, I was just that kind of an elephant, and nothing more. I was admired, also feared; but it was as an animal is admired and feared. The animal is not reverenced, neither was I; I was not even respected. I had no pedigree, no inherited title; so in the king's and nobles' eyes I was mere dirt; the people regarded me with wonder and awe, but there was no reverence mixed with it; through the force of inherited ideas they were not able to conceive of anything being entitled to that except pedigree and lordship. There you see the hand of that awful power, the Roman Catholic Church. In two or three little centuries it had converted a nation of men to a nation of worms. Before the day of the Church's supremacy in the world, men were men, and held their heads up, and had a man's pride and spirit and independence; and what of greatness and position a person got, he got mainly by achievement, not by birth. But then the Church came to the front, with an axe to grind; and she was wise, subtle, and knew more than one way to skin a cat — or a nation; she invented "divine right of kings," and propped it all around, brick by brick, with the Beatitudes — wrenching them from their good purpose to make them fortify an evil one; she preached (to the commoner) humility, obedience to superiors, the beauty of self-sacrifice; she preached (to the commoner) meekness under insult; preached (still to the commoner, always to the commoner) patience, meanness of spirit, non-resistance under oppression; and she introduced heritable ranks and aristocracies, and taught all the Christian populations of the earth to bow down to them and worship them.

Even down to my birth-century that poison was still in the blood of Christendom, and the best of English commoners was still content to see his inferiors impudently continuing to hold a number of positions, such as lordships and the throne, to which the grotesque laws of his country did not allow him to aspire; in fact, he was not merely contented with this strange condition of things, he was even able to persuade himself that he was proud of it. It seems to show that there isn't anything you can't stand, if you are only born and bred to it. Of course that taint, that reverence for rank and title, had been in our American blood, too — I know that; but when I left America it had disappeared — at least to all intents and purposes. The remnant of it was restricted to the dudes and dudesses. When a disease has worked its way down to that level, it may fairly be said to be out of the system.

But to return to my anomalous position in King Arthur's kingdom. Here I was, a giant among pigmies, a man among children, a master intelligence among intellectual moles: by all rational measurement the one and only actually great man in that whole British world; and yet there and then, just as in the remote England of my birth-time, the sheep-witted earl who could claim long descent from a king's leman, acquired at secondhand from the slums of London, was a better man than I was. Such a personage was fawned upon in Arthur's realm and reverently looked up to by everybody, even though his dispositions were as mean as his intelligence, and his morals as base as his lineage. There were times when *he* could sit down in the king's presence, but I couldn't. I could have got a title easily enough, and that would have raised me a large step in everybody's eyes; even in the king's, the giver of it. But I didn't ask for it; and I declined it when it was offered. I couldn't have enjoyed such a thing with my notions; and it wouldn't have been fair, anyway, because as far back as I could go, our tribe had always been short of the bar sinister. I couldn't have felt really and satisfactorily fine and proud and set-up over any title except one that should come from the nation itself, the only legitimate source; and such an one I hoped to win; and in the course of years of honest and honorable endeavor, I did win it and did wear it with a high and clean pride. This title fell casually from the lips of a blacksmith, one day, in a village, was caught up as a happy thought and tossed from mouth to mouth with a laugh and an affirmative vote; in ten days it had swept the kingdom, and was become as familiar as the king's name. I was never known by any other designation afterward, whether in the nation's talk or in grave debate upon matters of state at the council-board of the sovereign. This title, translated into modern speech, would be THE BOSS. Elected by the nation. That suited me. And it was a pretty high title. There were very few THE'S, and I was one of them. If you spoke of the duke, or the earl, or the bishop, how could anybody tell which one you meant? But if you spoke of The King or The Queen or The Boss, it was different.

Well, I liked the king, and as king I respected him — respected the office; at least respected it as much as I was capable of respecting any unearned supremacy; but as MEN I looked down upon him and his nobles — privately. And he and they liked me, and respected my office; but as an animal, without birth or sham title, they looked down upon me — and were not particularly private about it, either. I didn't charge for my opinion about them, and they didn't charge for their opinion about me: the account was square, the books balanced, everybody was satisfied.

Chapter IX. The Tournament

They were always having grand tournaments there at Camelot; and very stirring and picturesque and ridiculous human bullfights they were, too, but just a little wearisome to the practical mind. However, I was generally on hand — for two reasons: a man must not hold himself aloof from the things which his friends and his community have at heart if he would be liked — especially as a statesman; and both as business man and statesman I wanted to study the tournament and see if I couldn't invent an improvement on it. That reminds me to remark, in passing, that the very first official thing I did, in my administration — and it was on the very first day of it, too — was to start a patent office; for I knew that a country without a patent office and good patent laws was just a crab, and couldn't travel any way but sideways or backways.

Things ran along, a tournament nearly every week; and now and then the boys used to want me to take a hand — I mean Sir Launcelot and the rest — but I said I would by and by; no hurry yet, and too much government machinery to oil up and set to rights and start a-going.

We had one tournament which was continued from day to day during more than a week, and as many as five hundred knights took part in it, from first to last. They were weeks gathering. They came on horseback from everywhere; from the very ends of the country, and even from beyond the sea; and many brought ladies, and all brought squires and troops of servants. It was a most gaudy and gorgeous crowd, as to costumery, and very characteristic of the country and the time, in the way of high animal spirits, innocent indecencies of language, and happy-hearted indifference to morals. It was fight or look on, all day and every day; and sing, gamble, dance, carouse half the night every night. They had a most noble good time. You never saw such people. Those banks of beautiful ladies, shining in their barbaric splendors, would see a knight sprawl from his horse in the lists with a lanceshaft the thickness of your ankle clean through him and the blood spouting, and instead of fainting they would clap their hands and crowd each other for a better view; only sometimes one would dive into her handkerchief, and look ostentatiously brokenhearted, and then you could lay two to one that there was a scandal there somewhere and she was afraid the public hadn't found it out.

The noise at night would have been annoying to me ordinarily, but I didn't mind it in the present circumstances, because it kept me from hearing the quacks detaching legs and arms from the day's cripples. They ruined an uncommon good old cross-cut saw for me, and broke the saw-buck, too, but I let it pass. And as for my axe — well, I made up my mind that the next time I lent an axe to a surgeon I would pick my century.

I not only watched this tournament from day to day, but detailed an intelligent priest from my Department of Public Morals and Agriculture, and ordered him to report it; for it was my purpose by and by, when I should have gotten the people along far enough, to start a newspaper. The first thing you want in a new country, is a patent office; then work up your school system; and after that, out with your paper. A newspaper has its faults, and plenty of them, but no matter, it's hark from the tomb for a dead nation, and don't you forget it. You can't resurrect a dead nation without it; there isn't any way. So I wanted to sample things, and be finding out what sort of reporter-material I might be able to rake together out of the sixth century when I should come to need it.

Well, the priest did very well, considering. He got in all the details, and that is a good thing in a local item: you see, he had kept books for the undertaker-department of his church when he was younger, and there, you know, the money's in the details; the more details, the more swag: bearers, mutes, candles, prayers — everything counts; and if the bereaved don't buy prayers enough you mark up your candles with a forked pencil, and your bill shows up all right. And he had a good knack at getting in the complimentary thing here and there about a knight that was likely to advertise — no, I mean a knight that had influence; and he also had a neat gift of exaggeration, for in his time he had kept door for a pious hermit who lived in a sty and worked miracles.

Of course this novice's report lacked whoop and crash and lurid description, and therefore wanted the true ring; but its antique wording was quaint and sweet and simple, and full of the fragrances and flavors of the time, and these little merits made up in a measure for its more important lacks. Here is an extract from it:

Then Sir Brian de les Isles and Grummore Grummorsum, knights of the castle, encountered with Sir Aglovale and Sir Tor, and Sir Tor smote down Sir Grummore Grummorsum to the earth. Then came Sir Carados of the dolorous tower, and Sir Turquine, knights of the castle, and there encountered with them Sir Percivale de Galis and Sir Lamorak de Galis, that were two brethren, and there encountered Sir Percivale with Sir Carados, and either brake their spears unto their hands, and then Sir Turquine with Sir Lamorak, and either of them smote down other, horse and all, to the earth, and either parties rescued other and horsed them again. And Sir Arnold, and Sir Gauter, knights of the castle, encountered with Sir Brandiles and Sir Kay, and these four knights encountered mightily, and brake their spears to their hands. Then came Sir Pertolope from the castle, and there encountered with him Sir Lionel, and there Sir Pertolope the green knight smote down Sir Lionel, brother to Sir Launcelot. All this was marked by noble heralds, who bare him best, and their names. Then Sir Bleobaris brake his spear upon Sir Gareth, but of that stroke Sir Bleobaris fell to the earth. When Sir Galihodin saw that, he bad Sir Gareth keep him, and Sir Gareth smote him to the earth. Then Sir Galihud gat a spear to avenge his brother, and in the same wise Sir Gareth served him, and Sir Dinadan and his brother La Cote Male Taile, and Sir Sagramore le Disirous, and Sir Dodinas le Savage; all these he bare down with one spear. When King Aswisance of Ireland saw Sir Gareth fare so he marvelled what he might be, that one time seemed green, and another time, at his again coming, he seemed blue. And thus at every course that he rode to and fro he changed his color, so that there might neither king nor knight have ready cognizance of him. Then Sir Agwisance the King of Ireland encountered with Sir Gareth, and there Sir Gareth smote him from his horse, saddle and all. And then came King Carados of Scotland, and Sir Gareth smote him down horse and man. And in the same wise he served King Uriens of the land of Gore. And then there came in Sir Bagdemagus, and Sir Gareth smote him down horse and man to the earth. And Bagdemagus's son Meliganus brake a spear upon Sir Gareth mightily and knightly. And then Sir Galahault the noble prince cried on high, Knight with the many colors, well hast thou justed; now make thee ready that I may just with thee. Sir Gareth heard him, and he gat a great spear, and so they encountered together, and there the prince brake his spear; but Sir Gareth smote him upon the left side of the helm, that he reeled here and there, and he had fallen down had not his men recovered him. Truly, said King Arthur, that knight with the many colors is a good knight. Wherefore the king called unto him Sir Launcelot, and prayed him to encounter with that knight. Sir, said Launcelot, I may as well find in my heart for to forbear him at this time, for he hath had travail enough this day, and when a good knight doth so well upon some day, it is no good knight's part to let him of his worship, and, namely, when he seeth a knight hath done so great labour; for peradventure, said Sir Launcelot, his quarrel is here this day, and peradventure he is best beloved with this lady of all that be here, for I see well he paineth himself and enforceth him to do great deeds, and therefore, said Sir Launcelot, as for me, this day he shall have the honour; though it lay in my power to put him from it, I would not.

There was an unpleasant little episode that day, which for reasons of state I struck out of my priest's report. You will have noticed that Garry was doing some great fighting in the engagement. When I say Garry I mean Sir Gareth. Garry was my private pet name for him; it suggests that I had a deep affection for him, and that was the case. But it was a private pet name only, and never spoken aloud to any one, much less to him; being a noble, he would not have endured a familiarity like that from me. Well, to proceed: I sat in the private box set apart for me as the king's minister. While Sir Dinadan was waiting for his turn to enter the lists, he came in there and sat down and began to talk; for he was always making up to me, because I was a stranger and he liked to have a fresh market for his jokes, the most of them having reached that stage of wear where the teller has to do the laughing himself while the other person looks sick. I had always responded to his efforts as well as I could, and felt a very deep and real kindness for him, too, for the reason that if by malice of fate he knew the one particular anecdote which I had heard oftenest and had most hated and most loathed all my life, he had at least spared it me. It was one which I had heard attributed to every humorous person who had ever stood on American soil, from Columbus down to Artemus Ward. It was about a humorous lecturer who flooded an ignorant audience with the killingest jokes for an hour and never got a laugh; and then when he was leaving, some gray simpletons wrung him gratefully by the hand and said it had been the funniest thing they had ever heard, and "it was all they could do to keep from laughin' right out in meetin'." That anecdote never saw the day that it was worth the telling; and yet I had sat under the telling of it hundreds and thousands and millions and billions of times, and cried and cursed all the way through. Then who can hope to know what my feelings were, to hear this armor-plated ass start in on it again, in the murky twilight of tradition, before the dawn of history, while even Lactantius might be referred to as "the late Lactantius," and the Crusades wouldn't be born for five hundred years yet? Just as he finished, the call-boy came; so, haw-hawing like a demon, he went rattling and clanking out like a crate of loose castings, and I knew nothing more. It was some minutes before I came to, and then I opened my eyes just in time to see Sir Gareth fetch him an awful welt, and I unconsciously out with the prayer, "I hope to gracious he's killed!" But by ill-luck, before I had got half through with the words, Sir Gareth crashed into Sir Sagramor le Desirous and sent him thundering over his horse's crupper, and Sir Sagramor caught my remark and thought I meant it for *him* .

Well, whenever one of those people got a thing into his head, there was no getting it out again. I knew that, so I saved my breath, and offered no explanations. As soon as Sir Sagramor got well, he notified me that there was a little account to settle between us, and he named a day three or four years in the future; place of settlement, the lists where the offense had been given. I said I would be ready when he got back. You see, he was going for the Holy Grail. The boys all took a flier at the Holy Grail now and then. It was a several years' cruise. They always put in the long absence snooping around, in the most conscientious way, though none of them had any idea where the Holy Grail really was, and I don't think any of them actually expected to find it, or would have known what to do with it if he *had* run across it. You see, it was just the Northwest Passage of that day, as you may say; that was all. Every year expeditions went out holy grailing, and next year relief expeditions went out to hunt for *them* . There was worlds of reputation in it, but no money. Why, they actually wanted *me* to put in! Well, I should smile.

Chapter X. Beginnings of Civilization

The Round Table soon heard of the challenge, and of course it was a good deal discussed, for such things interested the boys. The king thought I ought now to set forth in quest of adventures, so that I might gain renown and be the more worthy to meet Sir Sagramor when the several years should have rolled away. I excused myself for the present; I said it would take me three or four years yet to get things well fixed up and going smoothly; then I should be ready; all the chances were that at the end of that time Sir Sagramor would still be out grailing, so no valuable time would be lost by the postponement; I should then have been in office six or seven years, and I believed my system and machinery would be so well developed that I could take a holiday without its working any harm.

I was pretty well satisfied with what I had already accomplished. In various quiet nooks and corners I had the beginnings of all sorts of industries under way — nuclei of future vast factories, the iron and steel missionaries of my future civilization. In these were gathered together the brightest young minds I could find, and I kept agents out raking the country for more, all the time. I was training a crowd of ignorant folk into experts — experts in every sort of handiwork and scientific calling. These nurseries of mine went smoothly and privately along undisturbed in their obscure country retreats, for nobody was allowed to come into their precincts without a special permit — for I was afraid of the Church.

I had started a teacher-factory and a lot of Sunday-schools the first thing; as a result, I now had an admirable system of graded schools in full blast in those places, and also a complete variety of Protestant congregations all in a prosperous and growing condition. Everybody could be any kind of a Christian he wanted to; there was perfect freedom in that matter. But I confined public religious teaching to the churches and the Sunday-schools, permitting nothing of it in my other educational buildings. I could have given my own sect the preference and made everybody a Presbyterian without any trouble, but that would have been to affront a law of human nature: spiritual wants and instincts are as various in the human family as are physical appetites, complexions, and features, and a man is only at his best, morally, when he is equipped with the religious garment whose color and shape and size most nicely accommodate themselves to the spiritual complexion, angularities, and stature of the individual who wears it; and, besides, I was afraid of a united Church; it makes a mighty power, the mightiest conceivable, and then when it by and by gets into selfish hands, as it is always bound to do, it means death to human liberty and paralysis to human thought.

All mines were royal property, and there were a good many of them. They had formerly been worked as savages always work mines — holes grubbed in the earth and the mineral brought up in sacks of hide by hand, at the rate of a ton a day; but I had begun to put the mining on a scientific basis as early as I could.

Yes, I had made pretty handsome progress when Sir Sagramor's challenge struck me.

Four years rolled by — and then! Well, you would never imagine it in the world. Unlimited power is the ideal thing when it is in safe hands. The despotism of heaven is the one absolutely perfect government. An earthly despotism would be the absolutely perfect earthly government, if the conditions were the same, namely, the despot the perfectest individual of the human race, and his lease of life perpetual. But as a perishable perfect man must die, and leave his despotism in the hands of an imperfect successor, an earthly despotism is not merely a bad form of government, it is the worst form that is possible.

My works showed what a despot could do with the resources of a kingdom at his command. Unsuspected by this dark land, I had the civilization of the nineteenth century booming under its very nose! It was fenced away from the public view, but there it was, a gigantic and unassailable fact — and to be heard from, yet, if I lived and had luck. There it was, as sure a fact and as substantial a fact as any serene volcano, standing innocent with its smokeless summit in the blue sky and giving no sign of the rising hell in its bowels. My schools and churches were children four years before; they were grownup now; my shops of that day were vast factories now; where I had a dozen trained men then, I had a thousand now; where I had one brilliant expert then, I had fifty now. I stood with my hand on the cock, so to speak, ready to turn it on and flood the midnight world with light at any moment. But I was not going to do the thing in that sudden way. It was not my policy. The people could not have stood it; and, moreover, I should have had the Established Roman Catholic Church on my back in a minute.

No, I had been going cautiously all the while. I had had confidential agents trickling through the country some time, whose office was to undermine knighthood by imperceptible degrees, and to gnaw a little at this and that and the other superstition, and so prepare the way gradually for a better order of things. I was turning on my light one-candle-power at a time, and meant to continue to do so.

I had scattered some branch schools secretly about the kingdom, and they were doing very well. I meant to work this racket more and more, as time wore on, if nothing occurred to frighten me. One of my deepest secrets was my West Point — my military academy. I kept that most jealously out of sight; and I did the same with my naval academy which I had established at a remote seaport. Both were prospering to my satisfaction.

Clarence was twenty-two now, and was my head executive, my right hand. He was a darling; he was equal to anything; there wasn't anything he couldn't turn his hand to. Of late I had been training him for journalism, for the time seemed about right for a start in the newspaper line; nothing big, but just a small weekly for experimental circulation in my civilization-nurseries. He took to it like a duck; there was an editor concealed in him, sure. Already he had doubled himself in one way; he talked sixth century and wrote nineteenth. His journalistic style was climbing, steadily; it was already up to the back settlement Alabama mark, and couldn't be told from the editorial output of that region either by matter or flavor.

We had another large departure on hand, too. This was a telegraph and a telephone; our first venture in this line. These wires were for private service only, as yet, and must be kept private until a riper day should come. We had a gang of men on the road, working mainly by night. They were stringing ground wires; we were afraid to put up poles, for they would attract too much inquiry. Ground wires were good enough, in both instances, for my wires were protected by an insulation of my own invention which was perfect. My men had orders to strike across country, avoiding roads, and establishing connection with any considerable towns whose lights betrayed their presence, and leaving experts in charge. Nobody could tell you how to find any place in the kingdom, for nobody ever went intentionally to any place, but only struck it by accident in his wanderings, and then generally left it without thinking to inquire what its name was. At one time and another we had sent out topographical expeditions to survey and map the kingdom, but the priests had always interfered and raised trouble. So we had given the thing up, for the present; it would be poor wisdom to antagonize the Church.

As for the general condition of the country, it was as it had been when I arrived in it, to all intents and purposes. I had made changes, but they were necessarily slight, and they were not noticeable. Thus far, I had not even meddled with taxation, outside of the taxes which provided the royal revenues. I had systematized those, and put the service on an effective and righteous basis. As a result, these revenues were already quadrupled, and yet the burden was so much more equably distributed than before, that all the kingdom felt a sense of relief, and the praises of my administration were hearty and general.

Personally, I struck an interruption, now, but I did not mind it, it could not have happened at a better time. Earlier it could have annoyed me, but now everything was in good hands and swimming right along. The king had reminded me several times, of late, that the postponement I had asked for, four years before, had about run out now. It was a hint that I ought to be starting out to seek adventures and get up a reputation of a size to make me worthy of the honor of breaking a lance with Sir Sagramor, who was still out grailing, but was being hunted for by various relief expeditions, and might be found any year, now. So you see I was expecting this interruption; it did not take me by surprise.

Chapter XI. The Yankee in Search of Adventures

There never was such a country for wandering liars; and they were of both sexes. Hardly a month went by without one of these tramps arriving; and generally loaded with a tale about some princess or other wanting help to get her out of some faraway castle where she was held in captivity by a lawless scoundrel, usually a giant. Now you would think that the first thing the king would do after listening to such a novelette from an entire stranger, would be to ask for credentials — yes, and a pointer or two as to locality of castle, best route to it, and so on. But nobody ever thought of so simple and commonsense a thing at that. No, everybody swallowed these people's lies whole, and never asked a question of any sort or about anything. Well, one day when I was not around, one of these people came along — it was a she one, this time — and told a tale of the usual pattern. Her mistress was a captive in a vast and gloomy castle, along with forty-four other young and beautiful girls, pretty much all of them princesses; they had been languishing in that cruel captivity for twenty-six years; the masters of the castle were three stupendous brothers, each with four arms and one eye — the eye in the center of the forehead, and as big as a fruit. Sort of fruit not mentioned; their usual slovenliness in statistics.

Would you believe it? The king and the whole Round Table were in raptures over this preposterous opportunity for adventure. Every knight of the Table jumped for the chance, and begged for it; but to their vexation and chagrin the king conferred it upon me, who had not asked for it at all.

By an effort, I contained my joy when Clarence brought me the news. But he — he could not contain his. His mouth gushed delight and gratitude in a steady discharge — delight in my good fortune, gratitude to the king for this splendid mark of his favor for me. He could keep neither his legs nor his body still, but pirouetted about the place in an airy ecstasy of happiness.

On my side, I could have cursed the kindness that conferred upon me this benefaction, but I kept my vexation under the surface for policy's sake, and did what I could to let on to be glad. Indeed, I *said* I was glad. And in a way it was true; I was as glad as a person is when he is scalped.

Well, one must make the best of things, and not waste time with useless fretting, but get down to business and see what can be done. In all lies there is wheat among the chaff; I must get at the wheat in this case: so I sent for the girl and she came. She was a comely enough creature, and soft and modest, but, if signs went for anything, she didn't know as much as a lady's watch. I said:

"My dear, have you been questioned as to particulars?"

She said she hadn't.

"Well, I didn't expect you had, but I thought I would ask, to make sure; it's the way I've been raised. Now you mustn't take it unkindly if I remind you that as we don't know you, we must go a little slow. You may be all right, of course, and we'll hope that you are; but to take it for granted isn't business. *You* understand that. I'm obliged to ask you a few questions; just answer up fair and square, and don't be afraid. Where do you live, when you are at home?"

"In the land of Moder, fair sir."

"Land of Moder. I don't remember hearing of it before. Parents living?"

"As to that, I know not if they be yet on live, sith it is many years that I have lain shut up in the castle."

"Your name, please?"

"I hight the Demoiselle Alisande la Carteloise, an it please you."

"Do you know anybody here who can identify you?"

"That were not likely, fair lord, I being come hither now for the first time."

"Have you brought any letters — any documents — any proofs that you are trustworthy and truthful?"

"Of a surety, no; and wherefore should I? Have I not a tongue, and cannot I say all that myself?"

"But *your* saying it, you know, and somebody else's saying it, is different."

"Different? How might that be? I fear me I do not understand."

"Don't *understand* ? Land of — why, you see — you see — why, great Scott, can't you understand a little thing like that? Can't you understand the difference between your — *why* do you look so innocent and idiotic!"

"I? In truth I know not, but an it were the will of God."

"Yes, yes, I reckon that's about the size of it. Don't mind my seeming excited; I'm not. Let us change the subject. Now as to this castle, with forty-five princesses in it, and three ogres at the head of it, tell me — where is this harem?"

"Harem?"

"The *castle* , you understand; where is the castle?"

"Oh, as to that, it is great, and strong, and well beseen, and lieth in a far country. Yes, it is many leagues."

"*How* many?"

"Ah, fair sir, it were woundily hard to tell, they are so many, and do so lap the one upon the other, and being made all in the same image and tincted with the same color, one may not know the one league from its fellow, nor how to count them except they be taken apart, and ye wit well it were God's work to do that, being not within man's capacity; for ye will note — "

"Hold on, hold on, never mind about the distance; *whereabouts* does the castle lie? What's the direction from here?"

"Ah, please you sir, it hath no direction from here; by reason that the road lieth not straight, but turneth evermore; wherefore the direction of its place abideth not, but is some time under the one sky and anon under another, whereso if ye be minded that it is in the east, and wend thitherward, ye shall observe that the way of the road doth yet again turn upon itself by the space of half a circle, and this marvel happing again and yet again and still again, it will grieve you that you had thought by vanities of the mind to thwart and bring to naught the will of Him that giveth not a castle a direction from a place except it pleaseth Him, and if it please Him not, will the rather that even all castles and all directions thereunto vanish out of the earth, leaving the places wherein they tarried desolate and vacant, so warning His creatures that where He will He will, and where He will not He — "

"Oh, that's all right, that's all right, give us a rest; never mind about the direction, *hang* the direction — I beg pardon, I beg a thousand pardons, I am not well to-day; pay no attention when I soliloquize, it is an old habit, an old, bad habit, and hard to get rid of when one's digestion is all disordered with eating food that was raised forever and ever before he was born; good land! a man can't keep his functions regular on spring chickens thirteen hundred years old. But come — never mind about that; let's — have you got such a thing as a map of that region about you? Now a good map — "

"Is it peradventure that manner of thing which of late the unbelievers have brought from over the great seas, which, being boiled in oil, and an onion and salt added thereto, doth — "

"What, a map? What are you talking about? Don't you know what a map is? There, there, never mind, don't explain, I hate explanations; they fog a thing up so that you can't tell anything about it. Run along, dear; good-day; show her the way, Clarence."

Oh, well, it was reasonably plain, now, why these donkeys didn't prospect these liars for details. It may be that this girl had a fact in her somewhere, but I don't believe you could have sluiced it out with a hydraulic; nor got it with the earlier forms of blasting, even; it was a case for dynamite. Why, she was a perfect ass; and yet the king and his knights had listened to her as if she had been a leaf out of the gospel. It kind of sizes up the whole party. And think of the simple ways of this court: this wandering wench hadn't any more trouble to get access to the king in his palace than she would have had to get into the poorhouse in my day and country. In fact, he was glad to see her, glad to hear her tale; with that adventure of hers to offer, she was as welcome as a corpse is to a coroner.

Just as I was ending-up these reflections, Clarence came back. I remarked upon the barren result of my efforts with the girl; hadn't got hold of a single point that could help me to find the castle. The youth looked a little surprised, or puzzled, or something, and intimated that he had been wondering to himself what I had wanted to ask the girl all those questions for.

"Why, great guns," I said, "don't I want to find the castle? And how else would I go about it?"

"La, sweet your worship, one may lightly answer that, I ween. She will go with thee. They always do. She will ride with thee."

"Ride with me? Nonsense!"

"But of a truth she will. She will ride with thee. Thou shalt see."

"What? She browse around the hills and scour the woods with me — alone — and I as good as engaged to be married? Why, it's scandalous. Think how it would look."

My, the dear face that rose before me! The boy was eager to know all about this tender matter. I swore him to secrecy and then whispered her name — "Puss Flanagan." He looked disappointed, and said he didn't remember the countess. How natural it was for the little courtier to give her a rank. He asked me where she lived.

"In East Har — " I came to myself and stopped, a little confused; then I said, "Never mind, now; I'll tell you some time."

And might he see her? Would I let him see her some day?

It was but a little thing to promise — thirteen hundred years or so — and he so eager; so I said Yes. But I sighed; I couldn't help it. And yet there was no sense in sighing, for she wasn't born yet. But that is the way we are made: we don't reason, where we feel; we just feel.

My expedition was all the talk that day and that night, and the boys were very good to me, and made much of me, and seemed to have forgotten their vexation and disappointment, and come to be as anxious for me to hive those ogres and set those ripe old virgins loose as if it were themselves that had the contract. Well, they *were* good children — but just children, that is all. And they gave me no end of points about how to scout for giants, and how to scoop them in; and they told me all sorts of charms against enchantments, and gave me salves and other rubbish to put on my wounds. But it never occurred to one of them to reflect that if I was such a wonderful necromancer as I was pretending to be, I ought not to need salves or instructions, or charms against enchantments, and, least of all, arms and armor, on a foray of any kind — even against fire-spouting dragons, and devils hot from perdition, let alone such poor adversaries as these I was after, these commonplace ogres of the back settlements.

I was to have an early breakfast, and start at dawn, for that was the usual way; but I had the demon's own time with my armor, and this delayed me a little. It is troublesome to get into, and there is so much detail. First you wrap a layer or two of blanket around your body, for a sort of cushion and to keep off the cold iron; then you put on your sleeves and shirt of chain mail — these are made of small steel links woven together, and they form a fabric so flexible that if you toss your shirt onto the floor, it slumps into a pile like a peck of wet fish-net; it is very heavy and is nearly the uncomfortablest material in the world for a night shirt, yet plenty used it for that — tax collectors, and reformers, and one-horse kings with a defective title, and those sorts of people; then you put on your shoes — flatboats roofed over with interleaving bands of steel — and screw your clumsy spurs into the heels. Next you buckle your greaves on your legs, and your cuisses on your thighs; then come your backplate and your breastplate, and you begin to feel crowded; then you hitch onto the breastplate the half-petticoat of broad overlapping bands of steel which hangs down in front but is scolloped out behind so you can sit down, and isn't any real improvement on an inverted coal scuttle, either for looks or for wear, or to wipe your hands on; next you belt on your sword; then you put your stovepipe joints onto your arms, your iron gauntlets onto your hands, your iron rattrap onto your head, with a rag of steel web hitched onto it to hang over the back of your neck — and there you are, snug as a candle in a candle-mould. This is no time to dance. Well, a man that is packed away like that is a nut that isn't worth the cracking, there is so little of the meat, when you get down to it, by comparison with the shell.

The boys helped me, or I never could have got in. Just as we finished, Sir Bedivere happened in, and I saw that as like as not I hadn't chosen the most convenient outfit for a long trip. How stately he looked; and tall and broad and grand. He had on his head a conical steel casque that only came down to his ears, and for visor had only a narrow steel bar that extended down to his upper lip and protected his nose; and all the rest of him, from neck to heel, was flexible chain mail, trousers and all. But pretty much all of him was hidden under his outside garment, which of course was of chain mail, as I said, and hung straight from his shoulders to his ankles; and from his middle to the bottom, both before and behind, was divided, so that he could ride and let the skirts hang down on each side. He was going grailing, and it was just the outfit for it, too. I would have given a good deal for that ulster, but it was too late now to be fooling around. The sun was just up, the king and the court were all on hand to see me off and wish me luck; so it wouldn't be etiquette for me to tarry. You don't get on your horse yourself; no, if you tried it you would get disappointed. They carry you out, just as they carry a sun-struck man to the drug store, and put you on, and help get you to rights, and fix your feet in the stirrups; and all the while you do feel so strange and stuffy and like somebody else — like somebody that has been married on a sudden, or struck by lightning, or something like that, and hasn't quite fetched around yet, and is sort of numb, and can't just get his bearings. Then they stood up the mast they called a spear, in its socket by my left foot, and I gripped it with my hand; lastly they hung my shield around my neck, and I was all complete and ready to up anchor and get to sea. Everybody was as good to me as they could be, and a maid of honor gave me the stirrup-cup her own self. There was nothing more to do now, but for that damsel to get up behind me on a pillion, which she did, and put an arm or so around me to hold on.

And so we started, and everybody gave us a goodbye and waved their handkerchiefs or helmets. And everybody we met, going down the hill and through the village was respectful to us, except some shabby little boys on the outskirts. They said:

"Oh, what a guy!" And hove clods at us.

In my experience boys are the same in all ages. They don't respect anything, they don't care for anything or anybody. They say "Go up, baldhead" to the prophet going his unoffending way in the gray of antiquity; they sass me in the holy gloom of the Middle Ages; and I had seen them act the same way in Buchanan's administration; I remember, because I was there and helped. The prophet had his bears and settled with his boys; and I wanted to get down and settle with mine, but it wouldn't answer, because I couldn't have got up again. I hate a country without a derrick.

Chapter XII. Slow Torture

Straight off, we were in the country. It was most lovely and pleasant in those sylvan solitudes in the early cool morning in the first freshness of autumn. From hilltops we saw fair green valleys lying spread out below, with streams winding through them, and island groves of trees here and there, and huge lonely oaks scattered about and casting black blots of shade; and beyond the valleys we saw the ranges of hills, blue with haze, stretching away in billowy perspective to the horizon, with at wide intervals a dim fleck of white or gray on a wave-summit, which we knew was a castle. We crossed broad natural lawns sparkling with dew, and we moved like spirits, the cushioned turf giving out no sound of footfall; we dreamed along through glades in a mist of green light that got its tint from the sun-drenched roof of leaves overhead, and by our feet the clearest and coldest of runlets went frisking and gossiping over its reefs and making a sort of whispering music, comfortable to hear; and at times we left the world behind and entered into the solemn great deeps and rich gloom of the forest, where furtive wild things whisked and scurried by and were gone before you could even get your eye on the place where the noise was; and where only the earliest birds were turning out and getting to business with a song here and a quarrel yonder and a mysterious far-off hammering and drumming for worms on a tree trunk away somewhere in the impenetrable remotenesses of the woods. And by and by out we would swing again into the glare.

About the third or fourth or fifth time that we swung out into the glare — it was along there somewhere, a couple of hours or so after sun-up — it wasn't as pleasant as it had been. It was beginning to get hot. This was quite noticeable. We had a very long pull, after that, without any shade. Now it is curious how progressively little frets grow and multiply after they once get a start. Things which I didn't mind at all, at first, I began to mind now — and more and more, too, all the time. The first ten or fifteen times I wanted my handkerchief I didn't seem to care; I got along, and said never mind, it isn't any matter, and dropped it out of my mind. But now it was different; I wanted it all the time; it was nag, nag, nag, right along, and no rest; I couldn't get it out of my mind; and so at last I lost my temper and said hang a man that would make a suit of armor without any pockets in it. You see I had my handkerchief in my helmet; and some other things; but it was that kind of a helmet that you can't take off by yourself. That hadn't occurred to me when I put it there; and in fact I didn't know it. I supposed it would be particularly convenient there. And so now, the thought of its being there, so handy and close by, and yet not get-at-able, made it all the worse and the harder to bear. Yes, the thing that you can't get is the thing that you want, mainly; every one has noticed that. Well, it took my mind off from everything else; took it clear off, and centered it in my helmet; and mile after mile, there it stayed, imagining the handkerchief, picturing the handkerchief; and it was bitter and aggravating to have the salt sweat keep trickling down into my eyes, and I couldn't get at it. It seems like a little thing, on paper, but it was not a little thing at all; it was the most real kind of misery. I would not say it if it was not so. I made up my mind that I would carry along a reticule next time, let it look how it might, and people say what they would. Of course these iron dudes of the Round Table would think it was scandalous, and maybe raise Sheol about it, but as for me, give me comfort first, and style afterwards. So we jogged along, and now and then we struck a stretch of dust, and it would tumble up in clouds and get into my nose and make me sneeze and cry; and of course I said things I oughtn't to have said, I don't deny that. I am not better than others.

We couldn't seem to meet anybody in this lonesome Britain, not even an ogre; and, in the mood I was in then, it was well for the ogre; that is, an ogre with a handkerchief. Most knights would have thought of nothing but getting his armor; but so I got his bandanna, he could keep his hardware, for all of me.

Meantime, it was getting hotter and hotter in there. You see, the sun was beating down and warming up the iron more and more all the time. Well, when you are hot, that way, every little thing irritates you. When I trotted, I rattled like a crate of dishes, and that annoyed me; and moreover I couldn't seem to stand that shield slatting and banging, now about my breast, now around my back; and if I dropped into a walk my joints creaked and screeched in that wearisome way that a wheelbarrow does, and as we didn't create any breeze at that gait, I was like to get fried in that stove; and besides, the quieter you went the heavier the iron settled down on you and the more and more tons you seemed to weigh every minute. And you had to be always changing hands, and passing your spear over to the other foot, it got so irksome for one hand to hold it long at a time.

Well, you know, when you perspire that way, in rivers, there comes a time when you — when you — well, when you itch. You are inside, your hands are outside; so there you are; nothing but iron between. It is not a light thing, let it sound as it may. First it is one place; then another; then some more; and it goes on spreading and spreading, and at last the territory is all occupied, and nobody can imagine what you feel like, nor how unpleasant it is. And when it had got to the worst, and it seemed to me that I could not stand anything more, a fly got in through the bars and settled on my nose, and the bars were stuck and wouldn't work, and I couldn't get the visor up; and I could only shake my head, which was baking hot by this time, and the fly — well, you know how a fly acts when he has got a certainty — he only minded the shaking enough to change from nose to lip, and lip to ear, and buzz and buzz all around in there, and keep on lighting and biting, in a way that a person, already so distressed as I was, simply could not stand. So I gave in, and got Alisande to unship the helmet and relieve me of it. Then she emptied the conveniences out of it and fetched it full of water, and I drank and then stood up, and she poured the rest down inside the armor. One cannot think how refreshing it was. She continued to fetch and pour until I was well soaked and thoroughly comfortable.

It was good to have a rest — and peace. But nothing is quite perfect in this life, at any time. I had made a pipe a while back, and also some pretty fair tobacco; not the real thing, but what some of the Indians use: the inside bark of the willow, dried. These comforts had been in the helmet, and now I had them again, but no matches.

Gradually, as the time wore along, one annoying fact was borne in upon my understanding — that we were weather-bound. An armed novice cannot mount his horse without help and plenty of it. Sandy was not enough; not enough for me, anyway. We had to wait until somebody should come along. Waiting, in silence, would have been agreeable enough, for I was full of matter for reflection, and wanted to give it a chance to work. I wanted to try and think out how it was that rational or even half-rational men could ever have learned to wear armor, considering its inconveniences; and how they had managed to keep up such a fashion for generations when it was plain that what I had suffered to-day they had had to suffer all the days of their lives. I wanted to think that out; and moreover I wanted to think out some way to reform this evil and persuade the people to let the foolish fashion die out; but thinking was out of the question in the circumstances. You couldn't think, where Sandy was.

She was a quite biddable creature and goodhearted, but she had a flow of talk that was as steady as a mill, and made your head sore like the drays and wagons in a city. If she had had a cork she would have been a comfort. But you can't cork that kind; they would die. Her clack was going all day, and you would think something would surely happen to her works, by and by; but no, they never got out of order; and she never had to slack up for words. She could grind, and pump, and churn, and buzz by the week, and never stop to oil up or blow out. And yet the result was just nothing but wind. She never had any ideas, any more than a fog has. She was a perfect blatherskite; I mean for jaw, jaw, jaw, talk, talk, talk, jabber, jabber, jabber; but just as good as she could be. I hadn't minded her mill that morning, on account of having that hornets' nest of other troubles; but more than once in the afternoon I had to say:

"Take a rest, child; the way you are using up all the domestic air, the kingdom will have to go to importing it by tomorrow, and it's a low enough treasury without that."

Chapter XIII. Freemen

Yes, it is strange how little a while at a time a person can be contented. Only a little while back, when I was riding and suffering, what a heaven this peace, this rest, this sweet serenity in this secluded shady nook by this purling stream would have seemed, where I could keep perfectly comfortable all the time by pouring a dipper of water into my armor now and then; yet already I was getting dissatisfied; partly because I could not light my pipe — for, although I had long ago started a match factory, I had forgotten to bring matches with me — and partly because we had nothing to eat. Here was another illustration of the childlike improvidence of this age and people. A man in armor always trusted to chance for his food on a journey, and would have been scandalized at the idea of hanging a basket of sandwiches on his spear. There was probably not a knight of all the Round Table combination who would not rather have died than been caught carrying such a thing as that on his flagstaff. And yet there could not be anything more sensible. It had been my intention to smuggle a couple of sandwiches into my helmet, but I was interrupted in the act, and had to make an excuse and lay them aside, and a dog got them.

Night approached, and with it a storm. The darkness came on fast. We must camp, of course. I found a good shelter for the demoiselle under a rock, and went off and found another for myself. But I was obliged to remain in my armor, because I could not get it off by myself and yet could not allow Alisande to help, because it would have seemed so like undressing before folk. It would not have amounted to that in reality, because I had clothes on underneath; but the prejudices of one's breeding are not gotten rid of just at a jump, and I knew that when it came to stripping off that bobtailed iron petticoat I should be embarrassed.

With the storm came a change of weather; and the stronger the wind blew, and the wilder the rain lashed around, the colder and colder it got. Pretty soon, various kinds of bugs and ants and worms and things began to flock in out of the wet and crawl down inside my armor to get warm; and while some of them behaved well enough, and snuggled up amongst my clothes and got quiet, the majority were of a restless, uncomfortable sort, and never stayed still, but went on prowling and hunting for they did not know what; especially the ants, which went tickling along in wearisome procession from one end of me to the other by the hour, and are a kind of creatures which I never wish to sleep with again. It would be my advice to persons situated in this way, to not roll or thrash around, because this excites the interest of all the different sorts of animals and makes every last one of them want to turn out and see what is going on, and this makes things worse than they were before, and of course makes you objurgate harder, too, if you can. Still, if one did not roll and thrash around he would die; so perhaps it is as well to do one way as the other; there is no real choice. Even after I was frozen solid I could still distinguish that tickling, just as a corpse does when he is taking electric treatment. I said I would never wear armor after this trip.

All those trying hours whilst I was frozen and yet was in a living fire, as you may say, on account of that swarm of crawlers, that same unanswerable question kept circling and circling through my tired head: How do people stand this miserable armor? How have they managed to stand it all these generations? How can they sleep at night for dreading the tortures of next day?

When the morning came at last, I was in a bad enough plight: seedy, drowsy, fagged, from want of sleep; weary from thrashing around, famished from long fasting; pining for a bath, and to get rid of the animals; and crippled with rheumatism. And how had it fared with the nobly born, the titled aristocrat, the Demoiselle Alisande la Carteloise? Why, she was as fresh as a squirrel; she had slept like the dead; and as for a bath, probably neither she nor any other noble in the land had ever had one, and so she was not missing it. Measured by modern standards, they were merely modified savages, those people. This noble lady showed no impatience to get to breakfast — and that smacks of the savage, too. On their journeys those Britons were used to long fasts, and knew how to bear them; and also how to freight up against probable fasts before starting, after the style of the Indian and the anaconda. As like as not, Sandy was loaded for a three-day stretch.

We were off before sunrise, Sandy riding and I limping along behind. In half an hour we came upon a group of ragged poor creatures who had assembled to mend the thing which was regarded as a road. They were as humble as animals to me; and when I proposed to breakfast with them, they were so flattered, so overwhelmed by this extraordinary condescension of mine that at first they were not able to believe that I was in earnest. My lady put up her scornful lip and withdrew to one side; she said in their hearing that she would as soon think of eating with the other cattle — a remark which embarrassed these poor devils merely because it referred to them, and not because it insulted or offended them, for it didn't. And yet they were not slaves, not chattels. By a sarcasm of law and phrase they were freemen. Seven-tenths of the free population of the country were of just their class and degree: small "independent" farmers, artisans, etc.; which is to say, they were the nation, the actual Nation; they were about all of it that was useful, or worth saving, or really respectworthy, and to subtract them would have been to subtract the Nation and leave behind some dregs, some refuse, in the shape of a king, nobility and gentry, idle, unproductive, acquainted mainly with the arts of wasting and destroying, and of no sort of use or value in any rationally constructed world.

And yet, by ingenious contrivance, this gilded minority, instead of being in the tail of the procession where it belonged, was marching head up and banners flying, at the other end of it; had elected itself to be the Nation, and these innumerable clams had permitted it so long that they had come at last to accept it as a truth; and not only that, but to believe it right and as it should be. The priests had told their fathers and themselves that this ironical state of things was ordained of God; and so, not reflecting upon how unlike God it would be to amuse himself with sarcasms, and especially such poor transparent ones as this, they had dropped the matter there and become respectfully quiet.

The talk of these meek people had a strange enough sound in a formerly American ear. They were freemen, but they could not leave the estates of their lord or their bishop without his permission; they could not prepare their own bread, but must have their corn ground and their bread baked at his mill and his bakery, and pay roundly for the same; they could not sell a piece of their own property without paying him a handsome percentage of the proceeds, nor buy a piece of somebody else's without remembering him in cash for the privilege; they had to harvest his grain for him gratis, and be ready to come at a moment's notice, leaving their own crop to destruction by the threatened storm; they had to let him plant fruit trees in their fields, and then keep their indignation to themselves when his heedless fruit-gatherers trampled the grain around the trees; they had to smother their anger when his hunting parties galloped through their fields laying waste the result of their patient toil; they were not allowed to keep doves themselves, and when the swarms from my lord's dovecote settled on their crops they must not lose their temper and kill a bird, for awful would the penalty be; when the harvest was at last gathered, then came the procession of robbers to levy their blackmail upon it: first the Church carted off its fat tenth, then the king's commissioner took his twentieth, then my lord's people made a mighty inroad upon the remainder; after which, the skinned freeman had liberty to bestow the remnant in his barn, in case it was worth the trouble; there were taxes, and taxes, and taxes, and more taxes, and taxes again, and yet other taxes — upon this free and independent pauper, but none upon his lord the baron or the bishop, none upon the wasteful nobility or the all-devouring Church; if the baron would sleep unvexed, the freeman must sit up all night after his day's work and whip the ponds to keep the frogs quiet; if the freeman's daughter — but no, that last infamy of monarchical government is unprintable; and finally, if the freeman, grown desperate with his tortures, found his life unendurable under such conditions, and sacrificed it and fled to death for mercy and refuge, the gentle Church condemned him to eternal fire, the gentle law buried him at midnight at the crossroads with a stake through his back, and his master the baron or the bishop confiscated all his property and turned his widow and his orphans out of doors.

And here were these freemen assembled in the early morning to work on their lord the bishop's road three days each — gratis; every head of a family, and every son of a family, three days each, gratis, and a day or so added for their servants. Why, it was like reading about France and the French, before the ever memorable and blessed Revolution, which swept a thousand years of such villany away in one swift tidal-wave of blood — one: a settlement of that hoary debt in the proportion of half a drop of blood for each hogshead of it that had been pressed by slow tortures out of that people in the weary stretch of ten centuries of wrong and shame and misery the like of which was not to be mated but in hell. There were two "Reigns of Terror," if we would but remember it and consider it; the one wrought murder in hot passion, the other in heartless cold blood; the one lasted mere months, the other had lasted a thousand years; the one inflicted death upon ten thousand persons, the other upon a hundred millions; but our shudders are all for the "horrors" of the minor Terror, the momentary Terror, so to speak; whereas, what is the horror of swift death by the axe, compared with lifelong death from hunger, cold, insult, cruelty, and heartbreak? What is swift death by lightning compared with death by slow fire at the stake? A city cemetery could contain the coffins filled by that brief Terror which we have all been so diligently taught to shiver at and mourn over; but all France could hardly contain the coffins filled by that older and real Terror — that unspeakably bitter and awful Terror which none of us has been taught to see in its vastness or pity as it deserves.

These poor ostensible freemen who were sharing their breakfast and their talk with me, were as full of humble reverence for their king and Church and nobility as their worst enemy could desire. There was something pitifully ludicrous about it. I asked them if they supposed a nation of people ever existed, who, with a free vote in every man's hand, would elect that a single family and its descendants should reign over it forever, whether gifted or boobies, to the exclusion of all other families — including the voter's; and would also elect that a certain hundred families should be raised to dizzy summits of rank, and clothed on with offensive transmissible glories and privileges to the exclusion of the rest of the nation's families — *including his own* .

They all looked unhit, and said they didn't know; that they had never thought about it before, and it hadn't ever occurred to them that a nation could be so situated that every man *could* have a say in the government. I said I had seen one — and that it would last until it had an Established Church. Again they were all unhit — at first. But presently one man looked up and asked me to state that proposition again; and state it slowly, so it could soak into his understanding. I did it; and after a little he had the idea, and he brought his fist down and said *he* didn't believe a nation where every man had a vote would voluntarily get down in the mud and dirt in any such way; and that to steal from a nation its will and preference must be a crime and the first of all crimes. I said to myself:

"This one's a man. If I were backed by enough of his sort, I would make a strike for the welfare of this country, and try to prove myself its loyalest citizen by making a wholesome change in its system of government."

You see my kind of loyalty was loyalty to one's country, not to its institutions or its office-holders. The country is the real thing, the substantial thing, the eternal thing; it is the thing to watch over, and care for, and be loyal to; institutions are extraneous, they are its mere clothing, and clothing can wear out, become ragged, cease to be comfortable, cease to protect the body from winter, disease, and death. To be loyal to rags, to shout for rags, to worship rags, to die for rags — that is a loyalty of unreason, it is pure animal; it belongs to monarchy, was invented by monarchy; let monarchy keep it. I was from Connecticut, whose Constitution declares "that all political power is inherent in the people, and all free governments are founded on their authority and instituted for their benefit; and that they have *at all times* an undeniable and indefeasible right to *alter their form of government* in such a manner as they may think expedient."

Under that gospel, the citizen who thinks he sees that the commonwealth's political clothes are worn out, and yet holds his peace and does not agitate for a new suit, is disloyal; he is a traitor. That he may be the only one who thinks he sees this decay, does not excuse him; it is his duty to agitate anyway, and it is the duty of the others to vote him down if they do not see the matter as he does.

And now here I was, in a country where a right to say how the country should be governed was restricted to six persons in each thousand of its population. For the nine hundred and ninety-four to express dissatisfaction with the regnant system and propose to change it, would have made the whole six shudder as one man, it would have been so disloyal, so dishonorable, such putrid black treason. So to speak, I was become a stockholder in a corporation where nine hundred and ninety-four of the members furnished all the money and did all the work, and the other six elected themselves a permanent board of direction and took all the dividends. It seemed to me that what the nine hundred and ninety-four dupes needed was a new deal. The thing that would have best suited the circus side of my nature would have been to resign the Boss-ship and get up an insurrection and turn it into a revolution; but I knew that the Jack Cade or the Wat Tyler who tries such a thing without first educating his materials up to revolution grade is almost absolutely certain to get left. I had never been accustomed to getting left, even if I do say it myself. Wherefore, the "deal" which had been for some time working into shape in my mind was of a quite different pattern from the Cade-Tyler sort.

So I did not talk blood and insurrection to that man there who sat munching black bread with that abused and mistaught herd of human sheep, but took him aside and talked matter of another sort to him. After I had finished, I got him to lend me a little ink from his veins; and with this and a sliver I wrote on a piece of bark —

Put him in the Man-factory —

and gave it to him, and said:

"Take it to the palace at Camelot and give it into the hands of Amyas le Poulet, whom I call Clarence, and he will understand."

"He is a priest, then," said the man, and some of the enthusiasm went out of his face.

"How — a priest? Didn't I tell you that no chattel of the Church, no bond-slave of pope or bishop can enter my Man-Factory? Didn't I tell you that *you* couldn't enter unless your religion, whatever it might be, was your own free property?"

"Marry, it is so, and for that I was glad; wherefore it liked me not, and bred in me a cold doubt, to hear of this priest being there."

"But he isn't a priest, I tell you."

The man looked far from satisfied. He said:

"He is not a priest, and yet can read?"

"He is not a priest and yet can read — yes, and write, too, for that matter. I taught him myself." The man's face cleared. "And it is the first thing that you yourself will be taught in that Factory — "

"I? I would give blood out of my heart to know that art. Why, I will be your slave, your — "

"No you won't, you won't be anybody's slave. Take your family and go along. Your lord the bishop will confiscate your small property, but no matter. Clarence will fix you all right."

Chapter XIV. "Defend Thee, Lord"

I paid three pennies for my breakfast, and a most extravagant price it was, too, seeing that one could have breakfasted a dozen persons for that money; but I was feeling good by this time, and I had always been a kind of spendthrift anyway; and then these people had wanted to give me the food for nothing, scant as their provision was, and so it was a grateful pleasure to emphasize my appreciation and sincere thankfulness with a good big financial lift where the money would do so much more good than it would in my helmet, where, these pennies being made of iron and not stinted in weight, my half-dollar's worth was a good deal of a burden to me. I spent money rather too freely in those days, it is true; but one reason for it was that I hadn't got the proportions of things entirely adjusted, even yet, after so long a sojourn in Britain — hadn't got along to where I was able to absolutely realize that a penny in Arthur's land and a couple of dollars in Connecticut were about one and the same thing: just twins, as you may say, in purchasing power. If my start from Camelot could have been delayed a very few days I could have paid these people in beautiful new coins from our own mint, and that would have pleased me; and them, too, not less. I had adopted the American values exclusively. In a week or two now, cents, nickels, dimes, quarters, and half-dollars, and also a trifle of gold, would be trickling in thin but steady streams all through the commercial veins of the kingdom, and I looked to see this new blood freshen up its life.

The farmers were bound to throw in something, to sort of offset my liberality, whether I would or no; so I let them give me a flint and steel; and as soon as they had comfortably bestowed Sandy and me on our horse, I lit my pipe. When the first blast of smoke shot out through the bars of my helmet, all those people broke for the woods, and Sandy went over backwards and struck the ground with a dull thud. They thought I was one of those fire-belching dragons they had heard so much about from knights and other professional liars. I had infinite trouble to persuade those people to venture back within explaining distance. Then I told them that this was only a bit of enchantment which would work harm to none but my enemies. And I promised, with my hand on my heart, that if all who felt no enmity toward me would come forward and pass before me they should see that only those who remained behind would be struck dead. The procession moved with a good deal of promptness. There were no casualties to report, for nobody had curiosity enough to remain behind to see what would happen.

I lost some time, now, for these big children, their fears gone, became so ravished with wonder over my awe-compelling fireworks that I had to stay there and smoke a couple of pipes out before they would let me go. Still the delay was not wholly unproductive, for it took all that time to get Sandy thoroughly wonted to the new thing, she being so close to it, you know. It plugged up her conversation mill, too, for a considerable while, and that was a gain. But above all other benefits accruing, I had learned something. I was ready for any giant or any ogre that might come along, now.

We tarried with a holy hermit, that night, and my opportunity came about the middle of the next afternoon. We were crossing a vast meadow by way of short-cut, and I was musing absently, hearing nothing, seeing nothing, when Sandy suddenly interrupted a remark which she had begun that morning, with the cry:

"Defend thee, lord! —peril of life is toward!"

And she slipped down from the horse and ran a little way and stood. I looked up and saw, far off in the shade of a tree, half a dozen armed knights and their squires; and straightway there was bustle among them and tightening of saddle-girths for the mount. My pipe was ready and would have been lit, if I had not been lost in thinking about how to banish oppression from this land and restore to all its people their stolen rights and manhood without disobliging anybody. I lit up at once, and by the time I had got a good head of reserved steam on, here they came. All together, too; none of those chivalrous magnanimities which one reads so much about — one courtly rascal at a time, and the rest standing by to see fair play. No, they came in a body, they came with a whirr and a rush, they came like a volley from a battery; came with heads low down, plumes streaming out behind, lances advanced at a level. It was a handsome sight, a beautiful sight — for a man up a tree. I laid my lance in rest and waited, with my heart beating, till the iron wave was just ready to break over me, then spouted a column of white smoke through the bars of my helmet. You should have seen the wave go to pieces and scatter! This was a finer sight than the other one.

But these people stopped, two or three hundred yards away, and this troubled me. My satisfaction collapsed, and fear came; I judged I was a lost man. But Sandy was radiant; and was going to be eloquent — but I stopped her, and told her my magic had miscarried, somehow or other, and she must mount, with all despatch, and we must ride for life. No, she wouldn't. She said that my enchantment had disabled those knights; they were not riding on, because they couldn't; wait, they would drop out of their saddles presently, and we would get their horses and harness. I could not deceive such trusting simplicity, so I said it was a mistake; that when my fireworks killed at all, they killed instantly; no, the men would not die, there was something wrong about my apparatus, I couldn't tell what; but we must hurry and get away, for those people would attack us again, in a minute. Sandy laughed, and said:

"Lack-a-day, sir, they be not of that breed! Sir Launcelot will give battle to dragons, and will abide by them, and will assail them again, and yet again, and still again, until he do conquer and destroy them; and so likewise will Sir Pellinore and Sir Aglovale and Sir Carados, and mayhap others, but there be none else that will venture it, let the idle say what the idle will. And, la, as to yonder base rufflers, think ye they have not their fill, but yet desire more?"

"Well, then, what are they waiting for? Why don't they leave? Nobody's hindering. Good land, I'm willing to let bygones be bygones, I'm sure."

"Leave, is it? Oh, give thyself easement as to that. They dream not of it, no, not they. They wait to yield them."

"Come — really, is that 'sooth' — as you people say? If they want to, why don't they?"

"It would like them much; but an ye wot how dragons are esteemed, ye would not hold them blamable. They fear to come."

"Well, then, suppose I go to them instead, and — "

"Ah, wit ye well they would not abide your coming. I will go."

And she did. She was a handy person to have along on a raid. I would have considered this a doubtful errand, myself. I presently saw the knights riding away, and Sandy coming back. That was a relief. I judged she had somehow failed to get the first innings — I mean in the conversation; otherwise the interview wouldn't have been so short. But it turned out that she had managed the business well; in fact, admirably. She said that when she told those people I was The Boss, it hit them where they lived: "smote them sore with fear and dread" was her word; and then they were ready to put up with anything she might require. So she swore them to appear at Arthur's court within two days and yield them, with horse and harness, and be my knights henceforth, and subject to my command. How much better she managed that thing than I should have done it myself! She was a daisy.

Chapter XV. Sandy's Tale

"And so I'm proprietor of some knights," said I, as we rode off. "Who would ever have supposed that I should live to list up assets of that sort. I shan't know what to do with them; unless I raffle them off. How many of them are there, Sandy?"

"Seven, please you, sir, and their squires."

"It is a good haul. Who are they? Where do they hang out?"

"Where do they hang out?"

"Yes, where do they live?"

"Ah, I understood thee not. That will I tell eftsoons." Then she said musingly, and softly, turning the words daintily over her tongue: "Hang they out — hang they out — where hang — where do they hang out; eh, right so; where do they hang out. Of a truth the phrase hath a fair and winsome grace, and is prettily worded withal. I will repeat it anon and anon in mine idlesse, whereby I may peradventure learn it. Where do they hang out. Even so! already it falleth trippingly from my tongue, and forasmuch as — "

"Don't forget the cowboys, Sandy."

"Cowboys?"

"Yes; the knights, you know: You were going to tell me about them. A while back, you remember. Figuratively speaking, game's called."

"Game — "

"Yes, yes, yes! Go to the bat. I mean, get to work on your statistics, and don't burn so much kindling getting your fire started. Tell me about the knights."

"I will well, and lightly will begin. So they two departed and rode into a great forest. And — "

"Great Scott!"

You see, I recognized my mistake at once. I had set her works a-going; it was my own fault; she would be thirty days getting down to those facts. And she generally began without a preface and finished without a result. If you interrupted her she would either go right along without noticing, or answer with a couple of words, and go back and say the sentence over again. So, interruptions only did harm; and yet I had to interrupt, and interrupt pretty frequently, too, in order to save my life; a person would die if he let her monotony drip on him right along all day.

"Great Scott!" I said in my distress. She went right back and began over again:

"So they two departed and rode into a great forest. And — "

"*Which* two?"

"Sir Gawaine and Sir Uwaine. And so they came to an abbey of monks, and there were well lodged. So on the morn they heard their masses in the abbey, and so they rode forth till they came to a great forest; then was Sir Gawaine ware in a valley by a turret, of twelve fair damsels, and two knights armed on great horses, and the damsels went to and fro by a tree. And then was Sir Gawaine ware how there hung a white shield on that tree, and ever as the damsels came by it they spit upon it, and some threw mire upon the shield — "

"Now, if I hadn't seen the like myself in this country, Sandy, I wouldn't believe it. But I've seen it, and I can just see those creatures now, parading before that shield and acting like that. The women here do certainly act like all possessed. Yes, and I mean your best, too, society's very choicest brands. The humblest hello-girl along ten thousand miles of wire could teach gentleness, patience, modesty, manners, to the highest duchess in Arthur's land."

"Hello-girl?"

"Yes, but don't you ask me to explain; it's a new kind of a girl; they don't have them here; one often speaks sharply to them when they are not the least in fault, and he can't get over feeling sorry for it and ashamed of himself in thirteen hundred years, it's such shabby mean conduct and so unprovoked; the fact is, no gentleman ever does it — though I — well, I myself, if I've got to confess — "

"Peradventure she — "

"Never mind her; never mind her; I tell you I couldn't ever explain her so you would understand."

"Even so be it, sith ye are so minded. Then Sir Gawaine and Sir Uwaine went and saluted them, and asked them why they did that despite to the shield. Sirs, said the damsels, we shall tell you. There is a knight in this country that owneth this white shield, and he is a passing good man of his hands, but he hateth all ladies and gentlewomen, and therefore we do all this despite to the shield. I will say you, said Sir Gawaine, it beseemeth evil a good knight to despise all ladies and gentlewomen, and peradventure though he hate you he hath some cause, and peradventure he loveth in some other places ladies and gentlewomen, and to be loved again, and he such a man of prowess as ye speak of — "

"Man of prowess — yes, that is the man to please them, Sandy. Man of brains — that is a thing they never think of. Tom Sayers — John Heenan — John L. Sullivan — pity but you could be here. You would have your legs under the Round Table and a 'Sir' in front of your names within the twenty-four hours; and you could bring about a new distribution of the married princesses and duchesses of the Court in another twenty-four. The fact is, it is just a sort of polished-up court of Comanches, and there isn't a squaw in it who doesn't stand ready at the dropping of a hat to desert to the buck with the biggest string of scalps at his belt."

" — and he be such a man of prowess as ye speak of, said Sir Gawaine. Now, what is his name? Sir, said they, his name is Marhaus the king's son of Ireland."

"Son of the king of Ireland, you mean; the other form doesn't mean anything. And look out and hold on tight, now, we must jump this gully.... There, we are all right now. This horse belongs in the circus; he is born before his time."

"I know him well, said Sir Uwaine, he is a passing good knight as any is on live."

"*On live*. If you've got a fault in the world, Sandy, it is that you are a shade too archaic. But it isn't any matter."

" — for I saw him once proved at a justs where many knights were gathered, and that time there might no man withstand him. Ah, said Sir Gawaine, damsels, methinketh ye are to blame, for it is to suppose he that hung that shield there will not be long therefrom, and then may those knights match him on horseback, and that is more your worship than thus; for I will abide no longer to see a knight's shield dishonored. And therewith Sir Uwaine and Sir Gawaine departed a little from them, and then were they ware where Sir Marhaus came riding on a great horse straight toward them. And when the twelve damsels saw Sir Marhaus they fled into the turret as they were wild, so that some of them fell by the way. Then the one of the knights of the tower dressed his shield, and said on high, Sir Marhaus defend thee. And so they ran together that the knight brake his spear on Marhaus, and Sir Marhaus smote him so hard that he brake his neck and the horse's back — "

"Well, that is just the trouble about this state of things, it ruins so many horses."

"That saw the other knight of the turret, and dressed him toward Marhaus, and they went so eagerly together, that the knight of the turret was soon smitten down, horse and man, stark dead — "

"*Another* horse gone; I tell you it is a custom that ought to be broken up. I don't see how people with any feeling can applaud and support it."

. . . .

"So these two knights came together with great random — "

I saw that I had been asleep and missed a chapter, but I didn't say anything. I judged that the Irish knight was in trouble with the visitors by this time, and this turned out to be the case.

" — that Sir Uwaine smote Sir Marhaus that his spear brast in pieces on the shield, and Sir Marhaus smote him so sore that horse and man he bare to the earth, and hurt Sir Uwaine on the left side — "

"The truth is, Alisande, these archaics are a little *too* simple; the vocabulary is too limited, and so, by consequence, descriptions suffer in the matter of variety; they run too much to level Saharas of fact, and not enough to picturesque detail; this throws about them a certain air of the monotonous; in fact the fights are all alike: a couple of people come together with great random — random is a good word, and so is exegesis, for that matter, and so is holocaust, and defalcation, and usufruct and a hundred others, but land! a body ought to discriminate — they come together with great random, and a spear is brast, and one party brake his shield and the other one goes down, horse and man, over his horse-tail and brake his neck, and then the next candidate comes randoming in, and brast *his* spear, and the other man brast his shield, and down *he* goes, horse and man, over his horse-tail, and brake *his* neck, and then there's another elected, and another and another and still another, till the material is all used up; and when you come to figure up results, you can't tell one fight from another, nor who whipped; and as a *picture* , of living, raging, roaring battle, sho! why, it's pale and noiseless — just ghosts scuffling in a fog. Dear me, what would this barren vocabulary get out of the mightiest spectacle? — the burning of Rome in Nero's time, for instance? Why, it would merely say, 'Town burned down; no insurance; boy brast a window, fireman brake his neck!' Why, *that* ain't a picture!"

It was a good deal of a lecture, I thought, but it didn't disturb Sandy, didn't turn a feather; her steam soared steadily up again, the minute I took off the lid:

"Then Sir Marhaus turned his horse and rode toward Gawaine with his spear. And when Sir Gawaine saw that, he dressed his shield, and they aventred their spears, and they came together with all the might of their horses, that either knight smote other so hard in the midst of their shields, but Sir Gawaine's spear brake — "

"I knew it would."

— "but Sir Marhaus's spear held; and therewith Sir Gawaine and his horse rushed down to the earth — "

"Just so — and brake his back."

— "and lightly Sir Gawaine rose upon his feet and pulled out his sword, and dressed him toward Sir Marhaus on foot, and therewith either came unto other eagerly, and smote together with their swords, that their shields flew in cantels, and they bruised their helms and their hauberks, and wounded either other. But Sir Gawaine, fro it passed nine of the clock, waxed by the space of three hours ever stronger and stronger and thrice his might was increased. All this espied Sir Marhaus, and had great wonder how his might increased, and so they wounded other passing sore; and then when it was come noon — "

The pelting singsong of it carried me forward to scenes and sounds of my boyhood days:

"N-e-e-ew Haven! ten minutes for refreshments — knductr'll strike the gong-bell two minutes before train leaves — passengers for the Shore-line please take seats in the rear k'yar, this k'yar don't go no furder — *ahh* -pls, *aw* -rnjz, b'*nan* ners, *s-a-n-d* 'ches, p — op-corn!"

— "and waxed past noon and drew toward evensong. Sir Gawaine's strength feebled and waxed passing faint, that unnethes he might dure any longer, and Sir Marhaus was then bigger and bigger — "

"Which strained his armor, of course; and yet little would one of these people mind a small thing like that."

— "and so, Sir Knight, said Sir Marhaus, I have well felt that ye are a passing good knight, and a marvelous man of might as ever I felt any, while it lasteth, and our quarrels are not great, and therefore it were a pity to do you hurt, for I feel you are passing feeble. Ah, said Sir Gawaine, gentle knight, ye say the word that I should say. And therewith they took off their helms and either kissed other, and there they swore together either to love other as brethren — "

But I lost the thread there, and dozed off to slumber, thinking about what a pity it was that men with such superb strength — strength enabling them to stand up cased in cruelly burdensome iron and drenched with perspiration, and hack and batter and bang each other for six hours on a stretch — should not have been born at a time when they could put it to some useful purpose. Take a jackass, for instance: a jackass has that kind of strength, and puts it to a useful purpose, and is valuable to this world because he is a jackass; but a nobleman is not valuable because he is a jackass. It is a mixture that is always ineffectual, and should never have been attempted in the first place. And yet, once you start a mistake, the trouble is done and you never know what is going to come of it.

When I came to myself again and began to listen, I perceived that I had lost another chapter, and that Alisande had wandered a long way off with her people.

"And so they rode and came into a deep valley full of stones, and thereby they saw a fair stream of water; above thereby was the head of the stream, a fair fountain, and three damsels sitting thereby. In this country, said Sir Marhaus, came never knight since it was christened, but he found strange adventures — "

"This is not good form, Alisande. Sir Marhaus the king's son of Ireland talks like all the rest; you ought to give him a brogue, or at least a characteristic expletive; by this means one would recognize him as soon as he spoke, without his ever being named. It is a common literary device with the great authors. You should make him say, 'In this country, be jabers, came never knight since it was christened, but he found strange adventures, be jabers.' You see how much better that sounds."

— "came never knight but he found strange adventures, be jabers. Of a truth it doth indeed, fair lord, albeit 'tis passing hard to say, though peradventure that will not tarry but better speed with usage. And then they rode to the damsels, and either saluted other, and the eldest had a garland of gold about her head, and she was threescore winter of age or more — "

"The *damsel* was?"

"Even so, dear lord — and her hair was white under the garland — "

"Celluloid teeth, nine dollars a set, as like as not — the loose-fit kind, that go up and down like a portcullis when you eat, and fall out when you laugh."

"The second damsel was of thirty winter of age, with a circlet of gold about her head. The third damsel was but fifteen year of age — "

Billows of thought came rolling over my soul, and the voice faded out of my hearing!

Fifteen! Break — my heart! oh, my lost darling! Just her age who was so gentle, and lovely, and all the world to me, and whom I shall never see again! How the thought of her carries me back over wide seas of memory to a vague dim time, a happy time, so many, many centuries hence, when I used to wake in the soft summer mornings, out of sweet dreams of her, and say "Hello, Central!" just to hear her dear voice come melting back to me with a "Hello, Hank!" that was music of the spheres to my enchanted ear. She got three dollars a week, but she was worth it.

I could not follow Alisande's further explanation of who our captured knights were, now — I mean in case she should ever get to explaining who they were. My interest was gone, my thoughts were far away, and sad. By fitful glimpses of the drifting tale, caught here and there and now and then, I merely noted in a vague way that each of these three knights took one of these three damsels up behind him on his horse, and one rode north, another east, the other south, to seek adventures, and meet again and lie, after year and day. Year and day — and without baggage. It was of a piece with the general simplicity of the country.

The sun was now setting. It was about three in the afternoon when Alisande had begun to tell me who the cowboys were; so she had made pretty good progress with it — for her. She would arrive some time or other, no doubt, but she was not a person who could be hurried.

We were approaching a castle which stood on high ground; a huge, strong, venerable structure, whose gray towers and battlements were charmingly draped with ivy, and whose whole majestic mass was drenched with splendors flung from the sinking sun. It was the largest castle we had seen, and so I thought it might be the one we were after, but Sandy said no. She did not know who owned it; she said she had passed it without calling, when she went down to Camelot.

Chapter XVI. Morgan Le Fay

If knights errant were to be believed, not all castles were desirable places to seek hospitality in. As a matter of fact, knights errant were *not* persons to be believed — that is, measured by modern standards of veracity; yet, measured by the standards of their own time, and scaled accordingly, you got the truth. It was very simple: you discounted a statement ninety-seven per cent; the rest was fact. Now after making this allowance, the truth remained that if I could find out something about a castle before ringing the doorbell — I mean hailing the warders — it was the sensible thing to do. So I was pleased when I saw in the distance a horseman making the bottom turn of the road that wound down from this castle.

As we approached each other, I saw that he wore a plumed helmet, and seemed to be otherwise clothed in steel, but bore a curious addition also — a stiff square garment like a herald's tabard. However, I had to smile at my own forgetfulness when I got nearer and read this sign on his tabard:

"Persimmon's Soap — All the Prime-Donna Use It."

That was a little idea of my own, and had several wholesome purposes in view toward the civilizing and uplifting of this nation. In the first place, it was a furtive, underhand blow at this nonsense of knight errantry, though nobody suspected that but me. I had started a number of these people out — the bravest knights I could get — each sandwiched between bulletin-boards bearing one device or another, and I judged that by and by when they got to be numerous enough they would begin to look ridiculous; and then, even the steel-clad ass that *hadn't* any board would himself begin to look ridiculous because he was out of the fashion.

Secondly, these missionaries would gradually, and without creating suspicion or exciting alarm, introduce a rudimentary cleanliness among the nobility, and from them it would work down to the people, if the priests could be kept quiet. This would undermine the Church. I mean would be a step toward that. Next, education — next, freedom — and then she would begin to crumble. It being my conviction that any Established Church is an established crime, an established slave-pen, I had no scruples, but was willing to assail it in any way or with any weapon that promised to hurt it. Why, in my own former day — in remote centuries not yet stirring in the womb of time — there were old Englishmen who imagined that they had been born in a free country: a "free" country with the Corporation Act and the Test still in force in it — timbers propped against men's liberties and dishonored consciences to shore up an Established Anachronism with.

My missionaries were taught to spell out the gilt signs on their tabards — the showy gilding was a neat idea, I could have got the king to wear a bulletin-board for the sake of that barbaric splendor — they were to spell out these signs and then explain to the lords and ladies what soap was; and if the lords and ladies were afraid of it, get them to try it on a dog. The missionary's next move was to get the family together and try it on himself; he was to stop at no experiment, however desperate, that could convince the nobility that soap was harmless; if any final doubt remained, he must catch a hermit — the woods were full of them; saints they called themselves, and saints they were believed to be. They were unspeakably holy, and worked miracles, and everybody stood in awe of them. If a hermit could survive a wash, and that failed to convince a duke, give him up, let him alone.

Whenever my missionaries overcame a knight errant on the road they washed him, and when he got well they swore him to go and get a bulletin-board and disseminate soap and civilization the rest of his days. As a consequence the workers in the field were increasing by degrees, and the reform was steadily spreading. My soap factory felt the strain early. At first I had only two hands; but before I had left home I was already employing fifteen, and running night and day; and the atmospheric result was getting so pronounced that the king went sort of fainting and gasping around and said he did not believe he could stand it much longer, and Sir Launcelot got so that he did hardly anything but walk up and down the roof and swear, although I told him it was worse up there than anywhere else, but he said he wanted plenty of air; and he was always complaining that a palace was no place for a soap factory anyway, and said if a man was to start one in his house he would be damned if he wouldn't strangle him. There were ladies present, too, but much these people ever cared for that; they would swear before children, if the wind was their way when the factory was going.

This missionary knight's name was La Cote Male Taile, and he said that this castle was the abode of Morgan le Fay, sister of King Arthur, and wife of King Uriens, monarch of a realm about as big as the District of Columbia — you could stand in the middle of it and throw bricks into the next kingdom. "Kings" and "Kingdoms" were as thick in Britain as they had been in little Palestine in Joshua's time, when people had to sleep with their knees pulled up because they couldn't stretch out without a passport.

La Cote was much depressed, for he had scored here the worst failure of his campaign. He had not worked off a cake; yet he had tried all the tricks of the trade, even to the washing of a hermit; but the hermit died. This was, indeed, a bad failure, for this animal would now be dubbed a martyr, and would take his place among the saints of the Roman calendar. Thus made he his moan, this poor Sir La Cote Male Taile, and sorrowed passing sore. And so my heart bled for him, and I was moved to comfort and stay him. Wherefore I said:

"Forbear to grieve, fair knight, for this is not a defeat. We have brains, you and I; and for such as have brains there are no defeats, but only victories. Observe how we will turn this seeming disaster into an advertisement; an advertisement for our soap; and the biggest one, to draw, that was ever thought of; an advertisement that will transform that Mount Washington defeat into a Matterhorn victory. We will put on your bulletin-board, '*Patronized by the elect* .' How does that strike you?"

"Verily, it is wonderly bethought!"

"Well, a body is bound to admit that for just a modest little oneline ad, it's a corker."

So the poor colporteur's griefs vanished away. He was a brave fellow, and had done mighty feats of arms in his time. His chief celebrity rested upon the events of an excursion like this one of mine, which he had once made with a damsel named Maledisant, who was as handy with her tongue as was Sandy, though in a different way, for her tongue churned forth only railings and insult, whereas Sandy's music was of a kindlier sort. I knew his story well, and so I knew how to interpret the compassion that was in his face when he bade me farewell. He supposed I was having a bitter hard time of it.

Sandy and I discussed his story, as we rode along, and she said that La Cote's bad luck had begun with the very beginning of that trip; for the king's fool had overthrown him on the first day, and in such cases it was customary for the girl to desert to the conqueror, but Maledisant didn't do it; and also persisted afterward in sticking to him, after all his defeats. But, said I, suppose the victor should decline to accept his spoil? She said that that wouldn't answer — he must. He couldn't decline; it wouldn't be regular. I made a note of that. If Sandy's music got to be too burdensome, some time, I would let a knight defeat me, on the chance that she would desert to him.

In due time we were challenged by the warders, from the castle walls, and after a parley admitted. I have nothing pleasant to tell about that visit. But it was not a disappointment, for I knew Mrs. le Fay by reputation, and was not expecting anything pleasant. She was held in awe by the whole realm, for she had made everybody believe she was a great sorceress. All her ways were wicked, all her instincts devilish. She was loaded to the eyelids with cold malice. All her history was black with crime; and among her crimes murder was common. I was most curious to see her; as curious as I could have been to see Satan. To my surprise she was beautiful; black thoughts had failed to make her expression repulsive, age had failed to wrinkle her satin skin or mar its bloomy freshness. She could have passed for old Uriens' granddaughter, she could have been mistaken for sister to her own son.

As soon as we were fairly within the castle gates we were ordered into her presence. King Uriens was there, a kind-faced old man with a subdued look; and also the son, Sir Uwaine le Blanchemains, in whom I was, of course, interested on account of the tradition that he had once done battle with thirty knights, and also on account of his trip with Sir Gawaine and Sir Marhaus, which Sandy had been aging me with. But Morgan was the main attraction, the conspicuous personality here; she was head chief of this household, that was plain. She caused us to be seated, and then she began, with all manner of pretty graces and graciousnesses, to ask me questions. Dear me, it was like a bird or a flute, or something, talking. I felt persuaded that this woman must have been misrepresented, lied about. She trilled along, and trilled along, and presently a handsome young page, clothed like the rainbow, and as easy and undulatory of movement as a wave, came with something on a golden salver, and, kneeling to present it to her, overdid his graces and lost his balance, and so fell lightly against her knee. She slipped a dirk into him in as matter-of-course a way as another person would have harpooned a rat!

Poor child! he slumped to the floor, twisted his silken limbs in one great straining contortion of pain, and was dead. Out of the old king was wrung an involuntary "O-h!" of compassion. The look he got, made him cut it suddenly short and not put any more hyphens in it. Sir Uwaine, at a sign from his mother, went to the anteroom and called some servants, and meanwhile madame went rippling sweetly along with her talk.

I saw that she was a good housekeeper, for while she talked she kept a corner of her eye on the servants to see that they made no balks in handling the body and getting it out; when they came with fresh clean towels, she sent back for the other kind; and when they had finished wiping the floor and were going, she indicated a crimson fleck the size of a tear which their duller eyes had overlooked. It was plain to me that La Cote Male Taile had failed to see the mistress of the house. Often, how louder and clearer than any tongue, does dumb circumstantial evidence speak.

Morgan le Fay rippled along as musically as ever. Marvelous woman. And what a glance she had: when it fell in reproof upon those servants, they shrunk and quailed as timid people do when the lightning flashes out of a cloud. I could have got the habit myself. It was the same with that poor old Brer Uriens; he was always on the ragged edge of apprehension; she could not even turn toward him but he winced.

In the midst of the talk I let drop a complimentary word about King Arthur, forgetting for the moment how this woman hated her brother. That one little compliment was enough. She clouded up like storm; she called for her guards, and said:

"Hale me these varlets to the dungeons."

That struck cold on my ears, for her dungeons had a reputation. Nothing occurred to me to say — or do. But not so with Sandy. As the guard laid a hand upon me, she piped up with the tranquilest confidence, and said:

"God's wounds, dost thou covet destruction, thou maniac? It is The Boss!"

Now what a happy idea that was! — and so simple; yet it would never have occurred to me. I was born modest; not all over, but in spots; and this was one of the spots.

The effect upon madame was electrical. It cleared her countenance and brought back her smiles and all her persuasive graces and blandishments; but nevertheless she was not able to entirely cover up with them the fact that she was in a ghastly fright. She said:

"La, but do list to thine handmaid! as if one gifted with powers like to mine might say the thing which I have said unto one who has vanquished Merlin, and not be jesting. By mine enchantments I foresaw your coming, and by them I knew you when you entered here. I did but play this little jest with hope to surprise you into some display of your art, as not doubting you would blast the guards with occult fires, consuming them to ashes on the spot, a marvel much beyond mine own ability, yet one which I have long been childishly curious to see."

The guards were less curious, and got out as soon as they got permission.

Chapter XVII. A Royal Banquet

Madame, seeing me pacific and unresentful, no doubt judged that I was deceived by her excuse; for her fright dissolved away, and she was soon so importunate to have me give an exhibition and kill somebody, that the thing grew to be embarrassing. However, to my relief she was presently interrupted by the call to prayers. I will say this much for the nobility: that, tyrannical, murderous, rapacious, and morally rotten as they were, they were deeply and enthusiastically religious. Nothing could divert them from the regular and faithful performance of the pieties enjoined by the Church. More than once I had seen a noble who had gotten his enemy at a disadvantage, stop to pray before cutting his throat; more than once I had seen a noble, after ambushing and despatching his enemy, retire to the nearest wayside shrine and humbly give thanks, without even waiting to rob the body. There was to be nothing finer or sweeter in the life of even Benvenuto Cellini, that rough-hewn saint, ten centuries later. All the nobles of Britain, with their families, attended divine service morning and night daily, in their private chapels, and even the worst of them had family worship five or six times a day besides. The credit of this belonged entirely to the Church. Although I was no friend to that Catholic Church, I was obliged to admit this. And often, in spite of me, I found myself saying, "What would this country be without the Church?"

After prayers we had dinner in a great banqueting hall which was lighted by hundreds of grease-jets, and everything was as fine and lavish and rudely splendid as might become the royal degree of the hosts. At the head of the hall, on a dais, was the table of the king, queen, and their son, Prince Uwaine. Stretching down the hall from this, was the general table, on the floor. At this, above the salt, sat the visiting nobles and the grown members of their families, of both sexes, — the resident Court, in effect — sixty-one persons; below the salt sat minor officers of the household, with their principal subordinates: altogether a hundred and eighteen persons sitting, and about as many liveried servants standing behind their chairs, or serving in one capacity or another. It was a very fine show. In a gallery a band with cymbals, horns, harps, and other horrors, opened the proceedings with what seemed to be the crude first-draft or original agony of the wail known to later centuries as "In the Sweet Bye and Bye." It was new, and ought to have been rehearsed a little more. For some reason or other the queen had the composer hanged, after dinner.

After this music, the priest who stood behind the royal table said a noble long grace in ostensible Latin. Then the battalion of waiters broke away from their posts, and darted, rushed, flew, fetched and carried, and the mighty feeding began; no words anywhere, but absorbing attention to business. The rows of chops opened and shut in vast unison, and the sound of it was like to the muffled burr of subterranean machinery.

The havoc continued an hour and a half, and unimaginable was the destruction of substantials. Of the chief feature of the feast — the huge wild boar that lay stretched out so portly and imposing at the start — nothing was left but the semblance of a hoopskirt; and he was but the type and symbol of what had happened to all the other dishes.

With the pastries and so on, the heavy drinking began — and the talk. Gallon after gallon of wine and mead disappeared, and everybody got comfortable, then happy, then sparklingly joyous — both sexes, — and by and by pretty noisy. Men told anecdotes that were terrific to hear, but nobody blushed; and when the nub was sprung, the assemblage let go with a horse-laugh that shook the fortress. Ladies answered back with historiettes that would almost have made Queen Margaret of Navarre or even the great Elizabeth of England hide behind a handkerchief, but nobody hid here, but only laughed — howled, you may say. In pretty much all of these dreadful stories, ecclesiastics were the hardy heroes, but that didn't worry the chaplain any, he had his laugh with the rest; more than that, upon invitation he roared out a song which was of as daring a sort as any that was sung that night.

By midnight everybody was fagged out, and sore with laughing; and, as a rule, drunk: some weepingly, some affectionately, some hilariously, some quarrelsomely, some dead and under the table. Of the ladies, the worst spectacle was a lovely young duchess, whose wedding-eve this was; and indeed she was a spectacle, sure enough. Just as she was she could have sat in advance for the portrait of the young daughter of the Regent d'Orleans, at the famous dinner whence she was carried, foul-mouthed, intoxicated, and helpless, to her bed, in the lost and lamented days of the Ancient Regime.

Suddenly, even while the priest was lifting his hands, and all conscious heads were bowed in reverent expectation of the coming blessing, there appeared under the arch of the far-off door at the bottom of the hall an old and bent and white-haired lady, leaning upon a crutch-stick; and she lifted the stick and pointed it toward the queen and cried out:

"The wrath and curse of God fall upon you, woman without pity, who have slain mine innocent grandchild and made desolate this old heart that had nor chick, nor friend nor stay nor comfort in all this world but him!"

Everybody crossed himself in a grisly fright, for a curse was an awful thing to those people; but the queen rose up majestic, with the death-light in her eye, and flung back this ruthless command:

"Lay hands on her! To the stake with her!"

The guards left their posts to obey. It was a shame; it was a cruel thing to see. What could be done? Sandy gave me a look; I knew she had another inspiration. I said:

"Do what you choose."

She was up and facing toward the queen in a moment. She indicated me, and said:

"Madame, *he* saith this may not be. Recall the commandment, or he will dissolve the castle and it shall vanish away like the instable fabric of a dream!"

Confound it, what a crazy contract to pledge a person to! What if the queen —

But my consternation subsided there, and my panic passed off; for the queen, all in a collapse, made no show of resistance but gave a countermanding sign and sunk into her seat. When she reached it she was sober. So were many of the others. The assemblage rose, whiffed ceremony to the winds, and rushed for the door like a mob; overturning chairs, smashing crockery, tugging, struggling, shouldering, crowding — anything to get out before I should change my mind and puff the castle into the measureless dim vacancies of space. Well, well, well, they *were* a superstitious lot. It is all a body can do to conceive of it.

The poor queen was so scared and humbled that she was even afraid to hang the composer without first consulting me. I was very sorry for her — indeed, any one would have been, for she was really suffering; so I was willing to do anything that was reasonable, and had no desire to carry things to wanton extremities. I therefore considered the matter thoughtfully, and ended by having the musicians ordered into our presence to play that Sweet Bye and Bye again, which they did. Then I saw that she was right, and gave her permission to hang the whole band. This little relaxation of sternness had a good effect upon the queen. A statesman gains little by the arbitrary exercise of ironclad authority upon all occasions that offer, for this wounds the just pride of his subordinates, and thus tends to undermine his strength. A little concession, now and then, where it can do no harm, is the wiser policy.

Now that the queen was at ease in her mind once more, and measurably happy, her wine naturally began to assert itself again, and it got a little the start of her. I mean it set her music going — her silver bell of a tongue. Dear me, she was a master talker. It would not become me to suggest that it was pretty late and that I was a tired man and very sleepy. I wished I had gone off to bed when I had the chance. Now I must stick it out; there was no other way. So she tinkled along and along, in the otherwise profound and ghostly hush of the sleeping castle, until by and by there came, as if from deep down under us, a faraway sound, as of a muffled shriek — with an expression of agony about it that made my flesh crawl. The queen stopped, and her eyes lighted with pleasure; she tilted her graceful head as a bird does when it listens. The sound bored its way up through the stillness again.

"What is it?" I said.

"It is truly a stubborn soul, and endureth long. It is many hours now."

"Endureth what?"

"The rack. Come — ye shall see a blithe sight. An he yield not his secret now, ye shall see him torn asunder."

What a silky smooth hellion she was; and so composed and serene, when the cords all down my legs were hurting in sympathy with that man's pain. Conducted by mailed guards bearing flaring torches, we tramped along echoing corridors, and down stone stairways dank and dripping, and smelling of mould and ages of imprisoned night — a chill, uncanny journey and a long one, and not made the shorter or the cheerier by the sorceress's talk, which was about this sufferer and his crime. He had been accused by an anonymous informer, of having killed a stag in the royal preserves. I said:

"Anonymous testimony isn't just the right thing, your Highness. It were fairer to confront the accused with the accuser."

"I had not thought of that, it being but of small consequence. But an I would, I could not, for that the accuser came masked by night, and told the forester, and straightway got him hence again, and so the forester knoweth him not."

"Then is this Unknown the only person who saw the stag killed?"

"Marry, *no* man *saw* the killing, but this Unknown saw this hardy wretch near to the spot where the stag lay, and came with right loyal zeal and betrayed him to the forester."

"So the Unknown was near the dead stag, too? Isn't it just possible that he did the killing himself? His loyal zeal — in a mask — looks just a shade suspicious. But what is your highness's idea for racking the prisoner? Where is the profit?"

"He will not confess, else; and then were his soul lost. For his crime his life is forfeited by the law — and of a surety will I see that he payeth it! — but it were peril to my own soul to let him die unconfessed and unabsolved. Nay, I were a fool to fling me into hell for *his* accommodation."

"But, your Highness, suppose he has nothing to confess?"

"As to that, we shall see, anon. An I rack him to death and he confess not, it will peradventure show that he had indeed naught to confess — ye will grant that that is sooth? Then shall I not be damned for an unconfessed man that had naught to confess — wherefore, I shall be safe."

It was the stubborn unreasoning of the time. It was useless to argue with her. Arguments have no chance against petrified training; they wear it as little as the waves wear a cliff. And her training was everybody's. The brightest intellect in the land would not have been able to see that her position was defective.

As we entered the rack-cell I caught a picture that will not go from me; I wish it would. A native young giant of thirty or thereabouts lay stretched upon the frame on his back, with his wrists and ankles tied to ropes which led over windlasses at either end. There was no color in him; his features were contorted and set, and sweat-drops stood upon his forehead. A priest bent over him on each side; the executioner stood by; guards were on duty; smoking torches stood in sockets along the walls; in a corner crouched a poor young creature, her face drawn with anguish, a half-wild and hunted look in her eyes, and in her lap lay a little child asleep. Just as we stepped across the threshold the executioner gave his machine a slight turn, which wrung a cry from both the prisoner and the woman; but I shouted, and the executioner released the strain without waiting to see who spoke. I could not let this horror go on; it would have killed me to see it. I asked the queen to let me clear the place and speak to the prisoner privately; and when she was going to object I spoke in a low voice and said I did not want to make a scene before her servants, but I must have my way; for I was King Arthur's representative, and was speaking in his name. She saw she had to yield. I asked her to indorse me to these people, and then leave me. It was not pleasant for her, but she took the pill; and even went further than I was meaning to require. I only wanted the backing of her own authority; but she said:

"Ye will do in all things as this lord shall command. It is The Boss."

It was certainly a good word to conjure with: you could see it by the squirming of these rats. The queen's guards fell into line, and she and they marched away, with their torchbearers, and woke the echoes of the cavernous tunnels with the measured beat of their retreating footfalls. I had the prisoner taken from the rack and placed upon his bed, and medicaments applied to his hurts, and wine given him to drink. The woman crept near and looked on, eagerly, lovingly, but timorously, — like one who fears a repulse; indeed, she tried furtively to touch the man's forehead, and jumped back, the picture of fright, when I turned unconsciously toward her. It was pitiful to see.

"Lord," I said, "stroke him, lass, if you want to. Do anything you're a mind to; don't mind me."

Why, her eyes were as grateful as an animal's, when you do it a kindness that it understands. The baby was out of her way and she had her cheek against the man's in a minute and her hands fondling his hair, and her happy tears running down. The man revived and caressed his wife with his eyes, which was all he could do. I judged I might clear the den, now, and I did; cleared it of all but the family and myself. Then I said:

"Now, my friend, tell me your side of this matter; I know the other side."

The man moved his head in sign of refusal. But the woman looked pleased — as it seemed to me — pleased with my suggestion. I went on —

"You know of me?"

"Yes. All do, in Arthur's realms."

"If my reputation has come to you right and straight, you should not be afraid to speak."

The woman broke in, eagerly:

"Ah, fair my lord, do thou persuade him! Thou canst an thou wilt. Ah, he suffereth so; and it is for me — for *me* ! And how can I bear it? I would I might see him die — a sweet, swift death; oh, my Hugo, I cannot bear this one!"

And she fell to sobbing and grovelling about my feet, and still imploring. Imploring what? The man's death? I could not quite get the bearings of the thing. But Hugo interrupted her and said:

"Peace! Ye wit not what ye ask. Shall I starve whom I love, to win a gentle death? I wend thou knewest me better."

"Well," I said, "I can't quite make this out. It is a puzzle. Now — "

"Ah, dear my lord, an ye will but persuade him! Consider how these his tortures wound me! Oh, and he will not speak! — whereas, the healing, the solace that lie in a blessed swift death — "

"What *are* you maundering about? He's going out from here a free man and whole — he's not going to die."

The man's white face lit up, and the woman flung herself at me in a most surprising explosion of joy, and cried out:

"He is saved! — for it is the king's word by the mouth of the king's servant — Arthur, the king whose word is gold!"

"Well, then you do believe I can be trusted, after all. Why didn't you before?"

"Who doubted? Not I, indeed; and not she."

"Well, why wouldn't you tell me your story, then?"

"Ye had made no promise; else had it been otherwise."

"I see, I see.... And yet I believe I don't quite see, after all. You stood the torture and refused to confess; which shows plain enough to even the dullest understanding that you had nothing to confess — "

"I, my lord? How so? It was I that killed the deer!"

"You *did* ? Oh, dear, this is the most mixed-up business that ever — "

"Dear lord, I begged him on my knees to confess, but — "

"You *did* ! It gets thicker and thicker. What did you want him to do that for?"

"Sith it would bring him a quick death and save him all this cruel pain."

"Well — yes, there is reason in that. But *he* didn't want the quick death."

"He? Why, of a surety he *did* ."

"Well, then, why in the world *didn't* he confess?"

"Ah, sweet sir, and leave my wife and chick without bread and shelter?"

"Oh, heart of gold, now I see it! The bitter law takes the convicted man's estate and beggars his widow and his orphans. They could torture you to death, but without conviction or confession they could not rob your wife and baby. You stood by them like a man; and *you* — true wife and the woman that you are — you would have bought him release from torture at cost to yourself of slow starvation and death — well, it humbles a body to think what your sex can do when it comes to self-sacrifice. I'll book you both for my colony; you'll like it there; it's a Factory where I'm going to turn groping and grubbing automata into *men* ."

Chapter XVIII. In the Queen's Dungeons

Well, I arranged all that; and I had the man sent to his home. I had a great desire to rack the executioner; not because he was a good, painstaking and paingiving official, — for surely it was not to his discredit that he performed his functions well — but to pay him back for wantonly cuffing and otherwise distressing that young woman. The priests told me about this, and were generously hot to have him punished. Something of this disagreeable sort was turning up every now and then. I mean, episodes that showed that not all priests were frauds and self-seekers, but that many, even the great majority, of these that were down on the ground among the common people, were sincere and right-hearted, and devoted to the alleviation of human troubles and sufferings. Well, it was a thing which could not be helped, so I seldom fretted about it, and never many minutes at a time; it has never been my way to bother much about things which you can't cure. But I did not like it, for it was just the sort of thing to keep people reconciled to an Established Church. We *must* have a religion — it goes without saying — but my idea is, to have it cut up into forty free sects, so that they will police each other, as had been the case in the United States in my time. Concentration of power in a political machine is bad; and and an Established Church is only a political machine; it was invented for that; it is nursed, cradled, preserved for that; it is an enemy to human liberty, and does no good which it could not better do in a split-up and scattered condition. That wasn't law; it wasn't gospel: it was only an opinion — my opinion, and I was only a man, one man: so it wasn't worth any more than the pope's — or any less, for that matter.

Well, I couldn't rack the executioner, neither would I overlook the just complaint of the priests. The man must be punished somehow or other, so I degraded him from his office and made him leader of the band — the new one that was to be started. He begged hard, and said he couldn't play — a plausible excuse, but too thin; there wasn't a musician in the country that could.

The queen was a good deal outraged, next morning when she found she was going to have neither Hugo's life nor his property. But I told her she must bear this cross; that while by law and custom she certainly was entitled to both the man's life and his property, there were extenuating circumstances, and so in Arthur the king's name I had pardoned him. The deer was ravaging the man's fields, and he had killed it in sudden passion, and not for gain; and he had carried it into the royal forest in the hope that that might make detection of the misdoer impossible. Confound her, I couldn't make her see that sudden passion is an extenuating circumstance in the killing of venison — or of a person — so I gave it up and let her sulk it out. I *did* think I was going to make her see it by remarking that her own sudden passion in the case of the page modified that crime.

"Crime!" she exclaimed. "How thou talkest! Crime, forsooth! Man, I am going to *pay* for him!"

Oh, it was no use to waste sense on her. Training — training is everything; training is all there is *to* a person. We speak of nature; it is folly; there is no such thing as nature; what we call by that misleading name is merely heredity and training. We have no thoughts of our own, no opinions of our own; they are transmitted to us, trained into us. All that is original in us, and therefore fairly creditable or discreditable to us, can be covered up and hidden by the point of a cambric needle, all the rest being atoms contributed by, and inherited from, a procession of ancestors that stretches back a billion years to the Adam-clam or grasshopper or monkey from whom our race has been so tediously and ostentatiously and unprofitably developed. And as for me, all that I think about in this plodding sad pilgrimage, this pathetic drift between the eternities, is to look out and humbly live a pure and high and blameless life, and save that one microscopic atom in me that is truly *me* : the rest may land in Sheol and welcome for all I care.

No, confound her, her intellect was good, she had brains enough, but her training made her an ass — that is, from a many-centuries-later point of view. To kill the page was no crime — it was her right; and upon her right she stood, serenely and unconscious of offense. She was a result of generations of training in the unexamined and unassailed belief that the law which permitted her to kill a subject when she chose was a perfectly right and righteous one.

Well, we must give even Satan his due. She deserved a compliment for one thing; and I tried to pay it, but the words stuck in my throat. She had a right to kill the boy, but she was in no wise obliged to pay for him. That was law for some other people, but not for her. She knew quite well that she was doing a large and generous thing to pay for that lad, and that I ought in common fairness to come out with something handsome about it, but I couldn't — my mouth refused. I couldn't help seeing, in my fancy, that poor old grandma with the broken heart, and that fair young creature lying butchered, his little silken pomps and vanities laced with his golden blood. How could she *pay* for him! *Whom* could she pay? And so, well knowing that this woman, trained as she had been, deserved praise, even adulation, I was yet not able to utter it, trained as I had been. The best I could do was to fish up a compliment from outside, so to speak — and the pity of it was, that it was true:

"Madame, your people will adore you for this."

Quite true, but I meant to hang her for it some day if I lived. Some of those laws were too bad, altogether too bad. A master might kill his slave for nothing — for mere spite, malice, or to pass the time — just as we have seen that the crowned head could do it with *his* slave, that is to say, anybody. A gentleman could kill a free commoner, and pay for him — cash or garden-truck. A noble could kill a noble without expense, as far as the law was concerned, but reprisals in kind were to be expected. *Any* body could kill *some* body, except the commoner and the slave; these had no privileges. If they killed, it was murder, and the law wouldn't stand murder. It made short work of the experimenter — and of his family, too, if he murdered somebody who belonged up among the ornamental ranks. If a commoner gave a noble even so much as a Damiens-scratch which didn't kill or even hurt, he got Damiens' dose for it just the same; they pulled him to rags and tatters with horses, and all the world came to see the show, and crack jokes, and have a good time; and some of the performances of the best people present were as tough, and as properly unprintable, as any that have been printed by the pleasant Casanova in his chapter about the dismemberment of Louis XV's poor awkward enemy.

I had had enough of this grisly place by this time, and wanted to leave, but I couldn't, because I had something on my mind that my conscience kept prodding me about, and wouldn't let me forget. If I had the remaking of man, he wouldn't have any conscience. It is one of the most disagreeable things connected with a person; and although it certainly does a great deal of good, it cannot be said to pay, in the long run; it would be much better to have less good and more comfort. Still, this is only my opinion, and I am only one man; others, with less experience, may think differently. They have a right to their view. I only stand to this: I have noticed my conscience for many years, and I know it is more trouble and bother to me than anything else I started with. I suppose that in the beginning I prized it, because we prize anything that is ours; and yet how foolish it was to think so. If we look at it in another way, we see how absurd it is: if I had an anvil in me would I prize it? Of course not. And yet when you come to think, there is no real difference between a conscience and an anvil — I mean for comfort. I have noticed it a thousand times. And you could dissolve an anvil with acids, when you couldn't stand it any longer; but there isn't any way that you can work off a conscience — at least so it will stay worked off; not that I know of, anyway.

There was something I wanted to do before leaving, but it was a disagreeable matter, and I hated to go at it. Well, it bothered me all the morning. I could have mentioned it to the old king, but what would be the use? — he was but an extinct volcano; he had been active in his time, but his fire was out, this good while, he was only a stately ash-pile now; gentle enough, and kindly enough for my purpose, without doubt, but not usable. He was nothing, this so-called king: the queen was the only power there. And she was a Vesuvius. As a favor, she might consent to warm a flock of sparrows for you, but then she might take that very opportunity to turn herself loose and bury a city. However, I reflected that as often as any other way, when you are expecting the worst, you get something that is not so bad, after all.

So I braced up and placed my matter before her royal Highness. I said I had been having a general jail-delivery at Camelot and among neighboring castles, and with her permission I would like to examine her collection, her bric-a-brac — that is to say, her prisoners. She resisted; but I was expecting that. But she finally consented. I was expecting that, too, but not so soon. That about ended my discomfort. She called her guards and torches, and we went down into the dungeons. These were down under the castle's foundations, and mainly were small cells hollowed out of the living rock. Some of these cells had no light at all. In one of them was a woman, in foul rags, who sat on the ground, and would not answer a question or speak a word, but only looked up at us once or twice, through a cobweb of tangled hair, as if to see what casual thing it might be that was disturbing with sound and light the meaningless dull dream that was become her life; after that, she sat bowed, with her dirt-caked fingers idly interlocked in her lap, and gave no further sign. This poor rack of bones was a woman of middle age, apparently; but only apparently; she had been there nine years, and was eighteen when she entered. She was a commoner, and had been sent here on her bridal night by Sir Breuse Sance Pite, a neighboring lord whose vassal her father was, and to which said lord she had refused what has since been called le droit du seigneur, and, moreover, had opposed violence to violence and spilt half a gill of his almost sacred blood. The young husband had interfered at that point, believing the bride's life in danger, and had flung the noble out into the midst of the humble and trembling wedding guests, in the parlor, and left him there astonished at this strange treatment, and implacably embittered against both bride and groom. The said lord being cramped for dungeon-room had asked the queen to accommodate his two criminals, and here in her bastile they had been ever since; hither, indeed, they had come before their crime was an hour old, and had never seen each other since. Here they were, kenneled like toads in the same rock; they had passed nine pitch dark years within fifty feet of each other, yet neither knew whether the other was alive or not. All the first years, their only question had been — asked with beseechings and tears that might have moved stones, in time, perhaps, but hearts are not stones: "Is he alive?" "Is she alive?" But they had never got an answer; and at last that question was not asked any more — or any other.

I wanted to see the man, after hearing all this. He was thirty-four years old, and looked sixty. He sat upon a squared block of stone, with his head bent down, his forearms resting on his knees, his long hair hanging like a fringe before his face, and he was muttering to himself. He raised his chin and looked us slowly over, in a listless dull way, blinking with the distress of the torchlight, then dropped his head and fell to muttering again and took no further notice of us. There were some pathetically suggestive dumb witnesses present. On his wrists and ankles were cicatrices, old smooth scars, and fastened to the stone on which he sat was a chain with manacles and fetters attached; but this apparatus lay idle on the ground, and was thick with rust. Chains cease to be needed after the spirit has gone out of a prisoner.

I could not rouse the man; so I said we would take him to her, and see — to the bride who was the fairest thing in the earth to him, once — roses, pearls, and dew made flesh, for him; a wonder-work, the masterwork of nature: with eyes like no other eyes, and voice like no other voice, and a freshness, and lithe young grace, and beauty, that belonged properly to the creatures of dreams — as he thought — and to no other. The sight of her would set his stagnant blood leaping; the sight of her —

But it was a disappointment. They sat together on the ground and looked dimly wondering into each other's faces a while, with a sort of weak animal curiosity; then forgot each other's presence, and dropped their eyes, and you saw that they were away again and wandering in some far land of dreams and shadows that we know nothing about.

I had them taken out and sent to their friends. The queen did not like it much. Not that she felt any personal interest in the matter, but she thought it disrespectful to Sir Breuse Sance Pite. However, I assured her that if he found he couldn't stand it I would fix him so that he could.

I set forty-seven prisoners loose out of those awful rat-holes, and left only one in captivity. He was a lord, and had killed another lord, a sort of kinsman of the queen. That other lord had ambushed him to assassinate him, but this fellow had got the best of him and cut his throat. However, it was not for that that I left him jailed, but for maliciously destroying the only public well in one of his wretched villages. The queen was bound to hang him for killing her kinsman, but I would not allow it: it was no crime to kill an assassin. But I said I was willing to let her hang him for destroying the well; so she concluded to put up with that, as it was better than nothing.

Dear me, for what trifling offenses the most of those forty-seven men and women were shut up there! Indeed, some were there for no distinct offense at all, but only to gratify somebody's spite; and not always the queen's by any means, but a friend's. The newest prisoner's crime was a mere remark which he had made. He said he believed that men were about all alike, and one man as good as another, barring clothes. He said he believed that if you were to strip the nation naked and send a stranger through the crowd, he couldn't tell the king from a quack doctor, nor a duke from a hotel clerk. Apparently here was a man whose brains had not been reduced to an ineffectual mush by idiotic training. I set him loose and sent him to the Factory.

Some of the cells carved in the living rock were just behind the face of the precipice, and in each of these an arrow-slit had been pierced outward to the daylight, and so the captive had a thin ray from the blessed sun for his comfort. The case of one of these poor fellows was particularly hard. From his dusky swallow's hole high up in that vast wall of native rock he could peer out through the arrow-slit and see his own home off yonder in the valley; and for twenty-two years he had watched it, with heartache and longing, through that crack. He could see the lights shine there at night, and in the daytime he could see figures go in and come out — his wife and children, some of them, no doubt, though he could not make out at that distance. In the course of years he noted festivities there, and tried to rejoice, and wondered if they were weddings or what they might be. And he noted funerals; and they wrung his heart. He could make out the coffin, but he could not determine its size, and so could not tell whether it was wife or child. He could see the procession form, with priests and mourners, and move solemnly away, bearing the secret with them. He had left behind him five children and a wife; and in nineteen years he had seen five funerals issue, and none of them humble enough in pomp to denote a servant. So he had lost five of his treasures; there must still be one remaining — one now infinitely, unspeakably precious, — but *which* one? wife, or child? That was the question that tortured him, by night and by day, asleep and awake. Well, to have an interest, of some sort, and half a ray of light, when you are in a dungeon, is a great support to the body and preserver of the intellect. This man was in pretty good condition yet. By the time he had finished telling me his distressful tale, I was in the same state of mind that you would have been in yourself, if you have got average human curiosity; that is to say, I was as burning up as he was to find out which member of the family it was that was left. So I took him over home myself; and an amazing kind of a surprise party it was, too — typhoons and cyclones of frantic joy, and whole Niagaras of happy tears; and by George! we found the aforetime young matron graying toward the imminent verge of her half century, and the babies all men and women, and some of them married and experimenting familywise themselves — for not a soul of the tribe was dead! Conceive of the ingenious devilishness of that queen: she had a special hatred for this prisoner, and she had *invented* all those funerals herself, to scorch his heart with; and the sublimest stroke of genius of the whole thing was leaving the family-invoice a funeral *short* , so as to let him wear his poor old soul out guessing.

But for me, he never would have got out. Morgan le Fay hated him with her whole heart, and she never would have softened toward him. And yet his crime was committed more in thoughtlessness than deliberate depravity. He had said she had red hair. Well, she had; but that was no way to speak of it. When red-headed people are above a certain social grade their hair is auburn.

Consider it: among these forty-seven captives there were five whose names, offenses, and dates of incarceration were no longer known! One woman and four men — all bent, and wrinkled, and mind-extinguished patriarchs. They themselves had long ago forgotten these details; at any rate they had mere vague theories about them, nothing definite and nothing that they repeated twice in the same way. The succession of priests whose office it had been to pray daily with the captives and remind them that God had put them there, for some wise purpose or other, and teach them that patience, humbleness, and submission to oppression was what He loved to see in parties of a subordinate rank, had traditions about these poor old human ruins, but nothing more. These traditions went but little way, for they concerned the length of the incarceration only, and not the names of the offenses. And even by the help of tradition the only thing that could be proven was that none of the five had seen daylight for thirty-five years: how much longer this privation has lasted was not guessable. The king and the queen knew nothing about these poor creatures, except that they were heirlooms, assets inherited, along with the throne, from the former firm. Nothing of their history had been transmitted with their persons, and so the inheriting owners had considered them of no value, and had felt no interest in them. I said to the queen:

"Then why in the world didn't you set them free?"

The question was a puzzler. She didn't know *why* she hadn't, the thing had never come up in her mind. So here she was, forecasting the veritable history of future prisoners of the Castle d'If, without knowing it. It seemed plain to me now, that with her training, those inherited prisoners were merely property — nothing more, nothing less. Well, when we inherit property, it does not occur to us to throw it away, even when we do not value it.

When I brought my procession of human bats up into the open world and the glare of the afternoon sun — previously blindfolding them, in charity for eyes so long untortured by light — they were a spectacle to look at. Skeletons, scarecrows, goblins, pathetic frights, every one;

legitimatest possible children of Monarchy by the Grace of God and the Established Church. I muttered absently:

"I *wish* I could photograph them!"

You have seen that kind of people who will never let on that they don't know the meaning of a new big word. The more ignorant they are, the more pitifully certain they are to pretend you haven't shot over their heads. The queen was just one of that sort, and was always making the stupidest blunders by reason of it. She hesitated a moment; then her face brightened up with sudden comprehension, and she said she would do it for me.

I thought to myself: She? why what can she know about photography? But it was a poor time to be thinking. When I looked around, she was moving on the procession with an axe!

Well, she certainly was a curious one, was Morgan le Fay. I have seen a good many kinds of women in my time, but she laid over them all for variety. And how sharply characteristic of her this episode was. She had no more idea than a horse of how to photograph a procession; but being in doubt, it was just like her to try to do it with an axe.

Chapter XIX. Knight-Errantry as a Trade

Sandy and I were on the road again, next morning, bright and early. It was so good to open up one's lungs and take in whole luscious barrels-ful of the blessed God's untainted, dew-fashioned, woodland-scented air once more, after suffocating body and mind for two days and nights in the moral and physical stenches of that intolerable old buzzard-roost! I mean, for me: of course the place was all right and agreeable enough for Sandy, for she had been used to high life all her days.

Poor girl, her jaws had had a wearisome rest now for a while, and I was expecting to get the consequences. I was right; but she had stood by me most helpfully in the castle, and had mightily supported and reinforced me with gigantic foolishnesses which were worth more for the occasion than wisdoms double their size; so I thought she had earned a right to work her mill for a while, if she wanted to, and I felt not a pang when she started it up:

"Now turn we unto Sir Marhaus that rode with the damsel of thirty winter of age southward — "

"Are you going to see if you can work up another half-stretch on the trail of the cowboys, Sandy?"

"Even so, fair my lord."

"Go ahead, then. I won't interrupt this time, if I can help it. Begin over again; start fair, and shake out all your reefs, and I will load my pipe and give good attention."

"Now turn we unto Sir Marhaus that rode with the damsel of thirty winter of age southward. And so they came into a deep forest, and by fortune they were nighted, and rode along in a deep way, and at the last they came into a courtelage where abode the duke of South Marches, and there they asked harbour. And on the morn the duke sent unto Sir Marhaus, and bad him make him ready. And so Sir Marhaus arose and armed him, and there was a mass sung afore him, and he brake his fast, and so mounted on horseback in the court of the castle, there they should do the battle. So there was the duke already on horseback, clean armed, and his six sons by him, and every each had a spear in his hand, and so they encountered, whereas the duke and his two sons brake their spears upon him, but Sir Marhaus held up his spear and touched none of them. Then came the four sons by couples, and two of them brake their spears, and so did the other two. And all this while Sir Marhaus touched them not. Then Sir Marhaus ran to the duke, and smote him with his spear that horse and man fell to the earth. And so he served his sons. And then Sir Marhaus alight down, and bad the duke yield him or else he would slay him. And then some of his sons recovered, and would have set upon Sir Marhaus. Then Sir Marhaus said to the duke, Cease thy sons, or else I will do the uttermost to you all. When the duke saw he might not escape the death, he cried to his sons, and charged them to yield them to Sir Marhaus. And they kneeled all down and put the pommels of their swords to the knight, and so he received them. And then they holp up their father, and so by their common assent promised unto Sir Marhaus never to be foes unto King Arthur, and thereupon at Whitsuntide after, to come he and his sons, and put them in the king's grace.[2]

"Even so standeth the history, fair Sir Boss. Now ye shall wit that that very duke and his six sons are they whom but few days past you also did overcome and send to Arthur's court!"

"Why, Sandy, you can't mean it!"

"An I speak not sooth, let it be the worse for me."

"Well, well, well, — now who would ever have thought it? One whole duke and six dukelets; why, Sandy, it was an elegant haul. Knight-errantry is a most chuckleheaded trade, and it is tedious hard work, too, but I begin to see that there *is* money in it, after all, if you have luck. Not that I would ever engage in it as a business, for I wouldn't. No sound and legitimate business can be established on a basis of speculation. A successful whirl in the knight-errantry line — now what is it when you blow away the nonsense and come down to the cold facts? It's just a corner in pork, that's all, and you can't make anything else out of it. You're rich — yes, — suddenly rich — for about a day, maybe a week; then somebody corners the market on *you* , and down goes your bucket-shop; ain't that so, Sandy?"

"Whethersoever it be that my mind miscarrieth, bewraying simple language in such sort that the words do seem to come endlong and overthwart — "

"There's no use in beating about the bush and trying to get around it that way, Sandy, it's *so* , just as I say. I *know* it's so. And, moreover, when you come right down to the bedrock, knight-errantry is *worse* than pork; for whatever happens, the pork's left, and so somebody's benefited anyway; but when the market breaks, in a knight-errantry whirl, and every knight in the pool passes in his checks, what have you got for assets? Just a rubbish-pile of battered corpses and a barrel or two of busted hardware. Can you call *those* assets? Give me pork, every time. Am I right?"

"Ah, peradventure my head being distraught by the manifold matters whereunto the confusions of these but late adventured haps and fortunings whereby not I alone nor you alone, but every each of us, meseemeth — "

"No, it's not your head, Sandy. Your head's all right, as far as it goes, but you don't know business; that's where the trouble is. It unfits you to argue about business, and you're wrong to be always trying. However, that aside, it was a good haul, anyway, and will breed a handsome crop of reputation in Arthur's court. And speaking of the cowboys, what a curious country this is for women and men that never get old. Now there's Morgan le Fay, as fresh and young as a Vassar pullet, to all appearances, and here is this old duke of the South Marches still slashing away with sword and lance at his time of life, after raising such a family as he has raised. As I understand it, Sir Gawaine killed seven of his sons, and still he had six left for Sir Marhaus and me to take into camp. And then there was that damsel of sixty winter of age still excursioning around in her frosty bloom — How old are you, Sandy?"

It was the first time I ever struck a still place in her. The mill had shut down for repairs, or something.

* * * * *

Chapter XX. The Ogre's Castle

Between six and nine we made ten miles, which was plenty for a horse carrying triple — man, woman, and armor; then we stopped for a long nooning under some trees by a limpid brook.

Right so came by and by a knight riding; and as he drew near he made dolorous moan, and by the words of it I perceived that he was cursing and swearing; yet nevertheless was I glad of his coming, for that I saw he bore a bulletin-board whereon in letters all of shining gold was writ:

"USE PETERSON'S PROPHYLACTIC TOOTHBRUSH — ALL THE GO."

I was glad of his coming, for even by this token I knew him for knight of mine. It was Sir Madok de la Montaine, a burly great fellow whose chief distinction was that he had come within an ace of sending Sir Launcelot down over his horse-tail once. He was never long in a stranger's presence without finding some pretext or other to let out that great fact. But there was another fact of nearly the same size, which he never pushed upon anybody unasked, and yet never withheld when asked: that was, that the reason he didn't quite succeed was, that he was interrupted and sent down over horse-tail himself. This innocent vast lubber did not see any particular difference between the two facts. I liked him, for he was earnest in his work, and very valuable. And he was so fine to look at, with his broad mailed shoulders, and the grand leonine set of his plumed head, and his big shield with its quaint device of a gauntleted hand clutching a prophylactic toothbrush, with motto: "Try Noyoudont." This was a tooth-wash that I was introducing.

He was aweary, he said, and indeed he looked it; but he would not alight. He said he was after the stove-polish man; and with this he broke out cursing and swearing anew. The bulletin-boarder referred to was Sir Ossaise of Surluse, a brave knight, and of considerable celebrity on account of his having tried conclusions in a tournament once, with no less a Mogul than Sir Gaheris himself — although not successfully. He was of a light and laughing disposition, and to him nothing in this world was serious. It was for this reason that I had chosen him to work up a stove-polish sentiment. There were no stoves yet, and so there could be nothing serious about stove-polish. All that the agent needed to do was to deftly and by degrees prepare the public for the great change, and have them established in predilections toward neatness against the time when the stove should appear upon the stage.

Sir Madok was very bitter, and brake out anew with cursings. He said he had cursed his soul to rags; and yet he would not get down from his horse, neither would he take any rest, or listen to any comfort, until he should have found Sir Ossaise and settled this account. It appeared, by what I could piece together of the unprofane fragments of his statement, that he had chanced upon Sir Ossaise at dawn of the morning, and been told that if he would make a short cut across the fields and swamps and broken hills and glades, he could head off a company of travelers who would be rare customers for prophylactics and tooth-wash. With characteristic zeal Sir Madok had plunged away at once upon this quest, and after three hours of awful crosslot riding had overhauled his game. And behold, it was the five patriarchs that had been released from the dungeons the evening before! Poor old creatures, it was all of twenty years since any one of them had known what it was to be equipped with any remaining snag or remnant of a tooth.

"Blank-blank-blank him," said Sir Madok, "an I do not stove-polish him an I may find him, leave it to me; for never no knight that hight Ossaise or aught else may do me this disservice and bide on live, an I may find him, the which I have thereunto sworn a great oath this day."

And with these words and others, he lightly took his spear and gat him thence. In the middle of the afternoon we came upon one of those very patriarchs ourselves, in the edge of a poor village. He was basking in the love of relatives and friends whom he had not seen for fifty years; and about him and caressing him were also descendants of his own body whom he had never seen at all till now; but to him these were all strangers, his memory was gone, his mind was stagnant. It seemed incredible that a man could outlast half a century shut up in a dark hole like a rat, but here were his old wife and some old comrades to testify to it. They could remember him as he was in the freshness and strength of his young manhood, when he kissed his child and delivered it to its mother's hands and went away into that long oblivion. The people at the castle could not tell within half a generation the length of time the man had been shut up there for his unrecorded and forgotten offense; but this old wife knew; and so did her old child, who stood there among her married sons and daughters trying to realize a father who had been to her a name, a thought, a formless image, a tradition, all her life, and now was suddenly concreted into actual flesh and blood and set before her face.

It was a curious situation; yet it is not on that account that I have made room for it here, but on account of a thing which seemed to me still more curious. To wit, that this dreadful matter brought from these downtrodden people no outburst of rage against these oppressors. They had been heritors and subjects of cruelty and outrage so long that nothing could have startled them but a kindness. Yes, here was a curious revelation, indeed, of the depth to which this people had been sunk in slavery. Their entire being was reduced to a monotonous dead level of patience, resignation, dumb uncomplaining acceptance of whatever might befall them in this life. Their very imagination was dead. When you can say that of a man, he has struck bottom, I reckon; there is no lower deep for him.

I rather wished I had gone some other road. This was not the sort of experience for a states- man to encounter who was planning out a peaceful revolution in his mind. For it could not help bringing up the unget-aroundable fact that, all gentle cant and philosophizing to the contrary notwithstanding, no people in the world ever did achieve their freedom by goody-goody talk and moral suasion: it being immutable law that all revolutions that will succeed must *begin* in blood, whatever may answer afterward. If history teaches anything, it teaches that. What this folk needed, then, was a Reign of Terror and a guillotine, and I was the wrong man for them.

Two days later, toward noon, Sandy began to show signs of excitement and feverish ex- pectancy. She said we were approaching the ogre's castle. I was surprised into an uncomfortable shock. The object of our quest had gradually dropped out of my mind; this sudden resurrec- tion of it made it seem quite a real and startling thing for a moment, and roused up in me a smart interest. Sandy's excitement increased every moment; and so did mine, for that sort of thing is catching. My heart got to thumping. You can't reason with your heart; it has its own laws, and thumps about things which the intellect scorns. Presently, when Sandy slid from the horse, motioned me to stop, and went creeping stealthily, with her head bent nearly to her knees, toward a row of bushes that bordered a declivity, the thumpings grew stronger and quicker. And they kept it up while she was gaining her ambush and getting her glimpse over the declivity; and also while I was creeping to her side on my knees. Her eyes were burning now, as she pointed with her finger, and said in a panting whisper:

"The castle! The castle! Lo, where it looms!"

What a welcome disappointment I experienced! I said:

"Castle? It is nothing but a pigsty; a pigsty with a wattled fence around it."

She looked surprised and distressed. The animation faded out of her face; and during many moments she was lost in thought and silent. Then:

"It was not enchanted aforetime," she said in a musing fashion, as if to herself. "And how strange is this marvel, and how awful — that to the one perception it is enchanted and dight in a base and shameful aspect; yet to the perception of the other it is not enchanted, hath suffered no change, but stands firm and stately still, girt with its moat and waving its banners in the blue air from its towers. And God shield us, how it pricks the heart to see again these gracious captives, and the sorrow deepened in their sweet faces! We have tarried along, and are to blame."

I saw my cue. The castle was enchanted to *me* , not to her. It would be wasted time to try to argue her out of her delusion, it couldn't be done; I must just humor it. So I said:

"This is a common case — the enchanting of a thing to one eye and leaving it in its proper form to another. You have heard of it before, Sandy, though you haven't happened to experience it. But no harm is done. In fact, it is lucky the way it is. If these ladies were hogs to everybody and to themselves, it would be necessary to break the enchantment, and that might be impossible if one failed to find out the particular process of the enchantment. And hazardous, too; for in attempting a disenchantment without the true key, you are liable to err, and turn your hogs into dogs, and the dogs into cats, the cats into rats, and so on, and end by reducing your materials to nothing finally, or to an odorless gas which you can't follow — which, of course, amounts to the same thing. But here, by good luck, no one's eyes but mine are under the enchantment, and so it is of no consequence to dissolve it. These ladies remain ladies to you, and to themselves, and to everybody else; and at the same time they will suffer in no way from my delusion, for when I know that an ostensible hog is a lady, that is enough for me, I know how to treat her."

"Thanks, oh, sweet my lord, thou talkest like an angel. And I know that thou wilt deliver them, for that thou art minded to great deeds and art as strong a knight of your hands and as brave to will and to do, as any that is on live."

"I will not leave a princess in the sty, Sandy. Are those three yonder that to my disordered eyes are starveling swineherds — "

"The ogres, Are *they* changed also? It is most wonderful. Now am I fearful; for how canst thou strike with sure aim when five of their nine cubits of stature are to thee invisible? Ah, go warily, fair sir; this is a mightier emprise than I wend."

"You be easy, Sandy. All I need to know is, how *much* of an ogre is invisible; then I know how to locate his vitals. Don't you be afraid, I will make short work of these bunco-steerers. Stay where you are."

I left Sandy kneeling there, corpse-faced but plucky and hopeful, and rode down to the pigsty, and struck up a trade with the swineherds. I won their gratitude by buying out all the hogs at the lump sum of sixteen pennies, which was rather above latest quotations. I was just in time; for the Church, the lord of the manor, and the rest of the tax-gatherers would have been along next day and swept off pretty much all the stock, leaving the swineherds very short of hogs and Sandy out of princesses. But now the tax people could be paid in cash, and there would be a stake left besides. One of the men had ten children; and he said that last year when a priest came and of his ten pigs took the fattest one for tithes, the wife burst out upon him, and offered him a child and said:

"Thou beast without bowels of mercy, why leave me my child, yet rob me of the wherewithal to feed it?"

How curious. The same thing had happened in the Wales of my day, under this same old Established Church, which was supposed by many to have changed its nature when it changed its disguise.

I sent the three men away, and then opened the sty gate and beckoned Sandy to come — which she did; and not leisurely, but with the rush of a prairie fire. And when I saw her fling herself upon those hogs, with tears of joy running down her cheeks, and strain them to her heart, and kiss them, and caress them, and call them reverently by grand princely names, I was ashamed of her, ashamed of the human race.

We had to drive those hogs home — ten miles; and no ladies were ever more fickle-minded or contrary. They would stay in no road, no path; they broke out through the brush on all sides, and flowed away in all directions, over rocks, and hills, and the roughest places they could find. And they must not be struck, or roughly accosted; Sandy could not bear to see them treated in ways unbecoming their rank. The troublesomest old sow of the lot had to be called my Lady, and your Highness, like the rest. It is annoying and difficult to scour around after hogs, in armor. There was one small countess, with an iron ring in her snout and hardly any hair on her back, that was the devil for perversity. She gave me a race of an hour, over all sorts of country, and then we were right where we had started from, having made not a rod of real progress. I seized her at last by the tail, and brought her along squealing. When I overtook Sandy she was horrified, and said it was in the last degree indelicate to drag a countess by her train.

We got the hogs home just at dark — most of them. The princess Nerovens de Morganore was missing, and two of her ladies in waiting: namely, Miss Angela Bohun, and the Demoiselle Elaine Courtemains, the former of these two being a young black sow with a white star in her forehead, and the latter a brown one with thin legs and a slight limp in the forward shank on the starboard side — a couple of the tryingest blisters to drive that I ever saw. Also among the missing were several mere baronesses — and I wanted them to stay missing; but no, all that sausage-meat had to be found; so servants were sent out with torches to scour the woods and hills to that end.

Of course, the whole drove was housed in the house, and, great guns! — well, I never saw anything like it. Nor ever heard anything like it. And never smelt anything like it. It was like an insurrection in a gasometer.

Chapter XXI. The Pilgrims

When I did get to bed at last I was unspeakably tired; the stretching out, and the relaxing of the long-tense muscles, how luxurious, how delicious! but that was as far as I could get — sleep was out of the question for the present. The ripping and tearing and squealing of the nobility up and down the halls and corridors was pandemonium come again, and kept me broad awake. Being awake, my thoughts were busy, of course; and mainly they busied themselves with Sandy's curious delusion. Here she was, as sane a person as the kingdom could produce; and yet, from my point of view she was acting like a crazy woman. My land, the power of training! of influence! of education! It can bring a body up to believe anything. I had to put myself in Sandy's place to realize that she was not a lunatic. Yes, and put her in mine, to demonstrate how easy it is to seem a lunatic to a person who has not been taught as you have been taught. If I had told Sandy I had seen a wagon, uninfluenced by enchantment, spin along fifty miles an hour; had seen a man, unequipped with magic powers, get into a basket and soar out of sight among the clouds; and had listened, without any necromancer's help, to the conversation of a person who was several hundred miles away, Sandy would not merely have supposed me to be crazy, she would have thought she knew it. Everybody around her believed in enchantments; nobody had any doubts; to doubt that a castle could be turned into a sty, and its occupants into hogs, would have been the same as my doubting among Connecticut people the actuality of the telephone and its wonders, — and in both cases would be absolute proof of a diseased mind, an unsettled reason. Yes, Sandy was sane; that must be admitted. If I also would be sane — to Sandy — I must keep my superstitions about unenchanted and unmiraculous locomotives, balloons, and telephones, to myself. Also, I believed that the world was not flat, and hadn't pillars under it to support it, nor a canopy over it to turn off a universe of water that occupied all space above; but as I was the only person in the kingdom afflicted with such impious and criminal opinions, I recognized that it would be good wisdom to keep quiet about this matter, too, if I did not wish to be suddenly shunned and forsaken by everybody as a madman.

The next morning Sandy assembled the swine in the diningroom and gave them their breakfast, waiting upon them personally and manifesting in every way the deep reverence which the natives of her island, ancient and modern, have always felt for rank, let its outward casket and the mental and moral contents be what they may. I could have eaten with the hogs if I had had birth approaching my lofty official rank; but I hadn't, and so accepted the unavoidable slight and made no complaint. Sandy and I had our breakfast at the second table. The family were not at home. I said:

"How many are in the family, Sandy, and where do they keep themselves?"

"Family?"

"Yes."

"Which family, good my lord?"

"Why, this family; your own family."

"Sooth to say, I understand you not. I have no family."

"No family? Why, Sandy, isn't this your home?"

"Now how indeed might that be? I have no home."

"Well, then, whose house is this?"

"Ah, wit you well I would tell you an I knew myself."

"Come — you don't even know these people? Then who invited us here?"

"None invited us. We but came; that is all."

"Why, woman, this is a most extraordinary performance. The effrontery of it is beyond admiration. We blandly march into a man's house, and cram it full of the only really valuable nobility the sun has yet discovered in the earth, and then it turns out that we don't even know the man's name. How did you ever venture to take this extravagant liberty? I supposed, of course, it was your home. What will the man say?"

"What will he say? Forsooth what can he say but give thanks?"

"Thanks for what?"

Her face was filled with a puzzled surprise:

"Verily, thou troublest mine understanding with strange words. Do ye dream that one of his estate is like to have the honor twice in his life to entertain company such as we have brought to grace his house withal?"

"Well, no — when you come to that. No, it's an even bet that this is the first time he has had a treat like this."

"Then let him be thankful, and manifest the same by grateful speech and due humility; he were a dog, else, and the heir and ancestor of dogs."

To my mind, the situation was uncomfortable. It might become more so. It might be a good idea to muster the hogs and move on. So I said:

"The day is wasting, Sandy. It is time to get the nobility together and be moving."

"Wherefore, fair sir and Boss?"

"We want to take them to their home, don't we?"

"La, but list to him! They be of all the regions of the earth! Each must hie to her own home; wend you we might do all these journeys in one so brief life as He hath appointed that created life, and thereto death likewise with help of Adam, who by sin done through persuasion of his helpmeet, she being wrought upon and bewrayed by the beguilements of the great enemy of man, that serpent hight Satan, aforetime consecrated and set apart unto that evil work by over-mastering spite and envy begotten in his heart through fell ambitions that did blight and mildew a nature erst so white and pure whenso it hove with the shining multitudes its brethren-born in glade and shade of that fair heaven wherein all such as native be to that rich estate and — "

"Great Scott!"

"My lord?"

"Well, you know we haven't got time for this sort of thing. Don't you see, we could distribute these people around the earth in less time than it is going to take you to explain that we can't. We mustn't talk now, we must act. You want to be careful; you mustn't let your mill get the start of you that way, at a time like this. To business now — and sharp's the word. Who is to take the aristocracy home?"

"Even their friends. These will come for them from the far parts of the earth."

This was lightning from a clear sky, for unexpectedness; and the relief of it was like pardon to a prisoner. She would remain to deliver the goods, of course.

"Well, then, Sandy, as our enterprise is handsomely and successfully ended, I will go home and report; and if ever another one — "

"I also am ready; I will go with thee."

This was recalling the pardon.

"How? You will go with me? Why should you?"

"Will I be traitor to my knight, dost think? That were dishonor. I may not part from thee until in knightly encounter in the field some overmatching champion shall fairly win and fairly wear me. I were to blame an I thought that that might ever hap."

"Elected for the long term," I sighed to myself. "I may as well make the best of it." So then I spoke up and said:

"All right; let us make a start."

While she was gone to cry her farewells over the pork, I gave that whole peerage away to the servants. And I asked them to take a duster and dust around a little where the nobilities had mainly lodged and promenaded; but they considered that that would be hardly worth while, and would moreover be a rather grave departure from custom, and therefore likely to make talk. A departure from custom — that settled it; it was a nation capable of committing any crime but that. The servants said they would follow the fashion, a fashion grown sacred through immemorial observance; they would scatter fresh rushes in all the rooms and halls, and then the evidence of the aristocratic visitation would be no longer visible. It was a kind of satire on Nature: it was the scientific method, the geologic method; it deposited the history of the family in a stratified record; and the antiquary could dig through it and tell by the remains of each period what changes of diet the family had introduced successively for a hundred years.

The first thing we struck that day was a procession of pilgrims. It was not going our way, but we joined it, nevertheless; for it was hourly being borne in upon me now, that if I would govern this country wisely, I must be posted in the details of its life, and not at second hand, but by personal observation and scrutiny.

This company of pilgrims resembled Chaucer's in this: that it had in it a sample of about all the upper occupations and professions the country could show, and a corresponding variety of costume. There were young men and old men, young women and old women, lively folk and grave folk. They rode upon mules and horses, and there was not a side-saddle in the party; for this specialty was to remain unknown in England for nine hundred years yet.

It was a pleasant, friendly, sociable herd; pious, happy, merry and full of unconscious coarsenesses and innocent indecencies. What they regarded as the merry tale went the continual round and caused no more embarrassment than it would have caused in the best English society twelve centuries later. Practical jokes worthy of the English wits of the first quarter of the far-off nineteenth century were sprung here and there and yonder along the line, and compelled the delightedest applause; and sometimes when a bright remark was made at one end of the procession and started on its travels toward the other, you could note its progress all the way by the sparkling spray of laughter it threw off from its bows as it plowed along; and also by the blushes of the mules in its wake.

Sandy knew the goal and purpose of this pilgrimage, and she posted me. She said:

"They journey to the Valley of Holiness, for to be blessed of the godly hermits and drink of the miraculous waters and be cleansed from sin."

"Where is this watering place?"

"It lieth a two-day journey hence, by the borders of the land that hight the Cuckoo Kingdom."

"Tell me about it. Is it a celebrated place?"

"Oh, of a truth, yes. There be none more so. Of old time there lived there an abbot and his monks. Belike were none in the world more holy than these; for they gave themselves to study of pious books, and spoke not the one to the other, or indeed to any, and ate decayed herbs and naught thereto, and slept hard, and prayed much, and washed never; also they wore the same garment until it fell from their bodies through age and decay. Right so came they to be known of all the world by reason of these holy austerities, and visited by rich and poor, and reverenced."

"Proceed."

"But always there was lack of water there. Whereas, upon a time, the holy abbot prayed, and for answer a great stream of clear water burst forth by miracle in a desert place. Now were the fickle monks tempted of the Fiend, and they wrought with their abbot unceasingly by beggings and beseechings that he would construct a bath; and when he was become aweary and might not resist more, he said have ye your will, then, and granted that they asked. Now mark thou what 'tis to forsake the ways of purity the which He loveth, and wanton with such as be worldly and an offense. These monks did enter into the bath and come thence washed as white as snow; and lo, in that moment His sign appeared, in miraculous rebuke! for His insulted waters ceased to flow, and utterly vanished away."

"They fared mildly, Sandy, considering how that kind of crime is regarded in this country."

"Belike; but it was their first sin; and they had been of perfect life for long, and differing in naught from the angels. Prayers, tears, torturings of the flesh, all was vain to beguile that water to flow again. Even processions; even burnt-offerings; even votive candles to the Virgin, did fail every each of them; and all in the land did marvel."

"How odd to find that even this industry has its financial panics, and at times sees its assignats and greenbacks languish to zero, and everything come to a standstill. Go on, Sandy."

"And so upon a time, after year and day, the good abbot made humble surrender and destroyed the bath. And behold, His anger was in that moment appeased, and the waters gushed richly forth again, and even unto this day they have not ceased to flow in that generous measure."

"Then I take it nobody has washed since."

"He that would essay it could have his halter free; yes, and swiftly would he need it, too."

"The community has prospered since?"

"Even from that very day. The fame of the miracle went abroad into all lands. From every land came monks to join; they came even as the fishes come, in shoals; and the monastery added building to building, and yet others to these, and so spread wide its arms and took them in. And nuns came, also; and more again, and yet more; and built over against the monastery on the yon side of the vale, and added building to building, until mighty was that nunnery. And these were friendly unto those, and they joined their loving labors together, and together they built a fair great foundling asylum midway of the valley between."

"You spoke of some hermits, Sandy."

"These have gathered there from the ends of the earth. A hermit thriveth best where there be multitudes of pilgrims. Ye shall not find no hermit of no sort wanting. If any shall mention a hermit of a kind he thinketh new and not to be found but in some far strange land, let him but scratch among the holes and caves and swamps that line that Valley of Holiness, and whatsoever be his breed, it skills not, he shall find a sample of it there."

I closed up alongside of a burly fellow with a fat good-humored face, purposing to make myself agreeable and pick up some further crumbs of fact; but I had hardly more than scraped acquaintance with him when he began eagerly and awkwardly to lead up, in the immemorial way, to that same old anecdote — the one Sir Dinadan told me, what time I got into trouble with Sir Sagramor and was challenged of him on account of it. I excused myself and dropped to the rear of the procession, sad at heart, willing to go hence from this troubled life, this vale of tears, this brief day of broken rest, of cloud and storm, of weary struggle and monotonous defeat; and yet shrinking from the change, as remembering how long eternity is, and how many have wended thither who know that anecdote.

Early in the afternoon we overtook another procession of pilgrims; but in this one was no merriment, no jokes, no laughter, no playful ways, nor any happy giddiness, whether of youth or age. Yet both were here, both age and youth; gray old men and women, strong men and women of middle age, young husbands, young wives, little boys and girls, and three babies at the breast. Even the children were smileless; there was not a face among all these half a hundred people but was cast down, and bore that set expression of hopelessness which is bred of long and hard trials and old acquaintance with despair. They were slaves. Chains led from their fettered feet and their manacled hands to a sole-leather belt about their waists; and all except the children were also linked together in a file six feet apart, by a single chain which led from collar to collar all down the line. They were on foot, and had tramped three hundred miles in eighteen days, upon the cheapest odds and ends of food, and stingy rations of that. They had slept in these chains every night, bundled together like swine. They had upon their bodies some poor rags, but they could not be said to be clothed. Their irons had chafed the skin from their ankles and made sores which were ulcerated and wormy. Their naked feet were torn, and none walked without a limp. Originally there had been a hundred of these unfortunates, but about half had been sold on the trip. The trader in charge of them rode a horse and carried a whip with a short handle and a long heavy lash divided into several knotted tails at the end. With this whip he cut the shoulders of any that tottered from weariness and pain, and straightened them up. He did not speak; the whip conveyed his desire without that. None of these poor creatures looked up as we rode along by; they showed no consciousness of our presence. And they made no sound but one; that was the dull and awful clank of their chains from end to end of the long file, as forty-three burdened feet rose and fell in unison. The file moved in a cloud of its own making.

All these faces were gray with a coating of dust. One has seen the like of this coating upon furniture in unoccupied houses, and has written his idle thought in it with his finger. I was reminded of this when I noticed the faces of some of those women, young mothers carrying babes that were near to death and freedom, how a something in their hearts was written in the dust upon their faces, plain to see, and lord, how plain to read! for it was the track of tears. One of these young mothers was but a girl, and it hurt me to the heart to read that writing, and reflect that it was come up out of the breast of such a child, a breast that ought not to know trouble yet, but only the gladness of the morning of life; and no doubt —

She reeled just then, giddy with fatigue, and down came the lash and flicked a flake of skin from her naked shoulder. It stung me as if I had been hit instead. The master halted the file and jumped from his horse. He stormed and swore at this girl, and said she had made annoyance enough with her laziness, and as this was the last chance he should have, he would settle the account now. She dropped on her knees and put up her hands and began to beg, and cry, and implore, in a passion of terror, but the master gave no attention. He snatched the child from her, and then made the men-slaves who were chained before and behind her throw her on the ground and hold her there and expose her body; and then he laid on with his lash like a madman till her back was flayed, she shrieking and struggling the while piteously. One of the men who was holding her turned away his face, and for this humanity he was reviled and flogged.

All our pilgrims looked on and commented — on the expert way in which the whip was handled. They were too much hardened by lifelong everyday familiarity with slavery to notice that there was anything else in the exhibition that invited comment. This was what slavery could do, in the way of ossifying what one may call the superior lobe of human feeling; for these pilgrims were kindhearted people, and they would not have allowed that man to treat a horse like that.

I wanted to stop the whole thing and set the slaves free, but that would not do. I must not interfere too much and get myself a name for riding over the country's laws and the citizen's rights roughshod. If I lived and prospered I would be the death of slavery, that I was resolved upon; but I would try to fix it so that when I became its executioner it should be by command of the nation.

Just here was the wayside shop of a smith; and now arrived a landed proprietor who had bought this girl a few miles back, deliverable here where her irons could be taken off. They were removed; then there was a squabble between the gentleman and the dealer as to which should pay the blacksmith. The moment the girl was delivered from her irons, she flung herself, all tears and frantic sobbings, into the arms of the slave who had turned away his face when she was whipped. He strained her to his breast, and smothered her face and the child's with kisses, and washed them with the rain of his tears. I suspected. I inquired. Yes, I was right; it was husband and wife. They had to be torn apart by force; the girl had to be dragged away, and she struggled and fought and shrieked like one gone mad till a turn of the road hid her from sight; and even after that, we could still make out the fading plaint of those receding shrieks. And the husband and father, with his wife and child gone, never to be seen by him again in life? — well, the look of him one might not bear at all, and so I turned away; but I knew I should never get his picture out of my mind again, and there it is to this day, to wring my heartstrings whenever I think of it.

We put up at the inn in a village just at nightfall, and when I rose next morning and looked abroad, I was ware where a knight came riding in the golden glory of the new day, and recognized him for knight of mine — Sir Ozana le Cure Hardy. He was in the gentlemen's furnishing line, and his missionarying specialty was plug hats. He was clothed all in steel, in the beautifulest armor of the time — up to where his helmet ought to have been; but he hadn't any helmet, he wore a shiny stovepipe hat, and was ridiculous a spectacle as one might want to see. It was another of my surreptitious schemes for extinguishing knighthood by making it grotesque and absurd. Sir Ozana's saddle was hung about with leather hat boxes, and every time he overcame a wandering knight he swore him into my service and fitted him with a plug and made him wear it. I dressed and ran down to welcome Sir Ozana and get his news.

"How is trade?" I asked.

"Ye will note that I have but these four left; yet were they sixteen whenas I got me from Camelot."

"Why, you have certainly done nobly, Sir Ozana. Where have you been foraging of late?"

"I am but now come from the Valley of Holiness, please you sir."

"I am pointed for that place myself. Is there anything stirring in the monkery, more than common?"

"By the mass ye may not question it!.... Give him good feed, boy, and stint it not, an thou valuest thy crown; so get ye lightly to the stable and do even as I bid.... Sir, it is parlous news I bring, and — be these pilgrims? Then ye may not do better, good folk, than gather and hear the tale I have to tell, sith it concerneth you, forasmuch as ye go to find that ye will not find, and seek that ye will seek in vain, my life being hostage for my word, and my word and message being these, namely: That a hap has happened whereof the like has not been seen no more but once this two hundred years, which was the first and last time that that said misfortune strake the holy valley in that form by commandment of the Most High whereto by reasons just and causes thereunto contributing, wherein the matter — "

"The miraculous fount hath ceased to flow!" This shout burst from twenty pilgrim mouths at once.

"Ye say well, good people. I was verging to it, even when ye spake."

"Has somebody been washing again?"

"Nay, it is suspected, but none believe it. It is thought to be some other sin, but none wit what."

"How are they feeling about the calamity?"

"None may describe it in words. The fount is these nine days dry. The prayers that did begin then, and the lamentations in sackcloth and ashes, and the holy processions, none of these have ceased nor night nor day; and so the monks and the nuns and the foundlings be all exhausted, and do hang up prayers writ upon parchment, sith that no strength is left in man to lift up voice. And at last they sent for thee, Sir Boss, to try magic and enchantment; and if you could not come, then was the messenger to fetch Merlin, and he is there these three days now, and saith he will fetch that water though he burst the globe and wreck its kingdoms to accomplish it; and right bravely doth he work his magic and call upon his hellions to hie them hither and help, but not a whiff of moisture hath he started yet, even so much as might qualify as mist upon a copper mirror an ye count not the barrel of sweat he sweateth betwixt sun and sun over the dire labors of his task; and if ye — "

Breakfast was ready. As soon as it was over I showed to Sir Ozana these words which I had written on the inside of his hat: "Chemical Department, Laboratory extension, Section G. Pxxp. Send two of first size, two of No. 3, and six of No. 4, together with the proper complementary details — and two of my trained assistants." And I said:

"Now get you to Camelot as fast as you can fly, brave knight, and show the writing to Clarence, and tell him to have these required matters in the Valley of Holiness with all possible dispatch."

"I will well, Sir Boss," and he was off.

Chapter XXII. The Holy Fountain

The pilgrims were human beings. Otherwise they would have acted differently. They had come a long and difficult journey, and now when the journey was nearly finished, and they learned that the main thing they had come for had ceased to exist, they didn't do as horses or cats or angle-worms would probably have done — turn back and get at something profitable — no, anxious as they had before been to see the miraculous fountain, they were as much as forty times as anxious now to see the place where it had used to be. There is no accounting for human beings.

We made good time; and a couple of hours before sunset we stood upon the high confines of the Valley of Holiness, and our eyes swept it from end to end and noted its features. That is, its large features. These were the three masses of buildings. They were distant and isolated temporalities shrunken to toy constructions in the lonely waste of what seemed a desert — and was. Such a scene is always mournful, it is so impressively still, and looks so steeped in death. But there was a sound here which interrupted the stillness only to add to its mournfulness; this was the faint far sound of tolling bells which floated fitfully to us on the passing breeze, and so faintly, so softly, that we hardly knew whether we heard it with our ears or with our spirits.

We reached the monastery before dark, and there the males were given lodging, but the women were sent over to the nunnery. The bells were close at hand now, and their solemn booming smote upon the ear like a message of doom. A superstitious despair possessed the heart of every monk and published itself in his ghastly face. Everywhere, these black-robed, soft-sandaled, tallow-visaged specters appeared, flitted about and disappeared, noiseless as the creatures of a troubled dream, and as uncanny.

The old abbot's joy to see me was pathetic. Even to tears; but he did the shedding himself. He said:

"Delay not, son, but get to thy saving work. An we bring not the water back again, and soon, we are ruined, and the good work of two hundred years must end. And see thou do it with enchantments that be holy, for the Church will not endure that work in her cause be done by devil's magic."

"When I work, Father, be sure there will be no devil's work connected with it. I shall use no arts that come of the devil, and no elements not created by the hand of God. But is Merlin working strictly on pious lines?"

"Ah, he said he would, my son, he said he would, and took oath to make his promise good."

"Well, in that case, let him proceed."

"But surely you will not sit idle by, but help?"

"It will not answer to mix methods, Father; neither would it be professional courtesy. Two of a trade must not underbid each other. We might as well cut rates and be done with it; it would arrive at that in the end. Merlin has the contract; no other magician can touch it till he throws it up."

"But I will take it from him; it is a terrible emergency and the act is thereby justified. And if it were not so, who will give law to the Church? The Church giveth law to all; and what she wills to do, that she may do, hurt whom it may. I will take it from him; you shall begin upon the moment."

"It may not be, Father. No doubt, as you say, where power is supreme, one can do as one likes and suffer no injury; but we poor magicians are not so situated. Merlin is a very good magician in a small way, and has quite a neat provincial reputation. He is struggling along, doing the best he can, and it would not be etiquette for me to take his job until he himself abandons it."

The abbot's face lighted.

"Ah, that is simple. There are ways to persuade him to abandon it."

"No-no, Father, it skills not, as these people say. If he were persuaded against his will, he would load that well with a malicious enchantment which would balk me until I found out its secret. It might take a month. I could set up a little enchantment of mine which I call the telephone, and he could not find out its secret in a hundred years. Yes, you perceive, he might block me for a month. Would you like to risk a month in a dry time like this?"

"A month! The mere thought of it maketh me to shudder. Have it thy way, my son. But my heart is heavy with this disappointment. Leave me, and let me wear my spirit with weariness and waiting, even as I have done these ten long days, counterfeiting thus the thing that is called rest, the prone body making outward sign of repose where inwardly is none."

Of course, it would have been best, all round, for Merlin to waive etiquette and quit and call it half a day, since he would never be able to start that water, for he was a true magician of the time; which is to say, the big miracles, the ones that gave him his reputation, always had the luck to be performed when nobody but Merlin was present; he couldn't start this well with all this crowd around to see; a crowd was as bad for a magician's miracle in that day as it was for a spiritualist's miracle in mine; there was sure to be some skeptic on hand to turn up the gas at the crucial moment and spoil everything. But I did not want Merlin to retire from the job until I was ready to take hold of it effectively myself; and I could not do that until I got my things from Camelot, and that would take two or three days.

My presence gave the monks hope, and cheered them up a good deal; insomuch that they ate a square meal that night for the first time in ten days. As soon as their stomachs had been properly reinforced with food, their spirits began to rise fast; when the mead began to go round they rose faster. By the time everybody was half-seas over, the holy community was in good shape to make a night of it; so we stayed by the board and put it through on that line. Matters got to be very jolly. Good old questionable stories were told that made the tears run down and cavernous mouths stand wide and the round bellies shake with laughter; and questionable songs were bellowed out in a mighty chorus that drowned the boom of the tolling bells.

At last I ventured a story myself; and vast was the success of it. Not right off, of course, for the native of those islands does not, as a rule, dissolve upon the early applications of a humorous thing; but the fifth time I told it, they began to crack in places; the eight time I told it, they began to crumble; at the twelfth repetition they fell apart in chunks; and at the fifteenth they disintegrated, and I got a broom and swept them up. This language is figurative. Those islanders — well, they are slow pay at first, in the matter of return for your investment of effort, but in the end they make the pay of all other nations poor and small by contrast.

I was at the well next day betimes. Merlin was there, enchanting away like a beaver, but not raising the moisture. He was not in a pleasant humor; and every time I hinted that perhaps this contract was a shade too hefty for a novice he unlimbered his tongue and cursed like a bishop — French bishop of the Regency days, I mean.

Matters were about as I expected to find them. The "fountain" was an ordinary well, it had been dug in the ordinary way, and stoned up in the ordinary way. There was no miracle about it. Even the lie that had created its reputation was not miraculous; I could have told it myself, with one hand tied behind me. The well was in a dark chamber which stood in the center of a cut-stone chapel, whose walls were hung with pious pictures of a workmanship that would have made a chromo feel good; pictures historically commemorative of curative miracles which had been achieved by the waters when nobody was looking. That is, nobody but angels; they are always on deck when there is a miracle to the fore — so as to get put in the picture, perhaps. Angels are as fond of that as a fire company; look at the old masters.

The well-chamber was dimly lighted by lamps; the water was drawn with a windlass and chain by monks, and poured into troughs which delivered it into stone reservoirs outside in the chapel — when there was water to draw, I mean — and none but monks could enter the well-chamber. I entered it, for I had temporary authority to do so, by courtesy of my professional brother and subordinate. But he hadn't entered it himself. He did everything by incantations; he never worked his intellect. If he had stepped in there and used his eyes, instead of his disordered mind, he could have cured the well by natural means, and then turned it into a miracle in the customary way; but no, he was an old numskull, a magician who believed in his own magic; and no magician can thrive who is handicapped with a superstition like that.

I had an idea that the well had sprung a leak; that some of the wall stones near the bottom had fallen and exposed fissures that allowed the water to escape. I measured the chain — 98 feet. Then I called in a couple of monks, locked the door, took a candle, and made them lower me in the bucket. When the chain was all paid out, the candle confirmed my suspicion; a considerable section of the wall was gone, exposing a good big fissure.

I almost regretted that my theory about the well's trouble was correct, because I had another one that had a showy point or two about it for a miracle. I remembered that in America, many centuries later, when an oil well ceased to flow, they used to blast it out with a dynamite torpedo. If I should find this well dry and no explanation of it, I could astonish these people most nobly by having a person of no especial value drop a dynamite bomb into it. It was my idea to appoint Merlin. However, it was plain that there was no occasion for the bomb. One cannot have everything the way he would like it. A man has no business to be depressed by a disappointment, anyway; he ought to make up his mind to get even. That is what I did. I said to myself, I am in no hurry, I can wait; that bomb will come good yet. And it did, too.

When I was above ground again, I turned out the monks, and let down a fishline; the well was a hundred and fifty feet deep, and there was forty-one feet of water in it. I called in a monk and asked:

"How deep is the well?"

"That, sir, I wit not, having never been told."

"How does the water usually stand in it?"

"Near to the top, these two centuries, as the testimony goeth, brought down to us through our predecessors."

It was true — as to recent times at least — for there was witness to it, and better witness than a monk; only about twenty or thirty feet of the chain showed wear and use, the rest of it was unworn and rusty. What had happened when the well gave out that other time? Without doubt some practical person had come along and mended the leak, and then had come up and told the abbot he had discovered by divination that if the sinful bath were destroyed the well would flow again. The leak had befallen again now, and these children would have prayed, and processioned, and tolled their bells for heavenly succor till they all dried up and blew away, and no innocent of them all would ever have thought to drop a fishline into the well or go down in it and find out what was really the matter. Old habit of mind is one of the toughest things to get away from in the world. It transmits itself like physical form and feature; and for a man, in those days, to have had an idea that his ancestors hadn't had, would have brought him under suspicion of being illegitimate. I said to the monk:

"It is a difficult miracle to restore water in a dry well, but we will try, if my brother Merlin fails. Brother Merlin is a very passable artist, but only in the parlor-magic line, and he may not succeed; in fact, is not likely to succeed. But that should be nothing to his discredit; the man that can do *this* kind of miracle knows enough to keep hotel."

"Hotel? I mind not to have heard — "

"Of hotel? It's what you call hostel. The man that can do this miracle can keep hostel. I can do this miracle; I shall do this miracle; yet I do not try to conceal from you that it is a miracle to tax the occult powers to the last strain."

"None knoweth that truth better than the brotherhood, indeed; for it is of record that aforetime it was parlous difficult and took a year. Natheless, God send you good success, and to that end will we pray."

As a matter of business it was a good idea to get the notion around that the thing was difficult. Many a small thing has been made large by the right kind of advertising. That monk was filled up with the difficulty of this enterprise; he would fill up the others. In two days the solicitude would be booming.

On my way home at noon, I met Sandy. She had been sampling the hermits. I said:

"I would like to do that myself. This is Wednesday. Is there a matinee?"

"A which, please you, sir?"

"Matinee. Do they keep open afternoons?"

"Who?"

"The hermits, of course."

"Keep open?"

"Yes, keep open. Isn't that plain enough? Do they knock off at noon?"

"Knock off?"

"Knock off? — yes, knock off. What is the matter with knock off? I never saw such a dunderhead; can't you understand anything at all? In plain terms, do they shut up shop, draw the game, bank the fires — "

"Shut up shop, draw — "

"There, never mind, let it go; you make me tired. You can't seem to understand the simplest thing."

"I would I might please thee, sir, and it is to me dole and sorrow that I fail, albeit sith I am but a simple damsel and taught of none, being from the cradle unbaptized in those deep waters of learning that do anoint with a sovereignty him that partaketh of that most noble sacrament, investing him with reverend state to the mental eye of the humble mortal who, by bar and lack of that great consecration seeth in his own unlearned estate but a symbol of that other sort of lack and loss which men do publish to the pitying eye with sackcloth trappings whereon the ashes of grief do lie bepowdered and bestrewn, and so, when such shall in the darkness of his mind encounter these golden phrases of high mystery, these shut-up-shops, and draw-the-game, and bank-the-fires, it is but by the grace of God that he burst not for envy of the mind that can beget, and tongue that can deliver so great and mellow-sounding miracles of speech, and if there do ensue confusion in that humbler mind, and failure to divine the meanings of these wonders, then if so be this miscomprehension is not vain but sooth and true, wit ye well it is the very substance of worshipful dear homage and may not lightly be misprized, nor had been, an ye had noted this complexion of mood and mind and understood that that I would I could not, and that I could not I might not, nor yet nor might *nor* could, nor might-not nor could-not, might be by advantage turned to the desired *would* , and so I pray you mercy of my fault, and that ye will of your kindness and your charity forgive it, good my master and most dear lord."

I couldn't make it all out — that is, the details — but I got the general idea; and enough of it, too, to be ashamed. It was not fair to spring those nineteenth century technicalities upon the untutored infant of the sixth and then rail at her because she couldn't get their drift; and when she was making the honest best drive at it she could, too, and no fault of hers that she couldn't fetch the home plate; and so I apologized. Then we meandered pleasantly away toward the hermit holes in sociable converse together, and better friends than ever.

I was gradually coming to have a mysterious and shuddery reverence for this girl; nowadays whenever she pulled out from the station and got her train fairly started on one of those horizon-less transcontinental sentences of hers, it was borne in upon me that I was standing in the awful presence of the Mother of the German Language. I was so impressed with this, that sometimes when she began to empty one of these sentences on me I unconsciously took the very attitude of reverence, and stood uncovered; and if words had been water, I had been drowned, sure. She had exactly the German way; whatever was in her mind to be delivered, whether a mere remark, or a sermon, or a cyclopedia, or the history of a war, she would get it into a single sentence or die. Whenever the literary German dives into a sentence, that is the last you are going to see of him till he emerges on the other side of his Atlantic with his verb in his mouth.

We drifted from hermit to hermit all the afternoon. It was a most strange menagerie. The chief emulation among them seemed to be, to see which could manage to be the uncleanest and most prosperous with vermin. Their manner and attitudes were the last expression of complacent self-righteousness. It was one anchorite's pride to lie naked in the mud and let the insects bite him and blister him unmolested; it was another's to lean against a rock, all day long, conspicuous to the admiration of the throng of pilgrims and pray; it was another's to go naked and crawl around on all fours; it was another's to drag about with him, year in and year out, eighty pounds of iron; it was another's to never lie down when he slept, but to stand among the thorn-bushes and snore when there were pilgrims around to look; a woman, who had the white hair of age, and no other apparel, was black from crown to heel with forty-seven years of holy abstinence from water. Groups of gazing pilgrims stood around all and every of these strange objects, lost in reverent wonder, and envious of the fleckless sanctity which these pious austerities had won for them from an exacting heaven.

By and by we went to see one of the supremely great ones. He was a mighty celebrity; his fame had penetrated all Christendom; the noble and the renowned journeyed from the remotest lands on the globe to pay him reverence. His stand was in the center of the widest part of the valley; and it took all that space to hold his crowds.

His stand was a pillar sixty feet high, with a broad platform on the top of it. He was now doing what he had been doing every day for twenty years up there — bowing his body ceaselessly and rapidly almost to his feet. It was his way of praying. I timed him with a stop watch, and he made 1,244 revolutions in 24 minutes and 46 seconds. It seemed a pity to have all this power going to waste. It was one of the most useful motions in mechanics, the pedal movement; so I made a note in my memorandum book, purposing some day to apply a system of elastic cords to him and run a sewing machine with it. I afterward carried out that scheme, and got five years' good service out of him; in which time he turned out upward of eighteen thousand first-rate tow-linen shirts, which was ten a day. I worked him Sundays and all; he was going, Sundays, the same as week days, and it was no use to waste the power. These shirts cost me nothing but just the mere trifle for the materials — I furnished those myself, it would not have been right to make him do that — and they sold like smoke to pilgrims at a dollar and a half apiece, which was the price of fifty cows or a blooded race horse in Arthurdom. They were regarded as a perfect protection against sin, and advertised as such by my knights everywhere, with the paint-pot and stencil-plate; insomuch that there was not a cliff or a bowlder or a dead wall in England but you could read on it at a mile distance:

"Buy the only genuine St. Stylite; patronized by the Nobility. Patent applied for."

There was more money in the business than one knew what to do with. As it extended, I brought out a line of goods suitable for kings, and a nobby thing for duchesses and that sort, with ruffles down the forehatch and the running-gear clewed up with a featherstitch to leeward and then hauled aft with a back-stay and triced up with a half-turn in the standing rigging forward of the weather-gaskets. Yes, it was a daisy.

But about that time I noticed that the motive power had taken to standing on one leg, and I found that there was something the matter with the other one; so I stocked the business and unloaded, taking Sir Bors de Ganis into camp financially along with certain of his friends; for the works stopped within a year, and the good saint got him to his rest. But he had earned it. I can say that for him.

When I saw him that first time — however, his personal condition will not quite bear description here. You can read it in the Lives of the Saints.*

[*All the details concerning the hermits, in this chapter, are from Lecky — but greatly modified. This book not being a history but only a tale, the majority of the historian's frank details were too strong for reproduction in it. — *Editor*]

Chapter XXIII. Restoration of the Fountain

Saturday noon I went to the well and looked on a while. Merlin was still burning smoke-powders, and pawing the air, and muttering gibberish as hard as ever, but looking pretty downhearted, for of course he had not started even a perspiration in that well yet. Finally I said:

"How does the thing promise by this time, partner?"

"Behold, I am even now busied with trial of the powerfulest enchantment known to the princes of the occult arts in the lands of the East; an it fail me, naught can avail. Peace, until I finish."

He raised a smoke this time that darkened all the region, and must have made matters uncomfortable for the hermits, for the wind was their way, and it rolled down over their dens in a dense and billowy fog. He poured out volumes of speech to match, and contorted his body and sawed the air with his hands in a most extraordinary way. At the end of twenty minutes he dropped down panting, and about exhausted. Now arrived the abbot and several hundred monks and nuns, and behind them a multitude of pilgrims and a couple of acres of foundlings, all drawn by the prodigious smoke, and all in a grand state of excitement. The abbot inquired anxiously for results. Merlin said:

"If any labor of mortal might break the spell that binds these waters, this which I have but just essayed had done it. It has failed; whereby I do now know that that which I had feared is a truth established; the sign of this failure is, that the most potent spirit known to the magicians of the East, and whose name none may utter and live, has laid his spell upon this well. The mortal does not breathe, nor ever will, who can penetrate the secret of that spell, and without that secret none can break it. The water will flow no more forever, good Father. I have done what man could. Suffer me to go."

Of course this threw the abbot into a good deal of a consternation. He turned to me with the signs of it in his face, and said:

"Ye have heard him. Is it true?"

"Part of it is."

"Not all, then, not all! What part is true?"

"That that spirit with the Russian name has put his spell upon the well."

"God's wounds, then are we ruined!"

"Possibly."

"But not certainly? Ye mean, not certainly?"

"That is it."

"Wherefore, ye also mean that when he saith none can break the spell — "

"Yes, when he says that, he says what isn't necessarily true. There are conditions under which an effort to break it may have some chance — that is, some small, some trifling chance — of success."

"The conditions — "

"Oh, they are nothing difficult. Only these: I want the well and the surroundings for the space of half a mile, entirely to myself from sunset to-day until I remove the ban — and nobody allowed to cross the ground but by my authority."

"Are these all?"

"Yes."

"And you have no fear to try?"

"Oh, none. One may fail, of course; and one may also succeed. One can try, and I am ready to chance it. I have my conditions?"

"These and all others ye may name. I will issue commandment to that effect."

"Wait," said Merlin, with an evil smile. "Ye wit that he that would break this spell must know that spirit's name?"

"Yes, I know his name."

"And wit you also that to know it skills not of itself, but ye must likewise pronounce it? Ha-ha! Knew ye that?"

"Yes, I knew that, too."

"You had that knowledge! Art a fool? Are ye minded to utter that name and die?"

"Utter it? Why certainly. I would utter it if it was Welsh."

"Ye are even a dead man, then; and I go to tell Arthur."

"That's all right. Take your gripsack and get along. The thing for *you* to do is to go home and work the weather, John W. Merlin."

It was a home shot, and it made him wince; for he was the worst weather-failure in the kingdom. Whenever he ordered up the danger-signals along the coast there was a week's dead calm, sure, and every time he prophesied fair weather it rained brickbats. But I kept him in the weather bureau right along, to undermine his reputation. However, that shot raised his bile, and instead of starting home to report my death, he said he would remain and enjoy it.

My two experts arrived in the evening, and pretty well fagged, for they had traveled double tides. They had pack-mules along, and had brought everything I needed — tools, pump, lead pipe, Greek fire, sheaves of big rockets, roman candles, colored fire sprays, electric apparatus, and a lot of sundries — everything necessary for the stateliest kind of a miracle. They got their supper and a nap, and about midnight we sallied out through a solitude so wholly vacant and complete that it quite overpassed the required conditions. We took possession of the well and its surroundings. My boys were experts in all sorts of things, from the stoning up of a well to the constructing of a mathematical instrument. An hour before sunrise we had that leak mended in shipshape fashion, and the water began to rise. Then we stowed our fireworks in the chapel, locked up the place, and went home to bed.

Before the noon mass was over, we were at the well again; for there was a deal to do yet, and I was determined to spring the miracle before midnight, for business reasons: for whereas a miracle worked for the Church on a weekday is worth a good deal, it is worth six times as much if you get it in on a Sunday. In nine hours the water had risen to its customary level — that is to say, it was within twenty-three feet of the top. We put in a little iron pump, one of the first turned out by my works near the capital; we bored into a stone reservoir which stood against the outer wall of the well-chamber and inserted a section of lead pipe that was long enough to reach to the door of the chapel and project beyond the threshold, where the gushing water would be visible to the two hundred and fifty acres of people I was intending should be present on the flat plain in front of this little holy hillock at the proper time.

We knocked the head out of an empty hogshead and hoisted this hogshead to the flat roof of the chapel, where we clamped it down fast, poured in gunpowder till it lay loosely an inch deep on the bottom, then we stood up rockets in the hogshead as thick as they could loosely stand, all the different breeds of rockets there are; and they made a portly and imposing sheaf, I can tell you. We grounded the wire of a pocket electrical battery in that powder, we placed a whole magazine of Greek fire on each corner of the roof — blue on one corner, green on another, red on another, and purple on the last — and grounded a wire in each.

About two hundred yards off, in the flat, we built a pen of scantlings, about four feet high, and laid planks on it, and so made a platform. We covered it with swell tapestries borrowed for the occasion, and topped it off with the abbot's own throne. When you are going to do a miracle for an ignorant race, you want to get in every detail that will count; you want to make all the properties impressive to the public eye; you want to make matters comfortable for your head guest; then you can turn yourself loose and play your effects for all they are worth. I know the value of these things, for I know human nature. You can't throw too much style into a miracle. It costs trouble, and work, and sometimes money; but it pays in the end. Well, we brought the wires to the ground at the chapel, and then brought them under the ground to the platform, and hid the batteries there. We put a rope fence a hundred feet square around the platform to keep off the common multitude, and that finished the work. My idea was, doors open at 10:30, performance to begin at 11:25 sharp. I wished I could charge admission, but of course that wouldn't answer. I instructed my boys to be in the chapel as early as 10, before anybody was around, and be ready to man the pumps at the proper time, and make the fur fly. Then we went home to supper.

The news of the disaster to the well had traveled far by this time; and now for two or three days a steady avalanche of people had been pouring into the valley. The lower end of the valley was become one huge camp; we should have a good house, no question about that. Criers went the rounds early in the evening and announced the coming attempt, which put every pulse up to fever heat. They gave notice that the abbot and his official suite would move in state and occupy the platform at 10:30, up to which time all the region which was under my ban must be clear; the bells would then cease from tolling, and this sign should be permission to the multitudes to close in and take their places.

I was at the platform and all ready to do the honors when the abbot's solemn procession hove in sight — which it did not do till it was nearly to the rope fence, because it was a starless black night and no torches permitted. With it came Merlin, and took a front seat on the platform; he was as good as his word for once. One could not see the multitudes banked together beyond the ban, but they were there, just the same. The moment the bells stopped, those banked masses broke and poured over the line like a vast black wave, and for as much as a half hour it continued to flow, and then it solidified itself, and you could have walked upon a pavement of human heads to — well, miles.

We had a solemn stage-wait, now, for about twenty minutes — a thing I had counted on for effect; it is always good to let your audience have a chance to work up its expectancy. At length, out of the silence a noble Latin chant — men's voices — broke and swelled up and rolled away into the night, a majestic tide of melody. I had put that up, too, and it was one of the best effects I ever invented. When it was finished I stood up on the platform and extended my hands abroad, for two minutes, with my face uplifted — that always produces a dead hush — and then slowly pronounced this ghastly word with a kind of awfulness which caused hundreds to tremble, and many women to faint:

"Constantinopolitanischerdudelsackspfeifenmachersgesellschafft!"

Just as I was moaning out the closing hunks of that word, I touched off one of my electric connections and all that murky world of people stood revealed in a hideous blue glare! It was immense — that effect! Lots of people shrieked, women curled up and quit in every direction, foundlings collapsed by platoons. The abbot and the monks crossed themselves nimbly and their lips fluttered with agitated prayers. Merlin held his grip, but he was astonished clear down to his corns; he had never seen anything to begin with that, before. Now was the time to pile in the effects. I lifted my hands and groaned out this word — as it were in agony:

"Nihilistendynamittheaterkaestchenssprengungsattentaetsversuchungen!"

— and turned on the red fire! You should have heard that Atlantic of people moan and howl when that crimson hell joined the blue! After sixty seconds I shouted:

"Transvaaltruppentropentransporttrampelthiertreibertrauungsthraenen-tragoedie!"

— and lit up the green fire! After waiting only forty seconds this time, I spread my arms abroad and thundered out the devastating syllables of this word of words:

"Mekkamuselmannenmassenmenchenmoerdermohrenmuttermarmormonumentenmacher!"

— and whirled on the purple glare! There they were, all going at once, red, blue, green, purple! — four furious volcanoes pouring vast clouds of radiant smoke aloft, and spreading a blinding rainbowed noonday to the furthest confines of that valley. In the distance one could see that fellow on the pillar standing rigid against the background of sky, his seesaw stopped for the first time in twenty years. I knew the boys were at the pump now and ready. So I said to the abbot:

"The time is come, Father. I am about to pronounce the dread name and command the spell to dissolve. You want to brace up, and take hold of something." Then I shouted to the people: "Behold, in another minute the spell will be broken, or no mortal can break it. If it break, all will know it, for you will see the sacred water gush from the chapel door!"

I stood a few moments, to let the hearers have a chance to spread my announcement to those who couldn't hear, and so convey it to the furthest ranks, then I made a grand exhibition of extra posturing and gesturing, and shouted:

"Lo, I command the fell spirit that possesses the holy fountain to now disgorge into the skies all the infernal fires that still remain in him, and straightway dissolve his spell and flee hence to the pit, there to lie bound a thousand years. By his own dread name I command it — BGWJJILLIGKKK!"

Then I touched off the hogshead of rockets, and a vast fountain of dazzling lances of fire vomited itself toward the zenith with a hissing rush, and burst in mid-sky into a storm of flashing jewels! One mighty groan of terror started up from the massed people — then suddenly broke into a wild hosannah of joy — for there, fair and plain in the uncanny glare, they saw the freed water leaping forth! The old abbot could not speak a word, for tears and the chokings in his throat; without utterance of any sort, he folded me in his arms and mashed me. It was more eloquent than speech. And harder to get over, too, in a country where there were really no doctors that were worth a damaged nickel.

You should have seen those acres of people throw themselves down in that water and kiss it; kiss it, and pet it, and fondle it, and talk to it as if it were alive, and welcome it back with the dear names they gave their darlings, just as if it had been a friend who was long gone away and lost, and was come home again. Yes, it was pretty to see, and made me think more of them than I had done before.

I sent Merlin home on a shutter. He had caved in and gone down like a landslide when I pronounced that fearful name, and had never come to since. He never had heard that name before, — neither had I — but to him it was the right one. Any jumble would have been the right one. He admitted, afterward, that that spirit's own mother could not have pronounced that name better than I did. He never could understand how I survived it, and I didn't tell him. It is only young magicians that give away a secret like that. Merlin spent three months working enchantments to try to find out the deep trick of how to pronounce that name and outlive it. But he didn't arrive.

When I started to the chapel, the populace uncovered and fell back reverently to make a wide way for me, as if I had been some kind of a superior being — and I was. I was aware of that. I took along a night shift of monks, and taught them the mystery of the pump, and set them to work, for it was plain that a good part of the people out there were going to sit up with the water all night, consequently it was but right that they should have all they wanted of it. To those monks that pump was a good deal of a miracle itself, and they were full of wonder over it; and of admiration, too, of the exceeding effectiveness of its performance.

It was a great night, an immense night. There was reputation in it. I could hardly get to sleep for glorying over it.

Chapter XXIV. A Rival Magician

My influence in the Valley of Holiness was something prodigious now. It seemed worth while to try to turn it to some valuable account. The thought came to me the next morning, and was suggested by my seeing one of my knights who was in the soap line come riding in. According to history, the monks of this place two centuries before had been worldly minded enough to want to wash. It might be that there was a leaven of this unrighteousness still remaining. So I sounded a Brother:

"Wouldn't you like a bath?"

He shuddered at the thought — the thought of the peril of it to the well — but he said with feeling:

"One needs not to ask that of a poor body who has not known that blessed refreshment sith that he was a boy. Would God I might wash me! but it may not be, fair sir, tempt me not; it is forbidden."

And then he sighed in such a sorrowful way that I was resolved he should have at least one layer of his real estate removed, if it sized up my whole influence and bankrupted the pile. So I went to the abbot and asked for a permit for this Brother. He blenched at the idea — I don't mean that you could see him blench, for of course you couldn't see it without you scraped him, and I didn't care enough about it to scrape him, but I knew the blench was there, just the same, and within a book-cover's thickness of the surface, too — blenched, and trembled. He said:

"Ah, son, ask aught else thou wilt, and it is thine, and freely granted out of a grateful heart — but this, oh, this! Would you drive away the blessed water again?"

"No, Father, I will not drive it away. I have mysterious knowledge which teaches me that there was an error that other time when it was thought the institution of the bath banished the fountain." A large interest began to show up in the old man's face. "My knowledge informs me that the bath was innocent of that misfortune, which was caused by quite another sort of sin."

"These are brave words — but — but right welcome, if they be true."

"They are true, indeed. Let me build the bath again, Father. Let me build it again, and the fountain shall flow forever."

"You promise this? — you promise it? Say the word — say you promise it!"

"I do promise it."

"Then will I have the first bath myself! Go — get ye to your work. Tarry not, tarry not, but go."

I and my boys were at work, straight off. The ruins of the old bath were there yet in the basement of the monastery, not a stone missing. They had been left just so, all these lifetimes, and avoided with a pious fear, as things accursed. In two days we had it all done and the water in — a spacious pool of clear pure water that a body could swim in. It was running water, too. It came in, and went out, through the ancient pipes. The old abbot kept his word, and was the first to try it. He went down black and shaky, leaving the whole black community above troubled and worried and full of bodings; but he came back white and joyful, and the game was made! another triumph scored.

It was a good campaign that we made in that Valley of Holiness, and I was very well satisfied, and ready to move on now, but I struck a disappointment. I caught a heavy cold, and it started up an old lurking rheumatism of mine. Of course the rheumatism hunted up my weakest place and located itself there. This was the place where the abbot put his arms about me and mashed me, what time he was moved to testify his gratitude to me with an embrace.

When at last I got out, I was a shadow. But everybody was full of attentions and kindnesses, and these brought cheer back into my life, and were the right medicine to help a convalescent swiftly up toward health and strength again; so I gained fast.

Sandy was worn out with nursing; so I made up my mind to turn out and go a cruise alone, leaving her at the nunnery to rest up. My idea was to disguise myself as a freeman of peasant degree and wander through the country a week or two on foot. This would give me a chance to eat and lodge with the lowliest and poorest class of free citizens on equal terms. There was no other way to inform myself perfectly of their everyday life and the operation of the laws upon it. If I went among them as a gentleman, there would be restraints and conventionalities which would shut me out from their private joys and troubles, and I should get no further than the outside shell.

One morning I was out on a long walk to get up muscle for my trip, and had climbed the ridge which bordered the northern extremity of the valley, when I came upon an artificial opening in the face of a low precipice, and recognized it by its location as a hermitage which had often been pointed out to me from a distance as the den of a hermit of high renown for dirt and austerity. I knew he had lately been offered a situation in the Great Sahara, where lions and sandflies made the hermit-life peculiarly attractive and difficult, and had gone to Africa to take possession, so I thought I would look in and see how the atmosphere of this den agreed with its reputation.

My surprise was great: the place was newly swept and scoured. Then there was another surprise. Back in the gloom of the cavern I heard the clink of a little bell, and then this exclamation:

"Hello Central! Is this you, Camelot? — Behold, thou mayst glad thy heart an thou hast faith to believe the wonderful when that it cometh in unexpected guise and maketh itself manifest in impossible places — here standeth in the flesh his mightiness The Boss, and with thine own ears shall ye hear him speak!"

Now what a radical reversal of things this was; what a jumbling together of extravagant incongruities; what a fantastic conjunction of opposites and irreconcilables — the home of the bogus miracle become the home of a real one, the den of a mediaeval hermit turned into a telephone office!

The telephone clerk stepped into the light, and I recognized one of my young fellows. I said:

"How long has this office been established here, Ulfius?"

"But since midnight, fair Sir Boss, an it please you. We saw many lights in the valley, and so judged it well to make a station, for that where so many lights be needs must they indicate a town of goodly size."

"Quite right. It isn't a town in the customary sense, but it's a good stand, anyway. Do you know where you are?"

"Of that I have had no time to make inquiry; for whenas my comradeship moved hence upon their labors, leaving me in charge, I got me to needed rest, purposing to inquire when I waked, and report the place's name to Camelot for record."

"Well, this is the Valley of Holiness."

It didn't take; I mean, he didn't start at the name, as I had supposed he would. He merely said:

"I will so report it."

"Why, the surrounding regions are filled with the noise of late wonders that have happened here! You didn't hear of them?"

"Ah, ye will remember we move by night, and avoid speech with all. We learn naught but that we get by the telephone from Camelot."

"Why *they* know all about this thing. Haven't they told you anything about the great miracle of the restoration of a holy fountain?"

"Oh, *that* ? Indeed yes. But the name of *this* valley doth woundily differ from the name of *that* one; indeed to differ wider were not pos — "

"What was that name, then?"

"The Valley of Hellishness."

"*That* explains it. Confound a telephone, anyway. It is the very demon for conveying similarities of sound that are miracles of divergence from similarity of sense. But no matter, you know the name of the place now. Call up Camelot."

He did it, and had Clarence sent for. It was good to hear my boy's voice again. It was like being home. After some affectionate interchanges, and some account of my late illness, I said:

"What is new?"

"The king and queen and many of the court do start even in this hour, to go to your valley to pay pious homage to the waters ye have restored, and cleanse themselves of sin, and see the place where the infernal spirit spouted true hell-flames to the clouds — an ye listen sharply ye may hear me wink and hear me likewise smile a smile, sith 'twas I that made selection of those flames from out our stock and sent them by your order."

"Does the king know the way to this place?"

"The king? — no, nor to any other in his realms, mayhap; but the lads that holp you with your miracle will be his guide and lead the way, and appoint the places for rests at noons and sleeps at night."

"This will bring them here — when?"

"Mid-afternoon, or later, the third day."

"Anything else in the way of news?"

"The king hath begun the raising of the standing army ye suggested to him; one regiment is complete and officered."

"The mischief! I wanted a main hand in that myself. There is only one body of men in the kingdom that are fitted to officer a regular army."

"Yes — and now ye will marvel to know there's not so much as one West Pointer in that regiment."

"What are you talking about? Are you in earnest?"

"It is truly as I have said."

"Why, this makes me uneasy. Who were chosen, and what was the method? Competitive examination?"

"Indeed, I know naught of the method. I but know this — these officers be all of noble family, and are born — what is it you call it? — chuckleheads."

"There's something wrong, Clarence."

"Comfort yourself, then; for two candidates for a lieutenancy do travel hence with the king — young nobles both — and if you but wait where you are you will hear them questioned."

"That is news to the purpose. I will get one West Pointer in, anyway. Mount a man and send him to that school with a message; let him kill horses, if necessary, but he must be there before sunset tonight and say — "

"There is no need. I have laid a ground wire to the school. Prithee let me connect you with it."

It sounded good! In this atmosphere of telephones and lightning communication with distant regions, I was breathing the breath of life again after long suffocation. I realized, then, what a creepy, dull, inanimate horror this land had been to me all these years, and how I had been in such a stifled condition of mind as to have grown used to it almost beyond the power to notice it.

I gave my order to the superintendent of the Academy personally. I also asked him to bring me some paper and a fountain pen and a box or so of safety matches. I was getting tired of doing without these conveniences. I could have them now, as I wasn't going to wear armor any more at present, and therefore could get at my pockets.

When I got back to the monastery, I found a thing of interest going on. The abbot and his monks were assembled in the great hall, observing with childish wonder and faith the performances of a new magician, a fresh arrival. His dress was the extreme of the fantastic; as showy and foolish as the sort of thing an Indian medicine-man wears. He was mowing, and mumbling, and gesticulating, and drawing mystical figures in the air and on the floor, — the regular thing, you know. He was a celebrity from Asia — so he said, and that was enough. That sort of evidence was as good as gold, and passed current everywhere.

How easy and cheap it was to be a great magician on this fellow's terms. His specialty was to tell you what any individual on the face of the globe was doing at the moment; and what he had done at any time in the past, and what he would do at any time in the future. He asked if any would like to know what the Emperor of the East was doing now? The sparkling eyes and the delighted rubbing of hands made eloquent answer — this reverend crowd *would* like to know what that monarch was at, just as this moment. The fraud went through some more mummery, and then made grave announcement:

"The high and mighty Emperor of the East doth at this moment put money in the palm of a holy begging friar — one, two, three pieces, and they be all of silver."

A buzz of admiring exclamations broke out, all around:

"It is marvelous!" "Wonderful!" "What study, what labor, to have acquired a so amazing power as this!"

Would they like to know what the Supreme Lord of Inde was doing? Yes. He told them what the Supreme Lord of Inde was doing. Then he told them what the Sultan of Egypt was at; also what the King of the Remote Seas was about. And so on and so on; and with each new marvel the astonishment at his accuracy rose higher and higher. They thought he must surely strike an uncertain place some time; but no, he never had to hesitate, he always knew, and always with unerring precision. I saw that if this thing went on I should lose my supremacy, this fellow would capture my following, I should be left out in the cold. I must put a cog in his wheel, and do it right away, too. I said:

"If I might ask, I should very greatly like to know what a certain person is doing."

"Speak, and freely. I will tell you."

"It will be difficult — perhaps impossible."

"My art knoweth not that word. The more difficult it is, the more certainly will I reveal it to you."

You see, I was working up the interest. It was getting pretty high, too; you could see that by the craning necks all around, and the half-suspended breathing. So now I climaxed it:

"If you make no mistake — if you tell me truly what I want to know — I will give you two hundred silver pennies."

"The fortune is mine! I will tell you what you would know."

"Then tell me what I am doing with my right hand."

"Ah-h!" There was a general gasp of surprise. It had not occurred to anybody in the crowd — that simple trick of inquiring about somebody who wasn't ten thousand miles away. The magician was hit hard; it was an emergency that had never happened in his experience before, and it corked him; he didn't know how to meet it. He looked stunned, confused; he couldn't say a word. "Come," I said, "what are you waiting for? Is it possible you can answer up, right off, and tell what anybody on the other side of the earth is doing, and yet can't tell what a person is doing who isn't three yards from you? Persons behind me know what I am doing with my right hand — they will indorse you if you tell correctly." He was still dumb. "Very well, I'll tell you why you don't speak up and tell; it is because you don't know. *You* a magician! Good friends, this tramp is a mere fraud and liar."

This distressed the monks and terrified them. They were not used to hearing these awful beings called names, and they did not know what might be the consequence. There was a dead silence now; superstitious bodings were in every mind. The magician began to pull his wits together, and when he presently smiled an easy, nonchalant smile, it spread a mighty relief around; for it indicated that his mood was not destructive. He said:

"It hath struck me speechless, the frivolity of this person's speech. Let all know, if perchance there be any who know it not, that enchanters of my degree deign not to concern themselves with the doings of any but kings, princes, emperors, them that be born in the purple and them only. Had ye asked me what Arthur the great king is doing, it were another matter, and I had told ye; but the doings of a subject interest me not."

"Oh, I misunderstood you. I thought you said 'anybody,' and so I supposed 'anybody' included — well, anybody; that is, everybody."

"It doth — anybody that is of lofty birth; and the better if he be royal."

"That, it meseemeth, might well be," said the abbot, who saw his opportunity to smooth things and avert disaster, "for it were not likely that so wonderful a gift as this would be conferred for the revelation of the concerns of lesser beings than such as be born near to the summits of greatness. Our Arthur the king — "

"Would you know of him?" broke in the enchanter.

"Most gladly, yea, and gratefully."

Everybody was full of awe and interest again right away, the incorrigible idiots. They watched the incantations absorbingly, and looked at me with a "There, now, what can you say to that?" air, when the announcement came:

"The king is weary with the chase, and lieth in his palace these two hours sleeping a dreamless sleep."

"God's benison upon him!" said the abbot, and crossed himself; "may that sleep be to the refreshment of his body and his soul."

"And so it might be, if he were sleeping," I said, "but the king is not sleeping, the king rides."

Here was trouble again — a conflict of authority. Nobody knew which of us to believe; I still had some reputation left. The magician's scorn was stirred, and he said:

"Lo, I have seen many wonderful soothsayers and prophets and magicians in my life days, but none before that could sit idle and see to the heart of things with never an incantation to help."

"You have lived in the woods, and lost much by it. I use incantations myself, as this good brotherhood are aware — but only on occasions of moment."

When it comes to sarcasming, I reckon I know how to keep my end up. That jab made this fellow squirm. The abbot inquired after the queen and the court, and got this information:

"They be all on sleep, being overcome by fatigue, like as to the king."

I said:

"That is merely another lie. Half of them are about their amusements, the queen and the other half are not sleeping, they ride. Now perhaps you can spread yourself a little, and tell us where the king and queen and all that are this moment riding with them are going?"

"They sleep now, as I said; but on the morrow they will ride, for they go a journey toward the sea."

"And where will they be the day after tomorrow at vespers?"

"Far to the north of Camelot, and half their journey will be done."

"That is another lie, by the space of a hundred and fifty miles. Their journey will not be merely half done, it will be all done, and they will be *here* , in this valley."

That was a noble shot! It set the abbot and the monks in a whirl of excitement, and it rocked the enchanter to his base. I followed the thing right up:

"If the king does not arrive, I will have myself ridden on a rail: if he does I will ride you on a rail instead."

Next day I went up to the telephone office and found that the king had passed through two towns that were on the line. I spotted his progress on the succeeding day in the same way. I kept these matters to myself. The third day's reports showed that if he kept up his gait he would arrive by four in the afternoon. There was still no sign anywhere of interest in his coming; there seemed to be no preparations making to receive him in state; a strange thing, truly. Only one thing could explain this: that other magician had been cutting under me, sure. This was true. I asked a friend of mine, a monk, about it, and he said, yes, the magician had tried some further enchantments and found out that the court had concluded to make no journey at all, but stay at home. Think of that! Observe how much a reputation was worth in such a country. These people had seen me do the very showiest bit of magic in history, and the only one within their memory that had a positive value, and yet here they were, ready to take up with an adventurer who could offer no evidence of his powers but his mere unproven word.

However, it was not good politics to let the king come without any fuss and feathers at all, so I went down and drummed up a procession of pilgrims and smoked out a batch of hermits and started them out at two o'clock to meet him. And that was the sort of state he arrived in. The abbot was helpless with rage and humiliation when I brought him out on a balcony and showed him the head of the state marching in and never a monk on hand to offer him welcome, and no stir of life or clang of joy-bell to glad his spirit. He took one look and then flew to rouse out his forces. The next minute the bells were dinning furiously, and the various buildings were vomiting monks and nuns, who went swarming in a rush toward the coming procession; and with them went that magician — and he was on a rail, too, by the abbot's order; and his reputation was in the mud, and mine was in the sky again. Yes, a man can keep his trademark current in such a country, but he can't sit around and do it; he has got to be on deck and attending to business right along.

Chapter XXV. A Competitive Examination

When the king traveled for change of air, or made a progress, or visited a distant noble whom he wished to bankrupt with the cost of his keep, part of the administration moved with him. It was a fashion of the time. The Commission charged with the examination of candidates for posts in the army came with the king to the Valley, whereas they could have transacted their business just as well at home. And although this expedition was strictly a holiday excursion for the king, he kept some of his business functions going just the same. He touched for the evil, as usual; he held court in the gate at sunrise and tried cases, for he was himself Chief Justice of the King's Bench.

He shone very well in this latter office. He was a wise and humane judge, and he clearly did his honest best and fairest, — according to his lights. That is a large reservation. His lights — I mean his rearing — often colored his decisions. Whenever there was a dispute between a noble or gentleman and a person of lower degree, the king's leanings and sympathies were for the former class always, whether he suspected it or not. It was impossible that this should be otherwise. The blunting effects of slavery upon the slaveholder's moral perceptions are known and conceded, the world over; and a privileged class, an aristocracy, is but a band of slaveholders under another name. This has a harsh sound, and yet should not be offensive to any — even to the noble himself — unless the fact itself be an offense: for the statement simply formulates a fact. The repulsive feature of slavery is the *thing* , not its name. One needs but to hear an aristocrat speak of the classes that are below him to recognize — and in but indifferently modified measure — the very air and tone of the actual slaveholder; and behind these are the slaveholder's spirit, the slaveholder's blunted feeling. They are the result of the same cause in both cases: the possessor's old and inbred custom of regarding himself as a superior being. The king's judgments wrought frequent injustices, but it was merely the fault of his training, his natural and unalterable sympathies. He was as unfitted for a judgeship as would be the average mother for the position of milk-distributor to starving children in famine-time; her own children would fare a shade better than the rest.

One very curious case came before the king. A young girl, an orphan, who had a considerable estate, married a fine young fellow who had nothing. The girl's property was within a seigniory held by the Church. The bishop of the diocese, an arrogant scion of the great nobility, claimed the girl's estate on the ground that she had married privately, and thus had cheated the Church out of one of its rights as lord of the seigniory — the one heretofore referred to as le droit du seigneur. The penalty of refusal or avoidance was confiscation. The girl's defense was, that the lordship of the seigniory was vested in the bishop, and the particular right here involved was not transferable, but must be exercised by the lord himself or stand vacated; and that an older law, of the Church itself, strictly barred the bishop from exercising it. It was a very odd case, indeed.

It reminded me of something I had read in my youth about the ingenious way in which the aldermen of London raised the money that built the Mansion House. A person who had not taken the Sacrament according to the Anglican rite could not stand as a candidate for sheriff of London. Thus Dissenters were ineligible; they could not run if asked, they could not serve if elected. The aldermen, who without any question were Yankees in disguise, hit upon this neat device: they passed a by-law imposing a fine of L400 upon any one who should refuse to be a candidate for sheriff, and a fine of L600 upon any person who, after being elected sheriff, refused to serve. Then they went to work and elected a lot of Dissenters, one after another, and kept it up until they had collected L15,000 in fines; and there stands the stately Mansion House to this day, to keep the blushing citizen in mind of a long past and lamented day when a band of Yankees slipped into London and played games of the sort that has given their race a unique and shady reputation among all truly good and holy peoples that be in the earth.

The girl's case seemed strong to me; the bishop's case was just as strong. I did not see how the king was going to get out of this hole. But he got out. I append his decision:

"Truly I find small difficulty here, the matter being even a child's affair for simpleness. An the young bride had conveyed notice, as in duty bound, to her feudal lord and proper master and protector the bishop, she had suffered no loss, for the said bishop could have got a dispensation making him, for temporary conveniency, eligible to the exercise of his said right, and thus would she have kept all she had. Whereas, failing in her first duty, she hath by that failure failed in all; for whoso, clinging to a rope, severeth it above his hands, must fall; it being no defense to claim that the rest of the rope is sound, neither any deliverance from his peril, as he shall find. Pardy, the woman's case is rotten at the source. It is the decree of the court that she forfeit to the said lord bishop all her goods, even to the last farthing that she doth possess, and be thereto mulcted in the costs. Next!"

Here was a tragic end to a beautiful honeymoon not yet three months old. Poor young creatures! They had lived these three months lapped to the lips in worldly comforts. These clothes and trinkets they were wearing were as fine and dainty as the shrewdest stretch of the sumptuary laws allowed to people of their degree; and in these pretty clothes, she crying on his shoulder, and he trying to comfort her with hopeful words set to the music of despair, they went from the judgment seat out into the world homeless, bedless, breadless; why, the very beggars by the roadsides were not so poor as they.

Well, the king was out of the hole; and on terms satisfactory to the Church and the rest of the aristocracy, no doubt. Men write many fine and plausible arguments in support of monarchy, but the fact remains that where every man in a State has a vote, brutal laws are impossible. Arthur's people were of course poor material for a republic, because they had been debased so long by monarchy; and yet even they would have been intelligent enough to make short work of that law which the king had just been administering if it had been submitted to their full and free vote. There is a phrase which has grown so common in the world's mouth that it has come to seem to have sense and meaning — the sense and meaning implied when it is used; that is the phrase which refers to this or that or the other nation as possibly being "capable of self-government"; and the implied sense of it is, that there has been a nation somewhere, some time or other which *wasn't* capable of it — wasn't as able to govern itself as some self-appointed specialists were or would be to govern it. The master minds of all nations, in all ages, have sprung in affluent multitude from the mass of the nation, and from the mass of the nation only — not from its privileged classes; and so, no matter what the nation's intellectual grade was; whether high or low, the bulk of its ability was in the long ranks of its nameless and its poor, and so it never saw the day that it had not the material in abundance whereby to govern itself. Which is to assert an always self-proven fact: that even the best governed and most free and most enlightened monarchy is still behind the best condition attainable by its people; and that the same is true of kindred governments of lower grades, all the way down to the lowest.

King Arthur had hurried up the army business altogether beyond my calculations. I had not supposed he would move in the matter while I was away; and so I had not mapped out a scheme for determining the merits of officers; I had only remarked that it would be wise to submit every candidate to a sharp and searching examination; and privately I meant to put together a list of military qualifications that nobody could answer to but my West Pointers. That ought to have been attended to before I left; for the king was so taken with the idea of a standing army that he couldn't wait but must get about it at once, and get up as good a scheme of examination as he could invent out of his own head.

I was impatient to see what this was; and to show, too, how much more admirable was the one which I should display to the Examining Board. I intimated this, gently, to the king, and it fired his curiosity. When the Board was assembled, I followed him in; and behind us came the candidates. One of these candidates was a bright young West Pointer of mine, and with him were a couple of my West Point professors.

When I saw the Board, I did not know whether to cry or to laugh. The head of it was the officer known to later centuries as Norroy King-at-Arms! The two other members were chiefs of bureaus in his department; and all three were priests, of course; all officials who had to know how to read and write were priests.

My candidate was called first, out of courtesy to me, and the head of the Board opened on him with official solemnity:

"Name?"

"Mal-ease."

"Son of?"

"Webster."

"Webster — Webster. H'm — I — my memory faileth to recall the name. Condition?"

"Weaver."

"Weaver! — God keep us!"

The king was staggered, from his summit to his foundations; one clerk fainted, and the others came near it. The chairman pulled himself together, and said indignantly:

"It is sufficient. Get you hence."

But I appealed to the king. I begged that my candidate might be examined. The king was willing, but the Board, who were all well-born folk, implored the king to spare them the indignity of examining the weaver's son. I knew they didn't know enough to examine him anyway, so I joined my prayers to theirs and the king turned the duty over to my professors. I had had a blackboard prepared, and it was put up now, and the circus began. It was beautiful to hear the lad lay out the science of war, and wallow in details of battle and siege, of supply, transportation, mining and countermining, grand tactics, big strategy and little strategy, signal service, infantry, cavalry, artillery, and all about siege guns, field guns, gatling guns, rifled guns, smooth bores, musket practice, revolver practice — and not a solitary word of it all could these catfish make head or tail of, you understand — and it was handsome to see him chalk off mathematical nightmares on the blackboard that would stump the angels themselves, and do it like nothing, too — all about eclipses, and comets, and solstices, and constellations, and mean time, and sidereal time, and dinner time, and bedtime, and every other imaginable thing above the clouds or under them that you could harry or bullyrag an enemy with and make him wish he hadn't come — and when the boy made his military salute and stood aside at last, I was proud enough to hug him, and all those other people were so dazed they looked partly petrified, partly drunk, and wholly caught out and snowed under. I judged that the cake was ours, and by a large majority.

Education is a great thing. This was the same youth who had come to West Point so ignorant that when I asked him, "If a general officer should have a horse shot under him on the field of battle, what ought he to do?" answered up naively and said:

"Get up and brush himself."

One of the young nobles was called up now. I thought I would question him a little myself. I said:

"Can your lordship read?"

His face flushed indignantly, and he fired this at me:

"Takest me for a clerk? I trow I am not of a blood that — "

"Answer the question!"

He crowded his wrath down and made out to answer "No."

"Can you write?"

He wanted to resent this, too, but I said:

"You will confine yourself to the questions, and make no comments. You are not here to air your blood or your graces, and nothing of the sort will be permitted. Can you write?"

"No."

"Do you know the multiplication table?"

"I wit not what ye refer to."

"How much is 9 times 6?"

"It is a mystery that is hidden from me by reason that the emergency requiring the fathoming of it hath not in my life-days occurred, and so, not having no need to know this thing, I abide barren of the knowledge."

"If A trade a barrel of onions to B, worth 2 pence the bushel, in exchange for a sheep worth 4 pence and a dog worth a penny, and C kill the dog before delivery, because bitten by the same, who mistook him for D, what sum is still due to A from B, and which party pays for the dog, C or D, and who gets the money? If A, is the penny sufficient, or may he claim consequential damages in the form of additional money to represent the possible profit which might have inured from the dog, and classifiable as earned increment, that is to say, usufruct?"

"Verily, in the all-wise and unknowable providence of God, who moveth in mysterious ways his wonders to perform, have I never heard the fellow to this question for confusion of the mind and congestion of the ducts of thought. Wherefore I beseech you let the dog and the onions and these people of the strange and godless names work out their several salvations from their piteous and wonderful difficulties without help of mine, for indeed their trouble is sufficient as it is, whereas an I tried to help I should but damage their cause the more and yet mayhap not live myself to see the desolation wrought."

"What do you know of the laws of attraction and gravitation?"

"If there be such, mayhap his grace the king did promulgate them whilst that I lay sick about the beginning of the year and thereby failed to hear his proclamation."

"What do you know of the science of optics?"

"I know of governors of places, and seneschals of castles, and sheriffs of counties, and many like small offices and titles of honor, but him you call the Science of Optics I have not heard of before; peradventure it is a new dignity."

"Yes, in this country."

Try to conceive of this mollusk gravely applying for an official position, of any kind under the sun! Why, he had all the earmarks of a typewriter copyist, if you leave out the disposition to contribute uninvited emendations of your grammar and punctuation. It was unaccountable that he didn't attempt a little help of that sort out of his majestic supply of incapacity for the job. But that didn't prove that he hadn't material in him for the disposition, it only proved that he wasn't a typewriter copyist yet. After nagging him a little more, I let the professors loose on him and they turned him inside out, on the line of scientific war, and found him empty, of course. He knew somewhat about the warfare of the time — bushwhacking around for ogres, and bullfights in the tournament ring, and such things — but otherwise he was empty and useless. Then we took the other young noble in hand, and he was the first one's twin, for ignorance and incapacity. I delivered them into the hands of the chairman of the Board with the comfortable consciousness that their cake was dough. They were examined in the previous order of precedence.

"Name, so please you?"

"Pertipole, son of Sir Pertipole, Baron of Barley Mash."

"Grandfather?"

"Also Sir Pertipole, Baron of Barley Mash."

"Great-grandfather?"

"The same name and title."

"Great-great-grandfather?"

"We had none, worshipful sir, the line failing before it had reached so far back."

"It mattereth not. It is a good four generations, and fulfilleth the requirements of the rule."

"Fulfills what rule?" I asked.

"The rule requiring four generations of nobility or else the candidate is not eligible."

"A man not eligible for a lieutenancy in the army unless he can prove four generations of noble descent?"

"Even so; neither lieutenant nor any other officer may be commissioned without that qualification."

"Oh, come, this is an astonishing thing. What good is such a qualification as that?"

"What good? It is a hardy question, fair sir and Boss, since it doth go far to impugn the wisdom of even our holy Mother Church herself."

"As how?"

"For that she hath established the selfsame rule regarding saints. By her law none may be canonized until he hath lain dead four generations."

"I see, I see — it is the same thing. It is wonderful. In the one case a man lies dead-alive four generations — mummified in ignorance and sloth — and that qualifies him to command live people, and take their weal and woe into his impotent hands; and in the other case, a man lies bedded with death and worms four generations, and that qualifies him for office in the celestial camp. Does the king's grace approve of this strange law?"

The king said:

"Why, truly I see naught about it that is strange. All places of honor and of profit do belong, by natural right, to them that be of noble blood, and so these dignities in the army are their property and would be so without this or any rule. The rule is but to mark a limit. Its purpose is to keep out too recent blood, which would bring into contempt these offices, and men of lofty lineage would turn their backs and scorn to take them. I were to blame an I permitted this calamity. *You* can permit it an you are minded so to do, for you have the delegated authority, but that the king should do it were a most strange madness and not comprehensible to any."

"I yield. Proceed, sir Chief of the Herald's College."

The chairman resumed as follows:

"By what illustrious achievement for the honor of the Throne and State did the founder of your great line lift himself to the sacred dignity of the British nobility?"

"He built a brewery."

"Sire, the Board finds this candidate perfect in all the requirements and qualifications for military command, and doth hold his case open for decision after due examination of his competitor."

The competitor came forward and proved exactly four generations of nobility himself. So there was a tie in military qualifications that far.

He stood aside a moment, and Sir Pertipole was questioned further:

"Of what condition was the wife of the founder of your line?"

"She came of the highest landed gentry, yet she was not noble; she was gracious and pure and charitable, of a blameless life and character, insomuch that in these regards was she peer of the best lady in the land."

"That will do. Stand down." He called up the competing lordling again, and asked: "What was the rank and condition of the great-grandmother who conferred British nobility upon your great house?"

"She was a king's leman and did climb to that splendid eminence by her own unholpen merit from the sewer where she was born."

"Ah, this, indeed, is true nobility, this is the right and perfect intermixture. The lieutenancy is yours, fair lord. Hold it not in contempt; it is the humble step which will lead to grandeurs more worthy of the splendor of an origin like to thine."

I was down in the bottomless pit of humiliation. I had promised myself an easy and zenith-scouring triumph, and this was the outcome!

I was almost ashamed to look my poor disappointed cadet in the face. I told him to go home and be patient, this wasn't the end.

I had a private audience with the king, and made a proposition. I said it was quite right to officer that regiment with nobilities, and he couldn't have done a wiser thing. It would also be a good idea to add five hundred officers to it; in fact, add as many officers as there were nobles and relatives of nobles in the country, even if there should finally be five times as many officers as privates in it; and thus make it the crack regiment, the envied regiment, the King's Own regiment, and entitled to fight on its own hook and in its own way, and go whither it would and come when it pleased, in time of war, and be utterly swell and independent. This would make that regiment the heart's desire of all the nobility, and they would all be satisfied and happy. Then we would make up the rest of the standing army out of commonplace materials, and officer it with nobodies, as was proper — nobodies selected on a basis of mere efficiency — and we would make this regiment toe the line, allow it no aristocratic freedom from restraint, and force it to do all the work and persistent hammering, to the end that whenever the King's Own was tired and wanted to go off for a change and rummage around amongst ogres and have a good time, it could go without uneasiness, knowing that matters were in safe hands behind it, and business going to be continued at the old stand, same as usual. The king was charmed with the idea.

When I noticed that, it gave me a valuable notion. I thought I saw my way out of an old and stubborn difficulty at last. You see, the royalties of the Pendragon stock were a long-lived race and very fruitful. Whenever a child was born to any of these — and it was pretty often — there was wild joy in the nation's mouth, and piteous sorrow in the nation's heart. The joy was questionable, but the grief was honest. Because the event meant another call for a Royal Grant. Long was the list of these royalties, and they were a heavy and steadily increasing burden upon the treasury and a menace to the crown. Yet Arthur could not believe this latter fact, and he would not listen to any of my various projects for substituting something in the place of the royal grants. If I could have persuaded him to now and then provide a support for one of these outlying scions from his own pocket, I could have made a grand to-do over it, and it would have had a good effect with the nation; but no, he wouldn't hear of such a thing. He had something like a religious passion for royal grant; he seemed to look upon it as a sort of sacred swag, and one could not irritate him in any way so quickly and so surely as by an attack upon that venerable institution. If I ventured to cautiously hint that there was not another respectable family in England that would humble itself to hold out the hat — however, that is as far as I ever got; he always cut me short there, and peremptorily, too.

But I believed I saw my chance at last. I would form this crack regiment out of officers alone — not a single private. Half of it should consist of nobles, who should fill all the places up to Major-General, and serve gratis and pay their own expenses; and they would be glad to do this when they should learn that the rest of the regiment would consist exclusively of princes of the blood. These princes of the blood should range in rank from Lieutenant-General up to Field Marshal, and be gorgeously salaried and equipped and fed by the state. Moreover — and this was the master stroke — it should be decreed that these princely grandees should be always addressed by a stunningly gaudy and awe-compelling title (which I would presently invent), and they and they only in all England should be so addressed. Finally, all princes of the blood should have free choice; join that regiment, get that great title, and renounce the royal grant, or stay out and receive a grant. Neatest touch of all: unborn but imminent princes of the blood could be *born* into the regiment, and start fair, with good wages and a permanent situation, upon due notice from the parents.

All the boys would join, I was sure of that; so, all existing grants would be relinquished; that the newly born would always join was equally certain. Within sixty days that quaint and bizarre anomaly, the Royal Grant, would cease to be a living fact, and take its place among the curiosities of the past.

Chapter XXVI. The First Newspaper

When I told the king I was going out disguised as a petty freeman to scour the country and familiarize myself with the humbler life of the people, he was all afire with the novelty of the thing in a minute, and was bound to take a chance in the adventure himself — nothing should stop him — he would drop everything and go along — it was the prettiest idea he had run across for many a day. He wanted to glide out the back way and start at once; but I showed him that that wouldn't answer. You see, he was billed for the king's-evil — to touch for it, I mean — and it wouldn't be right to disappoint the house and it wouldn't make a delay worth considering, anyway, it was only a one-night stand. And I thought he ought to tell the queen he was going away. He clouded up at that and looked sad. I was sorry I had spoken, especially when he said mournfully:

"Thou forgettest that Launcelot is here; and where Launcelot is, she noteth not the going forth of the king, nor what day he returneth."

Of course, I changed the Subject. Yes, Guenever was beautiful, it is true, but take her all around she was pretty slack. I never meddled in these matters, they weren't my affair, but I did hate to see the way things were going on, and I don't mind saying that much. Many's the time she had asked me, "Sir Boss, hast seen Sir Launcelot about?" but if ever she went fretting around for the king I didn't happen to be around at the time.

There was a very good lay-out for the king's-evil business — very tidy and creditable. The king sat under a canopy of state; about him were clustered a large body of the clergy in full canonicals. Conspicuous, both for location and personal outfit, stood Marinel, a hermit of the quack-doctor species, to introduce the sick. All abroad over the spacious floor, and clear down to the doors, in a thick jumble, lay or sat the scrofulous, under a strong light. It was as good as a tableau; in fact, it had all the look of being gotten up for that, though it wasn't. There were eight hundred sick people present. The work was slow; it lacked the interest of novelty for me, because I had seen the ceremonies before; the thing soon became tedious, but the proprieties required me to stick it out. The doctor was there for the reason that in all such crowds there were many people who only imagined something was the matter with them, and many who were consciously sound but wanted the immortal honor of fleshly contact with a king, and yet others who pretended to illness in order to get the piece of coin that went with the touch. Up to this time this coin had been a wee little gold piece worth about a third of a dollar. When you consider how much that amount of money would buy, in that age and country, and how usual it was to be scrofulous, when not dead, you would understand that the annual king's-evil appropriation was just the River and Harbor bill of that government for the grip it took on the treasury and the chance it afforded for skinning the surplus. So I had privately concluded to touch the treasury itself for the king's-evil. I covered six-sevenths of the appropriation into the treasury a week before starting from Camelot on my adventures, and ordered that the other seventh be inflated into five-cent nickels and delivered into the hands of the head clerk of the King's Evil Department; a nickel to take the place of each gold coin, you see, and do its work for it. It might strain the nickel some, but I judged it could stand it. As a rule, I do not approve of watering stock, but I considered it square enough in this case, for it was just a gift, anyway. Of course, you can water a gift as much as you want to; and I generally do. The old gold and silver coins of the country were of ancient and unknown origin, as a rule, but some of them were Roman; they were ill-shapen, and seldom rounder than a moon that is a week past the full; they were hammered, not minted, and they were so worn with use that the devices upon them were as illegible as blisters, and looked like them. I judged that a sharp, bright new nickel, with a first-rate likeness of the king on one side of it and Guenever on the other, and a blooming pious motto, would take the tuck out of scrofula as handy as a nobler coin and please the scrofulous fancy more; and I was right. This batch was the first it was tried on, and it worked to a charm. The saving in expense was a notable economy. You will see that by these figures: We touched a trifle over 700 of the 800 patients; at former rates, this would have cost the government about $240; at the new rate we pulled through for about $35, thus saving upward of $200 at one swoop. To appreciate the full magnitude of this stroke, consider these other figures: the annual expenses of a national government amount to the equivalent of a contribution of three days' average wages of every individual of the population, counting every individual as if he were a man. If you take a nation of 60,000,000, where average wages are $2 per day, three days' wages taken from each individual will provide $360,000,000 and pay the government's expenses. In my day, in my own country, this money was collected from imposts, and the citizen imagined that the foreign importer paid it, and it made him comfortable to think so; whereas, in fact, it was paid by the American people, and was so equally and exactly distributed among them that the annual cost to the 100-millionaire and the annual cost to the sucking child of the day-laborer was precisely the same — each paid $6. Nothing could be equaler than that, I reckon. Well, Scotland and Ireland were tributary to Arthur, and the united populations of the British Islands amounted to something less than 1,000,000. A mechanic's average wage was 3 cents a day, when he paid his own keep. By this rule the national government's expenses were $90,000 a year, or about $250 a day. Thus, by the substitution of nickels for gold on a king's-evil day, I not only injured no one, dissatisfied no one, but pleased all concerned and saved four-fifths of that day's national expense into the bargain — a saving which would have been the equivalent of $800,000 in my day in America. In making this substitution I had drawn upon the wisdom of a very remote source — the wisdom of my boyhood — for the true statesman does not despise any wisdom, howsoever lowly may be its origin: in my boyhood I had always saved my pennies and contributed buttons to the foreign missionary cause. The buttons would answer the ignorant savage as well as the coin, the coin would answer me better than the buttons; all hands were happy and nobody hurt.

Marinel took the patients as they came. He examined the candidate; if he couldn't qualify he was warned off; if he could he was passed along to the king. A priest pronounced the words, "They shall lay their hands on the sick, and they shall recover." Then the king stroked the ulcers, while the reading continued; finally, the patient graduated and got his nickel — the king hanging it around his neck himself — and was dismissed. Would you think that that would cure? It certainly did. Any mummery will cure if the patient's faith is strong in it. Up by Astolat there was a chapel where the Virgin had once appeared to a girl who used to herd geese around there — the girl said so herself — and they built the chapel upon that spot and hung a picture in it representing the occurrence — a picture which you would think it dangerous for a sick person to approach; whereas, on the contrary, thousands of the lame and the sick came and prayed before it every year and went away whole and sound; and even the well could look upon it and live. Of course, when I was told these things I did not believe them; but when I went there and saw them I had to succumb. I saw the cures effected myself; and they were real cures and not questionable. I saw cripples whom I had seen around Camelot for years on crutches, arrive and pray before that picture, and put down their crutches and walk off without a limp. There were piles of crutches there which had been left by such people as a testimony.

In other places people operated on a patient's mind, without saying a word to him, and cured him. In others, experts assembled patients in a room and prayed over them, and appealed to their faith, and those patients went away cured. Wherever you find a king who can't cure the king's-evil you can be sure that the most valuable superstition that supports his throne — the subject's belief in the divine appointment of his sovereign — has passed away. In my youth the monarchs of England had ceased to touch for the evil, but there was no occasion for this diffidence: they could have cured it forty-nine times in fifty.

Well, when the priest had been droning for three hours, and the good king polishing the evidences, and the sick were still pressing forward as plenty as ever, I got to feeling intolerably bored. I was sitting by an open window not far from the canopy of state. For the five hundredth time a patient stood forward to have his repulsivenesses stroked; again those words were being droned out: "they shall lay their hands on the sick" — when outside there rang clear as a clarion a note that enchanted my soul and tumbled thirteen worthless centuries about my ears: "Camelot *Weekly Hosannah and Literary Volcano!* — latest irruption — only two cents — all about the big miracle in the Valley of Holiness!" One greater than kings had arrived — the newsboy. But I was the only person in all that throng who knew the meaning of this mighty birth, and what this imperial magician was come into the world to do.

I dropped a nickel out of the window and got my paper; the Adam-newsboy of the world went around the corner to get my change; is around the corner yet. It was delicious to see a newspaper again, yet I was conscious of a secret shock when my eye fell upon the first batch of display headlines. I had lived in a clammy atmosphere of reverence, respect, deference, so long that they sent a quivery little cold wave through me:

— and so on, and so on. Yes, it was too loud. Once I could have enjoyed it and seen nothing out of the way about it, but now its note was discordant. It was good Arkansas journalism, but this was not Arkansas. Moreover, the next to the last line was calculated to give offense to the hermits, and perhaps lose us their advertising. Indeed, there was too lightsome a tone of flippancy all through the paper. It was plain I had undergone a considerable change without noticing it. I found myself unpleasantly affected by pert little irreverencies which would have seemed but proper and airy graces of speech at an earlier period of my life. There was an abundance of the following breed of items, and they discomforted me:

L OCAL SMOKE AND CINDERS.

Sir Launcelot met up with old King Agrivance of Ireland unexpectedly last weok over on the moor south of Sir Balmoral le Merveilleuse's hog dasture. The widow has been notified.

Expedition No. 3 will start adout the first of mext month on a search f8r Sir Sagramour le Desirous. It is in comand of the renowned Knight of the Red Lawns, assissted by Sir Persant of Inde, who is compete9t. intelligent, courteous, and in every way a brick, and further assisted by Sir Palamides the Saracen, who is no huckleberry hinself. This is no pic-nic, these boys mean busine&s.

The readers of the Hosannah will regret to learn that the hadndsome and popular Sir Charolais of Gaul, who during his four weeks' stay at the Bull and Halibut, this city, has won every heart by his polished manners and elegant cPnversation, will pUll out to-day for home. Give us another call, Charley!

The bdsiness end of the funeral of the late Sir Dalliance the duke's son of Cornwall, killed in an encounter with the Giant of the Knotted Bludgeon last Tuesday on the borders of the Plain of Enchantment was in the hands of the ever affable and efficient Mumble, prince of un3ertakers, then whom there exists none by whom it were a more satisfying pleasure to have the last sad offices performed. Give him a trial.

The cordial thanks of the Hosannah office are due, from editor down to devil, to the ever courteous and thoughtful Lord High Stew d of the Palace's Third Assistant V t for several saucets of ice crEam a quality calculated to make the ey of the recipients humid with grt ude; and it done it. When this administration wants to chalk up a desirable name for early promotion, the Hosannah would like a chance to sudgest.

The Demoiselle Irene Dewlap, of South Astolat, is visiting her uncle, the popular host of the Cattlemen's Boarding Ho&se, Liver Lane, this city.

Young Barker the bellows-mender is hoMe again, and looks much improved by his vacation round-up among the out- lying smithies. See his ad.

Of course it was good enough journalism for a beginning; I knew that quite well, and yet it was somehow disappointing. The "Court Circular" pleased me better; indeed, its simple and dignified respectfulness was a distinct refreshment to me after all those disgraceful familiarities. But even it could have been improved. Do what one may, there is no getting an air of variety into a court circular, I acknowledge that. There is a profound monotonousness about its facts that baffles and defeats one's sincerest efforts to make them sparkle and enthuse. The best way to manage — in fact, the only sensible way — is to disguise repetitiousness of fact under variety of form: skin your fact each time and lay on a new cuticle of words. It deceives the eye; you think it is a new fact; it gives you the idea that the court is carrying on like everything; this excites you, and you drain the whole column, with a good appetite, and perhaps never notice that it's a barrel of soup made out of a single bean. Clarence's way was good, it was simple, it was dignified, it was direct and businesslike; all I say is, it was not the best way:

However, take the paper by and large, I was vastly pleased with it. Little crudities of a me- chanical sort were observable here and there, but there were not enough of them to amount to anything, and it was good enough Arkansas proof-reading, anyhow, and better than was needed in Arthur's day and realm. As a rule, the grammar was leaky and the construction more or less lame; but I did not much mind these things. They are common defects of my own, and one mustn't criticise other people on grounds where he can't stand perpendicular himself.

I was hungry enough for literature to want to take down the whole paper at this one meal, but I got only a few bites, and then had to postpone, because the monks around me besieged me so with eager questions: What is this curious thing? What is it for? Is it a handkerchief? — saddle blanket? — part of a shirt? What is it made of? How thin it is, and how dainty and frail; and how it rattles. Will it wear, do you think, and won't the rain injure it? Is it writing that appears on it, or is it only ornamentation? They suspected it was writing, because those among them who knew how to read Latin and had a smattering of Greek, recognized some of the letters, but they could make nothing out of the result as a whole. I put my information in the simplest form I could:

"It is a public journal; I will explain what that is, another time. It is not cloth, it is made of paper; some time I will explain what paper is. The lines on it are reading matter; and not written by hand, but printed; by and by I will explain what printing is. A thousand of these sheets have been made, all exactly like this, in every minute detail — they can't be told apart." Then they all broke out with exclamations of surprise and admiration:

"A thousand! Verily a mighty work — a year's work for many men."

"No — merely a day's work for a man and a boy."

They crossed themselves, and whiffed out a protective prayer or two.

"Ah-h — a miracle, a wonder! Dark work of enchantment."

I let it go at that. Then I read in a low voice, to as many as could crowd their shaven heads within hearing distance, part of the account of the miracle of the restoration of the well, and was accompanied by astonished and reverent ejaculations all through: "Ah-h-h!" "How true!" "Amazing, amazing!" "These be the very haps as they happened, in marvelous exactness!" And might they take this strange thing in their hands, and feel of it and examine it? — they would be very careful. Yes. So they took it, handling it as cautiously and devoutly as if it had been some holy thing come from some supernatural region; and gently felt of its texture, caressed its pleasant smooth surface with lingering touch, and scanned the mysterious characters with fascinated eyes. These grouped bent heads, these charmed faces, these speaking eyes — how beautiful to me! For was not this my darling, and was not all this mute wonder and interest and homage a most eloquent tribute and unforced compliment to it? I knew, then, how a mother feels when women, whether strangers or friends, take her new baby, and close themselves about it with one eager impulse, and bend their heads over it in a tranced adoration that makes all the rest of the universe vanish out of their consciousness and be as if it were not, for that time. I knew how she feels, and that there is no other satisfied ambition, whether of king, conqueror, or poet, that ever reaches halfway to that serene far summit or yields half so divine a contentment.

During all the rest of the seance my paper traveled from group to group all up and down and about that huge hall, and my happy eye was upon it always, and I sat motionless, steeped in satisfaction, drunk with enjoyment. Yes, this was heaven; I was tasting it once, if I might never taste it more.

Chapter XXVII. The Yankee and the King Travel Incognito

About bedtime I took the king to my private quarters to cut his hair and help him get the hang of the lowly raiment he was to wear. The high classes wore their hair banged across the forehead but hanging to the shoulders the rest of the way around, whereas the lowest ranks of commoners were banged fore and aft both; the slaves were bangless, and allowed their hair free growth. So I inverted a bowl over his head and cut away all the locks that hung below it. I also trimmed his whiskers and mustache until they were only about a half-inch long; and tried to do it inartistically, and succeeded. It was a villainous disfigurement. When he got his lubberly sandals on, and his long robe of coarse brown linen cloth, which hung straight from his neck to his anklebones, he was no longer the comeliest man in his kingdom, but one of the unhandsomest and most commonplace and unattractive. We were dressed and barbered alike, and could pass for small farmers, or farm bailiffs, or shepherds, or carters; yes, or for village artisans, if we chose, our costume being in effect universal among the poor, because of its strength and cheapness. I don't mean that it was really cheap to a very poor person, but I do mean that it was the cheapest material there was for male attire — manufactured material, you understand.

We slipped away an hour before dawn, and by broad sun-up had made eight or ten miles, and were in the midst of a sparsely settled country. I had a pretty heavy knapsack; it was laden with provisions — provisions for the king to taper down on, till he could take to the coarse fare of the country without damage.

I found a comfortable seat for the king by the roadside, and then gave him a morsel or two to stay his stomach with. Then I said I would find some water for him, and strolled away. Part of my project was to get out of sight and sit down and rest a little myself. It had always been my custom to stand when in his presence; even at the council board, except upon those rare occasions when the sitting was a very long one, extending over hours; then I had a trifling little backless thing which was like a reversed culvert and was as comfortable as the toothache. I didn't want to break him in suddenly, but do it by degrees. We should have to sit together now when in company, or people would notice; but it would not be good politics for me to be playing equality with him when there was no necessity for it.

I found the water some three hundred yards away, and had been resting about twenty minutes, when I heard voices. That is all right, I thought — peasants going to work; nobody else likely to be stirring this early. But the next moment these comers jingled into sight around a turn of the road — smartly clad people of quality, with luggage-mules and servants in their train! I was off like a shot, through the bushes, by the shortest cut. For a while it did seem that these people would pass the king before I could get to him; but desperation gives you wings, you know, and I canted my body forward, inflated my breast, and held my breath and flew. I arrived. And in plenty good enough time, too.

"Pardon, my king, but it's no time for ceremony — jump! Jump to your feet — some quality are coming!"

"Is that a marvel? Let them come."

"But my liege! You must not be seen sitting. Rise! — and stand in humble posture while they pass. You are a peasant, you know."

"True — I had forgot it, so lost was I in planning of a huge war with Gaul" — he was up by this time, but a farm could have got up quicker, if there was any kind of a boom in real estate — "and rightso a thought came randoming overthwart this majestic dream the which — "

"A humbler attitude, my lord the king — and quick! Duck your head! — more! — still more! — droop it!"

He did his honest best, but lord, it was no great things. He looked as humble as the leaning tower at Pisa. It is the most you could say of it. Indeed, it was such a thundering poor success that it raised wondering scowls all along the line, and a gorgeous flunkey at the tail end of it raised his whip; but I jumped in time and was under it when it fell; and under cover of the volley of coarse laughter which followed, I spoke up sharply and warned the king to take no notice. He mastered himself for the moment, but it was a sore tax; he wanted to eat up the procession. I said:

"It would end our adventures at the very start; and we, being without weapons, could do nothing with that armed gang. If we are going to succeed in our emprise, we must not only look the peasant but act the peasant."

"It is wisdom; none can gainsay it. Let us go on, Sir Boss. I will take note and learn, and do the best I may."

He kept his word. He did the best he could, but I've seen better. If you have ever seen an active, heedless, enterprising child going diligently out of one mischief and into another all day long, and an anxious mother at its heels all the while, and just saving it by a hair from drowning itself or breaking its neck with each new experiment, you've seen the king and me.

If I could have foreseen what the thing was going to be like, I should have said, No, if anybody wants to make his living exhibiting a king as a peasant, let him take the layout; I can do better with a menagerie, and last longer. And yet, during the first three days I never allowed him to enter a hut or other dwelling. If he could pass muster anywhere during his early novitiate it would be in small inns and on the road; so to these places we confined ourselves. Yes, he certainly did the best he could, but what of that? He didn't improve a bit that I could see.

He was always frightening me, always breaking out with fresh astonishers, in new and un-expected places. Toward evening on the second day, what does he do but blandly fetch out a dirk from inside his robe!

"Great guns, my liege, where did you get that?"

"From a smuggler at the inn, yester eve."

"What in the world possessed you to buy it?"

"We have escaped divers dangers by wit — thy wit — but I have bethought me that it were but prudence if I bore a weapon, too. Thine might fail thee in some pinch."

"But people of our condition are not allowed to carry arms. What would a lord say — yes, or any other person of whatever condition — if he caught an upstart peasant with a dagger on his person?"

It was a lucky thing for us that nobody came along just then. I persuaded him to throw the dirk away; and it was as easy as persuading a child to give up some bright fresh new way of killing itself. We walked along, silent and thinking. Finally the king said:

"When ye know that I meditate a thing inconvenient, or that hath a peril in it, why do you not warn me to cease from that project?"

It was a startling question, and a puzzler. I didn't quite know how to take hold of it, or what to say, and so, of course, I ended by saying the natural thing:

"But, sire, how can I know what your thoughts are?"

The king stopped dead in his tracks, and stared at me.

"I believed thou wert greater than Merlin; and truly in magic thou art. But prophecy is greater than magic. Merlin is a prophet."

I saw I had made a blunder. I must get back my lost ground. After a deep reflection and careful planning, I said:

"Sire, I have been misunderstood. I will explain. There are two kinds of prophecy. One is the gift to foretell things that are but a little way off, the other is the gift to foretell things that are whole ages and centuries away. Which is the mightier gift, do you think?"

"Oh, the last, most surely!"

"True. Does Merlin possess it?"

"Partly, yes. He foretold mysteries about my birth and future kingship that were twenty years away."

"Has he ever gone beyond that?"

"He would not claim more, I think."

"It is probably his limit. All prophets have their limit. The limit of some of the great prophets has been a hundred years."

"These are few, I ween."

"There have been two still greater ones, whose limit was four hundred and six hundred years, and one whose limit compassed even seven hundred and twenty."

"Gramercy, it is marvelous!"

"But what are these in comparison with me? They are nothing."

"What? Canst thou truly look beyond even so vast a stretch of time as — "

"Seven hundred years? My liege, as clear as the vision of an eagle does my prophetic eye penetrate and lay bare the future of this world for nearly thirteen centuries and a half!"

My land, you should have seen the king's eyes spread slowly open, and lift the earth's entire atmosphere as much as an inch! That settled Brer Merlin. One never had any occasion to prove his facts, with these people; all he had to do was to state them. It never occurred to anybody to doubt the statement.

"Now, then," I continued, "I *could* work both kinds of prophecy — the long and the short — if I chose to take the trouble to keep in practice; but I seldom exercise any but the long kind, because the other is beneath my dignity. It is properer to Merlin's sort — stump-tail prophets, as we call them in the profession. Of course, I whet up now and then and flirt out a minor prophecy, but not often — hardly ever, in fact. You will remember that there was great talk, when you reached the Valley of Holiness, about my having prophesied your coming and the very hour of your arrival, two or three days beforehand."

"Indeed, yes, I mind it now."

"Well, I could have done it as much as forty times easier, and piled on a thousand times more detail into the bargain, if it had been five hundred years away instead of two or three days."

"How amazing that it should be so!"

"Yes, a genuine expert can always foretell a thing that is five hundred years away easier than he can a thing that's only five hundred seconds off."

"And yet in reason it should clearly be the other way; it should be five hundred times as easy to foretell the last as the first, for, indeed, it is so close by that one uninspired might almost see it. In truth, the law of prophecy doth contradict the likelihoods, most strangely making the difficult easy, and the easy difficult."

It was a wise head. A peasant's cap was no safe disguise for it; you could know it for a king's under a diving-bell, if you could hear it work its intellect.

I had a new trade now, and plenty of business in it. The king was as hungry to find out everything that was going to happen during the next thirteen centuries as if he were expecting to live in them. From that time out, I prophesied myself baldheaded trying to supply the demand. I have done some indiscreet things in my day, but this thing of playing myself for a prophet was the worst. Still, it had its ameliorations. A prophet doesn't have to have any brains. They are good to have, of course, for the ordinary exigencies of life, but they are no use in professional work. It is the restfulest vocation there is. When the spirit of prophecy comes upon you, you merely cake your intellect and lay it off in a cool place for a rest, and unship your jaw and leave it alone; it will work itself: the result is prophecy.

Every day a knight-errant or so came along, and the sight of them fired the king's martial spirit every time. He would have forgotten himself, sure, and said something to them in a style a suspicious shade or so above his ostensible degree, and so I always got him well out of the road in time. Then he would stand and look with all his eyes; and a proud light would flash from them, and his nostrils would inflate like a war-horse's, and I knew he was longing for a brush with them. But about noon of the third day I had stopped in the road to take a precaution which had been suggested by the whip-stroke that had fallen to my share two days before; a precaution which I had afterward decided to leave untaken, I was so loath to institute it; but now I had just had a fresh reminder: while striding heedlessly along, with jaw spread and intellect at rest, for I was prophesying, I stubbed my toe and fell sprawling. I was so pale I couldn't think for a moment; then I got softly and carefully up and unstrapped my knapsack. I had that dynamite bomb in it, done up in wool in a box. It was a good thing to have along; the time would come when I could do a valuable miracle with it, maybe, but it was a nervous thing to have about me, and I didn't like to ask the king to carry it. Yet I must either throw it away or think up some safe way to get along with its society. I got it out and slipped it into my scrip, and just then here came a couple of knights. The king stood, stately as a statue, gazing toward them — had forgotten himself again, of course — and before I could get a word of warning out, it was time for him to skip, and well that he did it, too. He supposed they would turn aside. Turn aside to avoid trampling peasant dirt under foot? When had he ever turned aside himself — or ever had the chance to do it, if a peasant saw him or any other noble knight in time to judiciously save him the trouble? The knights paid no attention to the king at all; it was his place to look out himself, and if he hadn't skipped he would have been placidly ridden down, and laughed at besides.

The king was in a flaming fury, and launched out his challenge and epithets with a most royal vigor. The knights were some little distance by now. They halted, greatly surprised, and turned in their saddles and looked back, as if wondering if it might be worth while to bother with such scum as we. Then they wheeled and started for us. Not a moment must be lost. I started for *them* . I passed them at a rattling gait, and as I went by I flung out a hair-lifting soul-scorching thirteen-jointed insult which made the king's effort poor and cheap by comparison. I got it out of the nineteenth century where they know how. They had such headway that they were nearly to the king before they could check up; then, frantic with rage, they stood up their horses on their hind hoofs and whirled them around, and the next moment here they came, breast to breast. I was seventy yards off, then, and scrambling up a great bowlder at the roadside. When they were within thirty yards of me they let their long lances droop to a level, depressed their mailed heads, and so, with their horse-hair plumes streaming straight out behind, most gallant to see, this lightning express came tearing for me! When they were within fifteen yards, I sent that bomb with a sure aim, and it struck the ground just under the horses' noses.

Yes, it was a neat thing, very neat and pretty to see. It resembled a steamboat explosion on the Mississippi; and during the next fifteen minutes we stood under a steady drizzle of microscopic fragments of knights and hardware and horse-flesh. I say we, for the king joined the audience, of course, as soon as he had got his breath again. There was a hole there which would afford steady work for all the people in that region for some years to come — in trying to explain it, I mean; as for filling it up, that service would be comparatively prompt, and would fall to the lot of a select few — peasants of that seignory; and they wouldn't get anything for it, either.

But I explained it to the king myself. I said it was done with a dynamite bomb. This information did him no damage, because it left him as intelligent as he was before. However, it was a noble miracle, in his eyes, and was another settler for Merlin. I thought it well enough to explain that this was a miracle of so rare a sort that it couldn't be done except when the atmospheric conditions were just right. Otherwise he would be encoring it every time we had a good subject, and that would be inconvenient, because I hadn't any more bombs along.

Chapter XXVIII. Drilling the King

On the morning of the fourth day, when it was just sunrise, and we had been tramping an hour in the chill dawn, I came to a resolution: the king *must* be drilled; things could not go on so, he must be taken in hand and deliberately and conscientiously drilled, or we couldn't ever venture to enter a dwelling; the very cats would know this masquerader for a humbug and no peasant. So I called a halt and said:

"Sire, as between clothes and countenance, you are all right, there is no discrepancy; but as between your clothes and your bearing, you are all wrong, there is a most noticeable discrepancy. Your soldierly stride, your lordly port — these will not do. You stand too straight, your looks are too high, too confident. The cares of a kingdom do not stoop the shoulders, they do not droop the chin, they do not depress the high level of the eyeglance, they do not put doubt and fear in the heart and hang out the signs of them in slouching body and unsure step. It is the sordid cares of the lowly born that do these things. You must learn the trick; you must imitate the trademarks of poverty, misery, oppression, insult, and the other several and common inhumanities that sap the manliness out of a man and make him a loyal and proper and approved subject and a satisfaction to his masters, or the very infants will know you for better than your disguise, and we shall go to pieces at the first hut we stop at. Pray try to walk like this."

The king took careful note, and then tried an imitation.

"Pretty fair — pretty fair. Chin a little lower, please — there, very good. Eyes too high; pray don't look at the horizon, look at the ground, ten steps in front of you. Ah — that is better, that is very good. Wait, please; you betray too much vigor, too much decision; you want more of a shamble. Look at me, please — this is what I mean.... Now you are getting it; that is the idea — at least, it sort of approaches it.... Yes, that is pretty fair. *But!* There is a great big something wanting, I don't quite know what it is. Please walk thirty yards, so that I can get a perspective on the thing.... Now, then — your head's right, speed's right, shoulders right, eyes right, chin right, gait, carriage, general style right — everything's right! And yet the fact remains, the aggregate's wrong. The account don't balance. Do it again, please.... *Now* I think I begin to see what it is. Yes, I've struck it. You see, the genuine spiritlessness is wanting; that's what's the trouble. It's all *amateur* — mechanical details all right, almost to a hair; everything about the delusion perfect, except that it don't delude."

"What, then, must one do, to prevail?"

"Let me think...I can't seem to quite get at it. In fact, there isn't anything that can right the matter but practice. This is a good place for it: roots and stony ground to break up your stately gait, a region not liable to interruption, only one field and one hut in sight, and they so far away that nobody could see us from there. It will be well to move a little off the road and put in the whole day drilling you, sire."

After the drill had gone on a little while, I said:

"Now, sire, imagine that we are at the door of the hut yonder, and the family are before us. Proceed, please — accost the head of the house."

The king unconsciously straightened up like a monument, and said, with frozen austerity:

"Varlet, bring a seat; and serve to me what cheer ye have."

"Ah, your grace, that is not well done."

"In what lacketh it?"

"These people do not call *each other* varlets."

"Nay, is that true?"

"Yes; only those above them call them so."

"Then must I try again. I will call him villein."

"No-no; for he may be a freeman."

"Ah — so. Then peradventure I should call him goodman."

"That would answer, your grace, but it would be still better if you said friend, or brother."

"Brother! — to dirt like that?"

"Ah, but *we* are pretending to be dirt like that, too."

"It is even true. I will say it. Brother, bring a seat, and thereto what cheer ye have, withal. Now 'tis right."

"Not quite, not wholly right. You have asked for one, not *us* — for one, not both; food for one, a seat for one."

The king looked puzzled — he wasn't a very heavy weight, intellectually. His head was an hour-glass; it could stow an idea, but it had to do it a grain at a time, not the whole idea at once.

"Would *you* have a seat also — and sit?"

"If I did not sit, the man would perceive that we were only pretending to be equals — and playing the deception pretty poorly, too."

"It is well and truly said! How wonderful is truth, come it in whatsoever unexpected form it may! Yes, he must bring out seats and food for both, and in serving us present not ewer and napkin with more show of respect to the one than to the other."

"And there is even yet a detail that needs correcting. He must bring nothing outside; we will go in — in among the dirt, and possibly other repulsive things, — and take the food with the household, and after the fashion of the house, and all on equal terms, except the man be of the serf class; and finally, there will be no ewer and no napkin, whether he be serf or free. Please walk again, my liege. There — it is better — it is the best yet; but not perfect. The shoulders have known no ignobler burden than iron mail, and they will not stoop."

"Give me, then, the bag. I will learn the spirit that goeth with burdens that have not honor. It is the spirit that stoopeth the shoulders, I ween, and not the weight; for armor is heavy, yet it is a proud burden, and a man standeth straight in it.... Nay, but me no buts, offer me no objections. I will have the thing. Strap it upon my back."

He was complete now with that knapsack on, and looked as little like a king as any man I had ever seen. But it was an obstinate pair of shoulders; they could not seem to learn the trick of stooping with any sort of deceptive naturalness. The drill went on, I prompting and correcting:

"Now, make believe you are in debt, and eaten up by relentless creditors; you are out of work — which is horseshoeing, let us say — and can get none; and your wife is sick, your children are crying because they are hungry — "

And so on, and so on. I drilled him as representing in turn all sorts of people out of luck and suffering dire privations and misfortunes. But lord, it was only just words, words — they meant nothing in the world to him, I might just as well have whistled. Words realize nothing, vivify nothing to you, unless you have suffered in your own person the thing which the words try to describe. There are wise people who talk ever so knowingly and complacently about "the working classes," and satisfy themselves that a day's hard intellectual work is very much harder than a day's hard manual toil, and is righteously entitled to much bigger pay. Why, they really think that, you know, because they know all about the one, but haven't tried the other. But I know all about both; and so far as I am concerned, there isn't money enough in the universe to hire me to swing a pickaxe thirty days, but I will do the hardest kind of intellectual work for just as near nothing as you can cipher it down — and I will be satisfied, too.

Intellectual "work" is misnamed; it is a pleasure, a dissipation, and is its own highest reward. The poorest paid architect, engineer, general, author, sculptor, painter, lecturer, advocate, legislator, actor, preacher, singer is constructively in heaven when he is at work; and as for the musician with the fiddle-bow in his hand who sits in the midst of a great orchestra with the ebbing and flowing tides of divine sound washing over him — why, certainly, he is at work, if you wish to call it that, but lord, it's a sarcasm just the same. The law of work does seem utterly unfair — but there it is, and nothing can change it: the higher the pay in enjoyment the worker gets out of it, the higher shall be his pay in cash, also. And it's also the very law of those transparent swindles, transmissible nobility and kingship.

Chapter XXIX. The Smallpox Hut

When we arrived at that hut at mid-afternoon, we saw no signs of life about it. The field near by had been denuded of its crop some time before, and had a skinned look, so exhaustively had it been harvested and gleaned. Fences, sheds, everything had a ruined look, and were eloquent of poverty. No animal was around anywhere, no living thing in sight. The stillness was awful, it was like the stillness of death. The cabin was a one-story one, whose thatch was black with age, and ragged from lack of repair.

The door stood a trifle ajar. We approached it stealthily — on tiptoe and at half-breath — for that is the way one's feeling makes him do, at such a time. The king knocked. We waited. No answer. Knocked again. No answer. I pushed the door softly open and looked in. I made out some dim forms, and a woman started up from the ground and stared at me, as one does who is wakened from sleep. Presently she found her voice:

"Have mercy!" she pleaded. "All is taken, nothing is left."

"I have not come to take anything, poor woman."

"You are not a priest?"

"No."

"Nor come not from the lord of the manor?"

"No, I am a stranger."

"Oh, then, for the fear of God, who visits with misery and death such as be harmless, tarry not here, but fly! This place is under his curse — and his Church's."

"Let me come in and help you — you are sick and in trouble."

I was better used to the dim light now. I could see her hollow eyes fixed upon me. I could see how emaciated she was.

"I tell you the place is under the Church's ban. Save yourself — and go, before some straggler see thee here, and report it."

"Give yourself no trouble about me; I don't care anything for the Church's curse. Let me help you."

"Now all good spirits — if there be any such — bless thee for that word. Would God I had a sup of water! — but hold, hold, forget I said it, and fly; for there is that here that even he that feareth not the Church must fear: this disease whereof we die. Leave us, thou brave, good stranger, and take with thee such whole and sincere blessing as them that be accursed can give."

But before this I had picked up a wooden bowl and was rushing past the king on my way to the brook. It was ten yards away. When I got back and entered, the king was within, and was opening the shutter that closed the window-hole, to let in air and light. The place was full of a foul stench. I put the bowl to the woman's lips, and as she gripped it with her eager talons the shutter came open and a strong light flooded her face. Smallpox!

I sprang to the king, and said in his ear:

"Out of the door on the instant, sire! the woman is dying of that disease that wasted the skirts of Camelot two years ago."

He did not budge.

"Of a truth I shall remain — and likewise help."

I whispered again:

"King, it must not be. You must go."

"Ye mean well, and ye speak not unwisely. But it were shame that a king should know fear, and shame that belted knight should withhold his hand where be such as need succor. Peace, I will not go. It is you who must go. The Church's ban is not upon me, but it forbiddeth you to be here, and she will deal with you with a heavy hand an word come to her of your trespass."

It was a desperate place for him to be in, and might cost him his life, but it was no use to argue with him. If he considered his knightly honor at stake here, that was the end of argument; he would stay, and nothing could prevent it; I was aware of that. And so I dropped the subject. The woman spoke:

"Fair sir, of your kindness will ye climb the ladder there, and bring me news of what ye find? Be not afraid to report, for times can come when even a mother's heart is past breaking — being already broke."

"Abide," said the king, "and give the woman to eat. I will go." And he put down the knapsack.

I turned to start, but the king had already started. He halted, and looked down upon a man who lay in a dim light, and had not noticed us thus far, or spoken.

"Is it your husband?" the king asked.

"Yes."

"Is he asleep?"

"God be thanked for that one charity, yes — these three hours. Where shall I pay to the full, my gratitude! for my heart is bursting with it for that sleep he sleepeth now."

I said:

"We will be careful. We will not wake him."

"Ah, no, that ye will not, for he is dead."

"Dead?"

"Yes, what triumph it is to know it! None can harm him, none insult him more. He is in heaven now, and happy; or if not there, he bides in hell and is content; for in that place he will find neither abbot nor yet bishop. We were boy and girl together; we were man and wife these five and twenty years, and never separated till this day. Think how long that is to love and suffer together. This morning was he out of his mind, and in his fancy we were boy and girl again and wandering in the happy fields; and so in that innocent glad converse wandered he far and farther, still lightly gossiping, and entered into those other fields we know not of, and was shut away from mortal sight. And so there was no parting, for in his fancy I went with him; he knew not but I went with him, my hand in his — my young soft hand, not this withered claw. Ah, yes, to go, and know it not; to separate and know it not; how could one go peace — fuller than that? It was his reward for a cruel life patiently borne."

There was a slight noise from the direction of the dim corner where the ladder was. It was the king descending. I could see that he was bearing something in one arm, and assisting himself with the other. He came forward into the light; upon his breast lay a slender girl of fifteen. She was but half conscious; she was dying of smallpox. Here was heroism at its last and loftiest possibility, its utmost summit; this was challenging death in the open field unarmed, with all the odds against the challenger, no reward set upon the contest, and no admiring world in silks and cloth of gold to gaze and applaud; and yet the king's bearing was as serenely brave as it had always been in those cheaper contests where knight meets knight in equal fight and clothed in protecting steel. He was great now; sublimely great. The rude statues of his ancestors in his palace should have an addition — I would see to that; and it would not be a mailed king killing a giant or a dragon, like the rest, it would be a king in commoner's garb bearing death in his arms that a peasant mother might look her last upon her child and be comforted.

He laid the girl down by her mother, who poured out endearments and caresses from an overflowing heart, and one could detect a flickering faint light of response in the child's eyes, but that was all. The mother hung over her, kissing her, petting her, and imploring her to speak, but the lips only moved and no sound came. I snatched my liquor flask from my knapsack, but the woman forbade me, and said:

"No — she does not suffer; it is better so. It might bring her back to life. None that be so good and kind as ye are would do her that cruel hurt. For look you — what is left to live for? Her brothers are gone, her father is gone, her mother goeth, the Church's curse is upon her, and none may shelter or befriend her even though she lay perishing in the road. She is desolate. I have not asked you, good heart, if her sister be still on live, here overhead; I had no need; ye had gone back, else, and not left the poor thing forsaken — "

"She lieth at peace," interrupted the king, in a subdued voice.

"I would not change it. How rich is this day in happiness! Ah, my Annis, thou shalt join thy sister soon — thou'rt on thy way, and these be merciful friends that will not hinder."

And so she fell to murmuring and cooing over the girl again, and softly stroking her face and hair, and kissing her and calling her by endearing names; but there was scarcely sign of response now in the glazing eyes. I saw tears well from the king's eyes, and trickle down his face. The woman noticed them, too, and said:

"Ah, I know that sign: thou'st a wife at home, poor soul, and you and she have gone hungry to bed, many's the time, that the little ones might have your crust; you know what poverty is, and the daily insults of your betters, and the heavy hand of the Church and the king."

The king winced under this accidental home-shot, but kept still; he was learning his part; and he was playing it well, too, for a pretty dull beginner. I struck up a diversion. I offered the woman food and liquor, but she refused both. She would allow nothing to come between her and the release of death. Then I slipped away and brought the dead child from aloft, and laid it by her. This broke her down again, and there was another scene that was full of heartbreak. By and by I made another diversion, and beguiled her to sketch her story.

"Ye know it well yourselves, having suffered it — for truly none of our condition in Britain escape it. It is the old, weary tale. We fought and struggled and succeeded; meaning by success, that we lived and did not die; more than that is not to be claimed. No troubles came that we could not outlive, till this year brought them; then came they all at once, as one might say, and overwhelmed us. Years ago the lord of the manor planted certain fruit trees on our farm; in the best part of it, too — a grievous wrong and shame — "

"But it was his right," interrupted the king.

"None denieth that, indeed; an the law mean anything, what is the lord's is his, and what is mine is his also. Our farm was ours by lease, therefore 'twas likewise his, to do with it as he would. Some little time ago, three of those trees were found hewn down. Our three grown sons ran frightened to report the crime. Well, in his lordship's dungeon there they lie, who saith there shall they lie and rot till they confess. They have naught to confess, being innocent, wherefore there will they remain until they die.

Ye know that right well, I ween. Think how this left us; a man, a woman and two children, to gather a crop that was planted by so much greater force, yes, and protect it night and day from pigeons and prowling animals that be sacred and must not be hurt by any of our sort. When my lord's crop was nearly ready for the harvest, so also was ours; when his bell rang to call us to his fields to harvest his crop for nothing, he would not allow that I and my two girls should count for our three captive sons, but for only two of them; so, for the lacking one were we daily fined. All this time our own crop was perishing through neglect; and so both the priest and his lordship fined us because their shares of it were suffering through damage. In the end the fines ate up our crop — and they took it all; they took it all and made us harvest it for them, without pay or food, and we starving. Then the worst came when I, being out of my mind with hunger and loss of my boys, and grief to see my husband and my little maids in rags and misery and despair, uttered a deep blasphemy — oh! a thousand of them! — against the Church and the Church's ways. It was ten days ago. I had fallen sick with this disease, and it was to the priest I said the words, for he was come to chide me for lack of due humility under the chastening hand of God. He carried my trespass to his betters; I was stubborn; wherefore, presently upon my head and upon all heads that were dear to me, fell the curse of Rome.

"Since that day we are avoided, shunned with horror. None has come near this hut to know whether we live or not. The rest of us were taken down. Then I roused me and got up, as wife and mother will. It was little they could have eaten in any case; it was less than little they had to eat. But there was water, and I gave them that. How they craved it! and how they blessed it! But the end came yesterday; my strength broke down. Yesterday was the last time I ever saw my husband and this youngest child alive. I have lain here all these hours — these ages, ye may say — listening, listening for any sound up there that — "

She gave a sharp quick glance at her eldest daughter, then cried out, "Oh, my darling!" and feebly gathered the stiffening form to her sheltering arms. She had recognized the death-rattle.

Chapter XXX. The Tragedy of the Manor-House

At midnight all was over, and we sat in the presence of four corpses. We covered them with such rags as we could find, and started away, fastening the door behind us. Their home must be these people's grave, for they could not have Christian burial, or be admitted to consecrated ground. They were as dogs, wild beasts, lepers, and no soul that valued its hope of eternal life would throw it away by meddling in any sort with these rebuked and smitten outcasts.

We had not moved four steps when I caught a sound as of footsteps upon gravel. My heart flew to my throat. We must not be seen coming from that house. I plucked at the king's robe and we drew back and took shelter behind the corner of the cabin.

"Now we are safe," I said, "but it was a close call — so to speak. If the night had been lighter he might have seen us, no doubt, he seemed to be so near."

"Mayhap it is but a beast and not a man at all."

"True. But man or beast, it will be wise to stay here a minute and let it get by and out of the way."

"Hark! It cometh hither."

True again. The step was coming toward us — straight toward the hut. It must be a beast, then, and we might as well have saved our trepidation. I was going to step out, but the king laid his hand upon my arm. There was a moment of silence, then we heard a soft knock on the cabin door. It made me shiver. Presently the knock was repeated, and then we heard these words in a guarded voice:

"Mother! Father! Open — we have got free, and we bring news to pale your cheeks but glad your hearts; and we may not tarry, but must fly! And — but they answer not. Mother! father! — "

I drew the king toward the other end of the hut and whispered:

"Come — now we can get to the road."

The king hesitated, was going to demur; but just then we heard the door give way, and knew that those desolate men were in the presence of their dead.

"Come, my liege! in a moment they will strike a light, and then will follow that which it would break your heart to hear."

He did not hesitate this time. The moment we were in the road I ran; and after a moment he threw dignity aside and followed. I did not want to think of what was happening in the hut — I couldn't bear it; I wanted to drive it out of my mind; so I struck into the first subject that lay under that one in my mind:

"I have had the disease those people died of, and so have nothing to fear; but if you have not had it also — "

He broke in upon me to say he was in trouble, and it was his conscience that was troubling him:

"These young men have got free, they say — but *how* ? It is not likely that their lord hath set them free."

"Oh, no, I make no doubt they escaped."

"That is my trouble; I have a fear that this is so, and your suspicion doth confirm it, you having the same fear."

"I should not call it by that name though. I do suspect that they escaped, but if they did, I am not sorry, certainly."

"I am not sorry, I *think* — but — "

"What is it? What is there for one to be troubled about?"

"*If* they did escape, then are we bound in duty to lay hands upon them and deliver them again to their lord; for it is not seemly that one of his quality should suffer a so insolent and highhanded outrage from persons of their base degree."

There it was again. He could see only one side of it. He was born so, educated so, his veins were full of ancestral blood that was rotten with this sort of unconscious brutality, brought down by inheritance from a long procession of hearts that had each done its share toward poisoning the stream. To imprison these men without proof, and starve their kindred, was no harm, for they were merely peasants and subject to the will and pleasure of their lord, no matter what fearful form it might take; but for these men to break out of unjust captivity was insult and outrage, and a thing not to be countenanced by any conscientious person who knew his duty to his sacred caste.

I worked more than half an hour before I got him to change the subject — and even then an outside matter did it for me. This was a something which caught our eyes as we struck the summit of a small hill — a red glow, a good way off.

"That's a fire," said I.

Fires interested me considerably, because I was getting a good deal of an insurance business started, and was also training some horses and building some steam fire-engines, with an eye to a paid fire department by and by. The priests opposed both my fire and life insurance, on the ground that it was an insolent attempt to hinder the decrees of God; and if you pointed out that they did not hinder the decrees in the least, but only modified the hard consequences of them if you took out policies and had luck, they retorted that that was gambling against the decrees of God, and was just as bad. So they managed to damage those industries more or less, but I got even on my Accident business. As a rule, a knight is a lummox, and some times even a labrick, and hence open to pretty poor arguments when they come glibly from a superstition-monger, but even *he* could see the practical side of a thing once in a while; and so of late you couldn't clean up a tournament and pile the result without finding one of my accident-tickets in every helmet.

We stood there awhile, in the thick darkness and stillness, looking toward the red blur in the distance, and trying to make out the meaning of a faraway murmur that rose and fell fitfully on the night. Sometimes it swelled up and for a moment seemed less remote; but when we were hopefully expecting it to betray its cause and nature, it dulled and sank again, carrying its mystery with it. We started down the hill in its direction, and the winding road plunged us at once into almost solid darkness — darkness that was packed and crammed in between two tall forest walls. We groped along down for half a mile, perhaps, that murmur growing more and more distinct all the time. The coming storm threatening more and more, with now and then a little shiver of wind, a faint show of lightning, and dull grumblings of distant thunder. I was in the lead. I ran against something — a soft heavy something which gave, slightly, to the impulse of my weight; at the same moment the lightning glared out, and within a foot of my face was the writhing face of a man who was hanging from the limb of a tree! That is, it seemed to be writhing, but it was not. It was a grewsome sight. Straightway there was an ear-splitting explosion of thunder, and the bottom of heaven fell out; the rain poured down in a deluge. No matter, we must try to cut this man down, on the chance that there might be life in him yet, mustn't we? The lightning came quick and sharp now, and the place was alternately noonday and midnight. One moment the man would be hanging before me in an intense light, and the next he was blotted out again in the darkness. I told the king we must cut him down. The king at once objected.

"If he hanged himself, he was willing to lose his property to his lord; so let him be. If others hanged him, belike they had the right — let him hang."

"But — "

"But me no buts, but even leave him as he is. And for yet another reason. When the lightning cometh again — there, look abroad."

Two others hanging, within fifty yards of us!

"It is not weather meet for doing useless courtesies unto dead folk. They are past thanking you. Come — it is unprofitable to tarry here."

There was reason in what he said, so we moved on. Within the next mile we counted six more hanging forms by the blaze of the lightning, and altogether it was a grisly excursion. That murmur was a murmur no longer, it was a roar; a roar of men's voices. A man came flying by now, dimly through the darkness, and other men chasing him. They disappeared. Presently another case of the kind occurred, and then another and another. Then a sudden turn of the road brought us in sight of that fire — it was a large manor-house, and little or nothing was left of it — and everywhere men were flying and other men raging after them in pursuit.

I warned the king that this was not a safe place for strangers. We would better get away from the light, until matters should improve. We stepped back a little, and hid in the edge of the wood. From this hiding-place we saw both men and women hunted by the mob. The fearful work went on until nearly dawn. Then, the fire being out and the storm spent, the voices and flying footsteps presently ceased, and darkness and stillness reigned again.

We ventured out, and hurried cautiously away; and although we were worn out and sleepy, we kept on until we had put this place some miles behind us. Then we asked hospitality at the hut of a charcoal burner, and got what was to be had. A woman was up and about, but the man was still asleep, on a straw shake-down, on the clay floor. The woman seemed uneasy until I explained that we were travelers and had lost our way and been wandering in the woods all night. She became talkative, then, and asked if we had heard of the terrible goings-on at the manor-house of Abblasoure. Yes, we had heard of them, but what we wanted now was rest and sleep. The king broke in:

"Sell us the house and take yourselves away, for we be perilous company, being late come from people that died of the Spotted Death."

It was good of him, but unnecessary. One of the commonest decorations of the nation was the waffle-iron face. I had early noticed that the woman and her husband were both so decorated. She made us entirely welcome, and had no fears; and plainly she was immensely impressed by the king's proposition; for, of course, it was a good deal of an event in her life to run across a person of the king's humble appearance who was ready to buy a man's house for the sake of a night's lodging. It gave her a large respect for us, and she strained the lean possibilities of her hovel to the utmost to make us comfortable.

We slept till far into the afternoon, and then got up hungry enough to make cotter fare quite palatable to the king, the more particularly as it was scant in quantity. And also in variety; it consisted solely of onions, salt, and the national black bread made out of horse-feed. The woman told us about the affair of the evening before. At ten or eleven at night, when everybody was in bed, the manor-house burst into flames. The countryside swarmed to the rescue, and the family were saved, with one exception, the master. He did not appear. Everybody was frantic over this loss, and two brave yeomen sacrificed their lives in ransacking the burning house seeking that valuable personage. But after a while he was found — what was left of him — which was his corpse. It was in a copse three hundred yards away, bound, gagged, stabbed in a dozen places.

Who had done this? Suspicion fell upon a humble family in the neighborhood who had been lately treated with peculiar harshness by the baron; and from these people the suspicion easily extended itself to their relatives and familiars. A suspicion was enough; my lord's liveried retainers proclaimed an instant crusade against these people, and were promptly joined by the community in general. The woman's husband had been active with the mob, and had not returned home until nearly dawn. He was gone now to find out what the general result had been. While we were still talking he came back from his quest. His report was revolting enough. Eighteen persons hanged or butchered, and two yeomen and thirteen prisoners lost in the fire.

"And how many prisoners were there altogether in the vaults?"

"Thirteen."

"Then every one of them was lost?"

"Yes, all."

"But the people arrived in time to save the family; how is it they could save none of the prisoners?"

The man looked puzzled, and said:

"Would one unlock the vaults at such a time? Marry, some would have escaped."

"Then you mean that nobody *did* unlock them?"

"None went near them, either to lock or unlock. It standeth to reason that the bolts were fast; wherefore it was only needful to establish a watch, so that if any broke the bonds he might not escape, but be taken. None were taken."

"Natheless, three did escape," said the king, "and ye will do well to publish it and set justice upon their track, for these murthered the baron and fired the house."

I was just expecting he would come out with that. For a moment the man and his wife showed an eager interest in this news and an impatience to go out and spread it; then a sudden something else betrayed itself in their faces, and they began to ask questions. I answered the questions myself, and narrowly watched the effects produced. I was soon satisfied that the knowledge of who these three prisoners were had somehow changed the atmosphere; that our hosts' continued eagerness to go and spread the news was now only pretended and not real. The king did not notice the change, and I was glad of that. I worked the conversation around toward other details of the night's proceedings, and noted that these people were relieved to have it take that direction.

The painful thing observable about all this business was the alacrity with which this oppressed community had turned their cruel hands against their own class in the interest of the common oppressor. This man and woman seemed to feel that in a quarrel between a person of their own class and his lord, it was the natural and proper and rightful thing for that poor devil's whole caste to side with the master and fight his battle for him, without ever stopping to inquire into the rights or wrongs of the matter. This man had been out helping to hang his neighbors, and had done his work with zeal, and yet was aware that there was nothing against them but a mere suspicion, with nothing back of it describable as evidence, still neither he nor his wife seemed to see anything horrible about it.

This was depressing — to a man with the dream of a republic in his head. It reminded me of a time thirteen centuries away, when the "poor whites" of our South who were always despised and frequently insulted by the slave-lords around them, and who owed their base condition simply to the presence of slavery in their midst, were yet pusillanimously ready to side with the slave-lords in all political moves for the upholding and perpetuating of slavery, and did also finally shoulder their muskets and pour out their lives in an effort to prevent the destruction of that very institution which degraded them. And there was only one redeeming feature connected with that pitiful piece of history; and that was, that secretly the "poor white" did detest the slave-lord, and did feel his own shame. That feeling was not brought to the surface, but the fact that it was there and could have been brought out, under favoring circumstances, was something — in fact, it was enough; for it showed that a man is at bottom a man, after all, even if it doesn't show on the outside.

Well, as it turned out, this charcoal burner was just the twin of the Southern "poor white" of the far future. The king presently showed impatience, and said:

"An ye prattle here all the day, justice will miscarry. Think ye the criminals will abide in their father's house? They are fleeing, they are not waiting. You should look to it that a party of horse be set upon their track."

The woman paled slightly, but quite perceptibly, and the man looked flustered and irresolute. I said:

"Come, friend, I will walk a little way with you, and explain which direction I think they would try to take. If they were merely resisters of the gabelle or some kindred absurdity I would try to protect them from capture; but when men murder a person of high degree and likewise burn his house, that is another matter."

The last remark was for the king — to quiet him. On the road the man pulled his resolution together, and began the march with a steady gait, but there was no eagerness in it. By and by I said:

"What relation were these men to you — cousins?"

He turned as white as his layer of charcoal would let him, and stopped, trembling.

"Ah, my God, how know ye that?"

"I didn't know it; it was a chance guess."

"Poor lads, they are lost. And good lads they were, too."

"Were you actually going yonder to tell on them?"

He didn't quite know how to take that; but he said, hesitatingly:

"Ye-s."

"Then I think you are a damned scoundrel!"

It made him as glad as if I had called him an angel.

"Say the good words again, brother! for surely ye mean that ye would not betray me an I failed of my duty."

"Duty? There is no duty in the matter, except the duty to keep still and let those men get away. They've done a righteous deed."

He looked pleased; pleased, and touched with apprehension at the same time. He looked up and down the road to see that no one was coming, and then said in a cautious voice:

"From what land come you, brother, that you speak such perilous words, and seem not to be afraid?"

"They are not perilous words when spoken to one of my own caste, I take it. You would not tell anybody I said them?"

"I? I would be drawn asunder by wild horses first."

"Well, then, let me say my say. I have no fears of your repeating it. I think devil's work has been done last night upon those innocent poor people. That old baron got only what he deserved. If I had my way, all his kind should have the same luck."

Fear and depression vanished from the man's manner, and gratefulness and a brave animation took their place:

"Even though you be a spy, and your words a trap for my undoing, yet are they such refreshment that to hear them again and others like to them, I would go to the gallows happy, as having had one good feast at least in a starved life. And I will say my say now, and ye may report it if ye be so minded. I helped to hang my neighbors for that it were peril to my own life to show lack of zeal in the master's cause; the others helped for none other reason. All rejoice to-day that he is dead, but all do go about seemingly sorrowing, and shedding the hypocrite's tear, for in that lies safety. I have said the words, I have said the words! the only ones that have ever tasted good in my mouth, and the reward of that taste is sufficient. Lead on, an ye will, be it even to the scaffold, for I am ready."

There it was, you see. A man is a man, at bottom. Whole ages of abuse and oppression cannot crush the manhood clear out of him. Whoever thinks it a mistake is himself mistaken. Yes, there is plenty good enough material for a republic in the most degraded people that ever existed — even the Russians; plenty of manhood in them — even in the Germans — if one could but force it out of its timid and suspicious privacy, to overthrow and trample in the mud any throne that ever was set up and any nobility that ever supported it. We should see certain things yet, let us hope and believe. First, a modified monarchy, till Arthur's days were done, then the destruction of the throne, nobility abolished, every member of it bound out to some useful trade, universal suffrage instituted, and the whole government placed in the hands of the men and women of the nation there to remain. Yes, there was no occasion to give up my dream yet a while.

Chapter XXXI. Marco

We strolled along in a sufficiently indolent fashion now, and talked. We must dispose of about the amount of time it ought to take to go to the little hamlet of Abblasoure and put justice on the track of those murderers and get back home again. And meantime I had an auxiliary interest which had never paled yet, never lost its novelty for me since I had been in Arthur's kingdom: the behavior — born of nice and exact subdivisions of caste — of chance passers-by toward each other. Toward the shaven monk who trudged along with his cowl tilted back and the sweat washing down his fat jowls, the coal-burner was deeply reverent; to the gentleman he was abject; with the small farmer and the free mechanic he was cordial and gossipy; and when a slave passed by with a countenance respectfully lowered, this chap's nose was in the air — he couldn't even see him. Well, there are times when one would like to hang the whole human race and finish the farce.

Presently we struck an incident. A small mob of half-naked boys and girls came tearing out of the woods, scared and shrieking. The eldest among them were not more than twelve or fourteen years old. They implored help, but they were so beside themselves that we couldn't make out what the matter was. However, we plunged into the wood, they skurrying in the lead, and the trouble was quickly revealed: they had hanged a little fellow with a bark rope, and he was kicking and struggling, in the process of choking to death. We rescued him, and fetched him around. It was some more human nature; the admiring little folk imitating their elders; they were playing mob, and had achieved a success which promised to be a good deal more serious than they had bargained for.

It was not a dull excursion for me. I managed to put in the time very well. I made various acquaintanceships, and in my quality of stranger was able to ask as many questions as I wanted to. A thing which naturally interested me, as a statesman, was the matter of wages. I picked up what I could under that head during the afternoon. A man who hasn't had much experience, and doesn't think, is apt to measure a nation's prosperity or lack of prosperity by the mere size of the prevailing wages; if the wages be high, the nation is prosperous; if low, it isn't. Which is an error. It isn't what sum you get, it's how much you can buy with it, that's the important thing; and it's that that tells whether your wages are high in fact or only high in name. I could remember how it was in the time of our great civil war in the nineteenth century. In the North a carpenter got three dollars a day, gold valuation; in the South he got fifty — payable in Confederate shinplasters worth a dollar a bushel. In the North a suit of overalls cost three dollars — a day's wages; in the South it cost seventy-five — which was two days' wages. Other things were in proportion. Consequently, wages were twice as high in the North as they were in the South, because the one wage had that much more purchasing power than the other had.

Yes, I made various acquaintances in the hamlet and a thing that gratified me a good deal was to find our new coins in circulation — lots of milrays, lots of mills, lots of cents, a good many nickels, and some silver; all this among the artisans and commonalty generally; yes, and even some gold — but that was at the bank, that is to say, the goldsmith's. I dropped in there while Marco, the son of Marco, was haggling with a shopkeeper over a quarter of a pound of salt, and asked for change for a twenty-dollar gold piece. They furnished it — that is, after they had chewed the piece, and rung it on the counter, and tried acid on it, and asked me where I got it, and who I was, and where I was from, and where I was going to, and when I expected to get there, and perhaps a couple of hundred more questions; and when they got aground, I went right on and furnished them a lot of information voluntarily; told them I owned a dog, and his name was Watch, and my first wife was a Free Will Baptist, and her grandfather was a Prohibitionist, and I used to know a man who had two thumbs on each hand and a wart on the inside of his upper lip, and died in the hope of a glorious resurrection, and so on, and so on, and so on, till even that hungry village questioner began to look satisfied, and also a shade put out; but he had to respect a man of my financial strength, and so he didn't give me any lip, but I noticed he took it out of his underlings, which was a perfectly natural thing to do. Yes, they changed my twenty, but I judged it strained the bank a little, which was a thing to be expected, for it was the same as walking into a paltry village store in the nineteenth century and requiring the boss of it to change a two thousand-dollar bill for you all of a sudden. He could do it, maybe; but at the same time he would wonder how a small farmer happened to be carrying so much money around in his pocket; which was probably this goldsmith's thought, too; for he followed me to the door and stood there gazing after me with reverent admiration.

Our new money was not only handsomely circulating, but its language was already glibly in use; that is to say, people had dropped the names of the former moneys, and spoke of things as being worth so many dollars or cents or mills or milrays now. It was very gratifying. We were progressing, that was sure.

I got to know several master mechanics, but about the most interesting fellow among them was the blacksmith, Dowley. He was a live man and a brisk talker, and had two journeymen and three apprentices, and was doing a raging business. In fact, he was getting rich, hand over fist, and was vastly respected. Marco was very proud of having such a man for a friend. He had taken me there ostensibly to let me see the big establishment which bought so much of his charcoal, but really to let me see what easy and almost familiar terms he was on with this great man. Dowley and I fraternized at once; I had had just such picked men, splendid fellows, under me in the Colt Arms Factory. I was bound to see more of him, so I invited him to come out to Marco's Sunday, and dine with us. Marco was appalled, and held his breath; and when the grandee accepted, he was so grateful that he almost forgot to be astonished at the condescension.

Marco's joy was exuberant — but only for a moment; then he grew thoughtful, then sad; and when he heard me tell Dowley I should have Dickon, the boss mason, and Smug, the boss wheelwright, out there, too, the coal-dust on his face turned to chalk, and he lost his grip. But I knew what was the matter with him; it was the expense. He saw ruin before him; he judged that his financial days were numbered. However, on our way to invite the others, I said:

"You must allow me to have these friends come; and you must also allow me to pay the costs."

His face cleared, and he said with spirit:

"But not all of it, not all of it. Ye cannot well bear a burden like to this alone."

I stopped him, and said:

"Now let's understand each other on the spot, old friend. I am only a farm bailiff, it is true; but I am not poor, nevertheless. I have been very fortunate this year — you would be astonished to know how I have thriven. I tell you the honest truth when I say I could squander away as many as a dozen feasts like this and never care *that* for the expense!" and I snapped my fingers. I could see myself rise a foot at a time in Marco's estimation, and when I fetched out those last words I was become a very tower for style and altitude. "So you see, you must let me have my way. You can't contribute a cent to this orgy, that's *settled* ."

"It's grand and good of you — "

"No, it isn't. You've opened your house to Jones and me in the most generous way; Jones was remarking upon it to-day, just before you came back from the village; for although he wouldn't be likely to say such a thing to you — because Jones isn't a talker, and is diffident in society — he has a good heart and a grateful, and knows how to appreciate it when he is well treated; yes, you and your wife have been very hospitable toward us — "

"Ah, brother, 'tis nothing — *such* hospitality!"

"But it *is* something; the best a man has, freely given, is always something, and is as good as a prince can do, and ranks right along beside it — for even a prince can but do his best. And so we'll shop around and get up this layout now, and don't you worry about the expense. I'm one of the worst spendthrifts that ever was born. Why, do you know, sometimes in a single week I spend — but never mind about that — you'd never believe it anyway."

And so we went gadding along, dropping in here and there, pricing things, and gossiping with the shopkeepers about the riot, and now and then running across pathetic reminders of it, in the persons of shunned and tearful and houseless remnants of families whose homes had been taken from them and their parents butchered or hanged. The raiment of Marco and his wife was of coarse tow-linen and linsey-woolsey respectively, and resembled township maps, it being made up pretty exclusively of patches which had been added, township by township, in the course of five or six years, until hardly a hand's-breadth of the original garments was surviving and present. Now I wanted to fit these people out with new suits, on account of that swell company, and I didn't know just how to get at it — with delicacy, until at last it struck me that as I had already been liberal in inventing wordy gratitude for the king, it would be just the thing to back it up with evidence of a substantial sort; so I said:

"And Marco, there's another thing which you must permit — out of kindness for Jones — because you wouldn't want to offend him. He was very anxious to testify his appreciation in some way, but he is so diffident he couldn't venture it himself, and so he begged me to buy some little things and give them to you and Dame Phyllis and let him pay for them without your ever knowing they came from him — you know how a delicate person feels about that sort of thing — and so I said I would, and we would keep mum. Well, his idea was, a new outfit of clothes for you both — "

"Oh, it is wastefulness! It may not be, brother, it may not be. Consider the vastness of the sum — "

"Hang the vastness of the sum! Try to keep quiet for a moment, and see how it would seem; a body can't get in a word edgeways, you talk so much. You ought to cure that, Marco; it isn't good form, you know, and it will grow on you if you don't check it. Yes, we'll step in here now and price this man's stuff — and don't forget to remember to not let on to Jones that you know he had anything to do with it. You can't think how curiously sensitive and proud he is. He's a farmer — pretty fairly well-to-do farmer — and I'm his bailiff; *but* — the imagination of that man! Why, sometimes when he forgets himself and gets to blowing off, you'd think he was one of the swells of the earth; and you might listen to him a hundred years and never take him for a farmer — especially if he talked agriculture. He *thinks* he's a Sheol of a farmer; thinks he's old Grayback from Wayback; but between you and me privately he don't know as much about farming as he does about running a kingdom — still, whatever he talks about, you want to drop your underjaw and listen, the same as if you had never heard such incredible wisdom in all your life before, and were afraid you might die before you got enough of it. That will please Jones."

It tickled Marco to the marrow to hear about such an odd character; but it also prepared him for accidents; and in my experience when you travel with a king who is letting on to be something else and can't remember it more than about half the time, you can't take too many precautions.

This was the best store we had come across yet; it had everything in it, in small quantities, from anvils and drygoods all the way down to fish and pinchbeck jewelry. I concluded I would bunch my whole invoice right here, and not go pricing around any more. So I got rid of Marco, by sending him off to invite the mason and the wheelwright, which left the field free to me. For I never care to do a thing in a quiet way; it's got to be theatrical or I don't take any interest in it. I showed up money enough, in a careless way, to corral the shopkeeper's respect, and then I wrote down a list of the things I wanted, and handed it to him to see if he could read it. He could, and was proud to show that he could. He said he had been educated by a priest, and could both read and write. He ran it through, and remarked with satisfaction that it was a pretty heavy bill. Well, and so it was, for a little concern like that. I was not only providing a swell dinner, but some odds and ends of extras. I ordered that the things be carted out and delivered at the dwelling of Marco, the son of Marco, by Saturday evening, and send me the bill at dinner-time Sunday. He said I could depend upon his promptness and exactitude, it was the rule of the house. He also observed that he would throw in a couple of miller-guns for the Marcos gratis — that everybody was using them now. He had a mighty opinion of that clever device. I said:

"And please fill them up to the middle mark, too; and add that to the bill."

He would, with pleasure. He filled them, and I took them with me. I couldn't venture to tell him that the miller-gun was a little invention of my own, and that I had officially ordered that every shopkeeper in the kingdom keep them on hand and sell them at government price —

which was the merest trifle, and the shopkeeper got that, not the government. We furnished them for nothing.

The king had hardly missed us when we got back at nightfall. He had early dropped again into his dream of a grand invasion of Gaul with the whole strength of his kingdom at his back, and the afternoon had slipped away without his ever coming to himself again.

Chapter XXXII. Dowley's Humiliation

Well, when that cargo arrived toward sunset, Saturday afternoon, I had my hands full to keep the Marcos from fainting. They were sure Jones and I were ruined past help, and they blamed themselves as accessories to this bankruptcy. You see, in addition to the dinner-materials, which called for a sufficiently round sum, I had bought a lot of extras for the future comfort of the family: for instance, a big lot of wheat, a delicacy as rare to the tables of their class as was ice-cream to a hermit's; also a sizeable deal dinner-table; also two entire pounds of salt, which was another piece of extravagance in those people's eyes; also crockery, stools, the clothes, a small cask of beer, and so on. I instructed the Marcos to keep quiet about this sumptuousness, so as to give me a chance to surprise the guests and show off a little. Concerning the new clothes, the simple couple were like children; they were up and down, all night, to see if it wasn't nearly daylight, so that they could put them on, and they were into them at last as much as an hour before dawn was due. Then their pleasure — not to say delirium — was so fresh and novel and inspiring that the sight of it paid me well for the interruptions which my sleep had suffered. The king had slept just as usual — like the dead. The Marcos could not thank him for their clothes, that being forbidden; but they tried every way they could think of to make him see how grateful they were. Which all went for nothing: he didn't notice any change.

It turned out to be one of those rich and rare fall days which is just a June day toned down to a degree where it is heaven to be out of doors. Toward noon the guests arrived, and we assembled under a great tree and were soon as sociable as old acquaintants. Even the king's reserve melted a little, though it was some little trouble to him to adjust himself to the name of Jones along at first. I had asked him to try to not forget that he was a farmer; but I had also considered it prudent to ask him to let the thing stand at that, and not elaborate it any. Because he was just the kind of person you could depend on to spoil a little thing like that if you didn't warn him, his tongue was so handy, and his spirit so willing, and his information so uncertain.

Dowley was in fine feather, and I early got him started, and then adroitly worked him around onto his own history for a text and himself for a hero, and then it was good to sit there and hear him hum. Self-made man, you know. They know how to talk. They do deserve more credit than any other breed of men, yes, that is true; and they are among the very first to find it out, too. He told how he had begun life an orphan lad without money and without friends able to help him; how he had lived as the slaves of the meanest master lived; how his day's work was from sixteen to eighteen hours long, and yielded him only enough black bread to keep him in a half-fed condition; how his faithful endeavors finally attracted the attention of a good blacksmith, who came near knocking him dead with kindness by suddenly offering, when he was totally unprepared, to take him as his bound apprentice for nine years and give him board and clothes and teach him the trade — or "mystery" as Dowley called it. That was his first great rise, his first gorgeous stroke of fortune; and you saw that he couldn't yet speak of it without a sort of eloquent wonder and delight that such a gilded promotion should have fallen to the lot of a common human being. He got no new clothing during his apprenticeship, but on his graduation day his master tricked him out in spang-new tow-linens and made him feel unspeakably rich and fine.

"I remember me of that day!" the wheelwright sang out, with enthusiasm.

"And I likewise!" cried the mason. "I would not believe they were thine own; in faith I could not."

"Nor other!" shouted Dowley, with sparkling eyes. "I was like to lose my character, the neighbors wending I had mayhap been stealing. It was a great day, a great day; one forgetteth not days like that."

Yes, and his master was a fine man, and prosperous, and always had a great feast of meat twice in the year, and with it white bread, true wheaten bread; in fact, lived like a lord, so to speak. And in time Dowley succeeded to the business and married the daughter.

"And now consider what is come to pass," said he, impressively. "Two times in every month there is fresh meat upon my table." He made a pause here, to let that fact sink home, then added — "and eight times salt meat."

"It is even true," said the wheelwright, with bated breath.

"I know it of mine own knowledge," said the mason, in the same reverent fashion.

"On my table appeareth white bread every Sunday in the year," added the master smith, with solemnity. "I leave it to your own consciences, friends, if this is not also true?"

"By my head, yes," cried the mason.

"I can testify it — and I do," said the wheelwright.

"And as to furniture, ye shall say yourselves what mine equipment is." He waved his hand in fine gesture of granting frank and unhampered freedom of speech, and added: "Speak as ye are moved; speak as ye would speak; an I were not here."

"Ye have five stools, and of the sweetest workmanship at that, albeit your family is but three," said the wheelwright, with deep respect.

"And six wooden goblets, and six platters of wood and two of pewter to eat and drink from withal," said the mason, impressively. "And I say it as knowing God is my judge, and we tarry not here alway, but must answer at the last day for the things said in the body, be they false or be they sooth."

"Now ye know what manner of man I am, brother Jones," said the smith, with a fine and friendly condescension, "and doubtless ye would look to find me a man jealous of his due of respect and but sparing of outgo to strangers till their rating and quality be assured, but trouble yourself not, as concerning that; wit ye well ye shall find me a man that regardeth not these matters but is willing to receive any he as his fellow and equal that carrieth a right heart in his body, be his worldly estate howsoever modest. And in token of it, here is my hand; and I say with my own mouth we are equals — equals" — and he smiled around on the company with the satisfaction of a god who is doing the handsome and gracious thing and is quite well aware of it.

The king took the hand with a poorly disguised reluctance, and let go of it as willingly as a lady lets go of a fish; all of which had a good effect, for it was mistaken for an embarrassment natural to one who was being called upon by greatness.

The dame brought out the table now, and set it under the tree. It caused a visible stir of surprise, it being brand new and a sumptuous article of deal. But the surprise rose higher still when the dame, with a body oozing easy indifference at every pore, but eyes that gave it all away by absolutely flaming with vanity, slowly unfolded an actual simon-pure tablecloth and spread it. That was a notch above even the blacksmith's domestic grandeurs, and it hit him hard; you could see it. But Marco was in Paradise; you could see that, too. Then the dame brought two fine new stools — whew! that was a sensation; it was visible in the eyes of every guest. Then she brought two more — as calmly as she could. Sensation again — with awed murmurs. Again she brought two — walking on air, she was so proud. The guests were petrified, and the mason muttered:

"There is that about earthly pomps which doth ever move to reverence."

As the dame turned away, Marco couldn't help slapping on the climax while the thing was hot; so he said with what was meant for a languid composure but was a poor imitation of it:

"These suffice; leave the rest."

So there were more yet! It was a fine effect. I couldn't have played the hand better myself.

From this out, the madam piled up the surprises with a rush that fired the general astonishment up to a hundred and fifty in the shade, and at the same time paralyzed expression of it down to gasped "Oh's" and "Ah's," and mute upliftings of hands and eyes. She fetched crockery — new, and plenty of it; new wooden goblets and other table furniture; and beer, fish, chicken, a goose, eggs, roast beef, roast mutton, a ham, a small roast pig, and a wealth of genuine white wheaten bread. Take it by and large, that spread laid everything far and away in the shade that ever that crowd had seen before. And while they sat there just simply stupefied with wonder and awe, I sort of waved my hand as if by accident, and the storekeeper's son emerged from space and said he had come to collect.

"That's all right," I said, indifferently. "What is the amount? give us the items."

Then he read off this bill, while those three amazed men listened, and serene waves of satisfaction rolled over my soul and alternate waves of terror and admiration surged over Marco's:

He ceased. There was a pale and awful silence. Not a limb stirred. Not a nostril betrayed the passage of breath.

"Is that all?" I asked, in a voice of the most perfect calmness.

"All, fair sir, save that certain matters of light moment are placed together under a head hight sundries. If it would like you, I will sepa — "

"It is of no consequence," I said, accompanying the words with a gesture of the most utter indifference; "give me the grand total, please."

The clerk leaned against the tree to stay himself, and said:

"Thirty-nine thousand one hundred and fifty milrays!"

The wheelwright fell off his stool, the others grabbed the table to save themselves, and there was a deep and general ejaculation of:

"God be with us in the day of disaster!"

The clerk hastened to say:

"My father chargeth me to say he cannot honorably require you to pay it all at this time, and therefore only prayeth you — "

I paid no more heed than if it were the idle breeze, but, with an air of indifference amounting almost to weariness, got out my money and tossed four dollars on to the table. Ah, you should have seen them stare!

The clerk was astonished and charmed. He asked me to retain one of the dollars as security, until he could go to town and — I interrupted:

"What, and fetch back nine cents? Nonsense! Take the whole. Keep the change."

There was an amazed murmur to this effect:

"Verily this being is *made* of money! He throweth it away even as if it were dirt."

The blacksmith was a crushed man.

The clerk took his money and reeled away drunk with fortune. I said to Marco and his wife:

"Good folk, here is a little trifle for you" — handing the miller-guns as if it were a matter of no consequence, though each of them contained fifteen cents in solid cash; and while the poor creatures went to pieces with astonishment and gratitude, I turned to the others and said as calmly as one would ask the time of day:

"Well, if we are all ready, I judge the dinner is. Come, fall to."

Ah, well, it was immense; yes, it was a daisy. I don't know that I ever put a situation together better, or got happier spectacular effects out of the materials available. The blacksmith — well, he was simply mashed. Land! I wouldn't have felt what that man was feeling, for anything in the world. Here he had been blowing and bragging about his grand meat-feast twice a year, and his fresh meat twice a month, and his salt meat twice a week, and his white bread every Sunday the year round — all for a family of three; the entire cost for the year not above 69.2.6 (sixty-nine cents, two mills and six milrays), and all of a sudden here comes along a man who slashes out nearly four dollars on a single blowout; and not only that, but acts as if it made him tired to handle such small sums. Yes, Dowley was a good deal wilted, and shrunk-up and collapsed; he had the aspect of a bladder-balloon that's been stepped on by a cow.

Chapter XXXIII. Sixth Century Political Economy

However, I made a dead set at him, and before the first third of the dinner was reached, I had him happy again. It was easy to do — in a country of ranks and castes. You see, in a country where they have ranks and castes, a man isn't ever a man, he is only part of a man, he can't ever get his full growth. You prove your superiority over him in station, or rank, or fortune, and that's the end of it — he knuckles down. You can't insult him after that. No, I don't mean quite that; of course you *can* insult him, I only mean it's difficult; and so, unless you've got a lot of useless time on your hands it doesn't pay to try. I had the smith's reverence now, because I was apparently immensely prosperous and rich; I could have had his adoration if I had had some little gimcrack title of nobility. And not only his, but any commoner's in the land, though he were the mightiest production of all the ages, in intellect, worth, and character, and I bankrupt in all three. This was to remain so, as long as England should exist in the earth. With the spirit of prophecy upon me, I could look into the future and see her erect statues and monuments to her unspeakable Georges and other royal and noble clothes-horses, and leave unhonored the creators of this world — after God — Gutenburg, Watt, Arkwright, Whitney, Morse, Stephenson, Bell.

The king got his cargo aboard, and then, the talk not turning upon battle, conquest, or ironclad duel, he dulled down to drowsiness and went off to take a nap. Mrs. Marco cleared the table, placed the beer keg handy, and went away to eat her dinner of leavings in humble privacy, and the rest of us soon drifted into matters near and dear to the hearts of our sort — business and wages, of course. At a first glance, things appeared to be exceeding prosperous in this little tributary kingdom — whose lord was King Bagdemagus — as compared with the state of things in my own region. They had the "protection" system in full force here, whereas we were working along down toward free-trade, by easy stages, and were now about half way. Before long, Dowley and I were doing all the talking, the others hungrily listening. Dowley warmed to his work, snuffed an advantage in the air, and began to put questions which he considered pretty awkward ones for me, and they did have something of that look:

"In your country, brother, what is the wage of a master bailiff, master hind, carter, shepherd, swineherd?"

"Twenty-five milrays a day; that is to say, a quarter of a cent."

The smith's face beamed with joy. He said:

"With us they are allowed the double of it! And what may a mechanic get — carpenter, dauber, mason, painter, blacksmith, wheelwright, and the like?"

"On the average, fifty milrays; half a cent a day."

"Ho-ho! With us they are allowed a hundred! With us any good mechanic is allowed a cent a day! I count out the tailor, but not the others — they are all allowed a cent a day, and in driving times they get more — yes, up to a hundred and ten and even fifteen milrays a day. I've paid a hundred and fifteen myself, within the week. 'Rah for protection — to Sheol with free-trade!"

And his face shone upon the company like a sunburst. But I didn't scare at all. I rigged up my pile-driver, and allowed myself fifteen minutes to drive him into the earth — drive him *all* in — drive him in till not even the curve of his skull should show above ground. Here is the way I started in on him. I asked:

"What do you pay a pound for salt?"

"A hundred milrays."

"We pay forty. What do you pay for beef and mutton — when you buy it?" That was a neat hit; it made the color come.

"It varieth somewhat, but not much; one may say seventy-five milrays the pound."

"*We* pay thirty-three. What do you pay for eggs?"

"Fifty milrays the dozen."

"We pay twenty. What do you pay for beer?"

"It costeth us eight and one-half milrays the pint."

"We get it for four; twenty-five bottles for a cent. What do you pay for wheat?"

"At the rate of nine hundred milrays the bushel."

"We pay four hundred. What do you pay for a man's tow-linen suit?"

"Thirteen cents."

"We pay six. What do you pay for a stuff gown for the wife of the laborer or the mechanic?"

"We pay eight cents, four mills."

"Well, observe the difference: you pay eight cents and four mills, we pay only four cents." I prepared now to sock it to him. I said: "Look here, dear friend, *what's become of your high wages you were bragging so about a few minutes ago?* " — and I looked around on the company with placid satisfaction, for I had slipped up on him gradually and tied him hand and foot, you see, without his ever noticing that he was being tied at all. "What's become of those noble high wages of yours? — I seem to have knocked the stuffing all out of them, it appears to me."

But if you will believe me, he merely looked surprised, that is all! he didn't grasp the situation at all, didn't know he had walked into a trap, didn't discover that he was *in* a trap. I could have shot him, from sheer vexation. With cloudy eye and a struggling intellect he fetched this out:

"Marry, I seem not to understand. It is *proved* that our wages be double thine; how then may it be that thou'st knocked therefrom the stuffing? — an miscall not the wonderly word, this being the first time under grace and providence of God it hath been granted me to hear it."

Well, I was stunned; partly with this unlooked-for stupidity on his part, and partly because his fellows so manifestly sided with him and were of his mind — if you might call it mind. My position was simple enough, plain enough; how could it ever be simplified more? However, I must try:

"Why, look here, brother Dowley, don't you see? Your wages are merely higher than ours in *name* , not in *fact* ."

"Hear him! They are the *double* — ye have confessed it yourself."

"Yes-yes, I don't deny that at all. But that's got nothing to do with it; the *amount* of the wages in mere coins, with meaningless names attached to them to know them by, has got nothing to do with it. The thing is, how much can you *buy* with your wages? — that's the idea. While it is true that with you a good mechanic is allowed about three dollars and a half a year, and with us only about a dollar and seventy-five — "

"There — ye're confessing it again, ye're confessing it again!"

"Confound it, I've never denied it, I tell you! What I say is this. With us *half* a dollar buys more than a *dollar* buys with you — and THEREFORE it stands to reason and the commonest kind of commonsense, that our wages are *higher* than yours."

He looked dazed, and said, despairingly:

"Verily, I cannot make it out. Ye've just said ours are the higher, and with the same breath ye take it back."

"Oh, great Scott, isn't it possible to get such a simple thing through your head? Now look here — let me illustrate. We pay four cents for a woman's stuff gown, you pay 8.4.0, which is four mills more than *double* . What do you allow a laboring woman who works on a farm?"

"Two mills a day."

"Very good; we allow but half as much; we pay her only a tenth of a cent a day; and — "

"Again ye're conf — "

"Wait! Now, you see, the thing is very simple; this time you'll understand it. For instance, it takes your woman 42 days to earn her gown, at 2 mills a day — 7 weeks' work; but ours earns hers in forty days — two days *short* of 7 weeks. Your woman has a gown, and her whole seven weeks wages are gone; ours has a gown, and two days' wages left, to buy something else with. There — *now* you understand it!"

He looked — well, he merely looked dubious, it's the most I can say; so did the others. I waited — to let the thing work. Dowley spoke at last — and betrayed the fact that he actually hadn't gotten away from his rooted and grounded superstitions yet. He said, with a trifle of hesitancy:

"But — but — ye cannot fail to grant that two mills a day is better than one."

Shucks! Well, of course, I hated to give it up. So I chanced another flyer:

"Let us suppose a case. Suppose one of your journeymen goes out and buys the following articles:

"1 pound of salt; 1 dozen eggs; 1 dozen pints of beer; 1 bushel of wheat; 1 tow-linen suit; 5 pounds of beef; 5 pounds of mutton.

"The lot will cost him 32 cents. It takes him 32 working days to earn the money — 5 weeks and 2 days. Let him come to us and work 32 days at *half* the wages; he can buy all those things for a shade under 14 1/2 cents; they will cost him a shade under 29 days' work, and he will have about half a week's wages over. Carry it through the year; he would save nearly a week's wages every two months, *your* man nothing; thus saving five or six weeks' wages in a year, your man not a cent. *Now* I reckon you understand that 'high wages' and 'low wages' are phrases that don't mean anything in the world until you find out which of them will *buy* the most!"

It was a crusher.

But, alas! it didn't crush. No, I had to give it up. What those people valued was *high wages* ; it didn't seem to be a matter of any consequence to them whether the high wages would buy anything or not. They stood for "protection," and swore by it, which was reasonable enough, because interested parties had gulled them into the notion that it was protection which had created their high wages. I proved to them that in a quarter of a century their wages had advanced but 30 per cent., while the cost of living had gone up 100; and that with us, in a shorter time, wages had advanced 40 per cent. while the cost of living had gone steadily down. But it didn't do any good. Nothing could unseat their strange beliefs.

Well, I was smarting under a sense of defeat. Undeserved defeat, but what of that? That didn't soften the smart any. And to think of the circumstances! the first statesman of the age, the capablest man, the best-informed man in the entire world, the loftiest uncrowned head that had moved through the clouds of any political firmament for centuries, sitting here apparently defeated in argument by an ignorant country blacksmith! And I could see that those others were sorry for me — which made me blush till I could smell my whiskers scorching. Put yourself in my place; feel as mean as I did, as ashamed as I felt — wouldn't *you* have struck below the belt to get even? Yes, you would; it is simply human nature. Well, that is what I did. I am not trying to justify it; I'm only saying that I was mad, and *anybody* would have done it.

Well, when I make up my mind to hit a man, I don't plan out a love-tap; no, that isn't my way; as long as I'm going to hit him at all, I'm going to hit him a lifter. And I don't jump at him all of a sudden, and risk making a blundering halfway business of it; no, I get away off yonder to one side, and work up on him gradually, so that he never suspects that I'm going to hit him at all; and by and by, all in a flash, he's flat on his back, and he can't tell for the life of him how it all happened. That is the way I went for brother Dowley. I started to talking lazy and comfortable, as if I was just talking to pass the time; and the oldest man in the world couldn't have taken the bearings of my starting place and guessed where I was going to fetch up:

"Boys, there's a good many curious things about law, and custom, and usage, and all that sort of thing, when you come to look at it; yes, and about the drift and progress of human opinion and movement, too. There are written laws — they perish; but there are also unwritten laws — *they* are eternal. Take the unwritten law of wages: it says they've got to advance, little by little, straight through the centuries. And notice how it works. We know what wages are now, here and there and yonder; we strike an average, and say that's the wages of to-day. We know what the wages were a hundred years ago, and what they were two hundred years ago; that's as far back as we can get, but it suffices to give us the law of progress, the measure and rate of the periodical augmentation; and so, without a document to help us, we can come pretty close to determining what the wages were three and four and five hundred years ago. Good, so far. Do we stop there? No. We stop looking backward; we face around and apply the law to the future. My friends, I can tell you what people's wages are going to be at any date in the future you want to know, for hundreds and hundreds of years."

"What, goodman, what!"

"Yes. In seven hundred years wages will have risen to six times what they are now, here in your region, and farm hands will be allowed 3 cents a day, and mechanics 6."

"I would't I might die now and live then!" interrupted Smug, the wheelwright, with a fine avaricious glow in his eye.

"And that isn't all; they'll get their board besides — such as it is: it won't bloat them. Two hundred and fifty years later — pay attention now — a mechanic's wages will be — mind you, this is law, not guesswork; a mechanic's wages will then be *twenty* cents a day!"

There was a general gasp of awed astonishment, Dickon the mason murmured, with raised eyes and hands:

"More than three weeks' pay for one day's work!"

"Riches! — of a truth, yes, riches!" muttered Marco, his breath coming quick and short, with excitement.

"Wages will keep on rising, little by little, little by little, as steadily as a tree grows, and at the end of three hundred and forty years more there'll be at least *one* country where the mechanic's average wage will be *two hundred* cents a day!"

It knocked them absolutely dumb! Not a man of them could get his breath for upwards of two minutes. Then the coal-burner said prayerfully:

"Might I but live to see it!"

"It is the income of an earl!" said Smug.

"An earl, say ye?" said Dowley; "ye could say more than that and speak no lie; there's no earl in the realm of Bagdemagus that hath an income like to that. Income of an earl — mf! it's the income of an angel!"

"Now, then, that is what is going to happen as regards wages. In that remote day, that man will earn, with *one* week's work, that bill of goods which it takes you upwards of *fifty* weeks to earn now. Some other pretty surprising things are going to happen, too. Brother Dowley, who is it that determines, every spring, what the particular wage of each kind of mechanic, laborer, and servant shall be for that year?"

"Sometimes the courts, sometimes the town council; but most of all, the magistrate. Ye may say, in general terms, it is the magistrate that fixes the wages."

"Doesn't ask any of those poor devils to *help* him fix their wages for them, does he?"

"Hm! That *were* an idea! The master that's to pay him the money is the one that's rightly concerned in that matter, ye will notice."

"Yes — but I thought the other man might have some little trifle at stake in it, too; and even his wife and children, poor creatures. The masters are these: nobles, rich men, the prosperous generally. These few, who do no work, determine what pay the vast hive shall have who *do* work. You see? They're a 'combine' — a trade union, to coin a new phrase — who band themselves together to force their lowly brother to take what they choose to give. Thirteen hundred years hence — so says the unwritten law — the 'combine' will be the other way, and then how these fine people's posterity will fume and fret and grit their teeth over the insolent tyranny of trade unions! Yes, indeed! the magistrate will tranquilly arrange the wages from now clear away down into the nineteenth century; and then all of a sudden the wage-earner will consider that a couple of thousand years or so is enough of this one-sided sort of thing; and he will rise up and take a hand in fixing his wages himself. Ah, he will have a long and bitter account of wrong and humiliation to settle."

"Do ye believe — "

"That he actually will help to fix his own wages? Yes, indeed. And he will be strong and able, then."

"Brave times, brave times, of a truth!" sneered the prosperous smith.

"Oh, — and there's another detail. In that day, a master may hire a man for only just one day, or one week, or one month at a time, if he wants to."

"What?"

"It's true. Moreover, a magistrate won't be able to force a man to work for a master a whole year on a stretch whether the man wants to or not."

"Will there be *no* law or sense in that day?"

"Both of them, Dowley. In that day a man will be his own property, not the property of magistrate and master. And he can leave town whenever he wants to, if the wages don't suit him! — and they can't put him in the pillory for it."

"Perdition catch such an age!" shouted Dowley, in strong indignation. "An age of dogs, an age barren of reverence for superiors and respect for authority! The pillory — "

"Oh, wait, brother; say no good word for that institution. I think the pillory ought to be abolished."

"A most strange idea. Why?"

"Well, I'll tell you why. Is a man ever put in the pillory for a capital crime?"

"No."

"Is it right to condemn a man to a slight punishment for a small offense and then kill him?"

There was no answer. I had scored my first point! For the first time, the smith wasn't up and ready. The company noticed it. Good effect.

"You don't answer, brother. You were about to glorify the pillory a while ago, and shed some pity on a future age that isn't going to use it. I think the pillory ought to be abolished. What usually happens when a poor fellow is put in the pillory for some little offense that didn't amount to anything in the world? The mob try to have some fun with him, don't they?"

"Yes."

"They begin by clodding him; and they laugh themselves to pieces to see him try to dodge one clod and get hit with another?"

"Yes."

"Then they throw dead cats at him, don't they?"

"Yes."

"Well, then, suppose he has a few personal enemies in that mob and here and there a man or a woman with a secret grudge against him — and suppose especially that he is unpopular in the community, for his pride, or his prosperity, or one thing or another — stones and bricks take the place of clods and cats presently, don't they?"

"There is no doubt of it."

"As a rule he is crippled for life, isn't he? — jaws broken, teeth smashed out? — or legs mutilated, gangrened, presently cut off? — or an eye knocked out, maybe both eyes?"

"It is true, God knoweth it."

"And if he is unpopular he can depend on *dying* , right there in the stocks, can't he?"

"He surely can! One may not deny it."

"I take it none of *you* are unpopular — by reason of pride or insolence, or conspicuous prosperity, or any of those things that excite envy and malice among the base scum of a village? *You* wouldn't think it much of a risk to take a chance in the stocks?"

Dowley winced, visibly. I judged he was hit. But he didn't betray it by any spoken word. As for the others, they spoke out plainly, and with strong feeling. They said they had seen enough of the stocks to know what a man's chance in them was, and they would never consent to enter them if they could compromise on a quick death by hanging.

"Well, to change the subject — for I think I've established my point that the stocks ought to be abolished. I think some of our laws are pretty unfair. For instance, if I do a thing which ought to deliver me to the stocks, and you know I did it and yet keep still and don't report me, *you* will get the stocks if anybody informs on you."

"Ah, but that would serve you but right," said Dowley, "for you *must* inform. So saith the law."

The others coincided.

"Well, all right, let it go, since you vote me down. But there's one thing which certainly isn't fair. The magistrate fixes a mechanic's wage at one cent a day, for instance. The law says that if any master shall venture, even under utmost press of business, to pay anything *over* that cent a day, even for a single day, he shall be both fined and pilloried for it; and whoever knows he did it and doesn't inform, they also shall be fined and pilloried. Now it seems to me unfair,

Dowley, and a deadly peril to all of us, that because you thoughtlessly confessed, a while ago, that within a week you have paid a cent and fifteen mil — "

Oh, I tell *you* it was a smasher! You ought to have seen them to go to pieces, the whole gang. I had just slipped up on poor smiling and complacent Dowley so nice and easy and softly, that he never suspected anything was going to happen till the blow came crashing down and knocked him all to rags.

A fine effect. In fact, as fine as any I ever produced, with so little time to work it up in.

But I saw in a moment that I had overdone the thing a little. I was expecting to scare them, but I wasn't expecting to scare them to death. They were mighty near it, though. You see they had been a whole lifetime learning to appreciate the pillory; and to have that thing staring them in the face, and every one of them distinctly at the mercy of me, a stranger, if I chose to go and report — well, it was awful, and they couldn't seem to recover from the shock, they couldn't seem to pull themselves together. Pale, shaky, dumb, pitiful? Why, they weren't any better than so many dead men. It was very uncomfortable. Of course, I thought they would appeal to me to keep mum, and then we would shake hands, and take a drink all round, and laugh it off, and there an end. But no; you see I was an unknown person, among a cruelly oppressed and suspicious people, a people always accustomed to having advantage taken of their helplessness, and never expecting just or kind treatment from any but their own families and very closest intimates. Appeal to *me* to be gentle, to be fair, to be generous? Of course, they wanted to, but they couldn't dare.

Chapter XXXIV. The Yankee and the King Sold as Slaves

Well, what had I better do? Nothing in a hurry, sure. I must get up a diversion; anything to employ me while I could think, and while these poor fellows could have a chance to come to life again. There sat Marco, petrified in the act of trying to get the hang of his miller-gun — turned to stone, just in the attitude he was in when my pile-driver fell, the toy still gripped in his unconscious fingers. So I took it from him and proposed to explain its mystery. Mystery! a simple little thing like that; and yet it was mysterious enough, for that race and that age.

I never saw such an awkward people, with machinery; you see, they were totally unused to it. The miller-gun was a little double-barreled tube of toughened glass, with a neat little trick of a spring to it, which upon pressure would let a shot escape. But the shot wouldn't hurt anybody, it would only drop into your hand. In the gun were two sizes — wee mustard-seed shot, and another sort that were several times larger. They were money. The mustard-seed shot represented milrays, the larger ones mills. So the gun was a purse; and very handy, too; you could pay out money in the dark with it, with accuracy; and you could carry it in your mouth; or in your vest pocket, if you had one. I made them of several sizes — one size so large that it would carry the equivalent of a dollar. Using shot for money was a good thing for the government; the metal cost nothing, and the money couldn't be counterfeited, for I was the only person in the kingdom who knew how to manage a shot tower. "Paying the shot" soon came to be a common phrase. Yes, and I knew it would still be passing men's lips, away down in the nineteenth century, yet none would suspect how and when it originated.

The king joined us, about this time, mightily refreshed by his nap, and feeling good. Anything could make me nervous now, I was so uneasy — for our lives were in danger; and so it worried me to detect a complacent something in the king's eye which seemed to indicate that he had been loading himself up for a performance of some kind or other; confound it, why must he go and choose such a time as this?

I was right. He began, straight off, in the most innocently artful, and transparent, and lubberly way, to lead up to the subject of agriculture. The cold sweat broke out all over me. I wanted to whisper in his ear, "Man, we are in awful danger! every moment is worth a principality till we get back these men's confidence; *don't* waste any of this golden time." But of course I couldn't do it. Whisper to him? It would look as if we were conspiring. So I had to sit there and look calm and pleasant while the king stood over that dynamite mine and mooned along about his damned onions and things. At first the tumult of my own thoughts, summoned by the danger-signal and swarming to the rescue from every quarter of my skull, kept up such a hurrah and confusion and fifing and drumming that I couldn't take in a word; but presently when my mob of gathering plans began to crystallize and fall into position and form line of battle, a sort of order and quiet ensued and I caught the boom of the king's batteries, as if out of remote distance:

" — were not the best way, methinks, albeit it is not to be denied that authorities differ as concerning this point, some contending that the onion is but an unwholesome berry when stricken early from the tree — "

The audience showed signs of life, and sought each other's eyes in a surprised and troubled way.

" — whileas others do yet maintain, with much show of reason, that this is not of necessity the case, instancing that plums and other like cereals do be always dug in the unripe state — "

The audience exhibited distinct distress; yes, and also fear.

" — yet are they clearly wholesome, the more especially when one doth assuage the asperities of their nature by admixture of the tranquilizing juice of the wayward cabbage — "

The wild light of terror began to glow in these men's eyes, and one of them muttered, "These be errors, every one — God hath surely smitten the mind of this farmer." I was in miserable apprehension; I sat upon thorns.

" — and further instancing the known truth that in the case of animals, the young, which may be called the green fruit of the creature, is the better, all confessing that when a goat is ripe, his fur doth heat and sore engame his flesh, the which defect, taken in connection with his several rancid habits, and fulsome appetites, and godless attitudes of mind, and bilious quality of morals — "

They rose and went for him! With a fierce shout, "The one would betray us, the other is mad! Kill them! Kill them!" they flung themselves upon us. What joy flamed up in the king's eye! He might be lame in agriculture, but this kind of thing was just in his line. He had been fasting long, he was hungry for a fight. He hit the blacksmith a crack under the jaw that lifted him clear off his feet and stretched him flat on his back. "St. George for Britain!" and he downed the wheelwright. The mason was big, but I laid him out like nothing. The three gathered themselves up and came again; went down again; came again; and kept on repeating this, with native British pluck, until they were battered to jelly, reeling with exhaustion, and so blind that they couldn't tell us from each other; and yet they kept right on, hammering away with what might was left in them. Hammering each other — for we stepped aside and looked on while they rolled, and struggled, and gouged, and pounded, and bit, with the strict and wordless attention to business of so many bulldogs. We looked on without apprehension, for they were fast getting past ability to go for help against us, and the arena was far enough from the public road to be safe from intrusion.

Well, while they were gradually playing out, it suddenly occurred to me to wonder what had become of Marco. I looked around; he was nowhere to be seen. Oh, but this was ominous! I pulled the king's sleeve, and we glided away and rushed for the hut. No Marco there, no Phyllis there! They had gone to the road for help, sure. I told the king to give his heels wings, and I would explain later. We made good time across the open ground, and as we darted into the shelter of the wood I glanced back and saw a mob of excited peasants swarm into view, with Marco and his wife at their head. They were making a world of noise, but that couldn't hurt anybody; the wood was dense, and as soon as we were well into its depths we would take to a tree and let them whistle. Ah, but then came another sound — dogs! Yes, that was quite another matter. It magnified our contract — we must find running water.

We tore along at a good gait, and soon left the sounds far behind and modified to a murmur. We struck a stream and darted into it. We waded swiftly down it, in the dim forest light, for as much as three hundred yards, and then came across an oak with a great bough sticking out over the water. We climbed up on this bough, and began to work our way along it to the body of the tree; now we began to hear those sounds more plainly; so the mob had struck our trail. For a while the sounds approached pretty fast. And then for another while they didn't. No doubt the dogs had found the place where we had entered the stream, and were now waltzing up and down the shores trying to pick up the trail again.

When we were snugly lodged in the tree and curtained with foliage, the king was satisfied, but I was doubtful. I believed we could crawl along a branch and get into the next tree, and I judged it worth while to try. We tried it, and made a success of it, though the king slipped, at the junction, and came near failing to connect. We got comfortable lodgment and satisfactory concealment among the foliage, and then we had nothing to do but listen to the hunt.

Presently we heard it coming — and coming on the jump, too; yes, and down both sides of the stream. Louder — louder — next minute it swelled swiftly up into a roar of shoutings, barkings, tramplings, and swept by like a cyclone.

"I was afraid that the overhanging branch would suggest something to them," said I, "but I don't mind the disappointment. Come, my liege, it were well that we make good use of our time. We've flanked them. Dark is coming on, presently. If we can cross the stream and get a good start, and borrow a couple of horses from somebody's pasture to use for a few hours, we shall be safe enough."

We started down, and got nearly to the lowest limb, when we seemed to hear the hunt returning. We stopped to listen.

"Yes," said I, "they're baffled, they've given it up, they're on their way home. We will climb back to our roost again, and let them go by."

So we climbed back. The king listened a moment and said:

"They still search — I wit the sign. We did best to abide."

He was right. He knew more about hunting than I did. The noise approached steadily, but not with a rush. The king said:

"They reason that we were advantaged by no parlous start of them, and being on foot are as yet no mighty way from where we took the water."

"Yes, sire, that is about it, I am afraid, though I was hoping better things."

The noise drew nearer and nearer, and soon the van was drifting under us, on both sides of the water. A voice called a halt from the other bank, and said:

"An they were so minded, they could get to yon tree by this branch that overhangs, and yet not touch ground. Ye will do well to send a man up it."

"Marry, that we will do!"

I was obliged to admire my cuteness in foreseeing this very thing and swapping trees to beat it. But, don't you know, there are some things that can beat smartness and foresight? Awkwardness and stupidity can. The best swordsman in the world doesn't need to fear the second best swordsman in the world; no, the person for him to be afraid of is some ignorant antagonist who has never had a sword in his hand before; he doesn't do the thing he ought to do, and so the expert isn't prepared for him; he does the thing he ought not to do; and often it catches the expert out and ends him on the spot. Well, how could I, with all my gifts, make any valuable preparation against a nearsighted, cross-eyed, pudding-headed clown who would aim himself at the wrong tree and hit the right one? And that is what he did. He went for the wrong tree, which was, of course, the right one by mistake, and up he started.

Matters were serious now. We remained still, and awaited developments. The peasant toiled his difficult way up. The king raised himself up and stood; he made a leg ready, and when the comer's head arrived in reach of it there was a dull thud, and down went the man floundering to the ground. There was a wild outbreak of anger below, and the mob swarmed in from all around, and there we were treed, and prisoners. Another man started up; the bridging bough was detected, and a volunteer started up the tree that furnished the bridge. The king ordered me to play Horatius and keep the bridge. For a while the enemy came thick and fast; but no matter, the head man of each procession always got a buffet that dislodged him as soon as he came in reach. The king's spirits rose, his joy was limitless. He said that if nothing occurred to mar the prospect we should have a beautiful night, for on this line of tactics we could hold the tree against the whole countryside.

However, the mob soon came to that conclusion themselves; wherefore they called off the assault and began to debate other plans. They had no weapons, but there were plenty of stones, and stones might answer. We had no objections. A stone might possibly penetrate to us once in a while, but it wasn't very likely; we were well protected by boughs and foliage, and were not visible from any good aiming point. If they would but waste half an hour in stone-throwing, the dark would come to our help. We were feeling very well satisfied. We could smile; almost laugh.

But we didn't; which was just as well, for we should have been interrupted. Before the stones had been raging through the leaves and bouncing from the boughs fifteen minutes, we began to notice a smell. A couple of sniffs of it was enough of an explanation — it was smoke! Our game was up at last. We recognized that. When smoke invites you, you have to come. They raised their pile of dry brush and damp weeds higher and higher, and when they saw the thick cloud begin to roll up and smother the tree, they broke out in a storm of joy-clamors. I got enough breath to say:

"Proceed, my liege; after you is manners."

The king gasped:

"Follow me down, and then back thyself against one side of the trunk, and leave me the other. Then will we fight. Let each pile his dead according to his own fashion and taste."

Then he descended, barking and coughing, and I followed. I struck the ground an instant after him; we sprang to our appointed places, and began to give and take with all our might. The powwow and racket were prodigious; it was a tempest of riot and confusion and thick-falling blows. Suddenly some horsemen tore into the midst of the crowd, and a voice shouted:

"Hold — or ye are dead men!"

How good it sounded! The owner of the voice bore all the marks of a gentleman: picturesque and costly raiment, the aspect of command, a hard countenance, with complexion and features marred by dissipation. The mob fell humbly back, like so many spaniels. The gentleman inspected us critically, then said sharply to the peasants:

"What are ye doing to these people?"

"They be madmen, worshipful sir, that have come wandering we know not whence, and — "

"Ye know not whence? Do ye pretend ye know them not?"

"Most honored sir, we speak but the truth. They are strangers and unknown to any in this region; and they be the most violent and bloodthirsty madmen that ever — "

"Peace! Ye know not what ye say. They are not mad. Who are ye? And whence are ye? Explain."

"We are but peaceful strangers, sir," I said, "and traveling upon our own concerns. We are from a far country, and unacquainted here. We have purposed no harm; and yet but for your brave interference and protection these people would have killed us. As you have divined, sir, we are not mad; neither are we violent or bloodthirsty."

The gentleman turned to his retinue and said calmly: "Lash me these animals to their kennels!"

The mob vanished in an instant; and after them plunged the horsemen, laying about them with their whips and pitilessly riding down such as were witless enough to keep the road instead of taking to the bush. The shrieks and supplications presently died away in the distance, and soon the horsemen began to straggle back. Meantime the gentleman had been questioning us more closely, but had dug no particulars out of us. We were lavish of recognition of the service he was doing us, but we revealed nothing more than that we were friendless strangers from a far country. When the escort were all returned, the gentleman said to one of his servants:

"Bring the led-horses and mount these people."

"Yes, my lord."

We were placed toward the rear, among the servants. We traveled pretty fast, and finally drew rein some time after dark at a roadside inn some ten or twelve miles from the scene of our troubles. My lord went immediately to his room, after ordering his supper, and we saw no more of him. At dawn in the morning we breakfasted and made ready to start.

My lord's chief attendant sauntered forward at that moment with indolent grace, and said:

"Ye have said ye should continue upon this road, which is our direction likewise; wherefore my lord, the earl Grip, hath given commandment that ye retain the horses and ride, and that certain of us ride with ye a twenty mile to a fair town that hight Cambenet, whenso ye shall be out of peril."

We could do nothing less than express our thanks and accept the offer. We jogged along, six in the party, at a moderate and comfortable gait, and in conversation learned that my lord Grip was a very great personage in his own region, which lay a day's journey beyond Cambenet. We loitered to such a degree that it was near the middle of the forenoon when we entered the market square of the town. We dismounted, and left our thanks once more for my lord, and then approached a crowd assembled in the center of the square, to see what might be the object of interest. It was the remnant of that old peregrinating band of slaves! So they had been dragging their chains about, all this weary time. That poor husband was gone, and also many others; and some few purchases had been added to the gang. The king was not interested, and wanted to move along, but I was absorbed, and full of pity. I could not take my eyes away from these worn and wasted wrecks of humanity. There they sat, grounded upon the ground, silent, uncomplaining, with bowed heads, a pathetic sight. And by hideous contrast, a redundant orator was making a speech to another gathering not thirty steps away, in fulsome laudation of "our glorious British liberties!"

I was boiling. I had forgotten I was a plebeian, I was remembering I was a man. Cost what it might, I would mount that rostrum and —

Click! the king and I were handcuffed together! Our companions, those servants, had done it; my lord Grip stood looking on. The king burst out in a fury, and said:

"What meaneth this ill-mannered jest?"

My lord merely said to his head miscreant, coolly:

"Put up the slaves and sell them!"

Slaves! The word had a new sound — and how unspeakably awful! The king lifted his manacles and brought them down with a deadly force; but my lord was out of the way when they arrived. A dozen of the rascal's servants sprang forward, and in a moment we were helpless, with our hands bound behind us. We so loudly and so earnestly proclaimed ourselves freemen, that we got the interested attention of that liberty-mouthing orator and his patriotic crowd, and they gathered about us and assumed a very determined attitude. The orator said:

"If, indeed, ye are freemen, ye have nought to fear — the God-given liberties of Britain are about ye for your shield and shelter! (Applause.) Ye shall soon see. Bring forth your proofs."

"What proofs?"

"Proof that ye are freemen."

Ah — I remembered! I came to myself; I said nothing. But the king stormed out:

"Thou'rt insane, man. It were better, and more in reason, that this thief and scoundrel here prove that we are *not* freemen."

You see, he knew his own laws just as other people so often know the laws; by words, not by effects. They take a *meaning* , and get to be very vivid, when you come to apply them to yourself.

All hands shook their heads and looked disappointed; some turned away, no longer interested. The orator said — and this time in the tones of business, not of sentiment:

"An ye do not know your country's laws, it were time ye learned them. Ye are strangers to us; ye will not deny that. Ye may be freemen, we do not deny that; but also ye may be slaves. The law is clear: it doth not require the claimant to prove ye are slaves, it requireth you to prove ye are not."

I said:

"Dear sir, give us only time to send to Astolat; or give us only time to send to the Valley of Holiness — "

"Peace, good man, these are extraordinary requests, and you may not hope to have them granted. It would cost much time, and would unwarrantably inconvenience your master — "

"*Master* , idiot!" stormed the king. "I have no master, I myself am the m — "

"Silence, for God's sake!"

I got the words out in time to stop the king. We were in trouble enough already; it could not help us any to give these people the notion that we were lunatics.

There is no use in stringing out the details. The earl put us up and sold us at auction. This same infernal law had existed in our own South in my own time, more than thirteen hundred years later, and under it hundreds of freemen who could not prove that they were freemen had been sold into lifelong slavery without the circumstance making any particular impression upon me; but the minute law and the auction block came into my personal experience, a thing which had been merely improper before became suddenly hellish. Well, that's the way we are made.

Yes, we were sold at auction, like swine. In a big town and an active market we should have brought a good price; but this place was utterly stagnant and so we sold at a figure which makes me ashamed, every time I think of it. The King of England brought seven dollars, and his prime minister nine; whereas the king was easily worth twelve dollars and I as easily worth fifteen. But that is the way things always go; if you force a sale on a dull market, I don't care what the property is, you are going to make a poor business of it, and you can make up your mind to it. If the earl had had wit enough to —

However, there is no occasion for my working my sympathies up on his account. Let him go, for the present; I took his number, so to speak.

The slave-dealer bought us both, and hitched us onto that long chain of his, and we constituted the rear of his procession. We took up our line of march and passed out of Cambenet at noon; and it seemed to me unaccountably strange and odd that the King of England and his chief minister, marching manacled and fettered and yoked, in a slave convoy, could move by all manner of idle men and women, and under windows where sat the sweet and the lovely, and yet never attract a curious eye, never provoke a single remark. Dear, dear, it only shows that there is nothing diviner about a king than there is about a tramp, after all. He is just a cheap and hollow artificiality when you don't know he is a king. But reveal his quality, and dear me it takes your very breath away to look at him. I reckon we are all fools. Born so, no doubt.

Chapter XXXV. A Pitiful Incident

It's a world of surprises. The king brooded; this was natural. What would he brood about, should you say? Why, about the prodigious nature of his fall, of course — from the loftiest place in the world to the lowest; from the most illustrious station in the world to the obscurest; from the grandest vocation among men to the basest. No, I take my oath that the thing that graveled him most, to start with, was not this, but the price he had fetched! He couldn't seem to get over that seven dollars. Well, it stunned me so, when I first found it out, that I couldn't believe it; it didn't seem natural. But as soon as my mental sight cleared and I got a right focus on it, I saw I was mistaken; it *was* natural. For this reason: a king is a mere artificiality, and so a king's feelings, like the impulses of an automatic doll, are mere artificialities; but as a man, he is a reality, and his feelings, as a man, are real, not phantoms. It shames the average man to be valued below his own estimate of his worth, and the king certainly wasn't anything more than an average man, if he was up that high.

Confound him, he wearied me with arguments to show that in anything like a fair market he would have fetched twenty-five dollars, sure — a thing which was plainly nonsense, and full or the baldest conceit; I wasn't worth it myself. But it was tender ground for me to argue on. In fact, I had to simply shirk argument and do the diplomatic instead. I had to throw conscience aside, and brazenly concede that he ought to have brought twenty-five dollars; whereas I was quite well aware that in all the ages, the world had never seen a king that was worth half the money, and during the next thirteen centuries wouldn't see one that was worth the fourth of it. Yes, he tired me. If he began to talk about the crops; or about the recent weather; or about the condition of politics; or about dogs, or cats, or morals, or theology — no matter what — I sighed, for I knew what was coming; he was going to get out of it a palliation of that tiresome seven-dollar sale. Wherever we halted where there was a crowd, he would give me a look which said plainly: "if that thing could be tried over again now, with this kind of folk, you would see a different result." Well, when he was first sold, it secretly tickled me to see him go for seven dollars; but before he was done with his sweating and worrying I wished he had fetched a hundred. The thing never got a chance to die, for every day, at one place or another, possible purchasers looked us over, and, as often as any other way, their comment on the king was something like this:

"Here's a two-dollar-and-a-half chump with a thirty-dollar style. Pity but style was marketable."

At last this sort of remark produced an evil result. Our owner was a practical person and he perceived that this defect must be mended if he hoped to find a purchaser for the king. So he went to work to take the style out of his sacred majesty. I could have given the man some valuable advice, but I didn't; you mustn't volunteer advice to a slave-driver unless you want to damage the cause you are arguing for. I had found it a sufficiently difficult job to reduce the king's style to a peasant's style, even when he was a willing and anxious pupil; now then, to undertake to reduce the king's style to a slave's style — and by force — go to! it was a stately contract. Never mind the details — it will save me trouble to let you imagine them. I will only remark that at the end of a week there was plenty of evidence that lash and club and fist had done their work well; the king's body was a sight to see — and to weep over; but his spirit? — why, it wasn't even phased. Even that dull clod of a slave-driver was able to see that there can be such a thing as a slave who will remain a man till he dies; whose bones you can break, but whose manhood you can't. This man found that from his first effort down to his latest, he couldn't ever come within reach of the king, but the king was ready to plunge for him, and did it. So he gave up at last, and left the king in possession of his style unimpaired. The fact is, the king was a good deal more than a king, he was a man; and when a man is a man, you can't knock it out of him.

We had a rough time for a month, tramping to and fro in the earth, and suffering. And what Englishman was the most interested in the slavery question by that time? His grace the king! Yes; from being the most indifferent, he was become the most interested. He was become the bitterest hater of the institution I had ever heard talk. And so I ventured to ask once more a question which I had asked years before and had gotten such a sharp answer that I had not thought it prudent to meddle in the matter further. Would he abolish slavery?

His answer was as sharp as before, but it was music this time; I shouldn't ever wish to hear pleasanter, though the profanity was not good, being awkwardly put together, and with the crash-word almost in the middle instead of at the end, where, of course, it ought to have been.

I was ready and willing to get free now; I hadn't wanted to get free any sooner. No, I cannot quite say that. I had wanted to, but I had not been willing to take desperate chances, and had always dissuaded the king from them. But now — ah, it was a new atmosphere! Liberty would be worth any cost that might be put upon it now. I set about a plan, and was straightway charmed with it. It would require time, yes, and patience, too, a great deal of both. One could invent quicker ways, and fully as sure ones; but none that would be as picturesque as this; none that could be made so dramatic. And so I was not going to give this one up. It might delay us months, but no matter, I would carry it out or break something.

Now and then we had an adventure. One night we were overtaken by a snowstorm while still a mile from the village we were making for. Almost instantly we were shut up as in a fog, the driving snow was so thick. You couldn't see a thing, and we were soon lost. The slave-driver lashed us desperately, for he saw ruin before him, but his lashings only made matters worse, for they drove us further from the road and from likelihood of succor. So we had to stop at last and slump down in the snow where we were. The storm continued until toward midnight, then ceased. By this time two of our feebler men and three of our women were dead, and others past moving and threatened with death. Our master was nearly beside himself. He stirred up the living, and made us stand, jump, slap ourselves, to restore our circulation, and he helped as well as he could with his whip.

Now came a diversion. We heard shrieks and yells, and soon a woman came running and crying; and seeing our group, she flung herself into our midst and begged for protection. A mob of people came tearing after her, some with torches, and they said she was a witch who had caused several cows to die by a strange disease, and practiced her arts by help of a devil in the form of a black cat. This poor woman had been stoned until she hardly looked human, she was so battered and bloody. The mob wanted to burn her.

Well, now, what do you suppose our master did? When we closed around this poor creature to shelter her, he saw his chance. He said, burn her here, or they shouldn't have her at all. Imagine that! They were willing. They fastened her to a post; they brought wood and piled it about her; they applied the torch while she shrieked and pleaded and strained her two young daughters to her breast; and our brute, with a heart solely for business, lashed us into position about the stake and warmed us into life and commercial value by the same fire which took away the innocent life of that poor harmless mother. That was the sort of master we had. I took *his* number. That snowstorm cost him nine of his flock; and he was more brutal to us than ever, after that, for many days together, he was so enraged over his loss.

We had adventures all along. One day we ran into a procession. And such a procession! All the riffraff of the kingdom seemed to be comprehended in it; and all drunk at that. In the van was a cart with a coffin in it, and on the coffin sat a comely young girl of about eighteen suckling a baby, which she squeezed to her breast in a passion of love every little while, and every little while wiped from its face the tears which her eyes rained down upon it; and always the foolish little thing smiled up at her, happy and content, kneading her breast with its dimpled fat hand, which she patted and fondled right over her breaking heart.

Men and women, boys and girls, trotted along beside or after the cart, hooting, shouting profane and ribald remarks, singing snatches of foul song, skipping, dancing — a very holiday of hellions, a sickening sight. We had struck a suburb of London, outside the walls, and this was a sample of one sort of London society. Our master secured a good place for us near the gallows. A priest was in attendance, and he helped the girl climb up, and said comforting words to her, and made the under-sheriff provide a stool for her. Then he stood there by her on the gallows, and for a moment looked down upon the mass of upturned faces at his feet, then out over the solid pavement of heads that stretched away on every side occupying the vacancies far and near, and then began to tell the story of the case. And there was pity in his voice — how seldom a sound that was in that ignorant and savage land! I remember every detail of what he said, except the words he said it in; and so I change it into my own words:

"Law is intended to mete out justice. Sometimes it fails. This cannot be helped. We can only grieve, and be resigned, and pray for the soul of him who falls unfairly by the arm of the law, and that his fellows may be few. A law sends this poor young thing to death — and it is right. But another law had placed her where she must commit her crime or starve with her child — and before God that law is responsible for both her crime and her ignominious death!

"A little while ago this young thing, this child of eighteen years, was as happy a wife and mother as any in England; and her lips were blithe with song, which is the native speech of glad and innocent hearts. Her young husband was as happy as she; for he was doing his whole duty, he worked early and late at his handicraft, his bread was honest bread well and fairly earned, he was prospering, he was furnishing shelter and sustenance to his family, he was adding his mite to the wealth of the nation. By consent of a treacherous law, instant destruction fell upon this holy home and swept it away! That young husband was waylaid and impressed, and sent to sea. The wife knew nothing of it. She sought him everywhere, she moved the hardest hearts with the supplications of her tears, the broken eloquence of her despair. Weeks dragged by, she watching, waiting, hoping, her mind going slowly to wreck under the burden of her misery. Little by little all her small possessions went for food. When she could no longer pay her rent, they turned her out of doors. She begged, while she had strength; when she was starving at last, and her milk failing, she stole a piece of linen cloth of the value of a fourth part of a cent, thinking to sell it and save her child. But she was seen by the owner of the cloth. She was put in jail and brought to trial. The man testified to the facts. A plea was made for her, and her sorrowful story was told in her behalf. She spoke, too, by permission, and said she did steal the cloth, but that her mind was so disordered of late by trouble that when she was overborne with hunger all acts, criminal or other, swam meaningless through her brain and she knew nothing rightly, except that she was so hungry! For a moment all were touched, and there was disposition to deal mercifully with her, seeing that she was so young and friendless, and her case so piteous, and the law that robbed her of her support to blame as being the first and only cause of her transgression; but the prosecuting officer replied that whereas these things were all true, and most pitiful as well, still there was much small theft in these days, and mistimed mercy here would be a danger to property — oh, my God, is there no property in ruined homes, and orphaned babes, and broken hearts that British law holds precious! — and so he must require sentence.

"When the judge put on his black cap, the owner of the stolen linen rose trembling up, his lip quivering, his face as gray as ashes; and when the awful words came, he cried out, 'Oh, poor child, poor child, I did not know it was death!' and fell as a tree falls. When they lifted him up his reason was gone; before the sun was set, he had taken his own life. A kindly man; a man whose heart was right, at bottom; add his murder to this that is to be now done here; and charge them both where they belong — to the rulers and the bitter laws of Britain. The time is come, my child; let me pray over thee — not *for* thee, dear abused poor heart and innocent, but for them that be guilty of thy ruin and death, who need it more."

After his prayer they put the noose around the young girl's neck, and they had great trouble to adjust the knot under her ear, because she was devouring the baby all the time, wildly kissing it, and snatching it to her face and her breast, and drenching it with tears, and half moaning, half shrieking all the while, and the baby crowing, and laughing, and kicking its feet with delight over what it took for romp and play. Even the hangman couldn't stand it, but turned away. When all was ready the priest gently pulled and tugged and forced the child out of the mother's arms, and stepped quickly out of her reach; but she clasped her hands, and made a wild spring toward him, with a shriek; but the rope — and the under-sheriff — held her short. Then she went on her knees and stretched out her hands and cried:

"One more kiss — oh, my God, one more, one more, — it is the dying that begs it!"

She got it; she almost smothered the little thing. And when they got it away again, she cried out:

"Oh, my child, my darling, it will die! It has no home, it has no father, no friend, no mother — "

"It has them all!" said that good priest. "All these will I be to it till I die."

You should have seen her face then! Gratitude? Lord, what do you want with words to express that? Words are only painted fire; a look is the fire itself. She gave that look, and carried it away to the treasury of heaven, where all things that are divine belong.

Chapter XXXVI. An Encounter in the Dark

London — to a slave — was a sufficiently interesting place. It was merely a great big village; and mainly mud and thatch. The streets were muddy, crooked, unpaved. The populace was an ever flocking and drifting swarm of rags, and splendors, of nodding plumes and shining armor. The king had a palace there; he saw the outside of it. It made him sigh; yes, and swear a little, in a poor juvenile sixth century way. We saw knights and grandees whom we knew, but they didn't know us in our rags and dirt and raw welts and bruises, and wouldn't have recognized us if we had hailed them, nor stopped to answer, either, it being unlawful to speak with slaves on a chain. Sandy passed within ten yards of me on a mule — hunting for me, I imagined. But the thing which clean broke my heart was something which happened in front of our old barrack in a square, while we were enduring the spectacle of a man being boiled to death in oil for counterfeiting pennies. It was the sight of a newsboy — and I couldn't get at him! Still, I had one comfort — here was proof that Clarence was still alive and banging away. I meant to be with him before long; the thought was full of cheer.

I had one little glimpse of another thing, one day, which gave me a great uplift. It was a wire stretching from housetop to housetop. Telegraph or telephone, sure. I did very much wish I had a little piece of it. It was just what I needed, in order to carry out my project of escape. My idea was to get loose some night, along with the king, then gag and bind our master, change clothes with him, batter him into the aspect of a stranger, hitch him to the slave-chain, assume possession of the property, march to Camelot, and —

But you get my idea; you see what a stunning dramatic surprise I would wind up with at the palace. It was all feasible, if I could only get hold of a slender piece of iron which I could shape into a lock-pick. I could then undo the lumbering padlocks with which our chains were fastened, whenever I might choose. But I never had any luck; no such thing ever happened to fall in my way. However, my chance came at last. A gentleman who had come twice before to dicker for me, without result, or indeed any approach to a result, came again. I was far from expecting ever to belong to him, for the price asked for me from the time I was first enslaved was exorbitant, and always provoked either anger or derision, yet my master stuck stubbornly to it — twenty-two dollars. He wouldn't bate a cent. The king was greatly admired, because of his grand physique, but his kingly style was against him, and he wasn't salable; nobody wanted that kind of a slave. I considered myself safe from parting from him because of my extravagant price. No, I was not expecting to ever belong to this gentleman whom I have spoken of, but he had something which I expected would belong to me eventually, if he would but visit us often enough. It was a steel thing with a long pin to it, with which his long cloth outside garment was fastened together in front. There were three of them. He had disappointed me twice, because he did not come quite close enough to me to make my project entirely safe; but this time I succeeded; I captured the lower clasp of the three, and when he missed it he thought he had lost it on the way.

I had a chance to be glad about a minute, then straightway a chance to be sad again. For when the purchase was about to fail, as usual, the master suddenly spoke up and said what would be worded thus — in modern English:

"I'll tell you what I'll do. I'm tired supporting these two for no good. Give me twenty-two dollars for this one, and I'll throw the other one in."

The king couldn't get his breath, he was in such a fury. He began to choke and gag, and meantime the master and the gentleman moved away discussing.

"An ye will keep the offer open — "

"'Tis open till the morrow at this hour."

"Then I will answer you at that time," said the gentleman, and disappeared, the master following him.

I had a time of it to cool the king down, but I managed it. I whispered in his ear, to this effect:

"Your grace *will* go for nothing, but after another fashion. And so shall I. Tonight we shall both be free."

"Ah! How is that?"

"With this thing which I have stolen, I will unlock these locks and cast off these chains tonight. When he comes about nine-thirty to inspect us for the night, we will seize him, gag him, batter him, and early in the morning we will march out of this town, proprietors of this caravan of slaves."

That was as far as I went, but the king was charmed and satisfied. That evening we waited patiently for our fellow-slaves to get to sleep and signify it by the usual sign, for you must not take many chances on those poor fellows if you can avoid it. It is best to keep your own secrets. No doubt they fidgeted only about as usual, but it didn't seem so to me. It seemed to me that they were going to be forever getting down to their regular snoring. As the time dragged on I got nervously afraid we shouldn't have enough of it left for our needs; so I made several premature attempts, and merely delayed things by it; for I couldn't seem to touch a padlock, there in the dark, without starting a rattle out of it which interrupted somebody's sleep and made him turn over and wake some more of the gang.

But finally I did get my last iron off, and was a free man once more. I took a good breath of relief, and reached for the king's irons. Too late! in comes the master, with a light in one hand and his heavy walking-staff in the other. I snuggled close among the wallow of snorers, to conceal as nearly as possible that I was naked of irons; and I kept a sharp lookout and prepared to spring for my man the moment he should bend over me.

But he didn't approach. He stopped, gazed absently toward our dusky mass a minute, evidently thinking about something else; then set down his light, moved musingly toward the door, and before a body could imagine what he was going to do, he was out of the door and had closed it behind him.

"Quick!" said the king. "Fetch him back!"

Of course, it was the thing to do, and I was up and out in a moment. But, dear me, there were no lamps in those days, and it was a dark night. But I glimpsed a dim figure a few steps away. I darted for it, threw myself upon it, and then there was a state of things and lively! We fought and scuffled and struggled, and drew a crowd in no time. They took an immense interest in the fight and encouraged us all they could, and, in fact, couldn't have been pleasanter or more cordial if it had been their own fight. Then a tremendous row broke out behind us, and as much as half of our audience left us, with a rush, to invest some sympathy in that. Lanterns began to swing in all directions; it was the watch gathering from far and near. Presently a halberd fell across my back, as a reminder, and I knew what it meant. I was in custody. So was my adversary. We were marched off toward prison, one on each side of the watchman. Here was disaster, here was a fine scheme gone to sudden destruction! I tried to imagine what would happen when the master should discover that it was I who had been fighting him; and what would happen if they jailed us together in the general apartment for brawlers and petty law-breakers, as was the custom; and what might —

Just then my antagonist turned his face around in my direction, the freckled light from the watchman's tin lantern fell on it, and, by George, he was the wrong man!

Chapter XXXVII. An Awful Predicament

Sleep? It was impossible. It would naturally have been impossible in that noisome cavern of a jail, with its mangy crowd of drunken, quarrelsome, and song-singing rapscallions. But the thing that made sleep all the more a thing not to be dreamed of, was my racking impatience to get out of this place and find out the whole size of what might have happened yonder in the slave-quarters in consequence of that intolerable miscarriage of mine.

It was a long night, but the morning got around at last. I made a full and frank explanation to the court. I said I was a slave, the property of the great Earl Grip, who had arrived just after dark at the Tabard inn in the village on the other side of the water, and had stopped there over night, by compulsion, he being taken deadly sick with a strange and sudden disorder. I had been ordered to cross to the city in all haste and bring the best physician; I was doing my best; naturally I was running with all my might; the night was dark, I ran against this common person here, who seized me by the throat and began to pummel me, although I told him my errand, and implored him, for the sake of the great earl my master's mortal peril —

The common person interrupted and said it was a lie; and was going to explain how I rushed upon him and attacked him without a word —

"Silence, sirrah!" from the court. "Take him hence and give him a few stripes whereby to teach him how to treat the servant of a nobleman after a different fashion another time. Go!"

Then the court begged my pardon, and hoped I would not fail to tell his lordship it was in no wise the court's fault that this highhanded thing had happened. I said I would make it all right, and so took my leave. Took it just in time, too; he was starting to ask me why I didn't fetch out these facts the moment I was arrested. I said I would if I had thought of it — which was true — but that I was so battered by that man that all my wit was knocked out of me — and so forth and so on, and got myself away, still mumbling.

I didn't wait for breakfast. No grass grew under my feet. I was soon at the slave quarters. Empty — everybody gone! That is, everybody except one body — the slave-master's. It lay there all battered to pulp; and all about were the evidences of a terrific fight. There was a rude board coffin on a cart at the door, and workmen, assisted by the police, were thinning a road through the gaping crowd in order that they might bring it in.

I picked out a man humble enough in life to condescend to talk with one so shabby as I, and got his account of the matter.

"There were sixteen slaves here. They rose against their master in the night, and thou seest how it ended."

"Yes. How did it begin?"

"There was no witness but the slaves. They said the slave that was most valuable got free of his bonds and escaped in some strange way — by magic arts 'twas thought, by reason that he had no key, and the locks were neither broke nor in any wise injured. When the master discovered his loss, he was mad with despair, and threw himself upon his people with his heavy stick, who resisted and brake his back and in other and divers ways did give him hurts that brought him swiftly to his end."

"This is dreadful. It will go hard with the slaves, no doubt, upon the trial."

"Marry, the trial is over."

"Over!"

"Would they be a week, think you — and the matter so simple? They were not the half of a quarter of an hour at it."

"Why, I don't see how they could determine which were the guilty ones in so short a time."

"*Which* ones? Indeed, they considered not particulars like to that. They condemned them in a body. Wit ye not the law? — which men say the Romans left behind them here when they went — that if one slave killeth his master all the slaves of that man must die for it."

"True. I had forgotten. And when will these die?"

"Belike within a four and twenty hours; albeit some say they will wait a pair of days more, if peradventure they may find the missing one meantime."

The missing one! It made me feel uncomfortable.

"Is it likely they will find him?"

"Before the day is spent — yes. They seek him everywhere. They stand at the gates of the town, with certain of the slaves who will discover him to them if he cometh, and none can pass out but he will be first examined."

"Might one see the place where the rest are confined?"

"The outside of it — yes. The inside of it — but ye will not want to see that."

I took the address of that prison for future reference and then sauntered off. At the first secondhand clothing shop I came to, up a back street, I got a rough rig suitable for a common seaman who might be going on a cold voyage, and bound up my face with a liberal bandage, saying I had a toothache. This concealed my worst bruises. It was a transformation. I no longer resembled my former self. Then I struck out for that wire, found it and followed it to its den. It was a little room over a butcher's shop — which meant that business wasn't very brisk in the telegraphic line. The young chap in charge was drowsing at his table. I locked the door and put the vast key in my bosom. This alarmed the young fellow, and he was going to make a noise; but I said:

"Save your wind; if you open your mouth you are dead, sure. Tackle your instrument. Lively, now! Call Camelot."

"This doth amaze me! How should such as you know aught of such matters as — "

"Call Camelot! I am a desperate man. Call Camelot, or get away from the instrument and I will do it myself."

"What — you?"

"Yes — certainly. Stop gabbling. Call the palace."

He made the call.

"Now, then, call Clarence."

"Clarence *who* ?"

"Never mind Clarence who. Say you want Clarence; you'll get an answer."

He did so. We waited five nerve-straining minutes — ten minutes — how long it did seem! — and then came a click that was as familiar to me as a human voice; for Clarence had been my own pupil.

"Now, my lad, vacate! They would have known *my* touch, maybe, and so your call was surest; but I'm all right now."

He vacated the place and cocked his ear to listen — but it didn't win. I used a cipher. I didn't waste any time in sociabilities with Clarence, but squared away for business, straight-off — thus:

"The king is here and in danger. We were captured and brought here as slaves. We should not be able to prove our identity — and the fact is, I am not in a position to try. Send a telegram for the palace here which will carry conviction with it."

His answer came straight back:

"They don't know anything about the telegraph; they haven't had any experience yet, the line to London is so new. Better not venture that. They might hang you. Think up something else."

Might hang us! Little he knew how closely he was crowding the facts. I couldn't think up anything for the moment. Then an idea struck me, and I started it along:

"Send five hundred picked knights with Launcelot in the lead; and send them on the jump. Let them enter by the southwest gate, and look out for the man with a white cloth around his right arm."

The answer was prompt:

"They shall start in half an hour."

"All right, Clarence; now tell this lad here that I'm a friend of yours and a deadhead; and that he must be discreet and say nothing about this visit of mine."

The instrument began to talk to the youth and I hurried away. I fell to ciphering. In half an hour it would be nine o'clock. Knights and horses in heavy armor couldn't travel very fast.

These would make the best time they could, and now that the ground was in good condition, and no snow or mud, they would probably make a seven-mile gait; they would have to change horses a couple of times; they would arrive about six, or a little after; it would still be plenty light enough; they would see the white cloth which I should tie around my right arm, and I would take command. We would surround that prison and have the king out in no time. It would be showy and picturesque enough, all things considered, though I would have preferred noonday, on account of the more theatrical aspect the thing would have.

Now, then, in order to increase the strings to my bow, I thought I would look up some of those people whom I had formerly recognized, and make myself known. That would help us out of our scrape, without the knights. But I must proceed cautiously, for it was a risky business. I must get into sumptuous raiment, and it wouldn't do to run and jump into it. No, I must work up to it by degrees, buying suit after suit of clothes, in shops wide apart, and getting a little finer article with each change, until I should finally reach silk and velvet, and be ready for my project. So I started.

But the scheme fell through like scat! The first corner I turned, I came plump upon one of our slaves, snooping around with a watchman. I coughed at the moment, and he gave me a sudden look that bit right into my marrow. I judge he thought he had heard that cough before. I turned immediately into a shop and worked along down the counter, pricing things and watching out of the corner of my eye. Those people had stopped, and were talking together and looking in at the door. I made up my mind to get out the back way, if there was a back way, and I asked the shopwoman if I could step out there and look for the escaped slave, who was believed to be in hiding back there somewhere, and said I was an officer in disguise, and my pard was yonder at the door with one of the murderers in charge, and would she be good enough to step there and tell him he needn't wait, but had better go at once to the further end of the back alley and be ready to head him off when I rousted him out.

She was blazing with eagerness to see one of those already celebrated murderers, and she started on the errand at once. I slipped out the back way, locked the door behind me, put the key in my pocket and started off, chuckling to myself and comfortable.

Well, I had gone and spoiled it again, made another mistake. A double one, in fact. There were plenty of ways to get rid of that officer by some simple and plausible device, but no, I must pick out a picturesque one; it is the crying defect of my character. And then, I had ordered my procedure upon what the officer, being human, would *naturally* do; whereas when you are least expecting it, a man will now and then go and do the very thing which it's *not* natural for him to do. The natural thing for the officer to do, in this case, was to follow straight on my heels; he would find a stout oaken door, securely locked, between him and me; before he could break it down, I should be far away and engaged in slipping into a succession of baffling disguises which would soon get me into a sort of raiment which was a surer protection from meddling law-dogs in Britain than any amount of mere innocence and purity of character. But instead of doing the natural thing, the officer took me at my word, and followed my instructions. And so, as I came trotting out of that cul de sac, full of satisfaction with my own cleverness, he turned the corner and I walked right into his handcuffs. If I had known it was a cul de sac — however, there isn't any excusing a blunder like that, let it go. Charge it up to profit and loss.

Of course, I was indignant, and swore I had just come ashore from a long voyage, and all that sort of thing — just to see, you know, if it would deceive that slave. But it didn't. He knew me. Then I reproached him for betraying me. He was more surprised than hurt. He stretched his eyes wide, and said:

"What, wouldst have me let thee, of all men, escape and not hang with us, when thou'rt the very *cause* of our hanging? Go to!"

"Go to" was their way of saying "I should smile!" or "I like that!" Queer talkers, those people.

Well, there was a sort of bastard justice in his view of the case, and so I dropped the matter. When you can't cure a disaster by argument, what is the use to argue? It isn't my way. So I only said:

"You're not going to be hanged. None of us are."

Both men laughed, and the slave said:

"Ye have not ranked as a fool — before. You might better keep your reputation, seeing the strain would not be for long."

"It will stand it, I reckon. Before tomorrow we shall be out of prison, and free to go where we will, besides."

The witty officer lifted at his left ear with his thumb, made a rasping noise in his throat, and said:

"Out of prison — yes — ye say true. And free likewise to go where ye will, so ye wander not out of his grace the Devil's sultry realm."

I kept my temper, and said, indifferently:

"Now I suppose you really think we are going to hang within a day or two."

"I thought it not many minutes ago, for so the thing was decided and proclaimed."

"Ah, then you've changed your mind, is that it?"

"Even that. I only *thought* , then; I *know* , now."

I felt sarcastical, so I said:

"Oh, sapient servant of the law, condescend to tell us, then, what you *know* ."

"That ye will all be hanged *to-day* , at mid-afternoon! Oho! that shot hit home! Lean upon me."

The fact is I did need to lean upon somebody. My knights couldn't arrive in time. They would be as much as three hours too late. Nothing in the world could save the King of England; nor me, which was more important. More important, not merely to me, but to the nation — the only nation on earth standing ready to blossom into civilization. I was sick. I said no more, there wasn't anything to say. I knew what the man meant; that if the missing slave was found, the postponement would be revoked, the execution take place to-day. Well, the missing slave was found.

Chapter XXXVIII. Sir Launcelot and Knights to the Rescue

Nearing four in the afternoon. The scene was just outside the walls of London. A cool, comfortable, superb day, with a brilliant sun; the kind of day to make one want to live, not die. The multitude was prodigious and far-reaching; and yet we fifteen poor devils hadn't a friend in it. There was something painful in that thought, look at it how you might. There we sat, on our tall scaffold, the butt of the hate and mockery of all those enemies. We were being made a holiday spectacle. They had built a sort of grand stand for the nobility and gentry, and these were there in full force, with their ladies. We recognized a good many of them.

The crowd got a brief and unexpected dash of diversion out of the king. The moment we were freed of our bonds he sprang up, in his fantastic rags, with face bruised out of all recognition, and proclaimed himself Arthur, King of Britain, and denounced the awful penalties of treason upon every soul there present if hair of his sacred head were touched. It startled and surprised him to hear them break into a vast roar of laughter. It wounded his dignity, and he locked himself up in silence. Then, although the crowd begged him to go on, and tried to provoke him to it by catcalls, jeers, and shouts of:

"Let him speak! The king! The king! his humble subjects hunger and thirst for words of wisdom out of the mouth of their master his Serene and Sacred Raggedness!"

But it went for nothing. He put on all his majesty and sat under this rain of contempt and insult unmoved. He certainly was great in his way. Absently, I had taken off my white bandage and wound it about my right arm. When the crowd noticed this, they began upon me. They said:

"Doubtless this sailorman is his minister — observe his costly badge of office!"

I let them go on until they got tired, and then I said:

"Yes, I am his minister, The Boss; and tomorrow you will hear that from Camelot which — "

I got no further. They drowned me out with joyous derision. But presently there was silence; for the sheriffs of London, in their official robes, with their subordinates, began to make a stir which indicated that business was about to begin. In the hush which followed, our crime was recited, the death warrant read, then everybody uncovered while a priest uttered a prayer.

Then a slave was blindfolded; the hangman unslung his rope. There lay the smooth road below us, we upon one side of it, the banked multitude wailing its other side — a good clear road, and kept free by the police — how good it would be to see my five hundred horsemen come tearing down it! But no, it was out of the possibilities. I followed its receding thread out into the distance — not a horseman on it, or sign of one.

There was a jerk, and the slave hung dangling; dangling and hideously squirming, for his limbs were not tied.

A second rope was unslung, in a moment another slave was dangling.

In a minute a third slave was struggling in the air. It was dreadful. I turned away my head a moment, and when I turned back I missed the king! They were blindfolding him! I was paralyzed; I couldn't move, I was choking, my tongue was petrified. They finished blindfolding him, they led him under the rope. I couldn't shake off that clinging impotence. But when I saw them put the noose around his neck, then everything let go in me and I made a spring to the rescue — and as I made it I shot one more glance abroad — by George! here they came, a-tilting! — five hundred mailed and belted knights on bicycles!

The grandest sight that ever was seen. Lord, how the plumes streamed, how the sun flamed and flashed from the endless procession of webby wheels!

I waved my right arm as Launcelot swept in — he recognized my rag — I tore away noose and bandage, and shouted:

"On your knees, every rascal of you, and salute the king! Who fails shall sup in hell tonight!"

I always use that high style when I'm climaxing an effect. Well, it was noble to see Launcelot and the boys swarm up onto that scaffold and heave sheriffs and such overboard. And it was fine to see that astonished multitude go down on their knees and beg their lives of the king they had just been deriding and insulting. And as he stood apart there, receiving this homage in rags, I thought to myself, well, really there is something peculiarly grand about the gait and bearing of a king, after all.

I was immensely satisfied. Take the whole situation all around, it was one of the gaudiest effects I ever instigated.

And presently up comes Clarence, his own self! and winks, and says, very modernly:

"Good deal of a surprise, wasn't it? I knew you'd like it. I've had the boys practicing this long time, privately; and just hungry for a chance to show off."

Chapter XXXIX. The Yankee's Fight with the Knights

Home again, at Camelot. A morning or two later I found the paper, damp from the press, by my plate at the breakfast table. I turned to the advertising columns, knowing I should find something of personal interest to me there. It was this:

DE PAR LE ROI.

> Know that the great lord and illus-
> trious Kni8ht, SIR SAGRAMOR LE
> DESIROUS having condescended to
> meet the King's Minister, Hank Mor-
> gan, the which is surnamed The Boss,
> for satisfgction of offence anciently given,
> these wilL engage in the lists by
> Camelot about the fourth hour of the
> morning of the sixteenth day of this
> next succeeding month. The battle
> will be a l outrance, sith the said offence

was of a deadly sort, admitting of no comPosition.

Clarence's editorial reference to this affair was to this effect:

It will be observed, by a gl7nce at our
advertising columns, that the community is to be favored with a treat of unusual interest in the tournament line.
The n ames of the artists are warrant of
good enterTemment. The box-office
will be open at noon of the 13th; admission 3 cents, reserved seatsh 5; proceeds to go to the hospital fund The
royal pair and all the Court will be present. With these exceptions, and the
press and the clergy, the free list is strictly susPended. Parties are hereby warned against buying tickets of speculators;
they will not be good at the door.
Everybody knows and likes The Boss,
everybody knows and likes Sir Sag.;
come, let us give the lads a good send-
off. ReMember, the proceeds go to a
great and free charity, and one whose
broad begevolence stretches out its helping hand, warm with the blood of a loving heart, to all that suffer, regardless of
race, creed, condition or color — the
only charity yet established in the earth
which has no politico-religious stop-
cock on its compassion, but says Here
flows the stream, let ALL come and
drink! Turn out, all hands! fetch along
your dou3hnuts and your gum-drops
and have a good time. Pie for sale on
the grounds, and rocks to crack it with;
and ciRcus-lemonade — three drops of
lime juice to a barrel of water.

N.B. This is the first tournament
under the new law, whidh allow each
combatant to use any weapon he may prefer. You may want to make a note of that.

Up to the day set, there was no talk in all Britain of anything but this combat. All other
topics sank into insignificance and passed out of men's thoughts and interest. It was not because
a tournament was a great matter, it was not because Sir Sagramor had found the Holy Grail, for
he had not, but had failed; it was not because the second (official) personage in the kingdom was

one of the duellists; no, all these features were commonplace. Yet there was abundant reason for the extraordinary interest which this coming fight was creating. It was born of the fact that all the nation knew that this was not to be a duel between mere men, so to speak, but a duel between two mighty magicians; a duel not of muscle but of mind, not of human skill but of superhuman art and craft; a final struggle for supremacy between the two master enchanters of the age. It was realized that the most prodigious achievements of the most renowned knights could not be worthy of comparison with a spectacle like this; they could be but child's play, contrasted with this mysterious and awful battle of the gods. Yes, all the world knew it was going to be in reality a duel between Merlin and me, a measuring of his magic powers against mine. It was known that Merlin had been busy whole days and nights together, imbuing Sir Sagramor's arms and armor with supernal powers of offense and defense, and that he had procured for him from the spirits of the air a fleecy veil which would render the wearer invisible to his antagonist while still visible to other men. Against Sir Sagramor, so weaponed and protected, a thousand knights could accomplish nothing; against him no known enchantments could prevail. These facts were sure; regarding them there was no doubt, no reason for doubt. There was but one question: might there be still other enchantments, *unknown* to Merlin, which could render Sir Sagramor's veil transparent to me, and make his enchanted mail vulnerable to my weapons? This was the one thing to be decided in the lists. Until then the world must remain in suspense.

So the world thought there was a vast matter at stake here, and the world was right, but it was not the one they had in their minds. No, a far vaster one was upon the cast of this die: *the life of knight-errantry* . I was a champion, it was true, but not the champion of the frivolous black arts, I was the champion of hard unsentimental commonsense and reason. I was entering the lists to either destroy knight-errantry or be its victim.

Vast as the show-grounds were, there were no vacant spaces in them outside of the lists, at ten o'clock on the morning of the 16th. The mammoth grandstand was clothed in flags, streamers, and rich tapestries, and packed with several acres of small-fry tributary kings, their suites, and the British aristocracy; with our own royal gang in the chief place, and each and every individual a flashing prism of gaudy silks and velvets — well, I never saw anything to begin with it but a fight between an Upper Mississippi sunset and the aurora borealis. The huge camp of beflagged and gay-colored tents at one end of the lists, with a stiff-standing sentinel at every door and a shining shield hanging by him for challenge, was another fine sight. You see, every knight was there who had any ambition or any caste feeling; for my feeling toward their order was not much of a secret, and so here was their chance. If I won my fight with Sir Sagramor, others would have the right to call me out as long as I might be willing to respond.

Down at our end there were but two tents; one for me, and another for my servants. At the appointed hour the king made a sign, and the heralds, in their tabards, appeared and made proclamation, naming the combatants and stating the cause of quarrel. There was a pause, then a ringing bugle-blast, which was the signal for us to come forth. All the multitude caught their breath, and an eager curiosity flashed into every face.

Out from his tent rode great Sir Sagramor, an imposing tower of iron, stately and rigid, his huge spear standing upright in its socket and grasped in his strong hand, his grand horse's face and breast cased in steel, his body clothed in rich trappings that almost dragged the ground — oh, a most noble picture. A great shout went up, of welcome and admiration.

And then out I came. But I didn't get any shout. There was a wondering and eloquent silence for a moment, then a great wave of laughter began to sweep along that human sea, but a warning bugle-blast cut its career short. I was in the simplest and comfortablest of gymnast costumes — flesh-colored tights from neck to heel, with blue silk puffings about my loins, and bareheaded. My horse was not above medium size, but he was alert, slender-limbed, muscled with watchsprings, and just a greyhound to go. He was a beauty, glossy as silk, and naked as he was when he was born, except for bridle and ranger-saddle.

The iron tower and the gorgeous bedquilt came cumbrously but gracefully pirouetting down the lists, and we tripped lightly up to meet them. We halted; the tower saluted, I responded; then we wheeled and rode side by side to the grandstand and faced our king and queen, to whom we made obeisance. The queen exclaimed:

"Alack, Sir Boss, wilt fight naked, and without lance or sword or — "

But the king checked her and made her understand, with a polite phrase or two, that this was none of her business. The bugles rang again; and we separated and rode to the ends of the lists, and took position. Now old Merlin stepped into view and cast a dainty web of gossamer threads over Sir Sagramor which turned him into Hamlet's ghost; the king made a sign, the bugles blew, Sir Sagramor laid his great lance in rest, and the next moment here he came thundering down the course with his veil flying out behind, and I went whistling through the air like an arrow to meet him — cocking my ear the while, as if noting the invisible knight's position and progress by hearing, not sight. A chorus of encouraging shouts burst out for him, and one brave voice flung out a heartening word for me — said:

"Go it, slim Jim!"

It was an even bet that Clarence had procured that favor for me — and furnished the language, too. When that formidable lance-point was within a yard and a half of my breast I twitched my horse aside without an effort, and the big knight swept by, scoring a blank. I got plenty of applause that time. We turned, braced up, and down we came again. Another blank for the knight, a roar of applause for me. This same thing was repeated once more; and it fetched such a whirlwind of applause that Sir Sagramor lost his temper, and at once changed his tactics and set himself the task of chasing me down. Why, he hadn't any show in the world at that; it was a game of tag, with all the advantage on my side; I whirled out of his path with ease whenever I chose, and once I slapped him on the back as I went to the rear. Finally I took the chase into my own hands; and after that, turn, or twist, or do what he would, he was never able to get behind me again; he found himself always in front at the end of his maneuver. So he gave up that business and retired to his end of the lists. His temper was clear gone now, and he forgot himself and flung an insult at me which disposed of mine. I slipped my lasso from the horn of my saddle, and grasped the coil in my right hand. This time you should have seen him come! — it was a business trip, sure; by his gait there was blood in his eye. I was sitting my horse at ease, and swinging the great loop of my lasso in wide circles about my head; the moment he was under way, I started for him; when the space between us had narrowed to forty feet, I sent the snaky spirals of the rope a-cleaving through the air, then darted aside and faced about and brought my trained animal to a halt with all his feet braced under him for a surge. The next moment the rope sprang taut and yanked Sir Sagramor out of the saddle! Great Scott, but there was a sensation!

Unquestionably, the popular thing in this world is novelty. These people had never seen anything of that cowboy business before, and it carried them clear off their feet with delight. From all around and everywhere, the shout went up:

"Encore! encore!"

I wondered where they got the word, but there was no time to cipher on philological matters, because the whole knight-errantry hive was just humming now, and my prospect for trade couldn't have been better. The moment my lasso was released and Sir Sagramor had been assisted to his tent, I hauled in the slack, took my station and began to swing my loop around my head again. I was sure to have use for it as soon as they could elect a successor for Sir Sagramor, and that couldn't take long where there were so many hungry candidates. Indeed, they elected one straight off — Sir Hervis de Revel.

Bzz ! Here he came, like a house afire; I dodged: he passed like a flash, with my horse-hair coils settling around his neck; a second or so later, *fst* ! his saddle was empty.

I got another encore; and another, and another, and still another. When I had snaked five men out, things began to look serious to the ironclads, and they stopped and consulted together. As a result, they decided that it was time to waive etiquette and send their greatest and best against me. To the astonishment of that little world, I lassoed Sir Lamorak de Galis, and after him Sir Galahad. So you see there was simply nothing to be done now, but play their right bower — bring out the superbest of the superb, the mightiest of the mighty, the great Sir Launcelot himself!

A proud moment for me? I should think so. Yonder was Arthur, King of Britain; yonder was Guenever; yes, and whole tribes of little provincial kings and kinglets; and in the tented camp yonder, renowned knights from many lands; and likewise the selectest body known to chivalry, the Knights of the Table Round, the most illustrious in Christendom; and biggest fact of all, the very sun of their shining system was yonder couching his lance, the focal point of forty thousand adoring eyes; and all by myself, here was I laying for him. Across my mind flitted the dear image of a certain hello-girl of West Hartford, and I wished she could see me now. In that moment, down came the Invincible, with the rush of a whirlwind — the courtly world rose to its feet and bent forward — the fateful coils went circling through the air, and before you could wink I was towing Sir Launcelot across the field on his back, and kissing my hand to the storm of waving kerchiefs and the thundercrash of applause that greeted me!

Said I to myself, as I coiled my lariat and hung it on my saddle-horn, and sat there drunk with glory, "The victory is perfect — no other will venture against me — knight-errantry is dead." Now imagine my astonishment — and everybody else's, too — to hear the peculiar bugle-call which announces that another competitor is about to enter the lists! There was a mystery here; I couldn't account for this thing. Next, I noticed Merlin gliding away from me; and then I noticed that my lasso was gone! The old sleight-of-hand expert had stolen it, sure, and slipped it under his robe.

The bugle blew again. I looked, and down came Sagramor riding again, with his dust brushed off and his veil nicely rearranged. I trotted up to meet him, and pretended to find him by the sound of his horse's hoofs. He said:

"Thou'rt quick of ear, but it will not save thee from this!" and he touched the hilt of his great sword. "An ye are not able to see it, because of the influence of the veil, know that it is no cumbrous lance, but a sword — and I ween ye will not be able to avoid it."

His visor was up; there was death in his smile. I should never be able to dodge his sword, that was plain. Somebody was going to die this time. If he got the drop on me, I could name the corpse. We rode forward together, and saluted the royalties. This time the king was disturbed. He said:

"Where is thy strange weapon?"

"It is stolen, sire."

"Hast another at hand?"

"No, sire, I brought only the one."

Then Merlin mixed in:

"He brought but the one because there was but the one to bring. There exists none other but that one. It belongeth to the king of the Demons of the Sea. This man is a pretender, and ignorant, else he had known that that weapon can be used in but eight bouts only, and then it vanisheth away to its home under the sea."

"Then is he weaponless," said the king. "Sir Sagramore, ye will grant him leave to borrow."

"And I will lend!" said Sir Launcelot, limping up. "He is as brave a knight of his hands as any that be on live, and he shall have mine."

He put his hand on his sword to draw it, but Sir Sagramor said:

"Stay, it may not be. He shall fight with his own weapons; it was his privilege to choose them and bring them. If he has erred, on his head be it."

"Knight!" said the king. "Thou'rt overwrought with passion; it disorders thy mind. Wouldst kill a naked man?"

"An he do it, he shall answer it to me," said Sir Launcelot.

"I will answer it to any he that desireth!" retorted Sir Sagramor hotly.

Merlin broke in, rubbing his hands and smiling his lowdownest smile of malicious gratification:

"'Tis well said, right well said! And 'tis enough of parleying, let my lord the king deliver the battle signal."

The king had to yield. The bugle made proclamation, and we turned apart and rode to our stations. There we stood, a hundred yards apart, facing each other, rigid and motionless, like horsed statues. And so we remained, in a soundless hush, as much as a full minute, everybody gazing, nobody stirring. It seemed as if the king could not take heart to give the signal. But at last he lifted his hand, the clear note of the bugle followed, Sir Sagramor's long blade described a flashing curve in the air, and it was superb to see him come. I sat still. On he came. I did not move. People got so excited that they shouted to me:

"Fly, fly! Save thyself! This is murther!"

I never budged so much as an inch till that thundering apparition had got within fifteen paces of me; then I snatched a dragoon revolver out of my holster, there was a flash and a roar, and the revolver was back in the holster before anybody could tell what had happened.

Here was a riderless horse plunging by, and yonder lay Sir Sagramor, stone dead.

The people that ran to him were stricken dumb to find that the life was actually gone out of the man and no reason for it visible, no hurt upon his body, nothing like a wound. There was a hole through the breast of his chain-mail, but they attached no importance to a little thing like that; and as a bullet wound there produces but little blood, none came in sight because of the clothing and swaddlings under the armor. The body was dragged over to let the king and the swells look down upon it. They were stupefied with astonishment naturally. I was requested to come and explain the miracle. But I remained in my tracks, like a statue, and said:

"If it is a command, I will come, but my lord the king knows that I am where the laws of combat require me to remain while any desire to come against me."

I waited. Nobody challenged. Then I said:

"If there are any who doubt that this field is well and fairly won, I do not wait for them to challenge me, I challenge them."

"It is a gallant offer," said the king, "and well beseems you. Whom will you name first?"

"I name none, I challenge all! Here I stand, and dare the chivalry of England to come against me — not by individuals, but in mass!"

"What!" shouted a score of knights.

"You have heard the challenge. Take it, or I proclaim you recreant knights and vanquished, every one!"

It was a "bluff" you know. At such a time it is sound judgment to put on a bold face and play your hand for a hundred times what it is worth; forty-nine times out of fifty nobody dares to "call," and you rake in the chips. But just this once — well, things looked squally! In just no time, five hundred knights were scrambling into their saddles, and before you could wink a widely scattering drove were under way and clattering down upon me. I snatched both revolvers from the holsters and began to measure distances and calculate chances.

Bang! One saddle empty. Bang! another one. Bang — bang, and I bagged two. Well, it was nip and tuck with us, and I knew it. If I spent the eleventh shot without convincing these people, the twelfth man would kill me, sure. And so I never did feel so happy as I did when my ninth downed its man and I detected the wavering in the crowd which is premonitory of panic. An instant lost now could knock out my last chance. But I didn't lose it. I raised both revolvers and pointed them — the halted host stood their ground just about one good square moment, then broke and fled.

The day was mine. Knight-errantry was a doomed institution. The march of civilization was begun. How did I feel? Ah, you never could imagine it.

And Brer Merlin? His stock was flat again. Somehow, every time the magic of fol-de-rol tried conclusions with the magic of science, the magic of fol-de-rol got left.

Chapter XL. Three Years Later

When I broke the back of knight-errantry that time, I no longer felt obliged to work in secret. So, the very next day I exposed my hidden schools, my mines, and my vast system of clandestine factories and workshops to an astonished world. That is to say, I exposed the nineteenth century to the inspection of the sixth.

Well, it is always a good plan to follow up an advantage promptly. The knights were temporarily down, but if I would keep them so I must just simply paralyze them — nothing short of that would answer. You see, I was "bluffing" that last time in the field; it would be natural for them to work around to that conclusion, if I gave them a chance. So I must not give them time; and I didn't.

I renewed my challenge, engraved it on brass, posted it up where any priest could read it to them, and also kept it standing in the advertising columns of the paper.

I not only renewed it, but added to its proportions. I said, name the day, and I would take fifty assistants and stand up *against the massed chivalry of the whole earth and destroy it* .

I was not bluffing this time. I meant what I said; I could do what I promised. There wasn't any way to misunderstand the language of that challenge. Even the dullest of the chivalry perceived that this was a plain case of "put up, or shut up." They were wise and did the latter. In all the next three years they gave me no trouble worth mentioning.

Consider the three years sped. Now look around on England. A happy and prosperous country, and strangely altered. Schools everywhere, and several colleges; a number of pretty good newspapers. Even authorship was taking a start; Sir Dinadan the Humorist was first in the field, with a volume of grayheaded jokes which I had been familiar with during thirteen centuries. If he had left out that old rancid one about the lecturer I wouldn't have said anything; but I couldn't stand that one. I suppressed the book and hanged the author.

Slavery was dead and gone; all men were equal before the law; taxation had been equalized. The telegraph, the telephone, the phonograph, the typewriter, the sewing-machine, and all the thousand willing and handy servants of steam and electricity were working their way into favor. We had a steamboat or two on the Thames, we had steam warships, and the beginnings of a steam commercial marine; I was getting ready to send out an expedition to discover America.

We were building several lines of railway, and our line from Camelot to London was already finished and in operation. I was shrewd enough to make all offices connected with the passenger service places of high and distinguished honor. My idea was to attract the chivalry and nobility, and make them useful and keep them out of mischief. The plan worked very well, the competition for the places was hot. The conductor of the 4.33 express was a duke; there wasn't a passenger conductor on the line below the degree of earl. They were good men, every one, but they had two defects which I couldn't cure, and so had to wink at: they wouldn't lay aside their armor, and they would "knock down" fare — I mean rob the company.

There was hardly a knight in all the land who wasn't in some useful employment. They were going from end to end of the country in all manner of useful missionary capacities; their penchant for wandering, and their experience in it, made them altogether the most effective spreaders of civilization we had. They went clothed in steel and equipped with sword and lance and battleaxe, and if they couldn't persuade a person to try a sewing-machine on the install-ment plan, or a melodeon, or a barbed-wire fence, or a prohibition journal, or any of the other thousand and one things they canvassed for, they removed him and passed on.

I was very happy. Things were working steadily toward a secretly longed-for point. You see, I had two schemes in my head which were the vastest of all my projects. The one was to overthrow the Catholic Church and set up the Protestant faith on its ruins — not as an Established Church, but a go-as-you-please one; and the other project was to get a decree issued by and by, commanding that upon Arthur's death unlimited suffrage should be introduced, and given to men and women alike — at any rate to all men, wise or unwise, and to all mothers who at middle age should be found to know nearly as much as their sons at twenty-one. Arthur was good for thirty years yet, he being about my own age — that is to say, forty — and I believed that in that time I could easily have the active part of the population of that day ready and eager for an event which should be the first of its kind in the history of the world — a rounded and complete governmental revolution without bloodshed. The result to be a republic. Well, I may as well confess, though I do feel ashamed when I think of it: I was beginning to have a base hankering to be its first president myself. Yes, there was more or less human nature in me; I found that out.

Clarence was with me as concerned the revolution, but in a modified way. His idea was a republic, without privileged orders, but with a hereditary royal family at the head of it instead of an elective chief magistrate. He believed that no nation that had ever known the joy of worshiping a royal family could ever be robbed of it and not fade away and die of melancholy. I urged that kings were dangerous. He said, then have cats. He was sure that a royal family of cats would answer every purpose. They would be as useful as any other royal family, they would know as much, they would have the same virtues and the same treacheries, the same disposition to get up shindies with other royal cats, they would be laughably vain and absurd and never know it, they would be wholly inexpensive; finally, they would have as sound a divine right as any other royal house, and "Tom VII, or Tom XI, or Tom XIV by the grace of God King," would sound as well as it would when applied to the ordinary royal tomcat with tights on. "And as a rule," said he, in his neat modern English, "the character of these cats would be considerably above the character of the average king, and this would be an immense moral advantage to the nation, for the reason that a nation always models its morals after its monarch's. The worship of royalty being founded in unreason, these graceful and harmless cats would easily become as sacred as any other royalties, and indeed more so, because it would presently be noticed that they hanged nobody, beheaded nobody, imprisoned nobody, inflicted no cruelties or injustices of any sort, and so must be worthy of a deeper love and reverence than the customary human king, and would certainly get it. The eyes of the whole harried world would soon be fixed upon this humane and gentle system, and royal butchers would presently begin to disappear; their subjects would fill the vacancies with catlings from our own royal house; we should become a factory; we should supply the thrones of the world; within forty years all Europe would be governed by cats, and we should furnish the cats. The reign of universal peace would begin then, to end no more forever.... Me-e-e-yow-ow-ow-ow — fzt! — wow!"

Hang him, I supposed he was in earnest, and was beginning to be persuaded by him, until he exploded that cat-howl and startled me almost out of my clothes. But he never could be in earnest. He didn't know what it was. He had pictured a distinct and perfectly rational and feasible improvement upon constitutional monarchy, but he was too featherheaded to know it, or care anything about it, either. I was going to give him a scolding, but Sandy came flying in at that moment, wild with terror, and so choked with sobs that for a minute she could not get her voice. I ran and took her in my arms, and lavished caresses upon her and said, beseechingly:

"Speak, darling, speak! What is it?"

Her head fell limp upon my bosom, and she gasped, almost inaudibly:

"HELLO-CENTRAL!"

"Quick!" I shouted to Clarence; "telephone the king's homeopath to come!"

In two minutes I was kneeling by the child's crib, and Sandy was dispatching servants here, there, and everywhere, all over the palace. I took in the situation almost at a glance — membranous croup! I bent down and whispered:

"Wake up, sweetheart! Hello-Central."

She opened her soft eyes languidly, and made out to say:

"Papa."

That was a comfort. She was far from dead yet. I sent for preparations of sulphur, I rousted out the croup-kettle myself; for I don't sit down and wait for doctors when Sandy or the child is sick. I knew how to nurse both of them, and had had experience. This little chap had lived in my arms a good part of its small life, and often I could soothe away its troubles and get it to laugh through the tear-dews on its eyelashes when even its mother couldn't.

Sir Launcelot, in his richest armor, came striding along the great hall now on his way to the stock-board; he was president of the stock-board, and occupied the Siege Perilous, which he had bought of Sir Galahad; for the stock-board consisted of the Knights of the Round Table, and they used the Round Table for business purposes now. Seats at it were worth — well, you would never believe the figure, so it is no use to state it. Sir Launcelot was a bear, and he had put up a corner in one of the new lines, and was just getting ready to squeeze the shorts to-day; but what of that? He was the same old Launcelot, and when he glanced in as he was passing the door and found out that his pet was sick, that was enough for him; bulls and bears might fight it out their own way for all him, he would come right in here and stand by little Hello-Central for all he was worth. And that was what he did. He shied his helmet into the corner, and in half a minute he had a new wick in the alcohol lamp and was firing up on the croup-kettle. By this time Sandy had built a blanket canopy over the crib, and everything was ready.

Sir Launcelot got up steam, he and I loaded up the kettle with unslaked lime and carbolic acid, with a touch of lactic acid added thereto, then filled the thing up with water and inserted the steam-spout under the canopy. Everything was shipshape now, and we sat down on either side of the crib to stand our watch. Sandy was so grateful and so comforted that she charged a couple of church-wardens with willow-bark and sumach-tobacco for us, and told us to smoke as much as we pleased, it couldn't get under the canopy, and she was used to smoke, being the first lady in the land who had ever seen a cloud blown. Well, there couldn't be a more contented or comfortable sight than Sir Launcelot in his noble armor sitting in gracious serenity at the end of a yard of snowy church-warden. He was a beautiful man, a lovely man, and was just intended to make a wife and children happy. But, of course Guenever — however, it's no use to cry over what's done and can't be helped.

Well, he stood watch-and-watch with me, right straight through, for three days and nights, till the child was out of danger; then he took her up in his great arms and kissed her, with his plumes falling about her golden head, then laid her softly in Sandy's lap again and took his stately way down the vast hall, between the ranks of admiring men-at-arms and menials, and so disappeared. And no instinct warned me that I should never look upon him again in this world! Lord, what a world of heartbreak it is.

The doctors said we must take the child away, if we would coax her back to health and strength again. And she must have sea-air. So we took a man-of-war, and a suite of two hundred and sixty persons, and went cruising about, and after a fortnight of this we stepped ashore on the French coast, and the doctors thought it would be a good idea to make something of a stay there. The little king of that region offered us his hospitalities, and we were glad to accept. If he had had as many conveniences as he lacked, we should have been plenty comfortable enough; even as it was, we made out very well, in his queer old castle, by the help of comforts and luxuries from the ship.

At the end of a month I sent the vessel home for fresh supplies, and for news. We expected her back in three or four days. She would bring me, along with other news, the result of a certain experiment which I had been starting. It was a project of mine to replace the tournament with something which might furnish an escape for the extra steam of the chivalry, keep those bucks entertained and out of mischief, and at the same time preserve the best thing in them, which was their hardy spirit of emulation. I had had a choice band of them in private training for some time, and the date was now arriving for their first public effort.

This experiment was baseball. In order to give the thing vogue from the start, and place it out of the reach of criticism, I chose my nines by rank, not capacity. There wasn't a knight in either team who wasn't a sceptered sovereign. As for material of this sort, there was a glut of it always around Arthur. You couldn't throw a brick in any direction and not cripple a king. Of course, I couldn't get these people to leave off their armor; they wouldn't do that when they bathed. They consented to differentiate the armor so that a body could tell one team from the other, but that was the most they would do. So, one of the teams wore chain-mail ulsters, and the other wore plate-armor made of my new Bessemer steel. Their practice in the field was the most fantastic thing I ever saw. Being ball-proof, they never skipped out of the way, but stood still and took the result; when a Bessemer was at the bat and a ball hit him, it would bound a hundred and fifty yards sometimes. And when a man was running, and threw himself on his stomach to slide to his base, it was like an ironclad coming into port. At first I appointed men of no rank to act as umpires, but I had to discontinue that. These people were no easier to please than other nines. The umpire's first decision was usually his last; they broke him in two with a bat, and his friends toted him home on a shutter. When it was noticed that no umpire ever survived a game, umpiring got to be unpopular. So I was obliged to appoint somebody whose rank and lofty position under the government would protect him.

Here are the names of the nines:

BESSEMERS

ULSTERS

KING ARTHUR.

EMPEROR LUCIUS.

KING LOT OF LOTHIAN.

KING LOGRIS.

KING OF NORTHGALIS.

KING MARHALT OF IRELAND.

KING MARSIL.

KING MORGANORE.

KING OF LITTLE BRITAIN.

KING MARK OF CORNWALL.

KING LABOR.

KING NENTRES OF GARLOT.

KING PELLAM OF LISTENGESE.

KING MELIODAS OF LIONES.

KING BAGDEMAGUS.

KING OF THE LAKE.

KING TOLLEME LA FEINTES.

THE SOWDAN OF SYRIA.

Umpire — CLARENCE.

The first public game would certainly draw fifty thousand people; and for solid fun would be worth going around the world to see. Everything would be favorable; it was balmy and beautiful spring weather now, and Nature was all tailored out in her new clothes.

Chapter XLI. The Interdict

However, my attention was suddenly snatched from such matters; our child began to lose ground again, and we had to go to sitting up with her, her case became so serious. We couldn't bear to allow anybody to help in this service, so we two stood watch-and-watch, day in and day out. Ah, Sandy, what a right heart she had, how simple, and genuine, and good she was! She was a flawless wife and mother; and yet I had married her for no other particular reasons, except that by the customs of chivalry she was my property until some knight should win her from me in the field. She had hunted Britain over for me; had found me at the hanging-bout outside of London, and had straightway resumed her old place at my side in the placidest way and as of right. I was a New Englander, and in my opinion this sort of partnership would compromise her, sooner or later. She couldn't see how, but I cut argument short and we had a wedding.

Now I didn't know I was drawing a prize, yet that was what I did draw. Within the twelve-month I became her worshiper; and ours was the dearest and perfectest comradeship that ever was. People talk about beautiful friendships between two persons of the same sex. What is the best of that sort, as compared with the friendship of man and wife, where the best impulses and highest ideals of both are the same? There is no place for comparison between the two friendships; the one is earthly, the other divine.

In my dreams, along at first, I still wandered thirteen centuries away, and my unsatisfied spirit went calling and harking all up and down the unreplying vacancies of a vanished world. Many a time Sandy heard that imploring cry come from my lips in my sleep. With a grand magnanimity she saddled that cry of mine upon our child, conceiving it to be the name of some lost darling of mine. It touched me to tears, and it also nearly knocked me off my feet, too, when she smiled up in my face for an earned reward, and played her quaint and pretty surprise upon me:

"The name of one who was dear to thee is here preserved, here made holy, and the music of it will abide alway in our ears. Now thou'lt kiss me, as knowing the name I have given the child."

But I didn't know it, all the same. I hadn't an idea in the world; but it would have been cruel to confess it and spoil her pretty game; so I never let on, but said:

"Yes, I know, sweetheart — how dear and good it is of you, too! But I want to hear these lips of yours, which are also mine, utter it first — then its music will be perfect."

Pleased to the marrow, she murmured:

"HELLO-CENTRAL!"

I didn't laugh — I am always thankful for that — but the strain ruptured every cartilage in me, and for weeks afterward I could hear my bones clack when I walked. She never found out her mistake. The first time she heard that form of salute used at the telephone she was surprised, and not pleased; but I told her I had given order for it: that henceforth and forever the telephone must always be invoked with that reverent formality, in perpetual honor and remembrance of my lost friend and her small namesake. This was not true. But it answered.

Well, during two weeks and a half we watched by the crib, and in our deep solicitude we were unconscious of any world outside of that sick-room. Then our reward came: the center of the universe turned the corner and began to mend. Grateful? It isn't the term. There isn't any term for it. You know that yourself, if you've watched your child through the Valley of the Shadow and seen it come back to life and sweep night out of the earth with one all-illuminating smile that you could cover with your hand.

Why, we were back in this world in one instant! Then we looked the same startled thought into each other's eyes at the same moment; more than two weeks gone, and that ship not back yet!

In another minute I appeared in the presence of my train. They had been steeped in troubled bodings all this time — their faces showed it. I called an escort and we galloped five miles to a hilltop overlooking the sea. Where was my great commerce that so lately had made these glistening expanses populous and beautiful with its white-winged flocks? Vanished, every one! Not a sail, from verge to verge, not a smoke-bank — just a dead and empty solitude, in place of all that brisk and breezy life.

I went swiftly back, saying not a word to anybody. I told Sandy this ghastly news. We could imagine no explanation that would begin to explain. Had there been an invasion? an earthquake? a pestilence? Had the nation been swept out of existence? But guessing was profitless. I must go — at once. I borrowed the king's navy — a "ship" no bigger than a steam launch — and was soon ready.

The parting — ah, yes, that was hard. As I was devouring the child with last kisses, it brisked up and jabbered out its vocabulary! — the first time in more than two weeks, and it made fools of us for joy. The darling mispronunciations of childhood! — dear me, there's no music that can touch it; and how one grieves when it wastes away and dissolves into correctness, knowing it will never visit his bereaved ear again. Well, how good it was to be able to carry that gracious memory away with me!

I approached England the next morning, with the wide highway of salt water all to myself. There were ships in the harbor, at Dover, but they were naked as to sails, and there was no sign of life about them. It was Sunday; yet at Canterbury the streets were empty; strangest of all, there was not even a priest in sight, and no stroke of a bell fell upon my ear. The mournfulness of death was everywhere. I couldn't understand it. At last, in the further edge of that town I saw a small funeral procession — just a family and a few friends following a coffin — no priest; a funeral without bell, book, or candle; there was a church there close at hand, but they passed it by weeping, and did not enter it; I glanced up at the belfry, and there hung the bell, shrouded in black, and its tongue tied back. Now I knew! Now I understood the stupendous calamity that had overtaken England. Invasion? Invasion is a triviality to it. It was the INTERDICT!

I asked no questions; I didn't need to ask any. The Church had struck; the thing for me to do was to get into a disguise, and go warily. One of my servants gave me a suit of clothes, and when we were safe beyond the town I put them on, and from that time I traveled alone; I could not risk the embarrassment of company.

A miserable journey. A desolate silence everywhere. Even in London itself. Traffic had ceased; men did not talk or laugh, or go in groups, or even in couples; they moved aimlessly about, each man by himself, with his head down, and woe and terror at his heart. The Tower showed recent war-scars. Verily, much had been happening.

Of course, I meant to take the train for Camelot. Train! Why, the station was as vacant as a cavern. I moved on. The journey to Camelot was a repetition of what I had already seen. The Monday and the Tuesday differed in no way from the Sunday. I arrived far in the night. From being the best electric-lighted town in the kingdom and the most like a recumbent sun of anything you ever saw, it was become simply a blot — a blot upon darkness — that is to say, it was darker and solider than the rest of the darkness, and so you could see it a little better; it made me feel as if maybe it was symbolical — a sort of sign that the Church was going to *keep* the upper hand now, and snuff out all my beautiful civilization just like that. I found no life stirring in the somber streets. I groped my way with a heavy heart. The vast castle loomed black upon the hilltop, not a spark visible about it. The drawbridge was down, the great gate stood wide, I entered without challenge, my own heels making the only sound I heard — and it was sepulchral enough, in those huge vacant courts.

Chapter XLII. War!

I found Clarence alone in his quarters, drowned in melancholy; and in place of the electric light, he had reinstituted the ancient rag-lamp, and sat there in a grisly twilight with all curtains drawn tight. He sprang up and rushed for me eagerly, saying:

"Oh, it's worth a billion milrays to look upon a live person again!"

He knew me as easily as if I hadn't been disguised at all. Which frightened me; one may easily believe that.

"Quick, now, tell me the meaning of this fearful disaster," I said. "How did it come about?"

"Well, if there hadn't been any Queen Guenever, it wouldn't have come so early; but it would have come, anyway. It would have come on your own account by and by; by luck, it happened to come on the queen's."

"*And* Sir Launcelot's?"

"Just so."

"Give me the details."

"I reckon you will grant that during some years there has been only one pair of eyes in these kingdoms that has not been looking steadily askance at the queen and Sir Launcelot — "

"Yes, King Arthur's."

" — and only one heart that was without suspicion — "

"Yes — the king's; a heart that isn't capable of thinking evil of a friend."

"Well, the king might have gone on, still happy and unsuspecting, to the end of his days, but for one of your modern improvements — the stock-board. When you left, three miles of the London, Canterbury and Dover were ready for the rails, and also ready and ripe for manipulation in the stock-market. It was wildcat, and everybody knew it. The stock was for sale at a giveaway. What does Sir Launcelot do, but — "

"Yes, I know; he quietly picked up nearly all of it for a song; then he bought about twice as much more, deliverable upon call; and he was about to call when I left."

"Very well, he did call. The boys couldn't deliver. Oh, he had them — and he just settled his grip and squeezed them. They were laughing in their sleeves over their smartness in selling stock to him at 15 and 16 and along there that wasn't worth 10. Well, when they had laughed long enough on that side of their mouths, they rested-up that side by shifting the laugh to the other side. That was when they compromised with the Invincible at 283!"

"Good land!"

"He skinned them alive, and they deserved it — anyway, the whole kingdom rejoiced. Well, among the flayed were Sir Agravaine and Sir Mordred, nephews to the king. End of the first act. Act second, scene first, an apartment in Carlisle castle, where the court had gone for a few days' hunting. Persons present, the whole tribe of the king's nephews. Mordred and Agravaine propose to call the guileless Arthur's attention to Guenever and Sir Launcelot. Sir Gawaine, Sir Gareth, and Sir Gaheris will have nothing to do with it. A dispute ensues, with loud talk; in the midst of it enter the king. Mordred and Agravaine spring their devastating tale upon him. *Tableau* . A trap is laid for Launcelot, by the king's command, and Sir Launcelot walks into it. He made it sufficiently uncomfortable for the ambushed witnesses — to wit, Mordred, Agravaine, and twelve knights of lesser rank, for he killed every one of them but Mordred; but of course that couldn't straighten matters between Launcelot and the king, and didn't."

"Oh, dear, only one thing could result — I see that. War, and the knights of the realm divided into a king's party and a Sir Launcelot's party."

"Yes — that was the way of it. The king sent the queen to the stake, proposing to purify her with fire. Launcelot and his knights rescued her, and in doing it slew certain good old friends of yours and mine — in fact, some of the best we ever had; to wit, Sir Belias le Orgulous, Sir Segwarides, Sir Griflet le Fils de Dieu, Sir Brandiles, Sir Aglovale — "

"Oh, you tear out my heartstrings."

" — wait, I'm not done yet — Sir Tor, Sir Gauter, Sir Gillimer — "

"The very best man in my subordinate nine. What a handy right-fielder he was!"

" — Sir Reynold's three brothers, Sir Damus, Sir Priamus, Sir Kay the Stranger — "

"My peerless short-stop! I've seen him catch a daisy-cutter in his teeth. Come, I can't stand this!"

" — Sir Driant, Sir Lambegus, Sir Herminde, Sir Pertilope, Sir Perimones, and — whom do you think?"

"Rush! Go on."

"Sir Gaheris, and Sir Gareth — both!"

"Oh, incredible! Their love for Launcelot was indestructible."

"Well, it was an accident. They were simply onlookers; they were unarmed, and were merely there to witness the queen's punishment. Sir Launcelot smote down whoever came in the way of his blind fury, and he killed these without noticing who they were. Here is an instantaneous photograph one of our boys got of the battle; it's for sale on every news-stand. There — the figures nearest the queen are Sir Launcelot with his sword up, and Sir Gareth gasping his latest breath. You can catch the agony in the queen's face through the curling smoke. It's a rattling battle-picture."

"Indeed, it is. We must take good care of it; its historical value is incalculable. Go on."

"Well, the rest of the tale is just war, pure and simple. Launcelot retreated to his town and castle of Joyous Gard, and gathered there a great following of knights. The king, with a great host, went there, and there was desperate fighting during several days, and, as a result, all the plain around was paved with corpses and cast-iron. Then the Church patched up a peace between Arthur and Launcelot and the queen and everybody — everybody but Sir Gawaine. He was bitter about the slaying of his brothers, Gareth and Gaheris, and would not be appeased. He notified Launcelot to get him thence, and make swift preparation, and look to be soon attacked. So Launcelot sailed to his Duchy of Guienne with his following, and Gawaine soon followed with an army, and he beguiled Arthur to go with him. Arthur left the kingdom in Sir Mordred's hands until you should return — "

"Ah — a king's customary wisdom!"

"Yes. Sir Mordred set himself at once to work to make his kingship permanent. He was going to marry Guenever, as a first move; but she fled and shut herself up in the Tower of London. Mordred attacked; the Bishop of Canterbury dropped down on him with the Interdict. The king returned; Mordred fought him at Dover, at Canterbury, and again at Barham Down. Then there was talk of peace and a composition. Terms, Mordred to have Cornwall and Kent during Arthur's life, and the whole kingdom afterward."

"Well, upon my word! My dream of a republic to *be* a dream, and so remain."

"Yes. The two armies lay near Salisbury. Gawaine — Gawaine's head is at Dover Castle, he fell in the fight there — Gawaine appeared to Arthur in a dream, at least his ghost did, and warned him to refrain from conflict for a month, let the delay cost what it might. But battle was precipitated by an accident. Arthur had given order that if a sword was raised during the consultation over the proposed treaty with Mordred, sound the trumpet and fall on! for he had no confidence in Mordred. Mordred had given a similar order to *his* people. Well, by and by an adder bit a knight's heel; the knight forgot all about the order, and made a slash at the adder with his sword. Inside of half a minute those two prodigious hosts came together with a crash! They butchered away all day. Then the king — however, we have started something fresh since you left — our paper has."

"No? What is that?"

"War correspondence!"

"Why, that's good."

"Yes, the paper was booming right along, for the Interdict made no impression, got no grip, while the war lasted. I had war correspondents with both armies. I will finish that battle by reading you what one of the boys says:

> 'Then the king looked about him, and then was he
> ware of all his host and of all his good knights
> were left no more on live but two knights, that
> was Sir Lucan de Butlere, and his brother Sir
> Bedivere: and they were full sore wounded. Jesu
> mercy, said the king, where are all my noble
> knights becomen? Alas that ever I should see this
> doleful day. For now, said Arthur, I am come to
> mine end. But would to God that I wist where were
> that traitor Sir Mordred, that hath caused all
> this mischief. Then was King Arthur ware where Sir

Mordred leaned upon his sword among a great heap
of dead men. Now give me my spear, said Arthur
unto Sir Lucan, for yonder I have espied the
traitor that all this woe hath wrought. Sir, let
him be, said Sir Lucan, for he is unhappy; and if
ye pass this unhappy day, ye shall be right well
revenged upon him. Good lord, remember ye of your
night's dream, and what the spirit of Sir Gawaine
told you this night, yet God of his great goodness
hath preserved you hitherto. Therefore, for God's
sake, my lord, leave off by this. For blessed be
God ye have won the field: for here we be three
on live, and with Sir Mordred is none on live.
And if ye leave off now, this wicked day of
destiny is past. Tide me death, betide me life,
saith the king, now I see him yonder alone, he
shall never escape mine hands, for at a better
avail shall I never have him. God speed you well,
said Sir Bedivere. Then the king gat his spear
in both his hands, and ran toward Sir Mordred
crying, Traitor, now is thy death day come. And
when Sir Mordred heard Sir Arthur, he ran until
him with his sword drawn in his hand. And then
King Arthur smote Sir Mordred under the shield,
with a foin of his spear throughout the body more
than a fathom. And when Sir Mordred felt that he
had his death's wound, he thrust himself, with
the might that he had, up to the butt of King
Arthur's spear. And right so he smote his father
Arthur with his sword holden in both his hands,
on the side of the head, that the sword pierced
the helmet and the brain-pan, and therewithal
Sir Mordred fell stark dead to the earth. And
the noble Arthur fell in a swoon to the earth,
and there he swooned oft-times — '"

"That is a good piece of war correspondence, Clarence; you are a first-rate newspaper man.
Well — is the king all right? Did he get well?"

"Poor soul, no. He is dead."

I was utterly stunned; it had not seemed to me that any wound could be mortal to him.

"And the queen, Clarence?"

"She is a nun, in Almesbury."

"What changes! and in such a short while. It is inconceivable. What next, I wonder?"

"I can tell you what next."

"Well?"

"Stake our lives and stand by them!"

"What do you mean by that?"

"The Church is master now. The Interdict included you with Mordred; it is not to be removed while you remain alive. The clans are gathering. The Church has gathered all the knights that are left alive, and as soon as you are discovered we shall have business on our hands."

"Stuff! With our deadly scientific war-material; with our hosts of trained — "

"Save your breath — we haven't sixty faithful left!"

"What are you saying? Our schools, our colleges, our vast workshops, our — "

"When those knights come, those establishments will empty themselves and go over to the enemy. Did you think you had educated the superstition out of those people?"

"I certainly did think it."

"Well, then, you may unthink it. They stood every strain easily — until the Interdict. Since then, they merely put on a bold outside — at heart they are quaking. Make up your mind to it — when the armies come, the mask will fall."

"It's hard news. We are lost. They will turn our own science against us."

"No they won't."

"Why?"

"Because I and a handful of the faithful have blocked that game. I'll tell you what I've done, and what moved me to it. Smart as you are, the Church was smarter. It was the Church that sent you cruising — through her servants, the doctors."

"Clarence!"

"It is the truth. I know it. Every officer of your ship was the Church's picked servant, and so was every man of the crew."

"Oh, come!"

"It is just as I tell you. I did not find out these things at once, but I found them out finally. Did you send me verbal information, by the commander of the ship, to the effect that upon his return to you, with supplies, you were going to leave Cadiz — "

"Cadiz! I haven't been at Cadiz at all!"

" — going to leave Cadiz and cruise in distant seas indefinitely, for the health of your family? Did you send me that word?"

"Of course not. I would have written, wouldn't I?"

"Naturally. I was troubled and suspicious. When the commander sailed again I managed to ship a spy with him. I have never heard of vessel or spy since. I gave myself two weeks to hear from you in. Then I resolved to send a ship to Cadiz. There was a reason why I didn't."

"What was that?"

"Our navy had suddenly and mysteriously disappeared! Also, as suddenly and as mysteriously, the railway and telegraph and telephone service ceased, the men all deserted, poles were cut down, the Church laid a ban upon the electric light! I had to be up and doing — and straight off. Your life was safe — nobody in these kingdoms but Merlin would venture to touch such a magician as you without ten thousand men at his back — I had nothing to think of but how to put preparations in the best trim against your coming. I felt safe myself — nobody would be anxious to touch a pet of yours. So this is what I did. From our various works I selected all the men — boys I mean — whose faithfulness under whatsoever pressure I could swear to, and I called them together secretly and gave them their instructions. There are fifty-two of them; none younger than fourteen, and none above seventeen years old."

"Why did you select boys?"

"Because all the others were born in an atmosphere of superstition and reared in it. It is in their blood and bones. We imagined we had educated it out of them; they thought so, too; the Interdict woke them up like a thunderclap! It revealed them to themselves, and it revealed them to me, too. With boys it was different. Such as have been under our training from seven to ten years have had no acquaintance with the Church's terrors, and it was among these that I found my fifty-two. As a next move, I paid a private visit to that old cave of Merlin's — not the small one — the big one — "

"Yes, the one where we secretly established our first great electric plant when I was projecting a miracle."

"Just so. And as that miracle hadn't become necessary then, I thought it might be a good idea to utilize the plant now. I've provisioned the cave for a siege — "

"A good idea, a first-rate idea."

"I think so. I placed four of my boys there as a guard — inside, and out of sight. Nobody was to be hurt — while outside; but any attempt to enter — well, we said just let anybody try it! Then I went out into the hills and uncovered and cut the secret wires which connected your bedroom with the wires that go to the dynamite deposits under all our vast factories, mills, workshops, magazines, etc., and about midnight I and my boys turned out and connected that wire with the cave, and nobody but you and I suspects where the other end of it goes to. We laid it under ground, of course, and it was all finished in a couple of hours or so. We sha'n't have to leave our fortress now when we want to blow up our civilization."

"It was the right move — and the natural one; military necessity, in the changed condition of things. Well, what changes *have* come! We expected to be besieged in the palace some time or other, but — however, go on."

"Next, we built a wire fence."

"Wire fence?"

"Yes. You dropped the hint of it yourself, two or three years ago."

"Oh, I remember — the time the Church tried her strength against us the first time, and presently thought it wise to wait for a hopefuler season. Well, how have you arranged the fence?"

"I start twelve immensely strong wires — naked, not insulated — from a big dynamo in the cave — dynamo with no brushes except a positive and a negative one — "

"Yes, that's right."

"The wires go out from the cave and fence in a circle of level ground a hundred yards in diameter; they make twelve independent fences, ten feet apart — that is to say, twelve circles within circles — and their ends come into the cave again."

"Right; go on."

"The fences are fastened to heavy oaken posts only three feet apart, and these posts are sunk five feet in the ground."

"That is good and strong."

"Yes. The wires have no ground-connection outside of the cave. They go out from the positive brush of the dynamo; there is a ground-connection through the negative brush; the other ends of the wire return to the cave, and each is grounded independently."

"No, no, that won't do!"

"Why?"

"It's too expensive — uses up force for nothing. You don't want any ground-connection except the one through the negative brush. The other end of every wire must be brought back into the cave and fastened independently, and *without* any ground-connection. Now, then, observe the economy of it. A cavalry charge hurls itself against the fence; you are using no power, you are spending no money, for there is only one ground-connection till those horses come against the wire; the moment they touch it they form a connection with the negative brush *through the ground* , and drop dead. Don't you see? — you are using no energy until it is needed; your lightning is there, and ready, like the load in a gun; but it isn't costing you a cent till you touch it off. Oh, yes, the single ground-connection — "

"Of course! I don't know how I overlooked that. It's not only cheaper, but it's more effectual than the other way, for if wires break or get tangled, no harm is done."

"No, especially if we have a telltale in the cave and disconnect the broken wire. Well, go on. The gatlings?"

"Yes — that's arranged. In the center of the inner circle, on a spacious platform six feet high, I've grouped a battery of thirteen gatling guns, and provided plenty of ammunition."

"That's it. They command every approach, and when the Church's knights arrive, there's going to be music. The brow of the precipice over the cave — "

"I've got a wire fence there, and a gatling. They won't drop any rocks down on us."

"Well, and the glass-cylinder dynamite torpedoes?"

"That's attended to. It's the prettiest garden that was ever planted. It's a belt forty feet wide, and goes around the outer fence — distance between it and the fence one hundred yards — kind of neutral ground that space is. There isn't a single square yard of that whole belt but is equipped with a torpedo. We laid them on the surface of the ground, and sprinkled a layer of sand over them. It's an innocent looking garden, but you let a man start in to hoe it once, and you'll see."

"You tested the torpedoes?"

"Well, I was going to, but — "

"But what? Why, it's an immense oversight not to apply a — "

"Test? Yes, I know; but they're all right; I laid a few in the public road beyond our lines and they've been tested."

"Oh, that alters the case. Who did it?"

"A Church committee."

"How kind!"

"Yes. They came to command us to make submission. You see they didn't really come to test the torpedoes; that was merely an incident."

"Did the committee make a report?"

"Yes, they made one. You could have heard it a mile."

"Unanimous?"

"That was the nature of it. After that I put up some signs, for the protection of future committees, and we have had no intruders since."

"Clarence, you've done a world of work, and done it perfectly."

"We had plenty of time for it; there wasn't any occasion for hurry."

We sat silent awhile, thinking. Then my mind was made up, and I said:

"Yes, everything is ready; everything is shipshape, no detail is wanting. I know what to do now."

"So do I; sit down and wait."

"No, *sir* ! rise up and *strike* !"

"Do you mean it?"

"Yes, indeed! The *de*fensive isn't in my line, and the *off*ensive is. That is, when I hold a fair hand — two-thirds as good a hand as the enemy. Oh, yes, we'll rise up and strike; that's our game."

"A hundred to one you are right. When does the performance begin?"

"*Now!* We'll proclaim the Republic."

"Well, that *will* precipitate things, sure enough!"

"It will make them buzz, I tell you! England will be a hornets' nest before noon tomorrow, if the Church's hand hasn't lost its cunning — and we know it hasn't. Now you write and I'll dictate thus:

" PROCLAMATION

"BE IT KNOWN UNTO ALL. Whereas the king having died and left no heir, it becomes my duty to continue the executive authority vested in me, until a government shall have been created and set in motion. The monarchy has lapsed, it no longer exists. By consequence, all political power has reverted to its original source, the people of the nation. With the monarchy, its several adjuncts died also; wherefore there is no longer a nobility, no longer a privileged class, no longer an Established Church; all men are become exactly equal; they are upon one common level, and religion is free.

A Republic is hereby proclaimed

, as being the natural estate of a nation when other authority has ceased. It is the duty of the British people to meet together immediately, and by their votes elect representatives and deliver into their hands the government."

I signed it "The Boss," and dated it from Merlin's Cave. Clarence said —

"Why, that tells where we are, and invites them to call right away."

"That is the idea. We *strike* — by the Proclamation — then it's their innings. Now have the thing set up and printed and posted, right off; that is, give the order; then, if you've got a couple of bicycles handy at the foot of the hill, ho for Merlin's Cave!"

"I shall be ready in ten minutes. What a cyclone there is going to be tomorrow when this piece of paper gets to work!... It's a pleasant old palace, this is; I wonder if we shall ever again — but never mind about that."

Chapter XLIII. The Battle of the Sand Belt

In Merlin's Cave — Clarence and I and fifty-two fresh, bright, well-educated, clean-minded young British boys. At dawn I sent an order to the factories and to all our great works to stop operations and remove all life to a safe distance, as everything was going to be blown up by secret mines, "*and no telling at what moment — therefore, vacate at once .*" These people knew me, and had confidence in my word. They would clear out without waiting to part their hair, and I could take my own time about dating the explosion. You couldn't hire one of them to go back during the century, if the explosion was still impending.

We had a week of waiting. It was not dull for me, because I was writing all the time. During the first three days, I finished turning my old diary into this narrative form; it only required a chapter or so to bring it down to date. The rest of the week I took up in writing letters to my wife. It was always my habit to write to Sandy every day, whenever we were separate, and now I kept up the habit for love of it, and of her, though I couldn't do anything with the letters, of course, after I had written them. But it put in the time, you see, and was almost like talking; it was almost as if I was saying, "Sandy, if you and Hello-Central were here in the cave, instead of only your photographs, what good times we could have!" And then, you know, I could imagine the baby goo-gooing something out in reply, with its fists in its mouth and itself stretched across its mother's lap on its back, and she a-laughing and admiring and worshipping, and now and then tickling under the baby's chin to set it cackling, and then maybe throwing in a word of answer to me herself — and so on and so on — well, don't you know, I could sit there in the cave with my pen, and keep it up, that way, by the hour with them. Why, it was almost like having us all together again.

I had spies out every night, of course, to get news. Every report made things look more and more impressive. The hosts were gathering, gathering; down all the roads and paths of England the knights were riding, and priests rode with them, to hearten these original Crusaders, this being the Church's war. All the nobilities, big and little, were on their way, and all the gentry. This was all as was expected. We should thin out this sort of folk to such a degree that the people would have nothing to do but just step to the front with their republic and —

Ah, what a donkey I was! Toward the end of the week I began to get this large and disenchanting fact through my head: that the mass of the nation had swung their caps and shouted for the republic for about one day, and there an end! The Church, the nobles, and the gentry then turned one grand, all-disapproving frown upon them and shriveled them into sheep! From that moment the sheep had begun to gather to the fold — that is to say, the camps — and offer their valueless lives and their valuable wool to the "righteous cause." Why, even the very men who had lately been slaves were in the "righteous cause," and glorifying it, praying for it, sentimentally slabbering over it, just like all the other commoners. Imagine such human muck as this; conceive of this folly!

Yes, it was now "Death to the Republic!" everywhere — not a dissenting voice. All England was marching against us! Truly, this was more than I had bargained for.

I watched my fifty-two boys narrowly; watched their faces, their walk, their unconscious attitudes: for all these are a language — a language given us purposely that it may betray us in times of emergency, when we have secrets which we want to keep. I knew that that thought would keep saying itself over and over again in their minds and hearts, *All England is marching against us!* and ever more strenuously imploring attention with each repetition, ever more sharply realizing itself to their imaginations, until even in their sleep they would find no rest from it, but hear the vague and flitting creatures of the dreams say, *All England* — ALL ENGLAND! — *is marching against you*! I knew all this would happen; I knew that ultimately the pressure would become so great that it would compel utterance; therefore, I must be ready with an answer at that time — an answer well chosen and tranquilizing.

I was right. The time came. They HAD to speak. Poor lads, it was pitiful to see, they were so pale, so worn, so troubled. At first their spokesman could hardly find voice or words; but he presently got both. This is what he said — and he put it in the neat modern English taught him in my schools:

"We have tried to forget what we are — English boys! We have tried to put reason before sentiment, duty before love; our minds approve, but our hearts reproach us. While apparently it was only the nobility, only the gentry, only the twenty-five or thirty thousand knights left alive out of the late wars, we were of one mind, and undisturbed by any troubling doubt; each and every one of these fifty-two lads who stand here before you, said, 'They have chosen — it is their affair.' But think! — the matter is altered — *All England is marching against us*! Oh, sir, consider! — reflect! — these people are our people, they are bone of our bone, flesh of our flesh, we love them — do not ask us to destroy our nation!"

Well, it shows the value of looking ahead, and being ready for a thing when it happens. If I hadn't foreseen this thing and been fixed, that boy would have had me! — I couldn't have said a word. But I was fixed. I said:

"My boys, your hearts are in the right place, you have thought the worthy thought, you have done the worthy thing. You are English boys, you will remain English boys, and you will keep that name unsmirched. Give yourselves no further concern, let your minds be at peace. Consider this: while all England is marching against us, who is in the van? Who, by the commonest rules of war, will march in the front? Answer me."

"The mounted host of mailed knights."

"True. They are thirty thousand strong. Acres deep they will march. Now, observe: none but *they* will ever strike the sand-belt! Then there will be an episode! Immediately after, the civilian multitude in the rear will retire, to meet business engagements elsewhere. None but nobles and gentry are knights, and *none but these* will remain to dance to our music after that episode. It is absolutely true that we shall have to fight nobody but these thirty thousand knights. Now speak, and it shall be as you decide. Shall we avoid the battle, retire from the field?"

"NO!!!"

The shout was unanimous and hearty.

"Are you — are you — well, afraid of these thirty thousand knights?"

That joke brought out a good laugh, the boys' troubles vanished away, and they went gaily to their posts. Ah, they were a darling fifty-two! As pretty as girls, too.

I was ready for the enemy now. Let the approaching big day come along — it would find us on deck.

The big day arrived on time. At dawn the sentry on watch in the corral came into the cave and reported a moving black mass under the horizon, and a faint sound which he thought to be military music. Breakfast was just ready; we sat down and ate it.

This over, I made the boys a little speech, and then sent out a detail to man the battery, with Clarence in command of it.

The sun rose presently and sent its unobstructed splendors over the land, and we saw a prodigious host moving slowly toward us, with the steady drift and aligned front of a wave of the sea. Nearer and nearer it came, and more and more sublimely imposing became its aspect; yes, all England was there, apparently. Soon we could see the innumerable banners fluttering, and then the sun struck the sea of armor and set it all aflash. Yes, it was a fine sight; I hadn't ever seen anything to beat it.

At last we could make out details. All the front ranks, no telling how many acres deep, were horsemen — plumed knights in armor. Suddenly we heard the blare of trumpets; the slow walk burst into a gallop, and then — well, it was wonderful to see! Down swept that vast horseshoe wave — it approached the sand-belt — my breath stood still; nearer, nearer — the strip of green turf beyond the yellow belt grew narrow — narrower still — became a mere ribbon in front of the horses — then disappeared under their hoofs. Great Scott! Why, the whole front of that host shot into the sky with a thundercrash, and became a whirling tempest of rags and fragments; and along the ground lay a thick wall of smoke that hid what was left of the multitude from our sight.

Time for the second step in the plan of campaign! I touched a button, and shook the bones of England loose from her spine!

In that explosion all our noble civilization-factories went up in the air and disappeared from the earth. It was a pity, but it was necessary. We could not afford to let the enemy turn our own weapons against us.

Now ensued one of the dullest quarter-hours I had ever endured. We waited in a silent solitude enclosed by our circles of wire, and by a circle of heavy smoke outside of these. We couldn't see over the wall of smoke, and we couldn't see through it. But at last it began to shred away lazily, and by the end of another quarter-hour the land was clear and our curiosity was enabled to satisfy itself. No living creature was in sight! We now perceived that additions had been made to our defenses. The dynamite had dug a ditch more than a hundred feet wide, all around us, and cast up an embankment some twenty-five feet high on both borders of it. As to destruction of life, it was amazing. Moreover, it was beyond estimate. Of course, we could not *count* the dead, because they did not exist as individuals, but merely as homogeneous protoplasm, with alloys of iron and buttons.

No life was in sight, but necessarily there must have been some wounded in the rear ranks, who were carried off the field under cover of the wall of smoke; there would be sickness among the others — there always is, after an episode like that. But there would be no reinforcements; this was the last stand of the chivalry of England; it was all that was left of the order, after the recent annihilating wars. So I felt quite safe in believing that the utmost force that could for the future be brought against us would be but small; that is, of knights. I therefore issued a congratulatory proclamation to my army in these words:

SOLDIERS, CHAMPIONS OF HUMAN LIBERTY AND EQUALITY:

Your General congratulates you! In the pride of his
strength and the vanity of his renown, an arrogant
enemy came against you. You were ready. The conflict
was brief; on your side, glorious. This mighty
victory, having been achieved utterly without loss,
stands without example in history. So long as the
planets shall continue to move in their orbits, the
BATTLE OF THE SAND-BELT will not perish out of the

memories of men.

THE BOSS.

I read it well, and the applause I got was very gratifying to me. I then wound up with these remarks:

"The war with the English nation, as a nation, is at an end. The nation has retired from the field and the war. Before it can be persuaded to return, war will have ceased. This campaign is the only one that is going to be fought. It will be brief — the briefest in history. Also the most destructive to life, considered from the standpoint of proportion of casualties to numbers engaged. We are done with the nation; henceforth we deal only with the knights. English knights can be killed, but they cannot be conquered. We know what is before us. While one of these men remains alive, our task is not finished, the war is not ended. We will kill them all." [Loud and long continued applause.]

I picketed the great embankments thrown up around our lines by the dynamite explosion — merely a lookout of a couple of boys to announce the enemy when he should appear again.

Next, I sent an engineer and forty men to a point just beyond our lines on the south, to turn a mountain brook that was there, and bring it within our lines and under our command, arranging it in such a way that I could make instant use of it in an emergency. The forty men were divided into two shifts of twenty each, and were to relieve each other every two hours. In ten hours the work was accomplished.

It was nightfall now, and I withdrew my pickets. The one who had had the northern outlook reported a camp in sight, but visible with the glass only. He also reported that a few knights had been feeling their way toward us, and had driven some cattle across our lines, but that the knights themselves had not come very near. That was what I had been expecting. They were feeling us, you see; they wanted to know if we were going to play that red terror on them again. They would grow bolder in the night, perhaps. I believed I knew what project they would attempt, because it was plainly the thing I would attempt myself if I were in their places and as ignorant as they were. I mentioned it to Clarence.

"I think you are right," said he; "it is the obvious thing for them to try."

"Well, then," I said, "if they do it they are doomed."

"Certainly."

"They won't have the slightest show in the world."

"Of course they won't."

"It's dreadful, Clarence. It seems an awful pity."

The thing disturbed me so that I couldn't get any peace of mind for thinking of it and worrying over it. So, at last, to quiet my conscience, I framed this message to the knights:

TO THE HONORABLE THE COMMANDER OF THE INSURGENT
CHIVALRY OF ENGLAND: YOU fight in vain. We know
your strength — if one may call it by that name.
We know that at the utmost you cannot bring
against us above five and twenty thousand knights.
Therefore, you have no chance — none whatever.
Reflect: we are well equipped, well fortified, we
number 54. Fifty-four what? Men? No, MINDS — the
capablest in the world; a force against which
mere animal might may no more hope to prevail than
may the idle waves of the sea hope to prevail
against the granite barriers of England. Be advised.
We offer you your lives; for the sake of your
families, do not reject the gift. We offer you
this chance, and it is the last: throw down your
arms; surrender unconditionally to the Republic,

and all will be forgiven.

(Signed) THE BOSS.

I read it to Clarence, and said I proposed to send it by a flag of truce. He laughed the sarcastic laugh he was born with, and said:

"Somehow it seems impossible for you to ever fully realize what these nobilities are. Now let us save a little time and trouble. Consider me the commander of the knights yonder. Now, then, you are the flag of truce; approach and deliver me your message, and I will give you your answer."

I humored the idea. I came forward under an imaginary guard of the enemy's soldiers, produced my paper, and read it through. For answer, Clarence struck the paper out of my hand, pursed up a scornful lip and said with lofty disdain:

"Dismember me this animal, and return him in a basket to the base-born knave who sent him; other answer have I none!"

How empty is theory in presence of fact! And this was just fact, and nothing else. It was the thing that would have happened, there was no getting around that. I tore up the paper and granted my mistimed sentimentalities a permanent rest.

Then, to business. I tested the electric signals from the gatling platform to the cave, and made sure that they were all right; I tested and retested those which commanded the fences — these were signals whereby I could break and renew the electric current in each fence independently of the others at will. I placed the brook-connection under the guard and authority of three of my best boys, who would alternate in two-hour watches all night and promptly obey my signal, if I should have occasion to give it — three revolver-shots in quick succession. Sentry-duty was discarded for the night, and the corral left empty of life; I ordered that quiet be maintained in the cave, and the electric lights turned down to a glimmer.

As soon as it was good and dark, I shut off the current from all the fences, and then groped my way out to the embankment bordering our side of the great dynamite ditch. I crept to the top of it and lay there on the slant of the muck to watch. But it was too dark to see anything. As for sounds, there were none. The stillness was deathlike. True, there were the usual night-sounds of the country — the whir of night-birds, the buzzing of insects, the barking of distant dogs, the mellow lowing of far-off kine — but these didn't seem to break the stillness, they only intensified it, and added a grewsome melancholy to it into the bargain.

I presently gave up looking, the night shut down so black, but I kept my ears strained to catch the least suspicious sound, for I judged I had only to wait, and I shouldn't be disappointed. However, I had to wait a long time. At last I caught what you may call in distinct glimpses of sound dulled metallic sound. I pricked up my ears, then, and held my breath, for this was the sort of thing I had been waiting for. This sound thickened, and approached — from toward the north. Presently, I heard it at my own level — the ridge-top of the opposite embankment, a hundred feet or more away. Then I seemed to see a row of black dots appear along that ridge — human heads? I couldn't tell; it mightn't be anything at all; you can't depend on your eyes when your imagination is out of focus. However, the question was soon settled. I heard that metallic noise descending into the great ditch. It augmented fast, it spread all along, and it unmistakably furnished me this fact: an armed host was taking up its quarters in the ditch. Yes, these people were arranging a little surprise party for us. We could expect entertainment about dawn, possibly earlier.

I groped my way back to the corral now; I had seen enough. I went to the platform and signaled to turn the current on to the two inner fences. Then I went into the cave, and found everything satisfactory there — nobody awake but the working-watch. I woke Clarence and told him the great ditch was filling up with men, and that I believed all the knights were coming for us in a body. It was my notion that as soon as dawn approached we could expect the ditch's ambuscaded thousands to swarm up over the embankment and make an assault, and be followed immediately by the rest of their army.

Clarence said:

"They will be wanting to send a scout or two in the dark to make preliminary observations. Why not take the lightning off the outer fences, and give them a chance?"

"I've already done it, Clarence. Did you ever know me to be inhospitable?"

"No, you are a good heart. I want to go and — "

"Be a reception committee? I will go, too."

We crossed the corral and lay down together between the two inside fences. Even the dim light of the cave had disordered our eyesight somewhat, but the focus straightway began to regulate itself and soon it was adjusted for present circumstances. We had had to feel our way before, but we could make out to see the fence posts now. We started a whispered conversation, but suddenly Clarence broke off and said:

"What is that?"

"What is what?"

"That thing yonder."

"What thing — where?"

"There beyond you a little piece — dark something — a dull shape of some kind — against the second fence."

I gazed and he gazed. I said:

"Could it be a man, Clarence?"

"No, I think not. If you notice, it looks a lit — why, it *is* a man! — leaning on the fence."

"I certainly believe it is; let us go and see."

We crept along on our hands and knees until we were pretty close, and then looked up. Yes, it was a man — a dim great figure in armor, standing erect, with both hands on the upper wire — and, of course, there was a smell of burning flesh. Poor fellow, dead as a door-nail, and never knew what hurt him. He stood there like a statue — no motion about him, except that his plumes swished about a little in the night wind. We rose up and looked in through the bars of his visor, but couldn't make out whether we knew him or not — features too dim and shadowed.

We heard muffled sounds approaching, and we sank down to the ground where we were. We made out another knight vaguely; he was coming very stealthily, and feeling his way. He was near enough now for us to see him put out a hand, find an upper wire, then bend and step under it and over the lower one. Now he arrived at the first knight — and started slightly when he discovered him. He stood a moment — no doubt wondering why the other one didn't move on; then he said, in a low voice, "Why dreamest thou here, good Sir Mar — " then he laid his hand on the corpse's shoulder — and just uttered a little soft moan and sunk down dead. Killed by a dead man, you see — killed by a dead friend, in fact. There was something awful about it.

These early birds came scattering along after each other, about one every five minutes in our vicinity, during half an hour. They brought no armor of offense but their swords; as a rule, they carried the sword ready in the hand, and put it forward and found the wires with it. We would now and then see a blue spark when the knight that caused it was so far away as to be invisible to us; but we knew what had happened, all the same; poor fellow, he had touched a charged wire with his sword and been electrocuted. We had brief intervals of grim stillness, interrupted with piteous regularity by the clash made by the falling of an ironclad; and this sort of thing was going on, right along, and was very creepy there in the dark and lonesomeness.

We concluded to make a tour between the inner fences. We elected to walk upright, for convenience's sake; we argued that if discerned, we should be taken for friends rather than enemies, and in any case we should be out of reach of swords, and these gentry did not seem to have any spears along. Well, it was a curious trip. Everywhere dead men were lying outside the second fence — not plainly visible, but still visible; and we counted fifteen of those pathetic statues — dead knights standing with their hands on the upper wire.

One thing seemed to be sufficiently demonstrated: our current was so tremendous that it killed before the victim could cry out. Pretty soon we detected a muffled and heavy sound, and next moment we guessed what it was. It was a surprise in force coming! whispered Clarence to go and wake the army, and notify it to wait in silence in the cave for further orders. He was soon back, and we stood by the inner fence and watched the silent lightning do its awful work upon that swarming host. One could make out but little of detail; but he could note that a black mass was piling itself up beyond the second fence. That swelling bulk was dead men! Our camp was enclosed with a solid wall of the dead — a bulwark, a breastwork, of corpses, you may say. One terrible thing about this thing was the absence of human voices; there were no cheers, no war cries; being intent upon a surprise, these men moved as noiselessly as they could; and always when the front rank was near enough to their goal to make it proper for them to begin to get a shout ready, of course they struck the fatal line and went down without testifying.

I sent a current through the third fence now; and almost immediately through the fourth and fifth, so quickly were the gaps filled up. I believed the time was come now for my climax; I believed that that whole army was in our trap. Anyway, it was high time to find out. So I touched a button and set fifty electric suns aflame on the top of our precipice.

Land, what a sight! We were enclosed in three walls of dead men! All the other fences were pretty nearly filled with the living, who were stealthily working their way forward through the wires. The sudden glare paralyzed this host, petrified them, you may say, with astonishment; there was just one instant for me to utilize their immobility in, and I didn't lose the chance. You see, in another instant they would have recovered their faculties, then they'd have burst into a cheer and made a rush, and my wires would have gone down before it; but that lost instant lost them their opportunity forever; while even that slight fragment of time was still unspent, I shot the current through all the fences and struck the whole host dead in their tracks! *There* was a groan you could *hear* ! It voiced the death-pang of eleven thousand men. It swelled out on the night with awful pathos.

A glance showed that the rest of the enemy — perhaps ten thousand strong — were between us and the encircling ditch, and pressing forward to the assault. Consequently we had them *all!* and had them past help. Time for the last act of the tragedy. I fired the three appointed revolver shots — which meant:

"Turn on the water!"

There was a sudden rush and roar, and in a minute the mountain brook was raging through the big ditch and creating a river a hundred feet wide and twenty-five deep.

"Stand to your guns, men! Open fire!"

The thirteen gatlings began to vomit death into the fated ten thousand. They halted, they stood their ground a moment against that withering deluge of fire, then they broke, faced about and swept toward the ditch like chaff before a gale. A full fourth part of their force never reached the top of the lofty embankment; the three-fourths reached it and plunged over — to death by drowning.

Within ten short minutes after we had opened fire, armed resistance was totally annihilated, the campaign was ended, we fifty-four were masters of England. Twenty-five thousand men lay dead around us.

But how treacherous is fortune! In a little while — say an hour — happened a thing, by my own fault, which — but I have no heart to write that. Let the record end here.

Chapter XLIV. A Postscript by Clarence

I, Clarence, must write it for him. He proposed that we two go out and see if any help could be accorded the wounded. I was strenuous against the project. I said that if there were many, we could do but little for them; and it would not be wise for us to trust ourselves among them, anyway. But he could seldom be turned from a purpose once formed; so we shut off the electric current from the fences, took an escort along, climbed over the enclosing ramparts of dead knights, and moved out upon the field. The first wounded mall who appealed for help was sitting with his back against a dead comrade. When The Boss bent over him and spoke to him, the man recognized him and stabbed him. That knight was Sir Meliagraunce, as I found out by tearing off his helmet. He will not ask for help any more.

We carried The Boss to the cave and gave his wound, which was not very serious, the best care we could. In this service we had the help of Merlin, though we did not know it. He was disguised as a woman, and appeared to be a simple old peasant goodwife. In this disguise, with brown-stained face and smooth shaven, he had appeared a few days after The Boss was hurt and offered to cook for us, saying her people had gone off to join certain new camps which the enemy were forming, and that she was starving. The Boss had been getting along very well, and had amused himself with finishing up his record.

We were glad to have this woman, for we were short handed. We were in a trap, you see — a trap of our own making. If we stayed where we were, our dead would kill us; if we moved out of our defenses, we should no longer be invincible. We had conquered; in turn we were conquered. The Boss recognized this; we all recognized it. If we could go to one of those new camps and patch up some kind of terms with the enemy — yes, but The Boss could not go, and neither could I, for I was among the first that were made sick by the poisonous air bred by those dead thousands. Others were taken down, and still others. Tomorrow —

Tomorrow. It is here. And with it the end. About midnight I awoke, and saw that hag making curious passes in the air about The Boss's head and face, and wondered what it meant. Everybody but the dynamo-watch lay steeped in sleep; there was no sound. The woman ceased from her mysterious foolery, and started tiptoeing toward the door. I called out:

"Stop! What have you been doing?"

She halted, and said with an accent of malicious satisfaction:

"Ye were conquerors; ye are conquered! These others are perishing — you also. Ye shall all die in this place — every one — except *him* . He sleepeth now — and shall sleep thirteen centuries. I am Merlin!"

Then such a delirium of silly laughter overtook him that he reeled about like a drunken man, and presently fetched up against one of our wires. His mouth is spread open yet; apparently he is still laughing. I suppose the face will retain that petrified laugh until the corpse turns to dust.

The Boss has never stirred — sleeps like a stone. If he does not wake to-day we shall understand what kind of a sleep it is, and his body will then be borne to a place in one of the remote recesses of the cave where none will ever find it to desecrate it. As for the rest of us — well, it is agreed that if any one of us ever escapes alive from this place, he will write the fact here, and loyally hide this Manuscript with The Boss, our dear good chief, whose property it is, be he alive or dead.

THE END OF THE MANUSCRIPT

FINAL P.S. BY M.T.

The dawn was come when I laid the Manuscript aside. The rain had almost ceased, the world was gray and sad, the exhausted storm was sighing and sobbing itself to rest. I went to the stranger's room, and listened at his door, which was slightly ajar. I could hear his voice, and so I knocked. There was no answer, but I still heard the voice. I peeped in. The man lay on his back in bed, talking brokenly but with spirit, and punctuating with his arms, which he thrashed about, restlessly, as sick people do in delirium. I slipped in softly and bent over him. His mutterings and ejaculations went on. I spoke — merely a word, to call his attention. His glassy eyes and his ashy face were alight in an instant with pleasure, gratitude, gladness, welcome:

"Oh, Sandy, you are come at last — how I have longed for you! Sit by me — do not leave me — never leave me again, Sandy, never again. Where is your hand? — give it me, dear, let me hold it — there — now all is well, all is peace, and I am happy again — *we* are happy again, isn't it so, Sandy? You are so dim, so vague, you are but a mist, a cloud, but you are *here* , and that is blessedness sufficient; and I have your hand; don't take it away — it is for only a little while, I shall not require it long.... Was that the child?... Hello-Central!... she doesn't answer. Asleep, perhaps? Bring her when she wakes, and let me touch her hands, her face, her hair, and tell her goodbye.... Sandy! Yes, you are there. I lost myself a moment, and I thought you were gone.... Have I been sick long? It must be so; it seems months to me. And such dreams! such strange and awful dreams, Sandy! Dreams that were as real as reality — delirium, of course, but *so* real! Why, I thought the king was dead, I thought you were in Gaul and couldn't get home, I thought there was a revolution; in the fantastic frenzy of these dreams, I thought that Clarence and I and a handful of my cadets fought and exterminated the whole chivalry of England! But even that was not the strangest. I seemed to be a creature out of a remote unborn age, centuries hence, and even *that* was as real as the rest! Yes, I seemed to have flown back out of that age into this of ours, and then forward to it again, and was set down, a stranger and forlorn in that strange England, with an abyss of thirteen centuries yawning between me and you! between me and my home and my friends! between me and all that is dear to me, all that could make life worth the living! It was awful — awfuler than you can ever imagine, Sandy. Ah, watch by me, Sandy — stay by me every moment — *don't* let me go out of my mind again; death is nothing, let it come, but not with those dreams, not with the torture of those hideous dreams — I cannot endure *that* again.... Sandy?..."

He lay muttering incoherently some little time; then for a time he lay silent, and apparently sinking away toward death. Presently his fingers began to pick busily at the coverlet, and by that sign I knew that his end was at hand with the first suggestion of the death-rattle in his throat he started up slightly, and seemed to listen: then he said:

"A bugle?... It is the king! The drawbridge, there! Man the battlements! — turn out the — "

He was getting up his last "effect"; but he never finished it.

H. Beam Piper

Flight from Tomorrow

1

But yesterday, a whole planet had shouted: *Hail Hradzka! Hail the Leader!* Today, they were screaming: *Death to Hradzka! Kill the tyrant!*

The Palace, where Hradzka, surrounded by his sycophants and guards, had lorded it over a solar system, was now an inferno. Those who had been too closely identified with the dictator's rule to hope for forgiveness were fighting to the last, seeking only a quick death in combat; one by one, their isolated points of resistance were being wiped out. The corridors and chambers of the huge palace were thronged with rebels, loud with their shouts, and with the rasping hiss of heat-beams and the crash of blasters, reeking with the stench of scorched plastic and burned flesh, of hot metal and charred fabric. The living quarters were overrun; the mob smashed down walls and tore up floors in search of secret hiding-places. They found strange things-the space-ship that had been built under one of the domes, in readiness for flight to the still-loyal colonies on Mars or the Asteroid Belt, for instance-but Hradzka himself they could not find.

At last, the search reached the New Tower which reared its head five thousand feet above the palace, the highest thing in the city. They blasted down the huge steel doors, cut the power from the energy-screens. They landed from antigrav-cars on the upper levels. But except for barriers of metal and concrete and energy, they met with no opposition. Finally, they came to the spiral stairway which led up to the great metal sphere which capped the whole structure.

General Zarvas, the Army Commander who had placed himself at the head of the revolt, stood with his foot on the lowest step, his followers behind him. There was Prince Burvanny, the leader of the old nobility, and Ghorzesko Orhm, the merchant, and between them stood Tobbh, the chieftain of the mutinous slaves. There were clerks; laborers; poor but haughty nobles: and wealthy merchants who had long been forced to hide their riches from the dictator's tax-gatherers, and soldiers, and spacemen.

"You'd better let some of us go first sir," General Zarvas' orderly, a blood-stained bandage about his head, his uniform in rags, suggested. "You don't know what might be up there."

The General shook his head. "I'll go first." Zarvas Pol was not the man to send subordinates into danger ahead of himself. "To tell the truth, I'm afraid we won't find anything at all up there."

"You mean...?" Ghorzesko Orhm began.

"The 'time-machine'," Zarvas Pol replied. "If he's managed to get it finished, the Great Mind only knows where he may be, now. Or when."

He loosened the blaster in his holster and started up the long spiral. His followers spread out, below; sharp-shooters took position to cover his ascent. Prince Burvanny and Tobbh the Slave started to follow him. They hesitated as each motioned the other to precede him; then the nobleman followed the general, his blaster drawn, and the brawny slave behind him.

The door at the top was open, and Zarvas Pol stepped through but there was nothing in the great spherical room except a raised dais some fifty feet in diameter, its polished metal top strangely clean and empty. And a crumpled heap of burned cloth and charred flesh that had, not long ago, been a man. An old man with a white beard, and the seven-pointed star of the Learned Brothers on his breast, advanced to meet the armed intruders.

"So he is gone, Kradzy Zago?" Zarvas Pol said, holstering his weapon. "Gone in the 'time-machine', to hide in yesterday or tomorrow. And you let him go?"

The old one nodded. "He had a blaster, and I had none." He indicated the body on the floor. "Zoldy Jarv had no blaster, either, but he tried to stop Hradzka. See, he squandered his life as a fool squanders his money, getting nothing for it. And a man's life is not money, Zarvas Pol."

"I do not blame you, Kradzy Zago," General Zarvas said. "But now you must get to work, and build us another 'time-machine', so that we can hunt him down."

"Does revenge mean so much to you, then?"

The soldier made an impatient gesture. "Revenge is for fools, like that pack of screaming beasts below. I do not kill for revenge; I kill because dead men do no harm."

"Hradzka will do us no more harm," the old scientist replied. "He is a thing of yesterday; of a time long past and half-lost in the mists of legend."

"No matter. As long as he exists, at any point in space-time, Hradzka is still a threat. Revenge means much to Hradzka; he will return for it, when we least expect him."

The old man shook his head. "No, Zarvas Pol, Hradzka will not return."

* * * * *

Hradzka holstered his blaster, threw the switch that sealed the "time-machine", put on the antigrav-unit and started the time-shift unit. He reached out and set the destination-dial for the mid-Fifty-Second Century of the Atomic Era. That would land him in the Ninth Age of Chaos, following the Two-Century War and the collapse of the World Theocracy. A good time for his purpose: the world would be slipping back into barbarism, and yet possess the technologies of former civilizations. A hundred little national states would be trying to regain social stability, competing and warring with one another. Hradzka glanced back over his shoulder at the cases of books, record-spools, tri-dimensional pictures, and scale-models. These people of the past would welcome him and his science of the future, would make him their leader.

He would start in a small way, by taking over the local feudal or tribal government, would arm his followers with weapons of the future. Then he would impose his rule upon neighboring tribes, or princedoms, or communes, or whatever, and build a strong sovereignty; from that he envisioned a world empire, a Solar System empire.

Then, he would build "time-machines", many "time-machines". He would recruit an army such as the universe had never seen, a swarm of men from every age in the past. At that point, he would return to the Hundredth Century of the Atomic Era, to wreak vengeance upon those who had risen against him. A slow smile grew on Hradzka's thin lips as he thought of the tortures with which he would put Zarvas Pol to death.

He glanced up at the great disc of the indicator and frowned. Already he was back to the year 7500, A.E., and the temporal-displacement had not begun to slow. The disc was turning even more rapidly—7000, 6000, 5500; he gasped slightly. Then he had passed his destination; he was now in the Fortieth Century, but the indicator was slowing. The hairline crossed the Thirtieth Century, the Twentieth, the Fifteenth, the Tenth. He wondered what had gone wrong, but he had recovered from his fright by this time. When this insane machine stopped, as it must around the First Century of the Atomic Era, he would investigate, make repairs, then shift forward to his target-point. Hradzka was determined upon the Fifty-Second Century; he had made a special study of the history of that period, had learned the language spoken then, and he understood the methods necessary to gain power over the natives of that time.

The indicator-disc came to a stop, in the First Century. He switched on the magnifier and leaned forward to look; he had emerged into normal time in the year 10 of the Atomic Era, a decade after the first uranium-pile had gone into operation, and seven years after the first atomic bombs had been exploded in warfare. The altimeter showed that he was hovering at eight thousand feet above ground-level.

Slowly, he cut out the antigrav, letting the "time machine" down easily. He knew that there had been no danger of materializing inside anything; the New Tower had been built to put it above anything that had occupied that space-point at any moment within history, or legend, or even the geological knowledge of man. What lay below, however, was uncertain. It was night-the visi-screen showed only a star-dusted, moonless-sky, and dark shadows below. He snapped another switch; for a few micro-seconds a beam of intense light was turned on, automatically photographing the landscape under him. A second later, the developed picture was projected upon another screen; it showed only wooded mountains and a barren, brush-grown valley.

* * * * *

The "time-machine" came to rest with a soft jar and a crashing of broken bushes that was audible through the sound pickup. Hradzka pulled the main switch; there was a click as the shielding went out and the door opened. A breath of cool night air drew into the hollow sphere.

Then there was a loud *bang* inside the mechanism, and a flash of blue-white light which turned to pinkish flame with a nasty crackling. Curls of smoke began to rise from the square black box that housed the "time-shift" mechanism, and from behind the instrument-board. In a moment, everything was glowing-hot: driblets of aluminum and silver were running down from the instruments. Then the whole interior of the "time-machine" was afire; there was barely time for Hradzka to leap through the open door.

The brush outside impeded him, and he used his blaster to clear a path for himself away from the big sphere, which was now glowing faintly on the outside. The heat grew in intensity, and the brush outside was taking fire. It was not until he had gotten two hundred yards from the machine that he stopped, realizing what had happened.

The machine, of course, had been sabotaged. That would have been young Zoldy, whom he had killed, or that old billy-goat, Kradzy Zago; the latter, most likely. He cursed both of them for having marooned him in this savage age, at the very beginning of atomic civilization, with all his printed and recorded knowledge destroyed. Oh, he could still gain mastery over these barbarians; he knew enough to fashion a crude blaster, or a heat-beam gun, or an atomic-electric conversion unit. But without his books and records, he could never build an antigrav unit, and the secret of the "temporal shift" was lost.

For "Time" is not an object, or a medium which can be travelled along. The "Time-Machine" was not a vehicle; it was a mechanical process of displacement within the space-time continuum, and those who constructed it knew that it could not be used with the sort of accuracy that the dials indicated. Hradzka had ordered his scientists to produce a "Time Machine", and they had combined the possible-displacement within the space-time continuum-with the sort of fiction the dictator demanded, for their own well-being. Even had there been no sabotage, his return to his own "time" was nearly of zero probability.

The fire, spreading from the "time-machine", was blowing toward him; he observed the wind-direction and hurried around out of the path of the flames. The light enabled him to pick his way through the brush, and, after crossing a small stream, he found a rutted road and followed it up the mountainside until he came to a place where he could rest concealed until morning.

2

It was broad daylight when he woke, and there was a strange throbbing sound; Hradzka lay motionless under the brush where he had slept, his blaster ready. In a few minutes, a vehicle came into sight, following the road down the mountainside.

It was a large thing, four-wheeled, with a projection in front which probably housed the engine and a cab for the operator. The body of the vehicle was simply an open rectangular box. There were two men in the cab, and about twenty or thirty more crowded into the box body. These were dressed in faded and nondescript garments of blue and gray and brown; all were armed with crude weapons-axes, bill-hooks, long-handled instruments with serrated edges, and what looked like broad-bladed spears. The vehicle itself, which seemed to be propelled by some sort of chemical-explosion engine, was dingy and mud-splattered; the men in it were ragged and unshaven. Hradzka snorted in contempt; they were probably warriors of the local tribe, going to the fire in the belief that it had been started by raiding enemies. When they found the wreckage of the "time-machine", they would no doubt believe that it was the chariot of some god and drag it home to be venerated.

A plan of action was taking shape in his mind. First, he must get clothing of the sort worn by these people, and find a safe hiding-place for his own things. Then, pretending to be a deaf-mute, he would go among them to learn something of their customs and pick up the language. When he had done that, he would move on to another tribe or village, able to tell a credible story for himself. For a while, it would be necessary for him to do menial work, but in the end, he would establish himself among these people. Then he could gather around him a faction of those who were dissatisfied with whatever conditions existed, organize a conspiracy, make arms for his followers, and start his program of power-seizure.

The matter of clothing was attended to shortly after he had crossed the mountain and descended into the valley on the other side. Hearing a clinking sound some distance from the road, as of metal striking stone, Hradzka stole cautiously through the woods until he came within sight of a man who was digging with a mattock, uprooting small bushes of a particular sort, with rough gray bark and three-pointed leaves. When he had dug one up, he would cut off the roots and then slice away the root-bark with a knife, putting it into a sack. Hradzka's lip curled contemptuously; the fellow was gathering the stuff for medicinal use. He had heard of the use of roots and herbs for such purposes by the ancient savages.

The blaster would be no use here; it was too powerful, and would destroy the clothing that the man was wearing. He unfastened a strap from his belt and attached it to a stone to form a hand-loop, then, inched forward behind the lone herb-gatherer. When he was close enough, he straightened and rushed forward, swinging his improvised weapon. The man heard him and turned, too late.

* * * * *

After undressing his victim, Hradzka used the mattock to finish him, and then to dig a grave. The fugitive buried his own clothes with the murdered man, and donned the faded blue shirt, rough shoes, worn trousers and jacket. The blaster he concealed under the jacket, and he kept a few other Hundredth Century gadgets; these he would hide somewhere closer to his center of operations.

He had kept, among other things, a small box of food-concentrate capsules, and in one pocket of the newly acquired jacket he found a package containing food. It was rough and unappetizing fare-slices of cold cooked meat between slices of some cereal substance. He ate these before filling in the grave, and put the paper wrappings in with the dead man. Then, his work finished, he threw the mattock into the brush and set out again, grimacing disgustedly and scratching himself. The clothing he had appropriated was verminous.

Crossing another mountain, he descended into a second valley, and, for a time, lost his way among a tangle of narrow ravines. It was dark by the time he mounted a hill and found himself looking down another valley, in which a few scattered lights gave evidence of human habitations. Not wishing to arouse suspicion by approaching these in the night-time, he found a place among some young evergreens where he could sleep.

The next morning, having breakfasted on a concentrate capsule, he found a hiding-place for his blaster in a hollow tree. It was in a sufficiently prominent position so that he could easily find it again, and at the same time unlikely to be discovered by some native. Then he went down into the inhabited valley.

He was surprised at the ease with which he established contact with the natives. The first dwelling which he approached, a cluster of farm-buildings at the upper end of the valley, gave him shelter. There was a man, clad in the same sort of rough garments Hradzka had taken from the body of the herb-gatherer, and a woman in a faded and shapeless dress. The man was thin and work-bent; the woman short and heavy. Both were past middle age.

He made inarticulate sounds to attract their attention, then gestured to his mouth and ears to indicate his assumed affliction. He rubbed his stomach to portray hunger. Looking about, he saw an ax sticking in a chopping-block, and a pile of wood near it, probably the fuel used by these people. He took the ax, split up some of the wood, then repeated the hunger-signs. The man and the woman both nodded, laughing; he was shown a pile of tree-limbs, and the man picked up a short billet of wood and used it like a measuring-rule, to indicate that all the wood was to be cut to that length.

Hradzka fell to work, and by mid-morning, he had all the wood cut. He had seen a circular stone, mounted on a trestle with a metal axle through it, and judged it to be some sort of a grinding-wheel, since it was fitted with a foot-pedal and a rusty metal can was set above it to spill water onto the grinding-edge. After chopping the wood, he carefully sharpened the ax, handing it to the man for inspection. This seemed to please the man; he clapped Hradzka on the shoulder, making commendatory sounds.

* * * * *

It required considerable time and ingenuity to make himself a more or less permanent member of the household. Hradzka had made a survey of the farmyard, noting the sorts of work that would normally be performed on the farm, and he pantomimed this work in its simpler operations. He pointed to the east, where the sun would rise, and to the zenith, and to the west. He made signs indicative of eating, and of sleeping, and of rising, and of working. At length, he succeeded in conveying his meaning.

There was considerable argument between the man and the woman, but his proposal was accepted, as he expected that it would. It was easy to see that the work of the farm was hard for this aging couple; now, for a place to sleep and a little food, they were able to acquire a strong and intelligent slave.

In the days that followed, he made himself useful to the farm people; he fed the chickens and the livestock, milked the cow, worked in the fields. He slept in a small room at the top of the house, under the eaves, and ate with the man and woman in the farmhouse kitchen.

It was not long before he picked up a few words which he had heard his employers using, and related them to the things or acts spoken of. And he began to notice that these people, in spite of the crudities of their own life, enjoyed some of the advantages of a fairly complex civilization. Their implements were not hand-craft products, but showed machine workmanship. There were two objects hanging on hooks on the kitchen wall which he was sure were weapons. Both had wooden shoulder-stocks, and wooden fore-pieces; they had long tubes extending to the front, and triggers like blasters. One had double tubes mounted side-by-side, and double triggers; the other had an octagonal tube mounted over a round tube, and a loop extension on the trigger-guard. Then, there was a box on the kitchen wall, with a mouthpiece and a cylindrical tube on a cord. Sometimes a bell would ring out of the box, and the woman would go to this instrument, take down the tube and hold it to her ear, and talk into the mouthpiece. There was another box from which voices would issue, of people conversing, or of orators, or of singing, and sometimes instrumental music. None of these were objects made by savages; these people probably traded with some fairly high civilization. They were not illiterate; he found printed matter, indicating the use of some phonetic alphabet, and paper pamphlets containing printed reproductions of photographs as well as verbal text.

There was also a vehicle on the farm, powered, like the one he had seen on the road, by an engine in which a hydrocarbon liquid-fuel was exploded. He made it his business to examine this minutely, and to study its construction and operation until he was thoroughly familiar with it.

It was not until the third day after his arrival that the chickens began to die. In the morning, Hradzka found three of them dead when he went to feed them, the rest drooping unhealthily; he summoned the man and showed him what he had found. The next morning, they were all dead, and the cow was sick. She gave bloody milk, that evening, and the next morning she lay in her stall and would not get up.

The man and the woman were also beginning to sicken, though both of them tried to continue their work. It was the woman who first noticed that the plants around the farmhouse were withering and turning yellow.

* * * * *

The farmer went to the stable with Hradzka and looked at the cow. Shaking his head, he limped back to the house, and returned carrying one of the weapons from the kitchen-the one with the single trigger and the octagonal tube. As he entered the stable, he jerked down and up on the loop extension of the trigger-guard, then put the weapon to his shoulder and pointed it at the cow. It made a flash, and roared louder even than a hand-blaster, and the cow jerked convulsively and was dead. The man then indicated by signs that Hradzka was to drag the dead cow out of the stable, dig a hole, and bury it. This Hradzka did, carefully examining the wound in the cow's head-the weapon, he decided, was not an energy-weapon, but a simple solid-missile projector.

By evening, neither the man nor the woman were able to eat, and both seemed to be suffering intensely. The man used the communicating-instrument on the wall, probably calling on his friends for help. Hradzka did what he could to make them comfortable, cooked his own meal, washed the dishes as he had seen the woman doing, and tidied up the kitchen.

It was not long before people, men and women whom he had seen on the road or who had stopped at the farmhouse while he had been there, began arriving, some carrying baskets of food; and shortly after Hradzka had eaten, a vehicle like the farmer's, but in better condition and of better quality, arrived and a young man got out of it and entered the house, carrying a leather bag. He was apparently some sort of a scientist; he examined the man and his wife, asked many questions, and administered drugs. He also took samples for blood-tests and urinalysis. This, Hradzka considered, was another of the many contradictions he had encountered among these people-this man behaved like an educated scientist, and seemingly had nothing in common with the peasant herb-gatherer on the mountainside.

The fact was that Hradzka was worried. The strange death of the animals, the blight which had smitten the trees and vegetables around the farm, and the sickness of the farmer and his woman, all mystified him. He did not know of any disease which would affect plants and animals and humans; he wondered if some poisonous gas might not be escaping from the earth near the farmhouse. However, he had not, himself, been affected. He also disliked the way in which the doctor and the neighbors seemed to be talking about him. While he had come to a considerable revision of his original opinion about the culture-level of these people, it was not impossible that they might suspect him of having caused the whole thing by witchcraft; at any moment, they might fall upon him and put him to death. In any case, there was no longer any use in his staying here, and it might be wise if he left at once.

Accordingly, he filled his pockets with food from the pantry and slipped out of the farmhouse; before his absence was discovered he was well on his way down the road.

3

That night, Hradzka slept under a bridge across a fairly wide stream; the next morning, he followed the road until he came to a town. It was not a large place; there were perhaps four or five hundred houses and other buildings in it. Most of these were dwellings like the farmhouse where he had been staying, but some were much larger, and seemed to be places of business. One of these latter was a concrete structure with wide doors at the front; inside, he could see men working on the internal-combustion vehicles which seemed to be in almost universal use. Hradzka decided to obtain employment here.

It would be best, he decided, to continue his pretense of being a deaf-mute. He did not know whether a world-language were in use at this time or not, and even if not, the pretense of being a foreigner unable to speak the local dialect might be dangerous. So he entered the vehicle-repair shop and accosted a man in a clean shirt who seemed to be issuing instructions to the workers, going into his pantomime of the homeless mute seeking employment.

The master of the repair-shop merely laughed at him, however. Hradzka became more insistent in his manner, making signs to indicate his hunger and willingness to work. The other men in the shop left their tasks and gathered around; there was much laughter and unmistakably ribald and derogatory remarks. Hradzka was beginning to give up hope of getting employment here when one of the workmen approached the master and whispered something to him.

The two of them walked away, conversing in low voices. Hradzka thought he understood the situation; no doubt the workman, thinking to lighten his own labor, was urging that the vagrant be employed, for no other pay than food and lodging. At length, the master assented to his employee's urgings; he returned, showed Hradzka a hose and a bucket and sponges and cloths, and set him to work cleaning the mud from one of the vehicles. Then, after seeing that the work was being done properly, he went away, entering a room at one side of the shop.

About twenty minutes later, another man entered the shop. He was not dressed like any of the other people whom Hradzka had seen; he wore a gray tunic and breeches, polished black boots, and a cap with a visor and a metal insignia on it; on a belt, he carried a holstered weapon like a blaster.

After speaking to one of the workers, who pointed Hradzka out to him, he approached the fugitive and said something. Hradzka made gestures at his mouth and ears and made gargling sounds; the newcomer shrugged and motioned him to come with him, at the same time producing a pair of handcuffs from his belt and jingling them suggestively.

In a few seconds, Hradzka tried to analyze the situation and estimate its possibilities. The newcomer was a soldier, or, more likely, a policeman, since manacles were a part of his equipment. Evidently, since the evening before, a warning had been made public by means of communicating devices such as he had seen at the farm, advising people that a man of his description, pretending to be a deaf-mute, should be detained and the police notified; it had been for that reason that the workman had persuaded his master to employ Hradzka. No doubt he would be accused of causing the conditions at the farm by sorcery.

* * * * *

Hradzka shrugged and nodded, then went to the water-tap to turn off the hose he had been using. He disconnected it, coiled it and hung it up, and then picked up the water-bucket. Then, without warning, he hurled the water into the policeman's face, sprang forward, swinging the bucket by the bale, and hit the man on the head. Releasing his grip on the bucket, he tore the blaster or whatever it was from the holster.

One of the workers swung a hammer, as though to throw it. Hradzka aimed the weapon at him and pulled the trigger; the thing belched fire and kicked back painfully in his hand, and the man fell. He used it again to drop the policeman, then thrust it into the waistband of his trousers and ran outside. The thing was not a blaster at all, he realized-only a missile-projector like the big weapons at the farm, utilizing the force of some chemical explosive.

The policeman's vehicle was standing outside. It was a small, single-seat, two wheeled affair. Having become familiar with the principles of these hydro-carbon engines from examination of the vehicle of the farm, and accustomed as he was to far more complex mechanisms than this crude affair, Hradzka could see at a glance how to operate it. Springing onto the saddle, he kicked away the folding support and started the engine. Just as he did, the master of the repair-shop ran outside, one of the small hand-weapons in his hand, and fired several shots. They all missed, but Hradzka heard the whining sound of the missiles passing uncomfortably close to him.

It was imperative that he recover the blaster he had hidden in the hollow tree at the head of the valley. By this time, there would be a concerted search under way for him, and he needed a better weapon than the solid-missile projector he had taken from the policeman. He did not know how many shots the thing contained, but if it propelled solid missiles by chemical explosion, there could not have been more than five or six such charges in the cylindrical part of the weapon which he had assumed to be the charge-holder. On the other hand, his blaster, a weapon of much greater power, contained enough energy for five hundred blasts, and with it were eight extra energy-capsules, giving him a total of four thousand five hundred blasts.

Handling the two-wheeled vehicle was no particular problem; although he had never ridden on anything of the sort before, it was child's play compared to controlling a Hundredth Century strato-rocket, and Hradzka was a skilled rocket-pilot.

Several times he passed vehicles on the road-the passenger vehicles with enclosed cabins, and cargo-vehicles piled high with farm produce. Once he encountered a large number of children, gathered in front of a big red building with a flagstaff in front, from which a queer flag, with horizontal red and white stripes and a white-spotted blue device in the corner, flew. They scattered off the road in terror at his approach; fortunately, he hit none of them, for at the speed at which he was traveling, such a collision would have wrecked his light vehicle.

* * * * *

As he approached the farm where he had spent the past few days, he saw two passenger-vehicles standing by the road. One was a black one, similar to the one in which the physician had come to the farm, and the other was white with black trimmings and bore the same device he had seen on the cap of the policeman. A policeman was sitting in the driver's seat of this vehicle, and another policeman was standing beside it, breathing smoke with one of the white paper cylinders these people used. In the farm-yard, two men were going about with a square black box; to this box, a tube was connected by a wire, and they were passing the tube about over the ground.

The policeman who was standing beside the vehicle saw him approach, and blew his whistle, then drew the weapon from his belt. Hradzka, who had been expecting some attempt to halt him, had let go the right-hand steering handle and drawn his own weapon; as the policeman drew, he fired at him. Without observing the effect of the shot, he sped on; before he had rounded the bend above the farm, several shots were fired after him.

A mile beyond, he came to the place where he had hidden the blaster. He stopped the vehicle and jumped off, plunging into the brush and racing toward the hollow tree. Just as he reached it, he heard a vehicle approach and stop, and the door of the police vehicle slam. Hradzka's fingers found the belt of his blaster; he dragged it out and buckled it on, tossing away the missile weapon he had been carrying.

Then, crouching behind the tree, he waited. A few moments later, he caught a movement in the brush toward the road. He brought up the blaster, aimed and squeezed the trigger. There was a faint bluish glow at the muzzle, and a blast of energy tore through the brush, smashing the molecular structure of everything that stood in the way. There was an involuntary shout of alarm from the direction of the road; at least one of the policemen had escaped the blast. Hradzka holstered his weapon and crept away for some distance, keeping under cover, then turned and waited for some sign of the presence of his enemies. For some time nothing happened; he decided to turn hunter against the men who were hunting him. He started back in the direction of the road, making a wide circle, flitting silently from rock to bush and from bush to tree, stopping often to look and listen.

This finally brought him upon one of the policemen, and almost terminated his flight at the same time. He must have grown over-confident and careless; suddenly a weapon roared, and a missile smashed through the brush inches from his face. The shot had come from his left and a little to the rear. Whirling, he blasted four times, in rapid succession, then turned and fled for a few yards, dropping and crawling behind a rock. When he looked back, he could see wisps of smoke rising from the shattered trees and bushes which had absorbed the energy-output of his weapon, and he caught a faint odor of burned flesh. One of his pursuers, at least, would pursue him no longer.

He slipped away, down into the tangle of ravines and hollows in which he had wandered the day before his arrival at the farm. For the time being, he felt safe, and finally confident that he was not being pursued, he stopped to rest. The place where he stopped seemed familiar, and he looked about. In a moment, he recognized the little stream, the pool where he had bathed his feet, the clump of seedling pines under which he had slept. He even found the silver-foil wrapping from the food concentrate capsule.

But there had been a change, since the night when he had slept here. Then the young pines had been green and alive; now they were blighted, and their needles had turned brown. Hradzka stood for a long time, looking at them. It was the same blight that had touched the plants around the farmhouse. And here, among the pine needles on the ground, lay a dead bird.

It took some time for him to admit, to himself, the implications of vegetation, the chickens, the cow, the farmer and his wife, had all sickened and died. He had been in this place, and now, when he had returned, he found that death had followed him here, too.

* * * * *

During the early centuries of the Atomic Era, he knew, there had been great wars, the stories of which had survived even to the Hundredth Century. Among the weapons that had been used, there had been artificial plagues and epidemics, caused by new types of bacteria developed in laboratories, against which the victims had possessed no protection. Those germs and viruses had persisted for centuries, and gradually had lost their power to harm mankind. Suppose, now, that he had brought some of them back with him, to a century before they had been developed. Suppose, that was, that he were a human plague-carrier. He thought of the vermin that had infested the clothing he had taken from the man he had killed on the other side of the mountain; they had not troubled him after the first day.

There was a throbbing mechanical sound somewhere in the air; he looked about, and finally identified its source. A small aircraft had come over the valley from the other side of the mountain and was circling lazily overhead. He froze, shrinking back under a pine-tree; as long as he remained motionless, he would not be seen, and soon the thing would go away. He was beginning to understand why the search for him was being pressed so relentlessly; as long as he remained alive, he was a menace to everybody in this First Century world.

He got out his supply of food concentrates, saw that he had only three capsules left, and put them away again. For a long time, he sat under the dying tree, chewing on a twig and thinking. There must be some way in which he could overcome, or even utilize, his inherent deadliness to these people. He might find some isolated community, conceal himself near it, invade it at night and infect it, and then, when everybody was dead, move in and take it for himself. But was there any such isolated community? The farmhouse where he had worked had been fairly remote, yet its inhabitants had been in communication with the outside world, and the physician had come immediately in response to their call for help.

The little aircraft had been circling overhead, directly above the place where he lay hidden. For a while, Hradzka was afraid it had spotted him, and was debating the advisability of using his blaster on it. Then it banked, turned and went away. He watched it circle over the valley on the other side of the mountain, and got to his feet.

4

Almost at once, there was a new sound —a multiple throbbing, at a quick, snarling tempo that hinted at enormous power, growing louder each second. Hradzka stiffened and drew his blaster; as he did, five more aircraft swooped over the crest of the mountain and came rushing down toward him; not aimlessly, but as though they knew exactly where he was. As they approached, the leading edges of their wings sparkled with light, branches began flying from the trees about him, and there was a loud hammering noise.

He aimed a little in front of them and began blasting. A wing flew from one of the aircraft, and it plunged downward. Another came apart in the air; a third burst into flames. The other two zoomed upward quickly. Hradzka swung his blaster after them, blasting again and again. He hit a fourth with a blast of energy, knocking it to pieces, and then the fifth was out of range. He blasted at it twice, but without effect; a hand-blaster was only good for a thousand yards at the most.

Holstering his weapon, he hurried away, following the stream and keeping under cover of trees. The last of the attacking aircraft had gone away, but the little scout-plane was still circling about, well out of blaster-range.

Once or twice, Hradzka was compelled to stay hidden for some time, not knowing the nature of the pilot's ability to detect him. It was during one of these waits that the next phase of the attack developed.

It began, like the last one, with a distant roar that swelled in volume until it seemed to fill the whole world. Then, fifteen or twenty thousand feet out of blaster-range, the new attackers swept into sight.

There must have been fifty of them, huge tapering things with wide-spread wings, flying in close formation, wave after V-shaped wave. He stood and stared at them, amazed; he had never imagined that such aircraft existed in the First Century. Then a high-pitched screaming sound cut through the roar of the propellers, and for an instant he saw countless small specks in the sky, falling downward.

The first bomb-salvo landed in the young pines, where he had fought against the first air attack. Great gouts of flame shot upward, and smoke, and flying earth and debris. Hradzka turned and started to run. Another salvo fell in front of him; he veered to the left and plunged on through the undergrowth. Now the bombs were falling all about him, deafening him with their thunder, shaking him with concussion. He dodged, frightened, as the trunk of a tree came crashing down beside him. Then something hit him across the back, knocking him flat. For a moment, he lay stunned, then tried to rise. As he did, a searing light filled his eyes and a wave of intolerable heat swept over him. Then darkness....

* * * * *

"No, Zarvas Pol," Kradzy Zago repeated. "Hradzka will not return; the 'time-machine' was sabotaged."

"So? By you?" the soldier asked.

The scientist nodded. "I knew the purpose for which he intended it. Hradzka was not content with having enslaved a whole Solar System: he hungered to bring tyranny and serfdom to all the past and all the future as well; he wanted to be master not only of the present but of the centuries that were and were to be, as well. I never took part in politics, Zarvas Pol; I had no hand in this revolt. But I could not be party to such a crime as Hradzka contemplated when it lay within my power to prevent it."

"The machine will take him out of our space-time continuum, or back to a time when this planet was a swirling cloud of flaming gas?" Zarvas Pol asked.

Kradzy Zago shook his head. "No, the unit is not powerful enough for that. It will only take him about ten thousand years into the past. But then, when it stops, the machine will destroy itself. It may destroy Hradzka with it or he may escape. But if he does, he will be left stranded ten thousand years ago, when he can do us no harm.

"Actually, it did not operate as he imagined and there is an infinitely small chance that he could have returned to our 'time', in any event. But I wanted to insure against even so small a chance."

"We can't be sure of that," Zarvas Pol objected. "He may know more about the machine than you think; enough more to build another like it. So you must build me a machine and I'll take back a party of volunteers and hunt him down."

"That would not be necessary, and you would only share his fate." Then, apparently changing the subject, Kradzy Zago asked: "Tell me, Zarvas Pol; have you never heard the legends of the Deadly Radiations?"

General Zarvas smiled. "Who has not? Every cadet at the Officers' College dreams of re-discovering them, to use as a weapon, but nobody ever has. We hear these tales of how, in the early days, atomic engines and piles and fission-bombs emitted particles which were utterly deadly, which would make anything with which they came in contact deadly, which would bring a horrible death to any human being. But these are only myths. All the ancient experiments have been duplicated time and again, and the deadly radiation effect has never been observed. Some say that it is a mere old-wives' terror tale; some say that the deaths were caused by fear of atomic energy, when it was still unfamiliar; others contend that the fundamental nature of atomic energy has altered by the degeneration of the fissionable matter. For my own part, I'm not enough of a scientist to have an opinion."

* * * * *

The old one smiled wanly. "None of these theories are correct. In the beginning of the Atomic Era, the Deadly Radiations existed. They still exist, but they are no longer deadly, because all life on this planet has adapted itself to such radiations, and all living things are now immune to them."

"And Hradzka has returned to a time when such immunity did not exist? But would that not be to his advantage?"

"Remember, General, that man has been using atomic energy for ten thousand years. Our whole world has become drenched with radioactivity. The planet, the seas, the atmosphere, and every living thing, are all radioactive, now. Radioactivity is as natural to us as the air we breathe. Now, you remember hearing of the great wars of the first centuries of the Atomic Era, in which whole nations were wiped out, leaving only hundreds of survivors out of millions. You, no doubt, think that such tales are products of ignorant and barbaric imagination, but I assure you, they are literally true. It was not the blast-effect of a few bombs which created such holocausts, but the radiations released by the bombs. And those who survived to carry on the race were men and women whose systems resisted the radiations, and they transmitted to their progeny that power of resistance. In many cases, their children were mutants-not monsters, although there were many of them, too, which did not survive-but humans who were immune to radioactivity."

"An interesting theory, Kradzy Zago," the soldier commented. "And one which conforms both to what we know of atomic energy and to the ancient legends. Then you would say that those radiations are still deadly-to the non-immune?"

"Exactly. And Hradzka, his body emitting those radiations, has returned to the First Century of the Atomic Era-to a world without immunity."

General Zarvas' smile vanished. "Man!" he cried in horror. "You have loosed a carrier of death among those innocent people of the past!"

Kradzy Zago nodded. "That is true. I estimate that Hradzka will probably cause the death of a hundred or so people, before he is dealt with. But dealt with he will be. Tell me, General; if a man should appear now, out of nowhere, spreading a strange and horrible plague wherever he went, what would you do?"

"Why, I'd hunt him down and kill him," General Zarvas replied. "Not for anything he did, but for the menace he was. And then, I'd cover his body with a mass of concrete bigger than this palace."

"Precisely." Kradzy Zago smiled. "And the military commanders and political leaders of the First Century were no less ruthless or efficient than you. You know how atomic energy was first used? There was an ancient nation, upon the ruins of whose cities we have built our own, which was famed for its idealistic humanitarianism. Yet that nation, treacherously attacked, created the first atomic bombs in self defense, and used them. It is among the people of that nation that Hradzka has emerged."

"But would they recognize him as the cause of the calamity he brings among them?"

"Of course. He will emerge at the time when atomic energy is first being used. They will have detectors for the Deadly Radiations-detectors we know nothing of, today, for a detection instrument must be free from the thing it is intended to detect, and today everything is radioactive. It will be a day or so before they discover what is happening to them, and not a few will die in that time, I fear; but once they have found out what is killing their people, Hradzka's days-no, his hours-will be numbered."

"A mass of concrete bigger than this place," Tobbh the Slave repeated General Zarvas' words. "*The Ancient Spaceport!*"

Prince Burvanny clapped him on the shoulder. "Tobbh, man! You've hit it!"

"You mean...?" Kradzy Zago began.

"Yes. You all know of it. It's stood for nobody knows how many millennia, and nobody's ever decided what it was, to begin with, except that somebody, once, filled a valley with concrete, level from mountain-top to mountain-top. The accepted theory is that it was done for a firing-stand for the first Moon-rocket. But gentlemen, our friend Tobbh's explained it. It is the tomb of Hradzka, and it has been the tomb of Hradzka for ten thousand years before Hradzka was born!"

Philip K. Dick

The Skull

"What is this opportunity?" Conger asked. "Go on. I'm interested."

The room was silent; all faces were fixed on Conger-still in the drab prison uniform. The Speaker leaned forward slowly.

"Before you went to prison your trading business was paying well-all illegal-all very profitable. Now you have nothing, except the prospect of another six years in a cell."

Conger scowled.

"There is a certain situation, very important to this Council, that requires your peculiar abilities. Also, it is a situation you might find interesting. You were a hunter, were you not? You've done a great deal of trapping, hiding in the bushes, waiting at night for the game? I imagine hunting must be a source of satisfaction to you, the chase, the stalking —"

Conger sighed. His lips twisted. "All right," he said. "Leave that out. Get to the point. Who do you want me to kill?"

The Speaker smiled. "All in proper sequence," he said softly.

* * * * *

The car slid to a stop. It was night; there was no light anywhere along the street. Conger looked out. "Where are we? What is this place?"

The hand of the guard pressed into his arm. "Come. Through that door."

Conger stepped down, onto the damp sidewalk. The guard came swiftly after him, and then the Speaker. Conger took a deep breath of the cold air. He studied the dim outline of the building rising up before them.

"I know this place. I've seen it before." He squinted, his eyes growing accustomed to the dark. Suddenly he became alert. "This is —"

"Yes. The First Church." The Speaker walked toward the steps. "We're expected."

"Expected? *Here?*"

"Yes." The Speaker mounted the stairs. "You know we're not allowed in their Churches, especially with guns!" He stopped. Two armed soldiers loomed up ahead, one on each side.

"All right?" The Speaker looked up at them. They nodded. The door of the Church was open. Conger could see other soldiers inside, standing about, young soldiers with large eyes, gazing at the ikons and holy images.

"I see," he said.

"It was necessary," the Speaker said. "As you know, we have been singularly unfortunate in the past in our relations with the First Church."

"This won't help."

"But it's worth it. You will see."

* * * * *

They passed through the hall and into the main chamber where the altar piece was, and the kneeling places. The Speaker scarcely glanced at the altar as they passed by. He pushed open a small side door and beckoned Conger through.

"In here. We have to hurry. The faithful will be flocking in soon."

Conger entered, blinking. They were in a small chamber, low-ceilinged, with dark panels of old wood. There was a smell of ashes and smoldering spices in the room. He sniffed. "What's that? The smell."

"Cups on the wall. I don't know." The Speaker crossed impatiently to the far side. "According to our information, it is hidden here by this —"

Conger looked around the room. He saw books and papers, holy signs and images. A strange low shiver went through him.

"Does my job involve anyone of the Church? If it does —"

The Speaker turned, astonished. "Can it be that you believe in the Founder? Is it possible, a hunter, a killer —"

"No. Of course not. All their business about resignation to death, non-violence —"

"What is it, then?"

Conger shrugged. "I've been taught not to mix with such as these. They have strange abilities. And you can't reason with them."

The Speaker studied Conger thoughtfully. "You have the wrong idea. It is no one here that we have in mind. We've found that killing them only tends to increase their numbers."

"Then why come here? Let's leave."

"No. We came for something important. Something you will need to identify your man. Without it you won't be able to find him." A trace of a smile crossed the Speaker's face. "We don't want you to kill the wrong person. It's too important."

"I don't make mistakes." Conger's chest rose. "Listen, Speaker —"

"This is an unusual situation," the Speaker said. "You see, the person you are after-the person that we are sending you to find-is known only by certain objects here. They are the only traces, the only means of identification. Without them —"

"What are they?"

He came toward the Speaker. The Speaker moved to one side. "Look," he said. He drew a sliding wall away, showing a dark square hole. "In there."

Conger squatted down, staring in. He frowned. "A skull! A skeleton!"

"The man you are after has been dead for two centuries," the Speaker said. "This is all that remains of him. And this is all you have with which to find him."

For a long time Conger said nothing. He stared down at the bones, dimly visible in the recess of the wall. How could a man dead centuries be killed? How could he be stalked, brought down?

Conger was a hunter, a man who had lived as he pleased, where he pleased. He had kept himself alive by trading, bringing furs and pelts in from the Provinces on his own ship, riding at high speed, slipping through the customs line around Earth.

He had hunted in the great mountains of the moon. He had stalked through empty Martian cities. He had explored —

The Speaker said, "Soldier, take these objects and have them carried to the car. Don't lose any part of them."

The soldier went into the cupboard, reaching gingerly, squatting on his heels.

"It is my hope," the Speaker continued softly, to Conger, "that you will demonstrate your loyalty to us, now. There are always ways for citizens to restore themselves, to show their devotion to their society. For you I think this would be a very good chance. I seriously doubt that a better one will come. And for your efforts there will be quite a restitution, of course."

The two men looked at each other; Conger, thin, unkempt, the Speaker immaculate in his uniform.

"I understand you," Conger said. "I mean, I understand this part, about the chance. But how can a man who has been dead two centuries be —"

"I'll explain later," the Speaker said. "Right now we have to hurry!" The soldier had gone out with the bones, wrapped in a blanket held carefully in his arms. The Speaker walked to the door. "Come. They've already discovered that we've broken in here, and they'll be coming at any moment."

They hurried down the damp steps to the waiting car. A second later the driver lifted the car up into the air, above the house-tops.

* * * * *

The Speaker settled back in the seat.

"The First Church has an interesting past," he said. "I suppose you are familiar with it, but I'd like to speak of a few points that are of relevancy to us.

"It was in the twentieth century that the Movement began-during one of the periodic wars. The Movement developed rapidly, feeding on the general sense of futility, the realization that each war was breeding greater war, with no end in sight. The Movement posed a simple answer to the problem: Without military preparations-weapons-there could be no war. And without machinery and complex scientific technocracy there could be no weapons.

"The Movement preached that you couldn't stop war by planning for it. They preached that man was losing to his machinery and science, that it was getting away from him, pushing him into greater and greater wars. Down with society, they shouted. Down with factories and science! A few more wars and there wouldn't be much left of the world.

"The Founder was an obscure person from a small town in the American Middle West. We don't even know his name. All we know is that one day he appeared, preaching a doctrine of non-violence, non-resistance; no fighting, no paying taxes for guns, no research except for medicine. Live out your life quietly, tending your garden, staying out of public affairs; mind your own business. Be obscure, unknown, poor. Give away most of your possessions, leave the city. At least that was what developed from what he told the people."

The car dropped down and landed on a roof.

"The Founder preached this doctrine, or the germ of it; there's no telling how much the faithful have added themselves. The local authorities picked him up at once, of course. Apparently they were convinced that he meant it; he was never released. He was put to death, and his body buried secretly. It seemed that the cult was finished."

The Speaker smiled. "Unfortunately, some of his disciples reported seeing him after the date of his death. The rumor spread; he had conquered death, he was divine. It took hold, grew. And here we are today, with a First Church, obstructing all social progress, destroying society, sowing the seeds of anarchy —"

"But the wars," Conger said. "About them?"

"The wars? Well, there were no more wars. It must be acknowledged that the elimination of war was the direct result of non-violence practiced on a general scale. But we can take a more objective view of war today. What was so terrible about it? War had a profound selective value, perfectly in accord with the teachings of Darwin and Mendel and others. Without war the mass of useless, incompetent mankind, without training or intelligence, is permitted to grow and expand unchecked. War acted to reduce their numbers; like storms and earthquakes and droughts, it was nature's way of eliminating the unfit.

"Without war the lower elements of mankind have increased all out of proportion. They threaten the educated few, those with scientific knowledge and training, the ones equipped to direct society. They have no regard for science or a scientific society, based on reason. And this Movement seeks to aid and abet them. Only when scientists are in full control can the —"

* * * * *

He looked at his watch and then kicked the car door open. "I'll tell you the rest as we walk."

They crossed the dark roof. "Doubtless you now know whom those bones belonged to, who it is that we are after. He has been dead just two centuries, now, this ignorant man from the Middle West, this Founder. The tragedy is that the authorities of the time acted too slowly. They allowed him to speak, to get his message across. He was allowed to preach, to start his cult. And once such a thing is under way, there's no stopping it.

"But what if he had died before he preached? What if none of his doctrines had ever been spoken? It took only a moment for him to utter them, that we know. They say he spoke just once, just one time. *Then* the authorities came, taking him away. He offered no resistance; the incident was small."

The Speaker turned to Conger.

"Small, but we're reaping the consequences of it today."

They went inside the building. Inside, the soldiers had already laid out the skeleton on a table. The soldiers stood around it, their young faces intense.

Conger went over to the table, pushing past them. He bent down, staring at the bones. "So these are his remains," he murmured. "The Founder. The Church has hidden them for two centuries."

"Quite so," the Speaker said. "But now we have them. Come along down the hall."

They went across the room to a door. The Speaker pushed it open. Technicians looked up. Conger saw machinery, whirring and turning; benches and retorts. In the center of the room was a gleaming crystal cage.

The Speaker handed a Slem-gun to Conger. "The important thing to remember is that the skull must be saved and brought back-for comparison and proof. Aim low-at the chest."

Conger weighed the gun in his hands. "It feels good," he said. "I know this gun-that is, I've seen them before, but I never used one."

The Speaker nodded. "You will be instructed on the use of the gun and the operation of the cage. You will be given all data we have on the time and location. The exact spot was a place called Hudson's field. About 1960 in a small community outside Denver, Colorado. And don't forget-the only means of identification you will have will be the skull. There are visible characteristics of the front teeth, especially the left incisor —"

Conger listened absently. He was watching two men in white carefully wrapping the skull in a plastic bag. They tied it and carried it into the crystal cage. "And if I should make a mistake?"

"Pick the wrong man? Then find the right one. Don't come back until you succeed in reaching this Founder. And you can't wait for him to start speaking; that's what we must avoid! You must act in advance. Take chances; shoot as soon as you think you've found him. He'll be someone unusual, probably a stranger in the area. Apparently he wasn't known."

Conger listened dimly.

"Do you think you have it all now?" the Speaker asked.

"Yes. I think so." Conger entered the crystal cage and sat down, placing his hands on the wheel.

"Good luck," the Speaker said.

"We'll be awaiting the outcome. There's some philosophical doubt as to whether one can alter the past. This should answer the question once and for all."

Conger fingered the controls of the cage.

"By the way," the Speaker said. "Don't try to use this cage for purposes not anticipated in your job. We have a constant trace on it. If we want it back, we can get it back. Good luck."

Conger said nothing. The cage was sealed. He raised his finger and touched the wheel control. He turned the wheel carefully.

He was still staring at the plastic bag when the room outside vanished.

For a long time there was nothing at all. Nothing beyond the crystal mesh of the cage. Thoughts rushed through Conger's mind, helter-skelter. How would he know the man? How could he be certain, in advance? What had he looked like? What was his name? How had he acted, before he spoke? Would he be an ordinary person, or some strange outlandish crank?

Conger picked up the Slem-gun and held it against his cheek. The metal of the gun was cool and smooth. He practiced moving the sight. It was a beautiful gun, the kind of gun he could fall in love with. If he had owned such a gun in the Martian desert-on the long nights when he had lain, cramped and numbed with cold, waiting for things that moved through the darkness —

He put the gun down and adjusted the meter readings of the cage. The spiraling mist was beginning to condense and settle. All at once forms wavered and fluttered around him.

Colors, sounds, movements filtered through the crystal wire. He clamped the controls off and stood up.

* * * * *

He was on a ridge overlooking a small town. It was high noon. The air was crisp and bright. A few automobiles moved along a road. Off in the distance were some level fields. Conger went to the door and stepped outside. He sniffed the air. Then he went back into the cage.

He stood before the mirror over the shelf, examining his features. He had trimmed his beard-they had not got him to cut it off-and his hair was neat. He was dressed in the clothing of the middle-twentieth century, the odd collar and coat, the shoes of animal hide. In his pocket was money of the times. That was important. Nothing more was needed.

Nothing, except his ability, his special cunning. But he had never used it in such a way before.

He walked down the road toward the town.

The first things he noticed were the newspapers on the stands. April 5, 1961. He was not too far off. He looked around him. There was a filling station, a garage, some taverns, and a ten-cent store. Down the street was a grocery store and some public buildings.

A few minutes later he mounted the stairs of the little public library and passed through the doors into the warm interior.

The librarian looked up, smiling.

"Good afternoon," she said.

He smiled, not speaking because his words would not be correct; accented and strange, probably. He went over to a table and sat down by a heap of magazines. For a moment he glanced through them. Then he was on his feet again. He crossed the room to a wide rack against the wall. His heart began to beat heavily.

Newspapers-weeks on end. He took a roll of them over to the table and began to scan them quickly. The print was odd, the letters strange. Some of the words were unfamiliar.

He set the papers aside and searched farther. At last he found what he wanted. He carried the *Cherrywood Gazette* to the table and opened it to the first page. He found what he wanted:

PRISONER HANGS SELF

An unidentified man, held by the county sheriff's office for suspicion of criminal syndicalism, was found dead this morning, by —

He finished the item. It was vague, uninforming. He needed more. He carried the *Gazette* back to the racks and then, after a moment's hesitation, approached the librarian.

"More?" he asked. "More papers. Old ones?"

She frowned. "How old? Which papers?"

"Months old. And-before."

"Of the *Gazette*? This is all we have. What did you want? What are you looking for? Maybe I can help you."

He was silent.

"You might find older issues at the *Gazette* office," the woman said, taking off her glasses. "Why don't you try there? But if you'd tell me, maybe I could help you —"

He went out.

The *Gazette* office was down a side street; the sidewalk was broken and cracked. He went inside. A heater glowed in the corner of the small office. A heavy-set man stood up and came slowly over to the counter.

"What did you want, mister?" he said.

"Old papers. A month. Or more."

"To buy? You want to buy them?"

"Yes." He held out some of the money he had. The man stared.

"Sure," he said. "Sure. Wait a minute." He went quickly out of the room. When he came back he was staggering under the weight of his armload, his face red. "Here are some," he grunted. "Took what I could find. Covers the whole year. And if you want more —"

Conger carried the papers outside. He sat down by the road and began to go through them.

What he wanted was four months back, in December. It was a tiny item, so small that he almost missed it. His hands trembled as he scanned it, using the small dictionary for some of the archaic terms.

MAN ARRESTED FOR UNLICENSED DEMONSTRATION

An unidentified man who refused to give his name was picked up in Cooper Creek by special agents of the sheriff's office, according to Sheriff Duff. It was said the man was recently noticed in this area and had been watched continually. It was —

Cooper Creek. December, 1960. His heart pounded. That was all he needed to know. He stood up, shaking himself, stamping his feet on the cold ground. The sun had moved across the sky to the very edge of the hills. He smiled. Already he had discovered the exact time and place. Now he needed only to go back, perhaps to November, to Cooper Creek —

He walked back through the main section of town, past the library, past the grocery store. It would not be hard; the hard part was over. He would go there; rent a room, prepare to wait until the man appeared.

He turned the corner. A woman was coming out of a doorway, loaded down with packages. Conger stepped aside to let her pass. The woman glanced at him. Suddenly her face turned white. She stared, her mouth open.

Conger hurried on. He looked back. What was wrong with her? The woman was still staring; she had dropped the packages to the ground. He increased his speed. He turned a second corner and went up a side street. When he looked back again the woman had come to the entrance of the street and was starting after him. A man joined her, and the two of them began to run toward him.

He lost them and left the town, striding quickly, easily, up into the hills at the edge of town. When he reached the cage he stopped. What had happened? Was it something about his clothing? His dress?

He pondered. Then, as the sun set, he stepped into the cage.

Conger sat before the wheel. For a moment he waited, his hands resting lightly on the control. Then he turned the wheel, just a little, following the control readings carefully.

The grayness settled down around him.

But not for very long.

* * * * *

The man looked him over critically. "You better come inside," he said. "Out of the cold."

"Thanks." Conger went gratefully through the open door, into the living-room. It was warm and close from the heat of the little kerosene heater in the corner. A woman, large and shapeless in her flowered dress, came from the kitchen. She and the man studied him critically.

"It's a good room," the woman said. "I'm Mrs. Appleton. It's got heat. You need that this time of year."

"Yes." He nodded, looking around.

"You want to eat with us?"

"What?"

"You want to eat with us?" The man's brows knitted. "You're not a foreigner, are you, mister?"

"No." He smiled. "I was born in this country. Quite far west, though."

"California?"

"No." He hesitated. "In Oregon."

"What's it like up there?" Mrs. Appleton asked. "I hear there's a lot of trees and green. It's so barren here. I come from Chicago, myself."

"That's the Middle West," the man said to her. "You ain't no foreigner."

"Oregon isn't foreign, either," Conger said. "It's part of the United States."

The man nodded absently. He was staring at Conger's clothing.

"That's a funny suit you got on, mister," he said. "Where'd you get that?"

Conger was lost. He shifted uneasily. "It's a good suit," he said. "Maybe I better go some other place, if you don't want me here."

They both raised their hands protestingly. The woman smiled at him. "We just have to look out for those Reds. You know, the government is always warning us about them."

"The Reds?" He was puzzled.

"The government says they're all around. We're supposed to report anything strange or unusual, anybody doesn't act normal."

"Like me?"

They looked embarrassed. "Well, you don't look like a Red to me," the man said. "But we have to be careful. The *Tribune* says —"

Conger half listened. It was going to be easier than he had thought. Clearly, he would know as soon as the Founder appeared. These people, so suspicious of anything different, would be buzzing and gossiping and spreading the story. All he had to do was lie low and listen, down at the general store, perhaps. Or even here, in Mrs. Appleton's boarding house.

"Can I see the room?" he said.

"Certainly." Mrs. Appleton went to the stairs. "I'll be glad to show it to you."

They went upstairs. It was colder upstairs, but not nearly as cold as outside. Nor as cold as nights on the Martian deserts. For that he was grateful.

* * * * *

He was walking slowly around the store, looking at the cans of vegetables, the frozen packages of fish and meats shining and clean in the open refrigerator counters.

Ed Davies came toward him. "Can I help you?" he said. The man was a little oddly dressed, and with a beard! Ed couldn't help smiling.

"Nothing," the man said in a funny voice. "Just looking."

"Sure," Ed said. He walked back behind the counter. Mrs. Hacket was wheeling her cart up.

"Who's he?" she whispered, her sharp face turned, her nose moving, as if it were sniffing. "I never seen him before."

"I don't know."

"Looks funny to me. Why does he wear a beard? No one else wears a beard. Must be something the matter with him."

"Maybe he likes to wear a beard. I had an uncle who —"

"Wait." Mrs. Hacket stiffened. "Didn't that-what was his name? The Red-that old one. Didn't he have a beard? Marx. He had a beard."

Ed laughed. "This ain't Karl Marx. I saw a photograph of him once."

Mrs. Hacket was staring at him. "You did?"

"Sure." He flushed a little. "What's the matter with that?"

"I'd sure like to know more about him," Mrs. Hacket said. "I think we ought to know more, for our own good."

* * * * *

"Hey, mister! Want a ride?"

Conger turned quickly, dropping his hand to his belt. He relaxed. Two young kids in a car, a girl and a boy. He smiled at them. "A ride? Sure."

Conger got into the car and closed the door. Bill Willet pushed the gas and the car roared down the highway.

"I appreciate a ride," Conger said carefully. "I was taking a walk between towns, but it was farther than I thought."

"Where are you from?" Lora Hunt asked. She was pretty, small and dark, in her yellow sweater and blue skirt.

"From Cooper Creek."

"Cooper Creek?" Bill said. He frowned. "That's funny. I don't remember seeing you before."

"Why, do you come from there?"

"I was born there. I know everybody there."

"I just moved in. From Oregon."

"From Oregon? I didn't know Oregon people had accents."

"Do I have an accent?"

"You use words funny."

"How?"

"I don't know. Doesn't he, Lora?"

"You slur them," Lora said, smiling. "Talk some more. I'm interested in dialects." She glanced at him, white-teethed. Conger felt his heart constrict.

"I have a speech impediment."

"Oh." Her eyes widened. "I'm sorry."

They looked at him curiously as the car purred along. Conger for his part was struggling to find some way of asking them questions without seeming curious. "I guess people from out of town don't come here much," he said. "Strangers."

"No." Bill shook his head. "Not very much."

"I'll bet I'm the first outsider for a long time."

"I guess so."

Conger hesitated. "A friend of mine-someone I know, might be coming through here. Where do you suppose I might —" He stopped. "Would there be anyone certain to see him? Someone I could ask, make sure I don't miss him if he comes?"

They were puzzled. "Just keep your eyes open. Cooper Creek isn't very big."

"No. That's right."

They drove in silence. Conger studied the outline of the girl. Probably she was the boy's mistress. Perhaps she was his trial wife. Or had they developed trial marriage back so far? He could not remember. But surely such an attractive girl would be someone's mistress by this time; she would be sixteen or so, by her looks. He might ask her sometime, if they ever met again.

* * * * *

The next day Conger went walking along the one main street of Cooper Creek. He passed the general store, the two filling stations, and then the post office. At the corner was the soda fountain.

He stopped. Lora was sitting inside, talking to the clerk. She was laughing, rocking back and forth.

Conger pushed the door open. Warm air rushed around him. Lora was drinking hot chocolate, with whipped cream. She looked up in surprise as he slid into the seat beside her.

"I beg your pardon," he said. "Am I intruding?"

"No." She shook her head. Her eyes were large and dark. "Not at all."

The clerk came over. "What do you want?"

Conger looked at the chocolate. "Same as she has."

Lora was watching Conger, her arms folded, elbows on the counter. She smiled at him. "By the way. You don't know my name. Lora Hunt."

She was holding out her hand. He took it awkwardly, not knowing what to do with it. "Conger is my name," he murmured.

"Conger? Is that your last or first name?"

"Last or first?" He hesitated. "Last. Omar Conger."

"Omar?" She laughed. "That's like the poet, Omar Khayyam."

"I don't know of him. I know very little of poets. We restored very few works of art. Usually only the Church has been interested enough —" He broke off. She was staring. He flushed. "Where I come from," he finished.

"The Church? Which church do you mean?"

"The Church." He was confused. The chocolate came and he began to sip it gratefully. Lora was still watching him.

"You're an unusual person," she said. "Bill didn't like you, but he never likes anything different. He's so-so prosaic. Don't you think that when a person gets older he should become broadened in his outlook?"

Conger nodded.

"He says foreign people ought to stay where they belong, not come here. But you're not so foreign. He means orientals; you know."

Conger nodded.

The screen door opened behind them. Bill came into the room. He stared at them. "Well," he said.

Conger turned. "Hello."

"Well." Bill sat down. "Hello, Lora." He was looking at Conger. "I didn't expect to see you here."

Conger tensed. He could feel the hostility of the boy. "Something wrong with that?"

"No. Nothing wrong with it."

There was silence. Suddenly Bill turned to Lora. "Come on. Let's go."

"Go?" She was astonished. "Why?"

"Just go!" He grabbed her hand. "Come on! The car's outside."

"Why, Bill Willet," Lora said. "You're jealous!"

"Who is this guy?" Bill said. "Do you know anything about him? Look at him, his beard —"

She flared. "So what? Just because he doesn't drive a Packard and go to Cooper High!"

Conger sized the boy up. He was big-big and strong. Probably he was part of some civil control organization.

"Sorry," Conger said. "I'll go."

"What's your business in town?" Bill asked. "What are you doing here? Why are you hanging around Lora?"

Conger looked at the girl. He shrugged. "No reason. I'll see you later."

He turned away. And froze. Bill had moved. Conger's fingers went to his belt. *Half pressure,* he whispered to himself. *No more. Half pressure.*

He squeezed. The room leaped around him. He himself was protected by the lining of his clothing, the plastic sheathing inside.

"My God —" Lora put her hands up. Conger cursed. He hadn't meant any of it for her. But it would wear off. There was only a half-amp to it. It would tingle.

Tingle, and paralyze.

He walked out the door without looking back. He was almost to the corner when Bill came slowly out, holding onto the wall like a drunken man. Conger went on.

* * * * *

As Conger walked, restless, in the night, a form loomed in front of him. He stopped, holding his breath.

"Who is it?" a man's voice came. Conger waited, tense.

"Who is it?" the man said again. He clicked something in his hand. A light flashed. Conger moved.

"It's me," he said.

"Who is 'me'?"

"Conger is my name. I'm staying at the Appleton's place. Who are you?"

The man came slowly up to him. He was wearing a leather jacket. There was a gun at his waist.

"I'm Sheriff Duff. I think you're the person I want to talk to. You were in Bloom's today, about three o'clock?"

"Bloom's?"

"The fountain. Where the kids hang out." Duff came up beside him, shining his light into Conger's face. Conger blinked.

"Turn that thing away," he said.

A pause. "All right." The light flickered to the ground. "You were there. Some trouble broke out between you and the Willet boy. Is that right? You had a beef over his girl —"

"We had a discussion," Conger said carefully.

"Then what happened?"

"Why?"

"I'm just curious. They say you did something."

"Did something? Did what?"

"I don't know. That's what I'm wondering. They saw a flash, and something seemed to happen. They all blacked out. Couldn't move."

"How are they now?"

"All right."

There was silence.

"Well?" Duff said. "What was it? A bomb?"

"A bomb?" Conger laughed. "No. My cigarette lighter caught fire. There was a leak, and the fluid ignited."

"Why did they all pass out?"

"Fumes."

Silence. Conger shifted, waiting. His fingers moved slowly toward his belt. The Sheriff glanced down. He grunted.

"If you say so," he said. "Anyhow, there wasn't any real harm done." He stepped back from Conger. "And that Willet is a trouble-maker."

"Good night, then," Conger said. He started past the Sheriff.

"One more thing, Mr. Conger. Before you go. You don't mind if I look at your identification, do you?"

"No. Not at all." Conger reached into his pocket. He held his wallet out. The Sheriff took it and shined his flashlight on it. Conger watched, breathing shallowly. They had worked hard on the wallet, studying historic documents, relics of the times, all the papers they felt would be relevant.

Duff handed it back. "Okay. Sorry to bother you." The light winked off.

When Conger reached the house he found the Appletons sitting around the television set. They did not look up as he came in. He lingered at the door.

"Can I ask you something?" he said. Mrs. Appleton turned slowly. "Can I ask you-what's the date?"

"The date?" She studied him. "The first of December."

"December first! Why, it was just November!"

They were all looking at him. Suddenly he remembered. In the twentieth century they still used the old twelve-month system. November fed directly into December; there was no Quartember between.

He gasped. Then it was tomorrow! The second of December! Tomorrow!

"Thanks," he said. "Thanks."

He went up the stairs. What a fool he was, forgetting. The Founder had been taken into captivity on the second of December, according to the newspaper records. Tomorrow, only twelve hours hence, the Founder would appear to speak to the people and then be dragged away.

* * * * *

The day was warm and bright. Conger's shoes crunched the melting crust of snow. On he went, through the trees heavy with white. He climbed a hill and strode down the other side, sliding as he went.

He stopped to look around. Everything was silent. There was no one in sight. He brought a thin rod from his waist and turned the handle of it. For a moment nothing happened. Then there was a shimmering in the air.

The crystal cage appeared and settled slowly down. Conger sighed. It was good to see it again. After all, it was his only way back.

He walked up on the ridge. He looked around with some satisfaction, his hands on his hips. Hudson's field was spread out, all the way to the beginning of town. It was bare and flat, covered with a thin layer of snow.

Here, the Founder would come. Here, he would speak to them. And here the authorities would take him.

Only he would be dead before they came. He would be dead before he even spoke.

Conger returned to the crystal globe. He pushed through the door and stepped inside. He took the Slem-gun from the shelf and screwed the bolt into place. It was ready to go, ready to fire. For a moment he considered. Should he have it with him?

No. It might be hours before the Founder came, and suppose someone approached him in the meantime? When he saw the Founder coming toward the field, then he could go and get the gun.

Conger looked toward the shelf. There was the neat plastic package. He took it down and unwrapped it.

He held the skull in his hands, turning it over. In spite of himself, a cold feeling rushed through him. This was the man's skull, the skull of the Founder, who was still alive, who would come here, this day, who would stand on the field not fifty yards away.

What if *he* could see this, his own skull, yellow and eroded? Two centuries old. Would he still speak? Would he speak, if he could see it, the grinning, aged skull? What would there be for him to say, to tell the people? What message could he bring?

What action would not be futile, when a man could look upon his own aged, yellowed skull? Better they should enjoy their temporary lives, while they still had them to enjoy.

A man who could hold his own skull in his hands would believe in few causes, few movements. Rather, he would preach the opposite —

A sound. Conger dropped the skull back on the shelf and took up the gun. Outside something was moving. He went quickly to the door, his heart beating. Was it *he*? Was it the Founder, wandering by himself in the cold, looking for a place to speak? Was he meditating over his words, choosing his sentences?

What if he could see what Conger had held!

He pushed the door open, the gun raised.

Lora!

He stared at her. She was dressed in a wool jacket and boots, her hands in her pockets. A cloud of steam came from her mouth and nostrils. Her breast was rising and falling.

Silently, they looked at each other. At last Conger lowered the gun.

"What is it?" he said. "What are you doing here?"

She pointed. She did not seem able to speak. He frowned; what was wrong with her?

"What is it?" he said. "What do you want?" He looked in the direction she had pointed. "I don't see anything."

"They're coming."

"They? Who? Who are coming?"

"They are. The police. During the night the Sheriff had the state police send cars. All around, everywhere. Blocking the roads. There's about sixty of them coming. Some from town, some around behind." She stopped, gasping. "They said-they said —"

"What?"

"They said you were some kind of a Communist. They said —"

* * * * *

Conger went into the cage. He put the gun down on the shelf and came back out. He leaped down and went to the girl.

"Thanks. You came here to tell me? You don't believe it?"

"I don't know."

"Did you come alone?"

"No. Joe brought me in his truck. From town."

"Joe? Who's he?"

"Joe French. The plumber. He's a friend of Dad's."

"Let's go." They crossed the snow, up the ridge and onto the field. The little panel truck was parked half way across the field. A heavy short man was sitting behind the wheel, smoking his pipe. He sat up as he saw the two of them coming toward him.

"Are you the one?" he said to Conger.

"Yes. Thanks for warning me."

The plumber shrugged. "I don't know anything about this. Lora says you're all right." He turned around. "It might interest you to know some more of them are coming. Not to warn you-just curious."

"More of them?" Conger looked toward the town. Black shapes were picking their way across the snow.

"People from the town. You can't keep this sort of thing quiet, not in a small town. We all listen to the police radio; they heard the same way Lora did. Someone tuned in, spread it around —"

The shapes were getting closer. Conger could, make out a couple of them. Bill Willet was there, with some boys from the high school. The Appletons were along, hanging back in the rear.

"Even Ed Davies," Conger murmured.

The storekeeper was toiling onto the field, with three or four other men from the town.

"All curious as hell," French said. "Well, I guess I'm going back to town. I don't want my truck shot full of holes. Come on, Lora."

She was looking up at Conger, wide-eyed.

"Come on," French said again. "Let's go. You sure as hell can't stay here, you know."

"Why?"

"There may be shooting. That's what they all came to see. You know that don't you, Conger?"

"Yes."

"You have a gun? Or don't you care?" French smiled a little. "They've picked up a lot of people in their time, you know. You won't be lonely."

He cared, all right! He had to stay here, on the field. He couldn't afford to let them take him away. Any minute the Founder would appear, would step onto the field. Would he be one of the townsmen, standing silently at the foot of the field, waiting, watching?

Or maybe he was Joe French. Or maybe one of the cops. Anyone of them might find himself moved to speak. And the few words spoken this day were going to be important for a long time.

And Conger had to be there, ready when the first word was uttered!

"I care," he said. "You go on back to town. Take the girl with you."

Lora got stiffly in beside Joe French. The plumber started up the motor. "Look at them, standing there," he said. "Like vultures. Waiting to see someone get killed."

* * * * *

The truck drove away, Lora sitting stiff and silent, frightened now. Conger watched for a moment. Then he dashed back into the woods, between the trees, toward the ridge.

He could get away, of course. Anytime he wanted to he could get away. All he had to do was to leap into the crystal cage and turn the handles. But he had a job, an important job. He had to be here, here at this place, at this time.

He reached the cage and opened the door. He went inside and picked up the gun from the shelf. The Slem-gun would take care of them. He notched it up to full count. The chain reaction from it would flatten them all, the police, the curious, sadistic people —

They wouldn't take him! Before they got him, all of them would be dead. *He* would get away. He would escape. By the end of the day they would all be dead, if that was what they wanted, and he —

He saw the skull.

Suddenly he put the gun down. He picked up the skull. He turned the skull over. He looked at the teeth. Then he went to the mirror.

He held the skull up, looking in the mirror. He pressed the skull against his cheek. Beside his own face the grinning skull leered back at him, beside *his* skull, against his living flesh.

He bared his teeth. And he knew.

It was his own skull that he held. He was the one who would die. He was the Founder.

After a time he put the skull down. For a few minutes he stood at the controls, playing with them idly. He could hear the sound of motors outside, the muffled noise of men. Should he go back to the present, where the Speaker waited? He could escape, of course —

Escape?

He turned toward the skull. There it was, his skull, yellow with age. Escape? Escape, when he had held it in his own hands?

What did it matter if he put it off a month, a year, ten years, even fifty? Time was nothing. He had sipped chocolate with a girl born a hundred and fifty years before his time. Escape? For a little while, perhaps.

But he could not *really* escape, no more so than anyone else had ever escaped, or ever would.

Only, he had held it in his hands, his own bones, his own death's-head.

They had not.

He went out the door and across the field, empty handed. There were a lot of them standing around, gathered together, waiting. They expected a good fight; they knew he had something. They had heard about the incident at the fountain.

And there were plenty of police-police with guns and tear gas, creeping across the hills and ridges, between the trees, closer and closer. It was an old story, in this century.

One of the men tossed something at him. It fell in the snow by his feet, and he looked down. It was a rock. He smiled.

"Come on!" one of them called. "Don't you have any bombs?"

"Throw a bomb! You with the beard! Throw a bomb!"

"Let 'em have it!"

"Toss a few A Bombs!"

* * * * *

They began to laugh. He smiled. He put his hands to his hips. They suddenly turned silent, seeing that he was going to speak.

"I'm sorry," he said simply. "I don't have any bombs. You're mistaken."

There was a flurry of murmuring.

"I have a gun," he went on. "A very good one. Made by science even more advanced than your own. But I'm not going to use that, either."

They were puzzled.

"Why not?" someone called. At the edge of the group an older woman was watching. He felt a sudden shock. He had seen her before. Where?

He remembered. The day at the library. As he had turned the corner he had seen her. She had noticed him and been astounded. At the time, he did not understand why.

Conger grinned. So he *would* escape death, the man who right now was voluntarily accepting it. They were laughing, laughing at a man who had a gun but didn't use it. But by a strange twist of science he would appear again, a few months later, after his bones had been buried under the floor of a jail.

And so, in a fashion, he would escape death. He would die, but then, after a period of months, he would live again, briefly, for an afternoon.

An afternoon. Yet long enough for them to see him, to understand that he was still alive. To know that somehow he had returned to life.

And then, finally, he would appear once more, after two hundred years had passed. Two centuries later.

He would be born again, born, as a matter of fact, in a small trading village on Mars. He would grow up, learning to hunt and trade —

A police car came on the edge of the field and stopped. The people retreated a little. Conger raised his hands.

"I have an odd paradox for you," he said. "Those who take lives will lose their own. Those who kill, will die. But he who gives his own life away will live again!"

They laughed, faintly, nervously. The police were coming out, walking toward him. He smiled. He had said everything he intended to say. It was a good little paradox he had coined. They would puzzle over it, remember it.

Smiling, Conger awaited a death foreordained.

The Variable Man

I

Security Commissioner Reinhart rapidly climbed the front steps and entered the Council building. Council guards stepped quickly aside and he entered the familiar place of great whirring machines. His thin face rapt, eyes alight with emotion, Reinhart gazed intently up at the central SRB computer, studying its reading.

"Straight gain for the last quarter," observed Kaplan, the lab organizer. He grinned proudly, as if personally responsible. "Not bad, Commissioner."

"We're catching up to them," Reinhart retorted. "But too damn slowly. We must finally go over-and soon."

Kaplan was in a talkative mood. "We design new offensive weapons, they counter with improved defenses. And nothing is actually made! Continual improvement, but neither we nor Centaurus can stop designing long enough to stabilize for production."

"It will end," Reinhart stated coldly, "as soon as Terra turns out a weapon for which Centaurus can build no defense."

"Every weapon has a defense. Design and discord. Immediate obsolescence. Nothing lasts long enough to —"

"What we count on is the *lag*," Reinhart broke in, annoyed. His hard gray eyes bored into the lab organizer and Kaplan slunk back. "The time lag between our offensive design and their counter development. The lag varies." He waved impatiently toward the massed banks of SRB machines. "As you well know."

At this moment, 9:30 AM, May 7, 2136, the statistical ratio on the SRB machines stood at 21-17 on the Centauran side of the ledger. All facts considered, the odds favored a successful repulsion by Proxima Centaurus of a Terran military attack. The ratio was based on the total information known to the SRB machines, on a gestalt of the vast flow of data that poured in endlessly from all sectors of the Sol and Centaurus systems.

21-17 on the Centauran side. But a month ago it had been 24-18 in the enemy's favor. Things were improving, slowly but steadily. Centaurus, older and less virile than Terra, was unable to match Terra's rate of technocratic advance. Terra was pulling ahead.

"If we went to war now," Reinhart said thoughtfully, "we would lose. We're not far enough along to risk an overt attack." A harsh, ruthless glow twisted across his handsome features, distorting them into a stern mask. "But the odds are moving in our favor. Our offensive designs are gradually gaining on their defenses."

"Let's hope the war comes soon," Kaplan agreed. "We're all on edge. This damn waiting...."

The war would come soon. Reinhart knew it intuitively. The air was full of tension, the *elan*. He left the SRB rooms and hurried down the corridor to his own elaborately guarded office in the Security wing. It wouldn't be long. He could practically feel the hot breath of destiny on his neck-for him a pleasant feeling. His thin lips set in a humorless smile, showing an even line of white teeth against his tanned skin. It made him feel good, all right. He'd been working at it a long time.

First contact, a hundred years earlier, had ignited instant conflict between Proxima Centauran outposts and exploring Terran raiders. Flash fights, sudden eruptions of fire and energy beams.

And then the long, dreary years of inaction between enemies where contact required years of travel, even at nearly the speed of light. The two systems were evenly matched. Screen against screen. Warship against power station. The Centauran Empire surrounded Terra, an iron ring that couldn't be broken, rusty and corroded as it was. Radical new weapons had to be conceived, if Terra was to break out.

Through the windows of his office, Reinhart could see endless buildings and streets, Terrans hurrying back and forth. Bright specks that were commute ships, little eggs that carried businessmen and white-collar workers around. The huge transport tubes that shot masses of workmen to factories and labor camps from their housing units. All these people, waiting to break out. Waiting for the day.

Reinhart snapped on his vidscreen, the confidential channel. "Give me Military Designs," he ordered sharply.

* * * * *

He sat tense, his wiry body taut, as the vidscreen warmed into life. Abruptly he was facing the hulking image of Peter Sherikov, director of the vast network of labs under the Ural Mountains.

Sherikov's great bearded features hardened as he recognized Reinhart. His bushy black eyebrows pulled up in a sullen line. "What do you want? You know I'm busy. We have too much work to do, as it is. Without being bothered by-politicians."

"I'm dropping over your way," Reinhart answered lazily. He adjusted the cuff of his immaculate gray cloak. "I want a full description of your work and whatever progress you've made."

"You'll find a regular departmental report plate filed in the usual way, around your office someplace. If you'll refer to that you'll know exactly what we —"

"I'm not interested in that. I want to *see* what you're doing. And I expect you to be prepared to describe your work fully. I'll be there shortly. Half an hour."

* * * * *

Reinhart cut the circuit. Sherikov's heavy features dwindled and faded. Reinhart relaxed, letting his breath out. Too bad he had to work with Sherikov. He had never liked the man. The big Polish scientist was an individualist, refusing to integrate himself with society. Independent, atomistic in outlook. He held concepts of the individual as an end, diametrically contrary to the accepted organic state Weltansicht.

But Sherikov was the leading research scientist, in charge of the Military Designs Department. And on Designs the whole future of Terra depended. Victory over Centaurus-or more waiting, bottled up in the Sol System, surrounded by a rotting, hostile Empire, now sinking into ruin and decay, yet still strong.

Reinhart got quickly to his feet and left the office. He hurried down the hall and out of the Council building.

A few minutes later he was heading across the mid-morning sky in his highspeed cruiser, toward the Asiatic land-mass, the vast Ural mountain range. Toward the Military Designs labs.

Sherikov met him at the entrance. "Look here, Reinhart. Don't think you're going to order me around. I'm not going to —"

"Take it easy." Reinhart fell into step beside the bigger man. They passed through the check and into the auxiliary labs. "No immediate coercion will be exerted over you or your staff. You're free to continue your work as you see fit-for the present. Let's get this straight. My concern is to integrate your work with our total social needs. As long as your work is sufficiently productive —"

Reinhart stopped in his tracks.

"Pretty, isn't he?" Sherikov said ironically.

"What the hell is it?"

"Icarus, we call him. Remember the Greek myth? The legend of Icarus. Icarus flew.... This Icarus is going to fly, one of these days." Sherikov shrugged. "You can examine him, if you want. I suppose this is what you came here to see."

Reinhart advanced slowly. "This is the weapon you've been working on?"

"How does he look?"

Rising up in the center of the chamber was a squat metal cylinder, a great ugly cone of dark gray. Technicians circled around it, wiring up the exposed relay banks. Reinhart caught a glimpse of endless tubes and filaments, a maze of wires and terminals and parts criss-crossing each other, layer on layer.

"What is it?" Reinhart perched on the edge of a workbench, leaning his big shoulders against the wall. "An idea of Jamison Hedge-the same man who developed our instantaneous interstellar vidcasts forty years ago. He was trying to find a method of faster than light travel when he was killed, destroyed along with most of his work. After that ftl research was abandoned. It looked as if there were no future in it."

"Wasn't it shown that nothing could travel faster than light?"

"The interstellar vidcasts do! No, Hedge developed a valid ftl drive. He managed to propel an object at fifty times the speed of light. But as the object gained speed, its length began to diminish and its mass increased. This was in line with familiar twentieth-century concepts of mass-energy transformation. We conjectured that as Hedge's object gained velocity it would continue to lose length and gain mass until its length became nil and its mass infinite. Nobody can imagine such an object."

"Go on."

"But what actually occurred is this. Hedge's object continued to lose length and gain mass until it reached the theoretical limit of velocity, the speed of light. At that point the object, still gaining speed, simply ceased to exist. Having no length, it ceased to occupy space. It disappeared. However, the object had not been *destroyed*. It continued on its way, gaining momentum each moment, moving in an arc across the galaxy, away from the Sol system. Hedge's object entered some other realm of being, beyond our powers of conception. The next phase of Hedge's experiment consisted in a search for some way to slow the ftl object down, back to a sub-ftl speed, hence back into our universe. This counterprinciple was eventually worked out."

"With what result?"

"The death of Hedge and destruction of most of his equipment. His experimental object, in re-entering the space-time universe, came into being in space already occupied by matter. Possessing an incredible mass, just below infinity level, Hedge's object exploded in a titanic cataclysm. It was obvious that no space travel was possible with such a drive. Virtually all space contains *some* matter. To re-enter space would bring automatic destruction. Hedge had found his ftl drive and his counterprinciple, but no one before this has been able to put them to any use."

Reinhart walked over toward the great metal cylinder. Sherikov jumped down and followed him. "I don't get it," Reinhart said. "You said the principle is no good for space travel."

"That's right."

"What's this for, then? If the ship explodes as soon as it returns to our universe —"

"This is not a ship." Sherikov grinned slyly. "Icarus is the first practical application of Hedge's principles. Icarus is a bomb."

"So this is our weapon," Reinhart said. "A bomb. An immense bomb."

"A bomb, moving at a velocity greater than light. A bomb which will not exist in our universe. The Centaurans won't be able to detect or stop it. How could they? As soon as it passes the speed of light it will cease to exist-beyond all detection."

"But —"

"Icarus will be launched outside the lab, on the surface. He will align himself with Proxima Centaurus, gaining speed rapidly. By the time he reaches his destination he will be traveling at ftl-100. Icarus will be brought back to this universe within Centaurus itself. The explosion should destroy the star and wash away most of its planets-including their central hub-planet, Armun. There is no way they can halt Icarus, once he has been launched. No defense is possible. Nothing can stop him. It is a real fact."

"When will he be ready?"

Sherikov's eyes flickered. "Soon."

"Exactly how soon?"

The big Pole hesitated. "As a matter of fact, there's only one thing holding us back."

Sherikov led Reinhart around to the other side of the lab. He pushed a lab guard out of the way.

"See this?" He tapped a round globe, open at one end, the size of a grapefruit. "This is holding us up."

"What is it?"

"The central control turret. This thing brings Icarus back to sub-ftl flight at the correct moment. It must be absolutely accurate. Icarus will be within the star only a matter of a microsecond. If the turret does not function exactly, Icarus will pass out the other side and shoot beyond the Centauran system."

"How near completed is this turret?"

Sherikov hedged uncertainly, spreading out his big hands. "Who can say? It must be wired with infinitely minute equipment-microscope grapples and wires invisible to the naked eye."

"Can you name any completion date?"

Sherikov reached into his coat and brought out a manila folder. "I've drawn up the data for the SRB machines, giving a date of completion. You can go ahead and feed it. I entered ten days as the maximum period. The machines can work from that."

Reinhart accepted the folder cautiously. "You're sure about the date? I'm not convinced I can trust you, Sherikov."

Sherikov's features darkened. "You'll have to take a chance, Commissioner. I don't trust you any more than you trust me. I know how much you'd like an excuse to get me out of here and one of your puppets in."

Reinhart studied the huge scientist thoughtfully. Sherikov was going to be a hard nut to crack. Designs was responsible to Security, not the Council. Sherikov was losing ground-but he was still a potential danger. Stubborn, individualistic, refusing to subordinate his welfare to the general good.

"All right." Reinhart put the folder slowly away in his coat. "I'll feed it. But you better be able to come through. There can't be any slip-ups. Too much hangs on the next few days."

"If the odds change in our favor are you going to give the mobilization order?"

"Yes," Reinhart stated. "I'll give the order the moment I see the odds change."

* * * * *

Standing in front of the machines, Reinhart waited nervously for the results. It was two o'clock in the afternoon. The day was warm, a pleasant May afternoon. Outside the building the daily life of the planet went on as usual.

As usual? Not exactly. The feeling was in the air, an expanding excitement growing every day. Terra had waited a long time. The attack on Proxima Centaurus had to come-and the sooner the better. The ancient Centauran Empire hemmed in Terra, bottled the human race up in its one system. A vast, suffocating net draped across the heavens, cutting Terra off from the bright diamonds beyond.... And it had to end.

The SRB machines whirred, the visible combination disappearing. For a time no ratio showed. Reinhart tensed, his body rigid. He waited.

The new ratio appeared.

Reinhart gasped. 7-6. Toward Terra!

Within five minutes the emergency mobilization alert had been flashed to all Government departments. The Council and President Duffe had been called to immediate session. Everything was happening fast.

But there was no doubt. 7-6. In Terra's favor. Reinhart hurried frantically to get his papers in order, in time for the Council session.

At histo-research the message plate was quickly pulled from the confidential slot and rushed across the central lab to the chief official.

"Look at this!" Fredman dropped the plate on his superior's desk. "Look at it!"

Harper picked up the plate, scanning it rapidly. "Sounds like the real thing. I didn't think we'd live to see it."

Fredman left the room, hurrying down the hall. He entered the time bubble office. "Where's the bubble?" he demanded, looking around.

One of the technicians looked slowly up. "Back about two hundred years. We're coming up with interesting data on the War of 1914. According to material the bubble has already brought up —"

"Cut it. We're through with routine work. Get the bubble back to the present. From now on all equipment has to be free for Military work."

"But-the bubble is regulated automatically."

"You can bring it back manually."

"It's risky." The technician hedged. "If the emergency requires it, I suppose we could take a chance and cut the automatic."

"The emergency requires *everything*," Fredman said feelingly.

"But the odds might change back," Margaret Duffe, President of the Council, said nervously. "Any minute they can revert."

"This is our chance!" Reinhart snapped, his temper rising. "What the hell's the matter with you? We've waited years for this."

The Council buzzed with excitement. Margaret Duffe hesitated uncertainly, her blue eyes clouded with worry. "I realize the opportunity is here. At least, statistically. But the new odds have just appeared. How do we know they'll last? They stand on the basis of a single weapon."

"You're wrong. You don't grasp the situation." Reinhart held himself in check with great effort. "Sherikov's weapon tipped the ratio in our favor. But the odds have been moving in our direction for months. It was only a question of time. The new balance was inevitable, sooner or later. It's not just Sherikov. He's only one factor in this. It's all nine planets of the Sol System-not a single man."

One of the Councilmen stood up. "The President must be aware the entire planet is eager to end this waiting. All our activities for the past eighty years have been directed toward —"

Reinhart moved close to the slender President of the Council. "If you don't approve the war, there probably will be mass rioting. Public reaction will be strong. Damn strong. And you know it."

Margaret Duffe shot him a cold glance. "You sent out the emergency order to force my hand. You were fully aware of what you were doing. You knew once the order was out there'd be no stopping things."

A murmur rushed through the Council, gaining volume. "We have to approve the war!... We're committed!... It's too late to turn back!"

Shouts, angry voices, insistent waves of sound lapped around Margaret Duffe. "I'm as much for the war as anybody," she said sharply. "I'm only urging moderation. An inter-system war is a big thing. We're going to war because a machine says we have a statistical chance of winning."

"There's no use starting the war unless we can win it," Reinhart said. "The SRB machines tell us whether we can win."

"They tell us our *chance* of winning. They don't guarantee anything."

"What more can we ask, beside a good chance of winning?"

Margaret Duffe clamped her jaw together tightly. "All right. I hear all the clamor. I won't stand in the way of Council approval. The vote can go ahead." Her cold, alert eyes appraised Reinhart. "Especially since the emergency order has already been sent out to all Government departments."

"Good." Reinhart stepped away with relief. "Then it's settled. We can finally go ahead with full mobilization."

Mobilization proceeded rapidly. The next forty-eight hours were alive with activity.

Reinhart attended a policy-level Military briefing in the Council rooms, conducted by Fleet Commander Carleton.

"You can see our strategy," Carleton said. He traced a diagram on the blackboard with a wave of his hand. "Sherikov states it'll take eight more days to complete the ftl bomb. During that time the fleet we have near the Centauran system will take up positions. As the bomb goes off the fleet will begin operations against the remaining Centauran ships. Many will no doubt survive the blast, but with Armun gone we should be able to handle them."

Reinhart took Commander Carleton's place. "I can report on the economic situation. Every factory on Terra is converted to arms production. With Armun out of the way we should be able to promote mass insurrection among the Centauran colonies. An inter-system Empire is hard to maintain, even with ships that approach light speed. Local war-lords should pop up all over the place. We want to have weapons available for them and ships starting *now* to reach them in time. Eventually we hope to provide a unifying principle around which the colonies can all collect. Our interest is more economic than political. They can have any kind of government they want, as long as they act as supply areas for us. As our eight system planets act now."

Carleton resumed his report. "Once the Centauran fleet has been scattered we can begin the crucial stage of the war. The landing of men and supplies from the ships we have waiting in all key areas throughout the Centauran system. In this stage —"

Reinhart moved away. It was hard to believe only two days had passed since the mobilization order had been sent out. The whole system was alive, functioning with feverish activity. Countless problems were being solved-but much remained.

He entered the lift and ascended to the SRB room, curious to see if there had been any change in the machines' reading. He found it the same. So far so good. Did the Centaurans know about Icarus? No doubt; but there wasn't anything they could do about it. At least, not in eight days.

Kaplan came over to Reinhart, sorting a new batch of data that had come in. The lab organizer searched through his data. "An amusing item came in. It might interest you." He handed a message plate to Reinhart.

It was from histo-research:

May 9, 2136

This is to report that in bringing the research time bubble up to the present the manual return was used for the first time. Therefore a clean break was not made, and a quantity of material from the past was brought forward. This material included an individual from the early twentieth century who escaped from the lab immediately. He has not yet been taken into protective custody. Histo-research regrets this incident, but attributes it to the emergency.

E. Fredman

Reinhart handed the plate back to Kaplan. "Interesting. A man from the past-hauled into the middle of the biggest war the universe has seen."

"Strange things happen. I wonder what the machines will think."

"Hard to say. Probably nothing." Reinhart left the room and hurried along the corridor to his own office.

As soon as he was inside he called Sherikov on the vidscreen, using the confidential line.

The Pole's heavy features appeared. "Good day, Commissioner. How's the war effort?"

"Fine. How's the turret wiring proceeding?"

A faint frown flickered across Sherikov's face. "As a matter of fact, Commissioner —"

"What's the matter?" Reinhart said sharply.

Sherikov floundered. "You know how these things are. I've taken my crew off it and tried robot workers. They have greater dexterity, but they can't make decisions. This calls for more than mere dexterity. This calls for —" He searched for the word. " —for an *artist.*"

Reinhart's face hardened. "Listen, Sherikov. You have eight days left to complete the bomb. The data given to the SRB machines contained that information. The 7-6 ratio is based on that estimate. If you don't come through —"

Sherikov twisted in embarrassment. "Don't get excited, Commissioner. We'll complete it."

"I hope so. Call me as soon as it's done." Reinhart snapped off the connection. If Sherikov let them down he'd have him taken out and shot. The whole war depended on the ftl bomb.

The vidscreen glowed again. Reinhart snapped it on. Kaplan's face formed on it. The lab organizer's face was pale and frozen. "Commissioner, you better come up to the SRB office. Something's happened."

"What is it?"

"I'll show you."

Alarmed, Reinhart hurried out of his office and down the corridor. He found Kaplan standing in front of the SRB machines. "What's the story?" Reinhart demanded. He glanced down at the reading. It was unchanged.

Kaplan held up a message plate nervously. "A moment ago I fed this into the machines. After I saw the results I quickly removed it. It's that item I showed you. From histo-research. About the man from the past."

"What happened when you fed it?"

Kaplan swallowed unhappily. "I'll show you. I'll do it again. Exactly as before." He fed the plate into a moving intake belt. "Watch the visible figures," Kaplan muttered.

Reinhart watched, tense and rigid. For a moment nothing happened. 7-6 continued to show. Then —

The figures disappeared. The machines faltered. New figures showed briefly. 4-24 for Centaurus. Reinhart gasped, suddenly sick with apprehension. But the figures vanished. New figures appeared. 16-38 for Centaurus. Then 48-86. 79-15 in Terra's favor. Then nothing. The machines whirred, but nothing happened.

Nothing at all. No figures. Only a blank.

"What's it mean?" Reinhart muttered, dazed.

"It's fantastic. We didn't think this could —"

"*What's happened?*"

"The machines aren't able to handle the item. No reading can come. It's data they can't integrate. They can't use it for prediction material, and it throws off all their other figures."

"Why?"

"It's —it's a variable." Kaplan was shaking, white-lipped and pale. "Something from which no inference can be made. The man from the past. The machines can't deal with him. The variable man!"

II

Thomas Cole was sharpening a knife with his whetstone when the tornado hit.

The knife belonged to the lady in the big green house. Every time Cole came by with his Fixit cart the lady had something to be sharpened. Once in awhile she gave him a cup of coffee, hot black coffee from an old bent pot. He liked that fine; he enjoyed good coffee.

The day was drizzly and overcast. Business had been bad. An automobile had scared his two horses. On bad days less people were outside and he had to get down from the cart and go to ring doorbells.

But the man in the yellow house had given him a dollar for fixing his electric refrigerator. Nobody else had been able to fix it, not even the factory man. The dollar would go a long way. A dollar was a lot.

He knew it was a tornado even before it hit him. Everything was silent. He was bent over his whetstone, the reins between his knees, absorbed in his work.

He had done a good job on the knife; he was almost finished. He spat on the blade and was holding it up to see-and then the tornado came.

All at once it was there, completely around him. Nothing but grayness. He and the cart and horses seemed to be in a calm spot in the center of the tornado. They were moving in a great silence, gray mist everywhere.

And while he was wondering what to do, and how to get the lady's knife back to her, all at once there was a bump and the tornado tipped him over, sprawled out on the ground. The horses screamed in fear, struggling to pick themselves up. Cole got quickly to his feet.

Where was he?

The grayness was gone. White walls stuck up on all sides. A deep light gleamed down, not daylight but something like it. The team was pulling the cart on its side, dragging it along, tools and equipment falling out. Cole righted the cart, leaping up onto the seat.

And for the first time saw the people.

Men, with astonished white faces, in some sort of uniforms. Shouts, noise and confusion. And a feeling of danger!

Cole headed the team toward the door. Hoofs thundered steel against steel as they pounded through the doorway, scattering the astonished men in all directions. He was out in a wide hall. A building, like a hospital.

The hall divided. More men were coming, spilling from all sides.

Shouting and milling in excitement, like white ants. Something cut past him, a beam of dark violet. It seared off a corner of the cart, leaving the wood smoking.

Cole felt fear. He kicked at the terrified horses. They reached a big door, crashing wildly against it. The door gave-and they were outside, bright sunlight blinking down on them. For a sickening second the cart tilted, almost turning over. Then the horses gained speed, racing across an open field, toward a distant line of green, Cole holding tightly to the reins.

Behind him the little white-faced men had come out and were standing in a group, gesturing frantically. He could hear their faint shrill shouts.

But he had got away. He was safe. He slowed the horses down and began to breathe again.

The woods were artificial. Some kind of park. But the park was wild and overgrown. A dense jungle of twisted plants. Everything growing in confusion.

The park was empty. No one was there. By the position of the sun he could tell it was either early morning or late afternoon. The smell of the flowers and grass, the dampness of the leaves, indicated morning. It had been late afternoon when the tornado had picked him up. And the sky had been overcast and cloudy.

Cole considered. Clearly, he had been carried a long way. The hospital, the men with white faces, the odd lighting, the accented words he had caught-everything indicated he was no longer in Nebraska-maybe not even in the United States.

Some of his tools had fallen out and gotten lost along the way. Cole collected everything that remained, sorting them, running his fingers over each tool with affection. Some of the little chisels and wood gouges were gone. The bit box had opened, and most of the smaller bits had been lost. He gathered up those that remained and replaced them tenderly in the box. He took a key-hole saw down, and with an oil rag wiped it carefully and replaced it.

Above the cart the sun rose slowly in the sky. Cole peered up, his horny hand over his eyes. A big man, stoop-shouldered, his chin gray and stubbled. His clothes wrinkled and dirty. But his eyes were clear, a pale blue, and his hands were finely made.

He could not stay in the park. They had seen him ride that way; they would be looking for him.

Far above something shot rapidly across the sky. A tiny black dot moving with incredible haste. A second dot followed. The two dots were gone almost before he saw them. They were utterly silent.

Cole frowned, perturbed. The dots made him uneasy. He would have to keep moving-and looking for food. His stomach was already beginning to rumble and groan.

Work. There was plenty he could do: gardening, sharpening, grinding, repair work on machines and clocks, fixing all kinds of household things. Even painting and odd jobs and carpentry and chores.

He could do anything. Anything people wanted done. For a meal and pocket money.

Thomas Cole urged the team into life, moving forward. He sat hunched over in the seat, watching intently, as the Fixit cart rolled slowly across the tangled grass, through the jungle of trees and flowers.

* * * * *

Reinhart hurried, racing his cruiser at top speed, followed by a second ship, a military escort. The ground sped by below him, a blur of gray and green.

The remains of New York lay spread out, a twisted, blunted ruin overgrown with weeds and grass. The great atomic wars of the twentieth century had turned virtually the whole seaboard area into an endless waste of slag.

Slag and weeds below him. And then the sudden tangle that had been Central Park.

Histo-research came into sight. Reinhart swooped down, bringing his cruiser to rest at the small supply field behind the main buildings.

Harper, the chief official of the department, came quickly over as soon as Reinhart's ship landed.

"Frankly, we don't understand why you consider this matter important," Harper said uneasily.

Reinhart shot him a cold glance. "I'll be the judge of what's important. Are you the one who gave the order to bring the bubble back manually?"

"Fredman gave the actual order. In line with your directive to have all facilities ready for —"

Reinhart headed toward the entrance of the research building. "Where is Fredman?"

"Inside."

"I want to see him. Let's go."

Fredman met them inside. He greeted Reinhart calmly, showing no emotion. "Sorry to cause you trouble, Commissioner. We were trying to get the station in order for the war. We wanted the bubble back as quickly as possible." He eyed Reinhart curiously. "No doubt the man and his cart will soon be picked up by your police."

"I want to know everything that happened, in exact detail."

Fredman shifted uncomfortably. "There's not much to tell. I gave the order to have the automatic setting canceled and the bubble brought back manually. At the moment the signal reached it, the bubble was passing through the spring of 1913. As it broke loose, it tore off a piece of ground on which this person and his cart were located. The person naturally was brought up to the present, inside the bubble."

"Didn't any of your instruments tell you the bubble was loaded?"

"We were too excited to take any readings. Half an hour after the manual control was thrown, the bubble materialized in the observation room. It was de-energized before anyone noticed what was inside. We tried to stop him but he drove the cart out into the hall, bowling us out of the way. The horses were in a panic."

"What kind of cart was it?"

"There was some kind of sign on it. Painted in black letters on both sides. No one saw what it was."

"Go ahead. What happened then?"

"Somebody fired a Slem-ray after him, but it missed. The horses carried him out of the building and onto the grounds. By the time we reached the exit the cart was half way to the park."

Reinhart reflected. "If he's still in the park we should have him shortly. But we must be careful." He was already starting back toward his ship, leaving Fredman behind. Harper fell in beside him.

Reinhart halted by his ship. He beckoned some Government guards over. "Put the executive staff of this department under arrest. I'll have them tried on a treason count, later on." He smiled ironically as Harper's face blanched sickly pale. "There's a war going on. You'll be lucky if you get off alive."

Reinhart entered his ship and left the surface, rising rapidly into the sky. A second ship followed after him, a military escort. Reinhart flew high above the sea of gray slag, the uncovered waste area. He passed over a sudden square of green set in the ocean of gray. Reinhart gazed back at it until it was gone.

Central Park. He could see police ships racing through the sky, ships and transports loaded with troops, heading toward the square of green. On the ground some heavy guns and surface cars rumbled along, lines of black approaching the park from all sides.

They would have the man soon. But meanwhile, the SRB machines were blank. And on the SRB machines' readings the whole war depended.

About noon the cart reached the edge of the park. Cole rested for a moment, allowing the horses time to crop at the thick grass. The silent expanse of slag amazed him. What had happened? Nothing stirred. No buildings, no sign of life. Grass and weeds poked up occasionally through it, breaking the flat surface here and there, but even so, the sight gave him an uneasy chill.

Cole drove the cart slowly out onto the slag, studying the sky above him. There was nothing to hide him, now that he was out of the park. The slag was bare and uniform, like the ocean. If he were spotted —

A horde of tiny black dots raced across the sky, coming rapidly closer. Presently they veered to the right and disappeared. More planes, wingless metal planes. He watched them go, driving slowly on.

Half an hour later something appeared ahead. Cole slowed the cart down, peering to see. The slag came to an end. He had reached its limits. Ground appeared, dark soil and grass. Weeds grew everywhere. Ahead of him, beyond the end of the slag, was a line of buildings, houses of some sort. Or sheds.

Houses, probably. But not like any he had ever seen.

The houses were uniform, all exactly the same. Like little green shells, rows of them, several hundred. There was a little lawn in front of each. Lawn, a path, a front porch, bushes in a meager row around each house. But the houses were all alike and very small.

Little green shells in precise, even rows. He urged the cart cautiously forward, toward the houses.

No one seemed to be around. He entered a street between two rows of houses, the hoofs of his two horses sounding loudly in the silence. He was in some kind of town. But there were no dogs or children. Everything was neat and silent. Like a model. An exhibit. It made him uncomfortable.

A young man walking along the pavement gaped at him in wonder. An oddly-dressed youth, in a toga-like cloak that hung down to his knees. A single piece of fabric. And sandals.

Or what looked like sandals. Both the cloak and the sandals were of some strange half-luminous material. It glowed faintly in the sunlight. Metallic, rather than cloth.

A woman was watering flowers at the edge of a lawn. She straightened up as his team of horses came near. Her eyes widened in astonishment-and then fear. Her mouth fell open in a soundless *O* and her sprinkling can slipped from her fingers and rolled silently onto the lawn.

Cole blushed and turned his head quickly away. The woman was scarcely dressed! He flicked the reins and urged the horses to hurry.

Behind him, the woman still stood. He stole a brief, hasty look back-and then shouted hoarsely to his team, ears scarlet. He had seen right. She wore only a pair of translucent shorts. Nothing else. A mere fragment of the same half-luminous material that glowed and sparkled. The rest of her small body was utterly naked.

He slowed the team down. She had been pretty. Brown hair and eyes, deep red lips. Quite a good figure. Slender waist, downy legs, bare and supple, full breasts —. He clamped the thought furiously off. He had to get to work. Business.

Cole halted the Fixit cart and leaped down onto the pavement. He selected a house at random and approached it cautiously. The house was attractive. It had a certain simple beauty. But it looked frail-and exactly like the others.

He stepped up on the porch. There was no bell. He searched for it, running his hand uneasily over the surface of the door. All at once there was a click, a sharp snap on a level with his eyes. Cole glanced up, startled. A lens was vanishing as the door section slid over it. He had been photographed.

While he was wondering what it meant, the door swung suddenly open. A man filled up the entrance, a big man in a tan uniform, blocking the way ominously.

"What do you want?" the man demanded.

"I'm looking for work," Cole murmured. "Any kind of work. I can do anything, fix any kind of thing. I repair broken objects. Things that need mending." His voice trailed off uncertainly. "Anything at all."

"Apply to the Placement Department of the Federal Activities Control Board," the man said crisply. "You know all occupational therapy is handled through them." He eyed Cole curiously. "Why have you got on those ancient clothes?"

"Ancient? Why, I —"

The man gazed past him at the Fixit cart and the two dozing horses. "What's that? What are those two animals? *Horses?*" The man rubbed his jaw, studying Cole intently. "That's strange," he said.

"Strange?" Cole murmured uneasily. "Why?"

"There haven't been any horses for over a century. All the horses were wiped out during the Fifth Atomic War. That's why it's strange."

Cole tensed, suddenly alert. There was something in the man's eyes, a hardness, a piercing look. Cole moved back off the porch, onto the path. He had to be careful. Something was wrong.

"I'll be going," he murmured.

"There haven't been any horses for over a hundred years." The man came toward Cole. "Who are you? Why are you dressed up like that? Where did you get that vehicle and pair of horses?"

"I'll be going," Cole repeated, moving away.

The man whipped something from his belt, a thin metal tube. He stuck it toward Cole.

It was a rolled-up paper, a thin sheet of metal in the form of a tube. Words, some kind of script. He could not make any of them out. The man's picture, rows of numbers, figures —

"I'm Director Winslow," the man said. "Federal Stockpile Conservation. You better talk fast, or there'll be a Security car here in five minutes."

Cole moved-fast. He raced, head down, back along the path to the cart, toward the street.

Something hit him. A wall of force, throwing him down on his face. He sprawled in a heap, numb and dazed. His body ached, vibrating wildly, out of control. Waves of shock rolled over him, gradually diminishing.

He got shakily to his feet. His head spun. He was weak, shattered, trembling violently. The man was coming down the walk after him. Cole pulled himself onto the cart, gasping and retching. The horses jumped into life. Cole rolled over against the seat, sick with the motion of the swaying cart.

He caught hold of the reins and managed to drag himself up in a sitting position. The cart gained speed, turning a corner. Houses flew past. Cole urged the team weakly, drawing great shuddering breaths. Houses and streets, a blur of motion, as the cart flew faster and faster along.

Then he was leaving the town, leaving the neat little houses behind. He was on some sort of highway. Big buildings, factories, on both sides of the highway. Figures, men watching in astonishment.

After awhile the factories fell behind. Cole slowed the team down. What had the man meant? Fifth Atomic War. Horses destroyed. It didn't make sense. And they had things he knew nothing about. Force fields. Planes without wings-soundless.

Cole reached around in his pockets. He found the identification tube the man had handed him. In the excitement he had carried it off. He unrolled the tube slowly and began to study it. The writing was strange to him.

For a long time he studied the tube. Then, gradually, he became aware of something. Something in the top right-hand corner.

A date. October 6, 2128.

Cole's vision blurred. Everything spun and wavered around him. October, 2128. Could it be?

But he held the paper in his hand. Thin, metal paper. Like foil. And it had to be. It said so, right in the corner, printed on the paper itself.

Cole rolled the tube up slowly, numbed with shock. Two hundred years. It didn't seem possible. But things were beginning to make sense. He was in the future, two hundred years in the future.

While he was mulling this over, the swift black Security ship appeared overhead, diving rapidly toward the horse-drawn cart, as it moved slowly along the road.

Reinhart's vidscreen buzzed. He snapped it quickly on. "Yes?"

"Report from Security."

"Put it through." Reinhart waited tensely as the lines locked in place. The screen re-lit.

"This is Dixon. Western Regional Command." The officer cleared his throat, shuffling his message plates. "The man from the past has been reported, moving away from the New York area."

"Which side of your net?"

"Outside. He evaded the net around Central Park by entering one of the small towns at the rim of the slag area."

"*Evaded?*"

"We assumed he would avoid the towns. Naturally the net failed to encompass any of the towns."

Reinhart's jaw stiffened. "Go on."

"He entered the town of Petersville a few minutes before the net closed around the park. We burned the park level, but naturally found nothing. He had already gone. An hour later we received a report from a resident in Petersville, an official of the Stockpile Conservation Department. The man from the past had come to his door, looking for work. Winslow, the official, engaged him in conversation, trying to hold onto him, but he escaped, driving his cart off. Winslow called Security right away, but by then it was too late."

"Report to me as soon as anything more comes in. We must have him-and damn soon." Reinhart snapped the screen off. It died quickly.

He sat back in his chair, waiting.

Cole saw the shadow of the Security ship. He reacted at once. A second after the shadow passed over him, Cole was out of the cart, running and falling. He rolled, twisting and turning, pulling his body as far away from the cart as possible.

There was a blinding roar and flash of white light. A hot wind rolled over Cole, picking him up and tossing him like a leaf. He shut his eyes, letting his body relax. He bounced, falling and striking the ground. Gravel and stones tore into his face, his knees, the palms of his hands.

Cole cried out, shrieking in pain. His body was on fire. He was being consumed, incinerated by the blinding white orb of fire. The orb expanded, growing in size, swelling like some monstrous sun, twisted and bloated. The end had come. There was no hope. He gritted his teeth —

The greedy orb faded, dying down. It sputtered and winked out, blackening into ash. The air reeked, a bitter acrid smell. His clothes were burning and smoking. The ground under him was hot, baked dry, seared by the blast. But he was alive. At least, for awhile.

Cole opened his eyes slowly. The cart was gone. A great hole gaped where it had been, a shattered sore in the center of the highway. An ugly cloud hung above the hole, black and ominous. Far above, the wingless plane circled, watching for any signs of life.

Cole lay, breathing shallowly, slowly. Time passed. The sun moved across the sky with agonizing slowness. It was perhaps four in the afternoon. Cole calculated mentally. In three hours it would be dark. If he could stay alive until then —

Had the plane seen him leap from the cart?

He lay without moving. The late afternoon sun beat down on him. He felt sick, nauseated and feverish. His mouth was dry.

Some ants ran over his outstretched hand. Gradually, the immense black cloud was beginning to drift away, dispersing into a formless blob.

The cart was gone. The thought lashed against him, pounding at his brain, mixing with his labored pulse-beat. *Gone*. Destroyed. Nothing but ashes and debris remained. The realization dazed him.

Finally the plane finished its circling, winging its way toward the horizon. At last it vanished. The sky was clear.

Cole got unsteadily to his feet. He wiped his face shakily. His body ached and trembled. He spat a couple times, trying to clear his mouth. The plane would probably send in a report. People would be coming to look for him. Where could he go?

To his right a line of hills rose up, a distant green mass. Maybe he could reach them. He began to walk slowly. He had to be very careful. They were looking for him-and they had weapons. Incredible weapons.

He would be lucky to still be alive when the sun set. His team and Fixit cart were gone-and all his tools. Cole reached into his pockets, searching through them hopefully. He brought out some small screwdrivers, a little pair of cutting pliers, some wire, some solder, the whetstone, and finally the lady's knife.

Only a few small tools remained. He had lost everything else. But without the cart he was safer, harder to spot. They would have more trouble finding him, on foot.

Cole hurried along, crossing the level fields toward the distant range of hills.

The call came through to Reinhart almost at once. Dixon's features formed on the vidscreen. "I have a further report, Commissioner." Dixon scanned the plate. "Good news. The man from the past was sighted moving away from Petersville, along highway 13, at about ten miles an hour, on his horse-drawn cart. Our ship bombed him immediately."

"Did-did you get him?"

"The pilot reports no sign of life after the blast."

Reinhart's pulse almost stopped. He sank back in his chair. "Then he's dead!"

"Actually, we won't know for certain until we can examine the debris. A surface car is speeding toward the spot. We should have the complete report in a short time. We'll notify you as soon as the information comes in."

Reinhart reached out and cut the screen. It faded into darkness. Had they got the man from the past? Or had he escaped again? Weren't they ever going to get him? Couldn't he be captured? And meanwhile, the SRB machines were silent, showing nothing at all.

Reinhart sat brooding, waiting impatiently for the report of the surface car to come in.

* * * * *

It was evening.

"Come on!" Steven shouted, running frantically after his brother. "Come on back!"

"Catch me." Earl ran and ran, down the side of the hill, over behind a military storage depot, along a neotex fence, jumping finally down into Mrs. Norris' back yard.

Steven hurried after his brother, sobbing for breath, shouting and gasping as he ran. "Come back! You come back with that!"

"What's he got?" Sally Tate demanded, stepping out suddenly to block Steven's way.

Steven halted, his chest rising and falling. "He's got my intersystemvidsender." His small face twisted with rage and misery. "He better give it back!"

Earl came circling around from the right. In the warm gloom of evening he was almost invisible. "Here I am," he announced. "What you going to do?"

Steven glared at him hotly. His eyes made out the square box in Earl's hands. "You give that back! Or-or I'll tell Dad."

Earl laughed. "Make me."

"Dad'll make you."

"You better give it to him," Sally said.

"Catch me." Earl started off. Steven pushed Sally out of the way, lashing wildly at his brother. He collided with him, throwing him sprawling. The box fell from Earl's hands. It skidded to the pavement, crashing into the side of a guide-light post.

Earl and Steven picked themselves up slowly. They gazed down at the broken box.

"See?" Steven shrilled, tears filling his eyes. "See what you did?"

"You did it. You pushed into me."

"You did it!" Steven bent down and picked up the box. He carried it over to the guide-light, sitting down on the curb to examine it.

Earl came slowly over. "If you hadn't pushed me it wouldn't have got broken."

Night was descending rapidly. The line of hills rising above the town were already lost in darkness. A few lights had come on here and there. The evening was warm. A surface car slammed its doors, some place off in the distance. In the sky ships droned back and forth, weary commuters coming home from work in the big underground factory units.

Thomas Cole came slowly toward the three children grouped around the guide-light. He moved with difficulty, his body sore and bent with fatigue. Night had come, but he was not safe yet.

He was tired, exhausted and hungry. He had walked a long way. And he had to have something to eat-soon.

A few feet from the children Cole stopped. They were all intent and absorbed by the box on Steven's knees. Suddenly a hush fell over the children. Earl looked up slowly.

In the dim light the big stooped figure of Thomas Cole seemed extra menacing. His long arms hung down loosely at his sides. His face was lost in shadow. His body was shapeless, indistinct. A big unformed statue, standing silently a few feet away, unmoving in the half-darkness.

"Who are you?" Earl demanded, his voice low.

"What do you want?" Sally said. The children edged away nervously. "Get away."

Cole came toward them. He bent down a little. The beam from the guide-light crossed his features. Lean, prominent nose, beak-like, faded blue eyes —

Steven scrambled to his feet, clutching the vidsender box. "You get out of here!"

"Wait." Cole smiled crookedly at them. His voice was dry and raspy. "What do you have there?" He pointed with his long, slender fingers. "The box you're holding."

The children were silent. Finally Steven stirred. "It's my inter-system vidsender."

"Only it doesn't work," Sally said.

"Earl broke it." Steven glared at his brother bitterly. "Earl threw it down and broke it."

Cole smiled a little. He sank down wearily on the edge of the curb, sighing with relief. He had been walking too long. His body ached with fatigue. He was hungry, and tired. For a long time he sat, wiping perspiration from his neck and face, too exhausted to speak.

"Who are you?" Sally demanded, at last. "Why do you have on those funny clothes? Where did you come from?"

"Where?" Cole looked around at the children. "From a long way off. A long way." He shook his head slowly from side to side, trying to clear it.

"What's your therapy?" Earl said.

"My therapy?"

"What do you do? Where do you work?"

Cole took a deep breath and let it out again slowly. "I fix things. All kinds of things. Any kind."

Earl sneered. "Nobody fixes things. When they break you throw them away."

Cole didn't hear him. Sudden need had roused him, getting him suddenly to his feet. "You know any work I can find?" he demanded. "Things I could do? I can fix anything. Clocks, type-writers, refrigerators, pots and pans. Leaks in the roof. I can fix anything there is."

Steven held out his inter-system vidsender. "Fix this."

There was silence. Slowly, Cole's eyes focussed on the box. "That?"

"My sender. Earl broke it."

Cole took the box slowly. He turned it over, holding it up to the light. He frowned, concentrating on it. His long, slender fingers moved carefully over the surface, exploring it.

"He'll steal it!" Earl said suddenly.

"No." Cole shook his head vaguely. "I'm reliable." His sensitive fingers found the studs that held the box together. He depressed the studs, pushing them expertly in. The box opened, revealing its complex interior.

"He got it open," Sally whispered.

"Give it back!" Steven demanded, a little frightened. He held out his hand. "I want it back."

The three children watched Cole apprehensively. Cole fumbled in his pocket. Slowly he brought out his tiny screwdrivers and pliers. He laid them in a row beside him. He made no move to return the box.

"I want it back," Steven said feebly.

Cole looked up. His faded blue eyes took in the sight of the three children standing before him in the gloom. "I'll fix it for you. You said you wanted it fixed."

"I want it back." Steven stood on one foot, then the other, torn by doubt and indecision. "Can you really fix it? Can you make it work again?"

"Yes."

"All right. Fix it for me, then."

A sly smile flickered across Cole's tired face. "Now, wait a minute. If I fix it, will you bring me something to eat? I'm not fixing it for nothing."

"Something to eat?"

"Food. I need hot food. Maybe some coffee."

Steven nodded. "Yes. I'll get it for you."

Cole relaxed. "Fine. That's fine." He turned his attention back to the box resting between his knees. "Then I'll fix it for you. I'll fix it for you good."

His fingers flew, working and twisting, tracing down wires and relays, exploring and examining. Finding out about the inter-system vidsender. Discovering how it worked.

Steven slipped into the house through the emergency door. He made his way to the kitchen with great care, walking on tip-toe. He punched the kitchen controls at random, his heart beating excitedly. The stove began to whir, purring into life. Meter readings came on, crossing toward the completion marks.

Presently the stove opened, sliding out a tray of steaming dishes. The mechanism clicked off, dying into silence. Steven grabbed up the contents of the tray, filling his arms. He carried everything down the hall, out the emergency door and into the yard. The yard was dark. Steven felt his way carefully along.

He managed to reach the guide-light without dropping anything at all.

Thomas Cole got slowly to his feet as Steven came into view. "Here," Steven said. He dumped the food onto the curb, gasping for breath. "Here's the food. Is it finished?"

Cole held out the inter-system vidsender. "It's finished. It was pretty badly smashed."

Earl and Sally gazed up, wide-eyed. "Does it work?" Sally asked.

"Of course not," Earl stated. "How could it work? He couldn't —"

"Turn it on!" Sally nudged Steven eagerly. "See if it works."

Steven was holding the box under the light, examining the switches. He clicked the main switch on. The indicator light gleamed. "It lights up," Steven said.

"Say something into it."

Steven spoke into the box. "Hello! Hello! This is operator 6-Z75 calling. Can you hear me? This is operator 6-Z75. Can you hear me?"

In the darkness, away from the beam of the guide-light, Thomas Cole sat crouched over the food. He ate gratefully, silently. It was good food, well cooked and seasoned. He drank a container of orange juice and then a sweet drink he didn't recognize. Most of the food was strange to him, but he didn't care. He had walked a long way and he was plenty hungry. And he still had a long way to go, before morning. He had to be deep in the hills before the sun came up. Instinct told him that he would be safe among the trees and tangled growth-at least, as safe as he could hope for.

He ate rapidly, intent on the food. He did not look up until he was finished. Then he got slowly to his feet, wiping his mouth with the back of his hand.

The three children were standing around in a circle, operating the inter-system vidsender. He watched them for a few minutes. None of them looked up from the small box. They were intent, absorbed in what they were doing.

"Well?" Cole said, at last. "Does it work all right?"

After a moment Steven looked up at him. There was a strange expression on his face. He nodded slowly. "Yes. Yes, it works. It works fine."

Cole grunted. "All right." He turned and moved away from the light. "That's fine."

The children watched silently until the figure of Thomas Cole had completely disappeared. Slowly, they turned and looked at each other. Then down at the box in Steven's hands. They gazed at the box in growing awe. Awe mixed with dawning fear.

Steven turned and edged toward his house. "I've got to show it to my Dad," he murmured, dazed. "He's got to know. *Somebody's* got to know!"

III

Eric Reinhart examined the vidsender box carefully, turning it around and around.

"Then he did escape from the blast," Dixon admitted reluctantly. "He must have leaped from the cart just before the concussion."

Reinhart nodded. "He escaped. He got away from you-twice." He pushed the vidsender box away and leaned abruptly toward the man standing uneasily in front of his desk. "What's your name again?"

"Elliot. Richard Elliot."

"And your son's name?"

"Steven."

"It was last night this happened?"

"About eight o'clock."

"Go on."

"Steven came into the house. He acted queerly. He was carrying his inter-system vidsender." Elliot pointed at the box on Reinhart's desk. "That. He was nervous and excited. I asked what was wrong. For awhile he couldn't tell me. He was quite upset. Then he showed me the vidsender." Elliot took a deep, shaky breath. "I could see right away it was different. You see I'm an electrical engineer. I had opened it once before, to put in a new battery. I had a fairly good idea how it should look." Elliot hesitated. "Commissioner, it had been *changed*. A lot of the wiring was different. Moved around. Relays connected differently. Some parts were missing. New parts had been jury rigged out of old. Then I discovered the thing that made me call Security. The vidsender-it really *worked*."

"Worked?"

"You see, it never was anything more than a toy. With a range of a few city blocks. So the kids could call back and forth from their rooms. Like a sort of portable vidscreen. Commissioner, I tried out the vidsender, pushing the call button and speaking into the microphone. I—I got a ship of the line. A battleship, operating beyond Proxima Centaurus-over eight light years away. As far out as the actual vidsenders operate. Then I called Security. Right away."

For a time Reinhart was silent. Finally he tapped the box lying on the desk. "You got a ship of the line-with *this?*"

"That's right."

"How big are the regular vidsenders?"

Dixon supplied the information. "As big as a twenty-ton safe."

"That's what I thought." Reinhart waved his hand impatiently. "All right, Elliot. Thanks for turning the information over to us. That's all."

Security police led Elliot outside the office.

Reinhart and Dixon looked at each other. "This is bad," Reinhart said harshly. "He has some ability, some kind of mechanical ability. Genius, perhaps, to do a thing like this. Look at the period he came from, Dixon. The early part of the twentieth century. Before the wars began. That was a unique period. There was a certain vitality, a certain ability. It was a period of incredible growth and discovery. Edison. Pasteur. Burbank. The Wright brothers. Inventions and machines. People had an uncanny ability with machines. A kind of intuition about machines-which we don't have."

"You mean —"

"I mean a person like this coming into our own time is bad in itself, war or no war. He's too different. He's oriented along different lines. He has abilities we lack. This fixing skill of his. It throws us off, out of kilter. And with the war...."

"Now I'm beginning to understand why the SRB machines couldn't factor him. It's impossible for us to understand this kind of person. Winslow says he asked for work, any kind of work. The man said he could do anything, fix anything. Do you understand what that means?"

"No," Dixon said. "What does it mean?"

"Can any of us fix anything? No. None of us can do that. We're specialized. Each of us has his own line, his own work. I understand my work, you understand yours. The tendency in evolution is toward greater and greater specialization. Man's society is an ecology that forces adaptation to it. Continual complexity makes it impossible for any of us to know anything outside our own personal field —I can't follow the work of the man sitting at the next desk over from me. Too much knowledge has piled up in each field. And there's too many fields.

"This man is different. He can fix anything, do anything. He doesn't work with knowledge, with science-the classified accumulation of facts. He *knows* nothing. It's not in his head, a form of learning. He works by intuition-his power is in his hands, not his head. Jack-of-all-trades. His hands! Like a painter, an artist. In his hands-and he cuts across our lives like a knife-blade."

"And the other problem?"

"The other problem is that this man, this variable man, has escaped into the Albertine Mountain range. Now we'll have one hell of a time finding him. He's clever-in a strange kind of way. Like some sort of animal. He's going to be hard to catch."

Reinhart sent Dixon out. After a moment he gathered up the handful of reports on his desk and carried them up to the SRB room. The SRB room was closed up, sealed off by a ring of armed Security police. Standing angrily before the ring of police was Peter Sherikov, his beard waggling angrily, his immense hands on his hips.

"What's going on?" Sherikov demanded. "Why can't I go in and peep at the odds?"

"Sorry." Reinhart cleared the police aside. "Come inside with me. I'll explain." The doors opened for them and they entered. Behind them the doors shut and the ring of police formed outside. "What brings you away from your lab?" Reinhart asked.

Sherikov shrugged. "Several things. I wanted to see you. I called you on the vidphone and they said you weren't available. I thought maybe something had happened. What's up?"

"I'll tell you in a few minutes." Reinhart called Kaplan over. "Here are some new items. Feed them in right away. I want to see if the machines can total them."

"Certainly, Commissioner." Kaplan took the message plates and placed them on an intake belt. The machines hummed into life.

"We'll know soon," Reinhart said, half aloud.

Sherikov shot him a keen glance. "We'll know what? Let me in on it. What's taking place?"

"We're in trouble. For twenty-four hours the machines haven't given any reading at all. Nothing but a blank. A total blank."

Sherikov's features registered disbelief. "But that isn't possible. *Some* odds exist at all times."

"The odds exist, but the machines aren't able to calculate them."

"Why not?"

"Because a variable factor has been introduced. A factor which the machines can't handle. They can't make any predictions from it."

"Can't they reject it?" Sherikov said slyly. "Can't they just-just *ignore* it?"

"No. It exists, as real data. Therefore it affects the balance of the material, the sum total of all other available data. To reject it would be to give a false reading. The machines can't reject any data that's known to be true."

Sherikov pulled moodily at his black beard. "I would be interested in knowing what sort of factor the machines can't handle. I thought they could take in all data pertaining to contemporary reality."

"They can. This factor has nothing to do with contemporary reality. That's the trouble. Histo-research in bringing its time bubble back from the past got overzealous and cut the circuit too quickly. The bubble came back loaded-with a man from the twentieth century. A man from the past."

"I see. A man from two centuries ago." The big Pole frowned. "And with a radically different Weltanschauung. No connection with our present society. Not integrated along our lines at all. Therefore the SRB machines are perplexed."

Reinhart grinned. "Perplexed? I suppose so. In any case, they can't do anything with the data about this man. The variable man. No statistics at all have been thrown up-no predictions have been made. And it knocks everything else out of phase. We're dependent on the constant showing of these odds. The whole war effort is geared around them."

"The horse-shoe nail. Remember the old poem? 'For want of a nail the shoe was lost. For want of the shoe the horse was lost. For want of the horse the rider was lost. For want —'"

"Exactly. A single factor coming along like this, one single individual, can throw everything off. It doesn't seem possible that one person could knock an entire society out of balance-but apparently it is."

"What are you doing about this man?"

"The Security police are organized in a mass search for him."

"Results?"

"He escaped into the Albertine Mountain Range last night. It'll be hard to find him. We must expect him to be loose for another forty-eight hours. It'll take that long for us to arrange the annihilation of the range area. Perhaps a trifle longer. And meanwhile —"

"Ready, Commissioner," Kaplan interrupted. "The new totals."

The SRB machines had finished factoring the new data. Reinhart and Sherikov hurried to take their places before the view windows.

For a moment nothing happened. Then odds were put up, locking in place.

Sherikov gasped. 99-2. In favor of Terra. "That's wonderful! Now we —"

The odds vanished. New odds took their places. 97-4. In favor of Centaurus. Sherikov groaned in astonished dismay. "Wait," Reinhart said to him. "I don't think they'll last."

The odds vanished. A rapid series of odds shot across the screen, a violent stream of numbers, changing almost instantly. At last the machines became silent.

Nothing showed. No odds. No totals at all. The view windows were blank.

"You see?" Reinhart murmured. "The same damn thing!"

Sherikov pondered. "Reinhart, you're too Anglo-Saxon, too impulsive. Be more Slavic. This man will be captured and destroyed within two days. You said so yourself. Meanwhile, we're all working night and day on the war effort. The warfleet is waiting near Proxima, taking up positions for the attack on the Centaurans. All our war plants are going full blast. By the time the attack date comes we'll have a full-sized invasion army ready to take off for the long trip to the Centauran colonies. The whole Terran population has been mobilized. The eight supply planets are pouring in material. All this is going on day and night, even without odds showing. Long before the attack comes this man will certainly be dead, and the machines will be able to show odds again."

Reinhart considered. "But it worries me, a man like that out in the open. Loose. A man who can't be predicted. It goes against science. We've been making statistical reports on society for two centuries. We have immense files of data. The machines are able to predict what each person and group will do at a given time, in a given situation. But this man is beyond all prediction. He's a variable. It's contrary to science."

"The indeterminate particle."

"What's that?"

"The particle that moves in such a way that we can't predict what position it will occupy at a given second. Random. The random particle."

"Exactly. It's —it's *unnatural.*"

Sherikov laughed sarcastically. "Don't worry about it, Commissioner. The man will be captured and things will return to their natural state. You'll be able to predict people again, like laboratory rats in a maze. By the way-why is this room guarded?"

"I don't want anyone to know the machines show no totals. It's dangerous to the war effort."

"Margaret Duffe, for example?"

Reinhart nodded reluctantly. "They're too timid, these parliamentarians. If they discover we have no SRB odds they'll want to shut down the war planning and go back to waiting."

"Too slow for you, Commissioner? Laws, debates, council meetings, discussions.... Saves a lot of time if one man has all the power. One man to tell people what to do, think for them, lead them around."

Reinhart eyed the big Pole critically. "That reminds me. How is Icarus coming? Have you continued to make progress on the control turret?"

A scowl crossed Sherikov's broad features. "The control turret?" He waved his big hand vaguely. "I would say it's coming along all right. We'll catch up in time."

Instantly Reinhart became alert. "Catch up? You mean you're still behind?"

"Somewhat. A little. But we'll catch up." Sherikov retreated toward the door. "Let's go down to the cafeteria and have a cup of coffee. You worry too much, Commissioner. Take things more in your stride."

"I suppose you're right." The two men walked out into the hall. "I'm on edge. This variable man. I can't get him out of my mind."

"Has he done anything yet?"

"Nothing important. Rewired a child's toy. A toy vidsender."

"Oh?" Sherikov showed interest. "What do you mean? What did he do?"

"I'll show you." Reinhart led Sherikov down the hall to his office. They entered and Reinhart locked the door. He handed Sherikov the toy and roughed in what Cole had done. A strange look crossed Sherikov's face. He found the studs on the box and depressed them. The box opened. The big Pole sat down at the desk and began to study the interior of the box. "You're sure it was the man from the past who rewired this?"

"Of course. On the spot. The boy damaged it playing. The variable man came along and the boy asked him to fix it. He fixed it, all right."

"Incredible." Sherikov's eyes were only an inch from the wiring. "Such tiny relays. How could he —"

"What?"

"Nothing." Sherikov got abruptly to his feet, closing the box carefully. "Can I take this along? To my lab? I'd like to analyze it more fully."

"Of course. But why?"

"No special reason. Let's go get our coffee." Sherikov headed toward the door. "You say you expect to capture this man in a day or so?"

"*Kill* him, not capture him. We've got to eliminate him as a piece of data. We're assembling the attack formations right now. No slip-ups, this time. We're in the process of setting up a cross-bombing pattern to level the entire Albertine range. He must be destroyed, within the next forty-eight hours."

Sherikov nodded absently. "Of course," he murmured. A preoccupied expression still remained on his broad features. "I understand perfectly."

* * * * *

Thomas Cole crouched over the fire he had built, warming his hands. It was almost morning. The sky was turning violet gray. The mountain air was crisp and chill. Cole shivered and pulled himself closer to the fire.

The heat felt good against his hands. *His hands.* He gazed down at them, glowing yellow-red in the firelight. The nails were black and chipped. Warts and endless calluses on each finger, and the palms. But they were good hands; the fingers were long and tapered. He respected them, although in some ways he didn't understand them.

Cole was deep in thought, meditating over his situation. He had been in the mountains two nights and a day. The first night had been the worst. Stumbling and falling, making his way uncertainly up the steep slopes, through the tangled brush and undergrowth —

But when the sun came up he was safe, deep in the mountains, between two great peaks. And by the time the sun had set again he had fixed himself up a shelter and a means of making a fire. Now he had a neat little box trap, operated by a plaited grass rope and pit, a notched stake. One rabbit already hung by his hind legs and the trap was waiting for another.

The sky turned from violet gray to a deep cold gray, a metallic color. The mountains were silent and empty. Far off some place a bird sang, its voice echoing across the vast slopes and ravines. Other birds began to sing. Off to his right something crashed through the brush, an animal pushing its way along.

Day was coming. His second day. Cole got to his feet and began to unfasten the rabbit. Time to eat. And then? After that he had no plans. He knew instinctively that he could keep himself alive indefinitely with the tools he had retained, and the genius of his hands. He could kill game and skin it. Eventually he could build himself a permanent shelter, even make clothes but of hides. In winter —

But he was not thinking that far ahead. Cole stood by the fire, staring up at the sky, his hands on his hips. He squinted, suddenly tense. Something was moving. Something in the sky, drifting slowly through the grayness. A black dot.

He stamped out the fire quickly. What was it? He strained, trying to see. A bird?

A second dot joined the first. Two dots. Then three. Four. Five. A fleet of them, moving rapidly across the early morning sky. Toward the mountains.

Toward him.

Cole hurried away from the fire. He snatched up the rabbit and carried it along with him, into the tangled shelter he had built. He was invisible, inside the shelter. No one could find him. But if they had seen the fire —

He crouched in the shelter, watching the dots grow larger. They were planes, all right. Black wingless planes, coming closer each moment. Now he could hear them, a faint dull buzz, increasing until the ground shook under him.

The first plane dived. It dropped like a stone, swelling into a great black shape. Cole gasped, sinking down. The plane roared in an arc, swooping low over the ground. Suddenly bundles tumbled out, white bundles falling and scattering like seeds.

The bundles drifted rapidly to the ground. They landed. They were men. Men in uniform.

Now the second plane was diving. It roared overhead, releasing its load. More bundles tumbled out, filling the sky. The third plane dived, then the fourth. The air was thick with drifting bundles of white, a blanket of descending weed spores, settling to earth.

On the ground the soldiers were forming into groups. Their shouts carried to Cole, crouched in his shelter. Fear leaped through him. They were landing on all sides of him. He was cut off. The last two planes had dropped men behind him.

He got to his feet, pushing out of the shelter. Some of the soldiers had found the fire, the ashes and coals. One dropped down, feeling the coals with his hand. He waved to the others. They were circling all around, shouting and gesturing. One of them began to set up some kind of gun. Others were unrolling coils of tubing, locking a collection of strange pipes and machinery in place.

Cole ran. He rolled down a slope, sliding and falling. At the bottom he leaped to his feet and plunged into the brush. Vines and leaves tore at his face, slashing and cutting him. He fell again, tangled in a mass of twisted shrubbery. He fought desperately, trying to free himself. If he could reach the knife in his pocket —

Voices. Footsteps. Men were behind him, running down the slope. Cole struggled frantically, gasping and twisting, trying to pull loose. He strained, breaking the vines, clawing at them with his hands.

A soldier dropped to his knee, leveling his gun. More soldiers arrived, bringing up their rifles and aiming.

Cole cried out. He closed his eyes, his body suddenly limp. He waited, his teeth locked together, sweat dripping down his neck, into his shirt, sagging against the mesh of vines and branches coiled around him.

Silence.

Cole opened his eyes slowly. The soldiers had regrouped. A huge man was striding down the slope toward them, barking orders as he came.

Two soldiers stepped into the brush. One of them grabbed Cole by the shoulder.

"Don't let go of him." The huge man came over, his black beard jutting out. "Hold on."

Cole gasped for breath. He was caught. There was nothing he could do. More soldiers were pouring down into the gulley, surrounding him on all sides. They studied him curiously, murmuring together. Cole shook his head wearily and said nothing.

The huge man with the beard stood directly in front of him, his hands on his hips, looking him up and down. "Don't try to get away," the man said. "You can't get away. Do you understand?"

Cole nodded.

"All right. Good." The man waved. Soldiers clamped metal bands around Cole's arms and wrists. The metal dug into his flesh, making him gasp with pain. More clamps locked around his legs. "Those stay there until we're out of here. A long way out."

"Where-where are you taking me?"

Peter Sherikov studied the variable man for a moment before he answered. "Where? I'm taking you to my labs. Under the Urals." He glanced suddenly up at the sky. "We better hurry.

The Security police will be starting their demolition attack in a few hours. We want to be a long way from here when that begins."

* * * * *

Sherikov settled down in his comfortable reinforced chair with a sigh. "It's good to be back." He signalled to one of his guards. "All right. You can unfasten him."

The metal clamps were removed from Cole's arms and legs. He sagged, sinking down in a heap. Sherikov watched him silently.

Cole sat on the floor, rubbing wrists and legs, saying nothing.

"What do you want?" Sherikov demanded. "Food? Are you hungry?"

"No."

"Medicine? Are you sick? Injured?"

"No."

Sherikov wrinkled his nose. "A bath wouldn't hurt you any. We'll arrange that later." He lit a cigar, blowing a cloud of gray smoke around him. At the door of the room two lab guards stood with guns ready. No one else was in the room beside Sherikov and Cole.

Thomas Cole sat huddled in a heap on the floor, his head sunk down against his chest. He did not stir. His bent body seemed more elongated and stooped than ever, his hair tousled and unkempt, his chin and jowls a rough stubbled gray. His clothes were dirty and torn from crawling through the brush. His skin was cut and scratched; open sores dotted his neck and cheeks and forehead. He said nothing. His chest rose and fell. His faded blue eyes were almost closed. He looked quite old, a withered, dried-up old man.

Sherikov waved one of the guards over. "Have a doctor brought up here. I want this man checked over. He may need intravenous injections. He may not have had anything to eat for awhile."

The guard departed.

"I don't want anything to happen to you," Sherikov said. "Before we go on I'll have you checked over. And deloused at the same time."

Cole said nothing.

Sherikov laughed. "Buck up! You have no reason to feel bad." He leaned toward Cole, jabbing an immense finger at him. "Another two hours and you'd have been dead, out there in the mountains. You know that?"

Cole nodded.

"You don't believe me. Look." Sherikov leaned over and snapped on the vidscreen mounted in the wall. "Watch, this. The operation should still be going on."

The screen lit up. A scene gained form.

"This is a confidential Security channel. I had it tapped several years ago–for my own protection. What we're seeing now is being piped in to Eric Reinhart." Sherikov grinned. "Reinhart arranged what you're seeing on the screen. Pay close attention. You were there, two hours ago."

Cole turned toward the screen. At first he could not make out what was happening. The screen showed a vast foaming cloud, a vortex of motion. From the speaker came a low rumble, a deep-throated roar. After a time the screen shifted, showing a slightly different view. Suddenly Cole stiffened.

He was seeing the destruction of a whole mountain range.

The picture was coming from a ship, flying above what had once been the Albertine Mountain Range. Now there was nothing but swirling clouds of gray and columns of particles and debris, a surging tide of restless material gradually sweeping off and dissipating in all directions.

The Albertine Mountains had been disintegrated. Nothing remained but these vast clouds of debris. Below, on the ground, a ragged plain stretched out, swept by fire and ruin. Gaping wounds yawned, immense holes without bottom, craters side by side as far as the eye could see.

Craters and debris. Like the blasted, pitted surface of the moon. Two hours ago it had been rolling peaks and gulleys, brush and green bushes and trees.

Cole turned away.

"You see?" Sherikov snapped the screen off. "You were down there, not so long ago. All that noise and smoke-all for you. All for you, Mr. Variable Man from the past. Reinhart arranged that, to finish you off. I want you to understand that. It's very important that you realize that."

Cole said nothing.

Sherikov reached into a drawer of the table before him. He carefully brought out a small square box and held it out to Cole. "You wired this, didn't you?"

Cole took the box in his hands and held it. For a time his tired mind failed to focus. What did he have? He concentrated on it. The box was the children's toy. The inter-system vidsender, they had called it.

"Yes. I fixed this." He passed it back to Sherikov. "I repaired that. It was broken."

Sherikov gazed down at him intently, his large eyes bright. He nodded, his black beard and cigar rising and falling. "Good. That's all I wanted to know." He got suddenly to his feet, pushing his chair back. "I see the doctor's here. He'll fix you up. Everything you need. Later on I'll talk to you again."

Unprotesting, Cole got to his feet, allowing the doctor to take hold of his arm and help him up.

After Cole had been released by the medical department, Sherikov joined him in his private dining room, a floor above the actual laboratory.

The Pole gulped down a hasty meal, talking as he ate. Cole sat silently across from him, not eating or speaking. His old clothing had been taken away and new clothing given him. He was shaved and rubbed down. His sores and cuts were healed, his body and hair washed. He looked much healthier and younger, now. But he was still stooped and tired, his blue eyes worn and faded. He listened to Sherikov's account of the world of 2136 AD without comment.

"You can see," Sherikov said finally, waving a chicken leg, "that your appearance here has been very upsetting to our program. Now that you know more about us you can see why Commissioner Reinhart was so interested in destroying you."

Cole nodded.

"Reinhart, you realize, believes that the failure of the SRB machines is the chief danger to the war effort. But that is nothing!" Sherikov pushed his plate away noisily, draining his coffee mug. "After all, wars *can* be fought without statistical forecasts. The SRB machines only describe. They're nothing more than mechanical onlookers. In themselves, they don't affect the course of the war. *We* make the war. They only analyze."

Cole nodded.

"More coffee?" Sherikov asked. He pushed the plastic container toward Cole. "Have some."

Cole accepted another cupful. "Thank you."

"You can see that our real problem is another thing entirely. The machines only do figuring for us in a few minutes that eventually we could do for our own selves. They're our servants, tools. Not some sort of gods in a temple which we go and pray to. Not oracles who can see into the future for us. They don't see into the future. They only make statistical predictions-not prophecies. There's a big difference there, but Reinhart doesn't understand it. Reinhart and his kind have made such things as the SRB machines into gods. But I have no gods. At least, not any I can see."

Cole nodded, sipping his coffee.

"I'm telling you all these things because you must understand what we're up against. Terra is hemmed in on all sides by the ancient Centauran Empire. It's been out there for centuries, thousands of years. No one knows how long. It's old-crumbling and rotting. Corrupt and venal. But it holds most of the galaxy around us, and we can't break out of the Sol system. I told you about Icarus, and Hedge's work in ftl flight. We must win the war against Centaurus. We've waited and worked a long time for this, the moment when we can break out and get room among the stars for ourselves. Icarus is the deciding weapon. The data on Icarus tipped the SRB odds in our favor-for the first time in history. Success in the war against Centaurus will depend on Icarus, not on the SRB machines. You see?"

Cole nodded.

"However, there is a problem. The data on Icarus which I turned over to the machines specified that Icarus would be completed in ten days. More than half that time has already passed. Yet, we are no closer to wiring up the control turret than we were then. The turret baffles us." Sherikov grinned ironically. "Even *I* have tried my hand at the wiring, but with no success. It's intricate-and small. Too many technical bugs not worked out. We are building only one, you understand. If we had many experimental models worked out before —"

"But this is the experimental model," Cole said.

"And built from the designs of a man dead four years-who isn't here to correct us. We've made Icarus with our own hands, down here in the labs. And he's giving us plenty of trouble." All at once Sherikov got to his feet. "Let's go down to the lab and look at him."

They descended to the floor below, Sherikov leading the way. Cole stopped short at the lab door.

"Quite a sight," Sherikov agreed. "We keep him down here at the bottom for safety's sake. He's well protected. Come on in. We have work to do."

In the center of the lab Icarus rose up, the gray squat cylinder that someday would flash through space at a speed of thousands of times that of light, toward the heart of Proxima Centaurus, over four light years away. Around the cylinder groups of men in uniform were laboring feverishly to finish the remaining work.

"Over here. The turret." Sherikov led Cole over to one side of the room. "It's guarded. Centauran spies are swarming everywhere on Terra. They see into everything. But so do we. That's how we get information for the SRB machines. Spies in both systems."

The translucent globe that was the control turret reposed in the center of a metal stand, an armed guard standing at each side. They lowered their guns as Sherikov approached.

"We don't want anything to happen to this," Sherikov said. "Everything depends on it." He put out his hand for the globe. Half way to it his hand stopped, striking against an invisible presence in the air.

Sherikov laughed. "The wall. Shut it off. It's still on."

One of the guards pressed a stud at his wrist. Around the globe the air shimmered and faded.

"Now." Sherikov's hand closed over the globe. He lifted it carefully from its mount and brought it out for Cole to see. "This is the control turret for our enormous friend here. This is what will slow him down when he's inside Centaurus. He slows down and re-enters this universe. Right in the heart of the star. Then-no more Centaurus." Sherikov beamed. "And no more Armun."

But Cole was not listening. He had taken the globe from Sherikov and was turning it over and over, running his hands over it, his face close to its surface. He peered down into its interior, his face rapt and intent.

"You can't see the wiring. Not without lenses." Sherikov signalled for a pair of micro-lenses to be brought. He fitted them on Cole's nose, hooking them behind his ears. "Now try it. You can control the magnification. It's set for 1000X right now. You can increase or decrease it."

Cole gasped, swaying back and forth. Sherikov caught hold of him. Cole gazed down into the globe, moving his head slightly, focussing the glasses.

"It takes practice. But you can do a lot with them. Permits you to do microscopic wiring. There are tools to go along, you understand." Sherikov paused, licking his lip. "We can't get it done correctly. Only a few men can wire circuits using the micro-lenses and the little tools. We've tried robots, but there are too many decisions to be made. Robots can't make decisions. They just react."

Cole said nothing. He continued to gaze into the interior of the globe, his lips tight, his body taut and rigid. It made Sherikov feel strangely uneasy.

"You look like one of those old fortune tellers," Sherikov said jokingly, but a cold shiver crawled up his spine. "Better hand it back to me." He held out his hand.

Slowly, Cole returned the globe. After a time he removed the micro-lenses, still deep in thought.

"Well?" Sherikov demanded. "You know what I want. I want you to wire this damn thing up." Sherikov came close to Cole, his big face hard. "You can do it, I think. I could tell by the way you held it-and the job you did on the children's toy, of course. You could wire it up right, and in five days. Nobody else can. And if it's not wired up Centaurus will keep on running the galaxy and Terra will have to sweat it out here in the Sol system. One tiny mediocre sun, one dust mote out of a whole galaxy."

Cole did not answer.

Sherikov became impatient. "Well? What do you say?"

"What happens if I don't wire this control for you? I mean, what happens to *me?*"

"Then I turn you over to Reinhart. Reinhart will kill you instantly. He thinks you're dead, killed when the Albertine Range was annihilated. If he had any idea I had saved you —"

"I see."

"I brought you down here for one thing. If you wire it up I'll have you sent back to your own time continuum. If you don't —"

Cole considered, his face dark and brooding.

"What do you have to lose? You'd already be dead, if we hadn't pulled you out of those hills."

"Can you really return me to my own time?"

"Of course!"

"Reinhart won't interfere?"

Sherikov laughed. "What can he do? How can he stop me? I have my own men. You saw them. They landed all around you. You'll be returned."

"Yes. I saw your men."

"Then you agree?"

"I agree," Thomas Cole said. "I'll wire it for you. I'll complete the control turret-within the next five days."

IV

Three days later Joseph Dixon slid a closed-circuit message plate across the desk to his boss.

"Here. You might be interested in this."

Reinhart picked the plate up slowly. "What is it? You came all the way here to show me this?"

"That's right."

"Why didn't you vidscreen it?"

Dixon smiled grimly. "You'll understand when you decode it. It's from Proxima Centaurus."

"Centaurus!"

"Our counter-intelligence service. They sent it direct to me. Here, I'll decode it for you. Save you the trouble."

Dixon came around behind Reinhart's desk. He leaned over the Commissioner's shoulder, taking hold of the plate and breaking the seal with his thumb nail.

"Hang on," Dixon said. "This is going to hit you hard. According to our agents on Armun, the Centauran High Council has called an emergency session to deal with the problem of Terra's impending attack. Centauran relay couriers have reported to the High Council that the Terran bomb Icarus is virtually complete. Work on the bomb has been rushed through final stages in the underground laboratories under the Ural Range, directed by the Terran physicist Peter Sherikov."

"So I understand from Sherikov himself. Are you surprised the Centaurans know about the bomb? They have spies swarming over Terra. That's no news."

"There's more." Dixon traced the message plate grimly, with an unsteady finger. "The Centauran relay couriers reported that Peter Sherikov brought an expert mechanic out of a previous time continuum to complete the wiring of the turret!"

Reinhart staggered, holding on tight to the desk. He closed his eyes, gasping.

"The variable man is still alive," Dixon murmured. "I don't know how. Or why. There's nothing left of the Albertines. And how the hell did the man get half way around the world?"

Reinhart opened his eyes slowly, his face twisting. "Sherikov! He must have removed him before the attack. I told Sherikov the attack was forthcoming. I gave him the exact hour. He had to get help from the variable man. He couldn't meet his promise otherwise."

Reinhart leaped up and began to pace back and forth. "I've already informed the SRB machines that the variable man has been destroyed. The machines now show the original 7-6 ratio in our favor. But the ratio is based on false information."

"Then you'll have to withdraw the false data and restore the original situation."

"No." Reinhart shook his head. "I can't do that. The machines must be kept functioning. We can't allow them to jam again. It's too dangerous. If Duffe should become aware that —"

"What are you going to do, then?" Dixon picked up the message plate. "You can't leave the machines with false data. That's treason."

"The data can't be withdrawn! Not unless equivalent data exists to take its place." Reinhart paced angrily back and forth. "Damn it, I was *certain* the man was dead. This is an incredible situation. He must be eliminated-at any cost."

Suddenly Reinhart stopped pacing. "The turret. It's probably finished by this time. Correct?"

Dixon nodded slowly in agreement. "With the variable man helping, Sherikov has undoubtedly completed work well ahead of schedule."

Reinhart's gray eyes flickered. "Then he's no longer of any use-even to Sherikov. We could take a chance.... Even if there were active opposition...."

"What's this?" Dixon demanded. "What are you thinking about?"

"How many units are ready for immediate action? How large a force can we raise without notice?"

"Because of the war we're mobilized on a twenty-four hour basis. There are seventy air units and about two hundred surface units. The balance of the Security forces have been transferred to the line, under military control."

"Men?"

"We have about five thousand men ready to go, still on Terra. Most of them in the process of being transferred to military transports. I can hold it up at any time."

"Missiles?"

"Fortunately, the launching tubes have not yet been disassembled. They're still here on Terra. In another few days they'll be moving out for the Colonial fracas."

"Then they're available for immediate use?"

"Yes."

"Good." Reinhart locked his hands, knotting his fingers harshly together in sudden decision. "That will do exactly. Unless I am completely wrong, Sherikov has only a half-dozen air units and no surface cars. And only about two hundred men. Some defense shields, of course —"

"What are you planning?"

Reinhart's face was gray and hard, like stone. "Send out orders for all available Security units to be unified under your immediate command. Have them ready to move by four o'clock this afternoon. We're going to pay a visit," Reinhart stated grimly. "A surprise visit. On Peter Sherikov."

* * * * *

"Stop here," Reinhart ordered.

The surface car slowed to a halt. Reinhart peered cautiously out, studying the horizon ahead.

On all sides a desert of scrub grass and sand stretched out. Nothing moved or stirred. To the right the grass and sand rose up to form immense peaks, a range of mountains without end, disappearing finally into the distance. The Urals.

"Over there," Reinhart said to Dixon, pointing. "See?"

"No."

"Look hard. It's difficult to spot unless you know what to look for. Vertical pipes. Some kind of vent. Or periscopes."

Dixon saw them finally. "I would have driven past without noticing."

"It's well concealed. The main labs are a mile down. Under the range itself. It's virtually impregnable. Sherikov had it built years ago, to withstand any attack. From the air, by surface cars, bombs, missiles —"

"He must feel safe down there."

"No doubt." Reinhart gazed up at the sky. A few faint black dots could be seen, moving lazily about, in broad circles. "Those aren't ours, are they? I gave orders —"

"No. They're not ours. All our units are out of sight. Those belong to Sherikov. His patrol."

Reinhart relaxed. "Good." He reached over and flicked on the vidscreen over the board of the car. "This screen is shielded? It can't be traced?"

"There's no way they can spot it back to us. It's non-directional."

The screen glowed into life. Reinhart punched the combination keys and sat back to wait.

After a time an image formed on the screen. A heavy face, bushy black beard and large eyes. Peter Sherikov gazed at Reinhart with surprised curiosity. "Commissioner! Where are you calling from? What —"

"How's the work progressing?" Reinhart broke in coldly. "Is Icarus almost complete?"

Sherikov beamed with expansive pride. "He's done, Commissioner. Two days ahead of time. Icarus is ready to be launched into space. I tried to call your office, but they told me —"

"I'm not at my office." Reinhart leaned toward the screen. "Open your entrance tunnel at the surface. You're about to receive visitors."

Sherikov blinked. "Visitors?"

"I'm coming down to see you. About Icarus. Have the tunnel opened for me at once."

"Exactly where are you, Commissioner?"

"On the surface."

Sherikov's eyes flickered. "Oh? But —"

"Open up!" Reinhart snapped. He glanced at his wristwatch. "I'll be at the entrance in five minutes. I expect to find it ready for me."

"Of course." Sherikov nodded in bewilderment. "I'm always glad to see you, Commissioner. But I —"

"Five minutes, then." Reinhart cut the circuit. The screen died. He turned quickly to Dixon. "You stay up here, as we arranged. I'll go down with one company of police. You understand the necessity of exact timing on this?"

"We won't slip up. Everything's ready. All units are in their places."

"Good." Reinhart pushed the door open for him. "You join your directional staff. I'll proceed toward the tunnel entrance."

"Good luck." Dixon leaped out of the car, onto the sandy ground. A gust of dry air swirled into the car around Reinhart. "I'll see you later."

Reinhart slammed the door. He turned to the group of police crouched in the rear of the car, their guns held tightly. "Here we go," Reinhart murmured. "Hold on."

The car raced across the sandy ground, toward the tunnel entrance to Sherikov's underground fortress.

Sherikov met Reinhart at the bottom end of the tunnel, where the tunnel opened up onto the main floor of the lab.

The big Pole approached, his hand out, beaming with pride and satisfaction. "It's a pleasure to see you, Commissioner. This is an historic moment."

Reinhart got out of the car, with his group of armed Security police. "Calls for a celebration, doesn't it?" he said.

"That's a good idea! We're two days ahead, Commissioner. The SRB machines will be interested. The odds should change abruptly at the news."

"Let's go down to the lab. I want to see the control turret myself."

A shadow crossed Sherikov's face. "I'd rather not bother the workmen right now, Commissioner. They've been under a great load, trying to complete the turret in time. I believe they're putting a few last finishes on it at this moment."

"We can view them by vidscreen. I'm curious to see them at work. It must be difficult to wire such minute relays."

Sherikov shook his head. "Sorry, Commissioner. No vidscreen on them. I won't allow it. This is too important. Our whole future depends on it."

Reinhart snapped a signal to his company of police. "Put this man under arrest."

Sherikov blanched. His mouth fell open. The police moved quickly around him, their gun tubes up, jabbing into him. He was searched rapidly, efficiently. His gun belt and concealed energy screen were yanked off.

"What's going on?" Sherikov demanded, some color returning to his face. "What are you doing?"

"You're under arrest for the duration of the war. You're relieved of all authority. From now on one of my men will operate Designs. When the war is over you'll be tried before the Council and President Duffe."

Sherikov shook his head, dazed. "I don't understand. What's this all about? Explain it to me, Commissioner. What's happened?"

Reinhart signalled to his police. "Get ready. We're going into the lab. We may have to shoot our way in. The variable man should be in the area of the bomb, working on the control turret."

Instantly Sherikov's face hardened. His black eyes glittered, alert and hostile.

Reinhart laughed harshly. "We received a counter-intelligence report from Centaurus. I'm surprised at you, Sherikov. You know the Centaurans are everywhere with their relay couriers. You should have known —"

Sherikov moved. Fast. All at once he broke away from the police, throwing his massive body against them. They fell, scattering. Sherikov ran-directly at the wall. The police fired wildly. Reinhart fumbled frantically for his gun tube, pulling it up.

Sherikov reached the wall, running head down, energy beams flashing around him. He struck against the wall-and vanished.

"Down!" Reinhart shouted. He dropped to his hands and knees. All around him his police dived for the floor. Reinhart cursed wildly, dragging himself quickly toward the door. They had to get out, and right away. Sherikov had escaped. A false wall, an energy barrier set to respond to his pressure. He had dashed through it to safety. He —

From all sides an inferno burst, a flaming roar of death surging over them, around them, on every side. The room was alive with blazing masses of destruction, bouncing from wall to wall. They were caught between four banks of power, all of them open to full discharge. A trap —a death trap.

* * * * *

Reinhart reached the hall gasping for breath. He leaped to his feet. A few Security police followed him. Behind them, in the flaming room, the rest of the company screamed and struggled, blasted out of existence by the leaping bursts of power.

Reinhart assembled his remaining men. Already, Sherikov's guards were forming. At one end of the corridor a snub-barreled robot gun was maneuvering into position. A siren wailed. Guards were running on all sides, hurrying to battle stations.

The robot gun opened fire. Part of the corridor exploded, bursting into fragments. Clouds of choking debris and particles swept around them. Reinhart and his police retreated, moving back along the corridor.

They reached a junction. A second robot gun was rumbling toward them, hurrying to get within range. Reinhart fired carefully, aiming at its delicate control. Abruptly the gun spun convulsively. It lashed against the wall, smashing itself into the unyielding metal. Then it collapsed in a heap, gears still whining and spinning.

"Come on." Reinhart moved away, crouching and running. He glanced at his watch. *Almost time.* A few more minutes. A group of lab guards appeared ahead of them. Reinhart fired. Behind him his police fired past him, violet shafts of energy catching the group of guards as they entered the corridor. The guards spilled apart, falling and twisting. Part of them settled into dust, drifting down the corridor. Reinhart made his way toward the lab, crouching and leaping, pushing past heaps of debris and remains, followed by his men. "Come on! Don't stop!"

* * * * *

Suddenly from around them the booming, enlarged voice of Sherikov thundered, magnified by rows of wall speakers along the corridor. Reinhart halted, glancing around.

"Reinhart! You haven't got a chance. You'll never get back to the surface. Throw down your guns and give up. You're surrounded on all sides. You're a mile, under the surface."

Reinhart threw himself into motion, pushing into billowing clouds of particles drifting along the corridor. "Are you sure, Sherikov?" he grunted.

Sherikov laughed, his harsh, metallic peals rolling in waves against Reinhart's eardrums. "I don't want to have to kill you, Commissioner. You're vital to the war: I'm sorry you found out about the variable man. I admit we overlooked the Centauran espionage as a factor in this. But now that you know about him —"

Suddenly Sherikov's voice broke off. A deep rumble had shaken the floor, a lapping vibration that shuddered through the corridor.

Reinhart sagged with relief. He peered through the clouds of debris, making out the figures on his watch. Right on time. Not a second late.

The first of the hydrogen missiles, launched from the Council buildings on the other side of the world, were beginning to arrive. The attack had begun.

At exactly six o'clock Joseph Dixon, standing on the surface four miles from the entrance tunnel, gave the sign to the waiting units.

The first job was to break down Sherikov's defense screens. The missiles had to penetrate without interference. At Dixon's signal a fleet of thirty Security ships dived from a height of ten miles, swooping above the mountains, directly over the underground laboratories. Within five minutes the defense screens had been smashed, and all the tower projectors leveled flat. Now the mountains were virtually unprotected.

"So far so good," Dixon murmured, as he watched from his secure position. The fleet of Security ships roared back, their work done. Across the face of the desert the police surface cars were crawling rapidly toward the entrance tunnel, snaking from side to side.

Meanwhile, Sherikov's counter-attack had begun to go into operation.

Guns mounted among the hills opened fire. Vast columns of flame burst up in the path of the advancing cars. The cars hesitated and retreated, as the plain was churned up by a howling vortex, a thundering chaos of explosions. Here and there a car vanished in a cloud of particles. A group of cars moving away suddenly scattered, caught up by a giant wind that lashed across them and swept them up into the air.

Dixon gave orders to have the cannon silenced. The police air arm again swept overhead, a sullen roar of jets that shook the ground below. The police ships divided expertly and hurtled down on the cannon protecting the hills.

The cannon forgot the surface cars and lifted their snouts to meet the attack. Again and again the airships came, rocking the mountains with titanic blasts.

The guns became silent. Their echoing boom diminished, died away reluctantly, as bombs took critical toll of them.

Dixon watched with satisfaction as the bombing came to an end. The airships rose in a thick swarm, black gnats shooting up in triumph from a dead carcass. They hurried back as emergency anti-aircraft robot guns swung into position and saturated the sky with blazing puffs of energy.

Dixon checked his wristwatch. The missiles were already on the way from North America. Only a few minutes remained.

The surface cars, freed by the successful bombing, began to regroup for a new frontal attack. Again they crawled forward, across the burning plain, bearing down cautiously on the battered wall of mountains, heading toward the twisted wrecks that had been the ring of defense guns. Toward the entrance tunnel.

An occasional cannon fired feebly at them. The cars came grimly on. Now, in the hollows of the hills, Sherikov's troops were hurrying to the surface to meet the attack. The first car reached the shadow of the mountains....

A deafening hail of fire burst loose. Small robot guns appeared everywhere, needle barrels emerging from behind hidden screens, trees and shrubs, rocks, stones. The police cars were caught in a withering cross-fire, trapped at the base of the hills.

Down the slopes Sherikov's guards raced, toward the stalled cars. Clouds of heat rose up and boiled across the plain as the cars fired up at the running men. A robot gun dropped like a slug onto the plain and screamed toward the cars, firing as it came.

Dixon twisted nervously. Only a few minutes. Any time, now. He shaded his eyes and peered up at the sky. No sign of them yet. He wondered about Reinhart. No signal had come up from below. Clearly, Reinhart had run into trouble. No doubt there was desperate fighting going on in the maze of underground tunnels, the intricate web of passages that honeycombed the earth below the mountains.

In the air, Sherikov's few defense ships were taking on the police raiders. Outnumbered, the defense ships darted rapidly, wildly, putting up a futile fight.

Sherikov's guards streamed out onto the plain. Crouching and running, they advanced toward the stalled cars. The police airships screeched down at them, guns thundering.

Dixon held his breath. When the missiles arrived —

The first missile struck. A section of the mountain vanished, turned to smoke and foaming gasses. The wave of heat slapped Dixon across the face, spinning him around. Quickly he re-entered his ship and took off, shooting rapidly away from the scene. He glanced back. A second and third missile had arrived. Great gaping pits yawned among the mountains, vast sections missing like broken teeth. Now the missiles could penetrate to the underground laboratories below.

On the ground, the surface cars halted beyond the danger area, waiting for the missile attack to finish. When the eighth missile had struck, the cars again moved forward. No more missiles fell.

Dixon swung his ship around, heading back toward the scene. The laboratory was exposed. The top sections of it had been ripped open. The laboratory lay like a tin can, torn apart by mighty explosions, its first floors visible from the air. Men and cars were pouring down into it, fighting with the guards swarming to the surface.

* * * * *

Dixon watched intently. Sherikov's men were bringing up heavy guns, big robot artillery. But the police ships were diving again. Sherikov's defensive patrols had been cleaned from the sky. The police ships whined down, arcing over the exposed laboratory. Small bombs fell, whistling down, pin-pointing the artillery rising to the surface on the remaining lift stages.

Abruptly Dixon's vidscreen clicked. Dixon turned toward it.

Reinhart's features formed. "Call off the attack." His uniform was torn. A deep bloody gash crossed his cheek. He grinned sourly at Dixon, pushing his tangled hair back out of his face. "Quite a fight."

"Sherikov —"

"He's called off his guards. We've agreed to a truce. It's all over. No more needed." Reinhart gasped for breath, wiping grime and sweat from his neck. "Land your ship and come down here at once."

"The variable man?"

"That comes next," Reinhart said grimly. He adjusted his gun tube. "I want you down here, for that part. I want you to be in on the kill."

Reinhart turned away from the vidscreen. In the corner of the room Sherikov stood silently, saying nothing. "Well?" Reinhart barked. "Where is he? Where will I find him?"

Sherikov licked his lips nervously, glancing up at Reinhart. "Commissioner, are you sure —"

"The attack has been called off. Your labs are safe. So is your life. Now it's your turn to come through." Reinhart gripped his gun, moving toward Sherikov. "*Where is he?*"

For a moment Sherikov hesitated. Then slowly his huge body sagged, defeated. He shook his head wearily. "All right. I'll show you where he is." His voice was hardly audible, a dry whisper. "Down this way. Come on."

Reinhart followed Sherikov out of the room, into the corridor. Police and guards were working rapidly, clearing the debris and ruins away, putting out the hydrogen fires that burned everywhere. "No tricks, Sherikov."

"No tricks." Sherikov nodded resignedly. "Thomas Cole is by himself. In a wing lab off the main rooms."

"Cole?"

"The variable man. That's his name." The Pole turned his massive head a little. "He has a name."

Reinhart waved his gun. "Hurry up. I don't want anything to go wrong. This is the part I came for."

"You must remember something, Commissioner."

"What is it?"

Sherikov stopped walking. "Commissioner, nothing must happen to the globe. The control turret. Everything depends on it, the war, our whole —"

"I know. Nothing will happen to the damn thing. Let's go."

"If it should get damaged —"

"I'm not after the globe. I'm interested only in-in Thomas Cole."

They came to the end of the corridor and stopped before a metal door. Sherikov nodded at the door. "In there."

Reinhart moved back. "Open the door."

"Open it yourself. I don't want to have anything to do with it."

Reinhart shrugged. He stepped up to the door. Holding his gun level he raised his hand, passing it in front of the eye circuit. Nothing happened.

Reinhart frowned. He pushed the door with his hand. The door slid open. Reinhart was looking into a small laboratory. He glimpsed a workbench, tools, heaps of equipment, measuring devices, and in the center of the bench the transparent globe, the control turret.

"Cole?" Reinhart advanced quickly into the room. He glanced around him, suddenly alarmed. "Where —"

The room was empty. Thomas Cole was gone.

When the first missile struck, Cole stopped work and sat listening.

Far off, a distant rumble rolled through the earth, shaking the floor under him. On the bench, tools and equipment danced up and down. A pair of pliers fell crashing to the floor. A box of screws tipped over, spilling its minute contents out.

Cole listened for a time. Presently he lifted the transparent globe from the bench. With carefully controlled hands he held the globe up, running his fingers gently over the surface, his faded blue eyes thoughtful. Then, after a time, he placed the globe back on the bench, in its mount.

The globe was finished. A faint glow of pride moved through the variable man. The globe was the finest job he had ever done.

The deep rumblings ceased. Cole became instantly alert. He jumped down from his stool, hurrying across the room to the door. For a moment he stood by the door listening intently. He could hear noise on the other side, shouts, guards rushing past, dragging heavy equipment, working frantically.

A rolling crash echoed down the corridor and lapped against his door. The concussion spun him around. Again a tide of energy shook the walls and floor and sent him down on his knees.

The lights flickered and winked out.

Cole fumbled in the dark until he found a flashlight. Power failure. He could hear crackling flames. Abruptly the lights came on again, an ugly yellow, then faded back out. Cole bent down and examined the door with his flashlight. A magnetic lock. Dependent on an externally induced electric flux. He grabbed a screwdriver and pried at the door. For a moment it held. Then it fell open.

Cole stepped warily out into the corridor. Everything was in shambles. Guards wandered everywhere, burned and half-blinded. Two lay groaning under a pile of wrecked equipment. Fused guns, reeking metal. The air was heavy with the smell of burning wiring and plastic. A thick cloud that choked him and made him bend double as he advanced.

"Halt," a guard gasped feebly, struggling to rise. Cole pushed past him and down the corridor. Two small robot guns, still functioning, glided past him hurriedly toward the drumming chaos of battle. He followed.

At a major intersection the fight was in full swing. Sherikov's guards fought Security police, crouched behind pillars and barricades, firing wildly, desperately. Again the whole structure shuddered as a great booming blast ignited some place above. Bombs? Shells?

Cole threw himself down as a violet beam cut past his ear and disintegrated the wall behind him. A Security policeman, wild-eyed, firing erratically. One of Sherikov's guards winged him and his gun skidded to the floor.

A robot cannon turned toward him as he made his way past the intersection. He began to run. The cannon rolled along behind him, aiming itself uncertainly. Cole hunched over as he shambled rapidly along, gasping for breath. In the flickering yellow light he saw a handful of Security police advancing, firing expertly, intent on a line of defense Sherikov's guards had hastily set up.

The robot cannon altered its course to take them on, and Cole escaped around a corner.

He was in the main lab, the big chamber where Icarus himself rose, the vast squat column.

Icarus! A solid wall of guards surrounded him, grim-faced, hugging guns and protection shields. But the Security police were leaving Icarus alone. Nobody wanted to damage him. Cole evaded a lone guard tracking him and reached the far side of the lab.

It took him only a few seconds to find the force field generator. There was no switch. For a moment that puzzled him-and then he remembered. The guard had controlled it from his wrist.

Too late to worry about that. With his screwdriver he unfastened the plate over the generator and ripped out the wiring in handfuls. The generator came loose and he dragged it away from the wall. The screen was off, thank God. He managed to carry the generator into a side corridor.

Crouched in a heap, Cole bent over the generator, deft fingers flying. He pulled the wiring to him and laid it out on the floor, tracing the circuits with feverish haste.

The adaptation was easier than he had expected. The screen flowed at right angles to the wiring, for a distance of six feet. Each lead was shielded on one side; the field radiated outward, leaving a hollow cone in the center. He ran the wiring through his belt, down his trouser legs, under his shirt, all the way to his wrists and ankles.

He was just snatching up the heavy generator when two Security police appeared. They raised their blasters and fired point-blank.

Cole clicked on the screen. A vibration leaped through him that snapped his jaw and danced up his body. He staggered away, half-stupefied by the surging force that radiated out from him. The violet rays struck the field and deflected harmlessly.

He was safe.

He hurried on down the corridor, past a ruined gun and sprawled bodies still clutching blasters. Great drifting clouds of radioactive particles billowed around him. He edged by one cloud nervously. Guards lay everywhere, dying and dead, partly destroyed, eaten and corroded by the hot metallic salts in the air. He had to get out-and fast.

At the end of the corridor a whole section of the fortress was in ruins. Towering flames leaped on all sides. One of the missiles had penetrated below ground level.

Cole found a lift that still functioned. A load of wounded guards was being raised to the surface. None of them paid any attention to him. Flames surged around the lift, licking at the wounded. Workmen were desperately trying to get the lift into action. Cole leaped onto the lift. A moment later it began to rise, leaving the shouts and the flames behind.

The lift emerged on the surface and Cole jumped off. A guard spotted him and gave chase. Crouching, Cole dodged into a tangled mass of twisted metal, still white-hot and smoking. He ran for a distance, leaping from the side of a ruined defense-screen tower, onto the fused ground and down the side of a hill. The ground was hot underfoot. He hurried as fast as he could, gasping for breath. He came to a long slope and scrambled up the side.

The guard who had followed was gone, lost behind in the rolling clouds of ash that drifted from the ruins of Sherikov's underground fortress.

Cole reached the top of the hill. For a brief moment he halted to get his breath and figure where he was. It was almost evening. The sun was beginning to set. In the darkening sky a few dots still twisted and rolled, black specks that abruptly burst into flame and fused out again.

Cole stood up cautiously, peering around him. Ruins stretched out below, on all sides, the furnace from which he had escaped. A chaos of incandescent metal and debris, gutted and wrecked beyond repair. Miles of tangled rubbish and half-vaporized equipment.

He considered. Everyone was busy putting out the fires and pulling the wounded to safety. It would be awhile before he was missed. But as soon as they realized he was gone they'd be after him. Most of the laboratory had been destroyed. Nothing lay back that way.

Beyond the ruins lay the great Ural peaks, the endless mountains, stretching out as far as the eye could see.

Mountains and green forests. A wilderness. They'd never find him there.

Cole started along the side of the hill, walking slowly and carefully, his screen generator under his arm. Probably in the confusion he could find enough food and equipment to last him indefinitely. He could wait until early morning, then circle back toward the ruins and load up. With a few tools and his own innate skill he would get along fine. A screwdriver, hammer, nails, odds and ends —

A great hum sounded in his ears. It swelled to a deafening roar. Startled, Cole whirled around. A vast shape filled the sky behind him, growing each moment. Cole stood frozen, utterly transfixed. The shape thundered over him, above his head, as he stood stupidly, rooted to the spot.

Then, awkwardly, uncertainly, he began to run. He stumbled and fell and rolled a short distance down the side of the hill. Desperately, he struggled to hold onto the ground. His hands dug wildly, futilely, into the soft soil, trying to keep the generator under his arm at the same time.

A flash, and a blinding spark of light around him.

The spark picked him up and tossed him like a dry leaf. He grunted in agony as searing fire crackled about him, a blazing inferno that gnawed and ate hungrily through his screen. He spun dizzily and fell through the cloud of fire, down into a pit of darkness, a vast gulf between two hills. His wiring ripped off. The generator tore out of his grip and was lost behind. Abruptly, his force field ceased.

Cole lay in the darkness at the bottom of the hill. His whole body shrieked in agony as the unholy fire played over him. He was a blazing cinder, a half-consumed ash flaming in a universe of darkness. The pain made him twist and crawl like an insect, trying to burrow into the ground. He screamed and shrieked and struggled to escape, to get away from the hideous fire. To reach the curtain of darkness beyond, where it was cool and silent, where the flames couldn't crackle and eat at him.

He reached imploringly out, into the darkness, groping feebly toward it, trying to pull himself into it. Gradually, the glowing orb that was his own body faded. The impenetrable chaos of night descended. He allowed the tide to sweep over him, to extinguish the searing fire.

Dixon landed his ship expertly, bringing it to a halt in front of an overturned defense tower. He leaped out and hurried across the smoking ground.

From a lift Reinhart appeared, surrounded by his Security police. "He got away from us! He escaped!"

"He didn't escape," Dixon answered. "I got him myself."

Reinhart quivered violently. "What do you mean?"

"Come along with me. Over in this direction." He and Reinhart climbed the side of a demolished hill, both of them panting for breath. "I was landing. I saw a figure emerge from a lift and run toward the mountains, like some sort of animal. When he came out in the open I dived on him and released a phosphorus bomb."

"Then he's —*dead?*"

"I don't see how anyone could have lived through a phosphorus bomb." They reached the top of the hill. Dixon halted, then pointed excitedly down into the pit beyond the hill. "There!"

They descended cautiously. The ground was singed and burned clean. Clouds of smoke hung heavily in the air. Occasional fires still flickered here and there. Reinhart coughed and bent over to see. Dixon flashed on a pocket flare and set it beside the body.

The body was charred, half destroyed by the burning phosphorus. It lay motionless, one arm over its face, mouth open, legs sprawled grotesquely. Like some abandoned rag doll, tossed in an incinerator and consumed almost beyond recognition.

"He's alive!" Dixon muttered. He felt around curiously. "Must have had some kind of protection screen. Amazing that a man could —"

"It's him? It's really him?"

"Fits the description." Dixon tore away a handful of burned clothing. "This is the variable man. What's left of him, at least."

Reinhart sagged with relief. "Then we've finally got him. The data is accurate. He's no longer a factor."

Dixon got out his blaster and released the safety catch thoughtfully. "If you want, I can finish the job right now."

At that moment Sherikov appeared, accompanied by two armed Security police. He strode grimly down the hillside, black eyes snapping. "Did Cole —" He broke off. "Good God."

"Dixon got him with a phosphorus bomb," Reinhart said noncommittally. "He had reached the surface and was trying to get into the mountains."

Sherikov turned wearily away. "He was an amazing person. During the attack he managed to force the lock on his door and escape. The guards fired at him, but nothing happened. He had rigged up some kind of force field around him. Something he adapted."

"Anyhow, it's over with," Reinhart answered. "Did you have SRB plates made up on him?"

Sherikov reached slowly into his coat. He drew out a manila envelope. "Here's all the information I collected about him, while he was with me."

"Is it complete? Everything previous has been merely fragmentary."

"As near complete as I could make it. It includes photographs and diagrams of the interior of the globe. The turret wiring he did for me. I haven't had a chance even to look at them." Sherikov fingered the envelope. "What are you going to do with Cole?"

"Have him loaded up, taken back to the city-and officially put to sleep by the Euthanasia Ministry."

"Legal murder?" Sherikov's lips twisted. "Why don't you simply do it right here and get it over with?"

Reinhart grabbed the envelope and stuck it in his pocket. "I'll turn this right over to the machines." He motioned to Dixon. "Let's go. Now we can notify the fleet to prepare for the attack on Centaurus." He turned briefly back to Sherikov. "When can Icarus be launched?"

"In an hour or so, I suppose. They're locking the control turret in place. Assuming it functions correctly, that's all that's needed."

"Good. I'll notify Duffe to send out the signal to the warfleet." Reinhart nodded to the police to take Sherikov to the waiting Security ship. Sherikov moved off dully, his face gray and haggard. Cole's inert body was picked up and tossed onto a freight cart. The cart rumbled into the hold of the Security ship and the lock slid shut after it.

"It'll be interesting to see how the machines respond to the additional data," Dixon said.

"It should make quite an improvement in the odds," Reinhart agreed. He patted the envelope, bulging in his inside pocket. "We're two days ahead of time."

* * * * *

Margaret Duffe got up slowly from her desk. She pushed her chair automatically back. "Let me get all this straight. You mean the bomb is finished? Ready to go?"

Reinhart nodded impatiently. "That's what I said. The Technicians are checking the turret locks to make sure it's properly attached. The launching will take place in half an hour."

"Thirty minutes! Then —"

"Then the attack can begin at once. I assume the fleet is ready for action."

"Of course. It's been ready for several days. But I can't believe the bomb is ready so soon." Margaret Duffe moved numbly toward the door of her office. "This is a great day, Commissioner. An old era lies behind us. This time tomorrow Centaurus will be gone. And eventually the colonies will be ours."

"It's been a long climb," Reinhart murmured.

"One thing. Your charge against Sherikov. It seems incredible that a person of his caliber could ever —"

"We'll discuss that later," Reinhart interrupted coldly. He pulled the manila envelope from his coat. "I haven't had an opportunity to feed the additional data to the SRB machines. If you'll excuse me, I'll do that now."

* * * * *

For a moment Margaret Duffe stood at the door. The two of them faced each other silently, neither speaking, a faint smile on Reinhart's thin lips, hostility in the woman's blue eyes.

"Reinhart, sometimes I think perhaps you'll go too far. And sometimes I think you've *already* gone too far...."

"I'll inform you of any change in the odds showing." Reinhart strode past her, out of the office and down the hall. He headed toward the SRB room, an intense thalamic excitement rising up inside him.

A few moments later he entered the SRB room. He made his way to the machines. The odds 7-6 showed in the view windows. Reinhart smiled a little. 7-6. False odds, based on incorrect information. Now they could be removed.

Kaplan hurried over. Reinhart handed him the envelope, and moved over to the window, gazing down at the scene below. Men and cars scurried frantically everywhere. Officials coming and going like ants, hurrying in all directions.

The war was on. The signal had been sent out to the warfleet that had waited so long near Proxima Centaurus. A feeling of triumph raced through Reinhart. He had won. He had destroyed the man from the past and broken Peter Sherikov. The war had begun as planned. Terra was breaking out. Reinhart smiled thinly. He had been completely successful.

"Commissioner."

Reinhart turned slowly. "All right."

Kaplan was standing in front of the machines, gazing down at the reading. "Commissioner —"

Sudden alarm plucked at Reinhart. There was something in Kaplan's voice. He hurried quickly over. "What is it?"

Kaplan looked up at him, his face white, his eyes wide with terror. His mouth opened and closed, but no sound came.

"*What is it?*" Reinhart demanded, chilled. He bent toward the machines, studying the reading.

And sickened with horror.

100-1. *Against* Terra!

He could not tear his gaze away from the figures. He was numb, shocked with disbelief. 100-1. *What had happened?* What had gone wrong? The turret was finished, Icarus was ready, the fleet had been notified —

There was a sudden deep buzz from outside the building. Shouts drifted up from below. Reinhart turned his head slowly toward the window, his heart frozen with fear.

Across the evening sky a trail moved, rising each moment. A thin line of white. Something climbed, gaining speed each moment. On the ground, all eyes were turned toward it, awed faces peering up.

The object gained speed. Faster and faster. Then it vanished. Icarus was on his way. The attack had begun; it was too late to stop, now.

And on the machines the odds read a hundred to one-for failure.

At eight o'clock in the evening of May 15, 2136, Icarus was launched toward the star Centaurus. A day later, while all Terra waited, Icarus entered the star, traveling at thousands of times the speed of light.

Nothing happened. Icarus disappeared into the star. There was no explosion. The bomb failed to go off.

At the same time the Terran warfleet engaged the Centauran outer fleet, sweeping down in a concentrated attack. Twenty major ships were seized. A good part of the Centauran fleet was destroyed. Many of the captive systems began to revolt, in the hope of throwing off the Imperial bonds.

Two hours later the massed Centauran warfleet from Armun abruptly appeared and joined battle. The great struggle illuminated half the Centauran system. Ship after ship flashed briefly and then faded to ash. For a whole day the two fleets fought, strung out over millions of miles of space. Innumerable fighting men died-on both sides.

At last the remains of the battered Terran fleet turned and limped toward Armun-defeated. Little of the once impressive armada remained. A few blackened hulks, making their way uncertainly toward captivity.

Icarus had not functioned. Centaurus had not exploded. The attack was a failure.

The war was over.

"We've lost the war," Margaret Duffe said in a small voice, wondering and awed. "It's over. Finished."

The Council members sat in their places around the conference table, gray-haired elderly men, none of them speaking or moving. All gazed up mutely at the great stellar maps that covered two walls of the chamber.

"I have already empowered negotiators to arrange a truce," Margaret Duffe murmured. "Orders have been sent out to Vice-Commander Jessup to give up the battle. There's no hope. Fleet Commander Carleton destroyed himself and his flagship a few minutes ago. The Centauran High Council has agreed to end the fighting. Their whole Empire is rotten to the core. Ready to topple of its own weight."

Reinhart was slumped over at the table, his head in his hands. "I don't understand.... *Why?* Why didn't the bomb explode?" He mopped his forehead shakily. All his poise was gone. He was trembling and broken. "*What went wrong?*"

Gray-faced, Dixon mumbled an answer. "The variable man must have sabotaged the turret. The SRB machines knew.... They analyzed the data. *They knew!* But it was too late."

Reinhart's eyes were bleak with despair as he raised his head a little. "I knew he'd destroy us. We're finished. A century of work and planning." His body knotted in a spasm of furious agony. "All because of Sherikov!"

* * * * *

Margaret Duffe eyed Reinhart coldly. "Why because of Sherikov?"

"He kept Cole alive! I wanted him killed from the start." Suddenly Reinhart jumped from his chair. His hand clutched convulsively at his gun. "And he's *still* alive! Even if we've lost I'm going to have the pleasure of putting a blast beam through Cole's chest!"

"Sit down!" Margaret Duffe ordered.

Reinhart was half way to the door. "He's still at the Euthanasia Ministry, waiting for the official —"

"No, he's not," Margaret Duffe said.

Reinhart froze. He turned slowly, as if unable to believe his senses. "*What?*"

"Cole isn't at the Ministry. I ordered him transferred and your instructions cancelled."

"Where-where is he?"

There was unusual hardness in Margaret Duffe's voice as she answered. "With Peter Sherikov. In the Urals. I had Sherikov's full authority restored. I then had Cole transferred there, put in Sherikov's safe keeping. I want to make sure Cole recovers, so we can keep our promise to him-our promise to return him to his own time."

Reinhart's mouth opened and closed. All the color had drained from his face. His cheek muscles twitched spasmodically. At last he managed to speak. "You've gone insane! The traitor responsible for Earth's greatest defeat —"

"We have lost the war," Margaret Duffe stated quietly. "But this is not a day of defeat. It is a day of victory. The most incredible victory Terra has ever had."

Reinhart and Dixon were dumbfounded. "What —" Reinhart gasped. "What do you —" The whole room was in an uproar. All the Council members were on their feet. Reinhart's words were drowned out.

"Sherikov will explain when he gets here," Margaret Duffe's calm voice came. "He's the one who discovered it." She looked around the chamber at the incredulous Council members. "Everyone stay in his seat. You are all to remain here until Sherikov arrives. It's vital you hear what he has to say. His news transforms this whole situation."

* * * * *

Peter Sherikov accepted the briefcase of papers from his armed technician. "Thanks." He pushed his chair back and glanced thoughtfully around the Council chamber. "Is everybody ready to hear what I have to say?"

"We're ready," Margaret Duffe answered. The Council members sat alertly around the table. At the far end, Reinhart and Dixon watched uneasily as the big Pole removed papers from his briefcase and carefully examined them.

"To begin, I recall to you the original work behind the ftl bomb. Jamison Hedge was the first human to propel an object at a speed greater than light. As you know, that object diminished in length and gained in mass as it moved toward light speed. When it reached that speed it vanished. It ceased to exist in our terms. Having no length it could not occupy space. It rose to a different order of existence.

"When Hedge tried to bring the object back, an explosion occurred. Hedge was killed, and all his equipment was destroyed. The force of the blast was beyond calculation. Hedge had placed his observation ship many millions of miles away. It was not far enough, however. Originally, he had hoped his drive might be used for space travel. But after his death the principle was abandoned.

"That is-until Icarus. I saw the possibilities of a bomb, an incredibly powerful bomb to destroy Centaurus and all the Empire's forces. The reappearance of Icarus would mean the annihilation of their System. As Hedge had shown, the object would re-enter space already occupied by matter, and the cataclysm would be beyond belief."

"But Icarus never came back," Reinhart cried. "Cole altered the wiring so the bomb kept on going. It's probably still going."

"Wrong," Sherikov boomed. "The bomb *did* reappear. But it didn't explode."

Reinhart reacted violently. "You mean —"

"The bomb came back, dropping below the ftl speed as soon as it entered the star Proxima. But it did not explode. There was no cataclysm. It reappeared and was absorbed by the sun, turned into gas at once."

"Why didn't it explode?" Dixon demanded.

"Because Thomas Cole solved Hedge's problem. He found a way to bring the ftl object back into this universe without collision. Without an explosion. The variable man found what Hedge was after...."

The whole Council was on its feet. A growing murmur filled the chamber, a rising pandemonium breaking out on all sides.

"I don't believe it!" Reinhart gasped. "It isn't possible. If Cole solved Hedge's problem that would mean —" He broke off, staggered.

"Faster than light drive can now be used for space travel," Sherikov continued, waving the noise down. "As Hedge intended. My men have studied the photographs of the control turret. They don't know *how* or *why*, yet. But we have complete records of the turret. We can duplicate the wiring, as soon as the laboratories have been repaired."

Comprehension was gradually beginning to settle over the room. "Then it'll be possible to build ftl ships," Margaret Duffe murmured, dazed. "And if we can do that —"

"When I showed him the control turret, Cole understood its purpose. Not *my* purpose, but the original purpose Hedge had been working toward. Cole realized Icarus was actually an incomplete spaceship, not a bomb at all. He saw what Hedge had seen, an ftl space drive. He set out to make Icarus work."

"We can go *beyond* Centaurus," Dixon muttered. His lips twisted. "Then the war was trivial. We can leave the Empire completely behind. We can go beyond the galaxy."

"The whole universe is open to us," Sherikov agreed. "Instead of taking over an antiquated Empire, we have the entire cosmos to map and explore, God's total creation."

Margaret Duffe got to her feet and moved slowly toward the great stellar maps that towered above them at the far end of the chamber. She stood for a long time, gazing up at the myriad suns, the legions of systems, awed by what she saw.

"Do you suppose he realized all this?" she asked suddenly. "What we can see, here on these maps?"

"Thomas Cole is a strange person," Sherikov said, half to himself. "Apparently he has a kind of intuition about machines, the way things are supposed to work. An intuition more in his hands than in his head. A kind of genius, such as a painter or a pianist has. Not a scientist. He has no verbal knowledge about things, no semantic references. He deals with the things themselves. Directly.

"I doubt very much if Thomas Cole understood what would come about. He looked into the globe, the control turret. He saw unfinished wiring and relays. He saw a job half done. An incomplete machine."

"Something to be fixed," Margaret Duffe put in.

"Something to be fixed. Like an artist, he saw his work ahead of him. He was interested in only one thing: turning out the best job he could, with the skill he possessed. For us, that skill has opened up a whole universe, endless galaxies and systems to explore. Worlds without end. Unlimited, *untouched* worlds."

Reinhart got unsteadily to his feet. "We better get to work. Start organizing construction teams. Exploration crews. We'll have to reconvert from war production to ship designing. Begin the manufacture of mining and scientific instruments for survey work."

"That's right," Margaret Duffe said. She looked reflectively up at him. "But you're not going to have anything to do with it."

Reinhart saw the expression on her face. His hand flew to his gun and he backed quickly toward the door. Dixon leaped up and joined him. "Get back!" Reinhart shouted.

Margaret Duffe signalled and a phalanx of Government troops closed in around the two men. Grim-faced, efficient soldiers with magnetic grapples ready.

Reinhart's blaster wavered-toward the Council members sitting shocked in their seats, and toward Margaret Duffe, straight at her blue eyes. Reinhart's features were distorted with insane fear. "Get back! Don't anybody come near me or she'll be the first to get it!"

Peter Sherikov slid from the table and with one great stride swept his immense bulk in front of Reinhart. His huge black-furred fist rose in a smashing arc. Reinhart sailed against the wall, struck with ringing force and then slid slowly to the floor.

The Government troops threw their grapples quickly around him and jerked him to his feet. His body was frozen rigid. Blood dripped from his mouth. He spat bits of tooth, his eyes glazed over. Dixon stood dazed, mouth open, uncomprehending, as the grapples closed around his arms and legs.

Reinhart's gun skidded to the floor as he was yanked toward the door. One of the elderly Council members picked the gun up and examined it curiously. He laid it carefully on the table. "Fully loaded," he murmured. "Ready to fire."

Reinhart's battered face was dark with hate. "I should have killed all of you. *All* of you!" An ugly sneer twisted across his shredded lips. "If I could get my hands loose —"

"You won't," Margaret Duffe said. "You might as well not even bother to think about it." She signalled to the troops and they pulled Reinhart and Dixon roughly out of the room, two dazed figures, snarling and resentful.

For a moment the room was silent. Then the Council members shuffled nervously in their seats, beginning to breathe again.

Sherikov came over and put his big paw on Margaret Duffe's shoulder. "Are you all right, Margaret?"

She smiled faintly. "I'm fine. Thanks...."

Sherikov touched her soft hair briefly. Then he broke away and began to pack up his briefcase busily. "I have to go. I'll get in touch with you later."

"Where are you going?" she asked hesitantly. "Can't you stay and —"

"I have to get back to the Urals." Sherikov grinned at her over his bushy black beard as he headed out of the room. "Some very important business to attend to."

Thomas Cole was sitting up in bed when Sherikov came to the door. Most of his awkward, hunched-over body was sealed in a thin envelope of transparent airproof plastic. Two robot attendants whirred ceaselessly at his side, their leads contacting his pulse, blood-pressure, respiration, body temperature.

Cole turned a little as the huge Pole tossed down his briefcase and seated himself on the window ledge.

"How are you feeling?" Sherikov asked him.

"Better."

"You see we've quite advanced therapy. Your burns should be healed in a few months."

"How is the war coming?"

"The war is over."

Cole's lips moved. "Icarus —"

"Icarus went as expected. As *you* expected." Sherikov leaned toward the bed. "Cole, I promised you something. I mean to keep my promise-as soon as you're well enough."

"To return me to my own time?"

"That's right. It's a relatively simple matter, now that Reinhart has been removed from power. You'll be back home again, back in your own time, your own world. We can supply you with some discs of platinum or something of the kind to finance your business. You'll need a new Fixit truck. Tools. And clothes. A few thousand dollars ought to do it."

Cole was silent.

"I've already contacted histo-research," Sherikov continued. "The time bubble is ready as soon as you are. We're somewhat beholden to you, as you probably realize. You've made it possible for us to actualize our greatest dream. The whole planet is seething with excitement. We're changing our economy over from war to —"

"They don't resent what happened? The dud must have made an awful lot of people feel downright bad."

"At first. But they got over it-as soon as they understood what was ahead. Too bad you won't be here to see it, Cole. A whole world breaking loose. Bursting out into the universe. They want me to have an ftl ship ready by the end of the week! Thousands of applications are already on file, men and women wanting to get in on the initial flight."

Cole smiled a little, "There won't be any band, there. No parade or welcoming committee waiting for them."

"Maybe not. Maybe the first ship will wind up on some dead world, nothing but sand and dried salt. But everybody wants to go. It's almost like a holiday. People running around and shouting and throwing things in the streets."

"Afraid I must get back to the labs. Lots of reconstruction work being started." Sherikov dug into his bulging briefcase. "By the way.... One little thing. While you're recovering here, you might like to look at these." He tossed a handful of schematics on the bed.

Cole picked them up slowly. "What's this?"

"Just a little thing I designed." Sherikov arose and lumbered toward the door. "We're realigning our political structure to eliminate any recurrence of the Reinhart affair. This will block any more one-man power grabs." He jabbed a thick finger at the schematics. "It'll turn power over to all of us, not to just a limited number one person could dominate-the way Reinhart dominated the Council.

"This gimmick makes it possible for citizens to raise and decide issues directly. They won't have to wait for the Council to verbalize a measure. Any citizen can transmit his will with one of these, make his needs register on a central control that automatically responds. When a large enough segment of the population wants a certain thing done, these little gadgets set up an active field that touches all the others. An issue won't have to go through a formal Council.

The citizens can express their will long before any bunch of gray-haired old men could get around to it."

* * * * *

Sherikov broke off, frowning.

"Of course," he continued slowly, "there's one little detail...."

"What's that?"

"I haven't been able to get a model to function. A few bugs.... Such intricate work never was in my line." He paused at the door. "Well, I hope I'll see you again before you go. Maybe if you feel well enough later on we could get together for one last talk. Maybe have dinner together sometime. Eh?"

But Thomas Cole wasn't listening. He was bent over the schematics, an intense frown on his weathered face. His long fingers moved restlessly over the schematics, tracing wiring and terminals. His lips moved as he calculated.

Sherikov waited a moment. Then he stepped out into the hall and softly closed the door after him.

He whistled merrily as he strode off down the corridor.

Fritz Leiber

The Big Time

Chapter 1. Enter Three Hussars

> When shall we three meet again
> In thunder, lightning, or in rain?

> When the hurlyburly's done.
> When the battle's lost and won.

> —Macbeth

My name is Greta Forzane. Twenty-nine and a party girl would describe me. I was born in Chicago, of Scandinavian parents, but now I operate chiefly outside space and time-not in Heaven or Hell, if there are such places, but not in the cosmos or universe you know either.

I am not as romantically entrancing as the immortal film star who also bears my first name, but I have a rough-and-ready charm of my own. I need it, for my job is to nurse back to health and kid back to sanity Soldiers badly roughed up in the biggest war going. This war is the Change War, a war of time travelers-in fact, our private name for being in this war is being on the Big Time. Our Soldiers fight by going back to change the past, or even ahead to change the future, in ways to help our side win the final victory a billion or more years from now. A long killing business, believe me.

You don't know about the Change War, but it's influencing your lives all the time and maybe you've had hints of it without realizing.

Have you ever worried about your memory, because it doesn't seem to be bringing you exactly the same picture of the past from one day to the next? Have you ever been afraid that your personality was changing because of forces beyond your knowledge or control? Have you ever felt sure that sudden death was about to jump you from nowhere? Have you ever been scared of Ghosts-not the story-book kind, but the billions of beings who were once so real and strong it's hard to believe they'll just sleep harmlessly forever? Have you ever wondered about those things you may call devils or Demons-spirits able to range through all time and space, through the hot hearts of stars and the cold skeleton of space between the galaxies? Have you ever thought that the whole universe might be a crazy, mixed-up dream? If you have, you've had hints of the Change War.

How I got recruited into the Change War, how it's conducted, what the two sides are, why you don't consciously know about it, what I really think about it-you'll learn in due course.

* * * * *

The place outside the cosmos where I and my pals do our nursing job I simply call the Place. A lot of my nursing consists of amusing and humanizing Soldiers fresh back from raids into time. In fact, my formal title is Entertainer and I've got my silly side, as you'll find out.

My pals are two other gals and three guys from quite an assortment of times and places. We're a pretty good team, and with Sid bossing, we run a pretty good Recuperation Station, though we have our family troubles. But most of our troubles come slamming into the Place with the beat-up Soldiers, who've generally just been going through hell and want to raise some of their own. As a matter of fact, it was three newly arrived Soldiers who started this thing I'm going to tell you about, this thing that showed me so much about myself and everything.

When it started, I had been on the Big Time for a thousand sleeps and two thousand nightmares, and working in the Place for five hundred-one thousand. This two-nightmares routine every time you lay down your dizzy little head is rough, but you pretend to get used to it because being on the Big Time is supposed to be worth it.

The Place is midway in size and atmosphere between a large nightclub where the Entertainers sleep in and a small Zeppelin hangar decorated for a party, though a Zeppelin is one thing we haven't had yet. You go out of the Place, but not often if you have any sense and if you are an Entertainer like me, into the cold light of a morning filled with anything from the earlier dinosaurs to the later spacemen, who look strangely similar except for size.

Solely on doctor's orders, I have been on cosmic leave six times since coming to work at the Place, meaning I have had six brief vacations, if you care to call them that, for believe me they are busman's holidays, considering what goes on in the Place all the time. The last one I spent in Renaissance Rome, where I got a crush on Cesare Borgia, but I got over it. Vacations are for the birds, anyway, because they have to be fitted by the Spiders into serious operations of the Change War, and you can imagine how restful that makes them.

"See those Soldiers changing the past? You stick along with them. Don't go too far up front, though, but don't wander off either. Relax and enjoy yourself."

Ha! Now the kind of recuperation Soldiers get when they come to the Place is a horse of a far brighter color, simply dazzling by comparison. Entertainment is our business and we give them a bang-up time and send them staggering happily back into action, though once in a great while something may happen to throw a wee shadow on the party.

* * * * *

I am dead in some ways, but don't let that bother you —I am lively enough in others. If you met me in the cosmos, you would be more apt to yak with me or try to pick me up than to ask a cop to do same or a father to douse me with holy water, unless you are one of those hard-boiled reformer types. But you are not likely to meet me in the cosmos, because (bar Basin Street and the Prater) 15th Century Italy and Augustan Rome-until they spoiled it-are my favorite (Ha!) vacation spots and, as I have said, I stick as close to the Place as I can. It is really the nicest Place in the whole Change World. (Crisis! I even *think* of it capitalized!)

Anyhoo, when this thing started, I was twiddling my thumbs on the couch nearest the piano and thinking it was too late to do my fingernails and whoever came in probably wouldn't notice them anyway.

The Place was jumpy like it always is on an approach and the gray velvet of the Void around us was curdled with the uneasy lights you see when you close your eyes in the dark.

Sid was tuning the Maintainers for the pick-up and the right shoulder of his gold-worked gray doublet was streaked where he'd been wiping his face on it with quick ducks of his head.

Beauregard was leaning as close as he could over Sid's other shoulder, one white-trousered knee neatly indenting the rose plush of the control divan, and he wasn't missing a single flicker of Sid's old fingers on the dials; Beau's co-pilot besides piano player. Beau's face had that dead blank look it must have had when every double eagle he owned and more he didn't were riding on the next card to be turned in the gambling saloon on one of those wedding-cake Mississippi steamboats.

Doc was soused as usual, sitting at the bar with his top hat pushed back and his knitted shawl pulled around him, his wide eyes seeing whatever horrors a life in Nazi-occupied Czarist Russia can add to being a drunk Demon in the Change World.

Maud, who is the Old Girl, and Lili-the New Girl, of course-were telling the big beads of their identical pearl necklaces.

You might say that all us Entertainers were a bit edgy; being Demons doesn't automatically make us brave.

Then the red telltale on the Major Maintainer went out and the Door began to darken in the Void facing Sid and Beau, and I felt Change Winds blowing hard and my heart missed a couple of beats, and the next thing three Soldiers had stepped out of the cosmos and into the Place, their first three steps hitting the floor hard as they changed times and weights.

They were dressed as officers of hussars, as we'd been advised, and-praise the Bonny Dew! —I saw that the first of them was Erich, my own dear little commandant, the pride of the von Hohenwalds and the Terror of the Snakes. Behind him was some hard-faced Roman or other, and beside Erich and shouldering into him as they stamped forward was a new boy, blond, with a face like a Greek god who's just been touring a Christian hell.

They were uniformed exactly alike in black-shakos, fur-edged pelisses, boots, and so forth-with white skull emblems on the shakos. The only difference between them was that Erich had a Caller on his wrist and the New Boy had a black-gauntleted glove on his left hand and was clenching the mate in it, his right hand being bare like both of Erich's and the Roman's.

"You've made it, lads, hearts of gold," Sid boomed at them, and Beau twitched a smile and murmured something courtly and Maud began to chant, "Shut the Door!" and the New Girl copied her and I joined in because the Change Winds do blow like crazy when the Door is open, even though it can't ever be shut tight enough to keep them from leaking through.

"Shut it before it blows wrinkles in our faces," Maud called in her gamin voice to break the ice, looking like a skinny teen-ager in the tight, knee-length frock she'd copied from the New Girl.

But the three Soldiers weren't paying attention. The Roman —I remembered his name was Mark-was blundering forward stiffly as if there were something wrong with his eyes, while Erich and the New Boy were yelling at each other about a kid and Einstein and a summer palace and a bloody glove and the Snakes having booby-trapped Saint Petersburg. Erich had that taut sadistic smile he gets when he wants to hit me.

The New Boy was in a tearing rage. "Why'd you pull us out so bloody fast? We fair chewed the Nevsky Prospekt to pieces galloping away."

"Didn't you feel their stun guns, *Dummkopf*, when they sprung the trap-too soon, *Gott sei Dank*?" Erich demanded.

"I did," the New Boy told him. "Not enough to numb a cat. Why didn't you show us action?"

"Shut up. I'm your leader. I'll show you action enough."

"You won't. You're a filthy Nazi coward."

"*Weibischer Engländer!*"

"Bloody Hun!"

"*Schlange!*"

The blond lad knew enough German to understand that last crack. He threw back his sable-edged pelisse to clear his sword arm and he swung away from Erich, which bumped him into Beau. At the first sign of the quarrel, Beau had raised himself from the divan as quickly and silently as a —no, I won't use that word-and slithered over to them.

"Sirs, you forget yourselves," he said sharply, off balance, supporting himself on the New Boy's upraised arm. "This is Sidney Lessingham's Place of Entertainment and Recuperation. There are ladies —"

* * * * *

With a contemptuous snarl, the New Boy shoved him off and snatched with his bare hand for his saber. Beau reeled against the divan, it caught him in the shins and he fell toward the Maintainers. Sid whisked them out of the way as if they were a couple of beach radios-simply nothing in the Place is nailed down-and had them back on the coffee table before Beau hit the floor. Meanwhile, Erich had his saber out and had parried the New Boy's first wild slash and lunged in return, and I heard the scream of steel and the rutch of his boot on the diamond-studded pavement.

* * * * *

Beau rolled over and came up pulling from the ruffles of his shirt bosom a derringer I knew was some other weapon in disguise —a stun gun or even an Atropos. Besides scaring me damp for Erich and everybody, that brought me up short: us Entertainers' nerves must be getting as naked as the Soldiers', probably starting when the Spiders canceled all cosmic leaves twenty sleeps back.

Sid shot Beau his look of command, rapped out, "I'll handle this, you whoreson firebrand," and turned to the Minor Maintainer. I noticed that the telltale on the Major was glowing a reassuring red again, and I found a moment to thank Mamma Devi that the Door was shut.

Maud was jumping up and down, cheering I don't know which-nor did she, I bet-and the New Girl was white and I saw that the sabers were working more businesslike. Erich's flicked, flicked, flicked again and came away from the blond lad's cheek spilling a couple of red drops. The blond lad lunged fiercely, Erich jumped back, and the next moment they were both floating helplessly in the air, twisting like they had cramps.

I realized quick enough that Sid had shut off gravity in the Door and Stores sectors of the Place, leaving the rest of us firm on our feet in the Refresher and Surgery sectors. The Place has sectional gravity to suit our Extraterrestrial buddies-those crazy ETs sometimes come whooping in for recuperation in very mixed batches.

From his central position, Sid called out, kindly enough but taking no nonsense, "All right, lads, you've had your fun. Now sheathe those swords."

For a second or so, the two black hussars drifted and contorted. Erich laughed harshly and neatly obeyed-the commandant is used to free fall. The blond lad stopped writhing, hesitated while he glared upside down at Erich and managed to get his saber into its scabbard, although he turned a slow somersault doing it. Then Sid switched on their gravity, slow enough so they wouldn't get sprained landing.

* * * * *

Erich laughed, lightly this time, and stepped out briskly toward us. He stopped to clap the New Boy firmly on the shoulder and look him in the face.

"So, now you get a good scar," he said.

The other didn't pull away, but he didn't look up and Erich came on. Sid was hurrying toward the New Boy, and as he passed Erich, he wagged a finger at him and gayly said, "You rogue." Next thing I was giving Erich my "Man, you're home" hug and he was kissing me and cracking my ribs and saying, "*Liebchen! Doppchen!*" —which was fine with me because I do love him and I'm a good lover and as much a Doubleganger as he is.

We had just pulled back from each other to get a breath-his blue eyes looked so sweet in his worn face-when there was a thud behind us. With the snapping of the tension, Doc had fallen off his bar stool and his top hat was over his eyes. As we turned to chuckle at him, Maud squeaked and we saw that the Roman had walked straight up against the Void and was marching along there steadily without gaining a foot, like it does happen, his black uniform melting into that inside-your-head gray.

Maud and Beau rushed over to fish him back, which can be tricky. The thin gambler was all courtly efficiency again. Sid supervised from a distance.

"What's wrong with him?" I asked Erich.

He shrugged. "Overdue for Change Shock. And he was nearest the stun guns. His horse almost threw him. *Mein Gott*, you should have seen Saint Petersburg, *Liebchen*: the Nevsky Prospekt, the canals flying by like reception carpets of blue sky, a cavalry troop in blue and gold that blundered across our escape, fine women in furs and ostrich plumes, a monk with a big tripod and his head under a hood-it gave me the horrors seeing all those Zombies flashing past and staring at me in that sick unawakened way they have, and knowing that some of them, say the photographer, might be Snakes."

Our side in the Change War is the Spiders, the other side is the Snakes, though all of us-Spiders and Snakes alike-are Doublegangers and Demons too, because we're cut out of our lifelines in the cosmos. Your lifeline is all of you from birth to death. We're Doublegangers because we can operate both in the cosmos and outside of it, and Demons because we act reasonably alive while doing so-which the Ghosts don't. Entertainers and Soldiers are all Demon-Double-gangers, whichever side they're on-though they say the Snake Places are simply ghastly. Zombies are dead people whose lifelines lie in the so-called past.

* * * * *

"What were you doing in Saint Petersburg before the ambush?" I asked Erich. "That is, if you can talk about it."

"Why not? We were kidnapping the infant Einstein back from the Snakes in 1883. Yes, the Snakes got him, *Liebchen*, only a few sleeps back, endangering the West's whole victory over Russia —"

" —which gave your dear little Hitler the world on a platter for fifty years and got me loved to death by your sterling troops in the Liberation of Chicago —"

" —but which leads to the ultimate victory of the Spiders and the West over the Snakes and Communism, *Liebchen*, remember that. Anyway, our counter-snatch didn't work. The Snakes had guards posted-most unusual and we weren't warned. The whole thing was a great mess. No wonder Bruce lost his head-not that it excuses him."

"The New Boy?" I asked. Sid hadn't got to him and he was still standing with hooded eyes where Erich had left him, a dark pillar of shame and rage.

"*Ja*, a lieutenant from World War One. An Englishman."

"I gathered that," I told Erich. "Is he really effeminate?"

"*Weibischer?*" He smiled. "I had to call him something when he said I was a coward. He'll make a fine Soldier-only needs a little more shaping."

"You men are so original when you spat." I lowered my voice. "But you shouldn't have gone on and called him a Snake, Erich mine."

"*Schlange?*" The smile got crooked. "Who knows-about any of us? As Saint Petersburg showed me, the Snakes' spies are getting cleverer than ours." The blue eyes didn't look sweet now. "Are you, *Liebchen*, really nothing more than a good loyal Spider?"

"Erich!"

"All right, I went too far-with Bruce and with you too. We're all hacked these days, riding with one leg over the breaking edge."

Maud and Beau were supporting the Roman to a couch, Maud taking most of his weight, with Sid still supervising and the New Boy still sulking by himself. The New Girl should have been with him, of course, but I couldn't see her anywhere and I decided she was probably having a nervous breakdown in the Refresher, the little jerk.

"The Roman looks pretty bad, Erich," I said.

"Ah, Mark's tough. Got virtue, as his people say. And our little starship girl will bring him back to life if anybody can and if..."

"...you call this living," I filled in dutifully.

* * * * *

He was right. Maud had fifty-odd years of psychomedical experience, 23rd Century at that. It should have been Doc's job, but that was fifty drunks back.

"Maud and Mark, that will be an interesting experiment," Erich said. "Reminiscent of Goering's with the frozen men and the naked gypsy girls."

"You are a filthy Nazi. She'll be using electrophoresis and deep suggestion, if I know anything."

"How will you be able to know anything, *Liebchen*, if she switches on the couch curtains, as I perceive she is preparing to do?"

"Filthy Nazi I said and meant."

"Precisely." He clicked his heels and bowed a millimeter. "Erich Friederich von Hohenwald, *Oberleutnant* in the army of the Third Reich. Fell at Narvik, where he was Recruited by the

Spiders. Lifeline lengthened by a Big Change after his first death and at latest report Commandant of Toronto, where he maintains extensive baby farms to provide him with breakfast meat, if you believe the handbills of the *voyageurs* underground. At your service."

"Oh, Erich, it's all so lousy," I said, touching his hand, reminded that he was one of the unfortunates Resurrected from a point in their lifelines well before their deaths-in his case, because the date of his death had been shifted forward by a Big Change after his Resurrection. And as every Demon finds out, if he can't imagine it beforehand, it is pure hell to remember your future, and the shorter the time between your Resurrection and your death back in the cosmos, the better. Mine, bless Bab-ed-Din, was only an action-packed ten minutes on North Clark Street.

Erich put his other hand lightly over mine. "Fortunes of the Change War, *Liebchen*. At least I'm a Soldier and sometimes assigned to future operations-though why we should have this monomania about our future personalities back there, I don't know. Mine is a stupid *Oberst*, thin as paper-and frightfully indignant at the *voyageurs*! But it helps me a little if I see him in perspective and at least I get back to the cosmos pretty regularly, *Gott sei Dank*, so I'm better off than you Entertainers."

I didn't say aloud that a Changing cosmos is worse than none, but I found myself sending a prayer to the Bonny Dew for my father's repose, that the Change Winds would blow lightly across the lifeline of Anton A. Forzane, professor of physiology, born in Norway and buried in Chicago. Woodlawn Cemetery is a nice gray spot.

"That's all right, Erich," I said. "We Entertainers Got Mittens too."

He scowled around at me suspiciously, as if he were wondering whether I had all my buttons on.

"Mittens?" he said. "What do you mean? I'm not wearing any. Are you trying to say something about Bruce's gloves-which incidentally seem to annoy him for some reason. No, seriously, Greta, why do you Entertainers need mittens?"

"Because we get cold feet sometimes. At least I do. Got Mittens, as I say."

* * * * *

A sickly light dawned in his Prussian puss. He muttered, "Got mittens ... *Gott mit uns* ... God with us," and roared softly, "Greta, I don't know how I put up with you, the way you murder a great language for cheap laughs."

"You've got to take me as I am," I told him, "mittens and all, thank the Bonny Dew —" and hastily explained, "That's French —*le bon Dieu* —the good God-don't hit me. I'm not going to tell you any more of my secrets."

He laughed feebly, like he was dying.

"Cheer up," I said. "I won't be here forever, and there are worse places than the Place."

He nodded grudgingly, looking around. "You know what, Greta, if you'll promise not to make some dreadful joke out of it: on operations, I pretend I'll soon be going backstage to court the world-famous ballerina Greta Forzane."

He was right about the backstage part. The Place is a regular theater-in-the-round with the Void for an audience, the Void's gray hardly disturbed by the screens masking Surgery (Ugh!), Refresher and Stores. Between the last two are the bar and kitchen and Beau's piano. Between Surgery and the sector where the Door usually appears are the shelves and taborets of the Art Gallery. The control divan is stage center. Spaced around at a fair distance are six big low couches-one with its curtains now shooting up into the gray-and a few small tables. It is like a ballet set and the crazy costumes and characters that turn up don't ruin the illusion. By no means. Diaghilev would have hired most of them for the Ballet Russe on first sight, without even asking them whether they could keep time to music.

Chapter 2. A Right-Hand Glove

Last week in Babylon,
Last night in Rome,

—Hodgson

Beau had gone behind the bar and was talking quietly at Doc, but with his eyes elsewhere, looking very sallow and professional in his white, and I thought-Damballa! —I'm in the French Quarter. I couldn't see the New Girl. Sid was at last getting to the New Boy after the fuss about Mark. He threw me a sign and I started over with Erich in tow.

"Welcome, sweet lad. Sidney Lessingham's your host, and a fellow Englishman. Born in King's Lynn, 1564, schooled at Cambridge, but London was the life and death of me, though I outlasted Bessie, Jimmie, Charlie, and Ollie almost. And what a life! By turns a clerk, a spy, a bawd-the two trades are hand in glove —a poet of no account, a beggar, and a peddler of resurrection tracts. Beau Lassiter, our throats are tinder!"

At the word "poet," the New Boy looked up, but resentfully, as if he had been tricked into it.

"And to spare your throat for drinking, sweet gallant, I'll be so bold as to guess and answer one of your questions," Sid rattled on. "Yes, I knew Will Shakespeare-we were of an age-and he was such a modest, mind-your-business rogue that we all wondered whether he really did write those plays. Your pardon, 'faith, but that scratch might be looked to."

Then I saw that the New Girl hadn't lost her head, but gone to Surgery (Ugh!) for a first-aid tray. She reached a swab toward the New Boy's sticky cheek, saying rather shrilly, "If I might..."

Her timing was bad. Sid's last words and Erich's approach had darkened the look in the young Soldier's face and he angrily swept her arm aside without even glancing at her. Erich squeezed my arm. The tray clattered to the floor-and one of the drinks that Beau was bringing almost followed it. Ever since the New Girl's arrival, Beau had been figuring that she was his responsibility, though I don't think the two of them had reached an agreement yet. Beau was especially set on it because I was thick with Sid at the time and Maud with Doc, she loving tough cases.

"Easy now, lad, and you love me!" Sid thundered, again shooting Beau the "Hold it" look. "She's just a poor pagan trying to comfort you. Swallow your bile, you black villain, and perchance it will turn to poetry. Ah, did I touch you there? Confess, you are a poet."

* * * * *

There isn't much gets by Sid, though for a second I forgot my psychology and wondered if he knew what he was doing with his insights.

"Yes, I'm a poet, all right," the New Boy roared. "I'm Bruce Marchant, you bloody Zombies. I'm a poet in a world where even the lines of the King James and your precious Will whom you use for laughs aren't safe from Snakes' slime and the Spiders' dirty legs. Changing our history, stealing our certainties, claiming to be so blasted all-knowing and best intentioned and efficient, and what does it lead to? This bloody SI glove!"

He held up his black-gloved left hand which still held the mate and he shook it.

"What's wrong with the Spider Issue gauntlet, heart of gold?" Sid demanded. "And you love us, tell us." While Erich laughed, "Consider yourself lucky, *Kamerad*. Mark and I didn't draw any gloves at all."

"What's wrong with it?" Bruce yelled. "The bloody things are both lefts!" He slammed it down on the floor.

We all howled, we couldn't help it. He turned his back on us and stamped off, though I guessed he would keep out of the Void. Erich squeezed my arm and said between gasps, *"Mein Gott, Liebchen*, what have I always told you about Soldiers? The bigger the gripe, the smaller the cause! It is infallible!"

One of us didn't laugh. Ever since the New Girl heard the name Bruce Marchant, she'd had a look in her eyes like she'd been given the sacrament. I was glad she'd got interested in something, because she'd been pretty much of a snoot and a wet blanket up until now, although she'd come to the Place with the recommendation of having been a real whoopee girl in London and New York in the Twenties. She looked disapprovingly at us as she gathered up the tray and stuff, not forgetting the glove, which she placed on the center of the tray like a holy relic.

* * * * *

Beau cut over and tried to talk to her, but she ghosted past him and once again he couldn't do anything because of the tray in his hands. He came over and got rid of the drinks quick. I took a big gulp right away because I saw the New Girl stepping through the screen into Surgery and I hate to be reminded we have it and I'm glad Doc is too drunk to use it, some of the Arachnoid surgical techniques being very sickening as I know only too well from a personal experience that is number one on my list of things to be forgotten.

By that time, Bruce had come back to us, saying in a carefully hard voice, "Look here, it's not the dashed glove itself, as you very well know, you howling Demons."

"What is it then, noble heart?" Sid asked, his grizzled gold beard heightening the effect of innocent receptivity.

"It's the principle of the thing," Bruce said, looking around sharply, but none of us cracked a smile. "It's this mucking inefficiency and death of the cosmos-and don't tell me that isn't in the cards! —masquerading as benign omniscient authority. The Spiders-and we don't know who they are ultimately; it's just a name; we see only agents like ourselves-the Spiders pluck us from the quiet graves of our lifelines —"

"Is that bad, lad?" Sid murmured, innocently straight-faced.

" —and Resurrect us if they can and then tell us we must fight another time-traveling power called the Snakes-just a name, too-which is bent on perverting and enslaving the whole cosmos, past, present and future."

"And isn't it, lad?"

"Before we're properly awake, we're Recruited into the Big Time and hustled into tunnels and burrows outside our space-time, these miserable closets, gray sacks, puss pockets-no offense to this Place-that the Spiders have created, maybe by gigantic implosions, but no one knows for certain, and then we're sent off on all sorts of missions into the past and future to change history in ways that are supposed to thwart the Snakes."

"True, lad."

"And from then on, the pace is so flaming hot and heavy, the shocks come so fast, our emotions are wrenched in so many directions, our public and private metaphysics distorted so insanely, the deepest thread of reality we cling to tied in such bloody knots, that we never can get things straight."

"We've all felt that way, lad," Sid said soberly; Beau nodded his sleek death's head; "You should have seen me, *Kamerad*, my first fifty sleeps," Erich put in; while I added, "Us girls, too, Bruce."

"Oh, I know I'll get hardened to it, and don't think I can't. It's not that," Bruce said harshly. "And I wouldn't mind the personal confusion, the mess it's made of my spirit, I wouldn't even mind remaking history and destroying priceless, once-called imperishable beauties of the past, if I felt it were for the best. The Spiders assure us that, to thwart the Snakes, it is all-important that the West ultimately defeat the East. But what have they done to achieve this? I'll give you some beautiful examples. To stabilize power in the early Mediterranean world, they have built up Crete at the expense of Greece, making Athens a ghost city, Plato a trivial fabulist, and putting all Greek culture in a minor key."

* * * * *

"You got time for culture?" I heard myself say and I clapped my hand over my mouth in gentle reproof.

"But *you* remember the dialogues, lad," Sid observed. "And rail not at Crete —I have a sweet Keftian friend."

"For how long will I remember Plato's dialogues? And who after me?" Bruce challenged. "Here's another. The Spiders want Rome powerful and, to date, they've helped Rome so much that she collapses in a blaze of German and Parthian invasions a few years after the death of Julius Caesar."

This time it was Beau who butted in. Most everybody in the Place loves these bull sessions. "You omit to mention, sir, that Rome's newest downfall is directly due to the Unholy Triple Alliance the Snakes have fomented between the Eastern Classical World, Mohammedanized Christianity, and Marxist Communism, trying to pass the torch of power futurewards by way of Byzantium and the Eastern Church, without ever letting it pass into the hands of the Spider West. That, sir, is the Snakes' Three-Thousand-Year Plan which we are fighting against, striving to revive Rome's glories."

"Striving is the word for it," Bruce snapped. "Here's yet another example. To beat Russia, the Spiders kept England and America out of World War Two, thereby ensuring a German invasion of the New World and creating a Nazi empire stretching from the salt mines of Siberia to the plantations of Iowa, from Nizhni Novgorod to Kansas City!"

He stopped and my short hairs prickled. Behind me, someone was chanting in a weird spiritless voice, like footsteps in hard snow.

"*Salz, Salz, bringe Salz. Kein' Peitsch', gnädige Herren. Salz, Salz, Salz.*"

I turned and there was Doc waltzing toward us with little tiny steps, bent over so low that the ends of his shawl touched the floor, his head crooked up sideways and looking through us.

I knew then, but Erich translated softly. "'Salt, salt, I bring salt. No whip, merciful sirs.' He is speaking to my countrymen in their language." Doc had spent his last months in a Nazi-operated salt mine.

* * * * *

He saw us and got up, straightening his top hat very carefully. He frowned hard while my heart thumped half a dozen times. Then his face slackened, he shrugged his shoulders and muttered, "*Nichevo.*"

"And it does not matter, sir," Beau translated, but directing his remark at Bruce. "True, great civilizations have been dwarfed or broken by the Change War. But others, once crushed in the bud, have bloomed. In the 1870s, I traveled a Mississippi that had never known Grant's gunboats. I studied piano, languages, and the laws of chance under the greatest European masters at the University of Vicksburg."

"And you think your pipsqueak steamboat culture is compensation for —" Bruce began but, "Prithee none of that, lad," Sid interrupted smartly. "Nations are as equal as so many madmen or drunkards, and I'll drink dead drunk the man who disputes me. Hear reason: nations are not so puny as to shrivel and vanish at the first tampering with their past, no, nor with the tenth. Nations are monsters, boy, with guts of iron and nerves of brass. Waste not your pity on them."

"True indeed, sir," Beau pressed, cooler and keener for the attack on his Greater South. "Most of us enter the Change World with the false metaphysic that the slightest change in the past —a grain of dust misplaced-will transform the whole future. It is a long while before we accept with our minds as well as our intellects the law of the Conservation of Reality: that when the past is changed, the future changes barely enough to adjust, barely enough to admit the new data. The Change Winds meet maximum resistance always. Otherwise the first operation in

Babylonia would have wiped out New Orleans, Sheffield, Stuttgart, and Maud Davies' birthplace on Ganymede!

"Note how the gap left by Rome's collapse was filled by the imperialistic and Christianized Germans. Only an expert Demon historian can tell the difference in most ages between the former Latin and the present Gothic Catholic Church. As you yourself, sir, said of Greece, it is as if an old melody were shifted into a slightly different key. In the wake of a Big Change, cultures and individuals are transposed, it's true, yet in the main they continue much as they were, except for the usual scattering of unfortunate but statistically meaningless accidents."

"All right, you bloody savants-maybe I pushed my point too far," Bruce growled. "But if you want variety, give a thought to the rotten methods we use in our wonderful Change War. Poisoning Churchill and Cleopatra. Kidnapping Einstein when he's a baby."

"The Snakes did it first," I reminded him.

"Yes, and we copied them. How resourceful does that make us?" he retorted, arguing like a woman. "If we need Einstein, why don't we Resurrect him, deal with him as a man?"

* * * * *

Beau said, serving his culture in slightly thicker slices, "*Pardonnez-moi*, but when you have enjoyed your status as Doubleganger a *soupcon* longer, you will understand that great men can rarely be Resurrected. Their beings are too crystallized, sir, their lifelines too tough."

"Pardon me, but I think that's rot. I believe that most great men refuse to make the bargain with the Snakes, or with us Spiders either. They scorn Resurrection at the price demanded."

"Brother, they ain't that great," I whispered, while Beau glided on with, "However that may be, you have accepted Resurrection, sir, and so incurred an obligation which you as a gentleman must honor."

"I accepted Resurrection all right," Bruce said, a glare coming into his eyes. "When they pulled me out of my line at Passchendaele in '17 ten minutes before I died, I grabbed at the offer of life like a drunkard grabs at a drink the morning after. But even then I thought I was also seizing a chance to undo historic wrongs, work for peace." His voice was getting wilder all the time. Just beyond our circle, I noticed the New Girl watching him worshipfully. "But what did I find the Spiders wanted me for? Only to fight more wars, over and over again, make them crueler and stinkinger, cut the swath of death a little wider with each Big Change, work our way a little closer to the death of the cosmos."

Sid touched my wrist and, as Bruce raved on, he whispered to me, "What kind of ball, think you, will please and so quench this fire-brained rogue? And you love me, discover it."

I whispered back without taking my eyes off Bruce either, "I know somebody who'll be happy to put on any kind of ball he wants, if he'll just notice her."

"The New Girl, sweetling? 'Tis well. This rogue speaks like an angry angel. It touches my heart and I like it not."

Bruce was saying hoarsely but loudly, "And so we're sent on operations in the past and from each of those operations the Change Winds blow futurewards, swiftly or slowly according to the opposition they breast, sometimes rippling into each other, and any one of those Winds may shift the date of our own death ahead of the date of our Resurrection, so that in an instant-even here, outside the cosmos-we may molder and rot or crumble to dust and vanish away. The wind with our name in it may leak through the Door."

* * * * *

Faces hardened at that, because it's bad form to mention Change Death, and Erich flared out with, "*Halt's Maul, Kamerad!* There's always another Resurrection."

But Bruce didn't keep his mouth shut. He said, "Is there? I know the Spiders promise it, but even if they do go back and cut another Doubleganger from my lifeline, is he me?" He slapped his chest with his bare hand. "I don't think so. And even if he is me, with unbroken conscious-ness, why's he been Resurrected again? Just to refight more wars and face more Change Death for the sake of an almighty power —" his voice was rising to a climax —"an almighty power so bloody ineffectual, it can't furnish one poor Soldier pulled out of the mud of Passchendaele, one miserable Change Commando, one Godforsaken Recuperee a proper issue of equipment!"

And he held out his bare right hand toward us, fingers spread a little, as if it were the most amazing object and most deserving of outraged sympathy in the whole world.

The New Girl's timing was perfect. She whisked through us, and before he could so much as wiggle the fingers, she whipped a black gauntleted glove on it and anyone could see that it fitted his hand perfectly.

This time our laughing beat the other. We collapsed and slopped our drinks and pounded each other on the back and then started all over.

"*Ach, der Handschuh, Liebchen!* Where'd she get it?" Erich gasped in my ear.

"Probably just turned the other one inside out-that turns a left into a right —I've done it myself," I wheezed, collapsing again at the idea.

"That would put the lining outside," he objected.

"Then I don't know," I said. "We got all sorts of junk in Stores."

"It doesn't matter, *Liebchen*," he assured me. "*Ach, der Handschuh!*"

All through it, Bruce just stood there admiring the glove, moving the fingers a little now and then, and the New Girl stood watching him as if he were eating a cake she'd baked.

* * * * *

When the hysteria quieted down, he looked up at her with a big smile. "What did you say your name was?"

"Lili," she said, and believe you me, she was Lili to me even in my thoughts from then on, for the way she'd handled that lunatic.

"Lilian Foster," she explained. "I'm English also. Mr. Marchant, I've read *A Young Man's Fancy* I don't know how many times."

"You have? It's wretched stuff. From the Dark Ages —I mean my Cambridge days. In the trenches, I was working up some poems that were rather better."

"I won't hear you say that. But I'd be terribly thrilled to hear the new ones. Oh, Mr. Marchant, it was so strange to hear you call it Passiondale."

"Why, if I may ask?"

"Because that's the way I pronounce it to myself. But I looked it up and it's more like Pas-ken-DA-luh."

"Bless you! All the Tommies called it Passiondale, just as they called Ypres Wipers."

"How interesting. You know, Mr. Marchant, I'll wager we were Recruited in the same operation, summer of 1917. I'd got to France as a Red Cross nurse, but they found out my age and were going to send me back."

"How old were you-are you? Same thing, I mean to say."

"Seventeen."

"Seventeen in '17," Bruce murmured, his blue eyes glassy.

It was real corny dialogue and I couldn't resent the humorous leer Erich gave me as we listened to them, as if to say, "Ain't it nice, *Liebchen*, Bruce has a silly little English schoolgirl to occupy him between operations?"

Just the same, as I watched Lili in her dark bangs and pearl necklace and tight little gray dress that reached barely to her knees, and Bruce hulking over her tenderly in his snazzy hussar's rig, I knew that I was seeing the start of something that hadn't been part of me since Dave died fighting Franco years before I got on the Big Time, the sort of thing that almost made me wish there could be children in the Change World. I wondered why I'd never thought of trying to work things so that Dave got Resurrected and I told myself: no, it's all changed, I've changed, better the Change Winds don't disturb Dave or I know about it.

"No, I didn't die in 1917 —I was merely Recruited then," Lili was telling Bruce. "I lived all through the Twenties, as you can see from the way I dress. But let's not talk about that, shall we? Oh, Mr. Marchant, do you think you can possibly remember any of those poems you started in the trenches? I can't fancy them bettering your sonnet that concludes with, 'The bough swings in the wind, the night is deep; Look at the stars, poor little ape, and sleep.'"

That one almost made me whoop-what monkeys we are, I thought-though I'd be the first to admit that the best line to use on a poet is one of his own-in fact, as many as possible. I decided I could safely forget our little Britons and devote myself to Erich or whatever needed me.

Chapter 3. Nine for a Party

> Hell is the place for me. For to Hell go the fine churchmen, and the fine knights, killed in the tourney or in some grand war, the brave soldiers and the gallant gentlemen. With them will I go. There go also the fair gracious ladies who have lovers two or three beside their lord. There go the gold and the silver, the sables and ermine. There go the harpers and the minstrels and the kings of the earth.

—Aucassin

I exchanged my drink for a new one from another tray Beau was bringing around. The gray of the Void was beginning to look real pleasant, like warm thick mist with millions of tiny diamonds floating in it. Doc was sitting grandly at the bar with a steaming tumbler of tea —a chaser, I guess, since he was just putting down a shot glass. Sid was talking to Erich and laughing at the same time and I said to myself it begins to feel like a party, but something's lacking.

It wasn't anything to do with the Major Maintainer; its telltale was glowing a steady red like a nice little home fire amid the tight cluster of dials that included all the controls except the lonely and frightening Introversion switch that was never touched. Then Maud's couch curtains winked out and there were she and the Roman sitting quietly side by side.

He looked down at his shiny boots and the rest of his black duds like he was just waking up and couldn't believe it all, and he said, "*Omnia mutantur, nos et mutamur in illis,*" and I raised my eyebrows at Beau, who was taking the tray back, and he did proud by old Vicksburg by translating: "All things change and we change with them."

Then Mark slowly looked around at us, and I can testify that a Roman smile is just as warm as any other nationality, and he finally said, "We are nine, the proper number for a party. The couches, too. It is good."

Maud chuckled proudly and Erich shouted, "Welcome back from the Void, *Kamerad*," and then, because he's German and thinks all parties have to be noisy and satirically pompous, he jumped on a couch and announced, "*Herren und Damen*, permit me to introduce the noblest Roman of them all, Marcus Vipsaius Niger, legate to Nero Claudius (called Germanicus in a former time stream) and who in 763 A.U.C. (Correct, Mark? It means 10 A.D., you meatheads!) died bravely fighting the Parthians and the Snakes in the Battle of Alexandria. *Hoch, hoch, hoch!*"

* * * * *

We all swung our glasses and cheered with him and Sid yelled at Erich, "Keep your feet off the furniture, you unschooled rogue," and grinned and boomed at all three hussars, "Take your ease, Recuperees," and Maud and Mark got their drinks, the Roman paining Beau by refusing Falernian wine in favor of scotch and soda, and right away everyone was talking a mile a minute.

We had a lot to catch up on. There was the usual yak about the war —"The Snakes are laying mine fields in the Void," "I don't believe it, how can you mine nothing?" —and the shortages-bourbon, bobby pins, and the stabilitin that would have brought Mark out of it faster-and what had become of people —"Marcia? Oh, she's not around any more," (She'd been caught in a Change Gale and green and stinking in five seconds, but I wasn't going to say that) —and Mark had to be told about Bruce's glove, which convulsed us all over again, and the Roman remembered a legionary who had carried a gripe all the way to Octavius because he'd accidentally been issued the unbelievable luxury item sugar instead of the usual salt, and Erich asked Sid if he had any new Ghostgirls in stock and Sid sucked his beard like the old goat he is. "Dost thou ask me, lusty Allemand? Nay, there are several great beauties, amongst them an Austrian countess from Strauss's Vienna, and if it were not for sweetling here ... Mnnnn."

I poked a finger in Erich's chest between two of the bright buttons with their tiny death's heads. "You, my little von Hohenwald, are a menace to us real girls. You have too much of a thing about the unawakened, ghost kind."

He called me his little Demon and hugged me a bit too hard to prove it wasn't so, and then he suggested we show Bruce the Art Gallery. I thought this was a real brilliant idea, but when I tried to argue him out of it, he got stubborn. Bruce and Lili were willing to do anything anyone wanted them to, though not so willing to pay any attention while doing it. The saber cut was just a thin red line on his cheek; she'd washed away all the dried blood.

The Gallery gets you, though. It's a bunch of paintings and sculptures and especially odd knick-knacks, all made by Soldiers recuperating here, and a lot of them telling about the Change War from the stuff they're made of-brass cartridges, flaked flint, bits of ancient pottery glued into futuristic shapes, mashed-up Incan gold rebeaten by a Martian, whorls of beady Lunan wire, a picture in tempera on a crinkle-cracked thick round of quartz that had filled a starship porthole, a Sumerian inscription chiseled into a brick from an atomic oven.

* * * * *

There are a lot of things in the Gallery and I can always find some I haven't ever seen before. It gets you, as I say, thinking about the guys that made them and their thoughts and the far times and places they came from, and sometimes, when I'm feeling low, I'll come and look at them so I'll feel still lower and get inspired to kick myself back into a good temper. It's the only history of the Place there is and it doesn't change a great deal, because the things in it and the feelings that went into them resist the Change Winds better than anything else.

Right now, Erich's witty lecture was bouncing off the big ears I hide under my pageboy bob and I was thinking how awful it is that for us that there's not only change but Change. You don't know from one minute to the next whether a mood or idea you've got is really new or just welling up into you because the past has been altered by the Spiders or Snakes.

Change Winds can blow not only death but anything short of it, down to the featheriest fancy. They blow thousands of times faster than time moves, but no one can say how much faster or how far one of them will travel or what damage it'll do or how soon it'll damp out. The Big Time isn't the little time.

And then, for the Demons, there's the fear that our personality will just fade and someone else climb into the driver's seat and us not even know. Of course, we Demons are supposed to be able to remember through Change and in spite of it; that's why we are Demons and not Ghosts like the other Doublegangers, or merely Zombies or Unborn and nothing more, and as Beau truly said, there aren't any great men among us-and blamed few of the masses, either-we're a rare sort of people and that's why the Spiders have to Recruit us where they find us without caring about our previous knowledge and background, a Foreign Legion of time, a strange kind of folk, bright but always in the background, with built-in nostalgia and cynicism, as adaptable as Centaurian shape-changers but with memories as long as a Lunan's six arms, a kind of Change People, you might say, the cream of the damned.

But sometimes I wonder if our memories are as good as we think they are and if the whole past wasn't once entirely different from anything we remember, and we've forgotten that we forgot.

As I say, the Gallery gets you feeling real low, and so now I said to myself, "Back to your lousy little commandant, kid," and gave myself a stiff boot.

Erich was holding up a green bowl with gold dolphins or spaceships on it and saying, "And, to my mind, this proves that Etruscan art is derived from Egyptian. Don't you agree, Bruce?"

Bruce looked up, all smiles from Lili, and said, "What was that, dear chap?"

* * * * *

Erich's forehead got dark as the Door and I was glad the hussars had parked their sabers along with their shakos, but before he could even get out a Jerry cussword, Doc breezed up in that plateau-state of drunkenness so like hypnotized sobriety, moving as if he were on a dolly, ghosted the bowl out of Erich's hand, said, "A beautiful specimen of Middle Systemic Venusian. When Eightaitch finished it, he told me you couldn't look at it and not feel the waves of the Northern Venusian Shallows rippling around your hoofs. But it might look better inverted. I wonder. Who are you, young officer? *Nichevo*," and he carefully put the bowl back on its shelf and rolled on.

It's a fact that Doc knows the Art Gallery better than any of us, really by heart, he being the oldest inhabitant, though he maybe picked a bad time to show off his knowledge. Erich was going to take out after him, but I said, "Nix, *Kamerad*, remember gloves and sugar," and he contented himself with complaining, "That *nichevo* —it's so gloomy and hopeless, *ungeheuer-lich*. I tell you, *Liebchen*, they shouldn't have Russians working for the Spiders, not even as Entertainers."

I grinned at him and squeezed his hand. "Not much entertainment in Doc these days, is there?" I agreed.

He grinned back at me a shade sheepishly and his face smoothed and his blue eyes looked sweet again for a second and he said, "I shouldn't want to claw out at people that way, Greta, but at times I am just a jealous old man," which is not entirely true, as he isn't a day over thirty-three, although his hair is nearly white.

Our lovers had drifted on a few steps until they were almost fading into the Surgery screen. It was the last spot I would have picked for the formal preliminaries to a little British smooching, but Lili probably didn't share my prejudices, though I remembered she'd told me she'd served a brief hitch in an Arachnoid Field Hospital before being transferred to the Place.

But she couldn't have had anything like the experience I'd had during my short and sour career as a Spider nurse, when I'd acquired my best-hated nightmare and flopped completely (jobwise, but on the floor, too) at seeing a doctor flick a switch and a being, badly injured but human, turn into a long cluster of glistening strange fruit-ugh, it always makes me want to toss my cookies and my buttons. And to think that dear old Daddy Anton wanted his Greta chile to be a doctor.

* * * * *

Well, I could see this wasn't getting me anywhere I wanted to go, and after all there was a party going on.

Doc was babbling something at a great rate to Sid —I just hoped Doc wouldn't get inspired to go into his animal imitations, which sound pretty fierce and once seriously offended some recuperating ETs.

Maud was demonstrating to Mark a 23rd Century two-step and Beau sat down at the piano and improvised softly on her rhythm.

As the deep-thrumming relaxing notes hit us, Erich's face brightened and he dragged me over. Pleasantly soon I had my feet off the diamond-rough floor, which we don't carpet because most of the ETs, the dear boys, like it hard, and I was shouldering back deep into the couch nearest the piano, with cushions all around me and a fresh drink in my hand, while my Nazi boy friend was getting ready to discharge his *Weltschmerz* as song, which didn't alarm me too much, as his baritone is passable.

Things felt real good, like the Maintainer was just idling to keep the Place in existence and moored to the cosmos, not exerting itself at all or at most taking an occasional lazy paddle stroke. At times the Place's loneliness can be happy and comfortable.

Then Beau raised an eyebrow at Erich, who nodded, and next thing they were launched into a song we all know, though I've never found out where it originally came from. This time it made me think of Lili, and I wondered why-and why it's a tradition at Recuperation Stations to call the new girl Lili, though in this case it happened to be her real name.

> Standing in the Doorway just outside of space,
> Winds of Change blow 'round you but don't touch your face;
> You smile as you whisper tenderly,
> "Please cross to me, Recuperee;
> The operation's over, come in and close the Door."

Chapter 4. Sos from Nowhere

> De Bailhache, Fresca, Mrs. Cammel, whirled
> Beyond the circuit of the shuddering Bear
> In fractured atoms.

—Eliot

I realized the piano had deserted Erich and I cranked my head up and saw Beau, Maud and Sid streaking for the control divan. The Major Maintainer was blinking emergency-green and fast, but the code was plain enough for even me to recognize the Spider distress call and for a second I felt just sick. Then Erich blew out his reserve breath in the middle of "Door" and I gave myself another of those helpful mental boots at the base of the spine and we hurried after them toward the center of the Place along with Mark.

The blinks faded as we got there and Sid told us not to move because we were making shadows. He glued an eye to the telltale and we held still as statues as he caressed the dials like he was making love.

One sensitive hand flicked out past the Introversion switch over to the Minor Maintainer and right away the Place was dark as your soul and there was nothing for me but Erich's arm and the knowledge that Sid was nursing a green light I couldn't even see, although my eyes had plenty time to accommodate.

Then the green light finally came back very slowly and I could see the dear reliable old face-the green-gold beard making him look like a merman-and then the telltale flared bright and Sid flicked on the Place lights and I leaned back.

"That nails them, lads, whoever and whenever they may be. Get ready for a pick-up."

Beau, who was closest of course, looked at him sharply. Sid shrugged uneasily. "Meseemed at first it was from our own globe a thousand years before our Lord, but that indication flickered and faded like witchfire. As it is, the call comes from something smaller than the Place and certes adrift from the cosmos. Meseemed too at one point I knew the fist of the caller-an antipodean atomicist named Benson-Carter —but that likewise changed."

Beau said, "We're not in the right phase of the cosmos-Places rhythm for a pick-up, are we, sir?"

Sid answered, "Ordinarily not, boy."

Beau continued, "I didn't think we had any pick-ups scheduled. Or stand-by orders."

Sid said, "We haven't."

Mark's eyes glowed. He tapped Erich on the shoulder. "An octavian denarius against ten Reichsmarks it is a Snake trap."

Erich's grin showed his teeth. "Make it first through the Door next operation and I'm on."

* * * * *

It didn't take that to tell me things were serious, or the thought that there's always a first time for bumping into something from really outside the cosmos. The Snakes have broken our code more than once. Maud was quietly serving out weapons and Doc was helping her. Only Bruce and Lili stood off. But they were watching.

The telltale brightened. Sid reached toward the Maintainer, saying, "All right, my hearties. Remember, through this Doorway pass the fishiest finaglers in and out of the cosmos."

The Door appeared to the left and above where it should be and darkened much too fast. There was a gust of stale salt seawind, if that makes sense, but no stepped-up Change Winds I could tell-and I had been bracing myself against them. The Door got inky and there was a flicker of gray fur whips and a flash of copper flesh and gilt and something dark and a clump of hoofs and Erich was sighting a stun gun across his left forearm, and then the Door had vanished like that and a tentacled silvery Lunan and a Venusian satyr were coming straight toward us.

The Lunan was hugging a pile of clothes and weapons. The satyr was helping a wasp-waisted woman carry a heavy-looking bronze chest. The woman was wearing a short skirt and high-collared bolero jacket of leather so dark brown it was almost black. She had a two-horned *petsofa* hairdress and she was boldly gilded here and there and wore sandals and copper anklets and wristlets-one of them a copper-plated Caller-and from her wide copper belt hung a short-handled double-headed ax. She was dark-complexioned and her forehead and chin receded, but the effect was anything but weak; she had a face like a beautiful arrowhead-and a familiar one, by golly!

But before I could say, "Kabysia Labrys," Maud shrilly beat me to it with, "It's Kaby with two friends. Break out a couple of Ghostgirls."

And then I saw it really was old-home week because I recognized my Lunan boy friend Ilhilihis, and in the midst of all the confusion I got a nice kick out of knowing I was getting so I could tell the personality of one silver-furred muzzle from another.

They reached the control divan and Illy dumped his load and the others let down the chest, and Kaby staggered but shook off the two ETs when they started to support her, and she looked daggers at Sid when he tried to do the same, although she's his "sweet Keftian friend" he'd mentioned to Bruce.

* * * * *

She leaned straight-armed on the divan and took two gasping breaths so deep that the ridges of her spine showed through her brown-skinned waist, and then she threw up her head and commanded, "Wine!"

While Beau was rushing it, Sid tried to take her hand again, saying, "Sweetling, I'd never heard you call before and knew not this pretty little fist," but she ripped out, "Save your comfort for the Lunan," and I looked and saw-Hey, Zeus! —that one of Ilhilihis' six tentacles was lopped off halfway.

That was for me, and, going to him, I fast briefed myself: "Remember, he only weighs fifty pounds for all he's seven feet high; he doesn't like low sounds or to be grabbed; the two legs aren't tentacles and don't act the same; uses them for long walks, tentacles for leaps; uses tentacles for close vision too and for manipulation, of course; extended, they mean he's at ease; retracted, on guard or nervous; sharply retracted, disgusted; greeting —"

Just then, one of them swept across my face like a sweet-smelling feather duster and I said, "Illy, man, it's been a lot of sleeps," and brushed my fingers across his muzzle. It still took a little self-control not to hug him, and I did reach a little cluckingly for his lopped tentacle, but he wafted it away from me and the little voice-box belted to his side squeaked, "Naughty, naughty. Papa will fix his little old self. Greta girl, ever bandaged even a Terra octopus?"

I had, an intelligent one from around a quarter billion A.D., but I didn't tell him so. I stood and let him talk to the palm of my hand with one of his tentacles —I don't savvy feather-talk but it feels good, though I've often wondered who taught him English-and watched him use a couple others to whisk a sort of Lunan band-aid out of his pouch and cap his wound with it.

Meanwhile, the satyr knelt over the bronze chest, which was decorated with little death's heads and crosses with hoops at the top and swastikas, but looking much older than Nazi, and the satyr said to Sid, "Quick thinkin, Gov, when ya saw the Door comin in high n soffened up gravty unner it, but cud I hav sum hep now?"

Sid touched the Minor Maintainer and we all got very light and my stomach did a flip-flop while the satyr piled on the chest the clothes and weapons that Illy had been carrying and pranced off with it all and carefully put it down at the end of the bar. I decided the satyr's English instructor must have been quite a character, too. Wish I'd met him-her-it.

Sid thought to ask Illy if he wanted Moon-normal gravity in one sector, but my boy likes to mix, and being such a lightweight, Earth-normal gravity doesn't bother him. As he said to me once, "Would Jovian gravity bother a beetle, Greta girl?"

* * * * *

I asked Illy about the satyr and he squeaked that his name was Sevensee and that he'd never met him before this operation. I knew the satyrs were from a billion years in the future, just as the Loonies were from a billion in the past, and I thought-Kreesed us! —but it must have been a real big or emergency-like operation to have the Spiders using those two for it, with two billion years between them —a time-difference that gives you a feeling of awe for a second, you know.

I started to ask Illy about it, but just then Beau came scampering back from the bar with a big red-and-black earthenware goblet of wine-we try to keep a variety of drinking tools in stock so folks will feel more at home. Kaby grabbed it from him and drained most of it in one swallow and then smashed it on the floor. She does things like that, though Sid's tried to teach her better. Then she stared at what she was thinking about until the whites showed all around her eyes and her lips pulled way back from her teeth and she looked a lot less human than the two ETs, just like a fury. Only a time traveler knows how like the wild murals and engravings of them some of the ancients can look.

My hair stood up at the screech she let out. She smashed a fist into the divan and cried, "Goddess! Must I see Crete destroyed, revived, and now destroyed again? It is too much for your servant."

Personally, I thought she could stand anything.

There was a rush of questions at what she said about Crete —I asked one of them, for the news certainly frightened me-but she shot up her arm straight for silence and took a deep breath and began.

"In the balance hung the battle. Rowing like black centipedes, the Dorian hulls bore down on our outnumbered ships. On the bright beach, masked by rocks, Sevensee and I stood by the needle gun, ready to give the black hulls silent wounds. Beside us was Ilhilihis, suited as a sea monster. But then ...then..."

Then I saw she wasn't altogether the iron babe, for her voice broke and she started to shake and to sob rackingly, although her face was still a mask of rage, and she threw up the wine. Sid stepped in and made her stop, which I think he'd been wanting to do all along.

Chapter 5. Sid Insists on Ghostgirls

> Whenever I take up a newspaper and read it, I fancy I see ghosts creeping between the lines. There must be ghosts all over the world. They must be as countless as the grains of the sands, it seems to me.

—Ibsen

My Elizabethan boy friend put his fists on his hips and laid down the law to us as if we were a lot of nervous children who'd been playing too hard.

"Look you, masters, this is a Recuperation Station and I am running it as such. A plague of all operations! I care not if the frame of things disjoints and the whole Change World goes to ruin, but you, warrior maid, are going to rest and drink more wine slowly before you tell your tale and your colleagues are going to be properly companioned. No questions, anyone. Beau, and you love us, give us a lively tune."

Kaby relaxed a little and let him put his hand carefully against her back in token of support and she said grudgingly, "All right, Fat Belly."

Then, so help me, to the tune of the Muskrat Ramble, which I'd taught Beau, we got girls for those two ETs and everybody properly paired up.

Right here I want to point out that a lot of the things they say in the Change World about Recuperation Stations simply aren't so-and anyway they always leave out nine-tenths of it. The Soldiers that come through the Door are looking for a good time, sure, but they're hurt real bad too, every one of them, deep down in their minds and hearts, if not always in their bodies or so you can see it right away.

Believe me, a temporal operation is no joke, and to start with, there isn't one person in a hundred who can endure to be cut from his lifeline and become a really wide-awake Double-ganger —a Demon, that is-let alone a Soldier. What does a badly hurt and mixed-up creature need who's been fighting hard? *One individual* to look out for him and feel for him and patch him up, and it helps if the one is of the opposite sex-that's something that goes beyond species.

There's your basis for the Place and the wild way it goes about its work, and also for most other Recuperation Stations or Entertainment Spots. The name Entertainer can be misleading, but I like it. She's got to be a lot more than a good party girl-or boy-though she's got to be that too. She's got to be a nurse and a psychologist and an actress and a mother and a practical ethnologist and a lot of things with longer names-and a reliable friend.

* * * * *

None of us are all those things perfectly or even near it. We just try. But when the call comes, Entertainers have to forget grudges and gripes and envies and jealousies-and remember, they're lively people with sharp emotions-because there isn't any time then for anything but *help and don't ask who*!

And, deep inside her, a good Entertainer doesn't care who. Take the way it shaped up this time. It was pretty clear to me I ought to shift to Illy, although I wasn't quite easy in my mind about leaving Erich, because the Lunan was a long time from home and, after all, Erich was among anthropoids. Ilhilihis needed someone who was *simpatico*.

I like Illy and not just because he is a sort of tall cross between a spider monkey and a persian cat-though that is a handsome combo when you come to think of it. I like him for himself. So when he came in all lopped and shaky after a mean operation, I was the right person to look out for him. Now I've made my little speech and know-nothings in the Change World can go on making their bum jokes. But I ask you, how could an arrangement between Illy and me be anything but Platonic?

We might have had some octopoid girls and nymphs in stock-Sid couldn't be sure until he checked-but Ilhilihis and Sevensee voted for real people and I knew Sid saw it their way.

Maud squeezed Mark's hand and tripped over to Sevensee ("Those are sharp hoofs you got, man" —she's picked up some of my language, like she has everything else), though Beau did frown over his shoulder at Lili from the piano, maybe to argue that she ought to take on the ET, as Mark had been a real casualty and could use live nursing. But it was plain as day to anybody but Beau that Bruce and Lili were a big thing and the last to be disturbed.

Erich acted stiffly hurt at losing me, but I knew he wasn't. He thinks he has a great technique with Ghostgirls and he likes to show it off, and he really is pretty slick at it, if you go for that sort of thing and-yang my yin! —who doesn't at times?

And when Sid formally wafted the Countess out of Stores —a real blonde stunner in a white satin hobble skirt with a white egret swaying up from her tiny hat, way ahead of Maud and Lili and me when it came to looks, though transparent as cigarette smoke-and when Erich clicked his heels and bowed over her hand and proudly conducted her to a couch, black Svengali to her Trilby, and started to German-talk some life into her with much head cocking and toothy smiling and a flow of witty flattery, and when she began to flirt back and the dream look in her eyes sharpened hungrily and focused on him-well, then I knew that Erich was happy and felt he was doing proud by the *Reichswehr*. No, my little commandant wasn't worrying me on that score.

* * * * *

Mark had drawn a Greek hetaera, name of Phryne; I suppose not the one who maybe still does the famous courtroom striptease back in Athens, and he was waking her up with little sips of his scotch and soda, though, from some looks he'd flashed, I got the idea Kaby was the kid he really went for. Sid was coaxing the fighting gal to take some high-energy bread and olives along with the wine, and, for a wonder, Doc seemed to be carrying on an animated and rational conversation with Sevensee and Maud, maybe comparing notes on the Northern Venusian Shallows, and Beau had got on to Panther Rag, and Bruce and Lili were leaning on the piano, smiling very appreciatively, but talking to each other a mile a minute.

Illy turned back from inspecting them all and squeaked, "Animals with clothes are so refreshing, dahling! Like you're all carrying banners!"

Maybe he had something there, though my banners were kind of Ash Wednesday, a charcoal gray sweater and skirt. He looked at my mouth with a tentacle to see how I was smiling and he squeaked softly, "Do I seem dull and commonplace to you, Greta girl, because I haven't got banners? Just another Zombie from a billion years in your past, as gray and lifeless as Luna is today, not as when she was a real dreamy sister planet simply bursting with air and water and feather forests. Or am I as strangely interesting to you as you are to me, girl from a billion years in my future?"

"Illy, you're sweet," I told him, giving him a little pat. I noticed his fur was still vibrating nervously and I decided the heck with Sid's orders, I'm going to pump him about what he was doing with Kaby and the satyr. Couldn't have him a billion years from home and bottled up, too. Besides, I was curious.

Chapter 6. Crete Circa 1300 B.C.

> Maiden, Nymph, and Mother are the eternal royal Trinity of the island, and the Goddess, who is worshipped there in each of these aspects, as New Moon, Full Moon, and Old Moon, is the sovereign Deity.

> —Graves

Kaby pushed back at Sid some seconds of bread and olives, and, when he raised his bushy eyebrows, gave him a curt nod that meant she knew what she was doing. She stood up and sort of took a position. All the talk quieted down fast, even Bruce's and Lili's. Kaby's face and voice weren't strained now, but they weren't relaxed either.

"Woe to Spider! Woe to Cretan! Heavy is the news I bring you. Bear it bravely, like strong women. When we got the gun unlimbered, I heard seaweed fry and crackle. We three leaped behind the rock wall, saw our gun grow white as sunlight in a heat-ray of the Serpents! Natch, we feared we were outnumbered and I called upon my Caller."

I don't know how she does it, but she does-in English too. That is, when she figures she's got something important to report, and maybe she needs a little time to get ready.

Beau claims that all the ancients fit their thoughts into measured lines as naturally as we pick a word that will do, but I'm not sure how good the Vicksburg language department is. Though why I should wonder about things like that when I've got Kaby spouting the stuff right in front of me, I don't know.

"But I didn't die there, kiddos. I still hoped to hurt the Greek ships, maybe with the Snake's own heat gun. So I quick tried to outflank them. My two comrades crawled beside me-they are males, but they have courage. Soon we spied the ambush-setters. They were Snakes and they were many, filthily disguised as Cretans."

There was an indignant murmur at this, for our cutthroat Change War has its code, the Soldiers tell me. Being an Entertainer, I don't have to say what I think.

"They had seen us when we saw them," Kaby swept on, "and they loosed a killing volley. Heat- and knife-rays struck about us in a storm of wind and fire, and the Lunan lost a feeler, fighting for Crete's Triple Goddess. So we dodged behind a sand hill, steered our flight back toward the water. It was awful, what we saw there: Crete's brave ships all sunk or sinking, blue sky sullied by their death-smoke. Once again the Greeks had licked us! —aided by the filthy Serpents.

"Round our wrecks, their black ships scurried, like black beetles, filth their diet, yet this day they dine on heroes. On the quiet sunlit beach there, I could feel a Change Gale blowing, working changes deep inside me, aches and pains that were a stranger's. Half my memories were doubled, half my lifeline crooked and twisted, three new moles upon my sword-hand. Goddess, Goddess, Triple Goddess —"

* * * * *

Her voice wavered and Sid reached out a hand, but she straightened her back.

"Triple Goddess, give me courage to tell everything that happened. We ran down into the water, hoping to escape by diving. We had hardly gotten under when the heat-rays hit above us, turning all the cool green surface to a roaring white inferno. But as I believe I told you, I was calling on my Caller, and a Door now opened to us, deep below the deadly steam-clouds. We dived in like frightened minnows and a lot of water with us."

Off Chicago's Gold Coast, Dave once gave me a lesson in skin-diving and, remembering it, I got a flash of Kaby's Door in the dark depths.

"For a moment, all was chaos. Then the Door slammed shut behind us. We'd been picked up in time's nick by-an Express Room of our Spiders! —sloshing two feet deep in water, much more cramped for space than this Place. It was manned by a magician, an old coot named Benson-Carter. He dispelled the water quickly and reported on his Caller. We'd got dry, were feeling human, Illy here had shed his swimsuit, when we looked at the Maintainer. It was glowing, changing, melting! And when Benson-Carter touched it, he fell backward-death was in him. Then the Void began to darken, narrow, shrink and close around us, so I called upon my Caller-without wasting time, let me tell you!

"We can't say for sure what was it slowly squeezed that sweet Express Room, but we fear the dirty Snakes have found a way to find our Places and attack outside the cosmos! —found the Spiderweb that links us in the Void's gray less-than-nothing."

No murmur this time. This reaction was genuine; we'd been hit where we lived and I could see everybody was scared as sick as I was. Except maybe Bruce and Lili, who were still holding hands and beaming gently. I decided they were the kind that love makes brave, which it doesn't do to me. It just gives me two people to worry about.

"I can see you dig our feelings," Kaby continued. "This thing scared the pants off of us. If we could have, we'd have even Introverted the Maintainer, broken all the ties that bind us, chanced it incommunicado. But the little old Maintainer was a seething red-hot puddle filled with bubbles big as handballs. We sat tight and watched the Void close. I kept calling on my Caller."

* * * * *

I squeezed my eyes shut, but that made it easier to see the three of them with the Void shutting down on them. (Was ours still behaving? Yes, Bibi Miriam.) Poetry or no poetry, it got me.

"Benson-Carter, lying dying, also thought the Snakes had done it. And he knew that death was in him, so he whispered me his mission, giving me precise instructions: how to press the seven death's hands, starting lockside counterclockwise, one, three, five, six, two, four, seven, then you have a half an hour; after you have pressed the seven, do not monkey with the buttons-get out fast and don't stop moving."

I wasn't getting this part and I couldn't see that anyone else was, though Bruce was whispering to Lili. I remembered seeing skulls engraved on the bronze chest. I looked at Illy and he nodded a tentacle and spread two to say, I guessed, that yes, Benson-Carter had said something like that, but no, Illy didn't know much about it.

"All these things and more he whispered," Kaby went on, "with the last gasps of his life-force, telling all his secret orders-for he'd not been sent to get us, he was on a separate mission, when he heard my SOSs. Sid, it's you he was to contact, as the first leg of his mission, pick up from you three black hussars, death's-head Demons, daring Soldiers, then to wait until the Places next match rhythm with the cosmos-matter of two mealtimes, barely-and to tune in northern Egypt in the age of the last Caesar, in the year of Rome's swift downfall, there to start an operation in a battle near a city named for Thrace's Alexander, there to change the course of battle, blow sky-high the stinking Serpents, all their agents, all their Zombies!

"Goddess, pardon, now I savvy how you've guided my least footstep, when I thought you'd gone and left me-for I flubbed your three-mole signal. We've found Sid's Place, that's the first leg, and I see the three black hussars, and we've brought with us the weapon and the Parthian disguises, salvaged from the doomed Express Room when your Door appeared in time's nick, and the Room around us closing spewed us through before it vanished with the corpse of Benson-Carter. Triple Goddess, draw the milk now from the womanhood I flaunt here and inject the blackest hatred! Vengeance now upon the Serpents, vengeance sweet in northern Egypt, for your island, Crete, Goddess! —and a victory for the Spiders! Goddess, Goddess, we can swing it!"

The roar that made me try to stop my ears with my shoulders didn't come from Kaby-she'd spoken her piece-but from Sid. The dear boy was purple enough to make me want to remind him you can die of high blood pressure just as easy in the Change World.

"Dump me with ops! 'Sblood, I'll not endure it! Is this a battle post? They'll be mounting operations from field hospitals next. Kabysia Labrys, thou art mad to suggest it. And what's this prattle of locks, clocks, and death's heads, buttons and monkeys? This brabble, this farrago, this hocus-pocus! And where's the weapon you prate of? In that whoreson bronze casket, I suppose."

She nodded, looking blank and almost a little shy as poetic possession faded from her. Her answer came like its faltering last echo.

"It is nothing but a tiny tactical atomic bomb."

Chapter 7. Time to Think

After about 0.1 millisecond (one ten-thousandth part of a second) has elapsed, the radius of the ball of fire is some 45 feet, and the temperature is then in the vicinity of 300,000 degrees Centigrade. At this instant, the luminosity, as observed at a distance of 100,000 yards (5.7 miles), is approximately 100 times that of the sun as seen at the earth's surface ... the ball of fire expands very rapidly to its maximum radius of 450 feet within less than a second from the explosion.

—Los Alamos

Brother, that was all we needed to make everybody but Kaby and the two ETs start yelping at once, me included. It may seem strange that Change People, able to whiz through time and space and roust around outside the cosmos and knowing at least by hearsay of weapons a billion years in the future, like the Mindbomb, should panic at being shut in with a little primitive mid-20th Century gadget. Well, they feel the same as atomic scientists would feel if a Bengal tiger were brought into their laboratory, neither more nor less scared.

I'm a moron at physics, but I do know the Fireball is bigger than the Place. Remember that, besides the bomb, we'd recently been presented with a lot of other fears we hadn't had time to cope with, especially the business of the Snakes having learned how to get at our Places and melt the Maintainers and collapse them. Not to mention the general impression-first Saint Petersburg, then Crete-that the whole Change War was going against the Spiders.

Yet, in a free corner of my mind, I was shocked at how badly we were all panicking. It made me admit what I didn't like to: that we were all in pretty much the same state as Doc, except that the bottle didn't happen to be our out.

And had the rest of us been controlling our drinking so well lately?

Maud yelled, "Jettison it!" and pulled away from the satyr and ran from the bronze chest. Beau, harking back to what they'd thought of doing in the Express Room when it was too late, hissed, "Sirs, we must Introvert," and vaulted over the piano bench and legged it for the control divan. Erich seconded him with a white-faced *"Gott in Himmel, ja!"* from beside the surly, forgotten Countess, holding, by its slim stem, an empty, rose-stained wine glass.

I felt my mind flinch, because Introverting a Place is several degrees worse than foxholing. It's supposed not only to keep the Door tight shut, but also to lock it so even the Change Winds can't get through-cut the Place loose from the cosmos altogether.

I'd never talked with anyone from a Place that had been Introverted.

* * * * *

Mark dumped Phryne off his lap and ran after Maud. The Greek Ghostgirl, quite solid now, looked around with sleepy fear and fumbled her apple-green chiton together at the throat. She wrenched my attention away from everyone else for a moment, and I couldn't help wondering whether the person or Zombie back in the cosmos, from whose lifeline the Ghost has been taken, doesn't at least have strange dreams or thoughts when something like this happens.

Sid stopped Beau, though he almost got bowled over doing it, and he held the gambler away from the Maintainer in a bear hug and bellowed over his shoulders, "Masters, are you mad? Have you lost your wits? Maud! Mark! Marcus! Magdalene! On your lives, unhand that casket!"

Maud had swept the clothes and bows and quivers and stuff off it and was dragging it out from the bar toward the Door sector, so as to dump it through fast when we got one, I guess, while Mark acted as if he were trying to help her and wrestle it away from her at the same time.

They kept on as if they hadn't heard a word Sid said, with Mark yelling, "Let go, *meretrix*! This holds Rome's answer to Parthia on the Nile."

Kaby watched them as if she wanted to help Mark but scorned to scuffle with a mere-well, Mark had said it in Latin, I guess-call girl.

Then, on the top of the bronze chest, I saw those seven lousy skulls starting at the lock as plain as if they'd been under a magnifying glass, though ordinarily they'd have been a vague circle to my eyes at the distance, and I lost my mind and started to run in the opposite direction, but Illy whipped three tentacles around me, gentle-like, and squeaked, "Easy now, Greta girl, don't you be doing it, too. Hold still or Papa spank. My, my, but you two-leggers can whirl about when you have a mind to."

My stampede had carried his featherweight body a couple of yards, but it stopped me and I got my mind back, partly.

"Unhand it, I say!" Sid repeated without accomplishing anything, and he released Beau, though he kept a hand near the gambler's shoulder.

Then my fat friend from Lynn Regis looked real distraught at the Void and blustered at no one in particular, "'Sdeath, think you I'd mutiny against my masters, desert the Spiders, go to ground like a spent fox and pull my hole in after me? A plague of such cowardice! Who suggests it? Introversion's no mere last-ditch device. Unless ordered, supervised and sanctioned, it means the end. And what if I'd Introverted ere we got Kaby's call for succor, hey?"

* * * * *

His warrior maid nodded with harsh approval and he noticed it and shook his free hand at her and scolded her, "Not that I say yea to your mad plan for that Devil's casket, you half-clad lackwit. And yet to jettison.... Oh, ye gods, ye gods —" he wiped his hand across his face — "grant me a minute in which I may think!"

Thinking time wasn't an item even on the strictly limited list at the moment, although Sevensee, squatting dourly on his hairy haunches where Maud had left him, threw in a dead-pan "Thas tellin em, Gov."

Then Doc at the bar stood up tall as Abe Lincoln in his top hat and shawl and 19th Century duds and raised an unwavering arm for silence and said something that sounded like: "Introversh, inversh, glovsh," and then his enunciation switched to better than perfect as he continued, "I know to an absolute certainty what we must do."

It showed me how rabbity we were that the Place got quiet as a church while we all stopped whatever we were doing and waited breathless for a poor drunk to tell us how to save ourselves.

He said something like, "Inversh ... bosh ..." and held our eyes for a moment longer. Then the light went out of his and he slobbered out a *"Nichevo"* and slid an arm far along the bar for a bottle and started to pour it down his throat without stopping sliding.

Before he completed his collapse to the floor, in the split second while our attention was still focused on the bar, Bruce vaulted up on top of it, so fast it was almost like he'd popped up from nowhere, though I'd seen him start from behind the piano.

"I've a question. Has anyone here triggered that bomb?" he said in a voice that was very clear and just loud enough. "So it can't go off," he went on after just the right pause, his easy grin and brisk manner putting more heart into me all the time. "What's more, if it were to be triggered, we'd still have half an hour. I believe you said it had that long a fuse?"

He stabbed a finger at Kaby. She nodded.

"Right," he said. "It'd have to be that long for whoever plants it in the Parthian camp to get away. There's another safety margin.

"Second question. Is there a locksmith in the house?"

* * * * *

For all Bruce's easiness, he was watching us like a golden eagle and he caught Beau's and Maud's affirmatives before they had a chance to explain or hedge them and said, "That's very good. Under certain circumstances, you two'd be the ones to go to work on the chest. But before we consider that, there's Question Three: Is anyone here an atomics technician?"

That one took a little conversation to straighten out, Illy having to explain that, yes, the Early Lunans had atomic power-hadn't they blasted the life off their planet with it and made all those ghastly craters? —but no, he wasn't a technician exactly, he was a "thinger" (I thought at first his squeakbox was lisping); what was a thinger? —well, a thinger was someone who manipulated things in a way that was truly impossible to describe, but no, you couldn't possibly thing atomics; the idea was quite ridiculous, so he couldn't be an atomics thinger; the term was worse than a contradiction, well, really! —while Sevensee, from his two-thousand-millennia advantage of the Lunan, grunted to the effect that his culture didn't rightly use any kind of power, but just sort of moved satyrs and stuff by wrestling space-time around, "or think em roun ef we hafta. Can't think em in the Void, tho, wus luck. Hafta have —I dunno wut. Dun havvit anyhow."

"So we don't have an A-tech," Bruce summed up, "which makes it worse than useless, down-right dangerous, to tamper with the chest. We wouldn't know what to do if we did get inside safely. One more question." He directed it toward Sid. "How long before we can jettison anything?"

Sid, looking a shade jealous, yet mostly grateful for the way Bruce had calmed his chickens, started to explain, but Bruce didn't seem to be taking any chance of losing his audience, and as soon as Sid got to the word "rhythm," he pulled the answer away from him.

"In brief, not until we can effectively tune in on the cosmos again. Thank you, Master Lessingham. That's at least five hours-two mealtimes, as the Cretan officer put it," and he threw Kaby a quick soldierly smile. "So, whether the bomb goes to Egypt or elsewhere, there's not a thing we can do about it for five hours. All right then!"

His smile blinked out like a light and he took a couple of steps up and down the bar, as if measuring the space he had. Two or three cocktail glasses sailed off and popped, but he didn't seem to notice them and we hardly did either. It was creepy the way he kept staring from one to another of us. We had to look up. Behind his face, with the straight golden hair flirting around it, was only the Void.

"All right then," he repeated suddenly. "We're twelve Spiders and two Ghosts, and we've time for a bit of a talk, and we're all in the same bloody boat, fighting the same bloody war, so we'll all know what we're talking about. I raised the subject a while back, but I was steamed up about a glove, and it was a big jest. All right! But now the gloves are off!"

* * * * *

Bruce ripped them out of his belt where they'd been tucked and slammed them down on the bar, to be kicked off the next time he paced back and forth, and it wasn't funny.

"Because," he went right on, "I've been getting a completely new picture of what this Spiders' war has been doing to each one of us. Oh, it's jolly good sport to slam around in space and time and then have a rugged little party outside both of them when the operation's over. It's sweet to know there's no cranny of reality so narrow, no privacy so intimate or sacred, no wall of was or will be strong enough, that we can't shoulder in. Knowledge is a glamorous thing, sweeter than lust or gluttony or the passion of fighting and including all three, the ultimate insatiable hunger, and it's great to be Faust, even in a pack of other Fausts.

"It's sweet to jigger reality, to twist the whole course of a man's life or a culture's, to ink out his or its past and scribble in a new one, and be the only one to know and gloat over the changes-hah! killing men or carrying off women isn't in it for glutting the sense of power. It's sweet to feel the Change Winds blowing through you and know the pasts that were and the past that is and the pasts that may be. It's sweet to wield the Atropos and cut a Zombie or Unborn out of his lifeline and look the Doubleganger in the face and see the Resurrection-glow in it and Recruit a brother, welcome a newborn fellow Demon into our ranks and decide whether he'll best fit as Soldier, Entertainer, or what.

"Or he can't stand Resurrection, it fries or freezes him, and you've got to decide whether to return him to his lifeline and his Zombie dreams, only they'll be a little grayer and horrider than they were before, or whether, if she's got that tantalizing something, to bring her shell along for a Ghostgirl-that's sweet, too. It's even sweet to have Change Death poised over your neck, to know that the past isn't the precious indestructible thing you've been taught it was, to know that there's no certainty about the future either, whether there'll even be one, to know that no part of reality is holy, that the cosmos itself may wink out like a flicked switch and God be not and nothing left but nothing!"

He threw out his arms against the Void. "And knowing all that, it's doubly sweet to come through the Door into the Place and be out of the worst of the Change Winds and enjoy a well-earned Recuperation and share the memories of all these sweetnesses I've been talking about, and work out all the fascinating feelings you've been accumulating back in the cosmos, layer by black layer, in the company of and with the help of the best bloody little band of fellow Fausts and Faustines going!

"Oh, it's a sweet life, all right, but I'm asking you —" and here his eyes stabbed us again, one by one, fast —"I'm asking you what it's done to us. I've been getting a completely new picture, as I said, of what my life was and what it could have been if there'd been changes of the sort that even we Demons can't make, and what my life is. I've been watching how we've all been responding to things just now, to the news of Saint Petersburg and to what the Cretan officer told beautifully-only it wasn't beautiful what she had to tell-and mostly to that bloody box of bomb. And I'm simply asking each one of you, what's happened to you?"

* * * * *

He stopped his pacing and stuck his thumbs in his belt and seemed to be listening to the wheels turning in at least eleven other heads-only I stopped mine pretty quick, with Dave and Father and the Rape of Chicago coming up out of the dark on the turn and Mother and the Indiana Dunes and Jazz Limited just behind them, followed by the unthinkable thing the Spider doctor had flicked into existence when I flopped as a nurse, because I can't stand that to be done to my mind by anybody but myself.

I stopped them by using the old infallible Entertainers' gimmick, a fast survey of the most interesting topic there is-other people's troubles.

* * * * *

Offhand, Beau looked as if he had most troubles, shamed by his boss and his girl given her heart to a Soldier; he was hugging them to himself very quiet.

I didn't stop for the two ETs-they're too hard to figure-or for Doc; nobody can tell whether a fallen-down drunk's at the black or bright end of his cycle; you just know it's cycling.

Maud ought to be suffering as much as Beau, called names and caught out in a panic, which always hurts her because she's plus three hundred years more future than the rest of us and figures she ought to be that much wiser, which she isn't always-not to mention she's over fifty years old, though her home-century cosmetic science keeps her looking and acting teenage most of the time. She'd backed away from the bronze chest so as not to stand out, and now Lili came from behind the piano and stood beside her.

Lili had the opposite of troubles, a great big glow for Bruce, proud as a promised princess watching her betrothed. Erich frowned when he saw her, for he seemed proud too, proud of the way his *Kamerad* had taken command of us panicky whacks *Führer*-fashion. Sid still looked mostly grateful and inclined to let Bruce keep on talking.

Even Kaby and Mark, those two dragons hot for battle, standing a little in front and to one side of us by the bronze chest, like its guardians, seemed willing to listen. They made me realize one reason Sid had for letting Bruce run on, although the path his talk was leading us down was flashing with danger signals: When it was over, there'd still be the problem of what to do with the bomb, and a real opposition shaping up between Soldiers and Entertainers, and Sid was hoping a solution would turn up in the meantime or at least was willing to put off the evil day.

But beyond all that, and like the rest of us, I could tell from the way Sid was squinting his browy eyes and chewing his beardy lip that he was shaken and moved by what Bruce had said. This New Boy had dipped into our hearts and counted our kicks so beautifully, better than most of us could have done, and then somehow turned them around so that we had to think of what messes and heels and black sheep and lost lambs we were-well, we wanted to keep on listening.

Chapter 8. A Place to Stand

> Give me a place to stand, and I will move the world.

> —Archimedes

Bruce's voice had a faraway touch and he was looking up left at the Void as he said, "Have you ever really wondered why the two sides of this war are called the Snakes and the Spiders? Snakes may be clear enough-you always call the enemy something dirty. But Spiders-our name for ourselves? Bear with me, Ilhilihis; I know that no being is created dirty or malignant by Nature, but this is a matter of anthropoid feelings and folkways. Yes, Mark, I know that some of your legions have nicknames like the Drunken Lions and the Snails, and that's about as insulting as calling the British Expeditionary Force the Old Contemptibles.

"No, you'd have to go to bands of vicious youths in cities slated for ruin to find a habit of naming like ours, and even they would try to brighten up the black a bit. But simply-Spiders. And Snakes, for that's their name for themselves too, you know. Spiders and Snakes. What are our masters, that we give them names like that?"

It gave me the shivers and set my mind working in a dozen directions and I couldn't stop it, although it made the shivers worse.

Illy beside me now —I'd never given it a thought before, but he did have eight legs of a sort, and I remembered thinking of him as a spider monkey, and hadn't the Lunans had wisdom and atomic power and a billion years in which to get the Change War rolling?

Or suppose, in the far future, Terra's own spiders evolved intelligence and a cruel cannibal culture. They'd be able to keep their existence secret. I had no idea of who or what would be on Earth in Sevensee's day, and wouldn't it be perfect black hairy poisoned spider-mentality to spin webs secretly through the world of thought and all of space and time?

And Beau-wasn't there something real Snaky about him, the way he moved and all?

Spiders and Snakes. *Spinne und Schlange*, as Erich called them. S & S. But SS stood for the Nazi *Schutzstaffel*, the Black Shirts, and what if some of those cruel, crazy Jerries had discovered time travel and —I brought myself up with a jerk and asked myself, "Greta, how nuts can you get?"

* * * * *

From where he was on the floor, the front of the bar his sounding board, Doc shrieked up at Bruce like one of the damned from the pit, "Don't speak against the Spiders! Don't blaspheme! They can hear the Unborn whisper. Others whip only the skin, but they whip the naked brain and heart," and Erich called out, "That's enough, Bruce!"

But Bruce didn't spare him a look and said, "But whatever the Spiders are and no matter how much whip they use, it's plain as the telltale on the Maintainer that the Change War is not only going against them, but getting away from them. Dwell for a bit on the current flurry of stupid slugging and panicky anachronism, when we all know that anachronism is what gets the Change Winds out of control. This punch-drunk pounding on the Cretan-Dorian fracas as if it were the only battle going and the only way to work things. Whisking Constantine from Britain to the Bosporus by rocket, sending a pocket submarine back to sail with the Armada against Drake's woodensides —I'll wager you hadn't heard those! And now, to save Rome, an atomic bomb.

"Ye gods, they could have used Greek fire or even dynamite, but a fission weapon....I leave you to imagine what gaps and scars that will make in what's left of history-the smothering of Greece and the vanishment of Provence and the troubadours and the Papacy's Irish Captivity won't be in it!"

The cut on his cheek had opened again and was oozing a little, but he didn't pay any attention to it, and neither did we, as his lips thinned in irony and he said, "But I'm forgetting that this is a cosmic war and that the Spiders are conducting operations on billions, trillions of planets and inhabited gas clouds through millions of ages and that we're just one little world-one little solar system, Sevensee-and we can hardly expect our inscrutable masters, with all their pressing preoccupations and far-flung responsibilities, to be especially understanding or tender in their treatment of our pet books and centuries, our favorite prophets and periods, or unduly concerned about preserving any of the trifles that we just happen to hold dear.

"Perhaps there are some sentimentalists who would rather die forever than go on living in a world without the *Summa*, the Field Equations, *Process and Reality*, *Hamlet*, Matthew, Keats, and the *Odyssey*, but our masters are practical creatures, ministering to the needs of those rugged souls who want to go on living no matter what."

* * * * *

Erich's "Bruce, I'm telling you that's enough," was lost in the quickening flow of the New Boy's words. "I won't spend much time on the minor signs of our major crack-up —the canceling of leaves, the sharper shortages, the loss of the Express Room, the use of Recuperation Stations for ops and all the other frantic patchwork-last operation but one, we were saddled with three Soldiers from outside the Galaxy and, no fault of theirs, they were no earthly use. Such little things might happen at a bad spot in any war and are perhaps only local. But there's a big thing."

He paused again, to let us wonder, I guess. Maud must have worked her way over to me, for I felt her dry little hand on my arm and she whispered out of the side of her mouth, "What do we do now?"

"We listen," I told her the same way. I felt a little impatient with her need to be doing something about things.

She cocked a gold-dusted eyebrow at me and murmured, "You, too?"

I didn't get to ask her me, too, what? Crush on Bruce? Nuts! —because just then Bruce's voice took up again in the faraway range.

"Have you ever asked yourselves how many operations the fabric of history can stand before it's all stitches, whether too much Change won't one day wear out the past? And the present and the future, too, the whole bleeding business. Is the law of the Conservation of Reality any more than a thin hope given a long name, a prayer of theoreticians? Change Death is as certain as Heat Death, and far faster. Every operation leaves reality a bit cruder, a bit uglier, a bit more makeshift, and a whole lot less rich in those details and feelings that are our heritage, like the crude penciled sketch on canvas when you've stripped off the paint.

"If that goes on, won't the cosmos collapse into an outline of itself, then nothing? How much thinning can reality stand, having more and more Doublegangers cut out of it? And there's another thing about every operation-it wakes up the Zombies a little more, and as its Change Winds die, it leaves them a little more disturbed and nightmare-ridden and frazzled. Those of you who have been on operations in heavily worked-over temporal areas will know what I mean-that look they give you out of the sides of their eyes as if to say, 'You again? For Christ's sake, go away. We're the dead. We're the ones who don't want to wake up, who don't want to be Demons and hate to be Ghosts. Stop torturing us.'"

* * * * *

I looked around at the Ghostgirls; I couldn't help it. They'd somehow got together on the control divan, facing us, their backs to the Maintainers. The Countess had dragged along the bottle of wine Erich had fetched her earlier and they were passing it back and forth. The Countess had a big rose splotch across the ruffled white lace of her blouse.

Bruce said, "There'll come a day when all the Zombies and all the Unborn wake up and go crazy together and figuratively come marching at us in their numberless hordes, saying, 'We've had enough.'"

But I didn't turn back to Bruce right away. Phryne's chiton had slipped off one shoulder and she and the Countess were sitting sagged forward, elbows on knees, legs spread-at least, as far as the Countess's hobble skirt would let her-and swayed toward each other a little. They were still surprisingly solid, although they hadn't had any personal attention for a half hour, and they were looking up over my head with half-shut eyes and they seemed, so help me, to be listening to what Bruce was saying and maybe hearing some of it.

"We make a careful distinction between Zombies and Unborn, between those troubled by our operations whose lifelines lie in the past and those whose lifelines lie in the future. But is there any distinction any longer? Can we tell the difference between the past and the future? Can we any longer locate the now, the real now of the cosmos? The Places have their own nows, the now of the Big Time we're on, but that's different and it's not made for real living.

"The Spiders tell us that the real now is somewhere in the last half of the 20th Century, which means that several of us here are also alive in the cosmos, have lifelines along which the now is traveling. But do you swallow that story quite so easily, Ilhilihis, Sevensee? How does it strike the servants of the Triple Goddess? The Spiders of Octavian Rome? The Demons of Good Queen Bess? The gentlemen Zombies of the Greater South? Do the Unborn man the starships, Maud?

"The Spiders also tell us that, although the fog of battle makes the now hard to pin down precisely, it will return with the unconditional surrender of the Snakes and the establishment of cosmic peace, and roll on as majestically toward the future as before, quickening the continuum with its passage. Do you really believe that? Or do you believe, as I do, that we've used up all the future as well as the past, wasted it in premature experience, and that we've had the real now smudged out of existence, stolen from us forever, the precious now of true growth, the child-moment in which all life lies, the moment like a newborn baby that is the only home for hope there is?"

* * * * *

He let that start to sink in, then took a couple of quick steps and went on, his voice rising over Erich's "Bruce, for the last time —" and seeming to pick up a note of hope from the very word he had used, "But although things look terrifyingly black, there remains a chance-the slimmest chance, but still a chance-of saving the cosmos from Change Death and restoring reality's richness and giving the Ghosts good sleep and perhaps even regaining the real now. We have the means right at hand. What if the power of time traveling were used not for war and destruction, but for healing, for the mutual enrichment of the ages, for quiet communication and growth, in brief, to bring a peace message —"

But my little commandant is quite an actor himself and knows a wee bit about the principles of scene-stealing, and he was not going to let Bruce drown him out as if he were just another extra playing a Voice from the Mob. He darted across our front, between us and the bar, took a running leap, and landed bang on the bloody box of bomb.

A bit later, Maud was silently showing me the white ring above her elbow where I'd grabbed her and Illy was teasing a clutch of his tentacles out of my other hand and squeaking reproachfully, "Greta girl, don't ever do that."

Erich was standing on the chest and I noticed that his boots carefully straddled the circle of skulls, and I should have known anyway you could hardly push them in the right order by jumping on them, and he was pointing at Bruce and saying, " —and that means mutiny, my young sir. *Um Gottes willen*, Bruce, listen to me and step down before you say anything worse. I'm older than you, Bruce. Mark's older. Trust in your *Kameraden*. Guide yourself by their knowledge."

He had got my attention, but I had much rather have him black my eye.

"You older than me?" Bruce was grinning. "When your twelve-years' advantage was spent in soaking up the wisdom of a race of sadistic dreamers gone paranoid, in a world whose thought-stream had already been muddied by one total war? Mark older than me? When all his ideas and loyalties are those of a wolf pack of unimaginative sluggers two thousand years younger than I am? Either of you older because you have more of the killing cynicism that is all the wisdom the Change World ever gives you? Don't make me laugh!

"I'm an Englishman, and I come from an epoch when total war was still a desecration and the flowers and buds of thoughts not yet whacked off or blighted. I'm a poet and poets are wiser than anyone because they're the only people who have the guts to think and feel at the same time. Right, Sid? When I talk to all of you about a peace message, I want you to think about it concretely in terms of using the Places to bring help across the mountains of time when help is really needed, not to bring help that's undeserved or knowledge that's premature or contaminating, sometimes not to bring anything at all, but just to check with infinite tenderness and concern that everything's safe and the glories of the universe unfolding as they were intended to —"

"Yes, you are a poet, Bruce," Erich broke in. "You can tootle soulfully on the flute and make us drip tears. You can let out the stops on the big organ pipes and make us tremble as if at Jehovah's footsteps. For the last twenty minutes, you have been giving us some very *charmante* poetry. But what are you? An Entertainer? Or are you a Soldier?"

* * * * *

Right then —I don't know what it was, maybe Sid clearing his throat —I could sense our feelings beginning to turn against Bruce. I got the strangest feeling of reality clamping down and bright colors going dull and dreams vanishing. Yet it was only then I also realized how much Bruce had moved us, maybe some of us to the verge of mutiny, even. I was mad at Erich for what he was doing, but I couldn't help admiring his cockiness.

I was still under the spell of Bruce's words and the more-than-words behind them, but then Erich would shift around a bit and one of his heels would kick near the death's-head pushbuttons and I wanted to stamp with spike heels on every death's-head button on his uniform. I didn't know exactly what I felt yet.

"Yes, I'm a Soldier," Bruce told him, "and I hope you won't ever have to worry about my courage, because it's going to take more courage than any operation we've ever planned, ever dreamed of, to carry the peace message to the other Places and to the wound-spots of the cosmos. Perhaps it will be a fast wicket and we'll be bowled down before we score a single run, but who cares? We may at least see our real masters when they come to smash us, and for me that will be a deep satisfaction. And we may do some smashing of our own."

"So you're a Soldier," Erich said, his smile showing his teeth. "Bruce, I'll admit that the half-dozen operations you've been on were rougher than anything I drew in my first hundred sleeps. For that, I am all honest sympathy. But that you should let them get you into such a state that love and a girl can turn you upside down and start you babbling about peace messages —"

"Yes, by God, love and a girl have changed me!" Bruce shouted at him, and I looked around at Lili and I remembered Dave saying, "I'm going to Spain," and I wondered if anything would ever again make my face flame like that. "Or, rather, they've made me stand up for what I've believed in all along. They've made me —"

"*Wunderbar*," Erich called and began to do a little sissy dance on the bomb that set my teeth on edge. He bent his wrists and elbows at arty angles and stuck out a hip and ducked his head simperingly and blinked his eyes very fast. "Will you invite me to the wedding, Bruce? You'll have to get another best man, but I will be the flower girl and throw pretty little posies to all the distinguished guests. Here, Mark. Catch, Kaby. One for you, Greta. *Danke schön. Ach, zwei Herzen in dreivierteltakt ... ta-ta ... ta-ta ... ta-ta-ta-ta-ta ...*"

"What the hell do you think a woman is?" Bruce raged. "Something to mess around with in your spare time?"

* * * * *

Erich kept on humming "Two Hearts in Waltz Time" —and jigging around to it, damn him-but he slipped in a nod to Bruce and a "Precisely." So I knew where I stood, but it was no news to me.

"Very well," Bruce said, "let's leave this Brown Shirt *maricón* to amuse himself and get down to business. I made all of you a proposal and I don't have to tell you how serious it is or how serious Lili and I are about it. We not only must infiltrate and subvert other Places, which luckily for us are made for infiltration, we also must make contact with the Snakes and establish working relationships with their Demons at our level as one of our first steps."

That stopped Erich's jig and got enough of a gasp from some of us to make it seem to come from practically everybody. Erich used it to work a change of pace.

"Bruce! We've let you carry this foolery further than we should. You seem to have the idea that because anything goes in the Place-dueling, drunkenness, *und so weiter* —you can say what you have and it will all be forgotten with the hangover. Not so. It is true that among such a set of monsters and free spirits as ourselves, and working as secret agents to boot, there cannot be the obvious military discipline that would obtain in a Terran army.

"But let me tell you, Bruce, let me grind it home into you-Sid and Kaby and Mark will bear me out in this, as officers of equivalent rank-that the Spider line of command stretches into and through this Place just as surely as the word of *der Führer* rules Chicago. And as I shouldn't have to emphasize to you, Bruce, the Spiders have punishments that would make my countrymen in Belsen and Buchenwald-well, pale a little. So while there is still a shadow of justification for our interpreting your remarks as utterly tasteless clowning —"

"Babble on," Bruce said, giving him a loose downward wave of his hand without looking. "I made you people a proposal." He paused. "How do you stand, Sidney Lessingham?"

Then I felt my legs getting weak, because Sid didn't answer right away. The old boy swallowed and started to look around at the rest of us. Then the feeling of reality clamping down got something awful, because he didn't look around, but straightened his back a little. Just then, Mark cut in fast.

"It grieves me, Bruce, but I think you are possessed. Erich, he must be confined."

* * * * *

Kaby nodded, almost absently. "Confine or kill the coward, whichever is easier, whip the woman, and let's get on to the Egyptian battle."

"Indeed, yes," Mark said. "I died in it. But now perhaps no longer."

Kaby said to him, "I like you, Roman."

Bruce was smiling, barely, and his eyes were moving and fixing. "You, Ilhilihis?"

Illy's squeak box had never sounded mechanical to me before, but it did as he answered, "I'm a lot deeper into borrowed time than the rest of you, tra-la-la, but Papa still loves living. Include me very much out, Brucie."

"Miss Davies?"

Beside me, Maud said flatly, "Do you think I'm a fool?" Beyond her, I saw Lili and I thought, "My God, I might look as proud if I were in her shoes, but I sure as hell wouldn't look as confident."

Bruce's eyes hadn't quite come to Beau when the gambler spoke up. "I have no cause to like you, sir, rather the opposite. But this Place has come to bore me more than Boston and I have always found it difficult to resist a long shot. A very long one, I fear. I am with you, sir."

There was a pain in my chest and a roaring in my ears and through it I heard Sevensee grunting, " —sicka these lousy Spiders. Deal me in."

And then Doc reared up in front of the bar and he'd lost his hat and his hair was wild and he grabbed an empty fifth by the neck and broke the bottom of it all jagged against the bar and he waved it and screeched, *"Ubivaytye Pauki —i Nyemetzi!"*

And right behind his words, Beau sang out fast the English of it, "Kill the Spiders-and the Germans!"

And Doc didn't collapse then, though I could see he was hanging onto the bar tight with his other hand, and the Place got stiller, inside and out, than I've ever known it, and Bruce's eyes were finally moving back toward Sid.

* * * * *

But the eyes stopped short of Sid and I heard Bruce say, "Miss Forzane?" and I thought, "That's funny," and I started to look around at the Countess, and felt all the eyes and I realized, "Hey, that's me! But this can't happen to me. To the others, yes, but not to me. I just work here. Not to Greta, no, no, no!"

But it had, and the eyes didn't let go, and the silence and the feeling of reality were Godawful, and I said to myself, "Greta, you've got to say something, if only a suitable four-letter word," and then suddenly I knew what the silence was like. It was like that of a big city if there were some way of shutting off all the noise in one second. It was like Erich's singing when the piano had deserted him. It was as if the Change Winds should ever die completely ... and I knew beforehand what had happened when I turned my back on them all.

The Ghostgirls were gone. The Major Maintainer hadn't merely been switched to Introvert. It was gone, too.

Chapter 9. A Locked Room

"We examined the moss between the bricks, and found it undisturbed."

"You looked among D — —'s papers, of course, and into the books of the library?"

"Certainly; we opened every package and parcel; we not only opened every book, but we turned over every leaf in each volume...."

—Poe

Three hours later, Sid and I plumped down on the couch nearest the kitchen, though too tired to want to eat for a while yet. A tighter search than I could ever have cooked up had shown that the Maintainer was not in the Place.

Of course it had to be in the Place, as we kept telling each other for the first two hours. It had to be, if circumstances and the theories we lived by in the Change World meant anything. A Maintainer is what maintains a Place. The Minor Maintainer takes care of oxygen, temperature, humidity, gravity, and other little life-cycle and matter-cycle things generally, but it's the Major Maintainer that keeps the walls from buckling and the ceiling from falling in. It is little, but oh my, it does so much.

It doesn't work by wires or radio or anything complicated like that. It just hooks into local space-time.

I have been told that its inside working part is made up of vastly tough, vastly hard giant molecules, each one of which is practically a vest-pocket cosmos in itself. Outside, it looks like a portable radio with a few more dials and some telltales and switches and plug-ins for earphones and a lot of other sensory thingumajigs.

But the Maintainer was gone and the Void hadn't closed in, yet. By this time, I was so fagged, I didn't care much whether it did or not.

One thing for sure, the Maintainer had been switched to Introvert before it was spirited away or else its disappearance automatically produced Introversion, take your choice, because we sure were Introverted-real nasty martinet-schoolmaster grip of reality on my thoughts that I knew, without trying, liquor wouldn't soften, not a breath of Change Wind, absolutely stifling, and the gray of the Void seeming so much inside my head that I think I got a glimmering of what the science boys mean when they explain to me that the Place is a kind of interweaving of the material and the mental—a Giant Monad, one of them called it.

Anyway, I said to myself, "Greta, if this is Introversion, I want no part of it. It is not nice to be cut adrift from the cosmos and know it. A lifeboat in the middle of the Pacific and a starship between galaxies are not in it for loneliness."

* * * * *

I asked myself why the Spiders had ever equipped Maintainers with Introversion switches anyway, when we couldn't drill with them and weren't supposed to use them except in an emergency so tight that it was either Introvert or surrender to the Snakes, and for the first time the obvious explanation came to me:

Introversion must be the same as scuttling, its main purpose to withhold secrets and materiel from the enemy. It put a place into a situation from which even the Spider high command couldn't rescue it, and there was nothing left but to sink down, down (out? up?), down into the Void.

If that was the case, our chances of getting back were about those of my being a kid again playing in the Dunes on the Small Time.

I edged a little closer to Sid and sort of squunched under his shoulder and rubbed my cheek against the smudged, gold-worked gray velvet. He looked down and I said, "A long way to Lynn Regis, eh, Siddy?"

"Sweetling, thou spokest a mouthful," he said. He knows very well what he is doing when he mixes his language that way, the wicked old darling.

"Siddy," I said, "why this gold-work? It'd be a lot smoother without it."

"Marry, men must prick themselves out and, 'faith I know not, but it helps if there's metal in it."

"And girls get scratched." I took a little sniff. "But don't put this doublet through the cleaner yet. Until we get out of the woods, I want as much you around as possible."

"Marry, and why should I?" he asked blankly, and I think he wasn't fooling me. The last thing time travelers find out is how they do or don't smell. Then his face clouded and he looked as though he wanted to squunch under my shoulder. "But 'faith, sweetling, your forest has a few more trees than Sherwood."

"Thou saidst it," I agreed, and wondered about the look. He oughtn't to be interested in my girlishness now. I knew I was a mess, but he had stuck pretty close to me during the hunt and you never can tell. Then I remembered that he was the other one who hadn't declared himself when Bruce was putting it to us, and it probably troubled his male vanity. Not me, though—I was still grateful to the Maintainer for getting me out of that spot, whatever other it had got us all into. It seemed ages ago.

* * * * *

We'd all jumped to the conclusion that the two Ghostgirls had run away with the Maintainer, I don't know where or why, but it looked so much that way. Maud had started yipping about how she'd never trusted Ghosts and always known that some day they'd start doing things on their own, and Kaby had got it firmly fixed in her head, right between the horns, that Phryne, being a Greek, was the ringleader and was going to wreak havoc on us all.

But when we were checking Stores the first time, I had noticed that the Ghostgirl envelopes looked flat. Ectoplasm doesn't take up much space when it's folded, but I had opened one anyway, then another, and then called for help.

Every last envelope was empty. We had lost over a thousand Ghostgirls, Sid's whole stock.

Well, at least it proved what none of us had ever seen or heard of being demonstrated: that there is a spooky link—a sort of Change Wind contact-between a Ghost and its lifeline; and when that umbilicus, I've heard it called, is cut, the part away from the lifeline dies.

Interesting, but what had bothered me was whether we Demons were going to evaporate too, because we are as much Doublegangers as the Ghosts and our apron strings had been cut just as surely. We're more solid, of course, but that would only mean we'd take a little longer. Very logical.

I remember I had looked up at Lili and Maud-us girls had been checking the envelopes; it's one of the proprieties we frequently maintain and anyway, if men check them, they're apt to trot out that old wheeze about "instant women" which I'm sick to death of hearing, thank you.

Anyway, I had looked up and said, "It's been nice knowing you," and Lili had said, "Twenty-three, skiddoo," and Maud had said, "Here goes nothing," and we had shook hands all around.

We figured that Phryne and the Countess had faded at the same time as the other Ghostgirls, but an idea had been nibbling at me and I said, "Siddy, do you suppose it's just barely possible that, while we were all looking at Bruce, those two Ghostgirls would have been able to work the Maintainer and get a Door and lam out of here with the thing?"

"Thou speakst my thoughts, sweetling. All weighs against it: Imprimis, 'tis well known that Ghosts cannot lay plots or act on them. Secundo, the time forbade getting a Door. Tercio-and here's the real meat of it-the Place folds without the Maintainer. Quadro, 'twere folly to depend on not one of-how many of us? ten, elf-not looking around in all the time it would have taken them—"

"I looked around once, Siddy. They were drinking and they had got to the control divan under their own power. Now when was that? Oh, yes, when Bruce was talking about Zombies."

"Yes, sweetling. And as I was about to cap my argument with quinquo when you 'gan prattle, I could have sworn none could touch the Maintainer, much less work it and purloin it, without my certain knowledge. Yet..."

"Eftsoons yet," I seconded him.

* * * * *

Somebody must have got a door and walked out with the thing. It certainly wasn't in the Place. The hunt had been a lulu. Something the size of a portable typewriter is not easy to hide and we had been inside everything from Beau's piano to the renewer link of the Refresher.

We had even fluoroscoped everybody, though it had made Illy writhe like a box of worms, as he'd warned us; he said it tickled terribly and I insisted on smoothing his fur for five minutes afterward, although he was a little standoffish toward me.

Some areas, like the bar, kitchen and Stores, took a long while, but we were thorough. Kaby helped Doc check Surgery: since she last made the Place, she has been stationed in a Field Hospital (it turns out the Spiders actually are mounting operations from them) and learned a few nice new wrinkles.

However, Doc put in some honest work on his own, though, of course, every check was observed by at least three people, not including Bruce or Lili. When the Maintainer vanished, Doc had pulled out of his glassy-eyed drunk in a way that would have surprised me if I hadn't seen it happen to him before, but when we finished Surgery and got on to the Art Gallery, he had started to putter and I noticed him hold out his coat and duck his head and whip out a flask and take a swig and by now he was well on his way toward another peak.

The Art Gallery had taken time too, because there's such a jumble of strange stuff, and it broke my heart but Kaby took her ax and split a beautiful blue woodcarving of a Venusian medusa because, although there wasn't a mark in the paw-polished surface, she claimed it was just big enough. Doc cried a little and we left him fitting the pieces together and mooning over the other stuff.

After we'd finished everything else, Mark had insisted on tackling the floor. Beau and Sid both tried to explain to him how this is a one-sided Place, that there is nothing, but nothing, under the floor; it just gets a lot harder than the diamonds crusting it as soon as you get a quarter inch down-that being the solid equivalent of the Void. But Mark was knuckle-headed (like all Romans, Sid assured me on the q.t.) and broke four diamond-plus drills before he was satisfied.

Except for some trick hiding places, that left the Void, and things don't vanish if you throw them at the Void-they half melt and freeze forever unless you can fish them out. Back of the Refresher, at about eye-level, are three Venusian coconuts that a Hittite strongman threw there during a major brawl. I try not to look at them because they are so much like witch heads they give me the woolies. The parts of the Place right up against the Void have strange spatial properties which one of the gadgets in Surgery makes use of in a way that gives me the worse woolies, but that's beside the point.

* * * * *

During the hunt, Kaby and Erich had used their Callers as direction finders to point out the Maintainer, just as they're used in the cosmos to locate the Door-and sometimes in the Big Places, people tell me. But the Callers only went wild-like a compass needle whirling around without stopping-and nobody knew what that meant.

The trick hiding places were the Minor Maintainer, a cute idea, but it is no bigger than the Major and has its own mysterious insides and had obviously kept on doing its own work, so that was out for several reasons, and the bomb chest, though it seemed impossible for anyone to have opened it, granting they knew the secret of its lock, even before Erich jumped on it and put it in the limelight double. But when you've ruled out everything else, the word impossible changes meaning.

Since time travel is our business, a person might think of all sorts of tricks for sending the Maintainer into the past or future, permanently or temporarily. But the Place is strictly on the Big Time and everybody that should know tells me that time traveling *through* the Big Time is out. It's this way: the Big Time is a train, and the Little Time is the countryside and we're on the train, unless we go out a Door, and as Gertie Stein might put it, you can't time travel through the time you time travel in when you time travel.

I'd also played around with the idea of some fantastically obvious hiding place, maybe something that several people could pass back and forth between them, which would mean a conspiracy, and, of course, if you assume a big enough conspiracy, you can explain anything, including the cosmos itself. Still, I'd got a sort of shell-game idea about the Soldiers' three big black shakos and I hadn't been satisfied until I'd got the three together and looked in them all at the same time.

"Wake up, Greta, and take something. I can't stand here forever." Maud had brought us a tray of hearty snacks from then and yon, and I must say they were tempting; she whips up a mean hors d'oeuvre.

I looked them over and said, "Siddy, I want a hot dog."

"And I want a venison pasty! Out upon you, you finical jill, you o'erscrupulous jade, you whimsic and tyrannous poppet!"

I grabbed a handful and snuggled back against him.

"Go on, call me some more, Siddy," I told him. "Real juicy ones."

Chapter 10. Motives and Opportunities

My thought, whose murder yet is but fantastical,
Shakes so my single state of man that function
Is smother'd in surmise, and nothing is
But what is not.

—Macbeth

My big bad waif from King's Lynn had set the tray on his knees and started to wolf the food down. The others were finishing up. Erich, Mark and Kaby were having a quietly furious argument I couldn't overhear at the end of the bar nearest the bronze chest, and Illy was draped over the piano like a real octopus, listening in.

Beau and Sevensee were pacing up and down near the control divan and throwing each other a word now and then. Beyond them, Bruce and Lili were sitting on the opposite couch from us, talking earnestly about something. Maud had sat down at the other end of the bar and was knitting-it's one of the habits like chess and quiet drinking, or learning to talk by squeak box, that we pick up to pass the time in the Place in the long stretches between parties. Doc was fiddling around the Gallery, picking things up and setting them down, still managing to stay on his feet at any rate.

* * * * *

Lili and Bruce stood up, still gabbing intensely at each other, and Illy began to pick out with one tentacle a little tune in the high keys that didn't sound like anything on God's earth. "Where do they get all the energy?" I wondered.

As soon as I asked myself that, I knew the answer and I began to feel the same way myself. It wasn't energy; it was nerves, pure and simple.

Change is like a drug, I realized-you get used to the facts never staying the same, and one picture of the past and future dissolving into another maybe not very different but still different, and your mind being constantly goosed by strange moods and notions, like nightclub lights of shifting color with weird shadows between shining right on your brain.

The endless swaying and jogging is restful, like riding on a train.

You soon get to like the movement and to need it without knowing, and when it suddenly stops and you're just you and the facts you think from and feel from are exactly the same when you go back to them-boy, that's rough, as I found out now.

The instant we got Introverted, everything that ordinarily leaks into the Place, wake or sleep, had stopped coming, and we were nothing but ourselves and what we meant to each other and what we could make of that, an awfully lonely, scratchy situation.

I decided I felt like I'd been dropped into a swimming pool full of cement and held under until it hardened.

I could understand the others bouncing around a bit. It was a wonder they didn't hit the Void. Maud seemed to be standing it the best; maybe she'd got a little preparation from the long watches between stars; and then she is older than all of us, even Sid, though with a small "o" in "older."

* * * * *

The restless work of the search for the Maintainer had masked the feeling, but now it was beginning to come full force. Before the search, Bruce's speech and Erich's interruptions had done a passable masking job too. I tried to remember when I'd first got the feeling and decided it was after Erich had jumped on the bomb, about the time he mentioned poetry. Though I couldn't be sure. Maybe the Maintainer had been Introverted even earlier, when I'd turned to look at the Ghostgirls. I wouldn't have known. Nuts!

Believe me, I could feel that hardened cement on every inch of me. I remembered Bruce's beautiful picture of a universe without Big Change and decided it was about the worst idea going. I went on eating, though I wasn't so sure now it was a good idea to keep myself strong.

"Does the Maintainer have an Introversion telltale? Siddy!"

"'Sdeath, chit, and you love me, speak lower. Of a sudden, I feel not well, as if I'd drunk a butt of Rhenish and slept inside it. Marry yes, blue. In short flashes, saith the manual. Why ask'st thou?"

"No reason. God, Siddy, what I'd give for a breath of Change Wind."

"Thou can'st say that eftsoons," he groaned. I must have looked pretty miserable myself, for he put his arm around my shoulders and whispered gruffly, "Comfort thyself, sweetling, that while we suffer thus sorely, we yet cannot die the Change Death."

"What's that?" I asked him.

I didn't want to bounce around like the others. I had a suspicion I'd carry it too far. So, to keep myself from going batty, I started to rework the business of who had done what to the Maintainer.

During the hunt, there had been some pretty wild suggestions tossed around as to its disappearance or at least its Introversion: a feat of Snake science amounting to sorcery; the Spider high command bunkering the Places from above, perhaps in reaction to the loss of the Express Room, in such a hurry that they hadn't even time to transmit warnings; the hand of the Late Cosmicians, those mysterious hypothetical beings who are supposed to have successfully resisted the extension of the Change War into the future much beyond Sevensee's epoch-unless the Late Cosmicians are the ones fighting the Change War.

One thing these suggestions had steered very clear of was naming any one of us as a suspect, whether acting as Snake spy, Spider political police, agent of-who knows, after Bruce? —a secret Change World Committee of Public Safety or Spider revolutionary underground, or strictly on our own. Just as no one had piped a word, since the Maintainer had been palmed, about the split between Erich's and Bruce's factions.

Good group thinking probably, to sink differences in the emergency, but that didn't apply to what I did with my own thoughts.

* * * * *

Who wanted to escape so bad they'd Introvert the Place, cutting off all possible contact and communication either way with the cosmos and running the very big risk of not getting back to the cosmos at all?

Leaving out what had happened since Bruce had arrived and stirred things up, Doc seemed to me to have the strongest motive. He knew that Sid couldn't keep covering up for him forever and that Spider punishments for derelictions of duty are not just the clink of a firing squad, as Erich had reminded us. But Doc had been flat on the floor in front of the bar from the time Bruce had jumped on top of it, though I certainly hadn't had my eye on him every second.

Beau? Beau had said he was bored with the Place at a time when what he said counted, so he'd hardly lock himself in it maybe forever, not to mention locking Bruce in with himself and the babe he had a yen for.

Sid loves reality, Changing or not, and every least thing in it, people especially, more than any man or woman I've ever known-he's like a big-eyed baby who wants to grab every object and put it in his mouth-and it was hard to imagine him ever cutting himself off from the cosmos.

Maud, Kaby, Mark and the two ETs? None of them had any motive I knew of, though Sevensee's being from the very far future did tie in with that idea about the Late Cosmicians, and there did seem to be something developing between the Cretan and the Roman that could make them want to be Introverted together.

"Stick to the facts, Greta," I reminded myself with a private groan.

That left Erich, Bruce, Lili and myself.

Erich, I thought-now we're getting somewhere. The little commandant has the nervous system of a coyote and the courage of a crazy tomcat, and if he thought it would help him settle his battle with Bruce better to be locked in with him, he'd do it in a second.

But even before Erich had danced on the bomb, he'd been heckling Bruce from the crowd. Still, there would have been time between heckles for him to step quietly back from us, Introvert the Maintainer and ...well, that was nine-tenths of the problem.

If I was the guilty party, I was nuts and that was the best explanation of all. Gr-r-r!

Bruce's motives seemed so obvious, especially the mortal (or was it immortal?) danger he'd put himself in by inciting mutiny, that it seemed a shame he'd been in full view on the bar so long. Surely, if the Maintainer had been Introverted before he jumped on the bar, we'd all have noticed the flashing blue telltale. For that matter, I'd have noticed it when I looked back at the Ghostgirls-if it worked as Sid claimed, and he said he had never seen it in operation, just read in the manual-oh, 'sdeath!

* * * * *

But Bruce didn't need opportunity, as I'm sure all the males in the Place would have told me right off, because he had Lili to pull the job for him and she had as much opportunity as any of the rest of us. Myself, I have large reservations to this woman-putty-in-the-hands-of-the-man-she-loves-madly theory, but I had to admit there was something to be said for it in this case, and it had seemed quite natural to me when the rest of us had decided, by unspoken agreement, that neither Lili's nor Bruce's checks counted when we were hunting for the Maintainer.

That took care of all of us and left only the mysterious stranger, intruding somehow through a Door (how'd he get it without using our Maintainer?) or from an unimaginable hiding place or straight out of the Void itself. I know that last is impossible-nothing can step out of nothing-but if anything ever looked like it was specially built for something not at all nice to come looming out of, it's the Void-misty, foggily churning, slimy gray....

"Wait a second," I told myself, "and hang onto this, Greta. It should have smacked you in the face at the start."

Whatever came out of the Void, or, more to the point, whoever slipped back from our crowd to the Maintainer, Bruce would have seen them. He was looking at the Maintainer past our heads the whole time, and whatever happened to it, he saw it.

Erich wouldn't have, even after he was on the bomb, because he'd been stagewise enough to face Bruce most of the time to build up his role as tribune of the people.

But Bruce would have-unless he got so caught up in what he was saying....

No, kid, a Demon is always an actor, no matter how much he believes in what he's saying, and there never was an actor yet who wouldn't instantly notice a member of the audience starting to walk out on his big scene.

So Bruce knew, which made him a better actor than I'd have been willing to grant, since it didn't look as if anyone else had thought of what had just occurred to me, or they'd have gone over and put it to him.

Not me, though —I don't work that way. Besides, I didn't feel up to it-Nervy Anna enfold me, I felt like pure hell.

"Maybe," I told myself encouragingly, "the Place is Hell," but added, "Be your age, Greta-be a real rootless, ruleless, ruthless twenty-nine."

Chapter 11. The Western Front, 1917

The barrage roars and lifts. Then, clumsily bowed
With bombs and guns and shovels and battle gear,
Men jostle and climb to meet the bristling fire.
Lines of gray, muttering faces, masked with fear,
They leave their trenches, going over the top,
While time ticks blank and busy on their wrists

—Sassoon

"Please don't, Lili."

"I shall, my love."

"Sweetling, wake up! Hast the shakes?"

I opened my eyes a little and lied to Siddy with a smile and locked my hands together tight and watched Bruce and Lili quarrel nobly near the control divan and wished I had a great love to blur my misery and provide me with a passable substitute for Change Winds.

Lili won the argument, judging from the way she threw her head back and stepped away from Bruce's arms while giving him a proud, tender smile. He walked off a few steps; praise be, he didn't shrug his shoulders at us like an old husband, though his nerves were showing and he didn't seem to be standing Introversion well at all, as who of us were?

Lili rested a hand on the head of the control divan and pressed her lips together and looked around at us, mostly with her eyes. She'd wound a gray silk bandeau around her bangs. Her short gray silk dress without a waistline made her look, not so much like a flapper, though she looked like that all right, as like a little girl, except the neckline was scooped low enough to show she wasn't.

Her gaze hesitated and then stopped at me and I got a sunk feeling of what was coming, because women are always picking on me for an audience. Besides, Sid and I were the centrist party of two in our fresh-out-of-the-shell Place politics.

She took a deep breath and stuck out her chin and said in a voice that was even a little higher and Britisher than she usually uses, "We girls have often cried, 'Shut the Door!' But now the Door is jolly well shut for keeps!"

I knew I'd guessed right and I felt crawly with embarrassment, because I know about this love business of thinking you're the other person and trying to live their life-and grab their glory, though you don't know that-and carry their message for them, and how it can foul things up. Still, I couldn't help admitting what she said wasn't too bad a start-unpleasantly apt to be true, at any rate.

"My fiancé believes we may yet be able to open the Door. I do not. He thinks it is a bit premature to discuss the peculiar pickle in which we all find ourselves. I do not."

There was a rasp of laughter from the bar. The militarists were reacting. Erich stepped out, looking very happy. "So now we have to listen to women making speeches," he called. "What is this Place, anyhow? Sidney Lessingham's Saturday Evening Sewing Circle?"

* * * * *

Beau and Sevensee, who'd stopped their pacing halfway between the bar and the control divan, turned toward Erich, and Sevensee looked a little burlier, a little more like half a horse, than satyrs in mythology book illustrations. He stamped-medium hard, I'd say-and said, "Ahh, go flya kite." I'd found out he'd learned English from a Demon who'd been a longshoreman with syndicalist-anarchist sympathies. Erich shut up for a moment and stood there grinning, his hands on his hips.

Lili nodded to the satyr and cleared her throat, looking scared. But she didn't speak; I could see she was thinking and feeling something, and her face got ugly and haggard, as if she were in a Change Wind that hadn't reached me yet, and her mouth went into a snarl to fight tears, but some spurted out, and when she did speak her voice was an octave lower and it wasn't just London talking but New York too.

"I don't know how Resurrection felt to you people, because I'm new and I loathe asking questions, but to me it was pure torture and I wished only I'd had the courage to tell Suzaku, 'I wish to remain a Zombie, if you don't mind. I'd rather the nightmares.' But I accepted Resurrection because I've been taught to be polite and because there is the Demon in me I don't understand that always wishes to live, and I found that I still felt like a Zombie, although I could flit about, and that I still had the nightmares, except they'd grown a deal vivider.

"I was a young girl again, seventeen, and I suppose every woman wishes to be seventeen, but I wasn't seventeen inside my head —I was a woman who had died of Bright's disease in New York in 1929 and also, because a Big Change blew my lifeline into a new drift, a woman who had died of the same disease in Nazi-occupied London in 1955, but rather more slowly because, as you can fancy, the liquor was in far shorter supply. I had to live with both those sets of memories and the Change World didn't blot them out any more than I'm told it does those of any Demon, and it didn't even push them into the background as I'd hoped it would.

"When some Change Fellow would say to me, 'Hallo, beautiful, how about a smile?' or 'That's a posh frock, kiddo,' I'd be back at Bellevue looking down at my swollen figure and the light getting like spokes of ice, or in that dreadful gin-steeped Stepney bedroom with Phyllis coughing herself to death beside me, or at best, for a moment, a little girl in Glamorgan looking at the Roman road and wondering about the wonderful life that lay ahead."

* * * * *

I looked at Erich, remembering he had a long nasty future back in the cosmos himself, and at any rate he wasn't smiling, and I thought maybe he's getting a little humility, knowing someone else has two of those futures, but I doubted it.

"Because, you see," Lili kept forcing it out, "all my three lives I'd been a girl who fell in love with a great young poet she'd never met, the voice of the new youth and all youth, and she'd told her first big lie to get in the Red Cross and across to France to be nearer him, and it was all danger and dark magics and a knight in armor, and she pictured how she'd find him wounded but not seriously, with a little bandage around his head, and she'd light a fag for him and smile lightly, never letting him guess what she felt, but only being her best self and watching to see if that made something happen to him....

"And then the Boche machine guns cut him down at Passchendaele and there couldn't ever have been bandages big enough and the girl stayed seventeen inside and messed about and tried to be wicked, though she wasn't very good at that, and to drink, and she had a bit more talent there, though drinking yourself to death is not nearly as easy as it sounds, even with a kidney weakness to help. But she turned the trick.

"Then a cock crows. She wakes with a tearing start from the gray dreams of death that fill her lifeline. It's cold daybreak. There's the smell of a French farm. She feels her ankles and they're not at all like huge rubber boots filled with water. They're not swollen the least bit. They're young legs.

"There's a little window and the tops of a row of trees that may be poplars when there's more light, and what there is shows cots like her own and heads under blankets, and hanging uniforms make large shadows and a girl is snoring. There's a very distant rumble and it moves the window a bit. Then she remembers they're Red Cross girls many, many kilometers from Passchendaele and that Bruce Marchant is going to die at dawn today.

"In a few more minutes, he's going over the top where there's a crop-headed machine-gunner in field gray already looking down the sights and swinging the gun a bit. But she isn't going to die today. She's going to die in 1929 and 1955.

"And just as she's going mad, there's a creaking and out of the shadows tiptoes a Jap with a woman's hairdo and the whitest face and the blackest eyebrows. He's wearing a rose robe and a black sash which belts to his sides two samurai swords, but in his right hand he has a strange silver pistol. And he smiles at her as if they were brother and sister and lovers at the same time and he says, 'Voulez-vous vivre, mademoiselle?' and she stares and he bobs his head and says, 'Missy wish live, yes, no?'"

* * * * *

Sid's paw closed quietly around my shaking hands. It always gets me to hear about anyone's Resurrection, and although mine was crazier, it also had the Krauts in it. I hoped she wouldn't go through the rest of the formula and she didn't.

"Five minutes later, he's gone down a stairs more like a ladder to wait below and she's dressing in a rush. Her clothes resist a little, as if they were lightly gummed to the hook and the stained wall, and she hates to touch them. It's getting lighter and her cot looks as if someone were still sleeping there, although it's empty, and she couldn't bring herself to put her hand on the place if her new life depended on it.

"She climbs down and her long skirt doesn't bother her because she knows how to swing it. Suzaku conducts her past a sentry who doesn't see them and a puffy-faced farmer in a smock coughing and spitting the night out of his throat. They cross the farmyard and it's filled with rose light and she sees the sun is up and she knows that Bruce Marchant has just bled to death.

"There's an empty open touring car chugging loudly, waiting for someone; it has huge muddy wheels with wooden spokes and a brass radiator that says 'Simplex.' But Suzaku leads her past it to a dunghill and bows apologetically and she steps through a Door."

I heard Erich say to the others at the bar, "How touching! Now shall I tell everyone about my operation?" But he didn't get much of a laugh.

"That's how Lilian Foster came into the Change World with its steel-engraved nightmares and its deadly pace and deadlier lassitudes. I was more alive than I ever had been before, but it was the kind of life a corpse might get from unending electrical shocks and I couldn't summon any purpose or hope and Bruce Marchant seemed farther away than ever.

"Then, not six hours ago, a Soldier in a black uniform came through the Door and I thought, 'It can't be, but it does look like his photographs,' and then I thought I heard someone say the name Bruce, and then he shouted as if to all the world that he was Bruce Marchant, and I knew there was a Resurrection beyond Resurrection, a true resurrection. Oh, Bruce —"

She looked at him and he was crying and smiling and all the young beauty flooded back into her face, and I thought, "It has to be Change Winds, but it can't be. Face it without slobbering, Greta-there's something that works bigger miracles than Change."

And she went on, "And then the Change Winds died when the Snakes vaporized the Maintainer or the Ghostgirls Introverted it and all three of them vanished so swiftly and silently that even Bruce didn't notice-those are the best explanations I can summon and I fancy one of them is true. At all events, the Change Winds died and my past and even my futures became something I could bear lightly, because I have someone to bear them with me, and because at last I have a true future stretching out ahead of me, an unknown future which I shall create by living. Oh, don't you see that all of us have it now, this big opportunity?"

"Hussa for Sidney's suffragettes and the W.C.T.U.!" Erich cheered. "Beau, will you play us a medley of 'Hearts and Flowers' and 'Onward, Christian Soldiers'? I'm deeply moved, Lili. Where do the rest of us queue up for the Great Love Affair of the Century?"

Chapter 12. A Big Opportunity

Now is a bearable burden. What buckles the back is the added weight of the past's mistakes and the future's fears.

I had to learn to close the front door to tomorrow and the back door to yesterday and settle down to here and now.

—Anonymous

Nobody laughed at Erich's screwball sarcasms and still I thought, "Yes, perish his hysterical little gray head, but he's half right-Lili's got the big thing now and she wants to serve it up to the rest of us on a platter, only love doesn't cook and cut that way."

Those weren't bad ideas she had about the Maintainer, though, especially the one about the Ghostgirls doing the Introverting-it would explain why there couldn't be Introversion drill, the manual stuff about blue flashes being window-dressing, and something disappearing without movement or transition is the sort of thing that might not catch the attention-and I guess they gave the others something to think about too, for there wasn't any follow-up to Erich's frantic sniping.

But I honestly didn't see where there was this big opportunity being stuck away in a gray sack in the Void and I began to wonder and I got the strangest feeling and I said to myself, "Hang onto your hat, Greta. It's hope."

"The dreadful thing about being a Demon is that you have all time to range through," Lili was saying with a smile. "You can never shut the back door to yesterday or the front door to tomorrow and simply live in the present. But now that's been done for us: the Door is shut, we need never again rehash the past or the future. The Spiders and Snakes can never find us, for who ever heard of a Place that was truly lost being rescued? And as those in the know have told me, Introversion is the end as far as those outside are concerned. So we're safe from the Spiders and Snakes, we need never be slaves or enemies again, and we have a Place in which to live our new lives, the Place prepared for us from the beginning."

She paused. "Surely you understand what I mean? Sidney and Beauregard and Dr. Pyeshkov are the ones who explained it to me. The Place is a balanced aquarium, just like the cosmos. No one knows how many ages of Big Time it has been in use, without a bit of new material being brought in-only luxuries and people-and not a bit of waste cast off. No one knows how many more ages it may not sustain life. I never heard of Minor Maintainers wearing out. We have all the future, all the security, anyone can hope for. We have a Place to live together."

* * * * *

You know, she was dead right and I realized that all the time I'd had the conviction in the back of my mind that we were going to suffocate or something if we didn't get a Door open pretty quick. I should have known differently, if anybody should, because I'd once been in the Place without a Door for as long as a hundred sleeps during a foxhole stretch of the Change War and we'd had to start cycling our food and it had been okay.

And then, because it is also the way my mind works, I started to picture in a flash the consequences of our living together all by ourselves like Lili said.

I began to pair people off; I couldn't help it. Let's see, four women, six men, two ETs.

"Greta," I said, "you're going to be Miss Polly Andry for sure. We'll have a daily newspaper and folk-dancing classes, we'll shut the bar except evenings, Bruce'll keep a rhymed history of the Place."

I even thought, though I knew this part was strictly silly, about schools and children. I wondered what Siddy's would look like, or my little commandant's. "Don't go near the Void, dears." Of course that would be specially hard on the two ETs, but Sevensee at least wasn't so different and the genetics boys had made some wonderful advances and Maud ought to know about them and there were some amazing gadgets in Surgery when Doc sobered up. The patter of little hoofs...

"My fiance spoke to you about carrying a peace message to the rest of the cosmos," Lili added, "and bringing an end to the Big Change, and healing all the wounds that have been made in the Little Time."

I looked at Bruce. His face was set and strained, as will happen to the best of them when a girl starts talking about her man's business, and I don't know why, but I said to myself, "She's crucifying him, she's nailing him to his purpose as a woman will, even when there's not much point to it, as now."

And Lili went on, "It was a wonderful thought, but now we cannot carry or send any message and I believe it is too late in any event for a peace message to do any good. The cosmos is too raveled by change, too far gone. It will dissolve, fade, 'leave not a rack behind.' We're the survivors. The torch of existence has been put in our hands.

"We may already be all that's left in the cosmos, for have you thought that the Change Winds may have died at their source? We may never reach another cosmos, we may drift forever in the Void, but who of us has been Introverted before and who knows what we can or cannot do? We're a seed for a new future to grow from. Perhaps all doomed universes cast off seeds like this Place. It's a seed, it's an embryo, let it grow."

She looked swiftly at Bruce and then at Sid and she quoted, " 'Come, my friends, 'tis not too late to seek a newer world'."

* * * * *

I squeezed Sid's hand and I started to say something to him, but he didn't know I was there; he was listening to Lili quote Tennyson with his eyes entranced and his mouth open, as if he were imagining new things to put into it-oh, Siddy!

And then I saw the others were looking at her the same way. Ilhilihis was seeing finer feather forests than long-dead Luna's grow. The greenhouse child Maud ap-Ares Davies was stowing away on a starship bound for another galaxy, or thinking how different her life might have been, the children she might have had, if she'd stayed on the planets and out of the Change World. Even Erich looked as though he might be blitzing new universes, and Mark subduing them, for an eight-legged *Führer-imperator*. Beau was throbbing up a wider Mississippi in a bigger-than-life sidewheeler.

Even I—well, I wasn't dreaming of a Greater Chicago. "Let's not go hog-wild on this sort of thing," I told myself, but I did look up at the Void and I got a shiver because I imagined it drawing away and the whole Place starting to grow.

"I truly meant what I said about a seed," Lili went on slowly. "I know, as you all do, that there are no children in the Change World, that there cannot be, that we all become instantly sterile, that what they call a curse is lifted from us girls and we are no longer in bondage to the moon."

She was right, all right-if there's one thing that's been proved a million times in the Change World, it's that.

"But we are no longer in the Change World," Lili said softly, "and its limitations should no longer apply to us, including that one. I feel deeply certain of it, but —" she looked around slowly —"we are four women here and I thought one of us might have a surer indication."

My eyes followed hers around like anybody's would. In fact, everybody was looking around except Maud, and she had the silliest look of surprise on her face and it stayed there, and then, very carefully, she got down from the bar stool with her knitting. She looked at the half-finished pink bra with the long white needles stuck in it and her eyes bugged bigger yet, as if she were expecting it to turn into a baby sweater right then and there. Then she walked across the Place to Lili and stood beside her. While she was walking, the look of surprise changed to a quiet smile. The only other thing she did was throw her shoulders back a little.

I was jealous of her for a second, but it was a double miracle for her, considering her age, and I couldn't grudge her that. And to tell the truth, I was a little frightened, too. Even with Dave, I'd been bothered about this business of having babies.

* * * * *

Yet I stood up with Siddy —I couldn't stop myself and I guess he couldn't either-and hand in hand we walked to the control divan. Beau and Sevensee were there and Bruce, of course, and then, so help me, those Soldiers to the death, Kaby and Mark, started over from the bar and I couldn't see anything in their eyes about the greater glory of Crete and Rome, but something, I think, about each other, and after a moment Illy slowly detached himself from the piano and followed, lightly trailing his tentacles on the floor.

I couldn't exactly see him hoping for little Illies in this company, unless it was true what the jokes said about Lunans, but maybe he was being really disinterested and maybe he wasn't; maybe he was simply figuring that Illy ought to be on the side with the biggest battalions.

I heard dragging footsteps behind us and here came Doc from the Gallery, carrying in his folded arms an abstract sculpture as big as a newborn baby. It was an agglomeration of perfect shiny gray spheres the size of golf balls, shaping up to something like a large brain, but with holes showing through here and there. He held it out to us like an infant to be admired and worked his lips and tongue as if he were trying very hard to say something, though not a word came out that you could understand, and I thought, "Maxey Aleksevich may be speechless drunk and have all sorts of holes in his head, but he's got the right instincts, bless his soulful little Russian heart."

We were all crowded around the control divan like a football team huddling. The Peace Packers, it came to me. Sevensee would be fullback or center and Illy left end-what a receiver! The right number, too. Erich was alone at the bar, but now even he —"Oh, no, this can't be," I thought-even he came toward us. Then I saw that his face was working the worst ever. He stopped halfway and managed to force a smile, but it was the worst, too. "That's my little commandant," I thought, "no team spirit."

"So now Lili and Bruce-yes, and *Grossmutterchen* Maud-have their little nest," he said, and he wouldn't have had to push his voice very hard to get a screech. "But what are the rest of us supposed to be-cowbirds?"

* * * * *

He crooked his neck and flapped his hands and croaked, "Cuc-koo! Cuc-koo!" And I said to myself, "I often thought you were crazy, boy, but now I know."

"*Teufelsdreck!* —yes, Devil's dirt! —but you all seem to be infected with this dream of children. Can't you see that the Change World is the natural and proper end of evolution? —a period of enjoyment and measuring, an ultimate working out of things, which women call destruction —'Help, I'm being raped!' 'Oh, what are they doing to my children?' —but which men know as fulfillment.

"You're given good parts in *Götterdämmerung* and you go up to the author and tap him on the shoulder and say, 'Excuse me, Herr Wagner, but this Twilight of the Gods is just a bit morbid. Why don't you write an opera for me about the little ones, the dear little blue-eyed curly-tops? A plot? Oh, boy meets girl and they settle down to breed, something like that.'

"Devil's dirt doubled and damned! Have you thought what life will be like without a Door to go out of to find freedom and adventure, to measure your courage and keenness? Do you want to grow long gray beards hobbling around this asteroid turned inside out? Putter around indoors to the end of your days, mooning about little baby cosmoses? —incidentally, with a live bomb for company. The cave, the womb, the little gray home in the nest-is that what you want? It'll grow? Oh, yes, like the city engulfing the wild wood, a proliferation of *Kinder, Kirche, Küche* —I should live so long!

"Women! —how I hate their bright eyes as they look at me from the fireside, bent-shouldered, rocking, deeply happy to be old, and say, 'He's getting weak, he's giving out, soon I'll have to put him to bed and do the simplest things for him.' Your filthy Triple Goddess, Kaby, the birther, bride, and burier of man! Woman, the enfeebler, the fetterer, the crippler! Woman! —and the curly-headed little cancers she wants!"

408

He lurched toward us, pointing at Lili. "I never knew one who didn't want to cripple a man if you gave her the chance. Cripple him, swaddle him, clip his wings, grind him to sausage to mold another man, hers, a doll man. You hid the Maintainer, you little smother-hen, so you could have your nest and your Brucie!"

He stopped, gasping, and I expected someone to bop him one on the schnozzle, and I think he did, too. I turned to Bruce and he was looking, I don't know how, sorry, guilty, anxious, angry, shaken, inspired, all at once, and I wished people sometimes had simple suburban reactions like magazine stories.

Then Erich made the mistake, if it was one, of turning toward Bruce and slowly staggering toward him, pawing the air with his hands as if he were going to collapse into his arms, and saying, "Don't let them get you, Bruce. Don't let them tie you down. Don't let them clip you-your words or your deeds. You're a Soldier. Even when you talked about a peace message, you talked about doing some smashing of your own. No matter what you think and feel, Bruce, no matter how much lying you do and how much you hide, you're really not on their side."

That did it.

* * * * *

It didn't come soon enough or, I think, in the right spirit to please me, but I will say it for Bruce that he didn't muck it up by tipping or softening his punch. He took one step forward and his shoulders spun and his fist connected sweet and clean.

As he did it, he said only one word, "Loki!" and darn if that didn't switch me back to a campfire in the Indiana Dunes and my mother telling me out of the Elder Saga about the malicious, sneering, all-spoiling Norse god and how, when the other gods came to trap him in his hideaway by the river, he was on the point of finishing knotting a mysterious net big enough, I had imagined, to snare the whole universe, and that if they'd come a minute later, he would have.

Erich was stretched on the floor, his head hitched up, rubbing his jaw and glaring at Bruce. Mark, who was standing beside me, moved a little and I thought he was going to do something, maybe even clobber Bruce in the old spirit of you can't do that to my buddy, but he just shook his head and said, "*Omnia vincit amor.*" I nudged him and said, "Meaning?" and he said, "Love licks everything."

I'd never have expected it from a Roman, but he was half right at any rate. Lili had her victory: Bruce clearing the field for the marriage by laying out the woman-hating boy friend who would be trying to get him to go out nights. At that moment, I think Bruce wanted Lili and a life with her more than he wanted to reform the Change World. Sure, us women have our little victories-until the legions come or the Little Corporal draws up his artillery or the Panzers roar down the road.

Erich scrambled to his feet and stood there in a half-slump, half-crouch, still rubbing his jaw and glaring at Bruce over his hand, but making no move to continue the fight, and I studied his face and said to myself, "If he can get a gun, he's going to shoot himself, I know."

Bruce started to say something and hesitated, like I would have in his shoes, and just then Doc got one of his unpredictable inspirations and went weaving out toward Erich, holding out the sculpture and making deaf-and-dumb noises like he had to us. Erich looked at him as if he were going to kill him, and then grabbed the sculpture and swung it up over his head and smashed it down on the floor, and for a wonder, it didn't shatter. It just skidded along in one piece and stopped inches from my feet.

That thing not breaking must have been the last straw for Erich. I swear I could see the red surge up through his eyes toward his brain. He swung around into the Stores sector and ran the few steps between him and the bronze bomb chest.

Everything got very slow motion for me, though I didn't do any moving. Almost every man started out after Erich. Bruce didn't, though, and Siddy turned back after the first surge forward, while Illy squunched down for a leap, and it was between Sevensee's hairy shanks and

Beau's scissoring white pants that I saw that under-the-microscope circle of death's heads and watched Erich's finger go down on them in the order Kaby had given: one, three, five, six, two, four, seven. I was able to pray seven distinct times that he'd make a mistake.

He straightened up. Illy landed by the box like a huge silver spider and his tentacles whipped futilely across its top. The others surged to a frightened halt around them.

Erich's chest was heaving, but his voice was cool and collected as he said, "You mentioned something about our having a future, Miss Foster. Now you can make that more specific. Unless we get back to the cosmos and dump this box, or find a Spider A-tech, or manage to call headquarters for guidance on disarming the bomb, we have a future exactly thirty minutes long."

Chapter 13. The Tiger is Loose

> But whence he was, or of what wombe ybore,
> Of beasts, or of the earth, I have not red:
> But certes was with milke of wolves and tygres fed.

—Spenser

I guess when they really push the button or throw the switch or spring the trap or focus the beam or what have you, you don't faint or go crazy or anything else convenient. I didn't. Everything, everybody, every move that was made, every word that was spoken, was painfully real to me, like a hand twisting and squeezing things deep inside me, and I saw every least detail spotlighted and magnified like I had the seven skulls.

Erich was standing beyond the bomb chest; little smiles were ruffling his lips. I'd never seen him look so sharp. Illy was beside him, but not on his side, you understand. Mark, Sevensee and Beau were around the chest to the nearer side. Beau had dropped to a knee and was scanning the chest minutely, terror-under-control making him bend his head a little closer than he needed to for clear vision, but with his hands locked together behind his back, I guess to restrain the impulse to push any and everything that looked like a disarming button.

Doc was sprawled face down on the nearest couch, out like a light, I suppose.

Us four girls were still by the control divan. With Kaby, that surprised me, because she didn't look scared or frozen, but almost as intensely alive as Erich.

Sid had turned back, as I'd said, and had one hand stretched out toward but not touching the Minor Maintainer, and a look on his beardy face as if he were calling down death and destruction on every boozy rogue who had ever gone up from King's Lynn to Cambridge and London, and I realized why: if he'd thought of the Minor Maintainer a second sooner, he could have pinned Erich down with heavy gravity before he could touch the buttons.

Bruce was resting one hand on the head of the control divan and was looking toward the group around the chest, toward Erich, I think, as if Erich had done something rather wonderful for him, though I can't imagine myself being tickled at being included in anybody's suicide surprise party. Bruce looked altogether too dreamy, Brahma blast him, for someone who must have the same steel-spiked thought in his head that I know darn well the rest of us had: that in twenty-nine minutes or so, the Place would be a sun in a bag.

* * * * *

Erich was the first to get down to business, as I'd have laid any odds he would be. He had the jump on us and he wasn't going to lose it.

"Well, when are you going to start getting Lili to tell us where she hid the Maintainer? It has to be her-she was too certain it was gone forever when she talked. And Bruce must have seen from the bar who took the Maintainer, and who would he cover up for but his girl?"

There he was plagiarizing my ideas, but I guess I was willing to sign them over to him in full if he got us the right pail of water for that time-bomb.

He glanced at his wrist. "According to my Caller, you have twenty-nine and a half minutes, including the time it will take to get a Door or contact headquarters. When are you going to get busy on the girl?"

Bruce laughed a little-deprecatingly, so help me-and started toward him. "Look here, old man," he said, "there's no need to trouble Lili, or to fuss with headquarters, even if you could. Really not at all. Not to mention that your surmises are quite unfounded, old chap, and I'm a bit surprised at your advancing them. But that's quite all right because, as it happens, I'm an atomics technician and I even worked on that very bomb. To disarm it, you just have to fiddle a bit with some of the ankhs, those hoopy little crosses. Here, let me —"

Allah il allah, but it must have struck everybody as it did me as being just too incredible an assertion, too bloody British a bare-faced bluff, for Erich didn't have to say a word; Mark and Sevensee grabbed Bruce by the arms, one on each side, as he stooped toward the bronze chest, and they weren't gentle about it. Then Erich spoke.

"Oh, no, Bruce. Very sporting of you to try to cover up for your girl friend, but we aren't going to let ourselves be blown to stripped atoms twenty-eight minutes too soon while you monkey with the buttons, the very thing Benson-Carter warned against, and pray for a guess-work miracle. It's too thin, Bruce, when you come from 1917 and haven't been on the Big Time for a hundred sleeps and were calling for an A-tech yourself a few hours ago. Much too thin. Bruce, something is going to happen that I'm afraid you won't like, but you're going to have to put up with it. That is, unless Miss Foster decides to be cooperative."

"I say, you fellows, let me go," Bruce demanded, struggling experimentally. "I know it's a bit thick to swallow and I did give you the wrong impression calling for an A-tech, but I just wanted to capture your attention then; I didn't want to have to work on the bomb. Really, Erich, would they have ordered Benson-Carter to pick us up unless one of us were an A-tech? They'd be sure to include one in the bally operation."

"When they're using patchwork tactics?" Erich grinningly quoted back at him.

* * * * *

Kaby spoke up beside me and said, "Benson-Carter was a magician of matter and he was going on the operation disguised as an old woman. We have the cloak and hood with the other garments," and I wondered how this cold fish of a she-officer could be the same girl who was giving Mark slurpy looks not ten minutes ago.

"Well?" Erich asked, glancing at his Caller and then swinging his eyes around at us as if there must be some of the old *Wehrmacht* iron somewhere. We all found ourselves looking at Lili and she was looking so sharp herself, so ready to jump and so at bay, that it was all *I* needed, at any rate, to make Erich's theory about the Maintainer a rock-bottom certainty.

Bruce must have realized the way our minds were working, for he started to struggle in earnest and at the same time called, "For God's sake, don't do anything to Lili! Let me loose, you idiots! Everything's true I told you —I can save you from that bomb. Sevensee, you took my side against the Spiders; you've nothing to lose. Sid, you're an Englishman. Beau, you're a gentleman and you love her, too-for God's sake, stop them!"

Beau glanced up over his shoulder at Bruce and the others surging around close to his ankles and he had on his poker face. Sid I could tell was once more going through the purgatory of decision. Beau reached his own decision first and I'll say it for him that he acted on it fast and intelligently. Right from his kneeling position and before he'd even turned his head quite back, he jumped Erich.

But other things in this cosmos besides Man can pick sides and act fast. Illy landed on Beau midway and whipped his tentacles around him tight and they went wobbling around like a drunken white-and-silver barber pole. Beau got his hands each around a tentacle, and at the same time his face began to get purple, and I winced at what they were both going through.

Maybe Sevensee had a hoof in Sid's purgatory, because Bruce shook loose from the satyr and tried to knock out Mark, but the Roman twisted his arm and kept him from getting in a good punch.

Erich didn't make a move to mix into either fight, which is my little commandant all over. Using his fists on anybody but me is beneath him.

* * * * *

Then Sid made his choice, but there was no way for me to tell what it was, for, as he reached for the Minor Maintainer, Kaby contemptuously snatched it away from his hands and gave him a knee in the belly that doubled me up in sympathy and sent him sprawling on his knees toward the fighters. On the return, Kaby gave Lili, who'd started to grab too, an effortless backhand smash that set her down on the divan.

Erich's face lit up like an electric sign and he kept his eyes fixed on Kaby.

She crouched a little, carrying her weight on the balls of her feet and firmly cradling the Minor Maintainer in her left arm, like a basketball captain planning an offensive. Then she waved her free hand decisively to the right. I didn't get it, but Erich did and Mark too, for Erich jumped for the Refresher sector and Mark let go of Bruce and followed him, ducking around Sevensee's arms, who was coming back into the fight on which side I don't know. Illy un-whipped from Beau and copied Erich and Mark with one big spring.

Then Kaby twisted a dial as far as it would go and Bruce, Beau, Sevensee and poor Siddy were slammed down and pinned to the floor by about eight gravities.

It should have been lighter near us—I hoped it was, but you couldn't tell from watching Siddy; he went flat on his face, spread-eagled, one hand stretched toward me so close, I could have touched it (but not let go!), and his mouth was open against the floor and he was gasping through a corner of it and I could see his spine trying to sink through his belly. Bruce just managed to get his head and one shoulder up a bit, and they all made me think of a Dore illustration of the *Inferno* where the cream of the damned are frozen up to their necks in ice in the innermost circle of Hell.

The gravity didn't catch me, although I could feel it in my left arm. I was mostly in the Refresher sector, but I dropped down flat too, partly out of a crazy compassion I have, but mostly because I didn't want to take a chance of having Kaby knock me down.

Erich, Mark and Illy had got clear and they headed toward us. Maud picked the moment to make her play; she hadn't much choice of times, if she wanted to make one. The Old Girl was looking it for once, but I guess the thought of her miracle must have survived alongside the fear of sacked sun and must have meant a lot to her, for she launched out fast, all set to straight-arm Kaby into the heavy gravity and grab the Minor Maintainer with the other hand.

Chapter 14. "Now Will You Talk?"

Like diamonds, we are cut with our own dust.

—Webster

412

Cretans have eyes under their back hair, or let's face it, Entertainers aren't Soldiers. Kaby weaved to one side and flicked a helpful hand and poor old Maud went where she'd been going to send Kaby. It sickened me to see the gravity take hold and yank her down.

I could have jumped up and made it four in a row for Kaby, but I'm not a bit brave when things like my life are at stake.

Lili was starting to get up, acting a little dazed. Kaby gently pushed her down again and quietly said, "Where is it?" and then hauled off and slapped her across the face. What got me was the matter-of-fact way Kaby did it. I can understand somebody getting mad and socking someone, or even deliberately working up a rage so as to be able to do something nasty, but this cold-blooded way turns my stomach.

Lili looked as if half her face were about to start bleeding, but she didn't look dazed any more and her jaw set. Kaby grabbed Lili's pearl necklace and twisted it around her neck and it broke and the pearls went bouncing around like ping-pong balls, so Kaby yanked down Lili's gray silk bandeau until it was around the neck and tightened that. Lili started to choke through her tight-pressed lips. Erich, Mark and Illy had come up and crowded around, but they seemed to be content with the job Kaby was doing.

"Listen, slut," she said, "we have no time. You have a healing room in this place. I can work the things."

"Here it comes," I thought, wishing I could faint. On top of everything, on top of death even, they had to drag in the nightmare personally stylized for me, the horror with my name on it. I wasn't going to be allowed to blow up peacefully. They weren't satisfied with an A-bomb. They had to write my private hell into the script.

"There is a thing called an Invertor," Kaby said exactly as I'd known she would, but as I didn't really hear it just then —a mental split I'll explain in a moment. "It opens you up so they can cure your insides without cutting your skin or making you bleed anywhere. It turns the big parts of you inside out, but not the blood tubes. All your skin-your eyes, ears, nose, toes, all of it-becoming the lining of a little hole that's half-filled with your hair.

"Meantime, your insides are exposed for whatever the healer wants to do to them. You live for a while on the air inside the hole. First the healer gives you an air that makes you sleep, or you go mad in about fifty heartbeats. We'll see what ten heartbeats do to you without the sleepy air. Now will you talk?"

* * * * *

I hadn't been listening to her, though, not the real me, or I'd have gone mad without getting the treatment. I once heard Doc say your liver is more mysterious and farther away from you than the stars, because although you live with your liver all your life, you never see it or learn to point to it instinctively, and the thought of someone messing around with that intimate yet unknown part of you is just too awful.

I knew I had to do something quick. Hell, at the first hint of Introversion, before Kaby had even named it, Illy had winced so that his tentacles were all drawn up like fat feather-sausages. Erich had looked at him questioningly, but that lousy Looney had un-endeared himself to me by squeaking, "Don't mind me, I'm just sensitive. Get on with the girl. Make her tell."

Yes, I knew I had to do something, and here on the floor that meant thinking hard and in high gear about something else. The screwball sculpture Erich had tried to smash was a foot from my nose and I saw a faint trail of white stuff where it had skidded. I reached out and touched the trail; it was finely gritty, like powdered glass. I tipped up the sculpture and the part on which it had skidded wasn't marred at all, not even dulled; the gray spheres were as glisteningly bright as ever. So I knew the trail was diamond dust rubbed off the diamonds in the floor by something even harder.

That told me the sculpture was something special and maybe Doc had had a real idea in his pickled brain when he'd been pushing the thing at all of us and trying to tell us something.

He hadn't managed to say anything then, but he had earlier when he'd been going to tell us what to do about the bomb, and maybe there was a connection.

I twisted my memory hard and let it spring back and I got "Inversh ... bosh ..." Bosh, indeed! Bosh and inverse bosh to all boozers, Russki or otherwise.

So I quick tried the memory trick again and this time I got "glovsh" and then I grasped and almost sneezed on diamond dust as I watched the pieces fit themselves together in my mind like a speeded-up movie reel.

It all hung on that black right-hand hussar's glove Lili had produced for Bruce. Only she couldn't have found it in Stores, because we'd searched every fractional pigeonhole later on and there hadn't been any gloves there, not even the left-hand mate there would have been. Also, Bruce had had two left-hand gloves to start with, and we had been through the whole Place with a fine-tooth comb, and there had been only the two black gloves on the floor where Bruce had kicked them off the bar-those two and those two only, the left-hand glove he'd brought from outside and the right-hand glove Lili had produced for him.

* * * * *

So a left-hand glove had disappeared-the last I'd seen of it, Lili had been putting it on her tray-and a right-hand glove had appeared. Which could only add up to one thing: Lili had turned the left-hand glove into an identical right. She couldn't have done it by turning it inside out the ordinary way, because the lining was different.

But as I knew only too sickeningly well, there was an extraordinary way to turn things inside out, things like human beings. You merely had to put them on the Invertor in Surgery and flick the switch for full Inversion.

Or you could flick it for partial Inversion and turn something into a perfect three-dimensional mirror image of itself, just what a right-hand glove is of a left. Rotation through the fourth dimension, the science boys call it; I've heard of it being used in surgery on the highly asymmetric Martians, and even to give a socially impeccable right hand to a man who'd lost one, by turning an amputated right arm into an amputated left.

Ordinarily, nothing but live things are ever Inverted in Surgery and you wouldn't think of doing it to an inanimate object, especially in a Place where the Doc's a drunk and the Surgery hasn't been used for hundreds of sleeps.

But when you've just fallen in love, you think of wonderful crazy things to do for people. Drunk with love, Lili had taken Bruce's extra left-hand glove into Surgery, partially Inverted it, and got a right-hand glove to give him.

What Doc had been trying to say with his "Inversh ... bosh ..." was "Invert the box," meaning we should put the bronze chest through full Inversion to get at the bomb inside to disarm it. Doc too had got the idea from Lili's trick with the glove. What an inside-out tactical atomic bomb would look like, I could not imagine and did not particularly care to see. I might have to, though, I realized.

But the fast-motion film was still running in my head. Later on, Lili had decided like I had that her lover was going to lose out in his plea for mutiny unless she could give him a really captive audience-and maybe, even then, she had been figuring on creating the nest for Bruce's chicks and ... all those other things we'd believed in for a while. So she'd taken the Major Maintainer and remembered the glove, and not many seconds later, she had set down on a shelf of the Art Gallery an object that no one would think of questioning-except someone who knew the Gallery by heart.

* * * * *

I looked at the abstract sculpture a foot from my nose, at the clustered gray spheres the size of golf balls. I had known that the inside of the Maintainer was made up of vastly tough, vastly hard giant molecules, but I hadn't realized they were quite *that* big.

I said to myself, "Greta, this is going to give you a major psychosis, but you're the one who has to do it, because no one is going to listen to your deductions when they're all practically living on negative time already."

I got up as quietly as if I were getting out of a bed I shouldn't have been in-there are some things Entertainers are good at-and Kaby was just saying "you go mad in about fifty heartbeats." Everybody on their feet was looking at Lili. Sid seemed to have moved, but I had no time for him except to hope he hadn't done anything that might attract attention to me.

I stepped out of my shoes and walked rapidly to Surgery-there's one good thing about this hardest floor anywhere, it doesn't creak. I walked through the Surgery screen that is like a wall of opaque, odorless cigarette smoke and I concentrated on remembering my snafued nurse's training, and before I had time to panic, I had the sculpture positioned on the gleaming table of the Invertor.

I froze for a moment when I reached for the Inversion switch, thinking of the other time and trying to remember what it had been that bothered me so much about an inside-out brain being bigger and not having eyes, but then I either thumbed my nose at my nightmare or kissed my sanity good-by, I don't know which, and twisted the switch all the way over, and there was the Major Maintainer winking blue about three times a second as nice as you could want it.

It must have been working as sweet and steady as ever, all the time it was Inverted, except that, being inside out, it had hocused the direction finders.

Chapter 15. Lord Spider

> black legged spiders
> with red hearts of hell

> —marquis

"Jesu!" I turned and Sid's face was sticking through the screen like a tinted bas-relief hanging on a gray wall and I got the impression he had peered unexpectedly through a slit in an arras into Queen Elizabeth's bedroom.

He didn't have any time to linger on the sensation, even if he'd wanted to, for an elbow with a copper band thrust through the screen and dug his ribs and Kaby marched Lili in by the neck. Erich, Mark and Illy were right behind. They caught the blue flashes and stopped dead, staring at the long-lost. Erich spared me one look which seemed to say, so you did it, not that it matters. Then he stepped forward and picked it up and held it solidly to his left side in the double right-angle made by fingers, forearm and chest, and reached for the Introversion switch with a look on his face as if he were opening a fifth of whisky.

The blue light died and Change Winds hit me like a stiff drink that had been a long, long time in coming, like a hot trumpet note out of nowhere.

I felt the changing pasts blowing through me, and the uncertainties whistling past, and ice-stiff reality softening with all its duties and necessities, and the little memories shredding away and dancing off like autumn leaves, leaving maybe not even ghosts behind, and all the crazy moods like Mardi Gras dancers pouring down an evening street, and something inside me had the nerve to say it didn't care whether Greta Forzane's death was riding in those Winds because they felt so good.

I could tell it was hitting the others the same way. Even battered, tight-lipped Lili seemed to be saying, you're making me drink the stuff and I hate you for it, but I do love it. I guess we'd all had the worry that even finding and Extroverting the Maintainer wouldn't put us back in touch with the cosmos and give us those Winds we hate and love.

The thing that cut through to us as we stood there glowing was not the thought of the bomb, though that would have come in a few seconds more, but Sid's voice. He was still standing in the screen, except that now his face was out the other side and we could just see parts of his gray-doubleted back, but, of course, his "Jesu!" came through the screen as if it weren't there.

At first I couldn't figure out who he could be talking to, but I swear I never heard his voice so courtly obsequious before, so strong and yet so filled with awe and an under-note of, yes, sheer terror.

"Lord, I am filled from top to toe with confusion that you should so honor my poor Place," he said. "Poor say I and mine, when I mean that I have ever busked it faithfully for you, not dreaming that you would ever condescend ... yet knowing that your eye was certes ever upon me ... though I am but as a poor pinch of dust adrift between the suns ... I abase myself. Prithee, how may I serve thee, sir? I know not e'en how most suitably to address thee, Lord ... King ... Emperor Spider!"

* * * * *

I felt like I was getting very small, but not a bit less visible, worse luck, and even with the Change Winds inside me to give me courage, I thought this was really too much, coming on top of everything else; it was simply unfair.

At the same time, I realized it was to be expected that the big bosses would have been watching us with their unblinking beady black eyes ever since we had Introverted waiting to pounce if we should ever come out of it. I tried to picture what was on the other side of the screen and I didn't like the assignment.

But in spite of being petrified, I had a hard time not giggling, like the zany at graduation exercises, at the way the other ones in Surgery were taking it.

I mean the Soldiers. They each stiffened up like they had the old ramrod inside them, and their faces got that important look, and they glanced at each other and the floor without lowering their heads, as if they were measuring the distance between their feet and mentally chalking alternate sets of footprints to step into. The way Erich and Kaby held the Major and Minor Maintainers became formal; the way they checked their Callers and nodded reassuringly was positively esoteric. Even Illy somehow managed to look as if he were on parade.

Then from beyond the screen came what was, under the circumstances, the worst noise I've ever heard, a seemingly wordless distant-sounding howling and wailing, with a note of menace that made me shake, although it also had a nasty familiarity about it I couldn't place. Sid's voice broke into it, loud, fast and frightened.

"Your pardon, Lord, I did not think ... certes, the gravity ... I'll attend to it on the instant." He whipped a hand and half a head back through the screen, but without looking back and snapped his fingers, and before I could blink, Kaby had put the Minor Maintainer in his hand.

Sid went completely out of sight then and the howling stopped, and I thought that if that was the way a Lord Spider expressed his annoyance at being subjected to incorrect gravity, I hoped the bosses wouldn't start any conversations with me.

Erich pursed his lips and threw the other Soldiers a nod and the four of them marched through the screen as if they'd drilled a lifetime for this moment. I had the wild idea that Erich might give me his arm, but he strode past me as if I were ... an Entertainer.

I hesitated a moment then, but I had to see what was happening outside, even if I got eaten up for it. Besides, I had a bit of the thought that if these formalities went on much longer, even a Lord Spider was going to discover just how immune he was to confined atomic blast.

I walked through the screen with Lili beside me.

* * * * *

The Soldiers had stopped a few feet in front of it. I looked around ahead for whatever it was going to turn out to be, prepared to drop a curtsy or whatever else, bar nothing, that seemed expected of me.

I had a hard time spotting the beast. Some of the others seemed to be having trouble too. I saw Doc weaving around foolishly by the control divan, and Bruce and Beau and Sevensee and Maud on their feet beyond it, and I wondered whether we were dealing with an invisible monster; ought to be easy enough for the bosses to turn a simple trick like invisibility.

Then I looked sharply left where everyone else, even glassy-eyed Doc, was coming to look, into the Door sector, only there wasn't any monster there or even a Door, but just Siddy holding the Minor Maintainer and grinning like when he is threatening to tickle me, only more fiendishly.

"Not a move, masters," he cried, his eyes dancing, "or I'll pin the pack of you down, marry and amen I will. It is my firm purpose to see the Place blasted before I let this instrument out of my hands again."

My first thought was, "'Sblood but Siddy is a real actor! I don't care if he didn't study under anyone later than Burbage, that just proves how good Burbage is."

Sid had convinced us not only that the real Spiders had arrived, but earlier that the gravity in the edge of Stores had been a lot heavier than it actually was. He completely fooled all those Soldiers, including my swelled-headed victorious little commandant, and I kind of filed away the timing of that business of reaching out the hand and snapping the fingers without looking, it was so good.

"Beauregard!" Sid called. "Get to the Major Maintainer and call headquarters. But don't come through Door, marry go by Refresher. I'll not trust a single Demon of you in this sector with me until much more has been shown and settled."

"Siddy, you're wonderful," I said, starting toward him. "As soon as I got the Maintainer unsnarled and looked around and saw your sweet old face —"

"Back, tricksy trull! Not the breadth of one scarlet toenail nearer me, you Queen of Sleights and High Priestess of Deception!" he bellowed. "You least of all do I trust. Why you hid the Maintainer, I know not, 'faith, but later you'll discover the truth to me or I'll have your gizzard."

I could see there was going to have to be a little explaining.

* * * * *

Doc, touched off, I guess, by Sid waving his hand at me, threw back his head and let off one of those shuddery Siberian wolf-howls he does so blamed well. Sid waved toward him sharply and he shut up, beaming toothily, but at least I knew who was responsible for the Spider wail of displeasure that Sid had either called for or more likely got as a gift of the gods and used in his act.

Beau came circling around fast and Erich shoved the Major Maintainer into his hands without making any fuss. The four Soldiers were looking pretty glum after losing their grand review.

Beau dumped some junk off one of the Art Gallery's sturdy taborets and set the Major Maintainer on it carefully but fast, and quickly knelt in front of it and whipped on some earphones and started to tune. The way he did it snatched away from me my inward glory at my big Inversion brainwave so fast, I might never have had it, and there was nothing in my mind again but the bronze bomb chest.

I wondered if I should suggest Inverting the thing, but I said to myself, "Uh-uh, Greta, you got no diploma to show them and there probably isn't time to try two things, anyway."

Then Erich for once did something I wanted him to, though I didn't care for its effect on my nerves, by looking at his Caller and saying quietly, "Nine minutes to go, if Place time and cosmic time are synching."

Beau was steady as a rock and working adjustments so fine that I couldn't even see his fingers move.

Then, at the other end of the Place, Bruce took a few steps toward us. Sevensee and Maud followed a bit behind him. I remembered Bruce was another of our nuts with a private program for blowing up the place.

"Sidney," he called, and then, when he'd got Sid's attention, "Remember, Sidney, you and I both came down to London from Peterhouse."

I didn't get it. Then Bruce looked toward Erich with a devil-may-care challenge and toward Lili as if he were asking her forgiveness for something. I couldn't read her expression; the bruises were blue on her throat and her cheek was puffy.

Then Bruce once more shot Erich that look of challenge and he spun and grabbed Sevensee by a wrist and stuck out a foot-even half-horses aren't too sharp about infighting, I guess, and the satyr had every right to feel at least as confused as I felt-and sent him stumbling into Maud, and the two of them tumbled to the floor in a jumble of hairy legs and pearl-gray frock. Bruce raced to the bomb chest.

* * * * *

Most of us yelled, "Stop him, Sid, pin him down," or something like that —I know I did because I was suddenly sure that he'd been asking Lili's pardon for blowing the two of them up-and all the rest of us too, the love-blinded stinker.

Sid had been watching him all the time and now he lifted his hand to the Minor Maintainer, but then he didn't touch any of the dials, just watched and waited, and I thought, "Shaitan shave us! Does Siddy want in on death, too? Ain't he satisfied with all he knows about life?"

Bruce had knelt and was twisting some things on the front of the chest, and it was all as bright as if he were under a bank of Klieg lights, and I was telling myself I wouldn't know anything when the fireball fired, and not believing it, and Sevensee and Maud had got unscrambled and were starting for Bruce, and the rest of us were yelling at Sid, except that Erich was just looking at Bruce very happily, and Sid was still not doing anything, and it was unbearable except just then I felt the little arteries start to burst in my brain like a string of fire-crackers and the old aorta pop, and for good measure, a couple of valves come unhinged in my ticker, and I was thinking, "Well, now I know what it's like to die of heart failure and high blood pressure," and having a last quiet smile at having cheated the bomb, when Bruce jumped up and back from the chest.

"That does it!" he announced cheerily. "She's as safe as the Bank of England."

Sevensee and Maud stopped themselves just short of knocking him down and I said to myself, "Hey, let's get a move on! I thought heart attacks were fast."

Before anyone else could speak, Beau did. He had turned around from the Major Maintainer and pulled aside one of the earphones.

"I got headquarters," he said crisply. "They told me how to disarm the bomb —I merely said I thought we ought to know. What did you do, sir?" he called to Bruce.

"There's a row of four ankhs just below the lock. The first to your left you give a quarter turn to the right, the second a quarter turn to the left, same for the fourth, and you don't touch the third."

"That is it, sir," Beau confirmed.

The long silence was too much for me; I guess I must have the shortest span for unspoken relief going. I drew some nourishment out of my restored arteries into my brain cells and yelled, "Siddy, I know I'm a tricksy trull and the High Vixen of all Foxes, but what the Hell is Peterhouse?"

"The oldest college at Cambridge," he told me rather coolly.

Chapter 16. The Possibility-Binders

"Familiar with infinite universe sheafs and open-ended postulate systems? —the notion that everything is possible-and I mean everything-and everything has happened. *Everything.*"

—Heinlein

An hour later, I was nursing a weak highball and a black eye in the sleepy-time darkness on the couch farthest from the piano, half watching the highlighted party going on around it and the bar, while the Place waited for rendezvous with Egypt and the Battle of Alexandria.

Sid had swept all our outstanding problems into one big bundle and, since his hand held the joker of the Minor Maintainer, he had settled them all as high-handedly as if they'd been those of a bunch of schoolkids.

It amounted to this:

We'd been Introverted when most of the damning things had happened, so presumably only we knew about them, and we were all in so deep one way or another that we'd all have to keep quiet to protect our delicate complexions.

Well, Erich's triggering the bomb did balance rather neatly Bruce's incitement to mutiny, and there was Doc's drinking, while everybody who had declared for the peace message had something to hide. Mark and Kaby I felt inclined to trust anywhere, Maud for sure, and Erich in this particular matter, damn him. Illy I didn't feel at all easy about, but I told myself there always has to be a fly in the ointment —a darn big one this time, and furry.

Sid didn't mention his own dirty linen, but he knew we knew he'd flopped badly as boss of the Place and only recouped himself by that last-minute flimflam.

Remembering Sid's trick made me think for a moment about the real Spiders. Just before I snuck out of Surgery, I'd had a vivid picture of what they must look like, but now I couldn't get it again. It depressed me, not being able to remember-oh, I probably just imagined I'd had a picture, like a hophead on a secret-of-the-universe kick. Me ever find out anything about the Spiders? —except for nervous notions like I'd had during the recent fracas? —what a laugh!

The funniest thing (ha-ha!) was that I had ended up the least-trusted person. Sid wouldn't give me time to explain how I'd deduced what had happened to the Maintainer, and even when Lili spoke up and admitted hiding it, she acted so bored I don't think everybody believed her-although she did spill the realistic detail that she hadn't used partial Inversion on the glove; she'd just turned it inside out to make it a right and then done a full Inversion to get the lining back inside.

* * * * *

I tried to get Doc to confirm that he'd reasoned the thing out the same way I had, but he said he had been blacked out the whole time, except during the first part of the hunt, and he didn't remember having any bright ideas at all. Right now, he was having Maud explain to him twice, in detail, everything that had happened. I decided that it was going to take a little more work before my reputation as a great detective was established.

I looked over the edge of the couch and just made out in the gloom one of Bruce's black gloves. It must have been kicked there. I fished it up. It was the right-hand one. My big clue, and was I sick of it! Got mittens, God forbid! I slung it away and, like a lurking octopus, Illy shot up a tentacle from the next couch, where I hadn't known he was resting, and snatched the glove like it was a morsel of underwater garbage. These ETs can seem pretty shuddery non-human at times.

I thought of what a cold-blooded, skin-saving louse Illy had been, and about Sid and his easy suspicions, and Erich and my black eye, and how, as usual, I'd got left alone in the end. My men!

Bruce had explained about being an A-tech. Like a lot of us, he'd had several widely different jobs during his first weeks in the Change World and one of them had been as secretary to a group of the minor atomics boys from the Manhattan-Project-Earth-Satellite days. I gathered he'd also absorbed some of his bothersome ideas from them. I hadn't quite decided yet what species of heroic heel he belonged to, but he was thick with Mark and Erich again. Everybody's men!

Sid didn't have to argue with anybody; all the wild compulsions and mighty resolves were dead now, anyway until they'd had a good long rest. I sure could use one myself, I knew.

The party at the piano was getting wilder. Lili had been dancing the black bottom on top of it and now she jumped down into Sid's and Sevensee's arms, taking a long time about it. She'd been drinking a lot and her little gray dress looked about as innocent on her as diapers would on Nell Gwyn. She continued her dance, distributing her marks of favor equally between Sid, Erich and the satyr. Beau didn't mind a bit, but serenely pounded out "Tonight's the Night" —which she'd practically shouted to him not two minutes ago.

I was glad to be out of the party. Who can compete with a highly experienced, utterly disillusioned seventeen-year-old really throwing herself away for the first time?

* * * * *

Something touched my hand. Illy had stretched a tentacle into a furry wire to return me the black glove, although he ought to have known I didn't want it. I pushed it away, privately calling Illy a washed-out moronic tarantula, and right away I felt a little guilty. What right had I to be critical of Illy? Would my own character have shown to advantage if I'd been locked in with eleven octopoids a billion years away? For that matter, where did I get off being critical of anyone?

Still, I was glad to be out of the party, though I kept on watching it. Bruce was drinking alone at the bar. Once Sid had gone over to him and they'd had one together and I'd heard Bruce reciting from Rupert Brooke those deliberately corny lines, "For England's the one land, I know, Where men with Splendid Hearts may go; and Cambridgeshire, of all England, The Shire for Men who Understand;" and I'd remembered that Brooke too had died young in World War One and my ideas had got fuzzy. But mostly Bruce was just calmly drinking by himself. Every once in a while Lili would look at him and stop dead in her dancing and laugh.

I'd figured out this Bruce-Lili-Erich business as well as I cared to. Lili had wanted the nest with all her heart and nothing else would ever satisfy her, and now she'd go to hell her own way and probably die of Bright's disease for a third time in the Change World. Bruce hadn't wanted the nest or Lili as much as he wanted the Change World and the chances it gave for Soldierly cavorting and poetic drunks; Lili's seed wasn't his idea of healing the cosmos; maybe he'd make a real mutiny some day, but more likely he'd stick to bar-room epics.

His and Lili's infatuation wouldn't die completely, no matter how rancid it looked right now. The real-love angle might go, but Change would magnify the romance angle and it might seem to them like a big thing of a sort if they met again.

Erich had his *Kamerad*, shaped to suit him, who'd had the guts and cleverness to disarm the bomb he'd had the guts to trigger. You have to hand it to Erich for having the nerve to put us all in a situation where we'd have to find the Maintainer or fry, but I don't know anything disgusting enough to hand to him.

I had tried a while back. I had gone up behind him and said, "Hey, how's my wicked little commandant? Forgotten your *und so weiter*?" and as he turned, I clawed my nails and slammed him across the cheek. That's how I got the black eye. Maud wanted to put an electronic leech on it, but I took the old handkerchief in ice water. Well, at any rate Erich had his scratches to match Bruce's, not as deep, but four of them, and I told myself maybe they'd get infected —I hadn't washed my hands since the hunt. Not that Erich doesn't love scars.

* * * * *

Mark was the one who helped me up after Erich knocked me down.

"You got any omnias for that?" I snapped at him.

"For what?" Mark asked.

"Oh, for everything that's been happening to us," I told him disgustedly.

He seemed to actually think for a moment and then he said, *"Omnia mutantur, nihil interit."*

"Meaning?" I asked him.

He said, "All things change, but nothing is really lost."

It would be a wonderful philosophy to stand with against the Change Winds. Also damn silly. I wondered if Mark really believed it. I wished I could. Sometimes I come close to thinking it's a lot of baloney trying to be any decent kind of Demon, even a good Entertainer. Then I tell myself, "That's life, Greta. You've got to love through it somehow." But there are times when some of these cookies are not too easy to love.

Something brushed the palm of my hand again. It was Illy's tentacle, with the tendrils of the tip spread out like a little bush. I started to pull my hand away, but then I realized the Loon was simply lonely. I surrendered my hand to the patterned gossamer pressures of feather-talk.

Right away I got the words, "Feeling lonely, Greta girl?"

It almost floored me, I tell you. Here I was understanding feather-talk, which I just didn't, and I was understanding it in English, which didn't make sense at all.

For a second, I thought Illy must have spoken, but I knew he hadn't, and for a couple more seconds I thought he was working telepathy on me, using the feather-talk as cues. Then I tumbled to what was happening: he was playing English on my palm like on the keyboard of his squeakbox, and since I could play English on a squeakbox myself, my mind translated automatically.

Realizing this almost gave my mind stage fright, but I was too fagged to be hocused by self-consciousness. I just lay back and let the thoughts come through. It's good to have someone talk to you, even an underweight octopus, and without the squeaks Illy didn't sound so silly; his phrasing was soberer.

* * * * *

"Feeling sad, Greta girl, because you'll never understand what's happening to us all," Illy asked me, "because you'll never be anything but a shadow fighting shadows-and trying to love shadows in between the battles? It's time you understood we're not really fighting a war at all, although it looks that way, but going through a kind of evolution, though not exactly the kind Erich had in mind.

"Your Terran thought has a word for it and a theory for it —a theory that recurs on many worlds. It's about the four orders of life: Plants, Animals, Men and Demons. Plants are energy-binders —they can't move through space or time, but they can clutch energy and transform it. Animals are space-binders —they can move through space. Man (Terran or ET, Lunan or non-Lunan) is a time-binder —he has memory.

"Demons are the fourth order of evolution, possibility-binders —they can make all of what might be part of what is, and that is their evolutionary function. Resurrection is like the metamorphosis of a caterpillar into a butterfly: a third-order being breaks out of the chrysalis of its lifeline into fourth-order life. The leap from the ripped cocoon of an unchanging reality is like the first animal's leap when he ceases to be a plant, and the Change World is the core of meaning behind the many myths of immortality.

"All evolution looks like a war at first-octopoids against monopoids, mammals against reptiles. And it has a necessary dialectic: there must be the thesis-we call it Snake-and the antithesis-Spider-before there can be the ultimate synthesis, when all possibilities are fully realized in one ultimate universe. The Change War isn't the blind destruction it seems.

"Remember that the Serpent is your symbol of wisdom and the Spider your sign for patience. The two names are rightly frightening to you, for all high existence is a mixture of horror and delight. And don't be surprised, Greta girl, at the range of my words and thoughts; in a way, I've had a billion years to study Terra and learn her languages and myths.

"Who are the real Spiders and Snakes, meaning who were the first possibility-binders? Who was Adam, Greta girl? Who was Cain? Who were Eve and Lilith?

"In binding all possibility, the Demons also bind the mental with the material. All fourth-order beings live inside and outside all minds, throughout the whole cosmos. Even this Place is, after its fashion, a giant brain: its floor is the brainpan, the boundary of the Void is the cortex of gray matter-yes, even the Major and Minor Maintainers are analogues of the pineal and pituitary glands, which in some form sustain all nervous systems.

"There's the real picture, Greta girl."

The feather-talk faded out and Illy's tendril tips merged into a soft pad on which I fingered, "Thanks, Daddy Longlegs."

* * * * *

Chewing over in my mind what Illy had just told me, I looked back at the gang around the piano. The party seemed to be breaking up; at least some of them were chopping away at it. Sid had gone to the control divan and was getting set to tune in Egypt. Mark and Kaby were there with him, all bursting with eagerness and the vision of tanks on ranks of mounted Zombie bowmen going up in a mushroom cloud; I thought of what Illy had told me and I managed a smile-seems we've got to win and lose all the battles, every which way.

Mark had just put on his Parthian costume, groaning cheerfully, "Trousers again!" and was striding around under a hat like a fur-lined ice-cream cone and with the sleeves of his metal-stuffed candys flapping over his hands. He waved a short sword with a heart-shaped guard at Bruce and Erich and told them to get a move on.

Kaby was going along on the operation wearing the old-woman disguise intended for Benson-Carter. I got a half-hearted kick out of knowing she was going to have to cover that chest and hobble.

Bruce and Erich weren't taking orders from Mark just yet. Erich went over and said something to Bruce at the bar, and Bruce got down and went over with Erich to the piano, and Erich tapped Beau on the shoulder and leaned over and said something to him, and Beau nodded and yanked "Limehouse Blues" to a fast close and started another piece, something slow and nostalgic.

Erich and Bruce waved to Mark and smiled, as if to show him that whether he came over and stood with them or not, the legate and the lieutenant and the commandant were very much together. And while Sevensee hugged Lili with a simple enthusiasm that made me wonder why I've wasted so much imagination on genetic treatments for him, Erich and Bruce sang:

> "To the legion of the lost ones, to the cohort of the damned,
> To our brothers in the tunnels outside time,
> Sing three Change-resistant Zombies, raised from death and robot-crammed,
> And Commandos of the Spiders —
> Here's to crime!
> We're three blind mice on the wrong time-track,
> Hush-hush-hush!
> We've lost our now and will never get back,
> Hush-hush-hush!
> Change Commandos out on the spree,
> Damned through all possibility,
> Ghostgirls, think kindly on such as we,
> Hush-hush-hush!"

While they were singing, I looked down at my charcoal skirt and over at Maud and Lili and I thought, "Three gray hustlers for three black hussars, that's our speed." Well, I'd never thought of myself as a high-speed job, winning all the races —I wouldn't feel comfortable that way. Come to think of it, we've got to lose and win all the races in the long run, the way the course is laid out.

I fingered to Illy, "That's the picture, all right, Spider boy."

Andre Norton

Key Out of Time

1. Lotus World

There was a shading of rose in the pearl arch of sky, deepening at the horizon meeting of sea and air in a rainbow tint of cloud. The lazy swells of the ocean held the same soft color, darkened with crimson veins where spirals of weed drifted. A rose world bathed in soft sunlight, knowing only gentle winds, peace, and-sloth.

Ross Murdock leaned forward over the edge of the rock ledge to peer down at a beach of fine sand, pale pink sand with here and there a glitter of a crystalline "shell" —or were those delicate, fluted ovals shells? Even the waves came in languidly. And the breeze which ruffled his hair, smoothed about his sun-browned, half-bare body, caressed it, did not buffet on its way inland to stir the growths which the Terran settlers called "trees" but which possessed long lacy fronds instead of true branches.

Hawaika-named for the old Polynesian paradise —a world seemingly without flaw except the subtle one of being too perfect, too welcoming, too wooing. Its long, uneventful, unchanging days enticed forgetfulness, offered a life without effort. Except for the mystery....

Because this world was not the one pictured on the tape which had brought the Terran settlement team here. A map, a directing guide, a description all in one, that was the ancient voyage tape. Ross himself had helped to loot a storehouse on an unknown planet for a cargo of such tapes. Once they had been the space-navigation guides for a race or races who had ruled the star lanes ten thousand years in his own world's past, a civilization which had long since sunk again into the dust of its beginning.

Those tapes returned to Terra after their chance discovery, were studied, probed, deciphered by the best brains of his time, shared out by lot between already suspicious Terran powers, bringing into the exploration of space bitter rivalries and old hatreds.

Such a tape had landed their ship on Hawaika, a world of shallow seas and archipelagoes instead of true continents. The settlement team had had all the knowledge contained on that tape crowded into them, only to discover that much they had learned from it was false!

Of course, none of them had expected to discover here still the cities, the civilization the tape had projected as existing in that long-ago period. But no present island string they had visited approximated those on the maps they had seen, and so far they had not found any trace that any intelligent beings had walked, built, lived, on these beautiful, slumberous atolls. So, what had happened to the Hawaika of the tape?

Ross's right hand rubbed across the ridged scars which disfigured his left one, to be carried for the rest of his life as a mark of his meeting with the star voyagers in the past of his own world. He had deliberately seared his own flesh to break the mental control they had asserted. Then the battle had gone to him. But from it he had brought another scar-the unease of that old terror when Ross Murdock, fighter, rebel, outlaw by the conventions of his own era, Ross Murdock who considered himself an exceedingly tough individual, that toughness steeled by the training for Time Agent sorties, had come up against a power he did not understand, instinctively hated and feared.

Now he breathed deeply of the wind-the smell of the sea, the scents of the land growths, strange but pleasant. So easy to relax, to drop into the soft, lulling swing of this world in which they had found no fault, no danger, no irritant. Yet, once those others had been here-the blue-suited, hairless ones he called "Baldies." And what had happened then ... or afterward?

A black head, brown shoulders, slender body, broke the sleepy slip of the waves. A shimmering mask covered the face, catching glitter-fire in the sun. Two hands freed a chin curved yet firmly set, a mouth made more for laughter than sternness, wide dark eyes. Karara Trehern of the Alii, the one-time Hawaiian god-chieftain line, was an exceedingly pretty girl.

But Ross regarded her aloofly, with a coldness which bordered on hostility, as she flipped her mask into its pocket on top of the gill-pack. Below his rocky perch she came to a halt, her feet slightly apart in the sand, an impish twist to her lips as she called mockingly:

"Why not come in? The water's fine."

"Perfect, like all the rest of this." Some of his impatience came out in the sour tone. "No luck, as usual?"

"As usual," Karara conceded. "If there ever was a civilization here, it's been gone so long we'll probably never find any traces. Why don't you just pick out a good place to set up that time-probe and try it blind?"

Ross scowled. "Because" —his patience was exaggerated to the point of insult —"we have only one peep-probe. Once it's set we can't tear it down easily for transport somewhere else, so we want to be sure there's something to look at beyond."

She began to wring the water out of her long hair. "Well, as far as we've explored ... nothing. Come yourself next time. Tino-rau and Taua aren't particular; they like company."

Putting two fingers to her mouth, Karara whistled. Twin heads popped out of the water, facing the shore and her. Projecting noses, mouths with upturned corners so they curved in a lasting pleasant grin at the mammals on the shore-the dolphin pair, mammals whose ancestors had chosen the sea, whistled back in such close counterfeit of the girl's signal that they could be an echo of her call. Years earlier their species' intelligence had surprised, almost shocked, men. Experiments, training, co-operation, had developed a tie which gave the water-limited race of mankind new eyes, ears, minds, to see, evaluate, and report concerning an element in which the bipeds were not free.

Hand in hand with that co-operation had gone other experiments. Just as the clumsy armored diving suits of the early twentieth century had allowed man to begin penetration into a weird new world, so had the frog-man equipment made him still freer in the sea. And now the gill-pack which separated the needed oxygen from the water made even that lighter burden of tanks obsolete. But there remained depths into which man could not descend, whose secrets were closed to him. There the dolphins operated, in a partnership of minds, equal minds-though that last fact had been difficult for man to accept.

Ross's irritation, unjustified as he knew it to be, did not rest on Tino-rau or Taua. He enjoyed the hours when he buckled on gill-pack and took to the sea with those two ten-foot, black-and-silver escorts sharing the action. But Karara ... Karara's presence was a different matter altogether.

The Agents' teams had always been strictly masculine. Two men partnered for an interlocking of abilities and temperaments, going through training together, becoming two halves of a strong and efficient whole. Before being summarily recruited into the Project, Ross had been a loner-living on the ragged edges of the law, an indigestible bit for the civilization which had become too ordered and "adjusted" to absorb his kind. But in the Project he had discovered others like himself-men born out of time, too ruthless, too individualistic for their own age, but able to operate with ease in the dangerous paths of the Time Agents.

And when the time search for the wrecked alien ships had succeeded and the first intact ship found, used, duplicated, the Agents had come from forays into the past to be trained anew for travel to the stars. First there had been Ross Murdock, criminal. Then there had been Ross Murdock and Gordon Ashe, Time Agents. Now there was still Ross and Gordon and a quest as perilous as any they had known. Yet this time they had to depend upon Karara and the dolphins.

"Tomorrow" —Ross was still not sorting out his thoughts, truly aware of the feeling which worked upon him as a thorn in the finger —"I will come."

"Good!" If she recognized his hostility for what it was, that did not bother her. Once more she whistled to the dolphins, waved a casual farewell with one hand, and headed up the beach toward the base camp. Ross chose a more rugged path over the cliff.

Suppose they did not find what they sought near here? Yet the old taped map suggested that this was approximately the site starred upon it. Marking a city? A star port?

Ashe had volunteered for Hawaika, demanded this job after the disastrous Topaz affair when the team of Apache volunteers had been sent out too soon to counter what might have been a Red sneak settlement. Ross was still unhappy over the ensuing months when only Major Kelgarries and maybe, in a lesser part, Ross had kept Gordon Ashe in the Project at all. That

Topaz had been a failure was accepted when the settlement ship did not return. And that had added to Ashe's sense of guilt for having recruited and partially trained the lost team.

Among those dispatched over Ashe's vehement protests had been Travis Fox who had shared with Ashe and Ross the first galactic flight in an age-old derelict spaceship. Travis Fox-the Apache archaeologist-had he ever reached Topaz? Or would he and his team wander forever between worlds? Did they set down on a planet where some inimical form of native life or a Red settlement had awaited them? The very uncertainty of their fate continued to ride Ashe.

So he insisted on coming out with the second settlement team, the volunteers of Samoan and Hawaiian descent, to carry on a yet more exciting and hazardous exploration. Just as the Project had probed into the past of Terra, so would Ashe and Ross now attempt to discover what lay in the past of Hawaika, to see this world as it had been at the height of the galactic civilization, and so to learn what they could about their fore-runners into space. And the mystery they had dropped into upon landing added to the necessity for that discovery or discoveries.

Their probe, if fortune favored them, might become a gate through time. The installation was a vast improvement over these passage points they had first devised. Technical information had taken a vast leap forward after Terran engineers and scientists had had access to the tapes of the stellar empire. Adaptations and shortcuts developed, so that a new hybrid technology came into use, woven from the knowledge and experimentation of two civilizations thousands of years apart in time.

If and when he or Ashe-or Karara and her dolphins-discovered the proper site, the two Agents could set up their own equipment. Both Ross and Ashe had had enough drill in the process. All they needed was the brick of discovery; then they could build their wall. But they must find some remainder of the past, the smallest trace of ancient ruin upon which to center their peep-probe. And since landing here the long days had flowed into weeks with no such discovery made.

Ross crossed the ridge of rock which formed a cocks-comb rise on the island's spine and descended to the village. As they had been trained, the Polynesian settlers adapted native products to their own heritage of building and tools. It was necessary that they live off the land, for their transport ship had had storage space only for a limited number of supplies and tools. After it took off to return home they would be wholly on their own for several years. Their ship, a silvery ball, rested on a rock ledge, its pilot and crew having lingered to learn the results of Ashe's search. Four days more and they would have to lift for home even if the Agents still had only negative results to report.

That disappointment was driving Ashe, the way that six months earlier his outrage and guilt feelings over the Topaz affair had driven him. Karara's suggestion carried weight the longer Ross thought about it. With more swimmers hunting, there was just that much increased chance of turning up some clue. So far the dolphins had not reported any dangerous native sea life or any perils except the natural ones any diver always had at his shoulder under the waves.

There were extra gill-packs, and all of the settlers were good swimmers. An organized hunt ought to shake the Polynesians out of their present do-it-tomorrow attitude. As long as they had had definite work before them-the unloading of the ship, the building of the village, all the labors incidental to the establishing of this base-they had shown energy and enthusiasm. It was only during the last couple of weeks that the languor which appeared part of the atmosphere here had crept up on them, so that now they were content to live at a slower and lazier pace. Ross remembered Ashe's comparison made the evening before, likening Hawaika to a legendary Terran island where the inhabitants lived a drugged existence, feeding upon the seeds of a native plant. Hawaika was fast becoming a lotus land for Terrans.

"Through here, then westward...." Ashe hunched over the crate table in the mat-walled house. He did not look up as Ross entered. Karara's still damp head was bowed until those black locks, now sleeked to her round skull, almost touched the man's close-cropped brown hair. They were both studying a map as if they saw not lines on paper but the actual inlets and lagoons which that drawing represented.

"You are sure, Gordon, that this *is* the modern point to match the site on the tape?" The girl brushed back straying hair.

Ashe shrugged. There were tight brackets about his mouth which had not been there six months ago. He moved jerkily, not with the fluid grace of those old days when he had faced the vast distance of time travel with unruffled calm and a self-confidence to steady and support the novice Ross.

"The general outline of these two islands could stand for the capes on this —" He pulled a second map, this on transparent plastic, to fit over the first. The capes marked on the much larger body of land did slip over the modern islands with a surprising fit. The once large island, shattered and broken, could have produced the groups of atolls and islets they now prospected.

"How long —" Karara mused aloud, "and why?"

Ashe shrugged. "Ten thousand years, five, two." He shook his head. "We have no idea. It's apparent that there must have been some world-wide cataclysm here to change the contours of the land masses so much. We may have to wait on a return space flight to bring a 'copter or a hydroplane to explore farther." His hand swept beyond the boundaries of the map to indicate the whole of Hawaika.

"A year, maybe two, before we could hope for that," Ross cut in. "Then we'll have to depend on whether the Council believes this important enough." The contrariness which spiked his tongue whenever Karara was present made him say that without thinking. Then the twitch of Ashe's lip brought home Ross's error. Gordon needed reassurance now, not a recitation of the various ways their mission could be doomed.

"Look here!" Ross came to the table, his hand sweeping past Karara, as he used his forefinger for a pointer. "We know that what we want could be easily overlooked, even with the dolphins helping us to check. This whole area's too big. And you know that it is certain that whatever might be down there would be hidden with sea growths. Suppose ten of us start out in a semi-circle from about here and go as far as this point, heading inland. Video-cameras here and here ... comb the whole sector inch by inch if we have to. After all, we have plenty of time and manpower."

Karara laughed softly. "Manpower-always manpower, Ross? But there is woman-power, too. And we have perhaps even sharper sight. But this is a good idea, Gordon. Let me see —" she began to tell off names on her fingers, "PaKeeKee, Vaeoha, Hori, Liliha, Taema, Ui, Hono'ura-they are the best in the water. Me ... you, Gordon, Ross. That makes ten with keen eyes to look, and always there are Tino-rau and Taua. We will take supplies and camp here on this island which looks so much like a finger crooked to beckon. Yes, somehow that beckoning finger seems to me to promise better fortune. Shall we plan it so?"

Some of the tight look was gone from Ashe's face, and Ross relaxed. This was what Gordon needed-not to be sitting in here going over maps, reports, reworking over and over their scant leads. Ashe had always been a field man; and the settlement work had been stultifying, a laborious chore for him.

When Karara had gone Ross dropped down on the bunk against the side wall.

"What *did* happen here, do you think?" Half was real interest in the mystery they had mulled over and over since they had landed on a Hawaika which diverged so greatly from the maps; the other half, a desire to keep Ashe thinking on a subject removed from immediate worries. "An atomic war?"

"Could be. There are old radiation traces. But these aliens had, I'm sure, progressed beyond atomics. Suppose, just suppose, they could tamper with the weather, with the balance of the planet's crust? We don't know the extent of their powers, how they would use them. They had a colony here once, or there would have been no guide tape. And that is all we are sure of."

"Suppose" —Ross rolled over on his stomach, pillowed his head on his arms —"we could uncover some of that knowledge —"

The twitch was back at Ashe's lips. "That's the risk we have to run now."

"Risk?"

"Would you give a child one of those hand weapons we found in the derelict?"

"Naturally not!" Ross snapped and then saw the point. "You mean —*we* aren't to be trusted?" The answer was plain to read in Ashe's expression.

"Then why this whole setup, this hunt for what might mean trouble?"

"The old pinch, the bad one. What if the Reds discover something first? They drew some planets in the tape lottery, remember. It's a seesaw between us-we advance here, they there. We have to keep up the race or lose it. They must be combing their stellar colonies for a few answers just as furiously as we are."

"So, we go into the past to hunt if we have to. Well, I think I could do without answers such as the Baldies would know. But I will admit that I would like to know what did happen here-two, five, ten thousand years ago."

Ashe stood up and stretched. For the first time he smiled. "Do you know, I rather like the idea of fishing off Karara's beckoning finger. Maybe she's right about that changing our luck."

Ross kept his face carefully expressionless as he got up to prepare their evening meal.

2. Lair of Mano-Nui

Just under the surface of the water the sea was warm, weird life showed colors Ross could name, shades he could not. The corals, the animals masquerading as plants, the plants disguised as animals which inhabited the oceans of Terra, had their counterparts here. And the settlers had given them the familiar names, though the crabs, the fish, the anemones, and weeds of the shallow lagoons and reefs were not identical with Terran creatures. The trouble was that there was too much, such a wealth of life to attract the eyes, hold attention, that it was difficult to keep to the job at hand-the search for what was not natural, for what had no normal place here.

As the land seduced the senses and bewitched the off-worlder, so did the sea have its enchantment to pull one from duty. Ross resolutely skimmed by a forest of weaving, waving lace which varied from a green which was almost black to a pale tint he could not truly identify. Among those waving fans lurked ghost-fish, finned swimmers transparent enough so that one could sight, through their pallid sides, the evidences of recently ingested meals.

The Terrans had begun their sweep-search a half hour ago, slipping overboard from a ferry canoe, heading in toward the checkpoint of the finger isle, forming an arc of expert divers, men and girls so at home in the ocean that they should be able to make the discovery Ashe needed-if such did exist.

Mystery built upon mystery on Hawaika, Ross thought as he used his spear-gun to push aside a floating banner of weed in order to peer below its curtain. The native life of this world must always have been largely aquatic. The settlers had discovered only a few small animals on the islands. The largest of which was the burrower, a creature not unlike a miniature monkey in that it had hind legs on which it walked erect and forepaws, well clawed for digging purposes, which it used with as much skill and dexterity as a man used hands. Its body was hairless and it was able to assume, chameleon-like, the color of the soil and rocks where it denned. The head was set directly on its bowed shoulders without vestige of neck; and it had round bubbles of eyes near the top of its skull, a nose which was a single vertical slit, and a wide mouth fanged for crushing the shelled creatures on which it fed. All in all, to Terran eyes, it was a vaguely repulsive creature, but as far as the settlers had been able to discover it was the highest form of land life. The smaller rodentlike things, the two species of wingless diving birds, and an odd assortment of reptiles and amphibians sharing the island were all the burrowers' prey.

A world of sea and islands, what type of native intelligent life had it once supported? Or had this been only a galactic colony, with no native population before the coming of the stellar explorers? Ross hovered above a dark pocket where the bottom had suddenly dipped into a saucer-shaped depression. The sea growth about the rim rippled in the water raggedly, but there was something about its general outline....

Ross began a circumference of that hollow. Allowing for the distortion of the growths which had formed lumpy excrescences or reached turrets toward the surface-yes, allowing for those-this was decidedly something out of the ordinary! The depression was too regular, too even, Ross was certain of that. With a thrill of excitement he began a descent into the cup, striving to trace signs which would prove his suspicion correct.

How many years, centuries, had the slow coverage of the sea life gathered there, flourished, died, with other creatures to build anew on the remains? Now there was only a hint that the depression had other than a natural beginning.

Anchoring with a one-handed grip on a spike of Hawaikan coral-smoother than the Terran species-Ross aimed the butt of his spear-gun at the nearest wall of the saucer, striving to reach into a crevice between two lumps of growth and so probe into what might lie behind. The spear rebounded; there was no breaking that crust with such a fragile tool. But perhaps he would have better luck lower down.

The depression was deeper than he had first judged. Now the light which existed in the shallows vanished. Red and yellow as colors went, but Ross was aware of blues and greens in shades and tints which were not visible above. He switched on his diving torch, and color returned within its beam. A swirl of weed, pink in the light, became darkly emerald beyond as if it possessed the chameleon ability of the burrowers.

He was distracted by that phenomenon, and so he transgressed the diver's rule of never becoming so absorbed in surroundings as to forget caution. Just when did Ross become aware of that shadow below? Was it when a school of ghost-fish burst unexpectedly between weed growths, and he turned to follow them with the torch? Then the outer edge of his beam caught the movement of a shape, a flutter in the water of the gloomy depths.

Ross swung around, his back to the wall of the saucer, as he aimed the torch down at what was arising there. The light caught and held for a long moment of horror something which might have come out of the nightmares of his own world. Afterward Ross knew that the monster was not as large as it seemed in that endless minute of fear, perhaps no bigger than the dolphins.

He had had training in shark-infested seas on Terra, been carefully briefed against the danger from such hunters of the deep and ocean jungles. But this kind of thing had only existed before in the fairy tales of his race as the dragon of old lore. A scaled head with wide eyes gleaming in the light beam with cold and sullen hate, a gaping mouth fang-filled, a horn-set muzzle, that long, undulating neck and, below it, the half-seen bulk of a monstrous body.

His spear-gun, the knife at his waist belt, neither were protection against this! Yet to turn his back on that rising head was more than Ross could do. He pulled himself back against the wall of the saucer. The thing before him did not rush to attack. Plainly it had seen him and now it moved with the leisure of a hunter having no fears concerning the eventual outcome of the hunt. But the light appeared to puzzle it and Ross kept the beam shining straight into those evil eyes.

The shock of the encounter was wearing off; now Ross edged his flipper into a crevice to hold him steady while his hand went to the sonic-com at his waist. He tapped out a distress call which the dolphins could relay to the swimmers. The swaying dragon head paused, held rigid on a stiff, scaled column in the center of the saucer. That sonic vibration either surprised or bothered the hunter, made it wary.

Ross tapped again. The belief that if he tried to escape, he was lost, that only while he faced it so had he any chance, grew stronger. The head was only inches below the level of his flippered feet as he held to the weeds.

Again that weaving movement, the rise of head, a tremor along the serpent neck, an agitation in the depths. The dragon was on the move again. Ross aimed the light directly at the head. The scales, as far as he could determine, were not horny plates but lapped, silvery ovals such as a fish possessed. And the underparts of the monster might even be vulnerable to his spear. But knowing the way a Terran shark could absorb the darts of that weapon and survive, Ross feared to attack except as a last resort.

Above and to his left there was a small hollow where in the past some portion of the growths had been ripped away. If he could fit himself into that crevice, perhaps he could keep the dragon at bay until help arrived. Ross moved with all the skill he had. His hand closed upon the edge of the niche and he whirled himself up, just making it into that refuge as the head lashed at him wickedly. His suspicion that the dragon would attack anything on the run was well founded, and he knew he had no hope of winning to the surface above.

Now he stood in the crevice, facing outward, watching the head darting in the water. He had switched off the torch, and the loss of light appeared to bewilder the reptile for some precious seconds. Ross pulled as far back into the niche as he could, until the point of one shoulder touched a surface which was sleek, smooth, and cold. The shock of that contact almost sent him hurtling out again.

Gripping the spear before him in his right hand, Ross cautiously felt behind him with the left. His finger tips glided over a seamless surface where the growths had been torn or peeled away. Though he could not, or dared not, turn his head to see, he was certain that this was his proof that the walls of the saucer had been fashioned and placed there by some intelligent creature.

The dragon had risen, hovering now in the water directly before the entrance to Ross's hole, its neck curled back against its bulk. It had wide flippers moving like planes to hold it poised. The body, sloping from a massive round of shoulders to a tapering rear, was vaguely familiar. If one provided a Terran seal with a gorgon head and scales in place of fur, the effect would be similar. But Ross was assuredly not facing a seal at this moment.

Slight movement of the flippers kept it as stabilized as if it sprawled on a supporting surface. With the neck flattened against the body, the head curved downward until the horn on its snout pointed the tip straight at Ross's middle. The Terran steadied his spear-gun. The dragon's eyes were its most vulnerable targets; if the creature launched the attack, Ross would aim for them.

Both man and dragon were so intent upon their duel that neither was conscious of the sudden swirl overhead. A sleek dark shape struck down, skimming across the humped-back ridge of the dragon. Some of the settlers had empathy with the dolphins to a high degree, but Ross's own powers of contact were relatively feeble.

Only now he was given an assurance of aid, and a suggestion to attack. The dragon head writhed, twisted as the reptile attempted to see above and behind its own length. But the dolphin was only a streak fast disappearing. And that writhing changed the balance the monster had maintained, pushing it toward Ross.

The Terran fired too soon and without proper aim, so the dart snaked past the head. But the harpoon line half hooked about the neck and seemed to confuse the creature. Ross squirmed as far back as he could into his refuge and drew his knife. Against those fangs the weapon was an almost useless toy, but it was all he had.

Again the dolphin dived in attack on the reptile, this time seizing in its mouth the floating cord of the harpoon and giving it a jerk which jolted the dragon even more off balance, pulling it away from Ross's niche and out into the center of the saucer.

There were two dolphins in action now, Ross saw, playing the dragon as matadors might play a bull, keeping the creature disturbed by their agile maneuvers. Whatever prey came naturally to the Hawaikan monster was not of this type, and the creature was not prepared to deal effectively with their teasing, dodging tactics. Neither had touched the beast, but they kept it constantly striving to get at them.

Though it swam in circles attempting to face its teasers, the dragon did not abandon the level before Ross's refuge, and now and then it darted its head at him, unwilling to give up its prey. Only one of the dolphins frisked and dodged above now as the sonic on Ross's belt vibrated against his lower ribs with its message warning to be prepared for further action. Somewhere above, his own kind gathered. Hurriedly he tapped out in code his warning in return.

Two dolphins busy again, their last dive over the dragon pushing the monster down past Ross's niche toward the saucer's depths. Then they flashed up and away. The dragon was rising in turn, but coming to meet the Hawaikan creature was a ball giving off light, bringing sharp vision and color with it.

Ross's arm swung up to shield his eyes. There was a flash; such answering vibration carried through the waves that even his nerves, far less sensitive than those of the life about him, reacted. He blinked behind his mask. A fish floated by, spiraling up, its belly exposed. And about him growths drooped, trailed lifelessly through the water; while there was a now motionless bulk sinking to the obscurity of the depression floor. A weapon perfected on Terra to use against sharks and barracuda had worked here to kill what could have been more formidable prey.

The Terran wriggled out of the niche, rose to meet another swimmer. As Ashe descended, Ross relayed his news via the sonic. The dolphins were already nosing into the depths in pursuit of their late enemy.

"Look here —" Ross guided Ashe to the crevice which had saved him, aimed the torch beam into it. He had been right! There was a long groove in the covering built up by the growths; a vertical strip some six feet long, of a uniform gray, showed. Ashe touched the find and then gave the alert via the sonic code.

"Metal or an alloy, we've found it!"

But what did they have? Even after an hour's exploration by the full company, Ashe's expert search with his knowledge of artifacts and ancient remains, they were still baffled. It would require labor and tools they did not have, to clear the whole of the saucer. They could be sure only of its size and shape, and the fact that its walls were of an unknown substance which the sea could cloak but not erode. For the length of gray surface showed not the slightest pitting or time wear.

Down at its centermost point they found the dragon's den, an arch coated with growth, before which sprawled the body of the creature. That was dragged aloft with the dolphins' aid, to be taken ashore for study. But the arch itself ... was that part of some old installation?

Torches to the fore, they entered its shadow, only to remain baffled. Here and there were patches of the same gray showing in its interior. Ashe dug the butt of his spear-gun into the sand on the flooring to uncover another oval depression. But what it all signified or what had been its purpose, they could not guess.

"Set up the peep-probe here?" Ross asked.

Ashe's head moved in a slow negative. "Look farther ... spread out," the sonic clicked.

Within a matter of minutes the dolphins reported new remains-two more saucers, each larger than the first, set in a line on the ocean floor, pointing directly to Karara's Finger Island. Cautiously explored, these were discovered to be free of any but harmless life; they stirred up no more dragons.

When the Terrans came ashore on Finger Island to rest and eat their midday meal one of the men paced along the beached dragon. Ashore it lost none of its frightening aspect. And seeing it, even beached and dead, Ross wondered at his luck in surviving the encounter without a scratch.

"I think that this one would be alone," PaKeeKee commented. "Where there is an eater of this size, there is usually only one."

"Mano-Nui!" The girl Taema shivered as she gave to this monster the name of the shark demon of her people. "Such a one is truly king shark in these waters! But why have we not sighted its like before? Tino-rau, Taua ... they have not reported such —"

"Probably because, as PaKeeKee says, these things are rare," Ashe returned. "A carnivore of size would have to have a fairly wide hunting range, yet there's evidence that this thing has laired in that den for some time. Which means that it must have a defined hunting territory allowing no trespassing from others of its species."

Karara nodded. "Also it may hunt only at intervals, eat heavily, and lie quiet until that meal is digested. There are large snakes on Terra that follow that pattern. Ross was in its front yard when it came after him —"

"From now on" —Ashe swallowed a quarter of fruit —"we know what to watch for, and the weapon which will finish it off. Don't forget that!"

The delicate mechanisms of their sonics had already registered the vibrations which would warn of a dragon's presence, and the depth globes would then do the rest.

"Big skull, oversize for the body." PaKeeKee squatted on his heels by the head lying on the sand at the end of the now fully extended neck.

Ross had heretofore been more aware of the armament of that head, the fangs set in the powerful jaws, the horn on the snout. But PaKeeKee's comment drew his attention to the fact that the scale-covered skull did dome up above the eye pits in a way to suggest ample brain room. Had the thing been intelligent? Karara put that into words:

"Rule One?" She went over to survey the carcass.

Ross resented her half question, whether it was addressed to him or mere thinking aloud on her part.

Rule One: Conserve native life to the fullest extent. Humanoid form may not be the only evidence of intelligence.

There were the dolphins to prove that point right on Terra. But did Rule One mean that you had to let a monster nibble at you because it might just be a high type of alien intelligence? Let Karara spout Rule One while backed into a crevice under water with that horn stabbing at her mid-section!

"Rule One does not mean to forego self-defense," Ashe commented mildly. "This thing is a hunter, and you can't stop to apply recognition techniques when you are being regarded as legitimate prey. If you are the stronger, or an equal, yes-stop and think before becoming aggressive. But in a situation like this-take no chances."

"Anyway, from now on," Karara pointed out, "it could be possible to shock instead of kill."

"Gordon" —PaKeeKee swung around —"what have we found here-besides this thing?"

"I can't even guess. Except that those depressions were made for a purpose and have been there for a long time. Whether they were originally in the water, or the land sank, that we don't know either. But now we have a site to set up the peep-probe."

"We do that right away?" Ross wanted to know. Impatience bit at him. But Ashe still had a trace of frown. He shook his head.

"Have to make sure of our site, very sure. I don't want to start any chain reaction on the other side of the time wall."

And he was right, Ross was forced to admit, remembering what had happened when the galactics had discovered the Red time gates and traced them forward to their twentieth-century source, ruthlessly destroying each station. The original colonists of Hawaika had been as giants to Terran pygmies when it came to technical knowledge. To use even a peep-probe indiscreetly near one of their outposts might bring swift and terrible retribution.

3. The Ancient Mariners

Another map spread out and this time pinned down with small stones on beach gravel.

"Here, here, and here —" Ashe's finger indicated the points marked in a pattern which flared out from three sides of Finger Island. Each marked a set of three undersea depressions in perfect alliance with the land which, according to the galactic map, had once been a cape on a much larger land mass. Though the Terrans had found the ruins, if those saucers in the sea could be so termed, the remains had no meaning for the explorers.

"Do we set up here?" Ross asked. "If we could just get a report to send back...." That might mean the difference between awakening the co-operation of the Project policy makers so that a flood of supplies and personnel would begin to head their way.

"We set up here," Ashe decided.

He had selected a point between two of the lines where a reef would provide them with a secure base. And once that decision was made, the Terrans went into action.

Two days to go, to install the peep-probe and take some shots before the ship had to clear with or without their evidence. Together Ross and Ashe floated the installation out to the reef, Ui and Karara helping to tow the equipment and parts, the dolphins lending pushing noses on occasion. The aquatic mammals were as interested as the human beings they aided. And in water their help was invaluable. Had dolphins developed hands, Ross wondered fleetingly, would they have long ago wrested control of their native world-or at least of its seas-from the human kind?

All the human beings worked with practiced ease, even while masked and submerged, to set the probe in place, aiming it landward at the check point of the Finger's protruding nail of rock. After Ashe made the final adjustments, tested each and every part of the assembly, he gestured them in.

Karara's swift hand movement asked a question, and Ashe's sonic code-clicked in reply: "At twilight."

Yes, dusk was the proper time for using a peep-probe. To see without risk of being sighted in return was their safeguard. Here Ashe had no historical data to guide him. Their search for the former inhabitants might be a long drawn-out process skipping across centuries as the machine was adjusted to Terran time eras.

"When were they here?" Back on shore Karara shook out her hair, spread it over her shoulders to dry. "How many hundred years back will the probe return?"

"More likely thousands," Ross commented. "Where will you start, Gordon?"

Ashe brushed sand from the page of the notebook he had steadied against one bent knee and gazed out at the reef where they had set the probe.

"Ten thousand years —"

"Why?" Karara wanted to know. "Why that exact figure?"

"We know that galactic ships crashed on Terra then. So their commerce and empire-if it was an empire-was far-flung at that time. Perhaps they were at the zenith of their civilization; perhaps they were already on the down slope. I do not think they were near the beginning. So that date is as good a starting place as any. If we don't hit what we're after, then we can move forward until we do."

"Do you think that there ever was a native population here?"

"Might have been."

"But without any large land animals, no modern traces of any," she protested.

"Of people?" Ashe shrugged. "Good answers for both. Suppose there was a world-wide epidemic of proportions to wipe out a species. Or a war in which they used forces beyond our comprehension to alter the whole face of this planet, which did happen-the alteration, I mean. Several things could have removed intelligent life. Then such species as the burrowers could have developed or evolved from smaller, more primitive types."

"Those ape-things we found on the desert planet." Ross thought back to their first voyage on the homing derelict. "Maybe they had once been men and were degenerating. And the winged people, they could have been less than men on their way up — —"

"Ape-things ... winged people?" Karara interrupted. "Tell me!"

There was something imperious in her demand, but Ross found himself describing in detail their past adventures, first on the world of sand and sealed structures where the derelict had rested for a purpose its involuntary passengers had never understood, and then of the Terrans' limited exploration of that other planet which might have been the capital world of a far-flung stellar empire. There they had made a pact with a winged people living in the huge buildings of a jungle-choked city.

"But you see" —the Polynesian girl turned to Ashe when Ross had finished —"you did find them-these ape-things and the winged people. But here there are only the dragons and the burrowers. Are they the start or the finish? I want to know —"

"Why?" Ashe asked.

"Not just because I am curious, though I am that also, but because we, too, must have a beginning and an end. Did we come up from the seas, rise to know and feel and think, just to return to such beginning at our end? If your winged people were climbing and your ape-things descending"—she shook her head—"it would be frightening to hold a cord of life, both ends in your hands. Is it good for us to see such things, Gordon?"

"Men have asked that question all their thinking lives, Karara. There have been those who have said no, who have turned aside and tried to halt the growth of knowledge here or there, attempted to make men stand still on one tread of a stairway. Only there is that in us which will not stop, ill-fitted as we may be for the climbing. Perhaps we shall be safe and untroubled here on Hawaika if I do not go out to that reef tonight. By that action I may bring real danger down on all of us. Yet I can not hold back for that. Could you?"

"No, I do not believe that I could," she agreed.

"We are here because we are of those who must know-volunteers. And being of that temperament, it is in us always to take the next step."

"Even if it leads to a fall," she added in a low tone.

Ashe gazed at her, though her own eyes were on the sea where a lace of waves marked the reef. Her words were ordinary enough, but Ross straightened to match Ashe's stare. Why had he felt that odd instant of uneasiness as if his heart had fluttered instead of beating true?

"I know of you Time Agents," Karara continued. "There were plenty of stories about you told while we were in training."

"Tall tales, I can imagine, most of them." Ashe laughed, but his amusement sounded forced to Ross.

"Perhaps. Though I do not believe that many could be any taller than the truth. And so also I have heard of that strict rule you follow, that you must do nothing which might alter the course of history. But suppose, suppose here that the course of history could be altered, that whatever catastrophe occurred might be averted? If that was done, what would happen to our settlement in the here and now?"

"I don't know. That is an experiment which we have never dared to try, which we won't try—"

"Not even if it would mean a chance of life for a whole native race?" she persisted.

"Alternate worlds then, maybe." Ross's imagination caught up that idea. "Two worlds from a change point in history," he elaborated, noting her look of puzzlement. "One stemming from one decision, another from the alternate."

"I've heard of that! But, Gordon, if you could return to the time of decision here and you had it in your power to say, 'Yes-live!' or 'No-die!' to the alien natives, what would you do?"

"I don't know. But neither do I think I shall ever be placed in that position. Why do you ask?"

She was twisting her still damp hair into a pony tail and tying it so with a cord. "Because ... because I feel....No, I can not really put it into words, Gordon. It is that feeling one has on the eve of some important event-anticipation, fear, excitement. You'll let me go with you tonight, please! I want to see it-not the Hawaika that is, but that other world with another name, the one they saw and knew!"

An instant protest was hot in Ross's throat, but he had no time to voice it. For Ashe was already nodding.

"All right. But we may have no luck at all. Fishing in time is a chancy thing, so don't be disappointed if we don't turn you up that other world. Now, I'm going to pamper these old bones for an hour or two. Amuse yourselves, children." He lay back and closed his eyes.

The past two days had wiped half the shadows from his lean, tanned face. He had dropped two years, three, Ross thought thankfully. Let them be lucky tonight, and Ashe's cure could be nearly complete.

"What do you think happened here?" Karara had moved so that her back was now to the wash of waves, her face more in the shadow.

438

"How do I know? Could be any of ten different things."

"And will I please shut up and leave you alone?" she countered swiftly. "Do you wish to savor the excitement then, explore a world upon world, or am I saying it right? We have Hawaika One which is a new world for us; now there is Hawaika Two which is removed in time, not distance. And to explore that —"

"We won't be exploring it really," Ross protested.

"Why? Did your agents not spend days, weeks, even months of time in the past on Terra? What is to prevent your doing the same here?"

"Training. We have no way of learning the drill."

"What do you mean?"

"Well, it wasn't as easy as you seem to think it was back on Terra," he began scornfully. "We didn't just stroll through one of those gates and set up business, say, in Nero's Rome or Montezuma's Mexico. An Agent was physically and psychologically fitted to the era he was to explore. Then he trained, and how he trained!" Ross remembered the weary hours spent learning how to use a bronze sword, the technique of Beaker trading, the hypnotic instruction in a language which was already dead centuries before his own country existed. "You learned the language, the customs, everything you could about your time and your cover. You were letter perfect before you took even a trial run!"

"And here you would have no guides," Karara said, nodding. "Yes, I can see the difficulty. Then you will just use the peep-probe?"

"Probably. Oh, maybe later on we can scout through a gate. We have the material to set one up. But it would be a strictly limited project, allowing no chance of being caught. Maybe the big brains back home can take peep-data and work out some basis of infiltration for us from it."

"But that would take years!"

"I suppose so. Only you begin to swim in the shallows, don't you-not by jumping off a cliff!"

She laughed. "True enough! However, even a look into the past might solve part of the big mystery."

Ross grunted and stretched out to follow Ashe's example. But behind his closed eyes his brain was busy, and he did not cultivate the patience he needed. Peep-probes were all right, but Karara had a point. You wanted more than a small window into a mystery, you wanted a part in solving it.

The setting of the sun deepened rose to red, made a dripping wine-hued banner of most of the sky, so that under it they moved in a crimson sea, looked back at an island where shadows were embers instead of ashes. Three humans, two dolphins, and a machine mounted on a reef which might not even have existed in the time they sought. Ashe made his final adjustments, and then his finger pressed a button and they watched the vista-plate no larger than the palms of two hands.

Nothing, a dull gray nothing! Something must have gone wrong with their assembly work. Ross touched Ashe's shoulder. But now there were shadows gathering on the plate, thickening, to sharpen into a distinct picture.

It was still the sunset hour they watched. But somehow the colors were paler, less red and sullen than the ones about them in the here and now. And they were not seeing the isle toward which the probe had been aimed; they were looking at a rugged coastline where cliffs lifted well above the beach-strand. While on those cliffs —! Ross had not realized Karara had reached out to grasp his arm until her nails bit into his flesh. And even then he was hardly aware of the pain. Because there was a building on the cliff!

Massive walls of native rock reared in outward defenses, culminating in towers. And from the high point of one tower the pointed tail of a banner cracked in the wind. There was a headland of rock reaching out, not toward them but to the north, and rounding that....

"War canoe!" Karara exclaimed, but Ross had another identification:

"Longboat!"

In reality, the vessel was neither one nor the other, not the double canoe of the Pacific which had transported warriors on raid from one island to another, or the shield-hung warship of the Vikings. But the Terrans were right in its purpose: That rakish, sharp-prowed ship had been fashioned for swift passage of the seas, for maneuverability as a weapon.

Behind the first nosed another and a third. Their sails were dyed by the sun, but there were devices painted on them, and the lines of those designs glittered as if they had been drawn with a metallic fluid.

"The castle!" Ashe's cry pulled their attention back to land.

There was movement along those walls. Then came a flash, a splash in the water close enough to the lead ship to wet her deck with spray.

"They're fighting!" Karara shouldered against Ross for a better look.

The ships were altering course, swinging away from land, out to sea.

"Moving too fast for sails alone, and I don't see any oars." Ross was puzzled. "How do you suppose...."

The bombardment from the castle continued but did not score any hits. Already the ships were out of range, the lead vessel off the screen of the peep as well. Then there was just the castle in the sunset. Ashe straightened up.

"Rocks!" he repeated wonderingly. "They were throwing rocks!"

"But those ships, they must have had engines. They weren't just depending on sails when they retreated." Ross added his own cause for bewilderment.

Karara looked from one to the other. "There is something here you do not understand. What is wrong?"

"Catapults, yes," Ashe said with a nod. "Those would fit periods corresponding from the Roman Empire into the Middle Ages. But you're right, Ross, those ships had power of some kind to take them offshore that quickly."

"A technically advanced race coming up against a more backward one?" hazarded the younger man.

"Could be. Let's go forward some." The incoming tide was washing well up on the reef. Ashe had to don his mask as he plunged head and shoulders under water to make the necessary adjustment.

Once more he pressed the button. And Ross's gasp was echoed by one from the girl. The cliff again, but there was no castle dominating it, only a ruin, hardly more than rubble. Now, above the sites of the saucer depressions great pylons of silvery metal, warmed into fire brilliance by the sunset, raked into the sky like gaunt, skeleton fingers. There were no ships, no signs of any life. Even the vegetation which had showed on shore had vanished. There was an atmosphere of stark abandonment and death which struck the Terrans forcibly.

Those pylons, Ross studied them. Something familiar in their construction teased his memory. That refuel planet where the derelict ship had set down twice, on the voyage out and on their return. That had been a world of metal structures, and he believed he could trace a kinship between his memory of those and these pylons. Surely they had no connection with the earlier castle on the cliff.

Once more Ashe ducked to reset the probe. And in the fast-fading light they watched a third and last picture. But now they might have been looking at the island of the present, save that it bore no vegetation and there was a rawness about it, a sharpness of rock outline now vanished.

Those pylons, were they the key to the change which had come upon this world? What were they? Who had set them there? For the last Ross thought he had an answer. They were certainly the product of the galactic empire. And the castle ... the ships ... natives ... settlers? Two widely different eras, and the mystery still, lay between them. Would they ever be able to bring the key to it out of time?

They swam for the shore where Ui had a fire blazing and their supper prepared.

"How many years lying between those probes?" Ross pulled broiled fish apart with his fingers.

"That first was ten thousand years ago, the second," Ashe paused, "only two hundred years later."

"But" —Ross stared at his superior —"that means — —"

"That there was a war or some drastic form of invasion, yes."

"You mean that the star people arrived and just took over this whole planet?" Karara asked. "But why? And those pylons, what were they for? How much later was that last picture?"

"Five hundred years."

"The pylons were gone, too, then," Ross commented. "But why —?" he echoed Karara's question.

Ashe had taken up his notebook, but he did not open it. "I think" —there was a sharp, grim note in his voice —"we had better find out."

"Put up a gate?"

Ashe broke all the previous rules of their service with his answer:

"Yes, a gate."

4. Storm Menace

"We have to know." Ashe leaned back against the crate they had just emptied. "Something was done here-in two hundred years-and then, an empty world."

"Pandora's box." Ross drew a hand across his forehead, smearing sweat and fine sand into a brand.

Ashe nodded. "Maybe we run that risk, loosing all the devils of the aliens. But what if the Reds open the box first on one of their settlement worlds?"

There it was again, the old thorn which prodded them into risks and recklessness. Danger ahead on both paths. Don't risk trying to learn galactic secrets, but don't risk your enemy's learning them either. You held a white-hot iron in both hands in this business. And Ashe was right, they had stumbled on something here which hinted that a whole world had been altered to suit some plan. Suppose the secret of that alteration was discovered by their enemies?

"Were the ship and castle people natives?" Ross wondered aloud.

"Just at a guess they were, or at least settlers who had been established here so long they had developed a local form of civilization which was about on the level of a feudal society."

"You mean because of the castle and the rock bombardment. But what about the ships?"

"Two separate phases of a society at war, perhaps a more progressive against a less technically advanced. American warships paying a visit to the Shogun's Japan, for example."

Ross grinned. "Those warships didn't seem to fancy their welcome. They steered out to sea fast enough when the rocks began to fall."

"Yes, but the ships could exist in the castle pattern; the pylons could not!"

"Which period are you aiming for first-the castle or the pylons?"

"Castle first, I think. Then if we can't pick up any hints, we'll take some jumps forward until we do connect. Only we'll be under severe handicaps. If we could only plant an analyzer somewhere in the castle as a beginning."

Ross did not show his surprise. If Ashe was talking on those terms, then he was intending to do more than just lurk around a little beyond the gate; he was really planning to pick up alien speech patterns, eventually assume an alien agent identity!

"Gordon!" Karara appeared between two of the lace trees. She came so hastily that the contents of the two cups she carried slopped over. "You must hear what Hori has to say —"

The tall Samoan who trailed her spoke quickly. For the first time since Ross had known him he was very serious, a frown line between his eyes. "There is a bad storm coming. Our instruments register it."

"How long away?" Ashe was on his feet.

"A day ... maybe two...."

Ross could see no change in the sky, islands, or sea. They had had idyllic weather for the six weeks since their planeting, no sign of any such trouble in the Hawaikan paradise.

"It's coming," Hori repeated.

"The gate is half up," Ashe thought aloud, "too much of it set to be dismantled again in a hurry."

"If it's completed," Hori wanted to know, "would it ride out a storm?"

"It might, behind that reef where we have it based. To finish it would be a fast job."

Hori flexed his hands. "We're more brawn than brain in these matters, Gordon, but you've all our help, for what it's worth. What about the ship, does it lift on schedule?"

"Check with Rimbault about that. This storm, how will it compare to a Pacific typhoon?"

The Samoan shook his head. "How do we know? We have not yet had to face the local variety."

"The islands are low," Karara commented. "Winds and water could —"

"Yes! We'd better see Rimbault about a shelter if needed."

If the settlement had drowsed, now its inhabitants were busy. It was decided that they could shelter in the spaceship should the storm reach hurricane proportions, but before its coming the gate must be finished. The final fitting was left to Ashe and Ross, and the older agent fastened the last bolt when the waters beyond the reef were already wind ruffled, the sky darkening fast. The dolphins swam back and forth in the lagoon and with them Karara, though Ashe had twice waved her to the shore.

There was no sunlight left, and they worked with torches. Ashe began his inspection of the relatively simple transfer-the two upright bars, the slab of opaque material forming a doorstep between them. This was only a skeleton of the gates Ross had used in the past. But continual experimentation had produced this more easily transported installation.

Piled in a net were several supply containers ready for an exploring run-extra gill-packs, the analyzer, emergency rations, a medical kit, all the basics. Was Ashe going to try now? He had activated the transfer, the rods were glowing faintly, the slab they guarded having an eerie blue glimmer. He probably only wanted to be sure it worked.

What happened at that moment Ross could never find any adequate words to describe, nor was he sure he could remember. The disorientation of the pass-through he had experienced before; this time he was whirled into a vortex of feeling in which his body, his identity, were rift from him and he lost touch with all stability.

Instinctively he lashed out, his reflexes more than his conscious will keeping him above water in the wild rage of a storm-whipped sea. The light was gone; here was only dark and beating water. Then a lightning flash ripped wide the heavens over Ross as his head broke the surface and he saw, with unbelieving eyes, that he was being thrust shoreward-not to the strand of Finger Island-but against a cliff where water pounded an unyielding wall of rock.

Ross comprehended that somehow he had been jerked through the gate, that he was now fronting the land that had been somewhere beneath the heights supporting the castle. Then he fought for his life to escape the hammer of the sea determined to crack him against the surface of the cliff.

A rough surface loomed up before him, and he threw himself in that direction, embracing a rock, striving to cling through the backwash of the wave which had brought him there. His nails grated and broke on the stone, and then the fingers of his right hand caught in a hole, and he held with all the strength in his gasping, beaten body. He had had no preparation, no warning, and only the tough survival will which had been trained and bred into him saved his life.

As the water washed back, Ross strove to pull up farther on his anchorage, to be above the strike of the next wave. Somehow he gained a foot before it came. The mask of the gill-pack saved him from being smothered in that curling torrent as he clung stubbornly, resisting again the pull of the retreating sea.

Inch by inch between waves he fought for footing and stable support. Then he was on the surface of the rock, out of all but the lash of spray. He crouched there, spent and gasping.

The thunder roar of the surf, and beyond it the deeper mutter of the rage in the heavens, was deafening, dulling his sense as much as the ordeal through which he had passed. He was content to cling where he was, hardly conscious of his surroundings.

Sparks of light along the shore to the north at last caught Ross's attention. They moved, some clustering along the wave line, a few strung up the cliff. And they were not part of the storm's fireworks. Men here-why at this moment?

Another bolt of lightning showed him the answer. On the reef fringe which ran a tongue of land into the sea hung a ship-two ships-pounded by every hammer wave. Shipwrecks ... and those lights must mark castle dwellers drawn to aid the survivors.

Ross crawled across his rock on his hands and knees, wavered along the cliff wall until he was again faced with angry water. To drop into that would be a mistake. He hesitated-and now more than his own predicament struck home to him.

Ashe! Ashe had been ahead of him at the time gate. If Ross had been jerked through to this past, then somewhere in the water, on the shore, Gordon was here too! But where to find him....

Setting his back to the cliff and holding to the rough stone, Ross got to his feet, trying to see through the welter of foam and water. Not only the sea poured here; now a torrential rain fell into the bargain, streaming down about him, battering his head and shoulders. A chill rain which made him shiver.

He wore gill-pack, weighted belt with its sheathed tool and knife, flippers, and the pair of swimming trunks which had been suitable for the Hawaika he knew; but this was a different world altogether. Dare he use his torch to see the way out of here? Ross watched the lights to the north, deciding they were not too unlike his own beam, and took the chance.

Now he stood on a shelf of rock pitted with depressions, all pools. To his left was a drop into a boiling, whirling caldron from which points of stone fanged. Ross shuddered. At least he had escaped being pulled into that!

To his right, northward, there was another space of sea, a narrow strip, and then a second ledge. He measured the distance between that and the one on which he perched. Staying where he was would not locate Ashe.

Ross stripped off his flippers, made them fast in his belt. Then he leaped and landed painfully, as his feet slipped and he skidded face down on the northern ledge.

As he sat up, rubbing a bruised and scraped knee, he saw lights advancing in his direction. And between them a shadow crawling from water to shore. Ross stumbled along the ledge hastening to reach that figure, who lay still now just out of the waves. Ashe?

Ross's limping pace became a trot. But he was too late; the other lights, two of them, had reached the shadow. A man-or at least a body which was humanoid-sprawled face down. Other men, three of them, gathered over the exhausted swimmer.

Those who held the torches were still partially in the dark, but the third stooped to roll over their find. Ross caught the glint of light on a metallic headcovering, the glisten of wet armor of some type on the fellow's back and shoulders as he made quick examination of the sea's victim.

Then.... Ross halted, his eyes wide. A hand rose and fell with expert precision. There had been a blade in that hand. Already the three were turning away from the man so ruthlessly dispatched. Ashe? Or some survivor of the wrecked ships?

Ross retreated to the end of the ledge. The narrow stream of water dividing it from the rock where he had won ashore washed into a cave in the cliff. Dare he try to work his way into that? Masked, with the gill-pack, he could go under surface if he were not smashed by the waves against some wall.

He glanced back. The lights were very close to the end of his ledge. To withdraw to the second rock would mean being caught in a dead end, for he dared not enter the whirlpool on its far side. There was really no choice: stay and be killed, or try for the cave. Ross fastened on his flippers and lowered his body into the narrow stream. The fact that it was narrow and guarded on either side by the ledges tamed the waves a little, and Ross found the tug against him not so great as he feared it would be.

Keeping hand-holds on the rock, he worked along, head and shoulders often under the wash of rolling water, but winning steadily to the break in the cliff wall. Then he was through, into a space much larger than the opening, water-filled but not with a wild turbulence of waves.

Had he been sighted? Ross kept a handhold to the left of that narrow entrance, his body floating with the rise and fall of the water. He could make out the gleam of light without. It might be that one of those hunters had leaned out over the runnel of the cave entrance, was flashing his torch down into the water there.

Behind mask plate Ross's lips writhed in the snarl of the hunted. In here he would have the advantage. Let one of them, or all three, try to follow through that rock entrance and....

But if he had been sighted at the mouth of the lair, none of his trackers appeared to wish to press the hunt. The light disappeared, and Ross was left in the dark. He counted a hundred slowly and then a second hundred before he dared use his own torch.

For all its slit entrance this was a good-sized hideaway he had chanced upon. And he discovered, when he ventured to release his wall hold and swim out into its middle, the bottom arose in a slope toward its rear.

Moments later Ross pulled out of the water once more, to crouch shivering on a ledge only lapped now and then by wavelets. He had found a temporary refuge, but his good fortune did not quiet his fears. Had that been Ashe on the shore? And why had the swimmer been so summarily executed by the men who found him?

The ships caught on the reef, the castle on the cliff above his head ... enemies ... ships' crews and castle men? But the callous act of the shore patrol argued a state of war carried to fanatic proportions, perhaps inter-racial conflict.

He could not hope to explore until the storm was over. To plunge back into the sea would not find Ashe. And to be hunted along the shore by an unknown enemy was simply asking to die without achieving any good in return. No, he must remain where he was for the present.

Ross unhooked the torch from his belt and used it on this higher portion of the cave. He was perched on a ledge which protruded into the water in the form of a wedge. At his back the wall of the cave was rough, and trails of weed were festooned on its projections. The smell of fishy decay was strong enough to register as Ross pulled off his mask. As far as he could now see there was no exit except by sea.

A movement in the water brought his light flashing down into the dark flood. Then a sleek head arose in the path of that ray. Not a man swimming, but one of the dolphins!

Ross's exclamation of surprise was half gasp, half cry. The second dolphin showed for a moment and between the shadow of their bodies, just under the surface, moved a third form.

"Ashe!" Ross had no idea how the dolphins had come through the time gate, but that they had guided to safety a Terran he did not doubt at all. "Ashe!"

But it was not Ashe who came wading to the ledge where Ross waited with hand outstretched. He had been so sure of the other's identity that he blinked in complete bewilderment as his eyes met Karara's and she half stumbled, half reeled against him.

His arms about her shoulders steadied her, and her shivering body was close to his as she leaned her full weight upon him. Her hands made a feeble movement to her mask, and he pulled it off. Uncovered, her face was pale and drawn, her eyes now closed, and her breath came in ragged, tearing sobs which shook her even more.

"How did you get here?" Ross demanded even as he pushed her down on the ledge.

Her head moved slowly, in a weak gesture of negation.

"I don't know ... we were close to the gate. There was a flash of light ... then —" Her voice sealed up with a note of hysteria in it. "Then ... I was here ... and Taua with me. Tino-rau came ... Ross, Ross ... there was a man swimming. He got ashore; he was getting to his feet and and they killed him!"

Ross's hold tightened; he stared into her face with fierce demand.

"Was it Gordon?"

She blinked, brought her hand up to her mouth, and wiped it back and forth across her chin. There was a small red trickle growing between her fingers, dripping down her arm.

"Gordon?" She repeated it as if she had never heard the name before.

"Yes, did they kill Gordon?"

In his grasp she was swaying back and forth. Then, realizing he was shaking her, Ross got himself under control.

But a measure of understanding had come into her eyes. "No, not Gordon. Where is Gordon?"

"You haven't seen him?" Ross persisted, knowing it was useless.

"Not since we were at the gate." Her words were less slurred. "Weren't you with him?"

"No. I was alone."

"Ross, where are we?"

"Better say-when are we," he replied. "We're through the gate and back in time. And we have to find Gordon!" He did not want to think of what might have happened out on the shore.

5. Time Wrecked

"Can we go back?" Karara was herself again, her voice crisp.

"I don't know." Ross gave her the truth. The force which had drawn them through the gate was beyond his experience. As far as he knew, there had never been such an involuntary passage by time gate, and what their trip might mean he did not know.

The main concern was that Ashe must have come through, too, and that he was missing. Just let the storm abate, and, with the dolphins' aid, Ross's chance for finding the missing agent was immeasurably better. He said so now, and Karara nodded.

"Do you suppose there is a war going on here?" She hugged her arms across her breast, her shoulders heaving in the torch light with shudders she could not control. The damp chill was biting, and Ross realized that was also danger.

"Could be." He got to his feet, switched the light from the girl to the walls. That seaweed, could it make them some form of protective covering?

"Hold this-aim it there!" He thrust the torch into her hands and went for one of the loops of kelp.

Ross reeled in lines of the stuff. It was rank-smelling but only slightly damp, and he piled it on the ledge in a kind of nest. At least in the hollow of that mound they would be sheltered after a fashion.

Karara crawled into the center of the mass, and Ross followed her. The smell of the stuff filled his nose, was almost like a visible cloud, but he had been right, the girl stopped shivering, and he felt a measure of warmth in his own shaking body. Ross snapped off the torch, and they lay together in the dark, the half-rotten pile of weed holding them.

He must have slept, Ross guessed, when he stirred, raising his head. His body was stiff, aching, as he braced himself up on his hands and peered over the edge of their kelp nest. There was light in the cave, a pale grayish wash which grew stronger toward the slit opening. It must be day. And that meant they could move.

Ross groped in the weed, his hand falling on a curve of shoulder.

"Wake up!" His voice was hoarse and held the snap of an order.

There was a startled gasp in answer, and the mound beside him heaved as the girl stirred.

"Day out —" Ross pointed.

"And the storm —" she stood up, "I think it is over."

It was true that the level of water within the cave had fallen, that wavelets no longer lapped with the same vigor. Morning ... the storm over ... and somewhere Ashe!

Ross was about to snap his mask into place when Karara caught at his arm.

"Be careful! Remember what I saw-last night they were killing swimmers!"

He shook her off impatiently. "I'm no fool! And with the packs on we do not have to surface. Listen —" he had another thought, one which would provide an excellent excuse for keeping her safely out of his company, reducing his responsibility for her, "you take the dolphins and try to find the gate. We'll want out as soon as I locate Ashe."

"And if you do not find him soon?"

Ross hesitated. She had not said the rest. What if he could not find Gordon at all? But he would-he had to!

"I'll be back here" —he checked his watch, no longer an accurate timekeeper, for Hawaikan days held an hour more than the Terran twenty-four, but the settlers kept the off-world measurement to check on work periods —"in, say, two hours. You should know by then about the gate, and I'll have some idea of the situation along the shore. But listen —" Ross caught her shoulders in a taut grip, pulled her around to face him, his eyes hot and almost angry as they held hers, "don't let yourself be seen —" He repeated the cardinal rule of Agents in new territory. "We don't dare risk discovery."

Karara nodded and he could see that she understood, was aware of the importance of that warning. "Do you want Tino-rau or Taua?"

"No, I'm going to search along the shore first. Ashe would have tried for that last night ... was probably driven in the way we were. He'd go to ground somewhere. And I have this —" Ross touched the sonic on his belt. "I'll set it on his call; you do the same with yours. Then if we get within distance, he'll pick us up. Back here in two hours —"

"Yes." Karara kicked free of the weed, was already wading down to where the dolphins circled in the cave pool waiting for her. Ross followed, and the four swam for the open sea.

It could not be much after dawn, Ross thought, as he clung by one hand to a rock and watched Karara and the dolphins on their way. Then he paddled along the shore northward for his own survey of the coast. There was a rose cast in the sky, warming the silver along the far reaches of the horizon. And about him bobbed storm flotsam, so that he had to pick a careful way through floating debris.

On the reef one of the wrecked ships had vanished entirely. Perhaps it had been battered to death by the waves, ground to splinters against the rocks. The other still held, its prow well out of the now receding waves, jagged holes in its sides through which spurts of water cascaded now and then.

The wreck which had been driven landward was composed of planks, boxes, and containers rolled by the waves' force. Much of this was already free of the sea, and on the beach figures moved examining it. In spite of the danger of chance discovery, Ross edged along rocks, seeking a vantage point from which he could watch that activity.

He was flat against a sea-girt boulder, a swell of floating weed draped about him, when the nearest of the foraging parties moved into good view.

Men ...at least they had the outward appearance of men much like himself, though their skin was dark and their limbs appeared disproportionately long and thin. There were two groups of them, four wearing only a scanty loincloth, busy turning over and hunting through the debris under the direction of the other two.

The workers had thick growths of hair which not only covered their heads, but down their spines and the outer sides of their thin arms and legs to elbow and knee. The hair was a pallid yellow-white in vivid contrast to their dark skins, and their chins protruded sharply, allowing the lower line of their faces to take on a vaguely disturbing likeness to an animal's muzzle.

Their overseers were more fully clothed, wearing not only helmets on their heads, whose helms had a protective visor over the face, but also breast- and back-plates molded to their bodies. Ross thought that these could not be solid metal since they adapted to the movements of the wearers.

Feet and legs were covered with casing combinations of shoe and leggings, colored dull red. They were armed with swords of an odd pattern; their points curved up so that the blade resembled a fishhook. Unsheathed, the blades were clipped to a waist belt by catches which glittered in the weak morning light as if gem set.

Ross could see little of their faces, for the beak visors overhung their features. But their skins were as dusky as those of the laborers, and their arms and legs of the same unusual length ... men of the same race, he deduced.

Under the orders of the armed overseers the laborers were reducing the beach to order, sorting out the flotsam into two piles. Once they gathered about a find, and the sound of excited speech reached Ross as an agitated clicking. The armored men came up, surveyed the discovery. One of them shrugged, and clicked an order.

Ross caught only a half glimpse of the thing two of the workers dragged away. A body! Ashe.... The Terran was about to move closer when he saw the green cloak dragging about the corpse. No, not Gordon, just another victim from the wrecks.

The aliens were working their way toward Ross, and perhaps it was time for him to go. He was pushing aside his well-arranged curtain of weed when he was startled by a shout. For a second he thought he might have been sighted, until resulting action on shore told him otherwise.

The furred workers shrank back against the mound to which they had just dragged the body. While the two guards took up a position before them, curved swords, snapped from their belt hooks, ready in their hands. Again that shout. Was it a warning or a threat? With the language barrier Ross could only wait to see.

Another party approached along the beach from the south. In the lead was a cloaked and hooded figure, so muffled in its covering of silver-gray that Ross had no idea of the form beneath. Silvery-gray —no, now that hue was deepening with blue tones, darkening rapidly. By the time the cloaked newcomer had passed the rock which sheltered the Terran the covering was a rich blue which seemed to glow.

Behind the leader were a dozen armed men. They wore the same beaked helmets, the supple encasing breast- and back-plates, but their leggings were gray. They, too, carried curved swords, but the weapons were still latched to their belts and they made no move to draw them in spite of the very patent hostility of the guards before them.

Blue cloak halted some three feet from the guards. The sea wind pulled at the cloak, wrapping it about the body beneath. But even so, the wearer remained well hidden. From under a flapping edge came a hand. The fingers, long and slender, were curled about an ivory-colored wand which ended in a knob. Sparks flashed from it in a continuous flickering.

Ross clapped his hand to his belt. To his complete amazement the sonic disk he wore was reacting to those flashes, pricking sharply in perfect beat to their blink-blink. The Terran cupped his scarred fingers over the disk as he waited to see what was going to happen, wondering if the holder of that wand might, in return, pick up the broadcast of the code set on Ashe's call.

The hand clasping the wand was not dusky-skinned but had much of the same ivory shade as the rod, so that to Ross the meeting between flesh and wand was hardly distinguishable. Now by one firm thrust the hand planted the rod into the sand, leaving it to stand sentinel between the two parties.

Retreating a step or two, the red-clad guards gave ground. But they did not reclasp their swords. Their attitude, Ross judged, was that of men in some awe of their opponent, but men urged to defiance, either by a belief in the righteousness of their cause, or strengthened by an old hatred.

Now the cloaked one began to speak-or was that speech? Certainly the flow of sound had little in common with the clicking tongue Ross had caught earlier. This trill of notes possessed the rise and fall of a chant or song which could have been a formula of greeting-or a warning. And the lines of warriors escorting the chanter stood to attention, their weapons still undrawn.

Ross caught his lower lip between his teeth and bit down on it. That chanting-it crawled into the mind, set up a pattern! He shook his head vigorously and then was shocked by that recklessness. Not that any of those on shore had glanced in his direction.

The chant ended on a high, broken note. It was followed by a moment of silence through which sounded only the wind and the beat of wave.

Then one of the laborers flung up his head and clicked a word or two. He and his fellows fell face down on the beach, cupping their hands to pour sand over their unkempt heads. One of the guards turned with a sharp yell to boot the nearest of the workers in the ribs.

But his companion cried out. The wand which had stood so erect when it was first planted, now inclined toward the working party, its sparks shooting so swiftly and with such slight break between that they were fast making a single beam. Ross jerked his hand from contact with the sonic; a distinct throb of pain answered that stepping up of the mysterious broadcast.

The laborers broke and ran, or rather crawled on their bellies until they were well away, before they got to their feet and pelted back down the strand. However, the guards were of sterner stuff. They were withdrawing all right, but slowly backing away, their swords held up before them as men might retreat before insurmountable odds.

When they were well gone the robed one took up the wand. Holding it out beyond, the cloaked leader of the second party approached the two piles of salvage the workers had heaped into rough order. There was a detailed inspection of both until the robed one came upon the body.

At a trilled order two of the warriors came up and laid out the corpse. When the robed one nodded they stood well back. The rod moved, the tip rather than the knobbed head being pointed at the body.

Ross's head snapped back. That bolt of light, energy, fire-whatever it was-issuing from the rod had dazzled him into momentary blindness. And a vibration of force through the air was like a blow.

When he was able to see once more there was nothing at all on the sand where the corpse had lain, nothing except a glassy trough from which some spirals of vapor arose. Ross clung to his rock support badly shaken.

Men with swords ... and now this-some form of controlled energy which argued of technical development and science. Just as the cliff castle had bombarded with rocks ships sailing with a speed which argued engine power of an unknown type. A mixture of barbaric and advanced knowledge. To assess this, he needed more experience, more knowledge than he possessed. Now Ashe could....

Ashe!

Ross was jerked back to his own quest. The rod was quiet, no more sparks were flung from its knob. And under Ross's touch his sonic was quiet also. He snapped off the broadcast. If that device had picked up the flickering of the rod, the reverse could well be true.

The cloaked one chose from the pile of goods, and its escort gathered up the designated boxes, a small cask or two. So laden, the party returned south the way they had come. Ross allowed his breath to expel in a sigh of relief.

He worked his way farther north along the coast, watching other parties of the furred workers and their guards. Lines of the former climbed the cliff, hauling their spoil, their destination the castle. But Ross saw no sign of Ashe, received no answer to the sonic code he had reset once the strangers were out of distance. And the Terran began to realize that his present search might well be fruitless, though he fought against accepting it.

When he turned back to the slit cave Ross's fear was ready to be expressed in anger, the anger of frustration over his own helplessness. With no chance of trying to penetrate the castle, he could not learn whether or not Ashe had been taken prisoner. And until the workers left the beach he could not prowl there hunting the grimmer evidence his mind flinched from considering.

Karara waited for him on the inner ledge. There was no sign of the dolphins and as Ross pulled out of the water, pushing aside his mask, her face in the thin light of the cave was deeply troubled.

"You did not find him," she made that a statement rather than a question.

"No."

"And I did not find it —"

Ross used a length of weed from the nest as a towel. But now he stood very still.

"The gate ... no sign of it?"

"Just this —" She reached behind her and brought up a sealed container. Ross recognized one of the supply cans they had had in the cache by the gate. "There are others ... scattered. Taua and Tino-rau seek them now. It is as if all that was on the other side was sucked through with us."

"You are sure you found the right place?"

"Is-is this not part of it?" Again the girl sought for something on the ledge. What she held out to him was a length of metal rod, twisted and broken at one end as if a giant hand had wrenched it loose from the installation.

Ross nodded dully. "Yes," his voice was harsh as if the words were pulled out of him against his will and against all hope —"that's part of a side bar. It-it must have been totally wrecked."

Yet, even though he held that broken length in his hands, Ross could not really believe the gate was gone. He swam out once more, heading for the reef where the dolphins joined him as guides. There was a second piece of broken tube, the scattered containers of supplies, that was all. The Terrans were wrecked in time as surely as those ships had been wrecked on the sea reef the night before!

Ross headed once again for the cave. Their immediate needs were of major importance now. The containers must be all gathered and taken into their hiding place, because upon their contents three human lives could depend.

He paused just at the entrance to adjust the net of containers he transported. And it was that slight chance which brought him knowledge of the intruder.

On the ledge Karara was heaping up the kelp of the nest. But to one side and on a level with the girl's head....

Ross dared not flash his torch, thus betraying his presence. Leaving the net hitched to the rock by its sling, he swam under water along the side of the cave by a route which should bring him out within striking distance of that hunched figure perching above to watch Karara's every move.

6. Loketh the Useless

The wash of waves covered Ross's advance until he came up against the wall not too far from the spy's perch. Whoever crouched there still leaned forward to watch Karara. And Ross's eyes, having adjusted to the gloom of the cavern, made out the outline of head and shoulders. The next two or three minutes were the critical ones for the Terran. He must emerge on the ledge in the open before he could attack.

Karara might almost have read his mind and given conscious help. For now she went out on the point of the ledge to whistle the dolphins' summons. Tino-rau's sleek head bobbed above water as he answered the girl with a bubbling squeak. Karara knelt and the dolphin came to butt against her out-held hand.

Ross heard a gasp from the watcher, a faint sound of movement. Karara began to sing softly, her voice rippling in one of the liquid chants of her own people, the dolphin interjecting a note or two. Ross had heard them at that before, and it made perfect cover for his move. He sprang.

His grasp tightened on flesh, fingers closed about thin wrists. There was a yell of astonishment and fear from the stranger as the Terran jerked him from his perch to the ledge. Ross had his opponent flattened under him before he realized that the other had offered no struggle, but lay still.

"What is it?" Karara's torch beam caught them both. Ross looked down into a thin brown face not too different from his own. The wide-set eyes were closed, and the mouth gaped open. Though he believed the Hawaikan unconscious, Ross still kept hold on those wrists as he moved from the sprawled body. With the girl's aid he used a length of kelp to secure the captive.

The stranger wore a garment of glistening skintight material which covered body, legs, and feet, but left his lanky arms bare. A belt about his waist had loops for a number of objects, among them a hook-pointed knife which Ross prudently removed.

"Why, he is only a boy," Karara said. "Where did he come from, Ross?"

The Terran pointed to the wall crevice. "He was up there, watching you."

Her eyes were wide and round. "Why?"

Ross dragged his prisoner back against the wall of the cave. After witnessing the fate of those who had swum ashore from the wreck, he did not like to think what motive might have brought the Hawaikan here. Again Karara's thoughts must have matched his, for she added:

"But he did not even draw his knife. What are you going to do with him, Ross?"

That problem already occupied the Terran. The wisest move undoubtedly was to kill the native out of hand. But such ruthlessness was more than he could stomach. And if he could learn anything from the stranger-gain some knowledge of this new world and its ways-he would be twice winner. Why, this encounter might even lead to Ashe!

"Ross ... his leg. See?" The girl pointed.

The tight fit of the alien's clothing made the defect clear; the right leg of the stranger was shrunken and twisted. He was a cripple.

"What of it?" Ross demanded sharply. This was no time for an appeal to the sympathies.

But Karara did not urge any modification of the bonds as he half feared she would. Instead, she sat back cross-legged, an odd, withdrawn expression making her seem remote though he could have put out his hand to touch her.

"His lameness-it could be a bridge," she observed, to Ross's mystification.

"A bridge-what do you mean?"

The girl shook her head. "This is only a feeling, not a true thought. But also it is important. Look, I think he is waking."

The lids above those large eyes were fluttering. Then with a shake of the head, the Hawaikan blinked up at them. Blank bewilderment was all Ross could read in the stranger's expression until the alien saw Karara. Then a flood of clicking speech poured from his lips.

He seemed utterly astounded when they made no answer. And the fluency of his first outburst took on a pleading note, while the expectancy of his first greeting faded away.

Karara spoke to Ross. "He is becoming afraid, very much afraid. At first, I think, he was pleased ... happy."

"But why?"

The girl shook her head. "I do not know; I can only feel. Wait!" Her hand rose in imperious command. She did not rise to her feet, but crawled on hands and knees to the edge of the ledge. Both dolphins were there, raising their heads well out of the water, their actions expressing unusual excitement.

"Ross!" Karara's voice rang loudly. "Ross, they can understand him! Tino-rau and Taua can understand him!"

"You mean, they understand this language?" Ross found that fantastic, awesome as the abilities of the dolphins were.

"No, his mind. It's his mind, Ross. Somehow he thinks in patterns they can pick up and read! They do that, you know, with a few of us, but not in the same way. This is more direct, clearer! They're so excited!"

Ross glanced at the prisoner. The alien had wriggled about, striving to raise his head against the wall as a support. His captor pulled the Hawaikan into a sitting position, but the native accepted that aid almost as if he were not even aware of Ross's hands on his body. He stared with a kind of horrified disbelief at the bobbing dolphin heads.

"He is afraid," Karara reported. "He has never known such communication before."

"Can they ask him questions?" demanded Ross. If this odd mental tie between Terran dolphin and Hawaikan did exist, then there was a chance to learn about this world.

"They can try. Now he only knows fear, and they must break through that."

What followed was the most unusual four-sided conversation Ross could have ever imagined. He put a question to Karara, who relayed it to the dolphins. In turn, they asked it mentally of the Hawaikan and conveyed his answer back via the same route.

It took some time to allay the fears of the stranger. But at last the Hawaikan entered wholeheartedly into the exchange.

"He is the son of the lord ruling the castle above." Karara produced the first rational and complete answer. "But for some reason he is not accepted by his own kind. Perhaps," she added on her own, "it is because he is crippled. The sea is his home, as he expresses it, and he believes me to be some mythical being out of it. He saw me swimming, masked, and with the dolphins, and he is sure I change shape at will."

She hesitated. "Ross, I get something odd here. He does know, or thinks he knows, creatures who can appear and disappear at will. And he is afraid of their powers."

"Gods and goddesses-perfectly natural."

Karara shook her head. "No, this is more concrete than a religious belief."

Ross had a sudden inspiration. Hurriedly he described the cloaked figure who had driven the castle people from the piles of salvage. "Ask him about that one."

She relayed the question. Ross saw the prisoner's head jerk around. The Hawaikan looked from Karara to her companion, a shade of speculation in his expression.

"He wants to know why you ask about the Foanna? Surely you must well know what manner of beings they are."

"Listen —" Ross was sure now that he had made a real discovery, though its importance he could not guess, "tell him we come from where there are no Foanna. That we have powers and must know of their powers."

If he could only carry on this interrogation straight and not have to depend upon a double translation! And could he even be sure his questions reached the alien undistorted?

Wearily Ross sat back on his heels. Then he glanced at Karara with a twinge of concern. If he was tired by their roundabout communication, she must be doubly so. There was a droop to her shoulders, and her last reply had come in a voice hoarse with fatigue. Abruptly he started up.

"That's enough-for now."

Which was true. He had to have time for evaluation, to adjust to what they had learned during the steady stream of questions passed back and forth. And in that moment he was conscious of his hunger, just as his voice was paper dry from lack of drink. The canister of supplies he had left by the cave entrance...

"We need food and drink." He fumbled with his mask, but Karara motioned him back from the water.

"Taua brings ... Wait!"

The dolphin trailed the net of containers to them. Ross unscrewed one, pulled out a bulb of fresh water. A second box yielded the dry wafers of emergency rations.

Then, after a moment's hesitation, Ross crossed to the prisoner, cut his wrist bonds, and pressed both a bulb and a wafer into his hold. The Hawaikan watched the Terrans eat before he bit into the wafer, chewing it with vigor, turning the bulb around in his fingers with alert interest before he sucked at its contents.

As Ross chewed and swallowed, mechanically and certainly with no relish, he fitted one fact to another to make a picture of this Hawaikan time period in which they were now marooned. Of course, his picture was based on facts they had learned from their captive. Perhaps he had purposely misled them or fogged some essentials. But could he have done that in a mental contact? Ross would simply have to accept everything with a certain amount of cautious skepticism.

Anyway, there were the Wreckers of the castle-petty lordlings setting up their holds along the coasts, preying upon the shipping which was the lifeblood of this island-water world. The Terrans had seen them in action last night and today. And if the captive's information was correct, it was not only the storm's fury which brought the waves' harvest. The Wreckers had some method of attracting ships to crack up on their reefs.

Some method of attraction....And that force which had pulled the Terrans through the time gate; could there be a connection? However, there remained the Wreckers on the cliff. And their prey, the seafarers of the ocean, with an understandably deep enmity between them.

Those two parties Ross could understand and be prepared to deal with, he thought. But there remained the Foanna. And, from their prisoner's explanation, the Foanna were a very different matter.

They possessed a power which did not depend upon swords or ships or the natural tools and weapons of men. No, they had strengths which were unearthly, to give them superiority in all but one way-numbers. Though the Foanna had their warriors and servants, as Ross had seen on the beach, they, themselves, were of another race —a very old and dying race of which few remained. How many, their enemies could not say, for the Foanna had no separate identities known to the outer world. They appeared, gave their orders, levied their demands, opposed or aided as they wished-always just one or two at a time-always so muffled in their cloaks that even their physical appearances remained a mystery. But there was no mystery about their powers. Ross gathered that no Wrecker lord, no matter how much a leader among his own kind, how ambitious, had yet dared to oppose actively one of the Foanna, though he might make a token protest against some demand from them.

And certainly the captive's description of those powers in action suggested a supernatural origin of Foanna knowledge, or at least for its application. But Ross thought that the answer might be that they possessed the remnants of some almost forgotten technical know-how, the heritage of a very old race. He had tried to learn something of the origin of the Foanna themselves, wondering if the robed ones could be from the galactic empire. But the answer had come that the Foanna were older than recorded time, that they had lived in the great citadel before the race of the Terrans' prisoner had risen from very primitive savagery.

"What do we do now?" Karara broke in upon Ross's thoughts as she refastened the containers.

"These slaves that the Wreckers take upon occasion ...Maybe Ashe...." Ross was catching at very fragile straws; he had to. And the stranger had said that able-bodied men who swam ashore relatively uninjured were taken captive. Several had been the night before.

"Loketh."

Ross and Karara looked around. The prisoner put down the water bulb, and one of his hands made a gesture they could not mistake; he pointed to himself and repeated that word, "Loketh."

The Terran touched his own chest. "Ross Murdock."

Perhaps the other was as impatient as he with their roundabout method of communication and had decided to try and speed it up. The analyzer! Ashe had included the analyzer with the equipment by the gate. If Ross could find that ...why, then the major problem could be behind them. Swiftly he explained to Karara, and with a vigorous nod of assent she called to Taua, ordering the rest of the salvage material from the gate be brought to them.

"Loketh." Ross pointed to the youth. "Ross." That was himself. "Karara." He indicated the girl.

"Rosss." The alien made a clicking hiss of the first name. "Karara —" He did better with the second.

Ross carefully unpacked the box Taua had located. He had only slight knowledge of how the device worked. It was intended to record a strange language, break it down into symbols already familiar to the Time Agents. But could it also be used as a translator with a totally alien tongue? He could only hope that the rough handling of its journey through the gate had not damaged it and that the experiment might possibly work.

Putting the box between them, he explained what he wanted; and Karara took up the small micro-disk, speaking slowly and distinctly the same liquid syllables she had used in the dolphin song. Ross clicked the lever when she was finished, and watched the small screen. The symbols which flashed there had meaning for him right enough; he could translate what she had just taped. The machine still worked to that extent.

Now he pushed the box into place before Loketh and made the visibly reluctant Hawaikan take the disk from Karara. Then through the dolphin link Ross passed on definite instructions. Would it work as well to translate a stellar tongue as it had with languages past and present of his own planet?

Reluctantly Loketh began to talk to the disk, at first in a very rapid mumble and then, as there was no frightening response, with less speed and more confidence. There were symbol lines on the vista-plate in accordance, and some of them made sense! Ross was elated.

"Ask him: Can one enter the castle unseen to check on the slaves?"

"For what reason?"

Ross was sure he had read those symbols correctly.

"Tell him-that one of our kind may be among them."

Loketh did not reply so quickly this time. His eyes, grave and measuring, studied Ross, then Karara, then Ross again.

"There is a way ... discovered by this useless one."

Ross did not pay attention to the odd adjective Loketh chose to describe himself. He pressed to the important matter.

"Can and will he show me that way?"

Again that long moment of appraisal on the part of Loketh before he answered. Ross found himself reading the reply symbols aloud.

"If you dare, then I will lead."

7. Witches' Meat

He might be recklessly endangering all of them, Ross knew. But if Ashe was immured somewhere in that rock pile over their heads, then the risk of trusting Loketh would be worth it. However, because Ross was chancing his own neck did not mean that Karara need be drawn into immediate peril too. With the dolphins at her command and the supplies, scanty as those were, she would have a good chance to hide here safely.

"Holding out for what?" she asked quietly after Ross elaborated on this subject, thus bringing him to silence.

Because her question was just. With the gate gone the Terrans were committed to this time, just as they had earlier been committed to Hawaika when on their home world they had entered the spaceship for the take-off. There was no escape from the past, which had become their present.

"The Foanna," she continued, "these Wreckers, the sea people-all at odds with one another. Do we join any, then their quarrels must also become ours."

Taua nosed the ledge behind the girl, squeaked a demand for attention. Karara looked around at Loketh; her look was as searching as the one the native had earlier turned on her and Ross.

"He" —the girl nodded at the Hawaikan —"wishes to know if you trust him. And he says to tell you this: Because the Shades chose to inflict upon him a twisted leg he is not one with those of the castle, but to them a broken, useless thing. Ross, I gather he thinks we have powers like the Foanna, and that we may be supernatural. But because we did not kill him out of hand and have fed him, he considers himself bound to us."

"Ritual of bread and salt ... could be." Though it might be folly to match alien customs to Terran, Ross thought of that very ancient pact on his own world. Eat a man's food, become his friend, or at least declare a truce between you. Stiff taboos and codes of behavior marked nations on Terra, especially warrior societies, and the same might be true here.

"Ask him," Ross told Karara, "what is the rule for food and drink between friends or enemies!" The more he could learn of such customs the better protection he might be able to weave for them.

Long moments for the relay of that message, and then Loketh spoke into the micro-disk of the analyzer, slowly, with pauses, as if trying to make sure Ross understood every word.

"To give bread into the hands of one you have taken in battle, makes him your man-not as a slave to labor, but as one who draws sword at your bidding. When I took your bread I accepted you as cup-lord. Between such there is no betrayal, for how may a man betray his lord? I, Loketh, am now a sword in your hands, a man in your service. And to me this is doubly good, for as a useless one I have never had a lord, nor one to swear to. Also, with this Sea Maid and her followers to listen to thoughts, how could any man speak with a double tongue were he one who consorted with the Shadow and wore the Cloak of Evil?"

"He's right," Karara added. "His mind is open; he couldn't hide his thoughts from Taua and Tino-rau even if he wished."

"All right, I'll accept that." Ross glanced about the ledge. They had piled the containers at the far end. For Karara to move might be safe. He said so.

"Move where?" she asked flatly. "Those men from the castle are still hunting drift out there. I don't think anyone knows of this cave."

Ross nodded to Loketh. "He did, didn't he? I wouldn't want you trapped here. And I don't want to lose those supplies. What is in those containers may be what saves us all."

"We can sink those over by the wall, weight them down in a net. Then, if we have to move, they will be ready. Do not worry-that is my department." She smiled at him with a slightly mocking lift of lips.

Ross subsided, though he was irritated because she was right. The management of the dolphin team and sea matters were her department. And while he resented her reminder of that point he could not deny the justice of her retort.

In spite of his crippled leg, Loketh displayed an agility which surprised Ross. Freed from his ankle bonds, he beckoned the Terran back to the very niche where he had hidden to watch Karara. Up he swung into that and in a second had vanished from sight.

Ross followed, to discover it was not a niche after all but the opening of a crevice, leading upward as a vent. And it had been used before as a passage. There was no light, but the native guided Ross's hands to the hollow climbing holds cut into the stone. Then Loketh pushed past and went up the crude ladder into the dark.

It was difficult to judge either time or distance in this black tube. Ross counted the holds for some check. His agent training made one part of his mind sharply aware of such things; the need for memorizing a passage which led into the enemy's territory was apparent. What the purpose of this slit had originally been he did not know, but strongholds on Terra had had their hidden ways in and out for use in times of siege, and he was beginning to believe that these aliens had much in common with his own kind.

He had reached twenty in his counting and his senses, alerted by training and instinct, told him there was an opening not too far above. But the darkness remained so thick it fell in tangible folds about his sweating body. Ross almost cried out as fingers clamped about his wrist when he reached for a new hold. Then urged by that grasp, he was up and out, sprawling into a vertical passage. Far ahead was a gray of faint light.

Ross choked and then sneezed as dust puffed up from between his scrabbling hands. The hold which had been on his wrist shifted to his shoulder, and with a surprising strength Loketh hauled the Terran to his feet.

The passage in which they stood was a slit extending in height well above their heads, but narrow, not much wider than Ross's shoulders. Whether it was a natural fault or had been cut he could not tell.

Loketh was ahead again, his rocking limp making the outline of his body a jerky up-and-down shadow. Again his speed and agility amazed the Terran. Loketh might be lame, but he had learned to adapt to his handicap very well.

The light increased and Ross marked slits in the walls to his right, no wider than the breadth of his two fingers. He peered out of one and was looking into empty air while below he heard the murmur of the sea. This way must run in the cliff face above the beach.

A click of impatient whisper drew him on to join Loketh. Here was a flight of stairs, narrow of tread and very steep. Loketh turned back and side against these to climb, his outspread hand flattened on the stone as if it possessed adhesive qualities to steady him. For the first time his twisted leg was a disadvantage.

Ross counted again–ten, fifteen of those steps, bringing them once more into darkness. Then they emerged from a well-like opening into a circular room. A sudden and dazzling flare of light made the Terran shade his eyes. Loketh set a pallid but glowing cone on a wall shelf, and the Terran discovered that the burst of light was only relative to the dark of the passage; indeed it was very weak illumination.

The Hawaikan braced his body against the far wall. The strain of his effort, whatever its purpose, was easy to read in the contorted line of his shoulders. Then the wall slid under Loketh's urging, a slow move as if the weight of the slab he strove to handle was almost too great for his slender arms, or else the need for caution was intensified here.

They now fronted a narrow opening, and the light of the cone shone only a few feet into the space. Loketh beckoned to Ross and they went on. Here the left wall was cut in many places emitting patches of light in a way which bore no resemblance to conventional windows. It was like walking behind a pierced screen which followed no logical pattern in the cutaway portions. Ross gazed out and gasped.

He was standing above the center core of the castle, and the life below and beyond drew his attention. He had seen drawings reproducing the life of a feudal castle. This resembled them and yet, as Ross studied the scene closer, the differences between the Terran past and this became more distinct.

In the first place there were those animals–or were they animals? —being hooked up to a cart. They had six limbs, walking on four, holding the remaining two folded under their necks. Their harness consisted of a network fitted over their shoulders, anchored to the folded limbs. Their grotesque heads, bobbing and weaving on lengthy necks, their bodies, were sleekly scaled. Ross was startled by a resemblance he traced to the sea dragon he had met in the future of this world.

But the creatures were subject to the men harnessing them. And the activity in other respects ...Ross had to fight a wayward and fascinated interest in all he could see, force himself to concentrate on learning what might be pertinent to his own mission. But Loketh did not allow him to watch for long. Instead, his hand on the Terran's arm urged the other down the gallery behind the screen and once more into the bulk of the fortress.

Another narrow way ran through the thickness of the walls. Then a patch of light, not that of outer day, but a reddish gleam from an opening waist high. There Loketh went awkwardly to his good knee, motioning Ross to follow his example.

What lay below was a hall furnished with a barbaric rawness of color and glitter. There were long strips of brightly hued woven stuff on the walls, touched here and there with sparkling glints which were jewel-like. And set at intervals among the hangings were oval objects perhaps Ross's height on which were designs and patterns picked out in paint and metal. Maybe the stylized representation of native plants and animals.

The whole gave an impression of clashing color, just as the garments of those gathered there were garish in turn.

There were three Hawaikans on the two-step dais. All wore robes fitting tightly to the upper portion of their bodies, girded to their waists with elaborate belts, then falling in long points to floor level, the points being finished off with tassels. Their heads were covered with tight caps which were a latticework of decorated strips, glittering as they moved. And the mixture of colors in their apparel was such as to offend Terran eyes with their harsh clash of shade against shade.

Drawn up below the dais were two rows of guards. But the reason for the assembly baffled Ross, since he could not understand the clicking speech.

There came a hollow echoing sound as from a gong. The three on the dais straightened, turned their attention to the other end of the hall. Ross did not need Loketh's gesture to know that something of importance was about to begin.

Down the hall was a somber note in the splash of clashing color. The Terran recognized the gray-blue robe of the Foanna. There were three of the robed ones this time, one slightly in advance of the other two. They came at a gliding pace as if they swept along above that paved flooring, not by planting feet upon it. As they halted below the dais the men there rose.

Ross could read their reluctance to make that concession in the slowness of their movements. They were plainly being compelled to render deference when they longed to refuse it. Then the middle one of the castle lords spoke first.

"Zahur —" Loketh breathed in Ross's ear, his pointed finger indicating the speaker.

Ross longed vainly for the ability to ask questions, a chance to know what was in progress. That the meeting of the two Hawaikan factions was important he did not doubt.

There was an interval of silence after the castle lord finished speaking. To the Terran this spun on and on and he sensed the mounting tension. This must be a showdown, perhaps even a declaration of open hostilities between Wreckers and the older race. Or perhaps the pause was a subtle weapon of the Foanna, used to throw a less-sophisticated enemy off balance, as a judo fighter might use an opponent's attack as part of his own defense.

When the Foanna did make answer it came in the singsong of chanted words. Ross felt Loketh shiver, felt the crawl of chill along his own spine. The words-if those were words and not just sounds intended to play upon the mind and emotions of a listener-cut into one. Ross wanted to close his ears, thrust his fingers into them to drown out that sound, yet he did not have the power to raise his hands.

It seemed to him that the men on the dais were swaying now as if the chant were a rope leashed about them, pulling them back and forth. There was a clatter; one of the guards had fallen to the floor and lay there, rolling, his hands to his head.

A shout from the dais. The chanting reached a note so high that Ross felt the torment in his ears. Below, the lines of guards had broken. A party of them were heading for the end of the hall, making a wide detour around the Foanna. Loketh gave a small choked cry; his fingers tightened on Ross's forearm with painful intensity as he whispered.

What was about to happen meant something important. To Loketh or to him? Ashe! Was this concerned with Ashe? Ross crowded against the opening, tried to see the direction in which the guards had disappeared.

The wait made him doubly impatient. One of the men on the dais had dropped on the bench there, his head forward on his hands, his shoulders quivering. But the one Loketh had identified as Zahur still fronted the Foanna spokesman, and Ross gave tribute to the strength of will which kept him there.

They were returning, the guards, and herded between their lines three men. Two were Hawaikans, their bare dark bodies easily identifiable. But the third-Ashe! Ross almost shouted his name aloud.

The Terran stumbled along and there was a bandage above his knee. He had been stripped to his swimming trunks, all his equipment taken from him. There was a dark bruise on his left temple, the angry weal of a lash mark on neck and shoulder.

Ross's hands clenched. Never in his life had he so desperately wanted a weapon as he did at that moment. To spray the company below with a machine gun would have given him great satisfaction. But he had nothing but the knife in his belt and he was as cut off from Ashe as if they were in separate cells of some prison.

The caution which had been one of his inborn gifts and which had been fostered by his training, clamped down on his first wild desire for action. There was not the slightest chance of his doing Ashe any good at the present. But he had this much-he knew that Gordon was alive and that he was in the aliens' hands. Faced by those facts Ross could plan his own moves.

The Foanna chant began again, and the three prisoners moved; the two Hawaikans turned, set themselves on either side of Ashe, and gave him support. Their actions had a mechanical quality as if they were directed by a will beyond their own. Ashe gazed about him at the Wreckers and the robed figures. His awareness of them both suggested to Ross that if the natives had come under the control of the Foanna, the Terran resisted their influence. But Ashe did not try to escape the assistance of his two fellow prisoners, and he limped with their aid back down the hall, following the Foanna.

Ross deduced that the captives had been transferred from the lord of the castle to the Foanna. Which meant Ashe was on his way to another destination. The Terran was on his feet and headed back, intent on returning to the sea cave and starting out after Ashe as soon as he could.

"You have found Gordon!" Karara read his news from his face.

"The Wreckers had him prisoner. Now they've turned him over to the Foanna —"

"What will *they* do with him?" the girl demanded of Loketh.

His answer came roundabout as usual as the native squatted by the analyzer and clicked his answer into it.

"They have claimed the wreck survivors for tribute. Your companion will be witches' meat."

"Witches' meat?" repeated Ross, uncomprehending.

Then Karara drew a gagged breath which was a gasp of horror.

"Sacrifice! Ross, he must mean they are going to use Gordon for a sacrifice."

Ross stiffened and then whirled to catch Loketh by the shoulders. The inability to question the native directly was an added disaster now.

"Where are they taking him? Where?" He began that fiercely, and then forced control on himself.

Karara's eyes were half closed, her head back; she was manifestly aiming that inquiry at the dolphins, to be translated to Loketh.

Symbols burned on the analyzer screen.

"The Foanna have their own fortress. It can be entered best by sea. There is a boat ...I can show you, for it is my own secret."

"Tell him-yes, as soon as we can!" Ross broke out. The old feeling that time was all-important worried at him. Witches' meat ... witches' meat ... the words were sharp as a lash.

8. The Free Rovers

Twilight made a gray world where one could not trace the true meeting of land and water, sea and sky. Surely the haze about them was more than just the normal dusk of coming night.

Ross balanced in the middle of the skiff as it bobbed along the swell of waves inside a barrier reef. To his mind the craft carrying the three of them and their net of supplies was too frail, rode too high. But Karara paddling in the bow, Loketh at the stern seemed to be content, and Ross could not, for pride's sake, question their competency. He comforted himself with the knowledge that no agent was able to absorb every primitive skill, and Karara's people had explored the Pacific in out-rigger canoes hardly more stable than their present vessel, navigating by currents and stars.

Smothering his feeling of helplessness and the slow anger that roused in him, the Terran busied himself with study of a sort. They had had the longer part of the day in the cave before

Loketh would agree to venture out of hiding and paddle south. Ross, using the analyzer, had, with Loketh's aid, set about learning what he could of the native tongue.

Now possessed of a working vocabulary of clicked words, he was able to follow Loketh's speech so that translation through the dolphins was not necessary except for complicated directions. Also, he had a more detailed briefing of the present situation on Hawaika.

Enough to know that they might be embarking on a mad venture. The citadel of the Foanna was distinctly forbidden ground, not only for Loketh's people but also for the Foanna's Hawaikan followers who were housed and labored in an outer ring of fortification-cum-village. Those natives were, Ross gathered, a hereditary corps of servants and warriors, born to that status and not recruited from the native population at large. As such, they were armored by the "magic" of their masters.

"If the Foanna are so powerful," Ross had demanded, "why do you go with us against them?" To depend so heavily on the native made him uneasy.

The Hawaikan looked to Karara. One of his hands raised; his fingers sketched a sign toward the girl.

"With the Sea Maid and her magic I do not fear." He paused before adding, "Always has it been said of me-and to me-that I am a useless one, fit only to do women's tasks. No word weaver shall ever chant my battle deeds in the great hall of Zahur. I who am Zahur's true son can not carry my sword in any lord's train. But now you offer me one of the great to-be-remembered quests. If I go, so may I prove that I am a man, even if I go limpingly. There is nothing the Foanna can do to me which is worse than what the Shadow has already done. Choosing to follow you I may stand up to face Zahur in his own hall, show him that the blood of his House has not been drained from my veins because I walk crookedly!"

There was such bitter fire, not only in the sputtering rush of Loketh's words, but in his eyes, his face, the wry twist of his lips, that Ross believed him. The Terran no longer had any doubts that the castle outcast was willing to brave the unknown terrors of the Foanna keep, not just to aid Ross whom he considered himself bound to serve by the customs of his people, but because he saw in this venture a chance to gain what he had never had, a place in his warrior culture.

Shut off from the normal life of his people, he had early turned to the sea. His twisted leg had not proved a handicap in the water, and he stated with confidence that he was the best swimmer in the castle. Not that the men of his father's following had taken greatly to the sea, which they looked upon merely as a way of preying upon the true sea rovers.

The reef on which the ships had been wrecked was a snare of sorts-first by the whim of nature when wind and current piled up the trading ships there. Then, Ross was startled when Loketh elaborated on a later development of that trap.

"So Zahur returned from this meeting and set up a great magic among the rock, according to the spells he was taught. Now ships are drawn there so the wrecks have been many and Zahur becomes an even greater lord with many men coming to take sword oath under him."

"This magic," asked Ross, "of what manner is it and where did Zahur obtain it?"

"It is fashioned so —" Loketh sketched two straight lines in the air, "not curved as a sword. And the color of water under a storm sky, both rods being as tall as a man. There was much care to set them in place, that was done by a man of Glicmas."

"A man of Glicmas?"

"Glicmas is now the high lord of the Iccio. He is blood kin to Zahur, yet Zahur must take sword oath to send to Glicmas a fourth of all his sea-gleanings for a year in payment for this magic."

"And Glicmas, where did he get it? From the Foanna?"

Loketh made an emphatic denial of that. "No, the Foanna have spoken out against their use, making even greater ill feeling between the Old Ones and the coast people. It is said that Glicmas saw a great wonder in the sky and followed it to a high place of his own country. A mountain broke in twain and a voice issued forth from the rent, calling that the lord of the country come and stand to hear it. When Glicmas did so he was told that the magic would be his. Then the mountain closed again and he found many strange things upon the ground. As he uses them they make him akin to the Foanna in power. Some he gives to those who are his blood kin, and together they will be great until they close their fists not only upon the sea rovers, but upon the Foanna also. This they have come to believe."

"But you do not?" Karara asked then.

"I do not know, Sea Maid. The time is coming when perhaps they shall have their chance to prove how strong is their magic. Already the Rovers gather in fleets as they never did before. And it seems that they, too, have found a new magic, for their ships fly through the water, depending no longer on wind-filling sails, or upon strong arms of men at long paddles. There is a struggle before us. But that you must know, being who and what you are, Sea Maid."

"And what do you think I am? What do you think Ross is?"

"If the Foanna dwell on land and hold old knowledge and power beyond our reckoning in their two hands," he replied, "then it is possible that the same could have roots in the sea. It is my belief that you are of the Shades, but not the Shadow. And this warrior is also of your kind-but perhaps in different degree, putting into action your desires and wishes. Thus, if you go up against the Foanna, you shall be well matched, kind to kind."

Nice to be so certain of that, Ross thought. He did not share Loketh's confidence on that subject.

"The Shades ... the Shadow ..." Karara persisted. "What are these, Loketh?"

An odd expression crossed the Hawaikan's face. "Are those not known to you, Sea Maid? Indeed, then you are of a breed different from the men of land. The Shades are those of power who may come to the aid of men should it be their desire to influence the future. And the Shadow ... the Shadow is That Which Ends All-man, hope, good. To Which there is no appeal, and Which holds a vast and enduring hatred for that which has life and full substance."

"So Zahur has this new magic. Is it the gift of Shades or Shadow?" Ross brought them back to the subject which had sparked in him a small warning signal.

"Zahur prospers mightily." Loketh's answer was ambiguous.

"And so the Shadow could not provide such magic?" The Terran pushed.

But before the Hawaikan had a chance to answer, Karara added another question:

"But you believe that it did?"

"I do not know. Only the magic has made Zahur a part of Glicmas, and Glicmas is now perhaps a part of that which spoke from the mountain. It is not well to accept gifts which tie one man to another unless there is from the first a saying of how deep that bond may run."

"I think you are wise in that, Loketh," Karara said.

But the uneasiness had grown in Ross. Alien powers, out of a mountain heart, passed from one lord to another. And on the other hand the Rovers' sudden magic in turn, lending their ships wings. The two facts balanced in an odd way. Back on Terra there had been those sudden and unaccountable jumps in technical knowledge on the part of the enemy, jumps which had set in action the whole Time Travel service of which he had become a part. And these jumps had not been the result of normal research; they had come from the looting of derelict spaceships wrecked on his world in the far past.

Could driblets of the same stellar knowledge have been here deliberately fed to warring communities? He asked Loketh about the possibility of space-borne explorers. But to the Hawaikan that was a totally foreign conception. The stars, for Loketh, were the doorways and windows of the Shades, and he treated the suggestion of space travel as perhaps natural to those all-powerful specters, but certainly not for beings like himself. There was no hint that Hawaika had been openly visited by a galactic ship. Though that did not bar such landings. The planet was, Ross thought, thinly populated. Whole sections of the interiors of the larger islands were wilderness, and this world must be in the same state of only partial occupation as his own earth had been in the Bronze Age when tribes on the march had fanned out into virgin wilderness, great forests, and steppes unwalked by man before their coming.

Now as he balanced in the canoe and tried to keep his mind off the queasiness in his middle and the insecurity of the one thickness of sea-creature hide stretched over a bone framework which made up the craft between his person and the water, Ross still mulled over what might be true. Had the galactic invaders for their own purposes begun to meddle here, leaking weapons or tools to upset what must be a very delicate balance of power? Why? To bring on a conflict which would occupy the native population to the point of exhaustion or depopulation? So they could win a world for their own purposes without effort or risk on their part? Such cold-blooded fishing in carefully troubled waters fitted very well with the persons of the Baldies as he had known them on Terra.

And he could not set aside that memory of this very coast as he had seen it through the peep, the castle in ruins, tall pylons reaching from the land into the sea. Was this the beginning of that change which would end in the Hawaika of his own time, empty of intelligent life, shattered into a loose network of islands?

"This fog is strange." Karara's words startled Ross to return to the here and now.

The haze he had been only half conscious of when they had put out from the tiny secret bay where Loketh kept his boat, was truly a fog, piling up in soft billows and cutting down visibility with speed.

"The Foanna!" Loketh's answer was sharp, a recognition of danger. "Their magic-they hide their place so! There is trouble, trouble on the move!"

"Do we land then?" Ross did not ascribe the present blotting out of the landscape to any real manipulation of nature on the part of the all-powerful Foanna. Too many times the reputations of "medicine men" had been so enhanced by coincidence. But he did doubt the wisdom of trying to bore ahead blindly in this murk.

"Taua and Tino-rau can guide us," Karara reminded him. "Throw out the rope, Ross. What is above water will not confuse them."

He moved cautiously, striving to adapt his actions to the swing of the boat. The line was ready coiled to hand and he tossed the loose end overboard, to feel the cord jerk taut as one of the dolphins caught it up.

They were being towed now, though both paddlers reinforced the forward tug with their efforts. The curtain gathering above the surface of the water did not hamper the swimmers beneath its surface, and Ross felt relief. He turned his head to speak to Loketh.

"How near are we?"

The mist had thickened to the point that, close as the native was, the lines of his body blurred. His clicking answer seemed distorted, too, almost as if the fog had altered not only his form but his personality.

"Maybe very soon now. We must see the sea gate before we are sure."

"And if we aren't able to see that?" challenged Ross.

"The sea gate is above and below the water. Those who obey the Sea Maid, who are able to speak thought to thought, will find it if we can not."

But they were never to reach that goal. Karara gave warning: "There are ships about."

Ross knew that the dolphins had told her. He demanded in turn: "What kind?"

"Larger, much larger than this."

Then Loketh broke in: "A Rover Raider-three of them!"

Ross frowned. He was the cripple here. The other two, with their ability to communicate with the dolphins, were the sighted, he the blind. And he resented his handicap in a burst of bitterness which must have colored his tone as he ordered, "Head inshore-now!"

Once on land, even in the fog, he felt that they had the advantage in any hide-and-seek which might ensue with this superior enemy force. But afloat he was helpless and vulnerable, a state Ross did not accept easily.

"No," Loketh returned as sharply. "There is no place to land along the cliff."

"We are between two of the ships," Karara reported.

"Your paddles —" Ross schooled his voice to a whisper, "hold them-don't use them. Let the dolphins take us on. In the fog, if we make no sound, we may get by the ships."

"Right!" Karara agreed, and he heard an assenting grunt from Loketh.

They were moving very slowly. Strong as the dolphins were, they dared not expend all their strength on towing the skiff too fast. Ross thought furiously. Perhaps the sea could be their way of escape if the need arose. He had no idea why raiding ships were moving under the cover of fog into the vicinity of the Foanna citadel. But the Terran's knowledge of tactics led him to guess that this impending visit was not anticipated by the Foanna, nor was it a friendly one. And, as veteran seamen who should normally be wary of fog as thick as this, the Rovers themselves must have a driving reason, or some safeguard which led them here now.

But dared the three spill out of their boat, trust to their swimming ability and that of the dolphins, and invade the Foanna sea gate so? Could they use the coming Rover attack as a cover for their own invasion of the hold? Ross considered that the odds in their favor were beginning to look better.

He whispered his idea and began to prepare their gear. The boat was still headed for the shore the three could not see. But they could hear sounds out of the white cotton wall which told them how completely they were boxed in by the raiders; creaks, whispers, noises, Ross could not readily identify, carried across the waves.

Before leaving the cave and beginning this voyage they had introduced Loketh to the use of the gill-pack, made him practice in the depths of the cave pool with one of the extras drawn through the gate among the supplies. Now all three were equipped with the water aid, and they could be gone in the sea before the trap closed.

"The supply net —" Ross warned Karara. A moment or two later there was a small bump against the skiff at his left hand. He cautiously raised the collection of containers and eased the burden into the water, knowing that one of the dolphins would take charge of it.

However, he was not prepared for what happened next. Under him the boat lurched first one way and then the other in sharp jerks as if the dolphins were trying to spill them into the sea. Ross heard Karara call out, her voice thin and frightened:

"Taua! Tino-rau! They have gone mad! They will not listen!"

The boat raced in a zigag path. Loketh clutched at Ross, striving to steady him, to keep the boat on an even keel.

"The Foanna —!" Just as Loketh cried out, Karara plunged over the prow of the boat, whether by design or chance Ross did not know.

And then the craft whirled about, smashed side against side with a dark bulk looming out of the fog. Above, Ross heard cries, knew that they had crashed against one of the raiders. He fought to retain his balance, but he had been knocked to the bottom of the boat against Loketh and they struggled together, unable to move during a precious second or two.

Out of the air over their heads dropped a mass of waving strands which enveloped both of them. The stuff was adhesive, slimy. Ross let out a choked cry as the lines tightened about his arms and body, pinioning him.

Those tightened, wove a net. Now he was being drawn up out of the plunging skiff, a helpless captive. His flailing legs, still free of the slimy cords, struck against the side of the larger ship. Then he swung in, over the well of the deck, thudded down on that surface with bruising force, unable to understand anything except that he had been taken prisoner by a very effective device.

Loketh dropped beside him. But Karara was not brought in, and Ross held to that small bit of hope. Had she made it to freedom by dropping into the water before the Rovers netted them? He could see men gathering about him, masked and distorted in the fog. Then he was rolled across the deck, boosted over the edge of a hatch and knew an instant of terror as he fell into the depth below.

How long was he unconscious? It could not have been very long, Ross decided, as he opened his eyes on dark, heard the small sounds of the ship. He lay very still, trying to remember, to gather his wits before he tried to flex his arms. They were held tight to his sides by strands which no longer seemed slimy, but were wrinkling as they dried. There was an odor from them which gagged him. But there was no loosening of those loops in spite of his struggles, which grew more intense as his strength returned. And at last he lay panting, knowing there was no easy way of escape from here.

9. Battle Test

Babble of speech, cries, sounded muffled to Ross, made a mounting clamor on the deck. Had the raiders' ship been boarded? Was it now under attack? He strove to hear and think through the pain in his head, the bewilderment.

"Loketh?" He was certain that the Hawaikan had been dumped into the same hold.

The only answer was a low moan, a mutter from the dark. Ross began to inch his way in that direction. He was no seaman, but during that worm's progress he realized that the ship itself had changed. The vibration which had carried through the planks on which he lay was stilled. Some engine shut off; one portion of his mind put that into familiar terms. Now the vessel rocked with the waves, did not bore through them.

Ross brought up against another body.

"Loketh!"

"Ahhhhh ... the fire ... the fire —!" The half-intelligible answer held no meaning for the Terran. "It burns in my head ... the fire —"

The rocking of the ship rolled Ross away from his fellow prisoner toward the opposite side of the hold. There was a roar of voice, bull strong above the noise on deck, then the sound of feet back and forth there.

"The fire ... ahhh —" Loketh's voice rose to a scream.

Ross was now wedged between two abutments he could not see and from which his best efforts could not free him. The pitching of the ship was more pronounced. Remembering the two vessels he had seen pounded to bits on the reef, Ross wondered if the same doom loomed for this one. But that disaster had occurred during a storm. And, save for the fog, this had been a calm night, the sea untroubled.

Unless-maybe the shaking his body had received during the past few moments had sharpened his thinking-unless the Foanna had their own means of protection at the sea gate and this was the result. The dolphins.... What had made Tino-rau and Taua react as they did? And if the Rover ship was out of control, it would be a good time to attempt escape.

"Loketh!" Ross dared to call louder. "Loketh!" He struggled against the drying strands which bound him from shoulder to mid thigh. There was no give in them.

More sounds from the upper deck. Now the ship was answering to direction again. The Terran heard sounds he could not identify, and the ship no longer rocked so violently. Loketh moaned.

As far as Ross could judge, they were heading out to sea.

"Loketh!" He wanted information; he must have it! To be so ignorant of what was going on was unbearable frustration. If they were now prisoners in a ship leaving the island behind.... The threat of that was enough to set Ross struggling with his bonds until he lay panting with exhaustion.

"Rossss?" Only a Hawaikan could make that name a hiss.

"Here! Loketh?" But of course it was Loketh.

"I am here." The other's voice sounded oddly weak as if it issued from a man drained by a long illness.

"What happened to you?" Ross demanded.

"The fire ... the fire in my head-eating ... eating...." Loketh's reply came with long pauses between the words.

The Terran was puzzled. What fire? Loketh had certainly reacted to something beyond the unceremonious handling they had received as captives. This whole ship had reacted. And the dolphins....But what fire was Loketh talking about?

"I did not feel anything," he stated to himself as well as to the Hawaikan.

"Nothing burning in your head? So you could not think—"

"No."

"It must have been the Foanna magic. Fire eating so that a man is nothing, only that which fire feeds upon!"

Karara! Ross's thoughts flashed back to those few seconds when the dolphins had seemed to go crazy. Karara had then called out something about the Foanna. So the dolphins must have felt this, and Karara, and Loketh. Whatever it was. But why not Ross Murdock?

Karara possessed an extra, undefinable sense which gave her contact with the dolphins. Loketh had a mind which those could read in turn. But such communication was closed to Ross.

At first that realization carried with it a feeling of shame and loss. That he did not have what these others possessed, a subtle power beyond the body, a part of mind, was humbling. Just as he had felt shut out and crippled when he had been forced to use the analyzer instead of the sense the others had, so did he suffer now.

Then Ross laughed shortly. All right, sometimes insensitivity could be a defense as it had at the sea gate. Suppose his lack could also be a weapon? He had not been knocked out as the others appeared to be. But for the bad luck of having been captured before the raiders had succumbed, Ross could, perhaps, have been master of this ship by now. He did not laugh now; he smiled sardonically at his own grandiose reaction. No use thinking about what might have been, just file this fact for future reference.

A creaking overhead heralded the opening of the hatch. Light lanced down into the cubby, and a figure swung over and down a side ladder, coming to stand over Ross, feet apart for balancing, accommodating to the swing of the vessel with the ease of long practice.

Thus Ross came face to face with his first representative of the third party in the Hawaikan tangle of power—a Rover.

The seaman was tall, with a heavier development of shoulder and upper arms than the landsmen. Like the guards he wore supple armor, but this had been colored or overlaid with a pearly hue in which other tints wove opaline lines. His head was bare except for a broad, scaled band running from the nape of his neck to the mid-point of his forehead, a band supporting a sharply serrated crest not unlike the erect fin of some Terran fish.

Now as he stood, fists planted on hips, the Rover presented a formidable figure, and Ross recognized in him the air of command. This must be one of the ship's officers.

Dark eyes surveyed Ross with interest. The light from the deck focused directly across the raider's shoulder to catch the Terran in its full glare, and Ross fought the need for squinting. But he tried to give back stare for stare, confidence for self-confidence.

On Terra in the past more than one adventurer's life had been saved simply because he had the will and nerve enough to face his captors without any display of anxiety. Such bravado might not hold here and now, but it was the only weapon Ross had to hand and he used it.

"You—" the Rover broke the silence first, "you are not of the Foanna—" He paused as if waiting an answer-denial or protest. Ross provided neither.

"No, not of the Foanna, nor of the scum of the coast either." Again a pause.

"So, what manner of fish has come to the net of Torgul?" He called an order aloft. "A rope here! We'll have this fish and its fellow out—"

Loketh and Ross were jerked up to the outer deck, dumped into the midst of a crowd of seamen. The Hawaikan was left to lie but, at a gesture from the officer, Ross was set on his feet. He could see the nature of his bonds now, a network of dull gray strands, shriveled and stinking, but not giving in the least when he made another try at moving his arms.

"Ho —" The officer grinned. "This fish does not like the net! You have teeth, fish. Use them, slash yourself free."

A murmur of applause from the crew answered that mild taunt. Ross thought it time for a countermove.

"I see you do not come too close to those teeth." He used the most defiant words his limited Hawaikan vocabulary offered.

There was a moment of silence, and then the officer clapped his hands together with a sharp explosion of sound.

"You would use your teeth, fish?" he asked and his tone could be a warning.

This was going it blind with a vengeance, but Ross took the next leap in the dark. He had the feeling, which often came to him in tight quarters, that he was being supplied from some hard core of endurance and determination far within him with the right words, the fortunate guess.

"On which one of you?" He drew his lips tight, displaying those same teeth, wondering for one startled moment if he should take the Rover's query literally.

"Vistur! Vistur!" More than one voice called.

One of the crew took a step or two forward. Like Torgul, he was tall and heavy, his over-long arms well muscled. There were scars on his forearms, the seam of one up his jaw. He looked what he was, a very tough fighting man, one who was judged so by peers as seasoned and dangerous.

"Do you choose to prove your words on Vistur, fish?" Again the officer had a formal note in his question, as if this was all part of some ceremony.

"If he meets with me as he stands-no other weapons." Ross flashed back.

Now he had another reaction from them. There were some jeers, a sprinkling of threats as to Vistur's intentions. But Ross caught also the fact that two or three of them had gone silent and were eyeing him in a new and more searching fashion and that Torgul was one of those.

Vistur laughed. "Well said, fish. So shall it be."

Torgul's hand came out, palm up, facing Ross. In its hollow was a small object the Terran could not see clearly. A new weapon? Only the officer made no move to touch it to Ross, the hand merely moved in a series of waves in mid-air. Then the Rover spoke.

"He carries no unlawful magic."

Vistur nodded. "He's no Foanna. And what need have I to fear the spells of any coast crawler? I am Vistur!"

Again the yells of his supporters arose in hearty answer. The statement held more complete and quiet confidence than any wordy boast.

"And I am Ross Murdock!" The Terran matched the Rover tone for tone. "But does a fish swim with its fins bound to its sides? Or does Vistur fear a free fish too greatly to face one?"

His taunt brought the result Ross wanted. The ties were cut from behind, to flutter down as withered, useless strings. Ross flexed his arms. Tight as those thongs had been they had not constricted circulation, and he was ready to meet Vistur. The Terran did not doubt that the Rover champion was a formidable fighter, but he had not had the advantage of going through one of the Agent training courses. Every trick of unarmed fighting known on his own world had been pounded into Ross long ago. His hands and feet could be as deadly weapons as any crook-bladed sword-or gun-provided he could get close enough to use them properly.

Vistur stripped off his weapon belt, put to one side his helmet, showing that under it his hair was plaited into a braid coiled about the crown of his head to provide what must be an extra padding for that strangely narrowed helm. Then he peeled off his armor, peeled it literally indeed, catching the lower edge of the scaled covering with his hands and pulling it up and over his head and shoulders as one might skin off a knitted garment. Now he stood facing Ross, wearing little more than the Terran's swimming trunks.

Ross had dropped his belt and gill-pack. He moved into the circle the crew had made. From above came a strong light, centering from a point on the mainmast and giving him good sight of his opponent.

Vistur was being urged to make a quick end of the reckless challenger, his supporters shouting directions and encouragement. But if the Rover had confidence, he also possessed the more intelligent and valuable trait of caution in the face of the unknown. He outweighed, apparently outmatched Ross, but he did not rush in rashly as his backers wished him to.

They circled, Ross studying every move of the Rover's muscles, every slight fraction of change in the other's balance. There would be something to telegraph an attack from the other. For he intended to fight purely in defense.

The charge came at last as the crew grew impatient and yelled their impatience to see the prisoner taught a lesson. But Ross did not believe it was that which sent Vistur at him. The Hawaikan simply thought he knew the best way to take the Terran.

Ross ducked so that a hammer blow merely grazed him. But the Terran's stiffened hand swept sidewise in a judo chop. Vistur gave a whooping cry and went to his knees and Ross swung again, sending the Rover flat to the deck. It had been quick but not so vicious as it might have been. The Terran had no desire to kill or even disable Vistur for more than a few minutes. His victim would carry a couple of aching bruises and perhaps a hearty respect for a new mode of fighting from this encounter. He could have as easily been dead had either of those blows landed other than where Ross chose to plant them.

"Ahhhh—"

The Terran swung around, setting his back to the foot of the mast. Had he guessed wrong? With their chosen champion down, would the crew now rush him? He had gambled on the element of fair play which existed in a primitive Terran warrior society after a man-to-man challenge. But he could be wrong. Ross waited, tense. Just let one of them pull a weapon, and it could be his end.

Two of them were aiding Vistur to his feet. The Rover's breath whistled in and out of him with that same whooping, and both of his hands rose unsteadily to his chest. The majority of his fellows stared from him to the slighter Terran as if unable to believe the evidence of their eyes.

Torgul gathered up from the deck the belt and gill-pack Ross had shed in preparation for the fight. He turned the belt around over his forearm until the empty knife sheath was uppermost. One of the crew came forward and slammed back into its proper place the long diver's knife which had been there when Ross was captured. Then the Rover offered belt and gill-pack to Ross. The Terran relaxed. His gamble had paid off; by the present signs he had won his freedom.

"And my swordsman?" As he buckled on the belt Ross nodded at Loketh still lying bound where they had pushed him at the beginning of the fight.

"He is sworn to you?" Torgul asked.

"He is."

"Loose the coast rat then," the Rover ordered. "Now—tell me, stranger, what manner of man are you? Do you come from the Foanna, after all? You have a magic which is not our magic, since the Stone of Phutka did not reveal it on you. Are you from the Shades?"

His fingers moved in the same sign Loketh had once made before Karara. Ross gave his chosen explanation.

"I am from the sea, Captain. As for the Foanna, they are no friend to me, since they hold captive in their keep one who is my brother-kin."

Torgul stared him up and down. "You say you are from the sea. I have been a Rover since I was able to stumble on my two feet across a deck, after the manner and custom of my people, yet I have never seen your like before. Perhaps your coming means ill to me and mine, but by the Law of Battle, you have won your freedom on this ship. I swear to you, however, stranger, that if ill comes from you, then the Law will not hold, and you shall match your magic against the Strength of Phutka. That you shall discover is another thing altogether."

"I will swear any oath you desire of me, Captain, that I have no ill toward you and yours. There is only one wish I hold: to bring him whom I seek out from the Foanna hold before they make him witches' meat."

"That will be a task worthy of any magic you may be able to summon, stranger. We have tasted this night of the power of the sea gate. Though we went in under the Will of Phutka, we were as weeds whirled about on the waves. Who enters that gate must have more force than any we now know."

"And you, too, then have a score to settle with the Foanna?"

"We have a score against the Foanna, or against their magic," Torgul admitted. "Three ships-one island fairing-are gone as if they never were! And those who went with them are of our fleet-clan. There is the work of the Shadow stretching dark and heavy across the sea, new come into these waters. But there remains nothing we can do this night. We have been lucky to win to sea again. Now, stranger, what shall we do with you? Or will you take to the sea again since you name it as home?"

"Not here," Ross countered swiftly. He must gain some idea of where they might be in relation to the island, how far from its shore. Karara and the dolphins-what had happened to them?

"You took no other prisoners?" Ross had to ask.

"There were more of you?" Torgul countered.

"Yes." No need to say how many, Ross decided.

"We saw no others. You ...all of you —" the Captain rounded on the still-clustered crew, "get about your work! We must raise Kyn Add by morning and report to the council."

He walked away and Ross, determined to learn all he could, followed him into the stern cabin. Here again the Terran was faced with barbaric splendor in carvings, hangings, a wealth of plate and furnishing not too different from the display he had seen in the Wreckers' castle. As Ross hesitated just within the doorway Torgul glanced back at him.

"You have your life and that of your man, stranger. Do not ask more of me, unless you have that within your hands to enforce the asking."

"I want nothing, save to be returned to where you took me, Captain."

Torgul smiled grimly. "You are the sea, you yourself said that. The sea is wide, but it is all one. Through it you must have your own paths. Take any you choose. But I do not risk my ship again into what lies in wait before the gates of the Foanna."

"Where do you go then, Captain?"

"To Kyn Add. You have your own choice, stranger-the sea or our fairing."

There would be no way of changing the Rover's decision, Ross thought. And even with the gill-pack he could not swim back to where he had been taken. There were no guideposts in the sea. But a longer acquaintance with Torgul might be helpful.

"Kyn Add then, Captain." He made the next move to prove equality and establish himself with this Rover, seating himself at the table as one who had the right to share the Captain's quarters.

10. Death at Kyn Add

The hour was close to dawn again and a need for sleep weighted Ross's eyelids, was a craving as strong as hunger. Still restlessness had brought him on deck, sent him to pacing, alert to this vessel and its crew.

He had seen the ships of the Terran Bronze Age traders-small craft compared to those of his own time, depending upon oarsmen when the wind failed their sails, creeping along coasts rather than venturing too far into dangerous seas, sometimes even tying up at the shore each night. There had been other ships, leaner, hardier. Those had plunged into the unknown, touching lands beyond the sea mists, sailed and oared by men plagued by the need to learn what lay beyond the horizon.

And here was such a ship, taut, well kept, larger than the Viking longboats Ross had watched on the tapes of the Project's collection, yet most like those far-faring Terran craft. The prow curved up in a mighty bowsprit where was the carved likeness of the sea dragon Ross had fought in the Hawaika of his own time. The eyes of that monster flashed with a regular blink of light which the Terran did not understand. Was it a signal or merely a device to threaten a possible enemy?

There were sails, now furled as this ship bored on, answering to the steady throb of what could only be an engine. And his puzzlement held. A Viking longboat powered by motor? The mixture was incongruous.

The crew were uniform as to face. All of them wore the flexible pearly armor, the skull-strip helmets. Though there were individual differences in ornaments and the choice of weapons. The majority of the men did carry curve-pointed swords, though those were broader and heavier than those the Terran had seen ashore. But several had axes with sickle-shaped heads, whose points curved so far back that they nearly met to form a circle.

Spaced at regular intervals on deck were boxlike objects fronting what resembled gun ports. And smaller ones of the same type were on the raised deck at the stern and mounted in the prow, their muzzles, if the square fronts might be deemed muzzles, flanking the blinking dragon head. Catapults of some type? Ross wondered.

"Rosss —" His name was given the hiss Loketh used, but it was not the Wrecker youth who joined him now at the stern of the ship. "Ho ... that was strong magic, that fighting knowledge of yours!"

Vistur rubbed his chest reminiscently. "You have big magic, sea man. But then you serve the Maid, do you not? Your swordsman has told us that even the great fish understand and obey her."

"Some fish," qualified Ross.

"Such fish as that, perhaps?" Vistur pointed to the curling wake of foam.

Startled, Ross stared in that direction. Torgul's command was the centermost in a trio of ships, and those cruised in a line, leaving three trails of troubled wave behind them. Coming up now to port in the comparative calm between two wakes was a dark object. In the limited light Ross could be sure of nothing save that it trailed the ships, appeared to rest on or only lightly in the water, and that its speed was less than that of the vessels it doggedly pursued.

"A fish-that?" Ross asked.

"Watch!" Vistur ordered.

But the Hawaikan's sight must have been keener than the Terran's. Had there been a quick movement back there? Ross could not be sure.

"What happened?" He turned to Vistur for enlightenment.

"As a salkar it leaps now and then above the surface. But that is no salkar. Unless, Ross, you who say you are from the sea have servants unlike any finned one we have drawn in by net or line before this day."

The dolphins! Could Tino-rau or Taua or both be in steady pursuit of the ships? But Karara ... Ross leaned against the rail, stared until his eyes began to water from the strain of trying to make out the nature of the black blot. No use, the distance was too great. He brought his fist down against the wood, trying to control his impatience. More than half of him wanted to burst into Torgul's quarters, demand that the Captain bring the ship about to pick up or contact that trailer or trailers.

"Yours?" again Vistur asked.

Ross had tight rein on himself now. "I do not know. It could well be."

It could well be also that the smart thing would be to encourage the Rovers to believe that he had a force of sea dwellers much larger than the four Time castaways. The leader of an army-or a navy-had more prestige in any truce discussion than a member of a lost scouting party. But the thought that the dolphins could be trailing held both promise and worry-promise of allies, and worry over what had happened to Karara. Had she, too, disappeared after Ashe into the hold of the Foanna?

The day did not continue to lighten. Though there was no cottony mist as had enclosed them the night before, there was an odd muting of sea and sky, limiting vision. Shortly Ross was unable to sight the follower or followers. Even Vistur admitted he had lost visual contact. Had the blot been hopelessly outdistanced, or was it still dogging the wakes of the Rover ships?

Ross shared the morning meal with Captain Torgul, a round of leathery substance with a salty, meaty flavor, and a thick mixture of what might be native fruit reduced to a tart paste. Once before he had tasted alien food when in the derelict spaceship it had meant eat or starve. And this was a like circumstance, since their emergency ration supplies had been lost in the net. But though he was apprehensive, no ill effects followed. Torgul had been uncommunicative earlier; now he was looser of tongue, volunteering that they were almost to their port-the fairing of Kyn Add.

The Terran had no idea how far he might question the Hawaikan, yet the fuller his information the better. He discovered that Torgul appeared willing to accept Ross's statement that he was from a distant part of the sea and that local customs differed from those he knew.

Living on and by the sea the Rovers were quick-witted, adaptive, with a highly flexible if loose-knit organization of fleet-clans. Each of these had control over certain islands which served them as "fairings," ports for refitting and anchorage between voyages, usually ruggedly wooded where the sea people could find the raw material for their ships. Colonies of clans took to the sea, not in the slim, swift cruisers like the ship Ross was now on, but in larger, deeper vessels providing living quarters and warehouses afloat. They lived by trade and raiding, spending only a portion of the year ashore to grow fast-sprouting crops on their fairing islands and indulge in some manufacture of articles the inhabitants of the larger and more heavily populated islands were not able to duplicate.

Their main article of commerce was, however, a sea-dwelling creature whose supple and well-tanned hide formed their defensive armor and served manifold other uses. This could only be hunted by men trained and fearless enough to brave more than one danger Torgul did not explain in detail. And a cargo of such skins brought enough in trade to keep a normal-sized fleet-clan for a year.

There was warfare among them. Rival clans tried to jump each other's hunting territories, raid fairings. But until the immediate past, Ross gathered, such encounters were relatively bloodless affairs, depending more upon craft and skillful planning to reduce the enemy to a position of disadvantage in which he was forced to acknowledge defeat, rather than ruthless battle of no quarter.

The shore-side Wrecker lords were always considered fair game, and there was no finesse in Rover raids upon them. Those were conducted with a cold-blooded determination to strike hard at a long-time foe. However, within the past year there had been several raids on fairings with the same blood-bath result of a foray on a Wrecker port. And, since all the fleet-clans denied the sneak-and-strike, kill-and-destroy tactics which had finished those Rover holdings, the seafarers were divided in their opinion as to whether the murderous raids were the work of Wreckers suddenly acting out of character and taking to the sea to bring war back to their enemies, or whether there was a rogue fleet moving against their own kind for some purpose no Rover could yet guess.

"And you believe?" Ross asked as Torgul finished his résumé of the new dangers besetting his people.

Torgul's hand, its long, slender fingers spidery to Terran eyes, rubbed back and forth across his chin before he answered:

"It is very hard for one who has fought them long to believe that suddenly those shore rats are entrusting themselves to the waves, venturing out to stir us with their swords. One does not descend into the depths to kick a salkar in the rump; not if one still has his wits safely encased under his skull braid. As for a rogue fleet ... what would turn brother against brother to the extent of slaying children and women? Raiding for a wife, yes, that is common among our youth. And there have been killings over such matters. But not the killing of a woman-never of a child!

We are a people who have never as many women as there are men who wish to bring them into the home cabin. And no clan has as many children as they hope the Shades will send them."

"Then who?"

When Torgul did not answer at once Ross glanced at the Captain, and what the Terran thought he saw showing for an instant in the other's eyes was a revelation of danger. So much so that he blurted out:

"You think that I —we —"

"You have named yourself of the sea, stranger, and you have magic which is not ours. Tell me this in truth: Could you not have killed Vistur easily with those two blows if you had wished it?"

Ross took the bold course. "Yes, but I did not. My people kill no more wantonly than yours."

"The coast rats I know, and the Foanna, as well as any man may know their kind and ways, and my people-But you I do not know, sea stranger. And I say to you as I have said before, make me regret that I suffered you to claim battle rights and I shall speedily correct that mistake!"

"Captain!"

That cry had come from the cabin door behind Ross. Torgul was on his feet with the swift movements of a man called many times in the past for an instant response to emergency.

The Terran was close on the Rover's heels as they reached the deck. A cluster of crewmen gathered on the port side near the narrow bow. That odd misty quality this day held provided a murk hard to pierce, but the men were gesturing at a low-riding object rolling with the waves.

That was near enough for even Ross to be able to distinguish a small boat akin to the one in which he, Karara, and Loketh had dared the sea gate of the Foanna.

Torgul took up a great curved shell hanging by a thong on the mainmast. Setting its narrow end to his lips, he blew. A weird booming note, like the coughing of a sea monster, carried over the waves. But there was no answer from the drifting boat, no sign it carried any passengers.

"Hou, hou, hou —" Torgul's signal was re-echoed by shell calls from the other two cruisers.

"Heave to!" the Captain ordered. "Wakti, Zimmon, Yoana-out and bring that in!"

Three of the crew leaped to the railing, poised there for a moment, and then dived almost as one into the water. A rope end was thrown, caught by one of them. And then they swam with powerful strokes toward the drifting boat. Once the rope was made fast the small craft was drawn toward Torgul's command, the crewmen swimming beside it. Ross longed to know the reason for the tense expectancy of the men around him. It was apparent the skiff had some ominous meaning for them.

Ross caught a glimpse of a body huddled within the craft. Under Torgul's orders a sling was dropped, to rise, weighted with a passenger. The Terran was shouldered back from the rail as the limp body was hurried into the Captain's cabin. Several crewmen slid down to make an examination of the boat itself.

Their heads came up, their eyes searched along the rail and centered on Ross. The hostility was so open the Terran braced himself to meet those cold stares as he would a rush from a challenger.

A slight sound behind sent Ross leaping to the right, wanting to get his back against solid protection. Loketh came up, his limp making him awkward so that he clutched at the rail for support. In his other hand was one of the hooked swords bared and ready.

"Get the murderers!" Someone in the back line of the massing crew yipped that.

Ross drew his diver's knife. Shaken at this sudden change in the crew's attitude, he was warily on the defensive. Loketh was beside him now and the Hawaikan nodded to the sea.

"Better go there," he cried. "Over before they try to gut you!"

"Kill!" The word shrilled into a roar from the Rovers. They started up the deck toward Ross and Loketh. Then someone leaped between, and Vistur fronted his own comrades.

"Stand away —" One of the others ran forward, thrusting at the tall Rover with a stiffened out-held arm to fend him out of their path.

Vistur rolled a shoulder, sending the fellow shunting away. He went down while two more, unable to halt, thudded on him. Vistur stamped on an outstretched hand and sent a sword spinning.

"What goes here!" Torgul's demand was loud enough to be heard. It stopped a few of the crew and two more went down as the Captain struck out with his fists. Then he was facing Ross, and the chill in his eyes was the threat the others had voiced.

"I told you, sea stranger, that if I found you were a danger to me or mine, you would meet the Justice of Phutka!"

"You did," Ross returned. "And in what way am I now a danger, Captain?"

"Kyn Add has been taken by those who are not Wreckers, not Rovers, not those who serve the Foanna-but strangers out of the sea!"

Ross could only stare back, confused. And then the full force of his danger struck home. Who those raiding sea strangers could be, he had no idea, but that he was now condemned out of his own mouth was true and he realized that these men were not going to listen to any argument from him in their present state of mind.

The growl of the crew was that of a hungry animal. Ross saw the wisdom in Loketh's choice. Far better chance the open sea than the mob before them.

But his time for choice had passed. Out of nowhere whirled a lacy gray-white net, slapping him back against a bulkhead to glue him there. Ross tried to twist loose, got his head around in time to see Loketh scramble to the top of the rail, turn as if to launch himself at the men speeding for the now helpless Terran. But the Hawaikan's crippled leg failed him and he toppled back overside.

"No!" Again Torgul's shout halted the crew. "He shall take the Black Curse with him when he goes to meet the Shadow-and only one can speak that curse. Bring him!"

Helpless, reeling under their blows, dragged along, Ross was thrown into the Captain's cabin, confronted by a figure braced up by coverings and cushions in Torgul's own chair.

A woman, her face a drawn death's head of skin pulled tight upon bone, yet a fiery inner strength holding her mind above the suffering of her body, looked at the Terran with narrowed eyes. She nursed a bandaged arm against her, and now and then her mouth quivered as if she could not altogether control some emotion or physical pain.

"Yours is the cursing, Lady Jazia. Make it heavy to bear for him as his kind has laid the burden of pain and remembering on all of us."

She brought her good hand up to her mouth, wiping its back across her lips as if to temper their quiver. And all the time her eyes held upon Ross.

"Why do you bring me this man?" Her voice was strained, high. "He is not of those who brought the Shadow to Kyn Add."

"What —?" Torgul began and then schooled his voice to a more normal tone. "Those were from the sea?" He was gentle in his questioning. "They came out of the sea, using weapons against which we had no defense?"

She nodded. "Yes, they made very sure that only the dead remained. But I had gone to the Shrine of Phutka, since it was my day of duty, and Phutka's power threw its shade over me. So I did not die, but I saw-yes, I saw!"

"Not those like me?" Ross dared to speak to her directly.

"No, not those like you. There were few ... only so many —" She spread out her five fingers. "And they were all of one like as if born in one birth. They had no hair on their heads, and their bodies were of this hue —" She plucked at one of the coverings they had heaped around her; it was a lavender-blue mixture.

Ross sucked in his breath, and Torgul was fast to pounce upon the understanding he read in the Terran's face.

"Not your kind-but still you know them!"

"I know them," Ross agreed. "They are the enemy!"

The Baldies from the ancient spaceships, that wholly alien race with whom he had once fought a desperate encounter on the edge of an unnamed sea in the far past of his own world. The galactic voyagers were here-and in active, if secret, conflict with the natives!

11. Weapon from the Depths

Jazia told her story with an attention to time and detail which amazed Ross and won his admiration for her breed. She had witnessed the death and destruction of all which was her life, and yet she had the wit to note and record mentally for possible future use all that she had been able to see of the raiders.

They had come out of the sea at dawn, walking with supreme confidence and lack of any fear. Axes flung when they did not reply to the sentries' challenges had never touched them, and a bombardment of heavier missiles had been turned aside. They proved invulnerable to any weapon the Rovers had. Men who made suicidal rushes to use sword or battle ax hand-to-hand had fallen, before they were in striking distance, under spraying tongues of fire from tubes the aliens carried.

Rovers were not fearful or easily cowed, but in the end they had fled from the five invaders, gone to ground in their halls, tried to reach their beached ships, only to die as they ran and hid. The slaughter had been remorseless and entire, leaving Jazia in the hill shrine as the only survivor. She had hidden for the rest of the day, seen the killing of a few fugitives, and that night had stolen to the shore, launched one of the ship's boats which was in a cove well away from the main harbor of the fairing, heading out to sea in hope of meeting the homing cruisers with her warning.

"They stayed there on the island?" Ross asked. That point of her story puzzled him. If the object of that murderous raid had been only to stir up trouble among the Hawaikan Rovers, perhaps turning one clan against the other, as he had deduced when he had listened to Torgul's report of similar happenings, then the star men should have withdrawn as soon as their mission was complete, leaving the dead to call for vengeance in the wrong direction. There would be no reason to court discovery of their true identity by lingering.

"When the boat was asea there were still lights at the fairing hall, and they were not our lights, nor did the dead carry them," she said slowly. "What have those to fear? They can not be killed!"

"If they are still there, that we can put to the test," Torgul replied grimly, and a murmur from his officers bore out his determination.

"And lose all the rest of you?" Ross retorted coldly. "I have met these before; they can will a man to obey them. Look you —" He slammed his left hand flat on the table. The ridges of scar tissue were plain against his tanned skin. He knew no better way of driving home the dangers of dealing with the star men than providing this graphic example. "I held my own hand in fire so that the hurt of it would work against their pull upon my thoughts, against their willing that I come and be easy meat for their butchering."

Jazia's fingers flickered out, smoothed across his old scars lightly as she gazed into his eyes.

"This, too, is true," she said slowly. "For it was also pain of body which kept me from their last snare. They stood by the hall and I saw Prahad, Okun, Mosaji, come out to them to be killed as if they were in a hold net and were drawn. And there was that which called me also so that I would go to them though I called upon the Power of Phutka to save. And the answer to that plea came in a strange way, for I fell as I went from the shrine and cut my arm on the rocks. The pain of that hurt was as a knife severing the net. Then I crawled for the wood and that calling did not come again —"

"If you know so much about them, tell us what weapons we may use to pull them down!" That demand came from Vistur.

Ross shook his head. "I do not know."

"Yet," Jazia mused, "all things which live must also die sooner or later. And it is in my mind that these have also a fate they dread and fear. Perhaps we may find and use it."

"They came from the sea-by a ship, then?" Ross asked. She shook her head.

"No, there was no ship; they came walking through the breaking waves as if they had followed some road across the sea bottom."

"A sub!"

"What is that?" Torgul demanded.

"A type of ship which goes under the waves, not through them, carrying air within its hull for the breathing of the crew."

Torgul's eyes narrowed. One of the other captains who had been summoned from the two companion cruisers gave a snort of disbelief.

"There are no such ships —" he began, to be silenced by a gesture from Torgul.

"We know of no such ships," the other corrected. "But then we know of no such devices as Jazia saw in operation either. How does one war upon these under-the-seas ships, Ross?"

The Terran hesitated. To describe to men who knew nothing of explosives the classic way of dealing with a sub via depth charges was close to impossible. But he did his best.

"Among my people one imprisons in a container a great power. Then the container is dropped near the sub and —"

"And how," broke in the skeptical captain, "do you know where such a ship lies? Can you see it through the water?"

"In a way-not see, but hear. There is a machine which makes for the captain of the above-seas ship a picture of where the sub lies or moves so that he may follow its course. Then when he is near enough he drops the container and the power breaks free-to also break apart the sub."

"Yet the making of such containers and the imprisoning of the power within them," Torgul said, "this is the result of a knowledge which is greater than any save the Foanna may possess. You do not have it?" His conclusion was half statement, half question.

"No. It took many years and the combined knowledge of many men among my people to make such containers, such a listening device. I do not have it."

"Why then think of what we do not have?" Torgul's return was decisive. "What *do* we have?"

Ross's head came up. He was listening, not to anything in that cabin, but to a sound which had come through the port just behind his head. There-it had come again! He was on his feet.

"What —?" Vistur's hand hovered over the ax at his belt. Ross saw their gaze centered on him.

"We may have reinforcements now!" The Terran was already on his way to the deck.

He hurried to the rail and whistled, the thin, shrill summons he had practiced for weeks before he had ever begun this fantastic adventure.

A sleek dark body broke water and the dolphin grin was exposed as Tino-rau answered his call. Though Ross's communication powers with the two finned scouts was very far from Karara's, he caught the message in part and swung around to face the Rovers who had crowded after him.

"We have a way now of learning more about your enemies."

"A boat-it comes without sail or oars!" One of the crew pointed.

Ross waved vigorously, but no hand replied from the skiff. Though it came steadily onward, the three cruisers its apparent goal.

"Karara!" Ross called.

Then side by side with Tino-rau were two wet heads, two masked faces showing as the swimmers trod water-Karara and Loketh.

"Drop ropes!" Ross gave that order as if he rather than Torgul commanded. And the Captain himself was one of those who moved to obey.

Loketh came out of the sea first and as he scrambled over the rail he had his sword ready, looking from Ross to Torgul. The Terran held up empty hands and smiled.

"No trouble now."

Loketh snapped up his mask. "So the Sea Maid said the finned ones reported. Yet before, these thirsted for your blood on their blades. What magic have you worked?"

"None. Just the truth has been discovered." Ross reached for Karara's hand as she came nimbly up the rope, swung her across the rail to the deck where she stood unmasked, brushing back her hair and looking around with a lively curiosity.

"Karara, this is Captain Torgul," Ross introduced the Rover commander who was staring round-eyed at the girl. "Karara is she who swims with the finned ones, and they obey her." Ross gestured to Tino-rau. "It is Taua who brings the skiff?" he asked the Polynesian.

She nodded. "We followed from the gate. Then Loketh came and said that ... that...." She paused and then added, "But you do not seem to be in danger. What has happened?"

"Much. Listen-this is important. There is trouble at an island ahead. The Baldies were there; they murdered the kin of these men. The odds are they reached there by some form of sub. Send one of the dolphins to see what is happening and if they are still there...."

Karara asked no more questions, but whistled to the dolphin. With a flip of tail Tino-rau took off.

Since they could make no concrete plan of action, the cruiser captains agreed to wait for Tino-rau's report and to cruise well out of sight of the fairing harbor until it came.

"This belief in magic," Ross remarked to Karara, "has one advantage. The natives seem able to take in their stride the fact the dolphins will scout for us."

"They have lived their lives on the sea; for it they must have a vast respect. Perhaps they know, as did my people, that the ocean has many secrets, some of which are never revealed except to the forms of life which claim their homes there. But, even if you discover this Baldy sub, what will the Rovers be able to do about it?"

"I don't know-yet." Ross could not tell why he clung to the idea that they could do anything to strike back at the superior alien force. He only knew that he was not yet willing to relinquish the thought that in some way they could.

"And Ashe?"

Yes, Ashe....

"I don't know." It hurt Ross to admit that.

"Back there, what really happened at the gate?" he asked Karara. "All at once the dolphins seemed to go crazy."

"I think for a moment or two they did. You felt nothing?"

"No."

"It was like a fire slashing through the head. Some protective device of the Foanna, I think."

A mental defense to which he was not sensitive. Which meant that he might be able to breach that gate if none of the others could. But he had to be there first. Suppose, just suppose Torgul could be persuaded that this attack on the gutted Kyn Add was useless. Would the Rover commander take them back to the Foanna keep? Or with the dolphins and the skiff could Ross himself return to make the try?

That he could make it on his own, Ross doubted. Excitement and will power had buoyed him up throughout the past Hawaikan day and night. Now fatigue closed in, past his conditioning and the built-in stimulant of the Terran rations, to enclose him in a groggy haze. He had been warned against this reaction, but that was just another item he had pushed out of his conscious mind. The last thing he remembered now was seeing Karara move through a fuzzy cloud.

Voices argued somewhere beyond, the force of that argument carried more by tone than any words Ross could understand. He was pulled sluggishly out of a slumber too deep for any dream to trouble, and lifted heavy eyelids to see Karara once again. There was a prick in his arm-or was that part of the unreality about him?

" —four-five-six —" she was counting, and Ross found himself joining in:

" —seven-eight-nine-ten!"

On reaching "ten" he was fully awake and knew that she had applied the emergency procedure they had been drilled in using, giving him a pep shot. When Ross sat up on the narrow bunk there was a light in the cabin and no sign of day outside the porthole. Torgul, Vistur, the two other cruiser captains, all there … and Jazia.

Ross swung his feet to the deck. A pep-shot headache was already beginning, but would wear off soon. There was, however, a concentration of tension in the cabin, and something must have driven Karara to use the drug.

"What is it?"

Karara fitted the medical kit into the compact carrying case.

"Tino-rau has returned. There *is* a sub in the bay. It emits energy waves on a shoreward beam."

"Then they are still there." Ross accepted the dolphin's report without question. Neither of the scouts would make a mistake in those matters. Energy waves beamed shoreward-power for some type of unit the Baldies were using? Suppose the Rovers could find a way of cutting off the power.

"The Sea Maid has told us that this ship sits on the bottom of the harbor. If we could board it —" began Torgul.

"Yes!" Vistur brought his fist down against the end of the bunk on which the Terran still sat, jarring the dull, drug-borne pain in Ross's head. "Take it-then turn it against its crew!"

There was an eagerness in all Rover faces. For that was a game the Hawaikan seafarers understood: Take an enemy ship and turn its armament against its companions in a fleet. But that plan would not work out. Ross had a healthy respect for the technical knowledge of the galactic invaders. Of course he, Karara, even Loketh might be able to reach the sub. Whether they could then board her was an entirely different matter.

Now the Polynesian girl shook her head. "The broadcast there-Tino-rau rates it as lethal. There are dead fish floating in the bay. He had warning at the reef entrance. Without a shield, there will be no way of getting in."

"Might as well wish for a depth bomb," Ross began and then stopped.

"You have thought of something?"

"A shield —" Ross repeated her words. It was so wild this thought of his, and one which might have no chance of working. He knew almost nothing about the resources of the invaders. Could that broadcast which protected the sub and perhaps activated the weapons of the invaders ashore be destroyed? A wall of fish-sea life herded in there as a shield … wild, yes, even so wild it might work. Ross outlined the idea, speaking more to Karara than to the Rovers.

"I do not know," she said doubtfully. "That would need many fish, too many to herd and drive — —"

"Not fish," Torgul cut in, "salkars!"

"Salkars?"

"You have seen the bow carving on this ship. That is a salkar. Such are larger than a hundred fish! Salkars driven in … they might even wreck this undersea ship with their weight and anger."

"And you can find these salkars near-by?" Ross began to take fire. That dragon which had hunted him-the bulk of the thing was well above any other sea life he had seen here. And to its ferocity he could give testimony.

"At the spawning reefs. We do not hunt at this season which is the time of the taking of mates. Now, too, they are easily angered so they will even attack a cruiser. To slay them at present is a loss, for their skins are not good. But they would be ripe for battle were they to be disturbed."

"And how would you get them from the spawning reefs to Kyn Add?"

"That is not too difficult; the reef lies here." Torgul drew lines with the point of his sword on the table top. "And here is Kyn Add. Salkars have a great hunger at this time. Show them bait and they will follow; especially will they follow swimming bait."

There were a great many holes in the plan which had only a halfway chance of working. But the Rovers seized upon it with enthusiasm, and so it was set up.

Perhaps some two hours later Ross swam toward the land mass of Kyn Add. Gleams of light pricked on the shore well to his left. Those must mark the Rover settlement. And again the Terran wondered why the invaders had remained there. Unless they knew that there had been three cruisers out on a raid and for some reason they were determined to make a complete mop-up.

Karara moved a little to his right, Taua between them, the dolphin's super senses their guide and warning. The swiftest of the cruisers had departed, Loketh on board to communicate with Tino-rau in the water. Since the male dolphin was the best equipped to provide a fox for salkar hounds, he was the bait for this weird fishing expedition.

"No farther!" Ross's sonic pricked a warning against his body. Through that he took a jolt which sent him back, away from the bay entrance.

"On the reef." Karara's tapped code drew him on a new course. Moments later they were both out of the water, though the wash of waves over their flippered feet was constant. The rocks among which they crouched were a rough harborage from which they could see the shore as a dark blot. But they were well away from the break in the reef through which, if their outlandish plan succeeded, the salkars would come.

"A one-in-a-million chance!" Ross commented as he put up his mask.

"Was not the whole Time Agent project founded on just such chances?" Karara asked the right question. This was Ross's kind of venture. Yes, one-in-a-million chances had been pulled off by the Time Agents. Why, it had been close to those odds against their ever finding what they had first sought along the back trails of time-the wrecked spaceships.

Just suppose this could be a rehearsal for another attack? If the salkars could be made to crack the guard of the Baldies, could they also be used against the Foanna gate? Maybe....But take one fight at a time.

"They come!" Karara's fingers gripped Ross's shoulder. Her hand was hard, bar rigid. He could see nothing, hear nothing. That warning must have come from the dolphins. But so far their plan was working; the monsters of the Hawaikan sea were on their way.

12. Baldies

"Ohhhh!" Karara clutched at Ross, her breath coming in little gasps, giving vent to her fear and horror. They had not known what might come from this plan; certainly neither had foreseen the present chaos in the lagoon.

Perhaps the broadcast energy of the enemy whipped the already vicious-tempered salkars into this insane fury. But now the moonlit water was beaten into foam as the creatures fought there, attacking each other with a ferocity neither Terran had witnessed before.

Lights gleamed along the shore where the alien invaders must have been drawn by the clamor of the fighting marine reptiles. Somewhere in the heights above the beach of the lagoon a picked band of Rovers should now be making their way from the opposite side of Kyn Add under strict orders not to go into attack unless signaled. Whether the independent sea warriors would hold to that command was a question which had worried Ross from the first.

Tino-rau and Taua in the waters to the seaward of the reef, the two Terrans on that barrier itself, and between them and the shore the wild melee of maddened salkars. Ross started. The sonic warning which had been pulsing steadily against his skin cut off sharply. The broadcast in the bay had been silenced! This was the time to move, but no swimmer could last in the lagoon itself.

"Along the reef," Karara said.

That would be the long way round, Ross knew, but the only one possible. He studied the cluster of lights ashore. Two or three figures moved there. Seemingly the attention of the aliens was well centered upon the battle still in progress in the lagoon.

"Stay here!" he ordered the girl. Adjusting his mask, Ross dropped into the water, cutting away from the reef and then turning to swim parallel with it. Tino-rau matched him as he went, guiding Ross to a second break in the reef, toward the shore some distance from where the conflict of the salkars still made a hideous din in the night.

The Terran waded in the shallows, stripping off his flippers and snapping them to his belt, letting his mask swing free on his chest. He angled toward the beach where the aliens had been. At least he was better armed for this than he had been when he had fronted the Rovers with only a diver's knife. From the Time Agent supplies he had taken the single hand weapon he had long ago found in the armory of the derelict spaceship. This could only be used sparingly, since they did not know how it could be recharged, and the secret of its beam still remained secret as far as Terran technicians were concerned.

Ross worked his way to a curtain of underbrush from which he had a free view of the beach and the aliens. Three of them he counted, and they were Baldies, all right-taller and thinner than his own species, their bald heads gray-white, the upper dome of their skulls overshadowing the features on their pointed chinned faces. They all wore the skintight blue-purple-green suits of the space voyagers-suits which Ross knew of old were insulated and protective for their wearers, as well as a medium for keeping in touch with one another. Just as he, wearing one, had once been trailed over miles of wilderness.

To him, all three of the invaders looked enough alike to have been stamped out from one pattern. And their movements suggested that they worked or went into action with drilled precision. They all faced seaward, holding tubes aimed at the salkar-infested lagoon. There was no sound of any explosion, but green spears of light struck at the scaled bodies plunging in the water. And where those beams struck, flesh seared. Methodically the trio raked the basin. But, Ross noted, those beams which had been steady at his first sighting, were now interrupted by flickers. One of the Baldies upended his tube, rapped its butt against a rock as if trying to correct a jamming. When the alien went into action once again his weapon flashed and failed. Within a matter of moments the other two were also finished. The lighted rods pushed into the sand, giving a glow to the scene, darkened as a fire might sink to embers. Power fading?

An ungainly shape floundered out of the churned water, lumbered over the shale of the beach, its supple neck outstretched, its horned nose down for a gore-threatening charge. Ross had not realized that the salkars could operate out of what he thought was their natural element, but this wild-eyed dragon was plainly bent on reaching its tormentors.

For a moment or two the Baldies continued to front the creature, almost, Ross thought, as if they could not believe that their weapons had failed them. Then they broke and ran back to the fairing which they had taken with such contemptuous ease. The salkar plowed along in their wake, but its movements grew more labored the farther it advanced, until at last it lay with only its head upraised, darting it back and forth, its fanged jaws well agape, voicing a coughing howl.

Its plaint was answered from the water as a second of its kind wallowed ashore. A terrible wound had torn skin and flesh just behind its neck; yet still it came on, hissing and bubbling a battle challenge. It did not attack its fellow; instead it dragged its bulk past the first comer, on its way after the Baldies.

The salkars continued to come ashore, two more, a third, a fourth, mangled and torn-pulling themselves as far as they could up the beach. To lie, facing inland, their necks weaving, their horned heads bobbing, their cries a frightful din. What had drawn them out of their preoccupation of battle among themselves into this attempt to reach the aliens, Ross could not determine. Unless the intelligence of the beasts was such that they had been able to connect the searing beams which the Baldies had turned on them so tellingly with the men on the beach, and had responded by striving to reach a common enemy.

But no desire could give them the necessary energy to pull far ashore. Almost helplessly beached, they continued to dig into the yielding sand with their flippers in a vain effort to pursue the aliens.

Ross skirted the clamoring barrier of salkars and headed for the fairing. A neck snapped about; a head was lowered in his direction. He smelled the rank stench of reptile combined with burned flesh. The nearest of the brutes must have scented the Terran in turn, as it was now trying vainly to edge around to cut across Ross's path. But it was completely outclassed on land, and the man dodged it easily.

Three Baldies had fled this way. Yet Jazia had reported five had come out of the sea to take Kyn Add. Two were missing. Where? Had they remained in the fairing? Were they now in the sub? And that sub-what had happened to it? The broadcast had been cut off; he had seen the failure of the weapons and the shore lights. Might the sub have suffered from salkar attack? Though Ross could hardly believe that the beasts could wreck it.

The Terran was traveling blindly, keeping well under cover of such brush as he could, knowing only that he must head inland. Under his feet the ground was rising, and he recalled the nature of this territory as Torgul and Jazia had pictured it for him. This had to be part of the ridge wall of the valley in which lay the buildings of the fairing. In these heights was the Shrine of Phutka where Jazia had hidden out. To the west now lay the Rover village, so he had to work his way left, downhill, in order to reach the hole where the Baldies had gone to ground. Ross made that progress with the stealth of a trained scout.

Hawaika's moon, triple in size to Terra's companion, was up, and the landscape was sharply clear, with shadows well defined. The glow, weird to Terran eyes, added to the effect of being abroad in a nightmare, and the bellowing of the grounded salkars continued a devils' chorus.

When the Rovers had put up the buildings of their fairing, they had cleared a series of small fields radiating outward from those structures. All of these were now covered with crops almost ready to harvest. The grain, if that Terran term could be applied to this Hawaikan product, was housed in long pods which dipped from shoulder-high bushes. And the pods were well equipped with horny projections which tore. A single try at making his way into one of those fields convinced Ross of the folly of such an advance. He sat back to nurse his scratched hands and survey the landscape.

To go down a very tempting lane would be making himself a clear target for anyone in those buildings ahead. He had seen the flamers of the Baldies fail on the beach, but that did not mean the aliens were now weaponless.

His best chance, Ross decided, was to circle north, come back down along the bed of a stream. And he was at the edge of that watercourse when a faint sound brought him to a frozen halt, weapon ready.

"Rosss —"

"Loketh!"

"And Torgul and Vistur."

This was the party from the opposite side of the island, gone expertly to earth. In the moonlight Ross could detect no sign of their presence, yet their voices sounded almost beside him.

"They are in there, in the great hall." That was Torgul. "But no longer are there any lights."

"Now —" An urgent exclamation drew their attention.

Light below. But not the glow of the rods Ross had seen on the beach. This was the warm yellow-red of honest fire, bursting up, the flames growing higher as if being fed with frantic haste.

Three figures were moving down there. Ross began to believe that there were only this trio ashore. He could sight no weapons in their hands, which did not necessarily mean they were unarmed. But the stream ran close behind the rear wall of one of the buildings, and Ross thought its bed could provide cover for a man who knew what he was doing. He pointed out as much to Torgul.

"And if their magic works and you are drawn out to be killed?" The Rover captain came directly to the point.

"That is a chance to be taken. But remember ... the magic of the Foanna at the sea gate did not work against me. Perhaps this won't either. Once, earlier, I won against it."

"Have you then another hand to give to the fire as your defense?" That was Vistur. "But no man has the right to order another's battle challenge."

"Just so," returned Ross sharply. "And this is a thing I have long been trained to do."

He slid down into the stream bed. Approaching from this angle, the structures of the fairing were between him and the fire. So screened he reached a log wall, got to his feet, and edged along it. Then he witnessed a wild scene. The fire raged in great, sky-touching tongues. And already the roof of one of the Rover buildings smoldered. Why the aliens had built up such a conflagration, Ross could not guess. A signal designed to reach some distance?

He did not doubt there was some urgent purpose. For the three were dragging in fuel with almost frenzied haste, bringing out of the Rover buildings bales of cloth to be ripped apart and whirled into the devouring flames, furniture, everything movable which would burn.

There was one satisfaction. The Baldies were so intent upon this destruction that they kept no watch save that now and then one of them would run to the head of the path leading to the lagoon and listen as if he expected a salkar to come pounding up the slope.

"They're ... they're rattled!" Ross could hardly believe it. The Baldies who had always occupied his mind and memory as practically invincible supermen were acting like badly frightened primitives! And when the enemy was so off balance you pushed-you pushed hard.

Ross thumbed the button on the grip of the strange weapon. He sighted with deliberation and fired. The blue figure at the top of the path wilted, and for a long moment neither of his companions noted his collapse. Then one of them whirled and started for the limp body, his colleague running after him. Ross allowed them to reach his first victim before he fired the second and third time.

All three lay quiet, but still Ross did not venture forth until he had counted off a dozen Terran seconds. Then he slipped forward keeping to cover until he came up to the bodies.

The blue-clad shoulder had a flaccid feel under his hand as if the muscles could not control the flesh about them. Ross rolled the alien over, looked down in the bright light of the fire into the Baldy's wide-open eyes. Amazement-the Terran thought he could read that in the dead stare which answered his intent gaze-and then anger, a cold and deadly anger which chilled into ice.

"Kill!"

Ross slewed around, still down on one knee, to face the charge of a Rover. In the firelight the Hawaikan's eyes were blazing with fanatical hatred. He had his hooked sword ready to deliver a finishing stroke. The Terran blocked with a shoulder to meet the Rover's knees, threw him back. Then Ross landed on top of the fighting crewman, trying to pin the fellow to earth and avoid that recklessly slashing blade.

"Loketh! Vistur!" Ross shouted as he struggled.

More of the Rovers appeared from between the buildings, bearing down on the limp aliens and the two fighting men. Ross recognized the limping gait of Loketh using a branch to aid him into a running scuttle across the open.

"Loketh-here!"

The Hawaikan covered the last few feet in a dive which carried him into Ross and the Rover. "Hold him," the Terran ordered and had just time enough to throw himself between the Baldies and the rest of the crew. There was a snarling from the Rovers; and Ross, knowing their temper, was afraid he could not save the captives which they considered, fairly, their legitimate prey. He must depend upon the hope that there were one or two cooler heads among them with enough authority to restrain the would-be avengers. Otherwise he would have to beam them into helplessness.

"Torgul!" he shouted.

There was a break in the line of runners speeding for him. The big man lunging straight across could only be Vistur; the other, yelling orders, was Torgul. It would depend upon how much control the Captain had over his men. Ross scrambled to his feet. He had clicked on the beamer to its lowest frequency. It would not kill, but would render its victim temporarily paralyzed; and how long that state would continue Ross had no way of knowing. Tried on Terran laboratory animals, the time had varied from days to weeks.

Vistur used the flat side of his war ax, clapping it against the foremost runners, setting his own bulk to impose a barrier. And now Torgul's orders appeared to be getting through, more and more of the men slacked, leaving a trio of hotheads, two of whom Vistur sent reeling with his fists.

The Captain came up to Ross. "They are alive then?" He leaned over to inspect the Baldy the Terran had rolled on his back, assessing the alien's frozen stare with thoughtful measurement.

"Yes, but they can not move."

"Well enough." Torgul nodded. "They shall meet the Justice of Phutka after the Law. I think they will wish that they had been left to the boarding axes of angry men."

"They are worth more alive than dead, Captain. Do you not wish to know why they have carried war to your people, how many of them there may yet be to attack-and other things? Also —" Ross nodded at the fire now catching the second building, "why have they built up that blaze? Is it a signal to others of their kind?"

"Very well said. Yes, it would be well for us to learn such things. Nor will Phutka be jealous of the time we take to ask questions and get answers, many answers." He prodded the Baldy with the toe of his sea boot.

"How long will they remain so? Your magic has a bite in it."

Ross smiled. "Not my magic, Captain. This weapon was taken from one of their own ships. As to how long they will remain so-that I do not know."

"Very well, we can take precautions." Under Torgul's orders the aliens were draped with capture nets like those Ross and Loketh had worn. The sea-grown plant adhered instantly, wet strands knitting in perfect restrainers as long as it was uncut.

Having seen to that, Torgul ordered the excavation of Kyn Add.

"As you say," he remarked to Ross, "that fire may well be a signal to bring down more of their kind. I think we have had the Favor of Phutka in this matter, but the prudent man stretches no favor of that kind too far. Also," he looked about him —"we have given to Phutka and the Shades our dead; there is nothing for us here now but hate and sorrow. In one day we have been broken from a clan of pride and ships to a handful of standardless men."

"You will join some other clan?" Karara had come with Jazia to stand on the stone ledge chipped to form a base for a column bearing a strange, brooding-eyed head looking seaward. The Rover woman was superintending the freeing of the head from the column.

At the Terran girl's question the Captain gazed down into the dreadful chaos of the valley. They could yet hear the roars of the dying salkars. The reptiles that had made their way to land had not withdrawn but still lay, some dead now, some with weaving heads reaching inland. And the whole of the fairing was ablaze with fire.

"We are now blood-sworn men, Sea Maid. For such there is no clan. There is only the hunting and the kill. With the magic of Phutka perhaps we shall have a short hunt and a good kill."

"There ... now ... so...." Jazia stepped back. The head which had faced the sea was lowered carefully to a wide strip of crimson-and-gold stuff she had brought from Torgul's ship. With her one usable hand the Rover woman drew the fabric about the carving, muffling it except for the eyes. Those were large ovals deeply carved, and in them Ross saw a glitter. Jewels set there? Yet, he had a queer, shivery feeling that something more than gems occupied those sockets-that he had actually been regarded for an instant of time, assessed and dismissed.

"We go now." Jazia waved and Torgul sent men forward. They lifted the wrapped carving to a board carried between them and started downslope.

Karara cried out and Ross looked around.

The pillar which had supported the head was crumbling away, breaking into a rubble which cascaded across the stone ledge. Ross blinked-this must be an illusion, but he was too tired to be more than dully amazed as he became one of the procession returning to the ships.

13. The Sea Gate of the Foanna

Ross raised a shell cup to his lips but hardly sipped the fiery brew it contained. This was a gesture of ceremony, but he wanted a steady head and a quick tongue for any coming argument. Torgul, Afrukta, Ongal-the three commanders of the Rover cruisers; Jazia, who represented the mysterious Power of Phutka; Vistur and some other subordinate officers; Karara; himself, with Loketh hovering behind: a council of war. But summoned against whom?

The Terran had come too far afield from his own purpose-to reach Ashe in the Foanna keep. And to further his own plans was a task he doubted his ability to perform. His attack on the Baldies had made him too important to the Rovers for them to allow him willingly to leave them on a quest of his own.

"These star men" —Ross set down the cup, tried to choose the most telling words in his limited Hawaikan vocabulary —"possess weapons and powers you can not dream of, that you have no defense against. Back at Kyn Add we were lucky. The salkars attacked their sub and halted the broadcast powering their flamers. Otherwise we could not have taken them, even though we were many against their few. Now you talk of hunting them in their own territory-on land and in the mountains where they have their base. That would be folly akin to swimming barehanded to front a salkar."

"So-then we must sit and wait for them to eat us up?" flared Ongal. "I say it is better to die fighting with one's blade wet!"

"Do you not also wish to take at least one of the enemy with you when you fight to that finish?" Ross countered. "These could kill you before you came in blade range."

"You had no trouble with that weapon of yours," Afrukta spoke up.

"I have told you-this weapon was stolen from them. I have only one and I do not know how long it will continue to serve me, or whether they have a defense against it. Those we took were naked to any force, for their broadcast had failed them. But to smash blindly against their main base would be the act of madmen."

"The salkars opened a way for us —" That was Torgul.

"But we can not move a pack of those inland to the mountains," Vistur pointed out reasonably.

Ross studied the Captain. That Torgul was groping for a plan and that it had to be a shrewd one, the Terran guessed. His respect for the Rover commander had been growing steadily since their first meeting. The cruiser-raiders had always been captained by the most daring men of the Rover clans. But Ross was also certain that a successful cruiser commander must possess a level-headed leaven of intelligence and be a strategist of parts.

The Hawaikan force needed a key which would open the Baldy base as the salkars had opened the lagoon. And all they had to aid them was a handful of facts gained from their prisoners.

Oddly enough the picklock to the captives' minds had been produced by the dolphins. Just as Tino-rau and Taua had formed a bridge of communication between the Terran and Loketh, so did they read and translate the thoughts of the galactic invaders. For the Baldies, among their own kind, were telepathic, vocalizing only to give orders to inferiors.

Their capture by these primitive "inferiors" had delivered the first shock, and the mind-probes of the dolphins had sent the "supermen" close to the edge of sanity. To accept an animal form as an equal had been shattering.

But the star men's thoughts and memories had been winnowed at last and the result spread before this impromptu council. Rovers and Terrans were briefed on the invaders' master plan for taking over a world. Why they desired to do so even the dolphins had not been able to discover; perhaps they themselves had not been told by their superiors.

It was a plan almost contemptuous in its simplicity, as if the galactic force had no reason to fear effective opposition. Except in one direction-one single direction.

Ross's fingers tightened on the shell cup. Had Torgul reached that conclusion yet, the belief that the Foanna could be their key? If so, they might be able to achieve their separate purposes in one action.

"It would seem that they are wary of the Foanna," he suggested, alert to any telltale response from Torgul. But it was Jazia who answered the Terran's half question.

"The Foanna have a powerful magic; they can order wind and wave, man and creature-if so be their will. Well might these killers fear the Foanna!"

"Yet now they move against them," Ross pointed out, still eyeing Torgul.

The Captain's reply was a small, quiet smile.

"Not directly, as you have heard. It is all a part of their plan to set one of us against the other, letting us fight many small wars and so use up our men while they take no risks. They wait the day when we shall be exhausted and then they will reveal themselves to claim all they wish. So today they stir up trouble between the Wreckers and the Foanna, knowing that the Foanna are few. Also they strive in turn to anger us by raids, allowing us to believe that either the Wreckers or Foanna have attacked. Thus —" he held up his left thumb, made a pincers of right thumb and forefinger to close upon it, "they hope to catch the Foanna, between Wreckers and Rovers. Because the Foanna are those they reckon the most dangerous they move against them now, using us and weakening our forces into the bargain. A plan which is clever, but the plan of men who do not like to fight with their own blades."

"They are worse than the coast scum, these cowards!" Ongal spat.

Torgul smiled again. "That is what they believe we will say, kinsman, and so underrate them. By our customs, yes, they are cowards. But what care they for our judgments? Did we think of the salkars when we used them to force the lagoon? No, they were only beasts to be our tools. So now it is the same with us, except that we know what they intend. And we shall not be such obedient tools. If the Foanna are our answer, then —" He paused, gazing into his cup as if he could read some shadowy future there.

"If the Foanna are the answer, then what?" Ross pushed.

"Instead of fighting the Foanna, we must warm, cherish, try to ally ourselves with them. And do all that while we still have time!"

"Just how do we do these things?" demanded Ongal. "The Foanna you would warn, cherish, claim as allies, are already our enemies. Were we not on the way to force their sea gate only days ago? There is no chance of seeking peace now. And have the finned ones not learned from the women-killers that already there is an army of Wreckers camped about the citadel to which these sons of the Shadow plan to lend certain weapons? Do we throw away three cruisers-all we have left-in a hopeless fight? Such is the council of one struck by loss of wits."

"There is a way-my way," Ross seized the opening. "In the Foanna citadel is my sword-lord, to whose service I am vowed. We were on our way to attempt his freeing when your ship picked us out of the waves. He is learned beyond me in the dealing with strange peoples, and if the Foanna are as clever as you say, they will already have discovered that he is not just a slave they claimed from Lord Zahur."

There it was in the open, his own somewhat tattered hope that Ashe had been able to impress his captors with his knowledge and potential. Trained to act as contact man with other races, there was a chance that Gordon had saved himself from whatever fate had been planned for the prisoners the Foanna had claimed. If that happened, Ashe could be their opening wedge in the Foanna stronghold.

"This also I know: That which guards the gate-which turns your minds whirling and sent you back from your raid-does not affect me. I may be able to win inside and find my clansman, and in that doing treat with the Foanna."

The Baldy prisoners had not underestimated the attack on the Foanna citadel. As the Rover cruisers beat in under the cover of night the fires and torches of both besieged and besiegers made a wild glow across the sky. Only on the sea side of the fortress there was no sign of involvement. Whatever guarded the gate must still be in force.

Ross stood with his feet well apart to balance his body against the swing of the deck. His suggestion had been argued over, protested, but at last carried with the support of Torgul and Jazia, and now he was to make his try. The sum of the Rovers' and Loketh's knowledge of the sea gate had been added for his benefit, but he knew that this venture must depend upon himself alone. Karara, the dolphins, the Hawaikans, were all too sensitive to the barrier.

Torgul moved in the faint light. "We are close; our power is ebbing. If we advance, we shall be drifting soon."

"It is time then." Ross crossed to the rope ladder, but another was there before him. Karara perched on the rail. He regarded her angrily.

"You can't go."

"I know. But we are still safe here. Just because you are free of one defense of the gate, Ross, do not believe that makes it easy."

He was stung by her assumption that he could be so self-assured.

"I know my business."

Ross pushed past her, swinging down the rope ladder, pausing only above water level to snap on flippers, make sure of the set of his weighted belt, and slide his gill-mask over his face. There was a splash beside him as the net containing spare belt, flippers, and mask hit the water and he caught at it. These could provide Ashe's escape from the fortress.

The lights on the shore made a wide arc of radiance across the sea. As Ross headed toward the wave-washed coast he began to hear shouting and other sounds which made him believe that the besiegers were in the midst of an all-out assault. Yet those distant fires and rocketlike blasts into the sky had a wavery blur. And Ross, making his way with the effortless water cleaving of the diver, surfaced now and then to spot film curling up from the surface of the sea between the two standing rock pillars which marked the sea gate.

He was startled by a thunderous crack, rending the air above the small bay. Ross pulled to one of the pillars, steadied himself with one hand against it. Those twists of film rising from the surging surface were thickening. More tendrils grew out from parent stems to creep along above the waves, raising up sprouts and branches in turn. A wall of mist was building between gate and shore.

Again a thunderclap overhead. Involuntarily the Terran ducked. Then he turned his face up to the sky, striving to see any evidence of storm. What hung there sped the growth of the fog on the water. Yet where the fog was gray-white, it was a darkness spouting from the highest point of the citadel. Ross could not explain how he was able to see one shade of darkness against equal dusk, but he did—or did he only sense it? He shook his head, willing himself to look away from the finger. Only it was a finger no longer; now it was a fist aimed at the stars it was fast blotting out. A fist rising to the heavens before it curled back, descended to press the fortress and its surroundings into rock and earth.

Fog curled about Ross, spilled outward through the sea gates. He loosed his grip on the pillar and dived, swimming on through the gap with the fortress of the Foanna before him.

There was a jetty somewhere ahead; that much he knew from Torgul's description. Those who served the Foanna sometimes took sea roads and they had slim, fast cutters for such coast-wise travel. Ross surfaced cautiously, to discover there was no visibility to wave level. Here the mist was thick, a smothering cover so bewildering he was confused as to direction. He ducked below again and flippered on.

Was his confusion born of the fog, or was it also in his head? Did he, after all, have this much reaction to the gate defense? Ross ducked that suspicion as he had ducked the moist blanket on the surface. He had come from the gate, which meant that the jetty must lie—there!

A few moments later Ross had proof that his sense of direction had not altogether failed him, when his shoulder grazed against a solid obstruction in the water and his exploring touch told him that he had found one of the jetty piles. He surfaced again and this time he heard not a thunder roll but the singsong chanting of the Foanna.

It was loud, almost directly above his head, but since the cotton mist held he was not afraid of being sighted. The chanter must be on the jetty. And to Ross's right was a dark bulk which he thought was one of the cutters. Was a sortie by the besieged being planned?

Then, out of the night, came a dazzling beam, well above the level of Ross's head where he clung to the piling. It centered on the cutter, slicing into the substance of the vessel with the ease of steel piercing clay. The chanting stopped on mid-note, broken by cries of surprise and alarm. Ross, pressing against the pile, received a jolt from his belt sonic.

There must be a Baldy sub in the basin inside the gate. Perhaps the flame beam now destroying the cutter was to be turned on the walls of the keep in turn.

Foanna chant again, low and clear. Splashes from the water as those on the jetty cast into the sea objects Ross could not define. The Terran's body jerked, his mask smothered a cry of pain. About his legs and middle, immersed in the waves, there was cold so intense that it seared. Fear goaded him to pull up on one of the under beams of the pier. He reached that refuge and rubbed his icy legs with what vigor he could summon.

Moments later he crept along toward the shore. The energy ray had found another target. Ross paused to watch a second cutter sliced. If the counter stroke of the Foanna would rout the invaders, it had not yet begun to work.

The net holding the extra gear brought along in hopes of Ashe's escape weighed the Terran down, but he would not abandon it as he felt his way from one foot- and hand-hold to the next. The waves below gave off an icy exudation which made him shiver uncontrollably. And he knew that as long as that effect lasted he dared not venture into the sea again.

Light ... along with the cold, there was a phosphorescence on the water-white patches floating, dipping, riding the waves. Some of them gathered under the pier, clustering about the pilings. And the fog thinned with their coming, as if those irregular blotches absorbed and fed upon the mist. The Terran could see now he had reached the land end of the jetty. He wedged his flippers into his belt, pulled on over his feet the covers of salkar-hide Torgul had provided.

Save for his belt, his trunks, and the gill-pack, Ross's body was bare and the cold caught at him. But, slinging the carry net over his shoulder, he dropped to the damp sand and stood listening.

The clamor of the attack which had carried all the way offshore to the Rover cruisers had died away. And there were no more claps of thunder. Instead, there was now a thick wash of rain.

No more fire rays as he faced seaward. And the fog was lifting, so Ross could distinguish the settling cutters, their bows still moored to the jetty. There was no movement there. Had those on the pier fled?

Dot ... dash ... dot ...

Ross did not drop the net. But he crouched back in the half protection of the piling. For a moment which stretched beyond Terran time measure he froze so, waiting.

Dot ... dash ... dot ...

Not the prickle induced by the enemy installations, it was a real coded call picked up by his sonic, and one he knew.

Don't rush, he told himself sharply-play it safe. By rights only two people in this time and place would know that call. And one would have no reason to use it. But —a trap? This could be a trap. Awe of the Foanna powers had touched him a little in spite of his off-world skepticism. He could be lured now by someone using Ashe's call.

Ross stripped for action after a fashion, bundling the net and its contents into a hollow he scooped behind a pile well above water level. The alien hand weapon he had left with Karara, not trusting it to the sea. But he had his diver's knife and his two hands which, by training, could be, and had been, deadly weapons.

With the sonic against the bare skin of his middle where it would register strongest, knife in hand, Ross moved into the open. The floating patches did not supply much light, but he was certain the call had come from the jetty.

There was movement there —a flash or two. And the sonic? Ross had to be sure, very sure. The broadcast was certainly stronger when he faced in that direction. Dared he come into the open? Perhaps in the dark he could cut Ashe away from his captors so they could swim for it together.

Ross clicked a code reply. Dot ...dot ...dot...

The answer was quick, imperative: "Where?"

Surely no one but Ashe could have sent that! Ross did not hesitate.

"Be ready-escape."

"No!" Even more imperative. "Friends here...."

Had he guessed rightly? Had Ashe established friendly relations with the Foanna? But Ross kept to the caution which had been his defense and armor so long. There was one question he thought only Ashe could answer, something out of the past they had shared when they had made their first journey into time disguised as Beaker traders of the Bronze Age. Deliberately he tapped that question.

"What did we kill in Britain?"

Tensely he waited. But when the reply came it did not pulse from the sonic under his fingers; instead, a well-remembered voice called out of the night.

"A white wolf." And the words were Terran English.

"Ashe!" Ross leaped forward, climbed toward the figure he could only dimly see.

14. The Foanna

"Ross!" Ashe's hands gripped his shoulders as if never intending to free him again. "Then you did come through —"

Ross understood. Gordon Ashe must have feared that he was the only one swept through the time door by that freak chance.

"And Karara and the dolphins!"

"Here-now?" In this black bowl of the citadel bay Ashe was only a shadow with voice and hands.

"No, out with the Rover cruisers. Ashe, do you know the Baldies are on Hawaika? They've organized this whole thing-the attack here-trouble all over. Right now they have one of their subs out there. That's what cut those cutters to pieces. Five days ago five of them wiped out a whole Rover fairing, just five of them!"

"Gordoon." Unlike the hissing speech of the Hawaikans, this new voice made a singing, lilting call of Ashe's name. "This is your swordsman in truth?" Another shadow drew near them, and Ross saw the flutter of cloak edge.

"This is my friend." There was a tone of correction in Ashe's reply. "Ross, this is the Guardian of the sea gate."

"And you come," the Foanna continued, "with those who gather to feast at the Shadow's table. But your Rovers will find little loot to their liking —"

"No." Ross hesitated. How did one address the Foanna? He had claimed equality with Torgul. But that approach was not the proper one here; instinct told him that. He fell back on the complete truth uttered simply. "We took three of the Baldy killers. From them we learned they move to wipe out the Foanna first. For you," he addressed himself to the cloaked shape, "they believe to be a threat. We heard that they urged the Wreckers to this attack and so —"

"And so the Rovers come, but not to loot? Then they are something new among their kind." The Foanna's reply was as chill as the sea bay's water.

"Loot does not summon men who want a blood price for their dead kin!" Ross retorted.

"No, and the Rovers are believers in the balance of hurt against hurt," the Foanna conceded. "Do they also believe in the balance of aid against aid? Now that is a thought upon which depends much. Gordoon, it would seem that we may not take to our ships. So let us return to council."

Ashe's hand was on Ross's arm guiding him through the murk. Though the fog which had choked the bay had vanished, thick darkness remained and Ross noted that even the fires and flares were dimmed and fewer. Then they were in a passage where a very faint light clung to the walls.

Robed Foanna, three of them, moved ahead with that particular gliding progress. Then Ashe and Ross, and bringing up the rear, a dozen of the mailed guards. The passageway became a ramp. Ross glanced at Ashe. Like the Foanna, the Terran Agent wore a cloak of gray, but his did not shift color from time to time as did those of the Hawaikan enigmas. And now Gordon shoved back its folds, revealing supple body armor.

Questions gathered in Ross. He wanted to know-needed desperately to know-Ashe's standing with the Foanna. What had happened to raise Gordon from the status of captive in Zahur's hold to familiar companionship with the most dreaded race on this planet?

The ramp's head faced blank wall with a sharp-angled turn to the right of a narrower passage. One of the Foanna made a slight sign to the guards, who turned with drilled precision to march off along the passage. Now the other Foanna held out their wands.

What a moment earlier had been unbroken surface showed an opening. The change had been so instantaneous that Ross had not seen any movement at all.

Beyond that door they passed from one world to another. Ross's senses, already acutely alert to his surroundings, could not supply him with any reason by sight, sound, or smell for his firm conviction that this hold was alien as neither the Wrecker castle nor the Rover ships had been. Surely the Foanna were not the same race, perhaps not even the same species as the other native Hawaikans.

Those robes which he had seen both silver gray and dark blue, now faded, pearled, thinned, until each of the three still gliding before him were opalescent columns without definite form.

Ashe's grasp fell on Ross's arm once more, and his whisper reached the younger man thinly. "They are mistresses of illusion. Be prepared not to believe all that you see."

Mistresses-Ross caught that first. Women, or at least female then. Illusion, yes, already he was convinced that here his eyes could play tricks on him. He could hardly determine what was robe, what was wall, or if more than shades of shades swept before him.

Another blank wall, then an opening, and flowing through it to touch him such a wave of alienness that Ross felt he was buffeted by a storm wind. Yet as he hesitated before it, reluctant in spite of Ashe's hold to go ahead, he also knew that this did not carry with it the cold hostility he had known while facing the Baldies. Alien-yes. Inimical to his kind-no.

"You are right, younger brother."

Spoken those words-or forming in his mind?

Ross was in a place which was sheer wonder. Under his feet dark blue-the blue of a Terran sky at dusk-caught up in it twinkling points of light as if he strode, not equal with stars, but above them! Walls-were there any walls here? Or shifting, swaying blue curtains on which silvery lines ran to form symbols and words which some bemused part of his brain almost understood, but not quite.

Constant motion, no quiet, until he came to a place where those swaying curtains were stilled, where he no longer strode above the sky but on soft surface, a mat of gray living sod where his steps released a spicy fragrance. And there he really saw the Foanna for the first time.

Where had their cloaks gone? Had they tossed them away during that walk or drift across this amazing room, or had the substance which had formed those coverings flowed away by itself? As Ross looked at the three in wonder he knew that he was seeing them as not even their servants and guards ever viewed them. And yet was he seeing them as they really were or as they wished him to see them?

"As we are, younger brother, as we are!" Again an answer which Ross was not sure was thought or speech.

In form they were humanoid, and they were undoubtedly women. The muffling cloaks gone, they wore sleeveless garments of silver which were girded at the waist with belts of blue gems. Only in their hair and their eyes did they betray alien blood. For the hair which flowed and wove about them, cascading down shoulders, rippling about their arms, was silver, too, and it swirled, moved as if it had a separate life of its own. While their eyes....Ross looked into those golden eyes and was lost for seconds until panic awoke in him, forcing him after sharp struggle to look away.

Laughter? No, he had not heard laughter. But a sense of amusement tinged with respect came to him.

"You are very right, Gordoon. This one is also of your kind. He is not witches' meat." Ross caught the distaste, the kind of haunting unhappiness which colored those words, remnants of an old hurt.

"These are the Foanna," Ashe's voice broke more of the spell. "The Lady Ynlan, The Lady Yngram, the Lady Ynvalda."

The Foanna-these three only?

She whom Ashe had named Ynlan, whose eyes had entrapped and almost held what was Ross Murdock, made a small gesture with her ivory hand. And in that gesture as well as in the words witches' meat the Terran read the unhappiness which was as much a part of this room as the rest of its mystery.

"The Foanna are now but three. They have been only three for many weary years, oh man from another world and time. And soon, if these enemies have their way, they will not be three-but none!"

"But —" Ross was still startled. He knew from Loketh that the Wreckers had deemed the Foanna few in number, an old and dying race. But that there were only three women left was hard to believe.

The response to his unspoken wonder came clear and determined. "We may be but three; however, our power remains. And sometimes power distilled by time becomes the stronger. Now it would seem that time is no longer our servant but perhaps among our enemies. So tell us this tale of yours as to why the Rovers would make one with the Foanna-tell us all, younger brother!"

Ross reported what he had seen, what Tino-rau and Taua had learned from the prisoners taken at Kyn Add. And when he had finished, the three Foanna stood very still, their hands clasped one to the other. Though they were only an arm's distance from him, Ross had the feeling they had withdrawn from his time and world.

So complete was their withdrawal that he dared to ask Ashe one of the many questions which had been boiling inside him.

"Who are they?" But Ross knew he really meant: What are they?

Gordon Ashe shook his head. "I don't really know-the last of a very old race which possesses powers and knowledge different from any we have believed in for centuries. We have heard of witches. In the modern day we discount the legends about them. The Foanna bring those legends alive. And I promise you this-if they turn those powers loose" —he paused —"it will be such a war as this world, perhaps any world has never seen!"

"That is so." The Foanna had returned from the place to which they had withdrawn. "And this is also the truth or one face of the truth. The Rovers are right in their belief that we have kept some measure of balance between one form of change and another on this world. If we were as many as we once were, then against us these invaders could not move at all. But we are three only and also-do we have the right to evoke disaster which will strike not only the enemy but perhaps recoil upon the innocent? There has been enough death here already. And those who are our servants shall no longer be asked to face battle to keep an empty shell inviolate. We would see with our own eyes these invaders, probe what they would do. There is ever change in life, and if a pattern grows too set, then the race caught in it may wither and die. Maybe our pattern has been too long in its old design. We shall make no decision until we see in whose hands the future may rest."

Against such finality of argument there was no appeal. These could not be influenced by words.

"Gordoon, there is much to be done. Do you take with you this younger brother and see to his needs. When all is in readiness we shall come."

One minute Ross had been standing on the carpet of living moss. Then ... he was in a more normal room with four walls, a floor, a ceiling, and light which came from rods set in the corners. He gasped.

"Stunned me, too, the first time they put me through it," he heard Ashe say. "Here, get some of this inside you, it'll steady your head."

There was a cup in his hand, a beautifully carved, rose-red container shaped in the form of a flower. Somehow Ross brought it to his lips with shaking hands, gulped down a good third of its contents. The liquid was a mixture of tart and sweet, cooling his mouth and throat, but warming as it went down, and that glow spread through him.

"What-how did they do that?" he demanded.

Ashe shrugged. "How do they do the hundred and one things I have seen happen here? We've been teleported. How it's done I don't know any more than I did the first time it happened. Simply a part of Foanna 'magic' as far as spectators are concerned." He sat down on a stool, his long legs stretched out before him. "Other worlds, other ways-even if they are confounded queer ones. As far as I know, there's no reason for their power to work, but it does. Now, have you seen the time gate? Is it in working order?"

Ross put down the now empty cup and sat down opposite Ashe. As concisely as he could, he outlined the situation with a quick résumé of all that had happened to him, Karara, and the dolphins since they had been sucked through the gate. Ashe asked no questions, but his expression was that of the Agent Ross had known, evaluating and listing all the younger man had to report. When the other was through he said only two words:

"No return."

So much had happened in so short a time that Ross's initial shock at the destruction of the gate had faded, been well overlaid by all the demands made upon his resources, skill, and strength. Even now, the fact Ashe voiced seemed of little consequence balanced against the struggle in progress.

"Ashe —" Ross rubbed his hands up and down his arms, brushing away grains of sand, "remember those pylons with the empty seacoast behind them? Does that mean the Baldies are going to win?"

"I don't know. No one has ever tried to change the course of history. Maybe it is impossible even if we dared to try." Ashe was on his feet again, pacing back and forth.

"Try what, Gordoon?"

Ross jerked around, Ashe halted. One of the Foanna stood there, her hair playing about her shoulders as if some breeze felt only by her stirred those long strands.

"Dare to try and change the course of the future," Ashe explained, accepting her materialization with the calm of one who had witnessed it before.

"Ah, yes, your traveling in time. And now you think that perhaps this poor world of ours has a choice as to which overlords it will welcome? I do not know either, Gordoon, whether the future may be altered nor if it be wise to try. But also ... well, perhaps we should see our enemy before we are set in any path. Now, it is time that we go. Younger brother, how did you plan to leave this place when you accomplished your mission?"

"By the sea gate. I have extra swimming equipment cached under the jetty."

"And the Rover ships await you at sea?"

"Yes."

"Then we shall take your way, since the cutters are sunk."

"There is only one extra gill-pack —and that Baldy sub is out there, too!"

"So? Then we shall try another road, though it will sap our power temporarily." Her head inclined slightly to the left as if she listened. "Good! Our people are now in the passage which will take them to safety. What those outside will find here when they break in will be of little aid to their plans. Secrets of the Foanna remain secrets past others' prying. Though they shall try, oh, how they shall try to solve them! There is knowledge that only certain types of minds can hold and use, and to others it remains for all time unlearnable. Now —"

Her hand reached out, flattened against Ross's forehead.

"Think of your Rover ship, younger brother, see it in your mind! And see well and clearly for me."

Torgul's cruiser was there; he could picture with details he had not thought he knew or remembered. The deck in the dark of the night with only a shaded light at the mast. The deck...

Ross gave a choked cry. He did not see this in his mind; he saw it with his eyes! His hand swung out in an involuntary gesture of repudiation and struck painfully against wood. He was on the cruiser!

A startled exclamation from behind him-then a shout. Ashe was here and beyond him three cloaked figures, the Foanna. They had their own road indeed and had taken it.

"You ... Rosss —" Vistur fronted them, his face a mixture of bewilderment and awe. "The Foanna —" said in a half whisper, echoed by crewmen gathering around, but not too close.

"Gordon!" Karara elbowed her way between two of the Hawaikans and ran across the deck. She caught the Agent's both hands as if to assure herself that he was alive and there before her. Then she turned to the three Foanna.

There was an odd expression on the Polynesian girl's face, first of measurement with some fear, and then of dawning wonder. From beneath the cloak of the middle Foanna came the rod of office with its sparking knob. Karara dropped Ashe's hands, took a tentative step forward and then another. The knob was directly before her, breast high. She brought up both hands, cupping them about the knob, but not touching it directly. The sparks it emitted could have been flashing against her flesh, but Karara displayed no awareness of that. Instead, she lifted both hands farther, palm up and cupped, as if she carried some invisible bounty, then flattened them, loosing what she held.

There was a sigh from the crewmen; Karara's gesture had been confident, as if she knew just what she was doing and why. And Ross heard Ashe draw a deep breath also as the Terran girl turned, allying herself with the Foanna.

"These Great Ones stand in peace," she said. "It is their will that no harm comes to this ship and those who sail in her."

"What do the Great Ones want of us?" Torgul advanced but not too near.

"To speak concerning those who are your prisoners."

"So be it." The Captain bowed. "The Great Ones' will is our will; let it be as they wish."

15. Return to the Battle

Ross lay listening to the even breathing from across the cabin. He had awakened in that quick transference from sleep to consciousness which was always his when on duty, but he made no attempt to move. Ashe was still sleeping.

Ashe, whom he thought or had thought he knew as well as one man could ever know another, who had taken the place of family for Ross Murdock the loner. Years-two ... four of them now since he had made half of that partnership.

His head turned, though he could not see that lean body, that quiet, controlled face. Ashe still looked the same, but ... Ross's sense of loss was hurt and anger mingled. What had they done to Gordon, those three? Bewitched? Tales Terrans had accepted as purest fantasy for centuries came into his mind. Could it be that his own world once had its Foanna?

Ross scowled. You couldn't refute their "magic," call it by what scientific name you wished-hypnotism ... telaporting. They got results, and the results were impressive. Now he remembered the warning the Foanna themselves had delivered hours earlier to the Rovers. There were limits to their abilities; because they were forced to draw on mental and physical energy, they could be exhausted. Thus, they had barriers, too.

Again Ross considered the subject of barriers. Karara had been able to meet the aliens, if not mind-to-mind, then in a closer way even than Ashe. The talent which tied her to the dolphins had in turn been a bond with the Foanna. Ashe and Karara could enter that circle, but not Ross Murdock. Along with his new separation from Ashe came that feeling of inferiority to bite on, and the taste was sour.

"This isn't going to be easy."

So Ashe was awake.

"What can they do?" Ross asked in return.

"I don't know. I don't believe that they can teleport an army into Baldy headquarters the way Torgul expects. And it wouldn't do such an army much good to get there and then be outclassed by the weapons the Baldies might have," Ashe said.

Ross had a moment of warmth and comfort; he knew that tone of old. Ashe was studying the problem, willing to talk out difficulties as he always had before.

"No, outright assault isn't the answer. We'll have to know more about the enemy. One thing puzzles me: Why have the Baldies suddenly stepped up their timing?"

"What makes you think they have?"

"Well, according to the accounts I've heard, it's been about three or four planet years here since some off-world devices have been infiltrating the native civilization —"

"You mean such things as those attractors set up on the reef at Zahur's castle?" Ross remembered Loketh's story.

"Those, and other things. The refinements added to the engine power on these ships.... Torgul said they spread from Rover fleet to fleet; no one's sure where they started. The Baldies began slowly, but they are speeding up now-those fairing attacks have all been recent. And this assault on the Foanna citadel blew up almost overnight on a flimsy excuse. Why the quick push after the slow beginning?"

"Maybe they decided the natives are easy pushovers and they no longer have to worry about any real opposition," Ross suggested.

"Could be. Self-confidence becoming arrogance when they didn't uncover any opponent strong enough to matter. Or else, they may be spurred by some need with a time limit. If we knew the reason for those pylons, we might guess their motives."

"Are you going to try to change the future?"

"That sounds arrogant, too. Can we if we wish to? We never dared to try it on Terra. And the risk may be worse than all our fears. Also, the choice is not ours."

"There's one thing I don't understand," Ross said. "Why did the Foanna walk out of the citadel and leave it undefended for their enemies? What about their guards? Did they just leave them too?" He was willing to make the most of any flaw in the aliens' character.

"Most of their people had already escaped through underground ways. The rest left when they knew the cutters had been sunk," Ashe returned. "As to why they deserted the citadel, I don't know. The decision was theirs."

There-up with the barrier between them again. But Ross refused to accept the cutoff this time, determined to pull Ashe back into the familiar world of the here and now.

"That keep could be a trap, about the best on this planet!" The idea was more than just a gambit to attract Ashe's attention, it was true! A perfect trap to catch Baldies.

"Don't you see," Ross sat up, slapped his feet down on the deck as he leaned forward eagerly. "Don't you see ... if the Baldies know anything at all about the Foanna, and I'm betting they do and want to learn all they can, they'll visit the citadel. They won't want to depend on second- and third-hand reports of the place, especially ones delivered by primitives such as the Wreckers. They had a sub there. I'll bet the crew are in picking over the loot right now!"

"If that's what they're hunting" —there was amusement in Ashe's tone —"they won't find much. The Foanna have better locks than their enemies have keys. You heard Ynlan before we left-any secrets left will remain secrets."

"But there's bait-bait for a trap!" argued Ross.

"You're right!" To the younger man's joy Ashe's enthusiasm was plain. "And if the Baldies could be led to believe that what they wanted was obtainable with just a little more effort, or the right tools —"

"The trap could net bigger catch than just underlings!" Ross's thought matched Ashe's. "Why, it might even pull in the VIP directing the whole operation! How can we set it up, and do we have time?"

"The trap would have to be of Foanna setting; our part would come after it was sprung." Ashe was thoughtful again. "But it is the only move which we can make at present with any hope of success. And it will only work if the Foanna are willing."

"Have to be done quickly," Ross pointed out.

"Yes, I'll see." Ashe was a dark figure against the thin light of the companionway as he slid back the cabin door. "If Ynvalda agrees...." As he went out Ross was right behind him.

The Foanna had been given, by their own choice, quarters on the bow deck of the cruiser where sailcloth had been used to form a tent. Not that any of the awe-stricken Rovers would venture too near them. Ashe reached for the flap of the fabric and a lilting voice called:

"You seek us, Gordoon?"

"This is important."

"Yes, it is important, for the thought which brings you both has merit. Enter then, brothers!"

The flap was looped aside and before them was a swirling of mist? ...light? ...sheets of pale color? Ross could not have described what he saw-save if the Foanna were there, he could not distinguish them from the rippling of their hair, the melting film of their robes.

"So, younger brother, you think that which was our home and our treasure box has now become a trap for the confounding of those who believe we are a threat to them?"

Somehow Ross was not surprised that they knew about his idea before he had said a word, before Ashe had given any explanations. Their omniscience was only a small portion of their other talents.

"Yes."

"And why do you believe so? We swear to you that the coast folk can not be driven into those parts of the castle which mean the most, any more than our sea gate can be breached unless we will it so."

"Yet I swam through the sea gate, and the sub was there also." Ross knew again a flash of-was it pleasure? —at being able to state this fact. There *were* chinks in the Foanna defenses.

"Again the truth. You have that within you, young brother, which is both a lack and a shield. True also that this underseas ship entered after you. Perhaps it has a shield as part of it; perhaps those from the stars have their own protection. But they can not reach the heart of what they wish, not unless we open the doors for them. It is your belief, younger brother, that they still strive to force such doors?"

"Yes. Knowing there is something to be learned, they will try for it. They will not dare not to." Ross was very certain on that point. His encounters with the Baldies had not led to any real understanding. But the way they had wiped out the line of Russian time stations made him sure that they dealt thoroughly with any situation they considered a threat.

From the prisoners taken at Kyn Add they had learned the invaders believed the Foanna their enemies here, even though the Old Ones had not repulsed them or their activities. Therefore, it followed that, having taken the stronghold, the Baldies would endeavor to rip open every one of its secrets.

"A trap with good bait —"

Ross wondered which one of the Foanna said that. To see nothing but the swirls of mist-color, listen to disembodied voices from it, was disconcerting. Part of the stage dressing, he decided, for building their prestige with the other races with whom they dealt. Three women alone would have to buttress their authority with such trappings.

"Ah, younger brother, indeed you are beginning to understand us!" Laughter, soft, but unmistakable.

Ross frowned. He did not feel the touch-go-touch of mental communication which the dolphins used. But he did not doubt that the Foanna read his thoughts, or at least a few of them.

"Some of them," echoed from the mist. "Not all-not as your older brother's or the maiden whose mind meets with ours. With you, younger brother, it is a thought here, a thought there, and only our intuition to connect them into a pattern. But now, there is serious planning to be done. And, knowing this enemy, you believe they will come to search for what they can not find. So you would set a trap. But they have weapons beyond your weapons, have they not, younger brother? Brave as are these Rover kind, they can not use swords against flame, their hands against a killer who may stand apart and slay. What remains, Gordoon? What remains in our favor?"

"You have your weapons, too," Ashe answered.

"Yes, we have our weapons, but long have they been used only in one pattern, and they are atuned to another race. Did our defenses hold against you, Gordoon, when you strove to prove that you were as you claimed to be? And did another repulse younger brother when he dared the sea gate? So can we trust them in turn against these other strangers with different brains? Only at the testing shall we know, and in such learning perhaps we shall also be forced to eat the sourness of defeat. To risk all may be to lose all."

"That may be true," Ashe assented.

"You mean the sight you have had into our future says that this happens? Yes, to stake all and to lose-not only for ourselves, but for all others here-that is a weighty decision to make, Gordoon. But the trap promises. Let us think on it for a space. Do you also consult with the Rovers if they wish to take part in what may be desperate folly."

Torgul paced the afterdeck, well away from the tent which sheltered the Foanna, but with his eyes turning to it as Ross explained what might be a good attack.

"Those women-killers would have no fear of Foanna magic, rather would they come to seek it out? It would be a chance to catch leaders in a trap?"

"You have heard what the prisoners said or thought. Yes, they would seek out such knowledge and we would have this chance to capture them —"

"With what?" Torgul demanded. "I am not Ongal to argue that it is better to die in pursuit of blood payment than to take an enemy or enemies with me! What chance have we against their powers?"

"Ask that of them!" Ross nodded toward the still silent tent.

Even as he spoke the three cloaked Foanna emerged, pacing down to mid-ship where Torgul and his lieutenants, Ross and Ashe came to meet them.

"We have thought on this." The lilting half chant which the Foanna used for ordinary communication was a song in the dawn wind. "It was in our minds to retreat, to wait out this troubling of the land, since we are few and that which we hold within us is worth the guarding. But now, what profit such guardianship when there may be none to whom we may pass it after us? And if you have seen the truth, elder brother" —the cowled heads swung to Ashe —"then there may be no future for any of us. But still there are our limitations. Rover," now they spoke directly to Torgul, "we can not put your men within the citadel by desiring-not without certain aids which lie sealed there now. No, we, ourselves, must win inside bodily and then ... then, perhaps, we can pull tight the lines of our net!"

"To run a cruiser through the gate —" Torgul began.

"No, not a ship, Captain. A handful of warriors in the water can risk the gate, but not a ship."

Ashe broke in, "How many gill-packs do we have?"

Ross counted hurriedly. "I left one cached ashore. But there's mine and Karara's and Loketh's —also two more —"

"To pass the gates," that was the Foanna, "we ourselves shall not need your underwater aids."

"You," Ross said to Ashe, "and I with Karara's pack——"

"For Karara!"

Both the Terrans looked around. The Polynesian girl stood close to the Foanna, smiling faintly.

"This venture is mine also," she spoke with conviction. "As it is Tino-rau's and Taua's. Is that not so, Daughters of the Alii of this world?"

"Yes, Sea Maid. There are weapons of many sorts, and not all of them fit into a warrior's hand or can be swung with the force of a man's arm and shoulder. Yes, this venture is yours, also, sister."

Ross's protests bubbled unspoken; he had to accept the finality of the Foanna decree. It seemed now that the make-up of their task force depended upon the whims of the three rather than the experience of those trained to such risks. And Ashe was apparently willing to accept their leadership.

So it was an odd company that took to the water just as dawn colored the sky. Loketh had clung fiercely to his pack, insisted that he be one of the swimmers, and the Foanna accepted him as well. Ross and Ashe, Loketh, and Baleku, a young under-officer of Ongal's, accorded the best swimmer of the fleet, Karara and the dolphins. And with them those three others, shapes sliding smoothly through the water, as difficult to define in this new element as they had been in their tent. Before them frisked the dolphins. Tino-rau and Taua played about the Foanna in an ecstatic joy and when all were in the sea they shot off shoreward.

That sub within the sea gate, had it unleashed the same lethal broadcast as the one at Kyn Add? But the dolphins could give warning if that were so.

Ross swam easily, Ashe next, Loketh on his left, Baleku a little behind and Karara to the fore as if in vain pursuit of the dolphins-the Foanna well to the left. A queer invasion party, even queerer when one totaled up the odds which might lie ahead.

There was no mist or storm this morning to hide the headlands where the Foanna citadel stood. And the promontories of the sea gate were starkly clear in the growing light. The same drive which always was a part of Ross when he was committed to action sustained him now, though he was visited by a small prick of doubt when he thought that the leadership did not lie with Ashe but with the Foanna.

No warning of any trouble ahead as they passed between the mighty, sea-sunk bases of the gate pillars. Ross depended upon his sonic, but there was no adverse report from the sensitive recorder. The terrible chill of the water during the night attack had been dissipated, but here and there dead sea things floated, being torn and devoured by hunters of the waves.

They were well past the pillars when Ross was aware that Loketh had changed place in the line, spurting ahead. After him went Baleku. They caught up with Karara, flashed past her.

Ross looked to Ashe, on to the Foanna, but saw nothing to explain the action of the two Hawaikans. Then his sonic beat out a signal from Ashe.

"Danger ... follow the Foanna ... left."

Karara had already changed course to head in that direction. Ahead of her he could see Loketh and Baleku both still bound for the mid-point of the shore where the jetty and the sunken cutters were. Ashe passed before him, and Ross reluctantly followed orders.

A shelf of rock reached out from the cliff wall, under it a dark opening. The Foanna sought this without hesitation, Ashe, Karara, and Ross following. Moments later they were out of the water where footing sloped back and up. Below them Tino-rau and Taua nosed the rise, their heads lifting out of the water as they "spoke." And Karara hastened to reply.

"Loketh ... Baleku ..." Ross began when he caught a mental stroke of anger so deadly that it was a chill lance into his brain. He faced the Foanna, startled and a little frightened.

"They will not come-now." A knob-crowned wand stretched out in the air, pointing to the upper reaches of the slope. "Nor can any of their blood-unless we win."

"What is wrong?" Ashe asked.

"You were right, very right, men out of time! These invaders are not to be lightly dismissed. They have turned one of our own defenses against us. Loketh, Baleku, all of their kind, can be made into tools for a master. They belong to the enemy now."

"And we have failed so early?" Karara wanted to know.

Again that piercing thrust of anger so vivid that it was no mere emotion but seemed a tangible force.

"Failed? No, not yet have we even begun to fight! You were very right; this is such an evil as must be faced and fought, even if we lose all in battle! Now we must do that which none of our own race has done for generations-we must open three locks, throw wide the Great Door, and seek out the Keeper of the Closed Knowledge!"

Light, a sharp ray sighting from the tip of the wand. And the Foanna following that beam, the three Terrans coming after ... into the unknown.

16. The Opening of the Great Door

It was not the general airlessness of the long-closed passage which wore on Ross's nerves, made Karara suddenly reach out and clasp fingers about the wrists of the two men she walked between; it was a crushing sensation of age, of a toll of years so long, so heavy, as to make time itself into a turgid flood which tugged at their bodies, mired their feet as they trudged after the Foanna. This sense of age, of a dead and heavy past, was so stifling that all three Terrans breathed in gasps.

Karara's breaths became sobs. Yet she matched her pace to Ashe and Ross, kept going. Ross himself had little idea of their surroundings, but one small portion of his brain asked answerless questions. The foremost being: Why did the past crush in on him here? He had traveled time, but never before had he been beaten with the feel of countless dead and dying years.

"Going back —" That hoarse whisper came from Ashe, and Ross thought he understood.

"A time gate!" He was eager to accept such an explanation. Time gates he could understand, but that the Foanna used one....

"Not our kind," Ashe replied.

But his words had pulled Ross out of a spell which had been as quicksand about him. And he began to fight back with a determination not to be sucked into what filled this place. In spite of Ross's efforts, his eyes could supply him with no definite impression of where they were. The ramp had led them out of the sea, but where they walked now, linked hand to hand, Ross could not say. He could see the glimmer of the Foanna; turning his head he could see his companions as shadows, but all beyond that was utter dark.

"Ahhhh —" Karara's sobs gave way to a whisper which was half moan. "This is a way of gods, old gods, gods who never dealt with men! It is not well to walk the road of the gods!"

Her fear lapped to Ross. He faced that emotion as he had faced so many different kinds of fear all his life. Sure, he felt that pressure on him, not the pressure of past centuries now-but a power beyond his ability to describe.

"Not our gods!" Ross put his stubborn defiance into words, more as a shield against his own wavering. "No power where there is no belief!" From what half-forgotten bit of reading had he dredged that knowledge? "No being without belief!" he repeated.

To his vast amazement he heard Ashe laugh, though the sound bordered on hysteria.

"No belief, no power," the older man replied. "You've speared the right fish, Ross! No gods of ours dwell here, Karara, and whatever god does has no rights over us. Hold to that, girl, hold tight!"

"Ah, ye forty thousand gods,

Ye gods of sea, of sky, of woods,

Of mountains, of valleys,

Ye assemblies of gods,

Ye elder brothers of the gods that are,

Ye gods that once were,

Ye that whisper. Ye that watch by night,

Ye that show your gleaming eyes,

Come down, awake, stir,

Walk this road, walk this road!"

She was singing, first softly and then more strongly, the liquid words of her own tongue repeated in English as if what she strove to call she would share with her companions. Now there was triumph in her singing and Ross found himself echoing her, "Walk this road!" as a demand.

It was still there, all of it, the crushing weight of the past, and that which brooded within that past, which had reached out for them, to possess or to alter. Only they were free of that reaching now. And they could see too! The fuzzy darkness was lighter and there were normal walls about them. Ross put out his free hand and rubbed finger tips along rough stone.

Once more their senses were assaulted by a stealthy attack from beyond the bounds of space and time as the walls fell away and they came out into a wide space whose boundaries they could not see. Here that which brooded was strong, a mighty weight poised aloft to strike them down.

"Come down, awake, stir...." Karara's pleading sank again to a whisper, her voice sounded hoarse as if her mouth were dry, her words formed by a shrunken tongue, issued from a parched throat.

Light spreading in channels along the floor, making a fiery pattern-patterns within patterns, intricate designs within designs. Ross jerked his eyes away from those patterns. To study them was danger, he knew without being warned. Karara's nails bit into his flesh and he welcomed that pain; it kept him alert, conscious of what was Ross Murdock, holding him safely apart from something greater than he, but entirely alien.

The designs and patterns were lines on a pavement. And now the three Foanna, swaying as if yielding to unseen winds, began to follow those patterns with small dancing steps. But the Terrans remained where they were, holding to one another for the sustaining strength their contact offered.

Back, forth, the Foanna danced-and once more their cloaks vanished or were discarded, so their silver-bright figures advanced, retreated, weaving a way from one arabesque to another. First about the outer rim and then in, by spirals and circles. No light except the crimson glowing rivulets on the floor, the silver bodies of the Foanna moving back and forth, in and out.

Then, suddenly, the three dancers halted, huddled together in an open space between the designs. And Ross was startled by the impression of confusion, doubt, almost despair wafted from them to the Terrans. Back across the patterned floor they came, their hands clasped even as the Terrans stood together, and now they fronted the three out of time.

"Too few ...we are too few...." she who was the mid one of the trio said. "We can not open the Great Door."

"How many do you need?" Karara's voice was no longer parched, frightened. She might have traveled through fear to a new serenity.

Why did he think that, Ross wondered fleetingly. Was it because he, too, had had the same release?

The Polynesian girl loosed her grip on her companions' hands, taking a step closer to the Foanna.

"Three can be four—"

"Or five." Ashe moved up beside her. "If we suit your purpose."

Was Gordon Ashe crazy? Or had he fallen victim to whatever filled this place? Yet it was Ashe's voice, sane, serene, as Ross had always heard it. The younger Agent wet his lips; it was his turn to have a dry mouth. This was not his game; it could not be. Yet he summoned voice enough to add in turn:

"Six—"

When it came the Foanna answer was a warning:

"To aid us you must cast aside your shields, allow your identities to become one with our forces. Having done so, it may be that you shall never be as you are now but changed."

"Changed...."

The word echoed, perhaps not in the place where they stood, but in Ross's head. This was a risk such as he had never taken before. His chances in the past had been matters of action where his own strength and wits were matched against the problem. Here, he would open a door to forces he and his kind should not meet-expose himself to danger such as did not exist on the plane where weapons and strength of arm could decide victory or defeat.

And this was not really his fight at all. What did it matter to Terrans ten thousand years or so in the future what happened to Hawaikans in this past? He was a fool; they were all fools to become embroiled in this. The Baldies and their stellar empire-if that ever had existed as the Terrans surmised-was long gone before his breed entered space.

"If you accomplish this with our aid," said Ashe, "will you be able to defeat the invaders?"

Again a lengthening moment of silence before the Foanna replied:

"We can not tell. We only know that there is a force laid up here, set behind certain gates in the far past, upon which we may call for some supreme effort. But this much we also know: The Evil of the Shadow reaches out from here now, and where that darkness falls men will no longer be men but things in the guise of men who obey and follow as mindless creatures. As yet this shadow of the Shadow is a small one. But it will spread, for that is the nature of those who have spawned it. They have chanced upon and corrupted a thing we know. Such power feeds upon the will to power. Having turned it to their bidding, they will not be able to resist using it, for it is so easy to do and the results exult the nature of those who employ it.

"You have said that you and those like you who travel the time trails fear to change the past. Here the first steps have been taken to alter the future, but unless we complete the defense it will be ill for all of us."

"And this is your only weapon?" Ashe asked once more.

"The only one strong enough to stand against that which is now unleashed."

In the pavement the fiery lines were bright and glowing. Even when Ross shut his eyes, parts of those designs were still visible against his eyelids.

"We don't know how." He made a last feeble protest on the side of prudence. "We couldn't move as you did."

"Apart, no-together, yes."

The silvery figures were once more swaying, the mist which was their hair flowing about them. Karara's hands went out, and the slender fingers of one of the Foanna lifted, closed about firm, brown Terran flesh. Ashe was doing the same!

Ross thought he cried out, but he could not be sure, as he watched Karara's head begin to sway in concert with her Foanna partner, her black hair springing out from her shoulders to rival the rippling strands of the alien's. Ashe was consciously matching steps with the companion who also drew him along a flowing line of fire.

In this last instant Ross realized the time for retreat was past-there was no place left to go. His hands went out, though he had to force that invitation because in him there was a shrinking horror of this surrender. But he could not let the others go without him.

The Foanna's touch was cool, and yet it seemed that flesh met his flesh, fingers as normal as his met fingers in that grasp. And when that hold was complete he gave a small gasp. For his horror was wiped away; he knew in its place a burst of energy which could be disciplined to use as a weapon or a tool in concentrated and complicated action. His feet so ...and then so....Did those directions flow without words from the Foanna's fingers to his and then along his nerves to his brain? He only knew which was the proper next step, and the next, and the next, as they wove their way along the pattern lines, with their going adding a necessary thread to a design.

Forward four steps, backward one-in and out. Did Ross actually hear that sweet thrumming, akin to the lilting speech of the Foanna, or was it a throbbing in his blood? In and out....What had become of the others he did not know; he was aware only of his own path, of the hand in his, of the silvery shape at his side to whom he was now tied as if one of the Rover capture nets enclosed them both.

The fiery lines under his feet were smoking, tendrils rising and twisting as the hair of the Foanna rippled and twisted. And the smoke clung, wreathed his body. They moved in a cocoon of smoke, thicker and thicker, until Ross could not even see the Foanna who accompanied him, was only assured of her presence by the hand which grasped his.

And a small part of him clung desperately to the awareness of that clasp as an anchorage against what might come, a tie between the world of reality and the place into which he was passing.

How did one find words to describe this? Ross wondered with that part of him which remained stubbornly Ross Murdock, Terran Time Agent. He thought that he did not see with his eyes, hear with his ears but used other senses his own kind did not recognize nor acknowledge.

Space ...not a room ...a cave-anything made by normal nature. Space which held something.

Pure energy? His Terran mind strove to give name to that which was nameless. Perhaps it was that spark of memory and consciousness which gave him that instant of "Seeing." Was it a throne? And on it a shimmering figure? He was regarded intently, measured, and-set aside.

There were questions or a question he could not hear, and perhaps an answer he would never be able to understand. Or had any of this happened at all?

Ross crouched on a cold floor, his head hanging, drained of energy, of all that feeling of power and well-being he had had when they had begun their dance across the symbols. About him those designs still glowed dully. When he looked at them too intently his head ached. He could almost understand, but the struggle was so exhausting he winced at the effort.

"Gordon —?"

There was no clasp on his hand; he was alone, alone between two glowing arabesques. That loneliness struck at him with the sharpness of a blow. His head came up; frantically he stared about him in search of his companions. "Gordon!" His plea and demand in one was answered:

"Ross?"

On his hands and knees, Ross used the rags of his strength to crawl in that direction, stopping now and then to shade his eyes with his hands, to peer through the cracks between his fingers for some sight of Ashe.

There he was, sitting quietly, his head up as if he were listening, or striving to listen. His cheeks were sunken; he had the drained, worn look of a man strained to the limit of physical energy. Yet there was a quiet peace in his face. Ross crawled on, put out a hand to Ashe's arm as if only by touching the other could he be sure he was not an illusion. And Ashe's fingers came up to cover the younger man's in a grasp as tight as the Foanna's hold had been.

"We did it; together we did it," Ashe said. "But where-why —?"

Those questions were not aimed at him, Ross knew. And at that moment the younger man did not care where they had been, what they had done. It was enough that his terrible loneliness was gone, that Ashe was here.

Still keeping his hold on Ross, Ashe turned his head and called into the wilderness of the symbol-glowing space about them, "Karara?"

She came to them, not crawling, not wrung almost dry of spirit and strength, but on her two feet. About her shoulders her dark hair waved and spun-or was it dark now? Along those strands there seemed to be threaded motes of light, giving a silvery sheen which was a faint echo of the Foanna's tresses. And was it only his bemused and bewildered sight, Ross mused, or was her skin fairer?

Karara smiled down at them and held out her hands, offering one to each. When they took them Ross knew again that surge of energy he had felt when he had followed the Foanna into the maze dance.

"Come! There is much to do."

He could not be mistaken; her voice held the singing lilt of the Foanna. Somehow she had crossed some barrier to become a paler, perhaps a lesser, but still a copy of the three aliens. Was this what they had meant when they warned of a change which might come to those who followed them into the ritual of this place?

Ross looked from the girl to Ashe with searching intensity. No, he could see no outward change in Gordon. And he felt none within himself.

"Come!" Some of Karara's old impetuousness returned as she tugged at them, urging them to their feet and drawing them with her. She appeared to know where they must go, and both men followed her guidance.

Once more they came out of the weird and alien into the normal, for here were the rock walls of a passage running up at an angle which became so steep they were forced to pull along by handholds hollowed in the walls.

"Where are we going?" Ashe asked.

"To cleanse." Karara's answer was ambiguous, and she sped along hardly touching the handholds. "But hurry!"

They finished their climb and were in another corridor where patches of sunlight came through a pierced wall to dazzle their eyes. This was similar to the way which had run beside the courtyard in Zahur's castle.

Ross looked out of the first opening down into a courtyard. But where Zahur's had held the busy life of a castle, this was silent. Silent, but not deserted. There were men below, armed, helmed. He recognized the uniform of the Wrecker warriors, saw one or two who wore the gray of the Foanna servants. They stood in lines, unmoving, without speech among themselves, men who might have been frozen into immobility and arranged so for some game in which they were the voiceless, will-less pieces.

And their immobility was a thing to arouse fear. Were they dead and still standing?

"Come!" Karara's voice had sunk to a whisper and her hand pulled at the men.

"What —?" began Ross.

Ashe shook his head. Those rows below drawn up as if in order to march, unliving rows. They could not be alive as the Terrans knew life!

Ross left his vantage point, ready to follow Karara. But he could not blot from his mind the picture of those lines, nor forget the terrible blankness which made their faces more unhuman, more frightenly alien than those of the Foanna.

17. Shades Against Shadow

The corridor ended in a narrow slit of room, and the wall before them was not the worked stone of the citadel but a single slab of what appeared to be glass curdled into creamy ridges and depressions.

Here were the Foanna, their robes once more cloaking them. Each held, point out, one of the rods. They moved slowly but with the precise gestures of those about a demanding and very important task as they traced each depression in the wall before them with the wand points. Down, up, around ... as their feet had moved in the dance pattern, so now their wands moved to cover each line.

"Now!"

The wands dropped points to the floor. The Foanna moved equidistant from one another. Then, as one, the rods were lifted vertically, brought down together with a single loud tap.

On the wall the blue lines they had traced with such care darkened, melted. The glassy slab shivered, shattered, fell outward in a lace of fragments. So the narrow room became a balcony above a large chamber.

Below a platform ran the full length of that hall, and on it were mounted a line of oval disks. These had been turned to different angles and each reflected light, a ray beam directed at them from a machine whose metallic casing, projecting antennae, was oddly out of place here.

Once more the three staffs of the Foanna raised as one in the air. This time, from the knobs held out over the hall blazed, not the usual whirl of small sparks, but strong beams of light-blue light darkening as it pierced downward until it became thrusting lines of almost tangible substance.

When those blue beams struck the nearest ovals they webbed with lines which cracked wide open. Shattered bits tinkled down to the platform. There was a stir at the end of the hall where the machine stood. Figures ran into plain sight. Baldies! Ross cried out a warning as he saw those star men raise weapon tubes aimed at the perch on which the Foanna stood.

Fire crackling with the speed and sound of lightning lashed up at the balcony. The lances of light met the spears of dark, and there was a flash which blinded Ross, a sound which split open the whole world.

The Terran's eyes opened, not upon darkness but on dazzling light, flashes of it which tore over him in great sweeping arcs. Dazed, sick, he tried to press his prone body into the unyielding surface on which he lay. But there was no way of burrowing out of this wild storm of light and clashing sound. Now under him the very fabric of the floor rocked and quivered as if it were being shaken apart into crumbling rubble.

All the will and ability to move was gone. Ross could only lie there and endure. What had happened, he did not know save that what raged about him now was a warring of inimical forces, perhaps both feeding on each other even as they strove for mastery.

The play of rays resembled sword blades crossing, fencing. Ross threw his arm over his eyes to shut out the intolerable brilliance of that thrust and counter. His body tingled and winced as the whirlwind of energy clashed and reclashed. He was beaten, stupid, as a man pinned down too long under a heavy shelling.

How did it end? In one terrific thunderclap of sound and blasting power? And when did it end-hours ...days later? Time was a thing set apart from this. Ross lay in the quiet which his body welcomed thirstily. Then he was conscious of the touch of wind on his face, wind carrying the hint of sea salt.

He opened his eyes and saw above him a patch of clouded sky. Shakily he levered himself up on his elbows. There were no complete walls any more, just jagged points of masonry, broken teeth set in a skull's jawbone. Open sky, dark clouds spattering rain.

"Gordon? Karara?" Ross's voice was a thin whisper. He licked his lips and tried again: "Gordon!"

Had there been an answering whimper? Ross crawled into a hollow between two fallen blocks. A pool of water? No, it was the cloak of one of the Foanna spread out across the flooring in this fragment of room. Then Ross saw that Ashe was there, the cloaked figure braced against the Terran's shoulder as he half supported, half embraced the Foanna.

"Ynvalda!" Ashe called that with an urgency which was demanding. Now the Foanna moved, raising an arm in the cloak's flowing sleeve.

Ross sat back on his heels.

"Ross-Ashe?" He turned his head. Karara stood here, then came forward, planting her feet with care, her hands outstretched, her eyes wide and unseeing. Ross pulled himself up and went to her, finding that the once solid floor seemed to dip and sway under him, until he, too, must balance and creep. His hands closed on her shoulders and he pulled her to him in mutual support.

"Gordon?"

"Over there. You all right?"

"I think so." Her voice was weak. "The Foanna ... Ynlan ... Ynvalda —" Steadying herself against him, she tried to look around.

The place which had once been a narrow room, then a balcony, was now a perch above stomach-turning space. The hall of the oval mirrors was gone, having disappeared into a hollow the depths of which were veiled by a vapor which boiled and bubbled as if, far below, some huge caldron hung above a blazing fire.

Karara cried out and Ross drew her back from that drop. He was clearer-headed now and looked about for some way down from this doubtful perch. Of the other two Foanna there was no sign. Had they been sucked up and out in the inferno they had created with their unleashing of energy against the Baldies' installation?

"Ross-look!" Karara's cry, her upflung arm directed his attention aloft.

Under the sullen gathering of the storm a sphere arose as a bubble might seek the surface of a pool before breaking. A ship — a Baldy ship taking off from the ruined citadel! So some of the enemy had survived that trial of strength!

The globe was small, a scout used for within-atmosphere exploration, Ross judged. It arose first, and then moved inland, fleeing the gathering storm, to be out of sight in moments. Inland, where the mountain base of the invaders was reputed to be. Retreating? Or bound to gather reinforcements?

"Baldies?" Karara asked.

"Yes."

She wiped her hand across her face, smearing dust and grime on her cheeks. As raindrops pattered about them, Ross drew the girl with him into the alcove where Ashe sheltered with the Foanna. The cowled alien was sitting up, her hand still gripping one of the wands, now a half-melted ruin.

Ashe glanced at them as if for the first time he remembered they might be there.

"Baldy ship just took off inland," Ross told him. "We didn't see either of the other Foanna."

"They have gone to do what is to be done," Ashe's companion replied. "So some of the enemy fled. Well, perhaps they have learned one lesson, not to meddle with others' devices. Ahh, so much gone which will never come again! Never again —"

She held up the half-melted wand, turning it back and forth before her, before she cast it away. It flew out, up, then dropped into the caldron of the hall which had been. A gust of rain, cold, chilling the lightly clad Terrans, swept across them.

The Foanna was helped to her feet by Ashe. For a moment she turned slowly, giving a lingering look to the ruins. Then she spoke: "Broken stone holds no value. Take hands, my brothers, my sister, it is time we go hence."

Karara's hand in Ross's right, Ashe's in his left, and both linked to Ynvalda in turn. Then-they were indeed elsewhere, in a courtyard where bodies lay flaccid under the drenching downpour of the rain. And moving among those bodies were the two other Foanna, bending to examine one man after another. Perhaps over one in three they so inspected they held consultation before a wand was used in tracing certain portions of the body between them. When they were finished, that man stirred, moaned, showed signs of life once more.

"Rosss —!" From behind a tumbled wall crept a Hawaikan who did not wear the guard armor of the others. Gill-pack, flippers, diver's belt, had been stripped from him. There was a bleeding gash down the side of his face, and he held his left arm against his body, supported by his right hand.

"Baleku!"

The Rover pulled himself up to his feet and stood swaying. Ross reached him quickly to catch him as he slumped forward.

"Loketh?" the Terran asked.

"The women-killers took him." Somehow the Rover got that out as Ross half supported, half led him to where the Foanna were gathering those they had been able to revive. "They wanted to learn" —Baleku was obviously making a great effort to tell his story —"about ... about where we came from ... where we got the packs."

"So now they will know of us, or will if they get the story out of Loketh." Ashe worked with Ross to splint the Rover's broken arm. "How many of them were here, Baleku?"

The Rover's head moved slowly from side to side. "I do not know in truth. It is-was-like a dream. I was in the water swimming through the sea gate. Then suddenly I was in another place where those from the stars waited about me. They had our packs and belts and these they showed us, demanding to know whereof these were. Loketh was like one deep in sleep and they left him so when they questioned me. Then there came a great noise and the floor under us shook, lightning flashed through the air. Two of the women-killers ran from the room and all of them were greatly excited. They took up Loketh and carried him away, with him the packs and other things. And I was left alone, though I could not move-as if they had left me in a net I could not see.

"More and more were the flashes. Then one of those slayers of women stood in the doorway. He raised his hand, and my feet were free, but I could not move otherwise than to follow after him. We came along a hall and into this court where men stood unstirring, although stones fell from the walls upon some of them and the ground shook —"

Baleku's voice grew shriller, his words ran together. "The one who pulled me after him by his will-he cried out and put his hands to his head. Back and forth he ran, bumping into the standing men, and once running into a wall as if he were blinded. And then he was gone and I was alone. There was more falling stone and one struck my shoulder so I was thrown to the ground. There I lay until you came."

"So few-out of many so few —" One of the Foanna stood beside them, her cloak streaming with the falling rain. "And for these" —she faced the lines of those they had not revived — "there was no chance. They died as helplessly as if they went into a meeting of swords with their arms bound to their sides! Evil have we wrought here."

Ashe shook his head. "Evil has been wrought here, Ynlan, but not by your seeking. And those who died here helplessly may be only a small portion of those yet to be sacrificed. Have you forgotten the slaughter at Kyn Add and those other fairings where women and children were also struck down to serve some purpose we do not even yet know?"

"Lady, Great One —" Baleku struggled to sit up and Ross slipped an arm behind him in aid. "She for whom I made a bride-cup was meat for them at Kyn Add, along with many others. If these slayers are not put to the sword's edge, there will be other fairings so used. And these Shadow ones possess a magic to draw men to them helplessly to be killed. Great One, you have powers; all men know that wind and wave obey your call. Do you now use your magic! It is better to fall with a power we know, than answer such spells as those killers have netted about the men here!"

"This is one weapon which they shall not use again." Ynvalda rose from a stone block where she had been sitting. "And perhaps in its way it was one of the most dangerous. But in defeating it we have by so much weakened ourselves also. And the strong place of these star men lies not on the coast, but inland. They will be warned by those who fled this place. Wind and wave, yes, those have served our purpose in the past. But now perhaps we have found that which our power will not best! Only-for this" —her gesture was for the ruins of the citadel and the dead —"there shall be a payment exacted-to the height of our desire!"

Whether the Foanna did have any control over the storm winds or not, the present deluge appeared not to accommodate them. The dazed, injured survivors of the courtyard were brought to shelter in some of the underground passages.

There appeared to be no other reminders of the Wrecker force which had earlier besieged the keep than those survivors. But within hours some of those who had served the Foanna for generations returned. And the Foanna themselves opened the sea gates so that the Rover cruisers anchored in the small bay below their ruined walls.

A small force, and one ill-equipped to go up against the Baldies. Some five star men's bodies had been found in the citadel, but the ship had gone off to warn their base. To Ross's thinking the advantage still lay with the invaders.

But the Hawaikans refused to accept the idea that the odds were against them. As soon as the storm blew out its force Ongal's cruiser headed northwest to other clan fairings where the Rovers could claim kinship. And Afrukta sailed on the same errand south. While some of the Wreckers were released to carry the warning to their lords. Just how great a force could be gathered through such means and how effective it would be, was a question to make the Terrans uneasy.

Karara disappeared with the Foanna into the surviving inner cliff-burrows below the citadel. But Ashe and Ross remained with Torgul and his officers, striving to bring organization out of the chaos about them.

"We must know just where their lair lies," Torgul stated the obvious. "The mountains you believe, and they can fly in sky ships to and from that point. Well" —he spread out a chart — "here are the mountains on this island, running so. An army marching hither could be sighted from sky ships. Also, there are many mountains. Which is the one or ones we must seek? It may take many tens of days to find that place, while they will always know where we are, watch us from above, prepare for our coming —"

Again Ross mentally paid tribute to the Captain's quick grasp of essentials.

"You have a solution, Captain?" Ashe asked.

"There is the river-here —" Torgul said reflectively. "Perhaps I think in terms of water because I am a sailor. But here it does run, and for this far along it our cruisers may ascend." He pointed with his finger tip. "This lies, however, in Glicmas's land, and he is now the mightiest of the Wrecker lords, his sword always drawn against us. I do not believe that we could talk him into — —"

"Glicmas!" Ross interrupted. They both looked at him inquiringly, and he repeated Loketh's story of the Wrecker lord who had had dealings with a "voice from the mountain" and so gained the wrecking devices to make him the dominant lord of the district.

"So!" Torgul exclaimed. "That is the evil of this Shadow in the mountains! No, under those circumstances I do not think we shall talk Glicmas into furthering any raid against those who have made him great over his fellows. Rather will he turn against us in their cause."

"And if we do not use the cruisers up the river" —Ashe conned the map —"then perhaps a small party or parties working overland could strike the stream here, nearer to the uplands."

Torgul frowned at the map. "I do not think so. Even small parties moving in that direction would be sighted by Glicmas's people. The more so if they headed inland. He will not wish to share his secrets with others."

"But, say —a party of Foanna."

The Captain glanced up swiftly to favor Ashe with a keen regard. "Then he would not dare. No, I am sure he would not dare to interfere. Not yet has he risen high enough to turn the hook of his sword against them. But would the Foanna do so?"

"If not the Foanna, then others wearing like robes," Ashe said slowly.

"Others wearing like robes?" repeated Torgul. Now his frown was heavy. "No man would take on the guise of the Foanna; he would be blasted by their power for so doing. If the Foanna will lead us in their persons, then we shall follow gladly, knowing that their magic will be with us."

"There is also this," Ross broke in. "The Baldies have the gill-packs they took from Baleku and Loketh, and they have Loketh. They will want to learn more about us. We hoped that the citadel would provide bait to draw them and it did. That our plan for a trap there was spoiled was ill fortune. But I am sure that if the Baldies believe we are coming to them, they will hold off an all-out attack against our march, hoping to gather us in intact. They'd risk that."

Ashe nodded. "I agree. We are the unknown they must solve now. And this much I am sure of-the future of this world and her people balances on a very narrow line of choice. It is my hope that such a choice is still to be made."

Torgul smiled thinly. "We live in perilous times when the Shades require our swords to go up against the Shadow!"

18. World in Doubt?

The day was dully overcast as all days had been since they had begun this sulk-and-march penetration into the mountain territory. Ross could not accept the idea that the Foanna might actually command wind and wave, storm and sun, as the Hawaikans firmly believed, but the gloomy weather *had* favored them so far. And now they had reached the last breathing point before they took the plunge into the heart of the enemy country. About the way in which they were to make that plunge, Ross had his own plan. One he did not intend to share with either Ashe or Karara. Though he had had to outline it to the one now waiting here with him.

"This is still your mind, younger brother?"

He did not turn his head to look at the cloaked figure. "It is still my mind!" Ross could be firm on that point.

The Terran backed out of the vantage place from which he had been studying the canyonlike valley cupping the Baldy spaceship. Now he got to his feet and faced Ynlan, his own gray cloak billowing out in the wind to reveal the Rover scale armor underneath.

"You can do it for me?" he asked in turn. During the past days the Foanna had admitted that the weird battle within the citadel had weakened and limited their "magic." Last night they had detected a force barrier ahead and to transport the whole party through that by teleporting was impossible.

"Yes, you alone. Then my wand would be drained for a space. But what can you do within their hold, save be meat for their taking?"

"There can not be too many of them left there. That's a small ship. They lost five at the citadel, and the Rovers have three prisoners. No sign of the scout ship we know they have-so more of them must be gone in it. I won't be facing an army. And what they have in the way of weapons may be powered by installations in the ship. A lot of damage done there. Or even if the ship lifted —" He was not sure of what he could do; this was a venture depending largely on improvisation at the last moment.

"You propose to send off the ship?"

"I don't know whether that is possible. No, perhaps I can only attract their attention, break through the force shield so the rest may attack."

Ross knew that he must attempt this independent action, that in order to remain the Ross Murdock he had always been, he must be an actor not a spectator.

The Foanna did not argue with him now. "Where —?" Her long sleeve rippled as she gestured to the canyon. Dull as the skies were overhead, there was light here-too much of it for his purpose as the ground about the ship was open. To appear there might be fatal.

Ross was grasped by another and much more promising idea. The Foanna had transported them all to the deck of Torgul's cruiser after asking him to picture it for her mentally. And to all outward appearances the Baldy ship before them now was twin to the one which had taken him once on a fantastic voyage across a long-vanished stellar empire. Such a ship he knew!

"Can you put me in the ship?"

"If you have a good memory of it, yes. But how know you these ships?"

"I was in one once for many days. If these are alike, then I know it well!"

"And if this is unlike, to try such may mean your death."

He had to accept her warning. Yet outwardly this ship was a duplicate. And before he had voyaged on the derelict he had also explored a Wrecker freighter on his own world thousands of years before his own race had evolved. There was one portion of both ships which had been identical-save for size-and that part was the best for his purpose.

"Send me-here!"

With closed eyes, Ross produced a mental picture of the control cabin. Those seats which were not really seats but webbing support swinging before banks of buttons and levers; all the other installations he had watched, studied, until they were as known to him as the plate bulkheads of the cabin below in which he had slept. Very vivid, that memory. He felt the touch of the Foanna's cool fingers on his forehead-then it was gone. He opened his eyes.

No more wind and gloom, he stood directly behind the pilot's web-sling, facing a vista-plate and rows of controls, just as he had stood so many times in the derelict. He had made it! This was the control cabin of the spacer. And it was alive-the faint thrumming in the air, the play of lights on the boards.

Ross pulled the cowl of his Foanna cloak up over his head. He had had days to accustom himself to the bulk of the robe, but still its swathings were sometimes a hindrance rather than a help. Slowly he turned. There were no Baldies here, but the well door to the lower levels was open, and from it came small sounds echoing up the communication ladder. The ship was occupied.

Not for the first time since he had started on this venture Ross wished for more complete information. Doubtless several of those buttons or levers before him controlled devices which could be the greatest aid to him now. But which and how he did not know. Once in just such a cabin he had meddled and, in activating a long silent installation, had called the attention of the Baldies to their wrecked ship, to the Terrans looting it. Only by the merest chance had the vengeance of the stellar spacemen fallen then on the Russian investigators and not on his own people.

He knew better than to touch anything before the pilot's station, but the banks of controls to one side were concerned with the inner well-being of the ship-and they tempted him. To go it blind was, however, more of a risk than he dared take. There was one future precaution for him.

From a very familiar case beside the pilot's seat Ross gathered up a collection of disks, sorted through them hastily for one which bore a certain symbol on its covering. There was only one of those. Slapping the rest back into their container, Ross pressed a button on the control board.

Again his guess paid off! Another disk was exposed as a small panel slid back. Ross clawed that out of the holder, put in its place the one he had found. Now, if his choice had been correct, the crew who took off in this ship, unless they checked their route tape first, would find themselves heading to another primitive planet and not returning to base. Perhaps exhaustion of fuel might ground them past hope of ever regaining their home port again. Next to damaging the ship, which he could not do, this was the best thing to assure that any enemy leaving Hawaika would not speedily return with a second expeditionary force.

Ross dropped the route disk he had taken out into a pocket on his belt, to be destroyed when he had the chance. Now he catfooted across the deck to look into the well and listen.

The walls glowed with a diffused light. From here the Terran could count at least four levels under him, with perhaps another. The bottom two ought to be supplies and general storage. Then the engine room, tech labs above, and next to the control cabin the living quarters.

Through the fabric of the ship, shivering up his body from the soles of his feet, he could feel the vibration of engines at work. One such must control the force field which ringed this canyon, perhaps even powered the weapons the invaders could turn against any assault.

Ross whirled about, his Foanna cloak in a wide swing. There was one control which he knew. Yes, again the board was the same as the one he was familiar with. His hand plunged out and down, raking the lever from one measure point to the very end of the slit in which it moved. Then he planted himself with his back to the wall. Whoever came up the well hunting the cause for the failure would be facing the other way. Ross crouched a little, pushing the cape well back on his shoulders to free his arms. There was a feline suppleness in his stance just as a jungle cat might wait coming of its prey.

What he heard was a shout below, the click of foot-gear on the rungs of the level ladder. Ross's lips drew back in a snarl which was also feline. He thought that would do it! Spacemen were ultra-sensitive to any failure in air flow.

White head, bare of any hair, thin shoulders a little hunched under the blue-green-lavender stuff of the Baldies' uniforms.... Head turning now so that the eyes could see the necessary switch. An exclamation from the alien and —

But the Baldy never had a chance to complete that turn, look behind him. Ross sprang and struck with the side of his hand. The hairless head snapped forward. His hands already hooked in the other's armpits, the Terran heaved the alien up and over onto the deck of the control cabin. It was only when he was about to bind his captive that Ross discovered the Baldy was dead. A blow calculated to stun the alien had been too severe. Breathing a little faster, the Terran rolled the body back and hoisted it into the navigator's swing-seat, fastening it with the take-off belts. One down-how many left?

He had little time to wonder, for before he could reach the well once again there was a call from below-sharp and demanding. The Terran searched his victim, but the Baldy was unarmed.

Again a shout. Then silence-too complete a silence. How could they have guessed trouble so quickly. Unless, unless the Baldies' mental communication had been at work ... they might even now know their fellow was dead.

But not how he died. Ross was prepared to grant the Baldies super-Terran abilities, but he did not see how they could know what had happened here. They could only suspect danger, not know the form it had taken. And sooner or later one of them must come to adjust the switch. This could be a duel of patience.

Ross squatted at the edge of the well, trying to make his ears supply him with hints of what might be happening below. Had there been an alteration in the volume of vibration? He set his palm flat to the deck, tried to deduce the truth. But he could not be sure. That there had been some slight change he was certain.

They could not wait much longer without making an attempt to reopen the air-supply regulator, or could they? Again Ross was hampered by lack of information. Perhaps the Baldies did not need the same amount of oxygen his own kind depended upon. And if that were true, Ross could be the first to suffer in playing a waiting game. Well, air was not the only thing he could cut off from here, though it had been the first and most important to his mind. Ross hesitated. Two-edged weapons cut in both directions. But he had to force a countermove from them. He pulled another switch. The control cabin, the whole of the ship, was plunged into darkness.

No sound from below this time. Ross pictured the interior layout of the ships he had known. Two levels down to reach the engine room. Could he descend undetected? There was only one way to test that-try it.

He pulled the Foanna cloak about him, was several rungs down on the ladder when the glow in the walls came on. An emergency switch? With a forward scramble, Ross swung into one of the radiating side corridors. The sliding-door panels along it were all closed; he could detect no sounds behind them. But the vibration in the ship's walls had returned to its steady beat.

Now the Terran realized the folly of his move. He was more securely trapped here than he had been in the control cabin. There was only one way out, up or down the ladder, and the enemy could have that under observation from below. All they would need to do was to use a flamer or a paralyzing ray such as the one he had turned over to Ashe several days ago.

Ross inched along to the stairwell. A faint pad of movement, a shadow of sound from the ladder. Someone on the way up. Could they mentally detect him, know him for an alien intruder by the broadcast of his thoughts? The Baldies had a certain respect for the Foanna and might desire to take one alive. He drew the robe about him, used it to muffle his figure completely as the true wearers did.

But the figure pulling painfully up from rung to rung was no Baldy. The lean Hawaikan arms, the thin Hawaikan face, drawn of feature, painfully blank of expression-Loketh-under the same dread spell as had held the warriors in the citadel courtyard. Could the aliens be using this Hawaikan captive as a defense shield, moving up behind him?

Loketh's head turned, those blank eyes regarded Ross. And their depths were troubled, recognition of a sort returning. The Hawaikan threw up one hand in a beseeching gesture and then went to his knees in the corridor.

"Great One! Great One!" The words came from his lips in a breathy hiss as he groveled. Then his body went flaccid, and he sprawled face down, his twisted leg drawn up as if he would run but could not.

"Foanna!" The one word came out of the walls themselves, or so it seemed.

"Foanna-the wise learn what lies before them when they walk alone in the dark." The Hawaikan speech was stilted, accented, but understandable.

Ross stood motionless. Had they somehow seen him through Loketh's eyes? Or had they been alerted merely by the Hawaikan's call? They believed he was one of the Foanna. Well, he would play that role.

"Foanna!" Sharper this time, demanding. "You lie in our hand. Let us clasp the fingers tightly and you shall be naught."

Out of somewhere the words Karara had chanted in the Foanna temple came to Ross-not in her Polynesian tongue but in the English she had repeated. And softening his voice to his best approximation of the Foanna singsong Ross sang:

"Ye forty thousand gods,

Ye gods of sea, of sky-of stars," he improvised.

"Ye elders of the gods that are,

Ye gods that once were,

Ye that whisper, yet that watch by night,

Ye that show your gleaming eyes."

"Foanna!" The summons was on the ragged edge of patience. "Your tricks will not move our mountains!"

"Ye gods of mountains," Ross returned, "of valleys, of Shades and not the Shadow," he wove in the beliefs of this world, too. "Walk now this world, between the stars!" His confidence was growing. And there was no use in remaining pent in this corridor. He would have to chance that they were not prepared to kill summarily one of the Foanna.

Ross went to the well, went down the ladder slowly, keeping his robe about him. Here at the next level there was a wider space about the opening, and three door panels. Behind one must be those he sought. He was buoyed up by a curious belief in himself, almost as if wearing this robe did give him in part the power attributed to the Foanna.

He laid his hand on the door to his right and sent it snapping back into its frame, stepped inside as if he entered here by right.

There were three Baldies. To his Terran eyes they were all superficially alike, but the one seated on a control stool had a cold arrogance in his expression, a pitiless half smile which made Ross face him squarely. The Terran longed for one of the Foanna staffs and the ability to use it. To spray that energy about this cabin might reduce the Baldy defenses to nothing. But now two of the paralyzing tubes were trained on him.

"You have come to us, Foanna, what have you to offer?" demanded the commander, if that was his rank.

"Offer?" For the first time Ross spoke. "There is no reason for the Foanna to make any offer, slayer of women and children. You have come from the stars to take, but that does not mean we choose to give."

He felt it now, that inner pulling, twisting in his mind, the willing which was their more subtle weapon. Once they had almost bent him with that willing because then he had worn their livery, a spacesuit taken from the wrecked freighter. Now he did not have that chink in his defense. And all that stubborn independence and determination to be himself alone resisted the influence with a fierce inner fire.

"We offer life to you, Foanna, freedom of the stars. These other dirt creepers are nothing to you, why take you weapons in their cause? You are not of the same race."

"Nor are you!" Ross's hands moved under the envelope of the robe, unloosing the two hidden clasps which held it. That bank of controls before which the commander sat-to silence that would cause trouble. And he depended upon Ynlan. The Rovers should now be massed at either end of the canyon waiting for the force field to fail and let them in.

Ross steadied himself, poised for action. "We have something for you, star men —" he tried to hold their attention with words, "have you not heard of the power of the Foanna-that they can command wind and wave? That they can be where they were not in a single movement of the eyelid? And this is so-behold!"

It was the oldest trick in the world, perhaps on any planet. But because it was so old maybe it had been forgotten by the aliens. For, as Ross pointed, those heads did turn for an instant.

He was in the air, the robe gathered in his arms wide spread as bat wings. And then they crashed in a tangle which bore them all back against the controls. Ross strove to enmesh them in the robe, using the pressure of his body to slam them all on the buttons and levers of the board. Whether that battering would accomplish his purpose, he could not tell. But that he had only these few seconds torn out of time to try, he knew, and determined to use them as best he could.

One of the Baldies had slithered down to the floor and another was aiming strangely ineffectual blows at him. But the third had wriggled free to bring up a paralyzer. Ross slewed around, dragging the alien he held across his body just as the other fired. But though the fighter went limp and heavy in Ross's hold, the Terran's own right arm fell to his side, his upper chest was numb, and his head felt as if one of the Rover's boarding axes had clipped it. Ross reeled back and fell, his left hand raking down the controls as he went. Then he lay on the cabin floor and saw the convulsed face of the commander above him, a paralyzer aiming at his middle.

To breathe was an effort Ross found torture to endure. The red haze in his head filled all the world. Pain-he strove to flee the pain but was held captive in it. And always the pressure on him kept that agony steady.

"Let ...be...." He wanted to scream that. Perhaps he had, but the pressure continued. Then he forced his eyes open. Ashe-Ashe and one of the Foanna bending over him, Ashe's hands on his chest, pressing, relaxing, pressing again.

"It is good —" He knew Ynvalda's voice. Her hand rested lightly on his forehead and from that touch Ross drew again the quickening of body and spirit he had felt on the dancing floor.

"How —?" He began and then changed to —"Where —?" For this was not the engine room of the spacer. He lay in the open, with sweet, rain-wet wind filling his starved lungs now without Ashe's force aid.

"It is over," Ashe told him, "all over-for now."

But not until the sun reached the canyon hours later and they sat in council, did Ross learn all the tale. Just as he had made his own plan for reaching the spacer, so had Ashe, Karara, and the dolphins worked on a similar attempt. The river running deep in those mountain gorges had provided a road for the dolphins and they found beneath its surface an entrance past the force barrier.

"The Baldies were so sure of their superiority on this primitive world they set no guards save that field," Ashe explained. "We slipped through five swimmers to reach the ship. And then the field went down, thanks to you."

"So I did help-that much." Ross grinned wryly. What had he proven by his sortie? Nothing much. But he was not sorry he had made it. For the very fact he had done it on his own had eased in part that small ache which was in him now when he looked at Ashe and remembered how it had once been. Ashe might be-always would be-his friend, but the old tight-locking comradeship of the Project was behind them, vanished like the time gate.

"And what will you do with them?" Ross nodded toward the captives, the three from the ship, two more taken from the small scouting globe which had homed to find their enemies ready for them.

"We wait," Ynvalda said, "for those on the Rover ship to be brought hither. By our laws they deserve death."

The Rovers at that council nodded vigorously, all save Torgul and Jazia. The Rover woman spoke first.

"They bear the Curse of Phutka heavy on them. To live under such a curse is worse than a clean, quick dying. Listen, it has come upon me that better this curse not only eat them up but be carried by them to rot those who sent them —"

Together the Foanna nodded. "There has been enough of killing," said Ynlan. "No, warriors, we do not say this because we shrink from rightful deaths. But Jazia speaks the truth in this matter. Let these depart. Perhaps they will bear that with them which will convince their leaders that this is not a world they may squeeze in their hands as one crushes a ripe quaya to eat its seeds. You believe in your cursing, Rovers, then let the fruit of it be made plain beyond the stars!"

Was this the time to speak of the switched tapes, Ross wondered. No, he did not really believe that the Rover curse or their treatment of the captives would, either one, influence the star leaders. But, if the invaders did not return to their base, their vanishing might also work to keep another expedition from invading Hawaikan skies. Leave it to chance, a curse, and time....

So it was decided.

"Have we won?" Ross asked Ashe later.

"Do you mean, have we changed the future? Who can answer that? They may return in force, this may have been a step which was taken before. Those pylons may still stand in the future above a deserted sea and island. We shall probably never know."

That was also their own truth. For them also there had been a substitution of journey tapes by Fate, and this was now their Hawaika. Ross Murdock, Gordon Ashe, Karara Trehern, Tino-rau, Taua-five Terrans forever lost in time-in the past with a dubious future. Would this be the barren, lotus world, or another now? Yes, no-either. They had found their key to the mystery out of time, but they could not turn it, and there was no key to the gate which had ceased to exist. Grasp tight the present. Ross looked about him. Yes, the present, which might be very satisfying after all....

The Time Traders

Chapter 1

To anyone who glanced casually inside the detention room the young man sitting there did not seem very formidable. In height he might have been a little above average, but not enough to make him noticeable. His brown hair was cropped conservatively; his unlined boy's face was not one to be remembered-unless one was observant enough to note those light-gray eyes and catch a chilling, measuring expression showing now and then for an instant in their depths.

Neatly and inconspicuously dressed, in this last quarter of the twentieth century his like was to be found on any street of the city ten floors below-to all outward appearances. But that other person under the protective coloring so assiduously cultivated could touch heights of encased and controlled fury which Murdock himself did not understand and was only just learning to use as a weapon against a world he had always found hostile.

He was aware, though he gave no sign of it, that a guard was watching him. The cop on duty was an old hand-he probably expected some reaction other than passive acceptance from the prisoner. But he was not going to get it. The law had Ross sewed up tight this time. Why didn't they get about the business of shipping him off? Why had he had that afternoon session with the skull thumper? Ross had been on the defensive then, and he had not liked it. He had given to the other's questions all the attention his shrewd mind could muster, but a faint, very faint, apprehension still clung to the memory of that meeting.

The door of the detention room opened. Ross did not turn his head, but the guard cleared his throat as if their hour of mutual silence had dried his vocal cords. "On your feet, Murdock! The judge wants to see you."

Ross rose smoothly, with every muscle under fluid control. It never paid to talk back, to allow any sign of defiance to show. He would go through the motions as if he were a bad little boy who had realized his errors. It was a meek-and-mild act that had paid off more than once in Ross's checkered past. So he faced the man seated behind the desk in the other room with an uncertain, diffident smile, standing with boyish awkwardness, respectfully waiting for the other to speak first.

Judge Ord Rawle. It was his rotten luck to pull old Eagle Beak on his case. Well, he would simply have to take it when the old boy dished it out. Not that he had to remain stuck with it later....

"You have a bad record, young man."

Ross allowed his smile to fade; his shoulders slumped. But under concealing lids his eyes showed an instant of cold defiance.

"Yes, sir," he agreed in a voice carefully cultivated to shake convincingly about the edges. Then suddenly all Ross's pleasure in the skill of his act was wiped away. Judge Rawle was not alone; that blasted skull thumper was sitting there, watching the prisoner with the same keenness he had shown the other day.

"A very bad record for the few years you have had to make it." Eagle Beak was staring at him, too, but without the same look of penetration, luckily for Ross. "By rights, you should be turned over to the new Rehabilitation Service...."

Ross froze inside. That was the "treatment," icy rumors of which had spread throughout his particular world. For the second time since he had entered the room his self-confidence was jarred. Then he clung with a degree of hope to the phrasing of that last sentence.

"Instead, I have been authorized to offer you a choice, Murdock. One which I shall state-and on record —I do not in the least approve."

Ross's twinge of fear faded. If the judge didn't like it, there must be something in it to the advantage of Ross Murdock. He'd grab it for sure!

"There is a government project in need of volunteers. It seems that you have tested out as possible material for this assignment. If you sign for it, the law will consider the time spent on it as part of your sentence. Thus you may aid the country which you have heretofore disgraced — —"

"And if I refuse, I go to this rehabilitation. Is that right, sir?"

"I certainly consider you a fit candidate for rehabilitation. Your record —" He shuffled through the papers on his desk.

"I choose to volunteer for the project, sir."

The judge snorted and pushed all the papers into a folder. He spoke to a man waiting in the shadows. "Here then is your volunteer, Major."

Ross bottled in his relief. He was over the first hump. And since his luck had held so far, he might be about to win all the way....

The man Judge Rawle called "Major" moved into the light. At the first glance Ross, to his hidden annoyance, found himself uneasy. To face up to Eagle Beak was all part of the game. But somehow he sensed one did not play such games with this man.

"Thank you, your honor. We will be on our way at once. This weather is not very promising."

Before he realized what was happening, Ross found himself walking meekly to the door. He considered trying to give the major the slip when they left the building, losing himself in a storm-darkened city. But they did not take the elevator downstairs. Instead, they climbed two or three flights up the emergency stairs. And to his humiliation Ross found himself panting and slowing, while the other man, who must have been a good dozen years his senior, showed no signs of discomfort.

They came out into the snow on the roof, and the major flashed a torch skyward, guiding in a dark shadow which touched down before them. A helicopter! For the first time Ross began to doubt the wisdom of his choice.

"On your way, Murdock!" The voice was impersonal enough, but that very impersonality got under one's skin.

Bundled into the machine between the silent major and an equally quiet pilot in uniform, Ross was lifted over the city, whose ways he knew as well as he knew the lines on his own palm, into the unknown he was already beginning to regard dubiously. The lighted streets and buildings, their outlines softened by the soft wet snow, fell out of sight. Now they could mark the outer highways. Ross refused to ask any questions. He could take this silent treatment; he *had* taken a lot of tougher things in the past.

The patches of light disappeared, and the country opened out. The plane banked. Ross, with all the familiar landmarks of his world gone, could not have said if they were headed north or south. But moments later not even the thick curtain of snowflakes could blot out the pattern of red lights on the ground, and the helicopter settled down.

"Come on!"

For the second time Ross obeyed. He stood shivering, engulfed in a miniature blizzard. His clothing, protection enough in the city, did little good against the push of the wind. A hand gripped his upper arm, and he was drawn forward to a low building. A door banged and Ross and his companion came into a region of light and very welcome heat.

"Sit down—over there!"

Too bewildered to resent orders, Ross sat. There were other men in the room. One, wearing a queer suit of padded clothing, a bulbous headgear hooked over his arm, was reading a paper. The major crossed to speak to him and after they conferred for a moment, the major beckoned Ross with a crooked finger. Ross trailed the officer into an inner room lined with lockers.

From one of the lockers the major pulled a suit like the pilot's, and began to measure it against Ross. "All right," he snapped. "Climb into this! We haven't all night."

Ross climbed into the suit. As soon as he fastened the last zipper his companion jammed one of the domed helmets on his head. The pilot looked in the door. "We'd better scramble, Kelgarries, or we may be grounded for the duration!"

They hurried back to the flying field. If the helicopter had been a surprising mode of travel, this new machine was something straight out of the future —a needle-slim ship poised on fins, its sharp nose lifting vertically into the heavens. There was a scaffolding along one side, which the pilot scaled to enter the ship.

Unwillingly, Ross climbed the same ladder and found that he must wedge himself in on his back, his knees hunched up almost under his chin. To make it worse, cramped as those quarters were, he had to share them with the major. A transparent hood snapped down and was secured, sealing them in.

During his short lifetime Ross had often been afraid, bitterly afraid. He had fought to toughen his mind and body against such fears. But what he experienced now was no ordinary fear; it was panic so strong that it made him feel sick. To be shut in this small place with the knowledge that he had no control over his immediate future brought him face to face with every terror he had ever known, all of them combined into one horrible whole.

How long does a nightmare last? A moment? An hour? Ross could not time his. But at last the weight of a giant hand clamped down on his chest, and he fought for breath until the world exploded about him.

He came back to consciousness slowly. For a second he thought he was blind. Then he began to sort out one shade of grayish light from another. Finally, Ross became aware that he no longer rested on his back, but was slumped in a seat. The world about him was wrung with a vibration that beat in turn through his body.

Ross Murdock had remained at liberty as long as he had because he was able to analyze a situation quickly. Seldom in the past five years had he been at a loss to deal with any challenging person or action. Now he was aware that he was on the defensive and was being kept there. He stared into the dark and thought hard and furiously. He was convinced that everything that was happening to him this day was designed with only one end in view-to shake his self-confidence and make him pliable. Why?

Ross had an enduring belief in his own abilities and he also possessed a kind of shrewd understanding seldom granted to one so young. He knew that while Murdock was important to Murdock, he was none too important in the scheme of things as a whole. He had a record —a record so bad that Rawle might easily have thrown the book at him. But it differed in one important way from that of many of his fellows; until now he had been able to beat most of the raps. Ross believed this was largely because he had always worked alone and taken pains to plan a job in advance.

Why now had Ross Murdock become so important to someone that they would do all this to shake him? He was a volunteer-for what? To be a guinea pig for some bug they wanted to learn how to kill cheaply and easily? They'd been in a big hurry to push him off base. Using the silent treatment, this rushing around in planes, they were really working to keep him groggy. So, all right, he'd give them a groggy boy all set up for their job, whatever it was. Only, was his act good enough to fool the major? Ross had a hunch that it might not be, and that really hurt.

It was deep night now. Either they had flown out of the path of the storm or were above it. There were stars shining through the cover of the cockpit, but no moon.

Ross's formal education was sketchy, but in his own fashion he had acquired a range of knowledge which would have surprised many of the authorities who had had to deal with him. All the wealth of a big city library had been his to explore, and he had spent much time there, soaking up facts in many odd branches of learning. Facts were very useful things. On at least three occasions assorted scraps of knowledge had preserved Ross's freedom, once, perhaps his life.

Now he tried to fit together the scattered facts he knew about his present situation into some proper pattern. He was inside some new type of super-super atomjet, a machine so advanced in design that it would not have been used for anything that was not an important mission. Which meant that Ross Murdock had become necessary to someone, somewhere. Knowing that fact should give him a slight edge in the future, and he might well need such an edge. He'd just have to wait, play dumb, and use his eyes and ears.

At the rate they were shooting along they ought to be out of the country in a couple of hours. Didn't the Government have bases half over the world to keep the "cold peace"? Well, there was nothing for it. To be planted abroad someplace might interfere with plans for escape, but he'd handle that detail when he was forced to face it.

Then suddenly Ross was on his back once more, the giant hand digging into his chest and middle. This time there were no lights on the ground to guide them in. Ross had no intimation that they had reached their destination until they set down with a jar which snapped his teeth together.

The major wriggled out, and Ross was able to stretch his cramped body. But the other's hand was already on his shoulder, urging him along. Ross crawled free and clung dizzily to a ladderlike disembarking structure.

Below there were no lights, only an expanse of open snow. Men were moving across that blank area, gathering at the foot of the ladder. Ross was hungry and very tired. If the major wanted to play games, he hoped that such action could wait until the next morning.

In the meantime he must learn where "here" was. If he had a chance to run, he wanted to know the surrounding territory. But that hand was on his arm, drawing him along toward a door that stood half-open. As far as Ross could see, it led to the interior of a hillock of snow. Either the storm or men had done a very good cover-up job, and somehow Ross knew the camouflage was intentional.

That was Ross's introduction to the base, and after his arrival his view of the installation was extremely limited. One day was spent in undergoing the most searching physical he had ever experienced. And after the doctors had poked and pried he was faced by a series of other tests no one bothered to explain. Thereafter he was introduced to solitary, that is, confined to his own company in a cell-like room with a bunk that was more comfortable than it looked and an announcer in a corner of the ceiling. So far he had been told exactly nothing. And so far he had asked no questions, stubbornly keeping up his end of what he believed to be a tug of wills. At the moment, safely alone and lying flat on his bunk he eyed the announcer, a very dangerous young man and one who refused to yield an inch.

"Now hear this...." The voice transmitted through that grill was metallic, but its rasp held overtones of Kelgarries' voice. Ross's lips tightened. He had explored every inch of the walls and knew that there was no trace of the door which had admitted him. With only his bare hands to work with he could not break out, and his only clothes were the shirt, sturdy slacks, and a pair of soft-soled moccasins that they had given him.

"...to identify ..." droned the voice. Ross realized that he must have missed something, not that it mattered. He was almost determined not to play along any more.

There was a click, signifying that Kelgarries was through braying. But the customary silence did not close in again. Instead, Ross heard a clear, sweet trilling which he vaguely associated with a bird. His acquaintance with all feathered life was limited to city sparrows and plump park pigeons, neither of which raised their voices in song, but surely those sounds were bird notes. Ross glanced from the mike in the ceiling to the opposite wall and what he saw there made him sit up, with the instant response of an alerted fighter.

For the wall was no longer there! Instead, there was a sharp slope of ground cutting down from peaks where the dark green of fir trees ran close to the snow line. Patches of snow clung to the earth in sheltered places, and the scent of those pines was in Ross's nostrils, real as the wind touching him with its chill.

He shivered as a howl sounded loudly and echoed, bearing the age-old warning of a wolf pack, hungry and a-hunt. Ross had never heard that sound before, but his human heritage subconsciously recognized it for what it was-death on four feet. Similarly, he was able to identify the gray shadows slinking about the nearest trees, and his hands balled into fists as he looked wildly about him for some weapon.

The bunk was under him and three of the four walls of the room enclosed him like a cave. But one of those gray skulkers had raised its head and was looking directly at him, its reddish eyes alight. Ross ripped the top blanket off the bunk with a half-formed idea of snapping it at the animal when it sprang.

Stiff-legged, the beast advanced, a guttural growl sounding deep in its throat. To Ross the animal, larger than any dog he had even seen and twice as vicious, was a monster. He had the blanket ready before he realized that the wolf was not watching him after all, and that its attention was focused on a point out of his line of vision.

The wolfs muzzle wrinkled in a snarl, revealing long yellow-white teeth. There was a singing twang, and the animal leaped into the air, fell back, and rolled on the ground, biting despairingly at a shaft protruding from just behind its ribs. It howled again, and blood broke from its mouth.

Ross was beyond surprise now. He pulled himself together and got up, to walk steadily toward the dying wolf. And he wasn't in the least amazed when his outstretched hands flattened against an unseen barrier. Slowly, he swept his hands right and left, sure that he was touching the wall of his cell. Yet his eyes told him he was on a mountain side, and every sight, sound, and smell was making it real to him.

Puzzled, he thought a moment and then, finding an explanation that satisfied him, he nodded once and went back to sit at ease on his bunk. This must be some superior form of TV that included odors, the illusion of wind, and other fancy touches to make it more vivid. The total effect was so convincing that Ross had to keep reminding himself that it was all just a picture.

The wolf was dead. Its pack mates had fled into the brush, but since the picture remained, Ross decided that the show was not yet over. He could still hear a click of sound, and he waited for the next bit of action. But the reason for his viewing it still eluded him.

A man came into view, crossing before Ross. He stooped to examine the dead wolf, catching it by the tail and hoisting its hindquarters off the ground. Comparing the beast's size with the hunter's, Ross saw that he had not been wrong in his estimation of the animal's unusually large dimensions. The man shouted over his shoulder, his words distinct enough, but unintelligible to Ross.

The stranger was oddly dressed-too lightly dressed if one judged the climate by the frequent snow patches and the biting cold. A strip of coarse cloth, extending from his armpit to about four inches above the knee, was wound about his body and pulled in at the waist by a belt. The belt, far more ornate than the cumbersome wrapping, was made of many small chains linking metal plates and supported a long dagger which hung straight in front. The man also wore a round blue cloak, now swept back on his shoulders to free his bare arms, which was fastened by a large pin under his chin. His footgear, which extended above his calves, was made of animal hide, still bearing patches of shaggy hair. His face was beardless, though a shadowy line along his chin suggested that he had not shaved that particular day. A fur cap concealed most of his dark-brown hair.

Was he an Indian? No, for although his skin was tanned, it was as fair as Ross's under that weathering. And his clothing did not resemble any Indian apparel Ross had ever seen. Yet, in spite of his primitive trappings, the man had such an aura of authority, of self-confidence, and competence that it was clear he was top dog in his own section of the world.

Soon another man, dressed much like the first, but with a rust-brown cloak, came along, pulling behind him two very reluctant donkeys, whose eyes rolled fearfully at sight of the dead wolf. Both animals wore packs lashed on their backs by ropes of twisted hide. Then another man came along, with another brace of donkeys. Finally, a fourth man, wearing skins for covering and with a mat of beard on his cheeks and chin, appeared. His uncovered head, a bush of uncombed flaxen hair, shone whitish as he knelt beside the dead beast, a knife with a dull-gray blade in his hand, and set to work skinning the wolf with appreciable skill. Three more pairs of donkeys, all heavily laden, were led past the scene before he finished his task. Finally, he rolled the bloody skin into a bundle and gave the flayed body a kick before he ran lightly after the disappearing train of pack animals.

Chapter 2

Ross, absorbed in the scene before him, was not prepared for the sudden and complete darkness which blotted out not only the action but the light in his own room as well.

514

"What —?" His startled voice rang loudly in his ears, too loudly, for all sound had been wiped out with the light. The faint swish of the ventilating system, of which he had not been actively aware until it had disappeared, was also missing. A trace of the same panic he had known in the cockpit of the atomjet tingled along his nerves. But this time he could meet the unknown with action.

Ross slowly moved through the dark, his hands outstretched before him to ward off contact with the wall. He was determined that somehow he would discover the hidden door, escape from this dark cell....

There! His palm struck flat against a smooth surface. He swept out his hand-and suddenly it passed over emptiness. Ross explored by touch. There *was* a door and now it was open. For a moment he hesitated, upset by a nagging little fear that if he stepped through he would be out on the hillside with the wolves.

"That's stupid!" Again he spoke aloud. And, just because he did feel uneasy, he moved. All the frustrations of the past hours built up in him a raging desire to do something-anything-just so long as it was what *he* wanted to do and not at another's orders.

Nevertheless, Ross continued to move slowly, for the space beyond that open door was as deep and dark a pit as the room he left. To squeeze along one wall, using an outstretched arm as a guide, was the best procedure, he decided.

A few feet farther on, his shoulder slipped from the surface and he half tumbled into another open door. But there was the wall again, and he clung to it thankfully. Another door ... Ross paused, trying to catch some faint sound, the slightest hint that he was not alone in this blindman's maze. But without even air currents to stir it, the blackness itself took on a thick solidity which encased him as a congealing jelly.

The wall ended. Ross kept his left hand on it, flailed out with his right, and felt his nails scrape across another surface. The space separating the two surfaces was wider than any doorway. Was it a cross-corridor? He was about to make a wider arm sweep when he heard a sound. He was not alone.

Ross went back to the wall, flattening himself against it, trying to control the volume of his own breathing in order to catch the slightest whisper of the other noise. He discovered that lack of sight can confuse the ear. He could not identify those clicks, the wisp of fluttering sound that might be air displaced by the opening of another door.

Finally, he detected something moving at floor level. Someone or something must be creeping, not walking, toward him. Ross pushed back around the corner. It never occurred to him to challenge that crawler. There was an element of danger in this strange encounter in the dark; it was not meant to be a meeting between fellow explorers.

The sound of crawling was not steady. There were long pauses, and Ross became convinced that each rest was punctuated by heavy breathing as if the crawler was finding progress a great and exhausting effort. He fought the picture that persisted in his imagination-that of a wolf snuffling along the blacked-out hall. Caution suggested a quick retreat, but Ross's urge to rebellion held him where he was, crouching, straining to see what crept toward him.

Suddenly there was a blinding flare of light, and Ross's hands went to cover his dazzled eyes. And he heard a despairing, choked exclamation from near to floor level. The same steady light that normally filled hall and room was bright again. Ross found himself standing at the juncture of two corridors-momentarily, he was absurdly pleased that he had deduced that correctly-and the crawler —?

A man-at least the figure was a two-legged, two-armed body reasonably human in outline-was lying several yards away. But the body was so wrapped in bandages and the head so totally muffled, that it lacked all identity. For that reason it was the more startling.

One of the mittened hands moved slightly, raising the body from the ground so it could squirm forward an inch or so. Before Ross could move, a man came running into the corridor from the far end. Murdock recognized Major Kelgarries. He wet his lips as the major went down on his knees beside the creature on the floor.

"Hardy! Hardy!" That voice, which carried the snap of command whenever it was addressed to Ross, was now warmly human. "Hardy, man!" The major's hands were on the bandaged body, lifting it, easing the head and shoulders back against his arm. "It's all right, Hardy. You're back-safe. This is the base, Hardy." He spoke slowly, soothingly, with the steadiness one would use to comfort a frightened child.

Those mittened paws which had beat feebly into the air fell onto the bandage-wreathed chest. "Back-safe —" The voice from behind the face mask was a rusty croak.

"Back, safe," the major assured him.

"Dark-dark all around again —" protested the croak.

"Just a power failure, man. Everything's all right now. We'll get you into bed."

The mitten pawed again until it touched Kelgarries' arm; then it flexed a little as if the hand under it was trying to grip.

"Safe —?"

"You bet you are!" The major's tone carried firm reassurance. Now Kelgarries looked up at Ross as if he knew the other had been there all the time.

"Murdock, get down to the end room. Call Dr. Farrell!"

"Yes, sir!" The "sir" came so automatically that Ross had already reached the end room before he realized he had used it.

Nobody explained matters to Ross Murdock. The bandaged Hardy was claimed by the doctor and two attendants and carried away, the major walking beside the stretcher, still holding one of the mittened hands in his. Ross hesitated, sure he was not supposed to follow, but not ready either to explore farther or return to his own room. The sight of Hardy, whoever he might be, had radically changed Ross's conception of the project he had too speedily volunteered to join.

That what they did here was important, Ross had never doubted. That it was dangerous, he had early suspected. But his awareness had been an abstract concept of danger, not connected with such concrete evidence as Hardy crawling through the dark. From the first, Ross had nursed vague plans for escape; now he knew he must get out of this place lest he end up a twin for Hardy.

"Murdock?"

Having heard no warning sound from behind, Ross whirled, ready to use his fists, his only weapons. But he did not face the major, or any of the other taciturn men he knew held positions of authority. The newcomer's brown skin was startling against the neutral shade of the walls. His hair and brows were only a few shades darker; but the general sameness of color was relieved by the vivid blue of his eyes.

Expressionless, the dark stranger stood quietly, his arms hanging loosely by his sides, studying Ross, as if the younger man was some problem he had been assigned to solve. When he spoke, his voice was a monotone lacking any modulation of feeling.

"I am Ashe." He introduced himself baldly; he might have been saying "This is a table and that is a chair."

Ross's quick temper took spark from the other's indifference. "All right-so you're Ashe!" He strove to make a challenge of it. "And what is that supposed to mean?"

But the other did not rise to the bait. He shrugged. "For the time being we have been partnered — —"

"Partnered for what?" demanded Ross, controlling his temper.

"We work in pairs here. The machine sorts us ..." he answered briefly and consulted his wrist watch. "Mess call soon."

Ashe had already turned away, and Ross could not stand the other's lack of interest. While Murdock refused to ask questions of the major or any others on that side of the fence, surely he could get some information from a fellow "volunteer."

"What is this place, anyway?" he asked.

The other glanced back over his shoulder. "Operation Retrograde."

Ross swallowed his anger. "Okay, but what do they do here? Listen, I just saw a fellow who'd been banged up as if he'd been in a concrete mixer, creeping along this hall. What sort of work do they do here? And what do we have to do?"

To his amazement Ashe smiled, at least his lips quirked faintly. "Hardy got under your skin, eh? Well, we have our percentage of failures. They are as few as it's humanly possible to make, and they give us every advantage that can be worked out for us — —"

"Failures at what?"

"Operation Retrograde."

Somewhere down the hall a buzzer gave a muted whirr.

"That's mess call. And I'm hungry, even if you're not." Ashe walked away as if Ross Murdock had ceased to exist.

But Ross Murdock did exist, and to him that was an important fact. As he trailed along behind Ashe he determined that he was going to continue to exist, in one piece and unharmed, Operation Retrograde or no Operation Retrograde. And he was going to pry a few enlightening answers out of somebody very soon.

To his surprise he found Ashe waiting for him at the door of a room from which came the sound of voices and a subdued clatter of trays and tableware.

"Not many in tonight," Ashe commented in a take-it-or-leave-it tone. "It's been a busy week."

The room was rather sparsely occupied. Five tables were empty, while the men gathered at the remaining two. Ross counted ten men, either already eating or coming back from a serving hatch with well-filled trays. All of them were dressed in slacks, shirt, and moccasins like himself-the outfit seemed to be a sort of undress uniform-and six of them were ordinary in physical appearance. The other four differed so radically that Ross could barely conceal his amazement.

Since their fellows accepted them without comment, Ross silently stole glances at them as he waited behind Ashe for a tray. One pair were clearly Oriental; they were small, lean men with thin brackets of long black mustache on either side of their mobile mouths. Yet he had caught a word or two of their conversation, and they spoke his own language with the facility of the native born. In addition to the mustaches, each wore a blue tattoo mark on the forehead and others of the same design on the backs of their agile hands.

The second duo were even more fantastic. The color of their flaxen hair was normal, but they wore it in braids long enough to swing across their powerful shoulders, a fashion unlike any Ross had ever seen. Yet any suggestion of effeminacy certainly did not survive beyond the first glance at their ruggedly masculine features.

"Gordon!" One of the braided giants swung halfway around from the table to halt Ashe as he came down the aisle with his tray. "When did you get back? And where is Sanford?"

One of the Orientals laid down the spoon with which he had been vigorously stirring his coffee and asked with real concern, "Another loss?"

Ashe shook his head. "Just reassignment. Sandy's holding down Outpost Gog and doing well." He grinned and his face came to life with an expression of impish humor Ross would not have believed possible. "He'll end up with a million or two if he doesn't watch out. He takes to trade as if he were born with a beaker in his fist."

The Oriental laughed and then glanced at Ross. "Your new partner, Ashe?"

Some of the animation disappeared from Ashe's brown face; he was noncommittal again. "Temporary assignment. This is Murdock." The introduction was flat enough to daunt Ross. "Hodaki, Feng," he indicated the two Easterners with a nod as he put down his tray. "Jansen, Van Wyke." That accounted for the blonds.

"Ashe!" A man arose at the other table and came to stand beside theirs. Thin, with a dark, narrow face and restless eyes, he was much younger than the others, younger and not so well controlled. He might answer questions if there was something in it for him, Ross decided, and filed the thought away.

"Well, Kurt?" Ashe's recognition was as dampening as it could be, and Ross's estimation of the younger man went up a fraction when the snub appeared to have no effect upon him.

"Did you hear about Hardy?"

Feng looked as if he were about to speak, and Van Wyke frowned. Ashe made a deliberate process of chewing and swallowing before he replied. "Naturally." His tone reduced whatever had happened to Hardy to a matter-of-fact proceeding far removed from Kurt's implied melodrama.

"He's smashed up ... kaput...." Kurt's accent, slight in the beginning, was thickening. "Tortured...."

Ashe regarded him levelly. "You aren't on Hardy's run, are you?"

Still Kurt refused to be quashed. "Of course, I'm not! You know the run I am in training for. But that is not saying that such can not happen as well on my run, or yours, or yours!" He pointed a stabbing finger at Feng and then at the blond men.

"You can fall out of bed and break your neck, too, if your number comes up that way," observed Jansen. "Go cry on Millaird's shoulder if it hurts you that much. You were told the score at your briefing. You know why you were picked...."

Ross caught a faint glance aimed at him by Ashe. He was still totally in the dark, but he would not try to pry any information from this crowd. Maybe part of their training was this hush-hush business. He would wait and see, until he could get Kurt aside and do a little pumping. Meanwhile he ate stolidly and tried to cover up his interest in the conversation.

"Then you are going to keep on saying 'Yes, sir,' 'No, sir,' to every order here ——?"

Hodaki slammed his tattooed hand on the table. "Why this foolishness, Kurt? You well know how and why we are picked for runs. Hardy had the deck stacked against him through no fault of the project. That has happened before; it will happen again ——"

"Which is what I have been saying! Do you wish it to happen to you? Pretty games those tribesmen on your run play with their prisoners, do they not?"

"Oh, shut up!" Jansen got to his feet. Since he loomed at least five inches above Kurt and probably could have broken him in two over one massive knee, his order was one to be considered. "If you have any complaints, go make them to Millaird. And, little man" —he poked a massive forefinger into Kurt's chest —"wait until you make that first run of yours before you sound off so loudly. No one is sent out without every ounce of preparation he can take. But we can't set up luck in advance, and Hardy was unlucky. That's that. We got him back, and that was lucky for him. He'd be the first to tell you so." He stretched. "I'm for a game–Ashe? Hodaki?"

"Always so energetic," murmured Ashe, but he nodded as did the small Oriental.

Feng smiled at Ross. "Always these three try to beat each other, and so far all the contests are draws. But we hope ...yes, we have hopes...."

So Ross had no chance to speak to Kurt. Instead, he was drawn into the knot of men who, having finished their meal, entered a small arena with a half circle of spectator seats at one side and a space for contestants at the other. What followed absorbed Ross as completely as the earlier scene of the wolf killing. This too was a fight, but not a physical struggle. All three contenders were not only unlike in body, but as Ross speedily came to understand, they were also unlike in their mental approach to any problem.

They seated themselves crosslegged at the three points of a triangle. Then Ashe looked from the tall blond to the small Oriental. "Territory?" he asked crisply.

"Inland plains!" That came almost in chorus, and each man, looking at his opponent, began to laugh.

Ashe himself chuckled. "Trying to be smart tonight, boys?" he inquired. "All right, plains it is."

He brought his hand down on the floor before him, and to Ross's astonishment the area around the players darkened and the floor became a stretch of miniature countryside. Grassy plains rippled under the wind of a fair day.

"Red!"

"Blue!"

"Yellow!"

The choices came quickly from the dusk masking the players. And upon those orders points of the designated color came into being as small lights.

"Red-caravan!" Ross recognized Jansen's boom.

"Blue-raiders!" Hodaki's choice was only an instant behind.

"Yellow-unknown factor."

Ross was sure that sigh came from Jansen. "Is the unknown factor a natural phenomenon?"

"No-tribe on the march."

"Ah!" Hodaki was considering that. Ross could picture his shrug.

The game began. Ross had heard of chess, of war games played with miniature armies or ships, of games on paper which demand from the players a quick wit and a trained memory. This game, however, was all those combined, and more. As his imagination came to life the moving points of light were transformed into the raiders, the merchants' caravan, the tribe on the march. There was ingenious deployment, a battle, a retreat, a small victory here, to be followed by a bigger defeat there. The game might have gone on for hours. The men about him muttered, taking sides and arguing heatedly in voices low enough not to drown out the moves called by the players. Ross was thrilled when the red traders avoided a very cleverly laid ambush, and indignant when the tribe was forced to withdraw or the caravan lost points. It was the most fascinating game he had ever seen, and he realized that the three men ordering those moves were all masters of strategy. Their respective skills checkmated each other so equally that an outright win was far away.

Then Jansen laughed, and the red line of the caravan gathered in a tight knot. "Camped at a spring," he announced, "but with plenty of sentries out." Red sparks showed briefly beyond that center core. "And they'll have to stay there for all of me. We could keep this up till doomsday, and nobody would crack."

"No"—Hodaki contradicted him—"someday one of you will make a little mistake and then——"

"And then whatever bully boys you're running will clobber us?" asked Jansen. "That'll be the day! Anyway, truce for now."

"Granted!"

The lights of the arena went on and the plains vanished into a dark, tiled floor. "Any time you want a return engagement it'll be fine with me," said Ashe, getting up.

Jansen grinned. "Put that off for a month or so, Gordon. We push into time tomorrow. Take care of yourselves, you two. I don't want to have to break in another set of players when I come back."

Ross, finding it difficult to shake off the illusion which had held him entranced, felt a slight touch on his shoulder and glanced up. Kurt stood behind him, apparently intent upon Jansen and Hodaki as they argued over some point of the game.

"See you tonight." The boy's lips hardly moved, a trick Ross knew from his own past. Yes, he *would* see Kurt tonight, or whenever he could. He was going to learn what it was this odd company seemed determined to keep as their own private secret.

Chapter 3

Ross stood cautiously against the wall of his darkened room, his head turned toward the slightly open door. A slight shuffling sound had awakened him, and he was now as ready as a cat before her spring. But he did not hurl himself at the figure now easing the door farther open. He waited until the visitor was approaching the bunk before he slid along the wall, closing the door and putting his shoulders against it.

"What's the pitch?" Ross demanded in a whisper.

There was a ragged breath, maybe two, then a little laugh out of the dark. "You are ready?" The visitor's accent left no doubt as to his identity. Kurt was paying him the promised visit.

"Did you think that I wouldn't be?"

"No." The dim figure sat without invitation on the edge of the bunk. "I would not be here otherwise, Murdock. You are plenty ... have plenty on the ball. You see, I have heard things about you. Like me, you were tricked into this game. Tell me, is it not true that you saw Hardy tonight."

"You hear a lot, don't you?" Ross was noncommittal.

"I hear, I see, I learn more than these big mouths, like the major with all his do's and don'ts. That I can tell you! You saw Hardy. Do *you* want to be a Hardy?"

"Is there any danger of that?"

"Danger!" Kurt snorted. "Danger-you have not yet known the meaning of danger, little man. Not until now. I ask you again, do you want to end like Hardy? They have not yet looped you in with all their big talk. That is why I came here tonight. If you know what is good for you, Murdock, you will make a break before they tape you ——"

"Tape me?"

Kurt's laugh was full of anger, not amusement. "Oh, yes. They have many tricks here. They are big brains, eggheads, all of them with their favorite gadgets. They put you through a machine to get you registered on a tape. Then, my boy, you cannot get outside the base without ringing all the alarms! Neat, eh? So if you want to make a break, you must try it before they tape you."

Ross did not trust Kurt, but he was listening to him attentively. The other's argument sounded convincing to one whose general ignorance of science led him to be as fearful of the whole field as his ancestors had been of black magic. As all his generation, he was conditioned to believe that all kinds of weird inventions were entirely possible and probable-usually to be produced in some dim future, but perhaps today.

"They must have you taped," Ross pointed out.

Kurt laughed again, but this time he was amused. "They believe that they have. Only they are not as smart as they believe, the major and the rest, including Millaird! No, I have a fighting chance to get out of this place, only I cannot do it alone. That is why I have been waiting for them to bring in a new guy I could get to before they had him pinned down for good. You are tough, Murdock. I saw your record, and I'm betting that you did not come here with the intention of staying. So-here is your chance to go along with one who knows the ropes. You will not have such a good one again."

The longer Kurt talked, the more convincing he was. Ross lost a few of his suspicions. It was true that he had come prepared to run at the first possible opportunity, and if Kurt had everything planned, so much the better. Of course, it was possible that Kurt was a stool pigeon, leading him on as a test. But that was a chance Ross would have to take.

"Look here, Murdock, maybe you think it's easy to break out of here. Do you know where we are, boy? We're near enough to the North Pole as makes no difference! Are you going to leg it back some hundreds of miles through thick ice and snow? A nice jaunt if you make it. I do not think that you can-not without plans and a partner who knows what he is about."

"And how *do* we go? Steal one of those atomjets? I'm no pilot-are you?"

"They have other things besides a-j's here. This place is strictly hush-hush. Even the a-j's do not set down too often for fear they will be tracked by radar. Where have you been, boy? Don't you know the Reds are circling around up here? These fellows watch for Red activity, and the Reds watch them. They play it under the table on both sides. We get our supplies overland by cats ——"

"Cats?"

"Snow sleds, like tractors," the other answered impatiently. "Our stuff is dumped miles to the south, and the cats go down once a month to bring it back. There's no trick to driving a cat, and they tear off the miles ——"

"How many miles to the south?" inquired Ross skeptically. Granted Kurt was speaking the truth, travel over an arctic wilderness in a stolen machine was risky, to say the least. Ross had only a very vague idea of the polar regions, but he was sure that they could easily swallow up the unwary forever.

"Maybe only a hundred or so, boy. But I have more than one plan, and I'm willing to risk *my* neck. Do you think I intend to start out blind?"

There was that, of course. Ross had early sized up his visitor as one who was first of all interested in his own welfare. He wouldn't risk his neck without a definite plan in mind.

"Well, what do you say, Murdock? Are you with me or not?"

"I'll take some time to chew it over — —"

"Time is what you do not have, boy. Tomorrow they will tape you. Then-no over the wall for you."

"Suppose you tell me your trick for fooling the tape," Ross countered.

"That I cannot do, seeing as how it lies in the way my brain is put together. Do you think I can break open my skull and hand you a piece of what is inside? No, you jump with me tonight or else I must wait to grab the next one who lands here."

Kurt stood up. His last words were spoken matter-of-factly, and Ross believed he meant exactly what he said. But Ross hesitated. He wanted to try for freedom, a desire fed by his suspicions of what was going on here. He neither liked nor trusted Kurt, but he thought he understood him-better than he understood Ashe or the others. Also, with Kurt he was sure he could hold his own; it would be the kind of struggle he had experienced before.

"Tonight...." he repeated slowly.

"Yes, tonight!" There was new eagerness in Kurt's voice, for he sensed that the other was wavering. "I have been preparing for a long time, but there must be two of us. We have to take turns driving the cat. There can be no rest until we are far to the south. I tell you it will be easy. There are food caches arranged along the route for emergencies. I have a map marked to show where they are. Are you coming?"

When Ross did not answer at once the other moved closer to him.

"Remember Hardy? He was not the first, and he will not be the last. They use us up fast here. That is why they brought you so quickly. I tell you, it is better to take your chance with me than on a run."

"And what is a run?"

"So they have not yet briefed you? Well, a run is a little jaunt back into history-not nice comfortable history such as you learned out of a book when you were a little kid. No, you are dropped back into some savage time before history — —"

"That's impossible!"

"Yes? You saw those two big blond boys tonight, did you not? Why do you suppose they sport those braids? Because they are taking a little trip into the time when he-men wore braids, and carried axes big enough to crack a man open! And Hodaki and his partner.... Ever hear of the Tartars? Maybe you have not, but once they nearly overran most of Europe."

Ross swallowed. He now knew where he had seen braids pictured on warriors-the Vikings! And Tartars, yes, that movie about someone named Khan, Genghis Khan! But to return into the past was impossible.

Yet, he remembered the picture he had watched today with the wolf slayer and the shaggy-haired man who wore skins. Neither of these was of his own world! Could Kurt be telling the truth? Ross's vivid memory of the scene he had witnessed made Kurt's story more convincing.

"Suppose you get sent back to a time where they do not like strangers," Kurt continued. "Then you are in for it. That is what happened to Hardy. And it is not good-not good at all!"

"But why?"

Kurt snorted. "*That* they do not tell you until just before you take your first run. I do not want to know why. But I do know that I am not going to be sent into any wilderness where a savage may run a spear through me just to prove something or other for Major John Kelgarries, or for Millaird either. I will try my plan first."

The urgency in Kurt's protest carried Ross past the wavering point. He, too, would try the cat. He was only familiar with this time and world; he had no desire to be sent into another one.

Once Ross had made his decision, Kurt hurried him into action. Kurt's knowledge of the secret procedures at the base proved excellent. Twice they were halted by locked doors, but only momentarily, for Kurt had a tiny gadget, concealed in the palm of his hand, which had only to be held over a latch to open a recalcitrant door.

There was enough light in the corridors to give them easy passage, but the rooms were dark, and twice Kurt had to lead Ross by the hand, avoiding furniture or installations with the surety of one who had practiced that same route often. Murdock's opinion of his companion's ability underwent several upward revisions during that tour, and he began to believe that he was really in luck to have found such a partner.

In the last room, Ross willingly followed Kurt's orders to put on the fur clothing Kurt passed to him. The fit was not exact, but he surmised that Kurt had chosen as well as possible. A final door opened, and they stepped out into the polar night of winter. Kurt's mittened hand grasped Ross's, pulling him along. Together, they pushed back the door of a hangar shed to get at their escape vehicle.

The cat was a strange machine, but Ross was given no time to study it. He was shoved into the cockpit, a bubble covering settled down over them, closing them in, and the engine came to life under Kurt's urging. The cat must be traveling at its best pace, Ross thought. Yet the crawl which took them away from the mounded snow covering the base seemed hardly better than a man could make afoot.

For a short time Kurt headed straight away from the starting point, but Ross soon heard him counting slowly to himself as if he were timing something. At the count of twenty the cat swung to the right and made a wide half circle which was copied at the next count of twenty by a similar sweep in the opposite direction. After this pattern had been repeated for six turns, Ross found it difficult to guess whether they had ever returned to their first course. When Kurt stopped counting he asked, "Why the dance pattern?"

"Would you rather be scattered in little pieces all over the landscape?" the other snapped. "The base doesn't need fences two miles high to keep us in, or others out; they take other precautions. You should thank fortune we got through that first mine field without blowing...."

Ross swallowed, but he refused to let Kurt know that he was rattled. "So it isn't as easy to get away as you said?"

"Shut up!" Kurt began counting again, and Ross had some cold apprehensive moments in which to reflect upon the folly of quick decisions and wonder bleakly why he had not thought things through before he leaped.

Again they sketched a weaving pattern in the snow, but this time the arcs formed acute angles. Ross glanced now and then at the intent man at the wheel. How had Kurt managed to memorize this route? His urge to escape the base must certainly be a strong one.

Back and forth they crawled, gaining only a few yards in each of those angled strikes to right or left.

"Good thing these cats are atomic powered," Kurt commented during one of the intervals between mine fields. "We'd run out of fuel otherwise."

Ross fought down the impulse to move his feet away from any possible contact point with the engine. These machines must be safe to ride in, but the bogy of radiation was frightening. Luckily, Kurt was now back to a straight track, with no more weaving.

"We are out!" Kurt said with exultation. But he added no more than just the reassurance of their escape.

The cat crawled on. To Ross's eyes there was no trail to follow, no guideposts, yet Kurt steered ahead with confidence. A little later he pulled to a stop and said to Ross, "We have to drive turn and turn about-your turn."

Ross was dubious. "Well, I can drive a car-but this ———"

"Is fool proof." Kurt caught him up. "The worst was getting through the mine fields, and we are out of that now. See here —" his hand made a shadow on the lighted instrument panel, "this will keep you straight. If you can steer a car, you can steer this. Watch!" He started up again and once more swung the cat to the left.

A light on the panel began to blink at a rate which increased rapidly as they veered farther away from their original course.

"See? You keep that light steady, and you are on course. If it begins to blink, you cast about until it steadies again. Simple enough for a baby. Take over and see."

It was hard to change places in the sealed cabin of the cat, but they were successful, and Ross took the wheel gingerly. Following Kurt's directions, he started ahead, his eyes focused on the light rather than the white expanse before him. And after a few minutes of strain he caught the hang of it. As Kurt had promised, it was very simple. After watching him for a while, his instructor gave a grunt of satisfaction and settled down for a nap.

Once the first excitement of driving the cat wore off, the operation tended to become monotonous. Ross caught himself yawning, but he kept at his post with dogged stubbornness. This had been Kurt's game all the way through-so far-and he was certainly not going to resign his first chance to show that he could be of use also. If there had only been some break in the eternal snow, some passing light or goal to be seen ahead, it would not have been so bad. Finally, every now and then, Ross had to jiggle off course just enough so that the warning blink of light would alert him and keep him from falling asleep. He was unaware that Kurt had awakened during one of those maneuvers until the other spoke. "Your own private alarm clock, Murdock? Okay, I do not quarrel with anyone who uses his head. But you had better get some shut-eye, or we will not keep rolling."

Ross was too tired to protest. They changed places, and he curled up as best he could on his small share of seat. Only now that he was free to sleep, he realized he no longer wanted to. Kurt must have thought Ross had fallen asleep, for after perhaps two miles of steady grinding along, he moved cautiously behind the wheel. Ross saw by the trace of light from the instrument panel that his companion was digging into the breast of his parka to bring out a small object which he held against the wheel of the cat with one hand, while with the other he tapped out an irregular rhythm.

To Ross the action made no sense. But he did not miss the other's sigh of relief as he restored his treasure to hiding once more, as if some difficult task was now behind him. Shortly afterward the cat ground to a stop, and Ross sat up, rubbing his eyes. "What's the matter? Engine trouble?"

Kurt had folded his arms across the wheel. "No. It is just that we are to wait here ———"

"Wait? For what? Kelgarries to come along and pick us up?"

Kurt laughed. "The major? How I wish that he *would* arrive presently. What a surprise he would receive! Not two little mice to be put back into their cages, but the tiger cat, all claws and fangs!"

Ross sat up straighter. This now had the bad smell of a frame, a frame with himself planted right in the middle. He figured out the possibilities and came up with an answer which would smear Ross Murdock all over any map. If Kurt were waiting to meet friends out here, they could only be of one brand.

For most of his short life Ross had been engaged in a private war against the restrictions imposed upon him by a set of legal rules to which something within him would not conform. And he had, during those same years filled with attacks, retreats, and strategic maneuvering, formulated a code of rules by which to play his dangerous game. He had not murdered, and he would never follow the path Kurt took. To one who was supremely impatient of restraint, the methods and aims of Kurt's employers were not only impossibly fantastic and illogical-they were to be opposed to the last ounce of any man's energy.

"Your friends late?" He tried to sound casual.

"Not yet, and if you now plan to play the hero, Murdock, think better of it!" Kurt's tone held the crack of an order-that note Ross had so much disliked in the major's voice. "This is an operation which has been most carefully planned and upon which a great deal depends. No one shall spoil it for us now — —"

"The Reds planted you on the project, eh?" Ross wanted to keep the other talking to give himself a chance to think. And this was one time he had to think, clearly and with speed.

"There is no need for me to tell you the sad tale of my life, Murdock. And you would doubtless find much of it boring. If you wish to continue to live-for a while, at least-you will remain quiet and do as you are told."

Kurt must be armed, for he would not be so confident unless he had a weapon he could now turn on Ross. On the other hand, if what Ross guessed were true, this *was* the time to play the hero-when there was only Kurt to handle. Better to be a dead hero than a live captive in the hands of Kurt's dear friends across the pole.

Without warning, Ross threw his body to the left, striving to pin Kurt against the driver's side of the cabin, his hands clawing at the fur ruff bordering the other's hood, trying for a throat hold. Perhaps it was Kurt's over-confidence which betrayed him and left him open to a surprise attack. He struggled hard to bring up his arm, but both his weight and Ross's held him tight. Ross caught at his wrist, noticing a gleam of metal.

They threshed about, the bulkiness of the fur clothing hampering them. Ross wondered fleetingly why the other had not made sure of him earlier. As it was he fought with all his vigor to keep Kurt immobile, to try and knock him out with a lucky blow.

In the end Kurt aided in his own defeat. When Ross relaxed somewhat, the other pushed against him, only to have Ross flinch to one side. Kurt could not stop himself, and his head cracked against the wheel of the cat. He went limp.

Ross made the most of the next few moments. He brought his belt from under his parka, twisting it around Kurt's wrists with no gentleness. Then he wriggled about, changing places with the unconscious man.

He had no idea of where to go, but he was sure he was going to get away-at the cat's top speed-from that point. And with that in mind and only a limited knowledge of how to manage the machine, Ross started up and turned in a wide circle until he was sure the cat was headed in the opposite direction.

The light which had guided them was still on. Would reversing its process take him back to the base? Lost in the immensity of the cold wilderness, he made the only choice possible and gunned the cat again.

Chapter 4

Once again Ross sat waiting for others to decide his future. He was as outwardly composed as he had been in Judge Rawle's chambers, but inwardly he was far more apprehensive. Out in the wilderness of the polar night he had had no chance for escape. Heading away from Kurt's rendezvous, Ross had run straight into the search party from the base, had seen in action that mechanical hound that Kurt had said they would put on the fugitives' trail-the thing which would have gone on hunting them until its metal rusted into powder. Kurt's boasted immunity to that tracker had not been as good as he had believed, though it had won them a start.

Ross did not know just how much it might count in his favor that he had been on his way back, with Kurt a prisoner in the cat. As his waiting hours wore on he began to think it might mean very little indeed. This time there was no show on the wall of his cell, nothing but time to think-too much of that-and no pleasant things to think about.

But he had learned one valuable lesson on that cold expedition. Kelgarries and the others at the base were the most formidable opponents he had ever met, and all the balance of luck and equipment lay on their side of the scales. Ross was now convinced that there could be no escape from this base. He had been impressed by Kurt's preparations, knowing that some of them were far beyond anything he himself could have devised. He did not doubt that Kurt had come here fully prepared with every ingenious device the Reds could supply.

At least Kurt's friends had had a rude welcome when they did arrive at the meeting place. Kelgarries had heard Ross out and then had sent ahead a team. Before Ross's party had reached the base there had been a blast which split the arctic night wide open. And Kurt, conscious by then, had shown his only sign of emotion when he realized what it meant.

The door to Ross's cell room clicked, and he swung his feet to the floor, sitting up on his bunk to face his future. This time he made no attempt to put on an act. He was not in the least sorry he had tried to get away. Had Kurt been on the level, it would have been a bright play. That Kurt was not, was just plain bad luck.

Kelgarries and Ashe entered, and at the sight of Ashe the taut feeling in Ross's middle loosened a bit. The major might come by himself to pass sentence, but he would not bring Ashe along if the sentence was a really harsh one.

"You got off to a bad start here, Murdock." The major sat down on the edge of the wall shelf which doubled as a table. "You're going to have a second chance, so consider yourself lucky. We know you aren't another plant of our enemies, a fact that saves your neck. Do you have anything to add to your story?"

"No, sir." He was not adding that "sir" to curry any favor; it came naturally when one answered Kelgarries.

"But you have some questions?"

Ross met that with the truth. "A lot of them."

"Why don't you ask them?"

Ross smiled thinly, an expression far removed and years older than his bashful boy's grin of the shy act. "A wise guy doesn't spill his ignorance. He uses his eyes and ears and keeps his trap shut — —"

"And goes off half cocked as a result...." the major added. "I don't think you would have enjoyed the company of Kurt's paymaster."

"I didn't know about him then-not when I left here."

"Yes, and when you discovered the truth, you took steps. Why?" For the first time there was a trace of feeling in the major's voice.

"Because I don't like the line-up on his side of the fence.'"

"That single fact has saved your neck this time, Murdock. Step out of line once more, and nothing will help you. But just so we won't have to worry about that, suppose you ask a few of those questions."

"How much of what Kurt fed me is the truth?" Ross blurted out. "I mean all that stuff about shooting back in time."

"All of it." The major said it so quietly that it carried complete conviction.

"But why-how —?"

"You have us on a spot, Murdock. Because of your little expedition, we have to tell you more now than we tell any of our men before the final briefing. Listen, and then forget all of it except what applies to the job at hand.

"The Reds shot up Sputnik and then Muttnik.... When —? Twenty-five years ago. We got up our answers a little later. There were a couple of spectacular crashes on the moon, then that space station that didn't stay in orbit, after that-stalemate. In the past quarter century we've had no voyages into space, nothing that was prophesied. Too many bugs, too many costly failures. Finally we began to get hints of something big, bigger than any football roaming the heavens.

"Any discovery in science comes about by steps. It can be traced back through those steps by another scientist. But suppose you were confronted by a result which apparently had been produced without any preliminaries. What would be your guess concerning it?"

Ross stared at the major. Although he didn't see what all this had to do with time-jumping, he sensed that Kelgarries was waiting for a serious answer, that somehow Ross would be judged by his reply.

"Either that the steps were kept strictly secret," he said slowly, "or that the result didn't rightfully belong to the man who said he discovered it."

For the first time the major regarded him with approval. "Suppose this discovery was vital to your life-what would you do?"

"Try to find the source!"

"There you have it! Within the past five years our friends across the way have come up with three such discoveries. One we were able to trace, duplicate, and use, with a few refinements of our own. The other two remain rootless; yet they are linked with the first. We are now attempting to solve that problem, and the time grows late. For some reason, though the Reds now have their super, super gadgets, they are not yet ready to use them. Sometimes the things work, and sometimes they fail. Everything points to the fact that the Reds are now experimenting with discoveries which are not basically their own — —"

"Where did they get them? From another world?" Ross's imagination came to life. Had a successful space voyage been kept secret? Had there been contact made with another intelligent race?

"In a way it's another world, but the world of time-not space. Seven years ago we got a man out of East Berlin. He was almost dead, but he lived long enough to record on tape some amazing data, so wild it was almost dismissed as the ravings of delirium. But that was after Sputnik, and we didn't dare disregard any hints from the other side of the Iron Curtain. So the recording was turned over to our scientists, who proved it had a core of truth.

"Time travel has been written up in fiction; it has been discussed otherwise as an impossibility. Then we discover that the Reds have it working — —"

"You mean, they go into the future and bring back machines to use now."

The major shook his head. "Not the future, the past."

Was this an elaborate joke? Somewhat heatedly Ross snapped out the answer to that. "Look here, I know I haven't the education of your big brains, but I do know that the farther back you go into history the simpler things are. We ride in cars; only a hundred years ago men drove horses. We have guns; go back a little and you'll find them waving swords and shooting guys with bows and arrows-those that don't wear tin plate on them to stop being punctured — —"

"Only they were, after all," commented Ashe. "Look at Agincourt, m'lad, and remember what arrows did to the French knights in armor."

Ross disregarded the interruption. "Anyway" —he stuck doggedly to his point —"the farther back you go, the simpler things are. How are the Reds going to find anything in history we can't beat today?"

"That is a point which has baffled us for several years now," the major returned. "Only it is not *how* they are going to find it, but *where*. Because somewhere in the past of this world they have contacted a civilization able to produce weapons and ideas so advanced as to baffle our experts. We have to find that source and either mine it ourselves or close it off. As yet we're still trying to find it."

Ross shook his head. "It must be a long way back. Those guys who discover tombs and dig up old cities-couldn't they give you some hints? Wouldn't a civilization like that have left something we could find today?"

"It depends," Ashe remarked, "upon the type of civilization. The Egyptians built in stone, grandly. They used tools and weapons of copper, bronze, and stone, and they were considerate enough to operate in a dry climate which preserved relics well. The cities of the Fertile Crescent built in mud brick and used stone, copper, and bronze tools. They also chose a portion of the world where climate was a factor in keeping their memory green.

"The Greeks built in stone, wrote their books, kept their history to bequeath it to their successors, and so did the Romans. And on this side of the ocean the Incas, the Mayas, the unknown races before them, and the Aztecs of Mexico all built in stone and worked in metal. And stone and metal survive. But what if there had been an early people who used plastics and brittle alloys, who had no desire to build permanent buildings, whose tools and artifacts were meant to wear out quickly, perhaps for economic reasons? What would they leave us-considering, perhaps, that an ice age had intervened between their time and ours, with glaciers to grind into dust what little they did possess?

"There is evidence that the poles of our world have changed and that this northern region was once close to being tropical. Any catastrophe violent enough to bring about a switch in the poles of this planet might well have wiped out all traces of a civilization, no matter how superior. We have good reason to believe that such a people must have existed, but we must find them.

"And Ashe is a convert from the skeptics—" the major slipped down from his perch on the wall shelf—"he is an archaeologist, one of your tomb discoverers, and knows what he is talking about. We must do our hunting in time earlier than the first pyramid, earlier than the first group of farmers who settled by the Tigris River. But we have to let the enemy guide us to it. That's where you come in."

"Why me?"

"That is a question to which our psychologists are still trying to find the answer, my young friend. It seems that the majority of the people of the several nations linked together in this project have become too civilized. The reactions of most men to given sets of circumstances have become set in regular patterns and they cannot break that conditioning, or if personal danger forces them to change those patterns, they are afterward so adrift they cannot function at their highest potential. Teach a man to kill, as in war, and then you have to recondition him later.

"But during these same wars we also develop another type. He is the born commando, the secret agent, the expendable man who lives on action. There are not many of this kind, and they are potent weapons. In peacetime that particular collection of emotions, nerve, and skills becomes a menace to the very society he has fought to preserve during a war. He is pressured by the peaceful environment into becoming a criminal or a misfit.

"The men we send out from here to explore the past are not only given the best training we can possibly supply for them, but they are all of the type once heralded as the frontiersman. History is sentimental about that type-when he is safely dead-but the present finds him difficult to live with. Our time agents are misfits in the modern world because their inherited abilities are born out of season now. They must be young enough and possess a certain brand of intelligence to take the stiff training and to adapt, and they must pass our tests. Do you understand?"

Ross nodded. "You want crooks because they are crooks — —"

"No, not because they are crooks, but because they are misfits in their time and place. Don't, I beg of you, Murdock, think that we are operating a penal institution here. You would never have been recruited if you hadn't tested out to suit us. But the man who may be labeled murderer in his own period might rank as a hero in another, an extreme example, but true. When we train a man he not only can survive in the period to which he is sent, but he can also pass as a native born in that era — —"

"What about Hardy?"

The major gazed into space. "There is no operation which is foolproof. We have never said that we don't run into trouble or that there is no danger in this. We have to deal with both natives of different times, and if we are lucky and hit a hot run, with the Reds. They suspect that we are casting about, hunting their trail. They managed to plant Kurt Vogel on us. He had an almost perfect cover and conditioning. Now you have it straight, Murdock. You satisfy our tests, and you'll be given a chance to say yes or no before your first run. If you say no and refuse duty, it means you must become an exile and stay here. No man who has gone through our training can return to normal life; there is too much chance of his being picked up and sweated by the opposition."

"Never?"

The major shrugged. "This may be a long-term operation. We hope not, but there is no way of telling now. You will be in exile until we either find what we want or fail entirely. That is the last card I have to lay on the table." He stretched. "You're slated for training tomorrow. Think it over and then let us know your answer when the time comes. Meanwhile, you are to be teamed with Ashe, who will see to putting you through the course."

It was a big hunk to swallow, but once down, Ross found it digestible. The training opened up a whole new world to him. Judo and wrestling were easy enough to absorb, and he thoroughly enjoyed the workouts. But the patient hours of archery practice, the strict instruction in the use of a long-bladed bronze dagger were more demanding. The mastering of one new language and then another, the intensive drill in unfamiliar social customs, the memorizing of strict taboos and ethics were difficult. Ross learned to keep records in knots on hide thongs and was inducted into the art of primitive bargaining and trade. He came to understand the worth of a cross-shaped tin ingot compared to a string of amber beads and some well-cured white furs. He now understood why he had been shown a traders' caravan during that first encounter with the purpose behind Operation Retrograde.

During the training days his feeling toward Ashe changed materially. A man could not work so closely with another and continue to resent his attitude; either he blew up entirely, or he learned to adjust. His awe at Ashe's vast amount of practical knowledge, freely offered to serve his own blundering ignorance, created a respect for the man which might have become friendship, had Ashe ever relaxed his own shield of impersonal efficiency. Ross did not try to breach the barrier between them mainly because he was sure that the reason for it was the fact that he was a "volunteer." It gave him an odd new feeling he avoided trying to analyze. He had always had a kind of pride in his record; now he had begun to wish sometimes that it was a record of a different type.

Men came and went. Hodaki and his partner disappeared, as did Jansen and his. One lost track of time within that underground warren which was the base. Ross gradually discovered that the whole establishment covered a large area under an external crust of ice and snow. There were laboratories, a well-appointed hospital, armories which stocked weapons usually seen only in museums, but which here were free of any signs of age, and ready for use. There were libraries with mile upon mile of tape recordings as well as films. Ross could not understand everything he heard and saw, but he soaked up all he could so that once or twice, when drifting off to sleep at night, he thought of himself as a sponge which had nearly reached its total limit of absorption.

He learned to wear naturally the clumsy kilt-tunic he had seen on the wolf slayer, to shave with practiced assurance, using a leaf-shaped bronze razor, to eat strange food until he relished the taste. Making lesson time serve a double duty, he lay under sunlamps while listening to tape recordings, until his skin darkened to a weathered hue resembling Ashe's. There was always talk to listen to, important talk which he was afraid to miss.

"Bronze." Ashe weighed a dagger in his hand one day. Its hilt, made of dark horn studded with an intricate pattern of tiny golden nail heads, had a gleam not unlike that of the blade. "Do you know, Murdock, that bronze can be tougher than steel? If it wasn't that iron is so much more plentiful and easier to work, we might never have come out of the Bronze Age? Iron is cheaper and easier found, and when the first smith learned to work it, an end came to one way of life, a beginning to another.

"Yes, bronze is important to us here, and so are the men who worked it. Smiths were sacred in the old days. We know that they made a secret of their trade which overrode the bounds of district, tribe, and race. A smith was welcome in any village, his person safe on the road. In fact, the roads themselves were under the protection of the gods; there was peace on them for all wayfarers. The land was wide then, and it was empty. The tribes were few and small, and there was plenty of room for the hunter, the farmer, the trader. Life was not such a scramble of man against man, but rather of man against nature — —"

"No wars?" asked Ross. "Then why the bow-and-dagger drill?"

"Wars were small affairs, disputes between family clans or tribes. As for the bow, there were formidable things in the forests-giant animals, wolves, wild boars — —"

"Cave bears?"

Ashe sighed with weary patience. "Get it through your head, Murdock, that history is much longer than you seem to think. Cave bears and the use of bronze weapons do not overlap. No, you will have to go back maybe several thousand years earlier and then hunt your bear with a flint-tipped spear in your hand if you are fool enough to try it."

"Or take a rifle with you." Ross made a suggestion he had longed to voice for some time.

Ashe rounded on him swiftly, and Ross knew him well enough now to realize that he was seriously displeased.

"That is just what you don't do, Murdock, not from this base, as you well know by now. You take no weapon from here which is not designed for the period in which your run lies. Just as you do not become embroiled while on that run in any action which might influence the course of history."

Ross went on polishing the blade he held. "What would happen if someone did break that rule?"

Ashe put down the dagger he had been playing with. "We don't know-we just don't know. So far we have operated in the fringe territory, keeping away from any district with a history which we can trace accurately. Maybe some day —" his eyes were on a wall of weapon racks he plainly did not see —"maybe some day we can stand and watch the rise of the pyramids, witness the march of Alexander's armies....But not yet. We stay away from history, and we are sure that the Reds are doing the same. It has become the old problem once presented by the atom bomb. Nobody wants to upset the balance and take the consequences. Let us find their outpost and we'll withdraw our men from all the other runs at once."

"What makes everyone so sure that they have an outpost somewhere? Couldn't they be working right at the main source, sir?"

"They could, but for some reason they are not. As for how we know that much, it's information received." Ashe smiled thinly. "No, the source is much farther back in time than their halfway post. But if we find that, then we can trail them. So we plant men in suitable eras and hope for the best. That's a good weapon you have there, Murdock. Are you willing to wear it in earnest?"

The inflection in that question caught Ross's full attention. His gray eyes met those blue ones. This was it-at long last.

"Right away?"

Ashe picked up a belt of bronze plates strung together with chains, a twin to that Ross had seen worn by the wolf slayer. He held it out to the younger man. "You can take your trial run any time-tomorrow."

Ross drew a deeper breath. "Where-to when?"

"An island which will later be Britain. When? About two thousand B.C. Beaker traders were beginning to open their stations there. This is your graduation exercise, Murdock."

Ross fitted the blade he had been polishing into the wooden sheath on the belt. "If you say I can do it, I'm willing to try."

He caught that glance Ashe shot at him, but he could not read its meaning. Annoyance? Impatience? He was still puzzling over it when the other turned abruptly and left him alone.

Chapter 5

He might have said yes, but that didn't mean, Ross discovered, that he was to be shipped off at once to early Britain. Ashe's "tomorrow" proved to be several days later. The cover was that of a Beaker trader, and Ross's impersonation was checked again and again by experts, making sure that the last detail was correct and that no suspicion of a tribesman, no mistake on Ross's part would betray him.

The Beaker people were an excellent choice for infiltration. They were not a closely knit clan, suspicious of strangers and alert to any deviation from the norm, as more race-conscious tribes might be. For they lived by trade, leaving to Ross's own time the mark of their far-flung "empire" in the beakers found in graves scattered in clusters of a handful or so from the Rhineland to Spain, and from the Balkans to Britain.

They did not depend only upon the taboo of the trade road for their safety, for the Beakermen were master bowmen. A roving people, they pushed into new territory to establish posts, living amicably among peoples with far different customs-the Downs farmers, horse herders, shore-side fisherfolk.

With Ashe, Ross passed a last inspection. Their hair had not grown long enough to require braiding, but they did have enough to hold it back from their faces with hide headbands. The kilt-tunics of coarse material, duplicating samples brought from the past, were harsh to the skin and poorly fitting. But the workmanship of their link-and-plate bronze belts, the sleek bow guards strapped to their wrists, and the bows themselves approached fine art. Ashe's round cloak was the blue of a master trader, and he wore wealth in a necklace of polished wolf's teeth alternating with amber beads. Ross's more modest position in the tribe was indicated not only by his red-brown cloak, but by the fact that his personal jewelry consisted only of a copper bracelet and a cloak pin with a jet head.

He had no idea how the time transition was to be made, nor how one might step from the polar regions of the Western Hemisphere to the island of Britain lying off the Eastern. And it was a complicated business as he discovered.

The transition itself was a fairly simple, though disturbing, process. One walked a short corridor and stood for an instant on a plate while the light centered there curled about in a solid core, shutting one off from floor and wall. Ross gasped for breath as the air was sucked out of his lungs. He experienced a moment of deathly sickness with the sensation of being lost in nothingness. Then he breathed again and looked through the dying wall of light to where Ashe waited.

Quick and easy as the trip through time had been, the journey to Britain was something else. There could be only one transfer point if the secret was to be preserved. But men from that point must be moved swiftly and secretly to their appointed stations. Ross, knowing the strict rules concerning the transportation of objects from one time to another, wondered how that travel could be effected. After all, they could not spend months, or even years, getting across continents and seas.

The answer was ingenious. Three days after they had stepped through the barrier of time at the outpost, Ross and Ashe balanced on the rounded back of a whale. It was a whale which would deceive anyone who did not test its hide with a harpoon, and whalers with harpoons large enough to trouble such a monster were yet well in the future.

Ashe slid a dugout into the water, and Ross climbed into that unsteady craft, holding it against the side of the disguised sub until his partner joined him. The day, misty and drizzling, made the shore they aimed for a half-seen line across the water. With a shiver born of more than cold, Ross dipped his paddle and helped Ashe send their crude boat toward that half-hidden strip of land.

There was no real dawn; the sky lightened somewhat, but the drizzle continued. Green patches showed among the winter-denuded trees back from the beach, but the countryside facing them gave an impression of untamed wilderness. Ross knew from his briefing that the whole of Britain was as yet only sparsely settled. The first wave of hunter-fishers to establish villages had been joined by other invaders who built massive tombs and had an elaborate religion. Small village-forts had been linked from hill to hill by trackways. There were "factories," which turned out in bulk such fine flint weapons and tools that a thriving industry was in full operation, not yet having been superseded by the metal imported by the Beaker merchants. Bronze was still so rare and costly that only the head man of a village could hope to own one of the long daggers. Even the arrowheads in Ross's quiver were chipped of flint.

They drew the dugout well up onto the shore and ran it into a shallow depression in the bank, heaping stones and brush about for its concealment. Then Ashe intently surveyed the surrounding country, seeking a landmark.

"Inland from here...." Ashe used the language of the Beakermen, and Ross knew that from now on he must not only live as a trader, but also think as one. All other memories must be buried under the false one he had learned; he must be interested in the present rate of exchange and the chance for profit. The two men were on their way to Outpost Gog, where Ashe's first partner, the redoubtable Sanford, was playing his role so well.

The rain squished in their hide boots, made sodden strings of their cloaks, plastered their woven caps to their thick mats of hair. Yet Ashe bore steadily on across the land with the certainty of one following a marked trail. His self-confidence was rewarded within the first half mile when they came out upon one of the link trackways, its beaten surface testifying to constant use.

Here Ashe turned eastward, stepping up the pace to a ground-covering trot. The peace of the road held-at least by day. By night only the most hardened and desperate outlaws would brave the harmful spirits roving in the dark.

All the lore that had been pounded into him at the base began to make some sense to Ross as he followed his guide, sniffing strange wet smells from the brush, the trees, and the damp earth; piecing together in his mind what he had been taught and what he now saw for himself, until it made a tight pattern.

The track they were following sloped slightly upward, and a change in the wind brought to them a sour odor, blanking out all normal scents. Ashe halted so suddenly that Ross almost plowed into him. But he was alerted by the older man's attitude.

Something had been burned! Ross drew in a deep lungful of the smell and then wished that he had not. It was wood-burned wood-and something else. Since this was not possibly normal, he was prepared for the way Ashe melted into cover in the brush.

They worked their way, sometimes crawling on their bellies, through the wet stands of dead grass, taking full advantage of all cover. They crouched at the top of the hill while Ashe parted the prickly branches of an evergreen bush to make them a window.

The black patch left by the fire, which had come from a ruin above, had spread downhill on the opposite side of the valley. Charred posts still stood like lone teeth in a skull to mark what must have once been one of the stockade walls of a post. But all they now guarded was a desolation from which came that overpowering stench.

"Our post?" Ross asked in a whisper.

Ashe nodded. He was studying the scene with an intent absorption which, Ross knew, would impress every important detail upon his mind. That the place had been burned was clear from the first. But why and by whom was a problem vital to the two lurking in the brush.

It took them almost an hour to cross the valley-an hour of hiding, casting about, searching. They had made a complete circle of the destroyed post and Ashe stood in the shadow of a copse, rubbing clots of mud from his hands and frowning up at the charred posts.

"They weren't rushed. Or if they were, the attackers covered their trail afterward —" Ross ventured.

The older man shook his head. "Tribesmen would not have muddled a trail if they had won. No, this was no regular attack. There have been no signs of a war party coming or leaving."

"Then what?" demanded Ross.

"Lightning for one thing-and we'd better hope it was that. Or —" Ashe's blue eyes were very cold and bleak, as cold and bleak as the countryside about them.

"Or —?" Ross dared to prompt him.

"Or we have made contact with the Reds in the wrong way!"

Ross's hand instinctively went to the dagger at his belt. Little help a dagger would be in an unequal struggle like this! They were only two in a thin web of men strung out through centuries of time with orders to seek out that which did not fit properly into the pattern of the past: to locate the enemy wherever in history or prehistory he had gone to earth. Had the Reds been searching, too, and was this first disaster their victory?

The time traders had their evidence when they at last ventured into what had been the heart of Outpost Gog. Ross, inexperienced as he was in such matters, could not mistake the signs of the explosion. There was a crater on the crown of the hill, and Ashe stood apart from it, eying the fragments about them—scorched wood, blackened stone.

"The Reds?"

"It must have been. This damage was done by explosives."

It was clear why Outpost Gog could not report the disaster. The attack had destroyed their one link with the post on this time level; the concealed communicator had gone up with the blast.

"Eleven —" Ashe's finger tapped on the ornate buckle of his wide belt. "We have about ten days to stick it out," he added, "and it seems we may be able to use them to better advantage than just letting you learn how it feels to walk about some four thousand years before you were born. We have to find out-if we can-what happened here and why!"

Ross gazed at the mess. "Dig?" he asked.

"Some digging is indicated."

So they dug. Finally, black with charcoal smudges and sick with the evidences of death they had chanced upon, they collapsed on the cleanest spot they could find.

"They must have hit at night," Ashe said slowly. "Only at that time would they find everyone here. Men don't trust a night filled with ghosts, and our agents conform to local custom as usual. All of the post people could be erased with one bomb at night."

All except two of them had been true Beaker traders, including women and children. No Beaker trading post was large, and this one was unusually small. The attacker had wiped out some twenty people, eighteen of them innocent victims.

"How long ago?" Ross wanted to know.

"Maybe two days. And this attack came without any warning, or Sandy would have sent a message. He had no suspicions at all; his last reports were all routine, which means that if they were on to him-and they must have been, judging by the results-he was not even aware of it."

"What do we do now?"

Ashe looked at him. "We wash-no —" he corrected himself—"we don't! We go to Nodren's village. We are frightened, grief-stricken. We have found our kinsmen dead under strange circumstances. We ask questions of one to whom I am known as an inhabitant of this post."

So, covered with dirt, they walked along the trackway toward the neighboring village with a weariness they did not have to counterfeit.

The dog sighted or perhaps scented them first. It was a rough-coated beast, showing its fangs with a wolflike ferocity. But it was smaller than a wolf, and it barked between its warning snarls. Ashe brought his bow from beneath the shelter of his cloak and held it ready.

"Ho, one comes to speak with Nodren-Nodren of the Hill!"

Only the dog snapped and snarled. Ashe rubbed his forearm across his face, the gesture of a weary and heartsick man, smearing the ash and grime into an awesome mask.

"Who speaks to Nodren —?" There was a different twist to the pronunciation of some words, but Ross was able to understand.

"One who has hunted with him and feasted with him. The one who gave into his hand the friendship gift of the ever-sharp knife. It is Assha of the traders — —"

"Go far from us, man of ill luck. You who are hunted by the evil spirits." The last was a shrill cry.

Ashe remained where he was, facing into the bushes which hid the tribesman.

"Who speaks for Nodren yet not with the voice of Nodren?" he demanded. "This is Assha who asks. We have drunk blood together and faced the white wolf and the wild boar in their fury. Nodren lets not others speak for him, for Nodren is a man and a chief!"

"And you are cursed!" A stone flew through the air, striking a rain pool and spattering mud on Ashe's boots. "Go and take your evil with you!"

"Is it from the hand of Nodren or Nodren's young men that doom came upon those of my blood? Have war arrows passed between the place of the traders and the town of Nodren? Is that why you hide in the shadows so that I, Assha, cannot look upon the face of one who speaks boldly and throws stones?"

"No war arrows between us, trader. *We* do not provoke the spirits of the hills. No fire comes from the sky at night to eat us up with a noise of many thunders. Lurgha speaks in such thunders; Lurgha's hand smites with such fire. You have the Wrath of Lurgha upon you, trader! Keep away from us lest Lurgha's wrath fall upon us also."

Lurgha was the local storm god, Ross recalled. The sound of thunder and fire coming out of the sky at night-the bomb! Perhaps the very method of attack on the post would defeat Ashe's attempt to learn anything from these neighbors. The superstitions of the people would lead them to shun both the site of the post and Ashe himself as cursed and taboo.

"If the Wrath of Lurgha had struck at Assha, would Assha still live to walk upon this road?" Ashe prodded the ground with the tip of his bowstave. "Yet Assha walks, as you see him; Assha talks, as you hear him. It is ridiculous to answer him with the nonsense of little children — —"

"Spirits so walk and talk to unlucky men," retorted the man in hiding. "It may be the spirit of Assha who does so now —"

Ashe made a sudden leap. There was a flurry of action behind the bush screen and he reappeared, dragging into the gray light of the rainy day a wriggling captive, whom he bumped without ceremony onto the beaten earth of the road.

The man was bearded, wearing his thick mop of black hair in a round topknot secured by a hide loop. He wore a skin tunic, now in considerable disarray, which was held in place with a woven, tasseled belt.

"Ho, so it is Lal of the Quick Tongue who speaks so loudly of spirits and the Wrath of Lurgha!" Ashe studied his captive. "Now, Lal, since you speak for Nodren-which I believe will greatly surprise him-you will continue to tell me of this Wrath of Lurgha from the night skies and what has happened to Sanfra, who was my brother, and those others of my kin. I am Assha, and you know of the wrath of Assha and how it ate up Twist-tooth, the outlaw, when he came in with his evil men. The Wrath of Lurgha is hot, but so too is the wrath of Assha." Ashe contorted his face in such a way that Lal squirmed and looked away. When the tribesman spoke, all his former authority and bluster had gone.

"Assha knows that I am as his dog. Let him not turn upon me his swift-cutting big knife, nor the arrows from his lightning bow. It was the Wrath of Lurgha which smote the place on the hill, first the thunder of his fist meeting the earth, and then the fire which he breathed upon those whom he would slay — —"

"And this you saw with your own eyes, Lal?"

The shaggy head shook an emphatic negative. "Assha knows that Lal is no chief who can stand and look upon the wonders of Lurgha's might and keep his eyes in his head. Nodren himself saw this wonder — —"

"And if Lurgha came in the night, when all men keep to their homes and leave the outer world to the restless spirits, how did Nodren see his coming?"

Lal crouched lower to the ground, his eyes darting to the bushes and the freedom they promised, then back to Ashe's firmly planted boots.

"I am not a chief, Assha. How could I know in what way or for what reason Nodren saw the coming of Lurgha — —?"

"Fool!" A second voice, that of a woman, spat the word from the brush which fringed the roadway. "Speak to Assha with a straight tongue. If he is a spirit, he will know that you do not tell him the truth. And if he has been spared by Lurgha...." She showed her wonderment with a hiss of indrawn breath.

So urged, Lal mumbled sullenly, "It is said that there came a message for one to witness the Wrath of Lurgha in its descent upon the outlanders so that Nodren and the men of Nodren would truly know that the traders were cursed, and should be put to the spear should they come here again — —"

"This message-how was it brought? Did the voice of Lurgha sound in Nodren's ear alone, or came it by the tongue of some man?"

"Ahee!" Lal lay flat on the ground, his hands over his ears.

"Lal is a fool and fears his own shadow as it skips before him on a sunny day!" Out of the bushes stepped a young woman, obviously of some importance in her own group. Walking with a proud stride, her eyes boldly met Ashe's. A shining disk hung about her neck on a thong, and another decorated the woven belt of her cloth tunic. Her hair was bound in a thread net fastened with jet pins.

"I greet Cassca, who is the First Sower." There was a formal note in Ashe's voice. "But why should Cassca hide from Assha?"

"There has been death on your hill, Assha —" she sniffed —"you smell of it now-Lurgha's death. Those who come from that hill may well be some who no longer walk in their bodies." Cassca placed her fingers momentarily on Ashe's outstretched palm before she nodded. "No spirit are you, Assha, for all know that a spirit is solid to the eye, but not to the touch. So it would seem that you were not burned up by Lurgha, after all."

"This matter of a message from Lurgha —" he prompted.

"It came out of the empty air in the hearing not only of Nodren, but also of Hangor, Effar, and myself, Cassca. For we stood at that time near the Old Place...." She made a curious gesture with the fingers of her right hand. "It will soon be the time of sowing, and though Lurgha brings sun and rain to feed the grain, yet it is in the Great Mother that the seed lies. Upon her business only women may go into the Inner Circle." She gestured again. "But as we met to make the first sacrifice there came music out of the air such as we have never heard, voices singing like birds in a strange tongue." Her face assumed an awesome expression. "Afterward a voice said that Lurgha was angered with the hill of the men-from-afar and that in the night he would send his Wrath against them, and that Nodren must witness this thing so that he could see what Lurgha did to those he would punish. So it was done by Nodren. And there was a sound in the air — —"

"What kind of a sound?" Ashe asked quietly.

"Nodren said it was a hum and there was the dark shadow of Lurgha's bird between him and the stars. Then came the smiting of the hill with thunder and lightning, and Nodren fled, for the Wrath of Lurgha is a fearsome thing. Now do the people come to the Great Mother's Place with many fine offerings that she may stand between them and that Wrath."

"Assha thanks Cassca, who is the handmaiden of the Great Mother. May the sowing prosper and the reaping be good this year!" Ashe said finally, ignoring Lal, who still groveled on the road.

"You go from this place, Assha?" she asked. "For though I stand under the protecting hand of the Mother and so do not fear, yet there are others who will raise their spears against you for the honor of Lurgha."

"We go, and again thanks be to you, Cassca."

He turned back the way they had come, and Ross fell in beside him as the woman watched them out of sight.

Chapter 6

"That bird of Lurgha's —" said Ross, once they were out of sight of Cassca and Lal, "could it have been a plane?"

"Sounds like it," snapped his companion. "If the Reds have done their work efficiently, and there's no reason to suppose otherwise, then there is no use in contacting either Dorhta's town or Munga's. The same announcement concerning the Wrath of Lurgha was probably made there-to their good purpose, not ours."

"Cassca didn't seem to be overly impressed with Lurgha's curse, not as much as the man was."

"She is the closest thing to a priestess that this tribe knows, and she serves a goddess older and more powerful than Lurgha-the Mother Earth, the Great Mother, goddess of fertility and growth. Nodren's people believe that unless Cassca performs her mysteries and sows part of the first field in the spring there won't be any harvest. Consequently, she is secure in her office and doesn't fear the Wrath of Lurgha too much. These people are now changing from one type of worship to another, but some of Cassca's beliefs will persist clear down to our day, taking on the coating of 'magic' and a lot of other enameling along the way."

Ashe had been talking as a man talks to cover up furious thinking. Now he paused again and turned toward the sea. "We have to stick it out somewhere until the sub comes to pick us up. We'll need shelter."

"Will the tribesmen be after us?"

"They may well be. Let the right men get to talking up a holy extermination of those upon whom the Wrath of Lurgha has fallen and we could be in for plenty of trouble. Some of those men are trained hunters and trackers, and the Reds may have planted an agent to report the return of anyone to our post. Just now we're about the most important time travelers out, for we know the Reds have appeared on this line. They must have a large post here, too, or they couldn't have sent a plane on that raid. You can't build a time transport large enough to take through a considerable amount of material. Everything used by us in this age has to be assembled on this side, and the use of all machines is limited to where they can not be seen by any natives. Luckily large sections of this world are mostly wilderness and unpopulated in the areas where we operate the base posts. So if the Reds have a plane, it was put together here, and that means a big post somewhere." Again Ashe was thinking aloud as he pushed ahead of Ross into the fringes of a wood. "Sandy and I scouted this territory pretty well last spring. There is a cave about half a mile to the west; it will shelter us for tonight."

Ashe's plans would probably have been easily accomplished if the cave had been unoccupied. Without incident they came down into a hollow through which trickled a small stream, its banks laced with a thin edging of ice. Under Ashe's direction Ross collected an armload of firewood. He was no woodsman and his prolonged exposure to the chilling drizzle made him eager for even the very rough shelter of a cave, so eager that he plunged forward carelessly. His foot came down on a slippery patch of mud, sending him sprawling on his face. There was a growl, and a white bulk rushed him. The cloak, rucked up about his throat and shoulders, then saved his life, for only stout cloth was caught between those fangs.

With a startled cry, Ross rolled as he might have to escape a man's attack, struggling to unsheath his dagger. A white-hot flash of pain scored his upper arm. The breath was driven out of him as a fight raged over his prone body; he heard grunts, snarls, and was severely pommeled. Then he was free as the bodies broke away. Shaken, he got to his knees. A short distance away the fight was still in progress. He saw Ashe straddle the body of a huge white wolf, his legs clamped about the animal's haunches, his hooked arm under the beast's head, forcing it up and back while his dagger rose and sank twice in the underparts of the heaving body.

Ross held his own weapon ready. He leaped from a half crouch, and his dagger sank cleanly home behind the short ribs. One of their blows must have reached the animal's heart. With an almost human cry the wolf stiffened convulsively. Then it was still. Ashe squatted near it, methodically driving his dagger into the moist soil to clean the blade.

A red rivulet trickled down his thigh where the lower edge of his kilt-tunic had been ripped up to the link belt. He was breathing hard, but otherwise he was as composed as always. "These sometimes hunt in pairs at this season," he observed. "Be ready with your bow —"

Ross strung his with the cord he had been keeping dry within the breast folds of his tunic. He fitted an arrow to the string, grateful to be a passable marksman. The slash on his arm smarted in protest as he moved, and he noted that Ashe did not try to get up.

"A bad one?" Ross indicated the blood now thickening into a stream along Ashe's thigh.

Ashe pulled away the torn tunic and exposed a nasty looking gash on the outside of his hip. He pressed his palm against the gaping wound and motioned Ross to scout ahead. "See if the cave is clear. We can't do anything until we know that."

Reluctantly Ross followed the stream until he found the cave, a snug-looking place with an overhang to keep it dry. The unpleasant smell of a lair hung about its mouth. He chose a stone from the stream, chucked it into the dark opening, and waited. The stone rattled as it struck an inner wall, but there was no other sound. A second stone from a different angle followed the first, with the same results. Ross was now certain that the cave was unoccupied. Once they were inside with a fire going at the entrance, they could hope to keep it free of intruders. A little heartened, he cast about a bit upstream and then turned back to where he had left Ashe.

"No male?" the other greeted him. "This is a female, and she was close to whelping —" He nudged the white wolf with his toe. His hands held a pad of rags against his hip, and his face was shaded with pain.

"Nothing in the cave anyway. Let's see about this...." Ross laid aside the bow and kneeled to examine Ashe's thigh wound. His own slash was more of a smarting graze, but this tear was deep and ugly.

"Second plate-belt —" Ashe got the words out between set teeth, and Ross clicked open the hidden recess in the other's bronze belt to bring out a small packet. Ashe made a wry face as he swallowed three of the pills within. Ross mashed another pill onto the bandage he prepared, and when the last cumbersome fold was secure Ashe relaxed.

"Let us hope that works," he commented a little bleakly. "Now come here where I can get my hands on you and let me see your scratch. Animal bites can be a nasty business."

Bandaged in turn, with the bitterness of the anti-septo pill on his tongue, Ross helped Ashe limp upstream to the cave. He left the older man outside while he cleaned up the floor of the cave and then made his companion as comfortable as he could on a bed of bracken. The fire Ross had longed for was built. They stripped off their sodden clothing and hung it to dry. Ross wrapped a bird he had shot in clay and tucked it under the hot coals to be roasted.

They had surely had bad luck, he thought, but they were now undercover, had a fire, and food of a sort. His arm ached, sharp pain shooting from fingers to elbow when he moved it. Though Ashe made no complaint, Ross gauged that the older man's discomfort was far worse than his own, and he carefully hid all signs of his own twinges.

They ate the bird, saltless, and with their fingers. Ross savored each greasy bite, licking his hands clean afterward while Ashe lay back on the improvised bed, his face gaunt in the half light of the fire.

"We are about five miles from the sea here. There is no way of raising our base now that Sandy's installation is gone. I'll have to lay up, since I can't risk any more loss of blood. And you're not too good in the woods —"

Ross accepted that valuation with a new humbleness. He was only too well aware that if it had not been for Ashe, he and not the white wolf would have died down in the valley. Yet a strange shyness kept him from trying to put his thanks into words. The only kind of amends he could make for the other's hurt was to provide hands, feet, and strength for the man who did know what to do and how to do it.

"We'll have to hunt —" he ventured.

"Deer," Ashe caught him up. "But the marsh at the mouth of this stream provides a better hunting ground than inland. If the wolf laired here very long, she has already frightened away any large game. It isn't the matter of food which bothers me — —"

"It is being tied up here," Ross filled in for him with some daring. "But look here, I'll take orders. This is your territory, and I'm green at the game. You tell me what to do, and I'll do it the best that I can." He glanced up to find Ashe surveying him intently, but as usual there was no readable expression on the other's brown face.

"The first thing to do is get the wolf's hide," Ashe said briskly. "Then bury the carcass. You'd better drag it up here to work on it. If her mate is hanging around, he might try to jump you."

Why Ashe should think it necessary to acquire the wolf skin puzzled Ross, but he asked no questions. His skinning task took four times as long and was far from being the neat job the shock-haired man of the record tape had accomplished. Ross had to wash himself off in the stream before piling stones over the corpse in temporary burial. When he pulled his bloody burden back to the cave, Ashe lay with his eyes closed. Ross thankfully sat on his own pile of bracken and tried not to notice the throbbing ache in his arm.

He must have fallen asleep, for when he roused it was to see Ashe crawl over to mend the dying fire from their store of wood. Ross, angry at himself, beat the other to the task.

"Get back," he said roughly. "This is my job. I didn't mean to fail."

Surprisingly, Ashe settled back without a word, leaving Ross to sit by the fire, a fire he was very glad to have a moment or so later when a wailing howl sounded down-wind. If this was not the white wolf's mate, then it was another of her kin who prowled the upper reaches of the small valley.

The next day, having provided Ashe with a supply of firewood, Ross went to try his luck in the marsh. The thick drizzle which had hung over the land the day before was gone, and he faced a clear, bright morning, though the breeze had an icy snap. But it was a good morning to be alive and out in the open, and Ross's spirits rose.

He tried to put to use all the woodlore he had learned at the base. But it was one thing to learn something academically and another to put that learning into practice. He was uncomfortably certain that Ashe would not have found his showing very good.

The marsh was a series of pools between rank growths of leafless willows and coarse tufts of grass, with hillocks of firmer soil rising like islands. Ross, approaching with caution, was glad of it, for from one of those hillocks arose a trail of white smoke, and he saw a black blot which was probably a rude hut. Why one should choose to live in the midst of such country he could not guess, though it might be merely the temporary camp of some hunter.

Ross also saw thousands of birds feeding greedily on the dried seed of the marsh grasses, paddling in the pools, and setting up a clamor to drive a man mad. They did not seem in the least disturbed by that distant camper.

Ross had reason to be proud of his marksmanship that morning. He had in his quiver perhaps half a dozen of the lighter shafts made for shooting birds. In place of the finely chipped and wickedly barbed flint points used for heavier game, these were tipped with needle-sharp, light bone heads. He had a string of four birds looped together by their feet within almost as many minutes. For the flocks rose in their first alarm only to settle again to feast.

Then he knocked over a hare —a fat giant of its race-that stared at him brazenly from a tussock. The hare kicked back into a pool in its death struggle, however, and Ross was forced to leave cover to retrieve its body. But he was alert and he stood up, dagger out and ready, to greet the man who parted the bushes to watch him.

For a long minute gray eyes stared into brown ones, and then Ross noted the other's bedraggled and tattered dress. The kilt-tunic smudged with mud, scorched and charred along one edge, was styled like his own. The fellow wore his hair fastened back with a band, unlike the topknot of the local tribesman.

Ross, his dagger still ready, broke the silence first. "I am a believer in the fire and the fashioned metal, the climbing sun, and the moving water." He repeated the recognition speech of the Beakermen.

"The fire warms by the grace of Tulden, the metal is fashioned by the mystery of the smith, the sun climbs without our aid, and who can stop the water from running?" The stranger's voice was hoarse. Now that Ross had time to examine him more closely he saw the dark bruise on his exposed shoulder, the raw red mark of a burn running across the man's broad chest. He dared to test his surmise concerning the other.

"I am of the kin of Assha. We returned to the hill — —"

"Ashe!"

Not "Assha" but "Ashe!" Ross, though sure of that pronunciation, was still cautious. "You are from the hill place, where Lurgha smote with thunder and fire?"

The man slid his long legs across the log which had been his shelter. The burn across his chest was not his only brand, for Ross noticed another red stripe, puffed and fiery looking, which swelled the calf of one leg. The man studied Ross closely, and then his fingers moved in a sign which to the uninitiated native might have been one for the warding off of evil, but which to Ross was the "thumbs up" of his own age.

"Sanford?"

At that name the man shook his head. "McNeil," he named himself. "Where is Ashe?"

He might really be what he seemed, but on the other hand, he could be a Red spy. Ross had not forgotten Kurt. "What happened?" he parried one question with another.

"Bomb. The Reds must have spotted us, and we didn't have a chance. We weren't expecting any trouble. I'd been down to see about a missing burden donkey and was about halfway back up the hill when she hit. When I came to I was all the way down the hill with part of the fort on top of me. The rest....Well, you saw the place, didn't you?"

Ross nodded. "What are you doing here?"

McNeil spread his hands in a tired little gesture. "I tried to talk to Nodren, but they stoned me away. I knew that Ashe was coming through and hoped to reach him when he hit the beach, but I was too late. Then I figured he would pass here to make contact with the sub, so I was waiting it out until I saw you. Where is Ashe?"

It all sounded logical enough. Still, with Ashe injured, Ross was taking no chances. He pushed his dagger back into its sheath and picked up the hare. "Stay here," he told McNeil, "I'll be back — —"

"But-wait! Where's Ashe, you young fool? We have to get together."

Ross went on. He was sure that the stranger was in no shape to race after him, and he would lay a muddled trail before he returned to the cave valley. If this man was a Red plant, he would have to reckon with one who had already met Kurt Vogel.

The laying of that muddled trail took time. It was past midday when Ross came back to Ashe, who was sitting up by the mouth of the cave at the fire, using his dagger to fashion a crutch out of a length of sapling. He surveyed Ross's burden with approval, but lost interest in the promise of food as soon as the other reported his meeting in the marsh.

"McNeil-chap with brown hair, brown eyes, a right eyebrow which quirks up toward his hairline when he smiles?"

"Brown hair and eyes, okay-and he didn't smile any."

"Chip broken off a front tooth-upper right?"

Ross shut his eyes to visualize the stranger. Yes, there had been a small break on a front tooth. He nodded.

"That's McNeil. Not that you didn't do right not to bring him here without being sure. What made you so watchful? Kurt?"

Again Ross nodded. "And what you said about the Reds' planting someone here to wait for us."

Ashe scratched the bristles on his chin. "Never underrate them-we don't dare do that. But the man you met is McNeil, and we'd better get him here. Can you bring him?"

"I think he's able to get about, in spite of that leg. From his story he's been stirring around."

Ashe bit absent-mindedly into a piece of hare and swore mildly when he burned his tongue. "Odd that Cassca didn't tell us about him. Unless she thought there was no use causing trouble by admitting they had driven him away. You going now?"

Ross moved around the fire. "Might as well. He didn't look too comfortable. And I'll bet he's hungry."

He took the direct route back to the marsh, but this time no thread of smoke spiraled into the air. Ross hesitated. That shelter on the small island was surely the place where McNeil had holed up. Should he try to work his way out to it now? Or had something happened to the man while he was gone?

Again that sixth sense of impending disaster, which is perhaps bred into some men, alerted Ross. Why he turned suddenly and backed against a bushy willow, he could not have explained. However, because he did so the loop of hide rope meant for his throat hit his shoulder harmlessly. It fell to the ground, and he stamped one boot down on it. Then it was the work of seconds to grasp it and give it a quick jerk. The surprised man who held the other end was brought sprawling into the open.

Ross had seen that round face before. "Lal of the town of Nodren." He found words to greet the ropeman even as his knee came up against the fellow's jaw, jarring Lal so that he dropped a flint knife. Ross kicked it into the willows. "What do you hunt here, Lal?"

"Traders!" The voice was weak, but it held heat.

The tribesman did not try to struggle against Ross's hold, and Ross, gripping him by the nape of the neck, moved through a screen of brush to a hollow. Luckily there was no water cupped there, for McNeil lay in the bottom of that dip, his arms tied tightly behind him and his ankles lashed together with no thought for the pain of his burned leg.

Chapter 7

Ross whirled the rope which had been meant to bring him down around Lal. He lashed the tribesman's arms tight to his body before he knelt to cut loose his fellow time traveler. Lal now huddled against the far wall of the cup, fear in every line of his small body. So apparent was this fear that Ross felt no satisfaction at turning the tables on him. Instead he felt increasingly uneasy.

"What is this all about?" he asked McNeil as he stripped off his bonds and helped him up.

McNeil massaged his wrists, took a step or two, and grimaced with pain. "Our friend seeks to be an obedient servant of Lurgha."

Ross picked up his bow. "The tribe is out to hunt us?"

"Lurgha has ordered-out of thin air again-that any traders who escaped are to be brought in and introduced to him personally at the sacrifice for the enrichment of the fields!"

The old, old gift of blood and life at the spring sowing. Ross recalled grisly details from his cram lessons. Any wandering stranger or enemy tribesman taken in a raid before that day would meet such a fate. On unlucky years when people were not available a deer or wolf might serve. But the best sacrifice of all was a man. So Lurgha had decreed-from the air-that traders were his meat? What of Ashe? Let any hunter from the village track him down.

"We have to move fast," Ross told McNeil as he took up the rope which made a leading cord for Lal. Ashe would want to question the tribesman about this second order from Lurgha.

Impatient as Ross was, he had to mend his pace to accommodate McNeil. The man from the hill post was close to the end of his strength. He had started off bravely enough, but now he wavered. Ross sent Lal ahead with a sharp push, ordering him to stay there, while he went to McNeil's aid. It was well into the afternoon before they came up the stream and saw the fire before the cave.

"Macna!" Ashe hailed Ross's companion with the native version of his name. "And Lal. But what do you here, Lal of Nodren's town?"

"Mischief." Ross helped McNeil within the cave and to the pile of brush which was his own bed. "He was hunting traders as a present for Lurgha."

"So —" Ashe turned upon the tribesman —"and by whose word did you go hunting my kinsman, Lal? Was it Nodren's? Has he forgotten the blood bond between us? For it was in the name of Lurgha himself that that bond was made — —"

"Aaaah —" The tribesman squatted down against the wall where Ross had shoved him. Unable to hide his head in his arms, he brought his face down upon his knees so that only his shaggy topknot of hair was exposed. Ross realized, with stupefaction, that the little man was crying like a child, his hunched shoulders rising and falling with the force of his sobs. "Aaaah —" he wailed.

Ashe allowed him a moment or two of noisy grief and then limped over to grasp his topknot and pull up his head. Lal's eyes were screwed tightly shut, but there were tears on his cheeks, and his mouth twisted in another wail.

"Be quiet!" Ashe shook him, but not too harshly. "Have you yet felt the bite of my sharp knife? Has an arrow holed your skin? You are alive, and you could be dead. Show that you are glad you live and continue to breathe by telling us what you know, Lal."

The woman Cassca had displayed a measure of intelligence and ease at their meeting upon the road. But it was very plain that Lal was of different stuff, a simple man in whose head few ideas could find house room at one time. And to him the present was all black. Little by little they dragged the story out of him.

Lal was poor, so poor that he had never dared dream of owning for himself some of the precious things the hill traders displayed to the wealthy of Nodren's town. But he was also a follower of the Great Mother's, rather than one who made sacrifices to Lurgha. Lurgha was the god for warriors and great men; he was too high to concern himself with such as Lal.

So when Nodren reported the end of the hill post under the storm fist of Lurgha, Lal had been impressed only to a point. He was still convinced it was none of his concern, and instead he began thinking of the treasures which might lie hidden in the destroyed buildings. It occurred to him that Lurgha's Wrath had been laid upon the men who had owned them, but perhaps it would not stretch to the fine things themselves. So he had gone secretly to the hill to explore.

What he had seen there had utterly converted him to a belief in the fury of Lurgha and he had been frightened out of his simple wits, fleeing without making the search he had intended. But Lurgha had seen him there, had read his impious thoughts....

At that point Ashe interrupted the stream of Lal's story. How had Lurgha seen Lal?

Because-Lal shuddered, began to cry again, and spoke the next few sentences haltingly-that very morning when he had gone out to hunt wild fowl in the marshes Lurgha had spoken to *him*, to Lal, who was less than a flea creeping upon a worn-out fur rug.

And how had Lurgha spoken? Ashe's voice was softer, gentle.

Out of the air, even as he had spoken to Nodren, who was a chief. He said that he had seen Lal in the hill post, and so Lal was his meat. But not yet would he eat him, not if Lal served him in other ways. And he, Lal, had lain flat on the ground before the bodiless voice of Lurgha and had sworn that he would serve Lurgha to the end of his life.

Then Lurgha had told him to hunt down one of the evil traders who was hiding in the marshes, and bind him with ropes. Then he was to call the men of the village and together they would carry the prisoner to the hill where Lurgha had loosed his wrath, and there they would leave him. Later they might return and take what they found there and use it to bless the fields at sowing time, and all would be well with Nodren's village. And Lal had sworn that he would do as Lurgha bade, but now he could not. So Lurgha would eat him up-he was a man without hope.

"Yet," Ashe said even more gently, "have you not served the Great Mother all these years, giving to her a portion of the first fruits even when the yield of your one field was small?"

Lal stared at him, his woebegone face still smeared with tears. It took a second or two for the question to penetrate his fear-clouded mind. Then he nodded timidly.

"Has she not dealt with you well in return, Lal? You are a poor man, that is true. But you are not gaunt of belly, even though this is the thin season when men fast before the coming of the new harvest. The Great Mother watches over her own. And it is she who has brought you to us now. For this I say to you, Lal, and I, Assha of the traders, speak with a straight tongue. The Lurgha who struck our post, who spoke to you from the air, means you no good ——"

"Aaaah!" wailed Lal. "So do I know, Assha. He is of the blackness and the wandering spirits of the dark!"

"Just so. Thus he is no kin to the mother, for she is of the light and of good things, of the new grain, and the newborn lambs for your flocks, of the maids who wed with men and bring forth sons to lift their fathers' spears, daughters to spin by the hearth and sow the yellow grain in the furrows. Lurgha's quarrel lies with us, Lal, not with Nodren nor with you. And we take upon us that quarrel." He limped into the outer air where the shadows of evening were beginning to creep across the ground.

"Hear me, Lurgha," he called into the coming night, "I am Assha of the traders, and upon myself I take your hate. Not upon Lal, nor upon Nodren, nor upon the people who live in Nodren's town, shall your wrath lie. Thus do I say it!"

Ross, noticing that Ashe concealed from Lal a wave of his hand, was prepared for some display meant to impress the tribesman. It came in a spectacular burst of green fire beyond the stream. Lal wailed again, but when that fire was followed by no other manifestation he ventured to raise his head once more.

"You have seen how Lurgha answered me, Lal. Toward me only will his wrath be turned. Now —" Ashe limped back and dragged out the white wolf skin, dropping it before Lal —"this you will give to Cassca that she may make a curtain for the Mother's home. See, it is white and so rare that the Mother will be pleased with such a fine gift. And you will tell her all that has chanced and how you believe in her powers over the powers of Lurgha, and the Mother will be well pleased with you. But you shall say nothing to the men of the village, for this quarrel is between Lurgha and Assha now and not for the meddling of others."

He unfastened the rope which bound Lal's arms. Lal reached out a hand to the wolf skin, his eyes filled with wonderment. "This is a fine thing you give me, Assha, and the Mother will be pleased, for in many years she has not had such a curtain for her secret place. Also, I am but a little man; the quarrels of great ones are not for me. Since Lurgha has accepted your words this is none of my affair. Yet I will not go back to the village for a while-with your permission, Assha. For I am a man of loose and wagging tongue and oftentimes I speak what I do not really wish to say. So if I am asked questions, I answer. If I am not there to be asked such questions, I cannot answer."

McNeil laughed, and Ashe smiled. "Well enough, Lal. Perhaps you are a wiser man than you think. But also I do not believe you should stay here."

The tribesman was already nodding. "That do I say, too, Assha. You are now facing the Wrath of Lurgha, and with that I wish no part. Thus I shall go into the marsh for a while. There are birds and hares to hunt, and I shall work upon this fine skin so that when I take it to the Mother it shall indeed be a gift worth her smiles. Now, Assha, I would go before the night comes if it pleases you."

"Go with good fortune, Lal." Ashe stood apart while the tribesman ducked his head in a shy, awkward farewell to the others, pattering out into the valley.

"What if they pick him up?" McNeil asked wearily.

"I don't think they can," Ashe returned. "And what would you do-keep him here? If we tried that, he'd scheme to escape and try to turn the tables on us. Now he'll keep away from Nodren's village and out of sight for the time being. Lal's not too bright in some ways, but he's a good hunter. If he has reason for hiding out, it'll take a better hunter to track him. At least we know now that the Reds are afraid they did not make a clean sweep here. What happened, McNeil?"

While he was telling his story in more detail both Ashe and Ross worked on his burns, making him comfortable. Then Ashe sat back as Ross prepared food.

"How did they spot the post?" Ashe rubbed his chin and frowned at the fire.

"Only way I can guess is that they picked up our post signal and pinpointed the source. That means they must have been hunting us for some time."

"No strangers about lately?"

McNeil shook his head. "Our cover wasn't broken that way. Sanford was a wonder. If I hadn't known better, I would have sworn he was born one of the Beaker folk. He had a network of informants running all the way from here into Brittany. Amazing how he was able to work without arousing any suspicions. I suppose his being a member of the smiths' guild was a big help. He could pick up a lot of news from any village where there was one at work. And I tell you," McNeil propped himself up on his elbow to exclaim more vehemently —"there wasn't a whisper of trouble from here clear across the channel and pretty far to the north. We were already sure the south was clean before we ever took cover as Beakers, especially since their clans are thick in Spain."

Ashe chewed a broiled wing reflectively. "Their permanent base with the transport *has* to be somewhere within the bounds of the territory they hold in our own time."

"They could plant it in Siberia and laugh at us," McNeil exploded. "No hope of our getting in there ——"

"No." Ashe threw the stripped bone into the fire and licked grease from his fingers. "Then they would be faced with the old problem of distance. If what they are exploiting lay within their modern boundaries, we would never have tumbled to the thing in the first place. What the Reds want must lie outside their twentieth century holdings, a slender point in our favor. Therefore they will plant their shift point as close to it as they can. Our transportation problem is more difficult than theirs will ever be.

"You know why we chose the arctic for our base; it lies in a section of the world never populated by other than roving hunters. But I'll wager anything you want to name that their point is somewhere in Europe where they have people to contend with. If they are using a plane, they can't risk its being seen ——"

"I don't see why not," Ross broke in. "These people couldn't possibly know what it was-Lurgha's bird-magic —"

Ashe shook his head. "They must have the interference-with-history worry as much as we have. Anything of our own time has to be hidden or disguised in such a way that the native who may stumble upon it will never know it is man-made. Our sub is a whale to all appearances. Possibly their plane is a bird, but neither can bear too close an examination. We don't know what could result from a leak of real knowledge in this or any primitive time ... how it might change history ——"

"But," Ross advanced what he believed to be the best argument against that reasoning, "suppose I handed Lal a gun and taught him to use it. He couldn't duplicate the weapon-the technology required lies so far beyond this age. These people couldn't reproduce such a thing."

"True enough. On the other hand, don't belittle the ingenuity of the smiths or the native intelligence of men in any era. These tribesmen might not be able to reproduce your gun, but it would set them thinking along new lines. We might find that they would think our time right out of being. No, we dare not play tricks with the past. This is the same situation we faced immediately after the discovery of the atom bomb. Everybody raced to produce that new weapon and then sat around and shivered for fear we'd be crazy enough to use it on each other.

"The Reds have made new discoveries which we have to match, or we will go under. But back in time we have to be careful, both of us, or perhaps destroy the world we do live in."

"What do we do now?" McNeil wanted to know.

"Murdock and I came here only for a trial run. It's his test. The sub is to call for us about nine days from now."

"So if we sit tight-if we *can* sit tight —" McNeil lay down again —"they will take us out. Meanwhile we have nine days."

They spent three more days in the cave. McNeil was on his feet and impatient to leave before Ashe was able to hobble well enough to travel. Though Ross and McNeil took turns at hunting and guard duty, they saw no signs that the tribesmen were tracking them. Apparently Lal had done as he promised, withdrawing to the marsh and hiding there apart from his people.

In the gray of pre-dawn on the fourth day Ashe wakened Ross. Their fire had been buried with earth, and already the cave seemed bleak. They ate venison roasted the night before and went out into the chill of a fog. A little way down the valley McNeil joined them out of the mist from his guard post. Keeping their pace to one which favored Ashe's healing wound, they made their way inland in the direction of the track linking the villages.

Crossing that road they continued northward, the land beginning to rise under them. Far away they heard the blatting of sheep, the bark of a dog. In the fog, Ross stumbled in a shallow ditch beyond which lay a stubbled field. Ashe paused to look about him, his nostrils expanding as if he were a hound smelling out their trail.

The three went on, crossing a whole series of small, irregular fields. Ross was sure that the yield from any of these cleared strips must be scanty. The fog was thickening. Ashe pressed the pace, using his handmade crutch carefully. He gave an audible sigh of relief when they were faced at last by two stone monoliths rising like pillars. A third stone lay across them, forming a rude arch through which they saw a narrow valley running back into the hills.

Through the fog Ross could sense the eerie strangeness of the valley beyond the massive gate. He would have said that he was not superstitious, that he had merely studied these tribal beliefs as lessons; he had not accepted them. Yet now, if he had been alone, he would have avoided that place and turned aside from the valley, for that which waited within was not for him. To his secret relief Ashe paused by the arch to wait.

The older man gestured the other two into cover. Ross obeyed willingly, though the dank drops of condensing fog dripped on his cloak and wet his face as he brushed against prickly-leafed shrubs. Here were walls of evergreen plants and dwarfed pines almost as if this tunnel of year-round greenery had been planted with some purpose in mind. Once his companions had concealed themselves, Ashe called, shrill but sweetly, with a bird's rising notes. Three times he made that sound before a figure moved in the fog, the rough gray-white of its long cloak melting in the wisps of mist.

Down that green tunnel, out of the heart of the valley, the other came, a loop of cloak concealing the entire figure. It halted right in back of the arch and Ashe, making a gesture to the others to stay where they were, faced the muffled stranger.

"Hands and feet of the Mother, she who sows what may be reaped — —"

"Outland stranger who is under the Wrath of Lurgha," the other mocked him in the voice of Cassca. "What do you want, outlander, that you dare to come here where no man may enter?"

"That which you know. For on the night when Lurgha came you also saw — —"

Ross heard the hiss of a sharply drawn breath. "How knew you that, outlander?"

"Because you serve the Mother and you are jealous for her and her service. If Lurgha is a mighty god, you wanted to see his acts with your own eyes."

When she finally answered, there was anger as well as frustration in her voice. "And you know of my shame then, Assha. For Lurgha came-on a bird he came, and he did even as he said he would. So now the village will make offerings to Lurgha and beg his favor, and the Mother will no more have those to harken to her words and offer her the first fruits — —"

"But from whence came this bird which was Lurgha, can you tell me that, she who waits upon the Mother?"

"What difference does it make from what direction Lurgha came? That does not add nor take from his power." Cassca moved beneath the arch. "Or does it in some strange way, Assha?"

"Perhaps it does. Only tell me."

She turned slowly and pointed over her right shoulder. "From that way he came, Assha. Well did I watch, knowing that I was the Mother's and that even Lurgha's thunderbolts could not eat me up. Does knowing that make Lurgha smaller in your eyes, Assha? When he has eaten up all that is yours and your kin with it?"

"Perhaps," Assha repeated. "I do not think Lurgha will come so again."

She shrugged, and the heavy cloak flapped. "That shall be as it shall be, Assha. Now go, for it is not good that any man come hither."

Cassca paced back into the heart of the green tunnel, and Ross and McNeil came out of concealment. McNeil faced in the direction she had pointed. "Northeast —" he commented thoughtfully, "the Baltic lies in that quarter."

Chapter 8

"...and that is about all." Ten days later Ashe, a dressing on his leg and a few of the pain lines smoothed from his face, sat on a bunk in the arctic time post nursing a mug of coffee in his hands and smiling, a little crookedly, at Nelson Millaird.

Millaird, Kelgarries, Dr. Webb, all the top brass of the project had not only come through the transfer point to meet the three from Britain but were now crammed into the room, nearly pushing Ross and McNeil through the wall. Because this was it! What they had hunted for months-years-now lay almost within their grasp.

Only Millaird, the director, did not seem so confident. A big man with a bushy thatch of coarse graying hair and a heavy, fleshy face, he did not look like a brain. Yet Ross had been on the roster long enough to know that it was Millaird's thick and hairy hands that gathered together all the loose threads of Operation Retrograde and deftly wove them into a workable pattern. Now the director leaned back in a chair which was too small for his bulk, chewing thoughtfully on a toothpick.

"So we have the first whiff of a trail," he commented without elation.

"A pretty strong lead!" Kelgarries broke in. Too excited to sit still, the major stood with his back against the door, as alert as if he were about to turn and face the enemy. "The Reds wouldn't have moved against Gog if they did not consider it a menace to them. Their big base must be in this time sector!"

"*A* big base," Millaird corrected. "The one we are after, no. And right now they may be switching times. Do you think they will sit here and wait for us to show up in force?" But Millaird's tone, intended to deflate, had no effect on the major.

"And just how long would it take them to dismantle a big base?" that officer countered. "At least a month. If we shoot a team in there in a hurry —"

Millaird folded his huge hands over his barrel-shaped body and laughed, without a trace of humor. "Just where do we send that team, Kelgarries? Northeast of a coastal point in Britain is a rather vague direction, to say the least. Not," he spoke to Ashe now, "that you didn't do all you could, Ashe. And you, McNeil, nothing to add?"

"No, sir. They jumped us out of the blue when Sandy thought he had every possible line tapped, every safeguard working. I don't know how they caught on to us, unless they located our beam to this post. If so, they must have been deliberately hunting us for some time, because we only used the beam as scheduled — —"

"The Reds have patience and brains and probably some more of their surprise gadgets to help them. We have the patience and the brains, but not the gadgets. And time is against us. Get anything out of this, Webb?" Millaird asked the hitherto silent third member of his ruling committee.

The quiet man adjusted his glasses on the bridge of his nose, a flattish nose which did not support them very well. "Just another point to add to our surmises. I would say that they are located somewhere near the Baltic Sea. There are old trade routes there, and in our own time it is a territory closed to us. We never did know too much about that section of Europe. Their installation may be close to the Finnish border. They could disguise their modern station under half a dozen covers; that is strange country."

Millaird's hands unfolded and he produced a notebook and pen from a shirt pocket. "Won't hurt to stir up some of the present-day agents of the M.I. and the rest. They might just come up with a useful hint. So you'd say the Baltic. But that is a big slice of country."

Webb nodded. "We have one advantage-the old trade routes. In the Beaker period they are pretty well marked. The major one into that section was established for the amber trade. The country is forested, but not so heavily as it was in an earlier period. The native tribes are mostly roving hunters, and fishermen along the coast. But they have had contact with traders." He shoved his glasses back into place with a nervous gesture. "The Reds may run into trouble themselves there at this time — —"

"How?" Kelgarries demanded.

"Invasion of the ax people. If they have not yet arrived, they are due very soon. They formed one of the big waves of migratory people, who flooded the country, settled there. Eventually they became the Norse or Celtic stock. We don't know whether they stamped out the native tribes they found there or assimilated them."

"That might be a nice point to have settled more definitely," McNeil commented. "It could mean the difference between getting your skull split and continuing to breathe."

"I don't think they would tangle with the traders. Evidence found today suggests that the Beaker folk simply went on about their business in spite of a change in customers," Webb returned.

"Unless they were pushed into violence." Ashe handed his empty mug to Ross. "Don't forget Lurgha's Wrath. From now on our enemies might take a very dim view of any Beaker trade posts near their property."

Webb shook his head slowly. "A wholesale attack on Beaker establishments would constitute a shift in history. The Reds won't dare that, not just on general suspicion. Remember, they are not any more eager to tinker with history than we are. No, they will watch for us. We will have to stop communication by radio — —"

"We can't!" snapped Millaird vehemently. "We can cut it down, but I won't send the boys out without some means of quick communication. You lab boys put your brains to work and see what you can turn out in the way of talk boxes that they can't snoop. Time!" He drummed on his knee with his thick fingers. "It all comes back to a question of time."

"Which we do not have," Ashe observed in his usual quiet voice. "If the Reds are afraid they have been spotted, they must be dismantling their post right now, working around the clock. We'll never again have such a good chance to nail them. We must move now."

Millaird's lids drooped almost shut; he might have been napping. Kelgarries stirred restlessly by the door, and Webb's round face had settled into what looked like permanent lines of disapproval.

"Doc," Millaird spoke over his shoulder to the fourth man of his following, "what is your report?"

"Ashe must be under treatment for at least five days. McNeil's burns aren't too bad, and Murdock's slash is almost healed."

"Five days —" Millaird droned, and then flashed a glance at the major. "Personnel. We're tied down without any useful personnel. Who in processing could be switched without tangling them up entirely?"

"No one. I can recall Jansen and Van Wyke. These ax people might be a good cover for them." The momentary light in Kelgarries' eyes faded. "No, we have no proper briefing and can't get it until the tribe does appear on the map. I won't send any men in cold. Their blunders would not only endanger them but might menace the whole project."

"So that leaves us with you three," Millaird said. "We'll recall what men we can and brief them again as fast as possible. But you know how long that will take. In the meantime——"

Ashe spoke directly to Webb. "You can't pinpoint the region closer than just the Baltic?"

"We can do this much," the other answered him slowly, and with obvious reluctance. "We can send the sub cruising offshore there for the next five days. If there is any radio activity-any communication-we should be able to trace the beams. It all depends upon whether the Reds have any parties operating from their post. Flimsy——"

"But something!" Kelgarries seized upon it with the relief of one who needed action.

"And they will be waiting for just such a move on our part," Webb continued deliberately.

"All right, so they'll be watching!" the major said, about to lose his temper, "but it is about the only move we can make to back up the boys when they do go in."

He whipped around the door and was gone. Webb got up slowly. "I will work over the maps again," he told Ashe. "We haven't scouted that area, and we don't dare send a photo-plane over it now. Any trip in will be a stab in the dark."

"When you have only one road, you take it," Ashe replied. "I'll be glad to see anything you can show me, Miles."

If Ross had believed that his pre-trial-run cramming had been a rigorous business, he was soon to laugh at that estimation. Since the burden of the next jump would rest on only three of them-Ashe, McNeil, and himself-they were plunged into a whirlwind of instruction, until Ross, dazed and too tired to sleep on the third night, believed that he was more completely bewildered than indoctrinated. He said as much sourly to McNeil.

"Base has pulled back three other teams," McNeil replied. "But the men have to go to school again, and they won't be ready to come on for maybe three, four weeks. To change runs means unlearning stuff as well as learning it——"

"What about new men?"

"Don't think Kelgarries isn't out now beating the bushes for some! Only, we have to be fitted to the physical type we are supposed to represent. For instance, set a small, dark-headed pugnose among your Norse sea rovers, and he's going to be noticed-maybe remembered too well. We can't afford to take that chance. So Kelgarries had to discover men who not only look the part but are also temperamentally fitted for this job. You can't plant a fellow who thinks as a seaman-not a seaman, you understand, but one whose mind works in that pattern-among a wandering tribe of cattle herders. The protection for the man and the project lies in his being fitted into the right spot at the right time."

Ross had never really thought of that point before. Now he realized that he and Ashe and McNeil were of a common mold. All about the same height, they shared brown hair and light eyes-Ashe's blue, his own gray, and McNeil's hazel-and they were of similar build, small-boned, lean, and quick-moving. He had not seen any of the true Beakermen except on the films. But now, recalling those, he could see that the three time traders were of the same general physical type as the far-roving people they used as a cover.

It was on the morning of the fifth day while the three were studying a map Webb had produced that Kelgarries, followed at his own weighty pace by Millaird, burst in upon them.

"We have it! This time *we* have the luck! The Reds slipped. Oh, how they slipped!"

Webb watched the major, a thin little smile pulling at his pursed mouth. "Miracles sometimes do happen," he remarked. "I suppose the sub has a fix for us."

Kelgarries passed over the flimsy strip of paper he had been waving as a banner of triumph. Webb read the notation on it and bent over the map, making a mark with one of those needle-sharp pencils which seemed to grow in his breast pocket, ready for use. Then he made a second mark.

"Well, it narrows it a bit," he conceded. Ashe looked in turn and laughed.

"I would like to hear your definition of 'narrow' sometime, Miles. Remember we have to cover this on foot, and a difference of twenty miles can mean a lot."

"That mark is quite a bit in from the sea." McNeil offered his own protest when he saw the marking. "We don't know that country —"

Webb shoved his glasses back for the hundredth time that morning. "I suppose we could consider this critical, condition red," he said in such a dubious tone that he might have been begging someone to protest his statement. But no one did. Millaird was busy with the map.

"I think we do, Miles!" He looked to Ashe. "You'll parachute in. The packs with which you will be equipped are special stuff. Once you have them off sprinkle them with a powder Miles will provide and in ten minutes there won't be enough of them left for anyone to identify. We haven't but a dozen of these, and we can't throw them away except in a crisis. Find the base and rig up the detector. Your fix in this time will be easy-but it is the other end of the line we must have. Until you locate that, stick to the job. Don't communicate with us until you have it!"

"There is the possibility," Ashe pointed out, "the Reds may have more than one intermediate post. They probably have played it smart and set up a series of them to spoil a direct trace, as each would lead only to another farther back in time — —"

"All right. If that proves true, just get us the next one back," Millaird returned. "From that we can trace them along if we must send in some of the boys wearing dinosaur skins later. We *have* to find their primary base, and if that hunt goes the hard way, well, we do it the hard way."

"How did you get the fix?" McNeil asked.

"One of their field parties ran into trouble and yelled for help."

"Did they get it?"

The major grinned. "What do you think? You know the rules-and the ones the Reds play by are twice as tough on their own men."

"What kind of trouble?" Ashe wanted to know.

"Some kind of a local religious dispute. We do our best with their code, but we're not a hundred per cent perfect in reading it. I gather they were playing with a local god and got their fingers burned."

"Lurgha again, eh?" Ashe smiled.

"Foolish," Webb said impatiently. "That is a silly thing to do. You were almost over the edge of prudence yourself, Gordon, with that Lurgha business. To use the Great Mother was a ticklish thing to try, and you were lucky to get out of it so easily."

"Once was enough," Ashe agreed. "Though using it may have saved our lives. But I assure you I am not starting a holy war or setting up as a prophet."

Ross had been taught something of map reading, but mentally he could not make what he saw on paper resemble the countryside. A few landmarks, if there were any outstanding ones, were all he could hope to impress upon his memory until he was actually on the ground.

Landing there according to Millaird's instruction was another experience he would not have chosen of his own accord. To jump was a matter of timing, and in the dark with a measure of rain thrown in, the action was anything but pleasant. Leaving the plane in a blind, follow-the-leader fashion, Ross found the descent into darkness one of the worst trials he had yet faced. But he did not make too bad a landing in the small parklike expanse they had chosen for their target.

Ross pulled loose his harness and chute, dragging them to what he judged to be the center of the clearing. Hearing a plaintive bray from the air, he dodged as one of the two burden asses sent to join them landed and began to kick at its trappings. The animals they had chosen were the most docile available and they had been given sedation before the jump so that now, feeling Ross's hands, the donkey stood quietly while Ross stripped it of its hanging straps.

"Rossa —" The sound of his Beaker name called through the dark brought Ross facing in the other direction.

"Here, and I have one of the donkeys."

"And I the other!" That was McNeil.

Their eyes adjusted to a gloom which was not as thick as it would be in the forest and they worked fast. Then they dragged the parachutes together in a heap. The rain would, Webb had assured them, add to the rapid destruction wrought by the chemical he had provided. Ashe shook it over the pile, and there was a faint greenish glow. Then they moved away to the woodland and made camp for the balance of the night.

So much of their whole exploit depended upon luck, and this small part had been successful. Unless some agent had been stationed to watch for their arrival Ross believed they could not be spotted.

The rest of their plan was elastic. Posing as traders who had come to open a new station, they were to stay near a river which drained a lake and then angled southward to the distant sea. They knew this section was only sparsely settled by small tribes, hardly larger than family clans. These people were generations behind the civilized level of the villagers of Britain-roving hunters who followed the sweep of game north or south with the seasons.

Along the seashore the fishermen had established more permanent holdings which were slowly becoming towns. There were perhaps a few hardy pioneer farmers on the southern fringes of the district, but the principle reason traders came to this region was to get amber and furs. The Beaker people dealt in both.

Now as the three sheltered under the wide branches of a towering pine Ashe fumbled with a pack and brought out the "beaker" which was the identifying mark of his adopted people. He measured into it a portion of the sour, stimulating drink which the traders introduced wherever they went. The cup passed from hand to hand, its taste unpleasant on the tongue, but comfortingly warm to one's middle.

They took turns keeping the watch until the gray of false dawn became the clearer light of morning. After breakfasting on flat cakes of meal, they packed the donkeys, using the same knots and cross lashing which were the mark of real Beaker traders. Their bows protected from dampness under their cloaks, they set out to find the river and their path southward.

Ashe led, Ross towed the donkeys, and McNeil brought up the rear. In the absence of a path they had to set a ragged course, keeping to the edge of the clearing until they saw the end of the lake.

"Woodsmoke," Ashe commented when they had completed two thirds of their journey. Ross sniffed and was able to smell it too. Nodding to Ashe, McNeil oozed into nothingness between the trees with an ease Murdock envied. As they waited for him to return, Ross became conscious of another life about them, one busy with its own concerns, which were in no way those of human beings, except that food and perhaps shelter were to be reckoned among them.

In Britain, Ross had known there were others of his kind about, but this was different. Here, he could have believed it if he had been told he was the first man to walk this way.

A squirrel ran out on a tree limb and surveyed the two men with curious beady eyes, then clung head down on the tree trunk to see them better. One of the donkeys tossed its head, and the squirrel was gone with a flirt of its tail. Although it was quiet, there was a hum underneath the surface which Ross tried to analyze, to identify the many small sounds which went into its making.

Perhaps because he was trying so hard, he noted the faint noise. His hand touched Ashe's arm and a slight movement of his head indicated the direction of the sound. Then, as fluidly as he had melted into the woods, McNeil returned. "Company," he said in a soft voice.

"What kind?"

"Tribesmen, but wilder than any I've seen, even on the tapes. We are certainly out on the fringes now. These people look about cave level. I don't think they've ever heard of traders."

"How many?"

"Three, maybe four families. Most of the males must be out hunting, but there're about ten children and six or seven women. I don't think they've had good luck lately by the look of them."

"Maybe their luck and ours are going to turn together," Ashe said, motioning Ross forward with the donkeys. "We will circle about them to the river and then try bartering later. But I do want to establish contact."

Chapter 9

"Not to be too hopeful —" McNeil rubbed his arm across his hot face —"so far, so good." After kicking from his path some of the branches Ross had lopped from the trees they had been felling, he went to help his companion roll another small log up to a shelter which was no longer temporary. If there had been any eyes other than the woodland hunters' to spy upon them, they would have seen only the usual procedure of the Beaker traders, busily constructing one of their posts.

That they were being watched by the hunters, all three were certain. That there might be other spies in the forest, they had to assume for their own safety. They might prowl at night, but in the daytime all of the time agents kept within the bounds of the roles they were acting.

Barter with the head men of the hunting clan had brought those shy people into the camp of the strangers who had such wonders to exchange for tanned deer hides and better furs. The news of the traders' arrival spread quickly during the short time they had been here, so that two other clans had sent men to watch the proceedings.

With the trade came news which the agents sifted and studied. Each of them had a list of questions to insert into their conversations with the tribesmen if and when that was possible. Although they did not share a common speech with the forest men, signs were informative and certain nouns could be quickly learned. In the meantime Ashe became friendly with the nearest and first of the clan groups they discovered, going hunting with the men as an excuse to penetrate the unknown section they must quarter in their search for the Red base.

Ross drank river water and mopped his own hot face. "If the Reds aren't traders," he mused aloud, "what *is* their cover?"

McNeil shrugged. "A hunting tribe-fishermen —"

"Where would they get the women and children?"

"The same way they get their men-recruit them in our own time. Or in the way lots of tribes grew during periods of stress."

Ross set down the water jug. "You mean, kill off the men, take over their families?" This was a cold-bloodedness he found sickening. Although he had always prided himself on his toughness, several times during his training at the project he had been confronted by things which shook his belief in his own strong stomach and nerve.

"It has been done," McNeil remarked bleakly, "hundreds of times by invaders. In this setup-small family clans, widely scattered-that move would be very easy."

"They would have to pose as farmers, not hunters," Ross pointed out. "They couldn't move a base around with them."

"All right, so they set up a farming village. Oh, I see what you mean-there isn't any village around here. Yet they are here, maybe underground."

How right their guesses were they learned that night when Ashe returned, a deer's haunch on his shoulder. Ross knew him well enough by now to sense his preoccupation. "You found something?"

"A new set of ghosts," Ashe replied with a strange little smile.

"Ghosts!" McNeil pounced upon that. "The Reds like to play the supernatural angle, don't they? First the voice of Lurgha and now ghosts. What do these ghosts do?"

"They inhabit a bit of mountainous territory southeast of here, a stretch strictly taboo for all hunters. We were following a bison track until the beast headed for the ghost country. Then Ulffa called us off in a hurry. It seems that the hunter who goes in there after his quarry never reappears, or if he does, it's in a damaged condition, blown upon by ghosts and burned to death! That's one point."

He sat down by the fire and stretched his arms wearily. "The second is a little more disturbing for us. A Beaker camp about twenty miles south of here, as far as I can judge, was exterminated just a week ago. The message was passed to me because I was thought to be a kinsman of the slain — —"

McNeil sat up. "Done because they were hunting us?"

"Might well be. On the other hand, the affair may have been just one of general precaution."

"The ghosts did it?" Ross wanted to know.

"I asked that. No, it seems that strange tribesmen overran it at night."

"At night?" McNeil whistled.

"Just so." Ashe's tone was dry. "The tribes do not fight that way. Either someone slipped up in his briefing, or the Reds are overconfident and don't care about the rules. But it was the work of tribesmen, or their counterfeits. There is also a nasty rumor speeding about that the ghosts do not relish traders and that they might protest intrusions of such with penalties all around — —"

"Like the Wrath of Lurgha," supplied Ross.

"There is a certain repetition in this which suggests a lot to the suspicious mind," Ashe agreed.

"I'd say no more hunting expeditions for the present," McNeil said. "It is too easy to mistake a friend for a deer and weep over his grave afterward."

"That is a thought which entered my mind several times this afternoon," Ashe agreed. "These people are deceptively simple on the surface, but their minds do not work along the same patterns as ours. We try to outwit them, but it takes only one slip to make it fatal. In the meantime, I think we'd better make this place a little more snug, and it might be well to post sentries as unobtrusively as possible."

"How about faking some signs of a ruined camp and heading into the blue ourselves?" McNeil asked. "We could strike for the ghost mountains, traveling by night, and Ulffa's crowd would think we were finished off."

"An idea to keep in mind. The point against it would be the missing bodies. It seems that the tribesmen who raided the Beaker camp left some very distasteful evidence of what happened to the camp's personnel. And those we can't produce to cover our trail."

McNeil was not yet convinced. "We might be able to fake something along that line, too — —"

"We may have to fake nothing," Ross cut in softly. He was standing close to the edge of the clearing where they were building their hut, his hand on one of the saplings in the palisade they had set up so laboriously that day. Ashe was beside him in an instant.

"What is it?"

Ross's hours of listening to the sounds of the wilderness were his measuring gauge now. "That bird has never called from inland before. It is the blue one we've seen fishing for frogs along the river."

Ashe, not even glancing at the forest, went for the water jug. "Get your trail supplies," he ordered.

Their leather pouches which held enough iron rations to keep them going were always at hand. McNeil gathered them from behind the fur curtain fronting their half-finished cabin. Again the bird called, its cry piercing and covering a long distance. Ross could understand why a careless man would select it for the signal. He crossed the clearing to the donkeys' shelter, slashing through their nose halters. Probably the patient little beasts would swiftly fall victims to some forest prowlers, but at least they would have their chance to escape.

McNeil, his cloak slung about him to conceal the ration bags, picked up the leather bucket as if he were merely going down to the river for water, and came to join Ross. They believed that they were carrying it off well, that the camp must appear normal to any lurkers in the woods. But either they had made some slip or the enemy was impatient. An arrow sped out of the night to flash across the fire, and Ashe escaped death only because he had leaned forward to feed the flames. His arm swung out and sent the water in the jar hissing onto the blaze as he himself rolled in the other direction.

Ross plunged for the brush with McNeil. Lying flat on the half-frozen ground, they started to work their way to the river bank where the open area would make surprise less possible.

"Ashe?" he whispered and felt McNeil's warm breath on his cheek as he replied:

"He'll make it the other way! He's the best we have for this sort of job."

They made a worm's progress, twice lying, with dagger in hand, while they listened to a faint rustle which betrayed the passing of one of the attackers. Both times Ross was tempted to rise and try to cut off the stranger, but he fought down the impulse. He had learned a control of himself that would have been impossible for him a few months earlier.

The glimmer of the river was pale through the clumps of bushes which sometimes grew into the flood. In this country winter still clung tenaciously in shadowy places with cups of leftover snow, and there was a bite in the wind and water. Ross rose to his knees with an involuntary gasp as a scream cut through the night. He wrenched around toward the camp, only to feel McNeil's hand clamp on his forearm.

"That was a donkey," whispered McNeil urgently. "Come on, let's go down to that ford we discovered!"

They turned south, daring now to trot, half bent to the ground. The river was swollen with spring floods which were only now beginning to subside, but two days earlier they had noticed a sandbar at one spot. By crossing that shelf across the bed, they might hope to put water between them and the unknown enemy tonight. It would give them a breathing space, even though Ross privately shrank from the thought of plowing into the stream. He had seen good-sized trees swirling along in the current only yesterday. And to make such a dash in the dark....

From McNeil's throat burst a startling sound which Ross had last heard in Britain-the questing howl of a hunting wolf. The cry was answered seconds later from downstream.

"Ashe!"

They worked their way along the edge of the water with continued care, until they came upon Ashe at last, so much a part of his background that Ross started when the lump he had taken for a bush hunched forward to join them. Together they made the river crossing and turned south again to head for the mountains. It was then that disaster struck.

Ross heard no birdcall warning this time. Though he was on guard, he never sensed the approach of the man who struck him down from behind. One moment he had been trailing McNeil and Ashe; the next moment was black nothingness.

He was aware of a throb of pain which carried throughout his body and then localized in his head. Forcing open his eyes, the dazzle of light was like a spear point striking directly into his head, intensifying his pain to agony. He brought his hand up to his face and felt stickiness there.

"Assha —" He believed he called that aloud, but he did not even hear his own voice. They were in a valley; a wolf had attacked him out of the bushes. Wolf? No, the wolf was dead, but then it came alive again to howl on a river bank.

Ross forced his eyes open once more, enduring the pain of beams he recognized as sunshine. He turned his head to avoid the glare. It was hard to focus, but he fought to steady himself. There was some reason why it was necessary to move, to get away. But away from what and where? When Ross tried to think he could only see muddled pictures which had no connection.

Then a moving object crossed his very narrow field of vision, passing between him and a thing he knew was a tree trunk. A four-footed creature with a red tongue hanging from its jaws. It came toward him stiff-legged, growling low in its throat, and sniffed at his body before barking in short excited bursts of sound.

The noise hurt his head so much that Ross closed his eyes. Then a shock of icy liquid thrown into his face aroused him to make a feeble protest and he saw, hanging over him in a strange upside-down way, a bearded face which he knew from the past.

Hands were laid on him and the roughness with which he was moved sent Ross spiraling back into the dark once again. When he aroused for the second time it was night and the pain in his head was dulled. He put out his hands and discovered that he lay on a pile of fur robes, and was covered by one.

"Assha —" Again he tried that name. But it was not Assha who came in answer to his feeble call. The woman who knelt beside him with a horn cup in her hand had neatly braided hair in which gray strands showed silver by firelight. Ross knew he had seen her before, but again where and when eluded him. She slipped a sturdy arm under his head and raised him while the world whirled about. The edge of the horn cup was pressed to his lips, and he drank bitter stuff which burned in his throat and lit a fire in his insides. Then he was left to himself once again and in spite of his pain and bewilderment he slept.

How many days he lay in the camp of Ulffa, tended by the chief's head wife, Ross found it hard to reckon. It was Frigga who had argued the tribe into caring for a man they believed almost dead when they found him, and who nursed Ross back to life with knowledge acquired through half a hundred exchanges between those wise women who were the doctors and priestesses of these roaming peoples.

Why Frigga had bothered with the injured stranger at all Ross learned when he was able to sit up and marshal his bewildered thoughts into some sort of order. The matriarch of the tribe thirsted for knowledge. That same urge which had led her to certain experiments with herbs, had made her consider Ross a challenge to her healing skill. When she knew that he would live she determined to learn from him all he had to give.

Ulffa and the men of the tribe might have eyed the metal weapons of the traders with awe and avid desire, but Frigga wanted more than trade goods. She wanted the secret of the making of such cloth as the strangers wore, everything she could learn of their lives and the lands through which they had come. She plied Ross with endless questions which he answered as best he could, for he lay in an odd dreamy state where only the present had any reality. The past was dim and far away, and while he was now and then dimly aware that he had something to do, he forgot it easily.

The chief and his men prowled the half-built station after the attackers had withdrawn, bringing back with them a handful of loot —a bronze razor, two skinning knives, some fishhooks, a length of cloth which Frigga appropriated. Ross eyed this spoil indifferently, making no claim upon it. His interest in everything about him was often blanked out by headaches which kept him limp on his bed, uncaring and stupid for hours or even full days.

He gathered that the tribe had been living in fear of an attack from the same raiders who had wiped out the trading post. But at last their scouts returned with the information that the enemy had gone south.

There was one change of which Ross was not aware but which might have startled both Ashe and McNeil. Ross Murdock had indeed died under that blow which had left him unconscious beside the river. The young man whom Frigga had drawn back to sense and a slow recovery was Rossa of the Beaker people. This same Rossa nursed a hot desire for vengeance against those who had struck him down and captured his kinsmen, a feeling which the family tribe who had rescued him could well understand.

There was the same old urgency pushing him to try his strength now, to keep to his feet even when they were unsteady. His bow was gone, but Ross spent hours fashioning another, and he traded his copper bracelet for the best dozen arrows in Ulffa's camp. The jet pin from his cloak he presented to Frigga with all his gratitude.

Now that his strength was coming back he could not rest easy in the camp. He was ready to leave, even though the gashes on his head were still tender to the touch. Ulffa indulgently planned a hunt southward, and Rossa took the trail with the tribesmen.

He broke with the clan hunters when they turned aside at the beginning of the taboo land. Ross, his own mind submerged and taken over by his Beaker cover, hesitated too. Yet he could not give up, and the others left him there, his eyes on the forbidden heights, unhappy and tormented by more than the headaches which still came and went with painful regularity. In the mountains lay what he sought —a hidden something within his brain told him that over and over-but the mountains were taboo, and he should not venture into them.

How long he might have hesitated there if he had not come upon the trail, Ross did not know. But on the day after the hunters of Ulffa's clan left, a glint of sunlight striking between two trees pointed out a woodsman's blaze on a third tree trunk. The two halves of Ross's memory clicked together for an instant as he examined that cut. He knew that it marked a trace and he pushed on, hunting a second cut and then a third. Convinced that these would lead him into the unknown territory, Ross's desire to explore overcame the grafted superstitions of his briefing.

There were other signs that this was an often-traveled route: a spring cleared of leaves and walled with stone, a couple of steps cut in the turf on a steep slope. Ross moved warily, alert to any sound. He might not be an expert woodsman, but he was learning fast, perhaps the faster because his false memories now supplanted the real ones.

That night he built no fire, crawling instead into the heart of a rotted log to sleep, awakening once to the call of a wolf and another time at the distant crash of a dead tree yielding to wind.

In the morning he was about to climb back to the trail he had prudently left the night before when he saw five bearded, fur-clad men looking much the same as Ulffa's people. Ross hugged the earth and watched them pass out of sight before he followed.

All that day he wove an up-and-down trail behind the small band, sometimes catching sight of them as they topped a rise well ahead or stopped to eat. It was late afternoon when he crept cautiously to the top of a ridge and gazed down into a valley.

There was a town in that valley, sturdy houses of logs behind a stockade. He had seen towns vaguely like it before, yet it had a dreamlike quality as if it were not as real as it appeared.

Ross rested his chin on his arms and watched that town and the people moving in it. Some were fur-clad hunters, but others dressed quite differently. He started up with a little cry at the sight of one of the men who had walked so swiftly from one house to the next; surely he was a Beaker trader!

His unease grew stronger with every moment he watched, but it was the oddness he sensed in that town which bothered him and not any warning that he, himself, was in danger. He had gotten to his knees to see better when out of nowhere a rope sang through the air, settling about his chest with a vicious jerk which not only drove the air from his lungs but pinioned his arms tight to his body.

Chapter 10

Having been cuffed and battered into submission more quickly than would have been possible three weeks earlier, Murdock now stood sullenly surveying the man who, though he dressed like a Beaker trader, persisted in using a language Ross did not know.

"We do not play as children here." At last the man spoke words Ross could understand. "You will answer me or else others shall ask the questions, and less gently. I say to you now-who are you and from where do you come?"

For a moment Ross glowered across the table at him, his inbred antagonism to authority aroused by that contemptuous demand, but then common sense cautioned. His initial introduction to this village had left him bruised and with one of his headaches. There was no reason to let them beat him until he was in no shape to make a break for freedom when and if there was an opportunity.

"I am Rossa of the traders," he returned, eying the man with a carefully measured stare. "I came into this land in search of my kinsmen who were taken by raiders in the night."

The man, who sat on a stool by the table, smiled slowly. Again he spoke in the strange tongue, and Ross merely stared solidly back. His words were short and explosive sounding, and the man's smile faded; his annoyance grew as he continued to speak.

One of Ross's two guards ventured to interrupt, using the Beaker language. "From where did you come?" He was a quiet-faced, slender man, not like his companion, who had roped Murdock from behind and was of the bully breed, able to subdue Ross's wildcat resistance in a very short struggle.

"I came to this land from the south," Ross answered, "after the manner of my people. This is a new land with furs and the golden tears of the sun to be gathered and bartered. The traders move in peace, and their hands are raised against no man. Yet in the darkness there came those who would slay without profit, for what reason I have no knowing."

The quiet man continued the questioning and Ross answered fully with details of the past of one Rossa, a Beaker merchant. Yes, he was from the south. His father was Gurdi, who had a trading post in the warm lands along the big river. This was Rossa's first trip to open new territory. He had come with his father's blood brother, Assha, who was a noted far voyager, and it was an honor to be chosen as donkey-leader for such a one as Assha. With Assha had been Macna, one who was also a far trader, though not as noted as Assha.

Of a certainty, Assha was of his own race! Ross blinked at that question. One need only to look upon him to know that he was of trader blood and no uncivilized woodsrunner. How long had he known Assha? Ross shrugged. Assha had come to his father's post the winter before and had stayed with them through the cold season. Gurdi and Assha had mingled blood after he pulled Gurdi free from the river in flood. Assha had lost his boat and trade goods in that rescue, so Gurdi had made good his loss this year. Detail by detail he gave the story. In spite of the fact that he provided these details glibly, sure that they were true, Ross continued to be haunted by an odd feeling that he was indeed reciting a tale of adventure which had happened long ago and to someone else. Perhaps that pain in his head made him think of these events as very colorless and far away.

"It would seem" —the quiet man turned to the one behind the table —"that this is indeed one Rossa, a Beaker trader."

But the man looked impatient, angry. He made a sign to the other guard, who turned Ross around roughly and sent him toward the door with a shove. Once again the leader gave an order in his own language, adding a few words more with a stinging snap that might have been a threat or a warning.

Ross was thrust into a small room with a hard floor and not even a skin rug to serve as a bed. Since the quiet man had ordered the removal of the ropes from Ross's arms, he leaned against the wall, rubbing the pain of returning circulation away from his wrists and trying to understand what had happened to him and where he was. Having spied upon it from the heights, he knew it wasn't an ordinary trading station, and he wanted to know what they did here. Also, somewhere in this village he hoped to find Assha and Macna.

At the end of the day his captors opened the door only long enough to push inside a bowl and a small jug. He felt for those in the dusk, dipping his fingers into a lukewarm mush of meal and drinking the water from the jug avidly. His headache dulled, and from experience Ross knew that this bout was almost over. If he slept, he would waken with a clearer mind and no pain. Knowing he was very tired, he took the precaution of curling up directly in front of the door so that no one could enter without arousing him.

It was still dark when he awoke with a curious urgency remaining from a dream he could not remember. Ross sat up, flexing his arms and shoulders to combat the stiffness which had come with his cramped sleep. He could not rid himself of a feeling that there was something to be done and that time was his enemy.

Assha! Gratefully he seized on that. He must find Assha and Macna, for the three of them could surely discover a way to get out of this village. That was what was so important!

He had been handled none too gently, and they were holding him a prisoner. But Ross believed that this was not the worst which could happen to him here, and he must be free before the worst did come. The question was, How could he escape? His bow and dagger were gone, and he did not even have his long cloak pin for a weapon, since he had given that to Frigga.

Running his hands over his body, Ross inventoried what remained of his clothing and posses-sions. He unfastened the bronze chain-belt still buckled in his kilt tunic, swinging the length speculatively in one hand. A masterpiece of craftsmanship, it consisted of patterned plates linked together with a series of five finely wrought chains and a front buckle in the form of a lion's head, its protruding tongue serving as a hook to support a dagger sheath. Its weight promised a weapon of sorts, which when added to the element of surprise might free him.

By rights they would be expecting him to produce some opposition, however. It was well known that only the best fighters, the shrewdest minds, followed the traders' roads. It was a proud thing to be a trader in the wilderness, a thought that warmed Ross now as he waited in the dark for what luck and Ba-Bal of the Bright Horns would send. Were he ever to return to Gurdi's post, Ba-Bal, whose boat rode across the sky from dawn to dusk, would have a fine ox, jars of the first brewing, and sweet-smelling amber laid upon his altar.

Ross had patience which he had learned from the mixed heritage of his two pasts, the real and the false graft. He could wait as he had waited many times before-quiet, and with outward ease-for the right moment to come. It came now with footsteps ringing sharply, halting before his cell door.

With the noiseless speed of a hunting cat, Ross flung himself from behind the door to a wall, where he would be hidden from the newcomer for that necessary instant or two. If his attack was to be successful, it must occur inside the room. He heard the sound of a bar being slid out of its brackets, and he poised himself, the belt rippling from his right hand.

The door was opening inward, and a man stood silhouetted against the outer light. He muttered, looking toward the corner where Ross had thrown his single garment in a roll which might just resemble, for the needed second or two, a man curled in slumber. The man in the doorway took the bait, coming forward far enough for Ross to send the door slamming shut as he himself sprang with the belt aimed for the other's head.

There was a startled cry, cut off in the middle as the belt plates met flesh and bone in a crushing force. Luck was with him! Ross caught up his kilt and belted it around him after he had made a hurried examination of the body now lying at his feet. He was not sure that the man was dead, but at any rate he was completely unconscious. Ross stripped off the man's cloak, located his dagger, freed it from the belt hook, and snapped it on his own.

Then inch by inch Ross edged open the door, peering through the crack. As far as he could see, the hall was empty, so he jerked the portal open, and dagger in hand, sprang out, ready for attack. He closed the door, slipping the bar back into its brackets. If the man inside revived and pounded for attention, his own friends might think it was Ross and delay investigating.

But the escape from the cell was the easiest part of what he planned to do, as Ross well knew. To find Assha and Macna in this maze of rooms occupied by the enemy was far more difficult. Although he had no idea in which of the village buildings they might be confined, this one was the largest and seemed to be the headquarters of the chief men, which meant it could also serve as their prison.

Light came from a torch in a bracket halfway down the hall. The wood burned smokily, giving off a resinous odor, and to Ross the glow was sufficient illumination. He slipped along as close to the wall as he could, ready to freeze at the slightest sound. But this portion of the building might well have been deserted, for he saw or heard no one. He tried the only two doors opening out of the hall, but they were secured on the other side. Then he came to a bend in the corridor, and stopped short, hearing a murmur of low voices.

If he had used a hunter's tricks of silent tread and vigilant wariness before, Ross was doubly on guard now as he wriggled to a point from which he could see beyond that turn. Mere luck prevented him from giving himself away a moment later.

Assha! Assha, alive, well, apparently under no restraint, was just turning away from the same quiet man who had had a part in Ross's interrogation. That was surely Assha's brown hair, his slender wiry body draped with a Beaker's kilt. A familiar tilt of the head convinced Ross, though he could not see the man's face. The quiet man went down the hall, leaving Assha before a door. As he passed through it Ross sped forward and followed him inside.

Assha had crossed the bare room and was standing on a glowing plate in the floor. Ross, aroused to desperate action by some fear he did not understand, leaped after him. His left hand fell upon Assha's shoulder, turning the man half around as Ross, too, stepped upon the patch of luminescence.

Murdock had only an instant to realize that he was staring into the face of an astonished stranger. His hand flashed up in an edgewise blow which caught the other on the side of the throat, and then the world came apart about them. There was a churning, whirling sickness which griped and bent Ross almost double across the crumpled body of his victim. He held his head lest it be torn from his shoulders by the spinning thing which seemed based behind his eyes.

The sickness endured only for a moment, and some buried part of Ross's mind accepted it as a phenomenon he had experienced before. He came out of it gasping, to focus his attention once more on the man at his feet.

The stranger was still breathing. Ross stooped to drag him from the plate and began binding and gagging him with lengths torn from his kilt. Only when his captive was secure did he begin looking about him curiously.

The room was bare of any furnishings and now, as he glanced at the floor, Ross saw that the plate had lost its glow. The Beaker trader Rossa rubbed sweating palms on his kilt and thought fleetingly of forest ghosts and other mysteries. Not that the traders bowed to those ghosts which were the plague of lesser men and tribes, but anything which suddenly appeared and then disappeared without any logical explanation, needed thinking on. Murdock pulled the prisoner, who was now reviving, to the far end of the room and then went back to the plate with the persistence of a man who refused to treat with ghosts and wanted something concrete to explain the unexplainable. Though he rubbed his hands across the smooth surface of the plate, it did not light up again.

His captive having writhed himself half out of the corner of the room, Ross debated the wisdom of another silencing—say a tap on the skull with the heavy hilt of his dagger. Deciding against it because he might need a guide, he freed the victim's ankle bonds and pulled him to his feet, holding the dagger ready where the man could see it. Were there any more surprises to be encountered in this place, Assha's double would test them first.

The door did not lead to the same corridor, or even the same kind of corridor Ross had passed through moments earlier. Instead they entered a short passage with walls of some smooth stuff which had almost the sheen of polished metal and were sleek and cold to the touch. In fact, the whole place was chill, chill as river water in the spring.

Still herding the prisoner before him, Ross came to the nearest door and looked within, to be faced by incomprehensible frames of metal rods and boxes. Rossa of the traders marveled and stared, but again, he realized that what he saw was not altogether strange. Part of one wall was a board on which small lights flashed and died, to flash again in winks of bright color. A mysterious object made of wire and disks hung across the back of a chair standing near-by.

The bound man lurched for the chair and fell, rolling toward the wall. Ross pushed him on until he was hidden behind one of the metal boxes. Then he made the rounds of the room, touching nothing, but studying what he could not understand. Puffs of warm air came in through grills near the floor, but the room had the same general chill as the hall outside.

Meanwhile the lights on the board had become more active, flashing on and off in complex patterns. Ross now heard a buzzing, as if a swarm of angry insects were gathered for an attack. Crouching beside his captive, Ross watched the lights, trying to discover the source of the sound.

The buzz grew shriller, almost demanding. Ross heard the tramp of heavy footgear in the corridor, and a man entered the room, crossing purposefully to the chair. He sat down and drew the wire-and-disk frame over his head. His hands moved under the lights, but Ross could not guess what he was doing.

The captive at Murdock's side tried to stir, but Ross's hand pinned him quiet. The shrill noise which had originally summoned the man at the lights was interrupted by a sharp pattern of long-and-short sounds, and his hands flew even more quickly while Ross took in every detail of the other's clothing and equipment. He was neither a shaggy tribesman nor a trader. He wore a dull-green outer garment cut in one piece to cover his arms and legs as well as his body, and his hair was so short that his round skull might have been shaven. Ross rubbed the back of his wrist across his eyes, experiencing again that dim other memory. Odd as this man looked, Murdock had seen his like before somewhere, yet the background had not been Gurdi's post on the southern river. Where and when had he, Rossa, ever been with such strange beings? And why could he not remember it all more clearly?

Boots sounded once more in the hall, and another figure strode in. This one wore furs, but he, too, was no woods hunter, Ross realized as he studied the newcomer in detail. The loose overshirt of thick fur with its hood thrown back, the high boots, and all the rest were not of any primitive fashioning. And the man had four eyes! One pair were placed normally on either side of his nose, and the other two, black-rimmed and murky, were set above on his forehead.

The fur-clad man tapped the one seated at the board. He freed his head partially from the wire cage so that they could talk together in a strange language while lights continued to flash and the buzzing died away. Ross's captive wriggled with renewed vigor and at last thrashed free a foot to kick at one of the metal installations. The resulting clang brought both men around. The one at the board tore his head cage off as he jumped to his feet, while the other brought out a gun.

Gun? One little fraction of Ross's mind wondered at his recognition of that black thing and of the danger it promised, even as he prepared for battle. He pushed his captive across the path of the man in fur and threw himself in the other direction. There was a blast to make a torment in his head as he hurled toward the door.

So intent was Ross upon escape that he did not glance behind but skidded out on his hands and knees, thus fortunately presenting a poor target to the third man coming down the hall. Ross's shoulder hit the newcomer at thigh level, and they tangled in a struggling mass which saved Ross's life as the others burst out behind them.

Ross fought grimly, his hands and feet moving in blows he was not conscious of planning. His opponent was no easy match and at last Ross was flattened, in spite of his desperate efforts. He was whirled over, his arms jerked behind him, and cold metal rings snapped about his wrists. Then he was rolled back, to lie blinking up at his enemies.

All three men gathered over him, barking questions which he could not understand. One of them disappeared and returned with Ross's former captive, his mouth a straight line and a light in his eyes Ross understood far better than words.

"You are the trader prisoner?" The man who looked like Assha leaned over Murdock, patches of red on his tanned skin where the gag and wrist bonds had been.

"I am Rossa, son of Gurdi, of the traders," Ross returned, meeting what he read in the other's expression with a ready defiance. "I was a prisoner, yes. But you did not keep me one for long then, nor shall you now."

The man's thin upper lip lifted. "You have done yourself ill, my young friend. We have a better prison here for you, one from which you shall not escape."

He spoke to the other men, and there was the ring of an order in his voice. They pulled Ross to his feet, pushing him ahead of them. During the short march Ross used his eyes, noticing things he could not identify in the rooms through which they passed. Men called questions and at last they paused long enough, Ross firmly in the hold of the fur-clad guard, for the other two to put on similar garments.

Ross had lost his cloak in the fight, but no fur shirt was given him. He shivered more and more as the chill which clung to that warren of rooms and halls bit into his half-clad body. He was certain of only one thing about this place; he could not possibly be in the crude buildings of the valley village. However, he was unable to guess where he was and how he had come there.

Finally, they went down a narrow room filled with bulky metal objects of bright scarlet or violet that gleamed weirdly and were equipped with rods along which all the colors of the rainbow ringed. Here was a round door, and when one of the guards used both hands to tug it open, the cold that swept in at them was a frigid breath that burned as it touched bare skin.

Chapter 11

It took Ross a while to learn that the dirty-white walls of this tunnel which were almost entirely opaque, with dark objects showing dimly through them here and there, were of solid ice. A black wire was hooked overhead and at regular intervals hung with lights which did nothing to break the sensation of glacial cold about them.

Ross shuddered. Every breath he drew stung in his lungs; his bare shoulders and arms and the exposed section of thigh between kilt and boot were numb. He could only move on stiffly, pushed ahead by his guards when he faltered. He guessed that were he to lose his footing here and surrender to the cold, he would forfeit the battle entirely and with it his life.

He had no way of measuring the length of the boring through the solid ice, but they were at last fronted by another opening, a ragged one which might have been hacked with an ax. They emerged from it into the wildest scene Ross had ever seen. Of course, he was familiar with ice and snow, but here was a world surrendered completely to the brutal force of winter in a strange, abnormal way. It was a still, dead white-gray world in which nothing moved save the wind which curled the drifts.

His guards covered their eyes with the murky lenses they had worn pushed up on their foreheads within the shelter, for above them sunlight dazzled on the ice crest. Ross, his eyes smarting, kept his gaze centered on his feet. He was given no time to look about. A rope was produced, a loop of it flipped in a noose about his throat, and he was towed along like a leashed dog. Before them was a path worn in the snow, not only by the passing of booted feet, but with more deeply scored marks as if heavy objects had been sledded there. Ross slipped and stumbled in the ruts, fearing to fall lest he be dragged. The numbness of his body reached into his head. He was dizzy, the world about him misting over now and again with a haze which arose from the long stretches of unbroken snow fields.

Tripping in a rut, he went down upon one knee, his flesh too numbed now to feel the additional cold of the snow, snow so hard that its crust delivered a knife's cut. Unemotionally, he watched a thin line of red trickle in a sluggish drop or two down the blue skin of his leg. The rope jerked him forward, and Ross scrambled awkwardly until one of his captors hooked a fur mitten in his belt and heaved him to his feet once more.

The purpose of that trek through the snow was obscure to Ross. In fact, he no longer cared, save that a hard rebel core deep inside him would not let him give up as long as his legs could move and he had a scrap of conscious will left in him. It was more difficult to walk now. He skidded and went down twice more. Then, the last time he slipped, he sledded past the man who led him, sliding down the slope of a glass-slick slope. He lay at the foot, unable to get up. Through the haze and deadening blanket of the cold he knew that he was being pulled about, shaken, generally mishandled; but this time he could not respond. Someone snapped open the rings about his wrists.

There was a call, echoing eerily across the ice. The fumbling about his body changed to a tugging and once more he was sent rolling down the slope. But the rope was now gone from his throat, and his arms were free. This time when he brought up hard against an obstruction he was not followed.

Ross's conscious mind-that portion of him that was Rossa, the trader-was content to lie there, to yield to the lethargy born of the frigid world about him. But the subconscious Ross Murdock of the Project prodded at him. He had always had a certain cold hatred which could crystalize and become a spur. Once it had been hatred of circumstances and authority; now it became hatred for those who had led him into this wilderness with the purpose, as he knew now, of leaving him to freeze and die.

Ross pulled his hands under him. Though there was no feeling in them, they obeyed his will clumsily. He levered himself up and looked around. He lay in a narrow crevicelike cut, partly walled in by earth so frozen as to resemble steel. Crusted over it in long streaks from above were tongues of ice. To remain here was to serve his captors' purpose.

Ross inched his way to his feet. This opening, which was intended as his grave, was not so deep as the men had thought it in their hurry to be rid of him. He believed that he could climb out if he could make his body answer to his determination.

Somehow Ross made that supreme effort and came again to the rutted path from which they had tumbled him. Even if he could, there was no sense in going along that rutted trail, for it led back to the ice-encased building from which he had been brought. They had thrust him out to die; they would not take him in.

But a road so well marked must have some goal, and in hopes that he might find shelter at the other end, Ross turned to the left. The trace continued down the slope. Now the towering walls of ice and snow were broken by rocky teeth as if they had bitten deep upon this land, only to be gnawed in return. Rounding one of those rock fangs, Ross looked at a stretch of level ground. Snow lay here, but the beaten-down trail led straight through it to the rounded side of a huge globe half buried in the ground, a globe of dark material which could only be man-made.

Ross was past caution. He must get to warmth and shelter or he was done for, and he knew it. Wavering and weaving, he went on, his attention fixed on the door ahead —a closed oval door. With a sob of exhausted effort, Ross threw himself against it. The barrier gave, letting him fall forward into a queer glimmering radiance of bluish light.

The light rousing him because it promised more, he crawled on past another door which was flattened back against the inner wall. It was like making one's way down a tube. Ross paused, pressing his lifeless hands against his bare chest under the edge of his tunic, suddenly realizing that there was warmth here. His breath did not puff out in frosty streamers before him, nor did the air sear his lungs when he ventured to draw in more than shallow gulps.

With that realization a measure of animal caution returned to him. To remain where he was, just inside the entrance, was to court disaster. He must find a hiding place before he collapsed, for he sensed he was very near the end of his ability to struggle. Hope had given him a flash of false strength, the impetus to move, and he must make the most of that gift.

His path ended at a wide ladder, coiling in slow curves into gloom below and shadows above. He sensed that he was in a building of some size. He was afraid to go down, for even looking in that direction almost finished his sense of balance, so he climbed up.

Step by step, Ross made that painful journey, passing levels from which three or four hallways ran out like the radii of a spider's web. He was close to the end of his endurance when he heard a sound, echoed, magnified, from below. It was someone moving. He dragged his body into the fourth level where the light was very faint, hoping to crawl far enough into one of the passages to remain unseen from the stair. But he had gone only part-way down his chosen road when he collapsed, panting, and fell back against the wall. His hands pawed vainly against that sleek surface. He was falling through it!

Ross had a second, perhaps two, of stupefied wonder. Lying on a soft surface, he was enfolded by a warmth which eased his bruised and frozen body. There was a sharp prick in his thigh, another in his arm, and the world was a hazy dream until he finally slept in the depths of exhaustion.

There were dreams, detailed ones, and Ross stirred uneasily as his sleep thinned to waking. He lay with his eyes closed, fitting together odd bits of-dreams? No, he was certain that they were memories. Rossa of the Beaker traders and Ross Murdock of the project were again fused into one and the same person. How it had happened he did not know, but it was true.

Opening his eyes, he noticed a curved ceiling of soft blue which misted at the edges into gray. The restful color acted on his troubled, waking mind like a soothing word. For the first time since he had been struck down in the night his headache was gone. He raised his hand to explore that old hurt near his hairline that had been so tender only yesterday that it could not bear pressure. There remained only a thin, rough line like a long-healed scar, that was all.

Ross lifted his head to look about him. His body lay supported in a cradlelike arrangement of metal, almost entirely immersed in a red gelatinous substance with a clean, aromatic odor. Just as he was no longer cold, neither was he hungry. He felt as fit as he ever had in his life.

Sitting up in the cradle, he stroked the jelly away from his shoulders and chest. It fell from him cleanly, leaving no trace of grease or dampness on his skin.

There were other fixtures in the small cylinderlike chamber besides that odd bed in which he had lain. Two bucket-shaped seats were placed at the narrow fore part of the room and before those seats was a system of controls he could not comprehend.

As Ross swung his feet to the floor there was a click from the side which brought him around, ready for trouble. But the noise had been caused by the opening of a door into a small cupboard. Inside the cupboard lay a fat package. Obviously this was an invitation to investigate the offering.

The package contained a much folded article of fabric, compressed and sealed in a transparent bag which he fumbled twice before he succeeded in releasing its fastening. Ross shook out a garment of material such as he had never seen before. Its sheen and satin-smooth surface suggested metal, but its stuff was as supple as fine silk. Color rippled across it with every twist and turn he gave to the length-dark blue fading to pale violet, accented with wavering streaks of vivid and startling green.

Ross experimented with a row of small, brilliant-green studs which made a transverse line from the right shoulder to the left hip, and they came apart. As he climbed into the suit the stuff modeled to his body in a tight but perfect fit. Across the shoulders were bands of green to match the studs, and the stockinglike tights were soled with a thick substance which formed a cushion for his feet.

He pressed the studs together, felt them lock, and then stood smoothing that strange, beautiful fabric, unable to account for either it or his surroundings. His head was clear; he could remember every detail of his flight up to the time he had fallen through the wall. And he was certain that he had passed through not only one, but two, of the Red time posts. Could this be the third? If so, was he still a captive? Why would they leave him to freeze in the open country one moment and then treat him this way later?

He could not connect the ice-encased building from which the Reds had taken him with this one. At the sound of another soft noise Ross glanced over his shoulder just in time to see the cradle of jelly, from which he had emerged, close in upon itself until its bulk was a third of its former size. Compact as a box, it folded up against the wall.

Ross, his cushioned feet making no sound, advanced to the bucket-chairs. But lowering his body into one of them for a better look at what vaguely resembled the control of a helicopter-like the one in which he had taken the first stage of his fantastic journey across space and time-he did not find it comfortable. He realized that it had not been constructed to accommodate a body shaped precisely like his own.

A body like his own....That jelly bath or bed or whatever it was....The clothing which adapted so skillfully to his measurements....

Ross leaned forward to study the devices on the control board, confirming his suspicions. He had made the final jump of them all! He was now in some building of that alien race upon whose existence Millaird and Kelgarries had staked the entire project. This was the source, or one of the sources, from which the Reds were getting the knowledge which fitted no modern pattern.

A world encased in ice and a building with strange machinery. This thing—a cylinder with a pilot's seat and a set of controls. Was it an alien place? But the jelly bath-and the rest of it.... Had his presence activated that cupboard to supply him with clothing? And what had become of the tunic he was wearing when he entered?

Ross got up to search the chamber. The bed-bath was folded against the wall, but there was no sign of his Beaker clothing, his belt, the hide boots. He could not understand his own state of well being, the lack of hunger and thirst.

There were two possible explanations for it all. One was that the aliens still lived here and for some reason had come to his aid. The other was that he stood in a place where robot machinery worked, though those who had set it up were no longer there. It was difficult to separate his memory of the half-buried globe he had seen from his sickness of that moment. Yet he knew that he had climbed and crawled through emptiness, neither seeing nor hearing any other life.

Now Ross restlessly paced up and down, seeking the door through which he must have come, but there was not even a line to betray such an opening.

"I want out," he said aloud, standing in the center of the cramped room, his fists planted on his hips, his eyes still searching for the vanished door. He had tapped, he had pushed, he had tried every possible way to find it. If he could only remember how he had come in! But all he could recall was leaning against a wall which moved inward and allowed him to fall. But where had he fallen? Into that jelly bath?

Ross, stung by a sudden idea, glanced at the ceiling. It was low enough so that by standing on tiptoes he could drum his fingers on its surface. Now he moved to the place directly above where the cradle had swung before it had folded itself away.

Rapping and poking, his efforts were rewarded at last. The blue curve gave under his assault. He pushed now, rising on his toes, though in that position he could exert little pressure. Then as if some faulty catch had been released, the ceiling swung up so that he lost his footing and would have fallen had he not caught the back of one of the bucket-seats.

He jumped and by hooking his hands over the edge of the opening, was able to work his way up and out, to face a small line of light. His fingers worked at that, and he opened a second door, entering a familiar corridor.

Holding the door open, Ross looked back, his eyes widening at what he saw. For it was plain now that he had just climbed out of a machine with the unmistakable outline of a snub-nosed rocket. The small flyer-or a jet, or whatever it was-had been fitted into a pocket in the side of the big structure as a ship into a berth, and it must have been set there to shoot from that enclosing chamber as a bullet is shot from a rifle barrel. But why?

Ross's imagination jumped from fact to theory. The torpedo craft could be an atomic jet. All right, he had been in bad shape when he fell into it by chance and the bed machine had caught him as if it had been created for just such a duty. What kind of a small plane would be equipped with a restorative apparatus? Only one intended to handle emergencies, to transport badly injured living things who had to leave the building in a hurry.

In other words, a lifeboat!

But why would a building need a lifeboat? That would be rather standard equipment for a ship. Ross stepped into the corridor and stared about him with open and incredulous wonder. Could this be some form of ship, grounded here, deserted and derelict, and now being plundered by the Reds? The facts fitted! They fitted so well with all he had been able to discover that Ross was sure it was true. But he determined to prove it beyond all doubt.

He closed the door leading to the lifeboat berth, but not so securely that he could not open it again. That was too good a hiding place. On his cushioned feet he padded back to the stairway, and he stood there listening. Far below were sounds, a rasp of metal against metal, a low murmur of muted voices. But from above there was nothing, so he would explore above before he ventured into that other danger zone.

Ross climbed, passing two more levels, to come out into a vast room with a curving roof which must fill the whole crown of the globe. Here was such a wealth of machines, controls, things he could not understand that he stood bewildered, content for the moment merely to look. There were-he counted slowly-five control boards like those he had seen in the small escape ship. Each of these was faced by two or three of the bucket-seats, only these swung in webbing. He put his hand on one, and it bobbed elastically.

The control boards were so complicated that the one in the lifeboat might have been a child's toy in comparison. The air in the ship had been good; in the lifeboat it had held the pleasant odor of the jelly; but here Ross sniffed a faint but persistent hint of corruption, of an old malodor.

He left the vantage point by the stairs and paced between the control boards and their empty swinging seats. This was the main control room, of that he was certain. From this point all the vast bulk beneath him had been set in motion, sailed here and there. Had it been on the sea, or through the air? The globe shape suggested an air-borne craft. But a civilization so advanced as this would surely have left some remains. Ross was willing to believe that he could be much farther back in time than 2000 B.C., but he was still sure that traces of those who could build a thing like this would have existed in the twentieth century A.D.

Maybe that was how the Reds had found this. Something they had turned up within their country-say, in Siberia, or some of the forgotten corners of Asia-had been a clue.

Having had little schooling other than the intensive cramming at the base and his own informal education, the idea of the race who had created this ship overawed Ross more than he would admit. If the project could find this, turn loose on it the guys who knew about such things....But that was just what they were striving for, and he was the only project man to have found the prize. Somehow, someway, he had to get back-out of this half-buried ship and its icebound world-back to where he could find his own people. Perhaps the job was impossible, but he had to try. His survival was considered impossible by the men who had thrown him into the crevice, but here he was. Thanks to the men who had built this ship, he was alive and well.

Ross sat down in one of the uncomfortable seats to think and thus avoided immediate disaster, for he was hidden from the stairs on which sounded the tap of boots. A climber, maybe two, were on their way up, and there was no other exit from the control cabin.

Chapter 12

Ross dropped from the web-slung chair to the floor and made himself as small as possible under the platform at the front of the cabin. Here, where there was a smaller control board and two seats placed closely together, the odd, unpleasant odor clung and became stronger to Ross's senses as he waited tensely for the climbers to appear. Though he had searched, there was nothing in sight even faintly resembling a weapon. In a last desperate bid for freedom he crept back to the stairwell.

He had been taught a blow during his training period, one which required a precise delivery and, he had been warned, was often fatal. He would use it now. The climber was very close. A cropped head arose through the floor opening, and Ross struck, knowing as his hand chopped against the folds of a fur hood that he had failed.

But the impetus of that unexpected blow saved him after all. With a choked cry the man disappeared, crashing down upon the one following him. A scream and shouts were heard from below, and a shot ripped up the well as Ross scrambled away from it. He might have delayed the final battle, but they had him cornered. He faced that fact bleakly. They need only sit below and let nature take its course. His session in the lifeboat had restored his strength, but a man could not live forever without food and water.

However, he had bought himself perhaps a yard of time which must be put to work. Turning to examine the seats, Ross discovered that they could be unhooked from their webbing swings. Freeing all of them, he dragged their weight to the stairwell and jammed them together to make a barricade. It could not hold long against any determined push from below, but, he hoped, it would deflect bullets if some sharpshooter tried to wing him by ricochet. Every so often there was the crash of a shot and some shouting, but Ross was not going to be drawn out of cover by that.

He paced around the control cabin, still hunting for a weapon. The symbols on the levers and buttons were meaningless to him. They made him feel frustrated because he imagined that among that countless array were some that might help him out of the trap if he could only guess their use.

Once more he stood by the platform thinking. This was the point from which the ship had been sailed-in the air or on some now frozen sea. These control boards must have given the ship's master the means not only of propelling the vast bulk, but of unloading and loading cargo, lighting, heating, ventilation, and perhaps defense! Of course, every control might be dead now, but he remembered that in the lifeboat the machines had worked successfully, fulfilled expertly the duty for which they had been constructed.

The only step remaining was to try his luck. Having made his decision, Ross simply shut his eyes as he had in a very short and almost forgotten childhood, turned around three times, and pointed. Then he looked to see where luck had directed him.

His finger indicated a board before which there had been three seats, and he crossed to it slowly, with a sense that once he touched the controls he might inaugurate a chain of events he could not stop. The crash of a shot underlined the fact that he had no other recourse.

Since the symbols meant nothing, Ross concentrated on the shapes of the various devices and chose one which vaguely resembled the type of light switch he had always known. Since it was up, he pressed it down, counting to twenty slowly as he waited for a reaction. Below the switch was an oval button marked with two wiggles and a double dot in red. Ross snapped it level with the panel, and when it did not snap back, he felt somehow encouraged. When the two levers flanking that button did not push in or move up and down, Ross pulled them out without even waiting to count off.

This time he had results! A crackling of noise with a singsong rhythm, the volume of which, low at first, arose to a drone filled the cabin. Ross, deafened by the din, twisted first one lever and then the other until he had brought the sound to a less piercing howl. But he needed action, not just noise; he moved from behind the first chair to the next one. Here were five oval buttons, marked in the same vivid green as that which trimmed his clothing-two wiggles, a dot, a double bar, a pair of entwined circles, and a crosshatch.

Why make a choice? Recklessness bubbled to the surface, and Ross pushed all the buttons in rapid succession. The results were, in a measure, spectacular. Out of the top of the control board rose a triangle of screen which steadied and stood firm while across it played a rippling wave of color. Meanwhile the singsong became an angry squawking as if in protest.

Well, he had something, even if he didn't know what it was! And he had also proved that the ship was alive. However, Ross wanted more than a squawk of exasperation, which was exactly what the noise had become. It almost sounded, Ross decided as he listened, as if he were being expertly chewed out in another language. Yes, he wanted more than a series of squawks and a fanciful display of light waves on a screen.

At the section of board before the third and last seat there was less choice-only two switches. As Ross flicked up the first the pattern on the screen dwindled into a brown color shot with cream in which there was a suggestion of a picture. Suppose one didn't put the switch all the way up? Ross examined the slot in which the bar moved and now noted a series of tiny point marks along it. Selective? It would not do any harm to see. First he hurried back to the cork of chairs he had jammed into the stairwell. The squawks were now coming only at intervals, and Ross could hear nothing to suggest that his barrier was being forced.

He returned to the lever and moved it back two notches, standing open-mouthed at the immediate result. The cream-and-brown streaks were making a picture! Moving another notch down caused the picture to skitter back and forth on the screen. With memories of TV tuning to guide him, Ross brought the other lever down to a matching position, and the dim and shadowy images leaped into clear and complete focus. But the color was still brown, not the black and white he had expected.

Only, he was also looking into a face! Ross swallowed, his hand grasping one of the strings of chair webbing for support. Perhaps because in some ways it did resemble his own, that face was more preposterously nonhuman. The visage on the screen was sharply triangular with a small, sharply pointed chin and a jaw line running at an angle from a broad upper face. The skin was dark, covered largely with a soft and silky down, out of which hooked a curved and shining nose set between two large round eyes. On top of that astonishing head the down rose to a peak not unlike a cockatoo's crest. Yet there was no mistaking the intelligence in those eyes, nor the other's amazement at sight of Ross. They might have been staring at each other through a window.

Squawk ...squeek ...squawk....The creature in the mirror-on the vision plate-or outside the window-moved its absurdly small mouth in time to those sounds. Ross swallowed again and automatically made answer.

"Hello." His voice was a weak whistle, and perhaps it did not reach the furry-faced one, for he continued his questions if questions they were. Meanwhile Ross, over his first stupefaction, tried to see something of the creature's background. Though the objects were slightly out of focus, he was sure he recognized fittings similar to those about him. He must be in communication with another ship of the same type and one which was not deserted!

Furry-face had turned his head away to squawk rapidly over his shoulder, a shoulder which was crossed by a belt or sash with an elaborate pattern. Then he got up from his seat and stood aside to make room for the one he had summoned.

If Furry-face had been a startling surprise, Ross was now to have another. The man who now faced him on the screen was totally different. His skin registered as pale-cream-colored-and his face was far more human in shape, though it was hairless as was the smooth dome of his skull. When one became accustomed to that egg slickness, the stranger was not bad-looking, and he was wearing a suit which matched the one Ross had taken from the lifeboat.

This one did not attempt to say anything. Instead, he stared at Ross long and measuringly, his eyes growing colder and less friendly with every second of that examination. Ross had resented Kelgarries back at the project, but the major could not match Baldy for the sheer weight of unpleasant warning he could pack into a look. Ross might have been startled by Furry-face, but now his stubborn streak arose to meet this implied challenge. He found himself breathing hard and glaring back with an intensity which he hoped would get across and prove to Baldy that he would not have everything his own way if he proposed to tangle with Ross.

His preoccupation with the stranger on the screen betrayed Ross into the hands of those from below. He heard their attack on the barricade too late. By the time he turned around, the cork of seats was heaved up and a gun was pointing at his middle. His hands went up in small reluctant jerks as that threat held him where he was. Two of the fur-clad Reds climbed into the control chamber.

Ross recognized the leader as Ashe's double, the man he had followed across time. He blinked for just an instant as he faced Ross and then shouted an order at his companion. The other spun Murdock around, bringing his hands down behind him to clamp his wrists together. Once again Ross fronted the screen and saw Baldy watching the whole scene with an expression suggesting that he had been shocked out of his complacent superiority.

"Ah...." Ross's captors were staring at the screen and the unearthly man there. Then one flung himself at the control panel and his hands whipped back and forth, restoring to utter silence both screen and room.

"What are you?" The man who might have been Ashe spoke slowly in the Beaker tongue, drilling Ross with his stare as if by the force of his will alone he could pull the truth out of his prisoner.

"What do you think I am?" Ross countered. He was wearing the uniform of Baldy, and he had clearly established contact with the time owners of this ship. Let that worry the Red!

But they did not try to answer him. At a signal he was led to the stair. To descend that ladder with his hands behind him was almost impossible, and they had to pause at the next level to unclasp the handcuffs and let him go free. Keeping a gun on him carefully, they hurried along, trying to push the pace while Ross delayed all he could. He realized that in his recognition of the power of the gun back in the control chamber, his surrender to its threat, he had betrayed his real origin. So he must continue to confuse the trail to the project in every possible way left to him. He was sure that this time they would not leave him in the first convenient crevice.

He knew he was right when they covered him with a fur parka at the entrance to the ship, once more manacling his hands and dropping a noose leash on him.

So, they were taking him back to their post here. Well, in the post was the time transporter which could return him to his own kind. It would be, it must be possible to get to that! He gave his captors no more trouble but trudged, outwardly dispirited, along the rutted way through the snow up the slope and out of the valley.

He did manage to catch a good look at the globe-ship. More than half of it, he judged, was below the surface of the ground. To be so buried it must either have lain there a long time or, if it were an air vessel, crashed hard enough to dig itself that partial grave. Yet Ross had established contact with another ship like it, and neither of the creatures he had seen were human, at least not human in any way he knew.

Ross chewed on that as he walked. He believed that those with him were looting the ship of its cargo, and by its size, that cargo must be a large one. But cargo from where? Made by what hands, what *kind* of hands? Enroute to what port? And how had the Reds located the ship in the first place? There were plenty of questions and very few answers. Ross clung to the hope that somehow he had endangered the Reds' job here by activating the communication system of the derelict and calling the attention of its probable owners to its fate.

He also believed that the owners might take steps to regain their property. Baldy had impressed him deeply during those few moments of silent appraisal, and he knew he would not like to be on the receiving end of any retaliation from the other. Well, now he had only one chance, to keep the Reds guessing as long as he could and hope for some turn of fate which would allow him to try for the time transport. How the plate operated he did not know, but he had been transferred here from the Beaker age and if he could return to that time, escape might be possible. He had only to reach the river and follow it down to the sea where the sub was to make rendezvous at intervals. The odds were overwhelmingly against him, and Ross knew it. But there was no reason, he decided, to lie down and roll over dead to please the Reds.

As they approached the post Ross realized how much skill had gone into its construction. It looked as if they were merely coming up to the outer edge of a glacier tongue. Had it not been for the track in the snow, there would have been no reason to suspect that the ice covered anything but a thick core of its own substance. Ross was shoved through the white-walled tunnel to the building beyond.

He was hurried through the chain of rooms to a door and thrust through, his hands still fastened. It was dark in the cubby and colder than it had been outside. Ross stood still, waiting for his eyes to adjust to the gloom. It was several moments after the door had slammed shut that he caught a faint thud, a dull and hollow sound.

"Who is here?" he used the Beaker speech, determining to keep to the rags of his cover, which probably was a cover no longer. There was no reply, but after a pause that distant beat began again. Ross stepped cautiously forward, and by the simple method of running fullface into the walls, discovered that he was in a bare cell. He also discovered that the noise lay behind the left-hand wall, and he stood with his ear flat against it, listening. The sound did not have the regular rhythm of a machine in use-there were odd pauses between some blows, others came in a quick rain. It was as if someone were digging!

Were the Reds engaged in enlarging their icebound headquarters? Having listened for a considerable time, Ross doubted that, for the sound was too irregular. It seemed almost as if the longer pauses were used to check up on the result of labor-was it the extent of the excavation or the continued preservation of secrecy?

Ross slipped down along the wall, his shoulders still resting against it, and rested with his head twisted so he could hear the tapping. Meanwhile he flexed his wrists inside the hoops which confined them, and folding his hands as small as possible, tried to slip them through the rings. The only result was that he chafed his skin raw to no advantage. They had not taken off his parka, and in spite of the chill about him, he was too warm. Only that part of his body covered by the suit he had taken from the ship was comfortable; he could almost believe that it possessed some built-in conditioning device.

With no hope of relief Ross rubbed his hands back and forth against the wall, scraping the hoops on his wrists. The distant pounding had ceased, and this time the pause lengthened into so long a period that Ross fell asleep, his head falling forward on his chest, his raw wrists still pushed against the surface behind him.

He was hungry when he awoke, and with that hunger his rebellion sparked into flame. Awkwardly he got to his feet and lurched along to the door through which he had been thrown, where he proceeded to kick at the barrier. The cushiony stuff forming the soles of his tights muffled most of the force of those blows, but some noise was heard outside, for the door opened and Ross faced one of the guards.

"Food! I want to eat!" He put into the Beaker language all the resentment boiling in him.

The fellow ignoring him, reached in a long arm, and nearly tossing the prisoner off balance, dragged him out of the cell. Ross was marched into another room to face what appeared to be a tribunal. Two of the men there he knew-Ashe's double and the quiet man who had questioned him back in the other time station. The third, clearly one of greater authority, regarded Ross bleakly.

"Who are you?" the quiet man asked.

"Rossa, son of Gurdi. And I would eat before I make talk with you. I have not done any wrong that you should treat me as a barbarian who has stolen salt from the trading post — —"

"You are an agent," the leader corrected him dispassionately, "of whom you will tell us in due time. But first you shall speak of the ship, of what you found there, and why you meddled with the controls.... Wait a moment before you refuse, my young friend." He raised his hand from his lap, and once again Ross faced an automatic. "Ah, I see that you know what I hold-odd knowledge for an innocent Bronze Age trader. And please have no doubts about my hesitation to use this. I shall not kill you, naturally," the man continued, "but there are certain wounds which supply a maximum of pain and little serious damage. Remove his parka, Kirschov."

Once more Ross was unmanacled, the fur stripped from him. His questioner carefully studied the suit he wore under it. "Now you will tell us exactly what we wish to hear."

There was a confidence in that statement which chilled Ross; Major Kelgarries had displayed its like. Ashe had it in another degree, and certainly it had been present in Baldy. There was no doubt that the speaker meant exactly what he said. He had at his command methods which would wring from his captive the full sum of what he wanted, and there would be no consideration for that captive during the process.

His implied threat struck as cold as the glacial air, and Ross tried to meet it with an outward show of uncracked defenses. He decided to pick and choose from his information, feeding them scraps to stave off the inevitable. Hope dies very hard, and Ross having been pushed into corners long before his work at the project, had had considerable training in verbal fencing with hostile authority. He would volunteer nothing.... Let it be pulled from him reluctant word by word! He would spin it out as long as he could and hope that time might fight for him.

"You are an agent...."

Ross accepted this statement as one he would neither affirm nor deny.

"You came to spy under the cover of a barbarian trader," smoothly, without pause, the man changed language in mid-sentence, slipping from the Beaker speech into English.

But long experience in meeting the dangerous with an expression of complete lack of comprehension was Ross's weapon now. He stared somewhat stupidly at his interrogator with that bewildered, boyish look he had so long cultivated to bemuse enemies in his past.

Whether he could have held out long against the other's skill-for Ross possessed no illusions concerning the type of examiner he now faced-he was never to know. Perhaps the drastic interruption that occurred the next moment saved for Ross a measure of self-esteem.

There was a distant boom, hollow and thunderous. Underneath and around them the floor, walls, and ceiling of the room moved as if they had been pried from their setting of ice and were being rolled about by the exploring thumb and forefinger of some impatient giant.

Chapter 13

Ross swayed against a guard, was fended off, and bounced against the wall as the man shouted words Ross could not understand. A determined roar from the leader brought a semblance of order, but it was plain that they had not been expecting this. Ross was hustled out of the room back to his cell. His guards were opening the cell door when a second shock was felt and he was thrust into safekeeping with no ceremony.

He half crouched against the questionable security of the wall, waiting through two more twisting earth waves, both of which were accompanied or preceded by dull sounds. Bombing! That last wrench was really bad. Ross found himself lying on the floor, feeling tremors rippling along the earth. His stomach knotted convulsively with a fear unlike any he had known before. It was as if the very security of the world had been jerked from under him.

But that last explosion-if it was an explosion-appeared to be the end. Ross sat up gingerly after several long moments during which no more shocks moved the floor and walls. A line of light marked the door, showing cracks where none had previously existed. Ross, not yet ready to try standing erect, was heading toward it on his hands and knees when a sharp noise behind him brought him to a stop.

There was no light to see by, but he was certain that the scrape of metal against metal sounded from the far side of the wall. He crawled back and put his ear to the surface. Now he heard not only that scraping, but an undercurrent of clicks, chippings....

Under his exploring hands the surface remained as smooth as ever, however. Then suddenly, perhaps a foot from his head, there sounded a rip of metal. The wall was being holed from the other side! Ross caught a flicker of very weak light, and moving in it was the point of a tool pulling at the smooth surface of the wall. It broke away with a brittle sound, and a hand holding a light reached through the aperture.

Ross wondered if he should catch that wrist, but the hope that the digger might just possibly be an ally kept him motionless. After the hand with the light whipped back beyond the wall, a wide section gave away and a hunched figure crawled through, followed by a second. In the limited glow he saw the first tunneler clearly enough.

"Assha!"

Ross was unprepared for what followed his cry. The lean brown man moved with a panther's striking speed, and Ross was forced back. A hand like a steel ring on his throat shut the breath away from his bursting lungs; the other's muscular body held him flat in spite of his struggles. The light of the small flash glowed inches beyond his eyes as he fought to fill his lungs. Then the hand on his throat was gone and he gasped, a little dizzy.

"Murdock! What are you doing —?" Ashe's clipped voice was muffled by another sudden explosion. This time the earth tremors not only hurled them from their feet, but seemed to run along the walls and across the ceiling. Ross, burying his face in the crook of his arm, could not rid himself of the fear that the building was being slowly twisted into scrap. When the shock was over he raised his head.

"What's going on?" He heard McNeil ask.

"Attack." That was Ashe. "But why, and by whom-don't ask me! You are a prisoner, I suppose, Murdock?"

"Yes, sir." Ross was glad that his voice sounded normal enough.

He heard someone sigh and guessed it was McNeil. "Another digging party." There was tired disgust in that.

"I don't understand," Ross appealed to that section of the dark where Ashe had been. "Have you been here all the time? Are you trying to dig your way out? I don't see how you can cut out of this glacier that we're parked under ——"

"Glacier!" Ashe's exclamation was as explosive as the tremors. "So we're inside a glacier! That explains it. Yes, we've been here —"

"On ice!" McNeil commented and then laughed. "Glacier-ice-that's right, isn't it?"

"We're collaborating," Ashe continued. "Supplying our dear friends with a lot of information they already have and some flights of fancy they never dreamed about. However, they didn't know we had a few surprise packets of our own strewn about. It's amazing what the boys back at the project can pack away in a belt, or between layers of hide in a boot. So we've been engaged in some research of our own — —"

"But I didn't have any escape gadgets." Ross was struck by the unfairness of that.

"No," Ashe agreed, his voice even and cold, "they are not entrusted to first-run men. You might slip up and use them at the wrong moment. However, you appear to have done fairly well...."

The heat of Ross's rising anger was chilled by the noise which cracked over their heads, ground to them through the walls, flattened and threatened them. He had thought those first shocks the end of this ice burrow and the world; he knew that this one was.

And the silence that followed was as threatening in its way as the clamor had been. Then there was a shout, a shriek. The space of light near the cell door was widening as that barrier, broken from its lock, swung open slowly. The fear of being trapped sent the men in that direction.

"Out!"

Ross was ready enough to respond to that order, but they were stopped by a crackle of sound that could be only one thing-rapid-fire guns. Somewhere in this warren a fight was in progress. Ross, remembering the arrogant face of the bald ship's officer, wondered if this was not an attack in force-the aliens against the looting Reds. If so, would the ship people distinguish between those found here. He feared not.

The room outside was clear, but not for long. As they lay watching, two men backed in, then whirled to stare at each other. A voice roared from beyond as if ordering them back to some post. One of them took a step forward in reluctant obedience, but the other grabbed his arm and pulled him away. They turned to run, and an automatic cracked.

The man nearest Ross gave a queer little cough and folded forward to his knees, sprawling on his face. His companion stared at him wildly for an instant, and then skidded into the passage beyond, escaping by inches a shot which clipped the door as he lunged through it.

No one followed, for outside there was a crescendo of noise-shouting, cries of pain, an unidentifiable hissing. Ashe darted into the room, taking cover by the body. Then he came back, the fellow's gun in his hand, and with a jerk of his head summoned the other two. He motioned them on in a direction away from the sounds of battle.

"I don't get all this," McNeil commented as they reached the next passage. "What's going on? Mutiny? Or have our boys gotten through?"

"It must be the ship people," Ross answered.

"What ship?" Ashe caught him up swiftly.

"The big one the Reds have been looting — —"

"Ship?" echoed McNeil. "And *where* did you get that rig?" In the bright light it was easy to see Ross's alien dress. McNeil fingered the elastic material wonderingly.

"From the ship," Ross returned impatiently. "But if the ship people are attacking, I don't think they will notice any difference between us and the Reds...."

There was a burst of ear-splitting sound. For the third time Ross was thrown from his feet. This time the burrow lights flickered, dimmed, and went out.

"Oh, fine," commented McNeil bitterly out of the dark. "I never did care for blindman's buff."

"The transfer plate —" Ross clung to his own plan of escape —"if we can reach that —"

The light which had served Ashe and McNeil in their tunneling clicked on. Since the earth shocks appeared to be over for a while, they moved on, with Ashe in the lead and McNeil bringing up the rear. Ross hoped Ashe knew the way. The sound of fighting had died out, so one side or the other must have gained the victory. They might have only a few moments left to pass undetected.

Ross's sense of direction was fairly acute, but he could not have gone so unerringly to what he sought as Ashe did. Only he did not lead them to the room with the glowing plate, and Ross stifled a protest as they came instead to a small record room.

On a table were three spools of tape which Ashe caught up avidly, thrusting two in the front of his baggy tunic, passing the third to McNeil. Then he sped about trying the cupboards on the walls, but all were locked. His hand falling from the last latch, Ashe came back to the door where Ross waited.

"To the plate!" Ross urged.

Ashe surveyed the cupboards once more regretfully. "If we could have just ten minutes here — —"

McNeil snorted. "Listen, you may yearn to be the filling in an ice sandwich, but I don't! Another shock and we'll be buried so deep even a drill couldn't find us. Let's get out now. The kid is right about that-if we still can."

Once more Ashe took the lead and they wove through ghostly rooms to what must have been the heart of the post-the transfer point. To Ross's unvoiced relief the plate was glowing. He had been nagged by the fear that when the lights blew out the transfer plate might also have been affected. He jumped for the plate.

Neither Ashe nor McNeil wasted time in joining him there. As they clung together there was a cry from behind them, underlined by a shot. Ross, feeling Ashe sag against him, caught him in his arms. By the reflected glow of the plate he saw the Red leader of the post and behind him, his hairless face hanging oddly bodiless in the gloom, was the alien. Were those two now allies? Before Ross could be sure that he had really seen them, the wracking of space time caught him and the rest of the room faded away.

"...free. Get a move on!"

Ross glanced across Ashe's bowed shoulders to McNeil's excited face. The other was pulling at Ashe, who was only half-conscious. A stream of blood from a hole in his bare shoulder soaked the upper edge of his Beaker tunic, but as they steadied him between them, he gained some measure of awareness and moved his feet as they pulled him off the plate.

Well, they were free if only for a few seconds, and there was no reception committee waiting for them. Ross gave thanks silently for those two small favors. But if they were now returned to the Bronze Age village, they were still in enemy territory. With Ashe wounded, the odds against them were so high it was almost hopeless.

Working hurriedly with strips torn from McNeil's kilt, they managed to stop the flow of blood from Ashe's wound. Although he was still groggy, he was fighting, driven by the fear which whipped them all-time was one of their foremost enemies. Ross, Ashe's gun in hand, kept watch on the transfer plate, ready to shoot at anything appearing there.

"That will have to do!" Ashe pulled free from McNeil. "We must move." He hesitated, and then pulling the spools of tape from his bloodstained tunic, passed them to McNeil. "You'd better carry these."

"All right," the other answered almost absently.

"Move!" The force of that order from Ashe sent them into the corridor beyond. "The plate...."

But the plate remained clear. And Ross noted that they must have returned to the proper time, for the walls about them were the logs and stone of the village he remembered.

"Someone coming through?"

"Should be-soon."

They fled, the hide boots of the other two making only the faintest whisper of sound, Ross's foam-soled feet none at all. He could not have found the door to the outer world, but again Ashe guided them, and only once did they have to seek cover. At last they faced a barred door. Ashe leaned against the wall, McNeil supporting him, as Ross pulled free the locking beam. They let themselves out into the night.

"Which way?" McNeil asked.

To Ross's surprise Ashe did not turn to the gate in the outer stockade. Instead he gestured at the mountain wall in the opposite direction. "They'll expect us to try for the valley pass. So we had better go up the slope there."

"That has the look of a tough climb," ventured McNeil.

Ashe stirred. "When it becomes too tough for me" —his voice was dry —"I shall say so, never fear."

He started out with some of his old ease of movement, but his companions closed in on either side, ready to offer aid. Ross often wondered later if they could have won free of the village on their own efforts that night. He was sure their resolution would have been equal to the attempt, but their escape would have depended upon a fabulous run of luck such as men seldom encounter.

As it was, they had just reached a pool of shadow beside a small hut some two buildings away from the one they had fled, when the fireworks began. As if on signal the three fugitives threw themselves flat. From the roof of the building at the center of the village a pencil of brilliant-green light pointed straight up into the sky, and around that spear of radiance the roof sprouted tongues of more natural red-and-yellow flames. Figures shot from doors as the fire lapped down the peak of the roof.

"Now!" In spite of the rising clamor, Ashe's voice carried to his two companions.

The three sprinted for the palisade, mingling with bewildered men who ran out of the other cabins. The waves of fire washed on, providing light, too much light. Ashe and McNeil could pass as part of the crowd, but Ross's unusual clothing might be easily marked.

Others were running for the wall. Ross and McNeil boosted Ashe to the top, saw him over in safety. McNeil followed. Ross was just reaching to draw himself up when he was enveloped in a beam of light.

A high, screeching call, unlike any shout he had heard, split the clamor. Frantically Ross tried for a hold, knowing that he was presenting a perfect target for those behind. He gained the top of the stockade, looked down into a black block of shadow, not knowing whether Ashe and McNeil were waiting for him or had gone ahead. Hearing that strange cry again, Ross leaped blindly out into the darkness.

He landed badly, hitting hard enough to bruise, but thanks to the skill he had learned for parachuting, he broke no bones. He got to his feet and blundered on in the general direction of the mountain Ashe had picked as their goal. There were others coming over the wall of the village and moving through the shadows, so he dared not call out for fear of alerting the enemy.

The village had been set in the widest part of the valley. Behind its stockade the open ground narrowed swiftly, like the point of a funnel, and all fugitives from the settlement had to pass through that channel to escape. Ross's worst fear was that he had lost contact with Ashe and McNeil, and that he would never be able to pick up their trail in the wilderness ahead.

Thankful for the dark suit he wore which was protective covering in the night, he twice ducked into the brush to allow parties of refugees to pass him. Hearing them speak the guttural clicking speech he had learned from Ulffa's people, Ross deduced that they were innocent of the village's real purpose. These people were convinced they had been attacked by night demons. Perhaps there had only been a handful of Reds in that hidden retreat.

Ross pulled himself up a hard climb, and pausing to catch his breath, looked back. He was not overly surprised to see figures moving leisurely about the village examining the cabins, perhaps in search of the inhabitants. Each of those searchers was clad in a form-fitting suit that matched his own, and their bulbous hairless heads gleamed white in the firelight. Ross was astonished to see that they passed straight through walls of flame, apparently unconcerned and unsinged by the heat.

The human beings trapped in the town wailed and ran, or lay and beat their heads and hands on the ground, supine before the invaders. Each captive was dragged back to a knot of aliens near the main building. Some were hurled out again into the dark, unharmed; a few others were retained. A sorting of prisoners was plainly in progress. There was no question that the ship people had followed through into this time, and that they had their own arrangements for the Reds.

Ross had no desire to learn the particulars. He started climbing again, finding the pass at last. Beyond, the ground fell away again, and Ross went forward into the full darkness of the night with a vast surge of thankfulness.

Finally, he stopped simply because he was too weary, too hungry, to keep on his feet without stumbling, and a fall in the dark on these heights could be costly. Ross discovered a small hollow behind a stunted tree and crept into it as best he could, his heart laboring against his ribs, a hot stab of pain cutting into his side with every breath he drew.

He awoke all at once with the snap of a fighting man who is alert to ever present danger. A hand lay warm and hard over his mouth, and above it his eyes met McNeil's. When he saw that Ross was awake McNeil withdraw his hand. The morning sunlight was warm about them. Moving clumsily because of his stiff, bruised body, Ross crawled out of the hollow. He looked around, but McNeil stood there alone. "Ashe?" Ross questioned him.

McNeil, showing a haggard face covered with several days' growth of rusty-brown beard, nodded his head toward the slope. Fumbling inside his kilt, he brought out something clenched in his fist and offered it to Ross. The latter held out his palm and McNeil covered it with a handful of coarse-ground grain. Just to look at the stuff made Ross long for a drink, but he mouthed it and chewed, getting up to follow McNeil down into the tree-grown lower slopes.

"It's not good." McNeil spoke jerkily, using Beaker speech. "Ashe is out of his head some of the time. That hole in his shoulder is worse than we thought it was, and there's always the threat of infection. This whole wood is full of people flushed out of that blasted village! Most of them-all I've seen-are natives. But they have it firmly planted in their minds now that there are devils after them. If they see you wearing that suit — —"

"I know, and I'd strip if I could," Ross agreed. "But I'll have to get other clothing first; I can't run bare in this cold."

"That might be safer," McNeil growled. "I don't know just what happened back there, but it certainly must have been plenty!"

Ross swallowed a very dry mouthful of grain and then stooped to scoop up some leftover snow in the shadow of a tree root. It was not as refreshing as a real drink, but it helped. "You said Ashe is out of his head. What do we do for him, and what are your plans?"

"We have to reach the river, somehow. It drains to the sea, and at its mouth we are supposed to make contact with the sub."

The proposal sounded impossible to Ross, but so many impossible things had happened lately he was willing to go along with the idea-as long as he could. Gathering up more snow, he stuffed it into his mouth before he followed the already disappearing McNeil.

Chapter 14

"... that's my half of it. The rest of it you know." Ross held his hands close to the small fire sheltered in the pit he had helped dig and flexed his cold-numbed fingers in the warmth.

From across the handful of flames Ashe's eyes, too bright in a fever-flushed face, watched him demandingly. The fugitives had taken cover in an angle where the massed remains of an old avalanche provided a cave-pocket. McNeil was off scouting in the gray drizzle of the day, and their escape from the village was now some forty-eight hours behind them.

"So the crackpots were right, after all. They only had their times mixed." Ashe shifted on the bed of brush and leaves they had raked together for his comfort.

"I don't understand — —"

"Flying saucers," Ashe returned with an odd little laugh. "It was a wild possibility, but it was on the books from the start. This certainly will make Kelgarries turn red — —"

"Flying saucers?"

Ashe must be out of his head from the fever, Ross supposed. He wondered what he should do if Ashe tried to get up and walk away. He could not tackle a man with a bad hole in his shoulder, nor was he certain he could wrestle Ashe down in a real fight.

"That globe-ship was never built on this world. Use your head, Murdock. Think about your furry-faced friend and the baldy with him. Did either look like normal Terrans to you?"

"But —a spaceship!" It was something that had so long been laughed to scorn. When men had failed to break into space after the initial excitement of the satellite launchings, space flight had become a matter for jeers. On the other hand, there was the evidence collected by his own eyes and ears, his own experience. The services of the lifeboat had been techniques outside of his experience.

"This was insinuated once" —Ashe was lying flat now, gazing speculatively up at the projection of logs and earth which made them a partial roof—"along with a lot of other bright ideas, by a gentleman named Charles Fort, who took a lot of pleasure in pricking what he considered to be vastly over-inflated scientific pomposity. He gathered together four book loads of reported incidents of unexplainable happenings which he dared the scientists of his day to explain. And one of his bright suggestions was that such phenomena as the vast artificial earthworks found in Ohio and Indiana were originally thrown up by space castaways to serve as SOS signals. An intriguing idea, and now perhaps we may prove it true."

"But if such spaceships were wrecked on this world, I still don't see why we didn't find traces of them in our own time."

"Because that wreck you explored was bedded in a glacial era. Do you have any idea how long ago that was, counting from our own time? There were at least three glacial periods-and we don't know in which one the Reds went visiting. That age began about a million years before we were born, and the last of the ice ebbed out of New York State some thirty-eight thousand years ago, boy. That was the early Stone Age, reckoning it by the scale of human development, with an extremely thin population of the first real types of man clinging to a few warmer fringes of wilderness.

"Climatic changes, geographical changes, all altered the face of our continents. There was a sea in Kansas; England was part of Europe. So, even though as many as fifty such ships were lost here, they could all have been ground to bits by the ice flow, buried miles deep in quakes, or rusted away generations before the first really intelligent man arrived to wonder at them. Certainly there couldn't be too many such wrecks to be found. What do you think this planet was, a flypaper to attract them?"

"But if ships crashed here once, why didn't they later when men were better able to understand them?" Ross countered.

"For several reasons-all of them possible and able to be fitted into the fabric of history as we know it on this world. Civilizations rise, exist, and fall, each taking with it into the limbo of forgotten things some of the discoveries which made it great. How did the Indian civilizations of the New World learn to harden gold into a useable point for a cutting weapon? What was the secret of building possessed by the ancient Egyptians? Today you will find plenty of men to argue these problems and half a hundred others.

"The Egyptians once had a well-traveled trade route to India. Bronze Age traders opened up roads down into Africa. The Romans knew China. Then came an end to each of these empires, and those trade routes were forgotten. To our European ancestors of the Middle Ages, China was almost a legend, and the fact that the Egyptians had successfully sailed around the Cape of Good Hope was unknown. Suppose our space voyagers represented some star-born confederacy or empire which lived, rose to its highest point, and fell again into planet-bound barbarism all before the first of our species painted pictures on a cave wall?

"Or take it that this world was an unlucky reef on which too many ships and cargoes were lost, so that our whole solar system was posted, and skippers of star ships thereafter avoided it? Or they might even have had some rule that when a planet developed a primitive race of its own, it was to be left strictly alone until it discovered space flight for itself."

"Yes." Every one of Ashe's suppositions made good sense, and Ross was able to believe them. It was easier to think that both Furry-face and Baldy were inhabitants of another world than to think their kind existed on this planet before his own species was born. "But how did the Reds locate that ship?"

"Unless that information is on the tapes we were able to bring along, we shall probably never know," Ashe said drowsily. "I might make one guess-the Reds have been making an all-out effort for the past hundred years to open up Siberia. In some sections of that huge country there have been great climatic changes almost overnight in the far past. Mammoths have been discovered frozen in the ice with half-digested tropical plants in their stomach. It's as if the beasts were given some deep-freeze treatment instantaneously. If in their excavations the Reds came across the remains of a spaceship, remains well enough preserved for them to realize what they had discovered, they might start questing back in time to find a better one intact at an earlier date. That theory fits everything we know now."

"But why would the aliens attack the Reds now?"

"No ship's officers ever thought gently of pirates." Ashe's eyes closed.

There were questions, a flood of them, that Ross wanted to ask. He smoothed the fabric on his arm, that stuff which clung so tightly to his skin yet kept him warm without any need for more covering. If Ashe were right, on what world, what kind of world, had that material been woven, and how far had it been brought that he could wear it now?

Suddenly McNeil slid into their shelter and dropped two hares at the edge of the fire.

"How goes it?" he said, as Ross began to clean them.

"Reasonably well," Ashe, his eyes still closed, replied to that before Ross could. "How far are we from the river? And do we have company?"

"About five miles-if we had wings." McNeil answered in a dry tone. "And we have company all right, lots of it!"

That brought Ashe up, leaning forward on his good elbow. "What kind?"

"Not from the village." McNeil frowned at the fire which he fed with economic handfuls of sticks. "Something's happening on this side of the mountains. It looks as if there's a mass migration in progress. I counted five family clans on their way west-all in just this one morning."

"The village refugees' stories about devils might send them packing," Ashe mused.

"Maybe." But McNeil did not sound convinced. "The sooner we head downstream, the better. And I hope the boys will have that sub waiting where they promised. We do possess one thing in our favor-the spring floods are subsiding."

"And the high water should have plenty of raft material." Ashe lay back again. "We'll make those five miles tomorrow."

McNeil stirred uneasily and Ross, having cleaned and spitted the hares, swung them over the flames to broil. "Five miles in this country," the younger man observed, "is a pretty good day's march" —he did not add as he wanted to —"for a well man."

"I will make it," Ashe promised, and both listeners knew that as long as his body would obey him he meant to keep that promise. They also knew the futility of argument.

Ashe proved to be a prophet to be honored on two counts. They did make the trek to the river the next day, and there was a wealth of raft material marking the high-water level of the spring flood. The migrations McNeil had reported were still in progress, and the three men hid twice to watch the passing of small family clans. Once a respectably sized tribe, including wounded men, marched across their route, seeking a ford at the river.

"They've been badly mauled," McNeil whispered as they watched the people huddled along the water's edge while scouts cast upstream and down, searching for a ford. When they returned with the news that there was no ford to be found, the tribesmen then sullenly went to work with flint axes and knives to make rafts.

"Pressure-they are on the run." Ashe rested his chin on his good forearm and studied the busy scene. "These are not from the village. Notice the dress and the red paint on their faces. They're not like Ulffa's kin either. I wouldn't say they were local at all."

"Reminds me of something I saw once-animals running before a forest fire. They can't all be looking for new hunting territory," McNeil returned.

"Reds sweeping them out," Ross suggested. "Or could the ship people —?"

Ashe started to shake his head and then winced. "I wonder...." The crease between his level brows deepened. "The ax people!" His voice was still a whisper, but it carried a note of triumph as if he had fitted some stubborn jigsaw piece into its proper place.

"Ax people?"

"Invasion of another people from the east. They turned up in prehistory about this period. Remember, Webb spoke of them. They used axes for weapons and tamed horses."

"Tartars" —McNeil was puzzled —"This far west?"

"Not Tartars, no. You needn't expect those to come boiling out of middle Asia for some thousands of years yet. We don't know too much about the ax people, save that they moved west from the interior plains. Eventually they crossed to Britain; perhaps they were the ancestors of the Celts who loved horses too. But in their time they were a tidal wave."

"The sooner we head downstream, the better." McNeil stirred restlessly, but they knew that they must keep to cover until the tribesmen below were gone. So they lay in hiding another night, witnessing on the next morning the arrival of a smaller party of the red-painted men, again with wounded among them. At the coming of this rear guard the activity on the river bank rose close to frenzy.

The three men out of time were doubly uneasy. It was not for them to merely cross the river. They had to build a raft which would be water-worthy enough to take them downstream-to the sea if they were lucky. And to build such a sturdy raft would take time, time they did not have now.

In fact, McNeil waited only until the last tribal raft was out of bow shot before he plunged down to the shore, Ross at his heels. Since they lacked even the stone tools of the tribesmen, they were at a disadvantage, and Ross found he was hands and feet for Ashe, working under the other's close direction. Before night closed in they had a good beginning and two sets of blistered hands, as well as aching backs.

When it was too dark to work any longer, Ashe pointed back over the track they had followed. Marking the mountain pass was a light. It looked like fire, and if it was, it must be a big one for them to be able to sight it across this distance.

"Camp?" McNeil wondered.

"Must be," Ashe agreed. "Those who built that blaze are in such numbers that they don't have to take precautions."

"Will they be here by tomorrow?"

"Their scouts might, but this is early spring, and forage can't have been too good on the march. If I were the chief of that tribe, I'd turn aside into the meadow land we skirted yesterday and let the herds graze for a day, maybe more. On the other hand, if they need water ——"

"They will come straight ahead!" McNeil finished grimly. "And we can't be here when they arrive."

Ross stretched, grimacing at the twinge of pain in his shoulders. His hands smarted and throbbed, and this was just the beginning of their task. If Ashe had been fit, they might have trusted to logs for support and swum downstream to hunt a safer place for their shipbuilding project. But he knew that Ashe could not stand such an effort.

Ross slept that night mainly because his body was too exhausted to let him lie awake and worry. Roused in the earliest dawn by McNeil, they both crawled down to the water's edge and struggled to bind stubbornly resisting saplings together with cords twisted from bark. They reinforced them at crucial points with some strings torn from their kilts, and strips of rabbit hide saved from their kills of the past few days. They worked with hunger gnawing at them, having no time now to hunt. When the sun was well westward they had a clumsy craft which floated sluggishly. Whether it would answer to either pole or improvised paddle, they could not know until they tried it.

Ashe, his face flushed and his skin hot to the touch, crawled on board and lay in the middle, on the thin heap of bedding they had put there for him. He eagerly drank the water they carried to him in cupped hands and gave a little sigh of relief as Ross wiped his face with wet grass, muttering something about Kelgarries which neither of his companions understood.

McNeil shoved off and the bobbing craft spun around dizzily as the current pulled it free from the shore. They made a brave start, but luck deserted them before they had gotten out of sight of the spot where they embarked.

Striving to keep them in mid-current, McNeil poled furiously, but there were too many rocks and snagged trees projecting from the banks. Sharing that sweep of water with them, and coming up fast, was a full-sized tree. Twice its mat of branches caught on some snag, holding it back, and Ross breathed a little more freely, but it soon tore free again and rolled on, as menacing as a battering ram.

"Get closer to shore!" Ross shouted the warning. Those great, twisted roots seemed aimed straight at the raft, and he was sure if that mass struck them fairly, they would not have a chance. He dug in with his own pole, but his hasty push did not meet bottom; the stake in his hands plunged into some pothole in the hidden river bed. He heard McNeil cry out as he toppled into the water, gasping as the murky liquid flooded his mouth, choking him.

Half dazed by the shock, Ross struck out instinctively. The training at the base had included swimming, but to fight water in a pool under controlled conditions was far different from fighting death in a river of icy water when one had already swallowed a sizable quantity of that flood.

Ross had a half glimpse of a dark shadow. Was it the edge of the raft? He caught at it desperately, skinning his hands on rough bark, dragged on by it. The tree! He blinked his eyes to clear them of water, to try to see. But he could not pull his exhausted body high enough out of the water to see past the screen of roots; he could only cling to the small safety he had won and hope that he could rejoin the raft somewhere downstream.

After what seemed like a very long time he wedged one arm between two water-washed roots, sure that the support would hold his head above the surface. The chill of the stream struck at his hands and head, but the protection of the alien clothing was still effective, and the rest of his body was not cold. He was simply too tired to wrest himself free and trust again to the haphazard chance of making shore through the gathering dusk.

Suddenly a shock jarred his body and strained the arm he had thrust among the roots, wringing a cry out of him. He swung around and brushed footing under the water; the tree had caught on a shore snag. Pulling loose from the roots, he floundered on his hands and knees, falling afoul of a mass of reeds whose roots were covered with stale-smelling mud. Like a wounded animal he dragged himself through the ooze to higher land, coming out upon an open meadow flooded with moonlight.

For a while he lay there, his cold, sore hands under him, plastered with mud and too tired to move. The sound of a sharp barking aroused him-an imperative, summoning bark, neither belonging to a wolf nor a hunting fox. He listened to it dully and then, through the ground upon which he lay, Ross felt as well as heard the pounding of hoofs.

Hoofs-horses! Horses from over the mountains-horses which might mean danger. His mind seemed as dull and numb as his hands, and it took quite a long time for him to fully realize the menace horses might bring.

Getting up, Ross noticed a winged shape sweeping across the disk of the moon like a silent dart. There was a single despairing squeak out of the grass about a hundred feet away, and the winged shape arose again with its prey. Then the barking sound once more-eager, excited barking.

Ross crouched back on his heels and saw a smoky brand of light moving along the edge of the meadow where the band of trees began. Could it be a herd guard? Ross knew he had to head back toward the river, but he had to force himself on the path, for he did not know whether he dared enter the stream again. But what would happen if they hunted him with the dog? Confused memories of how water spoiled scent spurred him on.

Having reached the rising bank he had climbed so laboriously before, Ross miscalculated and tumbled back, rolling down into the mud of the reed bed. Mechanically he wiped the slime from his face. The tree was still anchored there; by some freak the current had rammed its rooted end up on a sand spit.

Above in the meadow the barking sounded very close, and now it was answered by a second canine belling. Ross wormed his way back through the reeds to the patch of water between the tree and the bank. His few poor efforts at escape were almost half-consciously taken; he was too tired to really care now.

Soon he saw a four-footed shape running along the top of the bank, giving tongue. It was then joined by a larger and even more vocal companion. The dogs drew even with Ross, who wondered dully if the animals could sight him in the shadows below, or whether they only scented his presence. Had he been able, he would have climbed over the log and taken his chances in the open water, but now he could only lie where he was-the tangle of roots between him and the bank serving as a screen, which would be little enough protection when men came with torches.

Ross was mistaken, however, for his worm's progress across the reed bed had liberally besmeared his dark clothing and masked the skin of his face and hands, giving him better cover than any he could have wittingly devised. Though he felt naked and defenseless, the men who trailed the hounds to the river bank, thrusting out the torch over the edge to light the sand spit, saw nothing but the trunk of the tree wedged against a mound of mud.

Ross heard a confused murmur of voices broken by the clamor of the dogs. Then the torch was raised out of line of his dazzled eyes. He saw one of the indistinct figures above cuff away a dog and move off, calling the hounds after it. Reluctantly, still barking, the animals went. Ross, with a little sob, subsided limply in the uncomfortable net of roots, still undiscovered.

Chapter 15

It was such a small thing, a tag of ragged stuff looped about a length of splintered sapling. Ross climbed stiffly over the welter of drift caught on the sand spit and pulled it loose, recognizing the string even before he touched it. That square knot was of McNeil's tying, and as Murdock sat down weakly in the sand and mud, nervously fingering the twisted cord, staring vacantly at the river, his last small hope died. The raft must have broken up, and neither Ashe nor McNeil could have survived the ultimate disaster.

Ross Murdock was alone, marooned in a time which was not his own, with little promise of escape. That one thought blanked out his mind with its own darkness. What was the use of getting up again, of trying to find food for his empty stomach, or warmth and shelter?

He had always prided himself on being able to go it alone, had thought himself secure in that calculated loneliness. Now that belief had been washed away in the river along with most of the will power which had kept him going these past days. Before, there had always been some goal, no matter how remote. Now, he had nothing. Even if he managed to reach the mouth of the river, he had no idea of where or how to summon the sub from the overseas post. All three of the time travelers might already have been written off the rolls, since they had not reported in.

Ross pulled the rag free from the sapling and wreathed it in a tight bracelet about his grimed wrist for some unexplainable reason. Worn and tired, he tried to think ahead. There was no chance of again contacting Ulffa's tribe. Along with all the other woodland hunters they must have fled before the advance of the horsemen. No, there was no reason to go back, and why make the effort to advance?

The sun was hot. This was one of those spring days which foretell the ripeness of summer. Insects buzzed in the reed banks where a green sheen showed. Birds wheeled and circled in the sky, some flock disturbed, their cries reaching Ross in hoarse calls of warning.

He was still plastered with patches of dried mud and slime, the reek of it thick in his nostrils. Now Ross brushed at a splotch on his knee, picking loose flakes to expose the alien cloth of his suit underneath, seemingly unbefouled. All at once it became necessary to be clean again at least.

Ross waded into the stream, stooping to splash the brown water over his body and then rubbing away the resulting mud. In the sunlight the fabric had a brilliant glow, as if it not only drew the light but reflected it. Wading farther out into the water, he began to swim, not with any goal in view, but because it was easier than crawling back to land once more.

Using the downstream current to supplement his skill, he watched both banks. He could not really hope to see either the raft or indications that its passengers had won to shore, but somewhere deep inside him he had not yet accepted the probable.

The effort of swimming broke through that fog of inertia which had held him since he had awakened that morning. It was with a somewhat healthier interest in life that Ross came ashore again on an arm of what was a bay or inlet angling back into the land. Here the banks of the river were well above his head, and believing that he was well sheltered, he stripped, hanging his suit in the sunlight and letting the unusual heat of the day soothe his body.

A raw fish, cornered in the shallows and scooped out, furnished one of the best meals he had ever tasted. He had reached for the suit draped over a willow limb when the first and only warning that his fortunes had once again changed came, swiftly, silently, and with deadly promise.

One moment the willows had moved gently in the breeze, and then a spear suddenly set them all quivering. Ross, clutching the suit to him with a frantic grab, skated about in the sand, going to one knee in his haste.

He found himself completely at the mercy of the two men standing on the bank well above him. Unlike Ulffa's people or the Beaker traders, they were very tall, with heavy braids of light or sun-bleached hair swinging forward on their wide chests. Their leather tunics hung to mid-thigh above leggings which were bound to their limbs with painted straps. Cuff bracelets of copper ringed their forearms, and necklaces of animal teeth and beads displayed their personal wealth. Ross could not remember having seen their like on any of the briefing tapes at the base.

One spear had been a warning, but a second was held ready, so Ross made the age-old signal of surrender, reluctantly dropping his suit and raising his hands palm out and shoulder high.

"Friend?" Ross asked in the Beaker tongue. The traders ranged far, and perhaps there was a chance they had had contact with this tribe.

The spear twirled, and the younger stranger effortlessly leaped down the bank, paddling over to Ross to pick up the suit he had dropped, holding it up while he made some comment to his companion. He seemed fascinated by the fabric, pulling and smoothing it between his hands, and Ross wondered if there was a chance of trading it for his own freedom.

Both men were armed, not only with the long-bladed daggers favored by the Beaker folk, but also with axes. When Ross made a slight effort to lower his hands the man before him reached to his belt ax, growling what was plainly a warning. Ross blinked, realizing that they might well knock him out and leave him behind, taking the suit with them.

Finally, they decided in favor of including him in their loot. Throwing the suit over one arm, the stranger caught Ross by the shoulder and pushed him forward roughly. The pebbled beach was painful to Ross's feet, and the breeze which whipped about him as he reached the top of the bank reminded him only too forcibly of his ordeal in the glacial world.

Murdock was tempted to make a sudden dash out on the point of the bank and dive into the river, but it was already too late. The man who was holding the spear had moved behind him, and Ross's wrist, held in a vise grip at the small of his back, kept him prisoner as he was pushed on into the meadow. There three shaggy horses grazed, their nose ropes gathered into the hands of a third man.

A sharp stone half buried in the ground changed the pattern of the day. Ross's heel scraped against it, and the resulting pain triggered his rebellion into explosion. He threw himself backward, his bruised heel sliding between the feet of his captor, bringing them both to the ground with himself on top. The other expelled air from his lungs in a grunt of surprise, and Ross whipped over, one hand grasping the hilt of the tribesman's dagger while the other, free of that prisoning wrist-lock, chopped at the fellow's throat.

Dagger out and ready, Ross faced the men in a half crouch as he had been drilled. They stared at him in open-mouthed amazement, then too late the spears went up. Ross placed the point of his looted weapon at the throat of the now quiet man by whom he knelt, and he spoke the language he had learned from Ulffa's people.

"You strike-this one dies."

They must have read the determined purpose in his eyes, for slowly, reluctantly, the spears went down. Having gained so much of a victory, Ross dared more. "Take —" he motioned to the waiting horses —"take and go!"

For a moment he thought that this time they would meet his challenge, but he continued to hold the dagger above the brown throat of the man who was now moaning faintly. His threat continued to register, for the other man shrugged the suit from his arm, left it lying on the ground, and retreated. Holding the nose rope of his horse, he mounted, waved the herder up also, and both of them rode slowly away.

The prisoner was slowly coming around, so Ross only had time to pull on the suit; he had not even fastened the breast studs before those blue eyes opened. A sunburned hand flashed to a belt, but the dagger and ax which had once hung there were now in Ross's possession. He watched the tribesman carefully as he finished dressing.

"What you do?" The words were in the speech of the forest people, distorted by a new accent.

"You go —" Ross pointed to the third horse the others had left behind —"I go —" he indicated the river —"I take these" —he patted the dagger and the ax. The other scowled.

"Not good...."

Ross laughed, a little hysterically. "Not good you," he agreed, "good-me!"

To his surprise the tribesman's stiff face relaxed, and the fellow gave a bark of laughter. He sat up, rubbing at his throat, a big grin pulling at the corners of his mouth.

"You-hunter?" The man pointed northeast to the woodlands fringing the mountains.

Ross shook his head. "Trader, me."

"Trader," the other repeated. Then he tapped one of the wide metal cuffs at his wrist. "Trade-this?"

"That. More things."

"Where?"

Ross pointed downstream. "By bitter water-trade there."

The man appeared puzzled. "Why you here?"

"Ride river water, like you ride," he said, pointing to the horse. "Ride on trees-many trees tied together. Trees break apart —I come here."

The conception of a raft voyage apparently got across, for the tribesman was nodding. Getting to his feet, he walked across to take up the nose rope of the waiting horse. "You come camp-Foscar. Foscar chief. He like you show trick how you take Tulka, make him sleep-hold his ax, knife."

Ross hesitated. This Tulka seemed friendly now, but would that friendliness last? He shook his head. "I go to bitter water. My chief there."

Tulka was scowling again. "You speak crooked words-your chief there!" He pointed eastward with a dramatic stretch of the arm. "Your chief speak Foscar. Say he give much these —" he touched his copper cuffs —"good knives, axes-get you back."

Ross stared at him without understanding. Ashe? Ashe in this Foscar's camp offering a reward for him? But how could that be?

"How you know my chief?"

Tulka laughed, this time derisively. "You wear shining skin-your chief wear shiny skin. He say find other shiny skin-give many good things to man who bring you back."

Shiny skin! The suit from the alien ship! Was it the ship people? Ross remembered the light on him as he climbed out of the Red village. He must have been sighted by one of the spacemen. But why were they searching for him, alerting the natives in an effort to scoop him up? What made Ross Murdock so important that they must have him? He only knew that he was not going to be taken if he could help it, that he had no desire to meet this "chief" who had offered treasure for his capture.

"You will come!" Tulka went into action, his mount flashing forward almost in a running leap at Ross, who stumbled back when horse and rider loomed over him. He swung up the ax, but it was a weapon with which he had had no training, too heavy for him.

As his blow met only thin air the shoulder of the mount hit him, and Ross went down, avoiding by less than a finger's breadth the thud of an unshod hoof against his skull. Then the rider landed on him, crushing him flat. A fist connected with his jaw, and for Ross the sun went out.

He found himself hanging across a support which moved with a rocking gait, whose pounding hurt his head, keeping him half dazed. Ross tried to move, but he realized that his arms were behind his back, fastened wrist to wrist, and a warm weight centered in the small of his spine to hold him face down on a horse. He could do nothing except endure the discomfort as best he could and hope for a speedy end to the gallop.

Over his head passed the cackle of speech. He caught short glimpses of another horse matching pace to the one that carried him. Then they swept into a noisy place where the shouting of many men made a din. The horse stopped and Ross was pulled from its back and dropped to the trodden dust, to lie blinking up dizzily, trying to focus on the scene about him.

They had arrived at the camp of the horsemen, whose hide tents served as a backdrop for the fair long-haired giants and the tall women hovering about to view the captive. The circle about him then broke, and men stood aside for a newcomer. Ross had believed that his original captors were physically imposing, but this one was their master. Lying on the ground at the chieftain's feet, Ross felt like a small and helpless child.

Foscar, if Foscar this was, could not yet have entered middle age, and the muscles which moved along his arms and across his shoulders as he leaned over to study Tulka's prize made him bear-strong. Ross glared up at him, that same hot rage which had led to his attack on Tulka now urging him to the only defiance he had left-words.

"Look well, Foscar. Free me, and I would do more than *look* at you," he said in the speech of the woods hunters.

Foscar's blue eyes widened and he lowered a fist which could have swallowed in its grasp both of Ross's hands, linking those great fingers in the stuff of the suit and drawing the captive to his feet, with no sign that his act had required any effort. Even standing, Ross was a good eight inches shorter than the chieftain. Yet he put up his chin and eyed the other squarely, without giving ground.

"So-yet still my hands are tied." He put into that all the taunting inflection he could summon. His reception by Tulka had given him one faint clue to the character of these people; they might be brought to acknowledge the worth of one who stood up to them.

"Child —" The fist shifted from its grip on the fabric covering Ross's chest to his shoulder, and now under its compulsion Ross swayed back and forth.

"Child?" From somewhere Ross raised that short laugh. "Ask Tulka. I be no child, Foscar. Tulka's ax, Tulka's knife-they were in my hand. A horse Tulka had to use to bring me down."

Foscar regarded him intently and then grinned. "Sharp tongue," he commented. "Tulka lost knife-ax? So! Ennar," he called over his shoulder, and one of the men stepped out a pace beyond his fellows.

He was shorter and much younger than his chief, with a boy's rangy slimness and an open, good-looking face, his eyes bright on Foscar with a kind of eager excitement. Like the other tribesmen he was armed with belt dagger and ax, and since he wore two necklaces and both cuff bracelets and upper armlets as did Foscar, Ross thought he must be a relative of the older man.

"Child!" Foscar clapped his hand on Ross's shoulder and then withdrew the hold. "Child!" He indicated Ennar, who reddened. "You take from Ennar ax, knife," Foscar ordered, "as you took from Tulka." He made a sign, and someone cut the thongs about Ross's wrists.

Ross rubbed one numbed hand against the other, setting his jaw. Foscar had stung his young follower with that contemptuous "child," so the boy would be eager to match all his skill against the prisoner. This would not be as easy as his taking Tulka by surprise. But if he refused, Foscar might well order him killed out of hand. He had chosen to be defiant; he would have to do his best.

"Take ax, knife —" Foscar stepped back, waving at his men to open out a ring encircling the two young men.

Ross felt a little sick as he watched Ennar's hand go to the haft of the ax. Nothing had been said about Ennar's not using his weapons in defense, but Ross discovered that there was some sense of sportsmanship in the tribesmen, after all. It was Tulka who pushed to the chief's side and said something which made Foscar roar bull-voiced at his youthful champion.

Ennar's hand came away from the ax hilt as if that polished wood were white-hot, and he transferred his discomfiture to Ross as the other understood. Ennar had to win now for his own pride's sake, and Ross felt *he* had to win for his life. They circled warily, Ross watching his opponent's eyes rather than those half-closed hands held at waist level.

Back at the base he had been matched with Ashe, and before Ashe with the tough-bodied, skilled, and merciless trainers in unarmed combat. He had had beaten into his bruised flesh knowledge of holds and blows intended to save his skin in just such an encounter. But then he had been well-fed, alert, prepared. He had not been knocked silly and then transported for miles slung across a horse after days of exposure and hard usage. It remained to be learned—was Ross Murdock as tough as he always thought himself to be? Tough or not, he was in this until he won—or dropped.

Comments from the crowd aroused Ennar to the first definite action. He charged, stooping low in a wrestler's stance, but Ross squatted even lower. One hand flicked to the churned dust of the ground and snapped up again, sending a cloud of grit into the tribesman's face. Then their bodies met with a shock, and Ennar sailed over Ross's shoulder to skid along the earth.

Had Ross been fresh, the contest would have ended there and then in his favor. But when he tried to whirl and throw himself on his opponent he was too slow. Ennar was not waiting to be pinned flat, and it was Ross's turn to be caught at a disadvantage.

A hand shot out to catch his leg just above the ankle, and once again Ross obeyed his teaching, falling easily at that pull, to land across his opponent. Ennar, disconcerted by the too-quick success of his attack, was unprepared for this. Ross rolled, trying to escape steel-fingered hands, his own chopping out in edgewise blows, striving to serve Ennar as he had Tulka.

He had to take a lot of punishment, though he managed to elude the powerful bear's hug in which he knew the other was laboring to engulf him, a hold which would speedily crush him into submission. Clinging to the methods he had been taught, he fought on, only now he knew, with a growing panic, that his best was not good enough. He was too spent to make an end. Unless he had some piece of great good luck, he could only delay his own defeat.

Fingers clawed viciously at his eyes, and Ross did what he had never thought to do in any fight—he snapped wolfishly, his teeth closing on flesh as he brought up his knee and drove it home into the body wriggling on his. There was a gasp of hot breath in his face as Ross called upon the last few rags of his strength, tearing loose from the other's slackened hold. He scrambled to one knee. Ennar was also on his knees, crouching like a four-legged beast ready to spring. Ross risked everything on a last gamble. Clasping his hands together, he raised them as high as he could and brought them down on the nape of the other's neck. Ennar sprawled forward face-down in the dust where seconds later Ross joined him.

Chapter 16

Murdock lay on his back, gazing up at the laced hides which stretched to make the tent roofing. Having been battered just enough to feel all one aching bruise, Ross had lost interest in the future. Only the present mattered, and it was a dark one. He might have fought Ennar to a standstill, but in the eyes of the horsemen he had also been beaten, and he had not impressed them as he had hoped. That he still lived was a minor wonder, but he deduced that he continued to breathe only because they wanted to exchange him for the reward offered by the aliens from out of time, an unpleasant prospect to contemplate.

His wrists were lashed over his head to a peg driven deeply into the ground; his ankles were bound to another. He could turn his head from side to side, but any further movement was impossible. He ate only bits of food dropped into his mouth by a dirty-fingered slave, a cowed hunter captured from a tribe overwhelmed in the migration of the horsemen.

"Ho-taker of axes!" A toe jarred into his ribs, and Ross bit back the grunt of pain which answered that rude bid for his attention. He saw in the dim light Ennar's face and was savagely glad to note the discolorations about the right eye and along the jaw line, the signatures left by his own skinned knuckles.

"Ho-warrior!" Ross returned hoarsely, trying to lade that title with all the scorn he could summon.

Ennar's hand, holding a knife, swung into his limited range of vision. "To clip a sharp tongue is a good thing!" The young tribesman grinned as he knelt down beside the helpless prisoner.

Ross knew a thrill of fear worse than any pain. Ennar might be about to do just what he hinted! Instead, the knife swung up and Ross felt the sawing at the cords about his wrists, enduring the pain in the raw gouges they had cut in his flesh with gratitude that it was not mutilation which had brought Ennar to him. He knew that his arms were free, but to draw them down from over his head was almost more than he could do, and he lay quiet as Ennar loosed his feet.

"Up!"

Without Ennar's hands pulling at him, Ross could not have reached his feet. Nor did he stay erect once he had been raised, crashing forward on his face as the other let him go, hot anger eating at him because of his own helplessness.

In the end, Ennar summoned two slaves who dragged Ross into the open where a council assembled about a fire. A debate was in progress, sometimes so heated that the speakers fingered their knife or ax hilts when they shouted their arguments. Ross could not understand their language, but he was certain that he was the subject under discussion and that Foscar had the deciding vote and had not yet given the nod to either side.

Ross sat where the slaves had dumped him, rubbing his smarting wrists, so deathly weary in mind and beaten in body that he was not really interested in the fate they were planning for him. He was content merely to be free of his bonds, a small favor, but one he savored dully.

He did not know how long the debate lasted, but at length Ennar came to stand over him with a message. "Your chief-he give many good things for you. Foscar take you to him."

"My chief is not here," Ross repeated wearily, making a protest he knew they would not heed. "My chief sits by the bitter water and waits. He will be angry if I do not come. Let Foscar fear his anger — —"

Ennar laughed. "You run from your chief. He will be happy with Foscar when you lie again under his hand. You will not like that —I think it so!"

"I think so, too," Ross agreed silently.

He spent the rest of that night lying between the watchful Ennar and another guard, though they had the humanity not to bind him again. In the morning he was allowed to feed himself, and he fished chunks of venison out of a stew with his unwashed fingers. But in spite of the messiness, it was the best food he had eaten in days.

The trip, however, was not to be a comfortable one. He was mounted on one of the shaggy horses, a rope run under the animal's belly to loop one foot to the other. Fortunately, his hands were bound so he was able to grasp the coarse, wiry mane and keep his seat after a fashion. The nose rope of his mount was passed to Tulka, and Ennar rode beside him with only half an eye for the path of his own horse and the balance of his attention for the prisoner.

They headed northeast, with the mountains as a sharp green-and-white goal against the morning sky. Though Ross's sense of direction was not too acute, he was certain that they were making for the general vicinity of the hidden village, which he believed the ship people had destroyed. He tried to discover something of the nature of the contact which had been made between the aliens and the horsemen.

"How find other chief?" he asked Ennar.

The young man tossed one of his braids back across his shoulder and turned his head to face Ross squarely. "Your chief come our camp. Talk with Foscar-two-four sleeps ago."

"How talk with Foscar? With hunter talk?"

For the first time Ennar did not appear altogether certain. He scowled and then snapped, "He talk-Foscar, us. We hear right words-not woods creeper talk. He speak to us good."

Ross was puzzled. How could the alien out of time speak the proper language of a primitive tribe some thousands of years removed from his own era? Were the ship people also familiar with time travel? Did they have their own stations of transfer? Yet their fury with the Reds had been hot. This was a complete mystery.

"This chief-he look like me?"

Again Ennar appeared at a loss. "He wear covering like you."

"But was he like me?" persisted Ross. He didn't know what he was trying to learn, only that it seemed important at that moment to press home to at least one of the tribesmen that he *was* different from the man who had put a price on his head and to whom he was to be sold.

"Not like!" Tulka spoke over his shoulder. "You look like hunter people-hair, eyes-Strange chief no hair on head, eyes not like — —"

"You saw him too?" Ross demanded eagerly.

"I saw. I ride to camp-they come so. Stand on rock, call to Foscar. Make magic with fire-it jump up!" He pointed his arm stiffly at a bush before them on the trail. "They point little, little spear-fire come out of the ground and burn. They say burn our camp if we do not give them man. We say-not have man. Then they say many good things for us if we find and bring man — —"

"But they are not my people," Ross cut in. "You see, I have hair, I am not like them. They are bad — —"

"You may be taken in war by them-chief's slave." Ennar had a reply to that which was logical according to the customs of his own tribe. "They want slave back-it is so."

"My people strong too, much magic," Ross pushed. "Take me to bitter water and they pay much-more than stranger chief!"

Both tribesmen were amused. "Where bitter water?" asked Tulka.

Ross jerked his head to the west. "Some sleeps away — —"

"Some sleeps!" repeated Ennar jeeringly. "We ride some sleeps, maybe many sleeps where we know not the trails-maybe no people there, maybe no bitter water-all things you say with split tongue so that we not give you back to master. We go this way not even one sleep-find chief, get good things. Why we do hard thing when we can do easy?"

What argument could Ross offer in rebuttal to the simple logic of his captors? For a moment he raged inwardly at his own helplessness. But long ago he had learned that giving away to hot fury was no good unless one did it deliberately to impress, and then only when one had the upper hand. Now Ross had no hand at all.

For the most part they kept to the open, whereas Ross and the other two agents had skulked in wooded areas on their flight through this same territory. So they approached the mountains from a different angle, and though he tried, Ross could pick out no familiar landmarks. If by some miracle he was able to free himself from his captors, he could only head due west and hope to strike the river.

At midday their party made camp in a grove of trees by a spring. The weather was as unseasonably warm as it had been the day before, and flies, brought out of cold-weather hiding, attacked the stamping horses and crawled over Ross. He tried to keep them off with swings of his bound hands, for their bites drew blood.

Having been tumbled from his mount, he remained fastened to a tree with a noose about his neck while the horsemen built a fire and broiled strips of deer meat.

It would seem that Foscar was in no hurry to get on, since after they had eaten, the men continued to lounge at ease, some even dropping off to sleep. When Ross counted faces he learned that Tulka and another had both disappeared, possibly to contact and warn the aliens they were coming.

It was midafternoon before the scouts reappeared, as unobtrusively as they had gone. They went before Foscar with a report which brought the chief over to Ross. "We go. Your chief waits —"

Ross raised his swollen, bitten face and made his usual protest. "Not my chief!"

Foscar shrugged. "He say so. He give good things to get you back under his hand. So-he your chief!"

Once again Ross was boosted on his mount, and bound. But this time the party split into two groups as they rode off. He was with Ennar again, just behind Foscar, with two other guards bringing up the rear. The rest of the men, leading their mounts, melted into the trees. Ross watched that quiet withdrawal speculatively. It argued that Foscar did not trust those he was about to do business with, that he was taking certain precautions of his own. Only Ross could not see how that distrust, which might be only ordinary prudence on Foscar's part, could in any way be an advantage for him.

They rode at a pace hardly above a walk into a small open meadow narrowing at the east. Then for the first time Ross was able to place himself. They were at the entrance to the valley of the village, about a mile away from the narrow throat above which Ross had lain to spy and had been captured, for he had come from the north over the spurs of rising ridges.

Ross's horse was pulled up as Foscar drove his heel into the ribs of his own mount, sending it at a brisker pace toward the neck of the valley. There was a blot of blue there-more than one of the aliens were waiting. Ross caught his lip between his teeth and bit down on it hard. He had stood up to the Reds, to Foscar's tribesmen, but he shrank from meeting those strangers with an odd fear that the worst the men of his own species could do would be but a pale shadow to the treatment he might meet at their hands.

Foscar was now a toy man astride a toy horse. He halted his galloping mount to sit facing the handful of strangers. Ross counted four of them. They seemed to be talking, though there was still a good distance separating the mounted man and the blue suits.

Minutes passed before Foscar's arm raised in a wave to summon the party guarding Ross. Ennar kicked his horse to a trot, towing Ross's mount behind, the other two men thudding along more discreetly. Ross noted that they were both armed with spears which they carried to the fore as they rode.

They were perhaps three quarters of the way to join Foscar, and Ross could see plainly the bald heads of the aliens as their faces turned in his direction. Then the strangers struck. One of them raised a weapon shaped similarly to the automatic Ross knew, except that it was longer in the barrel.

Ross did not know why he cried out, except that Foscar had only an ax and dagger which were both still sheathed at his belt. The chief sat very still, and then his horse gave a swift sidewise swerve as if in fright. Foscar collapsed, limp, bonelessly, to the trodden turf, to lie unmoving face down.

Ennar whooped, a cry combining defiance and despair in one. He reined up with violence enough to set his horse rearing. Then, dropping his hold on the leading rope of Ross's mount, he whirled and set off in a wild dash for the trees to the left. A spear lanced across Ross's shoulder, ripping at the blue fabric, but his horse whirled to follow the other, taking him out of danger of a second thrust. Having lost his opportunity, the man who had wielded the spear dashed by at Ennar's back.

Ross clung to the mane with both hands. His greatest fear was that he might slip from the saddle pad and since he was tied by his feet, lie unprotected and helpless under those dashing hoofs. Somehow he managed to cling to the horse's neck, his face lashed by the rough mane while the animal pounded on. Had Ross been able to grasp the dangling nose rope, he might have had a faint chance of controlling that run, but as it was he could only hold fast and hope.

He had only broken glimpses of what lay ahead. Then a brilliant fire, as vivid as the flames which had eaten up the Red village, burst from the ground a few yards ahead, sending the horse wild. There was more fire and the horse changed course through the rising smoke. Ross realized that the aliens were trying to cut him off from the thin safety of the woodlands. Why they didn't just shoot him as they had Foscar he could not understand.

The smoke of the burning grass was thick, cutting between him and the woods. Might it also provide a curtain behind which he could hope to escape both parties? The fire was sending the horse back toward the waiting ship people. Ross could hear a confused shouting in the smoke. Then his mount made a miscalculation, and a tongue of red licked too close. The animal screamed, dashing on blindly straight between two of the blazes and away from the blue-clad men.

Ross coughed, almost choking, his eyes watering as the stench of singed hair thickened the smoke. But he had been carried out of the fire circle and was shooting back into the meadowland. Mount and unwilling rider were well away from the upper end of that cleared space when another horse cut in from the left, matching speed to the uncontrolled animal to which Ross clung. It was one of the tribesmen riding easily.

The trick worked, for the wild race slowed to a gallop and the other rider, in a feat of horsemanship at which Ross marveled, leaned from his seat to catch the dangling nose rope, bringing the runaway against his own steady steed. Ross shaken, still coughing from the smoke and unable to sit upright, held to the mane. The gallop slowed to a rocking pace and finally came to a halt, both horses blowing, white-foam patches on their chests and their riders' legs.

Having made his capture, the tribesman seemed indifferent to Ross, looking back instead at the wide curtain of grass smoke, frowning as he studied the swift spread of the fire. Muttering to himself, he pulled the lead rope and brought Ross's horse to follow in the direction from which Ennar had brought the captive less than a half hour earlier.

Ross tried to think. The unexpected death of their chief might well mean his own, should the tribe's desire for vengeance now be aroused. On the other hand, there was a faint chance that he could now better impress them with the thought that he was indeed of another clan and that to aid him would be to work against a common enemy.

But it was hard to plan clearly, though wits alone could save him now. The parley which had ended with Foscar's murder had brought Ross a small measure of time. He was still a captive, even though of the tribesmen and not the unearthly strangers. Perhaps to the ship people these primitives were hardly higher in scale than the forest animals.

Ross did not try to talk to his present guard, who towed him into the western sun of late afternoon. They halted at last in that same small grove where they had rested at noon. The tribesman fastened the mounts and then walked around to inspect the animal Ross had ridden. With a grunt he loosened the prisoner and spilled him unceremoniously on the ground while he examined the horse. Ross levered himself up to sight the mark of the burn across that roan hide where the fire had blistered the skin.

Thick handfuls of mud from the side of the spring were brought and plastered over the seared strip. Then, having rubbed down both animals with twists of grass, the man came over to Ross, pushed him back to the ground, and studied his left leg.

Ross understood. By rights, his thigh should also have been scorched where the flame had hit, yet he had felt no pain. Now as the tribesman examined him for a burn, he could not see even the faintest discoloration of the strange fabric. He remembered how the aliens had strolled unconcerned through the burning village. As the suit had insulated him against the cold of the ice, so it would seem that it had also protected him against the fire, for which he was duly thankful. His escape from injury was a puzzle to the tribesman, who, failing to find any trace of burn on him, left Ross alone and went to sit well away from his prisoner as if he feared him.

They did not have long to wait. One by one, those who had ridden in Foscar's company gathered at the grove. The very last to come were Ennar and Tulka, carrying the body of their chief. The faces of both men were smeared with dust and when the others sighted the body they, too, rubbed dust into their cheeks, reciting a string of words and going one by one to touch the dead chieftain's right hand.

Ennar, resigning his burden to the others, slid from his tired horse and stood for a long moment, his head bowed. Then he gazed straight at Ross and came across the tiny clearing to stand over the man of a later time. The boyishness which had been a part of him when he had fought at Foscar's command was gone. His eyes were merciless as he leaned down to speak, shaping each word with slow care so that Ross could understand the promise-that frightful promise:

"Woods rat, Foscar goes to his burial fire. And he shall take a slave with him to serve him beyond the sky —a slave to run at his voice, to shake when he thunders. Slave-dog, you shall run for Foscar beyond the sky, and he shall have you forever to walk upon as a man walks upon the earth. I, Ennar, swear that Foscar shall be sent to the chiefs in the sky in all honor. And that you, dog-one, shall lie at his feet in that going!"

He did not touch Ross, but there was no doubt in Ross's mind that he meant every word he spoke.

Chapter 17

The preparations for Foscar's funeral went on through the night. A wooden structure, made up of tied fagots dragged in from the woodland, grew taller beyond the big tribal camp. The constant crooning wail of the women in the tents produced a minor murmur of sound, enough to drive a man to the edge of madness. Ross had been left under guard where he could watch it all, a refinement of torture which he would earlier have believed too subtle for Ennar. Though the older men carried minor commands among the horsemen, because Ennar was the closest of blood kin among the adult males, he was in charge of the coming ceremony.

The pick of the horse herd, a roan stallion, was brought in to be picketed near Ross as sacrifice number two, and two of the hounds were in turn leashed close by. Foscar, his best weapons to hand and a red cloak lapped about him, lay waiting on a bier. Near-by squatted the tribal wizard, shaking his thunder rattle and chanting in a voice which approached a shriek. This wild activity might have been a scene lifted directly from some tape stored at the project base. It was very difficult for Ross to remember that this was reality, that he was to be one of the main actors in the coming event, with no timely aid from Operation Retrograde to snatch him to safety.

Sometime during that nightmare he slept, his weariness of body overcoming him. He awoke, dazed, to find a hand clutching his mop of hair, pulling his head up.

"You sleep-you do not fear, Foscar's dog-one?"

Groggily Ross blinked up. Fear? Sure, he was afraid. Fear, he realized with a clear thrust of consciousness such as he had seldom experienced before, had always stalked beside him, slept in his bed. But he had never surrendered to it, and he would not now if he could help it.

"I do not fear!" He threw that creed into Ennar's face in one hot boast. He *would* not fear!

"We shall see if you speak so loudly when the fire bites you!" The other spat, yet in that oath there was a reluctant recognition of Ross's courage.

"When the fire bites...." That sang in Ross's head. There was something else-if he could only remember! Up to that moment he had kept a poor little shadow of hope. It is always impossible-he was conscious again with that strange clarity of mind-for a man to face his own death honestly. A man always continues to believe to the last moment of his life that something will intervene to save him.

The men led the horse to the mound of fagots which was now crowned with Foscar's bier. The stallion went quietly, until a tall tribesman struck true with an ax, and the animal fell. The hounds were also killed and laid at their dead master's feet.

But Ross was not to fare so easily. The wizard danced about him, a hideous figure in a beast mask, a curled fringe of dried snakeskins swaying from his belt. Shaking his rattle, he squawked like an angry cat as they pulled Ross to the stacked wood.

Fire-there was something about fire-if he could only remember! Ross stumbled and nearly fell across one leg of the dead horse they were propping into place. Then he remembered that tongue of flame in the meadow grass which had burned the horse but not the rider. His hands and his head would have no protection, but the rest of his body was covered with the flame-resistant fabric of the alien suit. Could he do it? There was such a slight chance, and they were already pushing him onto that mound, his hands tied. Ennar stooped, and bound his ankles, securing him to the brush.

So fastened, they left him. The tribe ringed around the pyre at a safe distance, Ennar and five other men approaching from different directions, torches aflame. Ross watched those blazing knots thrust into the brush and heard the crackle of the fire. His eyes, hard and measuring, studied the flash of flame from dried brush to seasoned wood.

A tongue of yellow-red flame licked up at him. Ross hardly dared to breathe as it wreathed about his foot, his hide fetters smoldering. The insulation of the suit did not cut all the heat, but it allowed him to stay put for the few seconds he needed to make his escape spectacular.

The flame had eaten through his foot bonds, and yet the burning sensation on his feet and legs was no greater than it would have been from the direct rays of a bright summer sun. Ross moistened his lips with his tongue. The impact of heat on his hands and his face was different. He leaned down, held his wrists to the flame, taking in stoical silence the burns which freed him.

Then, as the fire curled up so that he seemed to stand in a frame of writhing red banners, Ross leaped through that curtain, protecting his bowed head with his arms as best he could. But to the onlookers it seemed he passed unhurt through the heart of a roaring fire.

He kept his footing and stood facing that part of the tribal ring directly before him. He heard a cry, perhaps of fear, and a blazing torch flew through the air and struck his hip. Although he felt the force of the blow, the burning bits of the head merely slid down his thigh and leg, leaving no mark on the smooth blue fabric.

"Ahhhhhhh!"

Now the wizard capered before him, shaking his rattle to make a deafening din. Ross struck out, slapping the sorcerer out of his path, and stooped to pick up the smoldering brand which had been thrown at him. Whirling it about his head, though every movement was torture to his scorched hands, he set it flaming once more. Holding it in front of him as a weapon, he stalked directly at the men and women before him.

The torch was a poor enough defense against spears and axes, but Ross did not care-he put into this last gamble all the determination he could summon. Nor did he realize what a figure he presented to the tribesmen. A man who had crossed a curtain of fire without apparent hurt, who appeared to wash in tongues of flame without harm, and who now called upon fire in turn as a weapon, was no man but a demon!

The wall of people wavered and broke. Women screamed and ran; men shouted. But no one threw a spear or struck with an ax. Ross walked on, a man possessed, looking neither to the right or left. He was in the camp now, stalking toward the fire burning before Foscar's tent. He did not turn aside for that either, but holding the torch high, strode through the heart of the flames, risking further burns for the sake of insuring his ultimate safety.

The tribesmen melted away as he approached the last line of tents, with the open land beyond. The horses of the herd, which had been driven to this side to avoid the funeral pyre, were shifting nervously, the scent of burning making them uneasy.

Once more Ross whirled the dying torch about his head. Recalling how the aliens had sent his horse mad, he tossed it behind him into the grass between the tents and the herd. The tinder-dry stuff caught immediately. Now if the men tried to ride after him, they would have trouble.

Without hindrance he walked across the meadow at the same even pace, never turning to look behind. His hands were two separate worlds of smarting pain; his hair and eyebrows were singed, and a finger of burn ran along the angle of his jaw. But he was free, and he did not believe that Foscar's men would be in any haste to pursue him. Somewhere before him lay the river, the river which ran to the sea. Ross walked on in the sunny morning while behind him black smoke raised a dark beacon to the sky.

Afterward he guessed that he must have been lightheaded for several days, remembering little save the pain in his hands and the fact that it was necessary to keep moving. Once he fell to his knees and buried both hands in the cool, moist earth where a thread of stream trickled from a pool. The muck seemed to draw out a little of the agony while he drank with a fever thirst.

Ross seemed to move through a haze which lifted at intervals during which he noted his surroundings, was able to recall a little of what lay behind him, and to keep to the correct route. However, the gaps of time in between were forever lost to him. He stumbled along the banks of a river and fronted a bear fishing. The massive beast rose on its hind legs, growled, and Ross walked by it uncaring, unmenaced by the puzzled animal.

Sometimes he slept through the dark periods which marked the nights, or he stumbled along under the moon, nursing his hands against his breast, whimpering a little when his foot slipped and the jar of that mishap ran through his body. Once he heard singing, only to realize that it was himself who sang hoarsely a melody which would be popular thousands of years later in the world through which he wavered. But always Ross knew that he must go on, using that thick stream of running water as a guide to his final goal, the sea.

After a long while those spaces of mental clarity grew longer, appearing closer together. He dug small shelled things from under stones along the river and ate them avidly. Once he clubbed a rabbit and feasted. He sucked birds' eggs from a nest hidden among some reeds—just enough to keep his gaunt body going, though his gray eyes were now set in what was almost a death's-head.

Ross did not know just when he realized that he was again being hunted. It started with an uneasiness which differed from his previous fever-bred hallucinations. This was an inner pulling, a growing compulsion to turn and retrace his way back toward the mountains to meet something, or someone, waiting for him on the backward path.

But Ross kept on, fearing sleep now and fighting it. For once he had lain down to rest and had wakened on his feet, heading back as if that compulsion had the power to take over his body when his waking will was off guard.

So he rested, but he dared not sleep, the desire constantly tearing at his will, striving to take over his weakened body and draw it back. Perhaps against all reason he believed that it was the aliens who were trying to control him. Ross did not even venture to guess why they were so determined to get him. If there were tribesmen on his trail as well, he did not know, but he was sure that this was now purely a war of wills.

As the banks of the river were giving way to marshes, he had to wade through mud and water, detouring the boggy sections. Great clouds of birds whirled and shrieked their protests at his coming, and sleek water animals paddled and poked curious heads out of the water as this two-legged thing walked mechanically through their green land. Always that pull was with him, until Ross was more aware of fighting it than of traveling.

Why did they want him to return? Why did they not follow him? Or were they afraid to venture too far from where they had come through the transfer? Yet the unseen rope which was tugging at him did not grow less tenuous as he put more distance between himself and the mountain valley. Ross could understand neither their motives nor their methods, but he could continue to fight.

The bog was endless. He found an island and lashed himself with his suit belt to the single willow which grew there, knowing that he must have sleep, or he could not hope to last through the next day. Then he slept, only to waken cold, shaking, and afraid. Shoulder deep in a pool, he was aware that in his sleep he must have opened the belt buckle and freed himself, and only the mishap of falling into the water had brought him around to sanity.

Somehow he got back to the tree, rehooked the buckle and twisted the belt around the branches so that he was sure he could not work it free until daybreak. He lapsed into a deepening doze, and awoke, still safely anchored, with the morning cries of the birds. Ross considered the suit as he untangled the belt. Could the strange clothing be the tie by which the aliens held to him? If he were to strip, leaving the garment behind, would he be safe?

He tried to force open the studs across his chest, but they would not yield to the slight pressure which was all his seared fingers could exert, and when he pulled at the fabric, he was unable to tear it. So, still wearing the livery of the off-world men, Ross continued on his way, hardly caring where he went or how. The mud plastered on him by his frequent falls was some protection against the swarm of insect life his passing stirred into attack. However, he was able to endure a swollen face and slitted eyes, being far more conscious of the wrenching feeling within him than the misery of his body.

The character of the marsh began to change once more. The river was splitting into a dozen smaller streams, shaping out fanlike. Looking down at this from one of the marsh hillocks, Ross knew a faint surge of relief. Such a place had been on the map Ashe had made them memorize. He was close to the sea at last, and for the moment that was enough.

A salt-sharpened wind cut at him with the force of a fist in the face. In the absence of sunlight the leaden clouds overhead set a winterlike gloom across the countryside. To the constant sound of birdcalls Ross tramped heavily through small pools, beating a path through tangles of marsh grass. He stole eggs from nests, sucking his nourishment eagerly with no dislike for the fishy flavor, and drinking from stagnant, brackish ponds.

Suddenly Ross halted, at first thinking that the continuous roll of sound he heard was thunder. Yet the clouds overhead were massed no more than before and there was no sign of lightning. Continuing on, he realized that the mysterious sound was the pounding of surf-he was near the sea!

Willing his body to run, he weaved forward at a reeling trot, pitting all his energy against the incessant pull from behind. His feet skidded out of marsh mud into sand. Ahead of him were dark rocks surrounded by the white lace of spray.

Ross headed straight toward that spray until he stood knee-deep in the curling, foam-edged water and felt its tug on his body almost as strong as that other tug upon his mind. He knelt, letting the salt water sting to life every cut, every burn, sputtering as it filled his mouth and nostrils, washing from him the slime of the bog lands. It was cold and bitter, but it was the sea! He had made it!

Ross Murdock staggered back and sat down suddenly in the sand. Glancing about, he saw that his refuge was a rough triangle between two of the small river arms, littered with the debris of the spring floods which had grounded here after rejection by the sea. Although there was plenty of material for a fire, he had no means of kindling a flame, having lost the flint all Beaker traders carried for such a purpose.

This was the sea, and against all odds he had reached it. He lay back, his self-confidence restored to the point where he dared once more to consider the future. He watched the swooping flight of gulls drawing patterns under the clouds above. For the moment he wanted nothing more than to lie here and rest.

But he did not surrender to this first demand of his over-driven body for long. Hungry and cold, sure that a storm was coming, he knew he had to build a fire —a fire on shore could provide him with the means of signaling the sub. Hardly knowing why-because one part of the coastline was as good as another-Ross began to walk again, threading a path in and out among the rocky outcrops.

So he found it, a hollow between two such windbreaks within which was a blackened circle of small stones holding charred wood, with some empty shells piled near-by. Here was unmistakable evidence of a camp! Ross plunged forward, thrusting a hand impetuously into the black mass of the dead fire. To his astonishment, he touched warmth!

Hardly daring to disturb those precious bits of charcoal, he dug around them, then carefully blew into what appeared to be dead ashes. There was an answering glow! He could not have just imagined it.

From a pile of wood that had been left behind, Ross snatched a small twig, poking it at the coal after he had rubbed it into a brush on the rough rock. He watched, all one ache of hope. The twig caught!

With his stiff fingers so clumsy, he had to be very careful, but Ross had learned patience in a hard school. Bit by bit he fed that tiny blaze until he had a real fire. Then, leaning back against the rock, he watched it.

It was now obvious that the placement of the original fire had been chosen with care, for the outcrops gave it wind shelter. They also provided a dark backdrop, partially hiding the flames on the landward side but undoubtedly making them more visible from the sea. The site seemed just right for a signal fire-but to what?

Ross's hands shook slightly as he fed the blaze. It was only too clear why anyone would make a signal on this shore. McNeil-or perhaps both he and Ashe-had survived the breakup of the raft, after all. They had reached this point-abandoned no earlier than this morning, judging by the life remaining in the coals-and put up the signal. Then, just as arranged, they had been collected by the sub, by now on its way back to the hidden North American post. There was no hope of any pickup for him now. Just as he had believed them dead after he had found that rag on the sapling, so they must have thought him finished after his fall in the river. He was just a few hours too late!

Ross folded his arms across his hunched knees and rested his head on them. There was no possible way he could ever reach the post or his own kind-ever again. Thousands of miles lay between him and the temporary installation in this time.

He was so sunk in his own complete despair that he was long unaware of finally being free of the pressure to turn back which had so long haunted him. But as he roused to feed the fire he got to wondering. Had those who hunted him given up the chase? Since he had lost his own race with time, he did not really care. What did it matter?

The pile of wood was getting low, but he decided that did not matter either. Even so, Ross got to his feet, moving over to the drifts of storm wrack to gather more. Why should he stay here by a useless beacon? But somehow he could not force himself to move on, as futile as his vigil seemed.

Dragging the sun-dried, bleached limbs of long-dead trees to his half shelter, he piled them up, working until he laughed at the barricade he had built. "A siege!" For the first time in days he spoke aloud. "I might be ready for a siege...." He pulled over another branch, added it to his pile, and kneeled down once more by the flames.

There were fisherfolk to be found along this coast, and tomorrow when he was rested he would strike south and try to find one of their primitive villages. Traders would be coming into this territory now that the Red-inspired raiders were gone. If he could contact them....

But that spark of interest in the future died almost as soon as it was born. To be a Beaker trader as an agent for the project was one thing, to live the role for the rest of his life was something else.

Ross stood by his fire, staring out to sea for a sign he knew he would never see again as long as he lived. Then, as if a spear had struck between his shoulder blades, he was attacked.

The blow was not physical, but came instead as a tearing, red pain in his head, a pressure so terrible he could not move. He knew instantly that behind him now lurked the ultimate danger.

Chapter 18

Ross fought to break that hold, to turn his head, to face the peril which crept upon him now. Unlike anything he had ever met before in his short lifetime, it could only have come from some alien source. This strange encounter was a battle of will against will! The same rebellion against authority which had ruled his boyhood, which had pushed him into the orbit of the project, stiffened him to meet this attack.

He was going to turn his head; he was going to see who stood there. He *was!* Inch by inch, Ross's head came around, though sweat stung his seared and bitten flesh, and every breath was an effort. He caught a half glimpse of the beach behind the rocks, and the stretch of sand was empty. Overhead the birds were gone-as if they had never existed. Or, as if they had been swept away by some impatient fighter, who wanted no distractions from the purpose at hand.

Having successfully turned his head, Ross decided to turn his body. His left hand went out, slowly, as if it moved some great weight. His palm gritted painfully on the rock and he savored that pain, for it pierced through the dead blanket of compulsion that was being used against him. Deliberately he ground his blistered skin against the stone, concentrating on the sharp torment in his hand as the agony shot up his arm. While he focused his attention on the physical pain, he could feel the pressure against him weaken. Summoning all his strength, Ross swung around in a movement which was only a shadow of his former feline grace.

The beach was still empty, except for the piles of driftwood, the rocks, and the other things he had originally found there. Yet he knew that something was waiting to pounce. Having discovered that for him pain was a defense weapon, he had that one resource. If they took him, it would be after besting him in a fight.

Even as he made this decision, Ross was conscious of a curious weakening of the force bent upon him. It was as if his opponents had been surprised, either at his simple actions of the past few seconds or at his determination. Ross leaped upon that surprise, adding it to his stock of unseen weapons.

He leaned forward, still grinding his torn hand against the rock as a steadying influence, took up a length of dried wood, and thrust its end into the fire. Having once used fire to save himself, he was ready and willing to do it again, although at the same time, another part of him shrank from what he intended.

Holding his improvised torch breast-high, Ross stared across it, searching the land for the faintest sign of his enemies. In spite of the fire and the light he held before him, the dusk prevented him from seeing too far. Behind him the crash of the surf could have covered the noise of a marching army.

"Come and get me!"

He whirled his brand into bursting life and then hurled it straight into the drift among the dunes. He was grabbing for a second brand almost before the blazing head of the first had fallen into the twisted, bleached roots of a dead tree.

He stood tense, a second torch now kindled in his hand. The sharp vise of another's will which had nipped him so tightly a moment ago was easing, slowly disappearing as water might trickle away. Yet he could not believe that this small act of defiance had so daunted his unseen opponent as to make him give up the struggle this easily. It was more likely the pause of a wrestler seeking for a deadlier grip.

The brand in his hand-Ross's second line of defense-was a weapon he was loath to use, but would use if he were forced to it. He kept his hand mercilessly flat against the rock as a reminder and a spur.

Fire twisted and crackled among the driftwood where the first torch had lodged, providing a flickering light yards from where he stood. He was grateful for it in the gloom of the gathering storm. If they would only come to open war before the rain struck....

Ross sheltered his torch with his body as spray, driven inward from the sea, spattered his shoulders and his back. If it rained, he would lose what small advantage the fire gave him, but then he would find some other way to meet them. They would neither break him nor take him, even if he had to wade into the sea and swim out into the lash of the cold northern waves until he could not move his tired limbs any longer.

Once again that steel-edge will struck at Ross, probing his stubbornness, assaulting his mind. He whirled the torch, brought the scorching breath of the flame across the hand resting on the rock. Unable to control his own cry of protest, he was not sure he had the fortitude to repeat such an act.

He had won again! The pressure had fallen away in a flick, almost as if some current had been snapped off. Through the red curtain of his torment Ross sensed a surprise and disbelief. He was unaware that in this queer duel he was using both a power of will and a depth of perception he had never known he possessed. Because of his daring, he had shaken his opponents as no physical attack could have affected them.

"Come and get me!" He shouted again at the barren shoreline where the fire ate at the drift and nothing stirred, yet something very much alive and conscious lay hidden. This time there was more than simple challenge in Ross's demand–there was a note of triumph.

The spray whipped by him, striking at his fire, at the brand he held. Let the sea water put both out! He would find another way of fighting. He was certain of that, and he sensed that those out there knew it too and were troubled.

The fire was being driven by the wind along the crisscross lines of bone-white wood left high on the beach, forming a wall of flame between him and the interior, not, however, an insurmountable barrier to whatever lurked there.

Again Ross leaned against the rock, studying the length of beach. Had he been wrong in thinking that they were within the range of his voice? The power they had used might carry over a greater distance.

"Yahhhh —" Instead of a demand, he now voiced a taunting cry, screaming his defiance. Some wild madness had been transmitted to him by the winds, the roaring sea, his own pain. Ready to face the worst they could send against him, he tried to hurl that thought back at them as they had struck with their united will at him. No answer came to his challenge, no rise to counter-attack.

Moving away from the rock, Ross began to walk forward toward the burning drift, his torch ready in his hand. "I am here!" he shouted into the wind. "Come out-face me!"

It was then that he saw those who had tracked him. Two tall thin figures, wearing dark clothes, were standing quietly watching him, their eyes dark holes in the white ovals of their faces.

Ross halted. Though they were separated by yards of sand and rock and a burning barrier, he could feel the force they wielded. The nature of that force had changed, however. Once it had struck with a vigorous spear point; now it formed a shield of protection. Ross could not break through that shield, and they dared not drop it. A stalemate existed between them in this strange battle, the like of which Ross's world had not known before.

He watched those expressionless white faces, trying to find some reply to the deadlock. There flashed into his mind the certainty that while he lived and moved, and they lived and moved, this struggle, this unending pursuit, would continue. For some mysterious reason they wanted to have him under their control, but that was never going to happen if they all had to remain here on this strip of water-washed sand until they starved to death! Ross tried to drive that thought across to them.

"Murrrrdock!" That croaking cry borne out of the sea by the wind might almost have come from the bill of a sea bird.

"Murrrrdock!"

Ross spun around. Visibility had been drastically curtailed by the lowering clouds and the dashing spray, but he could see a round dark thing bobbing on the waves. The sub? A raft?

Sensing a movement behind him, Ross wheeled about as one of the alien figures leaped the blazing drift, heedless of the flames, and ran light-footedly toward him in what could only be an all-out attempt at capture. The man had ready a weapon like the one that had felled Foscar. Ross threw himself at his opponent in a reckless dive, falling on him with a smashing impact.

In Ross's grasp the alien's body was fragile, but he moved fluidly as Murdock fought to break his grip on the hand weapon and pin him to the sand. Ross was too intent upon his own part of the struggle to heed the sounds of a shot over his head and a thin, wailing cry. He slammed his opponent's hand against a stone, and the white face, inches away from his own, twisted silently with pain.

Fumbling for a better hold, Ross was sent rolling. He came down on his left hand with a force which brought tears to his eyes and stopped him just long enough for the other to regain his feet.

The blue-suited man sprinted back to the body of his fellow where it lay by the drift. He slung his unconscious comrade over the barrier with more ease than Ross would have believed possible and vaulted the barrier after him. Ross, half crouched on the sand, felt unusually light and empty. The strange tie which had drawn and held him to the strangers had been broken.

"Murdock!"

A rubber raft rode in on the waves, two men aboard it. Ross got up, pulling at the studs of his suit with his right hand. He could believe in what he saw now-the sub had not left, after all. The two men running toward him through the dusk were of his own kind.

"Murdock!"

It did not seem at all strange that Kelgarries reached him first. Ross, caught up in this dream, appealed to the major for aid with the studs. If the strangers from the ship did trace him by the suit, they were not going to follow the sub back to the post and serve the project as they had the Reds.

"Got-to-get-this-off—" He pulled the words out one by one, tugging frantically at the stubborn studs. "They can trace this and follow us —"

Kelgarries needed no better explanation. Ripping loose the fastenings, he pulled the clinging fabric from Ross, sending him reeling with pain as he pulled the left sleeve down the younger man's arm.

The wind and spray were ice on his body as they dragged him down to the raft, bundling him aboard. He did not at all remember their arrival on board the sub. He was lying in the vibrating heart of the undersea ship when he opened his eyes to see Kelgarries regarding him intently. Ashe, a coat of bandage about his shoulder and chest, lay on a neighboring bunk. McNeil stood watching a medical corpsman lay out supplies.

"He needs a shot," the medic was saying as Ross blinked at the major.

"You left the suit-back there?" Ross demanded.

"We did. What's this about them tracing you by it? Who was tracing you?"

"Men from the space ship. That's the only way they could have trailed me down the river." He was finding it difficult to talk, and the protesting medic kept waving a needle in his direction, but somehow in bursts of half-finished sentences Ross got out his story-Foscar's death, his own escape from the chief's funeral pyre, and the weird duel of wills back on the beach. Even as he poured it out he thought how unlikely most of it must sound. Yet Kelgarries appeared to accept every word, and there was no expression of disbelief on Ashe's face.

"So that's how you got those burns," said the major slowly when Ross had finished his story. "Deliberately searing your hand in the fire to break their hold —" He crashed his fist against the wall of the tiny cabin and then, when Ross winced at the jar, he hurriedly uncurled those fingers to press Ross's shoulder with a surprisingly warm and gentle touch. "Put him to sleep," he ordered the medic. "He deserves about a month of it, I should judge. I think he has brought us a bigger slice of the future than we had hoped for...."

Ross felt the prick of the needle and then nothing more. Even when he was carried ashore at the post and later when he was transported into his proper time, he did not awaken. He only approached a strange dreamy state in which he ate and drowsed, not caring for the world beyond his own bunk.

But there came a day when he did care, sitting up to demand food with a great deal of his old self-assertion. The doctor looked him over, permitting him to get out of bed and try out his legs. They were exceedingly uncooperative at first, and Ross was glad he had tried to move only from his bunk to a waiting chair.

"Visitors welcome?"

Ross looked up eagerly and then smiled, somewhat hesitatingly, at Ashe. The older man wore his arm in a sling but otherwise seemed his usual imperturbable self.

"Ashe, tell me what happened. Are we back at the main base? What about the Reds? We weren't traced by the ship people, were we?"

Ashe laughed. "Did Doc just wind you up to let you spin, Ross? Yes, this is home, sweet home. As for the rest-well, it is a long story, and we are still picking up pieces of it here and there."

Ross pointed to the bunk in invitation. "Can you tell me what is known?" He was still somewhat at a loss, his old secret awe of Ashe tempering his outward show of eagerness. Ross still feared one of those snubs the other so well knew how to deliver to the bumptious. But Ashe did come in and sit down, none of his old formality now in evidence.

"You have been a surprise package, Murdock." His observation had some of the ring of the old Ashe, but there was no withdrawal behind the words. "Rather a busy lad, weren't you, after you were bumped off into that river?"

Ross's reply was a grimace. "You heard all about that!" He had no time for his own adventures, already receding into a past which made them both dim and unimportant. "What happened to you-and to the project-and — —"

"One thing at a time, and don't rush your fences." Ashe was surveying him with an odd intentness which Ross could not understand. He continued to explain in his "instructor" voice. "We made it down the river-how, don't ask me. That was something of a 'project' in itself," he laughed. "The raft came apart piece by piece, and we waded most of the last couple of miles, I think. I'm none too clear on the details; you'll have to get those out of McNeil, who was still among those present then. Other than that, we cannot compete with your adventures. We built a signal fire and sat by it toasting our shins for a few days, until the sub came to collect us — —"

"And took you off." Ross experienced a fleeting return of that hollow feeling he had known on the shore when the still-warm coals of the signal fire had told him the story of his too-late arrival.

"And took us off. But Kelgarries agreed to spin out our waiting period for another twenty-four hours, in case you did manage to survive that toss you took into the river. Then we sighted your spectacular display of fireworks on the beach, and the rest was easy."

"The ship people didn't trace us back to post?"

"Not that we know of. Anyway, we've closed down the post on that time level. You might be interested in a very peculiar tale our modern agents have picked up, floating over and under the iron curtain. A blast went off in the Baltic region of this time, wiping some installation clean off the map. The Reds have kept quiet as to the nature of the explosion and the exact place where it occurred."

"The aliens followed *them* all the way up to this time!" —Ross half rose from the chair —"But why? And why did they trail me?"

"That we can only guess. But I don't believe that they were moved by any private vengeance for the looting of their derelict. There is some more imperative reason why they don't want us to find or use anything from one of their cargoes — —"

"But they were in power thousands of years ago. Maybe they and their worlds are gone now. Why should things we do today matter to them?"

"Well, it does matter, and in some very important way. And we have to learn that reason."

"How?" Ross looked down at his left hand, encased in a mitten of bandage under which he very gingerly tried to stretch a finger. Maybe he should have been eager to welcome another meeting with the ship people, but if he were truly honest, he had to admit that he did not. He glanced up, sure that Ashe had read all that hesitation and scorned him for it. But there was no sign that his discomfiture had been noticed.

"By doing some looting of our own," Ashe answered. "Those tapes we brought back are going to be a big help. More than one derelict was located. We were right in our surmise that the Reds first discovered the remains of one in Siberia, but it was in no condition to be explored. They already had the basic idea of the time traveler, so they applied it to the hunting down of other ships, with several way stops to throw people like us off the scent. So they found an intact ship, and also several others. At least three are on *this* side of the Atlantic where they couldn't get at them very well. Those we can deal with now — —"

"Won't the aliens be waiting for us to try that?"

"As far as we can discover they don't know where any of these ships crashed. Either there were no survivors, or passengers and crew took off in lifeboats while they were still in space. They might never have known of the Reds' activities if you hadn't triggered that communicator on the derelict."

Ross was reduced to a small boy who badly needed an alibi for some piece of juvenile mischief. "I didn't mean to." That excuse sounded so feeble that he was surprised into a laugh, only to see Ashe grinning back at him.

"Seeing as how your action also put a very effective spike in the opposition's wheel, you are freely forgiven. Anyway, you have also provided us with a pretty good idea of what we may be up against with the aliens, and we'll be prepared for that next time."

"Then there will be a next time?"

"We are calling in all time agents, concentrating our forces in the right period. Yes, there will be a next time. We have to learn just what they are trying so hard to protect."

"What do you think it is?"

"Space!" Ashe spoke the word softly as if he relished the promise it held.

"Space?"

"That ship you explored was a derelict from a galactic fleet, but it was a ship and it used the principle of space flight. Do you understand now? In these lost ships lies the secret which will make us free of all the stars! We must claim it."

"Can we — —?"

"Can *we*?" Ashe was laughing at Ross again with his eyes, though his face remained sober. "Then *you* still want to be counted in on this game?"

Ross looked down again at his bandaged hand and remembered swiftly so many things-the coast of Britain on a misty morning, the excitement of prowling the alien ship, the fight with Ennar, even the long nightmare of his flight down the river, and lastly, the exultation he had tasted when he had faced the alien and had locked wills-to hold steady. He knew that he could not, would not, give up what he had found here in the service of the project as long as it was in his power to cling to it.

"Yes." It was a very simple answer, but when his eyes met Ashe's, Ross knew that it would serve better than any solemn oath.

The Defiant Agents

No windows broke any of the four plain walls of the office; there was no focus of outer-world sunlight on the desk there. Yet the five disks set out on its surface appeared to glow-perhaps the heat of the mischief they could cause ... had caused ... blazed in them.

But fanciful imaginings did not cushion or veil cold, hard fact. Dr. Gordon Ashe, one of the four men peering unhappily at the display, shook his head slightly as if to free his mind of such cobwebs.

His neighbor to the right, Colonel Kelgarries, leaned forward to ask harshly: "No chance of a mistake?"

"You saw the detector." The thin gray string of a man behind the desk answered with chill precision. "No, no possible mistake. These five have definitely been snooped."

"And two choices among them," Ashe murmured. That was the important point now.

"I thought these were under maximum security," Kelgarries challenged the gray man.

Florian Waldour's remote expression did not change. "Every possible precaution was in force. There was a sleeper —a hidden agent-planted — —"

"Who?" Kelgarries demanded.

Ashe glanced around at his three companions-Kelgarries, colonel in command of one sector of Project Star, Florian Waldour, the security head on the station, Dr. James Ruthven....

"Camdon!" he said, hardly able to believe this answer to which logic had led him.

Waldour nodded.

For the first time since he had known and worked with Kelgarries Ashe saw him display open astonishment.

"Camdon? But he was sent us by —" The colonel's eyes narrowed. "He must have been sent....There were too many cross checks to fake that!"

"Oh, he was sent, all right." For the first time there was a note of emotion in Waldour's voice. "He was a sleeper, a very deep sleeper. They must have planted him a full twenty-five or thirty years ago. He's been just what he claimed to be as long as that."

"Well, he certainly was worth their time and trouble, wasn't he?" James Ruthven's voice was a growling rumble. He sucked in thick lips, continuing to stare at the disks. "How long ago were these snooped?"

Ashe's thoughts turned swiftly from the enormity of the betrayal to that important point. The time element-that was the primary concern now that the damage was done, and they knew it.

"That's one thing we don't know." Waldour's reply came slowly as if he hated the admission.

"We'll be safer, then, if we presume the very earliest period." Ruthven's statement was as ruthless in its implications as the shock they had had when Waldour announced the disaster.

"Eighteen months ago?" Ashe protested.

But Ruthven was nodding. "Camdon was in on this from the very first. We've had the tapes in and out for study all that time, and the new detector against snooping was not put in service until two weeks ago. This case came up on the first checking round, didn't it?" he asked Waldour.

"First check," the security man agreed. "Camdon left the base six days ago. But he has been in and out on his liaison duties from the first."

"He had to go through those search points every time," Kelgarries protested. "Thought nothing could get through those." The colonel brightened. "Maybe he got his snooper films and then couldn't take them off base. Have his quarters been turned out?"

Waldour's lips lifted in a grimace of exasperation. "Please, Colonel," he said wearily, "this is not a kindergarten exercise. In confirmation of his success, listen...." He touched a button on his desk and out of the air came the emotionless chant of a newscaster.

"Fears for the safety of Lassiter Camdon, space expediter for the Western Conference Space Council, have been confirmed by the discovery of burned wreckage in the mountains. Mr.

Camdon was returning from a mission to the Star Laboratory when his plane lost contact with Ragnor Field. Reports of a storm in that vicinity immediately raised concern —" Waldour snapped off the voice.

"True-or a cover for his escape?" Kelgarries wondered aloud.

"Could be either. They may have deliberately written him off when they had all they wanted," Waldour acknowledged. "But to get back to our troubles-Dr. Ruthven is right to assume the worst. I believe we can only insure the recovery of our project by thinking that these tapes were snooped anywhere from eighteen months ago to last week. And we must work accordingly!"

There was silence in the room as they all considered that. Ashe slipped down in his chair, his thoughts enmeshed in memories. First there had been Operation Retrograde, when specially trained "time agents" had shuttled back and forth in history, striving to locate and track down the mysterious source of alien knowledge which the eastern Communistic nations had suddenly begun to use.

Ashe himself and a younger partner, Ross Murdock, had been part of the final action which had solved the mystery, having traced that source of knowledge not to an earlier and forgotten Terran civilization but to wrecked spaceships from an eon-old galactic empire-an empire which had flourished when glacial ice covered most of Europe and northern America and Terrans were cave-dwelling primitives. Murdock, trapped by the Reds in one of those wrecked ships, had inadvertently summoned its original owners, who had descended to trace-through the Russian time stations-the looters of their wrecks, destroying the whole Red time-travel system.

But the aliens had not chanced on the parallel western system. And a year later that had been put into Project Folsom One. Again Ashe, Murdock, and a newcomer, the Apache Travis Fox, had gone back into time to the Arizona of the Folsom hunters, discovering what they wanted-two ships, one wrecked, the other intact. And when the full efforts of the project had been centered on bringing the intact ship back into the present, chance had triggered controls set by the dead alien commander. A party of four, Ashe, Murdock, Fox, and a technician, had then made an involuntary voyage into space, touching three worlds on which the galactic civilization of the far past was now marked only by ruins.

Voyage tape fed into the controls of the ship had taken the men, and, when rewound, had-by a miracle-returned them to Terra with a cargo of similar tapes found in a building on a world which might have been the central capital for a government comprised not of countries or of worlds but of solar systems. Tapes-each one the key to another planet.

And that ancient galactic knowledge was treasure such as the Terrans had never dreamed of possessing, though there were the attendant fears that such discoveries could be weapons in enemy hands. There had been an enforced sharing with other nations of tapes chosen at random at a great drawing. And each nation secretly remained convinced that, in spite of the untold riches it might hold as a result of chance, its rivals had done better. Right at this moment, Ashe did not in the least doubt, there were agents of his own party intent on accomplishing at the Red project just what Camdon had done there. However, that did not help in solving their present dilemma concerning Operation Cochise, one part of their project, but perhaps the most important now.

Some of the tapes were duds, either too damaged to be useful, or set for worlds hostile to Terrans lacking the equipment the earlier star-traveling race had had at its command. Of the five tapes they now knew had been snooped, three would be useless to the enemy.

But one of the remaining two....Ashe frowned. One was the goal toward which they had been working feverishly for a full twelve months. To plant a colony across the gulf of space —a successful colony-later to be used as a steppingstone to other worlds....

"So we have to move faster." Ruthven's comment reached Ashe through his stream of memories.

"I thought you required at least three more months to conclude personnel training," Waldour observed.

Ruthven lifted a fat hand, running the nail of a broad thumb back and forth across his lower lip in a habitual gesture Ashe had learned to mistrust. As the latter stiffened, bracing for a battle of wills, he saw Kelgarries come alert too. At least the colonel more often than not was ready to counter Ruthven's demands.

"We test and we test," said the fat man. "Always we test. We move like turtles when it would be better to race like greyhounds. There is such a thing as overcaution, as I have said from the first. One would think" —his accusing glance included Ashe and Kelgarries —"that there had never been any improvising in this project, that all had always been done by the book. I say that this is the time we must take the big gamble, or else we may find we have been outbid for space entirely. Let those others discover even one alien installation they can master and —" his thumb shifted from his lip, grinding down on the desk top as if it were crushing some venturesome but entirely unimportant insect —"and we are finished before we really begin."

There were a number of men in the project who would agree with that, Ashe knew. And a greater number in the country and conference at large. The public was used to reckless gambles which paid off, and there had been enough of those in the past to give an impressive argument for that point of view. But Ashe, himself, could not agree to a speed-up. He had been out among the stars, shaved disaster too closely because the proper training had not been given.

"I shall report that I advise a take-off within a week," Ruthven was continuing. "To the council I shall say that —"

"And I do not agree!" Ashe cut in. He glanced at Kelgarries for the quick backing he expected, but instead there was a lengthening moment of silence. Then the colonel spread out his hands and said sullenly:

"I don't agree either, but I don't have the final say-so. Ashe, what would be needed to speed up any take-off?"

It was Ruthven who replied. "We can use the Redax, as I have said from the start."

Ashe straightened, his mouth tight, his eyes hard and angry.

"And I'll protest that ... to the council! Man, we're dealing with human beings-selected volunteers, men who trust us-not with laboratory animals!"

Ruthven's thick lips pouted into what was close to a smile of derision. "Always the sentimentalists, you experts in the past! Tell me, Dr. Ashe, were you always so thoughtful of your men when you sent agents back into time? And certainly a voyage into space is less a risk than time travel. These volunteers know what they have signed for. They will be ready— —"

"Then you propose telling them about the use of Redax-what it does to a man's mind?" countered Ashe.

"Certainly. They will receive all necessary instructions."

Ashe was not satisfied and he would have spoken again, but Kelgarries interrupted:

"If it comes to that, none of us here has any right to make final decisions. Waldour has already sent in his report about the snoop. We'll have to await orders from the council."

Ruthven levered himself out of his chair, his solid bulk stretching his uniform coveralls. "That is correct, Colonel. In the meantime I would suggest we all check to see what can be done to speed up each one's portion of labor." Without another word, he tramped to the door.

Waldour eyed the other two with mounting impatience. It was plain he had work to do and wanted them to leave. But Ashe was reluctant. He had a feeling that matters were slipping out of his control, that he was about to face a crisis which was somehow worse than just a major security leak. Was the enemy always on the other side of the world? Or could he wear the same uniform, even share the same goals?

In the outer corridor he still hesitated, and Kelgarries, a step or so in advance, looked back over his shoulder impatiently.

"There's no use fighting-our hands are tied." His words were slurred, almost as if he wanted to disown them.

"Then you'll agree to use the Redax?" For the second time within the hour Ashe felt as if he had taken a step only to have firm earth turn into slippery, shifting sand underfoot.

"It isn't a matter of my agreeing. It may be a matter of getting through or not getting through-now. If they've had eighteen months, or even twelve...!" The colonel's fingers balled into a fist. "And *they* won't be delayed by any humanitarian reasoning ——"

"Then you believe Ruthven will win the council's approval?"

"When you are dealing with frightened men, you're talking to ears closed to anything but what they want to hear. After all, we can't prove that the Redax will be harmful."

"But we've only used it under rigidly controlled conditions. To speed up the process would mean a total disregard of those controls. Snapping a party of men and women back into their racial past and holding them there for too long a period...." Ashe shook his head.

"You have been in Operation Retrograde from the start, and we've been remarkably successful ——"

"Operating in a different way, educating picked men to return to certain points in history where their particular temperaments and characteristics fitted the roles they were selected to play, yes. And even then we had our percentage of failures. But to try this-returning people not physically into time, but *mentally and emotionally* into prototypes of their ancestors-that's something else again. The Apaches have volunteered, and they've been passed by the psychologists and the testers. But they're Americans of today, not tribal nomads of two or three hundred years ago. If you break down some barriers, you might just end up breaking them all."

Kelgarries was scowling. "You mean-they might revert utterly, have no contact with the present at all?"

"That's just what I do mean. Education and training, yes, but full awakening of racial memories, no. The two branches of conditioning should go slowly and hand in hand, otherwise-real trouble!"

"Only we no longer have the time to go slow. I'm certain Ruthven will be able to push this through-with Waldour's report to back him."

"Then we'll have to warn Fox and the rest. They must be given a choice in the matter."

"Ruthven said that would be done." The colonel did not sound convinced of that.

Ashe snorted. "If I hear him telling them, I'll believe it!"

"I wonder whether we can...."

Ashe half turned and frowned at the colonel. "What do you mean?"

"You said yourself that we had our failures in time travel. We expected those, accepted them, even when they hurt. When we asked for volunteers for this project we had to make them understand that there was a heavy element of risk involved. Three teams of recruits-the Eskimos from Point Barren, the Apaches, and the Islanders-all picked because their people had a high survival rating in the past, to be colonists on widely different types of planets. Well, the Eskimos and the Islanders aren't matched to any of the worlds on those snooped tapes, but Topaz is waiting for the Apaches. And we may have to move them in there in a hurry. It's a rotten gamble any way you see it!"

"I'll appeal directly to the council."

Kelgarries shrugged. "All right. You have my backing."

"But you believe such an effort hopeless?"

"You know the red-tape merchants. You'll have to move fast if you want to beat Ruthven. He's probably on a straight line now to Stanton, Reese, and Margate. This is what he has been waiting for!"

"There are the news syndicates; public opinion would back us ——"

"You don't mean that, of course." Kelgarries was suddenly coldly remote.

Ashe flushed under the heavy brown which overlay his regular features. To threaten a silence break was near blasphemy here. He ran both hands down the fabric covering his thighs as if to rub away some soil on his palms.

"No," he replied heavily, his voice dull. "I guess I don't. I'll contact Hough and hope for the best."

"Meanwhile," Kelgarries spoke briskly, "we'll do what we can to speed up the program as it now stands. I suggest you take off for New York within the hour — —"

"Me? Why?" Ashe asked with a trace of suspicion.

"Because I can't leave without acting directly against orders, and that would put us wrong immediately. You see Hough and talk to him personally-put it to him straight. He'll have to have all the facts if he's going to counter any move from Stanton before the council. You know every argument we can use and all the proof on our side, and you're authority enough to make it count."

"If I can do all that, I will." Ashe was alert and eager. The colonel, seeing his change of expression, felt easier.

But Kelgarries stood a moment watching Ashe as he hurried down a side corridor, before he moved on slowly to his own box of office. Once inside he sat for a long unhappy time staring at the wall and seeing nothing but the pictures produced by his thoughts. Then he pressed a button and read off the symbols which flashed on a small visa-screen set in his desk. Another button pushed, and he picked up a hand mike to relay an order which might postpone trouble for a while. Ashe was far too valuable a man to lose, and his emotions could boil him straight into disaster over this.

"Bidwell-reschedule Team A. They are to go to the Hypno-Lab instead of the reserve in ten minutes."

Releasing the mike, he again stared at the wall. No one dared interrupt a hypno-training period, and this one would last three hours. Ashe could not possibly see the trainees before he left for New York. And that would remove one temptation from his path-he would not talk at the wrong time.

Kelgarries' mouth twisted sourly. He had no pride in what he was doing. And he was perfectly certain that Ruthven would win and that Ashe's fears of Redax were well founded. It all came back to the old basic tenet of the service: the end justified the means. They must use every method and man under their control to make sure that Topaz would remain a western possession, even though that strange planet now swung far beyond the sky which covered both the western and eastern alliances on Terra. Time had run out too fast; they were being forced to play what cards they held, even though those might be very low ones. Ashe would be back, but not, Kelgarries hoped, until this had been decided one way or another. Not until this was finished.

Finished! Kelgarries blinked at the wall. Perhaps *they* were finished, too. No one would know until the transport ship landed on that other world which appeared on the direction tape symbolized by a jewellike disk of gold-brown which had given it the code name of Topaz.

2

There were an even dozen of the air-borne guardians, each following the swing of its own orbital path just within the atmospheric envelope of the planet which glowed as a great bronze-golden gem in the four-world system of a yellow star. The globes had been launched to form a web of protection around Topaz six months earlier, and the highest skill had gone into their production. Just as contact mines sown in a harbor could close that landfall to ships not knowing the secret channel, so was this world supposedly closed to any spaceship not equipped with the signal to ward off the sphere missiles.

That was the theory of the new off-world settlers whose protection they were to be, already tested as well as possible, but as yet not put to the ultimate proof. The small bright globes spun undisturbed across a two-mooned sky at night and made reassuring blips on an installation screen by day.

Then a thirteenth object winked into being, began the encircling, closing spiral of descent. A sphere resembling the warden-globes, it was a hundred times their size, and its orbit was purposefully controlled by instruments under the eye and hand of a human pilot.

Four men were strapped down on cushioned sling-seats in the control cabin of the Western Alliance ship, two hanging where their fingers might reach buttons and levers, the others merely passengers, their own labor waiting for the time when they would set down on the alien soil of Topaz. The planet hung there in their visa-screen, richly beautiful in its amber gold, growing larger, nearer, so that they could pick out features of seas, continents, mountain ranges, which had been studied on tape until they were familiar, yet now were strangely unfamiliar too.

One of the warden-globes alerted, oscillated in its set path, whirled faster as its delicate interior mechanisms responded to the awakening spark which would send it on its mission of destruction. A relay clicked, but for the smallest fraction of a millimeter failed to set the proper course. On the instrument, far below, which checked the globe's new course the mistake was not noted.

The screen of the ship spiraling toward Topaz registered a path which would bring it into violent contact with the globe. They were still some hundreds of miles apart when the alarm rang. The pilot's hand clawed out at the bank of controls; under the almost intolerable pressure of their descent, there was so little he could do. His crooked fingers fell back powerlessly from the buttons and levers; his mouth was a twisted grimace of bleak acceptance as the beat of the signal increased.

One of the passengers forced his head around on the padded rest, fought to form words, to speak to his companion. The other was staring ahead at the screen, his thick lips wide and flat against his teeth in a snarl of rage.

"They …are …here.…"

Ruthven paid no attention to the obvious as stated by his fellow scientist. His fury was a red, pulsing thing inside him, fed by his own helplessness. To be pinned here so near his goal, fastened up as a target for an inanimate but cunningly fashioned weapon, ate into him like a stream of deadly acid. His big gamble would puff out in a blast of fire to light up Topaz's sky, with nothing left-nothing. On the armrest of his sling-seat his nails scratched deep.

The four men in the control cabin could only sit and watch, waiting for the rendezvous which would blot them out. Ruthven's flaming anger was a futile blaze. His companion in the passenger seat had closed his eyes, his lips moving soundlessly in an expression of his own scattered thoughts. The pilot and his assistant divided their attention between the screen, with its appalling message, and the controls they could not effectively use, feverishly seeking a way out in these last moments.

Below them in the bowl of the ship were those who would not know the end consciously-save in one compartment. In a padded cage a prick-eared head stirred where it rested on forepaws, slitted eyes blinked, aware not only of familiar surroundings, but also of the tension and fear generated by human minds and emotions levels above. A pointed nose raised, and there was a growling deep in a throat covered with thick buff-gray hair.

The growl aroused another similar captive. Knowing yellow eyes met yellow eyes. An intelligence, which was certainly not that of the animal body which contained it, fought down instinct raging to send both those bodies hurtling at the fastenings of the twin cages. Curiosity and the ability to adapt had been bred into both from time immemorial. Then something else had been added to sly and cunning brains. A step up had been taken-to weld intelligence to cunning, connect thought to instinct.

More than a generation earlier mankind had chosen barren desert-the "white sands" of New Mexico-as a testing ground for atomic experiments. Humankind could be barred, warded out of the radiation limits; the natural desert dwellers, four-footed and winged, could not be so controlled.

For thousands of years, since the first southward roving Amerindian tribes had met with their kind, there had been a hunter of the open country, a smaller cousin of the wolf, whose natural abilities had made an undeniable impression on the human mind. He was in countless Indian legends as the Shaper or the Trickster, sometimes friend, sometimes enemy. Godling for some tribes, father of all evil for others. In the wealth of tales the coyote, above all other animals, had a firm place.

Driven by the press of civilization into the badlands and deserts, fought with poison, gun, and trap, the coyote had survived, adapting to new ways with all his legendary cunning. Those who had reviled him as vermin had unwillingly added to the folklore which surrounded him, telling their own tales of robbed traps, skillful escapes. He continued to be a trickster, laughing on moonlit nights from the tops of ridges at those who would hunt him down.

Then, close to the end of the twentieth century, when myths were scoffed at, the stories of the coyote's slyness began once more on a fantastic scale. And finally scientists were sufficiently intrigued to seek out this creature that seemed to display in truth all the abilities credited to his immortal namesake by pre-Columbian tribes.

What they discovered was indeed shattering to certain closed minds. For the coyote had not only adapted to the country of the white sands; he had evolved into something which could not be dismissed as an animal, clever and cunning, but limited to beast range. Six cubs had been brought back on the first expedition, coyote in body, their developing minds different. The grandchildren of those cubs were now in the ship's cages, their mutated senses alert, ready for the slightest chance of escape. Sent to Topaz as eyes and ears for less keenly endowed humans, they were not completely under the domination of man. The range of their mental powers was still uncomprehended by those who had bred, trained, and worked with them from the days their eyes had opened and they had taken their first wobbly steps away from their dams.

The male growled again, his lips wrinkling back in a snarl as the emanations of fear from the men he could not see reached panic peak. He still crouched, belly flat, on the protecting pads of his cage; but he strove now to wriggle closer to the door, just as his mate made the same effort.

Between the animals and those in the control cabin lay the others-forty of them. Their bodies were cushioned and protected with every ingenious device known to those who had placed them there so many weeks earlier. Their minds were free of the ship, roving into places where men had not trod before, a territory potentially more dangerous than any solid earth could ever be.

Operation Retrograde had returned men bodily into the past, sending agents to hunt mammoths, follow the roads of the Bronze Age traders, ride with Attila and Genghis Khan, pull bows among the archers of ancient Egypt. But Redax returned men in mind to the paths of their ancestors, or this was the theory. And those who slept here and now in their narrow boxes, lay under its government, while the men who had arbitrarily set them so could only assume they were actually reliving the lives of Apache nomads in the wide southwestern wastes of the late eighteenth and early nineteenth centuries.

Above, the pilot's hand pushed out again, fighting the pressure to reach one particular button. That, too, had been a last-minute addition, an experiment which had only had partial testing. To use it was the final move he could make, and he was already half convinced of its uselessness.

With no faith and only a very wan hope, he sent that round of metal flush with the board. What followed no one ever lived to explain.

On the planet the installation which tracked the missiles flashed on a screen bright enough to blind momentarily the duty man on watch, and its tracker was shaken off course. When it jiggled back into line it was no longer the efficient eye-in-the-sky it had been, though its tenders were not to realize that for an important minute or two.

While the ship, now out of control, sped in dizzy whirls toward Topaz, engines fought blindly to stabilize, to re-establish their functions. Some succeeded, some wobbled in and out of the danger zone, two failed. And in the control cabin three dead men spun in prisoning seats.

Dr. James Ruthven, blood bubbling from his lips with every shallow breath he could draw, fought the stealthy tide of blackness which crept up his brain, his stubborn will holding to rags of consciousness, refusing to acknowledge the pain of his fatally injured body.

The orbiting ship was on an erratic path. Slowly the machines were correcting, relays clicking, striving to bring it to a landing under auto-pilot. All the ingenuity built into a mechanical brain was now centered in landing the globe.

It was not a good landing, in fact a very bad one, for the sphere touched a mountain side, scraped down rocks, shearing away a portion of its outer bulk. But the mountain barrier was now between it and the base from which the missiles had been launched, and the crash had not been recorded on that tracking instrument. So far as the watchers several hundred miles away knew, the warden in the sky had performed as promised. Their first line of defense had proven satisfactory, and there had been no unauthorized landing on Topaz.

In the wreckage of the control cabin Ruthven pawed at the fastenings of his sling-chair. He no longer tried to suppress the moans every effort tore out of him. Time held the whip, drove him. He rolled from his seat to the floor, lay there gasping, as again he fought doggedly to remain above the waves-those frightening, fast-coming waves of dark faintness.

Somehow he was crawling, crawling along a tilted surface until he gained the well where the ladder to the lower section hung, now at an acute angle. It was that angle which helped him to the next level.

He was too dazed to realize the meaning of the crumpled bulkheads. There was a spur of bare rock under his hands as he edged over and around twisted metal. The moans were now a gobbling, burbling, almost continuous cry as he reached his goal —a small cabin still intact.

For long moments of anguish he paused by the chair there, afraid that he could not make the last effort, raise his almost inert bulk up to the point where he could reach the Redax release. For a second of unusual clarity he wondered if there was any reason for this supreme ordeal, whether any of the sleepers could be aroused. This might now be a ship of the dead.

His right hand, his arm, and finally his bulk over the seat, he braced himself and brought his left hand up. He could not use any of the fingers; it was like lifting numb, heavy weights. But he lurched forward, swept the unfeeling lump of cold flesh down against the release in a gesture which he knew must be his final move. And, as he fell back to the floor, Dr. Ruthven could not be certain whether he had succeeded or failed. He tried to screw his head around, to focus his eyes upward at that switch. Was it down or still stubbornly up, locking the sleepers into confinement? But there was a fog between; he could not see it-or anything.

The light in the cabin flickered, was gone as another circuit in the broken ship failed. It was dark, too, in the small cubby below which housed the two cages. Chance, which had snuffed out nineteen lives in the space globe, had missed ripping open that cabin on the mountain side. Five yards down the corridor the outside fabric of the ship was split wide open, the crisp air native to Topaz entering, sending a message to two keen noses through the combination of odors now pervading the wreckage.

And the male coyote went into action. Days ago he had managed to work loose the lower end of the mesh which fronted his cage, but his mind had told him that a sortie inside the ship was valueless. The odd rapport he'd had with the human brains, unknown to them, had operated to keep him to the old role of cunning deception, which in the past had saved countless of his species from sudden and violent death. Now with teeth and paws he went diligently to work, urged on by the whines of his mate, that tantalizing smell of an outside world tickling their nostrils —a wild world, lacking the taint of man-places.

He slipped under the loosened mesh and stood up to paw at the front of the female's cage. One forepaw caught in the latch and pressed it down, and the weight of the door swung against him. Together they were free now to reach the corridor and see ahead the subdued light of a strange moon beckoning them on into the open.

The female, always more cautious than her mate, lingered behind as he trotted forward, his ears a-prick with curiosity. Their training had been the same since cubhood-to range and explore, but always in the company and at the order of man. This was not according to the pattern she knew, and she was suspicious. But to her sensitive nose the smell of the ship was an offense, and the puffs of breeze from without enticing. Her mate had already slipped through the break; now he barked with excitement and wonder, and she trotted on to join him.

Above, the Redax, which had never been intended to stand rough usage, proved to be a better survivor of the crash than most of the other installations. Power purred along a network of lines, activated beams, turned off and on a series of fixtures in those coffin-beds. For five of the sleepers-nothing. The cabin which had held them was a flattened smear against the mountain side. Three more half aroused, choked, fought for life and breath in a darkness which was a mercifully short nightmare, and succumbed.

But in the cabin nearest the rent through which the coyotes had escaped, a young man sat up abruptly, looking into the dark with wide-open, terror-haunted eyes. He clawed for purchase against the smooth edge of the box in which he had lain, somehow got to his knees, weaving weakly back and forth, and half fell, half pushed to the floor where he could stand only by keeping his hold on the box.

Dazed, sick, weak, he swayed there, aware only of himself and his own sensations. There were small sounds in the dark, a stilled moan, a gasping sigh. But that meant nothing. Within him grew a compulsion to be out of this place, his terror making him lurch forward.

His flailing hand rapped painfully against an upright surface which his questing fingers identified hazily as an exit. Unconsciously he fumbled along the surface of the door until it gave under that weak pressure. Then he was out, his head swimming, drawn by the light behind the wall rent.

He progressed toward that in a scrambling crawl, making his way over the splintered skin of the globe. Then he dropped with a jarring thud onto the mound of earth the ship had pushed before it during its downward slide. Limply he tumbled on in a small cascade of clods and sand, hitting against a less movable rock with force enough to roll him over on his back and stun him again.

The second and smaller moon of Topaz swung brightly through the sky, its weird green rays making the blood-streaked face of the explorer an alien mask. It had passed well on to the horizon, and its large yellow companion had risen when a yapping broke the small sounds of the night.

As the *yipp, yipp, yipp* arose in a crescendo, the man stirred, putting one hand to his head. His eyes opened, he looked vaguely about him and sat up. Behind him was the torn and ripped ship, but he did not look back at it.

Instead, he got to his feet and staggered out into the direct path of the moonlight. Inside his brain there was a whirl of thoughts, memories, emotions. Perhaps Ruthven or one of his assistants could have explained that chaotic mixture for what it was. But for all practical purposes Travis Fox-Amerindian Time Agent, member of Team A, Operation Cochise-was far less of a thinking animal now than the two coyotes paying their ritual addresses to a moon which was not the one of their vanished homeland.

Travis wavered on, drawn somehow by that howling. It was familiar, a thread of something real through all the broken clutter in his head. He stumbled, fell, crawled up again, but he kept on.

Above, the female coyote lowered her head, drew a test sniff of a new scent. She recognized that as part of the proper way of life. She yapped once at her mate, but he was absorbed in his night song, his muzzle pointed moonward as he voiced a fine wailing.

Travis tripped, pitched forward on his hands and knees, and felt the jar of such a landing shoot up his stiffened forearms. He tried to get up, but his body only twisted, so he landed on his back and lay looking up at the moon.

A strong, familiar odor ... then a shadow looming above him. Hot breath against his cheek, and the swift sweep of an animal tongue on his face. He flung up his hand, gripped thick fur, and held on as if he had found one anchor of sanity in a world gone completely mad.

3

Travis, one knee braced against the red earth, blinked as he parted a screen of tall rust-brown grass with cautious fingers to look out into a valley where golden mist clouded most of the landscape. His head ached with dull persistence, the pain fostered in some way by his own bewilderment. To study the land ahead was like trying to see through one picture interposed over another and far different one. He knew what ought to be there, but what was before him was very dissimilar.

A buff-gray shape flitted through the tall cover grass, and Travis tensed. *Mba'a*—coyote? Or were these companions of his actually *ga-n*, spirits who could choose their shape at will and had, oddly, this time assumed the bodies of man's tricky enemy? Were they *ndendai*—enemies-or *dalaanbiyat'i*, allies? In this mad world he did not know.

Ei'dik'e? His mind formed a word he did not speak: Friend?

Yellow eyes met his directly. Dimly he had been aware, ever since awaking in this strange wilderness with the coming of morning light, that the four-footed ones trotting with him as he walked aimlessly had unbeastlike traits. Not only did they face him eye-to-eye, but in some ways they appeared able to read his thoughts.

He had longed for water to ease the burning in his throat, the ever-present pain in his head, and the creatures had nudged him in another direction, bringing him to a pool where he had mouthed liquid with a strange sweet, but not unpleasant taste.

Now he had given them names, names which had come out of the welter of dreams which shadowed his stumbling journey across this weird country.

Nalik'ideyu (Maiden-Who-Walks-Ridges) was the female who continued to shepherd him along, never venturing too far from his side. Naginlta (He-Who-Scouts-Ahead) was the male who did just that, disappearing at long intervals and then returning to face the man and his mate as if conveying some report necessary to their journey.

It was Nalik'ideyu who sought out Travis now, her red tongue lolling from her mouth as she panted. Not from exertion, he was certain of that. No, she was excited and eager ... on the hunt! That was it—a hunt!

Travis' own tongue ran across his lips as an impression hit him with feral force. There was meat-rich, fresh-just ahead. Meat that lived, waiting to be killed. Inside him his own avid hunger roused, shaking him farther out of the crusting dream.

His hands went to his waist, but the groping fingers did not find what vague memory told him should be there—a belt, heavy with knife in sheath.

He examined his own body with attention to find he was adequately covered by breeches of a smooth, dull brown material which blended well with the vegetation about him. He wore a loose shirt, belted in at the narrow waist by a folded strip of cloth, the ends of which fluttered free. On his feet were tall moccasins, the leg pieces extending some distance up his calves, the toes turned up in rounded points.

Some of this he found familiar, but these were fragments of memory; again his mind fitted one picture above another. One thing he did know for sure-he had no weapons. And that realization struck home with a thrust of real and terrible fear which tore away more of the bewilderment cloaking his mind.

Nalik'ideyu was impatient. Having advanced a step or two, she now looked back at him over her shoulder, yellow eyes slitted, her demand on him as instant and real as if she had voiced understandable words. Meat was waiting, and she was hungry. Also she expected Travis to aid in the hunt-at once.

Though he could not match her fluid grace in moving through the grass, Travis followed her, keeping to cover. He shook his head vigorously, in spite of the stab of pain the motion cost him, and paid more attention to his surroundings. It was apparent that the earth under him, the grass around, the valley of the golden haze, were all real, not part of a dream. Therefore that other countryside which he kept seeing in a ghostly fashion was a hallucination.

Even the air which he drew into his lungs and expelled again, had a strange smell, or was it taste? He could not be sure which. He knew that hypno-training could produce queer side effects, but ... this....

Travis paused, staring unseeingly before him at the grass still waving from the coyote's passage. Hypno-training! What was that? Now three pictures fought to focus in his mind: the two landscapes which did not match and a shadowy third. He shook his head again, his hands to his temples. This-this only was real: the ground, the grass, the valley, the hunger in him, the hunt waiting....

He forced himself to concentrate on the immediate present and the portion of world he could see, feel, scent, which lay here and now about him.

The grass grew shorter as he proceeded in Nalik'ideyu's wake. But the haze was not thinning. It seemed to hang in patches, and when he ventured through the edge of a patch it was like creeping through a fog of golden, dancing motes with here and there a glittering speck whirling and darting like a living thing. Masked by the stuff, Travis reached a line of brush and sniffed.

It was a warm scent, a heavy odor he could not identify and yet one he associated with a living creature. Flat to earth, he pushed head and shoulders under the low limbs of the bush to look ahead.

Here was a space where the fog did not hold, a pocket of earth clear under the morning sun. And grazing there were three animals. Again shock cleared a portion of Travis' bemused brain.

They were about the size, he thought, of antelopes, and they had a general resemblance to those beasts in that they had four slender legs, a rounded body, and a head. But they had alien features, so alien as to hold him in open-mouthed amazement.

The bodies had bare spots here and there, and patches of creamy-fur? Or was it hair which hung in strips, as if the creatures had been partially plucked in a careless fashion? The necks were long and moved about in a serpentine motion, as though their spines were as limber as reptiles'. On the end of those long and twisting necks were heads which also appeared more suitable to another species-broad, rather flat, with a singular toadlike look-but furnished with horns set halfway down the nose, horns which began in a single root and then branched into two sharp points.

They were unearthly! Again Travis blinked, brought his hand up to his head as he continued to view the browsers. There were three of them: two larger and with horns, the other a smaller beast with less of the ragged fur and only the beginning button of a protuberance on the nose; it was probably a calf.

One of those mental alerts from the coyotes broke his absorption. Nalik'ideyu was not interested in the odd appearance of the grazing creatures; she was intent upon their usefulness in another way-as a full and satisfying meal-and she was again impatient with him for his dull response.

His examination took a more practical turn. An antelope's defense was speed, though it could be tricked into hunting range through its inordinate curiosity. The slender legs of these beasts suggested a like degree of speed, and Travis had no weapons at all.

Those nose horns had an ugly look; this thing might be a fighter rather than a runner. But the suggestion which had flashed from coyote to him had taken root. Travis was hungry, he was a hunter, and here was meat on the hoof, queer as it looked.

Again he received a message. Naginlta was on the opposite side of the clearing. If the creatures depended on speed, then Travis believed they could probably outrun not only him but the coyotes as well-which left cunning and some sort of plan.

Travis glanced at the cover where he knew Nalik'ideyu crouched and from which had come that flash of agreement. He shivered. These were truly no animals, but *ga-n*, *ga-n* of power! And as *ga-n* he must treat them, accede to their will. Spurred by that, the Apache gave only flicks of attention to the browsers while at the same time he studied the part of the landscape uncovered by mist.

Without weapons or speed, they must conceive a trap. Again Travis sensed that agreement which was *ga-n* magic, and with it the strong impression urging him to the right. He was making progress with skill he did not even recognize and which he had never been conscious of learning.

The bushes and small, droop-limbed trees, their branches not clothed with leaves from proper twigs but with a reddish bristly growth protruding directly from their surfaces, made a partial wall for the pocket-sized meadow. That screen reached a rocky cleft where the mist curled in a long tongue through a wall twice Travis' height. If the browsers could be maneuvered into taking the path through that cleft....

Travis searched about him, and his hands closed upon the oldest weapon of his species, a stone pulled from an earth pocket and balanced neatly in the palm of his hand. It was a long chance but his best one.

The Apache took the first step on a new and fearsome road. These *ga-n* had put their thoughts-or their desires-into his mind. Could he so contact them in return?

With the stone clenched in his fist, his shoulders back against the wall not too far from the cleft opening, Travis strove to think out, clearly and simply, this poor plan of his. He did not know that he was reacting the way scientists deep space away had hoped he might. Nor did Travis guess that at this point he had already traveled far beyond the expectations of the men who had bred and trained the two mutant coyotes. He only believed that this might be the one way he could obey the wishes of the two spirits he thought far more powerful than any man. So he pictured in his mind the cleft, the running creatures, and the part the *ga-n* could play if they so willed.

Assent-in its way as loud and clear as if shouted. The man fingered the stone, weighed it. There would probably be just one moment when he could use it to effect, and he must be ready.

From this point he could no longer see the small meadow where the grazers were. But Travis knew, as well as if he watched the scene, that the coyotes were creeping in, belly flat to earth, adding a feline stealth and patience to their own cunning.

There! Travis' head jerked, the alert had come, the drive was beginning. He tensed, gripping his stone.

A yapping bark was answered by a sound he could not describe, a noise which was neither cough nor grunt but a combination of both. Again a yap-yap....

A toad-head burst through the screen of brush, the double horn on its nose festooned with a length of grass torn up by the roots. Wide eyes-milky and seeming to be without pupils-fastened on Travis, but he could not be sure the thing saw him, for it kept on, picking up speed as it approached the cleft. Behind it ran the calf, and that guttural cry was bubbling from its broad flat lips.

The long neck of the adult writhed, the frog-head swung closer to the ground so that the twin points of the horn were at a slant-aimed now at Travis. He had been right in his guess at their deadliness, but he had only a fleeting chance to recognize that fact as the thing bore down, its whole attitude expressing the firm intention of goring him.

He hurled his stone and then flung his body to one side, stumbling and rolling into the brush where he fought madly to regain his feet, expecting at any moment to feel trampling hoofs and thrusting horns. There was a crash to his right, and the bushes and grass were wildly shaken.

On his hands and knees the Apache retreated, his head turned to watch behind him. He saw the flirt of a triangular flap-tail in the mouth of the cleft. The calf had escaped. And now the threshing in the bushes stilled.

Was the thing stalking him? He got to his feet, for the first time hearing clearly the continued yapping, as if a battle was in progress. Then the second of the adult beasts came into view, backing and turning, trying to keep lowered head with menacing double horn always pointed to the coyotes dancing a teasing, worrying circle about it.

One of the coyotes flung up its head, looked upslope, and barked. Then, as one, both rushed the fighting beast, but for the first time from the same side, leaving it a clear path to retreat. It made a rush before which they fled easily, and then it whirled with a speed and grace, which did not fit its ungainly, ill-proportioned body, and jumped toward the cleft, the coyotes making no effort to hinder its escape.

Travis came out of cover, approaching the brush which had concealed the crash of the other animal. The actions of the coyotes had convinced him that there was no danger now; they would never have allowed the escape of their prey had the first beast not been in difficulties.

His shot with the stone, the Apache decided as he stood moments later surveying the twitching crumpled body, must have hit the thing in the head, stunning it. Then the momentum of its charge had carried it full force against the rock to kill it. Blind luck-or the power of the *ga-n*? He pulled back as the coyotes came padding up shoulder to shoulder to inspect the kill. It was truly more theirs than his.

Their prey yielded not only food but a weapon for Travis. Instead of the belt knife he had remembered having, he was now equipped with two. The double horn had been easy to free from the shattered skull, and some careful work with stones had broken off one prong at just the angle he wanted. So now he had a short and a longer tool, defense. At least they were better than the stone with which he had entered the hunt.

Nalik'ideyu pushed past him to lap daintily at the water. Then she sat up on her haunches, watching Travis as he smoothed the horn with a stone.

"A knife," he said to her, "this will be a knife. And —" he glanced up, measuring the value of the wood represented by trees and bushes —"then a bow. With a bow we shall hunt better."

The coyote yawned, her yellow eyes half closed, her whole pose one of satisfaction and contentment.

"A knife," Travis repeated, "and a bow." He needed weapons; he had to have them!

Why? His hand stopped scraping. Why? The toad-faced double horn had been quick to attack, but Travis could have avoided it, and it had not hunted him first. Why was he ridden by this fear that he must not be unarmed?

He dipped his hand into the pool of the spring and lifted the water to cool his sweating face. The coyote moved, turned around in the grass, crushing down the growth into a nest in which she curled up, head on paws. But Travis sat back on his heels, his now idle hands hanging down between his knees, and forced himself to the task of sorting out jumbled memories.

This landscape was wrong-totally unlike what it should be-but it was real. He had helped kill this alien creature. He had eaten its meat, raw. Its horn lay within touch now. All that was real and unchangeable. Which meant that the rest of it, that other desert world in which he had wandered with his kind, ridden horses, raided invading men of another race, that was not real-or else far, far removed from where he now sat.

Yet there had been no dividing line between those two worlds. One moment he had been in the desert place, returning from a successful foray against the Mexicans. Mexicans! Travis caught at that identification, tried to use it as a thread to draw closer to the beginning of his mystery.

Mexicans....And he was an Apache, one of the Eagle people, one who rode with Cochise. No!

Sweat again beaded his face where the water had cooled it. He was not of that past. He was Travis Fox, of the very late twentieth century, not a nomad of the middle nineteenth! He was of Team A of the project!

The Arizona desert and then this! From one to the other in an instant. He looked about him in rising fear. Wait! He had been in the dark when he got out of the desert, lying in a box. Getting out, he had crawled down a passage to reach moonlight, strange moonlight.

A box in which he had lain, a passage with smooth metallic walls, and an alien world at the end of it.

The coyote's ears twitched, her head came up, she was staring at the man's drawn face, at his eyes with their core of fear. She whined.

Travis caught up the two pieces of horn, thrust them into his sash belt, and got to his feet. Nalik'ideyu sat up, her head cocked a little to one side. As the man turned to seek his own back trail she padded along in his wake and whined for Naginlta. But Travis was more intent now on what he must prove to himself than he was on the actions of the two animals.

It was a wandering trail, and now he did not question his skill in being able to follow it so unerringly. The sun was hot. Winged things buzzed from the bushes, small scuttling things fled from him through the tall grass. Once Naginlta growled a warning which led them all to a detour, and Travis might not have picked up the proper trace again had not the coyote scout led him to it.

"Who are you?" he asked once, and then guessed it would have better been said, "What are you?" These were not animals, or rather they were more than the animals he had always known. And one part of him, the part which remembered the desert rancherias where Cochise had ruled, said they were spirits. Yet that other part of him.... Travis shook his head, accepting them now for what they were-welcome company in an alien place.

The day wore on close to sunset, and still Travis followed that wandering trail. The need which drove him kept him going through the rough country of hills and ravines. Now the mist lifted above towering walls of mountains very near him, yet not the mountains of his memory. These were dull brown, with a forbidding look, like sun-dried skulls baring teeth in warning against all comers.

With great difficulty, Travis topped a rise. Ahead against the skyline stood both coyotes. And, as the man joined them, first one and then the other flung back its head and sounded the sobbing, shattering cry which had been a part of that other life.

The Apache looked down. His puzzle was answered in part. The wreckage crumpled on the mountain side was identifiable —a spaceship! Cold fear gripped him and his own head went back; from between his tight lips came a cry as desolate and despairing as the one the animals had voiced.

4

Fire, mankind's oldest ally, weapon, tool, leaped high before the naked stone of the mountain side. Men sat cross-legged about it, fifteen of them. And behind, guarded by the flames and that somber circle, were the women. There was a uniformity in this gathering. The members were plainly all of the same racial stock, of medium height, stocky yet fined down to the peak of stamina and endurance, their skin brown, their shoulder-length hair black. And they were all young-none over thirty, some still in their late teens. Alike, too, was a certain drawn look in their faces, a tenseness of the eyes and mouth as they listened to Travis.

"So we must be on Topaz. Do any of you remember boarding the ship?"

"No. Only that we awoke within it." Across the fire one chin lifted; the eyes which caught Travis' held a deep, smoldering anger. "This is more trickery of the Pinda-lick-o-yi, the White Eyes. Between us there has never been fair dealing. They have broken their promise as a man breaks a rotten stick, for their words are as rotten. And it was you, Fox, who brought us to listen to them."

A stir about the circle, a murmur from the women.

"And do I not also sit here with you in this strange wilderness?" he countered.

"I do not understand," another of the men held out his hand, palm up, in a gesture of asking —"what has happened to us. We were in the old Apache world....I, Jil-Lee, was riding with Cuchillo Negro as we went down to the taking of Ramos. And then I was here, in a broken ship and beside me a dead man who was once my brother. How did I come out of the past of our people into another world across the stars?"

"Pinda-lick-o-yi tricks!" The first speaker spat into the fire.

"It was the Redax, I think," Travis replied. "I heard Dr. Ashe discuss this. A new machine which could make a man remember not his own past, but the past of his ancestors. While we were on that ship we must have been under its influence, so we lived as our people lived a hundred years or more ago —"

"And the purpose of such a thing?" Jil-Lee asked.

"To make us more like our ancestors perhaps. It is part of what they told us at the project. To venture into these new worlds requires a different type of man than lives on Terra today. Traits we have forgotten are needed to face the dangers of wild places."

"You, Fox, have been beyond the stars before, and you found there were such dangers to face?"

"It is true. You have heard of the three worlds I saw when the ship from the old days took us off, unwilling, to the stars. Did you not all volunteer to pioneer in this manner so you could also see strange and new things?"

"But we did not agree to be returned to the past in medicine dreams and be sent unknowingly into space!"

Travis nodded. "Deklay is right. But I know no more than you why we were so sent, or why the ship crashed. We have found Dr. Ruthven's body in the cabin with that new installation. Only we have discovered nothing else which tells us why we were brought here. With the ship broken, we must stay."

They were silent now, men and women alike. Behind them lay several days of activity, nights of exhausted slumber. Against the cliff wall lay the packs of supplies they had salvaged from the wreck. By mutual consent they had left the vicinity of the broken globe, following their old custom of speedily withdrawing from a place of death.

"This is a world empty of men?" Jil-Lee wanted to know.

"So far we have found only animal signs, and the *ga-n* have not warned us of anything else — —"

"Those devil ones!" Again Deklay spat into the fire. "I say we should have no dealings with them. The *mba'a* is no friend to the People."

Again a murmur which seemed one of agreement answered that outburst. Travis stiffened. Just how much influence had the Redax had over them? He knew from his own experience that sometimes he had an odd double reaction-two different feelings which almost sickened him when they struck simultaneously. And he was beginning to suspect that with some of the others the return to the past had been far more deep and lasting. Now Jil-Lee was actually to reason out what had happened. While Deklay had reverted to an ancestor who had ridden with Victorio or Magnus Colorado! Travis had a flash of premonition, a chill which made him half foresee a time when the past and the present might well split them apart-fatally.

"Devil or *ga-n*." A man with a quiet face, rather deeply sunken eyes, spoke for the first time. "We are in two minds because of this Redax, so let us not do anything in haste. Back in the desert world of the People I have seen the *mba'a*, and he was very clever. With the badger he went hunting, and when the badger had dug up the rat's nest, so did the *mba'a* wait on the other side of the thorny bush and catch those who would escape that way. Between him and the badger there was no war. These two who sit over yonder now-they are also hunters and they seem friendly to us. In a strange place a man needs all the help he can find. Let us not call names out of old tales, which may mean nothing in fact."

"Buck speaks straightly," Jil-Lee agreed. "We seek a camp which can be defended. For perhaps there are men here whose hunting territory we have invaded, though we have not yet seen them. We are a people small in number and alone. Let us walk softly on trails which are strange to our feet."

Inwardly Travis sighed in relief. Buck, Jil-Lee ... for the moment their sensible words appeared to swing the opinions of the party. If either of them could be established as *haldzil*, or clan leader, they would all be safer. He himself had no aspirations in that direction and dared not push too hard. It had been his initial urging which had brought them as volunteers into the project. Now he was doubly suspect, and especially by those who thought as Deklay, he was considered too alien to their old ways.

So far their protests had been fewer than he anticipated. Although brothers and sisters had followed each other into the team after the immemorial desire of Apaches to cling to family ties, they were not a true clan with solidity of that to back them, but representatives of half a dozen.

Basically, back on Terra, they had all been among the most progressive of their people-progressive, that is, in the white man's sense of the word. Travis had a fleeting recognition of his now oblique way of thinking. He, too, had been marked by the Redax. They had all been educated in the modern fashion and all possessed a spirit of adventure which marked them over their fellows. They had volunteered for the team and successfully passed the tests to weed out the temperamentally unfit or fainthearted. But all that was before Redax....

Why had they been submitted to that? And why this flight? What had pushed Dr. Ashe and Murdock and Colonel Kelgarries, time agents he knew and trusted, into dispatching them without warning to Topaz? Something had happened, something which had given Dr. Ruthven ascendancy over those others and had started them on this wild trip.

Travis was conscious of a stir about the firelit circle. The men were rising, moving back into the shadows, stretching out on the blankets they had found among other stores on the ship. They had discovered weapons there-knives, bows, quivers of arrows, all of which they had been trained to use in the intensive schooling of the project and which needed no more repair than they themselves could give. And the rations they carried were field supplies, few of them. Tomorrow they must begin hunting in earnest....

"Why has this thing been done to us?" Buck was beside Travis, those quiet eyes sliding past him to seek the fire once more. "I do not think you were told when the rest of us were not — —"

Travis seized upon that. "There are those who say that I knew, agreed?"

"That is so. Once we stood at the same place in time-in our thoughts, our desires. Now we stand at many places, as if we climbed a stairway, each at his own speed —a stairway the Pinda-lick-o-yi has set us upon. Some here, some there, some yet farther above...." He sketched a series of step outlines in the air. "And in this there is trouble —"

"The truth," Travis agreed. "Yet it is also true that I knew nothing of this, that I climb with you on these stairs."

"So I believe. But there comes a time when it is best not to be a woman stirring a pot of boiling stew but rather one who stands quietly at a distance —"

"You mean?" Travis pressed.

"I say that alone among us you have crossed the stars before, therefore new things are not so hard to understand. And we need a scout. Also the coyotes run in your footsteps, and you do not fear them."

It made good sense. Let him scout ahead of the party, taking the coyotes with him. Stay away from the camp for a while and speak small-until the people on Buck's stairway were more closely united.

"I go in the morning," Travis agreed. He could slip away tonight, but just now he could not force himself away from the fire, from the companionship.

"You might take Tsoay with you," Buck continued.

Travis waited for him to enlarge on that suggestion. Tsoay was one of the youngest of their group, Buck's own cross-cousin and near-brother.

"It is well," Buck explained, "that we learn this land, and it has always been our custom that the younger walk in the footprints of the older. Also, not only should trails be learned, but also men."

Travis caught the thought behind that. Perhaps by taking the younger men as scouts, one after another, he could build up among them a following of sorts. Among the Apaches, leadership was wholly a matter of personality. Until the reservation days, chieftains had gained their position by force of character alone, though they might come successively from one family clan over several generations.

He did not want the chieftainship here. No, but neither did he want growing whispers working about him to cut him off from his people. To every Apache severance from the clan was a little death. He must have those who would back him if Deklay, or those who thought like Deklay, turned grumbling into open hostility.

"Tsoay is one quick to learn," Travis agreed. "We go at dawn —"

"Along the mountain range?" Buck inquired.

"If we seek a protected place for the rancheria, yes. The mountains have always provided good strongholds for the People."

"And you think there is need for a fort?"

Travis shrugged. "I have been one day's journey out into this world. I saw nothing but animals. But that is no promise that elsewhere there are no enemies. The planet was on the tapes we brought back from that other world, and so it was known to the others who once rode between star and star as we rode between ranch and town. If they had this world set on a journey tape, it was for a reason; that reason may still be in force."

"Yet it was long ago that these star people rode so...." Buck mused. "Would the reason last so long?"

Travis remembered two other worlds, one of weird desert inhabited by beast things-or had they once been human, human to the point of possessing intelligence? —that had come out of sand burrows at night to attack a spaceship. And the second world where the ruins of a giant city had stood choked with jungle vegetation, where he had made a blowgun from tubes of rustless metal as a weapon gift for small winged men-but were they men? Both had been remnants of that ancient galactic empire.

"Some things could so remain," he answered soberly. "If we find them, we must be careful. But first a good site for the rancheria."

"There is no return to home for us," Buck stated flatly.

"Why do you say that? There could be a rescue ship later —"

The other raised his eyes again to Travis. "When you slept under the Redax how did you ride?"

"As a warrior-raiding ... living...."

"And I —I was one with *go'ndi*," Buck returned simply.

"But —"

"But the white man has assured us that such power-the power of a chief-does not exist? Yes, the Pinda-lick-o-yi has told us so many things. He is busy, busy with his tools, his machines, always busy. And those who think in another fashion cannot be measured by his rules, so they are foolish dreamers. Not all white men think so. There was Dr. Ashe-he was beginning to understand a little.

"Perhaps I, too, am standing still, halfway up the stairway of the past. But of this I am very sure: For us, there will be no return to our own place. And the time will come when something new shall grow from the seed of the past. Also it is necessary that you be one of the tenders of that growth. So I urge you, take Tsoay, and the next time, Lupe. For the young who may be swayed this way and that by words-as the wind shakes a small tree-must be given firm roots."

In Travis education warred with instinct, just as the picture Redax had planted in his mind had warred with his awaking to this alien landscape. Yet now he believed he must be guided by what he felt. And he knew that no man of his race would claim *go'ndi*, the power of spirit known only to a great chief, unless he had actually felt it swell within him. It might have been fostered by hallucination in the past, but the aura of it carried into the here and now. And Travis had no doubts that Buck believed implicitly in what he said, and that belief carried credulity to others.

"This is wisdom, *Nantan* —"

Buck shook his head. "I am no *nantan*, no chief. But of some things I am sure. You also be sure of what lies within you, younger brother!"

On the third day, ranging eastward along the base of the mountain range, Travis found what he believed would be an acceptable camp site. There was a canyon with a good spring of water cut round by well-marked game trails. A series of ledges brought him up to a small plateau where scrub wood could be used to build the wickiups. Water and food lay within reach, and the ledge approach was easy to defend. Even Deklay and his fellow malcontents were forced to concede the value of the site.

His duty to the clan accomplished, Travis returned to his own concern, one which had haunted him for days. Topaz had been taped by men of the vanished star empire. Therefore, the planet was important, but why? As yet he had found no indication that anything above the intelligence level of the split horns was native to this world. But he was gnawed by the certainty that there *was* something here, waiting....And the desire to learn what it was became an ever-burning ache.

Perhaps he was what Deklay had accused him of being, one who had come to follow the road of the Pinda-lick-o-yi too closely. For Travis was content to scout with only the coyotes for company, and he did not find the loneliness of the unknown planet as intimidating as most of the others.

He was checking his small trail pack on the fourth day after they had settled on the plateau when Buck and Jil-Lee hunkered down beside him.

"You go to hunt —?" Buck broke the silence first.

"Not for meat."

"What do you fear? That *ndendai* —enemy people-have marked this as their land?" Jil-Lee questioned.

"That may be true, but now I hunt for what this world was at one time, the reason why the ancient star men marked it as their own."

"And this knowledge may be of value to us?" Jil-Lee asked slowly. "Will it bring food to our mouths, shelter for our bodies-mean life for us?"

"All that is possible. It is the unknowing which is bad."

"True. Unknowing is always bad," Buck agreed. "But the bow which is fitted to one hand and strength of arm, may not be suited to another. Remember that, younger brother. Also, do you go alone?"

"With Naginlta and Nalik'ideyu I am not alone."

"Take Tsoay with you also. The four-footed ones are indeed *ga-n* for the service of those they like, but it is not good that man walks alone from his kind."

There it was again, the feeling of clan solidarity which Travis did not always share. On the other hand, Tsoay would not be a hindrance. On other scouts the boy had proved to have a keen eye for the country and a liking for experimentation which was not a universal attribute even among those of his own age.

"I would go to find a path through the mountains; it may be a long trail," Travis half protested.

"You believe what you seek may lie to the north?"

Travis shrugged. "I do not know. How can I? But it will be another way of seeking."

"Tsoay shall go. He keeps silent before older warriors as is proper for the untried, but his thoughts fly free as do yours," Buck replied. "It is in him also, this need to see new places."

"There is this," Jil-Lee got to his feet, " —do not go so far, brother, that you may not easily find a way to return. This is a wide land, and within it we are but a handful of men alone — —"

"That, too, I know." Travis thought he could read more than one kind of warning in Jil-Lee's words.

* * * * *

They were the second day away from the plateau camp, and climbing, when they chanced upon the pass Travis had hoped might exist. Before them lay an abrupt descent to what appeared to be open plains country cloaked in a dusky amber Travis now knew was the thick grass found in the southern valleys. Tsoay pointed with his chin.

"Wide land-good for horses, cattle, ranches...."

But all those lay far beyond the black space surrounding them. Travis wondered if there was any native animal which could serve man in place of the horse.

"Do we go down?" Tsoay asked.

From this point Travis could sight no break far out on the amber plain, no sign of any building or any disturbance of its smooth emptiness. Yet it drew him. "We go," he decided.

Close as it had looked from the pass, the plain was yet a day and a night, spent in careful watching by turns, ahead of them. It was midmorning of the second day that they left the foothill breaks, and the grass of the open country was waist high about them. Travis could see it rippling where the coyotes threaded ahead. Then he was conscious of a persistent buzzing, a noise which irritated faintly until he was compelled to trace it to its source.

The grass had been trampled flat for an irregular patch, with a trail of broken stalks out of the heart of the plain. At one side was a buzzing, seething mass of glitter-winged insects which Travis already knew as carrion eaters. They arose reluctantly from their feast as he approached.

He drew a short breath which was close to a grunt of astounded recognition. What lay there was so impossible that he could not believe the evidence of his eyes. Tsoay gave a sharp exclamation, went down on one knee for a closer examination, then looked at Travis over his shoulder, his eyes wide, more than a trace of excitement in his voice.

"Horse dung-and fresh!"

5

"There was one horse, unshod but ridden. It came here from the plains and it had been ridden hard, going lame. There was a rest here, maybe shortly after dawn." Travis sorted out what they had learned by a careful examination of the ground.

Nalik'ideyu and Naginlta, Tsoay, watched and listened as if the coyotes as well as the boy could understand every word.

"There is that also —" Tsoay indicated the one trace left by the unknown rider, an impression blurred as if some attempt had been made to conceal it.

"Small and light, the rider is both. Also in fear, I think —"

"We follow?" Tsoay asked.

"We follow," Travis assented. He looked to the coyotes, and as he had learned to do, thought out his message. This trail was the one to be followed. When the rider was sighted they were to report back if the Apaches had not yet caught up.

There was no visible agreement; the coyotes simply vanished through the wall of grass.

"Then there are others here," Tsoay said as he and Travis began their return to the foothills. "Perhaps there was a second ship —"

"That horse," Travis said, shaking his head. "There was no provision in the project for the shipping of horses."

"Perhaps they have always been here."

"Not so. To each world its own species of beasts. But we shall know the truth when we look upon that horse-and its rider."

It was warmer this side of the mountains, and the heat of the plains beat at them. Travis thought that the horse might well be seeking water if allowed his head. Where did he come from? And why had his rider gone in haste and fear?

This was rough, broken country and the tired, limping horse seemed to have picked the easiest way through it, without any hindrance from the man with him. Travis spotted a soft patch of ground with a deep-set impression. This time there had been no attempt at erasure; the boot track was plain. The rider had dismounted and was leading the horse-yet he was moving swiftly.

They followed the tracks around the bend of a shallow cut and found Nalik'ideyu waiting for them. Between her forefeet was a bundle still covered with smears of soft earth, and behind her were drag marks from a hole under the overhang of a bush. The coyote had plainly just disinterred her find. Travis squatted down to examine it, using his eyes before his hands.

It was a bag made of hide, probably the hide of one of the split horns by its color and the scraps of long hair which had been left in a simple decorative fringe along the bottom. The sides had been laced together neatly by someone used to working in leather, the closing flap lashed down tightly with braided thong loops.

As the Apache leaned closer to it he could smell a mixture of odors-the hide itself, horse, wood smoke, and other scents-strange to him. He undid the fastenings and pulled out the contents.

There was a shirt, with long full sleeves, of a gray wool undyed from the sheep. Then a very bulky short jacket which, after fingering it doubtfully, Travis decided was made of felt. It was elaborately decorated with highly colorful embroidery, and there was no mistaking the design —a heavy antlered Terran deer in mortal combat with what might be a puma. It was bordered with a geometric pattern of beautiful, oddly familiar work. Travis smoothed it flat over his knee and tried to remember where he had seen its like before ...a book! An illustration in a book! But which book, when? Not recently, and it was not a pattern known to his own people.

Twisted into the interior of the jacket was a silklike scarf, clear, light blue-the blue of Terra's cloudless skies on certain days, so different from the yellow shield now hanging above them. A small case of leather, with silhouetted designs cut from hide and affixed to it, designs as intricate and complex as the embroidery on the jacket-art of a high standard. In the case a knife and spoon, the bowl and blade of dull metal, the handles of horn carved with horse heads, the tiny wide-open eyes set with glittering stones.

Personal possessions dear to the owner, so that when they must be abandoned for flight they were hidden with some hope of recovery. Travis slowly repacked them, trying to fold the garments into their original creases. He was still puzzled by those designs.

"Who?" Tsoay touched the edge of the jacket with one finger, his admiration for it plain to read.

"I don't know. But it is of our own world."

"That is a deer, though the horns are wrong," Tsoay agreed. "And the puma is very well done. The one who made this knows animals well."

Travis pushed the jacket back into the bag and laced it shut. But he did not return it to the hiding place. Instead, he made it a part of his own pack. If they did not succeed in running down the fugitive, he wanted an opportunity for closer study, a chance to remember just where he had seen that picture before.

The narrow valley where they had discovered the bag sloped upward, and there were signs that their quarry found the ground harder to cover. The second discard lay in open sight-again a leather bag which Nalik'ideyu sniffed and then began to lick eagerly, thrusting her nose into its flaccid interior.

Travis picked it up, finding it damp to the touch. It had an odd smell, like that of sour milk. He ran a finger around inside, brought it out wet; yet this was neither water bag nor canteen. And he was completely mystified when he turned it inside out, for though the inner surface was wet, the bag was empty. He offered it to the coyote, and she took it promptly.

Holding it firmly to the earth with her forepaws, she licked the surface, though Travis could see no deposit which might attract her. It was clear that the bag had once held some sort of food.

"Here they rested," Tsoay said. "Not too far ahead now —"

But now they were in the kind of country where a man could hide in order to check on his back trail. Travis studied the terrain and then made his own plans. They would leave the plainly marked trace of the fugitive, strike out upslope to the east and try to parallel the other's route. In that maze of rock outcrops and wood copses there was tricky going.

Nalik'ideyu gave a last lick to the bag as Travis signaled her. She regarded him, then turned her head to survey the country before them. At last she trotted on, her buff coat melting into the vegetation. With Naginlta she would scout the quarry and keep watch, leaving the men to take the longer way around.

Travis pulled off his shirt, folding it into a packet and tucking it beneath the folds of his sash-belt, just as his ancestors had always done before a fight. Then he cached his pack and Tsoay's. As they began the stiff climb they carried only their bows, the quivers slung on their shoulders, and the long-bladed knives. But they flitted like shadows and, like the coyotes, their red-brown bodies became indistinguishable against the bronze of the land.

They should be, Travis judged, not more than an hour away from sundown. And they had to locate the stranger before the dark closed in. His respect for their quarry had grown. The unknown might have been driven by fear, but he held to a good pace and headed intelligently for just the kind of country which would serve him best. If Travis could only remember where he had seen the like of that embroidery! It had a meaning which might be important now....

Tsoay slipped behind a wind-gnarled tree and disappeared. Travis stooped under a line of bush limbs. Both were working their way south, using the peak ahead as an agreed landmark, pausing at intervals to examine the landscape for any hint of a man and horse.

Travis squirmed snake fashion into an opening between two rock pillars and lay there, the westering sun hot on his bare shoulders and back, his chin propped on his forearm. In the band holding back his hair he had inserted some concealing tufts of wiry mountain grass, the ends of which drooped over his rugged features.

Only seconds earlier he had caught that fragmentary warning from one of the coyotes. What they sought was very close, it was right down there. Both animals were in ambush, awaiting orders. And what they found was familiar, another confirmation that the fugitive was Terran, not native to Topaz.

With searching eyes, Travis examined the site indicated by the coyotes. His respect for the stranger was raised another notch. In time either he or Tsoay might have sighted that hideaway without the aid of the animal scouts; on the other hand, they might have failed. For the fugitive had truly gone to earth, using some pocket or crevice in the mountain wall.

There was no sign of the horse, but a branch here and there had been pulled out of place, the scars of their removal readable when one knew where to look. Odd, Travis began to puzzle over what he saw. It was almost as if whatever pursuit the stranger feared would come not at ground level but from above; the precautions the stranger had taken were to veil his retreat to the reaches of the mountain side.

Had he expected any trailer to make a flanking move from up that slope where the Apaches now lay? Travis' teeth nipped the weathered skin of his forearm. Could it be that at some time during the day's journeying the fugitive had doubled back, having seen his trackers? But there had been no traces of any such scouting, and the coyotes would surely have warned them. Human eyes and ears could be tricked, but Travis trusted the senses of Naginlta and Nalik'ideyu far above his own.

No, he did not believe that the rider expected the Apaches. But the man did expect someone or something which would come upon him from the heights. The heights....Travis rolled his head slightly to look at the upper reaches of the hills about him-with suspicion.

In their own journey across the mountains and through the pass they had found nothing threatening. Dangerous animals might roam there. There had been some paw marks, one such trail the coyotes had warned against. But the type of precautions the stranger had taken were against intelligent, thinking beings, not against animals more likely to track by scent than by sight.

And if the stranger expected an attack from above, then Travis and Tsoay must be alert. Travis analyzed each feature of the hillside, setting in his mind a picture of every inch of ground they must cross. Just as he had wanted daylight as an ally before, so now was he willing to wait for the shadows of twilight.

He closed his eyes in a final check, able to recall the details of the hiding place, knowing that he could reach it when the conditions favored, without mistake. Then he edged back from his vantage point, and raising his fingers to his lips, made a small angry chittering, three times repeated. One of the species inhabiting these heights, as they had noted earlier, was a creature about as big as the palm of a man's hand, resembling nothing so much as a round ball of ruffled feathers, though its covering might actually have been a silky, fluffy fur. Its short legs could cover ground at an amazing speed, and it had the bold impudence of a creature with few natural enemies. This was its usual cry.

Tsoay's hand waved Travis on to where the younger man had taken position behind the bleached trunk of a fallen tree.

"He hides," Tsoay whispered.

"Against trouble from above." Travis added his own observation.

"But not us, I think."

So Tsoay had come to that conclusion too? Travis tried to gauge the nearness of twilight. There was a period after the passing of Topaz' sun when the dusky light played odd tricks with shadows. That would be the first time for their move. He said as much, and Tsoay nodded eagerly. They sat with their backs to a boulder, the tree trunk serving as a screen, and chewed methodically on ration tablets. There was energy and sustenance in the tasteless squares which would support men, even though their stomachs continued to demand the satisfaction of fresh meat.

Taking turns, they dozed a little. But the last banners of Topaz' sun were still in the sky when Travis judged the shadows cover enough. He had no way of knowing how the stranger was armed. Though he used a horse for transportation, he might well carry a rifle and the most modern Terran sidearms.

The Apaches' bows were little use for infighting, but they had their knives. However, Travis wanted to take the fugitive unharmed if he could. There was information he must have. So he did not even draw his knife as he started downhill.

When he reached a pool of violet dusk at the bottom of the small ravine Naginlta's eyes regarded him knowingly. Travis signaled with his hand and thought out what would be the coyotes' part in this surprise attack. The prick-eared silhouette vanished. Uphill the chitter of a fluff-fur sounded twice-Tsoay was in position.

A howl ...wailing ...sobbing ...was heard, one of the keening songs of the *mba'a*. Travis darted forward. He heard the nicker of a frightened horse, a clicking which could have marked the pawing of hoof on gravel, saw the brush hiding the stranger's hole tremble, a portion of it fall away.

Travis sped on, his moccasins making no sound on the ground. One of the coyotes gave tongue for the second time, the eerie wailing rising to a yapping which echoed from the rocks about them. Travis poised for a dive.

Another section of those artfully heaped branches had given way and a horse reared, its up-flung head plainly marked against the sky. A blurred figure weaved back and forth before it, trying to control the mount. The stranger had his hands full, certainly no weapon drawn-this was it!

Travis leaped. His hands found their mark, the shoulders of the stranger. There was a shrill cry from the other as he tried to turn in the Apache's hold, to face his attacker. But Travis bore them both on, rolling almost under the feet of the horse, sliding downhill, the unknown's writhing body pinned down by the Apache's weight and his clasp, tight as an iron grip, about the other's chest and upper arms.

He felt his opponent go limp, but was suspicious enough not to release that hold, for the heavy breathing of the stranger was not that of an unconscious man. They lay so, the unknown still tight in Travis' hold but no longer fighting. The Apache could hear Tsoay soothing the horse with the purring words of a practiced horseman.

Still the stranger did not resume the struggle. They could not lie in this position all night, Travis thought with a wry twist of amusement. He shifted his hold, and got the lightning-quick response he had expected. But it was not quite quick enough, for Travis had the other's hands behind his back, cupping slender, almost delicate wrists together.

"Throw me a cord!" he called to Tsoay.

The younger man ran up with an extra bow cord, and in a moment they had bonds on the struggling captive. Travis rolled their catch over, reaching down for a fistful of hair to pull the head into a patch of clearer light.

In his grasp that hair came loose, a braid unwinding. He grunted as he looked down into the stranger's face. Dust marks were streaked now with tear runnels, but the gray eyes which turned fiercely on him said that their owner cried more in rage than fear.

His captive might be wearing long trousers tucked into curved, toed boots, and a loose overblouse, but she was certainly not only a woman, but a very young and attractive one. Also, at the present moment, an exceedingly angry one. And behind that anger was fear, the fear of one fighting hopelessly against insurmountable odds. But as she eyed Travis now her expression changed.

He felt she had expected another captor altogether and was astounded at the sight of him. Her tongue touched her lips, moistening them, and now the fear in her was another kind-the wary fear of one facing a totally new and perhaps dangerous thing.

"Who are you?" Travis spoke in English, for he had no doubts that she was Terran.

Now she sucked in her breath with a gasp of pure astonishment.

"Who are *you*?" she parroted his question in a marked accent. English was not her native tongue, he was sure.

Travis reached out, and again his hands closed on her shoulders. She started to twist and then realized he was merely pulling her up to a sitting position. Some of the fear had left her eyes, an intent interest taking its place.

"You are not Sons of the Blue Wolf," she stated in her heavily accented speech.

Travis smiled. "I am the Fox, not the Wolf," he returned. "And the Coyote is my brother." He snapped his fingers at the shadows, and the two animals came noiselessly into sight. Her gaze widened even more at Naginlta and Nalik'ideyu, and she deduced the bond which must exist between her captor and the beasts.

"This woman is also of our world." Tsoay spoke in Apache, looking over their prisoner with frank interest. "Only she is not of the People."

Sons of the Blue Wolf? Travis thought again of the embroidery designs on the jacket. Who had called themselves by that picturesque title-where-and when in time?

"What do you fear, Daughter of the Blue Wolf?" he asked.

And with that question he seemed to touch some button activating terror. She flung back her head so that she could see the darkening sky.

"The flyer!" Her voice was muted as if more than a whisper would carry to the stars just coming into brilliance above them. "They will come ... tracking. I did not reach the inner mountains in time."

There was a despairing note in that which cut through to Travis, who found that he, too, was searching the sky, not knowing what he looked for or what kind of menace it promised, only that it was real danger.

6

"The night comes," Tsoay spoke slowly in English. "Do these you fear hunt in the dark?"

She shook her head to free her forehead from a coil of braid, pulled loose in her struggle with Travis.

"They do not need eyes or such noses as those four-footed hunters of yours. They have a machine to track —"

"Then what purpose is this brush pile of yours?" Travis raised his chin at the disturbed hiding place.

"They do not constantly use the machine, and one can hope. But at night they can ride on its beam. We are not far enough into the hills to lose them. Bahatur went lame, and so I was slowed...."

"And what lies in these mountains that those you fear dare not invade them?" Travis continued.

"I do not know, save if one can climb far enough inside, one is safe from pursuit."

"I ask it again: Who are you?" The Apache leaned forward, his face in the fast-fading light now only inches away from hers. She did not shrink from his close scrutiny but met him eye to eye. This was a woman of proud independence, truly a chief's daughter, Travis decided.

"I am of the People of the Blue Wolf. We were brought across the star lanes to make this world safe for ...for ...the...." She hesitated, and now there was a shade of puzzlement on her face. "There is a reason —a dream. No, there is the dream and there is reality. I am Kaydessa of the Golden Horde, but sometimes I remember other things-like this speech of strange words I am mouthing now — —"

"The Golden Horde!" Travis knew now. The embroidery, Sons of the Blue Wolf, all fitted into a special pattern. But what a pattern! Scythian art, the ornament that the warriors of Genghis Khan bore so proudly. Tatars, Mongols-the barbarians who had swept from the fastness of the steppes to change the course of history, not only in Asia but across the plains of middle Europe. The men of the Emperor Khans who had ridden behind the yak-tailed standards of Genghis Khan, Kublai Khan, Tamerlane —!

"The Golden Horde," Travis repeated once again. "That lies far back in the history of another world, Wolf Daughter."

She stared at him, a queer, lost expression on her dust-grimed face.

"I know." Her voice was so muted he could hardly distinguish the words. "My people live in two times, and many do not realize that."

Tsoay had crouched down beside them to listen. Now he put out his hand, touching Travis' shoulder.

"Redax?"

"Or its like." For Travis was sure of one point. The project, which had been training three teams for space colonization-one of Eskimos, one of Pacific Islanders, and one of his own Apaches-had no reason or chance to select Mongols from the wild past of the raiding Hordes. There was only one nation on Terra which could have picked such colonists.

"You are Russian." He studied her carefully, intent on noting the effect of his words.

But she did not lose that lost look. "Russian ...Russian ..." she repeated, as if the very word was strange.

Travis was alarmed. Any Russian colony planted here could well possess technicians with machines capable of tracking a fugitive, and if mountain heights were protection against such a hunt, he intended to gain them, even by night traveling. He said this to Tsoay, and the other emphatically agreed.

"The horse is too lame to go on," the younger man reported.

Travis hesitated for a long second. Since the time they had stolen their first mounts from the encroaching Spanish, horses had always been wealth to his people. To leave an animal which could well serve the clan was not right. But they dared not waste time with a lame beast.

"Leave it here, free," he ordered.

"And the woman?"

"She goes with us. We must learn all we can of these people and what they do here. Listen, Wolf Daughter," again Travis leaned close to make sure she was listening to him as he spoke with emphasis —"you will travel with us into these high places, and there will be no trouble from you." He drew his knife and held the blade warningly before her eyes.

"It was already in my mind to go to the mountains," she told him evenly. "Untie my hands, brave warrior, you have surely nothing to fear from a woman."

His hand made a swift sweep and plucked a knife as long and keen as his from the folds of the sash beneath her loose outer garment.

"Not now, Wolf Daughter, since I have drawn your fangs."

He helped her to her feet and slashed the cord about her wrists with her knife, which he then fastened to his own belt. Alerting the coyotes, he dispatched them ahead; and the three started on, the Mongol girl between the two Apaches. The abandoned horse nickered lonesomely and then began to graze on tufts of grass, moving slowly to favor his foot.

The two moons rode the sky as the hours advanced, their beams fighting the shadows. Travis felt reasonably safe from any attack at ground level, depending upon the coyotes for warning. But he held them all to a steady pace. And he did not question the girl again until all three of them hunkered down at a small mountain spring, to dash icy water over their faces and drink from cupped hands.

"Why do you flee your own people, Wolf Daughter?"

"My name is Kaydessa," she corrected him.

He chuckled with laughter at the prim tone of her voice. "And you see here Tsoay of the People-the Apaches-while I am Fox." He was giving her the English equivalent of his tribal name.

"Apaches." She tried to repeat the word with the same accent he had used. "And what are Apaches?"

"Indians-Amerindians," he explained. "But you have not answered my question, Kaydessa. Why do you run from your own people?"

"Not from my people," she said, shaking her head determinedly. "From those others. It is like this-Oh, how can I make you understand rightly?" She spread her wet hands out before her in the moonlight, the damp patches on her sleeves clinging to her arms. "There are my people of the Golden Horde, though once we were different and we can remember bits of that previous life. Then there are also the men who live in the sky ship and use the machine so that we think only the thoughts they would have us think. Now why," she looked at Travis intently —"do I wish to tell you all this? It is strange. You say you are Indian-American-are we then enemies? There is a part memory which says that we are ...were...."

"Let us rather say," he corrected her, "that the Apaches and the Horde are not enemies here and now, no matter what was before." That was the truth, Travis recognized. By all accounts his people had come out of Asia in the very dim beginnings of migrating peoples. For all her dark-red hair and gray eyes, this girl who had been arbitrarily returned to a past just as they had been by Redax, could well be a distant clan-cousin.

"You —" Kaydessa's fingers rested for a moment on his wrist —"you, too, were sent here from across the stars. Is this not so?"

"It is so."

"And there are those here who govern you now?"

"No. We are free."

"How did you become free?" she demanded fiercely.

Travis hesitated. He did not want to tell of the wrecked ship, the fact that his people possessed no real defenses against the Russian-controlled colony.

"We went to the mountains," he replied evasively.

"Your governing machine failed?" Kaydessa laughed. "Ah, they are so great, those men of the machines. But they are smaller and weaker when their machines cannot obey them."

"It is so with your camp?" Travis probed gently. He was not quite sure of her meaning, but he dared not ask more detailed questions without dangerously revealing his own ignorance.

"In some manner their control machine-it can only work upon those within a certain distance. They discovered that in the days of the first landing, when hunters went out freely and many of them did not return. After that when hunters were sent out to learn how lay this land, they went along in the flyer with a machine so that there would be no more escapes. But we knew!" Kaydessa's fingers curled into small fists. "Yes, we knew that if we could get beyond the machines, there was freedom for us. And we planned-many of us-planned. Then nine or ten sleeps ago those others were very excited. They gathered in their ship, watching their machines. And something happened. For a while all those machines went dead.

"Jagatai, Kuchar, my brother Hulagur, Menlik...." She was counting the names off on her fingers. "They raided the horse herd, rode out...."

"And you?"

"I, too, should have ridden. But there was Aljar, my sister-Kuchar's wife. She was very near her time and to ride thus, fleeing and fast, might kill her and the child. So I did not go. Her son was born that night, but the others had the machine at work once more. We might long to go here," she brought her fist up to her breast, and then raised it to her head —"but there was that *here* which kept us to the camp and their will. We only knew that if we could reach the mountains, we might find our people who had already gained their freedom."

"But you are here. How did you escape?" Tsoay wanted to know.

"They knew that I would have gone had it not been for Aljar. So they said they would make her ride out with them unless I played guide to lead them to my brother and the others. Then I knew I must take up the sword of duty and hunt with them. But I prayed that the spirits of the upper air look with favor upon me, and they granted aid...." Her eyes held a look of wonder. "For when we were out on the plains and well away from the settlement, a grass devil attacked the leader of the searching party, and he dropped the mind control and so it was broken. Then I rode. Blue Sky Above knows how I rode. And those others are not with their horses as are the people of the Wolf."

"When did this happen?"

"Three suns ago."

Travis counted back in his mind. Her date for the failure of the machine in the Russian camp seemed to coincide with the crash landing of the American ship. Had one thing any connection with the other? It was very possible. The planeting spacer might have fought some kind of weird duel with the other colony before it plunged to earth on the other side of the mountain range.

"Do you know where in these mountains your people hide?"

Kaydessa shook her head. "Only that I must head south, and when I reach the highest peak make a signal fire on the north slope. But that I cannot do now, for those in the flyer may see it. I know they are on my trail, for twice I have seen it. Listen, Fox, I ask this of you —I, Kaydessa, who am eldest daughter to the Khan-for you are like unto us, a warrior and a brave man, that I believe. It may be that you cannot be governed by their machine, for you have not rested under their spell, nor are of our blood. Therefore, if they come close enough to send forth the call, the call I must obey as if I were a slave dragged upon a horse rope, then do you bind my hands and feet and hold me here, no matter how much I struggle to follow that command. For that which is truly me does not want to go. Will you swear this by the fires which expel demons?"

The utter sincerity of her tone convinced Travis that she was pleading for aid against a danger she firmly believed in. Whether she was right about his immunity to the Russian mental control was another matter, and one he would rather not put to the test.

"We do not swear by your fires, Blue Wolf Maiden, but by the Path of the Lightning." His fingers moved as if to curl about the sacred charred wood his people had once carried as "medicine." "So do I promise!"

She looked at him for a long moment and then nodded in satisfaction.

They left the pool and pushed on toward the mountain slopes, working their way back to the pass. A low growl out of the dark brought them to an instant halt. Naginlta's warning was sharp; there was danger ahead, acute danger.

The moonlight from the moons made a weird pattern of light and dark on the stretch ahead. Anything from a slinking four-footed hunter to a war party of intelligent beings might have been lying in wait there.

A flitting shadow out of shadows. Nalik'ideyu pressed against Travis' legs, making a barrier of her warm body, attracting his attention to a spot at the left perhaps a hundred yards on. There was a great splotch of dark there, large enough to hide a really formidable opponent;

that wordless communication between animal and man told Travis that such an opponent was just what was lurking there.

Whatever lay in ambush beside the upper track was growing impatient as its destined prey ceased to advance, the coyotes reported.

"Your left-beyond that pointed rock-in the big shadow —"

"Do you see it?" Tsoay demanded.

"No. But the *mba'a* do."

The men had their bows ready, arrows set to the cords. But in this light such weapons were practically useless unless the enemy moved into the path of the moon.

"What is it?" Kaydessa asked in a half whisper.

"Something waits for us ahead."

Before he could stop her, she set her fingers to her lips and gave a piercing whistle.

There was answering movement in the shadow. Travis shot at that, his arrow followed instantly by one from Tsoay. There was a cry, scaling up in a throat-scalding scream which made Travis flinch. Not because of the sound, but because of the hint which lay behind it-could it have been a human cry?

The thing flopped out into a patch of moonlight. It was four-limbed, its body silvery-and it was large. But the worst was that it had been groveling on all fours when it fell, and now it was rising on its hind feet, one forepaw striking madly at the two arrows dancing head-deep in its upper shoulder. Man? No! But something sufficiently manlike to chill the three downtrail.

A whirling four-footed hunter dashed in, snapped at the creature's legs, and it squalled again, aiming a blow with a forepaw; but the attacking coyote was already gone. Together Naginlta and Nalik'ideyu were harassing the creature, just as they had fought the split horn, giving the hunters time to shoot. Travis, although he again felt that touch of horror and disgust he could not account for, shot again.

Between them the Apaches must have sent a dozen arrows into the raving beast before it went to its knees and Naginlta sprang for its throat. Even then the coyote yelped and flinched, a bleeding gash across its head from the raking talons of the dying thing. When it no longer moved, Travis approached to see more closely what they had brought down. That smell....

Just as the embroidery on Kaydessa's jacket had awakened memories from his Terran past, so did this stench remind him of something. Where-when-had he smelled it before? Travis connected it with dark, dark and danger. Then he gasped in a half exclamation.

Not on this world, no, but on two others: two worlds of that broken stellar empire where he had been an involuntary explorer two planet years ago! The beast things which had lived in the dark of the desert world the Terrans' wandering galactic derelict had landed upon. Yes, the beast things whose nature they had never been able to deduce. Were they the degenerate dregs of a once intelligent species? Or were they animals, akin to man, but still animals?

The ape-things had controlled the night of the desert world. And they had been met again-also in the dark-in the ruins of the city which had been the final goal of the ship's taped voyage. So they were a part of the vanished civilization. And Travis' own vague surmise concerning Topaz was proven correct. This had not been an empty world for the long-gone space people. This planet had a purpose and a use, or else this beast would not have been here.

"Devil!" Kaydessa made a face of disgust.

"You know it?" Tsoay asked Travis. "What is it?"

"That I do not know, but it is a thing left over from the star people's time. And I have seen it on two other of their worlds."

"A man?" Tsoay surveyed the body critically. "It wears no clothes, has no weapons, but it walks erect. It looks like an ape, a very big ape. It is not a good thing, I think."

"If it runs with a pack-as they do elsewhere-this could be a very bad thing." Travis, remembering how these creatures had attacked in force on the other worlds, looked about him apprehensively. Even with the coyotes on guard, they could not stand up to such a pack closing in through the dark. They had better hole up in some defendable place and wait out the rest of the night.

Naginlta brought them to a cliff overhang where they could set their backs to the hard rock of the mountain, face outward to a space they could cover with arrow flight if the need arose. And the coyotes, lying before them with their noses resting on paws, would, Travis knew, alert them long before the enemy could close in.

They huddled against the rock, Kaydessa between them, alert at first to every sound of the night, their hearts beating faster at a small scrape of gravel, the rustle of a bush. Slowly, they began to relax.

"It is well that two sleep while one guards," Travis observed. "By morning we must push on, out of this country."

So the two Apaches shared the watch in turn, the Tatar girl at first protesting, and then falling exhausted into a slumber which left her breathing heavily.

Travis, on the dawn watch, began to speculate about the ape-thing they had killed. The two previous times he had met this creature it had been in ruins of the old empire. Were there ruins somewhere here? He wanted to make sure about that. On the other hand, there was the problem of the Tatar-Mongol settlement controlled by the Reds. There was no doubt in his mind that, were the Reds to suspect the existence of the Apache camp, they would make every attempt to hunt down and kill or capture the survivors from the American ship. A warning must be carried to the rancheria as quickly as they could make the return trip.

Beside him the girl stirred, raising her head. Travis glanced at her and then watched with attention. She was looking straight ahead, her eyes as fixed as if she were in a trance. Now she inched forward from the mountain wall, wriggling out of its shelter.

"What —?" Tsoay had awakened again. But Travis was already moving. He pushed on, rushing up to stand beside her, shoulder to shoulder.

"What is it? Where do you go?" he asked.

She made no answer, did not even seem aware of his voice. He caught at her arm and she pulled to free herself. When he tightened his grip she did not fight him actively as during their first encounter, but merely pulled and twisted as if she were being compelled to go ahead.

Compulsion! He remembered her plea the night before, asking his help against recapture by the machine. Now he deliberately tripped her, twisted her hands behind her back. She swayed in his hold, trying to win to her feet, paying no attention to him save as a hindrance against her answering that demanding call he could not hear.

7

"What happened?" Tsoay took a swift stride, stood over the writhing girl whose strength was now such that Travis had to exert all his efforts to control her.

"I think that the machine she spoke about is holding her. She is being drawn to it out of hiding as one draws a calf on a rope."

Both coyotes had arisen and were watching the struggle with interest, but there was no warning from them. Whatever called Kaydessa into such mindless and will-less answer did not touch the animals. And neither Apache felt it. So perhaps only Kaydessa's people were subject to it, as she had thought. How far away was that machine? Not too near, for otherwise the coyotes would have traced the man or men operating it.

"We cannot move her," Tsoay brought the problem into the open —"unless we bind and carry her. She is one of their kind. Why not let her go to them, unless you fear she will talk." His hand went to the knife in his belt, and Travis knew what primitive impulse moved in the younger man.

In the old days a captive who was likely to give trouble was efficiently eliminated. In Tsoay that memory was awake now. Travis shook his head.

"She has said that others of her kin are in these hills. We must not set two wolf packs hunting us," Travis said, giving the more practical reason which might better appeal to that savage instinct for self-preservation. "But you are right, since she has tried to answer this summons, we cannot force her with us. Therefore, do you take the back trail. Tell Buck what we have discovered and have him make the necessary precautions against either these Mongol outlaws or a Red thrust over the mountains."

"And you?"

"I stay to discover where the outlaws hide and learn all I can of this settlement. We may have reason to need friends — —"

"Friends!" Tsoay spat. "The People need no friends! If we have warning, we can hold our own country! As the Pinda-lick-o-yi have discovered before."

"Bows and arrows against guns and machines?" Travis inquired bitingly. "We must know more before we make any warrior boasts for the future. Tell Buck what we have discovered. Also say I will join you before," Travis calculated —"ten suns. If I do not, send no search party; the clan is too small to risk more lives for one."

"And if these Reds take you —?"

Travis grinned, not pleasantly. "They shall learn nothing! Can their machines sort out the thoughts of a dead man?" He did not intend his future to end as abruptly as that, but also he would not be easy meat for any Red hunting party.

Tsoay took a share of their rations and refused the company of the coyotes. Travis realized that for all his seeming ease with the animals, the younger scout had little more liking for them than Deklay and the others back at the rancheria. Tsoay went at dawn, aiming at the pass.

Travis sat down beside Kaydessa. They had bound her to a small tree, and she strove incessantly to free herself, turning her head at an acute and painful angle, only to face the same direction in which she had been tied. There was no breaking the spell which held her. And she would soon wear herself out with that struggling. Then he struck an expert blow.

The girl sagged limply, and he untied her. It all depended now on the range of the beam or broadcast of that diabolical machine. From the attitude of the coyotes, he assumed that those using the machine had not made any attempt to come close. They might not even know where their quarry was; they would simply sit and wait in the foothills for the caller to reel in a helpless captive.

Travis thought that if he moved Kaydessa farther away from that point, sooner or later they would be out of range and she would awake from the knockout, free again. Although she was not light, he could manage to carry her for a while. So burdened, Travis started on, with the coyotes scouting ahead.

He speedily discovered that he had set himself an ambitious task. The going was rough, and carrying the girl reduced his advance to a snail-paced crawl. But it gave him time to make careful plans.

As long as the Reds held the balance of power on this side of the mountain range, the rancheria was in danger. Bows and knives against modern armament was no contest at all. And it would only be a matter of time before exploration on the part of the northern settlement-or some tracking down of Tatar fugitives-would bring the enemy across the pass.

The Apaches could move farther south into the unknown continent below the wrecked ship, thus prolonging the time before they were discovered. But that would only postpone the inevitable showdown. Whether Travis could make his clan believe that, was also a matter of concern.

On the other hand, if the Red overlords could be met in some practical way....Travis' mind fastened on that more attractive idea, worrying it as Naginlta worried a prey, tearing out and devouring the more delicate portions. Every bit of sense and prudence argued against such an approach, whose success could rest only between improbability and impossibility; yet that was the direction in which he longed to move.

Across his shoulder Kaydessa stirred and moaned. The Apache doubled his efforts to reach the outcrop of rock he could see ahead, chiseled into high relief by the winds. In its lee they would have protection from any sighting from below. Panting, he made it, lowering the girl into the guarded cup of space, and waited.

She moaned again, lifted one hand to her head. Her eyes were half open, and still he could not be sure whether they focused on him and her surroundings intelligently or not.

"Kaydessa!"

Her heavy eyelids lifted, and he had no doubt she could see him. But there was no recognition of his identity in her gaze, only surprise and fear-the same expression she had worn during their first meeting in the foothills.

"Daughter of the Wolf," he spoke slowly. "Remember!" Travis made that an order, an emphatic appeal to the mind under the influence of the caller.

She frowned, the struggle she was making naked on her face. Then she answered: "You-Fox —"

Travis grunted with relief, his alarm subsiding. Then she *could* remember.

"Yes," he responded eagerly.

But she was gazing about, her puzzlement growing. "Where is this —?"

"We are higher in the mountains."

Now fear was pushing out bewilderment. "How did I come here?"

"I brought you." Swiftly he outlined what had happened at their night camp.

The hand which had been at her head was now pressed tight across her lips as if she were biting furiously into its flesh to still some panic of her own, and her gray eyes were round and haunted.

"You are free now," Travis said.

Kaydessa nodded, and then dropped her hand to speak. "You brought me away from the hunters. You did not have to obey them?"

"I heard nothing."

"You do not hear-you feel!" She shuddered. "Please." She clawed at the stone beside her, pulling up to her feet. "Let us go-let us go quickly! They will try again-move farther in —"

"Listen," Travis had to be sure of one thing —"have they any way of knowing that they had you under control and that you have again escaped?"

Kaydessa shook her head, some of the panic again shadowing her eyes.

"Then we'll just go on —" his chin lifted to the wastelands before them —"try to keep out of their reach."

And away from the pass to the south, he told himself silently. He dared not lead the enemy to that secret, so he must travel west or hole up somewhere in this unknown wilderness until they could be sure Kaydessa was no longer susceptible to that call, or that they were safely beyond its beamed radius. There was the chance of contacting her outlaw kin, just as there was the chance of stumbling into a pack of the ape-things. Before dark they must discover a protected camp site.

They needed water, food. He had a bare half dozen ration tablets. But the coyotes could locate water.

"Come!" Travis beckoned to Kaydessa, motioning her to climb ahead of him so that he could watch for any indication of her succumbing once again to the influence of the enemy. But his burdened early morning flight had told on Travis more than he thought, and he discovered he could not spur himself on to a pace better than a walk. Now and again one of the coyotes, usually Nalik'ideyu, would come into view, express impatience in both stance and mental signal, and then be gone again. The Apache was increasingly aware that the animals were disturbed, yet to his tentative gropings at contact they did not reply. Since they gave no warning of hostile animal or man, he could only be on constant guard, watching the countryside about him.

They had been following a ledge for several minutes before Travis was aware of some strange features of that path. Perhaps he had actually noted them with a trained eye before his archaeological studies of the recent past gave him a reason for the faint marks. This crack in the mountain's skin might have begun as a natural fault, but afterward it had been worked with tools, smoothed, widened to serve the purpose of some form of intelligence!

Travis caught at Kaydessa's shoulder to slow her pace. He could not have told why he did not want to speak aloud here, but he felt the need for silence. She glanced around, perplexed, more so when he went down on his knees and ran his fingers along one of those ancient tool marks. He was certain it was very old. Inside of him anticipation bubbled. A road made with such labor could only lead to something of importance. He was going to make the discovery, the dream which had first drawn him into these mountains.

"What is it?" Kaydessa knelt beside him, frowning at the ledge.

"This was cut by someone, a long time ago," Travis half whispered and then wondered why. There was no reason to believe the road makers could hear him when perhaps a thousand years or more lay between the chipping of that stone and this day.

The Tatar girl looked over her shoulder. Perhaps she too was troubled by the sense that here time was subtly telescoped, that past and present might be meeting. Or was that feeling with them both because of their enforced conditioning?

"Who?" Now her voice sank in turn.

"Listen —" he regarded her intently —"did your people or the Reds ever find any traces of the old civilization here-ruins?"

"No." She leaned forward, tracing with her own finger the same almost-obliterated marks which had intrigued Travis. "But I think they have looked. Before they discovered that we could be free, they sent out parties-to hunt, they said-but afterward they always asked many questions about the country. Only they never asked about ruins. Is that what they wished us to find? But why? Of what value are old stones piled on one another?"

"In themselves, little, save for the knowledge they may give us of the people who piled them. But for what the stones might contain-much value!"

"And how do you know what they might contain, Fox?"

"Because I have seen such treasure houses of the star men," he returned absently. To him the marks on the ledge were a pledge of greater discoveries to come. He must find where that carefully constructed road ran-to what it led. "Let us see where this will take us."

But first he gave the chittering signal in four sharp bursts. And the tawny-gray bodies came out of the tangled brush, bounding up to the ledge. Together the coyotes faced him, their attention all for his halting communication.

Ruins might lie ahead; he hoped that they did. But on another planet such ruins had twice proved to be deadly traps, and only good fortune had prevented their closing on Terran explorers. If the ape-things or any other dangerous form of life had taken up residence before them, he wanted good warning.

Together the coyotes turned and loped along the now level way of the ledge, disappearing around a curve fitted to the mountain side while Travis and Kaydessa followed.

They heard it before they saw its source —a waterfall. Probably not a large one, but high. Rounding the curve, they came into a fine mist of spray where sunlight made rainbows of color across a filmy veil of water.

For a long moment they stood entranced. Kaydessa then gave a little cry, held out her hands to the purling mist and brought them to her lips again to suck the gathered moisture.

Water slicked the surface of the ledge, and Travis pushed her back against the wall of the cliff. As far as he could discern, their road continued behind the out-flung curtain of water, and footing on the wet stone was treacherous. With their backs to the solid security of the wall, facing outward into the solid drape of water, they edged behind it and came out into rainbowed sunlight again.

Here either provident nature or ancient art had hollowed a pocket in the stone which was filled with water. They drank. Then Travis filled his canteen while Kaydessa washed her face, holding the cold freshness of the moisture to her cheeks with both palms.

She spoke, but he could not hear her through the roar. She leaned closer and raised her voice to a half shout:

"This is a place of spirits! Do you not also feel their power, Fox?"

Perhaps for a space out of time he did feel something. This was a watering place, perhaps a never-ceasing watering place-and to his desert-born-and-bred race all water was a spirit gift never to be taken for granted. The rainbow-the Spirit People's sacred sign-old beliefs stirred in Travis, moving him. "I feel," he said, nodding in emphasis to his agreement.

They followed the ledge road to a section where a landslide of an earlier season had choked it. Travis worked a careful way across the debris, Kaydessa obeying his guidance in turn. Then they were on a sloping downward way which led to a staircase-the treads weather-worn and crumbling, the angle so steep Travis wondered if it had ever been intended for beings with a physique approximating the Terrans'.

They came to a cleft where an arch of stone was chiseled out as a roofing. Travis thought he could make out a trace of carving on the capstone, so worn by years and weather that it was now only a faint shadow of design.

The cleft was a door into another valley. Here, too, golden mist swirled in tendrils to disguise and cloak what stood there. Travis had found his ruins. Only the structures were intact, not breached by time.

Mist flowed in lapping tongues back and forth, confusing outlines, now shuttering, now baring oval windows which were spaced in diamonds of four on round tower surfaces. There were no visible cracks, no cloaking of climbing vegetation, nothing to suggest age and long roots in the valley. Nor did the architecture he could view match any he had seen on those other worlds.

Travis strode away from the cleft doorway. Under his moccasins was a block pavement, yellow and green stone set in a simple pattern of checks. This, too, was level, unchipped and undisturbed, save for a drift or two of soil driven in by the wind. And nowhere could he see any vegetation.

The towers were of the same green stone as half the pavement blocks, a glassy green which made him think of jade-if jade could be mined in such quantities as these five-story towers demanded.

Nalik'ideyu padded to him, and he could hear the faint click of her claws on the pavement. There was a deep silence in this place, as if the air itself swallowed and digested all sound. The wind which had been with them all the day of their journeying was left beyond the cleft.

Yet there was life here. The coyote told him that in her own way. She had not made up her mind concerning that life-wariness and curiosity warred in her now as her pointed muzzle lifted toward the windows overhead.

The windows were all well above ground level, but there was no opening in the first stories as far as Travis could see. He debated moving into the range of those windows to investigate the far side of the towers for doorways. The mist and the message from Nalik'ideyu nourished his suspicions. Out in the open he would be too good a target for whatever or whoever might be standing within the deep-welled frames.

The silence was shattered by a boom. Travis jumped, slewed half around, knife in hand.

Boom-boom ... a second heavy beat-beat ... then a clangor with a swelling echo.

Kaydessa flung back her head and called, her voice rising up as if tunneled by the valley walls. She then whistled as she had done when they fronted the ape-thing and ran on to catch at Travis' sleeve, her face eager.

"My people! Come-it is my people!"

She tugged him on before breaking into a run, weaving fearlessly around the base of one of the towers. Travis ran after her, afraid he might lose her in the mist.

Three towers, another stretch of open pavement, and then the mist lifted to show them a second carved doorway not two hundred yards ahead. The boom-boom seemed to pull Kaydessa, and Travis could do nothing but trail her, the coyotes now trotting beside him.

8

They burst through a last wide band of mist into a wilderness of tall grass and shrubs. Travis heard the coyotes give tongue, but it was too late. Out of nowhere whirled a leather loop, settling about his chest, snapping his arms tight to his body, taking him off his feet with a jerk to be dragged helplessly along the ground behind a galloping horse.

A tawny fury sprang in the air to snap at the horse's head. Travis kicked fruitlessly, trying to regain his feet as the horse reared, and fought against the control of his shouting rider. All through the melee the Apache heard Kaydessa shrilly screaming words he did not understand.

Travis was on his knees, coughing in the dust, exerting the muscles in his chest and shoulders to loosen the lariat. On either side of him the coyotes wove a snarling pattern of defiance, dashing back and forth to present no target for the enemy, yet keeping the excited horses so stirred up that their riders could use neither ropes nor blades.

Then Kaydessa ran between two of the ringing horses to Travis and jerked at the loop about him. The tough, braided leather eased its hold, and he was able to gasp in full lungfuls of air. She was still shouting, but the tone had changed from one of recognition to a definite scolding.

Travis won to his feet just as the rider who had lassoed him finally got his horse under rein and dismounted. Holding the rope, the man walked hand over hand toward them, as Travis back on the Arizona range would have approached a nervous, unschooled pony.

The Mongol was an inch or so shorter than the Apache, and his face was young, though he had a drooping mustache bracketing his mouth with slender spear points of black hair. His breeches were tucked into high red boots, and he wore a loose felt jacket patterned with the same elaborate embroidery Travis had seen on Kaydessa's. On his head was a hat with a wide fur border-in spite of the heat-and that too bore touches of scarlet and gold design.

Still holding his lariat, the Mongol reached Kaydessa and stood for a moment, eying her up and down before he asked a question. She gave an impatient twitch to the rope. The coyotes snarled, but the Apache thought the animals no longer considered the danger immediate.

"This is my brother Hulagur." Kaydessa made the introduction over her shoulder. "He does not have your speech."

Hulagur not only did not understand, he was also impatient. He jerked at the rope with such sudden force that Travis was almost thrown. Then Kaydessa dragged as fiercely on the lariat in the other direction and burst into a soaring harangue which drew the rest of the men closer.

Travis flexed his upper arms, and the slack gained by Kaydessa's action made the lariat give again. He studied the Tatar outlaws. There were five of them beside Hulagur, lean men, hard-faced, narrow-eyed, the ragged clothing of three pieced out with scraps of hide. Besides the swords with the curved blades, they were armed with bows, two to each man, one long, one shorter. One of the riders carried a lance, long tassels of woolly hair streaming from below its head. Travis saw in them a formidable array of barbaric fighting men, but he thought that man for man the Apaches could not only take on the Mongols with confidence, but might well defeat them.

The Apache had never been a hot-headed, ride-for-glory fighter like the Cheyenne, the Sioux, and the Comanche of the open plains. He estimated the odds against him, used ambush, trick, and every feature of the countryside as weapon and defense. Fifteen Apache fighting men under Chief Geronimo had kept five thousand American and Mexican troops in the field for a year and had come off victorious for the moment.

Travis knew the tales of Genghis Khan and his formidable generals who swept over Asia into Europe, unbeaten and seemingly undefeatable. But they had been a wild wave, fed by a reservoir of manpower from the steppes of their homeland, utilizing driven walls of captives to protect their own men in city assaults and attacks. He doubted if even that endless sea of men could have won the Arizona desert defended by Apaches under Cochise, Victorio, or Magnus Colorado. The white man had done it-by superior arms and attrition; but bow against bow, knife against sword, craft and cunning against craft and cunning-he did not think so....

Hulagur dropped the end of the lariat, and Kaydessa swung around, loosening the loop so that the rope fell to Travis' feet. The Apache stepped free of it, turned and passed between two of the horsemen to gather up the bow he had dropped. The coyotes had gone with him and when he turned again to face the company of Tatars, both animals crowded past him to the entrance of the valley, plainly urging him to retire there.

The horsemen had faced about also, and the warrior with the lance balanced the shaft of the weapon in his hand as if considering the possibility of trying to spear Travis. But just then Kaydessa came up, towing Hulagur by a firm hold on his sash-belt.

"I have told this one," she reported to Travis, "how it is between us and that you also are enemy to those who hunt us. It is well that you sit together beside a fire and talk of these things."

Again that boom-boom broke her speech, coming from farther out in the open land.

"You will do this?" She made of it a half question, half statement.

Travis glanced about him. He could dodge back into the misty valley of the towers before the Tatars could ride him down. However, if he could patch up some kind of truce between his people and the outlaws, the Apaches would have only the Reds from the settlement to watch. Too many times in Terran past had war on two fronts been disastrous.

"I come-carrying this-and not pulled by your ropes." He held up his bow in an exaggerated gesture so that Hulagur could understand.

Coiling the lariat, the Mongol looked from the Apache bow to Travis. Slowly, and with obvious reluctance, he nodded agreement.

At Hulagur's call the lancer rode up to the waiting Apache, stretched out a booted foot in the heavy stirrup, and held down a hand to bring Travis up behind him riding double. Kaydessa mounted in the same fashion behind her brother.

Travis looked at the coyotes. Together the animals stood in the door to the tower valley, and neither made any move to follow as the horses trotted off. He beckoned with his hand and called to them.

Heads up, they continued to watch him go in company with the Mongols. Then without any reply to his coaxing, they melted back into the mists. For a moment Travis was tempted to slide down and run the risk of taking a lance point between the shoulders as he followed Naginlta and Nalik'ideyu into retreat. He was startled, jarred by the new awareness of how much he had come to depend on the animals. Ordinarily, Travis Fox was not one to be governed by the wishes of a *mba'a*, intelligent and un-animallike as it might be. This was an affair of men, and coyotes had no part in it!

Half an hour later Travis sat in the outlaw camp. There were fifteen Mongols in sight, a half dozen women and two children adding to the count. On a hillock near their yurts, the round brush-and-hide shelters-not too different from the wickiups of Travis' own people-was a crude drum, a hide stretched taut over a hollowed section of log. And next to that stood a man wearing a tall pointed cap, a red robe, and a girdle from which swung a fringe of small bones, tiny animal skulls, and polished bits of stone and carved wood.

It was this man's efforts which sent the boom-boom sounding at intervals over the landscape. Was this a signal-part of a ritual? Travis was not certain, though he guessed that the drummer was either medicine man or shaman, and so of some power in this company. Such men were credited with the ability to prophesy and also endowed with mediumship between man and spirit in the old days of the great Hordes.

The Apache evaluated the rest of the company. As was true of his own party, these men were much the same age-young and vigorous. And it was also apparent that Hulagur held a position of some importance among them-if he were not their chief.

After a last resounding roll on the drum, the shaman thrust the sticks into his girdle and came down to the fire at the center of the camp. He was taller than his fellows, pole thin under his robes, his face narrow, clean-shaven, with brows arched by nature to give him an unchanging expression of scepticism. He strode along, his tinkling collection of charms providing him with a not unmusical accompaniment, and came to stand directly before Travis, eying him carefully.

Travis copied his silence in what was close to a duel of wills. There was that in the shaman's narrowed green eyes which suggested that if Hulagur did in fact lead these fighting men, he had an advisor of determination and intelligence behind him.

"This is Menlik." Kaydessa did not push past the men to the fireside, but her voice carried.

Hulagur growled at his sister, but his admonition made no impression on her, and she replied in as hot a tone. The shaman's hand went up, silencing both of them.

"You are-who?" Like Kaydessa, Menlik spoke a heavily accented English.

"I am Travis Fox, of the Apaches."

"The Apaches," the shaman repeated. "You are of the West, the American West, then."

"You know much, man of spirit talk."

"One remembers. At times one remembers," Menlik answered almost absently. "How does an Apache find his way across the stars?"

"The same way Menlik and his people did," Travis returned. "You were sent to settle this planet, and so were we."

"There are many more of you?" countered Menlik swiftly.

"Are there not many of the Horde? Would one man, or three, or four, be sent to hold a world?" Travis fenced. "You hold the north, we the south of this land."

"But *they* are not governed by a machine!" Kaydessa cut in. "They are free!"

Menlik frowned at the girl. "Woman, this is a matter for warriors. Keep your tongue silent between your jaws!"

She stamped one foot, standing with her fists on her hips.

"I am a Daughter of the Blue Wolf. And we are all warriors-men and women alike-so shall we be as long as the Horde is not free to ride where we wish! These men have won their freedom; it is well that we learn how."

Menlik's expression did not change, but his lids drooped over his eyes as a murmur of what might be agreement came from the group. More than one of them must have understood enough English to translate for the others. Travis wondered about that. Had these men and women who had outwardly reverted to the life of their nomad ancestors once been well educated in the modern sense, educated enough to learn the basic language of the nation their rulers had set up as their principal enemy?

"So you ride the land south of the mountains?" the shaman continued.

"That is true."

"Then why did you come hither?"

Travis shrugged. "Why does anyone ride or travel into new lands? There is a desire to see what may lie beyond — —"

"Or to scout before the march of warriors!" Menlik snapped. "There is no peace between your rulers and mine. Do you ride now to take the herds and pastures of the Horde-or to try to do so?"

Travis turned his head deliberately from side to side, allowing them all to witness his slow and openly contemptuous appraisal of their camp.

"*This* is your Horde, Shaman? Fifteen warriors? Much has changed since the days of Temujin, has it not?"

"What do you know of Temujin-you, who are a man of no ancestors, out of the West?"

"What do I know of Temujin? That he was a leader of warriors and became Genghis Khan, the great lord of the East. But the Apaches had their warlords also, rider of barren lands. And I am of those who raided over two nations when Victorio and Cochise scattered their enemies as a man scatters a handful of dust in the wind."

"You talk bold, Apache...." There was a hint of threat in that.

"I speak as any warrior, Shaman. Or are you so used to talking with spirits instead of men that you do not realize that?"

He might have been alienating the shaman by such a sharp reply, but Travis thought he judged the temper of these people. To face them boldly was the only way to impress them. They would not treat with an inferior, and he was already at a disadvantage coming on foot, without any backing in force, into a territory held by horsemen who were suspicious and jealous of their recently acquired freedom. His only chance was to establish himself as an equal and then try to convince them that Apache and Tatar-Mongol had a common cause against the Reds who controlled the settlement on the northern plains.

Menlik's right hand went to his sash-girdle and plucked out a carved stick which he waved between them, muttering phrases Travis could not understand. Had the shaman retreated so far along the road to his past that he now believed in his own supernatural powers? Or was this to impress his watching followers?

"You call upon your spirits for aid, Menlik? But the Apache has the companionship of the *ga-n*. Ask of Kaydessa: Who hunts with the Fox in the wilds?" Travis' sharp challenge stopped that wand in mid-air. Menlik's head swung to the girl.

"He hunts with wolves who think like men." She supplied the information the shaman would not openly ask for. "I have seen them act as his scouts. This is no spirit thing, but real and of this world!"

"Any man may train a dog to his bidding!" Menlik spat.

"Does a dog obey orders which are not said aloud? These brown wolves come and sit before him, look into his eyes. And then he knows what lies within their heads, and they know what he would have them do. This is not the way of a master of hounds with his pack!"

Again the murmur ran about the camp as one or two translated. Menlik frowned. Then he rammed his sorcerer's wand back into his sash.

"If you are a man of power-such powers," he said slowly, "then you may walk alone where those who talk with spirits go-into the mountains." He then spoke over his shoulder in his native tongue, and one of the women reached behind her into a hut, brought out a skin bag and a horn cup. Kaydessa took the cup from her and held it while the other woman poured a white liquid from the bag to fill it.

Kaydessa passed the cup to Menlik. He pivoted with it in his hand, dribbling expertly over its brim a few drops at each point of the compass, chanting as he moved. Then he sucked in a mouthful of the contents before presenting the vessel to Travis.

The Apache smelled the same sour scent that had clung to the emptied bag in the foothills. And another part of memory supplied him with the nature of the drink. This was kumiss, a fermented mare's milk which was the wine and water of the steppes.

He forced himself to swallow a draft, though it was alien to his taste, and passed the cup back to Menlik. The shaman emptied the horn and, with that, set aside ceremony. With an upraised hand he beckoned Travis to the fire again, indicating a pot set on the coals.

"Rest ... eat!" he bade abruptly.

Night was gathering in. Travis tried to calculate how far Tsoay must have backtracked to the rancheria. He thought that he could have already made the pass and be within a day and a half from the Apache camp if he pushed on, as he would. As to where the coyotes were, Travis had no idea. But it was plain that he himself must remain in this encampment for the night or risk rousing the Mongols' suspicion once more.

He ate of the stew, spearing chunks out of the pot with the point of his knife. And it was not until he sat back, his hunger appeased, that the shaman dropped down beside him.

"The Khatun Kaydessa says that when she was slave to the caller, you did not feel its chains," he began.

"Those who rule you are not my overlords. The bonds they set upon your minds do not touch me." Travis hoped that that was the truth and his escape that morning had not been just a fluke.

"This could be, for you and I are not of one blood," Menlik agreed. "Tell me-how did you escape your bonds?"

"The machine which held us so was broken," Travis replied with a portion of the truth, and Menlik sucked in his breath.

"The machines, always the machines!" he cried hoarsely. "A thing which can sit in a man's head and make him do what it will against his will; it is demon sent! There are other machines to be broken, Apache."

"Words will not break them," Travis pointed out.

"Only a fool rides to his death without hope of striking a single blow before he chokes on the blood in his throat," Menlik retorted. "We cannot use bow or tulwar against weapons which flame and kill quicker than any storm lightning! And always the mind machines can make a man drop his knife and stand helplessly waiting for the slave collar to be set on his neck!"

Travis asked a question of his own. "I know that they can bring a caller part way into this mountain, for this very day I saw its effect upon the maiden. But there are many places in the hills well set for ambushes, and those unaffected by the machine could be waiting there. Would there be many machines so that they could send out again and again?"

Menlik's bony hand played with his wand. Then a slow smile curved his lips into the guise of a hunting cat's noiseless snarl.

"There is meat in that pot, Apache, rich meat, good for the filling of a lean belly! So men whose minds the machine could not trouble-such men to be waiting in ambush for the taking of the men who use such a machine-yes. But here would have to be bait, very good bait for such a trap, Lord of Wiles. Never do those others come far into the mountains. Their flyer does not lift well here, and they do not trust traveling on horseback. They were greatly angered to come so far in to reach Kaydessa, though they could not have been too close, or you would not have escaped at all. Yes, strong bait."

"Such bait as perhaps the knowledge that there were strangers across the mountains?"

Menlik turned his wand about in his hands. He was no longer smiling, and his glance at Travis was sharp and swift.

"Do you sit as Khan in your tribe, Lord?"

"I sit as one they will listen to." Travis hoped that was so. Whether Buck and the moderates would hold clan leadership upon his return was a fact he could not count upon as certain.

"This is a thing which we must hold council over," Menlik continued. "But it is an idea of power. Yes, one to think about, Lord. And I shall think...."

He got up and moved away. Travis blinked at the fire. He was very tired, and he disliked sleeping in this camp. But he must not go without the rest his body needed to supply him with a clear head in the morning. And not showing uneasiness might be one way of winning Menlik's confidence.

9

Travis settled his back against the spire of rock and raised his right hand into the path of the sun, cradling in his palm a disk of glistening metal. Flash ...flash ...he made the signal pattern just as his ancestors a hundred years earlier and far across space had used trade mirrors to relay war alerts among the Chiricahua and White Mountain ranges. If Tsoay had returned safely, and if Buck had kept the agreed lookout on that peak a mile or so ahead, then the clan would know that he was coming and with what escort.

He waited now, rubbing the small metal mirror absently on the loose sleeve of his shirt, waiting for a reply. Mirrors were best, not smoke fires which would broadcast too far the presence of men in the hills. Tsoay must have returned....

"What is it that you do?"

Menlik, his shaman's robe pulled up so that his breeches and boots were dark against the golden rock, climbed up beside the Apache. Menlik, Hulagur, and Kaydessa were riding with Travis, offering him one of their small ponies to hurry the trip. He was still regarded warily by the Tatars, but he did not blame them for their cautious attitude.

"Ah —" A flicker of light from the point ahead. One ... two ... three flashes, a pause, then two more together. He had been read. Buck had dispatched scouts to meet them, and knowing his people's skill at the business, Travis was certain the Tatars would never suspect their flanking unless the Apaches purposefully revealed themselves. Also the Tatars were not to go to the rancheria, but would be met at a mid-point by a delegation of Apaches. This was no time for the Tatars to learn just how few the clan numbered.

Menlik watched Travis flash an acknowledgment to the sentry ahead. "In this way you speak to your men?"

"This way I speak."

"A thing good and to be remembered. We have the drum, but that is for the ears of all with hearing. This is for the eyes only of those on watch for it. Yes, a good thing. And your people-they will meet with us?"

"They wait ahead," Travis confirmed.

It was close to midday and the heat, gathered in the rocky ways, was like a heaviness in the air itself. The Tatars had shucked their heavy jackets and rolled the fur brims of their hats far up their heads away from their sweat-beaded faces. And at every halt they passed from hand to hand the skin bag of kumiss.

Now even the ponies shuffled on with drooping heads, picking a way in a cut which deepened into a canyon. Travis kept a watch for the scouts. And not for the first time he thought of the disappearance of the coyotes. Somehow, back in the Tatar camp, he had counted confidently on the animals' rejoining him once he had started his return over the mountains.

But he had seen nothing of either beast, nor had he felt that unexplainable mental contact with them which had been present since his first awakening on Topaz. Why they had left him so unceremoniously after defending him from the Mongol attack, and why they were keeping themselves aloof now, he did not know. But he was conscious of a thread of alarm for their continued absence, and he hoped he would find they had gone back to the rancheria.

The ponies thudded dispiritedly along a sandy wash which bottomed the canyon. Here the heat became a leaden weight and the men were panting like four-footed beasts running before hunters. Finally Travis sighted what he had been seeking, a flicker of movement on the wall well above. He flung up his hand, pulling his mount to a stand. Apaches stood in full view, bows ready, arrows on cords. But they made no sound.

Kaydessa cried out, booted her mount to draw equal with Travis.

"A trap!" Her face, flushed with heat, was also stark with anger.

Travis smiled slowly. "Is there a rope about you, Wolf Daughter?" he inquired softly. "Are you now dragged across this sand?"

Her mouth opened and then closed again. The quirt she had half raised to slash at him, flopped across her pony's neck.

The Apache glanced back at the two men. Hulagur's hand was on his sword hilt, his eyes darting from one of those silent watchers to the next. But the utter hopelessness of the Tatar position was too plain. Only Menlik made no move toward any weapon, even his spirit wand. Instead, he sat quietly in the saddle, displaying no emotion toward the Apaches save his usual self-confident detachment.

"We go on." Travis pointed ahead.

Just as suddenly as they had appeared from the heart of the golden cliffs, so did the scouts vanish. Most of them were already on their way to the point Buck had selected for the meeting place. There had been only six men up there, but the Tatars had no way of knowing just how large a portion of the whole clan that number was.

Travis' pony lifted his head, nickered, and achieved a stumbling trot. Somewhere ahead was water, one of those oases of growth and life which pocked the whole mountain range-to the preservation of all animals and all men.

Menlik and Hulagur pushed on until their mounts were hard on the heels of the two ridden by the girl and Travis. Travis wondered if they still waited for some arrow to strike home, though he saw that both men rode with outward disregard for the patrolling scouts.

A grass-leaf bush beckoned them on and again the ponies quickened pace, coming out into a tributary canyon which housed a small pool and a good stand of grass and brush. To one side of the water Buck stood, his arms folded across his chest, armed only with his belt knife. Grouped behind him were Deklay, Tsoay, Nolan, Manulito-Travis tabulated hurriedly. Manulito and Deklay were to be classed together-or had been when he was last in the rancheria. On Buck's stairway from the past, both had halted more than halfway down. Nolan was a quiet man who seldom spoke, and whose opinion Travis could not foretell. Tsoay would back Buck.

Probably such a divided party was the best Travis could have hoped to gather. A delegation composed entirely of those who were ready to leave the past of the Redax—a collection of Bucks and Jil-Lees—was outside the bounds of possibility. But Travis was none too happy to have Deklay in on this.

Travis dismounted, letting the pony push forward by himself to dip nose into the pool.

"This is," Travis pointed politely with his chin—"Menlik, one who talks with spirits....Hulagur, who is son to a chief ...and Kaydessa, who is daughter to a chief. They are of the horse people of the north." He made the introduction carefully in English.

Then he turned to the Tatars. "Buck, Deklay, Nolan, Manulito, Tsoay," he named them all, "these stand to listen, and to speak for the Apaches."

But sometime later when the two parties sat facing each other, he wondered whether a common decision could come from the clansmen on his side of that irregular circle. Deklay's expression was closed; he had even edged a short way back, as if he had no desire to approach the strangers. And Travis read into every line of Deklay's body his distrust and antagonism.

He himself began to speak, retelling his adventures since they had followed Kaydessa's trail, sketching in the situation at the Tatar-Mongol settlement as he had learned it from her and from Menlik. He was careful to speak in English so that the Tatars could hear all he was reporting to his own kind. And the Apaches listened blank-faced, though Tsoay must already have reported much of this. When Travis was done it was Deklay who asked a question:

"What have we to do with these people?"

"There is this —" Travis chose his words carefully, thinking of what might move a warrior still conditioned to riding with the raiders of a hundred years earlier, "the Pinda-lick-o-yi (whom we call 'Reds,') are never willing to live side by side with any who are not of their mind. And they have weapons such as make our bow cords bits of rotten string, our knives slivers of rust. They do not kill; they enslave. And when they discover that we live, then they will come against us —"

Deklay's lips moved in a wolf grin. "This is a large land, and we know how to use it. The Pinda-lick-o-yi will not find us —"

"With their eyes maybe not," Travis replied. "With their machines-that is another matter."

"Machines!" Deklay spat. "Always these machines ...Is that all you can talk about? It would seem that you are bewitched by these machines, which we have not seen-none of us!"

"It was a machine which brought you here," Buck observed. "Go you back and look upon the spaceship and remember, Deklay. The knowledge of the Pinda-lick-o-yi is greater than ours when it deals with metal and wire and things which can be made with both. Machines brought us along the road of the stars, and there is no tracker in the clan who could hope to do the same. But now I have this to ask: Does our brother have a plan?"

"Those who are Reds," Travis answered slowly, "they do not number many. But more may later come from our own world. Have you heard of such arriving?" he asked Menlik.

"Not so, but we are not told much. We live apart and no one of us goes to the ship unless he is summoned. For they have weapons to guard them, or long since they would have been dead. It is not proper for a man to eat from the pot, ride in the wind, sleep easy under the same sky with him who has slain his brother."

"They have then killed among your people?"

"They have killed," Menlik returned briefly.

Kaydessa stirred and muttered a word or two to her brother. Hulagur's head came up, and he exploded into violent speech.

"What does he say?" Deklay demanded.

The girl replied: "He speaks of our father who aided in the escape of three and so afterward was slain by the leader as a lesson to us-since he was our 'white beard,' the Khan."

"We have taken the oath in blood-under the Wolf Head Standard-that they will also die," Menlik added. "But first we must shake them out of their ship-shell."

"That is the problem," Travis elaborated for the benefit of his clansmen. "We must get these Reds away from their protected camp-out into the open. When they now go they are covered by this 'caller' which keeps the Tatars under their control, but it has no effect on us."

"So, again I say: What is all this to us?" Deklay got to his feet. "This machine does not hunt us, and we can make our camps in this land where no Pinda-lick-o-yi can find them — —"

"We are not *dobe-gusndhe-he* —invulnerable. Nor do we know the full range of machines they can use. It does no one well to say '*doxa-da*' —this is not so-when he does not know all that lies in an enemy's wickiup."

To Travis' relief he saw agreement mirrored on Buck's face, Tsoay's, Nolan's. From the beginning he had had little hope of swaying Deklay; he could only trust that the verdict of the majority would be the accepted one. It went back to the old, old Apache institution of prestige. A *nantan*-chief had the *go'ndi*, the high power, as a gift from birth. Common men could possess horse power or cattle power; they might have the gift of acquiring wealth so they could make generous gifts-be *ikadntl'izi*, the wealthy ones who spoke for their family groups within the loose network of the tribe. But there was no hereditary chieftainship or even an undivided rule within a rancheria. The *nagunlka-dnat'an*, or war chief, often led only on the warpath and had no voice in clan matters save those dealing with a raid.

And to have a split now would fatally weaken their small clan. Deklay and those of a like mind might elect to withdraw and not one of the rest could deny him that right.

"We shall think on this," Buck said. "Here is food, water, pasturage for horses, a camp for our visitors. They will wait here." He looked at Travis. "You will wait with them, Fox, since you know their ways."

Travis' immediate reaction was objection, but then he realized Buck's wisdom. To offer the proposition of alliance to the Apaches needed an impartial spokesman. And if he himself did it, Deklay might automatically oppose the idea. Let Buck talk and it would be a statement of fact.

"It is well," Travis agreed.

Buck looked about, as if judging time from the lie of sun and shadow on the ground. "We shall return in the morning when the shadow lies here." With the toe of his high moccasin he made an impression in the soft earth. Then, without any formal farewell, he strode off, the others fast on his heels.

"He is your chief, that one?" Kaydessa asked, pointing after Buck.

"He is one having a large voice in council," Travis replied. He set about building up the cooking fire, bringing out the body of a split-horn calf which had been left them. Menlik sat on his heels by the pool, dipping up drinking water with his hand. Now he squinted his eyes against the probe of the sun.

"It will require much talking to win over the short one," he observed. "That one does not like us or your plan. Just as there will be those among the Horde who will not like it either." He flipped water drops from his fingers. "But this I do know, man who calls himself Fox, if we do not make a common cause, then we have no hope of going against the Reds. It will be for them as a man crushing fleas." He brought his hand down on his knee in emphatic slaps. "So ... and so ... and so!"

"This do I think also," Travis admitted.

"So let us both hope that all men will be as wise as we," Menlik said, smiling. "And since we can take a hand in that decision, this remains a time for rest."

The shaman might be content to sleep the afternoon away, but after he had eaten, Hulagur wandered up and down the valley, making a lengthy business of rubbing down their horses with twists of last season's grass. Now and then he paused beside Kaydessa and spoke, his uneasiness plain to Travis although he could not understand the words.

Travis had settled down in the shade, half dozing, yet alert to every movement of the three Tatars. He tried not to think of what might be happening in the rancheria by switching his mind to that misty valley of the towers. Did any of those three alien structures contain such a grab bag of the past as he, Ashe, and Murdock had found on that other world where the winged people had gathered together for them the artifacts of an older civilization? At that time he had created for their hosts a new weapon of defense, turning metal tubes into blow-guns. It had been there, too, where he had chanced upon the library of tapes, one of which had eventually landed Travis and his people here on Topaz.

Even if he did find racks of such tapes in one of those towers, there would be no way of using them-with the ship wrecked on the mountain side. Only-Travis' fingers itched where they lay quiet on his knees-there might be other things waiting. If he were only free to explore!

He reached out to touch Menlik's shoulder. The shaman half turned, opening his eyes with the languid effort of a sleepy cat. But the spark of intelligence awoke in them quickly.

"What is it?"

For a moment Travis hesitated, already regretting his impulse. He did not know how much Menlik remembered of the present. Remember of the present-one part of the Apache's mind was wryly amused at that snarled estimate of their situation. Men who had been dropped into their racial and ancestral pasts until the present time was less real than the dreams conditioning them had a difficult job evaluating any situation. But since Menlik had clung to his knowledge of English, he must be less far down that stairway.

"When we met you, Kaydessa and I, it was outside that valley." Travis was still of two minds about this questioning, but the Tatar camp had been close to the towers and there was a good chance the Mongols had explored them. "And inside were buildings ... very old...."

Menlik was fully alert now. He took his wand, played with it as he spoke:

"That is, or was, a place of much power, Fox. Oh, I know that you question my kinship with the spirits and the powers they give. But one learns not to dispute what one feels here-and here —" His long, somewhat grimy fingers went to his forehead and then to the bare brown chest where his shirt fell open. "I have walked the stone path in that valley, and there have been the whispers —"

"Whispers?"

Menlik twirled the wand. "Whispers which are too low for many ears to distinguish. You can hear them as one hears the buzzing of an insect, but never the words-no, never the words! But that is a place of great power!"

"A place to explore!"

But Menlik watched only his wand. "That I wonder, Fox, truly do I wonder. This is not our world. And here there may be that which does not welcome us."

Tricks-in-trade of a shaman? Or was it true recognition of something beyond human description? Travis could not be sure, but he knew that he must return to the valley and see for himself.

"Listen," Menlik said, leaning closer, "I have heard your tale, that you were on that first ship, the one which brought you unwilling along the old star paths. Have you ever seen such a thing as this?"

He smoothed a space of soft earth and with the narrow tip of his wand began to draw. Whatever role Menlik had played in the present before he had been reconditioned into a shaman of the Horde, he had had the ability of an artist, for with a minimum of lines he created a figure in that sketch.

It was a man or at least a figure with general human outlines. But the round, slightly oversized skull was bare, the clothing skintight to reveal unnaturally thin limbs. There were large eyes, small nose and mouth, rather crowded into the lower third of the head, giving an impression of an over-expanded brain case above. And it was familiar.

Not the flying men of the other world, certainly not the nocturnal ape-things. Yet for all its alien quality Travis was sure he had seen its like before. He closed his eyes and tried to visualize it apart from lines in the soil.

Such a head, white, almost like the bone of a skull laid bare, such a head lying face down on a bone-thin arm clad in a blue-purple skintight sleeve. Where had he seen it?

The Apache gave a sharp exclamation as he remembered fully. The derelict spaceship as he had first found it-the dead alien officer had still been seated at its controls! The alien who had set the tape which took them out into that forgotten empire-he was the subject of Menlik's drawing!

"Where? When did you see such a one?" The Apache bent down over the Tatar.

Menlik looked troubled. "He came into my mind when I walked the valley. I thought I could almost see such a face in one of the tower windows, but of that I am not sure. Who is it?"

"Someone from the old days-those who once ruled the stars," Travis answered. But were they still here then, the remnant of a civilization which had flourished ten thousand years ago? Were the Baldies, who centuries ago had hunted down so ruthlessly the Russians who had dared to loot their wrecked ships, still on Topaz?

He remembered the story of Ross Murdock's escape from those aliens in the far past of Europe, and he shivered. Murdock was tough, steel tough, yet his own description of that epic chase and the final meeting had carried with it his terror. What could a handful of primitively armed and almost primitively minded Terrans do now if they had to dispute Topaz with the Baldies?

10

"Beyond this —" Menlik worked his way to the very lip of a drop, raising a finger cautiously — "beyond this we do not go."

"But you say that the camp of your people lies well out in the plains —" Jil-Lee was up on one knee, using the field glasses they had brought from the stores of the wrecked ship. He passed them along to Travis. There was nothing to be sighted but the rippling amber waves of the tall grasses, save for an occasional break of a copse of trees near the foothills.

They had reached this point in the early morning, threading through the pass, making their way across the section known to the outlaws. From here they could survey the debatable land where their temporary allies insisted the Reds were in full control.

The result of the conference in the south had been this uneasy alliance. From the start Travis realized that he could not hope to commit the clan to any set plan, that even to get this scouting party to come against the stubborn resistance of Deklay and his reactionaries was a major achievement. There was now an opening wedge of six Apaches in the north.

"Beyond this," Menlik repeated, "they keep watch and can control us with the caller."

"What do you think?" Travis passed the glasses to Nolan.

If they were ever to develop a war chief, this lean man, tall for an Apache and slow to speak, might fill that role. He adjusted the lenses and began a detailed study-sweep of the open territory. Then he stiffened; his mouth, below the masking of the glasses, was tight.

"What is it?" Jil-Lee asked.

"Riders-two ... four ... five.... Also something else-in the air."

Menlik jerked back and grabbed at Nolan's arm, dragging him down by the weight of his body.

"The flyer! Come back-back!" He was still pulling at Nolan, prodding at Travis with one foot, and the Apaches stared at him with amazement.

The shaman sputtered in his own language, and then, visibly regaining command of himself, spoke English once more.

"Those are hunters, and they carry a caller. Either some others have escaped or they are determined to find our mountain camp."

Jil-Lee looked at Travis. "You did not feel anything when the woman was under that spell?"

Travis shook his head. Jil-Lee nodded and then said to the shaman: "We shall stay here and watch. But since it is bad for you-do you go. And we shall meet you near this place of the towers. Agreed?"

For a moment Menlik's face held a shadowy expression Travis tried to read. Was it resentment-resentment that he was forced to retreat when the others could stand their ground? Did the Tatar believe that he lost face this way? But the shaman gave a grunt of what they took as assent and slipped over the edge of the lookout point. A moment later they heard him speaking the Mongol tongue, warning Hulagur and Lotchu, his companions on the scout. Then came the clatter of pony hoofs as they rode their mounts away.

The Apaches settled back in the cup, which gave them a wide view over the plains. Soon it was not necessary to use the glasses in order to sight the advancing party of hunters-five riders, four wearing Tatar dress. The fifth had such an odd outline that Travis was reminded of Menlik's sketch of the alien. Under the sharper vision of the glasses he saw that the rider was equipped with a pack strapped between his shoulders and a bulbous helmet covering most of his head. Highly specialized equipment for communication, Travis guessed.

"That is a 'copter up above," Nolan said. "Different shape from ours."

They had been familiar with helicopters back on Terra. Ranchers used them for range inspection, and all of the Apache volunteers had flown in them. But Nolan was correct; this one possessed several unfamiliar features.

"The Tatars say they don't bring those very far into the mountains," Jil-Lee mused. "That could explain their man on horseback; he gets in where they don't fly."

Nolan fingered his bow. "If these Reds depend upon their machine to control what they seek, then they may be taken by surprise —— "

"But not yet!" Travis spoke sharply. Nolan frowned at him.

Jil-Lee chuckled. "The way is not so dark for us, younger brother, that we need your torch held for our feet!"

Travis swallowed back any retort, accepting the fairness of that rebuke. He had no right to believe that he alone knew the best way of handling the enemy. Biting on the sourness of that realization, he lay quietly with the others, watching the riders enter the foothills perhaps a quarter of a mile to the west.

The helicopter was circling now over the men riding into a cut between two rises. When they were lost to view, the pilot made wider casts, and Travis thought the flyer's crew were probably in communication with the helmeted one of the quintet on the ground.

He stirred. "They are heading for the Tatar camp, just as if they know exactly where it is —"

"That also may be true," Nolan replied. "What do we know of these Tatars? They have freely said that the Reds can hold them in mind ropes when they wish. Already they may be so bound. I say-let us go back to our own country." He added to the decisiveness of that by handing Jil-Lee the glasses and sliding down from their perch.

Travis looked at the other. In a way he could understand the wisdom of Nolan's suggestion. But he was sure that withdrawal now would only postpone trouble. Sooner or later the Apaches would have to stand against the Reds, and if they could do it now while the enemy was occupied with trouble from the Tatars, so much the better.

Jil-Lee was following Nolan. But something in Travis rebelled. He watched the circling helicopter. If it was overhanging the action area of the horsemen, they had either reined in or were searching a relatively small section of the foothills.

Reluctantly Travis descended to the hollow where Jil-Lee stood with Nolan. Tsoay and Lupe and Rope were a little to one side as if the final orders would come from their seniors.

"It would be well," Jil-Lee said slowly, "if we saw what weapons they have. I want a closer look at the equipment of that one in the helmet. Also," he smiled straight at Nolan—"I do not think that they can detect the presence of warriors of the People unless we will it so."

Nolan ran a finger along the curve of his bow, shot a measuring glance right and left at the general contours of the country.

"There is wisdom in what you say, elder brother. Only this is a trail we shall take alone, not allowing the men with fur hats to know where we walk." He looked pointedly in Travis' direction.

"That is wisdom, *Ba'is'a*," Travis promptly replied, giving Nolan the old title accorded the leader of a war party. Travis was grateful for that much of a concession.

They swung into action, heading southeast at an angle which should bring them across the track of the enemy hunting party. The path was theirs at last, only moments after the passing of their quarry. None of the five riders was taking any precautions to cover his trail. Each moved with the confidence of one not having to fear any attack.

From cover the Apaches looked aloft. They could hear the faint hum of the helicopter. It was still circling, Tsoay reported from a higher check point, but those circles remained close over the plains area-the riders had already passed beyond the limits of that aerial sentry.

Three to a side, the Apaches advanced with the trail between them. They were carefully hidden when they caught up with the hunters. The four Tatars were grouped together; the fifth man, heavily burdened by his pack, had climbed from the saddle and was sitting on the ground, his hands busy with a flat plate which covered him from upper chest to belt.

Now that he had a chance to see them closely, Travis noted the lack of expression on the broad Tatar faces. The four men were blank of eye, astride their mounts with no apparent awareness of their present surroundings. Then as one, their heads swung around to the helmeted leader before they dismounted and stood motionless for a long moment in a way which reminded Travis of the coyotes' attitude when they endeavored to pass some message to him. But these men even lacked the signs of thinking intelligence the animals had.

The helmeted man's hand moved across his chest plate, and instantly his followers came into a measure of life. One put his hand to his forehead with an odd, half-dazed gesture. Another half crouched, his lips wrinkling back in a snarl. And the leader, watching him, laughed. Then he snapped an order, his hand poised over his control plate.

One of the four took the horse reins, made the mounts fast to near-by bushes. Then as one they began to walk forward, the Red bringing up the rear several paces behind the nearest Tatar. They were going upslope to the crest of a small ridge.

The Tatar who first reached the crest put his hands to cup his mouth, sent a ringing cry southward, and the faint "hu-hu-hu" echoed on and on through the hills.

Either Menlik had reached the camp in time, or his people were not to be so easily enticed. For though the hunters waited for a long time, there was no answer to that hail. At last the helmeted man called his captives, bringing them sullenly down to mount and ride again—a move which suited the Apaches.

They could not tell how close was the communication between the rider and the helicopter. And they were still too near the plains to attack unless it was necessary for their own protection. Travis dropped back to join Nolan.

"He controls them by that plate on his chest," he said. "If we would take them, we must get at that —"

"These Tatars use lariats in fighting. Did they not rope you as a calf is roped for branding? Then why do they not so take this Red, binding his arms to his sides?" The suspicion in Nolan's voice was plain.

"Perhaps in them is some conditioned control making it so that they cannot attack their rulers —"

"I do not like this matter of machines which can play this way and that with minds and bodies!" flared Nolan. "A man should only *use* a weapon, not be one!"

Travis could agree to that. Had they by the wreck of their own ship and the death of Ruthven, escaped just such an existence as these Tatars now endured? If so, why? He and all the Apaches were volunteers, eager and willing to form new world colonies. What had happened back on Terra that they had been so ruthlessly sent out without warning and under Redax? Another small piece of that puzzle, or maybe the heart of the whole picture snapped into place. Had the project learned in some way of the Tatar settlement on Topaz and so been forced to speed up that translation from late twentieth-century Americans to primitives? That would explain a lot!

Travis returned abruptly to the matter now at hand as he saw a peak ahead. The party they were trailing was heading directly for the outlaw hide-out. Travis hoped Menlik had warned them in time. There-that wall of cliff to his left must shelter the valley of the towers, though it was still miles ahead. Travis did not believe the hunters would be able to reach their goal unless they traveled at night. They might not know of the ape-things which could menace the dark.

But the enemy, whether he knew of such dangers or not, did not intend to press on. As the sun pulled away, leaving crevices and crannies shadow dark, the hunters stopped to make camp. The Apaches, after their custom on the war trail, gathered on the heights above.

"This Red seems to think that he shall find those he seeks sitting waiting for him, as if their feet were nipped tight in a trap," Tsoay remarked.

"It is the habit of the Pinda-lick-o-yi," Lupe added, "to believe they are greater than all others. Yet this one is a stupid fool walking into the arms of a she-bear with a cub." He chuckled.

"A man with a rifle does not fear a man armed only with a stick," Travis cut in quickly. "This one is armed with a weapon which he has good reason to believe makes him invulnerable to attack. If he rests tonight, he probably leaves his machine on guard."

"At least we are sure of one thing," Nolan said in half agreement. "This one does not suspect that there are any in these hills save those he can master. And his machine does not work against us. Thus at dawn —" He made a swift gesture, and they smiled in concert.

At dawn-the old time of attack. An Apache does not attack at night. Travis was not sure that any of them could break that old taboo and creep down upon the camp before the coming of new light.

But tomorrow morning they would take over this confident Red, strip him of his enslaving machine.

Travis' head jerked. It had come as suddenly as a blow between his eyes-to half stun him. What ...what was it? Not any physical impact-no, something which was dazing but still immaterial. He braced his whole body, awaiting its return, trying frantically to understand what had happened in that instant of vertigo and seeming disembodiment. Never had he experienced anything like it-or had he? Two years or more ago when he had gone through the time transfer to enter the Arizona of the Folsom Men some ten thousand years earlier-that moment of transfer had been something like this, a sensation of being awry in space and time with no stable footing to be found.

Yet he was lying here on very tangible rock and soil, and nothing about him in the shadow-hung landscape of Topaz had changed in the slightest. But that blow had left behind it a quivering residue of panic buried far inside him, a tender spot like an open wound.

Travis drew a deep breath which was almost a sob, levered himself up on one elbow to stare intently down into the enemy camp. Was this some attack from the other's unknown weapon? Suddenly he was not at all sure what might happen when the Apaches made that dawn rush.

Jil-Lee was in station on his right. Travis must compare notes with him to be sure that this was not indeed a trap. Better to retreat now than to be taken like fish in a net. He crept out of his place, gave the chittering signal call of the fluff-ball, and heard Jil-Lee's answer in a cleverly mimicked trill of a night insect.

"Did you feel something just now-in your head?" Travis found it difficult to put that sensation into words.

"Not so. But you did?"

He had-of course, he had! The remains of it were still in him, that point of panic. "Yes."

"The machine?"

"I don't know." Travis' confusion grew. It might be that he alone of the party had been struck. If so, he could be a danger to his own kind.

"This is not good. I think we had better hold council, away from here." Jil-Lee's whisper was the merest ghost of sound. He chirped again to be answered from Tsoay upslope, who passed on the signal.

The first moon was high in the sky as the Apaches gathered together. Again Travis asked his question: Had any of the others felt that odd blow? He was met by negatives.

But Nolan had the final word: "This is not good," he echoed Jil-Lee's comment. "If it was the Red machine at work, then we may all be swept into his net along with those he seeks. Perhaps the longer one remains close to that thing, the more influence it gains over him. We shall stay here until dawn. If the enemy would reach the place they seek, then they must pass below us, for that is the easiest road. Burdened with his machine, that Red has ever taken the easiest way. So, we shall see if he also has a defense against these when they come without warning." He touched the arrows in his quiver.

To kill from ambush meant that they might never learn the secret of the machine, but after his experience Travis was willing to admit that Nolan's caution was the wise way. Travis wanted no part of a second attack like that which had shaken him so. And Nolan had not ordered a general retreat. It must be in the war chief's thoughts as it was in Travis' that if the machine could have an influence over Apaches, it must cease to function.

They set their ambush with the age-old skill the Redax had grafted into their memories. Then there was nothing to do but wait.

It was an hour after dawn when Tsoay signaled that the enemy was coming, and shortly after, they heard the thud of ponies' hoofs. The first Tatar plodded into view, and by the stance of his body in the saddle, Travis knew the Red had him under full control. Two, then three Tatars passed between the teeth of the Apache trap. The fourth one had allowed a wider gap to open between himself and his fellows.

Then the Red leader came. His face below the bulge of the helmet was not happy. Travis believed the man was not a horseman by inclination. The Apache set arrow to bow cord, and at the chirp from Nolan, fired in concert with his clansmen.

Only one of those arrows found a target. The Red's pony gave a shrill scream of pain and terror, reared, pawing at the air, toppled back, pinning its shouting rider under it.

The Red had had a defense right enough, one which had somehow deflected the arrows. But he neither had protection against his own awkward seat in the saddle nor the arrow which had seriously wounded the now threshing pony.

Ahead the Tatars twisted and writhed, mouthed tortured cries, then dropped out of their saddles to lie limply on the ground as if the arrows aimed at the master had instead struck each to the heart.

Either the Red was lucky, or his reactions were quick. He had somehow rolled clear of the struggling horse as Lupe leaped from behind a boulder, knife out and ready. To the eyes of the Apaches the helmeted man lay easy prey to Lupe's attack. Nor did he raise an arm to defend himself, though one hand lay free across the plate on his chest.

But the young Apache stumbled, rebounding back as if he had run into an unseen wall-when his knife was still six inches away from the other. Lupe cried out, shook under a second impact as the Red fired an automatic with his other hand.

Travis dropped his bow, returned to the most primitive weapon of all. His hand closed around a stone and he hurled the fist-sized oval straight at the helmet so clearly outlined against the rocks below.

But even as Lupe's knife had never touched flesh, so was the rock deflected; the Red was covered by some protective field. This was certainly nothing the Apaches had seen before. Nolan's whistle summoned them to draw back.

The Red fired again, the sharp bark of the hand gun harsh and loud. He did not have any real target, for with the exception of Lupe the Apaches had gone to earth. Between the rocks the Red was struggling to his feet, but he moved slowly, favoring his side and one leg; he had not come totally unharmed from his tumble with the pony.

An armed enemy who could not be touched-one who knew there were more than outlaws in this region. The Red leader was far more of a threat to the Apaches now than he had ever been. He must not be allowed to escape.

He was holstering his gun, moving along with one hand against the rocks to steady himself, trying to reach one of the ponies that stood with trailing reins beside the inert Tatars.

But when the enemy reached the far side of that rock he would have to sacrifice either his steadying hold, or his touch on the chest plate where his other hand rested. Would he, then, for an instant be vulnerable?

The pony!

Travis put an arrow on bow cord and shot. Not at the Red, who had released his hold of the rock, preferring to totter instead of lose control of the chest plate-but into the air straight before the nose of the mount.

The pony neighed wildly, tried to turn, and its shoulder caught the free, groping hand of the Red and spun the man around and back, so that he flung up both hands in an effort to ward himself off the rocks. Then the pony stampeded down the break, its companions catching the same fever, trailing in a mad dash which kept the Red hard against the boulders.

He continued to stand there until the horses, save for the wounded one still kicking fruitlessly, were gone. Travis felt a sense of reprieve. They might not be able to get at the Red, but he was hurt and afoot, two strikes which might yet reduce him to a condition the Apaches could handle.

Apparently the other was also aware of that, for now he pushed out from the rocks and stumbled along after the ponies. But he went only a step or two. Then, settling back once more against a convenient boulder, he began to work at the plate on his chest.

Nolan appeared noiselessly beside Travis. "What does he do?" His lips were very close to the younger man's ear, his voice hardly more than a breath.

Travis shook his head slightly. The Red's actions were a complete mystery. Unless, now disabled and afoot, he was trying to summon aid. Though there was no landing place for a helicopter here.

Now was the time to try and reach Lupe. Travis had seen a slight movement in the fallen Apache's hand, the first indication that the enemy's shot had not been as fatal as it had looked. He touched Nolan's arm, pointed to Lupe; and then, discarding his bow and quiver beside the war leader, he stripped for action. There was cover down to the wounded Apache which would aid him. He must pass one of the Tatars on the way, but none of the tribesmen had shown any signs of life since they had fallen from their saddles at the first attack.

With infinite care, Travis lowered himself into a narrow passage, took a lizard's way between brush and boulder, pausing only when he reached the Tatar for a quick check on the potential enemy.

The lean brown face was half turned, one cheek in the sand, but the slack mouth, the closed eyes were those, Travis believed, of a dead man. By some action of his diabolic machine the Red must have snuffed out his four captives-perhaps in the belief that they were part of the Apache attack.

Travis reached the rock where Lupe lay. He knew that Nolan was watching the Red and would give him warning if he suddenly showed an interest in anything but his machine. The Apache reached out, his hands closing on Lupe's ankles. Beneath his touch, flesh and muscle tensed. Lupe's eyes were open, focused now on Travis. There was a bleeding furrow above his right ear. The Red had tried a difficult head shot, failing in his aim by a mere fraction of an inch.

Lupe made a swift move for which Travis was ready. His grip on the other's body helped to tumble them both around a rock which lay between them and the Red. There was the crack of another shot and dust spurted from the side of the boulder. But they lay together, safe for the present, as Travis was sure the enemy would not risk an open attack on their small fortress.

With Travis' aid Lupe struggled back up to the site where Nolan waited. Jil-Lee was there to make competent examination of the boy's wound.

"Creased," he reported. "A sore head, but no great damage. Perhaps a scar later, warrior!" He gave Lupe an encouraging thump on the shoulder, before plastering an aid pack over the cut.

"Now we go!" Nolan spoke with emphatic decision.

"He saw enough of us to know we are not Tatars."

Nolan's eyes were cold, his mouth grim as he faced Travis.

"And how can we fight him —?"

"There is a wall —a wall you cannot see-about him," Lupe broke in. "When I would strike at him, I could not!"

"A man with invisible protection and a gun," Jil-Lee took up the argument. "How would you deal with him, younger brother?"

"I don't know," Travis admitted. Yet he also believed that if they withdrew, left the Red here to be found by his own people, the enemy would immediately begin an investigation of the southern country. Perhaps, pushed by their need for learning more about the Apaches, they would bring the helicopter in over the mountains. The answer to all Apache dangers, for now, lay in the immediate future of this one man.

"He is hurt, he cannot go far on foot. And even if he calls the 'copter, there is no landing place. He will have to move elsewhere to be picked up." Travis thought aloud, citing the thin handful of points in their favor.

Tsoay nodded toward the rim of the ravine. "Rocks up there and rocks can roll. Start an earthslide...."

Something within Travis balked at that. From the first he had been willing enough to slug it out with the Red, weapon to weapon, man to man. Also, he had wanted to take a captive, not stand over a body. But to use the nature of the country against the enemy, that was the oldest Apache trick of all and one they would have to be forced to employ.

Nolan had already nodded in assent, and Tsoay and Jil-Lee started off. Even if the Red did possess a protective wall device, could it operate in full against a landslide? They all doubted that.

The Apaches reached the cliff rim without exposing themselves to the enemy's fire. The Red still sat there calmly, his back against the rock, his hands busy with his equipment as if he had all the time in the world.

Then suddenly came a scream from more than one throat.

"*Dar-u-gar!*" The ancient war cry of the Mongol Hordes.

Then over the lip of the other slope rose a wave of men-their curved swords out, a glazed set to their eyes-heading for the Amerindians with utter disregard for any personal safety. Menlik in the lead, his shaman's robe flapping wide below his belt like the wings of some oversized predatory bird. Hulagur ...Jagatai ...men from the outlaws' camp. And they were not striving to destroy their disabled overlord in the vale below, but to wipe out the Apaches!

Only the fact that the Apaches were already sheltered behind the rocks they were laboring to dislodge gave them a precious few moments of grace. There was no time to use their bows. They could only use knives to meet the swords of the Tatars, knives and the fact that they could fight with unclouded minds.

"He has them under control!" Travis pawed at Jil-Lee's shoulder. "Get him-they'll stop!"

He did not wait to see if the other Apache understood. Instead, he threw the full force of his own body against the rock they had made the center stone of their slide. It gave, rolled, carrying with it and before it the rest of the piled rubble. Travis stumbled, fell flat, and then a body thudded down upon him, and he was fighting for his life to keep a blade from his throat. Around him were the shouts and cries of embroiled warriors; then all was silenced by a roar from below.

Glazed eyes in a face only a foot from his own, the twisted, panting mouth sending gusts of breath into his nostrils. Suddenly there was reason back in those eyes, a bewilderment, which became fear ...panic.... The Tatar's body twisted in Travis' hold, striving now not to attack, but to win free. As the Apache loosened his grip the other jerked away, so that for a moment or two they lay gasping, side by side.

Men sat up to look at men. There was a spreading stain down Jil-Lee's side and one of the Tatars sprawled near him, both his hands on his chest, coughing violently.

Menlik clawed at the trunk of a wind-twisted mountain tree, pulled himself to his feet, and stood swaying as might a man long ill and recovering from severe exertion.

Insensibly both sides drew apart, leaving a space between Tatar and Apache. The faces of the Amerindians were grim, those of the Mongols bewildered and then harsh as they eyed their late opponents with dawning reason. What had begun in compulsion for the Tatars might well flare now into rational combat-and from that to a campaign of extermination.

Travis was on his feet. He looked over the lip of the drop. The Red was still in his place down there, a pile of rubble about him. His protection must have failed, for his head was back at an unnatural angle and the dent in his helmet could be easily seen.

"That one is dead-or helpless!" Travis cried out. "Do you still wish to fight for him, Shaman?"

Menlik came away from the tree and walked to the edge of the drop. The others, too, were moving forward. After the shaman looked down he stooped, picked up a small stone, and flung it at the motionless Red. There was a crack of sound. They all saw the tiny spurt of flame, a curl of smoke from the plate on the Red's chest. Not only the man, but his control was finished now.

A wolfish growl and two of the Tatars swung over, started down to the Red. Menlik shouted and they slackened pace.

"We want that," he cried in English. "Perhaps so we can learn —"

"The learning is yours," Jil-Lee replied. "Just as this land is yours, Shaman. But I warn you, from this day do not ride south!"

Menlik turned, the charms on his belt clicking. "So that is the way it is to be, Apache?"

"That is the way it shall be, Tatar! We do not ride to war with allies who may turn their knives against our backs because they are slaves to a machine the enemy controls."

The Tatar's long, slender-fingered hands opened and closed. "You are a wise man, Apache, but sometimes more than wisdom alone is needed — —"

"We are wise men, Shaman, let it rest there," Jil-Lee replied somberly.

Already the Apaches were on their way, putting two cliff ridges behind them before they halted to examine and cover their wounds.

"We go." Nolan's chin lifted, indicating the southern route. "Here we do not come again; there is too much witchcraft in this place."

Travis stirred, saw that Jil-Lee was frowning at him.

"Go —?" he repeated.

"Yes, younger brother? You would continue to run with these who are governed by a machine?"

"No. Only, eyes are needed on this side of the mountains."

"Why?" This time Jil-Lee was plainly on the side of the conservatives. "We have now seen this machine at work. It is fortunate that the Red is dead. He will carry no tales of us back to his people as you feared. Thus, if we remain south from now on, we are safe. And this fight between Tatar and Red is none of ours. What do you seek here?"

"I must go again to the place of the towers," Travis answered with the truth. But his friends were facing him with heavy disapproval-now a full row of Deklays.

"Did you not tell us that you felt this strange thing during the night we waited about the camp? What if you become one with these Tatars and are also controlled by the machine? Then you, too, can be made into a weapon against us-your clansmen!" Jil-Lee was almost openly hostile.

Sense was on his side. But in Travis was this other desire of which he was becoming more conscious by the minute. There was a reason for those towers, perhaps a reason important enough for him to discover and run the risk of angering his own people.

"There may be this —" Nolan's voice was remote and cold, "you may already be a piece of this thing, bound to the machines. If so, we do not want you among us."

There it was-an open hostility with more power behind it than Deklay's motiveless disapproval had carried. Travis was troubled. The family, the clan-they were important. If he took the wrong step now and was outlawed from that tight fortress, then as an Apache he would indeed be a lost man. In the past of his people there had been renegades from the tribe-men such as the infamous Apache Kid who had killed and killed again, not only white men but his own people. Wolf men living wolves' lives in the hills. Travis was threatened with that. Yet-up the ladder of civilization, down the ladder-why did this feverish curiosity ride him so cruelly now?

"Listen," Jil-Lee, his side padded with bandages, stepped closer —"and tell me, younger brother, what is it that you seek in these towers?"

"On another world there were secrets of the old ones to be found in such ancient buildings. Here that might also be true."

"And among the secrets of those old ones," Nolan's voice was still harsh —"were those which brought us to this world, is that not so?"

"Did any man drive you, Nolan, or you, Tsoay, or you, Jil-Lee, or any of us, to promise to go beyond the stars? You were told what might be done, and you were eager to try it. You were all volunteers!"

"Save for this voyage when we were told nothing," Jil-Lee answered, cutting straight to the heart of the matter. "Yet, Nolan, I do not believe that it is for more voyage tapes that our younger brother now searches, nor would those do us any good-as our ship will not rise again from here. What is it that you do seek?"

"Knowledge-weapons, maybe. Can we stand against these machines of the Reds? Yet many of the devices they now use are taken from the star ships they have looted through time. To every weapon there is a defense."

Nolan blinked and for the first time a hint of interest touched the mask of his face. "To the bow, the rifle," he said softly, "to the rifle, the machine gun, to the cannon, the big bomb. The defense can be far worse than the first weapon. So you think that in these towers there may be things which shall be to the Reds' machines as the bomb is to the cannon of the Horse Soldiers?"

Travis had an inspiration. "Did not our people lay aside the bow for the rifle when we went up against the Bluecoats?"

"We do not so go up against these Reds!" protested Lupe.

"Not now. But what if they come across the mountains, perhaps driving the Tatars before them to do their fighting —?"

"And you believe that if you find weapons in these towers, you will know how to use them?" Jil-Lee asked. "What will give you that knowledge, younger brother?"

"I do not claim such knowledge," Travis countered. "But this much I do have: Once I studied to be an archaeologist and I have seen other storehouses of these star people. Who else among us can say as much as that?"

"That is the truth," Jil-Lee acknowledged. "Also there is good sense in this seeking out of the tower things. Let the Reds find such first-if they exist at all-and then we may truly be caught in a box canyon with only death at our heels."

"And you would go to these towers now?" Nolan demanded.

"I can cut across country and then rejoin you on the other side of the pass!" The feeling of urgency which had been mounting in Travis was now so demanding that he wanted to race ahead through the wilderness. He was surprised when Jil-Lee put out his palm up as if to warn the younger man.

"Take care, younger brother! This is not a lucky business. And remember, if one goes too far down a wrong trail, there is sometimes no returning—"

"We shall wait on the other side of the pass for one day," Nolan added. "Then—" he shrugged —"where you go will be your own affair."

Travis did not understand that promise of trouble. He was already two steps down his chosen path.

12

Travis had taken a direct cross route through the heights, but not swiftly enough to reach his objective before nightfall. And he had no wish to enter the tower valley by moonlight. In him two emotions now warred. There was the urge to invade the towers, to discover their secret, and flaring higher and higher the beginnings of a new fear. Was he now a battlefield for the superstitions of his race reborn by the Redax and his modern education in the Pinda-lick-o-yi world-half Apache brave of the past, half modern archaeologist with a thirst for knowledge? Or was the fear rooted more deeply and for another reason?

Travis crouched in a hollow, trying to understand what he felt. Why was it suddenly so overwhelmingly important for him to investigate the towers? If he only had the coyotes with him....Why and where had they gone?

He was alive to every noise out of the night, every scent the wind carried to him. The night had its own life, just as the daylight hours held theirs. Only a few of those sounds could he identify, even less did he see. There was one wide-winged, huge flying thing which passed across the green-gold plate of the nearer moon. It was so large that for an instant Travis believed the helicopter had come. Then the wings flapped, breaking the glide, and the creature merged in the shadows of the night —a hunter large enough to be a serious threat, and one he had never seen before.

Relying on his own small defense, the strewing of brittle sticks along the only approach to the hollow, Travis dozed at intervals, his head down on his forearm across his bent knees. But the cold cramped him and he was glad to see the graying sky of pre-dawn. He swallowed two ration tablets and a couple of mouthfuls of water from his canteen and started on.

By sunup he had reached the ledge of the waterfall, and he hurried along the ancient road at a pace which increased to a run the closer he drew to the valley. Deliberately he slowed, his native caution now in control, so that he was walking as he passed through the gateway into the swirling mists which alternately exposed and veiled the towers.

There was no change in the scene from the time he had come there with Kaydessa. But now, rising from a comfortable sprawl on the yellow-and-green pavement, was a welcoming committee-Nalik'ideyu and Naginlta showing no more excitement at his coming than if they had parted only moments before.

Travis went down on one knee, holding out his hand to the female, who had always been the more friendly. She advanced a step or two, touched a cold nose to his knuckles, and whined.

"Why?" He voiced that one word, but behind it was a long list of questions. Why had they left him? Why were they here where there was no hunting? Why did they meet him now as if they had calmly expected his return?

Travis glanced from the animals to the towers, those windows set in diamond pattern. And again he was visited by the impression that he was under observation. With the mist floating across those openings, it would be easy for a lurker to watch him unseen.

He walked slowly on into the valley, his moccasins making no sound on the pavement, but he could hear the faint click of the coyotes' claws as they paced beside him, on each hand. The sun did not penetrate here, making merely a gilt fog of the mist. As he approached within touching distance of the first tower, it seemed to Travis that the mist was curling about him; he could no longer see the archway through which he had entered the valley.

"Naye'nezyani-Slayer of Monsters-give strength to the bow arm, to the knife wrist!" Out of what long-buried memory did that ancient plea come? Travis was hardly aware of the sense of the words until he spoke them aloud. "You who wait —*shi inday to-dah ishan* —an Apache is not food for you! I am Fox of the Itcatcudnde'yu-the Eagle People; and beside me walk *ga'ns* of power...."

Travis blinked and shook his head as one waking. Why had he spoken so, using words and phrases which were not part of any modern speech?

He moved on, around the base of the first tower, to find no door, no break in its surface below the second-story windows-to the next structure and the next, until he had encircled all three. If he were to enter any, he must find a way of reaching the lowest windows.

On he went to the other opening of the valley, the one which gave upon the territory of the Tatar camp. But he did not sight any of the Mongols as he hacked down a sapling, trimmed, and smoothed it into a blunt-pointed lance. His sash-belt, torn into even strips and knotted together, gave him a rope which he judged would be barely long enough for his purpose.

Then Travis made a chancy cast for the lower window of the nearest tower. On the second try the lance slipped in, and he gave a quick jerk, jamming the lance as a bar across the opening. It was a frail ladder but the best he could improvise. He climbed until the sill of the window was within reach and he could pull himself up and over.

The sill was a wide one, at least a twenty-four-inch span between the inner and outer surface of the tower. Travis sat there for a minute, reluctant to enter. Near the end of his dangling scarf-rope the two coyotes lay on the pavement, their heads up, their tongues lolling from their mouths, their expressions ones of detached interest.

Perhaps it was the width of the outer wall that subdued the amount of light in the room. The chamber was circular, and directly opposite him was a second window, the lowest of the matching diamond pattern. He took the four-foot drop from the sill to the floor but lingered in the light as he surveyed every inch of the room. There were no furnishings at all, but in the very center sank a well of darkness. A smooth pillar, glowing faintly, rose from its core. Travis' adjusting eyes noted how the light came in small ripples-green and purple, over a foundation shade of dark blue.

The pillar seemed rooted below and it extended up through a similar opening in the ceiling, providing the only possible exit up or down, save for climbing from window to window outside. Travis moved slowly to the well. Underfoot was a smooth surface overlaid with a velvet carpet of dust which arose in languid puffs as he walked. Here and there he sighted prints in the dust, strange triangular wedges which he thought might possibly have been made by the claws of birds. But there were no other footprints. This tower had been undisturbed for a long, long time.

He came to the well and looked down. There was dark there, dark in which the pulsations of light from the pillar shown the stronger. But that glow did not extend beyond the edge of the well through which the thick rod threaded. Even by close examination he could detect no break in the smooth surface of the pillar, nothing remotely resembling hand- or footholds. If it did serve the purpose of a staircase, there were no treads.

At last Travis put out his hand to touch the surface of the pillar. And then he jerked back-to no effect. There was no breaking contact between his fingers and an unknown material which had the sleekness of polished metal but-and the thought made him slightly queasy-the warmth and very slight give of flesh!

He summoned all his strength to pull free and could not. Not only did that hold grip him, but his other hand and arm were being drawn to join the first! Inside Travis primitive fears awoke full force, and he threw back his head, voicing a cry of panic as wild as that of a hunting beast.

An instant later, his left palm was as tight a prisoner as his right. And with both hands so held, his whole body was suddenly snapped forward, off the safe foundation of the floor, tight to the pillar.

In this position he was sucked down into the well. And while unable to free himself from the pillar, he did slip along its length easily enough. Travis shut his eyes in an involuntary protest against this weird form of capture, and a shiver ran through his body as he continued to descend.

After the first shock had subsided the Apache realized that he was not truly falling at all. Had the pillar been horizontal instead of vertical, he would have gauged its speed that of a walk. He passed through two more room enclosures; he must already be below the level of the valley floor outside. And he was still a prisoner of the pillar, now in total darkness.

His feet came down against a level surface, and he guessed he must have reached the end. Again he pulled back, arching his shoulders in a final desperate attempt at escape, and stumbled away as he was released.

He came up sideways against a wall and stood there panting. The light, which might have come from the pillar but which seemed more a part of the very air, was bright enough to reveal that he was in a corridor running into greater dark both right and left.

Travis took two strides back to the pillar, fitted his palms once again to its surface, with no result. This time his flesh did not adhere and there was no possible way for him to climb that slick pole. He could only hope that at some point the corridor would give him access to the surface. But which way to go —?

At last he chose the right-hand path and started along it, pausing every few steps to listen. But there was no sound except the soft pad of his own feet. The air was fresh enough, and he thought he could detect a faint current coming toward him from some point ahead-perhaps an exit.

Instead, he came into a room and a small gasp of astonishment was wrung out of him. The walls were blank, covered with the same ripples of blue-purple-green light which colored the pillar. Just before him was a table and behind it a bench, both carved from the native yellow-red mountain rock. And there was no exit except the doorway in which he now stood.

Travis walked to the bench. Immovable, it was placed so that whoever sat there must face the opposite wall of the chamber with the table before him. And on the table was an object Travis recognized immediately from his voyage in the alien star ship, one of the reader-viewers through which the involuntary explorers had learned what little they knew of the older galactic civilization.

A reader-and beside it a box of tapes. Travis touched the edge of that box gingerly, half expecting it to crumble into nothingness. This was a place long deserted. Stone table, bench, the towers could survive through centuries of abandonment, but these other objects....

The substance of the reader was firm under the film of dust; there was less dust here than had been in the upper tower chamber. Hardly knowing why, Travis threw one leg over the bench and sat down behind the table, the reader before him, the box of tapes just beyond his hand.

He surveyed the walls and then looked away hurriedly. The rippling colors caught at his eyes. He had a feeling that if he watched that ebb and flow too long, he would be captured in some subtle web of enchantment just as the Reds' machine had caught and held the Tatars. He turned his attention to the reader. It was, he believed, much like the one they had used on the ship.

This room, table, bench, had all been designed with a set purpose. And that purpose-Travis' fingers rested on the box of tapes he could not yet bring himself to open-that purpose was to use the reader, he would swear to that. Tapes so left must have had a great importance for those who left them. It was as if the whole valley was a trap to channel a stranger into this underground chamber.

Travis snapped open the box, fed the first disk into the reader, and applied his eyes to the vision tube at its apex.

The rippling walls looked just the same when he looked up once more, but the cramp in his muscles told Travis that time had passed-perhaps hours instead of minutes-since he had taken out the first disk. He cupped his hands over his eyes and tried to think clearly. There had been sheets of meaningless symbol writing, but also there had been many clear, three-dimensional pictures, accompanied by a singsong commentary in an alien tongue, seemingly voiced out of thin air. He had been stuffed with ragged bits and patches of information, to be connected only by guesses, and some wild guesses, too. But this much he did know-these towers had been built by the bald spacemen, and they were highly important to that vanished stellar civilization. The information in this room, as disjointed as it had been for him, led to a treasure trove on Topaz greater than he had dreamed.

Travis swayed on the bench. To know so much and yet so little! If Ashe were only here, or some other of the project technicians! A treasure such as Pandora's box had been, peril for one who opened it and did not understand. The Apache studied the three walls of blue-purple-green in turn and with new attention. There were ways through those walls; he was fairly sure he could unlock at least one of them. But not now-certainly not now!

And there was another thing he knew: The Reds must *not* find this. Such a discovery on their part would not only mean the end of his own people on Topaz, but the end of Terra as well. This could be a new and alien Black Death spread to destroy whole nations at a time!

If he could-much as his archaeologist's training would argue against it-he would blot out this whole valley above and below ground. But while the Reds might possess a means of such destruction, the Apaches did not. No, he and his people must prevent its discovery by the enemy by doing what he had seen as necessary from the first-wiping out the Red leaders! And that must be done before they chanced upon the towers!

Travis arose stiffly. His eyes ached, his head felt stuffed with pictures, hints, speculations. He wanted to get out, back into the open air where perhaps the clean winds of the heights would blow some of this frightening half knowledge from his benumbed mind. He lurched down the corridor, puzzled now by the problem of getting back to the window level.

Here, before him, was the pillar. Without hope, but still obeying some buried instinct, Travis again set his hands to its surface. There was a tug at his cramped arms; once more his body was sucked to the pillar. This time he was rising!

He held his breath past the first level and then relaxed. The principle of this weird form of transportation was entirely beyond his understanding, but as long as it worked in reverse he didn't care to find out. He reached the windowed chamber, but the sunlight had left it; instead, the clean cut of moon sweep lay on the dusty floor. He must have been hours in that underground place.

Travis pulled away from the embrace of the pillar. The bar of his wooden lance was still across the window and he ran for it. To catch the scouting party at the pass he must hurry. The report they would make to the clan now had to be changed radically in the face of his new discoveries. The Apaches dared not retreat southward and withdraw from the fight, leaving the Reds to use what treasure lay here.

As he hit the pavement below he looked about for the coyotes. Then he tried the mind call. But as mysteriously as they had met him in the valley, so now were they gone again. And Travis had no time to hunt for them. With a sigh, he began his race to the pass.

In the old days, Travis remembered, Apache warriors had been able to cover forty-five or fifty miles a day on foot and over rough territory. But perhaps his modern breeding had slowed him. He had been so sure he could catch up before the others were through the pass. But he stood now in the hollow where they had camped, read the sign of overturned stone and bent twig left for him, and knew they would reach the rancheria and report the decision Deklay and the others wanted before he could head them off.

Travis slogged on. He was so tired now that only the drug from the sustenance tablets he mouthed at intervals kept him going at a dogged pace, hardly more than a swift walk. And always his mind was haunted by fragments of pictures, pictures he had seen in the reader. The big bomb had been the nightmare of his own world for so long, and what was that against the forces the bald star rovers had been able to command?

He fell beside a stream and slept. There was sunshine about him as he arose to stagger on. What day was this? How long had he sat in the tower chamber? He was not sure of time any more. He only knew that he must reach the rancheria, tell his story, somehow win over Deklay and the other reactionaries to prove the necessity for invading the north in force.

A rocky point which was a familiar landmark came into focus. He padded on, his chest heaving, his breath whistling through parched, sun-cracked lips. He did not know that his face was now a mask of driven resolution.

"Hahhhhhh —"

The cry reached his dulled ears. Travis lifted his head, saw the men before him and tried to think what that show of weapons turned toward him could mean.

A stone thudded to earth only inches before his feet, to be followed by another. He wavered to a stop.

"*Ni'ilgac* —!"

Witch? Where was a witch? Travis shook his head. There was no witch.

"*Do ne'ilka da'!*"

The old death threat, but why-for whom?

Another stone, this one hitting him in the ribs with force enough to send him reeling back and down. He tried to get up again, saw Deklay grin widely and take aim-and at last Travis realized what was happening.

Then there was a bursting pain in his head and he was falling-falling into a well of black, this time with no pillar of blue to guide him.

13

The rasp of something wet and rough, persistent against his cheek; Travis tried to turn his head to avoid the contact and was answered by a burst of pain which trailed off into a giddiness, making him fear another move, no matter how minor. He opened his eyes and saw the pointed ears, the outline of a coyote head between him and a dull gray sky, was able to recognize Nalik'ideyu.

A wetness other than that from the coyote's tongue slid down his forehead now. The dull clouds overhead had released the first heavy rain Travis had experienced since their landing on Topaz. He shivered as the chill damp of his clothes made him aware that he must have been lying out in the full force of the downpour for some time.

It was a struggle to get to his knees, but Nalik'ideyu mouthed a hold on his shirt, tugging and pulling so that somehow he crept into a hollow beneath the branches of a tree where the spouting water was lessened to a few pattering drops.

There the Apache's strength deserted him again and he could only hunch over, his bent knees against his chest, trying to endure the throbbing misery in his head, the awful floating sensation which followed any movement. Fighting against that, he tried to remember just what had happened.

The meeting with Deklay and at least four or five others ... then the Apache accusation of witchcraft, a serious thing in the old days. Old days! To Deklay and his fellows, these *were* the old days! And the threat that Deklay or some other had shouted at him —"Do ne'ilka da'" —meant literally: "It won't dawn for you-death!"

Stones, the last thing Travis remembered were the stones. Slowly his hands went out to explore his body. There was more than one bruised area on his shoulders and ribs, even on his thighs. He must still have been a target after he had fallen under the stone which had knocked him unconscious. Stoned ... outlawed! But why? Surely Deklay's hostility could not have swept Buck, Jil-Lee, Tsoay, even Nolan, into agreeing to that? Now he could not think straight.

Travis became aware of warmth, not only of warmth and the soft touch of a furred body by his side, but a comforting communication of mind, a feeling he had no words to describe adequately. Nalik'ideyu was sitting crowded against him, her nose thrust up to rest on his shoulder. She breathed in soft puffs which stirred the loose locks of his rain-damp hair. And now he flung one arm about her, a gesture which brought a whisper of answering whine.

He was past wondering about the actions of the coyotes, only supremely thankful for Nalik'ideyu's present companionship. And a moment later when her mate squeezed under the low loop of a branch and joined them in this natural wickiup, Travis held out his other hand, drew it lovingly across Naginlta's wet hide.

"Now what?" he asked aloud. Deklay could only have taken such a drastic action with the majority of the clan solidly behind him. It could well be that this reactionary was the new chief, this act of Travis' expulsion merely adding to Deklay's growing prestige.

The shivering which had begun when Travis recovered consciousness, still shook him at intervals. Back on Terra, like all the others in the team, he had had every inoculation known to the space physicians, including several experimental ones. But the cold virus could still practically immobilize a man, and this was no time to give body room to chills and fever.

Catching his breath as his movements touched to life the pain in one bruise after another, Travis peeled off his soaked clothing, rubbed his body dry with handfuls of last year's leaves culled from the thick carpet under him, knowing there was nothing he could do until the whirling in his head disappeared. So he burrowed into the leaves until only his head was uncovered, and tried to sleep, the coyotes curling up one on either side of his nest.

He dreamed but later could not remember any incident from those dreams, save a certain frustration and fear. When he awoke, again to the sound of steady rain, it was dark. He reached out-both coyotes were gone. His head was clearer and suddenly he knew what must be done. As soon as his body was strong enough, he, too, would return to instincts and customs of the past. This situation was desperate enough for him to challenge Deklay.

In the dark Travis frowned. He was slightly taller, and three or four years younger than his enemy. But Deklay had the advantage in a stouter build and longer reach. However, Travis was sure that in his present life Deklay had never fought a duel-Apache fashion. And an Apache duel was not a meeting anyone entered into lightly. Travis had the right to enter the rancheria and deliver such a challenge. Then Deklay must meet him or admit himself in the wrong. That part of it was simple.

But in the past such duels had just one end, a fatal one for at least one of the fighters. If Travis took this trail, he must be prepared to go the limit. And he didn't want to kill Deklay! There were too few of them here on Topaz to make any loss less than a real catastrophe. While he had no liking for Deklay, neither did he nurse any hatred. However, he must challenge the other or remain a tribal outcast; and Travis had no right to gamble with time and the future, not after what he had learned in the tower. It might be his life and skill, or Deklay's, against the blotting out of them all-and their home world into the bargain.

First, he must locate the present camp of the clan. If Nolan's arguments had counted, they would be heading south away from the pass. And to follow would draw him farther from the tower valley. Travis' battered face ached as he grinned bitterly. This was another time when a man could wish he were two people, a scout on sentry duty at the valley, the fighter heading in the opposite direction to have it out with Deklay. But since he was merely one man he would have to gamble on time, one of the trickiest risks of all.

Before dawn Nalik'ideyu returned, carrying with her a bird-or at least birds must have been somewhere in the creature's ancestry, but the present representative of its kind had only vestigial remnants of wings, its trailing feet and legs well developed and far more powerful.

Travis skinned the corpse, automatically putting aside some spine quills to feather future arrows. Then he ate slivers of dusky meat raw, throwing the bones to Nalik'ideyu.

Though he was still stiff and sore, Travis was determined to be on his way. He tried mind contact with the coyote, picturing the Apaches, notably Deklay, as sharply as he could by mental image. And her assent was clear in return. She and her mate were willing to lead him to the tribe. He gave a light sigh of relief.

As he slogged on through the depressing drizzle, the Apache wondered again why the coyotes had left him before and waited in the tower valley. What link was there between the animals of Terra and the remains of the long-ago empire of the stars? For he was certain it was not by chance that Nalik'ideyu and Naginlta had lingered in that misty place. He longed to communicate with them directly, to ask questions and be answered.

Without their aid, Travis would never have been able to track the clan. The drizzle alternated with slashing bursts of rain, torrential enough to drive the trackers to the nearest cover. Overhead the sky was either dull bronze or night black. Even the coyotes paced nose to ground, often making wide casts for the trail while Travis waited.

The rain lasted for three days and nights, filling watercourses with rapidly rising streams. Travis could only hope that the others were having the same difficulty traveling that he was, perhaps the more so since they were burdened with packs. The fact that they kept on meant that they were determined to get as far from the northern mountains as they could.

On the fourth morning the bronze of the clouds slowly thinned into the usual gold, and the sun struck across hills where mist curled like steam from a hundred bubbling pots. Travis relaxed in the welcome warmth, feeling his shirt dry on his shoulders. It was still a waterlogged terrain ahead which should continue to slow the clan. He had high expectations of catching up with them soon, and now the worst of his bruises had faded. His muscles were limber, and he had worked out his plan as best he could.

Two hours later he sat in ambush, waiting for the scout who was walking into his hands. Under the direction of the coyotes, Travis had circled the line of march, come in ahead of the clan. Now he needed an emissary to state his challenge, and the fact that the scout he was about to jump was Manulito, one of Deklay's supporters, suited Travis' purpose perfectly. He gathered his feet under him as the other came opposite, and sprang.

The rush carried Manulito off his feet and face down on the sod while Travis made the best of his advantage and pinned the wildly fighting man under him. Had it been one of the older braves he might not have been so successful, but Manulito was still a boy by Apache standards.

"Lie still!" Travis ordered. "Listen well-so you can say to Deklay the words of the Fox!"

The frenzied struggles ceased. Manulito managed to wrench his head to the left so he could see his captor. Travis loosened his grip, got to his feet. Manulito sat up, his face darkly sullen, but he did not reach for his knife.

"You will say this to Deklay: The Fox says he is a man of little sense and less courage, preferring to throw stones rather than meet knife to knife as does a warrior. If he thinks as a warrior, let him prove it-his strength against my strength-after the ways of the People!"

Some of the sullenness left Manulito's expression. He was eager, excited.

"You would duel with Deklay after the old custom?"

"I would. Say this to Deklay, openly so that all men may hear. Then Deklay must also give answer openly."

Manulito flushed at that implication concerning his leader's courage, and Travis knew that he would deliver the challenge openly. To keep his hold on the clan the latter must accept it, and there would be an audience of his people to witness the success or defeat of their new chief and his policies.

As Manulito disappeared Travis summoned the coyotes, putting full effort into getting across one message. Any tribe led by Deklay would be hostile to the mutant animals. They must go into hiding, run free in the wilderness if the gamble failed Travis. Now they withdrew into the bushes but not out of reach of his mind.

He did not have too long to wait. First came Jil-Lee, Buck, Nolan, Tsoay, Lupe-those who had been with him on the northern scout. Then the others, the warriors first, the women making a half circle behind, leaving a free space in which Deklay walked.

"I am the Fox," Travis stated. "And this one has named me witch and *natdahe*, outlaw of the mountains. Therefore do I come to name names in my turn. Hear me, People: This Deklay-he would walk among you as *'izesnantan*, a great chief-but he does not have the *go'ndi*, the holy power of a chief. For this Deklay is a fool, with a head filled by nothing but his own wishes, not caring for his clan brothers. He says he leads you into safety; I say he leads you into the worst danger any living man can imagine-even in peyote dreams! He is one twisted in his thoughts, and he would make you twisted also — —"

Buck cut in sharply, hushing the murmur of the massed clan.

"These are bold words, Fox. Will you back them?"

Travis' hands were already peeling off his shirt. "I will back them," he stated between set teeth. He had known since his awakening after the stoning that this next move was the only one left for him to make. But now that the testing of his action came, he could not be certain of the outcome, of anything save that the final decision of this battle might affect more than the fate of two men. He stripped, noting that Deklay was doing the same.

Having stepped into the center of the glade, Nolan was using the point of his knife to score a deep-ridged circle there. Naked except for his moccasins, with only his knife in his hand, Travis took the two strides which put him in the circle facing Deklay. He surveyed his opponent's finely muscled body, realizing that his earlier estimate of Deklay's probable advantages were close to the mark. In sheer strength the other outmatched him. Whether Deklay was skillful with his knife was another question, one which Travis would soon be able to answer.

They circled, eyes intent upon each move, striving to weigh and measure each other's strengths and weaknesses. Knife dueling among the Pinda-lick-o-yi, Travis remembered, had once been an art close to finished swordplay, with two evenly matched fighters able to engage for a long time without seriously marking each other. But this was a far rougher and more deadly game, with none of the niceties of such a meeting.

He evaded a vicious thrust from Deklay.

"The bull charges," he laughed. "And the Fox snaps!" By some incredible stroke of good fortune, the point of his weapon actually grazed Deklay's arm, drawing a thin, red inch-long line across the skin.

"Charge again, bull. Feel once more the Fox's teeth!"

He strove to goad Deklay into a crippling loss of temper, knowing how the other could explode into violent rage. It was dangerous, that rage, but it could also make a man blindly careless.

There was an inarticulate sound from Deklay, a dusky swelling in the man's face. He spat, as might an enraged puma, and rushed at Travis who did not quite manage to avoid the lunge, falling back with a smarting slash across the ribs.

"The bull gores!" Deklay bellowed. "Horns toss the Fox!"

He rushed again, elated by the sight of the trickling wound on Travis' side. But the slighter man slipped away.

Travis knew he must be careful in such evasions. One foot across the ridged circle and he was finished as much as if Deklay's blade had found its mark. Travis tried a thrust of his own, and his foot came down hard on a sharp pebble. Through the sole of his moccasin pain shot upward, caused him to stumble. Again the scarlet flame of a wound, down his shoulder and forearm this time.

Well, there was one trick, he knew. Travis tossed the knife into the air, caught it with his left hand. Deklay was now facing a left-handed fighter and must adjust to that.

"Paw, bull, rattle your horns!" Travis cried. "The Fox still shows his teeth!"

Deklay recovered from his instant of surprise. With a cry which was indeed like the bellow of an old range bull, he rushed into grapple, sure of his superior strength against a younger and already wounded man.

Travis ducked, one knee thumping the ground. He groped out with his right hand, caught up a handful of earth, and flung it into the dusky brown face. Again it seemed that luck was on his side. That handful could not be as blinding as sand, but some bit of the shower landed in Deklay's eye.

For a space of seconds Deklay was wide open-open for a blow which would rip him up the middle, the blow Travis could not and would not deliver.

Instead, he took the offensive recklessly, springing straight for his opponent. As the earth-grimed fingers of one hand clawed into Deklay's face, he struck with the other, not with the point of the knife but with its shaft. But Deklay, already only half conscious from the blow, had his own chance. He fell to the ground, leaving his knife behind, two inches of steel between Travis' ribs.

Somehow-he didn't know from where he drew that strength-Travis kept his feet and took one step and then another, out of the circle until the comforting brace of a tree trunk was against his bare back. Was he finished —?

He fought to nurse his rags of consciousness. Had he summoned Buck with his eyes? Or had the urgency of what he had to say reached somehow from mind to mind? The other was at his side, but Travis put out a hand to ward him off.

"Towers —" He struggled to keep his wits through the pain and billowing weakness beginning to creep through him. "Reds mustn't get to the towers! Worse than the bomb ...end us all!"

He had a hazy glimpse of Nolan and Jil-Lee closing in about him. The desire to cough tore at him, but they had to know, to believe....

"Reds get to the towers-everything finished. Not only here ...maybe back home too...."

Did he read comprehension on Buck's face? Would Nolan and Jil-Lee and the rest believe him? Travis could not suppress the cough any longer, and the ripping pain which followed was the worst he had ever experienced. But still he kept his feet, tried to make them understand.

"Don't let them get to the towers. Find that storehouse!"

Travis stood away from the tree, reached out to Buck his earth and bloodstained hand. "I swear ...truth ...this must be done!"

He was going down, and he had a queer thought that once he reached the ground everything would end, not only for him but also for his mission. Trying to see the faces of the men about him was like attempting to identify the people in a dream.

"Towers!" He had meant to shout it, but he could not even hear for himself that last word as he fell.

14

Travis' back was braced against blanketed packs as he steadied a piece of light-yellow bark against one bent knee scowling at the lines drawn on it in faint green.

"We are here then ...and the ship there —" His thumb was set on one point of the crude map, forefinger on the other. Buck nodded.

"That is so. Tsoay, Eskelta, Kawaykle, they watch the trails. There is the pass, two other ways men can come on foot. But who can watch the air?"

"The Tatars say the Reds dare not bring the 'copter into the mountains. After they first landed they lost a flyer in a tricky air-current flow up there. They have only one left and won't risk it. If only they aren't reinforced before we can move!" There it was again, that constant gnawing fear of time, time shortening into a rope to strangle them all.

"You think that the knowledge of our ship will bring them into the open?"

"That-or information about the towers would be the only things important enough to pull out their experts. They could send a controlled Tatar party to explore the ship, sure. But that wouldn't give them the technical reports they need. No, I think if they knew a wrecked Western Confederation ship was here, it would bring them-or enough of them to lessen the odds. We have to catch them in the open. Otherwise, they can hole up forever in that ship-fort of theirs."

"And just how do we let them know our ship is here? Send out another scouting party and let them be trailed back?"

"That's our last resource." Travis continued to frown at the map. Yes, it would be possible to let the Reds sight and trail an Apache party. But there was none in the clan who were expendable. Surely there was some other way of laying the trap with the wrecked ship for bait. Capture one of the Reds, let him escape again, having seen what they wanted him to see? Again a time-wasting business. And how long would they have to wait and what risks would they take to pick up a Red prisoner?

"If the Tatars were dependable...." Buck was thinking aloud.

But that "if" was far too big. They could not trust the Tatars. No matter how much the Mongols wanted to aid in pulling down the Reds, as long as they could be controlled by the caller they were useless. Or were they?

"Thought of something?" Buck must have caught Travis' change of expression.

"Suppose a Tatar saw our ship and then was picked up by a Red hunting patrol and they got the information out of him?"

"Do you think any outlaw would volunteer to let himself be picked up again? And if he did, wouldn't the Reds also be able to learn that he had been set up for the trap?"

"An escaped prisoner?" Travis suggested.

Now Buck was plainly considering the possibilities of such a scheme. And Travis' own spirits rose a little. The idea was full of holes, but it could be worked out. Suppose they capture, say, Menlik, bring him here as a prisoner, let him think they were about to kill him because of that attack back in the foothills. Then let him escape, pursue him northward to a point where he could be driven into the hands of the Reds? Very chancy, but it just might work. Travis was favoring a gamble now, since his desperate one with the duel had paid off.

The risk he had accepted then had cost him two deep wounds, one of which might have been serious if Jil-Lee's project-sponsored medical training had not been to hand. But it had also made Travis one of the clan again, with his people willing to listen to his warning concerning the tower treasury.

"The girl-the Tatar girl!"

At first Travis did not understand Buck's ejaculation.

"We get the girl," the other elaborated, "let her escape, then hunt her to where they'll pick her up. Might even imprison her in the ship to begin with."

Kaydessa? Though something within him rebelled at that selection for the leading role in their drama, Travis could see the advantage of Buck's choice. Woman-stealing was an ancient pastime among primitive cultures. The Tatars themselves had found wives that way in the past, just as the Apache raiders of old had taken captive women into their wickiups. Yes, for raiders to steal a woman would be a natural act, accepted as such by the Reds. For the same woman to endeavor to escape and be hunted by her captors also was reasonable. And for such a woman, cut off from her outlaw kin, to eventually head back toward the Red settlement as the only hope of evading her enemies-logical all the way!

"She would have to be well frightened," Travis observed with reluctance.

"That can be done for us —"

Travis glanced at Buck with sharp annoyance. He would not allow certain games out of their common past to be played with Kaydessa. But Buck had something very different from old-time brutality in mind.

"Three days ago, while you were still flat on your back, Deklay and I went back to the ship —"

"Deklay?"

"You beat him openly, so he must restore his honor in his own sight. And the council has forbidden another duel or challenge," Buck replied. "Therefore he will continue to push for recognition in another way. And now that he has heard your story and knows we must face the Reds, not run from them, he is eager to take the war trail-too eager. So we returned to the ship to make another search for weapons — —"

"There were none there before except those we had...."

"Nor now either. But we discovered something else." Buck paused and Travis was shaken out of his absorption with the problem at hand by a note in the other's voice. It was as if Buck had come upon something he could not summon the right words to describe.

"First," Buck continued, "there was this dead thing there, near where we found Dr. Ruthven. It was something like a man ... but all silvery hair — —"

"The ape-things! The ape-things from the other worlds! What else did you see?" Travis had dropped the map. His side gave him a painful twinge as he caught at Buck's sleeve. The bald space rovers-did they still exist here somewhere? Had they come to explore the ship built on the pattern of their own but manned by Terrans?

"Nothing except tracks, a lot of them, in every open cabin and hole. I think there must have been a sizable pack of the things."

"What killed the dead one?"

Buck wet his lips. "I think-fear...." His voice dropped a little, almost apologetically, and Travis stared.

"The ship is changed. Inside, there is something wrong. When you walk the corridors your skin crawls, you think there is something behind you. You hear things, see things from the corners of your eyes....When you turn, there's nothing, nothing at all! And the higher you climb into the ship, the worse it is. I tell you, Travis, never have I felt anything like it before!"

"It was a ship of many dead," Travis reminded him. Had the age-old Apache fear of the dead been activated by the Redax into an acute phobia-to strike down such a level-headed man as Buck?

"No, at first that, too, was my thought. Then I discovered that it was worst not near that chamber where we lay our dead, but higher, in the Redax cabin. I think perhaps the machine is still running, but running in a wrong way-so that it does not awaken old memories of our ancestors now, but brings into being all the fears which have ever haunted us through the dark of the ages. I tell you, Travis, when I came out of that place Deklay was leading me by the hand as if I were a child. And he was shivering as a man who will never be warm again. There is an evil there beyond our understanding. I think that this Tatar girl, were she only to stay there a very short time, would be well frightened-so frightened that any trained scientist examining her later would know there was a mystery to be explored."

"The ape-things —could they have tried to run the Redax?" Travis wondered. To associate machines with the creatures was outwardly pure folly. But they had been discovered on two of the planets of the old civilization, and Ashe had thought that they might represent the degenerate remnants of a once intelligent species.

"That is possible. If so, they raised a storm which drove them out and killed one of them. The ship is a haunted place now."

"But for us to use the girl...." Travis had seen the logic in Buck's first suggestion, but now he differed. If the atmosphere of the ship was as terrifying as Buck said, to imprison Kaydessa there, even temporarily, was still wrong.

"She need not remain long. Suppose we should do this: We shall enter with her and then allow the disturbance we would feel to overcome us. We could run, leave her alone. When she left the ship, we could then take up the chase, shepherding her back to the country she knows. Within the ship we would be with her and could see she did not remain too long."

Travis could see a good prospect in that plan. There was one thing he would insist on-if Kaydessa was to be in that ship, he himself would be one of the "captors." He said as much, and Buck accepted his determination as final.

They dispatched a scouting party to infiltrate the territory to the north, to watch and wait their chance of capture. Travis strove to regain his feet, to be ready to move when the moment came.

Five days later he was able to reach the ridge beyond which lay the wrecked ship. With him were Jil-Lee, Lupe, and Manulito. They satisfied themselves that the globe had had no visitors since Buck and Deklay; there was no sign that the ape-things had returned.

"From here," Travis said, "the ship doesn't look too bad, almost as if it might be able to take off again."

"It might lift," Jil-Lee gestured to the mountaintop behind the curve of the globe —"about that far. The tubes on this side are intact."

"What would happen were the Reds to get inside and try to fly again?" Manulito wondered aloud.

Travis was struck by a sudden idea, one perhaps just as wild as the other inspirations he had had since landing on Topaz, but one to be studied and explored-not dismissed without consideration. Suppose enough power remained to lift the ship partially and then blow it up? With the Red technicians on board at the time....But he was no engineer, he had no idea whether any part of the globe might or might not work again.

"They are not fools; a close look would tell them it is a wreck," Jil-Lee countered.

Travis walked on. Not too far ahead a yellow-brown shape moved out of the brush, stood stiff-legged in his path, facing the ship and growling in a harsh rumble of sound. Whatever moved or operated in that wreck was picked up by the acute sense of the coyote, even at this distance.

"On!" Travis edged around the snarling animal. With one halting step and then another, it followed him. There was a sharp warning yelp from the brush, and a second coyote head appeared. Naginlta followed Travis, but Nalik'ideyu refused to approach the grounded globe.

Travis surveyed the ship closely, trying to remember the layout of its interior. To turn the whole sphere into a trap-was it possible? How had Ashe said the Redax worked? Something about high-frequency waves stimulating certain brain and nerve centers.

What if one were shielded from those rays? That tear in the side-he himself must have climbed through that the night they crashed. And the break was not too far from the space lock. Near the lock was a storage compartment. And if it had not been jammed, or its contents crushed, they might have something. He beckoned to Jil-Lee.

"Give me a hand-up there."

"Why?"

"I want to see if the space suits are intact."

Jil-Lee regarded Travis with open bewilderment, but Manulito pushed forward. "We do not need those suits to walk here, Travis. This air we can breathe —"

"Not for the air, and not in the open." Travis advanced at a deliberate pace. "Those suits may be insulated in more ways than one — —"

"Against a mixed-up Redax broadcast, you mean!" Jil-Lee exclaimed. "Yes, but you stay here, younger brother. This is a risky climb, and you are not yet strong."

Travis was forced to accede to that, waiting as Manulito and Lupe climbed up to the tear and entered. At least Buck and Deklay's experience had forewarned them and they would be prepared for the weird ghosts haunting the interior.

But when they returned, pulling between them the limp space suit, both men were pale, the shiny sheen of sweat on their foreheads, their hands shaking. Lupe sat down on the ground before Travis.

"Evil spirits," he said, giving to this modern phenomenon the old name. "Truly ghosts and witches walk in there."

Manulito had spread the suit on the ground and was examining it with a care which spoke of familiarity.

"This is unharmed," he reported. "Ready to wear."

The suits were all tailored for size, Travis knew. And this fitted a slender, medium-sized man. It would fit him, Travis Fox. But Manulito was already unbuckling the fastenings with practiced ease.

"I shall try it out," he announced. And Travis, seeing the awkward climb to the entrance of the ship, had to agree that the first test should be carried out by someone more agile at the moment.

Sealed into the suit, with the bubble helmet locked in place, the Apache climbed back into the globe. The only form of communication with him was the rope he had tied about him, and if he went above the first level, he would have to leave that behind.

In the first few moments they saw no twitch of alarm running along the rope. After counting fifty slowly, Travis gave it a tentative jerk, to find it firmly fastened within. So Manulito had tied it there and was climbing to the control cabin.

They continued to wait with what patience they could muster. Naginlta, pacing up and down a good distance from the ship, whined at intervals, the warning echoed each time by his mate upslope.

"I don't like it —" Travis broke off when the helmeted figure appeared again at the break. Moving slowly in his cumbersome clothing, Manulito reached the ground, fumbled with the catch of his head covering and then stood, taking deep, lung-filling gulps of air.

"Well?" Travis demanded.

"I see no ghosts," Manulito said, grinning. "This is ghost-proof!" He slapped his gloved hand against the covering over his chest. "There is also this-from what I know of these ships-some of the relays still work. I think this could be made into a trap. We could entice the Reds in and then...." His hand moved in a quick upward flip.

"But we don't know anything about the engines," Travis replied.

"No? Listen-you, Fox, are not the only one to remember useful knowledge." Manulito had lost his cheerful grin. "Do you think we are just the savages those big brains back at the project wished us to be? They have played a trick on us with their Redax. So, we can play a few tricks, too. Me —? I went to M.I.T., or is that one of the things you no longer remember, Fox?"

Travis swallowed hastily. He really had forgotten that fact until this very minute. From the beginning, the Apache team had been carefully selected and screened, not only for survival potential, which was their basic value to the project, but also for certain individual skills. Just as Travis' grounding in archaeology had been one advantage, so had Manulito's technical training made a valuable, though different, contribution. If at first the Redax, used without warning, had smothered that training, perhaps the effects were now fading.

"You can do something, then?" he asked eagerly.

"I can try. There is a chance to booby trap the control cabin at least. And that is where they would poke and pry. Working in this suit will be tough. How about my trying to smash up the Redax first?"

"Not until after we use it on our captive," Jil-Lee decided. "Then there would be some time before the Reds come — —"

"You talk as if they *will* come," cut in Lupe. "How can you be sure?"

"We can't," Travis agreed. "But we can count on this much, judging from the past. Once they know that there is a wrecked ship here, they will be forced to explore it. They cannot afford an enemy settlement on this side of the mountains. That would be, according to their way of thinking, an eternal threat."

Jil-Lee nodded. "That is true. This is a complicated plan, yes, and one in which many things may go wrong. But it is also one which covers all the loopholes we know of."

With Lupe's aid Manulito crawled out of the suit. As he leaned it carefully against a supporting rock he said:

"I have been thinking of this treasure house in the towers. Suppose we could find new weapons there...."

Travis hesitated. He still shrank from the thought of opening the secret places behind those glowing walls, to loose a new peril.

"If we took weapons from there and lost the fight...." He advanced his first objection and was glad to see the expression of comprehension on Jil-Lee's face.

"It would be putting the weapons straight into Red hands," the other agreed.

"We may have to chance it before we're through," Manulito warned. "Suppose we do get some of their technicians into this trap. That isn't going to open up their main defense for us. We may need a bigger nutcracker than we've ever seen."

With a return of that queasy feeling he had known in the tower, Travis knew Manulito was speaking sense. They might have to open Pandora's box before the end of this campaign.

15

They camped another two days near the wrecked ship while Manulito prowled the haunted corridors and cabins in his space suit, planning his booby trap. At night he drew diagrams on pieces of bark and discussed the possibility of this or that device, sometimes lapsing into technicalities his companions could not follow. But Travis was well satisfied that Manulito knew what he was doing.

On the morning of the third day Nolan slipped into their midst. He was dust-grimed, his face gaunt, the signs of hard travel plain to read. Travis handed him the nearest canteen, and they watched him drink sparingly in small sips before he spoke.

"They come ... with the girl —"

"You had trouble?" asked Jil-Lee.

"The Tatars had moved their camp, which was only wise, since the Reds must have had a line on the other one. And they are now farther to the west. But —" he wiped his lips with the back of his hand —"also we saw your towers, Fox. And that is a place of power!"

"No sign that the Reds are prowling there?"

Nolan shook his head. "To my mind the mists there conceal the towers from aerial view. Only one coming on foot could tell them from the natural crags of the hills."

Travis relaxed. Time still granted them a margin of grace. He glanced up to see Nolan smiling faintly.

"This maiden, she is a kin to the puma of the mountains," he announced. "She has marked Tsoay with her claws until he looks like the ear-clipped yearling fresh from the branding chute — —"

"She is not hurt?" Travis demanded.

This time Nolan chuckled openly. "Hurt? No, we had much to do to keep her from hurting us, younger brother. That one is truly as she claims, a daughter of wolves. And she is also keen-witted, marking a return trail all the way, though she does not know that is as we wish. Did we not pick the easiest way back for just that reason? Yes, she plans to escape."

Travis stood up. "Let us finish this quickly!" His voice came out on a rough note. This plan had never had his full approval. Now he found it less and less easy to think about taking Kaydessa into the ship, allowing the emotional torment lurking there to work upon her. Yet he knew that the girl would not be hurt, and he had made sure he would be beside her within the globe, sharing with her the horror of the unseen.

A rattling of gravel down the narrow valley opening gave warning to those by the campfire. Manulito had already stowed the space suit in hiding. To Kaydessa they must have seemed reverted entirely to savagery.

Tsoay came first, an angry raking of four parallel scratches down his left cheek. And behind him Buck and Eskelta shoved the prisoner, urging her on with a show of roughness which did not descend to actual brutality. Her long braids had shaken loose, and a sleeve was torn, leaving one slender arm bare. But none of the fighting spirit had left her.

They thrust her out into the circle of waiting men and she planted her feet firmly apart, glaring at them all indiscriminately until she sighted Travis. Then her anger became hotter and more deadly.

"Pig! Rooter in the dirt! Diseased camel —" she shouted at him in English and then reverted to her own tongue, her voice riding up and down the scale. Her hands were tied behind her back, but there were no bonds on her tongue.

"This is one who can speak thunders, and shoot lightnings from her mouth," Buck commented in Apache. "Put her well away from the wood, lest she set it aflame."

Tsoay held his hands over his ears. "She can deafen a man when she cannot set her mark on him otherwise. Let us speedily get rid of her."

Yet for all their jeering comments, their eyes held respect. Often in the past a defiant captive who stood up boldly to his captors had received more consideration than usual from Apache warriors; courage was a quality they prized. A Pinda-lick-o-yi such as Tom Jeffords, who rode into Cochise's camp and sat in the midst of his sworn enemies for a parley, won the friendship of the very chief he had been fighting. Kaydessa had more influence with her captors than she could dream of holding.

Now it was time for Travis to play his part. He caught the girl's shoulder and pushed her before him toward the wreck.

Some of the spirit seemed to have left her thin, tense body, and she went without any more fight. Only when they came into full view of the ship did she falter. Travis heard her breathe a gasp of surprise.

As they had planned, four of the Apaches-Jil-Lee, Tsoay, Nolan, and Buck-fanned out toward the heights about the ship. Manulito had already gone to cover, to don the space suit and prepare for any accident.

Resolutely Travis continued to propel Kaydessa ahead. At the moment he did not know which was worse, to enter the ship expecting the fear to strike, or to meet it unprepared. He was ready to refuse to enter, not to allow the girl, sullenly plodding on under his compulsion, to face that unseen but potent danger.

Only the memory of the towers and the threat of the Reds finding and exploiting the treasure there kept him going. Eskelta went first, climbing to the tear. Travis cut the ropes binding Kaydessa's wrists and gave her a slight slap between the shoulders.

"Climb, woman!" His anxiety made that a harsh order and she climbed.

Eskelta was inside now, heading for the cabin which might reasonably be selected as a prison. They planned to get the girl as far as that point and then stage their act of being overcome by fear, allowing her to escape.

Stage an act? Travis was not two feet along that corridor before he knew that there would be little acting needed on his part. The thing which pervaded the ship did not attack sharply, rather it seeped into his mind and body as if he drew in poison with every breath, sent it racing along his veins with every beat of a laboring heart. Yet he could not put any name to his feelings, except an awful, weakening fear which weighted him heavier with every step he took.

Kaydessa screamed. Not this time in rage, but with such fervor that Travis lost his hold, staggered back to the wall. She whirled about, her face contorted, and sprang at him.

It was indeed like trying to fight a wildcat and after the first second or two he was hard put to protect his eyes, his face, his side, without injuring her in return. She scrambled over him, running for the break in the wall, and disappeared. Travis gasped, and started to crawl for the break. Eskelta loomed over him, pulled him up in haste.

They reached the opening but did not climb through. Travis was uncertain as to whether he could make that descent yet, and Eskelta was obeying orders in not venturing out too soon.

Below, the ground was bare. There was no sign of the Apaches, though they were in hiding there-and none of Kaydessa. Travis was amazed that she had vanished so quickly.

Still uneasy from the emanation within, they perched within the shadow of the break until Travis thought that the fugitive had a good five-minute start. Then he nodded a signal to Eskelta.

By the time they reached ground level Travis felt a warm wetness spreading under his shielding palm and he knew the wound had opened. He spoke a word or two in hot protest against that mishap, knowing it would keep him from the trail. Kaydessa must be covered all the way back across the pass, not only to be shepherded away from her people and toward the plains where she could be picked up by a Red patrol, but also to keep her from danger. And he had planned from the first to be one of those shepherds.

Now he was about as much use as a trail-lame pony. However, he could send deputies. He thought out his call, and Nalik'ideyu's head appeared in a frame of bush.

"Go, both of you and run with her! Guard —!" He said the words in a whisper, thought them with a fierce intensity as he centered his gaze on the yellow eyes in the pointed coyote face. There was a feeling of assent, and then the animal was gone. Travis sighed.

The Apache scouts were subtle and alert, but the coyotes could far outdo any man. With Nalik'ideyu and Naginlta flanking her flight, Kaydessa would be well guarded. She would probably never see her guards or know that they were running protection for her.

"That was a good move," Jil-Lee said, coming out of concealment. "But what have you done to yourself?" He stepped closer, pulling Travis' hand away from his side. By the time Lupe came to report, Travis was again wound in a strapping bandage pulled tightly about his lower ribs, and reconciled to the fact that any trailing he would do must be well to the rear of the first party.

"The towers," he said to Jil-Lee. "If our plan works, we can catch part of the Reds here. But we still have their ship to take, and for that we need help which we may find at the towers. Or at least we can be on guard there if they return with Kaydessa on that path."

Lupe dropped down lightly from an upper ledge. He was grinning.

"That woman is one who thinks. She runs from the ship first as a rabbit with a wolf at her heels. Then she begins to think. She climbs —" He lifted one finger to the slope behind them. "She goes behind a rock to watch under cover. When Fox comes from the ship with Eskelta, again she climbs. Buck lets himself be seen, so she moves east, as we wish —"

"And now?" questioned Travis.

"She is keeping to the high ways; almost she thinks like one of the People on the war trail. Nolan believes she will hole up for the night somewhere above. He will make sure."

Travis licked his lips. "She has no food or water."

Jil-Lee's lips shaped a smile. "They will see that she comes upon both as if by chance. We have planned all of this, as you know, younger brother."

That was true. Travis knew that Kaydessa would be guided without her knowledge by the "accidental" appearance now and then of some pursuer-just enough to push her along.

"Then, too, she is now armed," Jil-Lee added.

"How?" demanded Travis.

"Look to your own belt, younger brother. Where is your knife?"

Startled, Travis glanced down. His sheath was empty, and he had not needed that blade since he had drawn it to cut meat at the morning meal. Lupe laughed.

"She had steel in her hand when she came out of that ghost ship."

"Took it from me while we struggled!" Travis was openly surprised. He had considered the frenzy displayed by the Tatar girl as an outburst of almost mindless terror. Yet Kaydessa had had wit enough to take his knife! Could this be another case where one race was less affected by a mind machine than the other? Just as the Apaches had not been governed by the Red caller, so the Tatars might not be as sensitive to the Redax.

"She is a strong one, that woman-one worth many ponies." Eskelta reverted to the old measure of a wife's value.

"That is true!" Travis agreed emphatically and then was annoyed at the broadening of Jil-Lee's smile. Abruptly he changed the subject.

"Manulito is setting the booby trap in the ship."

"That is well. He and Eskelta will remain here, and you with them."

"Not so! We must go to the towers — —" Travis protested.

"I thought," Jil-Lee cut in, "that you believed the weapons of the old ones too dangerous for us to use."

"Maybe they will be forced into our hands. But we must be sure the towers are not entered by the Reds on their way here."

"That is reasonable. But for you, younger brother, no trailing today, perhaps not tomorrow. If that wound opens again, you might have much bad trouble."

Travis was forced to accept that, in spite of his worry and impatience. And the next day when he did move on he had only the report that Kaydessa had sheltered beside a pool for the night and was doggedly moving back across the mountains.

Three days later Travis, Jil-Lee, and Buck came into the tower valley. Kaydessa was in the northern foothills, twice turned back from the west and the freedom of the outlaws by the Apache scouts. And only half an hour before, Tsoay had reported by mirror what should have been welcome news: the Red helicopter was cruising as it had on the day they watched the hunters enter the uplands. There was an excellent chance of the fugitive's being sighted and picked up soon.

Tsoay had also spotted a party of three Tatars watching the helicopter. But after one wide sweep of the flyer they had taken to their ponies and ridden away at the fastest pace their mounts could manage in this rough territory.

On a stretch of smooth earth Buck scratched a trail, and they studied it. The Reds would have to follow this route to seek the wrecked ship —a route covered by Apache sentinels. And following the chain of communication the result of the trap would be reported to the party at the towers.

The waiting was the most difficult; too many imponderables did not allow for unemotional thinking. Travis was down to the last shred of patience when word came on the second morning at the hidden valley that Kaydessa had been picked up by a Red patrol-drawn out to meet them by the caller.

"Now-the tower weapons!" Buck answered the report with an imperative order to Travis. And the other knew he could no longer postpone the inevitable. And only by action could he blot out the haunting mental picture of Kaydessa once more drawn into the bondage she so hated.

Flanked by Jil-Lee and Buck, he climbed back through the tower window and faced the glowing pillar.

He crossed the room, put out both hands to the sleek pole, uncertain if the weird transport would work again. He heard the sharp gasp from the others as his body was sucked against the pillar and carried downward through the well. Buck followed him, and Jil-Lee came last. Then Travis led the way along the underground corridor to the room with the table and the reader.

He sat down on the bench, fumbled with the pile of tape disks, knowing that the other two were watching him with almost hostile intentness. He snapped a disk into the reader, hoping he could correctly interpret the directions it gave.

He looked up at the wall before him. Three ... four steps, the correct move-and then an unlocking....

"You know?" Buck demanded.

"I can guess — —"

"Well?" Jil-Lee moved to the table. "What do we do?"

"This —" Travis came from behind the table, walked to the wall. He put out both hands, flattened his palms against the green-blue-purple surface and slid them slowly along. Under his touch, the material of the wall was cool and hard, unlike the live feel the pillar had. Cool until —

One palm, held at arm's length had found the right spot. He slid the other hand along in the opposite direction until his arms were level with his shoulders. His fingers were able now to press on those points of warmth. Travis tensed and pushed hard with all ten fingers.

16

At first, as one second and then two passed and there was no response to the pressure, Travis thought he had mistaken the reading of the tape. Then, directly before his eyes, a dark line cut vertically down the wall. He applied more pressure until his fingers were half numb with effort. The line widened slowly. Finally he faced a slit some eight feet in height, a little more than two in width, and there the opening remained.

Light beyond, a cold, gray gleam-like that of a cloudy winter day on Terra-and with it the chill of air out of some arctic wasteland. Favoring his still bandaged side, Travis scraped through the door ahead of the others, and came into the place of gray cold.

"Wauggh!" Travis heard that exclamation from Jil-Lee, could have echoed it himself except that he was too astounded by what he had seen to say anything at all.

The light came from a grid of bars set far above their heads into the native rock which roofed this storehouse, for storehouse it was. There were orderly lines of boxes, some large enough to contain a tank, others no bigger than a man's fist. Symbols in the same blue-green-purple lights of the outer wall shone from their sides.

"What —?" Buck began one question and then changed it to another: "Where do we begin to look?"

"Toward the far end." Travis started down the center aisle between rows of the massed spoils of another time and world-or worlds. The same tape which had given him the clue to the unlocking of the door, emphasized the importance of something stored at the far end, an object or objects which must be used first. He had wondered about that tape. A sensation of urgency, almost of despair, had come through the gabble of alien words, the quick sequence of diagrams and pictures. The message might have been taped under a threat of some great peril.

There was no dust on the rows of boxes or on the floor underfoot. A current of cold, fresh air blew at intervals down the length of the huge chamber. They could not see the next aisle across the barriers of stored goods, but the only noise was a whisper and the faint sounds of their own feet. They came out into an open space backed by the wall, and Travis saw what had been so important.

"No!" His protest was involuntary, but his denial loud enough to echo.

Six-six of them-tall, narrow cases set upright against the wall; and from their depths, five pairs of dark eyes staring back at him in cold measurement. These were the men of the ships-the men Menlik had dreamed of-their bald white heads, their thin bodies with the skintight covering of the familiar blue-green-purple. Five of them were here, alive-watching ... waiting....

Five men-and six boxes. That small fact broke the spell in which those eyes held Travis. He looked again at the sixth box to his right. Expecting to meet another pair of eyes this time, he was disconcerted to face only emptiness. Then, as his gaze traveled downward, he saw what lay on the floor there —a skull, a tangle of bones, tattered material cobwebbed into dusty rags by time. Whatever had preserved five of the star men intact, had failed the sixth of their company.

"They are alive!" Jil-Lee whispered.

"I do not think so," Buck answered. Travis took another step, reached out to touch the transparent front of the nearest coffin case. There was no change in the eyes of the alien who stood within, no indication that if the Apaches could see him, he would be able to return their interest. The five stares which had bemused the visitors at first, did not break to follow their movements.

But Travis knew! Whether it was some message on the tape which the sight of the sleepers made clear, or whether some residue of the driving purpose which had set them there now reached his mind, was immaterial. He knew the purpose of this room and its contents, why it had been made and the reason its six guardians had been left as prisoners-and what they wanted from anyone coming after them.

"They sleep," he said softly.

"Sleep?" Buck caught him up.

"They sleep in something like deep freeze."

"Do you mean they can be brought to life again!" Jil-Lee cried.

"Maybe not now-it must be too long-but they were meant to wait out a period and be restored."

"How do you know that?" Buck asked.

"I don't know for certain, but I think I understand a little. Something happened a long time ago. Maybe it was a war, a war between whole star systems, bigger and worse than anything we can imagine. I think this planet was an outpost, and when the supply ships didn't come any more, when they knew they might be cut off for some length of time, they closed down. Stacked their supplies and machines here and then went to sleep to wait for their rescuers...."

"For rescuers who never came," Jil-Lee said softly. "And there is a chance they could be revived even now?"

Travis shivered. "Not one I would want to take."

"No," Buck's tone was somber, "that I agree to, younger brother. These are not men as we know them, and I do not think they would be good *dalaanbiyat'i* —allies. They had *go'ndi* in plenty, these star men, but it is not the power of the People. No one but a madman or a fool would try to disturb this sleep of theirs."

"The truth you speak," Jil-Lee agreed. "But where in this," he turned his shoulder to the sleeping star men and looked back at the filled chamber —"do we find anything which will serve us here and now?"

Again Travis had only the scrappiest information to draw upon. "Spread out," he told them. "Look for the marking of a circle surrounding four dots set in a diamond pattern."

They went, but Travis lingered for a moment to look once more into the bleak and bitter eyes of the star men. How many planet years ago had they sealed themselves into those boxes? A thousand, ten thousand? Their empire was long gone, yet here was an outpost still waiting to be revived to carry on its mysterious duties. It was as if in Saxon-invaded Britain long ago a Roman garrison had been frozen to await the return of the legions. Buck was right; there was no common ground today between Terran man and these unknowns. They must continue to sleep undisturbed.

Yet when Travis also turned away and went back down the aisle, he was still aware of a persistent pull on him to return. It was as though those eyes had set locking cords to will him back to release the sleepers. He was glad to turn a corner, to know that they could no longer watch him plunder their treasury.

"Here!" That was Buck's voice, but it echoed so oddly across the big chamber that Travis had difficulty in deciding what part of the warehouse it was coming from. And Buck had to call several times before Travis and Jil-Lee joined him.

There was the circle-dot-diamond symbol shining on the side of a case. They worked it out of the pile, setting it in the open. Travis knelt to run his hands along the top. The container was an unknown alloy, tough, unmarked by the years-perhaps indestructible.

Again his fingers located what his eyes could not detect-the impressions on the edge, oddly shaped impressions into which his finger tips did not fit too comfortably. He pressed, bearing down with the full strength of his arms and shoulders, and then lifted up the lid.

The Apaches looked into a set of compartments, each holding an object with a barrel, a hand grip, a general resemblance to the sidearms of their own world and time, but sufficiently different to point up the essential strangeness. With infinite care Travis worked one out of the vise-support which held it. The weapon was light in weight, lighter than any automatic he had ever held. Its barrel was long, a good eighteen inches-the grip alien in shape so that it didn't fit comfortably into his hand, the trigger nonexistent, but in its place a button on the lower part of the barrel which could be covered by an outstretched finger.

"What does it do?" asked Buck practically.

"I'm not sure. But it is important enough to have a special mention on the tape." Travis passed the weapon along to Buck and worked another loose from its holder.

"No way of loading I can see," Buck said, examining the weapon with care and caution.

"I don't think it fires a solid projectile," Travis replied. "We'll have to test them outside to find out just what we do have."

The Apaches took only three of the weapons, closing the box before they left. And as they wriggled back through the crack door, Travis was visited again by that odd flash of compelling, almost possessive power he had experienced when they had lain in ambush for the Red hunting party. He took a step or two forward until he was able to catch the edge of the reading table and steady himself against it.

"What is the matter?" Both Buck and Jil-Lee were watching him; apparently neither had felt that sensation. Travis did not reply for a second. He was free of it now. But he was sure of its source; it had not been any backlash of the Red caller! It was rooted here —a compulsion triggered to make the original intentions of the outpost obeyed, a last drag from the sleepers. This place had been set up with a single purpose: to protect and preserve the ancient rulers of Topaz. And perhaps the very presence here of the intruding Terrans had released a force, started an unseen installation.

Now Travis answered simply: "They want out...."

Jil-Lee glanced back at the slit door, but Buck still watched Travis.

"They call?" he asked.

"In a way," Travis admitted. But the compulsion had already ebbed; he was free. "It is gone now."

"This is not a good place," Buck observed somberly. "We touch that which should not be held by men of our earth." He held out the weapon.

"Did not the People take up the rifles of the Pinda-lick-o-yi for their defense when it was necessary?" Jil-Lee demanded. "We do what we must. After seeing that," his chin indicated the slit and what lay behind it —"do you wish the Reds to forage here?"

"Still," Buck's words came slowly, "this is a choice between two evils, rather than between an evil and a good —"

"Then let us see how powerful this evil is!" Jil-Lee headed for the corridor leading to the pillar.

* * * * *

It was late afternoon when they made their way through the swirling mists of the valley under the archway giving on the former site of the outlaw Tatar camp. Travis sighted the long barrel of the weapon at a small bush backed by a boulder, and he pressed the firing button. There was no way of knowing whether the weapon was loaded except to try it.

The result of his action was quick-quick and terrifying. There was no sound, no sign of any projectile ... ray-gas ... or whatever might have issued in answer to his finger movement. But the bush-the bush was no more!

A black smear made a ragged outline of the extinguished branches and leaves on the rock which had stood behind. The earth might still enclose roots under a thin coating of ash, but the bush was gone!

"The breath of Naye'nezyani-powerful beyond belief!" Buck broke their horrified silence first. "In truth evil is here!"

Jil-Lee raised his gun-if gun it could be called-aimed at the rock with the bush silhouette plain to see and fired.

This time they were able to witness disintegration in progress, the crumble of the stone as if its substance was no more than sand lapped by river water. A pile of blackened rubble remained-nothing more.

"To use this on a living thing?" Buck protested, horror basing the doubt in his voice.

"We do not use it against living things," Travis promised, "but against the ship of the Reds-to cut that to pieces. This will open the shell of the turtle and let us at its meat."

Jil-Lee nodded. "Those are true words. But now I agree with your fears of this place, Travis. This is a devil thing and must not be allowed to fall into the hands of those who —"

"Will use it more freely than we plan to?" Buck wanted to know. "We reserve to ourselves that right because we hold our motives higher? To think that way is also a crooked trail. We will use this means because we must, but afterward...."

Afterward that warehouse must be closed, the tapes giving the entrance clue destroyed. One part of Travis fought that decision, right though he knew it to be. The towers were the menace he had believed. And what was more discouraging than the risk they now ran, was the belief that the treasure was a poison which could not be destroyed but which might spread from Topaz to Terra.

Suppose the Western Conference had discovered that storehouse and explored its riches, would they have been any less eager to exploit them? As Buck had pointed out, one's own ideals could well supply reasons for violence. In the past Terra had been racked by wars of religion, one fanatically held opinion opposed to another. There was no righteousness in such struggles, only fatal ends. The Reds had no right to this new knowledge-but neither did they. It must be locked against the meddling of fools and zealots.

"Taboo —" Buck spoke that word with an emphasis they could appreciate. Knowledge must be set behind the invisible barriers of taboo, and that could work.

"These three-no more-we found no other weapons!" Jil-Lee added a warning suggestion.

"No others," Buck agreed and Travis echoed, adding:

"We found tombs of the space people, and these were left with them. Because of our great need we borrowed them, but they must be returned to the dead or trouble will follow. And they may only be used against the fortress of the Reds by us, who first found them and have taken unto ourselves the wrath of disturbed spirits."

"Well thought! That is an answer to give the People. The towers are the tombs of dead ones. When we return these they shall be taboo. We are agreed?" Buck asked.

"We are agreed!"

Buck tried his weapon on a sapling, saw it vanish into nothingness. None of the Apaches wanted to carry the strange guns against their bodies; the power made them objects of fear, rather than arms to delight a warrior. And when they returned to their temporary camp, they laid all three on a blanket and covered them up. But they could not cover up the memories of what had happened to bush, rock, and tree.

"If such are their small weapons," Buck observed that evening, "then what kind of things did they have to balance our heavy armament? Perhaps they were able to burn up worlds!"

"That may be what happened elsewhere," Travis replied. "We do not know what put an end to their empire. The capital-planet we found on the first voyage had not been destroyed, but it had been evacuated in haste. One building had not even been stripped of its furnishings." He remembered the battle he had fought there, he and Ross Murdock and the winged native, standing up to an attack of the ape-things while the winged warrior had used his physical advantage to fly above and bomb the enemies with boxes snatched from the piles....

"And here they went to sleep in order to wait out some danger-time or disaster-they did not believe would be permanent," Buck mused.

Travis thought he would flee from the eyes of the sleepers throughout his dreams that night, but on the contrary he slept heavily, finding it hard to rouse when Jil-Lee awakened him for his watch. But he was alert when he saw a four-footed shape flit out of the shadows, drink water from the stream, and shake itself vigorously in a spray of drops.

"Naginlta!" he greeted the coyote. Trouble? He could have shouted that question, but he put a tight rein on his impatience and strove to communicate in the only method possible.

No, what the coyote had come to report was not trouble but the fact that the one he had been set to guard was headed back into the mountains, though others came with her-four others. Nalik'ideyu still watched their camp. Her mate had come for further orders.

Travis squatted before the animal, cupped the coyote's jowls between his palms. Naginlta suffered his touch with only a small whine of uneasiness. With all his power of mental suggestion, Travis strove to reach the keen brain he knew was served by the yellow eyes looking into his.

The others with Kaydessa were to be led on, taken to the ship. But Kaydessa must not suffer harm. When they reached a spot near-by—Travis thought of a certain rock beyond the pass-then one of the coyotes was to go ahead to the ship. Let the Apaches there know....

Manulito and Eskelta should also be warned by the sentry along the peaks, but additional alerting would not go amiss. Those four with Kaydessa-they must reach the trap!

"What was that?" Buck rolled out of his blanket.

"Naginlta —" The coyote sped back into the dark again. "The Reds have taken the bait, a party of at least four with Kaydessa are moving into the foothills, heading south."

But the enemy party was not the only one on the move. In the light of day a sentry's mirror from a point in the peaks sent another warning down to their camp.

Out in their mountain meadows the Tatar outlaws were on horseback, moving toward the entrance of the tower valley. Buck knelt by the blanket covering the alien weapons.

"Now what?"

"We'll have to stop them," Travis replied, but he had no idea of just how they would halt those determined Mongol horsemen.

17

There were ten of them riding on small, wiry steppe ponies-men and women both, and well armed. Travis recalled it was the custom of the Horde that the women fought as warriors when necessary. Menlik-there was no mistaking the flapping robe of their leader. And they were singing! The rider behind the shaman thumped with violent energy a drum fastened beside his saddle horn, its heavy boom, boom the same call the Apache had heard before. The Mongols were working themselves into the mood for some desperate effort, Travis deduced. And if they were too deeply under the Red spell, there would be no arguing with them. He could wait no longer.

The Apache swung down from a ledge near the valley gate, moved into the open and stood waiting, the alien weapon resting across his forearm. If necessary, he intended to give a demonstration with it for an object lesson.

"*Dar-u-gar!*" The war cry which had once awakened fear across a quarter of Terra. Thin here, and from only a few throats, but just as menacing.

Two of the horsemen aimed lances, preparing to ride him down. Travis sighted a tree midway between them and pressed the firing button. This time there was a flash, a flicker of light, to mark the disappearance of a living thing.

One of the lancers' ponies reared, squealed in fear. The other kept on his course.

"Menlik!" Travis shouted. "Hold up your man! I do not want to kill!"

The shaman called out, but the lancer was already level with the vanished tree, his head half turned on his shoulders to witness the blackened earth where it had stood. Then he dropped his lance, sawed on the reins. A rifle bullet might not have halted his charge, unless it killed or wounded, but what he had just seen was a thing beyond his understanding.

The tribesmen sat their horses, facing Travis, watching him with the feral eyes of the wolves they claimed as forefathers, wolves that possessed the cunning of the wild, cunning enough not to rush breakneck into unknown danger.

Travis walked forward. "Menlik, I would talk —"

There was an outburst from the horsemen, protests from Hulagur and one or two of the others. But the shaman urged his mount into a walking pace toward the Apache until they stood only a few feet from each other-the warrior of the steppes and the Horde facing the warrior of the desert and the People.

"You have taken a woman from our yurts," Menlik said, but his eyes were more on the alien gun than on the man who held it. "Brave are you to come again into our land. He who sets foot in the stirrup must mount into the saddle; he who draws blade free of the scabbard must be prepared to use it."

"The Horde is not here —I see only a handful of people," Travis replied. "Does Menlik propose to go up against the Apaches so? Yet there are those who are his greater enemies."

"A stealer of women is not such a one as needs a regiment under a general to face him."

Suddenly Travis was impatient of the ceremonious talking; there was so little time.

"Listen, and listen well, Shaman!" He spoke curtly now. "I have not your woman. She is already crossing the mountains southward," he pointed with his chin —"leading the Reds into a trap."

Would Menlik believe him? There was no need, Travis decided, to tell him now that Kaydessa's part in this affair was involuntary.

"And you?" The shaman asked the question the Apache had hoped to hear.

"*We*," Travis emphasized that, "march now against those hiding behind in their ship out there." He indicated the northern plains.

Menlik raised his head, surveying the land about them with disbelieving, contemptuous appraisal.

"You are chief then of an army, an army equipped with magic to overcome machines?"

"One needs no army when he carries this." For the second time Travis displayed the power of the weapon he carried, this time cutting into shifting rubble an outcrop of cliff wall. Menlik's expression did not change, though his eyes narrowed.

The shaman signaled his small company, and they dismounted. Travis was heartened by this sign that Menlik was willing to talk. The Apache made a similar gesture, and Jil-Lee and Buck, their own weapons well in sight, came out to back him. Travis knew that the Tatar had no way of knowing that the three were alone; he well might have believed an unseen troop of Apaches were near-by and so armed.

"You would talk-then talk!" Menlik ordered.

This time Travis outlined events with an absence of word embroidery. "Kaydessa leads the Reds into a trap we have set beyond the peaks-four of them ride with her. How many now remain in the ship near the settlement?"

"There are at least two in the flyer, perhaps eight more in the ship. But there is no getting at them in there."

"No?" Travis laughed softly, shifted the weapon on his arm. "Do you not think that this will crack the shell of that nut so that we can get at the meat?"

Menlik's eyes flickered to the left, to the tree which was no longer a tree but a thin deposit of ash on seared ground.

"They can control us with the caller as they did before. If we go up against them, then we are once more gathered into their net-before we reach their ship."

"That is true for you of the Horde; it does not affect the People," Travis returned. "And suppose we burn out their machines? Then will you not be free?"

"To burn up a tree? Lightning from the skies can do that."

"Can lightning," Buck asked softly, "also make rock as sand of the river?"

Menlik's eyes turned to the second example of the alien weapon's power.

"Give us proof that this will act against their machines!"

"What proof, Shaman?" asked Jil-Lee. "Shall we burn down a mountain that you may believe? This is now a matter of time."

Travis had a sudden inspiration. "You say that the 'copter is out. Suppose we use that as a target?"

"That-that can sweep the flyer from the sky?" Menlik's disbelief was open.

Travis wondered if he had gone too far. But they needed to rid themselves of that spying flyer before they dared to move out into the plain. And to use the destruction of the helicopter as an example, would be the best proof he could give of the invincibility of the new Apache arms.

"Under the right conditions," he replied stoutly, "yes."

"And those conditions?" Menlik demanded.

"That it must be brought within range. Say, below the level of a neighboring peak where a man may lie in wait to fire."

Silent Apaches faced silent Mongols, and Travis had a chance to taste what might be defeat. But the helicopter must be taken before they advanced toward the ship and the settlement.

"And, maker of traps, how do you intend to bait this one?" Menlik's question was an open challenge.

"You know these Reds better than we," Travis counterattacked. "How would you bait it, Son of the Blue Wolf?"

"You say Kaydessa is leading the Reds south; we have but your word for that," Menlik replied. "Though how it would profit you to lie on such a matter —" He shrugged. "If you do speak the truth, then the 'copter will circle about the foothills where they entered."

"And what would bring the pilot nosing farther in?" the Apache asked.

Menlik shrugged again. "Any manner of things. The Reds have never ventured too far south; they are suspicious of the heights-with good cause." His fingers, near the hilt of his tulwar, twitched. "Anything which might suggest that their party is in difficulty would bring them in for a closer look —"

"Say a fire, with much smoke?" Jil-Lee suggested.

Menlik spoke over his shoulder to his own party. There was a babble of answer, two or three of the men raising their voices above those of their companions.

"If set in the right direction, yes," the shaman conceded. "When do you plan to move, Apaches?"

"At once!"

But they did not have wings, and the cross-country march they had to make was a rough journey on foot. Travis' "at once" stretched into night hours filled with scrambling over rocks, and an early morning of preparations, with always the threat that the helicopter might not return to fly its circling mission over the scene of operations. All they had was Menlik's assurance that while any party of the Red overlords was away from their well-defended base, the flyer did just that.

"Might be relaying messages on from a walkie-talkie or something like that," Buck commented.

"They should reach our ship in two days ... three at the most ... if they are pushing," Travis said thoughtfully. "It would be a help-if that flyer is a link in any com unit-to destroy it before its crew picks up and relays any report of what happens back there."

Jil-Lee grunted. He was surveying the heights above the pocket in which Menlik and two of the Mongols were piling brush. "There ... there ... and there...." The Apache's chin made three juts. "If the pilot swoops for a quick look, our cross fire will take out his blades."

They held a last conference with Menlik and then climbed to the perches Jil-Lee had selected. Sentries on lookout reported by mirror flash that Tsoay, Deklay, Lupe, and Nolan were now on the move to join the other three Apaches. If and when Manulito's trap closed its jaws on the Reds at the western ship, the news would pass and the Apaches would move out to storm the enemy fort on the prairie. And should they blast any caller the helicopter might carry, Menlik and his riders would accompany them.

There it was, just as Menlik had foretold: The wasp from the open country was flying into the hills. Menlik, on his knees, struck flint to steel, sparking the fire they hoped would draw the pilot to a closer investigation.

The brush caught, and smoke, thick and white, came first in separate puffs and then gathered into a murky pillar to form a signal no one could overlook. In Travis' hands the grip of the gun was slippery. He rested the end of the barrel on the rock, curbing his rising tension as best he could.

To escape any caller on the flyer, the Tatars had remained in the valley below the Apaches' lookout. And as the helicopter circled in, Travis sighted two men in its cockpit, one wearing a helmet identical to the one they had seen on the Red hunter days ago. The Reds' long undisputed sway over the Mongol forces would make them overconfident. Travis thought that even if they sighted one of the waiting Apaches, they would not take warning until too late.

Menlik's bush fire was performing well and the flyer was heading straight for it. The machine buzzed the smoke once, too high for the Apaches to trust raying its blades. Then the pilot came back in a lower sweep which carried him only yards above the smoldering brush, on a level with the snipers.

Travis pressed the button on the barrel, his target the fast-whirling blades. Momentum carried the helicopter on, but at least one of the marksmen, if not all three, had scored. The machine plowed through the smoke to crack up beyond.

Was their caller working, bringing in the Mongols to aid the Reds trapped in the wreck?

Travis watched Menlik make his way toward the machine, reach the cracked cover of the cockpit. But in the shaman's hand was a bare blade on which the sun glinted. The Mongol wrenched open the sprung door, thrust inward with the tulwar, and the howl of triumph he voiced was as wordless and wild as a wolf's.

More Mongols flooding down ... Hulagur ... a woman ... centering on the helicopter. This time a spear plunged into the interior of the broken flyer. Payment was being extracted for long slavery.

The Apaches dropped from the heights, waiting for Menlik to leave the wild scene. Hulagur had dragged out the body of the helmeted man and the Mongols were stripping off his equipment, smashing it with rocks, still howling their war cry. But the shaman came to the dying smudge fire to meet the Apaches.

He was smiling, his upper lip raised in a curve suggesting the victory purr of a snow tiger. And he saluted with one hand.

"There are two who will not trap men again! We believe you now, *andas*, comrades of battle, when you say you can go up against their fort and make it as nothing!"

Hulagur came up behind the shaman, a modern automatic in his hand. He tossed the weapon into the air, caught it again, laughing-disclaiming something in his own language.

"From the serpents we take two fangs," Menlik translated. "These weapons may not be as dangerous as yours, but they can bite deeper, quicker, and with more force than our arrows."

It did not take the Mongols long to strip the helicopter and the Reds of what they could use, deliberately smashing all the other equipment which had survived the wreck. They had accomplished one important move: The link between the southbound exploring party and the Red headquarters-if that was the role the helicopter had played-was now gone. And the "eyes" operating over the open territory of the plains had ceased to exist. The attacking war party could move against the ship near the Red settlement, knowing they had only controlled Mongol scouts to watch for. And to penetrate enemy territory under those conditions was an old, old game the Apaches had played for centuries.

While they waited for the signals from the peaks, a camp was established and a Mongol dispatched to bring up the rest of the outlaws and all extra mounts. Menlik carried to the Apaches a portion of the dried meat which had been transported Horde fashion-under the saddle to soften it for eating.

"We do not skulk any longer like rats or city men in dark holes," he told them. "This time we ride, and we shall take an accounting from those out there —a fine accounting!"

"They still have other controllers," Travis pointed out.

"And you have that which is an answer to all their machines," blazed Menlik in return.

"They will send against us your own people if they can," Buck warned.

Menlik pulled at his upper lip. "That is also truth. But now they have no eyes in the sky, and with so many of their men away, they will not patrol too far from camp. I tell you, *andas*, with these weapons of yours a man could rule a world!"

Travis looked at him bleakly. "Which is why they are taboo!"

"Taboo?" Menlik repeated. "In what manner are these forbidden? Do you not carry them openly, use them as you wish? Are they not weapons of your own people?"

Travis shook his head. "These are the weapons of dead men-if we can name them men at all. These we took from a tomb of the star race who held Topaz when our world was only a hunting ground of wild men wearing the skins of beasts and slaying mammoths with stone spears. They are from a tomb and are cursed, a curse we took upon ourselves with their use."

There was a strange light deep in the shaman's eyes. Travis did not know who or what Menlik had been before the Red conditioner had returned him to the role of Horde shaman. He might have been a technician or scientist-and deep within him some remnants of that training could now be dismissing everything Travis said as fantastic superstition.

Yet in another way the Apache spoke the exact truth. There was a curse on these weapons, on every bit of knowledge gathered in that warehouse of the towers. As Menlik had already noted, that curse was power, the power to control Topaz, and then perhaps to reach back across the stars to Terra.

When the shaman spoke again his words were a half whisper. "It will take a powerful curse to keep these out of the hands of men."

"With the Reds gone or powerless," Buck asked, "what need will anyone have for them?"

"And if another ship comes from the skies-to begin all over again?"

"To that we shall have an answer, also, if and when we must find it," Travis replied. That could well be true ... other weapons in the warehouse powerful enough to pluck a spaceship out of the sky, but they did not have to worry about that now.

"Arms from a tomb. Yes, this is truly dead men's magic. I shall say so to my people. When do we move out?"

"When we know whether or not the trap to the south is sprung," Buck answered.

The report came an hour after sunrise the next morning when Tsoay, Nolan, and Deklay padded into camp. The war chief made a slight gesture with one hand.

"It is done?" Travis wanted confirmation in words.

"It is done. The Pinda-lick-o-yi entered the ship eagerly. Then they blew it and themselves up. Manulito did his work well."

"And Kaydessa?"

"The woman is safe. When the Reds saw the ship, they left their machine outside to hold her captive. That mechanical caller was easily destroyed. She is now free and with the *mba'a* she comes across the mountains, Manulito and Eskelta with her also. Now —" he looked from his own people to the Mongols, "why are you here with these?"

"We wait, but the waiting is over," Jil-Lee said. "Now we go north!"

18

They lay along the rim of a vast basin, a scooping out of earth so wide they could not sight its other side. The bed of an ancient lake, Travis speculated, or perhaps even the arm of a long-dried sea. But now the hollow was filled with rolling waves of golden grass, tossing heavy heads under the flowing touch of a breeze with the exception of a space about a mile ahead where round domes-black, gray, brown-broke the yellow in an irregular oval around the globular silver bead of a spacer: a larger ship than that which had brought the Apaches, but of the same shape.

"The horse herd ... to the west." Nolan evaluated the scene with the eyes of an experienced raider. "Tsoay, Deklay, you take the horses!"

They nodded, and began the long crawl which would take them two miles or more from the party to stampede the horses.

To the Mongols in those domelike yurts horses were wealth, life itself. They would come running to investigate any disturbance among the grazing ponies, thus clearing the path to the ship and the Reds there. Travis, Jil-Lee, and Buck, armed with the star guns, would spearhead that attack-cutting into the substance of the ship itself until it was a sieve through which they could shake out the enemy. Only when the installations it contained were destroyed, might the Apaches hope for any assistance from the Mongols, either the outlaw pack waiting well back on the prairie or the people in the yurts.

The grass rippled and Naginlta poked out a nose, parting stems before Travis. The Apache beamed an order, sending the coyotes with the horse-raiding party. He had seen how the animals could drive hunted split-horns; they would do as well with the ponies.

Kaydessa was safe, the coyotes had made that clear by the fact that they had joined the attacking party an hour earlier. With Eskelta and Manulito she was on her way back to the north.

Travis supposed he should be well pleased that their reckless plan had succeeded as well as it had. But when he thought of the Tatar girl, all he could see was her convulsed face close to his in the ship corridor, her raking nails raised to tear his cheek. She had an excellent reason to hate him, yet he hoped....

They continued to watch both horse herd and domes. There were people moving about the yurts, but no signs of life at the ship. Had the Reds shut themselves in there, warned in some way of the two disasters which had whittled down their forces?

"Ah —!" Nolan breathed.

One of the ponies had raised its head and was facing the direction of the camp, suspicion plain to read in its stance. The Apaches must have reached the point between the herd and the domes which had been their goal. And the Mongol guard, who had been sitting cross-legged, the reins of his mount dangling close to his hand, got to his feet.

"Ahhhuuuuu!" The ancient Apache war cry that had sounded across deserts, canyons, and southwestern Terran plains to ice the blood, ripped just as freezingly through the honey-hued air of Topaz.

The horses wheeled, racing upslope away from the settlement. A figure broke from the grass, flapped his arms at one of the mounts, grabbed at flying mane, and pulled himself up on the bare back. Only a master horseman would have done that, but the whooping rider now drove the herd on, assisted by the snapping and snarling coyotes.

"Deklay —" Jil-Lee identified the reckless rider, "that was one of his rodeo tricks."

Among the yurts it was as if someone had ripped up a rotten log to reveal an ants' nest and sent the alarmed insects into a frenzy. Men boiled out of the domes, the majority of them running for the horse pasture. One or two were mounted on ponies that must have been staked out in the settlement. The main war party of Apaches skimmed silently through the grass on their way to the ship.

The three who were armed with the alien weapons had already tested their range by experimentation back in the hills, but the fear of exhausting whatever powered those barrels had curtailed their target practice. Now they snaked to the edge of the bare ground between them and the ladder hatch of the spacer. To cross that open space was to provide targets for lances and arrows-or the superior armament of the Reds.

"A chance we can hit from here." Buck laid his weapon across his bent knee, steadied the long barrel of the burner, and pressed the firing button.

The closed hatch of the ship shimmered, dissolved into a black hole. Behind Travis someone let out the yammer of a war whoop.

"Fire-cut the walls to pieces!"

Travis did not need that order from Jil-Lee. He was already beaming unseen destruction at the best target he could ask for-the side of the sphere. If the globe was armed, there was no weapon which could be depressed far enough to reach the marksmen at ground level.

Holes appeared, irregular gaps and tears in the fabric of the ship. The Apaches were turning the side of the globe into lacework. How far those rays penetrated into the interior they could not guess.

Movement at one of the holes, the chattering burst of machine-gun fire, spatters of soil and gravel into their faces; they could be cut to pieces by that! The hole enlarged, a scream ... cut off....

"They will not be too quick to try that again," Nolan observed with cold calm from behind Travis' post.

Methodically they continued to beam the ship. It would never be space-borne again; there were neither the skills nor materials here to repair such damage.

"It is like laying a knife to fat," Lupe said as he crawled up beside Travis. "Slice, slice —!"

"Move!" Travis reached to the left, pulled at Jil-Lee's shoulder.

Travis did not know whether it was possible or not, but he had a heady vision of their combined fire power cutting the globe in half, slicing it crosswise with the ease Lupe admired.

They scurried through cover just as someone behind yelled a warning. Travis threw himself down, rolled into a new firing position. An arrow sang over his head; the Reds were doing what the Apaches had known they would-calling in the controlled Mongols to fight. The attack on the ship must be stepped up, or the Amerindians would be forced to retreat.

Already a new lacing of holes appeared under their concentrated efforts. With the gun held tight to his middle, Travis found his feet, zigzagged across the bare ground for the nearest of those openings. Another arrow clanged harmlessly against the fabric of the ship a foot from his goal.

He made it in, over jagged metal shards which glowed faintly and reeked of ozone. The weapons' beams had penetrated well past both the outer shell and the wall of insulation webbing. He climbed a second and smaller break into a corridor enough like those of the western ship to be familiar. The Red spacer, based on the general plan of the alien derelict ship as his own had been, could not be very different.

Travis tried to subdue his heavy breathing and listen. He heard a confused shouting and the burr of what might be an alarm system. The ship's brain was the control cabin. Even if the Reds dared not try to lift now, that was the core of their communication lines. He started along the corridor, trying to figure out its orientation in relation to that all-important nerve center.

The Apache shoved open each door he passed with one shoulder, and twice he played a light beam on installations within cabins. He had no idea of their use, but the wholesale destruction of each and every machine was what good sense and logic dictated.

There was a sound behind. Travis whirled, saw Jil-Lee and beyond him Buck.

"Up?" Jil-Lee asked.

"And down," Buck added. "The Tatars say they have hollowed a bunker beneath."

"Separate and do as much damage as you can," Travis suggested.

"Agreed!"

Travis sped on. He passed another door and then backtracked hurriedly as he realized it had given on to an engine room. With the gun he blasted two long lines cutting the fittings into ragged lumps. Abruptly the lights went out; the burr of the alarms was silenced. Part of the ship, if not all, was dead. And now it might come to hunter and hunted in the dark. But that was an advantage as far as the Apaches were concerned.

Back in the corridor again, Travis crept through a curiously lifeless atmosphere. The shouting was stilled as if the sudden failure of the machines had stunned the Reds.

A tiny sound-perhaps the scrape of a boot on a ladder. Travis edged back into a compartment. A flash of light momentarily lighted the corridor; the approaching figure was using a torch.

Travis drew his knife with one hand, reversed it so he could use the heavy hilt as a silencer. The other was hurrying now, on his way to investigate the burned-out engine cabin. Travis could hear the rasp of his fast breathing. Now!

The Apache had put down the gun, his left arm closed about a shoulder, and the Red gasped as Travis struck with the knife hilt. Not clean-he had to hit a second time before the struggles of the man were over. Then, using his hands for eyes, he stripped the limp body on the floor of automatic and torch.

With the Red's weapon in the front of his sash, the burner in one hand and the torch in the other, Travis prowled on. There was a good chance that those above might believe him to be their comrade returning. He found the ladder leading to the next level, began to climb, pausing now and then to listen.

Shock preceded sound. Under him the ladder swayed and the globe itself rocked a little. A blast of some kind must have been set off at or under the level of the ground. The bunker Buck had mentioned?

Travis clung to the ladder, waited for the vibrations to subside. There was a shouting above, a questioning.... Hurriedly he ascended to the next level, scrambled out and away from the ladder just in time to avoid the light from another torch flashed down the well. Again that call of inquiry, then a shot-the boom of the explosion loud in the confined space.

To climb into the face of that light with a waiting marksman above was sheer folly. Could there be another way up? Travis retreated down one of the corridors raying out from the ladder well. A quick inspection of the cabins along that route told him he had reached a section of living quarters. The pattern was familiar; the control cabin would be on the next level.

Suddenly the Apache remembered something: On each level there should be an emergency opening giving access to the insulation space between the inner and outer skins of the ship through which repairs could be made. If he could find that and climb up to the next level....

The light shining down the well remained steady, and there was the echoing crack of another shot. But Travis was far enough away from the ladder now to dare use his own torch, seeking the door he needed on the wall surface. With a leap of heart he sighted the outline-his luck was in! The Russian and western ships were alike.

Once the panel was open he flashed his torch up, finding the climbing rungs and, above, the shadow outline of the next level opening. Securing the alien gun in his sash beside the automatic and holding the torch in his mouth, Travis climbed, not daring to think of the deep drop below. Four ... five ... ten rungs, and he could reach the other door.

His fingers slid over it, searching for the release catch. But there was no answering give. Balling his fist, he struck down at an awkward angle and almost lost his balance as the panel fell away beneath his blow. The door swung and he pulled through.

Darkness! Travis snapped on the torch for an instant, saw about him the relays of a com system, and gave it a full spraying as he pivoted, destroying the eyes and ears of the ship-unless the burnout he had effected below had already done that. A flash of automatic fire from his left, a searing burn along his arm an inch or so below the shoulder —

Travis' action was purely reflex. He swung the burner around, even as his mind gave a frantic No! To defend himself with automatic, knife, arrow-yes; but not this way. He huddled against the wall.

An instant earlier there had been a man there, a living, breathing man-one of his own species, if not of his own beliefs. Then because his own muscles had unconsciously obeyed warrior training, there was this. So easy-to deal death without really meaning to. The weapon in his hands was truly the devil gift they were right to fear. Such weapons were not to be put into the hands of men-any men-no matter how well intentioned.

Travis gulped in great mouthfuls of air. He wanted to throw the burner away, hurl it from him. But the task he could rightfully use it for was not yet done.

Somehow he reeled on into the control cabin to render the ship truly a dead thing and free himself of the heavy burden of guilt and terror between his hands. That weight could be laid aside; memory could not. And no one of his kind must ever have to carry such memories again.

* * * * *

The booming of the drums was like a pulse quickening the blood to a rhythm which bit at the brain, made a man's eyes shine, his muscles tense as if he held an arrow to bow cord or arched his fingers about a knife hilt. A fire blazed high and in its light men leaped and whirled in a mad dance with tulwar blades catching and reflecting the red gleam of flames. Mad, wild, the Mongols were drunk with victory and freedom. Beyond them, the silver globe of the ship showed the black holes of its death, which was also the death of the past-for all of them.

"What now?" Menlik, the dangling of amulets and charms tinkling as he moved, came up to Travis. There was none of the wild fervor in the shaman's face; instead, it was as if he had taken several strides out of the life of the Horde, was emerging into another person, and the question he asked was one they all shared.

Travis felt drained, flattened. They had achieved their purpose. The handful of Red overlords were dead, their machines burned out. There were no controls here any more; men were free in mind and body. What were they to do with that freedom?

"First," the Apache spoke his own thoughts —"we must return these."

The three alien weapons were lashed into a square of Mongol fabric, hidden from sight, although they could not be so easily shut out of mind. Only a few of the others, Apache or Mongol, had seen them; and they must be returned before their power was generally known.

"I wonder if in days to come," Buck mused, "they will not say that we pulled lightning out of the sky, as did the Thunder Slayer, to aid us. But this is right. We must return them and make that valley and what it holds taboo."

"And what if another ship comes-one of *yours*?" Menlik asked shrewdly.

Travis stared beyond the Tatar shaman to the men about the fire. His nightmare dragged into the open....What if a ship did come in, one with Ashe, Murdock, men he knew and liked, friends on board? What then of his guardianship of the towers and their knowledge? Could he be as sure of what to do then? He rubbed his hand across his forehead and said slowly:

"We shall take steps when-or if-that happens —"

But could they, would they? He began to hope fiercely that it would not happen, at least in his lifetime, and then felt the cold bleakness of the exile they must will themselves into.

"Whether we like it or not," (was he talking to the others or trying to argue down his own rebellion?) "we cannot let what lies under the towers be known ... found ... used ... unless by men who are wiser and more controlled than we are in our time."

Menlik drew his shaman's wand, twiddled it between his fingers, and beneath his drooping lids watched the three Apaches with a new kind of measurement.

"Then I say to you this: Such a guardianship must be a double charge, shared by my people as well. For if they suspect that you alone control these powers and their secret, there will be envy, hatred, fear, a division between us from the first-war ... raids....This is a large land and neither of our groups numbers many. Shall we split apart fatally from this day when there is room for all? If these ancient things are evil, then let us both guard them with a common taboo."

He was right, of course. And they would have to face the truth squarely. To both Apache and Mongol any off-world ship, no matter from which side, would be a menace. Here was where they would remain and set roots. The sooner they began thinking of themselves as people with a common bond, the better it would be. And Menlik's suggestion provided a tie.

"You speak well," Buck was saying. "This shall be a thing we share. We are three who know. Do you be three also, but choose well, Menlik!"

"Be assured that I will!" the Tatar returned. "We start a new life here; there is no going back. But as I have said: The land is wide. We have no quarrel with one another, and perhaps our two peoples shall become one; after all, we do not differ too greatly...." He smiled and gestured to the fire and the dancers.

Among the Mongols another man had gone into action, his head thrown back as he leaped and twirled, voicing a deep war cry. Travis recognized Deklay. Apache, Mongol-both raiders, horsemen, hunters, fighters when the need arose. No, there was no great difference. Both had been tricked into coming here, and they had no allegiance now for those who had sent them.

Perhaps clan and Horde would combine or perhaps they would drift apart-time would tell. But there would be the bond of the guardianship, the determination that what slept in the towers would not be roused-in their lifetime or many lifetimes!

Travis smiled a bit crookedly. A new religion of sorts, a priesthood with sacred and forbidden knowledge ... in time a whole new life and civilization stemming from this night. The bleak cold of his early thought cut less deep. There was a different kind of adventure here.

He reached out and gathered up the bundle of the burners, glancing from Buck to Jil-Lee to Menlik. Then he stood up, the weight of the burden in his arms, the feeling of a greater weight inside him.

"Shall we go?"

To get the weapons back-that was of first importance. Maybe then he could sleep soundly, to dream of riding across the Arizona range at dawn under a blue sky with a wind in his face, a wind carrying the scent of piñon pine and sage, a wind which would never caress or hearten him again, a wind his sons and sons' sons would never know. To dream troubled dreams, and hope in time those dreams would fade and thin-that a new world would blanket out the old. Better so, Travis told himself with defiance and determination-better so!

Lester Del Rey

Pursuit

I

Fear cut through the unconscious mind of Wilbur Hawkes. With almost physical violence, it tightened his throat and knifed at his heart. It darted into his numbed brain, screaming at him.

He was a soft egg in a vast globe of elastic gelatine. Two creatures swam menacingly through the resisting globe toward him. The gelatine fought against them, but they came on. One was near, and made a mystic pass. He screamed at it, and the gelatine grew stronger, throwing them back and away. Suddenly, the creatures drew back. A door opened, and they were gone. But he couldn't let them go. If they escaped....

Hawkes jerked upright in his bed, gasping out a hoarse cry, and the sound of his own voice completed the awakening. He opened his eyes to a murky darkness that was barely relieved by the little night-light. For a second, the nightmare was so strong on his mind that he seemed to see two shadows beyond the door, rushing down the steps. He fought off the illusion, and with straining senses jerked his head around the room. There was nothing there.

Sweat was beading his forehead, and he could feel his pulse racing. He had to get out-had to leave-at once!

He forced the idea aside. There was something cloudy in his mind, but he made reason take over and shove away some of the heavy fear. His fingers found a cigarette and lighted it automatically. The first familiar breath of smoke in his lungs helped. He drew in deeply again, while the tiny sounds in the room became meaningful. There was the insistent ticking of a clock and the soft shushing sound of a tape recorder. He stared at the machine, running on fast rewind, and reversed it to play. But the tape seemed to be blank, or erased.

He crushed the cigarette out on a table-top where other butts lay in disorder. It looked wrong, and his mind leaped up in sudden frantic fear, before he could calm it again. This time, reason echoed his emotional unease.

Hawkes had never smoked before!

But his fingers were already lighting another by old habit. His thoughts lurched, seeking for an answer. There was only a vague sense of something missing —a period of time seemed to have passed. It felt like a long period, but he had no memory of it. There had been the final fight with Irma, when he'd gone stalking out of the house, telling her to get a divorce any way she wanted. He'd opened the mail-box and taken out a letter —a letter from a Professor....

His mind refused to go further. There was only a complete blank after that. But it had been in midwinter, and now he could make out the faint outlines of full-leafed trees against the sky through the window! Months had gone by-and there was no faintest trace of them in his mind.

They'll get you! You can't escape! Hurry, go, GO!...

The cigarette fell from his shaking hands, and he was half out of the bed before the rational part of his mind could cut off the fear thoughts. He flipped on the lights, afraid of the dimness. It didn't help. The room was dusty, as if unused for months, and there was a cobweb in one corner by the mirror.

His own face shocked him. It was the same lean, sharp-featured face as ever, under the shock of nondescript, sandy hair. His ears still stuck out too much, and his lips were a trifle too thin. It looked no more than his thirty years; but it was a strained face, now-painted with weeks of fatigue, and grayish with fear, sweat-streaked and with nervous tension in every corded tendon of his throat. His somewhat bony, average-height figure shook visibly as he climbed from the bed.

Hawkes stood fighting himself, trying to get back in the bed, but it was a losing battle. Something seemed to swing up in the corner of the room, as if a shadow moved. He jerked his head toward it, but there was nothing there.

He heard his breath gasping harshly, and his knuckles whitened. There was the taste of blood in the corner of his mouth where he was biting his lips.

Get out! They'll be here at once! Leave-GO!

His hands were already fumbling with his under-clothing. He drew on briefs jerkily, and grabbed for the shirt and suit he had never seen before. He was no longer thinking, now. Blind panic was winning. He thrust his feet into shoes, not bothering with socks.

A slip of paper fell from his coat, with big sprawled Greek letters. He saw only the last line as it fell to the floor-some equation that ended with an infinity sign. Then psi and alpha, connected by a dash. The alpha sign had been scratched out, and something written over it. He tried to reach it, and more papers spilled from his coat pocket. The fear washed up more strongly. He forgot the papers. Even the cigarettes were too far away for him to return to them. His wallet lay on the chair, and he barely grabbed it before the urge overpowered him completely.

The doorknob slipped in his sweating hands, but he managed to turn it. The elevator wasn't at his floor, and he couldn't stop for it. His feet pounded on the stairs, taking him down the three floors to the street at a breakneck pace. The walls of the stairway seemed to be rushing together, as if trying to close the way. He screamed at them, until they were behind, and he was charging out of the front door.

A half-drunken couple was coming in —a fat, older man and a slim girl he barely saw. He hit them, throwing them aside. He jerked from the entrance. Cars were streaming down West End Avenue. He dashed across, paying no attention to them. His rush carried him onto the opposite sidewalk. Then, finally, the blind panic left him, and he was leaning against a building, gasping for breath, and wondering whether his heart could endure the next beat.

Across the street, the fat man he had hit was coming after him. Hawkes gathered himself together to apologize, but the words never came. A second blinding horror hit at him, and his eyes darted up towards the windows of his apartment.

It was only a tiny glow, at first, like a drop from the heart of a sun. Then, before he could more than blink, it spread, until the whole apartment seemed to blaze. A gout of smoke poured from the shattering window, and a dull concussion struck his ears.

The infernally bright flame flickered, leaped outward from the window, and died down almost as quickly as it had come, leaving twisted, half-molten metal where the window frames had been.

They'd almost gotten him! Hawkes felt his legs weaken and quiver, while his eyes remained glued to the spot that had lighted the whole street a second before. They'd tried-but he'd escaped in time.

It must have been a thermite bomb-nothing but thermite could be that hot. He had never imagined that even such a bomb could give so much heat so quickly. Where? In the tape-recorder?

He waited numbly, expecting more fire, but the brief flame seemed to have died out completely. He shook his head, unbelieving, and started to cross the street again, to survey the damage or to join the crowd that was beginning to collect.

The fear surged up in him again, halting his step as if he'd struck a physical barrier. With it came the sound of an auto-horn, the button held down permanently. His eyes darted down the street, to see a long, gray sedan with old-fashioned running-boards come around the corner on two wheels. Its brakes screeched, and it skidded to a halt beside Hawkes' apartment building.

A slim young man in gray tweeds leaped out of it and came to a stop. He threw back heavy black hair with a toss of his head and ran into the crowd that parted to let him through. Someone began pointing towards Hawkes.

Hawkes tried to slide around the corner without being seen, but a flashlight in the young man's hands pinpointed him. A yell went up.

"There he goes!"

His feet sounded hopelessly on the sidewalk as he dashed up toward Broadway, but behind came the sound of others in pursuit, and the shouting was becoming a meaningless babble as others took it up. There was no longer any doubt. Someone was certainly after him-there'd been no time to turn in an alarm over the fire in his apartment. They'd been coming for him before that started.

What hideous crime could he have committed during the period he couldn't remember? Or what spy-ring had encircled him?

He had no time to think of the questions, even. He ducked into the thin swarm of a few people leaving a theater just as the pursuing group rounded the corner, with the slim young man in the lead.

Their cries were enough. Hands reached for him from the theater crowd, and a foot stretched out to trip him up. Terror lent speed to his legs, but he could never outdistance them, as long as others picked up the chase.

A sudden blast of heat struck down, and the air was golden and hazy above him. He staggered sideways, blinded by the glare. The crowd was screaming in fear now, no longer holding him back. He felt the edge of a subway entrance. There was no other choice. He ducked down the steps, while his vision slowly returned, and risked a glance back at the street-just as the whole entrance came down in a wreck of broken wood and metal.

A clap of thundering noise sounded above him, drowning the hoarse screams of the people. The few persons in the station rushed for the fallen entrance, to mill about it crazily, just as a train pulled in. Hawkes started toward it, and then realized his pursuers would suspect that. Whatever frightful weapon had been used against him had back-fired on them-but they'd catch him at the next stop.

He found space at the end of the platform and dropped off, skirting behind the train, and avoiding the the high-voltage rails.

The uptown platform held only three people, and they seemed to be too busy at the other end, trying to see the wreckage, to notice him. He vaulted onto it, and dashed into the men's room. The few contents of his coat pocket came out quickly, and he began to stuff them into his trousers. He shoved the coat into a garbage can, wet his hair and slicked it back, and opened his shirt collar. The change didn't make much of a disguise, but they wouldn't be expecting him to show up so near where he entered.

His skin prickled as he came out, but he fought down the sickness in his stomach. A few drops of rain were beginning to fall, and the crowd around the accident was thinning out. That might help him-or it might prove more dangerous. He had to chance it.

He stopped to buy a paper, maintaining an air of casual interest in the crowd.

"What happened?" he asked.

The newsstand attendant jerked his eyes back from they excitement reluctantly. "Damned if I know. Someone, says a ball lightning came down and broke over there. Caved in the entrance. Nobody's hurt seriously, they say. I was just stacking up to go home when I heard it go off. Didn't see it. Just saw the entrance falling in."

Hawkes picked up his change and turned back across Broadway, pretending he was studying the paper. The dateline showed it was July 10, just seven months from the beginning of his memory lapse. He couldn't believe that there had been time enough for any group to invent a heat-ray, if such a thing could exist. Yet nothing else would explain the two sudden bursts of flame he had seen. Even if it could be invented, it would hardly be used in public for anything less than a National Emergency.

What had happened in the seven blanked-out months?

II

The room was smelly and cheap, with dirty walls and no carpet on the floor, but it was a relief after the hours of tramping and riding about the city. Hawkes sat on the rickety chair, letting the wetness dry out of his clothes. He looked at the bed, trying to convince himself he could strip and warm up there while his clothes dried. But something in his head warned him that he couldn't —he'd have to be ready to run again. The same urge had made him demand a room on the ground floor, where he could escape through the window if they found him. They could never find him here-but they would! Sooner or later, whatever was after him would come!

It had seemed simple enough, before. There had been three friends he could trust. Seven months, he had felt, couldn't have killed their faith in him, no matter what he'd done. And perhaps he'd been right, though there'd been no chance to test it.

He'd almost been caught at the first place. The two men outside had seemed to be no more than a couple of friends awaiting for a bus. Only the approach of another man who resembled Hawkes had tipped him off, by the quick interest they had shown.

The other places had also been posted-and beyond the third, he'd seen the gray sedan with the running boards, parked back in the shadows, waiting.

There had been less than ten dollars in his wallet, and most of that had gone for cab fares. He'd barely had enough left for this dingy room, the later edition of the newspaper, and the coffee and donuts that lay beside him, half-consumed.

He glanced toward the door, listening with quick fear as steps sounded on the stairs. Then he drew his breath in again, and reached for the newspaper. But it told him as little as the first one had.

This one mentioned the two mysterious explosions of "ball lightning" in a feature on the first page, but only as curiosities. They even gave his address and listed the apartment as being in his name, though apparently not currently occupied. But no other reference was made to him, or to the chase.

He shook his head at that. He couldn't see a newspaper-man refusing to make a story of it, if there was any other news about him to which they could tie the burning of his apartment. Apparently it was not the police who were after him, and he hadn't been guilty of anything so ordinary as murder.

Outside the window, a sudden scream sounded, and he jerked from the chair, reaching the door before he realized it was only a cat on the prowl. He shuddered, his old hatred of cats coming to the surface. For a minute, he thought of shutting the window. But he couldn't cut off his chance to retreat through the garbage-littered back-yard.

He returned to his search, beginning an inventory of the few belongings that had been in his pocket. There was a notebook, and he scanned it rapidly. A few pages were missing, and most were blank. There was only a shopping list. That puzzled him for a minute-he couldn't believe he'd taken to using lipstick as well as cigarettes, though both were listed in his handwriting. The notebook contained nothing else.

He stuffed it back into his pockets, along with his keyring. There were more keys than he'd expected, some of which were strange to him, but none held any mark that would identify them. He put a few pennies into another pocket-his entire wealth, now, in a world where no more money would be available to him. He grimaced, dropping a comb into the same pocket.

Then there was only his wallet left. His identification card was there, unchanged. Behind it, where his wife's picture had always been, there was only a folded clipping. He drew it out, hoping for a clew. It was only an announcement of people killed in an airplane crash-and among those found dead was Mrs. Wilbur Hawkes, of New York. It seemed that Irma had never reached Reno for the divorce.

He tried to feel some sorrow at that, but time must have healed whatever hurt there had been, even though he couldn't remember. She had hated him ever since she'd found that he really wasn't willing to please his father by becoming another of the vice-presidents in the old man's bank, with an unearned but fancy salary. He'd preferred teaching mathematics and dabbling with a bit of research into the probable value of the ESP work being done at Duke University. He'd explained why he hated banking; Irma had made it clear that she really needed the mink coat no assistant professor could afford. It had been stalemate —a bitter, seven-year stalemate, until she finally gave up hope and demanded a divorce.

He threw the clipping away, and pulled out the final bit of paper. It was a rent receipt for a cold-water apartment on the poorer section of West End-from the price of eighteen dollars a month, it had to be a cold-water place. He frowned, considering it. Apartment 12. That might explain why his own apartment had been unused, though it made little sense to him. It would probably be watched by now, anyway.

He jerked to his feet at a sound on the window-sill, but it was only a cat, eyeing the unfinished donut. He threw the food out, and the cat dived after it. Hawkes waited for the touch of ice along his backbone to go away. It didn't.

This time, he tried to ignore it. He picked up the paper and began going through it, looking for something that might give him some slight clew. But there was nothing there. Only a heading on an inside page that stirred his curiosity.

Scientist Seeks Confinement

He glanced at it, noting that a Professor Meinzer, formerly of City College, had appeared at Bellevue, asking to be put away in a padded cell, preferably with a strait-jacket. The Professor had only explained that he considered himself dangerous to society. No other reason was found. Professor Meinzer had been doing private work, believed to relate to his theory that....

The panic was back, thick in Hawkes' throat. He jerked back against the wall, his heart racing, while he tried to fight it down. There was no sound from the hall or outside. He forced his eyes back to the paper.

And the paper was surrounded by a golden haze. It burst into a momentary flame as the haze flickered out. Hawkes dropped the ashes from his clammy hands. He hadn't been burned!

You can't escape. Run. They'll get you!

He heard the outside door open, as it had opened a hundred times. But now it could only mean that more were coming. He jerked for the open window.

Something came sailing through the air to hit the sill. Hawkes screamed weakly, far down in his throat, before his eyes could register the fact that it was only the cat again.

Then the cat let out a horrible beginning of a sound, and its poor, half-starved body seemed to turn inside out, with a churning motion that Hawkes could barely see. Blood and gore spattered from it, striking his face and clothes.

He froze, unable to move. Either they were outside in the yard, or whatever frightful weapon they used could work through a closed door. He tried to move, first one way, then the other. His feet remained frozen.

Then steps sounded in the hallway, and he waited no longer. His legs came to sudden life, hurling him over the carcass of the cat and outside. He went charging through the refuse, and then leaped and clawed his way over the fence. The alley was deserted, and he shot down it, to swing right, and into another alley.

It wasn't until his muscles began to fail that he could control himself enough to stop and stumble into a darkened spot among the garbage cans, spent and gasping for breath.

There was no sign of anyone following. Hawkes had no idea of how they could trace him—but he was beginning to suspect that nothing was impossible, judging by the results of their weapons. For the moment, though, he seemed to have shaken off pursuit. And the physical fatigue had apparently eased some of his terror.

What had shocked him into losing seven months out of his memory, and still could drive him into absolute terror at the first sign of them?

He couldn't go back to the room, and his own apartment was out of the question. The rain had stopped, mercifully, but he couldn't walk the streets indefinitely, dirty and bedraggled as he was. He tried to think of something to do, but all of his schemes took money which he no longer had.

Finally, he arose wearily. Maybe the apartment for which he had the rent receipt was watched—but he'd have to chance it. There was no place else.

He'd been accidentally heading toward it, and he continued now, sticking to the alleys until he reached West End Avenue. He tried to hurry, but the best his tired muscles could do was a slow shuffle.

Light was beginning to show faintly in the sky, but it was still too early for more than a few cars and a chance pedestrian. At this hour, the avenue was used by only a few cruising cabs, heading toward better sections. He shuffled along, trying to look like a man on his way home after too much night out. The cat blood on his clothes bothered him, until he tried weaving a little as he walked, imitating the drunks he had seen often enough.

He passed an all night diner, and fished for his pennies. But there were several men inside. He went on, past Fifty-ninth Street, heading for the apartment, which should be near Sixty-seventh.

He was just reaching the top of the hill near Sixty-fourth when a gray sedan sped along, heading downtown. There were running boards on it, and behind the wheel sat the slim young man who'd given chase to Hawkes before.

Hawkes tried to duck, but the sedan was already braking and swinging back. It was beside him before he could realize more than the old clamor of his brain, telling him to run, that he couldn't escape.

The car matched his speed, and the driver leaned far to the right. "Will Hawkes," the young man called. "How about a lift?"

The smile was pleasant, and the voice was casual, as if they were old friends. There was no gun in the man's hands. It might have been any honest offer of a ride.

Hawkes braced himself, just as a patrol car turned onto the Avenue ahead. He opened his mouth to scream, but his vocal cords were frozen. The young man followed his eyes to the patrol car, and frowned.

Then the gray sedan lifted smoothly upwards to a height of twenty feet, turned sharply in mid-air, lifted again, and seemed to make a smooth landing on top of a huge garage building!

There had been no roar of jets and no evidence of any means of propulsion.

The patrol car went on down the Avenue, heading for the diner. The officers inside apparently had missed the whole affair.

Hawkes' cowardly legs suddenly came unfrozen. He was conscious of them churning madly. With an effort, he got partial control of himself, managing to focus on the house numbers.

There were no watchers outside the number he wanted, though they could have been in rooms across the street. He had no choice, now. He leaped up the steps and into the hallway. His eyes darted around, spotting a door that led out to the side, probably into an alley. He drew himself together, hiding behind the stairs.

But there was no further pursuit for the moment. The fear that seemed to come before each attack was missing. Maybe it meant he was safe for the moment-though it hadn't warned him of the car the young man was driving.

Heat rays! Levitation! Hawkes dropped to his knees as fatigue and reaction caught up with him again, but his mind churned over the new evidence. As a mathematician, he was sure such things could not exist. If they did, there would have been extension of math well in advance of the perfection of the machines, and he'd have known of it as speculative theory, at least. Yet, without such evidence, the devices apparently existed.

The police weren't in on it, that much was certain. It was more than a hunt for a criminal. What had been going on during the months he had missed?

His mind shuttled over the spy-thrillers he had seen. If some nation had the secrets, and he had discovered them....But the heat ray would never have been used openly, then; they wouldn't tip their hand. Anyhow, the cold war was still going on, and that would have been pointless when any nation had such power.

And if the secret belonged to the United States, the young man would never have levitated to avoid police at the greater risk of tipping off anyone who saw that such things could be done.

Nothing made sense-not even the crazy feeling of fear that had warned him on some occasions and failed him this last time. The only explanation that was credible was the totally incredible idea that some life, alien to earth and with strange unearthly powers, was after him-or that he was insane.

He fumbled through a pack of cigarettes until he located the last one, streaked with sweat that was still pouring down from his armpit, and lighted it. It was all answer-less —just as his sudden need for smoking was.

III

Hawkes crushed out the cigarette and began climbing the wide stairs slowly. It was probably an ambush into which he was heading-but without this place, he had no chance of resting. He stared at the numbers painted on the dirty red doors, and went on up a second flight of stairs. The number he wanted was at the end of the hall, dimly lighted. He dropped to the keyhole, but found it had been filled long ago, probably when the Yale lock was installed.

He put his ear against the door and listened. There was no sound from inside except a monotonous noise that must be water dripping from a leaky faucet. Finally, he climbed to his feet and reached for his keys. The third one he tried fitted, and the door swung open.

He fumbled about, looking for a light switch, and finally struck a match. The switch was a string hanging down from a bare bulb. He pulled it, to find he stood inside one of the old monstrosities with which New York is filled —a combination kitchen and bathroom, with a tiny closet for the toilet in one corner. There was an ice-box, a dirty stove, a Franklin heater connected to the chimney, a small sink, and a rickety table with four folding chairs. In a closet, cheap china showed.

He went through that, into the seven-by-twelve living room. There was a cheap radio, a worn sofa, two more folding chairs and a big typing table. The rug on the floor had been patched together. Then he breathed more easily. Over the back of one of the chairs was a sports jacket which he recognized as his own. He jerked it up suddenly and began going through the pockets, but they had already been emptied.

It didn't matter-he no longer cared why he should be in a place so totally unlike any his usually neat habits would have led him to. It was his.

Then, as he came into the bedroom, he hesitated. It was smaller than the living room, with a bed that took up half of one wall, and two dressers jammed into the remaining space. One corner held a cardboard closet-and hanging on the hook was a man's raincoat and hat, both at least five sizes too big for him. His eyes darted about, to find a strange mixture of things he remembered as his and possessions which he would never have owned. On one of the dressers was a small traveling case, filled with the cosmetics and appliances which only a woman would use.

He jerked open the closet, and his nose told him before his eyes that it held only female clothing! Yet on the shelf his old hat rested happily.

He could make no sense of it-the place looked as if several people lived in it, and yet it wasn't really fitted for anyone to spend his whole time there. There was none of the accumulation of property that would fit any permanent residence. He went out of the bedroom, passing the typewriter desk. The typewriter was an old, standard Olympia —a German machine he'd refitted with the Dvorak keyboard which he had learned for greater efficiency. He was sure nobody else would want it.

The dishes were dusty, and there was no food in the ice-box.

Now, though, it began to fit —a place where it was convenient to stop in, but not a place to live. And perhaps he had been in the habit of lending it to others. Though why he shouldn't have used his own apartment was something he still couldn't understand.

But it was possible there was no record of this place.

He began shucking off his shirt as he went back through the living room-until the marks on the rug caught his eyes. Something heavy had rested there recently-there had been other desks about, or heavily laden tables. And a bit of paper under the sofa could only have come from one of the complicated computing machines used in high-power mathematics. He scanned the fragment, making no sense of it, except that it was esoteric enough to belong to any new branch of theory. For a second, the heat-rays and levitations entered his head-but none of the symbols fitted such a branch of physical development.

What had been going on here-and why had the machines been removed so recently that their traces still looked fresh?

He shook his head-and froze, as a key turned in the lock.

There was no time for flight. She stood in the doorway, blinking at the light before he could turn. She, of course, was the girl whom he'd barely noticed when he knocked the couple down as he charged out of his apartment.

Of course? He puzzled over that. He'd almost expected it-and yet, now that he looked more closely, he couldn't even be sure that she was the same. She wore the same green jacket, but nothing else he could be sure of, because he had no other memory of that girl. This one was two inches shorter than he was, with dark red hair and the deepest blue eyes he had seen. She looked like an artist's conception of an Irish colleen, except that her mouth was open half an inch, and she was studying him with the look of being about ready to scream.

"Who are you?" He forced the words out at her.

She shook her head, and then smiled doubtfully. "Ellen Ibañez, naturally. You startled me! But you must be Wilbur Hawkes, of course. Didn't you get my wire?"

He watched her, but there had been no stumbling over his name, and no effort to make it sound too casual. Apparently, the name meant nothing to her. He shook his head. "What wire?" Then he plunged ahead, quickly. "You've heard of amnesia? Good. Well, I've got it-partially. If you can tell me anything about myself before yesterday, Miss, I'll never be anything but...."

He choked on that, unable to finish. And behind the surface emotions, his mind was poised, sniffing for danger. There was no feeling of it, though he kept telling himself alternately that she had been the girl at the door and that she obviously had not been.

He'd seen her before. The tilt of her head, that unmatchable hair....

"You poor man!" Her voice was all sympathy, and the bag she was carrying dropped to the floor as she came over. "You mean you *really* can't remember-at all?"

"Not for the last seven months!"

She seemed surprised. "But that was when you answered my advertisement. I never saw you-though you did call me, and your voice sounds familiar. You sent me the check, and I mailed you the key. That was all."

"But I must have given you references-told you something —"

Again, she shook her head. "Nothing. You said you were a teacher at CCNY, but that you were quitting, and wanted a place to use as an office. You didn't care what it was like. That's all."

Hawkes felt she was lying-but it could have been true. And in his present state, he probably believed everyone was other than they seemed. He remembered the gray sedan rising to the roof-and the cat turning inside out —

Sickness hit at him. He groped back towards a chair, sinking into it. He'd almost found a refuge, and even hoped that he could find some of the missing past. Now....

He must have partially fainted. He heard vague sounds, and then she was putting something against his lips. It was bitter and hot, though it only remotely resembled coffee. He gulped it gratefully, not caring that it was sweet and black. He saw the bottle of old coffee powder, caked with age, and heard the water boiling on the stove. Idly, he wondered whether he'd bought the jar originally or she had. Then his senses snapped back.

"Thanks," he muttered thickly. He groped his way to his feet, his head slowly clearing. "I guess I'd better go now."

She forced him back into the chair. "You're in no condition to leave here, Will Hawkes. Ugh! Your shoes are filthy. Let me help you ...there, isn't that better? Whatever you've been doing to yourself, you should be ashamed. You're going straight to bed while I clean some of this up!"

His head had sunk back on the table, and everything reached him through a thick fog. It wasn't right-girls didn't act that way to strange men who looked as if they'd come from a Bowery fight. Girls didn't take a man's clothes off. Girls didn't....

He let her half carry him into the bedroom, and tried to protest as she put him between clean sheets. He stared at the view of his lavender shorts against the fresh whiteness, while things seemed far away. He'd played with a girl named Ellen, once when he was eleven and she was nine. She'd had bright copper hair, and her name had been-what had it been? Not Ibañez. Bennett, that was it. Ellen Bennett.

He must have said it aloud. She chuckled. "Of course, Will. Though I never thought you'd be the same Will Hawkes. I knew it when I saw that scar on your shoulder, where you cut yourself sliding down our cellar door. Go to sleep."

Sliding down, sliding down into clouds of sleep. Sleep! She'd drugged him! Something in the coffee!

He jerked up, reaching for her, but she ducked aside, drawing on the tops to a pair of frilly pajamas. "Ellen, you —"

"Shh!" She pulled a robe over the pajamas and lay down, outside the blankets. "Shh, Will. You have to sleep. You're *so* tired, *so* sleepy...."

Her voice was soothing, and the fingers along the base of his neck was relaxing. He reached out a last inquiring finger of doubt for the feeling of danger, and couldn't find it. This was as wrong as the other things had been wrong-but his mind let go, and he was suddenly asleep.

He awoke slowly, with a thick feeling in his mouth. Drugged! And the sense of danger had failed him again! He swung over sharply, reaching for her, but she was gone.

His clothes lay beside him, neatly pressed, and he grabbed for them. There was a pair of socks, too large, but better than none. His muscles felt wrong as he began dressing, but the feeling wore away. The clock said that less than two hours had passed. If she'd put a drug in the coffee, it must have been one to which he was less sensitive than the average. She'd probably never suspected that he would waken.

A trace of fear struck through him, but it was weaker than before, and it seemed normal enough, under the circumstances. He fumbled over the shoelaces, and then grabbed up his coat.

She'd bring *them* back! Maybe they'd used her as a spy!

But he couldn't understand why she'd bothered to press his clothes. And the apartment still puzzled him. Even if her story was true, it simply wasn't the sort of a place where a girl like her would live. Nor was it fixed as she might have arranged a place, even allowing for what he might have done to it in seven months.

He reached automatically for the lock in the dim hall, and realized his hands knew the door, whatever else was true. Then he went out and down the stairs. He heard a babble of kids' voices, part in English and part in a sort of Spanish. That meant that things were normal, to the casual observer along the street. But he knew it was poor evidence that things really were as they should be. He stood in the comparative darkness of the hall, staring out. Nothing was wrong, so far as he could see. He had to risk it.

Hawkes shoved past the women on the steps and headed down West End, trying not to seem in a hurry. His eyes turned up to the roof of the garage, but he could see nothing there; he'd half-expected that the slim young man would be parked up on the roof, waiting.

Then the fear began, mounting slowly. He jerked around quickly, scanning the street. For a second, he thought he saw the slim figure, but it was only a back turned to him, and it disappeared into a barber-shop. Probably someone else.

The fear mounted a little, and he found his steps quickening. He cut around the corner, where men were crowded into a little restaurant. He was heading into a dead-end street, but there was an alley leading from it. He had to keep off the main streets.

Footsteps sounded behind him.

He moved faster, and the footsteps also speeded up. He slowed, and they kept on. Then they were nearly behind him, just as he reached the alley and jerked back into it, grabbing for a broken bottle he had spotted.

"Will!" It was a gasping wheeze. "Will! For God's sake, it's only me. I know everything-your amnesia. But let me explain!"

It stopped him. He held the bottle carefully, as the fat figure of an old man stepped softly around the corner, fear written on every aged wrinkle. It was the man he'd stumbled into when he dashed out of his apartment.

But the fear there matched his own so completely that he dropped the bottle. The other man stood trembling, gasping for breath. Then he gathered himself together, though his pudgy hands still clenched tightly, showing white knuckles.

"Will," he repeated. "You must believe me. I know about you. I want to help you-if there's any help for you, God forgive us both. And God have mercy on Earth. It's worse than you can believe-and different. It's...."

Horror washed over the old man's face. He stood, fighting within himself. Hawkes felt his own back hairs lift, and he drew back. For a second, the fat man seemed to waver before him, as if his body was only a projection. Then it quieted.

"It-it almost had me for a second."

He turned back to Hawkes, trying to control the quivering muscles in his face. But his victory was still incomplete when he suddenly leaped up.

"Get back, Will. Oh, God, O God!"

He leaped outwards, his fat old legs pumping savagely. Then the air seemed to quiver.

Where he had been, there was only a dark cloud of smoke, spreading outwards in a rough equivalent of his shape. A spurt of steam leaped upwards savagely, and the smoke seemed darker. It began to drift on the air, touched a building, and left a spot of smudginess, before it drifted on, getting thinner with each gust of wind. It was as if every atom of his body had suddenly disassociated itself from every other atom.

Hawkes found his fingernails cutting his palms, and there was blood flowing from his bitten tongue. He heard a hacking moan in his throat. He struggled against something that seemed to be holding him down, and then leaped at least ten feet, to land running.

The alley was twisted and narrow. He shot down it and around a corner. An ice-house stood there, and he barely avoided the loading trucks. He was back near the apartment building where he'd found the girl, and he doubled to a door that showed. It seemed to be locked, but somehow, he got through it. He seemed to melt through the door, though he wasn't sure whether his lunge smashed it or whether his fingers had found the latch in time.

He ducked around loose-hanging electric wires, under twisted pipes, and across a pile of coal around a hot-water heater. He twisted and turned, to come into complete darkness, and halt short, listening.

The fear was going-and there were again no sounds of pursuit. But he couldn't be sure. He'd heard no sounds when the fat man had leaped out, but they had been there.

Silently and thickly, he cursed. To find a man who seemed to be his friend, and who knew about him-and then to have them kill that man with such horrible efficiency before he could learn what it was all about!

He gagged in the darkness, almost fainting again.

Then, slowly, it was too much. For the moment, he could run no more, and nothing seemed to matter. He understood his sudden bravado no better than the unnatural cowardice that had been riding his shoulders, but he shrugged, and moved forward.

The dark passage led out to steps, that carried him up to the sidewalk, in front of the building. Ellen Ibañez-or Bennett-was less than five feet from him, and her eyes were fixed firmly on his face.

IV

She seemed surprised, but tried to smile. "I thought I left you asleep, Will," she said, in a tone that was meant to be bantering. "'Smatter, the fuse blow?"

He accepted the excuse for his presence in the basement. "Yeah, it did. You left the iron on. I wondered what happened to you?"

"Nothing. Just shopping. There wasn't a bit of food in the place-and I must say, Will, you aren't much of a housekeeper. I bought pounds of soap!"

He followed her up the stairs, and his key opened the door. He was still operating on the general belief that they'd be least likely to spot him where they had already found him once. If the girl had tipped them off, then they had it figured out that he had run off, and probably wouldn't be back.

He hoped so, at any rate.

She was talking too briskly, and she was too careful not to mention that the iron was cool, with its cord wrapped neatly around the handle. He offered no explanation, but let her babble on about the strange coincidence of his being *the* Will Hawkes, and how she'd almost forgotten the childhood days.

"How come the Ibañez?" he asked, finally.

"Stage name! I tried to make a go of the musicals, but it wasn't my line, I found. But the name stuck."

"And where'd you learn how to drug coffee that way?"

She didn't change expression. There was even a touch of a twinkle in her eye. "Waitress in a combination bar and restaurant. You needed the sleep, Will. And I guess I still feel as much of a mother to you as I did when you used to get hurt, so long ago."

She had things out of the bags now, and he saw that she had been doing a lot of shopping. There had still been time enough to call the slim young man, though-or, he suddenly realized, the fat man. He had no more reason to believe her an enemy than a friend. Then he corrected that. If she'd known enough to call the fat man, and had been his friend, she could have told him things. She'd denied knowing anything, though.

He couldn't understand why he trusted her-and yet, somehow, he did. Even if he knew she'd called them, he would still have to trust her. He was sure now that she was lying, and that she had been the girl at the door-but that meant she'd been with the fat man. And the fat man had seemed to be his friend. Or, had the man been set to lure him out, but miscalculated, and gotten only what had been meant for him?

His head was spinning, and he gave it up. He was a fool to trust her simply because the fear feeling subsided around her-but he had nothing better to do than to follow his hunches, and then try to play the odds as best he could.

"Cigarettes," she said, handing him a pack of his brand. "And for me. Shoe dye-your shoes need it, and I couldn't find a shoe store. I did get a shirt though, and a tie. You'll find a hat in that bag. Size seven and a quarter?"

He nodded gratefully, and went in to change. His old shirt had caught most of the cat's blood, and he needed a fresh one. There were a couple of spots on his trousers, but they'd do. And the sports jacket matched well enough. He daubed the dye onto his shoes-one of the combined polish and dye things.

"Cold-cuts all right?" she asked, and he called back a vague answer that seemed to satisfy her. He was staring at the shoe dye.

It worked fairly well, when he experimented. He daubed it onto his hair with a wisp of cotton. His hair began to mat down, but he found that combing it out as he went along removed the worst of the wax and still left some of the color. It worked better than it should have done.

He found a bottle of something that smelled of alcohol and belonged in her cosmetics, and began removing most of the mess. By being careful, he got the wax and most of the dye smell off, while leaving his hair darker.

"Better wash up," she called.

There was a razor among the things she had bought. He daubed some of the dye on his upper lip, where the stubble of a mustache was showing. It was easier there, if it didn't wash off in soap and water.

Some of it did, but when he finished shaving, he felt better. It wouldn't pass close inspection, but he now seemed to have darker hair, and the dye had exaggerated the little beginning of a mustache enough to make some change in his appearance.

He waited for her to comment, but she said nothing. He waited for her questions about what he was going to do, and her explanations that of course he couldn't stay there. She merely went on talking idly, while they ate. It didn't fit.

Finally he stood up and began taking down the rope that was strung up over one end of the room, to use as a clothes line, he supposed. She looked up at that. "What —"

"You can fight, if you want to," he told her. "Or you can save yourself the headache of being knocked out. Take your choice. People don't pay much attention to screams in a place like this. And I'm not going to harm you, if you'll take it easily."

"You mean it!" Her eyes were huge in her face, and there was a touch of fright now. She gulped visibly, and then seemed to go limp. "All right, Will. In the bedroom?"

He nodded, and she went ahead of him. She didn't struggle, until he was about to gag her. Then she drew her head aside. "There's money in my bag, if you're going out."

He swore, hotly and sickly. If she'd only act just once as a normal female should! Maybe Irma had been a hysterical, cold-blooded fool, but she couldn't have been that much different from other women-even the books indicated Ellen should be anything but so damned coöperative!

"If you'll tell me what's going on, I'll still let you go," he suggested, drawing her hands tighter together.

"I can't, Will. I don't know."

He had to believe her-he knew she was telling the truth, at least to some extent. And that made it just so much worse. He bound the gag over her mouth as gently as he could, and closed the door behind him. Her big eyes haunted him as he turned to the telephone.

The information girl at CCNY could only tell him that Wilbur Hawkes had resigned abruptly seven months before, and no one knew where he was-they had heard he was doing government research. He snorted at that-it was always the excuse, when nobody knew anything.

He tried a few other numbers, and gave up. Nobody knew-and nobody seemed to react to his name any differently from what they would have done had he remained a quiet, professorish man, minding his own business, instead of being chased by....

He couldn't complete that. The idea was still too fantastic. Even if there were alien life-forms that were subtly invading Earth, why should they pick on him? What good could a little, unimportant mathematician do them-particularly if they had the powers he already knew they possessed? It was a poor answer, though no harder to believe than that any group on Earth could so suddenly come up with miracles.

Anyhow, men knew enough already to be pretty sure that Mars and Venus wouldn't have creatures that could invade Earth-and the other planets were hopeless. Perhaps from another star-but that would mean violating the theories of mass-increase with the speed of light, and he was not ready to accept that, yet.

This time, he went out of the building without looking first. It could do no good-they could hide from him, he knew, and he would only call attention to himself by looking around. With the change in appearance, he might get by. He moved rapidly up to Broadway, where he found a little clothing store and a ready-made suit that nearly fitted him. The tailor there seemed unconcerned when he insisted the cuffs be turned up at once, and that he wanted to wear it immediately. It took nearly an hour, but he felt safe, for a change. A five-and-ten furnished a pair of heavy-rimmed glasses that seemed to have blanks in them, and he decided he might get by.

There was no evidence of pursuit. He caught a cab, and headed for the library. Ellen had been well-heeled —suspiciously so for a girl who lived in a cold-water flat like that; he'd peeled fifteen tens from her wallet, and there'd been more, not to mention the twenties. His conscience bothered him a bit, but he was in no position to worry too much.

The library was still the puzzle of the ages to him-he'd used it half his life, and still found it impossible to guess why such a building had been chosen. But eventually, he found the periodical room, and managed to get through the red tape enough to be given a small table with a stack of newspapers and magazines.

The mathematics magazines interested him most. He pored through them, looking for a single hint of the things he had seen. Einstein's work with gravity stood out, but no real advances had come from it. It was still a philosophical rather than an actual attack on physics-as beautiful as a new theology, and about as hard to utilize. He skimmed, through the pages, but nothing showed. No real advance had been made since his memory blanked out, except for one paper on variable stars which was interesting, but unhelpful.

He threw them aside in disgust. He knew that it was useless to look in other languages. Work couldn't be done without some first stages that would be reported, and any significant new theory would be picked up and spread. Science wasn't yet completely under political wraps.

For a second, he stopped as he came to a paper bearing his by-line. Then he grimaced-it was an old one, just published-his attempt to find how the phenomena of poltergeists could be fitted into the conservation of energy, and his final proof that the whole business was sheer rubbish. It would be nice to be able to get back to a life where he could fool around with such learned jokes.

The newspapers, beginning with the last day he could remember, were almost as barren of results. There was the story of the cold war, without the strange overtones that should be there if any of the major powers-where all the major scientists would tend to be-had found something new. He'd studied the statistical analysis of mob psychology at times, and felt sure he could spot the signs.

He skimmed on, without results, until he finally came to the current paper. This he read more carefully. There was no mention of him. But he found something on the fat man. It was a simple followup to the story about the scientist who'd turned himself in at Bellevue-the man had mysteriously disappeared, three hours later. And there was a picture-the face of the fat man, with "Professor Arthur Meinzer" under it.

It didn't help.

Hawkes shoved the magazines and papers back, and went through the series of halls and stairs that led him to the main reference room, inconveniently located on the top floor. He found the book he wanted, and thumbed rapidly through it. Meinzer was listed on the bottom of page 972 —but as he looked for 973, a pile of ashes dribbled onto the floor.

There was no use. They'd gotten there ahead of him.

He made one final attempt. He called the college, asking for Meinzer, to find that nobody even knew the name! He knew they were lying-but he could do nothing about that. Maybe it was only because of the publicity-or maybe because someone or something had gotten to them first!

Fear was growing with him as he came out on the street. He ducked into a crowd, and headed slowly into a corner drug store, trying to seem inconspicuous, but the fear mounted. They were near-they would get him! Run, GO!

He fought it down, and found that it was weakened, either by his becoming used to it or because the urgency was less than it had been.

He ducked into a phone-booth and called the newspaper, keeping his eye on both entrances to the store. It seemed to take forever to locate the proper man there, but finally he had his connection.

"Meinzer," the voice said, with a curious doubtfulness.

"Oh, yeah. Mister, that story's dead! Call up...."

The telephone melted slowly, dropping into a little cold puddle on the floor!

Hawkes had felt the tension mounting, and he was prepared for anything. Now he found himself on the street, darting across Forty-second Street against the light, without even remembering having left the booth. He stole a quick glance back, to see people staring at him with open mouths. He thought he saw a slim figure in gray tweeds, but he couldn't be sure-and there were probably thousands of such men in New York.

He ducked into a bank, wormed his way around the various aisles, and out the back entrance. A cab was waiting there, and he held out a bill.

"I'm late, buddy. Penn Station!"

The cab-driver took the bill and the hint, and darted out, just as the light was changing.

Penn Station was as good a place to try to get lost from pursuit as any. Hawkes examined his wallet, considering trying to get a train out-but he'd used up nearly all he had taken from Ellen.

And all his careful disguise had proved useless. They weren't fooled-and this business of dodging was wearing thin. By now, they'd know his habits!

He drew out a coin, flipping it. It came up heads. He frowned, but there was nothing else to do. He moved down the ramp toward the subway that would carry him back to Sixty-sixth and Broadway. He was probably walking into their trap by now, but the coin was right. He had to free Ellen. If they got him, it couldn't be much worse for him.

Then he shuddered. He couldn't know whether it would be worse for his country, or even his world. He couldn't really know anything.

V

It was growing dark as he walked down Sixty-sixth, eyeing every man suspiciously, and knowing his suspicion would do no good. He was still trying to think, though he knew his thoughts were as useless as his suspicions.

If he could remember! His mind came up sharply against leaving Irma and taking out the mail; then it went abruptly blank. What had been in the letter? It had been from a professor-it might have been from Professor Meinzer. That would tie in neatly. But Meinzer was dead, and he couldn't remember. They'd stripped him of his memory. How? Why? Were they trying to prevent his giving information to others-or were they trying to get something from him? And what could he know?

He'd dabbled with ESP mathematically, but now he found himself wondering if it could exist. Could they be tracking him by some natural or mechanical ability to read his mind? He strained his own mind to find a whisper of foreign thought, outside his brain. He drew a blank, of course, as he'd expected.

There were no answers. They could play with him, like a cat juggling a mouse, letting him almost learn something-and then, always, they arrived just in time to prevent his success!

Put a rat in a maze where it can't learn the path, and it goes insane. But what good would he be to anyone if they drove him insane? And why bother with all that when they could silence him as well by killing him?

He'd forgotten to watch, and was surprised to find his feet on the steps of the apartment building. He jerked back, and bumped into someone.

"Sorry." The words came from behind him, automatically, and he turned to see the slim young man stepping aside. For a second, their eyes met squarely. A row of teeth flashed in a brief smile as the man started around him. "Guess I was thinking. Should have watched where I was going."

The man went on down the street, and turned in at the restaurant entrance.

Hawkes lifted a foot that weighed a ton and slowly closed his mouth. He'd been facing away from the street light-and his face might have been hard to see. Yet....

It didn't fit. The young man must have known him!

He blanked it from his mind. He couldn't believe that it was anything but lack of recognition. It was hard to see here, where the other was facing the light, and he was in the shadow.

But it still meant that they were waiting, nearby.

He dashed up the stairs, expecting a rush at both landings. The normal sounds of the apartment house went on. He listened at his door, but he could hear nothing except the same drip he had heard before. Slowly, he inserted the key and went in. The small bulb was still on. He crept along, trying to move silently on floors that insisted on creaking. The living room was as he had left it, and he caught sight of Ellen on the bed.

He spotted a mirror over one of the dressers, and used that to study more of the bedroom. It seemed as empty as before.

Finally, he stepped inside. There was no one there but Ellen, and she seemed to be asleep, doubled up in a position that might have made the unkind cords easier to stand. She moaned slightly as he untied her gently, but didn't awaken. Her breathing was regular, and her breath had the odd muskiness of someone who has slept for several hours.

He found a bottle of liquor on the shelf where she had put it, and rinsed out a couple of glasses. It was good liquor-good enough to take without mixers, as they'd have to do.

She came awake when he called her, rubbing her eyes and then her wrists, where the cords had left a mark. But she was smiling. "Hi, Will. I knew you'd come back. Hey, not on an empty stomach."

"You need it-and so do I," he told her. "Bottoms up!"

They were big glasses. She gasped over it, but she downed it, then reached for the water he had brought as a chaser. She swallowed, and blinked tears out of her eyes. "I don't usually drink."

He made no comment, but refilled the glass. The liquor had less effect on him than he'd expected, though he'd always had a good head for it. It took some of the edge off his worrying, though.

She giggled suddenly, and he frowned. She couldn't take much on an empty stomach, it seemed. Then he shrugged. Let her drink-maybe if he could get her drunk, he could find something out; at least he might learn whether the slim young man had been there during the day.

"Like when you found your dad's cider," she said, and giggled again. "You got awful-hp! — awful drunk, Willy, din't you? You were-so-funny!"

She was trying to be careful with her words already. She slid around, doing things that brought more honestly beautiful thigh into the light than Will had seen in ten years. He reached to adjust her dress, and she giggled again, sliding against him.

"You kissed me then, Willy. Remember? Bet you don' remember!"

He began it coldly, deliberately. If he could work on her emotions enough, he'd crack the wall of evasion and lies, somehow. He reached for her, calculating what would arouse her without causing any shock to bring her back to her senses.

He hadn't counted on the quickness of her reponse, nor the complete acceptance of his right with which she took it. The liquor had reduced her to the stage of a little girl who competely trusted her companion. She seemed as unconscious of her body as a child might be.

Instead of protesting, she reached down and began unfastening the buttons on her dress. "'Syour turn now, Willy. Put you to bed last night, you put me to bed t'-night. Then you gotta kiss me good-night. Nighty-night, nighty-night."

He felt like a heel at first. And then he began to feel like a man-any man around a beautiful girl half-undressed, and getting more so.

She slipped under the sheets, tossing out the last of her clothing, and crooning happily. "Gotta kiss me good-night, Willy. Nighty-night!"

He yanked the pull-cord savagely, cutting off the light, and fumbling in the darkness. After what seemed hours of awkwardness, he slid in beside her, feeling her arms go around him in complete acceptance. To hell with *them*! They could chase him some other time!

He pulled her to him, while his blood beat in his neck, and he began to lose any conscious volition of what he was doing. He drew her tighter, while a great clot of emotion set fire to his brain. He —

Cold beyond anything he had known bit at him. A tremendous pressure within him seemed about to force him to explode outwards, and the shock jerked him into full awareness.

In a split second, he swung his eyes from the great, jagged landscape on which he stood, up an impossible range of mountains that were all harsh blacks and cold whites, to a cold black sky in which the stars were blazing specks without a flicker. He saw the Earth above him, bigger than the moon had ever been, and with the dim outlines of continents showing through the soft stuff that must be clouds.

He was on the moon! And naked, without air!

Almost at once, something clapped down around him, and the pressure let up, while heat seemed to leap into the rocks under his feet and make them comfortable. He gulped down the air that somehow seemed to stay close to him, instead of evaporating into the vacuum.

The moon! Now they had him!

Fear blazed in him —a stark, unreasoning terror that was like a physical thing. *Run-but you can't run! They've got you! You can't escape!*

The light blotted out, and then snapped on, more strongly. He stood in the kitchen of the cold-water apartment, still naked, with bits of chalky dust between his toes.

He had no time for reason. His brain seemed to have jumped over a hurdle and come down in a puddle beyond, foul with the stuff it had found there. He heard Ellen shriek, and then cry out again.

He lurched into the bedroom, while she let out another gurgling cry as the light showed him in the doorway. She came out of the bed, leaping for him, crying his name-cold sober! But he wanted none of her act. He shook her off.

"You damned alien! You filthy monster, disguised as a girl! When you get in a spot where I'm sure to find you out, you have a cute trick up your sleeve-but it won't work. You can send me back there-back to the rest of your kind, from wherever they came. But you won't fool me into thinking you're human again. You can't pass one test!"

He wouldn't be fooled into thinking it was a dream, either. He'd been physically on the moon-the very dust on his feet proved that. They might drive him insane, but they wouldn't do it that way.

She was crying now, gasping out words that he only half heard. "I'm human, Will. Oh, I'm human!"

"Then prove it! Come here, and prove it!"

She cried again at that, as he pulled her down with him. But slowly her crying quieted.

He awoke slowly, with sun-light streaming in the windows, and reached for her. He owed her more apologies than one, though he wasn't too sorry about most of it. She had proven herself human. And virginally so. Her complete surrender still left something warm inside him, where only the madness and the fear had been before.

Then he jerked upright, as he found her gone. He cursed himself for a fool, and listened for a stir and bustle from the kitchen, but there was none.

He was getting used to dressing with a feeling of dire pressure driving him on. He finished rapidly, and yanked the bedroom door open, just as he heard the outer lock click. She was coming in with a bottle of cream and a package of sausage as he reached the kitchen, and there was a smile tucked into the corner of her mouth.

And this time, he knew she wouldn't have betrayed him. Yet the fear increased in him. He darted past her as she leaned to kiss him, heading for the door. The room seemed to quiver. The hall was filled with a faint golden haze!

He had to get out! He jerked backwards, caught her hand, and pulled her. "Ellen! We've got to get out!"

It was a half-articulate shout, and she resisted, but he began dragging her after him. Something fumbled at the lock, and a key slipped into it. The door opened.

Hawkes didn't know what kind of an alien he expected. He knew that men could never have thrown him to the moon and back, not in another thousand years. It had to be a monster.

But he should have known that monsters here came in human form-they'd have to.

The fear rose to a shriek in his brain, and then died down as the human form entered. It was too normal-too familiar. A medium-sized man, dressed in a suit as inconspicuous as his own, wearing a silly little mustache that no outland monster should ever wear.

The creature jumped in, slamming the door behind it. "Stay there! You can't risk it outside now! We've got to —"

Hawkes hit the figure with his shoulder, in the best football fashion he could muster. It could try-but it couldn't keep him and Ellen here to be burned in their heat-ray bath, or treated to whatever alien torture they had in mind. He felt his shoulder hit. And he knew he'd missed. It was an arm that he struck against, and the arm brought him upright, while a second arm drew back and came forward with a savage right to his jaw.

He went out with a dull plopping sound in his brain. Then, slowly, an ache came out of the blackness, and the beginning of sound. He was fighting out of the unconsciousness, fighting against time and the monster who'd try to steal Ellen.

But Ellen's hands were on his head, and an ice-cold towel was wet against his forehead. "Will! Will!"

He groaned and sat up. The other-alien or human-was gone.

"Where —?" he began.

She was trying to help him to his feet, and he got up groggily, with his head beginning to clear.

"He just ran out, Will." Ellen was crying, this time almost silently, with the words coming out between shakes of her shoulders. "Will, we've got to get out. We've got to. The men are coming for you. They'll be here any minute. And it's wrong-it won't work! Oh, Will, hurry!"

"Men? Men are coming?" He'd almost forgotten that it could be men who were after him.

"I called them, Will. I thought I had to. But it won't work. Will, do anything you like, but *get* out! They are fools. They...."

He opened the door and peered out the doorway into the hall, which seemed quiet. He'd been a fool again. He'd trusted her for some reason, as if a body and loyalty had to go together. They'd been smart, picking a virgin for the job. It must have cost them plenty, unless they'd twisted her mind somehow. Maybe they could do it.

But he knew that whatever they looked like, it couldn't be real men who'd meet him out there.

"Why?" he asked, and was surprised at the flatness of his voice.

She shook her head. "Because I'm a fool, Will. Because I thought they could help you-until *he* came! And because I'm still in love with you, even if you'd forgotten me."

But the fear inside him was drowning out her words, and the golden haze was faint in the air again.

"Okay," he said finally. "Okay, don't burn her, too, now that she's done your dirty work. I'm coming."

The haze disappeared slowly, and he started down the stairs, still holding her hand.

VI

There were men with guns in the street. He'd heard two shots as he came down the stairs, and had shoved Ellen behind him. But it was silent now. People with dazed, frightened faces were still darting into the houses, leaving the street to the men with the guns.

Hawkes marched forward grimly, perversely stripped of fear, even though he was sure some of the men out there were monsters and others were their dupes. He tapped one of the men on the shoulder.

"Okay, here I am. The girl goes free!"

The man spun around as if mounted on a ball bearing and pulled by strings. The gun fell from his hands. His emotion-taut face loosened suddenly, seemed to run like melted wax, and congealed again in an expression of utter idiocy. He gargled frothily, and then screamed-high and shrill, like a tortured woman.

Suddenly he was a lunging maniac, tearing up the street.

Now the others were running-some toward cars, and some toward the corners, running flat and desperately on the flat of their feet, without any spring to their motions.

Hawkes jerked his eyes down toward the big gas-storage tanks where most of them had been, and the glow that had been in the corner of his vision was gone. Men seemed to be coming out of a trance. They were breaking away, forgetting about their guns and fleeing.

Three men alone were left.

Hawkes ducked back into the hall of the apartment, dragging Ellen with him. The glass of the door was somewhat dirty, but it made a dim mirror. He could see the slim young man and two others still there. The two men darted into a waiting car, and the leader turned up the street, running smoothly toward the apartment house.

Hawkes could make no sense of it-unless it was another of the seeming tricks designed to drive him out of his mind. He had decided he was one of the rats in the maze that didn't go crazy-the pressure could drive him somewhat mad, but it couldn't keep him that way.

He didn't wait to see what had happened, or whether the sirens that were sounding now were reinforcements for the men with guns or the police. He didn't bother with the slim young man any more. They'd apparently used their dupes to frighten out the people, and then had scared off the dupes-the poor humans who didn't know what it was all about. Now two of the three were gone, and the third monster was coming for him.

He'd escaped before. But sooner or later, they'd catch him-once they were sure he wouldn't be driven insane.

Or was this the beginning of insanity —a delusion of power, a feeling that he could escape? He could never know, if it was. He had to assume that he was sane.

He crouched back behind the stairs, while the young man in the gray tweeds dashed up them. Then he headed out into the street. The siren was near now-and tardily, he realized that the siren might herald the coming of the real monsters. It was as easy to look like a cop as any other human!

He jerked open the door of the nearest car, pulled Ellen in, and kicked the motor to life. He gunned away from the curb, tossed it into second, and twisted around the corner, straight toward the siren that was nearest. At the last minute, he jerked to the side of the street, to let the police car shoot by. "Never run from a tiger-run toward it. It sometimes works, and it's no worse."

The car was a big one, and the motor purred smoothly. He glanced down at the dash, and frowned. There was no key in the switch. For a second, he stared at it, and then grinned. He'd picked a monster's car, apparently-they'd done a neat job of duplicating, but they didn't need all the safeguards that humans used, and the switch had obviously been a dummy.

He looked at the buttons on the dash, wondering which would make it levitate. But he had no desire to test it, nor to stay in an auto which could probably be traced so easily.

He braked to a halt outside the subway and led Ellen down.

"We're down to the last hole," he told her as the train pulled out of the station. "How much money do you have?"

She shook her head, and held up her arm. "I left it, Will."

They were beyond the last hole, then. He realized now that as long as they'd been in a crowded apartment house, filled with other humans, it had proved a tough nut to crack for the aliens. But on the move....

"Maybe we have a chance," he told her. "If humans were after me, it'd be tough-but these things have to avoid the police."

She looked at him, misery on her face. "There are no aliens, Will. Those men you saw were F. B. I. men. That's where I reported you."

"You...."

He stared at her, but she was serious.

"But there was nothing about me in the papers, Ellen."

She pointed across the aisle. Spread over two columns on the front page, an older picture of him showed plainly. And even at the distance, the heading was boldly legible.

$100,000 REWARD FOR
THIS MAN!

He stared at the figure twice, unbelieving. He was no longer alone against a small group of humans or aliens. Now every living human on the face of the planet would be looking for him!

He could feel their hot breath on his neck, feel eyes staring at him through the papers. Fear began to rise in him, to be halted as the train ground to a new station. Ellen jerked him out, and he moved with her. It wasn't safe to be too long with one group, until they began to wonder and compare faces!

"But what —"

She shook her head. "Nothing, Will. I don't know. What can we do?"

He'd been wondering, while they moved quietly through the groups of people, and up the stairs. There was no place left. He had about a dollar in change, and that would be of no use to them. They'd have to dig a hole in the ground and pull it over them....

It joggled his memory, and he grabbed her hand and jerked open the door of a cab that was waiting for the light. He barked out an address — —the corner of Tenth Avenue and one of the streets below Twentieth. The driver got into motion, not bothering to look back. The address was near enough to where Hawkes wanted to be-an old warehouse, with a loading platform. He'd played there as a kid, climbing back under it and digging holes down into the damp, soft earth, as kids have always done. He'd been by there since, and it had remained unchanged.

Sooner or later, the aliens would locate them. But it would give Ellen and him a chance to rest-perhaps long enough for him to waylay someone at night and steal enough for them to leave town. That wouldn't be much help-but it was all he had left to count on.

He saw trucks loading there, as he paid the cab-driver. His heart sank abruptly, until he studied the way the big trailer was parked. If he watched carefully, he could slip under it from the side, and there was a chance he wouldn't be seen.

He darted beneath it.

Luck, for once was with him as he drew Ellen under the trailer and the platform. The old opening was covered with rubble, but he scraped it aside, and found an entrance barely big enough for them to wiggle through. Then they were back in a dark pocket under the back of the platform, barely big enough for them to sit upright. The hole had seemed bigger when he was a kid.

Outside, he heard a boy's voice yelling. "Monster attacks cops! Monster kills five cops! Extra Paper!"

Now he was a monster, to be shot on sight, probably.

"I shouldn't have brought you into this, Ellen," he said bitterly. "I should have left you. You don't even know what's going on-you haven't the faintest idea. If it were just humans, as you think...."

She snuggled against him in the coldness of the little cave. "Shh. I got you into it. I —I ratted on you, Scarface!"

But he couldn't reply to her attempt at humor. There was no fear now-not even the relief of fear. He'd felt brave for a few minutes, back in the hallway of the apartment. Now the chips were down, and sunk. They were here, in a dank hole, without food, and without a chance, while all the world searched for him to kill him-and while still-unknown aliens with unknown reasons played out their little game with consummate skill that would inevitably locate him.

It might take them a day-they probably would do nothing to him until night came, and the warehouse street was deserted! Ten more hours!

If he only knew what they wanted of him, or why! If he could remember!

He sat there, numbed within himself. Ellen leaned her head forward onto his lap, and he began stroking her hair softly. He'd have liked to have had a chance with her. One night wasn't enough for a whole life. He reached down to draw her face to his....

Fear hit him, as something rustled behind him. He tried to turn and look, but his neck refused. The fear grew to panic, and swelled higher as the golden haze began to spread over the little cave. Then his muscles snapped his head around sharply. The slim young man was crawling toward them, holding something that looked like a flashlight. Behind it, he could see the tense lips drawn back over clenched teeth. The man wasn't smiling now. He opened his mouth, just as the thing like a flashlight sprang into light.

No time seemed to elapse, but suddenly Ellen and the young man were both gone, and he sat in the dark hole, alone. He let out an animal cry, and dashed out, crawling through the opening, and kicking the rubble back as he went. He slipped out, and under the trailer. But there was no sign. They'd taken her, and left him unconscious!

He groaned, trying to figure. He'd always gone back to the same place to hide, since he'd found it. They must expect him back there. They'd take Ellen there and wait for him, drugging her, changing her mind, setting her up to use against him. The first time hadn't worked, but they'd try it again. It had to be that. If they hadn't taken her there, he had no way of finding her, and he had to find her.

He began running down the street, forcing himself to believe she was there. Then he slowed. It would do no good to have them all notice him, here on the street. Someone might recognize him then. He turned around, walking back to the bus stop. There were still two dimes and a nickel in his pocket.

He hunched down on the seat of the bus that seemed to crawl up Tenth Avenue. But no one noticed him in the almost empty vehicle. He got off at Sixty-Sixth and forced himself to walk to West End, up that to the apartment-house.

Men were drawing up in cars-men with guns in their hands. He made a final dash for the apartment entrance. This must be the real show-for which the other had been only a dress rehearsal to throw him off balance. They could wait.

He fumbled with the lock, until he finally got it open. Then he jumped in, slamming the door shut behind him. Ellen stood there, and the creature that had assaulted him before was pawing at her. But he had no time for the monster.

"Stay there!" he shouted at her. "You can't risk it outside now! We've got to —"

He saw she wasn't listening to him. He had to get rid of the creature somehow, if he could get it far enough away from her. Then they'd find some way to get outside, without going out through the entrance.

The creature sprang at him awkwardly. His arm darted down to catch one shoulder, and his right hand swung back and up. There was a savage satisfaction in seeing the creature crumple.

Ellen's voice reached him. "Will! Will, before I go crazy...."

"You're free," he told her. "Go down the fire escape and leave that here. I'll get rid of them out front somehow."

He shut the door again, and went down. The words had sounded brave enough, but there had been no courage behind them. Fear still rode him, like the little golden haze that again hovered over him, showing they had spotted him.

He walked out, with it thick around him, rising slowly in temperature. They had him-but Ellen might get away. He walked down the steps, his hands up. They drew back, surprise and something else on their features, their eyes on the haze that surrounded him. They were shouting, but he couldn't hear the words over the shrieks of the people along the street, rushing inside or trying to drag their kids to safety.

Hawkes doubled his legs under him and leaped. He was still attacking the tiger-the slim young man, down by the big gas-storage tanks, directing the new crop of human dupes.

His charge carried him there, while the young man slipped aside. Then someone fired a gun. He heard the young man yell hoarsely. "No shooting! Stop it! Damn it, NO SHOOTING!"

They weren't paying any attention to the shouts. Bullets ticked against the tanks. Hawkes ducked frantically, physical fear knotting his stomach.

Suddenly, he seemed to jerk upwards, to find himself suspended in mid-air, fifty feet off the ground, just beyond the tanks. He stared down at the men, dizzy with the height, but no longer surprised by anything. The men were pointing their guns upwards, while the young man leaped about among them. Bullets were splatting out, though none came near Hawkes. They seemed to ricochet off the air a few feet in front of him.

The slim young man drew back. And now, the rubble and stones along the street began to lift, and to drive savagely at the attackers. A gale swept along the street, though Hawkes could feel no breath of air, and the force of it was enough to knock most of them down.

They got up and began running, dashing away from the super-science that the young man now seemed bent on turning against his own troop of dupes, now that they were out of control.

Hawkes came drifting downward. He started to cry out in fear, until he noticed that the ground was coming up at him slowly, and that he was slipping sideways. He landed on a street back of the tanks, as gently as a feather.

Surprisingly, everyone was gone when he risked a glance back at the scene of the fight, with the back of the slim man just darting into the apartment house. Then Hawkes cursed, as the creature came darting out, with Ellen behind him, to leap into a car and drive off. The sound of sirens grew louder, and a police car swung onto West End.

Hawkes straightened up slowly, as it hit him. It had been the same scene he'd gone through before that morning-but with himself in the middle! He shot a glance at the sun, to see it still to the east, though his memory of the day indicated it should have been after noon.

Time! They'd twisted him back through time-the weapon that had looked like a flashlight must have tossed him hours backwards, instead of knocking him out. He'd been attacking himself there in the hallway of his apartment! He'd knocked himself out. And the fight he had just been through was the same fight that he had seen come to its end before!

Now, his younger self and Ellen must be just fleeing toward the hideout under the loading platform, with the slim man still following. If he could get there in time, before the man could run off with Ellen....

VII

The paper he'd found kept the other passengers on the bus from seeing him, but he was too deep in his own thoughts to read it. His eyes roamed back to the story of the cop-killing monster —a seemingly harmless florist in Brooklyn who'd suddenly gone berserk and rushed down the streets with a knife; he'd been wrong in thinking that concerned him. And he'd been wrong in thinking anyone would try to kill him on sight. The reward notice and picture were in front of his eyes-but it was a reward for information, and there was a huge box that proclaimed he was *not* a criminal and must not be harmed, or even allowed to know he was recognized.

The new facts only confused the issue. He twisted about in his mind, trying to explain why the young man had left him to drift down, and gone rushing into the apartment. He was ready for the collecting-and he'd been left uncollected!

The girl had said there were no aliens. Now he wondered. She had known more than he'd found from her-she'd known his brand of cigarettes, even. And there had been that shopping list, with the lipstick on it-the same type he now remembered her using. He'd known her before-and not just as a little girl. That tied him in with Meinzer, who was a mystery in himself.

He puzzled over it. The things that had happened to him had always been preceded by violent emotion, instead of followed by it. Usually, it had been fear-but sometimes some other emotion, as had been the case just before he was suddenly shifted to the Moon. Whenever he seemed on the verge of discovering something or emotionally upset, it hit at him. Did that mean he was only susceptible to the phenomena when off balance? It still didn't account for the fact that some of the things hadn't directly affected him, at all.

The more he knew, the less he knew.

He got off the bus and headed for the warehouse. This time, he had to wait before he could see a chance to dart under the trailer and into the entrance. He noticed that the gray sedan was parked nearby.

He darted in.

They were still there! He heard Ellen's voice, sounding as if she had been crying, and then an answer from the other. He felt his way carefully over the rubble, working as close as he could. Now, if he sprang the few feet....

"...must be a time-jump," the man's voice said, doubtfully. "I tell you, Ellen, those damned fools were firing at him, up there in the air, while you were still with him in the apartment. That's an angle on this psi factor stuff we hadn't expected."

The voice stopped for a moment. Then it picked up again. "Drat it! I wish you hadn't called the F. B. I. on him-they got rattled when he came out looking like a saint in a halo and jumped fifty feet up to float around. Some fool started shooting, and the rest joined in."

"I had to-he was talking about alien monsters. I thought he was going crazy, Dan. I couldn't tell him anything —I promised him I wouldn't, and I kept my promise. But I thought enough of them might catch him, somehow....Dan, can't we find him now? He needs us!"

Hawkes lay frozen. He tried to move forward, but his body was tensed, waiting for more. If something happened now....

"Alien monsters?" Dan's voice grew bitter. "It is alien-and a monster. This psi factor...."

The words blurred, and seemed to echo and re-echo inside Hawkes' head. That made twice he'd heard them mention the psi factor-the strange ability a few human minds had to perform seeming miracles. Men who had it could make dice roll the way they wanted. Young girls sometimes had it before puberty, and could throw heavy objects around a room without touching them; they did not even know they were the cause of the motion, but blamed it on poltergeists. Other men caused strange accidents-fires, for instance-the old salamander legend!

There'd been a piece of paper-psi equals alpha, the psi factor was the beginning of infinity for mankind. But it had been wrong. He'd changed that, on the other side. It should have read psi equals omega, the absolute end.

He gasped hoarsely, and heard their startled voices stop, while the flashlight beam swung around, to pick him out in the darkness. He felt Ellen and her younger brother, Dan, pulling him forward into the little cave with them, and he heard their voices questioning him. But his head was spinning madly under the sudden flood of memories that the missing key word had suddenly brought back.

The letter from Professor Meinzer had been about his paper on poltergeists which the old man had seen before publication. He'd been doing research on the psi factor for the government, and he needed a mathematician-even one who proved something which he knew wasn't true, provided the mathematics could handle his theories.

Hawkes' head was suddenly brimming with mental images of the seven months, while he worked on the mathematics to tie down the strange pattern of brain waves the old professor had found in the minds of those who had the mysterious psi factor. Dan had worked with them, in the little cluttered apartment, building the apparatus they needed. It was through Dan that Ellen was hired, as a general assistant and secretary.

There had been only the four of them, working in deepest secrecy in the three rooms which the government had felt were more suitable to maintain complete security than any deeply buried laboratory could have been. Ellen made a pretense of living there, and it was a neighborhood where no landlady worried about the men who went to a girl's place, provided everything was quiet.

They'd succeeded, too-they had found the tiny bundle of cells that controlled the psi factor, and learned to stimulate them by artificial wave trains and hypnosis. But the small group in the top division of the government to whom they were responsible had demanded more proof.

Hawkes had treated himself secretly, not knowing that Meinzer had done the same two days before. And both had learned the same thing. The wild talents appeared, but they couldn't be controlled. Meinzer hadn't found security in the hospital, hard as he'd tried to find it. He'd gotten up in the middle of the night and walked through the solid wall, unable to stop until he was back with the group.

Hawkes had tried another way to stop the wild abilities that operated without his conscious control. He'd prepared a new hypnotic tape, worded to make him forget everything he knew, or even the fact that he had worked on the psi factor. He'd put in commands that would make him avoid any reference to it, so that he couldn't learn accidentally. He'd ordered his brain to have nothing to do with it. Then he'd drugged himself with a combination of opiates and hypnotics that should have knocked out a horse. Then he'd telephoned Dan to have men pick him up in an hour and keep him drugged. He'd turned on the tape recorder and stumbled back to the bed.

He groaned, as he remembered his failure. "It's the ultimate, absolute alien, all right-the back of a man's own mind. It's Freud's unconsciousness, or id. The psi factor is controlled by that, and not by the conscious mind. And the id is a primitive beast-it operates on raw impulse, without reason or social consciousness. Every man's unconsciousness is back in the jungle, before civilization-and we've given that alien thing the greatest power that could exist when we wake up the psi power."

"Meinzer thought it was controlled, for a while," Ellen said. "He came when Dan and I called him. I went with him up to your apartment, while Dan got the men to carry you away. But we couldn't reach you-Meinzer barely touched the tape-recorder when something seemed to pick us up and drive us out of the room and down the stairs. We were just going back when you came out."

She shuddered, and Hawkes nodded. He'd obviously used that psi factor to throw off the drugs at the first sign of anyone near him. He told them sickly what had happened to the old man.

"So I killed him," he finished bitterly.

Dan shook his head. "No. Your psi factor works differently. You control heat and radiation, you can move yourself or any object in space for almost any distance, instantly if you want, and it seems you can do the same through time. But you can't disintegrate things, as Meinzer could. He had a suicide urge-we knew that before. When it got out of control again, he blew himself up-just as your dominant urge to protect yourself did all those things around you."

Hawkes grimaced. It wasn't pleasant to know, that he'd been doing all the things he'd blamed on monsters. He'd somehow remembered that someone was supposed to come to get him, and he'd run out in wild fear, while his unconscious mind blasted the apartment with heat to destroy all traces. He'd blasted down the subway entrance with another bolt of energy to make his getaway. The poor cat had surprised him, and been killed. His unconsciousness gone wild had tossed Dan's car two hundred feet to the roof of the garage. When it found him losing control emotionally with Ellen, it hadn't let his conscious brain give it the information it needed-it had simply thrown him completely off Earth, pulled air to him, and warmed the rocks. Then, when it found the Moon unfit for life, it had thrown him back to his own world. It had tossed him hours back in time this morning, and lifted him into the air while it pelted his "enemies" with rocks, and built a wall around him by throwing the bullets back instantly.

And it had somehow clung to the implanted idea that he must not find out about himself. It had destroyed anything where the written word might give him a hint, and had even melted the telephone so that he couldn't continue listening to other evidence.

It had probably done a thousand other things that he couldn't even remember, whenever its wild, reasonless fears were aroused and it decided that he had to be protected!

"You should have killed me," he told them. But he knew that they couldn't have done it.

"We had to let you sweat it out. You made us promise not to tell you anything, and we thought you might be right," Ellen told him. "We thought that it might adjust after awhile. All we did was to try to pick you up, until we knew it was impossible."

"Until Sis tipped off the Government men," Dan added. Hawkes could imagine what their reaction had been to having a man with his power running wild. He was surprised that they had bothered to make even an attempt to see that he wasn't harmed.

He shrugged helplessly. "And where does it leave us now-beyond this hole in the ground?"

"The Government's put about fifty specialists on the notes you and Meinzer left," Dan answered, but there was no assurance in his voice. "They're trying to find some way to bring the psi factor under the control of your logical, rational mind."

He got to his knees and began crawling out of the little cave, while Hawkes tried to help Ellen follow him. Outside, Dan knocked off the dirt from his clothes and headed for the sedan he'd, somehow gotten off the roof.

Hawkes followed, for want of anything better to do.

He knew the answers now-and he was worse off than ever. Instead of a horde of outside aliens, he had one single monster in his own skull, where he could never fight it, or even hope to escape it.

The power had been meant as a hope for the world. A man who could work such seeming miracles might have ended the threat of war; he'd have been the perfect spy, or better at attack than a hundred hydrogen bombs that had to smash whole cities to remove a few men and weapons. But now the world was better off without him. So long as he still lived, there would be nothing but danger from the alien monster in his head. He had no idea of his limits-but he was sure that it could trigger the energies of the universe to move the whole world out of its orbit, if that seemed necessary for his personal survival!

VIII

Hawkes leaned forward cautiously as the gray sedan moved up Tenth Avenue. His finger found the gun in Dan's coat pocket; and he pulled it out stealthily.

He knew that the only answer for him was suicide. He had to destroy himself, since no one else could!

He propped it up, pointing at his head, and his thumb pressed back on the trigger, further and further, until he felt sure the smallest change would set it off. Then he waited for the rough spot in the street or the sudden stop at a light that would do the trick before he could stop it.

The car lurched-and the gun suddenly vanished, leaving his hand empty.

His responses were too quick-and his mind wasn't waiting, once it knew there was danger. He slumped back on the rear seat, trying to think. Drugs were out-he knew his system could throw them off.

But he couldn't remove himself!

He lifted his wrist-to his teeth, and bit down savagely. If he could sever an artery....Pain shot through him, and he stared down at the blood.

Then the blood was gone, and the wound was closing before his eyes, until only smooth flesh remained. His mind could juggle the cells back into their original form.

It would have to be sudden, complete death.

And no death was that sudden! For a fraction of a second, there'd be life left-and during that split second, the damage would be repaired, or he would be shifted from danger.

There was no way out-unless he could pull himself to another planet, or throw himself back into the dim past. But that would take voluntary control, and he knew now that hours of effort had shown him how impossible that was. He hadn't been able to lift a crumb of bread from the table deliberately, in his original tests after he had treated himself.

He was faced with a problem that had to be solved-and there was no possible solution that he could find.

No man could face that dilemma forever without going insane. Hawkes shuddered, trying to picture what would happen if he went mad, and the wild talents began operating at every whim of his crazed mind!

Ellen shouted suddenly, grabbing for the wheel. Hawkes felt himself tense, and began lifting from the seat of the car. But there was no visible danger, and Dan was slowing to a halt at the curb, Hawkes' body dropped back slowly.

"Dan," Ellen was whispering hoarsely. "Dan, we can't. If we take him back, they'll find him, and they'll know what he can do. They'll kill him. Eventually, they'll kill Will!"

Hawkes started to protest, but Dan's words cut him short.

"You're right, Sis. They'll wait their time, until he won't know when to expect it-and then they'll drop an H-bomb on him, if they have to. That's faster than any nerve impulse!"

He swung back to face Hawkes, reaching for the door of the car. "Get out, Will-and get as far away as you can. I'm not going to drive you to your death. They'll get you eventually, but I won't be the one to make it easier for them!"

Hawkes jerked. The old fear came back suddenly.

You can't escape! They'll get you. Run! GO!

He screamed, as the golden haze flickered again. He could wipe out the Earth, but he couldn't survive, then. He could move back in time, but it would only mean other dangers-no man could stay awake forever, and he was used to civilized living.

The haze hesitated, while the sense of danger mounted. Then it was gone, as if the beast in his head had found no answer.

Suddenly the gray sedan lifted again, to a height of fifty feet above the tallest building. It shot forward, hesitated, and came down softly on a deserted side-road in Central Park.

His mind felt as if it were going to split. Dan and Ellen stared at him speechlessly.

You can't survive alone! No power is enough by itself! They'll get you! You are your own death-sentence! RUN! DON'T RUN!

Hawkes put his hand to his splitting skull, trying to force words through the agonies of pain, while slow understanding began to reach him.

"Dan! The scientists ...get me there!"

Then his mind seemed to clamp down on itself, and he was unconscious. He could protect himself from almost anything-except his own brain!

He was conscious of no pain, but only of irritation. There was a needle in his arm, and he removed it!

He opened his eyes slowly, to find himself the center of a group of men, while a white-clothed doctor stood staring at an empty hand that must have held a hypodermic.

Ellen cried out suddenly, and ran to him, cradling his head in her hands. He found her arm with his own hand, and stroked it slowly.

"You've found the answer?" he asked. Then he nodded, while the weight that had lain on him so long began to lift. His voice was suddenly positive. "You found it!"

One of the men pushed forward, but Dan shook his head, and came over to stand beside the cot where Hawkes lay. "No, Will. They didn't find it-you did! You found what we should have known-your unconscious mind may be a wild beast, but it isn't insane. When it was shocked into realizing that it couldn't save you by itself, it looked for help from your consciousness. And then it knocked you out-knocked itself out-until we could work on you."

"I guessed it," Hawkes said slowly. "But in that case, a psychotic with his id out in the driver's seat should become normal when they lock him up. Or wait-maybe his unconsciousness is a bit insane. Maybe. But you still have to communicate with that unconscious part of the brain, to make it understand that it has to surrender. And all the psychiatrists have been driving themselves crazy trying to solve that!"

"*Touché*," an older man said, and there was a faint sound of amusement from some of the others. "But this psi factor is the means of communication! You told us that yourself, while you were undergoing our hastily improvised hypnotic education of your brain. It always has been. The minute a girl bothered with poltergeists finds she is the cause of them, they stop. It's a faint, weak channel between consciousness and unconsciousness-or subconsciousness, if you prefer. And yours was widened by the treatment, even if it wasn't ready to work yet. We simply used your own technique to improve the relationship. All you ever needed was a longer, harder treatment than you and Meinzer had given yourselves. You just stopped too soon."

Hawkes dropped back comfortably onto the cot. He reached out for a glass of water, lifted it to his lips, and put it back-without using his hands. He thought of his clothes, and they were suddenly on him, over the single white garment he had been wearing. Another thought took that away, to leave him normally dressed.

Whether they were entirely correct or not in their theories, the psi factor was no longer wild. He had it under full control!

He sat up, just as three men entered the crowded room. One wore the uniform of a four-star general, but the familiar faces of the two civilians told Hawkes at once that they were more important than any general could be.

He was about to become officially the National Arsenal and replacement for all the armies, navies, and air-corps they had ever dreamed of having. He'd also become their bridge into space, their means of solving the secrets of the planets, and probably their chief historical tool, since nothing could ever be secret from him.

It was going to be a busy life for him and for the others like him who would now be carefully selected and treated!

He grinned faintly, as he realized that they didn't know yet just how important he was. He wasn't going to be a National Resource-he'd be a World Resource. This power was too great for any local political use, and no man who had it along with the full correlation of his conscious and subconscious mind could ever see it any other way.

But right now, he had other pressing business. He grinned at Ellen. "You don't mind a small wedding, do you?" he asked.

She shook her head, beginning to smile. He reached for her hand. This psi factor was going to be a handy thing to have around, with its complete control of space and time.

"I'm taking a two-week honeymoon before we talk business," he told the approaching three men. "But don't go away. We'll be back in ten minutes!"

Honolulu looked lovely in the moonlight, and June was the perfect month for a wedding.

...And It Comes Out Here

> There is one fact no sane man can quarrel
> with ... everything has a beginning and an end.
> But some men aren't sane; thus it isn't always so!

* * * * *

No, you're wrong. I'm not your father's ghost, even if I do look a bit like him. But it's a longish story, and you might as well let me in. You will, you know, so why quibble about it? At least, you always have ... or do ... or will. I don't know, verbs get all mixed up. We don't have the right attitude toward tenses for a situation like this.

Anyhow, you'll let me in. I did, so you will.

Thanks. You think you're crazy, of course, but you'll find out you aren't. It's just that things are a bit confused. And don't look at the machine out there too long-until you get used to it, you'll find it's hard on the eyes, trying to follow where the vanes go. You'll get used to it, of course, but it will take about thirty years.

You're wondering whether to give me a drink, as I remember it. Why not? And naturally, since we have the same tastes, you can make the same for me as you're having. Of course we have the same tastes-we're the same person. I'm you thirty years from now, or you're me. I remember just how you feel; I felt the same way when he-that is, of course, I or we-came back to tell me about it, thirty years ago.

Here, have one of these. You'll get to like them in a couple more years. And you can look at the revenue stamp date, if you still doubt my story. You'll believe it eventually, though, so it doesn't matter.

Right now, you're shocked. It's a real wrench when a man meets himself for the first time. Some kind of telepathy seems to work between two of the same people. You *sense* things. So I'll simply go ahead talking for half an hour or so, until you get over it. After that you'll come along with me. You know, I could try to change things around by telling what happened to me; but he —I—told me what I was going to do, so I might as well do the same. I probably couldn't help telling you the same thing in the same words, even if I tried-and I don't intend to try. I've gotten past that stage in worrying about all this.

So let's begin when you get up in half an hour and come out with me. You'll take a closer look at the machine, then. Yes, it'll be pretty obvious it must be a time machine. You'll sense that, too. You've seen it, just a small little cage with two seats, a luggage compartment, and a few buttons on a dash. You'll be puzzling over what I'll tell you, and you'll be getting used to the idea that you are the man who makes atomic power practical. Jerome Boell, just a plain engineer, the man who put atomic power in every home. You won't exactly believe it, but you'll want to go along.

* * * * *

I'll be tired of talking by then, and in a hurry to get going. So I cut off your questions, and get you inside. I snap on a green button, and everything seems to cut off around us. You can see a sort of foggy nothing surrounding the cockpit; it is probably the field that prevents passage through time from affecting us. The luggage section isn't protected, though.

* * * * *

You start to say something, but by then I'm pressing a black button, and everything outside will disappear. You look for your house, but it isn't there. There is exactly nothing there-in fact, there is no *there*. You are completely outside of time and space, as best you can guess how things are.

You can't feel any motion, of course. You try to reach a hand out through the field into the nothing around you and your hand goes out, all right, but nothing happens. Where the screen ends, your hand just turns over and pokes back at you. Doesn't hurt, and when you pull your arm back, you're still sound and uninjured. But it looks frightening and you don't try it again.

Then it comes to you slowly that you're actually traveling in time. You turn to me, getting used to the idea. "So this is the fourth dimension?" you ask.

Then you feel silly, because you'll remember that I said you'd ask that. Well, I asked it after I was told, then I came back and told it to you, and I still can't help answering when you speak.

"Not exactly," I try to explain. "Maybe it's no dimension-or it might be the fifth; if you're going to skip over the so-called fourth without traveling along it, you'd need a fifth. Don't ask me. I didn't invent the machine and I don't understand it."

"But...."

I let it go, and so do you. If you don't, it's a good way of going crazy. You'll see later why I couldn't have invented the machine. Of course, there may have been a start for all this once. There may have been a time when you did invent the machine-the atomic motor first, then the time-machine. And when you closed the loop by going back and saving yourself the trouble, it got all tangled up. I figured out once that such a universe would need some seven or eight time and space dimensions. It's simpler just to figure that this is the way time got bent back on itself. Maybe there is no machine, and it's just easier for us to imagine it. When you spend thirty years thinking about it, as I did-and you will-you get further and further from an answer.

Anyhow, you sit there, watching nothing all around you, and no time, apparently, though there is a time effect back in the luggage space. You look at your watch and it's still running. That means you either carry a small time field with you, or you are catching a small increment of time from the main field. I don't know, and you won't think about that then, either.

* * * * *

I'm smoking, and so are you, and the air in the machine is getting a bit stale. You suddenly realize that everything in the machine is wide open, yet you haven't seen any effects of air loss.

"Where are we getting our air?" you ask. "Or why don't we lose it?"

"No place for it to go," I explain. There isn't. Out there is neither time nor space, apparently. How could the air leak out? You still feel gravity, but I can't explain that, either. Maybe the machine has a gravity field built in, or maybe the time that makes your watch run is responsible for gravity. In spite of Einstein, you have always had the idea that time is an effect of gravity, and I sort of agree, still.

Then the machine stops-at least, the field around us cuts off. You feel a dankish sort of air replace the stale air, and you breathe easier, though we're in complete darkness, except for the weak light in the machine, which always burns, and a few feet of rough dirty cement floor around. You take another cigaret from me and you get out of the machine, just as I do.

I've got a bundle of clothes and I start changing. It's a sort of simple, short-limbed, one-piece affair I put on, but it feels comfortable.

"I'm staying here," I tell you. "This is like the things they wear in this century, as near as I can remember it, and I should be able to pass fairly well. I've had all my fortune-the one you make on that atomic generator-invested in such a way I can get it on using some identification I've got with me, so I'll do all right. I know they still use some kind of money, you'll see evidence of that. And it's a pretty easygoing civilization, from what I could see. We'll go up and I'll leave you. I like the looks of things here, so I won't be coming back with you."

You nod, remembering I've told you about it. "What century is this, anyway?"

I'd told you that, too, but you've forgotten. "As near as I can guess, it's about 2150. He told me, just as I'm telling you, that it's an interstellar civilization."

You take another cigaret from me, and follow me. I've got a small flashlight and we grope through a pile of rubbish, out into a corridor. This is a sub-sub-sub-basement. We have to walk up a flight of stairs, and there is an elevator waiting, fortunately with the door open.

"What about the time machine?" you ask.

"Since nobody ever stole it, it's safe."

* * * * *

We get in the elevator, and I say "first" to it. It gives out a coughing noise and the basement openings begin to click by us. There's no feeling of acceleration-some kind of false gravity they use in the future. Then the door opens, and the elevator says "first" back at us.

It's obviously a service elevator and we're in a dim corridor, with nobody around. I grab your hand and shake it. "You go that way. Don't worry about getting lost; you never did, so you can't. Find the museum, grab the motor, and get out. And good luck to you."

You act as if you're dreaming, though you can't believe it's a dream. You nod at me and I move out into the main corridor. A second later, you see me going by, mixed into a crowd that is loafing along toward a restaurant, or something like it, that is just opening. I'm asking questions of a man, who points, and I turn and move off.

You come out of the side corridor and go down a hall, away from the restaurant. There are quiet little signs along the hall. You look at them, realizing for the first time that things have changed.

Steij:neri, Faunten, Z:rgat Dispenseri. The signs are very quiet and dignified. Some of them can be decoded to stationery shops, fountains, and the like. What a zergot is, you don't know. You stop at a sign that announces: *Trav:l Biwrou —F:rst-Clas Twrz-Marz, Viin*s, and x: Trouj:n Planets. Spej:l reits tu aol s*nz wixin 60 lyt iirz!* But there is only a single picture of a dull-looking metal sphere, with passengers moving up a ramp, and the office is closed. You begin to get the hang of the spelling they use, though.

Now there are people around you, but nobody pays much attention to you. Why should they? You wouldn't care if you saw a man in a leopard-skin suit; you'd figure it was some part in a play and let it go. Well, people don't change much.

You get up your courage and go up to a boy selling something that might be papers on tapes.

"Where can I find the Museum of Science?"

"Downayer rien turn lefa the sign. Stoo bloss," he tells you. Around you, you hear some pretty normal English, but there are others using stuff as garbled as his. The educated and uneducated? I don't know.

You go right until you find a big sign built into the rubbery surface of the walk: *Miuzi:m *v Syens.* There's an arrow pointing and you turn left. Ahead of you, two blocks on, you can see a pink building, with faint aqua trimming, bigger than most of the others. They are building lower than they used to, apparently. Twenty floors up seems about the maximum. You head for it, and find the sidewalk is marked with the information that it is the museum.

* * * * *

You go up the steps, but you see that it seems to be closed. You hesitate for a moment, then. You're beginning to think the whole affair is complete nonsense, and you should get back to the time machine and go home. But then a guard comes to the gate. Except for the short legs in his suit and the friendly grin on his face, he looks like any other guard.

What's more, he speaks pretty clearly. Everyone says things in a sort of drawl, with softer vowels and slurred consonants, but it's rather pleasant.

"Help you, sir? Oh, of course. You must be playing in 'Atoms and Axioms.' The museum's closed, but I'll be glad to let you study whatever you need for realism in your role. Nice show. I saw it twice."

"Thanks," you mutter, wondering what kind of civilization can produce guards as polite as that. "I —I'm told I should investigate your display of atomic generators."

He beams at that. "Of course." The gate is swung to behind you, but obviously he isn't locking it. In fact, there doesn't seem to be a lock. "Must be a new part. You go down that corridor, up one flight of stairs and left. Finest display in all the known worlds. We've got the original of the first thirteen models. Professor Jonas was using them to check his latest theory of how they work. Too bad he could not explain the principle, either. Someone will, some day, though. Lord, the genius of that twentieth century inventor! It's quite a hobby with me, sir. I've read everything I could get on the period. Oh-congratulations on your pronunciation. Sounds just like some of our oldest tapes."

You get away from him, finally, after some polite thanks. The building seems deserted and you wander up the stairs. There's a room on your right filled with something that proclaims itself the first truly plastic diamond former, and you go up to it. As you come near, it goes through a crazy wiggle inside, stops turning out a continual row of what seem to be bearings, and slips something the size of a penny toward you.

"Souvenir," it announces in a well-modulated voice. "This is a typical gem of the twentieth century, properly cut to 58 facets, known technically as a Jaegger diamond, and approximately twenty carats in size. You can have it made into a ring on the third floor during morning hours for one-tenth credit. If you have more than one child, press the red button for the number of stones you desire."

You put it in your pocket, gulping a little, and get back to the corridor. You turn left and go past a big room in which models of spaceships-from the original thing that looks like a V-2, and is labeled first Lunar rocket, to a ten-foot globe, complete with miniature manikins-are sailing about in some kind of orbits. Then there is one labeled *Wep:nz*, filled with everything from a crossbow to a tiny rod four inches long and half the thickness of a pencil, marked *Fynal Hand Arm*. Beyond is the end of the corridor, and a big place that bears a sign, *Mad:lz *v Atamic Pau:r Sorsez.*

* * * * *

By that time, you're almost convinced. And you've been doing a lot of thinking about what you can do. The story I'm telling has been sinking in, but you aren't completely willing to accept it.

You notice that the models are all mounted on tables and that they're a lot smaller than you thought. They seem to be in chronological order, and the latest one, marked *2147 —Rincs Dyn*pat:*, is about the size of a desk telephone. The earlier ones are larger, of course, clumsier, but with variations, probably depending on the power output. A big sign on the ceiling gives a lot of dope on atomic generators, explaining that this is the first invention which leaped full blown into basically final form.

You study it, but it mentions casually the inventor, without giving his name. Either they don't know it, or they take it for granted that everyone does, which seems more probable. They call attention to the fact that they have the original model of the first atomic generator built, complete with design drawings, original manuscript on operation, and full patent application.

They state that it has all major refinements, operating on any fuel, producing electricity at any desired voltage up to five million, any chosen cyclic rate from direct current to one thousand megacycles, and any amperage up to one thousand, its maximum power output being fifty kilowatts, limited by the current-carrying capacity of the outputs. They also mention that the operating principle is still being investigated, and that only such refinements as better alloys and the addition of magnetric and nucleatric current outlets have been added since the original.

So you go to the end and look over the thing. It's simply a square box with a huge plug on each side, and a set of vernier controls on top, plus a little hole marked, in old-style spelling, *Drop BBs or wire here.* Apparently that's the way it's fueled. It's about one foot on each side.

"Nice," the guard says over your shoulder. "It finally wore out one of the cathogrids and we had to replace that, but otherwise it's exactly as the great inventor made it. And it still operates as well as ever. Like to have me tell you about it?"

"Not particularly," you begin, and then realize bad manners might be conspicuous here. While you're searching for an answer, the guard pulls something out of his pocket and stares at it.

"Fine, fine. The mayor of Altasecarba-Centaurian, you know-is arriving, but I'll be back in about ten minutes. He wants to examine some of the weapons for a monograph on Centaurian primitives compared to nineteenth century man. You'll pardon me?"

You pardon him pretty eagerly and he wanders off happily. You go up to the head of the line, to that Rinks Dynapattuh, or whatever it transliterates to. That's small and you can carry it. But the darned thing is absolutely fixed. You can't see any bolts, but you can't budge it, either.

* * * * *

You work down the line. It'd be foolish to take the early model if you can get one with built-in magnetic current terminals-Ehrenhaft or some other principle? —and nuclear binding-force energy terminals. But they're all held down by the same whatchamaycallem effect.

And, finally, you're right back beside the original first model. It's probably bolted down, too, but you try it tentatively and you find it moves. There's a little sign under it, indicating you shouldn't touch it, since the gravostatic plate is being renewed.

Well, you won't be able to change the time cycle by doing anything I haven't told you, but a working model such as that is a handy thing. You lift it; it only weighs about fifty pounds! Naturally, it can be carried.

You expect a warning bell, but nothing happens. As a matter of fact, if you'd stop drinking so much of that scotch and staring at the time machine out there now, you'd hear what I'm saying and know what will happen to you. But of course, just as I did, you're going to miss a lot of what I say from now on, and have to find out for yourself. But maybe some of it helps. I've tried to remember how much I remembered, after he told me, but I can't be sure. So I'll keep on talking. I probably can't help it, anyhow. Pre-set, you might say.

Well, you stagger down the corridor, looking out for the guard, but all seems clear. Then you hear his voice from the weapons room. You bend down and try to scurry past, but you know you're in full view. Nothing happens, though.

You stumble down the stairs, feeling all the futuristic rays in the world on your back, and still nothing happens. Ahead of you, the gate is closed. You reach it and it opens obligingly by itself. You breathe a quick sigh of relief and start out onto the street.

Then there's a yell behind you. You don't wait. You put one leg in front of the other and you begin racing down the walk, ducking past people, who stare at you with expressions you haven't time to see. There's another yell behind you.

Something goes over your head and drops on the sidewalk just in front of your feet, with a sudden ringing sound. You don't wait to find out about that, either. Somebody reaches out a hand to catch you and you dart past.

* * * * *

The street is pretty clear now and you jolt along, with your arms seeming to come out of the sockets, and that atomic generator getting heavier at every step.

Out of nowhere, something in a blue uniform about six feet tall and on the beefy side appears-and the badge hasn't changed much. The cop catches your arm and you know you're not going to get away, so you stop.

"You can't exert yourself that hard in this heat, fellow," the cop says. "There are laws against that, without a yellow sticker. Here, let me grab you a taxi."

* * * * *

Reaction sets in a bit and your knees begin to buckle, but you shake your head and come up for air.

"I —I left my money home," you begin.

The cop nods. "Oh, that explains it. Fine, I won't have to give you an appearance schedule. But you should have come to me." He reaches out and taps a pedestrian lightly on the shoulder. "Sir, an emergency request. Would you help this gentleman?"

* * * * *

The pedestrian grins, looks at his watch, and nods. "How far?"

You did notice the name of the building from which you came and you mutter it. The stranger nods again, reaches out and picks up the other side of the generator, blowing a little whistle the cop hands him. Pedestrians begin to move aside, and you and the stranger jog down the street at a trot, with a nice clear path, while the cop stands beaming at you both.

That way, it isn't so bad. And you begin to see why I decided I might like to stay in the future. But all the same, the organized cooperation here doesn't look too good. The guard can get the same and be there before you.

And he is. He stands just inside the door of the building as you reach it. The stranger lifts an eyebrow and goes off at once when you nod at him, not waiting for thanks. And the guard comes up, holding some dinkus in his hand, about the size of a big folding camera and not too dissimilar in other ways. He snaps it open and you get set to duck.

"You forgot the prints, monograph, and patent applications," he says. "They go with the generator-we don't like to have them separated. A good thing I knew the production office of 'Atoms and Axioms' was in this building. Just let us know when you're finished with the model and we'll pick it up."

You swallow several sets of tonsils you had removed years before, and take the bundle of papers he hands you out of the little case. He pumps you for some more information, which you give him at random. It seems to satisfy your amiable guard friend. He finally smiles in satisfaction and heads back to the museum.

You still don't believe it, but you pick up the atomic generator and the information sheets, and you head down toward the service elevator. There is no button on it. In fact, there's no door there.

You start looking for other doors or corridors, but you know this is right. The signs along the halls are the same as they were.

* * * * *

Then there's a sort of cough and something dilates in the wall. It forms a perfect door and the elevator stands there waiting. You get in, gulping out something about going all the way down, and then wonder how a machine geared for voice operation can make anything of that. What the deuce would that lowest basement be called? But the elevator has closed and is moving downward in a hurry. It coughs again and you're at the original level. You get out-and realize you don't have a light.

You'll never know what you stumbled over, but, somehow, you move back in the direction of the time machine, bumping against boxes, staggering here and there, and trying to find the right place by sheer feel. Then a shred of dim light appears; it's the weak light in the time machine. You've located it.

You put the atomic generator in the luggage space, throw the papers down beside it, and climb into the cockpit, sweating and mumbling. You reach forward toward the green button and hesitate. There's a red one beside it and you finally decide on that.

Suddenly, there's a confused yell from the direction of the elevator and a beam of light strikes against your eyes, with a shout punctuating it. Your finger touches the red button.

You'll never know what the shouting was about-whether they finally doped out the fact that they'd been robbed, or whether they were trying to help you. You don't care which it is. The field springs up around you and the next button you touch-the one on the board that hasn't been used so far-sends you off into nothingness. There is no beam of light, you can't hear a thing, and you're safe.

It isn't much of a trip back. You sit there smoking and letting your nerves settle back to normal. You notice a third set of buttons, with some pencil marks over them —"Press these to return to yourself 30 years" —and you begin waiting for the air to get stale. It doesn't because there is only one of you this time.

Instead, everything flashes off and you're sitting in the machine in your own back yard.

You'll figure out the cycle in more details later. You get into the machine in front of your house, go to the future in the sub-basement, land in your back yard, and then hop back thirty years to pick up yourself, landing in front of your house. Just that. But right then, you don't care. You jump out and start pulling out that atomic generator and taking it inside.

* * * * *

It isn't hard to disassemble, but you don't learn a thing; just some plates of metal, some spiral coils, and a few odds and ends-all things that can be made easily enough, all obviously of common metals. But when you put it together again, about an hour later, you notice something.

Everything in it is brand-new and there's one set of copper wires missing! It won't work. You put some #12 house wire in, exactly like the set on the other side, drop in some iron filings, and try it again.

And with the controls set at 120 volts, 60 cycles and 15 amperes, you get just that. You don't need the power company any more. And you feel a little happier when you realize that the luggage space wasn't insulated from time effects by a field, so the motor has moved backward in time, somehow, and is back to its original youth-minus the replaced wires the guard mentioned-which probably wore out because of the makeshift job you've just done.

But you begin getting more of a jolt when you find that the papers are all in your own writing, that your name is down as the inventor, and that the date of the patent application is 1951.

It will begin to soak in, then. You pick up an atomic generator in the future and bring it back to the past-your present-so that it can be put in the museum with you as the inventor so you can steal it to be the inventor. And you do it in a time machine which you bring back to yourself to take yourself into the future to return to take back to yourself....

Who invented what? And who built which?

Before long, your riches from the generator are piling in. Little kids from school are coming around to stare at the man who changed history and made atomic power so common that no nation could hope to be anything but a democracy and a peaceful one-after some of the worst times in history for a few years. Your name eventually becomes as common as Ampere, or Faraday, or any other spelled without a capital letter.

But you're thinking of the puzzle. You can't find any answer.

One day you come across an old poem-something about some folks calling it evolution and others calling it God. You go out, make a few provisions for the future, and come back to climb into the time machine that's waiting in the building you had put around it. Then you'll be knocking on your own door, thirty years back-or right now, from your view-and telling your younger self all these things I'm telling you.

But now....

Well, the drinks are finished. You're woozy enough to go along with me without protest, and I want to find out just why those people up there came looking for you and shouting, before the time machine left.

Let's go.

August Derleth

A Traveler in Time

YOU CAN'T ALWAYS ESCAPE EVILS BY RUNNING AWAY FROM THEM...BUT IT
MAY HELP!

"Tell me what time is," said Harrigan one late summer afternoon in a Madison Street bar. "I'd
like to know."

"A dimension," I answered. "Everybody knows that."

"All right, granted. I know space is a dimension and you can move forward or back in space.
And, of course, you keep on aging all the time."

"Elementary," I said.

"But what happens if you can move backward or forward in time? Do you age or get younger,
or do you keep the status quo?"

"I'm not an authority on time, Tex. Do you know anyone who traveled in time?"

Harrigan shrugged aside my question. "That was the thing I couldn't get out of Vanderkamp,
either. He presumed to know everything else."

"Vanderkamp?"

"He was another of those strange people a reporter always runs into. Lived in New York-
downtown, near the Bowery. Man of about forty, I'd say, but a little on the old-fashioned side.
Dutch background, and hipped on the subject of New Amsterdam, which, in case you don't
know, was the original name of New York City."

"Don't mind my interrupting," I cut in. "But I'm not quite straight on what Vanderkamp
has to do with time as dimension."

"Oh, he was touched on the subject. He claimed to travel in it. The fact is, he invented a
time-traveling machine."

"You certainly meet the whacks, Tex!"

"Don't I!" He grinned appreciatively and leaned reminiscently over the bar. "But Vanderkamp
had the wildest dreams of the lot. And in the end he managed the neatest conjuring trick of
them all. I was on the Brooklyn *Enterprise* at that time; I spent about a year there. Special
features, though I was on a reporter's salary. Vanderkamp was something of a local celebrity
in a minor way; he wrote articles on the early Dutch in New York, the nomenclature of the
Dutch, the history of Dutch place-names, and the like. He was handy with a pen, and even
handier with tools. He was an amateur electrician, carpenter, house-painter, and claimed to be
an expert in genealogy."

"And he built a time-traveling machine?"

"So he said. He gave me a rather hard time of it. He was a glib talker and half the time
I didn't know whether I was coming or going. He kept me on my toes by taking for granted
that I accepted his basic premises. I got next to him on a tip. He could be close-mouthed as
a clam, but his sister let things slip from time to time, and on this occasion she passed the
word to one of her friends in a grocery store that her brother had invented a machine that
took him off on trips into the past. It seemed like routine whack stuff, but Blake, who decided
what went into the *Enterprise* and what didn't, sent me over to Manhattan to get something
for the paper, on the theory that since Vanderkamp was well-known in Brooklyn, it was good
neighborhood copy.

"Vanderkamp was a sharp-eyed little fellow, about five feet or so in height, and I hit him at
a good time. His sister said he had just come back from a trip-she left me to draw my own
conclusions about what kind of trip-and I found him in a mild fit of temper. He was too upset,
in fact, to be truculent, which was more like his nature.

"Was it true, I wanted to know, that he'd invented a machine that traveled in time?

"He didn't make any bones about it. 'Certainly,' he said. 'I've been using it for the last month, and if my sister hadn't decided to blab nobody would know about it yet. What about it?'

"'You believe it can take you backwards or forwards into the past or the future?'

"'Do I look crazy? I said so, didn't I?'

"Now, as a matter of fact, he *did* look crazy. Unlike most of the candidates for my file of queer people, Vanderkamp actually looked like a nut. He had a wild eye and a constantly working mouth; he blinked a good deal and stammered when he was excited. In features he was as Dutch as his name implied. Well, we talked back and forth for some time, but I stuck with him and in the end he took me out into a shed adjoining his house and showed me the contraption he'd built.

"It looked like a top. The first thing I thought of was Brick Bradford, and before I could catch myself, I'd asked, 'Is that pure Brick Bradford?'

"He didn't turn a hair. 'Not by a long shot,' he answered. 'H. G. Wells was there first. I owe it to Wells.'

"'I see,' I said.

"'The hell you do!' he shot back. 'You think I'm as nutty as a fruit-cake.'

"'The idea of time travel is a little hard to swallow,' I said.

"'Sure it is. But me, I'm doing it. So that's all there is to it.'

"'If you don't mind, Mr. Vanderkamp,' I said, 'I'm a dummy in scientific matters. I have all I can do to tell a nut from a bolt.'

"'That I believe,' he said.

"'So how do you time travel?'

"'Look,' he said, 'time is a dimension like space. You can go up or down this ruler,' he snatched a steel ruler and waved it in front of me, 'from any given point. But you move. In the dimension of time, you only seem to move. You stand still; time moves. Do you get it?'

"I had to confess that I didn't.

"He tried again, with obviously strained patience. Judging by what I could gather from what he said, it was possible for him-so he believed-to get into his machine, twirl a few knobs, push a few buttons, relax for any given period, and end up just where he liked-back in the past, or ahead in the future. But wherever he ended up, he was still in this same spot. In other words, whether he was back in 1492 or ahead in 2092, the place he got out of his time machine was still his present address.

"It was beyond me, frankly, but I figured that as long as he was a little touched, it wouldn't do any harm to humor him. I intimated that I understood and asked him where he'd been last.

"His face fell, his brow clouded, and he said, 'I've been ahead thirty years.' He shook his head angrily. 'What a time! I'll be seventy, and you won't even be that, Mr. Harrigan. But we'll be in the middle of the worst atomic war you ever dreamed about.'

"Now this was before Hiroshima, quite a bit. I didn't know what he was talking about, but it gives me a queer feeling now and then when I think of what he said, especially since it's still short of thirty years since that time.

"'It's no time to be living here,' he went on. 'Direct hits on the entire area. What would you do?'

"'I'd get out,' I said.

"'That's what I thought,' he said. 'But that kind of warfare carries a long way. A long way. And I'm a man who loves his comforts, reasonably. I don't intend to set up housekeeping in equatorial Africa or the forests of Brazil.'

"'What did you see thirty years from now, Mr. Vanderkamp?' I asked him.

"'Everything blown to hell,' he answered. 'Not a building in all Manhattan.' He leered and added, 'And everybody who'll be living here at that time will be scattered into the atmosphere in fragments no bigger than an amoeba.'

"'You fill me with anticipation,' I said.

"So I went back to my desk and wrote the story. You could guess what kind it had to be. 'Time Travel Is Possible, Says Amateur Scientist!' —that kind of thing. You can see it every week, in large doses, in the feature sections of some of the biggest chain papers. It went over like an average feature about life on the moon or prehistoric animals surviving in remote mountain valleys, or what have you. Just what Vanderkamp went back to after I left, I don't know, but I have an idea that he gave his sister a devil of a time."

* * * * *

Vanderkamp stalked into the house and confronted his sister.

"You see, Julie —a reporter. Can't you learn to hold your tongue?"

She threw him a scornful glance. "What difference does it make?" she cried. "You're gone all the time."

"Maybe I'll take you along sometime. Just wait."

"Wait, wait! That's all I've been doing. Since I was ten years old I've been waiting on you!"

"Oh, the hell with it!" He turned on his heel and left the house.

She followed him to the door and shouted after him, "Where are you going now?"

"To New Amsterdam for a little peace and quiet," he said testily.

He threw open the thick-walled door of his time-machine and pulled it shut behind him. He sat down before the controls and began to chart his course for 1650. If his calculations were correct, he would shortly find himself in the vicinity of that sturdy if autocratic first citizen of the Dutch colony of New Amsterdam, Peter Stuyvesant, as well as Governor Stuyvesant's friend and neighbor, Heinrich Vanderkamp. He gave not even a figurative glance over his shoulder before he started out.

When he emerged at last from his machine, he was in what appeared to be the backyard of a modest residence on a street which, though he did not know it, he suspected might be the Bouwerie. At the moment of his emergence, a tall, angular woman stood viewing him, open-mouthed and aghast, from the wooden stoop at the back door of her home. He looked at her in astonishment himself. The resemblance to his sister Julie was uncanny.

With only the slightest hesitation, he addressed her in fluent Dutch. "Pray do not be disturbed, young lady."

"A fine way for a gentleman to call!" she exclaimed in a voice considerably more forceful than her appearance. "I suppose my father sent you. And where did you get that outlandish costume?"

"I bought it," he answered, truthfully enough.

"A likely tale," she said. "And if my father sent you, just go back and tell him I'm satisfied the way I am. No woman needs a man to manage her."

"I don't have the honor of your father's acquaintance," he answered.

She gazed at him suspiciously from narrowed eyes. "Everyone in New Amsterdam knows Henrik Van Tromp. He's as unloved as yonder bumblebee. Stand where you are and say whence you came."

"I am a visitor in New Amsterdam," he said, standing obediently still. "I confess I don't know my way about very well, and I chose to stop at this attractive home."

"I know it's attractive," she said tartly. "And it's plain to see you're a stranger here, or you'd never be wearing such clothes. Or is it the fashion where you come from?" She gave him no opportunity to answer, but added, after a moment of indecision, "Well, you look respectable enough, though much like my rascally cousin Pieter Vanderkamp. Do you know him?"

"No."

"Well, no matter. He's much older than you-near forty blessed years. You're no more than twenty, I don't doubt."

Involuntarily Vanderkamp put his hand to his cheek, and smiled as he felt its smooth roundness. "You may be right, at that," he said cryptically.

"You might as well come in," she said grudgingly. "What with the traffic on the road outside, the Indians, and people who come in such flighty vehicles as yours, I might as well live in the heart of the colony."

He looked around. "And still," he said, "it is a pleasant spot-peaceful, comfortable. I'm sure a man could live out his days here in contentment."

"Oh, could he?" she said belligerently. "And where would I be while this went on?"

He gazed at her beetling nose, her jutting chin. "A good question," he muttered thoughtfully.

He followed her into the house. It was a treasury of antiquities, filling him with delight. Miss Anna Van Tromp offered him a cup of milk, which he accepted, thanking her profusely. She talked volubly, eyeing him all the while with the utmost curiosity, and he gathered presently that her father had made several attempts to marry her off, disapproving of her solitary residence so far from the center of the city; but she had frowned upon one and all of the suitors he had encouraged to call on her. She was undeniably impressive, almost formidable, he conceded privately, with a touch of the shrew and harridan. Life with Miss Anna Van Tromp would not be easy, he reflected. But then, life with his sister Julie was not easy, either. Miss Anna, however, had not to face atomic warfare; all she had to look forward to in fourteen years was surrender to the besieging British, which she would have no trouble in surviving.

He settled down to his ingratiating best and succeeded in making a most favorable impression on Miss Anna Van Tromp before at last he took his leave, carrying with him a fine, hand-wrought bowl with which the lady had presented him. He had a hunch he might come back. Of all the times he had visited since finishing the machine, he knew that old New Amsterdam in the 1650s was the one period most likely to keep him contented-provided Miss Van Tromp didn't turn out to be a nuisance. So he took careful note of the set of his controls, jotting them down so that he would not be likely to forget them.

It was late when he found himself back in his own time.

His sister was waiting up for him. "Two o'clock in the morning!" she screamed at him. "What are you doing to me? Oh, God, why didn't I marry when I had the chance, instead of throwing away my life on a worthless brother!"

"Why don't you? It's not too late," he sighed wearily.

"How can you say that?" she snapped bitterly. "Here I am thirty nearly, and worn out from working for you. Who would marry me now? Oh, if only I could have another chance! If I could be young again, and do it all over, I'd know how to have a better life!"

In spite of his boredom with her, Vanderkamp felt the effect of this cry from a lonely heart. He looked at her pityingly; it was true, after all, that she had worked faithfully for him, without pay, since their parents died. "Take a look at this," he said gently, offering her the bowl.

"Hah! Can we eat bowls?"

He raised his eyes heavenward and went wearily to bed.

* * * * *

"I saw Vanderkamp again about a fortnight later," Harrigan went on. "Ran into him in a tavern on the Bowery. He recognized me and came over.

"'That was some story you did,' he said.

"'Been bothered by cranks?' I asked.

"'Hell, yes! Not too badly, though. They want to ride off somewhere just to get away. I get that feeling myself sometimes. But, tell me, have you seen the morning papers?'

"Now, by coincidence, the papers that morning had carried a story from some local nuclear physicist about the increasing probability that the atom would be smashed. I told him I'd seen it.

"'What did I tell you?' he said.

"I just smiled and asked where he'd been lately. He didn't hesitate to talk, perhaps because his sister had been giving him a hard time with her nagging. So I listened. It appeared, to hear him tell it, that he had been off visiting the Dutch in New Amsterdam. You could almost believe what he said, listening to him, except for that wild look he had. Anyway, he'd been in New Amsterdam about 1650, and he'd brought back a few trifling souvenirs of the trips. Would I like to see them? I said I would.

"I figured he'd got his hands on some nice antiques and wanted an appreciative audience. His sister wasn't home; so he took me around and showed me his pieces, one by one —a bowl, a pair of wooden candlesticks, wooden shoes, and more, all in all a fine collection. He even had a chair that looked pretty authentic, and I wondered where he'd dug up so many nice things of the New Amsterdam period-though, of course, I had to take his word as to where they belonged historically; I didn't know. But I imagine he got them somewhere in the city or perhaps up in the Catskill country.

"Well, after a while I got another look at his contraption. It didn't appear to have been moved at all; it was still sitting where it had been before, without a sign to say that it had been used to go anywhere, least of all into past time.

"'Tell me,' I said to him at last, 'when you go back in time do you get younger?'

"'Yes and no,' he said. 'Obviously.'

"It wasn't obvious to me, but I couldn't get any more than that out of him. The thing I couldn't figure out was the reason for his claim. He wasn't trying to sell anything to anybody, as far as I could see; he wasn't anxious to tell the world about his time-machine, either. He didn't mind talking in his oblique fashion about his trips. He did talk about New Amsterdam as if he had a pretty good acquaintance with the place. But then, he was known as a minor authority on the customs of the Dutch colony.

"He was touched, obviously. Just the same, he challenged me, in a way. I wanted to know something more about him, how his machine worked, how he took off, and so on. I made up my mind the next time I was in the neighborhood to look him up, hoping he wouldn't be home.

"When I made it, his sister was alone, and in fine fettle, as cantankerous as a flea-bitten mastiff.

"'He's gone again,' she complained bitterly.

"Clearly the two of them were at odds. I asked her whether she had seen him go. She hadn't; he had just marched out to his shop and that was an end to him as far as she was concerned.

"I haggled around quite a lot and finally got her permission to go out and see what I could see for myself. Of course, the shop was locked. I had counted on that and had brought along a handy little skeleton key. I was inside in no time. The machine wasn't there. Not a sign of it, or of Vanderkamp either.

"Now, I looked around all over, but I couldn't for the life of me figure out how he could have taken it out of that place; it was too big for doors or windows, and the walls and roof were solid and immovable. I figured that he couldn't have got such a large machine away without his sister's seeing him; so I locked the place up and went back to the house.

"But she was immovable; she hadn't seen a thing. If he had taken anything larger than pocket-size out of that shop of his, she had missed it. I could hardly doubt her sincerity. There was nothing to be had from that source; so I had no alternative but to wait for him another time."

* * * * *

Anna Van Tromp, considerably chastened, watched her strange suitor-she looked upon all men as suitors, without exception; for so her father had conditioned her to do-as he reached into his sack and brought out another wonder.

"Now this," said Vanderkamp, "is an alarm clock. You wind it up like this, you see; set it, and off it goes. Listen to it ring! That will wake you up in the morning."

"More magic," she cried doubtfully.

"No, no," he explained patiently. "It is an everyday thing in my country. Perhaps some day you would like to join me in a little visit there, Anna?"

"Ja, maybe," she agreed, looking out the window to his weird and frightening carriage, which had no animal to draw it and which vanished so strangely, fading away into the air, whenever Vanderkamp went into it. "This clothes-washing machine you talk about," she admitted. "This I would like to see."

"I must go now," said Vanderkamp, gazing at her with well-simulated coyness. "I'll leave these things here with you, and I'll just take along that bench over there."

"Ja, ja," said Anna, blushing.

"Six of one and half a dozen of the other," muttered Vanderkamp, comparing Anna with his sister.

He got into his time-machine and set out for home in the twentieth century. There was some reluctance in his going. Here all was somnolent peace and quiet, despite the rigors of living; in his own time there were wars and turmoil and the ultimate threat of the greatest war of all. New Amsterdam had one drawback, however-the presence of Anna Von Tromp. She had grown fond of him, undeniably, perhaps because he was so much more interested in her circumstances than in herself. What was a man to do? Julie at one end, Anna at the other. But even getting rid of Julie would not allow him to escape the warfare to come.

He thought deeply of his problem all the way home.

When he got back, he found his sister waiting up, as usual, ready to deliver the customary diatribe.

He forestalled her. "I've been thinking things over, Julie. I believe you'd be much happier if you were living with brother Carl. I'll give you as much money as you need, and you can pack your things and I'll take you down to Louisiana."

"Take me!" she exclaimed. *"How? In that crazy contraption of yours?"*

"Precisely."

"Oh no!" she said. *"You don't get me into that machine! How do I know what it will do to me? It's a time machine, isn't it? It might make an old hag of me-or a baby!"*

"You said that you wanted to be young again, didn't you?" he said softly. *"You said you'd like another chance...."*

A faraway look came into her eyes. "Oh, if I only could! If I only could be a girl again, with a chance to get married...."

"Pack your things," Vanderkamp said quietly.

* * * * *

"It must have been all of a month before I saw Vanderkamp again," Harrigan continued, waving for another scotch and soda. "I was down in the vicinity on an assignment and I took a run over to his place.

"He was home this time. He came to the door, which he had chained on the inside. He recognized me, and it was plain at the same time that he had no intention of letting me in.

"I came right out with the first question I had in mind. 'The thing that bothers me,' I said to him, 'is how you get that time machine of yours in and out of that shed.'

"'Mr. Harrigan,' he answered, 'newspaper reporters ought to have at least elementary scientific knowledge. You don't. How in hell could even a time machine be in two places at once, I ask you? If I take that machine back three centuries, that's where it is-not here. And three centuries ago that shop wasn't standing there. So you don't go in or out; you don't move at all, remember? It's time that moves.'

"'I called the other day,' I went on. 'Your sister spoke to me. Give her my regards.'

"'My sister's left me,' he said shortly, 'to stew, as you might say, in my own time machine.'

"'Really?' I said. 'Just what do you have in mind to do next?'

"'Let me ask *you* something, Mr. Harrigan,' he answered. 'Would you sit around here waiting for an atomic war if you could get away?'

"'Certainly not,' I answered.

"'Well, then, I don't intend to, either.'

"All this while he was standing at the door, refusing to open it any wider or to let me in. He was making it pretty plain that there wasn't much he had to say to me. And he seemed to be in a hurry.

"'Remember me to the inquiring public thirty years hence, Mr. Harrigan,' he said at last, and closed the door.

"That was the last I saw of him."

Harrigan finished his scotch and soda appreciatively and looked around for the bartender.

"Did he take off then?" I asked.

"Like a rocket," said Harrigan. "Queerest thing was that there wasn't a trace of him. The machine was gone, too-the same way as the last time, without a disturbance in the shop. He and his machine had simply vanished off the face of the earth and were never heard from again.

"Matter of fact, though," Harrigan went on thoughtfully, "Vanderkamp's disappearance wasn't the really queer angle on the pitch. The other thing broke in the papers the week after he left. The neighbors got pretty worked up about it. They called the police to tell them that Vanderkamp's sister Julie was back, only she was off her nut-and a good deal changed in appearance, too.

"Gal going blarmy was no news, of course, but that last bit about her appearance-they said she looked about twenty years older, all of a sudden-sort of rang a bell. So I went over there. It was Julie, all right; at least, she looked a hell of a lot like Julie had when I last saw her-provided you could grant that a woman could age twenty years in the few weeks it had been. And she was off her rocker, sure enough-or hysterical. Or at least madder than a wet hen. She made out like she couldn't speak a word of English, and they finally had to get an interpreter to understand her. She wouldn't speak anything but Dutch-and an old-fashioned kind, too.

"She made a lot of extravagant claims and kept insisting that she would bring the whole matter up in a complaint before Governor Stuyvesant. Said she wasn't Julie Vanderkamp, by God, but was named Anna Van Tromp-which is an old Dutch name thereabouts-and claimed that she had been abducted from her home on the Bowery. We pointed out the Third Avenue El and told her *that* was the Bowery, but she just sniffed and looked at us as though *we* were crazy."

I toyed with my drink. "You mean you actually listened to the poor girl's story?" I asked.

"Sure," Harrigan said. "Maybe she was as crazy as a bedbug, but I've listened to whackier stories from supposedly sane people. Sure, I listened to her." He paused thoughtfully for a moment, then went on.

"She claimed that this fellow Vanderkamp had come to her house and filled her with a lot of guff about the wonderful country he lived in, and how she ought to let him take her to see it. Apparently he waxed especially eloquent about an automatic washing-machine and dryer, and that had fascinated her, for some reason. Then, she said, he'd brought a ten-year-old girl along-though where in the world old Vanderkamp could have picked up a tot like that is beyond me-and the kid had added her blandishments to the plot. Between them, they had managed to lure her into the old guy's machine. From what she said, it was obviously the time machine she was talking about, and if she was Julie there was no reason why she shouldn't know about it. But she talked as though it was a complete mystery to her, as though she'd no idea what the purpose of it was. Well, anyway, here she was-and very unhappy, too. Wanted to go back to old New Amsterdam, but bad.

"It was a beautiful act, even if she was nuts. The strange thing was, though, that there were some things even a gal going whacky couldn't explain. For instance, the house was filled with what the experts said were priceless antiques from Dutch New Amsterdam, of the period just prior to the British siege. You'd think those things would make poor Julie feel more at home, seeing as she claimed to belong in that period, but apparently they just made her homesick. And, curiously enough, all the modern gadgets were gone. All those handy little items that make the twentieth century so livable had been taken away-including the washing-machine and dryer, by the way. Julie-or Anna, as she called herself-claimed that Vanderkamp had taken it back with him, wherever he'd gone to, after he'd brought her there."

"Poor woman," I said sympathetically. "They toted her off to the booby hatch, I suppose."

"No...." Harrigan said slowly. "They didn't, as a matter of fact. Since she was harmless, they let her stay in the house a while. Which was a mistake, it seems. Of course, she *wasn't* from the seventeenth century. That's impossible. All the same —." He broke off abruptly and stared moodily into his glass.

"What happened to her?" I asked.

"She was found one morning about two weeks after she got there," he said. "Dead. Electro-cuted. It seems she'd stuck her finger into a light socket while standing in a bathtub full of water.

An accident, obviously. As the Medical Examiner said, it was an accident any six-year-old child would have known enough about electricity to avoid.

"That is," Harrigan added, "a *twentieth-century* child...."

Frederik Pohl

The Tunnel Under the World

I

Pinching yourself is no way to see if you are dreaming. Surgical instruments? Well, yes-but a mechanic's kit is best of all!

* * * * *

On the morning of June 15th, Guy Burckhardt woke up screaming out of a dream.

It was more real than any dream he had ever had in his life. He could still hear and feel the sharp, ripping-metal explosion, the violent heave that had tossed him furiously out of bed, the searing wave of heat.

He sat up convulsively and stared, not believing what he saw, at the quiet room and the bright sunlight coming in the window.

He croaked, "Mary?"

His wife was not in the bed next to him. The covers were tumbled and awry, as though she had just left it, and the memory of the dream was so strong that instinctively he found himself searching the floor to see if the dream explosion had thrown her down.

But she wasn't there. Of course she wasn't, he told himself, looking at the familiar vanity and slipper chair, the uncracked window, the unbuckled wall. It had only been a dream.

"Guy?" His wife was calling him querulously from the foot of the stairs. "Guy, dear, are you all right?"

He called weakly, "Sure."

There was a pause. Then Mary said doubtfully, "Breakfast is ready. Are you sure you're all right? I thought I heard you yelling —"

Burckhardt said more confidently, "I had a bad dream, honey. Be right down."

* * * * *

In the shower, punching the lukewarm-and-cologne he favored, he told himself that it had been a beaut of a dream. Still, bad dreams weren't unusual, especially bad dreams about explosions. In the past thirty years of H-bomb jitters, who had not dreamed of explosions?

Even Mary had dreamed of them, it turned out, for he started to tell her about the dream, but she cut him off. "You *did*?" Her voice was astonished. "Why, dear, I dreamed the same thing! Well, almost the same thing. I didn't actually *hear* anything. I dreamed that something woke me up, and then there was a sort of quick bang, and then something hit me on the head. And that was all. Was yours like that?"

Burckhardt coughed. "Well, no," he said. Mary was not one of these strong-as-a-man, brave-as-a-tiger women. It was not necessary, he thought, to tell her all the little details of the dream that made it seem so real. No need to mention the splintered ribs, and the salt bubble in his throat, and the agonized knowledge that this was death. He said, "Maybe there really was some kind of explosion downtown. Maybe we heard it and it started us dreaming."

Mary reached over and patted his hand absently. "Maybe," she agreed. "It's almost half-past eight, dear. Shouldn't you hurry? You don't want to be late to the office."

He gulped his food, kissed her and rushed out-not so much to be on time as to see if his guess had been right.

But downtown Tylerton looked as it always had. Coming in on the bus, Burckhardt watched critically out the window, seeking evidence of an explosion. There wasn't any. If anything, Tylerton looked better than it ever had before: It was a beautiful crisp day, the sky was cloudless, the buildings were clean and inviting. They had, he observed, steam-blasted the Power & Light Building, the town's only skyscraper-that was the penalty of having Contro Chemical's main plant on the outskirts of town; the fumes from the cascade stills left their mark on stone buildings.

None of the usual crowd were on the bus, so there wasn't anyone Burckhardt could ask about the explosion. And by the time he got out at the corner of Fifth and Lehigh and the bus rolled away with a muted diesel moan, he had pretty well convinced himself that it was all imagination.

He stopped at the cigar stand in the lobby of his office building, but Ralph wasn't behind the counter. The man who sold him his pack of cigarettes was a stranger.

"Where's Mr. Stebbins?" Burckhardt asked.

The man said politely, "Sick, sir. He'll be in tomorrow. A pack of Marlins today?"

"Chesterfields," Burckhardt corrected.

"Certainly, sir," the man said. But what he took from the rack and slid across the counter was an unfamiliar green-and-yellow pack.

"Do try these, sir," he suggested. "They contain an anti-cough factor. Ever notice how ordinary cigarettes make you choke every once in a while?"

* * * * *

Burckhardt said suspiciously, "I never heard of this brand."

"Of course not. They're something new." Burckhardt hesitated, and the man said persuasively, "Look, try them out at my risk. If you don't like them, bring back the empty pack and I'll refund your money. Fair enough?"

Burckhardt shrugged. "How can I lose? But give me a pack of Chesterfields, too, will you?"

He opened the pack and lit one while he waited for the elevator. They weren't bad, he decided, though he was suspicious of cigarettes that had the tobacco chemically treated in any way. But he didn't think much of Ralph's stand-in; it would raise hell with the trade at the cigar stand if the man tried to give every customer the same high-pressure sales talk.

The elevator door opened with a low-pitched sound of music. Burckhardt and two or three others got in and he nodded to them as the door closed. The thread of music switched off and the speaker in the ceiling of the cab began its usual commercials.

No, not the *usual* commercials, Burckhardt realized. He had been exposed to the captive-audience commercials so long that they hardly registered on the outer ear any more, but what was coming from the recorded program in the basement of the building caught his attention. It wasn't merely that the brands were mostly unfamiliar; it was a difference in pattern.

There were jingles with an insistent, bouncy rhythm, about soft drinks he had never tasted. There was a rapid patter dialogue between what sounded like two ten-year-old boys about a candy bar, followed by an authoritative bass rumble: "Go right out and get a DELICIOUS Choco-Bite and eat your TANGY Choco-Bite *all up*. That's *Choco-Bite!*" There was a sobbing female whine: "I *wish* I had a Feckle Freezer! I'd do *anything* for a Feckle Freezer!" Burckhardt reached his floor and left the elevator in the middle of the last one. It left him a little uneasy. The commercials were not for familiar brands; there was no feeling of use and custom to them.

But the office was happily normal-except that Mr. Barth wasn't in. Miss Mitkin, yawning at the reception desk, didn't know exactly why. "His home phoned, that's all. He'll be in tomorrow."

"Maybe he went to the plant. It's right near his house."

She looked indifferent. "Yeah."

A thought struck Burckhardt. "But today is June 15th! It's quarterly tax return day-he has to sign the return!"

Miss Mitkin shrugged to indicate that that was Burckhardt's problem, not hers. She returned to her nails.

Thoroughly exasperated, Burckhardt went to his desk. It wasn't that he couldn't sign the tax returns as well as Barth, he thought resentfully. It simply wasn't his job, that was all; it was a responsibility that Barth, as office manager for Contro Chemicals' downtown office, should have taken.

* * * * *

He thought briefly of calling Barth at his home or trying to reach him at the factory, but he gave up the idea quickly enough. He didn't really care much for the people at the factory and the less contact he had with them, the better. He had been to the factory once, with Barth; it had been a confusing and, in a way, a frightening experience. Barring a handful of executives and engineers, there wasn't a soul in the factory-that is, Burckhardt corrected himself, remembering what Barth had told him, not a *living* soul-just the machines.

According to Barth, each machine was controlled by a sort of computer which reproduced, in its electronic snarl, the actual memory and mind of a human being. It was an unpleasant thought. Barth, laughing, had assured him that there was no Frankenstein business of robbing graveyards and implanting brains in machines. It was only a matter, he said, of transferring a man's habit patterns from brain cells to vacuum-tube cells. It didn't hurt the man and it didn't make the machine into a monster.

But they made Burckhardt uncomfortable all the same.

He put Barth and the factory and all his other little irritations out of his mind and tackled the tax returns. It took him until noon to verify the figures-which Barth could have done out of his memory and his private ledger in ten minutes, Burckhardt resentfully reminded himself.

He sealed them in an envelope and walked out to Miss Mitkin. "Since Mr. Barth isn't here, we'd better go to lunch in shifts," he said. "You can go first."

"Thanks." Miss Mitkin languidly took her bag out of the desk drawer and began to apply makeup.

Burckhardt offered her the envelope. "Drop this in the mail for me, will you? Uh-wait a minute. I wonder if I ought to phone Mr. Barth to make sure. Did his wife say whether he was able to take phone calls?"

"Didn't say." Miss Mitkin blotted her lips carefully with a Kleenex. "Wasn't his wife, anyway. It was his daughter who called and left the message."

"The kid?" Burckhardt frowned. "I thought she was away at school."

"She called, that's all I know."

Burckhardt went back to his own office and stared distastefully at the unopened mail on his desk. He didn't like nightmares; they spoiled his whole day. He should have stayed in bed, like Barth.

* * * * *

A funny thing happened on his way home. There was a disturbance at the corner where he usually caught his bus-someone was screaming something about a new kind of deep-freeze —so he walked an extra block. He saw the bus coming and started to trot. But behind him, someone was calling his name. He looked over his shoulder; a small harried-looking man was hurrying toward him.

Burckhardt hesitated, and then recognized him. It was a casual acquaintance named Swanson. Burckhardt sourly observed that he had already missed the bus.

He said, "Hello."

Swanson's face was desperately eager. "Burckhardt?" he asked inquiringly, with an odd intensity. And then he just stood there silently, watching Burckhardt's face, with a burning eagerness that dwindled to a faint hope and died to a regret. He was searching for something, waiting for something, Burckhardt thought. But whatever it was he wanted, Burckhardt didn't know how to supply it.

Burckhardt coughed and said again, "Hello, Swanson."

Swanson didn't even acknowledge the greeting. He merely sighed a very deep sigh.

"Nothing doing," he mumbled, apparently to himself. He nodded abstractedly to Burckhardt and turned away.

Burckhardt watched the slumped shoulders disappear in the crowd. It was an *odd* sort of day, he thought, and one he didn't much like. Things weren't going right.

Riding home on the next bus, he brooded about it. It wasn't anything terrible or disastrous; it was something out of his experience entirely. You live your life, like any man, and you form a network of impressions and reactions. You *expect* things. When you open your medicine chest, your razor is expected to be on the second shelf; when you lock your front door, you expect to have to give it a slight extra tug to make it latch.

It isn't the things that are right and perfect in your life that make it familiar. It is the things that are just a little bit wrong-the sticking latch, the light switch at the head of the stairs that needs an extra push because the spring is old and weak, the rug that unfailingly skids underfoot.

It wasn't just that things were wrong with the pattern of Burckhardt's life; it was that the *wrong* things were wrong. For instance, Barth hadn't come into the office, yet Barth *always* came in.

Burckhardt brooded about it through dinner. He brooded about it, despite his wife's attempt to interest him in a game of bridge with the neighbors, all through the evening. The neighbors were people he liked-Anne and Farley Dennerman. He had known them all their lives. But they were odd and brooding, too, this night and he barely listened to Dennerman's complaints about not being able to get good phone service or his wife's comments on the disgusting variety of television commercials they had these days.

Burckhardt was well on the way to setting an all-time record for continuous abstraction when, around midnight, with a suddenness that surprised him-he was strangely *aware* of it happening-he turned over in his bed and, quickly and completely, fell asleep.

II

On the morning of June 15th, Burckhardt woke up screaming.

It was more real than any dream he had ever had in his life. He could still hear the explosion, feel the blast that crushed him against a wall. It did not seem right that he should be sitting bolt upright in bed in an undisturbed room.

His wife came pattering up the stairs. "Darling!" she cried. "What's the matter?"

He mumbled, "Nothing. Bad dream."

She relaxed, hand on heart. In an angry tone, she started to say: "You gave me such a shock —"

But a noise from outside interrupted her. There was a wail of sirens and a clang of bells; it was loud and shocking.

The Burckhardts stared at each other for a heartbeat, then hurried fearfully to the window.

There were no rumbling fire engines in the street, only a small panel truck, cruising slowly along. Flaring loudspeaker horns crowned its top. From them issued the screaming sound of sirens, growing in intensity, mixed with the rumble of heavy-duty engines and the sound of bells. It was a perfect record of fire engines arriving at a four-alarm blaze.

Burckhardt said in amazement, "Mary, that's against the law! Do you know what they're doing? They're playing records of a fire. What are they up to?"

"Maybe it's a practical joke," his wife offered.

"Joke? Waking up the whole neighborhood at six o'clock in the morning?" He shook his head. "The police will be here in ten minutes," he predicted. "Wait and see."

But the police weren't —not in ten minutes, or at all. Whoever the pranksters in the car were, they apparently had a police permit for their games.

The car took a position in the middle of the block and stood silent for a few minutes. Then there was a crackle from the speaker, and a giant voice chanted:

"Feckle Freezers!

Feckle Freezers!

Gotta have a

Feckle Freezer!

Feckle, Feckle, Feckle,

Feckle, Feckle, Feckle —"

It went on and on. Every house on the block had faces staring out of windows by then. The voice was not merely loud; it was nearly deafening.

Burckhardt shouted to his wife, over the uproar, "What the hell is a Feckle Freezer?"

"Some kind of a freezer, I guess, dear," she shrieked back unhelpfully.

* * * * *

Abruptly the noise stopped and the truck stood silent. It was still misty morning; the Sun's rays came horizontally across the rooftops. It was impossible to believe that, a moment ago, the silent block had been bellowing the name of a freezer.

"A crazy advertising trick," Burckhardt said bitterly. He yawned and turned away from the window. "Might as well get dressed. I guess that's the end of —"

The bellow caught him from behind; it was almost like a hard slap on the ears. A harsh, sneering voice, louder than the arch-angel's trumpet, howled:

"Have you got a freezer? *It stinks!* If it isn't a Feckle Freezer, *it stinks!* If it's a last year's Feckle Freezer, *it stinks!* Only this year's Feckle Freezer is any good at all! You know who owns an Ajax Freezer? Fairies own Ajax Freezers! You know who owns a Triplecold Freezer? Commies own Triplecold Freezers! Every freezer but a brand-new Feckle Freezer *stinks!*"

The voice screamed inarticulately with rage. "I'm warning you! Get out and buy a Feckle Freezer right away! Hurry up! Hurry for Feckle! Hurry for Feckle! Hurry, hurry, hurry, Feckle, Feckle, Feckle, Feckle, Feckle, Feckle...."

It stopped eventually. Burckhardt licked his lips. He started to say to his wife, "Maybe we ought to call the police about —" when the speakers erupted again. It caught him off guard; it was intended to catch him off guard. It screamed:

"Feckle, Feckle, Feckle, Feckle, Feckle, Feckle, Feckle, Feckle. Cheap freezers ruin your food. You'll get sick and throw up. You'll get sick and die. Buy a Feckle, Feckle, Feckle, Feckle! Ever take a piece of meat out of the freezer you've got and see how rotten and moldy it is? Buy a Feckle, Feckle, Feckle, Feckle, Feckle. Do you want to eat rotten, stinking food? Or do you want to wise up and buy a Feckle, Feckle, Feckle —"

That did it. With fingers that kept stabbing the wrong holes, Burckhardt finally managed to dial the local police station. He got a busy signal-it was apparent that he was not the only one with the same idea-and while he was shakingly dialing again, the noise outside stopped.

He looked out the window. The truck was gone.

* * * * *

Burckhardt loosened his tie and ordered another Frosty-Flip from the waiter. If only they wouldn't keep the Crystal Cafe so *hot!* The new paint job-searing reds and blinding yellows-was bad enough, but someone seemed to have the delusion that this was January instead of June; the place was a good ten degrees warmer than outside.

He swallowed the Frosty-Flip in two gulps. It had a kind of peculiar flavor, he thought, but not bad. It certainly cooled you off, just as the waiter had promised. He reminded himself to pick up a carton of them on the way home; Mary might like them. She was always interested in something new.

He stood up awkwardly as the girl came across the restaurant toward him. She was the most beautiful thing he had ever seen in Tylerton. Chin-height, honey-blonde hair and a figure that-well, it was all hers. There was no doubt in the world that the dress that clung to her was the only thing she wore. He felt as if he were blushing as she greeted him.

"Mr. Burckhardt." The voice was like distant tomtoms. "It's wonderful of you to let me see you, after this morning."

He cleared his throat. "Not at all. Won't you sit down, Miss —"

"April Horn," she murmured, sitting down-beside him, not where he had pointed on the other side of the table. "Call me April, won't you?"

She was wearing some kind of perfume, Burckhardt noted with what little of his mind was functioning at all. It didn't seem fair that she should be using perfume as well as everything else. He came to with a start and realized that the waiter was leaving with an order for *filets mignon* for two.

"Hey!" he objected.

"Please, Mr. Burckhardt." Her shoulder was against his, her face was turned to him, her breath was warm, her expression was tender and solicitous. "This is all on the Feckle Corporation. Please let them-it's the *least* they can do."

He felt her hand burrowing into his pocket.

"I put the price of the meal into your pocket," she whispered conspiratorially. "Please do that for me, won't you? I mean I'd appreciate it if you'd pay the waiter —I'm old-fashioned about things like that."

She smiled meltingly, then became mock-businesslike. "But you must take the money," she insisted. "Why, you're letting Feckle off lightly if you do! You could sue them for every nickel they've got, disturbing your sleep like that."

* * * * *

With a dizzy feeling, as though he had just seen someone make a rabbit disappear into a top hat, he said, "Why, it really wasn't so bad, uh, April. A little noisy, maybe, but —"

"Oh, Mr. Burckhardt!" The blue eyes were wide and admiring. "I knew you'd understand. It's just that-well, it's such a *wonderful* freezer that some of the outside men get carried away, so to speak. As soon as the main office found out about what happened, they sent representatives around to every house on the block to apologize. Your wife told us where we could phone you-and I'm so very pleased that you were willing to let me have lunch with you, so that I could apologize, too. Because truly, Mr. Burckhardt, it is a *fine* freezer.

"I shouldn't tell you this, but —" the blue eyes were shyly lowered —"I'd do almost anything for Feckle Freezers. It's more than a job to me." She looked up. She was enchanting. "I bet you think I'm silly, don't you?"

Burckhardt coughed. "Well, I —"

"Oh, you don't want to be unkind!" She shook her head. "No, don't pretend. You think it's silly. But really, Mr. Burckhardt, you wouldn't think so if you knew more about the Feckle. Let me show you this little booklet —"

Burckhardt got back from lunch a full hour late. It wasn't only the girl who delayed him. There had been a curious interview with a little man named Swanson, whom he barely knew, who had stopped him with desperate urgency on the street-and then left him cold.

But it didn't matter much. Mr. Barth, for the first time since Burckhardt had worked there, was out for the day-leaving Burckhardt stuck with the quarterly tax returns.

What did matter, though, was that somehow he had signed a purchase order for a twelve-cubic-foot Feckle Freezer, upright model, self-defrosting, list price $625, with a ten per cent "courtesy" discount —"Because of that *horrid* affair this morning, Mr. Burckhardt," she had said.

And he wasn't sure how he could explain it to his wife.

* * * * *

He needn't have worried. As he walked in the front door, his wife said almost immediately, "I wonder if we can't afford a new freezer, dear. There was a man here to apologize about that noise and-well, we got to talking and —"

She had signed a purchase order, too.

It had been the damnedest day, Burckhardt thought later, on his way up to bed. But the day wasn't done with him yet. At the head of the stairs, the weakened spring in the electric light switch refused to click at all. He snapped it back and forth angrily and, of course, succeeded in jarring the tumbler out of its pins. The wires shorted and every light in the house went out.

"Damn!" said Guy Burckhardt.

"Fuse?" His wife shrugged sleepily. "Let it go till the morning, dear."

Burckhardt shook his head. "You go back to bed. I'll be right along."

It wasn't so much that he cared about fixing the fuse, but he was too restless for sleep. He disconnected the bad switch with a screwdriver, stumbled down into the black kitchen, found the flashlight and climbed gingerly down the cellar stairs. He located a spare fuse, pushed an empty trunk over to the fuse box to stand on and twisted out the old fuse.

When the new one was in, he heard the starting click and steady drone of the refrigerator in the kitchen overhead.

He headed back to the steps, and stopped.

Where the old trunk had been, the cellar floor gleamed oddly bright. He inspected it in the flashlight beam. It was metal!

"Son of a gun," said Guy Burckhardt. He shook his head unbelievingly. He peered closer, rubbed the edges of the metallic patch with his thumb and acquired an annoying cut-the edges were *sharp*.

The stained cement floor of the cellar was a thin shell. He found a hammer and cracked it off in a dozen spots-everywhere was metal.

The whole cellar was a copper box. Even the cement-brick walls were false fronts over a metal sheath!

* * * * *

Baffled, he attacked one of the foundation beams. That, at least, was real wood. The glass in the cellar windows was real glass.

He sucked his bleeding thumb and tried the base of the cellar stairs. Real wood. He chipped at the bricks under the oil burner. Real bricks. The retaining walls, the floor-they were faked.

It was as though someone had shored up the house with a frame of metal and then laboriously concealed the evidence.

The biggest surprise was the upside-down boat hull that blocked the rear half of the cellar, relic of a brief home workshop period that Burckhardt had gone through a couple of years before. From above, it looked perfectly normal. Inside, though, where there should have been thwarts and seats and lockers, there was a mere tangle of braces, rough and unfinished.

"But I *built* that!" Burckhardt exclaimed, forgetting his thumb. He leaned against the hull dizzily, trying to think this thing through. For reasons beyond his comprehension, someone had taken his boat and his cellar away, maybe his whole house, and replaced them with a clever mock-up of the real thing.

"That's crazy," he said to the empty cellar. He stared around in the light of the flash. He whispered, "What in the name of Heaven would anybody do that for?"

Reason refused an answer; there wasn't any reasonable answer. For long minutes, Burckhardt contemplated the uncertain picture of his own sanity.

He peered under the boat again, hoping to reassure himself that it was a mistake, just his imagination. But the sloppy, unfinished bracing was unchanged. He crawled under for a better look, feeling the rough wood incredulously. Utterly impossible!

He switched off the flashlight and started to wriggle out. But he didn't make it. In the moment between the command to his legs to move and the crawling out, he felt a sudden draining weariness flooding through him.

Consciousness went-not easily, but as though it were being taken away, and Guy Burckhardt was asleep.

III

On the morning of June 16th, Guy Burckhardt woke up in a cramped position huddled under the hull of the boat in his basement-and raced upstairs to find it was June 15th.

The first thing he had done was to make a frantic, hasty inspection of the boat hull, the faked cellar floor, the imitation stone. They were all as he had remembered them-all completely unbelievable.

The kitchen was its placid, unexciting self. The electric clock was purring soberly around the dial. Almost six o'clock, it said. His wife would be waking at any moment.

Burckhardt flung open the front door and stared out into the quiet street. The morning paper was tossed carelessly against the steps-and as he retrieved it, he noticed that this was the 15th day of June.

But that was impossible. *Yesterday* was the 15th of June. It was not a date one would forget-it was quarterly tax-return day.

He went back into the hall and picked up the telephone; he dialed for Weather Information, and got a well-modulated chant: " —and cooler, some showers. Barometric pressure thirty point zero four, rising ... United States Weather Bureau forecast for June 15th. Warm and sunny, with high around —"

He hung the phone up. June 15th.

"Holy heaven!" Burckhardt said prayerfully. Things were very odd indeed. He heard the ring of his wife's alarm and bounded up the stairs.

Mary Burckhardt was sitting upright in bed with the terrified, uncomprehending stare of someone just waking out of a nightmare.

"Oh!" she gasped, as her husband came in the room. "Darling, I just had the most *terrible* dream! It was like an explosion and —"

"Again?" Burckhardt asked, not very sympathetically. "Mary, something's funny! I *knew* there was something wrong all day yesterday and —"

He went on to tell her about the copper box that was the cellar, and the odd mock-up some-one had made of his boat. Mary looked astonished, then alarmed, then placatory and uneasy.

She said, "Dear, are you *sure*? Because I was cleaning that old trunk out just last week and I didn't notice anything."

"Positive!" said Guy Burckhardt. "I dragged it over to the wall to step on it to put a new fuse in after we blew the lights out and —"

"After we what?" Mary was looking more than merely alarmed.

"After we blew the lights out. You know, when the switch at the head of the stairs stuck. I went down to the cellar and —"

Mary sat up in bed. "Guy, the switch didn't stick. I turned out the lights myself last night."

Burckhardt glared at his wife. "Now I *know* you didn't! Come here and take a look!"

He stalked out to the landing and dramatically pointed to the bad switch, the one that he had unscrewed and left hanging the night before....

Only it wasn't. It was as it had always been. Unbelieving, Burckhardt pressed it and the lights sprang up in both halls.

* * * * *

Mary, looking pale and worried, left him to go down to the kitchen and start breakfast. Burck-hardt stood staring at the switch for a long time. His mental processes were gone beyond the point of disbelief and shock; they simply were not functioning.

He shaved and dressed and ate his breakfast in a state of numb introspection. Mary didn't disturb him; she was apprehensive and soothing. She kissed him good-by as he hurried out to the bus without another word.

Miss Mitkin, at the reception desk, greeted him with a yawn. "Morning," she said drowsily. "Mr. Barth won't be in today."

Burckhardt started to say something, but checked himself. She would not know that Barth hadn't been in yesterday, either, because she was tearing a June 14th pad off her calendar to make way for the "new" June 15th sheet.

He staggered to his own desk and stared unseeingly at the morning's mail. It had not even been opened yet, but he knew that the Factory Distributors envelope contained an order for twenty thousand feet of the new acoustic tile, and the one from Finebeck & Sons was a complaint.

After a long while, he forced himself to open them. They were.

By lunchtime, driven by a desperate sense of urgency, Burckhardt made Miss Mitkin take her lunch hour first-the June-fifteenth-that-was-yesterday, *he* had gone first. She went, looking vaguely worried about his strained insistence, but it made no difference to Burckhardt's mood.

The phone rang and Burckhardt picked it up abstractedly. "Contro Chemicals Downtown, Burckhardt speaking."

The voice said, "This is Swanson," and stopped.

Burckhardt waited expectantly, but that was all. He said, "Hello?"

Again the pause. Then Swanson asked in sad resignation, "Still nothing, eh?"

"Nothing what? Swanson, is there something you want? You came up to me yesterday and went through this routine. You —"

The voice crackled: "Burckhardt! Oh, my good heavens, *you remember*! Stay right there —I'll be down in half an hour!"

"What's this all about?"

"Never mind," the little man said exultantly. "Tell you about it when I see you. Don't say any more over the phone-somebody may be listening. Just wait there. Say, hold on a minute. Will you be alone in the office?"

"Well, no. Miss Mitkin will probably —"

"Hell. Look, Burckhardt, where do you eat lunch? Is it good and noisy?"

"Why, I suppose so. The Crystal Cafe. It's just about a block —"

"I know where it is. Meet you in half an hour!" And the receiver clicked.

* * * * *

The Crystal Cafe was no longer painted red, but the temperature was still up. And they had added piped-in music interspersed with commercials. The advertisements were for Frosty-Flip, Marlin Cigarettes —"They're sanitized," the announcer purred-and something called Choco-Bite candy bars that Burckhardt couldn't remember ever having heard of before. But he heard more about them quickly enough.

While he was waiting for Swanson to show up, a girl in the cellophane skirt of a nightclub cigarette vendor came through the restaurant with a tray of tiny scarlet-wrapped candies.

"Choco-Bites are *tangy*," she was murmuring as she came close to his table. "Choco-Bites are *tangier* than tangy!"

Burckhardt, intent on watching for the strange little man who had phoned him, paid little attention. But as she scattered a handful of the confections over the table next to his, smiling at the occupants, he caught a glimpse of her and turned to stare.

"Why, Miss Horn!" he said.

The girl dropped her tray of candies.

Burckhardt rose, concerned over the girl. "Is something wrong?"

But she fled.

The manager of the restaurant was staring suspiciously at Burckhardt, who sank back in his seat and tried to look inconspicuous. He hadn't insulted the girl! Maybe she was just a very strictly reared young lady, he thought-in spite of the long bare legs under the cellophane skirt-and when he addressed her, she thought he was a masher.

Ridiculous idea. Burckhardt scowled uneasily and picked up his menu.

"Burckhardt!" It was a shrill whisper.

Burckhardt looked up over the top of his menu, startled. In the seat across from him, the little man named Swanson was sitting, tensely poised.

"Burckhardt!" the little man whispered again. "Let's get out of here! They're on to you now. If you want to stay alive, come on!"

There was no arguing with the man. Burckhardt gave the hovering manager a sick, apologetic smile and followed Swanson out. The little man seemed to know where he was going. In the street, he clutched Burckhardt by the elbow and hurried him off down the block.

"Did you see her?" he demanded. "That Horn woman, in the phone booth? She'll have them here in five minutes, believe me, so hurry it up!"

* * * * *

Although the street was full of people and cars, nobody was paying any attention to Burckhardt and Swanson. The air had a nip in it-more like October than June, Burckhardt thought, in spite of the weather bureau. And he felt like a fool, following this mad little man down the street, running away from some "them" toward-toward what? The little man might be crazy, but he was afraid. And the fear was infectious.

"In here!" panted the little man.

It was another restaurant-more of a bar, really, and a sort of second-rate place that Burckhardt had never patronized.

"Right straight through," Swanson whispered; and Burckhardt, like a biddable boy, side-stepped through the mass of tables to the far end of the restaurant.

It was "L"-shaped, with a front on two streets at right angles to each other. They came out on the side street, Swanson staring coldly back at the question-looking cashier, and crossed to the opposite sidewalk.

They were under the marquee of a movie theater. Swanson's expression began to relax.

"Lost them!" he crowed softly. "We're almost there."

He stepped up to the window and bought two tickets. Burckhardt trailed him in to the theater. It was a weekday matinee and the place was almost empty. From the screen came sounds of gunfire and horse's hoofs. A solitary usher, leaning against a bright brass rail, looked briefly at them and went back to staring boredly at the picture as Swanson led Burckhardt down a flight of carpeted marble steps.

They were in the lounge and it was empty. There was a door for men and one for ladies; and there was a third door, marked "MANAGER" in gold letters. Swanson listened at the door, and gently opened it and peered inside.

"Okay," he said, gesturing.

Burckhardt followed him through an empty office, to another door —a closet, probably, because it was unmarked.

But it was no closet. Swanson opened it warily, looked inside, then motioned Burckhardt to follow.

It was a tunnel, metal-walled, brightly lit. Empty, it stretched vacantly away in both directions from them.

Burckhardt looked wondering around. One thing he knew and knew full well:

No such tunnel belonged under Tylerton.

* * * * *

There was a room off the tunnel with chairs and a desk and what looked like television screens. Swanson slumped in a chair, panting.

"We're all right for a while here," he wheezed. "They don't come here much any more. If they do, we'll hear them and we can hide."

"Who?" demanded Burckhardt.

The little man said, "Martians!" His voice cracked on the word and the life seemed to go out of him. In morose tones, he went on: "Well, I think they're Martians. Although you could be right, you know; I've had plenty of time to think it over these last few weeks, after they got you, and it's possible they're Russians after all. Still —"

"Start from the beginning. Who got me when?"

Swanson sighed. "So we have to go through the whole thing again. All right. It was about two months ago that you banged on my door, late at night. You were all beat up-scared silly. You begged me to help you —"

"*I* did?"

"Naturally you don't remember any of this. Listen and you'll understand. You were talking a blue streak about being captured and threatened, and your wife being dead and coming back to life, and all kinds of mixed-up nonsense. I thought you were crazy. But-well, I've always had a lot of respect for you. And you begged me to hide you and I have this darkroom, you know. It locks from the inside only. I put the lock on myself. So we went in there-just to humor you-and along about midnight, which was only fifteen or twenty minutes after, we passed out."

"Passed out?"

Swanson nodded. "Both of us. It was like being hit with a sandbag. Look, didn't that happen to you again last night?"

"I guess it did," Burckhardt shook his head uncertainly.

"Sure. And then all of a sudden we were awake again, and you said you were going to show me something funny, and we went out and bought a paper. And the date on it was June 15th."

"June 15th? But that's today! I mean —"

"You got it, friend. It's *always* today!"

It took time to penetrate.

Burckhardt said wonderingly, "You've hidden out in that darkroom for how many weeks?"

"How can I tell? Four or five, maybe. I lost count. And every day the same-always the 15th of June, always my landlady, Mrs. Keefer, is sweeping the front steps, always the same headline in the papers at the corner. It gets monotonous, friend."

IV

It was Burckhardt's idea and Swanson despised it, but he went along. He was the type who always went along.

"It's dangerous," he grumbled worriedly. "Suppose somebody comes by? They'll spot us and —"

"What have we got to lose?"

Swanson shrugged. "It's dangerous," he said again. But he went along.

Burckhardt's idea was very simple. He was sure of only one thing-the tunnel went some-where. Martians or Russians, fantastic plot or crazy hallucination, whatever was wrong with Tylerton had an explanation, and the place to look for it was at the end of the tunnel.

They jogged along. It was more than a mile before they began to see an end. They were in luck-at least no one came through the tunnel to spot them. But Swanson had said that it was only at certain hours that the tunnel seemed to be in use.

Always the fifteenth of June. Why? Burckhardt asked himself. Never mind the how. *Why?*

And falling asleep, completely involuntarily-everyone at the same time, it seemed. And not remembering, never remembering anything-Swanson had said how eagerly he saw Burckhardt again, the morning after Burckhardt had incautiously waited five minutes too many before retreating into the darkroom. When Swanson had come to, Burckhardt was gone. Swanson had seen him in the street that afternoon, but Burckhardt had remembered nothing.

And Swanson had lived his mouse's existence for weeks, hiding in the woodwork at night, stealing out by day to search for Burckhardt in pitiful hope, scurrying around the fringe of life, trying to keep from the deadly eyes of *them*.

Them. One of "them" was the girl named April Horn. It was by seeing her walk carelessly into a telephone booth and never come out that Swanson had found the tunnel. Another was the man at the cigar stand in Burckhardt's office building. There were more, at least a dozen that Swanson knew of or suspected.

They were easy enough to spot, once you knew where to look-for they, alone in Tylerton, changed their roles from day to day. Burckhardt was on that 8:51 bus, every morning of every day-that-was-June-15th, never different by a hair or a moment. But April Horn was sometimes gaudy in the cellophane skirt, giving away candy or cigarettes; sometimes plainly dressed; sometimes not seen by Swanson at all.

Russians? Martians? Whatever they were, what could they be hoping to gain from this mad masquerade?

Burckhardt didn't know the answer-but perhaps it lay beyond the door at the end of the tunnel. They listened carefully and heard distant sounds that could not quite be made out, but nothing that seemed dangerous. They slipped through.

And, through a wide chamber and up a flight of steps, they found they were in what Burckhardt recognized as the Contro Chemicals plant.

* * * * *

Nobody was in sight. By itself, that was not so very odd-the automatized factory had never had very many persons in it. But Burckhardt remembered, from his single visit, the endless, ceaseless busyness of the plant, the valves that opened and closed, the vats that emptied themselves and filled themselves and stirred and cooked and chemically tasted the bubbling liquids they held inside themselves. The plant was never populated, but it was never still.

Only-now it *was* still. Except for the distant sounds, there was no breath of life in it. The captive electronic minds were sending out no commands; the coils and relays were at rest.

Burckhardt said, "Come on." Swanson reluctantly followed him through the tangled aisles of stainless steel columns and tanks.

They walked as though they were in the presence of the dead. In a way, they were, for what were the automatons that once had run the factory, if not corpses? The machines were controlled by computers that were really not computers at all, but the electronic analogues of living brains. And if they were turned off, were they not dead? For each had once been a human mind.

Take a master petroleum chemist, infinitely skilled in the separation of crude oil into its fractions. Strap him down, probe into his brain with searching electronic needles. The machine scans the patterns of the mind, translates what it sees into charts and sine waves. Impress these same waves on a robot computer and you have your chemist. Or a thousand copies of your chemist, if you wish, with all of his knowledge and skill, and no human limitations at all.

Put a dozen copies of him into a plant and they will run it all, twenty-four hours a day, seven days of every week, never tiring, never overlooking anything, never forgetting....

Swanson stepped up closer to Burckhardt. "I'm scared," he said.

They were across the room now and the sounds were louder. They were not machine sounds, but voices; Burckhardt moved cautiously up to a door and dared to peer around it.

It was a smaller room, lined with television screens, each one —a dozen or more, at least-with a man or woman sitting before it, staring into the screen and dictating notes into a recorder. The viewers dialed from scene to scene; no two screens ever showed the same picture.

The pictures seemed to have little in common. One was a store, where a girl dressed like April Horn was demonstrating home freezers. One was a series of shots of kitchens. Burckhardt caught a glimpse of what looked like the cigar stand in his office building.

It was baffling and Burckhardt would have loved to stand there and puzzle it out, but it was too busy a place. There was the chance that someone would look their way or walk out and find them.

* * * * *

They found another room. This one was empty. It was an office, large and sumptuous. It had a desk, littered with papers. Burckhardt stared at them, briefly at first-then, as the words on one of them caught his attention, with incredulous fascination.

He snatched up the topmost sheet, scanned it, and another, while Swanson was frenziedly searching through the drawers.

Burckhardt swore unbelievingly and dropped the papers to the desk.

Swanson, hardly noticing, yelped with delight: "Look!" He dragged a gun from the desk. "And it's loaded, too!"

Burckhardt stared at him blankly, trying to assimilate what he had read. Then, as he realized what Swanson had said, Burckhardt's eyes sparked. "Good man!" he cried. "We'll take it. We're getting out of here with that gun, Swanson. And we're going to the police! Not the cops in Tylerton, but the F.B.I., maybe. Take a look at this!"

The sheaf he handed Swanson was headed: "Test Area Progress Report. Subject: Marlin Cigarettes Campaign." It was mostly tabulated figures that made little sense to Burckhardt and Swanson, but at the end was a summary that said:

> Although Test 47-K3 pulled nearly double the number of new users of any of the other tests conducted, it probably cannot be used in the field because of local sound-truck control ordinances.
>
> The tests in the 47-K12 group were second best and our recommendation is that retests be conducted in this appeal, testing each of the three best campaigns with and without the addition of sampling techniques.
>
> An alternative suggestion might be to proceed directly with the top appeal in the K12 series, if the client is unwilling to go to the expense of additional tests.
>
> All of these forecast expectations have an 80% probability of being within one-half of one per cent of results forecast, and more than 99% probability of coming within 5%.

Swanson looked up from the paper into Burckhardt's eyes. "I don't get it," he complained.

Burckhardt said, "I don't blame you. It's crazy, but it fits the facts, Swanson, *it fits the facts.* They aren't Russians and they aren't Martians. These people are advertising men! Somehow-heaven knows how they did it-they've taken Tylerton over. They've got us, all of us, you and me and twenty or thirty thousand other people, right under their thumbs.

"Maybe they hypnotize us and maybe it's something else; but however they do it, what happens is that they let us live a day at a time. They pour advertising into us the whole damned day long. And at the end of the day, they see what happened-and then they wash the day out of our minds and start again the next day with different advertising."

* * * * *

Swanson's jaw was hanging. He managed to close it and swallow. "Nuts!" he said flatly.

Burckhardt shook his head. "Sure, it sounds crazy-but this whole thing is crazy. How else would you explain it? You can't deny that most of Tylerton lives the same day over and over again. You've *seen* it! And that's the crazy part and we have to admit that that's true-unless we are the crazy ones. And once you admit that somebody, somehow, knows how to accomplish that, the rest of it makes all kinds of sense.

"Think of it, Swanson! They test every last detail before they spend a nickel on advertising! Do you have any idea what that means? Lord knows how much money is involved, but I know for a fact that some companies spend twenty or thirty million dollars a year on advertising. Multiply it, say, by a hundred companies. Say that every one of them learns how to cut its advertising cost by only ten per cent. And that's peanuts, believe me!

"If they know in advance what's going to work, they can cut their costs in half-maybe to less than half, I don't know. But that's saving two or three hundred million dollars a year-and if they pay only ten or twenty per cent of that for the use of Tylerton, it's still dirt cheap for them and a fortune for whoever took over Tylerton."

Swanson licked his lips. "You mean," he offered hesitantly, "that we're a —well, a kind of captive audience?"

Burckhardt frowned. "Not exactly." He thought for a minute. "You know how a doctor tests something like penicillin? He sets up a series of little colonies of germs on gelatine disks and he tries the stuff on one after another, changing it a little each time. Well, that's us-we're the germs, Swanson. Only it's even more efficient than that. They don't have to test more than one colony, because they can use it over and over again."

It was too hard for Swanson to take in. He only said: "What do we do about it?"

"We go to the police. They can't use human beings for guinea pigs!"

"How do we get to the police?"

Burckhardt hesitated. "I think —" he began slowly. "Sure. This place is the office of some-body important. We've got a gun. We'll stay right here until he comes along. And he'll get us out of here."

Simple and direct. Swanson subsided and found a place to sit, against the wall, out of sight of the door. Burckhardt took up a position behind the door itself—

And waited.

* * * * *

The wait was not as long as it might have been. Half an hour, perhaps. Then Burckhardt heard approaching voices and had time for a swift whisper to Swanson before he flattened himself against the wall.

It was a man's voice, and a girl's. The man was saying, " —reason why you couldn't report on the phone? You're ruining your whole day's test! What the devil's the matter with you, Janet?"

"I'm sorry, Mr. Dorchin," she said in a sweet, clear tone. "I thought it was important."

The man grumbled, "Important! One lousy unit out of twenty-one thousand."

"But it's the Burckhardt one, Mr. Dorchin. Again. And the way he got out of sight, he must have had some help."

"All right, all right. It doesn't matter, Janet; the Choco-Bite program is ahead of schedule anyhow. As long as you're this far, come on in the office and make out your worksheet. And don't worry about the Burckhardt business. He's probably just wandering around. We'll pick him up tonight and —"

They were inside the door. Burckhardt kicked it shut and pointed the gun.

"That's what you think," he said triumphantly.

It was worth the terrified hours, the bewildered sense of insanity, the confusion and fear. It was the most satisfying sensation Burckhardt had ever had in his life. The expression on the man's face was one he had read about but never actually seen: Dorchin's mouth fell open and his eyes went wide, and though he managed to make a sound that might have been a question, it was not in words.

The girl was almost as surprised. And Burckhardt, looking at her, knew why her voice had been so familiar. The girl was the one who had introduced herself to him as April Horn.

Dorchin recovered himself quickly. "Is this the one?" he asked sharply.

The girl said, "Yes."

Dorchin nodded. "I take it back. You were right. Uh, you-Burckhardt. What do you want?"

* * * * *

Swanson piped up, "Watch him! He might have another gun."

"Search him then," Burckhardt said. "I'll tell you what we want, Dorchin. We want you to come along with us to the FBI and explain to them how you can get away with kidnapping twenty thousand people."

"Kidnapping?" Dorchin snorted. "That's ridiculous, man! Put that gun away-you can't get away with this!"

Burckhardt hefted the gun grimly. "I think I can."

Dorchin looked furious and sick-but, oddly, not afraid. "Damn it —" he started to bellow, then closed his mouth and swallowed. "Listen," he said persuasively, "you're making a big mistake. I haven't kidnapped anybody, believe me!"

"I don't believe you," said Burckhardt bluntly. "Why should I?"

"But it's true! Take my word for it!"

Burckhardt shook his head. "The FBI can take your word if they like. We'll find out. Now how do we get out of here?"

Dorchin opened his mouth to argue.

Burckhardt blazed: "Don't get in my way! I'm willing to kill you if I have to. Don't you understand that? I've gone through two days of hell and every second of it I blame on you. Kill you? It would be a pleasure and I don't have a thing in the world to lose! Get us out of here!"

Dorchin's face went suddenly opaque. He seemed about to move; but the blonde girl he had called Janet slipped between him and the gun.

"Please!" she begged Burckhardt. "You don't understand. You mustn't shoot!"

"Get out of my way!"

"But, Mr. Burckhardt —"

She never finished. Dorchin, his face unreadable, headed for the door. Burckhardt had been pushed one degree too far. He swung the gun, bellowing. The girl called out sharply. He pulled the trigger. Closing on him with pity and pleading in her eyes, she came again between the gun and the man.

Burckhardt aimed low instinctively, to cripple, not to kill. But his aim was not good.

The pistol bullet caught her in the pit of the stomach.

* * * * *

Dorchin was out and away, the door slamming behind him, his footsteps racing into the distance.

Burckhardt hurled the gun across the room and jumped to the girl.

Swanson was moaning. "That finishes us, Burckhardt. Oh, why did you do it? We could have got away. We could have gone to the police. We were practically out of here! We —"

Burckhardt wasn't listening. He was kneeling beside the girl. She lay flat on her back, arms helter-skelter. There was no blood, hardly any sign of the wound; but the position in which she lay was one that no living human being could have held.

Yet she wasn't dead.

She wasn't dead-and Burckhardt, frozen beside her, thought: *She isn't alive, either.*

There was no pulse, but there was a rhythmic ticking of the outstretched fingers of one hand.

There was no sound of breathing, but there was a hissing, sizzling noise.

The eyes were open and they were looking at Burckhardt. There was neither fear nor pain in them, only a pity deeper than the Pit.

She said, through lips that writhed erratically, "Don't —worry, Mr. Burckhardt. I'm — all right."

Burckhardt rocked back on his haunches, staring. Where there should have been blood, there was a clean break of a substance that was not flesh; and a curl of thin golden-copper wire.

Burckhardt moistened his lips.

"You're a robot," he said.

The girl tried to nod. The twitching lips said, "I am. And so are you."

V

Swanson, after a single inarticulate sound, walked over to the desk and sat staring at the wall. Burckhardt rocked back and forth beside the shattered puppet on the floor. He had no words.

The girl managed to say, "I'm —sorry all this happened." The lovely lips twisted into a rictus sneer, frightening on that smooth young face, until she got them under control. "Sorry," she said again. "The-nerve center was right about where the bullet hit. Makes it difficult to-control this body."

Burckhardt nodded automatically, accepting the apology. Robots. It was obvious, now that he knew it. In hindsight, it was inevitable. He thought of his mystic notions of hypnosis or Martians or something stranger still-idiotic, for the simple fact of created robots fitted the facts better and more economically.

All the evidence had been before him. The automatized factory, with its transplanted minds-why not transplant a mind into a humanoid robot, give it its original owner's features and form?

Could it know that it was a robot?

"All of us," Burckhardt said, hardly aware that he spoke out loud. "My wife and my secretary and you and the neighbors. All of us the same."

"No." The voice was stronger. "Not exactly the same, all of us. I chose it, you see. I —" this time the convulsed lips were not a random contortion of the nerves —"I was an ugly woman, Mr. Burckhardt, and nearly sixty years old. Life had passed me. And when Mr. Dorchin offered me the chance to live again as a beautiful girl, I jumped at the opportunity. Believe me, I *jumped*, in spite of its disadvantages. My flesh body is still alive-it is sleeping, while I am here. I could go back to it. But I never do."

"And the rest of us?"

"Different, Mr. Burckhardt. I work here. I'm carrying out Mr. Dorchin's orders, mapping the results of the advertising tests, watching you and the others live as he makes you live. I do it by choice, but you have no choice. Because, you see, you are dead."

"Dead?" cried Burckhardt; it was almost a scream.

The blue eyes looked at him unwinkingly and he knew that it was no lie. He swallowed, marveling at the intricate mechanisms that let him swallow, and sweat, and eat.

He said: "Oh. The explosion in my dream."

"It was no dream. You are right-the explosion. That was real and this plant was the cause of it. The storage tanks let go and what the blast didn't get, the fumes killed a little later. But almost everyone died in the blast, twenty-one thousand persons. You died with them and that was Dorchin's chance."

"The damned ghoul!" said Burckhardt.

* * * * *

The twisted shoulders shrugged with an odd grace. "Why? You were gone. And you and all the others were what Dorchin wanted —a whole town, a perfect slice of America. It's as easy to transfer a pattern from a dead brain as a living one. Easier-the dead can't say no. Oh, it took work and money-the town was a wreck-but it was possible to rebuild it entirely, especially because it wasn't necessary to have all the details exact.

"There were the homes where even the brains had been utterly destroyed, and those are empty inside, and the cellars that needn't be too perfect, and the streets that hardly matter. And anyway, it only has to last for one day. The same day-June 15th-over and over again; and if someone finds something a little wrong, somehow, the discovery won't have time to snowball, wreck the validity of the tests, because all errors are canceled out at midnight."

The face tried to smile. "That's the dream, Mr. Burckhardt, that day of June 15th, because you never really lived it. It's a present from Mr. Dorchin, a dream that he gives you and then takes back at the end of the day, when he has all his figures on how many of you responded to what variation of which appeal, and the maintenance crews go down the tunnel to go through the whole city, washing out the new dream with their little electronic drains, and then the dream starts all over again. On June 15th.

"Always June 15th, because June 14th is the last day any of you can remember alive. Sometimes the crews miss someone-as they missed you, because you were under your boat. But it doesn't matter. The ones who are missed give themselves away if they show it-and if they don't, it doesn't affect the test. But they don't drain us, the ones of us who work for Dorchin. We sleep when the power is turned off, just as you do. When we wake up, though, we remember." The face contorted wildly. "If I could only forget!"

Burckhardt said unbelievingly, "All this to sell merchandise! It must have cost millions!"

The robot called April Horn said, "It did. But it has made millions for Dorchin, too. And that's not the end of it. Once he finds the master words that make people act, do you suppose he will stop with that? Do you suppose —"

The door opened, interrupting her. Burckhardt whirled. Belatedly remembering Dorchin's flight, he raised the gun.

"Don't shoot," ordered the voice calmly. It was not Dorchin; it was another robot, this one not disguised with the clever plastics and cosmetics, but shining plain. It said metallically: "Forget it, Burckhardt. You're not accomplishing anything. Give me that gun before you do any more damage. Give it to me *now*."

* * * * *

Burckhardt bellowed angrily. The gleam on this robot torso was steel; Burckhardt was not at all sure that his bullets would pierce it, or do much harm if they did. He would have put it to the test —

But from behind him came a whimpering, scurrying whirlwind; its name was Swanson, hysterical with fear. He catapulted into Burckhardt and sent him sprawling, the gun flying free.

"Please!" begged Swanson incoherently, prostrate before the steel robot. "He would have shot you-please don't hurt me! Let me work for you, like that girl. I'll do anything, anything you tell me —"

The robot voice said. "We don't need your help." It took two precise steps and stood over the gun-and spurned it, left it lying on the floor.

The wrecked blonde robot said, without emotion, "I doubt that I can hold out much longer, Mr. Dorchin."

"Disconnect if you have to," replied the steel robot.

Burckhardt blinked. "But you're not Dorchin!"

The steel robot turned deep eyes on him. "I am," it said. "Not in the flesh-but this is the body I am using at the moment. I doubt that you can damage this one with the gun. The other robot body was more vulnerable. Now will you stop this nonsense? I don't want to have to damage you; you're too expensive for that. Will you just sit down and let the maintenance crews adjust you?"

Swanson groveled. "You-you won't punish us?"

The steel robot had no expression, but its voice was almost surprised. "Punish you?" it repeated on a rising note. "How?"

Swanson quivered as though the word had been a whip; but Burckhardt flared: "Adjust *him*, if he'll let you-but not me! You're going to have to do me a lot of damage, Dorchin. I don't care what I cost or how much trouble it's going to be to put me back together again. But I'm going out of that door! If you want to stop me, you'll have to kill me. You won't stop me any other way!"

The steel robot took a half-step toward him, and Burckhardt involuntarily checked his stride. He stood poised and shaking, ready for death, ready for attack, ready for anything that might happen.

Ready for anything except what did happen. For Dorchin's steel body merely stepped aside, between Burckhardt and the gun, but leaving the door free.

"Go ahead," invited the steel robot. "Nobody's stopping you."

* * * * *

Outside the door, Burckhardt brought up sharp. It was insane of Dorchin to let him go! Robot or flesh, victim or beneficiary, there was nothing to stop him from going to the FBI or whatever law he could find away from Dorchin's synthetic empire, and telling his story. Surely the corporations who paid Dorchin for test results had no notion of the ghoul's technique he used; Dorchin would have to keep it from them, for the breath of publicity would put a stop to it. Walking out meant death, perhaps-but at that moment in his pseudo-life, death was no terror for Burckhardt.

There was no one in the corridor. He found a window and stared out of it. There was Tylerton-an ersatz city, but looking so real and familiar that Burckhardt almost imagined the whole episode a dream. It was no dream, though. He was certain of that in his heart and equally certain that nothing in Tylerton could help him now.

It had to be the other direction.

It took him a quarter of an hour to find a way, but he found it-skulking through the corridors, dodging the suspicion of footsteps, knowing for certain that his hiding was in vain, for Dorchin was undoubtedly aware of every move he made. But no one stopped him, and he found another door.

It was a simple enough door from the inside. But when he opened it and stepped out, it was like nothing he had ever seen.

First there was light-brilliant, incredible, blinding light. Burckhardt blinked upward, unbelieving and afraid.

He was standing on a ledge of smooth, finished metal. Not a dozen yards from his feet, the ledge dropped sharply away; he hardly dared approach the brink, but even from where he stood he could see no bottom to the chasm before him. And the gulf extended out of sight into the glare on either side of him.

* * * * *

No wonder Dorchin could so easily give him his freedom! From the factory, there was nowhere to go-but how incredible this fantastic gulf, how impossible the hundred white and blinding suns that hung above!

A voice by his side said inquiringly, "Burckhardt?" And thunder rolled the name, mutteringly soft, back and forth in the abyss before him.

Burckhardt wet his lips. "Y-yes?" he croaked.

"This is Dorchin. Not a robot this time, but Dorchin in the flesh, talking to you on a hand mike. Now you have seen, Burckhardt. Now will you be reasonable and let the maintenance crews take over?"

Burckhardt stood paralyzed. One of the moving mountains in the blinding glare came toward him.

It towered hundreds of feet over his head; he stared up at its top, squinting helplessly into the light.

It looked like —

Impossible!

The voice in the loudspeaker at the door said, "Burckhardt?" But he was unable to answer.

A heavy rumbling sigh. "I see," said the voice. "You finally understand. There's no place to go. You know it now. I could have told you, but you might not have believed me, so it was better for you to see it yourself. And after all, Burckhardt, why would I reconstruct a city just the way it was before? I'm a businessman; I count costs. If a thing has to be full-scale, I build it that way. But there wasn't any need to in this case."

From the mountain before him, Burckhardt helplessly saw a lesser cliff descend carefully toward him. It was long and dark, and at the end of it was whiteness, five-fingered whiteness....

"Poor little Burckhardt," crooned the loudspeaker, while the echoes rumbled through the enormous chasm that was only a workshop. "It must have been quite a shock for you to find out you were living in a town built on a table top."

VI

It was the morning of June 15th, and Guy Burckhardt woke up screaming out of a dream.

It had been a monstrous and incomprehensible dream, of explosions and shadowy figures that were not men and terror beyond words.

He shuddered and opened his eyes.

Outside his bedroom window, a hugely amplified voice was howling.

Burckhardt stumbled over to the window and stared outside. There was an out-of-season chill to the air, more like October than June; but the scent was normal enough-except for the sound-truck that squatted at curbside halfway down the block. Its speaker horns blared:

"Are you a coward? Are you a fool? Are you going to let crooked politicians steal the country from you? NO! Are you going to put up with four more years of graft and crime? NO! Are you going to vote straight Federal Party all up and down the ballot? YES! *You just bet you are!*"

Sometimes he screams, sometimes he wheedles, threatens, begs, cajoles ... but his voice goes on and on through one June 15th after another.

The Day of the Boomer Dukes

I. Foraminifera 9

Paptaste udderly, semped sempsemp dezhavoo, qued schmerz-Excuse me. I mean to say that it was like an endless diet of days, boring, tedious....

No, it loses too much in the translation. Explete my reasons, I say. Do my reasons matter? No, not to you, for you are troglodytes, knowing nothing of causes, understanding only acts. Acts and facts, I will give you acts and facts.

First you must know how I am called. My "name" is Foraminifera 9-Hart Bailey's Beam, and I am of adequate age and size. (If you doubt this, I am prepared to fight.) Once the-the tediety of life, as you might say, had made itself clear to me, there were, of course, only two alternatives. I do not like to die, so that possibility was out; and the remaining alternative was flight.

Naturally, the necessary machinery was available to me. I arrogated a small viewing machine, and scanned the centuries of the past in the hope that a sanctuary might reveal itself to my aching eyes. Kwel tediety that was! Back, back I went through the ages. Back to the Century of the Dog, back to the Age of the Crippled Men. I found no time better than my own. Back and back I peered, back as far as the Numbered Years. The Twenty-Eighth Century was boredom unendurable, the Twenty-Sixth a morass of dullness. Twenty-Fifth, Twenty-Fourth —wherever I looked, tediety was what I found.

* * * * *

I snapped off the machine and considered. Put the problem thus: Was there in all of the pages of history no age in which a 9-Hart Bailey's Beam might find adventure and excitement? There had to be! It was not possible, I told myself, despairing, that from the dawn of the dreaming primates until my own time there was no era at all in which I could be-happy? Yes, I suppose happiness is what I was looking for. But where was it? In my viewer, I had fifty centuries or more to look back upon. And that was, I decreed, the trouble; I could spend my life staring into the viewer, and yet never discover the time that was right for me. There were simply too many eras to choose from. It was like an enormous library in which there must, there had to be, contained the one fact I was looking for-that, lacking an index, I might wear my life away and never find.

"*Index!*"

I said the word aloud! For, to be sure, it was the answer. I had the freedom of the Learning Lodge, and the index in the reading room could easily find for me just what I wanted.

Splendid, splendid! I almost felt cheerful. I quickly returned the viewer I had been using to the keeper, and received my deposit back. I hurried to the Learning Lodge and fed my specifications into the index, as follows, that is to say: Find me a time in recent past where there is adventure and excitement, where there is a secret, colorful band of desperadoes with whom I can ally myself. I then added two specifications-second, that it should be before the time of the high radiation levels; and first, that it should be after the discovery of anesthesia, in case of accident-and retired to a desk in the reading room to await results.

It took only a few moments, which I occupied in making a list of the gear I wished to take with me. Then there was a hiss and a crackle, and in the receiver of the desk a book appeared. I unzipped the case, took it out, and opened it to the pages marked on the attached reading tape.

I had found my wonderland of adventure!

* * * * *

Ah, hours and days of exciting preparation! What a round of packing and buying; what a filling out of forms and a stamping of visas; what an orgy of injections and inoculations and preventive therapy! Merely getting ready for the trip made my pulse race faster and my adrenalin balance rise to the very point of paranoia; it was like being given a true blue new chance to live.

At last I was ready. I stepped into the transmission capsule; set the dials; unlocked the door, stepped out; collapsed the capsule and stored it away in my carry-all; and looked about at my new home.

Pyew! Kwel smell of staleness, of sourness, above all of coldness! It was a close matter then if I would be able to keep from a violent eructative stenosis, as you say. I closed my eyes and remembered warm violets for a moment, and then it was all right.

The coldness was not merely a smell; it was a physical fact. There was a damp grayish substance underfoot which I recognized as snow; and in a hard-surfaced roadway there were a number of wheeled vehicles moving, which caused the liquefying snow to splash about me. I adjusted my coat controls for warmth and deflection, but that was the best I could do. The reek of stale decay remained. Then there were also the buildings, painfully almost vertical. I believe it would not have disturbed me if they had been truly vertical; but many of them were minutes of arc from a true perpendicular, all of them covered with a carbonaceous material which I instantly perceived was an inadvertent deposit from the air. It was a bad beginning!

However, I was not *bored*.

* * * * *

I made my way down the "street," as you say, toward where a group of young men were walking toward me, five abreast. As I came near, they looked at me with interest and kwel respect, conversing with each other in whispers.

I addressed them: "Sirs, please direct me to the nearest recruiting office, as you call it, for the dread Camorra."

They stopped and pressed about me, looking at me intently. They were handsomely, though crudely dressed in coats of a striking orange color, and long trousers of an extremely dark material.

I decreed that I might not have made them understand me-it is always probable, it is understood, that a quicknik course in dialects of the past may not give one instant command of spoken communication in the field. I spoke again: "I wish to encounter a representative of the Camorra, in other words the Black Hand, in other words the cruel and sinister Sicilian terrorists named the Mafia. Do you know where these can be found?"

One of them said, "Nay. What's that jive?"

I puzzled over what he had said for a moment, but in the end decreed that his message was sensefree. As I was about to speak, however, he said suddenly: "Let's rove, man." And all five of them walked quickly away a few "yards." It was quite disappointing. I observed them conferring among themselves, glancing at me, and for a time proposed terminating my venture, for I then believed that it would be better to return "home," as you say, in order to more adequately research the matter.

* * * * *

However, the five young men came toward me again. The one who had spoken before, who I now detected was somewhat taller and fatter than the others, spoke as follows: "You're wanting the Mafia?" I agreed. He looked at me for a moment. "Are you holding?"

He was inordinately hard to understand. I said, slowly and with patience, "Keska that 'holding' say?"

"Money, man. You going to slip us something to help you find these cats?"

"Certainly, money. I have a great quantity of money instantly available," I rejoined him. This appeared to relieve his mind.

There was a short pause, directly after which this first of the young men spoke: "You're on, man. Yeah, come with us. What's to call you?" I queried this last statement, and he expanded: "The name. What's the name?"

"You may call me Foraminifera 9," I directed, since I wished to be incognito, as you put it, and we proceeded along the "street." All five of the young men indicated a desire to serve me, offering indeed to take my carry-all. I rejected this, politely.

I looked about me with lively interest, as you may well believe. Kwel dirt, kwel dinginess, kwel cold! And yet there was a certain charm which I can determine no way of expressing in this language. Acts and facts, of course. I shall not attempt to capture the subjectivity which is the charm, only to transcribe the physical datum-perhaps even data, who knows? My companions, for example: They were in appearance overwrought, looking about them continually, stopping entirely and drawing me with them into the shelter of a "door" when another man, this one wearing blue clothing and a visored hat appeared. Yet they were clearly devoted to me, at that moment, since they had put aside their own projects in order to escort me without delay to the Mafia.

* * * * *

Mafia! Fortunate that I had found them to lead me to the Mafia! For it had been clear in the historical work I had consulted that it was not ultimately easy to gain access to the Mafia. Indeed, so secret were they that I had detected no trace of their existence in other histories of the period. Had I relied only on the conventional work, I might never have known of their great underground struggle against what you term society. It was only in the actual contemporary volume itself, the curiosity titled *U.S.A. Confidential* by one Lait and one Mortimer, that I had descried that, throughout the world, this great revolutionary organization flexed its tentacles, the plexus within a short distance of where I now stood, battling courageously. With me to help them, what heights might we not attain! Kwel dramatic delight!

My meditations were interrupted. "Boomers!" asserted one of my five escorts in a loud, frightened tone. "Let's cut, man!" he continued, leading me with them into another entrance. It appeared, as well as I could decree, that the cause of his ejaculative outcry was the discovery of perhaps three, perhaps four, other young men, in coats of the same shiny material as my escorts. The difference was that they were of a different color, being blue.

* * * * *

We hastened along a lengthy chamber which was quite dark, immediately after which the large, heavy one opened a way to a serrated incline leading downward. It was extremely dark, I should say. There was also an extreme smell, quite like that of the outer air, but enormously intensified; one would suspect that there was an incomplete combustion of, perhaps, wood or coal, as well as a certain quantity of general decay. At any rate, we reached the bottom of the incline, and my escort behaved quite badly. One of them said to the other four, in these words: "Them jumpers follow us sure. Yeah, there's much trouble. What's to prime this guy now and split?"

Instantly they fell upon me with violence. I had fortunately become rather alarmed at their visible emotion of fear, and already had taken from my carry-all a Stollgratz 16, so that I quickly turned it on them. I started to replace the Stollgratz 16 as they fell to the floor, yet I realized that there might be an additional element of danger. Instead of putting the Stollgratz 16 in with the other trade goods, which I had brought to assist me in negotiating with the Mafia, I transferred it to my jacket. It had become clear to me that the five young men of my escort had intended to abduct and rob me-indeed had intended it all along, perhaps having never intended to convoy me to the office of the Mafia. And the other young men, those who wore the blue jackets in place of the orange, were already descending the incline toward me, quite rapidly.

"Stop," I directed them. "I shall not entrust myself to you until you have given me evidence that you entirely deserve such trust."

* * * * *

They all halted, regarding me and the Stollgratz 16. I detected that one of them said to another: "That cat's got a zip."

The other denied this, saying: "That no zip, man. Yeah, look at them Leopards. Say, you bust them flunkies with that thing?"

I perceived his meaning quite quickly. "You are 'correct'," I rejoined. "Are you associated in friendship with them flunkies?"

"Hell, no. Yeah, they're Leopards and we're Boomer Dukes. You cool them, you do us much good." I received this information as indicating that the two socio-economic units were inimical, and unfortunately lapsed into an example of the Bivalent Error. Since p implied not-q, I sloppily assumed that not-q implied r (with, you understand, r being taken as the class of phenomena pertinently favorable to me). This was a very poor construction, and of course resulted in certain difficulties. Qued, after all. I stated:

"Them flunkies offered to conduct me to a recruiting office, as you say, of the Mafia, but instead tried to take from me the much money I am holding." I then went on to describe to them my desire to attain contact with the said Mafia; meanwhile they descended further and grouped about me in the very little light, examining curiously the motionless figures of the Leopards.

They seemed to be greatly impressed; and at the same time, very much puzzled. Naturally. They looked at the Leopards, and then at me.

They gave every evidence of wishing to help me; but of course if I had not forgotten that one cannot assume from the statements "not-Leopard implies Boomer Duke" and "not-Leopard implies Foraminifera 9" that, qued, "Boomer Duke implies Foraminifera 9" ... if I had not forgotten this, I say, I should not have been "deceived." For in practice they were as little favorable to me as the Leopards. A certain member of their party reached a position behind me.

I quickly perceived that his intention was not favorable, and attempted to turn around in order to discharge at him with the Stollgratz 16, but he was very rapid. He had a metallic cylinder, and with it struck my head, knocking "me" unconscious.

II. Shield 8805

This candy store is called Chris's. There must be ten thousand like it in the city. A marble counter with perhaps five stools, a display case of cigars and a bigger one of candy, a few dozen girlie magazines hanging by clothespin-sort-of things from wire ropes along the wall. It has a couple of very small glass-topped tables under the magazines. And a juke —I can't imagine a place like Chris's without a juke.

I had been sitting around Chris's for a couple of hours, and I was beginning to get edgy. The reason I was sitting around Chris's was not that I liked Cokes particularly, but that it was one of the hanging-out places of a juvenile gang called The Leopards, with whom I had been trying to work for nearly a year; and the reason I was becoming edgy was that I didn't see any of them there.

The boy behind the counter-he had the same first name as I, Walter in both cases, though my last name is Hutner and his is, I believe, something Puerto Rican-the boy behind the counter was dummying up, too. I tried to talk to him, on and off, when he wasn't busy. He wasn't busy most of the time; it was too cold for sodas. But he just didn't want to talk. Now, these kids love to talk. A lot of what they say doesn't make sense-either bullying, or bragging, or purposeless swearing-but talk is their normal state; when they quiet down it means trouble. For instance, if you ever find yourself walking down Thirty-Fifth Street and a couple of kids pass you, talking, you don't have to bother looking around; but if they stop talking, turn quickly. You're about to be mugged. Not that Walt was a mugger-as far as I know; but that's the pattern of the enclave.

* * * * *

So his being quiet was a bad sign. It might mean that a rumble was brewing-and that meant that my work so far had been pretty nearly a failure. Even worse, it might mean that somehow the Leopards had discovered that I had at last passed my examinations and been appointed to the New York City Police Force as a rookie patrolman, Shield 8805.

Trying to work with these kids is hard enough at best. They don't like outsiders. But they particularly hate cops, and I had been trying for some weeks to decide how I could break the news to them.

The door opened. Hawk stood there. He didn't look at me, which was a bad sign. Hawk was one of the youngest in the Leopards, a skinny, very dark kid who had been reasonably friendly to me. He stood in the open door, with snow blowing in past him. "Walt. Out here, man."

It wasn't me he meant-they call me "Champ," I suppose because I beat them all shooting eight-ball pool. Walt put down the comic he had been reading and walked out, also without looking at me. They closed the door.

* * * * *

Time passed. I saw them through the window, talking to each other, looking at me. It was something, all right. They were scared. That's bad, because these kids are like wild animals; if you scare them, they hit first-it's the only way they know to defend themselves. But on the other hand, a rumble wouldn't scare them-not where they would show it; and finding out about the shield in my pocket wouldn't scare them, either. They hated cops, as I say; but cops were a part of their environment. It was strange, and baffling.

Walt came back in, and Hawk walked rapidly away. Walt went behind the counter, lit a cigaret, wiped at the marble top, picked up his comic, put it down again and finally looked at me. He said: "Some punk busted Fayo and a couple of the boys. It's real trouble."

I didn't say anything.

He took a puff on his cigaret. "They're chilled, Champ. Five of them."

"Chilled? Dead?" It sounded bad; there hadn't been a real rumble in months, not with a killing.

He shook his head. "Not dead. You're wanting to see, you go down Gomez's cellar. Yeah, they're all stiff but they're breathing. I be along soon as the old man comes back in the store."

He looked pretty sick. I left it at that and hurried down the block to the tenement where the Gomez family lived, and then I found out why.

* * * * *

They were sprawled on the filthy floor of the cellar like winoes in an alley. Fayo, who ran the gang; Jap; Baker; two others I didn't know as well. They were breathing, as Walt had said, but you just couldn't wake them up.

Hawk and his twin brother, Yogi, were there with them, looking scared. I couldn't blame them. The kids looked perfectly all right, but it was obvious that they weren't. I bent down and smelled, but there was no trace of liquor or anything else on their breath.

I stood up. "We'd better get a doctor."

"Nay. You call the meat wagon, and a cop comes right with it, man," Yogi said, and his brother nodded.

I laid off that for a moment. "What happened?"

Hawk said, "You know that witch Gloria, goes with one of the Boomer Dukes? She opened her big mouth to my girl. Yeah, opened her mouth and much bad talk came out. Said Fayo primed some jumper with a zip and the punk cooled him, and then a couple of the Boomers moved in real cool. Now they got the punk with the zip and much other stuff, real stuff."

"What kind of stuff?"

Hawk looked worried. He finally admitted that he didn't know what kind of stuff, but it was something dangerous in the way of weapons. It had been the "zip" that had knocked out the five Leopards.

I sent Hawk out to the drug-store for smelling salts and containers of hot black coffee-not that I knew what I was doing, of course, but they were dead set against calling an ambulance. And the boys didn't seem to be in any particular danger, only sleep.

* * * * *

However, even then I knew that this kind of trouble was something I couldn't handle alone. It was a tossup what to do-the smart thing was to call the precinct right then and there; but I couldn't help feeling that that would make the Leopards clam up hopelessly. The six months I had spent trying to work with them had not been too successful —a lot of the other neighborhood workers had made a lot more progress than I —but at least they were willing to talk to me; and they wouldn't talk to uniformed police.

Besides, as soon as I had been sworn in, the day before, I had begun the practice of carrying my .38 at all times, as the regulations say. It was in my coat. There was no reason for me to feel I needed it. But I did. If there was any truth to the story of a "zip" knocking out the boys-and I had all five of them right there for evidence —I had the unpleasant conviction that there was real trouble circulating around East Harlem that afternoon.

"Champ. They all waking up!"

I turned around, and Hawk was right. The five Leopards, all of a sudden, were stirring and opening their eyes. Maybe the smelling salts had something to do with it, but I rather think not.

We fed them some of the black coffee, still reasonably hot. They were scared; they were more scared than anything I had ever seen in those kids before. They could hardly talk at first, and when finally they came around enough to tell me what had happened I could hardly believe them. This man had been small and peculiar, and he had been looking for, of all things, the "Mafia," which he had read about in history books —old history books.

Well, it didn't make sense, unless you were prepared to make a certain assumption that I refused to make. Man from Mars? Nonsense. Or from the future? Equally ridiculous....

* * * * *

Then the five Leopards, reviving, began to walk around. The cellar was dark and dirty, and packed with the accumulation of generations in the way of old furniture and rat-inhabited mattresses and piles of newspapers; it wasn't surprising that we hadn't noticed the little gleaming thing that had apparently rolled under an abandoned potbelly stove.

Jap picked it up, squalled, dropped it and yelled for me.

I touched it cautiously, and it tingled. It wasn't painful, but it was an odd, unexpected feeling-perhaps you've come across the "buzzers" that novelty stores sell which, concealed in the palm, give a sudden, surprising tingle when the owner shakes hands with an unsuspecting friend. It was like that, like a mild electric shock. I picked it up and held it. It gleamed brightly, with a light of its own; it was round; it made a faint droning sound; I turned it over, and it spoke to me. It said in a friendly, feminine whisper: *Warning, this portatron attuned only to Bailey's Beam percepts. Remain quiescent until the Adjuster comes.*

That settled it. Any time a lit-up cue ball talks to me, I refer the matter to higher authority. I decided on the spot that I was heading for the precinct house, no matter what the Leopards thought.

But when I turned and headed for the stairs, I couldn't move. My feet simply would not lift off the ground. I twisted, and stumbled, and fell in a heap; I yelled for help, but it didn't do any good. The Leopards couldn't move either.

We were stuck there in Gomez's cellar, as though we had been nailed to the filthy floor.

III. Cow

When I see what this flunky has done to them Leopards, I call him a cool cat right away. But then we jump him and he ain't so cool. Angel and Tiny grab him under the arms and I'm grabbing the stuff he's carrying. Yeah, we get out of there.

There's bulls on the street, so we cut through the back and over the fences. Tiny don't like that. He tells me, "Cow. What's to leave this cat here? He must weigh eighteen tons." "You're bringing him," I tell him, so he shuts up. That's how it is in the Boomer Dukes. When Cow talks, them other flunkies shut up fast.

We get him in the loft over the R. and I. Social Club. Damn, but it's cold up there. I can hear the pool balls clicking down below so I pass the word to keep quiet. Then I give this guy the foot and pretty soon he wakes up.

As soon as I talk to him a little bit I figure we had luck riding with us when we see them Leopards. This cat's got real bad stuff. Yeah, I never hear of anything like it. But what it takes to make a fight he's got. I take my old pistol and give it to Tiny. Hell, it makes him happy and what's it cost me? Because what this cat's got makes that pistol look like something for babies.

* * * * *

First he don't want to talk. "Stomp him," I tell Angel, but he's scared. He says, "Nay. This is a real weird cat, Cow. I'm for cutting out of here."

"Stomp him," I tell him again, pretty quiet, but he does it. He don't have to tell me this cat's weird, but when the cat gets the foot a couple of times he's willing to talk. Yeah, he talks real funny, but that don't matter to me. We take all the loot out of his bag, and I make this cat tell me what it's to do. Damn, I don't know what he's talking about one time out of six, but I know enough. Even Tiny catches on after a while, because I see him put down that funky old pistol I gave him that he's been loving up.

I'm feeling pretty good. I wish a couple of them chicken Leopards would turn up so I could show them what they missed out on. Yeah, I'll take on them, and the Black Dogs, and all the cops in the world all at once-that's how good I'm feeling. I feel so good that I don't even like it when Angel lets out a yell and comes up with a wad of loot. It's like I want to prime the U.S. Mint for chickenfeed, I don't want it to come so easy.

But money's on hand, so I take it off Angel and count it. This cat was really loaded; there must be a thousand dollars here.

I take a handful of it and hand it over to Angel real cool. "Get us some charge," I tell him. "There's much to do and I'm feeling ready for some charge to do it with."

"How many sticks you want me to get?" he asks, holding on to that money like he never saw any before.

I tell him: "Sticks? Nay. I'm for real stuff tonight. You find Four-Eye and get us some horse." Yeah, he digs me then. He looks like he's pretty scared and I know he is, because this punk hasn't had anything bigger than reefers in his life. But I'm for busting a couple of caps of H, and what I do he's going to do. He takes off to find Four-Eye and the rest of us get busy on this cat with the funny artillery until he gets back.

* * * * *

It's like I'm a million miles down Dream Street. Hell, I don't want to wake up.

But the H is wearing off and I'm feeling mean. Damn, I'll stomp my mother if she talks big to me right then.

I'm the first one on my feet and I'm looking for trouble. The whole place is full now. Angel must have passed the word to everybody in the Dukes, but I don't even remember them coming in. There's eight or ten cats lying around on the floor now, not even moving. This won't do, I decide.

If I'm on my feet, they're all going to be on their feet. I start to give them the foot and they begin to move. Even the weirdie must've had some H. I'm guessing that somebody slipped him some to see what would happen, because he's off on Cloud Number Nine. Yeah, they're feeling real mean when they wake up, but I handle them cool. Even that little flunky Sailor starts to go up against me but I look at him cool and he chickens. Angel and Pete are real sick, with the shakes and the heaves, but I ain't waiting for them to feel good. "Give me that loot," I tell Tiny, and he hands over the stuff we took off the weirdie. I start to pass out the stuff.

"What's to do with this stuff?" Tiny asks me, looking at what I'm giving him.

I tell him, "Point it and shoot it." He isn't listening when the weirdie's telling me what the stuff is. He wants to know what it does, but I don't know that. I just tell him, "Point it and shoot it, man." I've sent one of the cats out for drinks and smokes and he's back by then, and we're all beginning to feel a little better, only still pretty mean. They begin to dig me.

"Yeah, it sounds like a rumble," one of them says, after a while.

I give him the nod, cool. "You're calling it," I tell him. "There's much fighting tonight. The Boomer Dukes is taking on the world!"

IV. Sandy Van Pelt

The front office thought the radio car would give us a break in spot news coverage, and I guessed as wrong as they did. I had been covering City Hall long enough, and that's no place to build a career-the Press Association is very tight there, there's not much chance of getting any kind of exclusive story because of the sharing agreements. So I put in for the radio car. It meant taking the night shift, but I got it.

I suppose the front office got their money's worth, because they played up every lousy auto smash the radio car covered as though it were the story of the Second Coming, and maybe it helped circulation. But I had been on it for four months and, wouldn't you know it, there wasn't a decent murder, or sewer explosion, or running gun fight between six P.M. and six A.M. any night I was on duty in those whole four months. What made it worse, the kid they gave me as photographer-Sol Detweiler, his name was-couldn't drive worth a damn, so I was stuck with chauffeuring us around.

We had just been out to LaGuardia to see if it was true that Marilyn Monroe was sneaking into town with Aly Khan on a night plane-it wasn't —and we were coming across the Triborough Bridge, heading south toward the East River Drive, when the office called. I pulled over and parked and answered the radiophone.

* * * * *

It was Harrison, the night City Editor. "Listen, Sandy, there's a gang fight in East Harlem. Where are you now?"

It didn't sound like much to me, I admit. "There's always a gang fight in East Harlem, Harrison. I'm cold and I'm on my way down to Night Court, where there may or may not be a story; but at least I can get my feet warm."

"*Where are you now?*" Harrison wasn't fooling. I looked at Sol, on the seat next to me; I thought I had heard him snicker. He began to fiddle with his camera without looking at me. I pushed the "talk" button and told Harrison where I was. It pleased him very much; I wasn't more than six blocks from where this big rumble was going on, he told me, and he made it very clear that I was to get on over there immediately.

I pulled away from the curb, wondering why I had ever wanted to be a newspaperman; I could have made five times as much money for half as much work in an ad agency. To make it worse, I heard Sol chuckle again. The reason he was so amused was that when we first teamed up I made the mistake of telling him what a hot reporter I was, and I had been visibly cooling off before his eyes for a better than four straight months.

Believe me, I was at the very bottom of my career that night. For five cents cash I would have parked the car, thrown the keys in the East River, and taken the first bus out of town. I was absolutely positive that the story would be a bust and all I would get out of it would be a bad cold from walking around in the snow.

And if that doesn't show you what a hot newspaperman I really am, nothing will.

* * * * *

Sol began to act interested as we reached the corner Harrison had told us to go to. "That's Chris's," he said, pointing at a little candy store. "And that must be the pool hall where the Leopards hang out."

"You know this place?"

He nodded. "I know a man named Walter Hutner. He and I went to school together, until he dropped out, couple weeks ago. He quit college to go to the Police Academy. He wanted to be a cop."

I looked at him. "You're going to college?"

"Sure, Mr. Van Pelt. Wally Hutner was a sociology major —I'm journalism-but we had a couple of classes together. He had a part-time job with a neighborhood council up here, acting as a sort of adult adviser for one of the gangs."

"They need advice on how to be gangs?"

"No, that's not it, Mr. Van Pelt. The councils try to get their workers accepted enough to bring the kids in to the social centers, that's all. They try to get them off the streets. Wally was working with a bunch called the Leopards."

I shut him up. "Tell me about it later!" I stopped the car and rolled down a window, listening.

* * * * *

Yes, there was something going on all right. Not at the corner Harrison had mentioned-there wasn't a soul in sight in any direction. But I could hear what sounded like gunfire and yelling, and, my God, even bombs going off! And it wasn't too far away. There were sirens, too-squad cars, no doubt.

"It's over that way!" Sol yelled, pointing. He looked as though he was having the time of his life, all keyed up and delighted. He didn't have to tell me where the noise was coming from, I could hear for myself. It sounded like D-Day at Normandy, and I didn't like the sound of it.

I made a quick decision and slammed on the brakes, then backed the car back the way we had come. Sol looked at me. "What —"

"Local color," I explained quickly. "This the place you were talking about? Chris's? Let's go in and see if we can find some of these hoodlums."

"But, Mr. Van Pelt, all the pictures are over where the fight's going on!"

"Pictures, shmictures! Come on!" I got out in front of the candy store, and the only thing he could do was follow me.

Whatever they were doing, they were making the devil's own racket about it. Now that I looked a little more closely I could see that they must have come this way; the candy store's windows were broken; every other street light was smashed; and what had at first looked like a flight of steps in front of a tenement across the street wasn't anything of the kind-it was a pile of bricks and stone from the false-front cornice on the roof! How in the world they had managed to knock that down I had no idea; but it sort of convinced me that, after all, Harrison had been right about this being a *big* fight. Over where the noise was coming from there were queer flashing lights in the clouds overhead-reflecting exploding flares, I thought.

* * * * *

No, I didn't want to go over where the pictures were. I like living. If it had been a normal Harlem rumble with broken bottles and knives, or maybe even home-made zip guns —I might have taken a chance on it, but this was for real.

"Come on," I yelled to Sol, and we pushed the door open to the candy store.

At first there didn't seem to be anyone in, but after we called a couple times a kid of about sixteen, coffee-colored and scared-looking, stuck his head up above the counter.

"You. What's going on here?" I demanded. He looked at me as if I was some kind of a two-headed monster. "Come on, kid. Tell us what happened."

"Excuse me, Mr. Van Pelt." Sol cut in ahead of me and began talking to the kid in Spanish. It got a rise out of him; at least Sol got an answer. My Spanish is only a little bit better than my Swahili, so I missed what was going on, except for an occasional word. But Sol was getting it all. He reported: "He knows Walt; that's what's bothering him. He says Walt and some of the Leopards are in a basement down the street, and there's something wrong with them. I can't exactly figure out what, but —"

"The hell with them. What about *that*?"

"You mean the fight? Oh, it's a big one all right, Mr. Van Pelt. It's a gang called the Boomer Dukes. They've got hold of some real guns somewhere —I can't exactly understand what kind of guns he means, but it sounds like something serious. He says they shot that parapet down across the street. Gosh, Mr. Van Pelt, you'd think it'd take a cannon for something like that. But it has something to do with Walt Hutner and all the Leopards, too."

I said enthusiastically, "Very good, Sol. That's fine. Find out where the cellar is, and we'll go interview Hutner."

"But Mr. Van Pelt, the pictures —"

"Sorry. I have to call the office." I turned my back on him and headed for the car.

* * * * *

The noise was louder, and the flashes in the sky brighter-it looked as though they were moving this way. Well, I didn't have any money tied up in the car, so I wasn't worried about leaving it in the street. And somebody's cellar seemed like a very good place to be. I called the office and started to tell Harrison what we'd found out; but he stopped me short. "Sandy, where've you been? I've been trying to call you for-Listen, we got a call from Fordham. They've detected radiation coming from the East Side-it's got to be what's going on up there! Radiation, do you hear me? That means atomic weapons! Now, you get th —"

Silence.

"Hello?" I cried, and then remembered to push the talk button. "Hello? Harrison, you there?"

Silence. The two-way radio was dead.

I got out of the car; and maybe I understood what had happened to the radio and maybe I didn't. Anyway, there was something new shining in the sky. It hung below the clouds in parts, and I could see it through the bottom of the clouds in the middle; it was a silvery teacup upside down, a hemisphere over everything.

It hadn't been there two minutes before.

* * * * *

I heard firing coming closer and closer. Around a corner a bunch of cops came, running, turning, firing; running, turning and firing again. It was like the retreat from Caporetto in miniature. And what was chasing them? In a minute I saw. Coming around the corner was a kid with a lightning-blue satin jacket and two funny-looking guns in his hand; there was a silvery aura around him, the same color as the lights in the sky; and I swear I saw those cops' guns hit him twenty times in twenty seconds, but he didn't seem to notice.

Sol and the kid from the candy store were right beside me. We took another look at the one-man army that was coming down the street toward us, laughing and prancing and firing those odd-looking guns. And then the three of us got out of there, heading for the cellar. Any cellar.

V. Priam's Maw

My occupation was "short-order cook", as it is called. I practiced it in a locus entitled "The White Heaven," established at Fifth Avenue, Newyork, between 1949 and 1962 C.E. I had created rapport with several of the aboriginals, who addressed me as Bessie, and presumed to approve the manner in which I heated specimens of minced ruminant quadruped flesh (deceased to be sure). It was a satisfactory guise, although tiring.

Using approved techniques, I was compiling anthropometric data while "I" was, as they say, "brewing coffee." I deem the probability nearly conclusive that it was the double duty, plus the datum that, as stated, "I" was physically tired, which caused me to overlook the first signal from my portatron. Indeed, I might have overlooked the second as well except that the aboriginal named Lester stated: "Hey, Bessie. Ya got an alarm clock in ya pocketbook?" He had related the annunciator signal of the portatron to the only significant datum in his own experience which it resembled, the ringing of a bell.

I annotated his dossier to provide for his removal in case it eventuated that he had made an undesirable intuit (this proved unnecessary) and retired to the back of the "store" with my carry-all. On identifying myself to the portatron, I received information that it was attuned to a Bailey's Beam, identified as Foraminifera 9-Hart, who had refused treatment for systemic weltschmerz and instead sought to relieve his boredom by adventuring into this era.

I thereupon compiled two recommendations which are attached: 2, a proposal for reprimand to the Keeper of the Learning Lodge for failure to properly annotate a volume entitled *U.S.A. Confidential* and, 1, a proposal for reprimand to the Transport Executive, for permitting Bailey's Beam-class personnel access to temporal transport. Meanwhile, I left the "store" by a rear exit and directed myself toward the locus of the transmitting portatron.

* * * * *

I had proximately left when I received an additional information, namely that developed weapons were being employed in the area toward which I was directing. This provoked that I abandon guise entirely. I went transparent and quickly examined all aboriginals within view, to determine if any required removal; but none had observed this. I rose to perhaps seventy-five meters and sped at full atmospheric driving speed toward the source of the alarm. As I crossed a "park" I detected the drive of another Adjuster, whom I determined to be Alephplex Priam's Maw-that is, my father. He bespoke me as follows: "Hurry, Besplex Priam's Maw. That crazy Foraminifera has been captured by aboriginals and they have taken his weapons away from him." "Weapons?" I inquired. "Yes, weapons," he stated, "for Foraminifera 9-Hart brought with him more than forty-three kilograms of weapons, ranging up to and including electronic."

I recorded this datum and we landed, went opaque in the shelter of a doorway and examined our percepts. "Quarantine?" asked my father, and I had to agree. "Quarantine," I voted, and he opened his carry-all and set-up a quarantine shield on the console. At once appeared the silvery quarantine dome, and the first step of our adjustment was completed. Now to isolate, remove, replace.

Queried Alephplex: "An Adjuster?" I observed the phenomenon to which he was referring. A young, dark aboriginal was coming toward us on the "street," driving a group of police aboriginals before him. He was armed, it appeared, with a fission-throwing weapon in one hand and some sort of tranquilizer —I deem it to have been a Stollgratz 16 —in the other; moreover, he wore an invulnerability belt. The police aboriginals were attempting to strike him with missile weapons, which the belt deflected. I neutralized his shield, collapsed him and stored him in my carry-all. "Not an Adjuster," I asserted my father, but he had already perceived that this was so. I left him to neutralize and collapse the police aboriginals while I zeroed in on the portatron. I did not envy him his job with the police aboriginals, for many of them were "dead," as they say. It required the most delicate adjustments.

* * * * *

The portatron developed to be in a "cellar" and with it were some nine or eleven aboriginals which it had immobilized pending my arrival. One spoke to me thus: "Young lady, please call the cops! We're stuck here, and —" I did not wait to hear what he wished to say further, but neutralized and collapsed him with the other aboriginals. The portatron apologized for having caused me inconvenience; but of course it was not its fault, so I did not neutralize it. Using it for d-f, I quickly located the culprit, Foraminifera 9-Hart Bailey's Beam, nearby. He spoke despairingly in the dialect of the locus, "Besplex Priam's Maw, for God's sake get me out of this!" "Out!" I spoke to him, "you'll wish you never were 'born,' as they say!" I neutralized but did not collapse him, pending instructions from the Central Authority. The aboriginals who were with him, however, I did collapse.

Presently arrived Alephplex, along with four other Adjusters who had arrived before the quarantine shield made it not possible for anyone else to enter the disturbed area. Each one of us had had to abandon guise, so that this locus of Newyork 1939-1986 must require new Adjusters to replace us —a matter to be charged against the guilt of Foraminifera 9-Hart Bailey's Beam, I deem.

* * * * *

This concluded Steps 3 and 2 of our Adjustment, the removal and the isolation of the disturbed specimens. We are transmitting same disturbed specimens to you under separate cover herewith, in neutralized and collapsed state, for the manufacture of simulacra thereof. One regrets to say that they number three thousand eight hundred forty-six, comprising all aboriginals within the quarantined area who had first-hand knowledge of the anachronisms caused by Foraminifera's importation of contemporary weapons into this locus.

Alephplex and the four other Adjusters are at present reconstructing such physical damage as was caused by the use of said weapons. Simultaneously, while I am preparing this report, "I" am maintaining the quarantine shield which cuts off this locus, both physically and temporally, from the remainder of its environment. I deem that if replacements for the attached aboriginals can be fabricated quickly enough, there will be no significant outside percept of the shield itself, or of the happenings within it-that is, by maintaining a quasi-stasis of time while the repairs are being made, an outside aboriginal observer will see, at most, a mere flicker of silver in the sky. All Adjusters here present are working as rapidly as we can to make sure the shield can be withdrawn, before so many aboriginals have observed it as to make it necessary to replace the entire city with simulacra. We do not wish a repetition of the California incident, after all.

Footnotes

1.   from M.T.: No matter.

2.   The story is borrowed, language and all, from the Morte d'Arthur. — M.T.

www.ingramcontent.com/pod-product-compliance
Lightning Source LLC
Chambersburg PA
CBHW070341030726
47504CB00001B/24